The Lord of the Rings cannot be described in a few words. J. R. R. Tolkien's great work has been labelled both a heroic romance and a classic of science fiction. It is, however, impossible to convey to the new reader all of the book's qualities, and the range of its creation. By turns comic, homely, epic, monstrous and diabolic, the narrative moves through countless changes of scenes and character in an imaginary world which is totally convincing in its detail. Tolkien created a new mythology in an invented world which has proved timeless in its appeal.

This one volume paperback edition includes the complete unabridged text of the three books, *The Fellowship of the Ring, The Two Towers* and *The Return of the King*, that together make up *The Lord of the Rings*; the Index and full Appendices. This reset edition contains newly drawn maps by Stephen Raw, based on Christopher Tolkien's original maps.

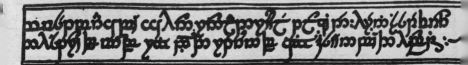

TOLKIEN

The Lord
of the Rings

BY

J.R.R. TOLKIEN

HarperCollins*Publishers*

HarperCollins*Publishers*
77–85 Fulham Palace Road,
Hammersmith, London W6 8JB
www.tolkien.co.uk

This film tie-in edition 2001
10

This edition has been reset and the maps
have been redrawn by Stephen Raw

Previously published in paperback by
HarperCollins*Publishers* 1995
Reprinted eighteen times
and in 1993
Reprinted four times
and by Grafton 1992
Reprinted four times

First published by HarperCollins*Publishers* 1991

THE FELLOWSHIP OF THE RING first published in
Great Britain by George Allen & Unwin 1954, second edition 1966
THE TWO TOWERS first published in Great Britain
by George Allen & Unwin 1954, second edition 1966
THE RETURN OF THE KING first published in
Great Britain by George Allen & Unwin 1955, second edition 1966

THE FELLOWSHIP OF THE RING
© The Trustees of The J.R.R Tolkien 1967 Settlement 1954, 1966
THE TWO TOWERS
© The Trustees of The J.R.R Tolkien 1967 Settlement 1954, 1966
THE RETURN OF THE KING
© The Trustees of The J.R.R Tolkien 1967 Settlement 1955, 1966

First published in one volume 1968

ISBN 0 00 712381 7

Printed and bound in Great Britain by
Clays Ltd, St Ives plc

Three Rings for the Elven-kings under the sky,
    Seven for the Dwarf-lords in their halls of stone,
Nine for Mortal Men doomed to die,
    One for the Dark Lord on his dark throne
In the Land of Mordor where the Shadows lie.
    One Ring to rule them all, One Ring to find them,
    One Ring to bring them all and in the darkness bind them
In the Land of Mordor where the Shadows lie.

CONTENTS

THE FELLOWSHIP OF THE RING

BOOK ONE

BOOK TWO

THE TWO TOWERS

BOOK THREE

BOOK FOUR

THE RETURN OF THE KING

BOOK FIVE

NOTE ON THE TEXT

The Lord of the Rings is often erroneously called a trilogy, when it is in fact a single novel, consisting of six books plus appendices, sometimes published in three volumes.

The first volume, *The Fellowship of the Ring*, was published in Great Britain by the London firm George Allen & Unwin on 29 July 1954; an American edition followed on 21 October of the same year, published by Houghton Mifflin Company of Boston. In the production of this first volume, Tolkien experienced what became for him a continual problem: printer's errors and compositor's mistakes, including well-intentioned 'corrections' of his sometimes idiosyncratic usage. These 'corrections' include the altering of *dwarves* to *dwarfs*, *elvish* to *elfish*, *further* to *farther*, *nasturtians* to *nasturtiums*, *try and say* to *try to say* and ('worst of all' to Tolkien) *elven* to *elfin*. In a work such as *The Lord of the Rings*, containing invented languages and delicately constructed nomenclatures, errors and inconsistencies impede both the understanding and the appreciation of serious readers – and Tolkien had many such readers from very early on. Even before the publication of the third volume, which contained much hitherto unrevealed information on the invented languages and writing systems, Tolkien received many letters from readers written in these systems, in addition to numerous enquiries on the finer points of their usage.

The second volume, *The Two Towers*, was published in England on 11 November 1954 and in the United States on 21 April 1955. Meanwhile Tolkien worked to keep a promise he had made in the foreword to volume one: that 'an index of names and strange words' would appear in the third volume. As originally planned, this index would contain much etymological information on the languages, particularly in the elven tongues, with a large vocabulary. It proved the chief cause of the delay in publishing volume three, which in the end contained no index at all, only an apology from the publisher for its absence. For Tolkien had abandoned work on it after indexing volumes one and two, believing its size and therefore its cost to be ruinous.

Volume three, *The Return of the King*, finally appeared in England on 20 October 1955 and in the United States on 5 January 1956. With the appearance of the third volume, *The Lord of the Rings* was published in its entirety, and its first edition text remained virtually unchanged for a decade. (Tolkien made a few small corrections, but further errors entered *The Fellowship of the Ring* in its second impression when the printer, having distributed the type after the first printing, reset the book without informing the author or publisher.)

In 1965, stemming from what then appeared to be copyright problems in the United States, an American paperback firm published an unauthorized and non-royalty-paying edition of *The Lord of the Rings*. For this new edition by Ace Books the text of the narrative was reset, thus introducing new typographical errors; the appendices, however, were reproduced photographically from the hardcover edition, and remain consistent with it.

Tolkien set to work on his first revision of the text so that a newly revised and authorized edition could successfully compete on the American market. This first revision of the text was published in America in paperback by Ballantine Books in

October 1965. In addition to revisions within the text itself, Tolkien replaced his original foreword with a new one. He was pleased to remove the original foreword; in his check copy, he wrote of it: 'confusing (as it does) real personal matters with the "machinery" of the Tale, is a serious mistake'. Tolkien also added an extension to the prologue and an index – not the detailed index of names promised in the first edition, but, rather, a bald index with only names and page references. Additionally, at this time the appendices were greatly revised.

Tolkien received his copies of the Ballantine edition in late January 1966, and in early February he recorded in his diary that he had 'worked for some hours on the Appendices in Ballantine version & found more errors than I at first expected'. Soon after this he sent a small number of further revisions to Ballantine for the appendices, including the now well-known addition of 'Estella Bolger' as wife of Meriadoc in the family trees in Appendix C. Most of these revisions, which entered variously in the third and fourth impressions (June and August 1966) of volume three, and which were not always inserted correctly (thereby causing further confusion in the text), somehow never made it into the main sequence of revision in the three-volume British hardcover edition, and for long remained an anomaly. Tolkien once wrote, concerning the revising of *The Lord of the Rings*, that perhaps he had failed to keep his notes in order; this errant branch of revision seems likely to be an example of that disorder.

The revised text first appeared in Great Britain in a three-volume hardcover 'Second Edition' from Allen & Unwin on 27 October 1966. But again there were problems. Although the revisions Tolkien sent to America of the text itself were available to be utilized in the new British edition, his extensive revisions to the appendices were lost after being entered into the Ballantine edition. Allen & Unwin were forced to reset the appendices using the copy as published in the first Ballantine edition. This did not include Tolkien's second, small set of revisions sent to Ballantine; but, more significantly, it did include a great number of errors and omissions, many of which were not discovered until long afterwards. Thus, in the appendices, a close scrutiny of the first edition text and of the much later corrected impressions of the second edition is necessary to discern whether any particular change in this edition is authorial or erroneous.

In America, the revised text appeared in hardcover in the three-volume edition published by Houghton Mifflin on 27 February 1967. This text was evidently photo-offset from the 1966 Allen & Unwin three-volume hardcover, and is thus consistent with it. Aside from the first printing of this second Houghton Mifflin edition, which has a 1967 date on the title page, none of the many reprintings is dated. After the initial printings of this edition, which bore a 1966 copyright notice, the date of copyright was changed to 1965 to match the statement in the Ballantine edition. This change has caused a great deal of confusion for librarians and other researchers who have tried to sort out the sequence of publications of these editions.

Meanwhile, Tolkien spent much of the summer of 1966 further revising the text. In June he learned that any more revisions were too late for inclusion in the 1966 Allen & Unwin second edition, and he recorded in his diary: 'But I am attempting to complete my work [on the revisions] – I cannot leave it while it is all in my mind. So much time has been wasted in all my work by this constant breaking of threads.' This was the last major set of revisions Tolkien himself made to the text during his lifetime. (Some small alterations were made by Tolkien in the 1969 one-volume India paper edition.) They were added to the second impression (1967) of the three-volume hardcover Allen & Unwin second edition. The revisions themselves mostly include corrections of nomenclature and attempts at consistency of usage throughout the three volumes.

J.R.R. Tolkien died in 1973. His third son and literary executor, Christopher Tolkien, sent a large set of further corrections of misprints, mainly in the appendices and index, to Allen & Unwin for use in their editions in 1974. Most of these corrections were typographical, and in line with his father's expressed intent in his own check copies.

Since 1974, Christopher Tolkien has sent additional corrections, as errors have been discovered, to the British publishers of *The Lord of the Rings* (Allen & Unwin, later Unwin Hyman, and now HarperCollins), who have tried to be conscientious in the impossible task of maintaining a textual integrity in whichever editions of *The Lord of the Rings* they have published. However, every time the text has been reset for publication in a new format (e.g. the various paperback editions published in England in the 1970s and 1980s), huge numbers of new misprints have crept in, though at times some of these errors have been observed and corrected in later printings. Still, throughout these years the three-volume British hardcover edition has retained the highest textual integrity.

In the United States, the text of the Ballantine paperback has remained unchanged since Tolkien added his few revisions in 1966. The text in all of the Houghton Mifflin editions remained unchanged from 1967 until 1987, when Houghton Mifflin photo-offset the then current three-volume British hardcover edition in order to update the text used in their editions. In those new reprintings a number of further corrections (overseen by Christopher Tolkien) were added, and the errant Ballantine branch of revision (including the 'Estella Bolger' addition) was integrated into the main branch of textual descent. Beginning in 1987, the Houghton Mifflin editions also included an earlier version of this 'Note on the Text', which contains some slight errors and simplifications based upon what I then understood to be true. This revision of the 'Note on the Text', undertaken for a new reset edition of *The Lord of the Rings* (to be published in various formats), replaces and supersedes the earlier version.

This new edition also contains a number of new corrections (again supervised by Christopher Tolkien), as well as a reconfigured index of names and page references. For this 'best possible' version, the text of *The Lord of the Rings* is being entered into computers, which should allow for a greater uniformity of text in future editions. Rayner Unwin, for much of his life Tolkien's publisher, has reminisced that as a child he was told, as an incentive to improve his religious knowledge, 'that the University Presses would pay five pounds to anyone who detected a printer's error in one of their authorized Bibles. I never heard of anyone who earned this small fortune, but I have often imagined an equivalent reward being offered three centuries after the first publication of *The Lord of the Rings*. It would take at least that long to achieve typographical perfection.'

It may indeed, but this new edition makes a significant stride towards such perfection, as well as achieving a desirable conformity of the text in the various formats in which it is published.

The textual history of *The Lord of the Rings*, merely in its published form, is a vast and complex web. In this brief note I have given only a glimpse of the overall sequence and structure. Further details on the revisions and corrections made over the years to the published text of *The Lord of the Rings*, and a fuller account of its publishing history, may be found in *J. R. R. Tolkien: A Descriptive Bibliography*, by Wayne G. Hammond, with the assistance of Douglas A. Anderson (1993).

For those interested in observing the gradual evolving of *The Lord of the Rings* from its earliest drafts to its published form, I highly recommend Christopher Tolkien's account in volumes six to nine of his series *The History of Middle-earth*: *The Return of the Shadow* (1988); *The Treason of Isengard* (1989); *The War of the Ring* (1990); and *Sauron Defeated* (1992). These volumes contain an engrossing over-the-shoulder look at the growth and unfolding of a masterpiece-in-progress, unparalleled in literature.

Last, I must acknowledge with great pleasure the friendly assistance and co-operation over many years of Christopher Tolkien and Wayne G. Hammond.

Douglas A. Anderson
Ithaca, New York
April 1993

FOREWORD TO THE SECOND EDITION

This tale grew in the telling, until it became a history of the Great War of the Ring and included many glimpses of the yet more ancient history that preceded it. It was begun soon after *The Hobbit* was written and before its publication in 1937; but I did not go on with this sequel, for I wished first to complete and set in order the mythology and legends of the Elder Days, which had then been taking shape for some years. I desired to do this for my own satisfaction, and I had little hope that other people would be interested in this work, especially since it was primarily linguistic in inspiration and was begun in order to provide the necessary background of 'history' for Elvish tongues.

When those whose advice and opinion I sought corrected *little hope* to *no hope*, I went back to the sequel, encouraged by requests from readers for more information concerning hobbits and their adventures. But the story was drawn irresistibly towards the older world, and became an account, as it were, of its end and passing away before its beginning and middle had been told. The process had begun in the writing of *The Hobbit*, in which there were already some references to the older matter: Elrond, Gondolin, the High-elves, and the orcs, as well as glimpses that had arisen unbidden of things higher or deeper or darker than its surface: Durin, Moria, Gandalf, the Necromancer, the Ring. The discovery of the significance of these glimpses and of their relation to the ancient histories revealed the Third Age and its culmination in the War of the Ring.

Those who had asked for more information about hobbits eventually got it, but they had to wait a long time; for the composition of *The Lord of the Rings* went on at intervals during the years 1936 to 1949, a period in which I had many duties that I did not neglect, and many other interests as a learner and teacher that often absorbed me. The delay was, of course, also increased by the outbreak of war in 1939, by the end of which year the tale had not yet reached the end of Book One. In spite of the darkness of the next five years I found that the story could not now be wholly abandoned, and I plodded on, mostly by night, till I stood by Balin's tomb in Moria. There I halted for a long while. It was almost a year later when I went on and so came to Lothlórien and the Great River late in 1941. In the next year I wrote the first drafts of the matter that now stands as Book Three, and the beginnings of chapters I and III of Book Five; and there as the beacons flared in Anórien and Théoden came to Harrowdale I stopped. Foresight had failed and there was no time for thought.

It was during 1944 that, leaving the loose ends and perplexities of a war which it was my task to conduct, or at least to report, I forced myself to tackle the journey of Frodo to Mordor. These chapters, eventually to become Book

Four, were written and sent out as a serial to my son, Christopher, then in South Africa with the RAF. Nonetheless it took another five years before the tale was brought to its present end; in that time I changed my house, my chair, and my college, and the days though less dark were no less laborious. Then when the 'end' had at last been reached the whole story had to be revised, and indeed largely re-written backwards. And it had to be typed, and re-typed: by me; the cost of professional typing by the ten-fingered was beyond my means.

The Lord of the Rings has been read by many people since it finally appeared in print; and I should like to say something here with reference to the many opinions or guesses that I have received or have read concerning the motives and meaning of the tale. The prime motive was the desire of a tale-teller to try his hand at a really long story that would hold the attention of readers, amuse them, delight them, and at times maybe excite them or deeply move them. As a guide I had only my own feelings for what is appealing or moving, and for many the guide was inevitably often at fault. Some who have read the book, or at any rate have reviewed it, have found it boring, absurd, or contempt-ible; and I have no cause to complain, since I have similar opinions of their works, or of the kinds of writing that they evidently prefer. But even from the points of view of many who have enjoyed my story there is much that fails to please. It is perhaps not possible in a long tale to please everybody at all points, nor to displease everybody at the same points; for I find from the letters that I have received that the passages or chapters that are to some a blemish are all by others specially approved. The most critical reader of all, myself, now finds many defects, minor and major, but being fortunately under no obligation either to review the book or to write it again, he will pass over these in silence, except one that has been noted by others: the book is too short.

As for any inner meaning or 'message', it has in the intention of the author none. It is neither allegorical nor topical. As the story grew it put down roots (into the past) and threw out unexpected branches: but its main theme was settled from the outset by the inevitable choice of the Ring as the link between it and *The Hobbit*. The crucial chapter, 'The Shadow of the Past', is one of the oldest parts of the tale. It was written long before the foreshadow of 1939 had yet become a threat of inevitable disaster, and from that point the story would have developed along essentially the same lines, if that disaster had been averted. Its sources are things long before in mind, or in some cases already written, and little or nothing in it was modified by the war that began in 1939 or its sequels.

The real war does not resemble the legendary war in its process or its conclusion. If it had inspired or directed the development of the legend, then certainly the Ring would have been seized and used against Sauron; he would not have been annihilated but enslaved, and Barad-dûr would not have been destroyed but occupied. Saruman, failing to get possession of the Ring, would in the confusion and treacheries of the time have found in Mordor the missing links in his own researches into Ring-lore, and before long he would have made a Great Ring of his own with which to challenge the self-styled Ruler of Middle-earth. In that conflict both sides would have held hobbits in hatred and contempt: they would not long have survived even as slaves.

Other arrangements could be devised according to the tastes or views of those who like allegory or topical reference. But I cordially dislike allegory in all its manifestations, and always have done so since I grew old and wary enough to detect its presence. I much prefer history, true or feigned, with its varied applicability to the thought and experience of readers. I think that many confuse 'applicability' with 'allegory'; but the one resides in the freedom of the reader, and the other in the purposed domination of the author.

An author cannot of course remain wholly unaffected by his experience, but the ways in which a story-germ uses the soil of experience are extremely complex, and attempts to define the process are at best guesses from evidence that is inadequate and ambiguous. It is also false, though naturally attractive, when the lives of an author and critic have overlapped, to suppose that the movements of thought or the events of times common to both were necessarily the most powerful influences. One has indeed personally to come under the shadow of war to feel fully its oppression; but as the years go by it seems now often forgotten that to be caught in youth by 1914 was no less hideous an experience than to be involved in 1939 and the following years. By 1918 all but one of my close friends were dead. Or to take a less grievous matter: it has been supposed by some that 'The Scouring of the Shire' reflects the situation in England at the time when I was finishing my tale. It does not. It is an essential part of the plot, foreseen from the outset, though in the event modified by the character of Saruman as developed in the story without, need I say, any allegorical significance or contemporary political reference whatsoever. It has indeed some basis in experience, though slender (for the economic situation was entirely different), and much further back. The country in which I lived in childhood was being shabbily destroyed before I was ten, in days when motor-cars were rare objects (I had never seen one) and men were still building suburban railways. Recently I saw in a paper a picture of the last decrepitude of the once thriving corn-mill beside its pool that long ago seemed to me so important. I never liked the looks of the Young miller, but his father, the Old miller, had a black beard, and he was not named Sandyman.

The Lord of the Rings is now issued in a new edition, and the opportunity has been taken of revising it. A number of errors and inconsistencies that still remained in the text have been corrected, and an attempt has been made to provide information on a few points which attentive readers have raised. I have considered all their comments and enquiries, and if some seem to have been passed over that may be because I have failed to keep my notes in order; but many enquiries could only be answered by additional appendices, or indeed by the production of an accessory volume containing much of the material that I .did not include in the original edition, in particular more detailed linguistic information. In the meantime this edition offers this Foreword, an addition to the Prologue, some notes, and an index of the names of persons and places. This index is in intention complete in items but not in references, since for the present purpose it has been necessary to reduce its bulk. A complete index, making full use of the material prepared for me by Mrs. N. Smith, belongs rather to the accessory volume.

PROLOGUE

I
Concerning Hobbits

This book is largely concerned with Hobbits, and from its pages a reader may discover much of their character and a little of their history. Further information will also be found in the selection from the Red Book of Westmarch that has already been published, under the title of *The Hobbit*. That story was derived from the earlier chapters of the Red Book, composed by Bilbo himself, the first Hobbit to become famous in the world at large, and called by him *There and Back Again*, since they told of his journey into the East and his return: an adventure which later involved all the Hobbits in the great events of that Age that are here related.

Many, however, may wish to know more about this remarkable people from the outset, while some may not possess the earlier book. For such readers a few notes on the more important points are here collected from Hobbit-lore, and the first adventure is briefly recalled.

Hobbits are an unobtrusive but very ancient people, more numerous formerly than they are today; for they love peace and quiet and good tilled earth: a well-ordered and well-farmed countryside was their favourite haunt. They do not and did not understand or like machines more complicated than a forge-bellows, a water-mill, or a hand-loom, though they were skilful with tools. Even in ancient days they were, as a rule, shy of 'the Big Folk', as they call us, and now they avoid us with dismay and are becoming hard to find. They are quick of hearing and sharp-eyed, and though they are inclined to be fat and do not hurry unnecessarily, they are nonetheless nimble and deft in their movements. They possessed from the first the art of disappearing swiftly and silently, when large folk whom they do not wish to meet come blundering by; and this art they have developed until to Men it may seem magical. But Hobbits have never, in fact, studied magic of any kind, and their elusiveness is due solely to a professional skill that heredity and practice, and a close friendship with the earth, have rendered inimitable by bigger and clumsier races.

For they are a little people, smaller than Dwarves: less stout and stocky, that is, even when they are not actually much shorter. Their height is variable, ranging between two and four feet of our measure. They seldom now reach three feet; but they have dwindled, they say, and in ancient days they were taller. According to the Red Book, Bandobras Took (Bullroarer), son of Isengrim the Second, was four foot five and able to ride a horse. He was surpassed in all Hobbit records only by two famous characters of old; but that curious matter is dealt with in this book.

As for the Hobbits of the Shire, with whom these tales are concerned, in the days of their peace and prosperity they were a merry folk. They dressed in bright colours, being notably fond of yellow and green; but they seldom wore shoes, since their feet had tough leathery soles and were clad in a thick curling hair, much like the hair of their heads, which was commonly brown. Thus, the only craft little practised among them was shoe-making; but they had long and skilful fingers and could make many other useful and comely things. Their faces were as a rule good-natured rather than beautiful, broad, bright-eyed, red-cheeked, with mouths apt to laughter, and to eating and drinking. And laugh they did, and eat, and drink, often and heartily, being fond of simple jests at all times, and of six meals a day (when they could get them). They were hospitable and delighted in parties, and in presents, which they gave away freely and eagerly accepted.

It is plain indeed that in spite of later estrangement Hobbits are relatives of ours: far nearer to us than Elves, or even than Dwarves. Of old they spoke the languages of Men, after their own fashion, and liked and disliked much the same things as Men did. But what exactly our relationship is can no longer be discovered. The beginning of Hobbits lies far back in the Elder Days that are now lost and forgotten. Only the Elves still preserve any records of that vanished time, and their traditions are concerned almost entirely with their own history, in which Men appear seldom and Hobbits are not mentioned at all. Yet it is clear that Hobbits had, in fact, lived quietly in Middle-earth for many long years before other folk became even aware of them. And the world being after all full of strange creatures beyond count, these little people seemed of very little importance. But in the days of Bilbo, and of Frodo his heir, they suddenly became, by no wish of their own, both important and renowned, and troubled the counsels of the Wise and the Great.

Those days, the Third Age of Middle-earth, are now long past, and the shape of all lands has been changed; but the regions in which Hobbits then lived were doubtless the same as those in which they still linger: the North-West of the Old World, east of the Sea. Of their original home the Hobbits in Bilbo's time preserved no knowledge. A love of learning (other than genealogical lore) was far from general among them, but there remained still a few in the older families who studied their own books, and even gathered reports of old times and distant lands from Elves, Dwarves, and Men. Their own records began only after the settlement of the Shire, and their most ancient legends hardly looked further back than their Wandering Days. It is clear, nonetheless, from these legends, and from the evidence of their peculiar words and customs, that like many other folk Hobbits had in the distant past moved westward. Their earliest tales seem to glimpse a time when they dwelt in the upper vales of Anduin, between the eaves of Greenwood the Great and the Misty Mountains. Why they later undertook the hard and perilous crossing of the mountains into Eriador is no longer certain. Their own accounts speak of the multiplying of Men in the land, and of a shadow that fell on the forest, so that it became darkened and its new name was Mirkwood.

Before the crossing of the mountains the Hobbits had already become divided into three somewhat different breeds: Harfoots, Stoors, and Fallohides. The Harfoots were browner of skin, smaller, and shorter, and they were beardless and bootless; their hands and feet were neat and nimble; and they preferred highlands and hillsides. The Stoors were broader, heavier in build; their feet and hands were larger, and they preferred flat lands and riversides. The Fallohides were fairer of skin and also of hair, and they were taller and slimmer than the others; they were lovers of trees and of woodlands.

The Harfoots had much to do with Dwarves in ancient times, and long lived in the foothills of the mountains. They moved westward early, and roamed over Eriador as far as Weathertop while the others were still in the Wilderland. They were the most normal and representative variety of Hobbit, and far the most numerous. They were the most inclined to settle in one place, and longest preserved their ancestral habit of living in tunnels and holes.

The Stoors lingered long by the banks of the Great River Anduin, and were less shy of Men. They came west after the Harfoots and followed the course of the Loudwater southwards; and there many of them long dwelt between Tharbad and the borders of Dunland before they moved north again.

The Fallohides, the least numerous, were a northerly branch. They were more friendly with Elves than the other Hobbits were, and had more skill in language and song than in handicrafts; and of old they preferred hunting to tilling. They crossed the mountains north of Rivendell and came down the River Hoarwell. In Eriador they soon mingled with the other kinds that had preceded them, but being somewhat bolder and more adventurous, they were often found as leaders or chieftains among clans of Harfoots or Stoors. Even in Bilbo's time the strong Fallohidish strain could still be noted among the greater families, such as the Tooks and the Masters of Buckland.

In the westlands of Eriador, between the Misty Mountains and the

Mountains of Lune, the Hobbits found both Men and Elves. Indeed, a remnant still dwelt there of the Dúnedain, the kings of Men that came over the Sea out of Westernesse; but they were dwindling fast and the lands of their North Kingdom were falling far and wide into waste. There was room and to spare for incomers, and ere long the Hobbits began to settle in ordered communities. Most of their earlier settlements had long disappeared and been forgotten in Bilbo's time; but one of the first to become important still endured, though reduced in size; this was at Bree and in the Chetwood that lay round about, some forty miles east of the Shire.

It was in these early days, doubtless, that the Hobbits learned their letters and began to write after the manner of the Dúnedain, who had in their turn long before learned the art from the Elves. And in those days also they forgot whatever languages they had used before, and spoke ever after the Common Speech, the Westron as it was named, that was current through all the lands of the kings from Arnor to Gondor, and about all the coasts of the Sea from Belfalas to Lune. Yet they kept a few words of their own, as well as their own names of months and days, and a great store of personal names out of the past.

About this time legend among the Hobbits first becomes history with a reckoning of years. For it was in the one thousand six hundred and first year of the Third Age that the Fallohide brothers, Marcho and Blanco, set out from Bree; and having obtained permission from the high king at Fornost,* they crossed the brown river Baranduin with a great following of Hobbits. They passed over the Bridge of Stonebows, that had been built in the days of the power of the North Kingdom, and they took all the land beyond to dwell in, between the river and the Far Downs. All that was demanded of them was that they should keep the Great Bridge in repair, and all other bridges and roads, speed the king's messengers, and acknowledge his lordship.

Thus began the *Shire-reckoning*, for the year of the crossing of the Brandywine (as the Hobbits turned the name) became Year One of the Shire, and all later dates were reckoned from it.† At once the western Hobbits fell in love with their new land, and they remained there, and soon passed once more out of the history of Men and of Elves. While there was still a king they were in name his subjects, but they were, in fact, ruled by their own chieftains and meddled not at all with events in the world outside. To the last battle at Fornost with the Witch-lord of Angmar they sent some

---

* As the records of Gondor relate this was Argeleb II, the twentieth of the Northern line, which came to an end with Arvedui three hundred years later.

† Thus, the years of the Third Age in the reckoning of the Elves and the Dúnedain may be found by adding 1600 to the dates of Shire-reckoning.

bowmen to the aid of the king, or so they maintained, though no tales of Men record it. But in that war the North Kingdom ended; and then the Hobbits took the land for their own, and they chose from their own chiefs a Thain to hold the authority of the king that was gone. There for a thousand years they were little troubled by wars, and they prospered and multiplied after the Dark Plague (S.R. 37) until the disaster of the Long Winter and the famine that followed it. Many thousands then perished, but the Days of Dearth (1158-60) were at the time of this tale long past and the Hobbits had again become accustomed to plenty. The land was rich and kindly, and though it had long been deserted when they entered it, it had before been well tilled, and there the king had once had many farms, cornlands, vineyards, and woods.

Forty leagues it stretched from the Far Downs to the Brandywine Bridge, and fifty from the northern moors to the marshes in the south. The Hobbits named it the Shire, as the region of the authority of their Thain, and a district of well-ordered business; and there in that pleasant corner of the world they plied their well-ordered business of living, and they heeded less and less the world outside where dark things moved, until they came to think that peace and plenty were the rule in Middle-earth and the right of all sensible folk. They forgot or ignored what little they had ever known of the Guardians, and of the labours of those that made possible the long peace of the Shire. They were, in fact, sheltered, but they had ceased to remember it.

At no time had Hobbits of any kind been warlike, and they had never fought among themselves. In olden days they had, of course, been often obliged to fight to maintain themselves in a hard world; but in Bilbo's time that was very ancient history. The last battle, before this story opens, and indeed the only one that had ever been fought within the borders of the Shire, was beyond living memory: the Battle of Greenfields, S.R. 1147, in which Bandobras Took routed an invasion of Orcs. Even the weathers had grown milder, and the wolves that had once come ravening out of the North in bitter white winters were now only a grandfather's tale. So, though there was still some store of weapons in the Shire, these were used mostly as trophies, hanging above hearths or on walls, or gathered into the museum at Michel Delving. The Mathom-house it was called; for anything that Hobbits had no immediate use for, but were unwilling to throw away, they called a *mathom*. Their dwellings were apt to become rather crowded with mathoms, and many of the presents that passed from hand to hand were of that sort.

Nonetheless, ease and peace had left this people still curiously tough. They were, if it came to it, difficult to daunt or to kill; and they were, perhaps, so unwearyingly fond of good things not least because they could, when put to it, do without them, and could survive rough handling by grief, foe, or weather in a way that astonished those who did not know them well and looked no further than their bellies and their well-fed faces. Though slow to quarrel, and for sport killing nothing that lived, they were doughty at bay, and at need could still handle arms. They shot well with the bow, for they were keen-eyed and sure at the mark. Not only with bows and arrows. If any Hobbit stooped for a stone, it was well to get quickly under cover, as all trespassing beasts knew very well.

All Hobbits had originally lived in holes in the ground, or so they believed, and in such dwellings they still felt most at home; but in the course of time they had been obliged to adopt other forms of abode. Actually in the Shire in Bilbo's days it was, as a rule, only the richest and the poorest Hobbits that maintained the old custom. The poorest went on living in burrows of the most primitive kind, mere holes indeed, with only one window or none; while the well-to-do still constructed more luxurious versions of the simple diggings of old. But suitable sites for these large and ramifying tunnels (or *smials* as they called them) were not everywhere to be found; and in the flats and the low-lying districts the Hobbits, as they multiplied, began to build above ground. Indeed, even in the hilly regions and the older villages, such as Hobbiton or Tuckborough, or in the chief township of the Shire, Michel Delving on the White Downs, there were now many houses of wood, brick, or stone. These were specially favoured by millers, smiths, ropers, and cartwrights, and others of that sort; for even when they had holes to live in, Hobbits had long been accustomed to build sheds and workshops.

The habit of building farmhouses and barns was said to have begun among the inhabitants of the Marish down by the Brandywine. The Hobbits of that quarter, the Eastfarthing, were rather large and heavy-legged, and they wore dwarf-boots in muddy weather. But they were well known to be Stoors in a large part of their blood, as indeed was shown by the down that many grew on their chins. No Harfoot or Fallohide had any trace of a beard. Indeed, the folk of the Marish, and of Buckland, east of the River, which they afterwards occupied, came for the most part later into the Shire up from south-away; and they still had many peculiar names and strange words not found elsewhere in the Shire.

It is probable that the craft of building, as many other crafts beside, was derived from the Dúnedain. But the Hobbits may have learned it direct from the Elves, the teachers of Men in their youth. For the Elves of the High Kindred had not yet forsaken Middle-earth, and they dwelt still at that time at the Grey Havens away to the west, and in other places within reach of the Shire. Three Elf-towers of immemorial age were still to be seen on the Tower Hills beyond the western marches. They shone far off in the moonlight. The tallest was furthest away, standing alone upon a green mound. The Hobbits of the Westfarthing said that one could see the

Sea from the top of that tower; but no Hobbit had ever been known to climb it. Indeed, few Hobbits had ever seen or sailed upon the Sea, and fewer still had ever returned to report it. Most Hobbits regarded even rivers and small boats with deep misgivings, and not many of them could swim. And as the days of the Shire lengthened they spoke less and less with the Elves, and grew afraid of them, and distrustful of those that had dealings with them; and the Sea became a word of fear among them, and a token of death, and they turned their faces away from the hills in the west.

The craft of building may have come from Elves or Men, but the Hobbits used it in their own fashion. They did not go in for towers. Their houses were usually long, low, and comfortable. The oldest kind were, indeed, no more than built imitations of *smials*, thatched with dry grass or straw, or roofed with turves, and having walls somewhat bulged. That stage, however, belonged to the early days of the Shire, and hobbit-building had long since been altered, improved by devices, learned from Dwarves, or discovered by themselves. A preference for round windows, and even round doors, was the chief remaining peculiarity of hobbit-architecture.

The houses and the holes of Shire-hobbits were often large, and inhabited by large families. (Bilbo and Frodo Baggins were as bachelors very exceptional, as they were also in many other ways, such as their friendship with the Elves.) Sometimes, as in the case of the Tooks of Great Smials, or the Brandybucks of Brandy Hall, many generations of relatives lived in (comparative) peace together in one ancestral and many-tunnelled mansion. All Hobbits were, in any case, clannish and reckoned up their relationships with great care. They drew long and elaborate family-trees with innumerable branches. In dealing with Hobbits it is important to remember who is related to whom, and in what degree. It would be impossible in this book to set out a family-tree that included even the more important members of the more important families at the time which these tales tell of. The genealogical trees at the end of the Red Book of Westmarch are a small book in themselves, and all but Hobbits would find them exceedingly dull. Hobbits delighted in such things, if they were accurate: they liked to have books filled with things that they already knew, set out fair and square with no contradictions.

2

Concerning Pipe-weed

There is another astonishing thing about Hobbits of old that must be mentioned, an astonishing habit: they imbibed or inhaled, through pipes of clay or wood, the smoke of the burning leaves of a herb, which they called *pipe-weed* or *leaf*, a variety probably of *Nicotiana*. A great deal of mystery surrounds the origin of this peculiar custom, or 'art' as the Hobbits preferred to call it. All that could be discovered about it in antiquity was put together by Meriadoc Brandybuck (later Master of Buckland), and since he and the tobacco of the Southfarthing play a part in the history that follows, his remarks in the introduction to his *Herblore of the Shire* may be quoted.

'This,' he says, 'is the one art that we can certainly claim to be our own invention. When Hobbits first began to smoke is not known, all the legends and family histories take it for granted; for ages folk in the Shire smoked various herbs, some fouler, some sweeter. But all accounts agree that Tobold Hornblower of Longbottom in the Southfarthing first grew the true pipe-weed in his gardens in the days of Isengrim the Second, about the year 1070 of Shire-reckoning. The best home-grown still comes from that district, especially the varieties now known as Longbottom Leaf, Old Toby, and Southern Star.

'How Old Toby came by the plant is not recorded, for to his dying day he would not tell. He knew much about herbs, but he was no traveller. It is said that in his youth he went often to Bree, though he certainly never went further from the Shire than that. It is thus quite possible that he learned of this plant in Bree, where now, at any rate, it grows well on the south slopes of the hill. The Bree-hobbits claim to have been the first actual smokers of the pipe-weed. They claim, of course, to have done everything before the people of the Shire, whom they refer to as "colonists"; but in this case their claim is, I think, likely to be true. And certainly it was from Bree that the art of smoking the genuine weed spread in the recent centuries among Dwarves and such other folk, Rangers, Wizards, or wanderers, as still passed to and fro through that ancient road-meeting. The home and centre of the art is thus to be found in the old inn of Bree, *The Prancing Pony*, that has been kept by the family of Butterbur from time beyond record.

'All the same, observations that I have made on my own many journeys south have convinced me that the weed itself is not native to our parts of the world, but came northward from the lower Anduin, whither it was, I suspect, originally brought over Sea by the Men of Westernesse. It grows abundantly in Gondor, and there is richer and larger than in the North, where it is never found wild, and flourishes only in warm sheltered places like Longbottom. The Men of Gondor call it *sweet galenas*, and esteem it only for the fragrance of its flowers. From that land it must have been carried up the Greenway during the long centuries between the coming of Elendil and our own days. But even the Dúnedain of Gondor allow us this credit: Hobbits first put it into pipes. Not even the Wizards first thought of that before we did. Though one Wizard that I knew took up the art long ago, and became as skilful in it as in all other things that he put his mind to.'

3
Of the Ordering of the Shire

The Shire was divided into four quarters, the Farthings already referred to, North, South, East, and West; and these again each into a number of folklands, which still bore the names of some of the old leading families, although by the time of this history these names were no longer found only in their proper folklands. Nearly all Tooks still lived in the Tookland, but that was not true of many other families, such as the Bagginses or the Boffins. Outside the Farthings were the East and West Marches: the Buckland (p. 96); and the Westmarch added to the Shire in S.R. 1462.

The Shire at this time had hardly any 'government'. Families for the most part managed their own affairs. Growing food and eating it occupied most of their time. In other matters they were, as a rule, generous and not greedy, but contented and moderate, so that estates, farms, workshops, and small trades tended to remain unchanged for generations.

There remained, of course, the ancient tradition concerning the high king at Fornost, or Norbury as they called it, away north of the Shire. But there had been no king for nearly a thousand years, and even the ruins of Kings' Norbury were covered with grass. Yet the Hobbits still said of wild folk and wicked things (such as trolls) that they had not heard of the king. For they attributed to the king of old all their essential laws; and usually they kept the laws of free will, because they were The Rules (as they said), both ancient and just.

It is true that the Took family had long been pre-eminent; for the office of Thain had passed to them (from the Oldbucks) some centuries before, and the chief Took had borne that title ever since. The Thain was the master of the Shire-moot, and captain of the Shire-muster and the Hobbitry-in-arms, but as muster and moot were only held in times of emergency, which no longer occurred, the Thainship had ceased to be more than a nominal dignity. The Took family was still, indeed, accorded a special respect, for it remained both numerous and exceedingly wealthy, and was liable to produce in every generation strong characters of peculiar habits and even adventurous temperament. The latter qualities, however, were now rather tolerated (in the rich) than generally approved. The custom endured, nonetheless, of referring to the head of the family as The Took, and of adding to his name, if required, a number: such as Isengrim the Second, for instance.

The only real official in the Shire at this date was the Mayor of Michel Delving (or of the Shire), who was elected every seven years at the Free Fair on the White Downs at the Lithe, that is at Midsummer. As mayor almost his only duty was to preside at banquets, given on the Shire-holidays, which occurred at frequent intervals. But the offices of Postmaster and First Shirriff were attached to the mayoralty, so that he managed both the Messenger Service and the Watch. These were the only Shire-services, and the Messengers were the most numerous, and much the busier of the two. By no means all Hobbits were lettered, but those who were wrote constantly to all their friends (and a selection of their relations) who lived further off than an afternoon's walk.

The Shirriffs was the name that the Hobbits gave to their police, or the nearest equivalent that they possessed. They had, of course, no uniforms (such things being quite unknown), only a feather in their caps; and they were in practice rather haywards than policemen, more concerned with the strayings of beasts than of people. There were in all the Shire only twelve of them, three in each Farthing, for Inside Work. A rather larger body, varying at need, was employed to 'beat the bounds', and to see that Outsiders of any kind, great or small, did not make themselves a nuisance.

At the time when this story begins the Bounders, as they were called, had been greatly increased. There were many reports and complaints of strange persons and creatures prowling about the borders, or over them: the first sign that all was not quite as it should be, and always had been except in tales and legends of long ago. Few heeded the sign, and not even Bilbo yet had any notion of what it portended. Sixty years had passed since he set out on his memorable journey, and he was old even for Hobbits, who reached a hundred as often as not; but much evidently still remained of the considerable wealth that he had brought back. How much or how little he revealed to no one, not even to Frodo his favourite 'nephew'. And he still kept secret the ring that he had found.

4

Of the Finding of the Ring

As is told in *The Hobbit*, there came one day to Bilbo's door the great Wizard, Gandalf the Grey, and thirteen dwarves with him: none other, indeed, than Thorin Oakenshield, descendant of kings, and his twelve companions in exile. With them he set out, to his own lasting astonishment, on a morning of April, it being then the year 1341 Shire-reckoning, on a quest of great treasure, the dwarf-hoards of the Kings under the Mountain, beneath Erebor in Dale, far off in the East. The quest was successful, and the Dragon that guarded the hoard was destroyed. Yet, though before all was won the Battle of Five Armies was fought, and Thorin was slain, and many deeds of renown were done, the matter would scarcely have concerned later history, or earned more than a note in the long annals of the Third Age, but for an 'accident' by the way. The party was assailed by Orcs in a high pass of the Misty Mountains as they went towards Wilderland; and so it happened that Bilbo was lost for a while in the black orc-mines deep under the mountains, and there, as he groped in vain in the dark, he put his hand on a ring, lying on the floor of a tunnel. He put it in his pocket. It seemed then like mere luck.

Trying to find his way out, Bilbo went on down to the roots of the mountains, until he could go no further. At the bottom of the tunnel lay a cold lake far from the light, and on an island of rock in the water lived Gollum. He was a loathsome little creature: he paddled a small boat with his large flat feet, peering with pale luminous eyes and catching blind fish with his long fingers, and eating them raw. He ate any living thing, even orc, if he could catch it and strangle it without a struggle. He possessed a secret treasure that had come to him long ages ago, when he still lived in the light: a ring of gold that made its wearer invisible. It was the one thing he loved, his 'precious', and he talked to it, even when it was not with him. For he kept it hidden safe in a hole on his island, except when he was hunting or spying on the orcs of the mines.

Maybe he would have attacked Bilbo at once, if the ring had been on him when they met; but it was not, and the hobbit held in his hand an Elvish knife, which served him as a sword. So to gain time Gollum challenged Bilbo to the Riddle-game, saying that if he asked a riddle which Bilbo could not guess, then he would kill him and eat him; but if Bilbo defeated him, then he would do as Bilbo wished: he would lead him to a way out of the tunnels.

Since he was lost in the dark without hope, and could neither go on nor back, Bilbo accepted the challenge; and they asked one another many riddles. In the end Bilbo won the game, more by luck (as it seemed) than by wits; for he was stumped at last for a riddle to ask, and cried out, as his hand came upon the ring he had picked up and forgotten: *What have I got in my pocket?* This Gollum failed to answer, though he demanded three guesses.

The Authorities, it is true, differ whether this last question was a mere 'question' and not a 'riddle' according to the strict rules of the Game; but all agree that, after accepting it and trying to guess the answer, Gollum was bound by his promise. And Bilbo pressed him to keep his word; for

the thought came to him that this slimy creature might prove false, even
though such promises were held sacred, and of old all but the wickedest
things feared to break them. But after ages alone in the dark Gollum's heart
was black, and treachery was in it. He slipped away, and returned to his
island, of which Bilbo knew nothing, not far off in the dark water. There,
he thought, lay his ring. He was hungry now, and angry, and once his
'precious' was with him he would not fear any weapon at all.

But the ring was not on the island; he had lost it, it was gone. His screech
sent a shiver down Bilbo's back, though he did not yet understand what
had happened. But Gollum had at last leaped to a guess, too late. *What
has it got in its pocketses?* he cried. The light in his eyes was like a green
flame as he sped back to murder the hobbit and recover his 'precious'. Just
in time Bilbo saw his peril, and he fled blindly up the passage away from
the water; and once more he was saved by his luck. For just as he ran he
put his hand in his pocket, and the ring slipped quietly on to his finger.
So it was that Gollum passed him without seeing him, and went to guard
the way out, lest the 'thief' should escape. Warily Bilbo followed him, as
he went along, cursing, and talking to himself about his 'precious'; from
which talk at last even Bilbo guessed the truth, and hope came to him in
the darkness: he himself had found the marvellous ring and a chance of
escape from the orcs and from Gollum.

At length they came to a halt before an unseen opening that led to the
lower gates of the mines, on the eastward side of the mountains. There
Gollum crouched at bay, smelling and listening; and Bilbo was tempted to
slay him with his sword. But pity stayed him, and though he kept the ring,
in which his only hope lay, he would not use it to help him kill the wretched
creature at a disadvantage. In the end, gathering his courage, he leaped
over Gollum in the dark, and fled away down the passage, pursued by his
enemy's cries of hate and despair: *Thief, thief! Baggins! We hates it for ever!*

Now it is a curious fact that this is not the story as Bilbo first told it to
his companions. To them his account was that Gollum had promised to
give him a *present*, if he won the game; but when Gollum went to fetch it
from his island he found the treasure was gone: a magic ring, which had
been given to him long ago on his birthday. Bilbo guessed that this was
the very ring that he had found, and as he had won the game, it was already
his by right. But being in a tight place, he said nothing about it, and made
Gollum show him the way out, as a reward instead of a present. This
account Bilbo set down in his memoirs, and he seems never to have altered
it himself, not even after the Council of Elrond. Evidently it still appeared
in the original Red Book, as it did in several of the copies and abstracts.
But many copies contain the true account (as an alternative), derived no

doubt from notes by Frodo or Samwise, both of whom learned the truth, though they seem to have been unwilling to delete anything actually written by the old hobbit himself.

Gandalf, however, disbelieved Bilbo's first story, as soon as he heard it, and he continued to be very curious about the ring. Eventually he got the true tale out of Bilbo after much questioning, which for a while strained their friendship; but the wizard seemed to think the truth important. Though he did not say so to Bilbo, he also thought it important, and disturbing, to find that the good hobbit had not told the truth from the first: quite contrary to his habit. The idea of a 'present' was not mere hobbitlike invention, all the same. It was suggested to Bilbo, as he confessed, by Gollum's talk that he overheard; for Gollum did, in fact, call the ring his 'birthday present', many times. That also Gandalf thought strange and suspicious; but he did not discover the truth in this point for many more years, as will be seen in this book.

Of Bilbo's later adventures little more need be said here. With the help of the ring he escaped from the orc-guards at the gate and rejoined his companions. He used the ring many times on his quest, chiefly for the help of his friends; but he kept it secret from them as long as he could. After his return to his home he never spoke of it again to anyone, save Gandalf and Frodo; and no one else in the Shire knew of its existence, or so he believed. Only to Frodo did he show the account of his Journey that he was writing.

His sword, Sting, Bilbo hung over his fireplace, and his coat of marvellous mail, the gift of the Dwarves from the Dragon-hoard, he lent to a museum, to the Michel Delving Mathom-house in fact. But he kept in a drawer at Bag End the old cloak and hood that he had worn on his travels; and the ring, secured by a fine chain, remained in his pocket.

He returned to his home at Bag End on June the 22nd in his fifty-second year (S.R. 1342), and nothing very notable occurred in the Shire until Mr. Baggins began the preparations for the celebration of his hundred-and-eleventh birthday (S.R. 1401). At this point this History begins.

NOTE ON THE SHIRE RECORDS

At the end of the Third Age the part played by the Hobbits in the great events that led to the inclusion of the Shire in the Reunited Kingdom awakened among them a more widespread interest in their own history; and many of their traditions, up to that time still mainly oral, were collected and written down. The greater families were also concerned with events in the Kingdom at large, and many of their members studied its ancient histories and legends. By the end of the first century of the Fourth

Age there were already to be found in the Shire several libraries that contained many historical books and records.

The largest of these collections were probably at Undertowers, at Great Smials, and at Brandy Hall. This account of the end of the Third Age is drawn mainly from the Red Book of Westmarch. That most important source for the history of the War of the Ring was so called because it was long preserved at Undertowers, the home of the Fairbairns, Wardens of the Westmarch.* It was in origin Bilbo's private diary, which he took with him to Rivendell. Frodo brought it back to the Shire, together with many loose leaves of notes, and during S.R. 1420–1 he nearly filled its pages with his account of the War. But annexed to it and preserved with it, probably in a single red case, were the three large volumes, bound in red leather, that Bilbo gave to him as a parting gift. To these four volumes there was added in Westmarch a fifth containing commentaries, genealogies, and various other matter concerning the hobbit members of the Fellowship.

The original Red Book has not been preserved, but many copies were made, especially of the first volume, for the use of the descendants of the children of Master Samwise. The most important copy, however, has a different history. It was kept at Great Smials, but it was written in Gondor, probably at the request of the great-grandson of Peregrin, and completed in S.R. 1592 (F.A. 172). Its southern scribe appended this note: Findegil, King's Writer, finished this work in IV 172. It is an exact copy in all details of the Thain's Book in Minas Tirith. That book was a copy, made at the request of King Elessar, of the Red Book of the Periannath, and was brought to him by the Thain Peregrin when he retired to Gondor in IV 64.

The Thain's Book was thus the first copy made of the Red Book and contained much that was later omitted or lost. In Minas Tirith it received much annotation, and many corrections, especially of names, words, and quotations in the Elvish languages; and there was added to it an abbreviated version of those parts of *The Tale of Aragorn and Arwen* which lie outside the account of the War. The full tale is stated to have been written by Barahir, grandson of the Steward Faramir, some time after the passing of the King. But the chief importance of Findegil's copy is that it alone contains the whole of Bilbo's 'Translations from the Elvish'. These three volumes were found to be a work of great skill and learning in which, between 1403 and 1418, he had used all the sources available to him in Rivendell, both living and written. But since they were little used by Frodo, being almost entirely concerned with the Elder Days, no more is said of them here.

Since Meriadoc and Peregrin became the heads of their great families, and at the same time kept up their connexions with Rohan and Gondor, the libraries at Bucklebury and Tuckborough contained much that did not appear in the Red Book. In Brandy Hall there were many works dealing with Eriador and the history of Rohan. Some of these were composed or begun by Meriadoc himself, though in the Shire he was chiefly remembered for his *Herblore of the Shire*, and for his *Reckoning of Years* in which he discussed the relation of the calendars of the Shire and Bree to those of Rivendell, Gondor, and Rohan. He also wrote a short treatise

---

* See Appendix B: annals 1451, 1462, 1482; and note at end of Appendix C.

on *Old Words and Names in the Shire*, showing special interest in discovering the kinship with the language of the Rohirrim of such 'shire-words' as *mathom* and old elements in place names.

At Great Smials the books were of less interest to Shire-folk, though more important for larger history. None of them was written by Peregrin, but he and his successors collected many manuscripts written by scribes of Gondor: mainly copies or summaries of histories or legends relating to Elendil and his heirs. Only here in the Shire were to be found extensive materials for the history of Númenor and the arising of Sauron. It was probably at Great Smials that *The Tale of Years** was put together, with the assistance of material collected by Meriadoc. Though the dates given are often conjectural, especially for the Second Age, they deserve attention. It is probable that Meriadoc obtained assistance and information from Rivendell, which he visited more than once. There, though Elrond had departed, his sons long remained, together with some of the High-elven folk. It is said that Celeborn went to dwell there after the departure of Galadriel; but there is no record of the day when at last he sought the Grey Havens, and with him went the last living memory of the Elder Days in Middle-earth.

* Represented in much reduced form in Appendix B as far as the end of the Third Age.

THE FELLOWSHIP
OF THE RING

BEING THE FIRST PART

OF

The Lord of the Rings

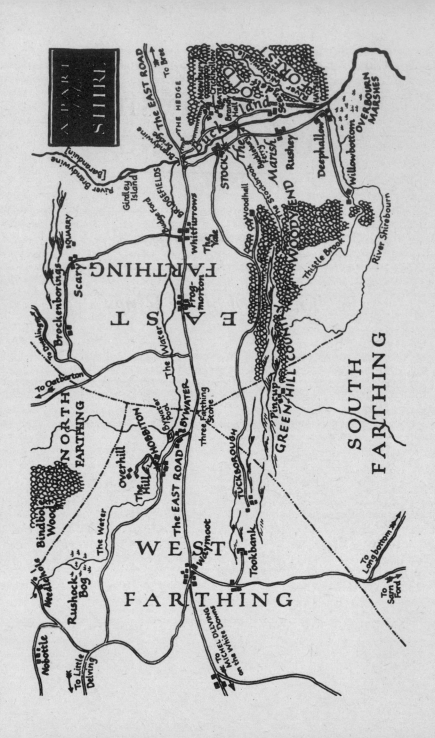

BOOK ONE

CHAPTER I

A LONG-EXPECTED PARTY

When Mr. Bilbo Baggins of Bag End announced that he would shortly be celebrating his eleventy-first birthday with a party of special magnificence, there was much talk and excitement in Hobbiton.

Bilbo was very rich and very peculiar, and had been the wonder of the Shire for sixty years, ever since his remarkable disappearance and unexpected return. The riches he had brought back from his travels had now become a local legend, and it was popularly believed, whatever the old folk might say, that the Hill at Bag End was full of tunnels stuffed with treasure. And if that was not enough for fame, there was also his prolonged vigour to marvel at. Time wore on, but it seemed to have little effect on Mr. Baggins. At ninety he was much the same as at fifty. At ninety-nine they began to call him *well-preserved*; but *unchanged* would have been nearer the mark. There were some that shook their heads and thought this was too much of a good thing; it seemed unfair that anyone should possess (apparently) perpetual youth as well as (reputedly) inexhaustible wealth.

'It will have to be paid for,' they said. 'It isn't natural, and trouble will come of it!'

But so far trouble had not come; and as Mr. Baggins was generous with his money, most people were willing to forgive him his oddities and his good fortune. He remained on visiting terms with his relatives (except, of course, the Sackville-Bagginses), and he had many devoted admirers among the hobbits of poor and unimportant families. But he had no close friends, until some of his younger cousins began to grow up.

The eldest of these, and Bilbo's favourite, was young Frodo Baggins. When Bilbo was ninety-nine he adopted Frodo as his heir, and brought him to live at Bag End; and the hopes of the Sackville-Bagginses were finally dashed. Bilbo and Frodo happened to have the same birthday, September 22nd. 'You had better come and live here, Frodo my lad,' said Bilbo one day; 'and then we can celebrate our birthday-parties comfortably together.' At that time Frodo was still in his *tweens*, as the hobbits called the irresponsible twenties between childhood and coming of age at thirty-three.

Twelve more years passed. Each year the Bagginses had given very lively combined birthday-parties at Bag End; but now it was understood that something quite exceptional was being planned for that autumn. Bilbo was going to be *eleventy-one*, 111, a rather curious number, and a very respectable age for a hobbit (the Old Took himself had only reached 130); and Frodo was going to be *thirty-three*, 33, an important number: the date of his 'coming of age'.

Tongues began to wag in Hobbiton and Bywater; and rumour of the coming event travelled all over the Shire. The history and character of Mr. Bilbo Baggins became once again the chief topic of conversation; and the older folk suddenly found their reminiscences in welcome demand.

No one had a more attentive audience than old Ham Gamgee, commonly known as the Gaffer. He held forth at *The Ivy Bush*, a small inn on the Bywater road; and he spoke with some authority, for he had tended the garden at Bag End for forty years, and had helped old Holman in the same job before that. Now that he was himself growing old and stiff in the joints, the job was mainly carried on by his youngest son, Sam Gamgee. Both father and son were on very friendly terms with Bilbo and Frodo. They lived on the Hill itself, in Number 3 Bagshot Row just below Bag End.

'A very nice well-spoken gentlehobbit is Mr. Bilbo, as I've always said,' the Gaffer declared. With perfect truth: for Bilbo was very polite to him, calling him 'Master Hamfast', and consulting him constantly upon the growing of vegetables – in the matter of 'roots', especially potatoes, the Gaffer was recognized as the leading authority by all in the neighbourhood (including himself).

'But what about this Frodo that lives with him?' asked Old Noakes of Bywater. 'Baggins is his name, but he's more than half a Brandybuck, they say. It beats me why any Baggins of Hobbiton should go looking for a wife away there in Buckland, where folks are so queer.'

'And no wonder they're queer,' put in Daddy Twofoot (the Gaffer's next-door neighbour), 'if they live on the wrong side of the Brandywine River, and right agin the Old Forest. That's a dark bad place, if half the tales be true.'

'You're right, Dad!' said the Gaffer. 'Not that the Brandybucks of Buckland live *in* the Old Forest; but they're a queer breed, seemingly. They fool about with boats on that big river – and that isn't natural. Small wonder that trouble came of it, I say. But be that as it may, Mr. Frodo is as nice a young hobbit as you could wish to meet. Very much like Mr. Bilbo, and in more than looks. After all his father was a Baggins. A decent respectable hobbit was Mr. Drogo Baggins; there was never much to tell of him, till he was drownded.'

'Drownded?' said several voices. They had heard this and other darker rumours before, of course; but hobbits have a passion for family history, and they were ready to hear it again.

'Well, so they say,' said the Gaffer. 'You see: Mr. Drogo, he married poor

Miss Primula Brandybuck. She was our Mr. Bilbo's first cousin on the mother's side (her mother being the youngest of the Old Took's daughters); and Mr. Drogo was his second cousin. So Mr. Frodo is his first *and* second cousin, once removed either way, as the saying is, if you follow me. And Mr. Drogo was staying at Brandy Hall with his father-in-law, old Master Gorbadoc, as he often did after his marriage (him being partial to his vittles, and old Gorbadoc keeping a mighty generous table); and he went out *boating* on the Brandywine River; and he and his wife were drownded, and poor Mr. Frodo only a child and all.'

'I've heard they went on the water after dinner in the moonlight,' said Old Noakes; 'and it was Drogo's weight as sunk the boat.'

'And *I* heard she pushed him in, and he pulled her in after him,' said Sandyman, the Hobbiton miller.

'You shouldn't listen to all you hear, Sandyman,' said the Gaffer, who did not much like the miller. 'There isn't no call to go talking of pushing and pulling. Boats are quite tricky enough for those that sit still without looking further for the cause of trouble. Anyway: there was this Mr. Frodo left an orphan and stranded, as you might say, among those queer Bucklanders, being brought up anyhow in Brandy Hall. A regular warren, by all accounts. Old Master Gorbadoc never had fewer than a couple of hundred relations in the place. Mr. Bilbo never did a kinder deed than when he brought the lad back to live among decent folk.

'But I reckon it was a nasty shock for those Sackville-Bagginses. They thought they were going to get Bag End, that time when he went off and was thought to be dead. And then he comes back and orders them off; and he goes on living and living, and never looking a day older, bless him! And suddenly he produces an heir, and has all the papers made out proper. The Sackville-Bagginses won't never see the inside of Bag End now, or it is to be hoped not.'

'There's a tidy bit of money tucked away up there, I hear tell,' said a stranger, a visitor on business from Michel Delving in the Westfarthing. 'All the top of your hill is full of tunnels packed with chests of gold and silver, *and* jools, by what I've heard.'

'Then you've heard more than I can speak to,' answered the Gaffer. 'I know nothing about *jools*. Mr. Bilbo is free with his money, and there seems no lack of it; but I know of no tunnel-making. I saw Mr. Bilbo when he came back, a matter of sixty years ago, when I was a lad. I'd not long come prentice to old Holman (him being my dad's cousin), but he had me up at Bag End helping him to keep folks from trampling and trapessing all over the garden while the sale was on. And in the middle of it all Mr. Bilbo comes up the Hill with a pony and some mighty big bags and a couple of chests. I don't doubt they were mostly full of treasure he had picked up in foreign parts, where there be mountains of gold, they say; but there wasn't enough to fill tunnels. But my lad Sam will know more about that. He's in and out of Bag End. Crazy about stories of the old days he is, and he listens to all Mr. Bilbo's tales. Mr. Bilbo has learned him his letters – meaning no harm, mark you, and I hope no harm will come of it.

'*Elves and Dragons!* I says to him. *Cabbages and potatoes are better for me and you. Don't go getting mixed up in the business of your betters, or you'll land in trouble too big for you*, I says to him. And I might say it to others,' he added with a look at the stranger and the miller.

But the Gaffer did not convince his audience. The legend of Bilbo's wealth was now too firmly fixed in the minds of the younger generation of hobbits.

'Ah, but he has likely enough been adding to what he brought at first,' argued the miller, voicing common opinion. 'He's often away from home. And look at the outlandish folk that visit him: dwarves coming at night, and that old wandering conjuror, Gandalf, and all. You can say what you like, Gaffer, but Bag End's a queer place, and its folk are queerer.'

'And you can say what *you* like, about what you know no more of than you do of boating, Mr. Sandyman,' retorted the Gaffer, disliking the miller even more than usual. 'If that's being queer, then we could do with a bit more queerness in these parts. There's some not far away that wouldn't offer a pint of beer to a friend, if they lived in a hole with golden walls. But they do things proper at Bag End. Our Sam says that *everyone's* going to be invited to the party, and there's going to be presents, mark you, presents for all – this very month as is.'

That very month was September, and as fine as you could ask. A day or two later a rumour (probably started by the knowledgeable Sam) was spread about that there were going to be fireworks – fireworks, what is more, such as had not been seen in the Shire for nigh on a century, not indeed since the Old Took died.

Days passed and The Day drew nearer. An odd-looking waggon laden with odd-looking packages rolled into Hobbiton one evening and toiled up the Hill to Bag End. The startled hobbits peered out of lamplit doors to gape at it. It was driven by outlandish folk, singing strange songs: dwarves with long beards and deep hoods. A few of them remained at Bag End. At the end of the second week in September a cart came in through Bywater from the direction of the Brandywine Bridge in broad daylight. An old man was driving it all alone. He wore a tall pointed blue hat, a long grey cloak, and a silver scarf. He had a long white beard and bushy eyebrows that stuck out beyond the brim of his hat. Small hobbit-children ran after the cart all through Hobbiton and right up the hill. It had a cargo of fireworks, as they rightly guessed. At Bilbo's front door the old man began to unload: there were great bundles of fireworks of all sorts and shapes, each labelled with a large red G ᚷ and the elf-rune, ᚠ.

That was Gandalf's mark, of course, and the old man was Gandalf the Wizard, whose fame in the Shire was due mainly to his skill with fires, smokes, and lights. His real business was far more difficult and dangerous, but the Shire-folk knew nothing about it. To them he was just one of the 'attractions' at the Party. Hence the excitement of the hobbit-children. 'G for Grand!' they shouted, and the old man smiled. They knew him by sight, though he only appeared in Hobbiton occasionally and never stopped long; but neither they nor any but the oldest of their elders had seen one of his firework displays – they now belonged to the legendary past.

When the old man, helped by Bilbo and some dwarves, had finished unloading, Bilbo gave a few pennies away; but not a single squib or cracker was forthcoming, to the disappointment of the onlookers.

'Run away now!' said Gandalf. 'You will get plenty when the time comes.' Then he disappeared inside with Bilbo, and the door was shut. The young hobbits stared at the door in vain for a while, and then made off, feeling that the day of the party would never come.

Inside Bag End, Bilbo and Gandalf were sitting at the open window of a small room looking out west on to the garden. The late afternoon was bright and peaceful. The flowers glowed red and golden: snap-dragons and sun-flowers, and nasturtians trailing all over the turf walls and peeping in at the round windows.

'How bright your garden looks!' said Gandalf.

'Yes,' said Bilbo. 'I am very fond indeed of it, and of all the dear old Shire; but I think I need a holiday.'

'You mean to go on with your plan then?'

'I do. I made up my mind months ago, and I haven't changed it.'

'Very well. It is no good saying any more. Stick to your plan – your whole plan, mind – and I hope it will turn out for the best, for you, and for all of us.'

'I hope so. Anyway I mean to enjoy myself on Thursday, and have my little joke.'

'Who will laugh, I wonder?' said Gandalf, shaking his head.

'We shall see,' said Bilbo.

The next day more carts rolled up the Hill, and still more carts. There might have been some grumbling about 'dealing locally', but that very week orders began to pour out of Bag End for every kind of provision, commodity, or luxury that could be obtained in Hobbiton or Bywater or anywhere in the neighbourhood. People became enthusiastic; and they began to tick off the days on the calendar; and they watched eagerly for the postman, hoping for invitations.

Before long the invitations began pouring out, and the Hobbiton post-office was blocked, and the Bywater post-office was snowed under, and voluntary assistant postmen were called for. There was a constant stream of them going up the Hill, carrying hundreds of polite variations on *Thank you, I shall certainly come.*

A notice appeared on the gate at Bag End: NO ADMITTANCE EXCEPT ON PARTY BUSINESS. Even those who had, or pretended to have Party Business were seldom allowed inside. Bilbo was busy: writing invitations, ticking off answers, packing up presents, and making some private preparations of his own. From the time of Gandalf's arrival he remained hidden from view.

One morning the hobbits woke to find the large field, south of Bilbo's front door, covered with ropes and poles for tents and pavilions. A special entrance was cut into the bank leading to the road, and wide steps and a large white gate were built there. The three hobbit-families of Bagshot Row, adjoining the field, were intensely interested and generally envied. Old Gaffer Gamgee stopped even pretending to work in his garden.

The tents began to go up. There was a specially large pavilion, so big that the tree that grew in the field was right inside it, and stood proudly near one end, at the head of the chief table. Lanterns were hung on all its branches. More promising still (to the hobbits' mind): an enormous open-air kitchen was erected in the north corner of the field. A draught of cooks, from every inn and eating-house for miles around, arrived to supplement the dwarves and other odd folk that were quartered at Bag End. Excitement rose to its height.

Then the weather clouded over. That was on Wednesday the eve of the Party. Anxiety was intense. Then Thursday, September the 22nd, actually dawned. The sun got up, the clouds vanished, flags were unfurled and the fun began.

Bilbo Baggins called it a *party*, but it was really a variety of entertainments rolled into one. Practically everybody living near was invited. A very few were overlooked by accident, but as they turned up all the same, that did not matter. Many people from other parts of the Shire were also asked; and there were even a few from outside the borders. Bilbo met the guests (and additions) at the new white gate in person. He gave away presents to all and sundry – the latter were those who went out again by a back way and came in again by the gate. Hobbits give presents to other people on their own birth-days. Not very expensive ones, as a rule, and not so lavishly as on this occasion; but it was not a bad system. Actually in Hobbiton and Bywater every day in the year it was somebody's birthday, so that every hobbit in those parts had a fair chance of at least one present at least once a week. But they never got tired of them.

On this occasion the presents were unusually good. The hobbit-children were so excited that for a while they almost forgot about eating. There were toys the like of which they had never seen before, all beautiful and some obviously magical. Many of them had indeed been ordered a year before, and had come all the way from the Mountain and from Dale, and were of real dwarf-make.

When every guest had been welcomed and was finally inside the gate, there were songs, dances, music, games, and, of course, food and drink. There were three official meals: lunch, tea, and dinner (or supper). But lunch and tea were marked chiefly by the fact that at those times all the guests were sitting down and eating together. At other times there were merely lots of people eating and drinking – continuously from elevenses until six-thirty, when the fireworks started.

The fireworks were by Gandalf: they were not only brought by him, but designed and made by him; and the special effects, set pieces, and flights of rockets were let off by him. But there was also a generous distribution of squibs, crackers, backarappers, sparklers, torches, dwarf-candles, elf-fountains, goblin-barkers and thunder-claps. They were all superb. The art of Gandalf improved with age.

There were rockets like a flight of scintillating birds singing with sweet voices. There were green trees with trunks of dark smoke: their leaves opened like a whole spring unfolding in a moment, and their shining branches dropped glowing flowers down upon the astonished hobbits, disappearing with a sweet scent just before they touched their upturned faces. There were fountains of butterflies that flew glittering into the trees; there were pillars of coloured fires that rose and turned into eagles, or sailing ships, or a phalanx of flying swans; there was a red thunderstorm and a shower of yellow rain; there was a forest of silver spears that sprang suddenly into the air with a yell like an embattled army, and came down again into the Water with a hiss like a hundred hot snakes. And there was also one last surprise, in honour of Bilbo, and it startled the hobbits exceedingly, as Gandalf intended. The lights went out. A great smoke went up. It shaped itself like a mountain seen in the distance, and began to glow at the summit. It spouted green and scarlet flames. Out flew a red-golden dragon – not life-size, but terribly life-like: fire came from his jaws, his eyes glared down; there was a roar, and he whizzed three times over the heads of the crowd. They all ducked, and many fell flat on their faces. The dragon passed like an express train, turned a somersault, and burst over Bywater with a deafening explosion.

'That is the signal for supper!' said Bilbo. The pain and alarm vanished at once, and the prostrate hobbits leaped to their feet. There was a splendid supper for everyone; for everyone, that is, except those invited to the special family dinner-party. This was held in the great pavilion with the tree. The invitations were limited to twelve dozen (a number also called by the hobbits one Gross, though the word was not considered proper to use of people); and the guests were selected from all the families to which Bilbo and Frodo were related, with the addition of a few special unrelated friends (such as Gandalf). Many young hobbits were included, and present by parental permission; for hobbits were easy-going with their children in the matter of sitting up late, especially when there was a chance of getting them a free meal. Bringing up young hobbits took a lot of provender.

There were many Bagginses and Boffins, and also many Tooks and Brandybucks; there were various Grubbs (relations of Bilbo Baggins' grand-mother), and various Chubbs (connexions of his Took grandfather); and a selection of Burrowses, Bolgers, Bracegirdles, Brockhouses, Goodbodies, Hornblowers and Proudfoots. Some of these were only very distantly connec-ted with Bilbo, and some of them had hardly ever been in Hobbiton before, as they lived in remote corners of the Shire. The Sackville-Bagginses were not forgotten. Otho and his wife Lobelia were present. They disliked Bilbo and detested Frodo, but so magnificent was the invitation card, written in golden ink, that they had felt it was impossible to refuse. Besides, their cousin, Bilbo, had been specializing in food for many years and his table had a high reputation.

All the one hundred and forty-four guests expected a pleasant feast; though they rather dreaded the after-dinner speech of their host (an inevitable item). He was liable to drag in bits of what he called poetry; and sometimes, after a glass or two, would allude to the absurd adventures of his mysterious journey. The guests were not disappointed: they had a *very* pleasant feast, in fact an engrossing entertainment: rich, abundant, varied, and prolonged. The pur-chase of provisions fell almost to nothing throughout the district in the ensu-ing weeks; but as Bilbo's catering had depleted the stocks of most stores, cellars and warehouses for miles around, that did not matter much.

After the feast (more or less) came the Speech. Most of the company were, however, now in a tolerant mood, at that delightful stage which they called 'filling up the corners'. They were sipping their favourite drinks, and nib-bling at their favourite dainties, and their fears were forgotten. They were prepared to listen to anything, and to cheer at every full stop.

My dear People, began Bilbo, rising in his place. 'Hear! Hear! Hear!' they shouted, and kept on repeating it in chorus, seeming reluctant to follow their own advice. Bilbo left his place and went and stood on a chair under the illuminated tree. The light of the lanterns fell on his beaming face; the golden buttons shone on his embroidered silk waistcoat. They could all see him standing, waving one hand in the air, the other was in his trouser-pocket.

My dear Bagginses and Boffins, he began again; *and my dear Tooks and Brandybucks, and Grubbs, and Chubbs, and Burrowses, and Hornblowers, and Bolgers, Bracegirdles, Goodbodies, Brockhouses and Proudfoots.* 'Proud FEET!' shouted an elderly hobbit from the back of the pavilion. His name, of course, was Proudfoot, and well merited; his feet were large, exceptionally furry, and both were on the table.

Proudfoots, repeated Bilbo. *Also my good Sackville-Bagginses that I welcome back at last to Bag End. Today is my one hundred and eleventh birthday: I am eleventy-one today!* 'Hurray! Hurray! Many Happy Returns!' they shouted, and they hammered joyously on the tables. Bilbo was doing splendidly. This was the sort of stuff they liked: short and obvious.

I hope you are all enjoying yourselves as much as I am. Deafening cheers. Cries of *Yes* (and *No*). Noises of trumpets and horns, pipes and flutes, and other musical instruments. There were, as has been said, many young hobbits present. Hundreds of musical crackers had been pulled. Most of them bore the mark DALE on them; which did not convey much to most of the hobbits, but they all agreed they were marvellous crackers. They contained instruments, small, but of perfect make and enchanting tones. Indeed, in one corner some of the young Tooks and Brandybucks, supposing Uncle Bilbo to have finished (since he had plainly said all that was necessary), now got up an impromptu orchestra, and began a merry dance-tune. Master Everard Took and Miss Melilot Brandybuck got on a table and with bells in their hands began to dance the Springle-ring: a pretty dance, but rather vigorous.

But Bilbo had not finished. Seizing a horn from a youngster near by, he blew three loud hoots. The noise subsided. *I shall not keep you long,* he cried. Cheers from all the assembly. *I have called you all together for a Purpose.* Something in the way that he said this made an impression. There was almost silence, and one or two of the Tooks pricked up their ears.

Indeed, for Three Purposes! First of all, to tell you that I am immensely fond of you all, and that eleventy-one years is too short a time to live among such excellent and admirable hobbits. Tremendous outburst of approval.

I don't know half of you half as well as I should like; and I like less than half of you half as well as you deserve. This was unexpected and rather difficult. There was some scattered clapping, but most of them were trying to work it out and see if it came to a compliment.

Secondly, to celebrate my birthday. Cheers again. *I should say: OUR birthday.* For it is, of course, also the birthday of my heir and nephew, Frodo. He comes of age and into his inheritance today.* Some perfunctory clapping by the elders; and some loud shouts of 'Frodo! Frodo! Jolly old Frodo,' from the juniors. The Sackville-Bagginses scowled, and wondered what was meant by 'coming into his inheritance'.

Together we score one hundred and forty-four. Your numbers were chosen to fit this remarkable total: One Gross, if I may use the expression. No cheers. This was ridiculous. Many of his guests, and especially the Sackville-Bagginses, were insulted, feeling sure they had only been asked to fill up the required number, like goods in a package. 'One Gross, indeed! Vulgar expression.'

It is also, if I may be allowed to refer to ancient history, the anniversary of my arrival by barrel at Esgaroth on the Long Lake; though the fact that it was my birthday slipped my memory on that occasion. I was only fifty-one then, and birthdays did not seem so important. The banquet was very splendid, however, though I had a bad cold at the time, I remember, and could only say 'thag you very buch'. I now repeat it more correctly: Thank you very much for coming to my little party. Obstinate silence. They all feared that a song or some poetry was now imminent; and they were getting bored. Why couldn't he stop talking and let them drink his health? But Bilbo did not sing or recite. He paused for a moment.

Thirdly and finally, he said, *I wish to make an ANNOUNCEMENT.* He spoke this last word so loudly and suddenly that everyone sat up who still could. *I regret to announce that – though, as I said, eleventy-one years is far too short a time to spend among you – this is the END. I am going. I am leaving NOW. GOOD-BYE!*

He stepped down and vanished. There was a blinding flash of light, and the guests all blinked. When they opened their eyes Bilbo was nowhere to be seen. One hundred and forty-four flabbergasted hobbits sat back speechless. Old Odo Proudfoot removed his feet from the table and stamped. Then there was a dead silence, until suddenly, after several deep breaths, every Baggins, Boffin, Took, Brandybuck, Grubb, Chubb, Burrows, Bolger, Bracegirdle, Brockhouse, Goodbody, Hornblower, and Proudfoot began to talk at once.

It was generally agreed that the joke was in very bad taste, and more food and drink were needed to cure the guests of shock and annoyance. 'He's mad. I always said so,' was probably the most popular comment. Even the Tooks (with a few exceptions) thought Bilbo's behaviour was absurd. For the moment most of them took it for granted that his disappearance was nothing more than a ridiculous prank.

But old Rory Brandybuck was not so sure. Neither age nor an enormous dinner had clouded his wits, and he said to his daughter-in-law, Esmeralda: 'There's something fishy in this, my dear! I believe that mad Baggins is off again. Silly old fool. But why worry? He hasn't taken the vittles with him.' He called loudly to Frodo to send the wine round again.

Frodo was the only one present who had said nothing. For some time he had sat silent beside Bilbo's empty chair, and ignored all remarks and questions. He had enjoyed the joke, of course, even though he had been in the know. He had difficulty in keeping from laughter at the indignant surprise of the guests. But at the same time he felt deeply troubled: he realized suddenly that he loved the old hobbit dearly. Most of the guests went on eating and drinking and discussing Bilbo Baggins' oddities, past and present; but the Sackville-Bagginses had already departed in wrath. Frodo did not want to have any more to do with the party. He gave orders for more wine to be served; then he got up and drained his own glass silently to the health of Bilbo, and slipped out of the pavilion.

As for Bilbo Baggins, even while he was making his speech, he had been fingering the golden ring in his pocket: his magic ring that he had kept secret for so many years. As he stepped down he slipped it on his finger, and he was never seen by any hobbit in Hobbiton again.

He walked briskly back to his hole, and stood for a moment listening with a smile to the din in the pavilion and to the sounds of merrymaking in other parts of the field. Then he went in. He took off his party clothes, folded up and wrapped in tissue-paper his embroidered silk waistcoat, and put it away. Then he put on quickly some old untidy garments, and fastened round his waist a worn leather belt. On it he hung a short sword in a battered black-leather scabbard. From a locked drawer, smelling of moth-balls, he took out an old cloak and hood. They had been locked up as if they were very precious, but they were so patched and weatherstained that their original colour could hardly be guessed: it might have been dark green. They were rather too large for him. He then went into his study, and from a large strong-box took out a bundle wrapped in old cloths, and a leather-bound manuscript; and also a large bulky envelope. The book and bundle he stuffed into the top of a heavy bag that was standing there, already nearly full. Into the envelope he slipped his golden ring, and its fine chain, and then sealed it, and addressed it to Frodo. At first he put it on the mantelpiece, but suddenly he removed it and stuck it in his pocket. At that moment the door opened and Gandalf came quickly in.

'Hullo!' said Bilbo. 'I wondered if you would turn up.'

'I am glad to find you visible,' replied the wizard, sitting down in a chair, 'I wanted to catch you and have a few final words. I suppose you feel that everything has gone off splendidly and according to plan?'

'Yes, I do,' said Bilbo. 'Though that flash was surprising: it quite startled me, let alone the others. A little addition of your own, I suppose?'

'It was. You have wisely kept that ring secret all these years, and it seemed to me necessary to give your guests something else that would seem to explain your sudden vanishment.'

'And would spoil my joke. You are an interfering old busybody,' laughed Bilbo, 'but I expect you know best, as usual.'

'I do – when I know anything. But I don't feel too sure about this whole affair. It has now come to the final point. You have had your joke, and alarmed or offended most of your relations, and given the whole Shire something to talk about for nine days, or ninety-nine more likely. Are you going any further?'

'Yes, I am. I feel I need a holiday, a very long holiday, as I have told you before. Probably a permanent holiday: I don't expect I shall return. In fact, I don't mean to, and I have made all arrangements.

'I am old, Gandalf. I don't look it, but I am beginning to feel it in my heart of hearts. *Well-preserved* indeed!' he snorted. 'Why, I feel all thin, sort of *stretched*, if you know what I mean: like butter that has been scraped over too much bread. That can't be right. I need a change, or something.'

Gandalf looked curiously and closely at him. 'No, it does not seem right,' he said thoughtfully. 'No, after all I believe your plan is probably the best.'

'Well, I've made up my mind, anyway. I want to see mountains again, Gandalf – *mountains*; and then find somewhere where I can *rest*. In peace and quiet, without a lot of relatives prying around, and a string of confounded visitors hanging on the bell. I might find somewhere where I can finish my book. I have thought of a nice ending for it: *and he lived happily ever after to the end of his days.*'

Gandalf laughed. 'I hope he will. But nobody will read the book, however it ends.'

'Oh, they may, in years to come. Frodo has read some already, as far as it has gone. You'll keep an eye on Frodo, won't you?'

'Yes, I will – two eyes, as often as I can spare them.'

'He would come with me, of course, if I asked him. In fact he offered to once, just before the party. But he does not really want to, yet. I want to see the wild country again before I die, and the Mountains; but he is still in love with the Shire, with woods and fields and little rivers. He ought to be comfortable here. I am leaving everything to him, of course, except a few oddments. I hope he will be happy, when he gets used to being on his own. It's time he was his own master now.'

'Everything?' said Gandalf. 'The ring as well? You agreed to that, you remember.'

'Well, er, yes, I suppose so,' stammered Bilbo.

'Where is it?'

'In an envelope, if you must know,' said Bilbo impatiently. 'There on the mantelpiece. Well, no! Here it is in my pocket!' He hesitated. 'Isn't that odd now?' he said softly to himself. 'Yet after all, why not? Why shouldn't it stay there?'

Gandalf looked again very hard at Bilbo, and there was a gleam in his eyes. 'I think, Bilbo,' he said quietly, 'I should leave it behind. Don't you want to?'

'Well yes – and no. Now it comes to it, I don't like parting with it at all, I may say. And I don't really see why I should. Why do you want me to?' he asked, and a curious change came over his voice. It was sharp with suspicion and annoyance. 'You are always badgering me about my ring; but you have never bothered me about the other things that I got on my journey.'

'No, but I had to badger you,' said Gandalf. 'I wanted the truth. It was important. Magic rings are – well, magical; and they are rare and curious. I was professionally interested in your ring, you may say; and I still am. I should like to know where it is, if you go wandering again. Also I think *you* have had it quite long enough. You won't need it any more, Bilbo, unless I am quite mistaken.'

Bilbo flushed, and there was an angry light in his eyes. His kindly face grew hard. 'Why not?' he cried. 'And what business is it of yours, anyway, to know what I do with my own things? It is my own. I found it. It came to me.'

'Yes, yes,' said Gandalf. 'But there is no need to get angry.'

'If I am it is your fault,' said Bilbo. 'It is mine, I tell you. My own. My precious. Yes, my precious.'

The wizard's face remained grave and attentive, and only a flicker in his deep eyes showed that he was startled and indeed alarmed. 'It has been called that before,' he said, 'but not by you.'

'But I say it now. And why not? Even if Gollum said the same once. It's not his now, but mine. And I shall keep it, I say.'

Gandalf stood up. He spoke sternly. 'You will be a fool if you do, Bilbo,' he said. 'You make that clearer with every word you say. It has got far too much hold on you. Let it go! And then you can go yourself, and be free.'

'I'll do as I choose and go as I please,' said Bilbo obstinately.

'Now, now, my dear hobbit!' said Gandalf. 'All your long life we have been friends, and you owe me something. Come! Do as you promised: give it up!'

'Well, if you want my ring yourself, say so!' cried Bilbo. 'But you won't get it. I won't give my precious away, I tell you.' His hand strayed to the hilt of his small sword.

Gandalf's eyes flashed. 'It will be my turn to get angry soon,' he said. 'If you say that again, I shall. Then you will see Gandalf the Grey uncloaked.' He took a step towards the hobbit, and he seemed to grow tall and menacing; his shadow filled the little room.

Bilbo backed away to the wall, breathing hard, his hand clutching at his pocket. They stood for a while facing one another, and the air of the room tingled. Gandalf's eyes remained bent on the hobbit. Slowly his hands relaxed, and he began to tremble.

'I don't know what has come over you, Gandalf,' he said. 'You have never been like this before. What is it all about? It is mine isn't it? I found it, and

Gollum would have killed me, if I hadn't kept it. I'm not a thief, whatever he said.'

'I have never called you one,' Gandalf answered. 'And I am not one either. I am not trying to rob you, but to help you. I wish you would trust me, as you used.' He turned away, and the shadow passed. He seemed to dwindle again to an old grey man, bent and troubled.

Bilbo drew his hand over his eyes. 'I am sorry,' he said. 'But I felt so queer. And yet it would be a relief in a way not to be bothered with it any more. It has been so growing on my mind lately. Sometimes I have felt it was like an eye looking at me. And I am always wanting to put it on and disappear, don't you know; or wondering if it is safe, and pulling it out to make sure. I tried locking it up, but I found I couldn't rest without it in my pocket. I don't know why. And I don't seem able to make up my mind.'

'Then trust mine,' said Gandalf. 'It is quite made up. Go away and leave it behind. Stop possessing it. Give it to Frodo, and I will look after him.'

Bilbo stood for a moment tense and undecided. Presently he sighed. 'All right,' he said with an effort. 'I will.' Then he shrugged his shoulders, and smiled rather ruefully. 'After all that's what this party business was all about, really: to give away lots of birthday presents, and somehow make it easier to give it away at the same time. It hasn't made it any easier in the end, but it would be a pity to waste all my preparations. It would quite spoil the joke.'

'Indeed it would take away the only point I ever saw in the affair,' said Gandalf.

'Very well,' said Bilbo, 'it goes to Frodo with all the rest.' He drew a deep breath. 'And now I really must be starting, or somebody else will catch me. I have said good-bye, and I couldn't bear to do it all over again.' He picked up his bag and moved to the door.

'You have still got the ring in your pocket,' said the wizard.

'Well, so I have!' cried Bilbo. 'And my will and all the other documents too. You had better take it and deliver it for me. That will be safest.'

'No, don't give the ring to me,' said Gandalf. 'Put it on the mantelpiece. It will be safe enough there, till Frodo comes. I shall wait for him.'

Bilbo took out the envelope, but just as he was about to set it by the clock, his hand jerked back, and the packet fell on the floor. Before he could pick it up, the wizard stooped and seized it and set it in its place. A spasm of anger passed swiftly over the hobbit's face again. Suddenly it gave way to a look of relief and a laugh.

'Well, that's that,' he said. 'Now I'm off!'

They went out into the hall. Bilbo chose his favourite stick from the stand; then he whistled. Three dwarves came out of different rooms where they had been busy.

'Is everything ready?' asked Bilbo. 'Everything packed and labelled?'

'Everything,' they answered.

'Well, let's start then!' He stepped out of the front-door.

It was a fine night, and the black sky was dotted with stars. He looked up, sniffing the air. 'What fun! What fun to be off again, off on the Road with dwarves! This is what I have really been longing for, for years! Good-bye!' he said, looking at his old home and bowing to the door. 'Good-bye, Gandalf!'

'Good-bye, for the present, Bilbo. Take care of yourself! You are old enough, and perhaps wise enough.'

'Take care! I don't care. Don't you worry about me! I am as happy now as I have ever been, and that is saying a great deal. But the time has come. I am being swept off my feet at last,' he added, and then in a low voice, as if to himself, he sang softly in the dark:

> *The Road goes ever on and on*
> *Down from the door where it began.*
> *Now far ahead the Road has gone,*
> *And I must follow, if I can,*
> *Pursuing it with eager feet,*
> *Until it joins some larger way*
> *Where many paths and errands meet.*
> *And whither then? I cannot say.*

He paused, silent for a moment. Then without another word he turned away from the lights and voices in the fields and tents, and followed by his three companions went round into his garden, and trotted down the long sloping path. He jumped over a low place in the hedge at the bottom, and took to the meadows, passing into the night like a rustle of wind in the grass.

Gandalf remained for a while staring after him into the darkness. 'Good-bye, my dear Bilbo – until our next meeting!' he said softly and went back indoors.

Frodo came in soon afterwards, and found him sitting in the dark, deep in thought. 'Has he gone?' he asked.

'Yes,' answered Gandalf, 'he has gone at last.'

'I wish – I mean, I hoped until this evening that it was only a joke,' said Frodo. 'But I knew in my heart that he really meant to go. He always used to joke about serious things. I wish I had come back sooner, just to see him off.'

'I think really he preferred slipping off quietly in the end,' said Gandalf. 'Don't be too troubled. He'll be all right – now. He left a packet for you. There it is!'

Frodo took the envelope from the mantelpiece, and glanced at it, but did not open it.

'You'll find his will and all the other documents in there, I think,' said the wizard. 'You are the master of Bag End now. And also, I fancy, you'll find a golden ring.'

'The ring!' exclaimed Frodo. 'Has he left me that? I wonder why. Still, it may be useful.'

'It may, and it may not,' said Gandalf. 'I should not make use of it, if I were you. But keep it secret, and keep it safe! Now I am going to bed.'

As master of Bag End Frodo felt it his painful duty to say good-bye to the guests. Rumours of strange events had by now spread all over the field, but Frodo would only say *no doubt everything will be cleared up in the morning*. About midnight carriages came for the important folk. One by one they rolled away, filled with full but very unsatisfied hobbits. Gardeners came by arrangement, and removed in wheel-barrows those that had inadvertently remained behind.

Night slowly passed. The sun rose. The hobbits rose rather later. Morning went on. People came and began (by orders) to clear away the pavilions and the tables and the chairs, and the spoons and knives and bottles and plates, and the lanterns, and the flowering shrubs in boxes, and the crumbs and cracker-paper, the forgotten bags and gloves and handkerchiefs, and the uneaten food (a very small item). Then a number of other people came (without orders): Bagginses, and Boffins, and Bolgers, and Tooks, and other guests that lived or were staying near. By mid-day, when even the best-fed were out and about again, there was a large crowd at Bag End, uninvited but not unexpected.

Frodo was waiting on the step, smiling, but looking rather tired and worried. He welcomed all the callers, but he had not much more to say than before. His reply to all inquiries was simply this: 'Mr. Bilbo Baggins has gone away; as far as I know, for good.' Some of the visitors he invited to come inside, as Bilbo had left 'messages' for them.

Inside in the hall there was piled a large assortment of packages and parcels and small articles of furniture. On every item there was a label tied. There were several labels of this sort:

For ADELARD TOOK, for his VERY OWN, from Bilbo; on an umbrella. Adelard had carried off many unlabelled ones.

For DORA BAGGINS in memory of a LONG correspondence, with love from Bilbo; on a large waste-paper basket. Dora was Drogo's sister and the eldest surviving female relative of Bilbo and Frodo; she was ninety-nine, and had written reams of good advice for more than half a century.

For MILO BURROWS, hoping it will be useful, from B.B.; on a gold pen and ink-bottle. Milo never answered letters.

For ANGELICA'S use, from Uncle Bilbo; on a round convex mirror. She was a young Baggins, and too obviously considered her face shapely.

For the collection of HUGO BRACEGIRDLE, from a contributor; on an (empty) book-case. Hugo was a great borrower of books, and worse than usual at returning them.

For LOBELIA SACKVILLE-BAGGINS, as a PRESENT; on a case of silver spoons. Bilbo believed that she had acquired a good many of his spoons, while he was away on his former journey. Lobelia knew that quite well. When she arrived later in the day, she took the point at once, but she also took the spoons.

This is only a small selection of the assembled presents. Bilbo's residence had got rather cluttered up with things in the course of his long life. It was a tendency of hobbit-holes to get cluttered up: for which the custom of giving so many birthday-presents was largely responsible. Not, of course, that the birthday-presents were always *new*; there were one or two old *mathoms* of forgotten uses that had circulated all around the district; but Bilbo had usually given new presents, and kept those that he received. The old hole was now being cleared a little.

Every one of the various parting gifts had labels, written out personally by Bilbo, and several had some point, or some joke. But, of course, most of the things were given where they would be wanted and welcome. The poorer hobbits, and especially those of Bagshot Row, did very well. Old Gaffer Gamgee got two sacks of potatoes, a new spade, a woollen waistcoat, and a bottle of ointment for creaking joints. Old Rory Brandybuck, in return for much hospitality, got a dozen bottles of Old Winyards: a strong red wine from the Southfarthing, and now quite mature, as it had been laid down by Bilbo's father. Rory quite forgave Bilbo, and voted him a capital fellow after the first bottle.

There was plenty of everything left for Frodo. And, of course, all the chief treasures, as well as the books, pictures, and more than enough furniture, were left in his possession. There was, however, no sign nor mention of money or jewellery: not a penny-piece or a glass bead was given away.

Frodo had a very trying time that afternoon. A false rumour that the whole household was being distributed free spread like wildfire; and before long the place was packed with people who had no business there, but could not be kept out. Labels got torn off and mixed, and quarrels broke out. Some people tried to do swaps and deals in the hall; and others tried to make off with minor items not addressed to them, or with anything that seemed unwanted or unwatched. The road to the gate was blocked with barrows and handcarts.

In the middle of the commotion the Sackville-Bagginses arrived. Frodo had retired for a while and left his friend Merry Brandybuck to keep an eye on things. When Otho loudly demanded to see Frodo, Merry bowed politely.

'He is indisposed,' he said. 'He is resting.'

'Hiding, you mean,' said Lobelia. 'Anyway we want to see him and we mean to see him. Just go and tell him so!'

Merry left them a long while in the hall, and they had time to discover their parting gift of spoons. It did not improve their tempers. Eventually they were shown into the study. Frodo was sitting at a table with a lot of papers in front of him. He looked indisposed – to see Sackville-Bagginses at any rate; and he stood up, fidgeting with something in his pocket. But he spoke quite politely.

The Sackville-Bagginses were rather offensive. They began by offering him bad bargain-prices (as between friends) for various valuable and unlabelled things. When Frodo replied that only the things specially directed by Bilbo were being given away, they said the whole affair was very fishy.

'Only one thing is clear to me,' said Otho, 'and that is that you are doing exceedingly well out of it. I insist on seeing the will.'

Otho would have been Bilbo's heir, but for the adoption of Frodo. He read the will carefully and snorted. It was, unfortunately, very clear and correct (according to the legal customs of hobbits, which demand among other things seven signatures of witnesses in red ink).

'Foiled again!' he said to his wife. 'And after waiting *sixty* years. Spoons? Fiddlesticks!' He snapped his fingers under Frodo's nose and stumped off. But Lobelia was not so easily got rid of. A little later Frodo came out of the study to see how things were going on and found her still about the place, investigating nooks and corners and tapping the floors. He escorted her firmly off the premises, after he had relieved her of several small (but rather valuable) articles that had somehow fallen inside her umbrella. Her face looked as if she was in the throes of thinking out a really crushing parting remark; but all she found to say, turning round on the step, was:

'You'll live to regret it, young fellow! Why didn't you go too? You don't belong here; you're no Baggins – you – you're a Brandybuck!'

'Did you hear that, Merry? That was an insult, if you like,' said Frodo as he shut the door on her.

'It was a compliment,' said Merry Brandybuck, 'and so, of course, not true.'

Then they went round the hole, and evicted three young hobbits (two Boffins and a Bolger) who were knocking holes in the walls of one of the cellars. Frodo also had a tussle with young Sancho Proudfoot (old Odo Proudfoot's grandson), who had begun an excavation in the larger pantry, where he thought there was an echo. The legend of Bilbo's gold excited both curiosity and hope; for legendary gold (mysteriously obtained, if not positively ill-gotten), is, as every one knows, any one's for the finding – unless the search is interrupted.

When he had overcome Sancho and pushed him out, Frodo collapsed on a chair in the hall. 'It's time to close the shop, Merry,' he said. 'Lock the door, and don't open it to anyone today, not even if they bring a battering ram.' Then he went to revive himself with a belated cup of tea.

He had hardly sat down, when there came a soft knock at the front-door. 'Lobelia again most likely,' he thought. 'She must have thought of something really nasty, and have come back again to say it. It can wait.'

He went on with his tea. The knock was repeated, much louder, but he took no notice. Suddenly the wizard's head appeared at the window.

'If you don't let me in, Frodo, I shall blow your door right down your hole and out through the hill,' he said.

'My dear Gandalf! Half a minute!' cried Frodo, running out of the room to the door. 'Come in! Come in! I thought it was Lobelia.'

'Then I forgive you. But I saw her some time ago, driving a pony-trap towards Bywater with a face that would have curdled new milk.'

'She had already nearly curdled me. Honestly, I nearly tried on Bilbo's ring. I longed to disappear.'

'Don't do that!' said Gandalf, sitting down. 'Do be careful of that ring, Frodo! In fact, it is partly about that that I have come to say a last word.'

'Well, what about it?'

'What do you know already?'

'Only what Bilbo told me. I have heard his story: how he found it, and how he used it: on his journey, I mean.'

'Which story, I wonder,' said Gandalf.

'Oh, not what he told the dwarves and put in his book,' said Frodo. 'He told me the true story soon after I came to live here. He said you had pestered him till he told you, so I had better know too. "No secrets between us, Frodo," he said; "but they are not to go any further. It's mine anyway."'

'That's interesting,' said Gandalf. 'Well, what did you think of it all?'

'If you mean, inventing all that about a "present", well, I thought the true story much more likely, and I couldn't see the point of altering it at all. It was very unlike Bilbo to do so, anyway; and I thought it rather odd.'

'So did I. But odd things may happen to people that have such treasures

– if they use them. Let it be a warning to you to be very careful with it. It may have other powers than just making you vanish when you wish to.'

'I don't understand,' said Frodo.

'Neither do I,' answered the wizard. 'I have merely begun to wonder about the ring, especially since last night. No need to worry. But if you take my advice you will use it very seldom, or not at all. At least I beg you not to use it in any way that will cause talk or rouse suspicion. I say again: keep it safe, and keep it secret!'

'You are very mysterious! What are you afraid of?'

'I am not certain, so I will say no more. I may be able to tell you something when I come back. I am going off at once: so this is good-bye for the present.' He got up.

'At once!' cried Frodo. 'Why, I thought you were staying on for at least a week. I was looking forward to your help.'

'I did mean to – but I have had to change my mind. I may be away for a good while; but I'll come and see you again, as soon as I can. Expect me when you see me! I shall slip in quietly. I shan't often be visiting the Shire openly again. I find that I have become rather unpopular. They say I am a nuisance and a disturber of the peace. Some people are actually accusing me of spiriting Bilbo away, or worse. If you want to know, there is supposed to be a plot between you and me to get hold of his wealth.'

'Some people!' exclaimed Frodo. 'You mean Otho and Lobelia. How abominable! I would give them Bag End and everything else, if I could get Bilbo back and go off tramping in the country with him. I love the Shire. But I begin to wish, somehow, that I had gone too. I wonder if I shall ever see him again.'

'So do I,' said Gandalf. 'And I wonder many other things. Good-bye now! Take care of yourself! Look out for me, especially at unlikely times! Good-bye!'

Frodo saw him to the door. He gave a final wave of his hand, and walked off at a surprising pace; but Frodo thought the old wizard looked unusually bent, almost as if he was carrying a great weight. The evening was closing in, and his cloaked figure quickly vanished into the twilight. Frodo did not see him again for a long time.

CHAPTER II

THE SHADOW OF THE PAST

The talk did not die down in nine or even ninety-nine days. The second disappearance of Mr. Bilbo Baggins was discussed in Hobbiton, and indeed all over the Shire, for a year and a day, and was remembered much longer than that. It became a fireside-story for young hobbits; and eventually Mad Baggins, who used to vanish with a bang and a flash and reappear with bags of jewels and gold, became a favourite character of legend and lived on long after all the true events were forgotten.

But in the meantime, the general opinion in the neighbourhood was that Bilbo, who had always been rather cracked, had at last gone quite mad, and had run off into the Blue. There he had undoubtedly fallen into a pool or a river and come to a tragic, but hardly an untimely, end. The blame was mostly laid on Gandalf.

'If only that dratted wizard will leave young Frodo alone, perhaps he'll settle down and grow some hobbit-sense,' they said. And to all appearance the wizard did leave Frodo alone, and he did settle down, but the growth of hobbit-sense was not very noticeable. Indeed, he at once began to carry on Bilbo's reputation for oddity. He refused to go into mourning; and the next year he gave a party in honour of Bilbo's hundred-and-twelfth birthday, which he called Hundred-weight Feast. But that was short of the mark, for twenty guests were invited and there were several meals at which it snowed food and rained drink, as hobbits say.

Some people were rather shocked; but Frodo kept up the custom of giving Bilbo's Birthday Party year after year until they got used to it. He said that he did not think Bilbo was dead. When they asked: 'Where is he then?' he shrugged his shoulders.

He lived alone, as Bilbo had done; but he had a good many friends, especially among the younger hobbits (mostly descendants of the Old Took) who had as children been fond of Bilbo and often in and out of Bag End. Folco Boffin and Fredegar Bolger were two of these; but his closest friends were Peregrin Took (usually called Pippin), and Merry Brandybuck (his real name was Meriadoc, but that was seldom remembered). Frodo went tramping all over the Shire with them; but more often he wandered by himself, and to the amazement of sensible folk he was sometimes seen far from home walking in the hills and woods under the starlight. Merry and Pippin suspected that he visited the Elves at times, as Bilbo had done.

As time went on, people began to notice that Frodo also showed signs of good 'preservation': outwardly he retained the appearance of a robust and energetic hobbit just out of his tweens. 'Some folk have all the luck,' they said; but it was not until Frodo approached the usually more sober age of fifty that they began to think it queer.

Frodo himself, after the first shock, found that being his own master and *the* Mr. Baggins of Bag End was rather pleasant. For some years he was quite happy and did not worry much about the future. But half unknown to himself the regret that he had not gone with Bilbo was steadily growing. He found himself wondering at times, especially in the autumn, about the wild lands, and strange visions of mountains that he had never seen came into his dreams. He began to say to himself: 'Perhaps I shall cross the River myself one day.' To which the other half of his mind always replied: 'Not yet.'

So it went on, until his forties were running out, and his fiftieth birthday was drawing near: fifty was a number that he felt was somehow significant (or ominous); it was at any rate at that age that adventure had suddenly befallen Bilbo. Frodo began to feel restless, and the old paths seemed too well-trodden. He looked at maps, and wondered what lay beyond their edges: maps made in the Shire showed mostly white spaces beyond its borders. He took to wandering further afield and more often by himself; and Merry and his other friends watched him anxiously. Often he was seen walking and talking with the strange wayfarers that began at this time to appear in the Shire.

There were rumours of strange things happening in the world outside; and as Gandalf had not at that time appeared or sent any message for several years, Frodo gathered all the news he could. Elves, who seldom walked in the Shire, could now be seen passing westward through the woods in the evening, passing and not returning; but they were leaving Middle-earth and were no longer concerned with its troubles. There were, however, dwarves on the road in unusual numbers. The ancient East–West Road ran through the Shire to its end at the Grey Havens, and dwarves had always used it on their way to their mines in the Blue Mountains. They were the hobbits' chief source of news from distant parts – if they wanted any: as a rule dwarves said little and hobbits asked no more. But now Frodo often met strange dwarves of far countries, seeking refuge in the West. They were troubled, and some spoke in whispers of the Enemy and of the Land of Mordor.

That name the hobbits only knew in legends of the dark past, like a shadow in the background of their memories; but it was ominous and disquieting. It seemed that the evil power in Mirkwood had been driven out by the White Council only to reappear in greater strength in the old strongholds of Mordor. The Dark Tower had been rebuilt, it was said. From there the power was spreading far and wide, and away far east and south there were wars and growing fear. Orcs were multiplying again in the mountains. Trolls were abroad, no longer dull-witted, but cunning and armed with dreadful weapons. And there were murmured hints of creatures more terrible than all these, but they had no name.

Little of all this, of course, reached the ears of ordinary hobbits. But even the deafest and most stay-at-home began to hear queer tales; and those whose business took them to the borders saw strange things. The conversation in *The Green Dragon* at Bywater, one evening in the spring of Frodo's fiftieth year, showed that even in the comfortable heart of the Shire rumours had been heard, though most hobbits still laughed at them.

Sam Gamgee was sitting in one corner near the fire, and opposite him was Ted Sandyman, the miller's son; and there were various other rustic hobbits listening to their talk.

'Queer things you do hear these days, to be sure,' said Sam.

'Ah,' said Ted, 'you do, if you listen. But I can hear fireside-tales and children's stories at home, if I want to.'

'No doubt you can,' retorted Sam, 'and I daresay there's more truth in some of them than you reckon. Who invented the stories anyway? Take dragons now.'

'No thank 'ee,' said Ted, 'I won't. I heard tell of them when I was a youngster, but there's no call to believe in them now. There's only one Dragon in Bywater, and that's Green,' he said, getting a general laugh.

'All right,' said Sam, laughing with the rest. 'But what about these Tree-men, these giants, as you might call them? They do say that one bigger than a tree was seen up away beyond the North Moors not long back.'

'Who's *they*?'

'My cousin Hal for one. He works for Mr. Boffin at Overhill and goes up to the Northfarthing for the hunting. He *saw* one.'

'Says he did, perhaps. Your Hal's always saying he's seen things; and maybe he sees things that ain't there.'

'But this one was as big as an elm tree, and walking – walking seven yards to a stride, if it was an inch.'

'Then I bet it wasn't an inch. What he saw *was* an elm tree, as like as not.'

'But this one was *walking*, I tell you; and there ain't no elm tree on the North Moors.'

'Then Hal can't have seen one,' said Ted. There was some laughing and clapping: the audience seemed to think that Ted had scored a point.

'All the same,' said Sam, 'you can't deny that others besides our Halfast have seen queer folk crossing the Shire – crossing it, mind you: there are more that are turned back at the borders. The Bounders have never been so busy before.

'And I've heard tell that Elves are moving west. They do say they are going to the harbours, out away beyond the White Towers.' Sam waved his arm vaguely: neither he nor any of them knew how far it was to the Sea, past the old towers beyond the western borders of the Shire. But it was an old tradition that away over there stood the Grey Havens, from which at times elven-ships set sail, never to return.

'They are sailing, sailing, sailing over the Sea, they are going into the West and leaving us,' said Sam, half chanting the words, shaking his head sadly and solemnly. But Ted laughed.

'Well, that isn't anything new, if you believe the old tales. And I don't see what it matters to me or you. Let them sail! But I warrant you haven't seen them doing it; nor any one else in the Shire.'

'Well I don't know,' said Sam thoughtfully. He believed he had once seen an Elf in the woods, and still hoped to see more one day. Of all the legends that he had heard in his early years such fragments of tales and half-remembered stories about the Elves as the hobbits knew, had always moved him most deeply. 'There are some, even in these parts, as know the Fair Folk and get news of them,' he said. 'There's Mr. Baggins now, that I work for. He told me that they were sailing and he knows a bit about Elves. And old Mr. Bilbo knew more: many's the talk I had with him when I was a little lad.'

'Oh, they're both cracked,' said Ted. 'Leastways old Bilbo was cracked, and Frodo's cracking. If that's where you get your news from, you'll never want for moonshine. Well, friends, I'm off home. Your good health!' He drained his mug and went out noisily.

Sam sat silent and said no more. He had a good deal to think about. For one thing, there was a lot to do up in the Bag End garden, and he would have a busy day tomorrow, if the weather cleared. The grass was growing fast. But Sam had more on his mind than gardening. After a while he sighed, and got up and went out.

It was early April and the sky was now clearing after heavy rain. The sun was down, and a cool pale evening was quietly fading into night. He walked home under the early stars through Hobbiton and up the Hill, whistling softly and thoughtfully.

It was just at this time that Gandalf reappeared after his long absence. For three years after the Party he had been away. Then he paid Frodo a brief visit, and after taking a good look at him he went off again. During the next year or two he had turned up fairly often, coming unexpectedly after dusk, and going off without warning before sunrise. He would not discuss his own business and journeys, and seemed chiefly interested in small news about Frodo's health and doings.

Then suddenly his visits had ceased. It was over nine years since Frodo had seen or heard of him, and he had begun to think that the wizard would never return and had given up all interest in hobbits. But that evening, as Sam was walking home and twilight was fading, there came the once familiar tap on the study window.

Frodo welcomed his old friend with surprise and great delight. They looked hard at one another.

'Ah well eh?' said Gandalf. 'You look the same as ever, Frodo!'

'So do you,' Frodo replied; but secretly he thought that Gandalf looked older and more careworn. He pressed him for news of himself and of the wide world, and soon they were deep in talk, and they stayed up far into the night.

Next morning after a late breakfast, the wizard was sitting with Frodo by the open window of the study. A bright fire was on the hearth, but the sun was warm, and the wind was in the South. Everything looked fresh, and the new green of Spring was shimmering in the fields and on the tips of the trees' fingers.

Gandalf was thinking of a spring, nearly eighty years before, when Bilbo had run out of Bag End without a handkerchief. His hair was perhaps whiter than it had been then, and his beard and eyebrows were perhaps longer, and his face more lined with care and wisdom; but his eyes were as bright as ever, and he smoked and blew smoke-rings with the same vigour and delight.

He was smoking now in silence, for Frodo was sitting still, deep in thought. Even in the light of morning he felt the dark shadow of the tidings that Gandalf had brought. At last he broke the silence.

'Last night you began to tell me strange things about my ring, Gandalf,' he said. 'And then you stopped, because you said that such matters were best left until daylight. Don't you think you had better finish now? You say the ring is dangerous, far more dangerous than I guess. In what way?'

'In many ways,' answered the wizard. 'It is far more powerful than I ever dared to think at first, so powerful that in the end it would utterly overcome anyone of mortal race who possessed it. It would possess him.

'In Eregion long ago many Elven-rings were made, magic rings as you call them, and they were, of course, of various kinds: some more potent and some less. The lesser rings were only essays in the craft before it was full-grown, and to the Elven-smiths they were but trifles – yet still to my mind dangerous for mortals. But the Great Rings, the Rings of Power, they were perilous.

'A mortal, Frodo, who keeps one of the Great Rings, does not die, but he does not grow or obtain more life, he merely continues, until at last every minute is a weariness. And if he often uses the Ring to make himself invisible, he *fades*: he becomes in the end invisible permanently, and walks in the twilight under the eye of the dark power that rules the Rings. Yes, sooner or later – later, if he is strong or well-meaning to begin with, but neither strength nor good purpose will last – sooner or later the dark power will devour him.'

'How terrifying!' said Frodo. There was another long silence. The sound of Sam Gamgee cutting the lawn came in from the garden.

'How long have you known this?' asked Frodo at length. 'And how much did Bilbo know?'

'Bilbo knew no more than he told you, I am sure,' said Gandalf. 'He would certainly never have passed on to you anything that he thought would be a danger, even though I promised to look after you. He thought the ring was very beautiful, and very useful at need; and if anything was wrong or queer, it was himself. He said that it was "growing on his mind", and he was always worrying about it; but he did not suspect that the ring itself was to blame. Though he had found out that the thing needed looking after; it did not seem always of the same size or weight; it shrank or expanded in an odd way, and might suddenly slip off a finger where it had been tight.'

'Yes, he warned me of that in his last letter,' said Frodo, 'so I have always kept it on its chain.'

'Very wise,' said Gandalf. 'But as for his long life, Bilbo never connected it with the ring at all. He took all the credit for that to himself, and he was very proud of it. Though he was getting restless and uneasy. *Thin and stretched* he said. A sign that the ring was getting control.'

'How long have you known all this?' asked Frodo again.

'Known?' said Gandalf. 'I have known much that only the Wise know, Frodo. But if you mean "known about *this* ring", well, I still do not *know*, one might say. There is a last test to make. But I no longer doubt my guess.

'When did I first begin to guess?' he mused, searching back in memory. 'Let me see – it was in the year that the White Council drove the dark power from Mirkwood, just before the Battle of Five Armies, that Bilbo found his ring. A shadow fell on my heart then, though I did not know yet what I feared. I wondered often how Gollum came by a Great Ring, as plainly it was – that at least was clear from the first. Then I heard Bilbo's strange story of how he had "won" it, and I could not believe it. When I at last got the truth out of him, I saw at once that he had been trying to put his claim to the ring beyond doubt. Much like Gollum with his "birthday present". The lies were too much alike for my comfort. Clearly the ring had an unwholesome power that set to work on its keeper at once. That was the first real warning I had that all was not well. I told Bilbo often that such rings were better left unused; but he resented it, and soon got angry. There was little else that I could do. I could not take it from him without doing greater harm; and I had no right to do so anyway. I could only watch and wait. I might perhaps have consulted Saruman the White, but something always held me back.'

'Who is he?' asked Frodo. 'I have never heard of him before.'

'Maybe not,' answered Gandalf. 'Hobbits are, or were, no concern of his. Yet he is great among the Wise. He is the chief of my order and the head of the Council. His knowledge is deep, but his pride has grown with it, and he takes ill any meddling. The lore of the Elven-rings, great and small, is his province. He has long studied it, seeking the lost secrets of their making; but when the Rings were debated in the Council, all that he would reveal to us of his ring-lore told against my fears. So my doubt slept – but uneasily. Still I watched and I waited.

'And all seemed well with Bilbo. And the years passed. Yes, they passed, and they seemed not to touch him. He showed no signs of age. The shadow fell on me again. But I said to myself: "After all he comes of a long-lived family on his mother's side. There is time yet. Wait!"

'And I waited. Until that night when he left this house. He said and did things then that filled me with a fear that no words of Saruman could allay. I knew at last that something dark and deadly was at work. And I have spent most of the years since then in finding out the truth of it.'

'There wasn't any permanent harm done, was there?' asked Frodo anxiously. 'He would get all right in time, wouldn't he? Be able to rest in peace, I mean?'

'He felt better at once,' said Gandalf. 'But there is only one Power in this world that knows all about the Rings and their effects; and as far as I know there is no Power in the world that knows all about hobbits. Among the Wise I am the only one that goes in for hobbit-lore: an obscure branch of knowledge, but full of surprises. Soft as butter they can be, and yet sometimes as tough as old tree-roots. I think it likely that some would resist the Rings far longer than most of the Wise would believe. I don't think you need worry about Bilbo.

'Of course, he possessed the ring for many years, and used it, so it might take a long while for the influence to wear off – before it was safe for him to see it again, for instance. Otherwise, he might live on for years, quite happily: just stop as he was when he parted with it. For he gave it up in the end of his own accord: an important point. No, I was not troubled about dear Bilbo any more, once he had let the thing go. It is for *you* that I feel responsible.

'Ever since Bilbo left I have been deeply concerned about you, and about all these charming, absurd, helpless hobbits. It would be a grievous blow to the world, if the Dark Power overcame the Shire; if all your kind, jolly, stupid Bolgers, Hornblowers, Boffins, Bracegirdles, and the rest, not to mention the ridiculous Bagginses, became enslaved.'

Frodo shuddered. 'But why should we be?' he asked. 'And why should he want such slaves?'

'To tell you the truth,' replied Gandalf, 'I believe that hitherto – *hitherto*, mark you – he has entirely overlooked the existence of hobbits. You should be thankful. But your safety has passed. He does not need you – he has many more useful servants – but he won't forget you again. And hobbits as miserable slaves would please him far more than hobbits happy and free. There is such a thing as malice and revenge.'

'Revenge?' said Frodo. 'Revenge for what? I still don't understand what all this has to do with Bilbo and myself, and our ring.'

'It has everything to do with it,' said Gandalf. 'You do not know the real peril yet; but you shall. I was not sure of it myself when I was last here; but the time has come to speak. Give me the ring for a moment.'

Frodo took it from his breeches-pocket, where it was clasped to a chain that hung from his belt. He unfastened it and handed it slowly to the wizard. It felt suddenly very heavy, as if either it or Frodo himself was in some way reluctant for Gandalf to touch it.

Gandalf held it up. It looked to be made of pure and solid gold. 'Can you see any markings on it?' he asked.

'No,' said Frodo. 'There are none. It is quite plain, and it never shows a scratch or sign of wear.'

'Well then, look!' To Frodo's astonishment and distress the wizard threw it suddenly into the middle of a glowing corner of the fire. Frodo gave a cry and groped for the tongs; but Gandalf held him back.

'Wait!' he said in a commanding voice, giving Frodo a quick look from under his bristling brows.

No apparent change came over the ring. After a while Gandalf got up, closed the shutters outside the window, and drew the curtains. The room became dark and silent, though the clack of Sam's shears, now nearer to the windows, could still be heard faintly from the garden. For a moment the wizard stood looking at the fire; then he stooped and removed the ring to the hearth with the tongs, and at once picked it up. Frodo gasped.

'It is quite cool,' said Gandalf. 'Take it!' Frodo received it on his shrinking palm: it seemed to have become thicker and heavier than ever.

'Hold it up!' said Gandalf. 'And look closely!'

As Frodo did so, he now saw fine lines, finer than the finest pen-strokes, running along the ring, outside and inside: lines of fire that seemed to form the letters of a flowing script. They shone piercingly bright, and yet remote, as if out of a great depth.

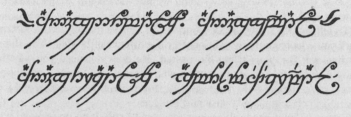

'I cannot read the fiery letters,' said Frodo in a quavering voice.

'No,' said Gandalf, 'but I can. The letters are Elvish, of an ancient mode, but the language is that of Mordor, which I will not utter here. But this in the Common Tongue is what is said, close enough:

> *One Ring to rule them all, One Ring to find them,*
> *One Ring to bring them all and in the darkness bind them.*

It is only two lines of a verse long known in Elven-lore:

> *Three Rings for the Elven-kings under the sky,*
>   *Seven for the Dwarf-lords in their halls of stone,*
> *Nine for Mortal Men doomed to die,*
>   *One for the Dark Lord on his dark throne*
> *In the Land of Mordor where the Shadows lie.*
>   *One Ring to rule them all, One Ring to find them,*
>   *One Ring to bring them all and in the darkness bind them*
> *In the Land of Mordor where the Shadows lie.'*

He paused, and then said slowly in a deep voice: 'This is the Master-ring, the One Ring to rule them all. This is the One Ring that he lost many ages ago, to the great weakening of his power. He greatly desires it – but he must *not* get it.'

Frodo sat silent and motionless. Fear seemed to stretch out a vast hand, like a dark cloud rising in the East and looming up to engulf him. 'This ring!' he stammered. 'How, how on earth did it come to me?'

'Ah!' said Gandalf. 'That is a very long story. The beginnings lie back in the Black Years, which only the lore-masters now remember. If I were to tell you all that tale, we should still be sitting here when Spring had passed into Winter.

'But last night I told you of Sauron the Great, the Dark Lord. The rumours that you have heard are true: he has indeed arisen again and left his hold in Mirkwood and returned to his ancient fastness in the Dark Tower of Mordor. That name even you hobbits have heard of, like a shadow on the borders of old stories. Always after a defeat and a respite, the Shadow takes another shape and grows again.'

'I wish it need not have happened in my time,' said Frodo.

'So do I,' said Gandalf, 'and so do all who live to see such times. But that is not for them to decide. All we have to decide is what to do with the time that is given us. And already, Frodo, our time is beginning to look black. The Enemy is fast becoming very strong. His plans are far from ripe, I think, but they are ripening. We shall be hard put to it. We should be very hard put to it, even if it were not for this dreadful chance.

'The Enemy still lacks one thing to give him strength and knowledge to beat down all resistance, break the last defences, and cover all the lands in a second darkness. He lacks the One Ring.

'The Three, fairest of all, the Elf-lords hid from him, and his hand never touched them or sullied them. Seven the Dwarf-kings possessed, but three he has recovered, and the others the dragons have consumed. Nine he gave to Mortal Men, proud and great, and so ensnared them. Long ago they fell under the dominion of the One, and they became Ringwraiths, shadows under his great Shadow, his most terrible servants. Long ago. It is many a year since the Nine walked abroad. Yet who knows? As the Shadow grows once more, they too may walk again. But come! We will not speak of such things even in the morning of the Shire.

'So it is now: the Nine he has gathered to himself; the Seven also, or else they are destroyed. The Three are hidden still. But that no longer troubles him. He only needs the One; for he made that Ring himself, it is his, and he let a great part of his own former power pass into it, so that he could rule all the others. If he recovers it, then he will command them all again, wherever they be, even the Three, and all that has been wrought with them will be laid bare, and he will be stronger than ever.

'And this is the dreadful chance, Frodo. He believed that the One had perished; that the Elves had destroyed it, as should have been done. But he knows now that it has *not* perished, that it has been found. So he is seeking it, seeking it, and all his thought is bent on it. It is his great hope and our great fear.'

'Why, why wasn't it destroyed?' cried Frodo. 'And how did the Enemy ever come to lose it, if he was so strong, and it was so precious to him?' He clutched the Ring in his hand, as if he saw already dark fingers stretching out to seize it.

'It was taken from him,' said Gandalf. 'The strength of the Elves to resist him was greater long ago; and not all Men were estranged from them. The Men of Westernesse came to their aid. That is a chapter of ancient history which it might be good to recall; for there was sorrow then too, and gathering dark, but great valour, and great deeds that were not wholly vain. One day, perhaps, I will tell you all the tale, or you shall hear it told in full by one who knows it best.

'But for the moment, since most of all you need to know how this thing came to you, and that will be tale enough, this is all that I will say. It was Gil-galad, Elven-king and Elendil of Westernesse who overthrew Sauron, though they themselves perished in the deed; and Isildur Elendil's son cut the Ring from Sauron's hand and took it for his own. Then Sauron was vanquished and his spirit fled and was hidden for long years, until his shadow took shape again in Mirkwood.

'But the Ring was lost. It fell into the Great River, Anduin, and vanished. For Isildur was marching north along the east banks of the River, and near the Gladden Fields he was waylaid by the Orcs of the Mountains, and almost all his folk were slain. He leaped into the waters, but the Ring slipped from his finger as he swam, and then the Orcs saw him and killed him with arrows.'

Gandalf paused. 'And there in the dark pools amid the Gladden Fields,' he said, 'the Ring passed out of knowledge and legend; and even so much of its history is known now only to a few, and the Council of the Wise could discover no more. But at last I can carry on the story, I think.

'Long after, but still very long ago, there lived by the banks of the Great River on the edge of Wilderland a clever-handed and quiet-footed little people. I guess they were of hobbit-kind; akin to the fathers of the fathers of the Stoors, for they loved the River, and often swam in it, or made little boats of reeds. There was among them a family of high repute, for it was large and wealthier than most, and it was ruled by a grandmother of the folk, stern and wise in old lore, such as they had. The most inquisitive and curious-minded of that family was called Sméagol. He was interested in roots and beginnings; he dived into deep pools; he burrowed under trees and growing plants; he tunnelled into green mounds; and he ceased to look up at the hill-tops, or the leaves on trees, or the flowers opening in the air: his head and his eyes were downward.

'He had a friend called Déagol, of similar sort, sharper-eyed but not so quick and strong. On a time they took a boat and went down to the Gladden Fields, where there were great beds of iris and flowering reeds. There Sméagol got out and went nosing about the banks but Déagol sat in the boat and fished. Suddenly a great fish took his hook, and before he knew where he was, he was dragged out and down into the water, to the bottom. Then he let go of his line, for he thought he saw something shining in the river-bed; and holding his breath he grabbed at it.

'Then up he came spluttering, with weeds in his hair and a handful of mud; and he swam to the bank. And behold! when he washed the mud away, there in his hand lay a beautiful golden ring; and it shone and glittered in the sun, so that his heart was glad. But Sméagol had been watching him from behind a tree, and as Déagol gloated over the ring, Sméagol came softly up behind.

'"Give us that, Déagol, my love," said Sméagol, over his friend's shoulder.

'"Why?" said Déagol.

'"Because it's my birthday, my love, and I wants it," said Sméagol.

'"I don't care," said Déagol. "I have given you a present already, more than I could afford. I found this, and I'm going to keep it."

'"Oh, are you indeed, my love," said Sméagol; and he caught Déagol by the throat and strangled him, because the gold looked so bright and beautiful. Then he put the ring on his finger.

'No one ever found out what had become of Déagol; he was murdered far from home, and his body was cunningly hidden. But Sméagol returned alone; and he found that none of his family could see him, when he was wearing the ring. He was very pleased with his discovery and he concealed it; and he used it to find out secrets, and he put his knowledge to crooked and malicious uses. He became sharp-eyed and keen-eared for all that was hurtful. The ring had given him power according to his stature. It is not to be wondered at that he became very unpopular and was shunned (when visible) by all his relations. They kicked him, and he bit their feet. He took to thieving, and going about muttering to himself, and gurgling in his throat. So they called him *Gollum*, and cursed him, and told him to go far away; and his grandmother, desiring peace, expelled him from the family and turned him out of her hole.

'He wandered in loneliness, weeping a little for the hardness of the world, and he journeyed up the River, till he came to a stream that flowed down from the mountains, and he went that way. He caught fish in deep pools with invisible fingers and ate them raw. One day it was very hot, and as he was bending over a pool, he felt a burning on the back of his head, and a dazzling light from the water pained his wet eyes. He wondered at it, for he had almost forgotten about the Sun. Then for the last time he looked up and shook his fist at her.

'But as he lowered his eyes, he saw far above the tops of the Misty Mountains, out of which the stream came. And he thought suddenly: "It would be cool and shady under those mountains. The Sun could not watch me there. The roots of those mountains must be roots indeed; there must be great secrets buried there which have not been discovered since the beginning."

'So he journeyed by night up into the highlands, and he found a little cave out of which the dark stream ran; and he wormed his way like a maggot into the heart of the hills, and vanished out of all knowledge. The Ring went into the shadows with him, and even the maker, when his power had begun to grow again, could learn nothing of it.'

'Gollum!' cried Frodo. 'Gollum? Do you mean that this is the very Gollum-creature that Bilbo met? How loathsome!'

'I think it is a sad story,' said the wizard, 'and it might have happened to others, even to some hobbits that I have known.'

'I can't believe that Gollum was connected with hobbits, however distantly,' said Frodo with some heat. 'What an abominable notion!'

'It is true all the same,' replied Gandalf. 'About their origins, at any rate, I know more than hobbits do themselves. And even Bilbo's story suggests the kinship. There was a great deal in the background of their minds and memories that was very similar. They understood one another remarkably well, very much better than a hobbit would understand, say, a Dwarf, or an Orc, or even an Elf. Think of the riddles they both knew, for one thing.'

'Yes,' said Frodo. 'Though other folks besides hobbits ask riddles, and of much the same sort. And hobbits don't cheat. Gollum meant to cheat all the time. He was just trying to put poor Bilbo off his guard. And I daresay it amused his wickedness to start a game which might end in providing him with an easy victim, but if he lost would not hurt him.'

'Only too true, I fear,' said Gandalf. 'But there was something else in it, I think, which you don't see yet. Even Gollum was not wholly ruined. He had proved tougher than even one of the Wise would have guessed – as a hobbit might. There was a little corner of his mind that was still his own, and light came through it, as through a chink in the dark: light out of the past. It was actually pleasant, I think, to hear a kindly voice again, bringing up memories of wind, and trees, and sun on the grass, and such forgotten things.

'But that, of course, would only make the evil part of him angrier in the end – unless it could be conquered. Unless it could be cured.' Gandalf sighed. 'Alas! there is little hope of that for him. Yet not no hope. No, not though he possessed the Ring so long, almost as far back as he can remember. For it was long since he had worn it much: in the black darkness it was seldom needed. Certainly he had never "faded". He is thin and tough still. But the thing was eating up his mind, of course, and the torment had become almost unbearable.

'All the "great secrets" under the mountains had turned out to be just empty night: there was nothing more to find out, nothing worth doing, only nasty furtive eating and resentful remembering. He was altogether wretched. He hated the dark, and he hated light more: he hated everything, and the Ring most of all.'

'What do you mean?' said Frodo. 'Surely the Ring was his precious and the only thing he cared for? But if he hated it, why didn't he get rid of it, or go away and leave it?'

'You ought to begin to understand, Frodo, after all you have heard,' said Gandalf. 'He hated it and loved it, as he hated and loved himself. He could not get rid of it. He had no will left in the matter.

'A Ring of Power looks after itself, Frodo. *It* may slip off treacherously, but its keeper never abandons it. At most he plays with the idea of handing it on to someone else's care – and that only at an early stage, when it first begins to grip. But as far as I know Bilbo alone in history has ever gone beyond playing, and really done it. He needed all my help, too. And even so he would never have just forsaken it, or cast it aside. It was not Gollum, Frodo, but the Ring itself that decided things. The Ring left *him*.'

'What, just in time to meet Bilbo?' said Frodo. 'Wouldn't an Orc have suited it better?'

'It is no laughing matter,' said Gandalf. 'Not for you. It was the strangest event in the whole history of the Ring so far: Bilbo's arrival just at that time, and putting his hand on it, blindly, in the dark.

'There was more than one power at work, Frodo. The Ring was trying to get back to its master. It had slipped from Isildur's hand and betrayed him; then when a chance came it caught poor Déagol, and he was murdered; and after that Gollum, and it had devoured him. It could make no further use of him: he was too small and mean; and as long as it stayed with him he would never leave his deep pool again. So now, when its master was awake once more and sending out his dark thought from Mirkwood, it abandoned Gollum. Only to be picked up by the most unlikely person imaginable: Bilbo from the Shire!

'Behind that there was something else at work, beyond any design of the Ring-maker. I can put it no plainer than by saying that Bilbo was *meant* to find the Ring, and *not* by its maker. In which case you also were *meant* to have it. And that may be an encouraging thought.'

'It is not,' said Frodo. 'Though I am not sure that I understand you. But how have you learned all this about the Ring, and about Gollum? Do you really know it all, or are you just guessing still?'

Gandalf looked at Frodo, and his eyes glinted. 'I knew much and I have learned much,' he answered. 'But I am not going to give an account of all my doings to *you*. The history of Elendil and Isildur and the One Ring is known to all the Wise. Your ring is shown to be that One Ring by the fire-writing alone, apart from any other evidence.'

'And when did you discover that?' asked Frodo, interrupting.

'Just now in this room, of course,' answered the wizard sharply. 'But I expected to find it. I have come back from dark journeys and long search to make that final test. It is the last proof, and all is now only too clear. Making out Gollum's part, and fitting it into the gap in the history, required some thought. I may have started with guesses about Gollum, but I am not guessing now. I know. I have seen him.'

'You have seen Gollum?' exclaimed Frodo in amazement.

'Yes. The obvious thing to do, of course, if one could. I tried long ago; but I have managed it at last.'

'Then what happened after Bilbo escaped from him? Do you know that?'

'Not so clearly. What I have told you is what Gollum was willing to tell – though not, of course, in the way I have reported it. Gollum is a liar, and you have to sift his words. For instance, he called the Ring his "birthday present", and he stuck to that. He said it came from his grandmother, who had lots of beautiful things of that kind. A ridiculous story. I have no doubt that Sméagol's grandmother was a matriarch, a great person in her way, but to talk of her possessing many Elven-rings was absurd, and as for giving them away, it was a lie. But a lie with a grain of truth.

'The murder of Déagol haunted Gollum, and he had made up a defence, repeating it to his "precious" over and over again, as he gnawed bones in the dark, until he almost believed it. It *was* his birthday. Déagol ought to have given the ring to him. It had previously turned up just so as to be a present. It *was* his birthday present, and so on, and on.

'I endured him as long as I could, but the truth was desperately important, and in the end I had to be harsh. I put the fear of fire on him, and wrung the true story out of him, bit by bit, together with much snivelling and snarling. He thought he was misunderstood and ill-used. But when he had at last told me his history, as far as the end of the Riddle-game and Bilbo's escape, he would not say any more, except in dark hints. Some other fear was on him greater than mine. He muttered that he was going to get his own back. People would see if he would stand being kicked, and driven into a hole and then *robbed*. Gollum had good friends now, good friends and very strong. They would help him. Baggins would pay for it. That was his chief thought. He hated Bilbo and cursed his name. What is more, he knew where he came from.'

'But how did he find that out?' asked Frodo.

'Well, as for the name, Bilbo very foolishly told Gollum himself; and after that it would not be difficult to discover his country, once Gollum came out. Oh yes, he came out. His longing for the Ring proved stronger than his fear of the Orcs, or even of the light. After a year or two he left the mountains. You see, though still bound by desire of it, the Ring was no longer devouring him; he began to revive a little. He felt old, terribly old, yet less timid, and he was mortally hungry.

'Light, light of Sun and Moon, he still feared and hated, and he always will, I think; but he was cunning. He found he could hide from daylight and moonshine, and make his way swiftly and softly by dead of night with his pale cold eyes, and catch small frightened or unwary things. He grew stronger and bolder with new food and new air. He found his way into Mirkwood, as one would expect.'

'Is that where you found him?' asked Frodo.

'I saw him there,' answered Gandalf, 'but before that he had wandered far, following Bilbo's trail. It was difficult to learn anything from him for certain, for his talk was constantly interrupted by curses and threats. "What had it got in its pocketses?" he said. "It wouldn't say, no precious. Little cheat. Not a fair question. It cheated first, it did. It broke the rules. We ought to have squeezed it, yes precious. And we will, precious!"

'That is a sample of his talk. I don't suppose you want any more. I had weary days of it. But from hints dropped among the snarls I even gathered that his padding feet had taken him at last to Esgaroth, and even to the streets of Dale, listening secretly and peering. Well, the news of the great events went far and wide in Wilderland, and many had heard Bilbo's name and knew where he came from. We had made no secret of our return journey to his home in the West. Gollum's sharp ears would soon learn what he wanted.'

'Then why didn't he track Bilbo further?' asked Frodo. 'Why didn't he come to the Shire?'

'Ah,' said Gandalf, 'now we come to it. I think Gollum tried to. He set out and came back westward, as far as the Great River. But then he turned aside. He was not daunted by the distance, I am sure. No, something else drew him away. So my friends think, those that hunted him for me.

'The Wood-elves tracked him first, an easy task for them, for his trail was still fresh then. Through Mirkwood and back again it led them, though they never caught him. The wood was full of the rumour of him, dreadful tales even among beasts and birds. The Woodmen said that there was some new terror abroad, a ghost that drank blood. It climbed trees to find nests; it crept into holes to find the young; it slipped through windows to find cradles.

'But at the western edge of Mirkwood the trail turned away. It wandered off southwards and passed out of the Wood-elves' ken, and was lost. And then I made a great mistake. Yes, Frodo, and not the first; though I fear it may prove the worst. I let the matter be. I let him go; for I had much else to think of at that time, and I still trusted the lore of Saruman.

'Well, that was years ago. I have paid for it since with many dark and dangerous days. The trail was long cold when I took it up again, after Bilbo left here. And my search would have been in vain, but for the help that I had from a friend: Aragorn, the greatest traveller and huntsman of this age of the world. Together we sought for Gollum down the whole length of Wilderland, without hope, and without success. But at last, when I had given up the chase and turned to other parts, Gollum was found. My friend returned out of the great perils bringing the miserable creature with him.

'What he had been doing he would not say. He only wept and called us cruel, with many a *gollum* in his throat; and when we pressed him he whined and cringed, and rubbed his long hands, licking his fingers as if they pained him, as if he remembered some old torture. But I am afraid there is no possible doubt: he had made his slow, sneaking way, step by step, mile by mile, south, down at last to the Land of Mordor.'

A heavy silence fell in the room. Frodo could hear his heart beating. Even outside everything seemed still. No sound of Sam's shears could now be heard.

'Yes, to Mordor,' said Gandalf. 'Alas! Mordor draws all wicked things, and the Dark Power was bending all its will to gather them there. The Ring of the Enemy would leave its mark, too, leave him open to the summons. And all folk were whispering then of the new Shadow in the South, and its hatred of the West. There were his fine new friends, who would help him in his revenge!

'Wretched fool! In that land he would learn much, too much for his comfort. And sooner or later as he lurked and pried on the borders he would be caught, and taken – for examination. That was the way of it, I fear. When he was found he had already been there long, and was on his way back. On some errand of mischief. But that does not matter much now. His worst mischief was done.

'Yes, alas! through him the Enemy has learned that the One has been found again. He knows where Isildur fell. He knows where Gollum found his ring. He knows that it is a Great Ring, for it gave long life. He knows that it is not one of the Three, for they have never been lost, and they endure no evil. He knows that it is not one of the Seven, or the Nine, for they are accounted for. He knows that it is the One. And he has at last heard, I think, of *hobbits* and the *Shire*.

'The Shire – he may be seeking for it now, if he has not already found out where it lies. Indeed, Frodo, I fear that he may even think that the long-unnoticed name of *Baggins* has become important.'

'But this is terrible!' cried Frodo. 'Far worse than the worst that I imagined from your hints and warnings. O Gandalf, best of friends, what am I to do? For now I am really afraid. What am I to do? What a pity that Bilbo did not stab that vile creature, when he had a chance!'

'Pity? It was Pity that stayed his hand. Pity, and Mercy: not to strike without need. And he has been well rewarded, Frodo. Be sure that he took so little hurt from the evil, and escaped in the end, because he began his ownership of the Ring so. With Pity.'

'I am sorry,' said Frodo. 'But I am frightened; and I do not feel any pity for Gollum.'

'You have not seen him,' Gandalf broke in.

'No, and I don't want to,' said Frodo. 'I can't understand you. Do you mean to say that you, and the Elves, have let him live on after all those horrible deeds? Now at any rate he is as bad as an Orc, and just an enemy. He deserves death.'

'Deserves it! I daresay he does. Many that live deserve death. And some that die deserve life. Can you give it to them? Then do not be too eager to deal out death in judgement. For even the very wise cannot see all ends. I have not much hope that Gollum can be cured before he dies, but there is a chance of it. And he is bound up with the fate of the Ring. My heart tells me that he has some part to play yet, for good or ill, before the end; and when that comes, the pity of Bilbo may rule the fate of many – yours not least. In any case we did not kill him: he is very old and very wretched. The Wood-elves have him in prison, but they treat him with such kindness as they can find in their wise hearts.'

'All the same,' said Frodo, 'even if Bilbo could not kill Gollum, I wish he had not kept the Ring. I wish he had never found it, and that I had not got it! Why did you let me keep it? Why didn't you make me throw it away, or, or destroy it?'

'Let you? Make you?' said the wizard. 'Haven't you been listening to all that I have said? You are not thinking of what you are saying. But as for throwing it away, that was obviously wrong. These Rings have a way of being found. In evil hands it might have done great evil. Worst of all, it might have fallen into the hands of the Enemy. Indeed it certainly would;

for this is the One, and he is exerting all his power to find it or draw it to himself.

'Of course, my dear Frodo, it was dangerous for you; and that has troubled me deeply. But there was so much at stake that I had to take some risk – though even when I was far away there has never been a day when the Shire has not been guarded by watchful eyes. As long as you never used it, I did not think that the Ring would have any lasting effect on you, not for evil, not at any rate for a very long time. And you must remember that nine years ago, when I last saw you, I still knew little for certain.'

'But why not destroy it, as you say should have been done long ago?' cried Frodo again. 'If you had warned me, or even sent me a message, I would have done away with it.'

'Would you? How would you do that? Have you ever tried?'

'No. But I suppose one could hammer it or melt it.'

'Try!' said Gandalf. 'Try now!'

Frodo drew the Ring out of his pocket again and looked at it. It now appeared plain and smooth, without mark or device that he could see. The gold looked very fair and pure, and Frodo thought how rich and beautiful was its colour, how perfect was its roundness. It was an admirable thing and altogether precious. When he took it out he had intended to fling it from him into the very hottest part of the fire. But he found now that he could not do so, not without a great struggle. He weighed the Ring in his hand, hesitating, and forcing himself to remember all that Gandalf had told him; and then with an effort of will he made a movement, as if to cast it away – but he found that he had put it back in his pocket.

Gandalf laughed grimly. 'You see? Already you too, Frodo, cannot easily let it go, nor will to damage it. And I could not "make" you – except by force, which would break your mind. But as for breaking the Ring, force is useless. Even if you took it and struck it with a heavy sledge-hammer, it would make no dint in it. It cannot be unmade by your hands, or by mine.

'Your small fire, of course, would not melt even ordinary gold. This Ring has already passed through it unscathed, and even unheated. But there is no smith's forge in this Shire that could change it at all. Not even the anvils and furnaces of the Dwarves could do that. It has been said that dragon-fire could melt and consume the Rings of Power, but there is not now any dragon left on earth in which the old fire is hot enough; nor was there ever any dragon, not even Ancalagon the Black, who could have harmed the One Ring, the Ruling Ring, for that was made by Sauron himself.

'There is only one way: to find the Cracks of Doom in the depths of

Orodruin, the Fire-mountain, and cast the Ring in there, if you really wish to destroy it, to put it beyond the grasp of the Enemy for ever.'

'I do really wish to destroy it!' cried Frodo. 'Or, well, to have it destroyed. I am not made for perilous quests. I wish I had never seen the Ring! Why did it come to me? Why was I chosen?'

'Such questions cannot be answered,' said Gandalf. 'You may be sure that it was not for any merit that others do not possess: not for power or wisdom, at any rate. But you have been chosen, and you must therefore use such strength and heart and wits as you have.'

'But I have so little of any of these things! You are wise and powerful. Will you not take the Ring?'

'No!' cried Gandalf, springing to his feet. 'With that power I should have power too great and terrible. And over me the Ring would gain a power still greater and more deadly.' His eyes flashed and his face was lit as by a fire within. 'Do not tempt me! For I do not wish to become like the Dark Lord himself. Yet the way of the Ring to my heart is by pity, pity for weakness and the desire of strength to do good. Do not tempt me! I dare not take it, not even to keep it safe, unused. The wish to wield it would be too great for my strength. I shall have such need of it. Great perils lie before me.'

He went to the window and drew aside the curtains and the shutters. Sunlight streamed back again into the room. Sam passed along the path outside whistling. 'And now,' said the wizard, turning back to Frodo, 'the decision lies with you. But I will always help you.' He laid his hand on Frodo's shoulder. 'I will help you bear this burden, as long as it is yours to bear. But we must do something, soon. The Enemy is moving.'

There was a long silence. Gandalf sat down again and puffed at his pipe, as if lost in thought. His eyes seemed closed, but under the lids he was watching Frodo intently. Frodo gazed fixedly at the red embers on the hearth, until they filled all his vision, and he seemed to be looking down into profound wells of fire. He was thinking of the fabled Cracks of Doom and the terror of the Fiery Mountain.

'Well!' said Gandalf at last. 'What are you thinking about? Have you decided what to do?'

'No!' answered Frodo, coming back to himself out of darkness, and finding to his surprise that it was not dark, and that out of the window he could see the sunlit garden. 'Or perhaps, yes. As far as I understand what you have said, I suppose I must keep the Ring and guard it, at least for the present, whatever it may do to me.'

'Whatever it may do, it will be slow, slow to evil, if you keep it with that purpose,' said Gandalf.

'I hope so,' said Frodo. 'But I hope that you may find some other better keeper soon. But in the meanwhile it seems that I am a danger, a danger to all that live near me. I cannot keep the Ring and stay here. I ought to leave Bag End, leave the Shire, leave everything and go away.' He sighed.

'I should like to save the Shire, if I could – though there have been times when I thought the inhabitants too stupid and dull for words, and have felt that an earthquake or an invasion of dragons might be good for them. But I don't feel like that now. I feel that as long as the Shire lies behind, safe and comfortable, I shall find wandering more bearable: I shall know that somewhere there is a firm foothold, even if my feet cannot stand there again.

'Of course, I have sometimes thought of going away, but I imagined that as a kind of holiday, a series of adventures like Bilbo's or better, ending in peace. But this would mean exile, a flight from danger into danger, drawing it after me. And I suppose I must go alone, if I am to do that and save the Shire. But I feel very small, and very uprooted, and well – desperate. The Enemy is so strong and terrible.'

He did not tell Gandalf, but as he was speaking a great desire to follow Bilbo flamed up in his heart – to follow Bilbo, and even perhaps to find him again. It was so strong that it overcame his fear: he could almost have run out there and then down the road without his hat, as Bilbo had done on a similar morning long ago.

'My dear Frodo!' exclaimed Gandalf. 'Hobbits really are amazing creatures, as I have said before. You can learn all that there is to know about their ways in a month, and yet after a hundred years they can still surprise you at a pinch. I hardly expected to get such an answer, not even from you. But Bilbo made no mistake in choosing his heir, though he little thought how important it would prove. I am afraid you are right. The Ring will not be able to stay hidden in the Shire much longer; and for your own sake, as well as for others, you will have to go, and leave the name of Baggins behind you. That name will not be safe to have, outside the Shire or in the Wild. I will give you a travelling name now. When you go, go as Mr. Underhill.

'But I don't think you need go alone. Not if you know of anyone you can trust, and who would be willing to go by your side – and that you would be willing to take into unknown perils. But if you look for a companion, be careful in choosing! And be careful of what you say, even to your closest friends! The enemy has many spies and many ways of hearing.'

Suddenly he stopped as if listening. Frodo became aware that all was very quiet, inside and outside. Gandalf crept to one side of the window. Then with a dart he sprang to the sill, and thrust a long arm out and downwards. There was a squawk, and up came Sam Gamgee's curly head hauled by one ear.

'Well, well, bless my beard!' said Gandalf. 'Sam Gamgee is it? Now what may you be doing?'

'Lor bless you, Mr. Gandalf, sir!' said Sam. 'Nothing! Leastways I was just trimming the grass-border under the window, if you follow me.' He picked up his shears and exhibited them as evidence.

'I don't,' said Gandalf grimly. 'It is some time since I last heard the sound of your shears. How long have you been eavesdropping?'

'Eavesdropping, sir? I don't follow you, begging your pardon. There ain't no eaves at Bag End, and that's a fact.'

'Don't be a fool! What have you heard, and why did you listen?' Gandalf's eyes flashed and his brows stuck out like bristles.

'Mr. Frodo, sir!' cried Sam quaking. 'Don't let him hurt me, sir! Don't let him turn me into anything unnatural! My old dad would take on so. I meant no harm, on my honour, sir!'

'He won't hurt you,' said Frodo, hardly able to keep from laughing, although he was himself startled and rather puzzled. 'He knows, as well as I do, that you mean no harm. But just you up and answer his questions straight away!'

'Well, sir,' said Sam dithering a little. 'I heard a deal that I didn't rightly understand, about an enemy, and rings, and Mr. Bilbo, sir, and dragons, and a fiery mountain, and – and Elves, sir. I listened because I couldn't help myself, if you know what I mean. Lor bless me, sir, but I do love tales of that sort. And I believe them too, whatever Ted may say. Elves, sir! I would dearly love to see *them*. Couldn't you take me to see Elves, sir, when you go?'

Suddenly Gandalf laughed. 'Come inside!' he shouted, and putting out both his arms he lifted the astonished Sam, shears, grass-clippings and all, right through the window and stood him on the floor. 'Take you to see Elves, eh?' he said, eyeing Sam closely, but with a smile flickering on his face. 'So you heard that Mr. Frodo is going away?'

'I did, sir. And that's why I choked: which you heard seemingly. I tried not to, sir, but it burst out of me: I was so upset.'

'It can't be helped, Sam,' said Frodo sadly. He had suddenly realized that flying from the Shire would mean more painful partings than merely saying farewell to the familiar comforts of Bag End. 'I shall have to go. But' – and here he looked hard at Sam – 'if you really care about me, you will keep that *dead* secret. See? If you don't, if you even breathe a word of what you've heard here, then I hope Gandalf will turn you into a spotted toad and fill the garden full of grass-snakes.'

Sam fell on his knees, trembling. 'Get up, Sam!' said Gandalf. 'I have thought of something better than that. Something to shut your mouth, and punish you properly for listening. You shall go away with Mr. Frodo!'

'Me, sir!' cried Sam, springing up like a dog invited for a walk. 'Me go and see Elves and all! Hooray!' he shouted, and then burst into tears.

CHAPTER III

THREE IS COMPANY

'You ought to go quietly, and you ought to go soon,' said Gandalf. Two or three weeks had passed, and still Frodo made no sign of getting ready to go.

'I know. But it is difficult to do both,' he objected. 'If I just vanish like Bilbo, the tale will be all over the Shire in no time.'

'Of course you mustn't vanish!' said Gandalf. 'That wouldn't do at all! I said *soon*, not *instantly*. If you can think of any way of slipping out of the Shire without its being generally known, it will be worth a little delay. But you must not delay too long.'

'What about the autumn, on or after Our Birthday?' asked Frodo. 'I think I could probably make some arrangements by then.'

To tell the truth, he was very reluctant to start, now that it had come to the point. Bag End seemed a more desirable residence than it had for years, and he wanted to savour as much as he could of his last summer in the Shire. When autumn came, he knew that part at least of his heart would think more kindly of journeying, as it always did at that season. He had indeed privately made up his mind to leave on his fiftieth birthday: Bilbo's one hundred and twenty-eighth. It seemed somehow the proper day on which to set out and follow him. Following Bilbo was uppermost in his mind, and the one thing that made the thought of leaving bearable. He thought as little as possible about the Ring, and where it might lead him in the end. But he did not tell all his thoughts to Gandalf. What the wizard guessed was always difficult to tell.

He looked at Frodo and smiled. 'Very well,' he said. 'I think that will do – but it must not be any later. I am getting very anxious. In the meanwhile, do take care, and don't let out any hint of where you are going! And see that Sam Gamgee does not talk. If he does, I really shall turn him into a toad.'

'As for *where I* am going,' said Frodo, 'it would be difficult to give that away, for I have no clear idea myself, yet.'

'Don't be absurd!' said Gandalf. 'I am not warning you against leaving an address at the post-office! But you are leaving the Shire – and that should not be known, until you are far away. And you must go, or at least set out, either North, South, West or East – and the direction should certainly not be known.'

'I have been so taken up with the thoughts of leaving Bag End, and of saying farewell, that I have never even considered the direction,' said Frodo. 'For where am I to go? And by what shall I steer? What is to be my quest? Bilbo went to find a treasure, there and back again; but I go to lose one, and not return, as far as I can see.'

'But you cannot see very far,' said Gandalf. 'Neither can I. It may be your task to find the Cracks of Doom; but that quest may be for others: I do not know. At any rate you are not ready for that long road yet.'

'No indeed!' said Frodo. 'But in the meantime what course am I to take?'

'Towards danger; but not too rashly, nor too straight,' answered the wizard. 'If you want my advice, make for Rivendell. That journey should not prove too perilous, though the Road is less easy than it was, and it will grow worse as the year fails.'

'Rivendell!' said Frodo. 'Very good: I will go east, and I will make for Rivendell. I will take Sam to visit the Elves; he will be delighted.' He spoke lightly; but his heart was moved suddenly with a desire to see the house of Elrond Halfelven, and breathe the air of that deep valley where many of the Fair Folk still dwelt in peace.

One summer's evening an astonishing piece of news reached the *Ivy Bush* and *Green Dragon*. Giants and other portents on the borders of the Shire were forgotten for more important matters: Mr. Frodo was selling Bag End, indeed he had already sold it – to the Sackville-Bagginses!

'For a nice bit, too,' said some. 'At a bargain price,' said others, 'and that's more likely when Mistress Lobelia's the buyer.' (Otho had died some years before, at the ripe but disappointed age of 102.)

Just why Mr. Frodo was selling his beautiful hole was even more debatable than the price. A few held the theory – supported by the nods and hints of Mr. Baggins himself – that Frodo's money was running out: he was going to leave Hobbiton and live in a quiet way on the proceeds of the sale down in Buckland among his Brandybuck relations. 'As far from the Sackville-Bagginses as may be,' some added. But so firmly fixed had the notion of the immeasurable wealth of the Bagginses of Bag End become that most found this hard to believe, harder than any other reason or unreason that their fancy could suggest: to most it suggested a dark and yet unrevealed plot by Gandalf. Though he kept himself very quiet and did not go about by day, it was well known that he was 'hiding up in the Bag End'. But however a removal might fit in with the designs of his wizardry, there was no doubt about the fact: Frodo Baggins was going back to Buckland.

'Yes, I shall be moving this autumn,' he said. 'Merry Brandybuck is looking out for a nice little hole for me, or perhaps a small house.'

As a matter of fact with Merry's help he had already chosen and bought a little house at Crickhollow in the country beyond Bucklebury. To all but Sam he pretended he was going to settle down there permanently. The decision to set out eastwards had suggested the idea to him; for Buckland was on the eastern borders of the Shire, and as he had lived there in childhood his going back would at least seem credible.

Gandalf stayed in the Shire for over two months. Then one evening, at the end of June, soon after Frodo's plan had been finally arranged, he suddenly announced that he was going off again next morning. 'Only for a short while, I hope,' he said. 'But I am going down beyond the southern borders to get some news, if I can. I have been idle longer than I should.'

He spoke lightly, but it seemed to Frodo that he looked rather worried. 'Has anything happened?' he asked.

'Well no; but I have heard something that has made me anxious and needs looking into. If I think it necessary after all for you to get off at once, I shall come back immediately, or at least send word. In the meanwhile stick to your plan; but be more careful than ever, especially of the Ring. Let me impress on you once more: *don't use it!*'

He went off at dawn. 'I may be back any day,' he said. 'At the very latest I shall come back for the farewell party. I think after all you may need my company on the Road.'

At first Frodo was a good deal disturbed, and wondered often what Gandalf could have heard; but his uneasiness wore off, and in the fine weather he forgot his troubles for a while. The Shire had seldom seen so fair a summer, or so rich an autumn: the trees were laden with apples, honey was dripping in the combs, and the corn was tall and full.

Autumn was well under way before Frodo began to worry about Gandalf again. September was passing and there was still no news of him. The Birthday, and the removal, drew nearer, and still he did not come, or send word. Bag End began to be busy. Some of Frodo's friends came to stay and help him with the packing: there was Fredegar Bolger and Folco Boffin, and of course his special friends Pippin Took and Merry Brandybuck. Between them they turned the whole place upside-down.

On September 20th two covered carts went off laden to Buckland, conveying the furniture and goods that Frodo had not sold to his new home, by way of the Brandywine Bridge. The next day Frodo became really anxious, and kept a constant look-out for Gandalf. Thursday, his birthday morning, dawned as fair and clear as it had long ago for Bilbo's great party. Still Gandalf did not appear. In the evening Frodo gave his farewell feast: it was quite small, just a dinner for himself and his four helpers; but he was troubled and felt in no mood for it. The thought that he would so soon have to part with his young friends weighed on his heart. He wondered how he would break it to them.

The four younger hobbits were, however, in high spirits, and the party soon became very cheerful in spite of Gandalf's absence. The dining-room was bare except for a table and chairs, but the food was good, and there was good wine: Frodo's wine had not been included in the sale to the Sackville-Bagginses.

'Whatever happens to the rest of my stuff, when the S.-B.s get their claws on it, at any rate I have found a good home for this!' said Frodo, as he drained his glass. It was the last drop of Old Winyards.

When they had sung many songs, and talked of many things they had done together, they toasted Bilbo's birthday, and they drank his health and Frodo's together according to Frodo's custom. Then they went out for a sniff of air, and glimpse of the stars, and then they went to bed. Frodo's party was over, and Gandalf had not come.

The next morning they were busy packing another cart with the remainder of the luggage. Merry took charge of this, and drove off with Fatty (that is Fredegar Bolger). 'Someone must get there and warm the house before you arrive,' said Merry. 'Well, see you later – the day after tomorrow, if you don't go to sleep on the way!'

Folco went home after lunch, but Pippin remained behind. Frodo was restless and anxious, listening in vain for a sound of Gandalf. He decided to wait until nightfall. After that, if Gandalf wanted him urgently, he would go to Crickhollow, and might even get there first. For Frodo was going on foot. His plan – for pleasure and a last look at the Shire as much as any other reason – was to walk from Hobbiton to Bucklebury Ferry, taking it fairly easy.

'I shall get myself a bit into training, too,' he said, looking at himself in a dusty mirror in the half-empty hall. He had not done any strenuous walking for a long time, and the reflection looked rather flabby, he thought.

After lunch, the Sackville-Bagginses, Lobelia and her sandy-haired son, Lotho, turned up, much to Frodo's annoyance. 'Ours at last!' said Lobelia, as she stepped inside. It was not polite; nor strictly true, for the sale of Bag End did not take effect until midnight. But Lobelia can perhaps be forgiven: she had been obliged to wait about seventy-seven years longer for Bag End than she once hoped, and she was now a hundred years old. Anyway, she had come to see that nothing she had paid for had been carried off; and she wanted the keys. It took a long while to satisfy her, as she had brought a complete inventory with her and went right through it. In the end she departed with Lotho and the spare key and the promise that the other key would be left at the Gamgees' in Bagshot Row. She snorted, and showed plainly that she thought the Gamgees capable of plundering the hole during the night. Frodo did not offer her any tea.

He took his own tea with Pippin and Sam Gamgee in the kitchen. It had been officially announced that Sam was coming to Buckland 'to do for Mr. Frodo and look after his bit of garden'; an arrangement that was approved by the Gaffer, though it did not console him for the prospect of having Lobelia as a neighbour.

'Our last meal at Bag End!' said Frodo, pushing back his chair. They left the washing up for Lobelia. Pippin and Sam strapped up their three packs and piled them in the porch. Pippin went out for a last stroll in the garden. Sam disappeared.

The sun went down. Bag End seemed sad and gloomy and dishevelled. Frodo wandered round the familiar rooms, and saw the light of the sunset fade on the walls, and shadows creep out of the corners. It grew slowly dark indoors. He went out and walked down to the gate at the bottom of the path, and then on a short way down the Hill Road. He half expected to see Gandalf come striding up through the dusk.

The sky was clear and the stars were growing bright. 'It's going to be a fine night,' he said aloud. 'That's good for a beginning. I feel like walking. I can't bear any more hanging about. I am going to start, and Gandalf must follow me.' He turned to go back, and then stopped, for he heard voices, just round the corner by the end of Bagshot Row. One voice was certainly the old Gaffer's; the other was strange, and somehow unpleasant. He could not make out what it said, but he heard the Gaffer's answers, which were rather shrill. The old man seemed put out.

'No, Mr. Baggins has gone away. Went this morning, and my Sam went with him: anyway all his stuff went. Yes, sold out and gone, I tell'ee. Why? Why's none of my business, or yours. Where to? That ain't no secret. He's moved to Bucklebury or some such place, away down yonder. Yes it is – a tidy way. I've never been so far myself; they're queer folks in Buckland. No, I can't give no message. Good night to you!'

Footsteps went away down the Hill. Frodo wondered vaguely why the fact that they did not come on up the Hill seemed a great relief. 'I am sick of questions and curiosity about my doings, I suppose,' he thought. 'What an inquisitive lot they all are!' He had half a mind to go and ask the Gaffer who the inquirer was; but he thought better (or worse) of it, and turned and walked quickly back to Bag End.

Pippin was sitting on his pack in the porch. Sam was not there. Frodo stepped inside the dark door. 'Sam!' he called. 'Sam! Time!'

'Coming, sir!' came the answer from far within, followed soon by Sam himself, wiping his mouth. He had been saying farewell to the beer-barrel in the cellar.

'All aboard, Sam?' said Frodo.

'Yes, sir. I'll last for a bit now, sir.'

Frodo shut and locked the round door, and gave the key to Sam. 'Run down with this to your home, Sam!' he said. 'Then cut along the Row and meet us as quick as you can at the gate in the lane beyond the meadows. We are not going through the village tonight. Too many ears pricking and eyes prying.' Sam ran off at full speed.

'Well, now we're off at last!' said Frodo. They shouldered their packs and took up their sticks, and walked round the corner to the west side of Bag End. 'Good-bye!' said Frodo, looking at the dark blank windows. He waved his hand, and then turned and (following Bilbo, if he had known it) hurried after Peregrin down the garden-path. They jumped over the low place in the hedge at the bottom and took to the fields, passing into the darkness like a rustle in the grasses.

At the bottom of the Hill on its western side they came to the gate opening on to a narrow lane. There they halted and adjusted the straps of their packs. Presently Sam appeared, trotting quickly and breathing hard; his heavy pack was hoisted high on his shoulders, and he had put on his head a tall shapeless felt bag, which he called a hat. In the gloom he looked very much like a dwarf.

'I am sure you have given me all the heaviest stuff,' said Frodo. 'I pity snails, and all that carry their homes on their backs.'

'I could take a lot more yet, sir. My packet is quite light,' said Sam stoutly and untruthfully.

'No, you don't, Sam!' said Pippin. 'It is good for him. He's got nothing except what he ordered us to pack. He's been slack lately, and he'll feel the weight less when he's walked off some of his own.'

'Be kind to a poor old hobbit!' laughed Frodo. 'I shall be as thin as a willow-wand, I'm sure, before I get to Buckland. But I was talking nonsense. I suspect you have taken more than your share, Sam, and I shall look into it at our next packing.' He picked up his stick again. 'Well, we all like walking in the dark,' he said, 'so let's put some miles behind us before bed.'

For a short way they followed the lane westwards. Then leaving it they turned left and took quietly to the fields again. They went in single file along hedgerows and the borders of coppices, and night fell dark about them. In their dark cloaks they were as invisible as if they all had magic rings. Since they were all hobbits, and were trying to be silent, they made no noise that even hobbits would hear. Even the wild things in the fields and woods hardly noticed their passing.

After some time they crossed the Water, west of Hobbiton, by a narrow plank-bridge. The stream was there no more than a winding black ribbon, bordered with leaning alder-trees. A mile or two further south they hastily crossed the great road from the Brandywine Bridge; they were now in the Tookland and bending south-eastwards they made for the Green Hill Country. As they began to climb its first slopes they looked back and saw the lamps in Hobbiton far off twinkling in the gentle valley of the Water. Soon it disappeared in the folds of the darkened land, and was followed by Bywater beside its grey pool. When the light of the last farm was far behind, peeping among the trees, Frodo turned and waved a hand in farewell.

'I wonder if I shall ever look down into that valley again,' he said quietly.

When they had walked for about three hours they rested. The night was clear, cool, and starry, but smoke-like wisps of mist were creeping up the hill-sides from the streams and deep meadows. Thin-clad birches, swaying in a light wind above their heads, made a black net against the pale sky. They ate a very frugal supper (for hobbits), and then went on again. Soon they struck a narrow road, that went rolling up and down, fading grey into the darkness ahead: the road to Woodhall, and Stock, and the Bucklebury Ferry. It climbed away from the main road in the Water-valley, and wound over the skirts of the Green Hills towards Woody-End, a wild corner of the Eastfarthing.

After a while they plunged into a deeply cloven track between tall trees that rustled their dry leaves in the night. It was very dark. At first they talked, or hummed a tune softly together, being now far away from inquisitive ears. Then they marched on in silence, and Pippin began to lag behind. At last, as they began to climb a steep slope, he stopped and yawned.

'I am so sleepy,' he said, 'that soon I shall fall down on the road. Are you going to sleep on your legs? It is nearly midnight.'

'I thought you liked walking in the dark,' said Frodo. 'But there is no great hurry. Merry expects us some time the day after tomorrow; but that leaves us nearly two days more. We'll halt at the first likely spot.'

'The wind's in the West,' said Sam. 'If we get to the other side of this hill, we shall find a spot that is sheltered and snug enough, sir. There is a dry fir-wood just ahead, if I remember rightly.' Sam knew the land well within twenty miles of Hobbiton, but that was the limit of his geography.

Just over the top of the hill they came on the patch of fir-wood. Leaving the road they went into the deep resin-scented darkness of the trees, and gathered dead sticks and cones to make a fire. Soon they had a merry crackle of flame at the foot of a large fir-tree and they sat round it for a while, until they began to nod. Then, each in an angle of the great tree's roots, they curled up in their cloaks and blankets, and were soon fast asleep. They set no watch; even Frodo feared no danger yet, for they were still in the heart of the Shire. A few creatures came and looked at them when the fire had died away. A fox passing through the wood on business of his own stopped several minutes and sniffed.

'Hobbits!' he thought. 'Well, what next? I have heard of strange doings in this land, but I have seldom heard of a hobbit sleeping out of doors under a tree. Three of them! There's something mighty queer behind this.' He was quite right, but he never found out any more about it.

The morning came, pale and clammy. Frodo woke up first, and found that a tree-root had made a hole in his back, and that his neck was stiff. 'Walking for pleasure! Why didn't I drive?' he thought, as he usually did at the beginning of an expedition. 'And all my beautiful feather beds are sold to the Sackville-Bagginses! These tree-roots would do them good.' He stretched. 'Wake up, hobbits!' he cried. 'It's a beautiful morning.'

'What's beautiful about it?' said Pippin, peering over the edge of his blanket with one eye. 'Sam! Get breakfast ready for half-past nine! Have you got the bath-water hot?'

Sam jumped up, looking rather bleary. 'No, sir, I haven't, sir!' he said.

Frodo stripped the blankets from Pippin and rolled him over, and then walked off to the edge of the wood. Away eastward the sun was rising red out of the mists that lay thick on the world. Touched with gold and red the autumn trees seemed to be sailing rootless in a shadowy sea. A little below him to the left the road ran down steeply into a hollow and disappeared.

When he returned Sam and Pippin had got a good fire going. 'Water!' shouted Pippin. 'Where's the water?'

'I don't keep water in my pockets,' said Frodo.

'We thought you had gone to find some,' said Pippin, busy setting out the food, and cups. 'You had better go now.'

'You can come too,' said Frodo, 'and bring all the water-bottles.' There was a stream at the foot of the hill. They filled their bottles and the small camping kettle at a little fall where the water fell a few feet over an outcrop of grey stone. It was icy cold; and they spluttered and puffed as they bathed their faces and hands.

When their breakfast was over, and their packs all trussed up again, it was after ten o'clock, and the day was beginning to turn fine and hot. They went down the slope, and across the stream where it dived under the road, and up the next slope, and up and down another shoulder of the hills; and by that time their cloaks, blankets, water, food, and other gear already seemed a heavy burden.

The day's march promised to be warm and tiring work. After some miles, however, the road ceased to roll up and down: it climbed to the top of a steep bank in a weary zig-zagging sort of way, and then prepared to go down for the last time. In front of them they saw the lower lands dotted with small clumps of trees that melted away in the distance to a brown woodland haze. They were looking across the Woody End towards the Brandywine River. The road wound away before them like a piece of string.

'The road goes on for ever,' said Pippin; 'but I can't without a rest. It is high time for lunch.' He sat down on the bank at the side of the road and looked away east into the haze, beyond which lay the River, and the end of the Shire in which he had spent all his life. Sam stood by him. His round eyes were wide open – for he was looking across lands he had never seen to a new horizon.

'Do Elves live in those woods?' he asked.

'Not that I ever heard,' said Pippin. Frodo was silent. He too was gazing eastward along the road, as if he had never seen it before. Suddenly he spoke, aloud but as if to himself, saying slowly:

> The Road goes ever on and on
>   Down from the door where it began.
> Now far ahead the Road has gone,
>   And I must follow, if I can,
> Pursuing it with weary feet,
>   Until it joins some larger way,
> Where many paths and errands meet.
>   And whither then? I cannot say.

'That sounds like a bit of old Bilbo's rhyming,' said Pippin. 'Or is it one of your imitations? It does not sound altogether encouraging.'

'I don't know,' said Frodo. 'It came to me then, as if I was making it up; but I may have heard it long ago. Certainly it reminds me very much of Bilbo in the last years, before he went away. He used often to say there was only one Road; that it was like a great river: its springs were at every doorstep, and every path was its tributary. "It's a dangerous business, Frodo, going out of your door," he used to say. "You step into the Road, and if you don't keep your feet, there is no knowing where you might be swept off to. Do you realize that this is the very path that goes through Mirkwood, and that if you let it, it might take you to the Lonely Mountain or even further and to worse places?" He used to say that on the path outside the front door at Bag End, especially after he had been out for a long walk.'

'Well, the Road won't sweep me anywhere for an hour at least,' said Pippin, unslinging his pack. The others followed his example, putting their packs against the bank and their legs out into the road. After a rest they had a good lunch, and then more rest.

The sun was beginning to get low and the light of afternoon was on the land as they went down the hill. So far they had not met a soul on the road. This way was not much used, being hardly fit for carts, and there was little traffic to the Woody End. They had been jogging along again for an hour or more when Sam stopped a moment as if listening. They were now on level ground, and the road after much winding lay straight ahead through grass-land sprinkled with tall trees, outliers of the approaching woods.

'I can hear a pony or a horse coming along the road behind,' said Sam.

They looked back, but the turn of the road prevented them from seeing far. 'I wonder if that is Gandalf coming after us,' said Frodo; but even as he said it, he had a feeling that it was not so, and a sudden desire to hide from the view of the rider came over him.

'It may not matter much,' he said apologetically, 'but I would rather not be seen on the road – by anyone. I am sick of my doings being noticed and discussed. And if it is Gandalf,' he added as an afterthought, 'we can give him a little surprise, to pay him out for being so late. Let's get out of sight!'

The other two ran quickly to the left and down into a little hollow not far from the road. There they lay flat. Frodo hesitated for a second: curiosity or some other feeling was struggling with his desire to hide. The sound of hoofs drew nearer. Just in time he threw himself down in a patch of long grass behind a tree that overshadowed the road. Then he lifted his head and peered cautiously above one of the great roots.

Round the corner came a black horse, no hobbit-pony but a full-sized horse; and on it sat a large man, who seemed to crouch in the saddle, wrapped in a great black cloak and hood, so that only his boots in the high stirrups showed below; his face was shadowed and invisible.

When it reached the tree and was level with Frodo the horse stopped. The riding figure sat quite still with its head bowed, as if listening. From inside the hood came a noise as of someone sniffing to catch an elusive scent; the head turned from side to side of the road.

A sudden unreasoning fear of discovery laid hold of Frodo, and he thought of his Ring. He hardly dared to breathe, and yet the desire to get it out of his pocket became so strong that he began slowly to move his hand. He felt that he had only to slip it on, and then he would be safe. The advice of Gandalf seemed absurd. Bilbo had used the Ring. 'And I am still in the Shire,' he thought, as his hand touched the chain on which it hung. At that moment the rider sat up, and shook the reins. The horse stepped forward, walking slowly at first, and then breaking into a quick trot.

Frodo crawled to the edge of the road and watched the rider, until he dwindled into the distance. He could not be quite sure, but it seemed to him that suddenly, before it passed out of sight, the horse turned aside and went into the trees on the right.

'Well, I call that very queer, and indeed disturbing,' said Frodo to himself, as he walked towards his companions. Pippin and Sam had remained flat in the grass, and had seen nothing; so Frodo described the rider and his strange behaviour.

'I can't say why, but I felt certain he was looking or *smelling* for me; and also I felt certain that I did not want him to discover me. I've never seen or felt anything like it in the Shire before.'

'But what has one of the Big People got to do with us?' said Pippin. 'And what is he doing in this part of the world?'

'There are some Men about,' said Frodo. 'Down in the Southfarthing they have had trouble with Big People, I believe. But I have never heard of anything like this rider. I wonder where he comes from.'

'Begging your pardon,' put in Sam suddenly, 'I know where he comes from. It's from Hobbiton that this here black rider comes, unless there's more than one. And I know where he's going to.'

'What do you mean?' said Frodo sharply, looking at him in astonishment. 'Why didn't you speak up before?'

'I have only just remembered, sir. It was like this: when I got back to our hole yesterday evening with the key, my dad, he says to me: *Hallo, Sam!* he says. *I thought you were away with Mr. Frodo this morning. There's been a strange customer asking for Mr. Baggins of Bag End, and he's only just gone. I've sent him on to Bucklebury. Not that I liked the sound of him. He seemed mighty put out, when I told him Mr. Baggins had left his old home for good. Hissed at me, he did. It gave me quite a shudder. What sort of a fellow was he? says I to the Gaffer. I don't know, says he; but he wasn't a hobbit. He was tall and black-like, and he stooped over me. I reckon it was one of the Big Folk from foreign parts. He spoke funny.*

'I couldn't stay to hear more, sir, since you were waiting; and I didn't give much heed to it myself. The Gaffer is getting old, and more than a bit blind, and it must have been near dark when this fellow come up the Hill and found him taking the air at the end of our Row. I hope he hasn't done no harm, sir, nor me.'

'The Gaffer can't be blamed anyway,' said Frodo. 'As a matter of fact I heard him talking to a stranger, who seemed to be inquiring for me, and

I nearly went and asked him who it was. I wish I had, or you had told me
about it before. I might have been more careful on the road.'

'Still, there may be no connexion between this rider and the Gaffer's
stranger,' said Pippin. 'We left Hobbiton secretly enough, and I don't see
how he could have followed us.'

'What about the *smelling*, sir?' said Sam. 'And the Gaffer said he was a
black chap.'

'I wish I had waited for Gandalf,' Frodo muttered. 'But perhaps it would
only have made matters worse.'

'Then you know or guess something about this rider?' said Pippin, who
had caught the muttered words.

'I don't know, and I would rather not guess,' said Frodo.

'All right, cousin Frodo! You can keep your secret for the present, if
you want to be mysterious. In the meanwhile what are we to do? I should
like a bite and a sup, but somehow I think we had better move on from
here. Your talk of sniffing riders with invisible noses has unsettled me.'

'Yes, I think we will move on now,' said Frodo; 'but not on the road –
in case that rider comes back, or another follows him. We ought to do a
good step more today. Buckland is still miles away.'

The shadows of the trees were long and thin on the grass, as they started
off again. They now kept a stone's throw to the left of the road, and kept
out of sight of it as much as they could. But this hindered them; for the
grass was thick and tussocky, and the ground uneven, and the trees began
to draw together into thickets.

The sun had gone down red behind the hills at their backs, and evening
was coming on before they came back to the road at the end of the long
level over which it had run straight for some miles. At that point it bent
left and went down into the lowlands of the Yale making for Stock; but a
lane branched right, winding through a wood of ancient oak-trees on its
way to Woodhall. 'That is the way for us,' said Frodo.

Not far from the road-meeting they came on the huge hulk of a tree: it
was still alive and had leaves on the small branches that it had put out
round the broken stumps of its long-fallen limbs; but it was hollow, and
could be entered by a great crack on the side away from the road. The
hobbits crept inside, and sat there upon a floor of old leaves and decayed
wood. They rested and had a light meal, talking quietly and listening from
time to time.

Twilight was about them as they crept back to the lane. The West wind
was sighing in the branches. Leaves were whispering. Soon the road began
to fall gently but steadily into the dusk. A star came out above the trees in
the darkening East before them. They went abreast and in step, to keep

up their spirits. After a time, as the stars grew thicker and brighter, the feeling of disquiet left them, and they no longer listened for the sound of hoofs. They began to hum softly, as hobbits have a way of doing as they walk along, especially when they are drawing near to home at night. With most hobbits it is a supper-song or a bed-song; but these hobbits hummed a walking-song (though not, of course, without any mention of supper and bed). Bilbo Baggins had made the words, to a tune that was as old as the hills, and taught it to Frodo as they walked in the lanes of the Water-valley and talked about Adventure.

> *Upon the hearth the fire is red,*
> *Beneath the roof there is a bed;*
> *But not yet weary are our feet,*
> *Still round the corner we may meet*
> *A sudden tree or standing stone*
> *That none have seen but we alone.*
> > *Tree and flower and leaf and grass,*
> > *Let them pass! Let them pass!*
> > *Hill and water under sky,*
> > *Pass them by! Pass them by!*

> *Still round the corner there may wait*
> *A new road or a secret gate,*
> *And though we pass them by today,*
> *Tomorrow we may come this way*
> *And take the hidden paths that run*
> *Towards the Moon or to the Sun.*
> > *Apple, thorn, and nut and sloe,*
> > *Let them go! Let them go!*
> > *Sand and stone and pool and dell,*
> > *Fare you well! Fare you well!*

> *Home is behind, the world ahead,*
> *And there are many paths to tread*
> *Through shadows to the edge of night,*
> *Until the stars are all alight.*
> *Then world behind and home ahead,*
> *We'll wander back to home and bed.*
> > *Mist and twilight, cloud and shade,*
> > *Away shall fade! Away shall fade!*
> > *Fire and lamp, and meat and bread,*
> > *And then to bed! And then to bed!*

The song ended. 'And *now* to bed! And *now* to bed!' sang Pippin in a high voice.

'Hush!' said Frodo. 'I think I hear hoofs again.'

They stopped suddenly and stood as silent as tree-shadows, listening. There was a sound of hoofs in the lane, some way behind, but coming slow and clear down the wind. Quickly and quietly they slipped off the path, and ran into the deeper shade under the oak-trees.

'Don't let us go too far!' said Frodo. 'I don't want to be seen, but I want to see if it is another Black Rider.'

'Very well!' said Pippin. 'But don't forget the sniffing!'

The hoofs drew nearer. They had no time to find any hiding-place better than the general darkness under the trees; Sam and Pippin crouched behind a large tree-bole, while Frodo crept back a few yards towards the lane. It showed grey and pale, a line of fading light through the wood. Above it the stars were thick in the dim sky, but there was no moon.

The sound of hoofs stopped. As Frodo watched he saw something dark pass across the lighter space between two trees, and then halt. It looked like the black shade of a horse led by a smaller black shadow. The black shadow stood close to the point where they had left the path, and it swayed from side to side. Frodo thought he heard the sound of snuffling. The shadow bent to the ground, and then began to crawl towards him.

Once more the desire to slip on the Ring came over Frodo; but this time it was stronger than before. So strong that, almost before he realized what he was doing, his hand was groping in his pocket. But at that moment there came a sound like mingled song and laughter. Clear voices rose and fell in the starlit air. The black shadow straightened up and retreated. It climbed on to the shadowy horse and seemed to vanish across the lane into the darkness on the other side. Frodo breathed again.

'Elves!' exclaimed Sam in a hoarse whisper. 'Elves, sir!' He would have burst out of the trees and dashed off towards the voices, if they had not pulled him back.

'Yes, it is Elves,' said Frodo. 'One can meet them sometimes in the Woody End. They don't live in the Shire, but they wander into it in Spring and Autumn, out of their own lands away beyond the Tower Hills. I am thankful that they do! You did not see, but that Black Rider stopped just here and was actually crawling towards us when the song began. As soon as he heard the voices he slipped away.'

'What about the Elves?' said Sam, too excited to trouble about the rider. 'Can't we go and see them?'

'Listen! They are coming this way,' said Frodo. 'We have only to wait.'

The singing drew nearer. One clear voice rose now above the others. It was singing in the fair elven-tongue, of which Frodo knew only a little, and the others knew nothing. Yet the sound blending with the melody seemed to shape itself in their thought into words which they only partly understood. This was the song as Frodo heard it:

> *Snow-white! Snow-white! O Lady clear!*
> *O Queen beyond the Western Seas!*
> *O Light to us that wander here*
> *Amid the world of woven trees!*
>
> *Gilthoniel! O Elbereth!*
> *Clear are thy eyes and bright thy breath!*
> *Snow-white! Snow-white! We sing to thee*
> *In a far land beyond the Sea.*
>
> *O stars that in the Sunless Year*
> *With shining hand by her were sown,*
> *In windy fields now bright and clear*
> *We see your silver blossom blown!*
>
> *O Elbereth! Gilthoniel!*
> *We still remember, we who dwell*
> *In this far land beneath the trees,*
> *Thy starlight on the Western Seas.*

The song ended. 'These are High Elves! They spoke the name of Elbereth!' said Frodo in amazement. 'Few of that fairest folk are ever seen in the Shire. Not many now remain in Middle-earth, east of the Great Sea. This is indeed a strange chance!'

The hobbits sat in shadow by the wayside. Before long the Elves came down the lane towards the valley. They passed slowly, and the hobbits could see the starlight glimmering on their hair and in their eyes. They bore no lights, yet as they walked a shimmer, like the light of the moon above the rim of the hills before it rises, seemed to fall about their feet. They were now silent, and as the last Elf passed he turned and looked towards the hobbits and laughed.

'Hail, Frodo!' he cried. 'You are abroad late. Or are you perhaps lost?' Then he called aloud to the others, and all the company stopped and gathered round.

'This is indeed wonderful!' they said. 'Three hobbits in a wood at night! We have not seen such a thing since Bilbo went away. What is the meaning of it?'

'The meaning of it, fair people,' said Frodo, 'is simply that we seem to be going the same way as you are. I like walking under the stars. But I would welcome your company.'

'But we have no need of other company, and hobbits are so dull,' they laughed. 'And how do you know that we go the same way as you, for you do not know whither we are going?'

'And how do you know my name?' asked Frodo in return.

'We know many things,' they said. 'We have seen you often before with Bilbo, though you may not have seen us.'

'Who are you, and who is your lord?' asked Frodo.

'I am Gildor,' answered their leader, the Elf who had first hailed him. 'Gildor Inglorion of the House of Finrod. We are Exiles, and most of our kindred have long ago departed and we too are now only tarrying here a while, ere we return over the Great Sea. But some of our kinsfolk dwell still in peace in Rivendell. Come now, Frodo, tell us what you are doing? For we see that there is some shadow of fear upon you.'

'O Wise People!' interrupted Pippin eagerly. 'Tell us about the Black Riders!'

'Black Riders?' they said in low voices. 'Why do you ask about Black Riders?'

'Because two Black Riders have overtaken us today, or one has done so twice,' said Pippin; 'only a little while ago he slipped away as you drew near.'

The Elves did not answer at once, but spoke together softly in their own tongue. At length Gildor turned to the hobbits. 'We will not speak of this here,' he said. 'We think you had best come now with us. It is not our custom, but for this time we will take you on our road, and you shall lodge with us tonight, if you will.'

'O Fair Folk! This is good fortune beyond my hope,' said Pippin. Sam was speechless. 'I thank you indeed, Gildor Inglorion,' said Frodo bowing. '*Elen síla lúmenn' omentielvo*, a star shines on the hour of our meeting,' he added in the high-elven speech.

'Be careful, friends!' cried Gildor laughing. 'Speak no secrets! Here is a scholar in the Ancient Tongue. Bilbo was a good master. Hail, Elf-friend!' he said, bowing to Frodo. 'Come now with your friends and join our company! You had best walk in the middle so that you may not stray. You may be weary before we halt.'

'Why? Where are you going?' asked Frodo.

'For tonight we go to the woods on the hills above Woodhall. It is some miles, but you shall have rest at the end of it, and it will shorten your journey tomorrow.'

They now marched on again in silence, and passed like shadows and faint lights: for Elves (even more than hobbits) could walk when they wished without sound or footfall. Pippin soon began to feel sleepy, and staggered once or twice; but each time a tall Elf at his side put out his arm and saved him from a fall. Sam walked along at Frodo's side, as if in a dream, with an expression on his face half of fear and half of astonished joy.

The woods on either side became denser; the trees were now younger and thicker; and as the lane went lower, running down into a fold of the hills, there were many deep brakes of hazel on the rising slopes at either hand. At last the Elves turned aside from the path. A green ride lay almost unseen through the thickets on the right; and this they followed as it wound away back up the wooded slopes on to the top of a shoulder of the hills that stood out into the lower land of the river-valley. Suddenly they came out of the shadow of the trees, and before them lay a wide space of grass, grey under the night. On three sides the woods pressed upon it; but east-ward the ground fell steeply and the tops of the dark trees, growing at the bottom of the slope, were below their feet. Beyond, the low lands lay dim and flat under the stars. Nearer at hand a few lights twinkled in the village of Woodhall.

The Elves sat on the grass and spoke together in soft voices; they seemed to take no further notice of the hobbits. Frodo and his companions wrapped themselves in cloaks and blankets, and drowsiness stole over them. The night grew on, and the lights in the valley went out. Pippin fell asleep, pillowed on a green hillock.

Away high in the East swung Remmirath, the Netted Stars, and slowly above the mists red Borgil rose, glowing like a jewel of fire. Then by some shift of airs all the mist was drawn away like a veil, and there leaned up, as he climbed over the rim of the world, the Swordsman of the Sky, Menelvagor with his shining belt. The Elves all burst into song. Suddenly under the trees a fire sprang up with a red light.

'Come!' the Elves called to the hobbits. 'Come! Now is the time for speech and merriment!'

Pippin sat up and rubbed his eyes. He shivered. 'There is a fire in the hall, and food for hungry guests,' said an Elf standing before him.

At the south end of the greensward there was an opening. There the green floor ran on into the wood, and formed a wide space like a hall, roofed by the boughs of trees. Their great trunks ran like pillars down each side. In the middle there was a wood-fire blazing, and upon the tree-pillars torches with lights of gold and silver were burning steadily. The Elves sat round the fire upon the grass or upon the sawn rings of old trunks. Some went to and fro bearing cups and pouring drink; others brought food on heaped plates and dishes.

'This is poor fare,' they said to the hobbits; 'for we are lodging in the greenwood far from our halls. If ever you are our guests at home, we will treat you better.'

'It seems to me good enough for a birthday-party,' said Frodo.

Pippin afterwards recalled little of either food or drink, for his mind was filled with the light upon the elf-faces, and the sound of voices so various and so beautiful that he felt in a waking dream. But he remembered that there was bread, surpassing the savour of a fair white loaf to one who is starving; and fruits sweet as wildberries and richer than the tended fruits of gardens; he drained a cup that was filled with a fragrant draught, cool as a clear fountain, golden as a summer afternoon.

Sam could never describe in words, nor picture clearly to himself, what he felt or thought that night, though it remained in his memory as one of the chief events of his life. The nearest he ever got was to say: 'Well, sir, if I could grow apples like that, I would call myself a gardener. But it was the singing that went to my heart, if you know what I mean.'

Frodo sat, eating, drinking, and talking with delight; but his mind was chiefly on the words spoken. He knew a little of the elf-speech and listened eagerly. Now and again he spoke to those that served him and thanked them in their own language. They smiled at him and said laughing: 'Here is a jewel among hobbits!'

After a while Pippin fell fast asleep, and was lifted up and borne away to a bower under the trees; there he was laid upon a soft bed and slept the rest of the night away. Sam refused to leave his master. When Pippin had gone, he came and sat curled up at Frodo's feet, where at last he nodded and closed his eyes. Frodo remained long awake, talking with Gildor.

They spoke of many things, old and new, and Frodo questioned Gildor much about happenings in the wide world outside the Shire. The tidings were mostly sad and ominous: of gathering darkness, the wars of Men, and the flight of the Elves. At last Frodo asked the question that was nearest to his heart:

'Tell me, Gildor, have you ever seen Bilbo since he left us?'

Gildor smiled. 'Yes,' he answered. 'Twice. He said farewell to us on this very spot. But I saw him once again, far from here.' He would say no more about Bilbo, and Frodo fell silent.

'You do not ask me or tell me much that concerns yourself, Frodo,' said Gildor. 'But I already know a little, and I can read more in your face and in the thought behind your questions. You are leaving the Shire, and yet you doubt that you will find what you seek, or accomplish what you intend, or that you will ever retu.n. Is not that so?'

'It is,' said Frodo; 'but I thought my going was a secret known only to Gandalf and my faithful Sam.' He looked down at Sam, who was snoring gently.

'The secret will not reach the Enemy from us,' said Gildor.

'The Enemy?' said Frodo. 'Then you know why I am leaving the Shire?'

'I do not know for what reason the Enemy is pursuing you,' answered Gildor; 'but I perceive that he is – strange indeed though that seems to me. And I warn you that peril is now both before you and behind you, and upon either side.'

'You mean the Riders? I feared that they were servants of the Enemy. What *are* the Black Riders?'

'Has Gandalf told you nothing?'

'Nothing about such creatures.'

'Then I think it is not for me to say more – lest terror should keep you from your journey. For it seems to me that you have set out only just in time, if indeed you are in time. You must now make haste, and neither stay nor turn back; for the Shire is no longer any protection to you.'

'I cannot imagine what information could be more terrifying than your hints and warnings,' exclaimed Frodo. 'I knew that danger lay ahead, of course; but I did not expect to meet it in our own Shire. Can't a hobbit walk from the Water to the River in peace?'

'But it is not your own Shire,' said Gildor. 'Others dwelt here before hobbits were; and others will dwell here again when hobbits are no more. The wide world is all about you: you can fence yourselves in, but you cannot for ever fence it out.'

'I know – and yet it has always seemed so safe and familiar. What can I do now? My plan was to leave the Shire secretly, and make my way to Rivendell; but now my footsteps are dogged, before ever I get to Buckland.'

'I think you should still follow that plan,' said Gildor. 'I do not think the Road will prove too hard for your courage. But if you desire clearer counsel, you should ask Gandalf. I do not know the reason for your flight, and therefore I do not know by what means your pursuers will assail you. These things Gandalf must know. I suppose that you will see him before you leave the Shire?'

'I hope so. But that is another thing that makes me anxious. I have been expecting Gandalf for many days. He was to have come to Hobbiton at the latest two nights ago; but he has never appeared. Now I am wondering what can have happened. Should I wait for him?'

Gildor was silent for a moment. 'I do not like this news,' he said at last. 'That Gandalf should be late, does not bode well. But it is said: *Do not meddle in the affairs of Wizards, for they are subtle and quick to anger.* The choice is yours: to go or wait.'

'And it is also said,' answered Frodo: '*Go not to the Elves for counsel, for they will say both no and yes.*'

'Is it indeed?' laughed Gildor. 'Elves seldom give unguarded advice, for advice is a dangerous gift, even from the wise to the wise, and all courses may run ill. But what would you? You have not told me all concerning yourself; and how then shall I choose better than you? But if you demand advice, I will for friendship's sake give it. I think you should now go at once, without delay; and if Gandalf does not come before you set out, then I also advise this: do not go alone. Take such friends as are trusty and willing. Now you should be grateful, for I do not give this counsel gladly. The Elves have their own labours and their own sorrows, and they are little concerned with the ways of hobbits, or of any other creatures upon earth. Our paths cross theirs seldom, by chance or purpose. In this meeting there may be more than chance; but the purpose is not clear to me, and I fear to say too much.'

'I am deeply grateful,' said Frodo; 'but I wish you would tell me plainly what the Black Riders are. If I take your advice I may not see Gandalf for a long while, and I ought to know what is the danger that pursues me.'

'Is it not enough to know that they are servants of the Enemy?' answered Gildor. 'Flee them! Speak no words to them! They are deadly. Ask no more of me! But my heart forbodes that, ere all is ended, you, Frodo son of Drogo, will know more of these fell things than Gildor Inglorion. May Elbereth protect you!'

'But where shall I find courage?' asked Frodo. 'That is what I chiefly need.'

'Courage is found in unlikely places,' said Gildor. 'Be of good hope! Sleep now! In the morning we shall have gone; but we will send our messages through the lands. The Wandering Companies shall know of your journey, and those that have power for good shall be on the watch. I name you Elf-friend; and may the stars shine upon the end of your road! Seldom have we had such delight in strangers, and it is fair to hear words of the Ancient Speech from the lips of other wanderers in the world.'

Frodo felt sleep coming upon him, even as Gildor finished speaking. 'I will sleep now,' he said; and the Elf led him to a bower beside Pippin, and he threw himself upon a bed and fell at once into a dreamless slumber.

CHAPTER IV

A SHORT CUT TO MUSHROOMS

In the morning Frodo woke refreshed. He was lying in a bower made by a living tree with branches laced and drooping to the ground; his bed was of fern and grass, deep and soft and strangely fragrant. The sun was shining through the fluttering leaves, which were still green upon the tree. He jumped up and went out.

Sam was sitting on the grass near the edge of the wood. Pippin was standing studying the sky and weather. There was no sign of the Elves.

'They have left us fruit and drink, and bread,' said Pippin. 'Come and have your breakfast. The bread tastes almost as good as it did last night. I did not want to leave you any, but Sam insisted.'

Frodo sat down beside Sam and began to eat. 'What is the plan for today?' asked Pippin.

'To walk to Bucklebury as quickly as possible,' answered Frodo, and gave his attention to the food.

'Do you think we shall see anything of those Riders?' asked Pippin cheerfully. Under the morning sun the prospect of seeing a whole troop of them did not seem very alarming to him.

'Yes, probably,' said Frodo, not liking the reminder. 'But I hope to get across the river without their seeing us.'

'Did you find out anything about them from Gildor?'

'Not much – only hints and riddles,' said Frodo evasively.

'Did you ask about the sniffing?'

'We didn't discuss it,' said Frodo with his mouth full.

'You should have. I am sure it is very important.'

'In that case I am sure Gildor would have refused to explain it,' said Frodo sharply. 'And now leave me in peace for a bit! I don't want to answer a string of questions while I am eating. I want to think!'

'Good heavens!' said Pippin. 'At breakfast?' He walked away towards the edge of the green.

From Frodo's mind the bright morning – treacherously bright, he thought – had not banished the fear of pursuit; and he pondered the words of Gildor. The merry voice of Pippin came to him. He was running on the green turf and singing.

'No! I could not!' he said to himself. 'It is one thing to take my young friends walking over the Shire with me, until we are hungry and weary, and food and bed are sweet. To take them into exile, where hunger and weariness may have no cure, is quite another – even if they are willing to come. The inheritance is mine alone. I don't think I ought even to take Sam.' He looked at Sam Gamgee, and discovered that Sam was watching him.

'Well, Sam!' he said. 'What about it? I am leaving the Shire as soon as ever I can – in fact I have made up my mind now not even to wait a day at Crickhollow, if it can be helped.'

'Very good, sir!'

'You still mean to come with me?'

'I do.'

'It is going to be very dangerous, Sam. It is already dangerous. Most likely neither of us will come back.'

'If you don't come back, sir, then I shan't, that's certain,' said Sam. '*Don't you leave him!* they said to me. *Leave him!* I said. *I never mean to. I am going with him, if he climbs to the Moon, and if any of those Black Riders try to stop him, they'll have Sam Gamgee to reckon with*, I said. They laughed.'

'Who are *they*, and what are you talking about?'

'The Elves, sir. We had some talk last night; and they seemed to know you were going away, so I didn't see the use of denying it. Wonderful folk, Elves, sir! Wonderful!'

'They are,' said Frodo. 'Do you like them still, now you have had a closer view?'

'They seem a bit above my likes and dislikes, so to speak,' answered Sam slowly. 'It don't seem to matter what I think about them. They are quite different from what I expected – so old and young, and so gay and sad, as it were.'

Frodo looked at Sam rather startled, half expecting to see some outward sign of the odd change that seemed to have come over him. It did not sound like the voice of the old Sam Gamgee that he thought he knew. But it looked like the old Sam Gamgee sitting there, except that his face was unusually thoughtful.

'Do you feel any need to leave the Shire now – now that your wish to see them has come true already?' he asked.

'Yes, sir. I don't know how to say it, but after last night I feel different. I seem to see ahead, in a kind of way. I know we are going to take a very long road, into darkness; but I know I can't turn back. It isn't to see Elves now, nor dragons, nor mountains, that I want – I don't rightly know what I want: but I have something to do before the end, and it lies ahead, not in the Shire. I must see it through, sir, if you understand me.'

'I don't altogether. But I understand that Gandalf chose me a good companion. I am content. We will go together.'

Frodo finished his breakfast in silence. Then standing up he looked over the land ahead, and called to Pippin.

'All ready to start?' he said as Pippin ran up. 'We must be getting off at once. We slept late; and there are a good many miles to go.'

'*You* slept late, you mean,' said Pippin. 'I was up long before; and we are only waiting for you to finish eating and thinking.'

'I have finished both now. And I am going to make for Bucklebury Ferry as quickly as possible. I am not going out of the way, back to the road we left last night: I am going to cut straight across country from here.'

'Then you are going to fly,' said Pippin. 'You won't cut straight on foot anywhere in this country.'

'We can cut straighter than the road anyway,' answered Frodo. 'The Ferry is east from Woodhall; but the hard road curves away to the left – you can see a bend of it away north over there. It goes round the north end of the Marish so as to strike the causeway from the Bridge above Stock. But that is miles out of the way. We could save a quarter of the distance if we made a line for the Ferry from where we stand.'

'*Short cuts make long delays*,' argued Pippin. 'The country is rough round here, and there are bogs and all kinds of difficulties down in the Marish – I know the land in these parts. And if you are worrying about Black Riders, I can't see that it is any worse meeting them on a road than in a wood or a field.'

'It is less easy to find people in the woods and fields,' answered Frodo. 'And if you are supposed to be on the road, there is some chance that you will be looked for on the road and not off it.'

'All right!' said Pippin. 'I will follow you into every bog and ditch. But it is hard! I had counted on passing the *Golden Perch* at Stock before sundown. The best beer in the Eastfarthing, or used to be: it is a long time since I tasted it.'

'That settles it!' said Frodo. 'Short cuts make delays, but inns make longer ones. At all costs we must keep you away from the *Golden Perch*. We want to get to Bucklebury before dark. What do you say, Sam?'

'I will go along with you, Mr. Frodo,' said Sam (in spite of private misgiving and a deep regret for the best beer in the Eastfarthing).

'Then if we are going to toil through bog and briar, let's go now!' said Pippin.

It was already nearly as hot as it had been the day before; but clouds were beginning to come up from the West. It looked likely to turn to rain. The hobbits scrambled down a steep green bank and plunged into the thick trees below. Their course had been chosen to leave Woodhall to their left, and to cut slanting through the woods that clustered along the eastern side of the hills, until they reached the flats beyond. Then they could make straight for the Ferry over country that was open, except for a few ditches and fences. Frodo reckoned they had eighteen miles to go in a straight line.

He soon found that the thicket was closer and more tangled than it had appeared. There were no paths in the undergrowth, and they did not get on very fast. When they had struggled to the bottom of the bank, they found a stream running down from the hills behind in a deeply dug bed with steep slippery sides overhung with brambles. Most inconveniently it cut across the line they had chosen. They could not jump over it, nor indeed get across it at all without getting wet, scratched, and muddy. They halted, wondering what to do. 'First check!' said Pippin, smiling grimly.

Sam Gamgee looked back. Through an opening in the trees he caught a glimpse of the top of the green bank from which they had climbed down. 'Look!' he said, clutching Frodo by the arm. They all looked, and on the edge high above them they saw against the sky a horse standing. Beside it stooped a black figure.

They at once gave up any idea of going back. Frodo led the way, and plunged quickly into the thick bushes beside the stream. 'Whew!' he said to Pippin. 'We were both right! The short cut has gone crooked already; but we got under cover only just in time. You've got sharp ears, Sam: can you hear anything coming?'

They stood still, almost holding their breath as they listened; but there was no sound of pursuit. 'I don't fancy he would try bringing his horse down that bank,' said Sam. 'But I guess he knows we came down it. We had better be going on.'

Going on was not altogether easy. They had packs to carry, and the bushes and brambles were reluctant to let them through. They were cut off from the wind by the ridge behind, and the air was still and stuffy. When they forced their way at last into more open ground, they were hot and tired and very scratched, and they were also no longer certain of the direction in which they were going. The banks of the stream sank, as it reached the levels and became broader and shallower, wandering off towards the Marish and the River.

'Why, this is the Stock-brook!' said Pippin. 'If we are going to try and get back on to our course, we must cross at once and bear right.'

They waded the stream, and hurried over a wide open space, rush-grown and treeless, on the further side. Beyond that they came again to a belt of trees: tall oaks, for the most part, with here and there an elm tree or an ash. The ground was fairly level, and there was little undergrowth; but the trees were too close for them to see far ahead. The leaves blew upwards in sudden gusts of wind, and spots of rain began to fall from the overcast sky. Then the wind died away and the rain came streaming down. They trudged along as fast as they could, over patches of grass, and through thick drifts of old leaves; and all about them the rain pattered and trickled. They did not talk, but kept glancing back, and from side to side.

After half an hour Pippin said: 'I hope we have not turned too much towards the south, and are not walking longwise through this wood! It is not a very broad belt – I should have said no more than a mile at the widest – and we ought to have been through it by now.'

'It is no good our starting to go in zig-zags,' said Frodo. 'That won't mend matters. Let us keep on as we are going! I am not sure that I want to come out into the open yet.'

They went on for perhaps another couple of miles. Then the sun gleamed out of ragged clouds again and the rain lessened. It was now past mid-day, and they felt it was high time for lunch. They halted under an elm tree: its leaves though fast turning yellow were still thick, and the ground at its feet was fairly dry and sheltered. When they came to make their meal, they found that the Elves had filled their bottles with a clear drink, pale golden in colour: it had the scent of a honey made of many flowers, and was wonderfully refreshing. Very soon they were laughing, and snapping their fingers at rain, and at Black Riders. The last few miles, they felt, would soon be behind them.

Frodo propped his back against the tree-trunk, and closed his eyes. Sam and Pippin sat near, and they began to hum, and then to sing softly:

> Ho! Ho! Ho! to the bottle I go
> To heal my heart and drown my woe.
> Rain may fall and wind may blow,
> And many miles be still to go,
> But under a tall tree I will lie,
> And let the clouds go sailing by.

Ho! Ho! Ho! they began again louder. They stopped short suddenly. Frodo sprang to his feet. A long-drawn wail came down the wind, like the cry of some evil and lonely creature. It rose and fell, and ended on a high piercing note. Even as they sat and stood, as if suddenly frozen, it was answered by another cry, fainter and further off, but no less chilling to the blood. There was then a silence, broken only by the sound of the wind in the leaves.

'And what do you think that was?' Pippin asked at last, trying to speak lightly, but quavering a little. 'If it was a bird, it was one that I never heard in the Shire before.'

'It was not bird or beast,' said Frodo. 'It was a call, or a signal – there were words in that cry, though I could not catch them. But no hobbit has such a voice.'

No more was said about it. They were all thinking of the Riders, but no one spoke of them. They were now reluctant either to stay or go on; but sooner or later they had got to get across the open country to the Ferry, and it was best to go sooner and in daylight. In a few moments they had shouldered their packs again and were off.

Before long the wood came to a sudden end. Wide grass-lands stretched before them. They now saw that they had, in fact, turned too much to the south. Away over the flats they could glimpse the low hill of Bucklebury across the River, but it was now to their left. Creeping cautiously out from the edge of the trees, they set off across the open as quickly as they could.

At first they felt afraid, away from the shelter of the wood. Far back behind them stood the high place where they had breakfasted. Frodo half expected to see the small distant figure of a horseman on the ridge dark against the sky; but there was no sign of one. The sun escaping from the breaking clouds, as it sank towards the hills they had left, was now shining brightly again. Their fear left them, though they still felt uneasy. But the land became steadily more tame and well-ordered. Soon they came into well-tended fields and meadows: there were hedges and gates and dikes for drainage. Everything seemed quiet and peaceful, just an ordinary corner of the Shire. Their spirits rose with every step. The line of the River grew nearer; and the Black Riders began to seem like phantoms of the woods now left far behind.

They passed along the edge of a huge turnip-field, and came to a stout gate. Beyond it a rutted lane ran between low well-laid hedges towards a distant clump of trees. Pippin stopped.

'I know these fields and this gate!' he said. 'This is Bamfurlong, old Farmer Maggot's land. That's his farm away there in the trees.'

'One trouble after another!' said Frodo, looking nearly as much alarmed as if Pippin had declared the lane was the slot leading to a dragon's den. The others looked at him in surprise.

'What's wrong with old Maggot?' asked Pippin. 'He's a good friend to all the Brandybucks. Of course he's a terror to trespassers, and keeps ferocious dogs – but after all, folk down here are near the border and have to be more on their guard.'

'I know,' said Frodo. 'But all the same,' he added with a shamefaced laugh, 'I am terrified of him and his dogs. I have avoided his farm for years and years. He caught me several times trespassing after mushrooms, when I was a youngster at Brandy Hall. On the last occasion he beat me, and then took me and showed me to his dogs. "See, lads," he said, "next time this young varmint sets foot on my land, you can eat him. Now see him off!' They chased me all the way to the Ferry. I have never got over the fright – though I daresay the beasts knew their business and would not really have touched me.'

Pippin laughed. 'Well, it's time you made it up. Especially if you are coming back to live in Buckland. Old Maggot is really a stout fellow – if you leave his mushrooms alone. Let's get into the lane and then we shan't be trespassing. If we meet him, I'll do the talking. He is a friend of Merry's, and I used to come here with him a good deal at one time.'

They went along the lane, until they saw the thatched roofs of a large house and farm-buildings peeping out among the trees ahead. The Maggots, and the Puddifoots of Stock, and most of the inhabitants of the Marish, were house-dwellers; and this farm was stoutly built of brick and had a high wall all round it. There was a wide wooden gate opening out of the wall into the lane.

Suddenly as they drew nearer a terrific baying and barking broke out, and a loud voice was heard shouting: 'Grip! Fang! Wolf! Come on, lads!'

Frodo and Sam stopped dead, but Pippin walked on a few paces. The gate opened and three huge dogs came pelting out into the lane, and dashed towards the travellers, barking fiercely. They took no notice of Pippin; but Sam shrank against the wall, while two wolvish-looking dogs sniffed at him suspiciously, and snarled if he moved. The largest and most ferocious of the three halted in front of Frodo, bristling and growling.

Through the gate there now appeared a broad thick-set hobbit with a round red face. 'Hallo! Hallo! And who may you be, and what may you be wanting?' he asked.

'Good afternoon, Mr. Maggot!' said Pippin.

The farmer looked at him closely. 'Well, if it isn't Master Pippin – Mr. Peregrin Took, I should say!' he cried, changing from a scowl to a grin. 'It's a long time since I saw you round here. It's lucky for you that I know you. I was just going out to set my dogs on any strangers. There are some funny things going on today. Of course, we do get queer folk wandering in these parts at times. Too near the River,' he said, shaking his head. 'But this fellow was the most outlandish I have ever set eyes on. He won't cross my land without leave a second time, not if I can stop it.'

'What fellow do you mean?' asked Pippin.

'Then you haven't seen him?' said the farmer. 'He went up the lane towards the causeway not a long while back. He was a funny customer and asking funny questions. But perhaps you'll come along inside, and we'll pass the news more comfortable. I've a drop of good ale on tap, if you and your friends are willing, Mr. Took.'

It seemed plain that the farmer would tell them more, if allowed to do it in his own time and fashion, so they all accepted the invitation. 'What about the dogs?' asked Frodo anxiously.

The farmer laughed. 'They won't harm you – not unless I tell 'em to. Here, Grip! Fang! Heel!' he cried. 'Heel, Wolf!' To the relief of Frodo and Sam, the dogs walked away and let them go free.

Pippin introduced the other two to the farmer. 'Mr. Frodo Baggins,' he said. 'You may not remember him, but he used to live at Brandy Hall.' At the name Baggins the farmer started, and gave Frodo a sharp glance. For a moment Frodo thought that the memory of stolen mushrooms had been aroused, and that the dogs would be told to see him off. But Farmer Maggot took him by the arm.

'Well, if that isn't queerer than ever?' he exclaimed. 'Mr. Baggins is it? Come inside! We must have a talk.'

They went into the farmer's kitchen, and sat by the wide fire-place. Mrs. Maggot brought out beer in a huge jug, and filled four large mugs. It was a good brew, and Pippin found himself more than compensated for missing the *Golden Perch*. Sam sipped his beer suspiciously. He had a natural mistrust of the inhabitants of other parts of the Shire; and also he was not disposed to be quick friends with anyone who had beaten his master, however long ago.

After a few remarks about the weather and the agricultural prospects (which were no worse than usual), Farmer Maggot put down his mug and looked at them all in turn.

'Now, Mr. Peregrin,' he said, 'where might you be coming from, and where might you be going to? Were you coming to visit me? For, if so, you had gone past my gate without my seeing you.'

'Well, no,' answered Pippin. 'To tell you the truth, since you have guessed it, we got into the lane from the other end: we had come over your fields. But that was quite by accident. We lost our way in the woods, back near Woodhall, trying to take a short cut to the Ferry.'

'If you were in a hurry, the road would have served you better,' said the farmer. 'But I wasn't worrying about that. You have leave to walk over my land, if you have a mind, Mr. Peregrin. And you, Mr. Baggins – though I daresay you still like mushrooms.' He laughed. 'Ah yes, I recognized the name. I recollect the time when young Frodo Baggins was one of the worst young rascals of Buckland. But it wasn't mushrooms I was thinking of. I had just heard the name Baggins before you turned up. What do you think that funny customer asked me?'

They waited anxiously for him to go on. 'Well,' the farmer continued, approaching his point with slow relish, 'he came riding on a big black horse in at the gate, which happened to be open, and right up to my door.

All black he was himself, too, and cloaked and hooded up, as if he did not want to be known. "Now what in the Shire can he want?" I thought to myself. We don't see many of the Big Folk over the border; and anyway I had never heard of any like this black fellow.

'"Good-day to you!" I says, going out to him. "This lane don't lead anywhere, and wherever you may be going, your quickest way will be back to the road." I didn't like the looks of him; and when Grip came out, he took one sniff and let out a yelp as if he had been stung: he put down his tail and bolted off howling. The black fellow sat quite still.

'"I come from yonder," he said, slow and stiff-like, pointing back west, over *my* fields, if you please. "Have you seen *Baggins*?" he asked in a queer voice, and bent down towards me. I could not see any face, for his hood fell down so low; and I felt a sort of shiver down my back. But I did not see why he should come riding over my land so bold.

'"Be off!" I said. "There are no Bagginses here. You're in the wrong part of the Shire. You had better go back west to Hobbiton – but you can go by road this time."

'"Baggins has left," he answered in a whisper. "He is coming. He is not far away. I wish to find him. If he passes will you tell me? I will come back with gold."

'"No you won't," I said. "You'll go back where you belong, double quick. I give you one minute before I call all my dogs."

'He gave a sort of hiss. It might have been laughing, and it might not. Then he spurred his great horse right at me, and I jumped out of the way only just in time. I called the dogs, but he swung off, and rode through the gate and up the lane towards the causeway like a bolt of thunder. What do you think of that?'

Frodo sat for a moment looking at the fire, but his only thought was how on earth would they reach the Ferry. 'I don't know what to think,' he said at last.

'Then I'll tell you what to think,' said Maggot. 'You should never have gone mixing yourself up with Hobbiton folk, Mr. Frodo. Folk are queer up there.' Sam stirred in his chair, and looked at the farmer with an unfriendly eye. 'But you were always a reckless lad. When I heard you had left the Brandybucks and gone off to that old Mr. Bilbo, I said that you were going to find trouble. Mark my words, this all comes of those strange doings of Mr. Bilbo's. His money was got in some strange fashion in foreign parts, they say. Maybe there is some that want to know what has become of the gold and jewels that he buried in the hill of Hobbiton, as I hear?'

Frodo said nothing: the shrewd guesses of the farmer were rather disconcerting.

'Well, Mr. Frodo,' Maggot went on, 'I'm glad that you've had the sense to come back to Buckland. My advice is: stay there! And don't get mixed up with these outlandish folk. You'll have friends in these parts. If any of these black fellows come after you again, I'll deal with them. I'll say you're dead, or have left the Shire, or anything you like. And that might be true enough; for as like as not it is old Mr. Bilbo they want news of.'

'Maybe you're right,' said Frodo, avoiding the farmer's eye and staring at the fire.

Maggot looked at him thoughtfully. 'Well, I see you have ideas of your own,' he said. 'It is as plain as my nose that no accident brought you and that rider here on the same afternoon; and maybe my news was no great news to you, after all. I am not asking you to tell me anything you have a mind to keep to yourself; but I see you are in some kind of trouble. Perhaps you are thinking it won't be too easy to get to the Ferry without being caught?'

'I was thinking so,' said Frodo. 'But we have got to try and get there; and it won't be done by sitting and thinking. So I am afraid we must be going. Thank you very much indeed for your kindness! I've been in terror of you and your dogs for over thirty years, Farmer Maggot, though you may laugh to hear it. It's a pity: for I've missed a good friend. And now I'm sorry to leave so soon. But I'll come back, perhaps, one day – if I get a chance.'

'You'll be welcome when you come,' said Maggot. 'But now I've a notion. It's near sundown already, and we are going to have our supper; for we mostly go to bed soon after the Sun. If you and Mr. Peregrin and all could stay and have a bite with us, we would be pleased!'

'And so should we!' said Frodo. 'But we must be going at once, I'm afraid. Even now it will be dark before we can reach the Ferry.'

'Ah! but wait a minute! I was going to say: after a bit of supper, I'll get out a small waggon, and I'll drive you all to the Ferry. That will save you a good step, and it might also save you trouble of another sort.'

Frodo now accepted the invitation gratefully, to the relief of Pippin and Sam. The sun was already behind the western hills, and the light was failing. Two of Maggot's sons and his three daughters came in, and a generous supper was laid on the large table. The kitchen was lit with candles and the fire was mended. Mrs. Maggot bustled in and out. One or two other hobbits belonging to the farm-household came in. In a short while fourteen sat down to eat. There was beer in plenty, and a mighty dish of mushrooms and bacon, besides much other solid farmhouse fare. The dogs lay by the fire and gnawed rinds and cracked bones.

When they had finished, the farmer and his sons went out with a lantern and got the waggon ready. It was dark in the yard, when the guests came out. They threw their packs on board and climbed in. The farmer sat in the driving-seat, and whipped up his two stout ponies. His wife stood in the light of the open door.

'You be careful of yourself, Maggot!' she called. 'Don't go arguing with any foreigners, and come straight back!'

'I will!' said he, and drove out of the gate. There was now no breath of wind stirring; the night was still and quiet, and a chill was in the air. They went without lights and took it slowly. After a mile or two the lane came to an end, crossing a deep dike, and climbing a short slope up on to the high-banked causeway.

Maggot got down and took a good look either way, north and south, but nothing could be seen in the darkness, and there was not a sound in the still air. Thin strands of river-mist were hanging above the dikes, and crawling over the fields.

'It's going to be thick,' said Maggot; 'but I'll not light my lantern till I turn for home. We'll hear anything on the road long before we meet it tonight.'

It was five miles or more from Maggot's lane to the Ferry. The hobbits wrapped themselves up, but their ears were strained for any sound above the creak of the wheels and the slow *clop* of the ponies' hoofs. The waggon seemed slower than a snail to Frodo. Beside him Pippin was nodding towards sleep; but Sam was staring forwards into the rising fog.

They reached the entrance to the Ferry lane at last. It was marked by two tall white posts that suddenly loomed up on their right. Farmer Maggot drew in his ponies and the waggon creaked to a halt. They were just beginning to scramble out, when suddenly they heard what they had all been dreading: hoofs on the road ahead. The sound was coming towards them.

Maggot jumped down and stood holding the ponies' heads, and peering forward into the gloom. *Clip-clop, clip-clop* came the approaching rider. The fall of the hoofs sounded loud in the still, foggy air.

'You'd better be hidden, Mr. Frodo,' said Sam anxiously. 'You get down in the waggon and cover up with blankets, and we'll send this rider to the rightabouts!' He climbed out and went to the farmer's side. Black Riders would have to ride over him to get near the waggon.

Clop-clop, clop-clop. The rider was nearly on them.

'Hallo there!' called Farmer Maggot. The advancing hoofs stopped short. They thought they could dimly guess a dark cloaked shape in the mist, a yard or two ahead.

'Now then!' said the farmer, throwing the reins to Sam and striding forward. 'Don't you come a step nearer! What do you want, and where are you going?'

'I want Mr. Baggins. Have you seen him?' said a muffled voice – but the voice was the voice of Merry Brandybuck. A dark lantern was uncovered, and its light fell on the astonished face of the farmer.

'Mr. Merry!' he cried.

'Yes, of course! Who did you think it was?' said Merry coming forward. As he came out of the mist and their fears subsided, he seemed suddenly to diminish to ordinary hobbit-size. He was riding a pony, and a scarf was swathed round his neck and over his chin to keep out the fog.

Frodo sprang out of the waggon to greet him. 'So there you are at last!' said Merry. 'I was beginning to wonder if you would turn up at all today, and I was just going back to supper. When it grew foggy I came across and rode up towards Stock to see if you had fallen in any ditches. But I'm blest if I know which way you have come. Where did you find them, Mr. Maggot? In your duck-pond?'

'No, I caught 'em trespassing,' said the farmer, 'and nearly set my dogs on 'em; but they'll tell you all the story, I've no doubt. Now, if you'll excuse me, Mr. Merry and Mr. Frodo and all, I'd best be turning for home. Mrs. Maggot will be worriting with the night getting thick.'

He backed the waggon into the lane and turned it. 'Well, good night to you all,' he said. 'It's been a queer day, and no mistake. But all's well as ends well; though perhaps we should not say that until we reach our own doors. I'll not deny that I'll be glad now when I do.' He lit his lanterns, and got up. Suddenly he produced a large basket from under the seat. 'I was nearly forgetting,' he said. 'Mrs. Maggot put this up for Mr. Baggins, with her compliments.' He handed it down and moved off, followed by a chorus of thanks and good-nights.

They watched the pale rings of light round his lanterns as they dwindled into the foggy night. Suddenly Frodo laughed: from the covered basket he held, the scent of mushrooms was rising.

CHAPTER V

A CONSPIRACY UNMASKED

'Now we had better get home ourselves,' said Merry. 'There's something funny about all this, I see; but it must wait till we get in.'

They turned down the Ferry lane, which was straight and well-kept and edged with large white-washed stones. In a hundred yards or so it brought them to the river-bank, where there was a broad wooden landing-stage. A large flat ferry-boat was moored beside it. The white bollards near the water's edge glimmered in the light of two lamps on high posts. Behind them the mists in the flat fields were now above the hedges; but the water before them was dark, with only a few curling wisps like steam among the reeds by the bank. There seemed to be less fog on the further side.

Merry led the pony over a gangway on to the ferry, and the others followed. Merry then pushed slowly off with a long pole. The Brandywine flowed slow and broad before them. On the other side the bank was steep, and up it a winding path climbed from the further landing. Lamps were twinkling there. Behind loomed up the Buck Hill; and out of it, through stray shrouds of mist, shone many round windows, yellow and red. They were the windows of Brandy Hall, the ancient home of the Brandybucks.

Long ago Gorhendad Oldbuck, head of the Oldbuck family, one of the oldest in the Marish or indeed in the Shire, had crossed the river, which was the original boundary of the land eastwards. He built (and excavated) Brandy Hall, changed his name to Brandybuck, and settled down to become master of what was virtually a small independent country. His family grew and grew, and after his days continued to grow, until Brandy Hall occupied the whole of the low hill, and had three large front-doors, many side-doors, and about a hundred windows. The Brandybucks and their numerous dependants then began to burrow, and later to build, all round about. That was the origin of Buckland, a thickly inhabited strip between the river and the Old Forest, a sort of colony from the Shire. Its chief village was Bucklebury, clustering in the banks and slopes behind Brandy Hall.

The people in the Marish were friendly with the Bucklanders, and the authority of the Master of the Hall (as the head of the Brandybuck family was called) was still acknowledged by the farmers between Stock and Rushey. But most of the folk of the old Shire regarded the Bucklanders as peculiar, half foreigners as it were. Though, as a matter of fact, they were not very different from the other hobbits of the Four Farthings. Except in one point: they were fond of boats, and some of them could swim.

Their land was originally unprotected from the East; but on that side they had built a hedge: the High Hay. It had been planted many generations ago, and was now thick and tall, for it was constantly tended. It ran all the way from Brandywine Bridge, in a big loop curving away from the river, to Haysend (where the Withywindle flowed out of the Forest into the Brandywine): well over twenty miles from end to end. But, of course, it was not a complete protection. The Forest drew close to the hedge in many places. The Bucklanders kept their doors locked after dark, and that also was not usual in the Shire.

The ferry-boat moved slowly across the water. The Buckland shore drew nearer. Sam was the only member of the party who had not been over the river before. He had a strange feeling as the slow gurgling stream slipped by: his old life lay behind in the mists, dark adventure lay in front. He scratched his head, and for a moment had a passing wish that Mr. Frodo could have gone on living quietly at Bag End.

The four hobbits stepped off the ferry. Merry was tying it up, and Pippin was already leading the pony up the path, when Sam (who had been looking back, as if to take farewell of the Shire) said in a hoarse whisper:

'Look back, Mr. Frodo! Do you see anything?'

On the far stage, under the distant lamps, they could just make out a figure: it looked like a dark black bundle left behind. But as they looked it seemed to move and sway this way and that, as if searching the ground. It then crawled, or went crouching, back into the gloom beyond the lamps.

'What in the Shire is that?' exclaimed Merry.

'Something that is following us,' said Frodo. 'But don't ask any more now! Let's get away at once!' They hurried up the path to the top of the bank, but when they looked back the far shore was shrouded in mist, and nothing could be seen.

'Thank goodness you don't keep any boats on the west-bank!' said Frodo. 'Can horses cross the river?'

'They can go twenty miles north to Brandywine Bridge – or they might swim,' answered Merry. 'Though I never heard of any horse swimming the Brandywine. But what have horses to do with it?'

'I'll tell you later. Let's get indoors and then we can talk.'

'All right! You and Pippin know your way; so I'll just ride on and tell Fatty Bolger that you are coming. We'll see about supper and things.'

'We had our supper early with Farmer Maggot,' said Frodo; 'but we could do with another.'

'You shall have it! Give me that basket!' said Merry, and rode ahead into the darkness.

It was some distance from the Brandywine to Frodo's new house at Crickhollow. They passed Buck Hill and Brandy Hall on their left, and on the outskirts of Bucklebury struck the main road of Buckland that ran south from the Bridge. Half a mile northward along this they came to a lane opening on their right. This they followed for a couple of miles as it climbed up and down into the country.

At last they came to a narrow gate in a thick hedge. Nothing could be seen of the house in the dark: it stood back from the lane in the middle of a wide circle of lawn surrounded by a belt of low trees inside the outer hedge. Frodo had chosen it, because it stood in an out-of-the-way corner of the country, and there were no other dwellings close by. You could get in and out without being noticed. It had been built a long while before by the Brandybucks, for the use of guests, or members of the family that wished to escape from the crowded life of Brandy Hall for a time. It was an old-fashioned countrified house, as much like a hobbit-hole as possible: it was long and low, with no upper storey; and it had a roof of turf, round windows, and a large round door.

As they walked up the green path from the gate no light was visible; the windows were dark and shuttered. Frodo knocked on the door, and Fatty Bolger opened it. A friendly light streamed out. They slipped in quickly and shut themselves and the light inside. They were in a wide hall with doors on either side; in front of them a passage ran back down the middle of the house.

'Well, what do you think of it?' asked Merry coming up the passage. 'We have done our best in a short time to make it look like home. After all Fatty and I only got here with the last cart-load yesterday.'

Frodo looked round. It did look like home. Many of his own favourite things – or Bilbo's things (they reminded him sharply of him in their new setting) – were arranged as nearly as possible as they had been at Bag End. It was a pleasant, comfortable, welcoming place; and he found himself wishing that he was really coming here to settle down in quiet retirement. It seemed unfair to have put his friends to all this trouble; and he wondered again how he was going to break the news to them that he must leave them so soon, indeed at once. Yet that would have to be done that very night, before they all went to bed.

'It's delightful!' he said with an effort. 'I hardly feel that I have moved at all.'

The travellers hung up their cloaks, and piled their packs on the floor. Merry led them down the passage and threw open a door at the far end. Firelight came out, and a puff of steam.

'A bath!' cried Pippin. 'O blessed Meriadoc!'

'Which order shall we go in?' said Frodo. 'Eldest first, or quickest first? You'll be last either way, Master Peregrin.'

'Trust me to arrange things better than that!' said Merry. 'We can't begin life at Crickhollow with a quarrel over baths. In that room there are *three* tubs, and a copper full of boiling water. There are also towels, mats and soap. Get inside, and be quick!'

Merry and Fatty went into the kitchen on the other side of the passage, and busied themselves with the final preparations for a late supper. Snatches of competing songs came from the bathroom mixed with the sound of splashing and wallowing. The voice of Pippin was suddenly lifted up above the others in one of Bilbo's favourite bath-songs.

> *Sing hey! for the bath at close of day*
> *that washes the weary mud away!*
> *A loon is he that will not sing:*
> *O! Water Hot is a noble thing!*
>
> *O! Sweet is the sound of falling rain,*
> *and the brook that leaps from hill to plain;*
> *but better than rain or rippling streams*
> *is Water Hot that smokes and steams.*
>
> *O! Water cold we may pour at need*
> *down a thirsty throat and be glad indeed;*
> *but better is Beer, if drink we lack,*
> *and Water Hot poured down the back.*
>
> *O! Water is fair that leaps on high*
> *in a fountain white beneath the sky;*
> *but never did fountain sound so sweet*
> *as splashing Hot Water with my feet!*

There was a terrific splash, and a shout of *Whoa!* from Frodo. It appeared that a lot of Pippin's bath had imitated a fountain and leaped on high.

Merry went to the door: 'What about supper and beer in the throat?' he called. Frodo came out drying his hair.

'There's so much water in the air that I'm coming into the kitchen to finish,' he said.

'Lawks!' said Merry, looking in. The stone floor was swimming. 'You ought to mop all that up before you get anything to eat, Peregrin,' he said. 'Hurry up, or we shan't wait for you.'

They had supper in the kitchen on a table near the fire. 'I suppose you three won't want mushrooms again?' said Fredegar without much hope.

'Yes we shall!' cried Pippin.

'They're mine!' said Frodo. 'Given to *me* by Mrs. Maggot, a queen among farmers' wives. Take your greedy hands away, and I'll serve them.'

Hobbits have a passion for mushrooms, surpassing even the greediest likings of Big People. A fact which partly explains young Frodo's long expeditions to the renowned fields of the Marish, and the wrath of the injured Maggot. On this occasion there was plenty for all, even according to hobbit standards. There were also many other things to follow, and when they had finished even Fatty Bolger heaved a sigh of content. They pushed back the table, and drew chairs round the fire.

'We'll clear up later,' said Merry. 'Now tell me all about it! I guess that you have been having adventures, which was not quite fair without me. I want a full account; and most of all I want to know what was the matter with old Maggot, and why he spoke to me like that. He sounded almost as if he was *scared*, if that is possible.'

'We have all been scared,' said Pippin after a pause, in which Frodo stared at the fire and did not speak. 'You would have been, too, if you had been chased for two days by Black Riders.'

'And what are they?'

'Black figures riding on black horses,' answered Pippin. 'If Frodo won't talk, I will tell you the whole tale from the beginning.' He then gave a full account of their journey from the time when they left Hobbiton. Sam gave various supporting nods and exclamations. Frodo remained silent.

'I should think you were making it all up,' said Merry, 'if I had not seen that black shape on the landing-stage – and heard the queer sound in Maggot's voice. What do you make of it all, Frodo?'

'Cousin Frodo has been very close,' said Pippin. 'But the time has come for him to open out. So far we have been given nothing more to go on than Farmer Maggot's guess that it has something to do with old Bilbo's treasure.'

'That was only a guess,' said Frodo hastily. 'Maggot does not *know* anything.'

'Old Maggot is a shrewd fellow,' said Merry. 'A lot goes on behind his round face that does not come out in his talk. I've heard that he used to go into the Old Forest at one time, and he has the reputation of knowing a good many strange things. But you can at least tell us, Frodo, whether you think his guess good or bad.'

'I *think*,' answered Frodo slowly, 'that it was a good guess, as far as it goes. There *is* a connexion with Bilbo's old adventures, and the Riders are looking, or perhaps one ought to say *searching*, for him or for me. I also fear, if you want to know, that it is no joke at all; and that I am not safe here or anywhere else.' He looked round at the windows and walls, as if he was afraid they would suddenly give way. The others looked at him in silence, and exchanged meaning glances among themselves.

'It's coming out in a minute,' whispered Pippin to Merry. Merry nodded.

'Well!' said Frodo at last, sitting up and straightening his back, as if he had made a decision. 'I can't keep it dark any longer. I have got something to tell you all. But I don't know quite how to begin.'

'I think I could help you,' said Merry quietly, 'by telling you some of it myself.'

'What do you mean?' said Frodo, looking at him anxiously.

'Just this, my dear old Frodo: you are miserable, because you don't know how to say good-bye. You meant to leave the Shire, of course. But danger has come on you sooner than you expected, and now you are making up your mind to go at once. And you don't want to. We are very sorry for you.'

Frodo opened his mouth and shut it again. His look of surprise was so comical that they laughed. 'Dear old Frodo!' said Pippin. 'Did you really think you had thrown dust in all our eyes? You have not been nearly careful or clever enough for that! You have obviously been planning to go and saying farewell to all your haunts all this year since April. We have constantly heard you muttering: "Shall I ever look down into that valley again, I wonder", and things like that. And pretending that you had come to the end of your money, and actually selling your beloved Bag End to those Sackville-Bagginses! And all those close talks with Gandalf.'

'Good heavens!' said Frodo. 'I thought I had been both careful and clever. I don't know what Gandalf would say. Is all the Shire discussing my departure then?'

'Oh no!' said Merry. 'Don't worry about that! The secret won't keep for long, of course; but at present it is, I think, only known to us conspirators. After all, you must remember that we know you well, and are often with you. We can usually guess what you are thinking. I knew Bilbo, too. To tell you the truth, I had been watching you rather closely ever since he left. I thought you would go after him sooner or later; indeed I expected you to go sooner, and lately we have been very anxious. We have been terrified that you might give us the slip, and go off suddenly, all on your own like he did. Ever since this spring we have kept our eyes open, and done a good deal of planning on our own account. You are not going to escape so easily!'

'But I must go,' said Frodo. 'It cannot be helped, dear friends. It is wretched for us all, but it is no use your trying to keep me. Since you have guessed so much, please help me and do not hinder me!'

'You do not understand!' said Pippin. 'You must go – and therefore we must, too. Merry and I are coming with you. Sam is an excellent fellow, and would jump down a dragon's throat to save you, if he did not trip over his own feet; but you will need more than one companion in your dangerous adventure.'

'My dear and most beloved hobbits!' said Frodo deeply moved. 'But I could not allow it. I decided that long ago, too. You speak of danger, but you do not understand. This is no treasure-hunt, no there-and-back journey. I am flying from deadly peril into deadly peril.'

'Of course we understand,' said Merry firmly. 'That is why we have decided to come. We know the Ring is no laughing-matter; but we are going to do our best to help you against the Enemy.'

'The Ring!' said Frodo, now completely amazed.

'Yes, the Ring,' said Merry. 'My dear old hobbit, you don't allow for the inquisitiveness of friends. I have known about the existence of the Ring for years – before Bilbo went away, in fact; but since he obviously regarded it as secret, I kept the knowledge in my head, until we formed our conspiracy. I did not know Bilbo, of course, as well as I know you; I was too young, and he was also more careful – but he was not careful enough. If you want to know how I first found out, I will tell you.'

'Go on!' said Frodo faintly.

'It was the Sackville-Bagginses that were his downfall, as you might expect. One day, a year before the Party, I happened to be walking along the road, when I saw Bilbo ahead. Suddenly in the distance the S.-B.s appeared, coming towards us. Bilbo slowed down, and then hey presto! he vanished. I was so startled that I hardly had the wits to hide myself in a more ordinary fashion; but I got through the hedge and walked along the field inside. I was peeping through into the road, after the S.-B.s had passed, and was looking straight at Bilbo when he suddenly reappeared. I caught a glint of gold as he put something back in his trouser-pocket.

'After that I kept my eyes open. In fact, I confess that I spied. But you must admit that it was very intriguing, and I was only in my teens. I must be the only one in the Shire, besides you Frodo, that has ever seen the old fellow's secret book.'

'You have read his book!' cried Frodo. 'Good heavens above! Is nothing safe?'

'Not too safe, I should say,' said Merry. 'But I have only had one rapid glance, and that was difficult to get. He never left the book about. I wonder what became of it. I should like another look. Have you got it, Frodo?'

'No. It was not at Bag End. He must have taken it away.'

'Well, as I was saying,' Merry proceeded, 'I kept my knowledge to myself, till this Spring when things got serious. Then we formed our conspiracy; and as we were serious, too, and meant business, we have not been too scrupulous. You are not a very easy nut to crack, and Gandalf is worse. But if you want to be introduced to our chief investigator, I can produce him.'

'Where is he?' said Frodo, looking round, as if he expected a masked and sinister figure to come out of a cupboard.

'Step forward, Sam!' said Merry; and Sam stood up with a face scarlet up to the ears. 'Here's our collector of information! And he collected a lot, I can tell you, before he was finally caught. After which, I may say, he seemed to regard himself as on parole, and dried up.'

'Sam!' cried Frodo, feeling that amazement could go no further, and quite unable to decide whether he felt angry, amused, relieved, or merely foolish.

'Yes, sir!' said Sam. 'Begging your pardon, sir! But I meant no wrong to you, Mr. Frodo, nor to Mr. Gandalf for that matter. *He* has some sense, mind you; and when you said *go alone*, he said *no! take someone as you can trust.*'

'But it does not seem that I can trust anyone,' said Frodo.

Sam looked at him unhappily. 'It all depends on what you want,' put in Merry. 'You can trust us to stick to you through thick and thin – to the bitter end. And you can trust us to keep any secret of yours – closer than you keep it yourself. But you cannot trust us to let you face trouble alone, and go off without a word. We are your friends, Frodo. Anyway: there it is. We know most of what Gandalf has told you. We know a good deal about the Ring. We are horribly afraid – but we are coming with you; or following you like hounds.'

'And after all, sir,' added Sam, 'you did ought to take the Elves' advice. Gildor said you should take them as was willing, and you can't deny it.'

'I don't deny it,' said Frodo, looking at Sam, who was now grinning. 'I don't deny it, but I'll never believe you are sleeping again, whether you snore or not. I shall kick you hard to make sure.

'You are a set of deceitful scoundrels!' he said, turning to the others. 'But bless you!' he laughed, getting up and waving his arms, 'I give in. I will take Gildor's advice. If the danger were not so dark, I should dance for joy. Even so, I cannot help feeling happy; happier than I have felt for a long time. I had dreaded this evening.'

'Good! That's settled. Three cheers for Captain Frodo and company!'

they shouted; and they danced round him. Merry and Pippin began a song, which they had apparently got ready for the occasion.

It was made on the model of the dwarf-song that started Bilbo on his adventure long ago, and went to the same tune:

> *Farewell we call to hearth and hall!*
> *Though wind may blow and rain may fall,*
> *We must away ere break of day*
> *Far over wood and mountain tall.*

> *To Rivendell, where Elves yet dwell*
> *In glades beneath the misty fell,*
> *Through moor and waste we ride in haste,*
> *And whither then we cannot tell.*

> *With foes ahead, behind us dread,*
> *Beneath the sky shall be our bed,*
> *Until at last our toil be passed,*
> *Our journey done, our errand sped.*

> *We must away! We must away!*
> *We ride before the break of day!*

'Very good!' said Frodo. 'But in that case there are a lot of things to do before we go to bed – under a roof, for tonight at any rate.'

'Oh! That was poetry!' said Pippin. 'Do you really mean to start before the break of day?'

'I don't know,' answered Frodo. 'I fear those Black Riders, and I am sure it is unsafe to stay in one place long, especially in a place to which it is known I was going. Also Gildor advised me not to wait. But I should very much like to see Gandalf. I could see that even Gildor was disturbed when he heard that Gandalf had never appeared. It really depends on two things. How soon could the Riders get to Bucklebury? And how soon could we get off? It will take a good deal of preparation.'

'The answer to the second question,' said Merry, 'is that we could get off in an hour. I have prepared practically everything. There are six ponies in a stable across the fields; stores and tackle are all packed, except for a few extra clothes, and the perishable food.'

'It seems to have been a very efficient conspiracy,' said Frodo. 'But what about the Black Riders? Would it be safe to wait one day for Gandalf?'

'That all depends on what you think the Riders would do, if they found you here,' answered Merry. 'They *could* have reached here by now, of course, if they were not stopped at the North-gate, where the Hedge runs down to the river-bank, just this side of the Bridge. The gate-guards would not let them through by night, though they might break through. Even in the daylight they would try to keep them out, I think, at any rate until they got a message through to the Master of the Hall – for they would not like the look of the Riders, and would certainly be frightened by them. But, of course, Buckland cannot resist a determined attack for long. And it is possible that in the morning even a Black Rider that rode up and asked for Mr. Baggins would be let through. It is pretty generally known that you are coming back to live at Crickhollow.'

Frodo sat for a while in thought. 'I have made up my mind,' he said finally. 'I am starting tomorrow, as soon as it is light. But I am not going by road: it would be safer to wait here than that. If I go through the North-gate my departure from Buckland will be known at once, instead of being secret for several days at least, as it might be. And what is more, the Bridge and the East Road near the borders will certainly be watched, whether any Rider gets into Buckland or not. We don't know how many there are; but there are at least two, and possibly more. The only thing to do is to go off in a quite unexpected direction.'

'But that can only mean going into the Old Forest!' said Fredegar horrified. 'You can't be thinking of doing that. It is quite as dangerous as Black Riders.'

'Not quite,' said Merry. 'It sounds very desperate, but I believe Frodo is right. It is the only way of getting off without being followed at once. With luck we might get a considerable start.'

'But you won't have any luck in the Old Forest,' objected Fredegar. 'No one ever has luck in there. You'll get lost. People don't go in there.'

'Oh yes they do!' said Merry. 'The Brandybucks go in – occasionally when the fit takes them. We have a private entrance. Frodo went in once, long ago. I have been in several times: usually in daylight, of course, when the trees are sleepy and fairly quiet.'

'Well, do as you think best!' said Fredegar. 'I am more afraid of the Old Forest than of anything I know about: the stories about it are a nightmare; but my vote hardly counts, as I am not going on the journey. Still, I am very glad someone is stopping behind, who can tell Gandalf what you have done, when he turns up, as I am sure he will before long.'

Fond as he was of Frodo, Fatty Bolger had no desire to leave the Shire, nor to see what lay outside it. His family came from the Eastfarthing, from Budgeford in Bridgefields in fact, but he had never been over the Brandywine Bridge. His task, according to the original plans of the conspirators, was to stay behind and deal with inquisitive folk, and to keep up as long as possible the pretence that Mr. Baggins was still living at Crickhollow. He had even brought along some old clothes of Frodo's to help him in playing the part. They little thought how dangerous that part might prove.

'Excellent!' said Frodo, when he understood the plan. 'We could not have left any message behind for Gandalf otherwise. I don't know whether these Riders can read or not, of course, but I should not have dared to risk a written message, in case they got in and searched the house. But if Fatty is willing to hold the fort, and I can be sure of Gandalf knowing the way we have gone, that decides me. I am going into the Old Forest first thing tomorrow.'

'Well, that's that,' said Pippin. 'On the whole I would rather have our job than Fatty's – waiting here till Black Riders come.'

'You wait till you are well inside the Forest,' said Fredegar. 'You'll wish you were back here with me before this time tomorrow.'

'It's no good arguing about it any more,' said Merry. 'We have still got to tidy up and put the finishing touches to the packing, before we get to bed. I shall call you all before the break of day.'

When at last he had got to bed, Frodo could not sleep for some time. His legs ached. He was glad that he was riding in the morning. Eventually he fell into a vague dream, in which he seemed to be looking out of a high window over a dark sea of tangled trees. Down below among the roots there was the sound of creatures crawling and snuffling. He felt sure they would smell him out sooner or later.

Then he heard a noise in the distance. At first he thought it was a great wind coming over the leaves of the forest. Then he knew that it was not leaves, but the sound of the Sea far-off; a sound he had never heard in waking life, though it had often troubled his dreams. Suddenly he found he was out in the open. There were no trees after all. He was on a dark heath, and there was a strange salt smell in the air. Looking up he saw before him a tall white tower, standing alone on a high ridge. A great desire came over him to climb the tower and see the Sea. He started to struggle up the ridge towards the tower: but suddenly a light came in the sky, and there was a noise of thunder.

CHAPTER VI

THE OLD FOREST

Frodo woke suddenly. It was still dark in the room. Merry was standing there with a candle in one hand, and banging on the door with the other. 'All right! What is it?' said Frodo, still shaken and bewildered.

'What is it!' cried Merry. 'It is time to get up. It is half past four and very foggy. Come on! Sam is already getting breakfast ready. Even Pippin is up. I am just going to saddle the ponies, and fetch the one that is to be the baggage-carrier. Wake that sluggard Fatty! At least he must get up and see us off.'

Soon after six o'clock the five hobbits were ready to start. Fatty Bolger was still yawning. They stole quietly out of the house. Merry went in front leading a laden pony, and took his way along a path that went through a spinney behind the house, and then cut across several fields. The leaves of trees were glistening, and every twig was dripping; the grass was grey with cold dew. Everything was still, and far-away noises seemed near and clear: fowls chattering in a yard, someone closing a door of a distant house.

In their shed they found the ponies; sturdy little beasts of the kind loved by hobbits, not speedy, but good for a long day's work. They mounted, and soon they were riding off into the mist, which seemed to open reluctantly before them and close forbiddingly behind them. After riding for about an hour, slowly and without talking, they saw the Hedge looming suddenly ahead. It was tall and netted over with silver cobwebs.

'How are you going to get through this?' asked Fredegar.

'Follow me!' said Merry, 'and you will see.' He turned to the left along the Hedge, and soon they came to a point where it bent inwards, running along the lip of a hollow. A cutting had been made, at some distance from the Hedge, and went sloping gently down into the ground. It had walls of brick at the sides, which rose steadily, until suddenly they arched over and formed a tunnel that dived deep under the Hedge and came out in the hollow on the other side.

Here Fatty Bolger halted. 'Good-bye, Frodo!' he said. 'I wish you were not going into the Forest. I only hope you will not need rescuing before the day is out. But good luck to you – today and every day!'

'If there are no worse things ahead than the Old Forest, I shall be lucky,' said Frodo. 'Tell Gandalf to hurry along the East Road: we shall soon be back on it and going as fast as we can.' 'Good-bye!' they cried, and rode down the slope and disappeared from Fredegar's sight into the tunnel.

It was dark and damp. At the far end it was closed by a gate of thick-set iron bars. Merry got down and unlocked the gate, and when they had all passed through he pushed it to again. It shut with a clang, and the lock clicked. The sound was ominous.

'There!' said Merry. 'You have left the Shire, and are now outside, and on the edge of the Old Forest.'

'Are the stories about it true?' asked Pippin.

'I don't know what stories you mean,' Merry answered. 'If you mean the old bogey-stories Fatty's nurses used to tell him, about goblins and wolves and things of that sort, I should say no. At any rate I don't believe them. But the Forest *is* queer. Everything in it is very much more alive, more aware of what is going on, so to speak, than things are in the Shire. And the trees do not like strangers. They watch you. They are usually content merely to watch you, as long as daylight lasts, and don't do much. Occasionally the most unfriendly ones may drop a branch, or stick a root out, or grasp at you with a long trailer. But at night things can be most alarming, or so I am told. I have only once or twice been in here after dark, and then only near the hedge. I thought all the trees were whispering to each other, passing news and plots along in an unintelligible language; and the branches swayed and groped without any wind. They do say the trees do actually move, and can surround strangers and hem them in. In fact long ago they attacked the Hedge: they came and planted themselves right by it, and leaned over it. But the hobbits came and cut down hundreds of trees, and made a great bonfire in the Forest, and burned all the ground in a long strip east of the Hedge. After that the trees gave up the attack, but they became very unfriendly. There is still a wide bare space not far inside where the bonfire was made.'

'Is it only the trees that are dangerous?' asked Pippin.

'There are various queer things living deep in the Forest, and on the far side,' said Merry, 'or at least I have heard so; but I have never seen any of them. But something makes paths. Whenever one comes inside one finds open tracks; but they seem to shift and change from time to time in a queer fashion. Not far from this tunnel there is, or was for a long time, the beginning of quite a broad path leading to the Bonfire Glade, and then on more or less in our direction, east and a little north. That is the path I am going to try and find.'

The hobbits now left the tunnel-gate and rode across the wide hollow. On the far side was a faint path leading up on to the floor of the Forest, a hundred yards and more beyond the Hedge; but it vanished as soon as it brought them under the trees. Looking back they could see the dark line of the Hedge through the stems of trees that were already thick about them.

Looking ahead they could see only tree-trunks of innumerable sizes and shapes: straight or bent, twisted, leaning, squat or slender, smooth or gnarled and branched; and all the stems were green or grey with moss and slimy, shaggy growths.

Merry alone seemed fairly cheerful. 'You had better lead on and find that path,' Frodo said to him. 'Don't let us lose one another, or forget which way the Hedge lies!'

They picked a way among the trees, and their ponies plodded along, carefully avoiding the many writhing and interlacing roots. There was no undergrowth. The ground was rising steadily, and as they went forward it seemed that the trees became taller, darker, and thicker. There was no sound, except an occasional drip of moisture falling through the still leaves. For the moment there was no whispering or movement among the branches; but they all got an uncomfortable feeling that they were being watched with disapproval, deepening to dislike and even enmity. The feeling steadily grew, until they found themselves looking up quickly, or glancing back over their shoulders, as if they expected a sudden blow.

There was not as yet any sign of a path, and the trees seemed constantly to bar their way. Pippin suddenly felt that he could not bear it any longer, and without warning let out a shout. 'Oi! Oi!' he cried. 'I am not going to do anything. Just let me pass through, will you!'

The others halted startled; but the cry fell as if muffled by a heavy curtain. There was no echo or answer though the wood seemed to become more crowded and more watchful than before.

'I should not shout, if I were you,' said Merry. 'It does more harm than good.'

Frodo began to wonder if it were possible to find a way through, and if he had been right to make the others come into this abominable wood. Merry was looking from side to side, and seemed already uncertain which way to go. Pippin noticed it. 'It has not taken you long to lose us,' he said. But at that moment Merry gave a whistle of relief and pointed ahead.

'Well, well!' he said. 'These trees *do* shift. There is the Bonfire Glade in front of us (or I hope so), but the path to it seems to have moved away!'

The light grew clearer as they went forward. Suddenly they came out of the trees and found themselves in a wide circular space. There was sky above them, blue and clear to their surprise, for down under the Forest-roof they had not been able to see the rising morning and the lifting of the mist. The sun was not, however, high enough yet to shine down into the clearing, though its light was on the tree-tops. The leaves were all thicker and greener about the edges of the glade, enclosing it with an almost solid wall. No tree grew there, only rough grass and many tall plants: stalky and faded hemlocks and wood-parsley, fire-weed seeding into fluffy ashes, and rampant nettles and thistles. A dreary place: but it seemed a charming and cheerful garden after the close Forest.

The hobbits felt encouraged, and looked up hopefully at the broadening daylight in the sky. At the far side of the glade there was a break in the wall of trees, and a clear path beyond it. They could see it running on into the wood, wide in places and open above, though every now and again the trees drew in and overshadowed it with their dark boughs. Up this path they rode. They were still climbing gently, but they now went much quicker, and with better heart; for it seemed to them that the Forest had relented, and was going to let them pass unhindered after all.

But after a while the air began to get hot and stuffy. The trees drew close again on either side, and they could no longer see far ahead. Now stronger than ever they felt again the ill will of the wood pressing on them. So silent was it that the fall of their ponies' hoofs, rustling on dead leaves and occasionally stumbling on hidden roots, seemed to thud in their ears. Frodo tried to sing a song to encourage them, but his voice sank to a murmur.

> *O! Wanderers in the shadowed land*
> *despair not! For though dark they stand,*
> *all woods there be must end at last,*
> *and see the open sun go past:*
> *the setting sun, the rising sun,*
> *the day's end, or the day begun.*
> *For east or west all woods must fail . . .*

Fail – even as he said the word his voice faded into silence. The air seemed heavy and the making of words wearisome. Just behind them a large branch fell from an old overhanging tree with a crash into the path. The trees seemed to close in before them.

'They do not like all that about ending and failing,' said Merry. 'I should not sing any more at present. Wait till we do get to the edge, and then we'll turn and give them a rousing chorus!'

He spoke cheerfully, and if he felt any great anxiety, he did not show it. The others did not answer. They were depressed. A heavy weight was settling steadily on Frodo's heart, and he regretted now with every step forward that he had ever thought of challenging the menace of the trees. He was, indeed, just about to stop and propose going back (if that was still possible), when things took a new turn. The path stopped climbing, and became for a while nearly level. The dark trees drew aside, and ahead they could see the path going almost straight forward. Before them, but some

distance off, there stood a green hill-top, treeless, rising like a bald head
out of the encircling wood. The path seemed to be making directly for it.

They now hurried forward again, delighted with the thought of climbing
out for a while above the roof of the Forest. The path dipped, and then
again began to climb upwards, leading them at last to the foot of the steep
hillside. There it left the trees and faded into the turf. The wood stood all
round the hill like thick hair that ended sharply in a circle round a shaven
crown.

The hobbits led their ponies up, winding round and round until they
reached the top. There they stood and gazed about them. The air was
gleaming and sunlit, but hazy; and they could not see to any great distance.
Near at hand the mist was now almost gone; though here and there it lay
in hollows of the wood, and to the south of them, out of a deep fold cutting
right across the Forest, the fog still rose like steam or wisps of white smoke.

'That,' said Merry, pointing with his hand, 'that is the line of the Withywindle. It comes down out of the Downs and flows south-west through the
midst of the Forest to join the Brandywine below Haysend. We don't want
to go *that* way! The Withywindle valley is said to be the queerest part of
the whole wood – the centre from which all the queerness comes, as it
were.'

The others looked in the direction that Merry pointed out, but they
could see little but mists over the damp and deep-cut valley; and beyond
it the southern half of the Forest faded from view.

The sun on the hill-top was now getting hot. It must have been about
eleven o'clock; but the autumn haze still prevented them from seeing much
in other directions. In the west they could not make out either the line of
the Hedge or the valley of the Brandywine beyond it. Northward, where
they looked most hopefully, they could see nothing that might be the line
of the great East Road, for which they were making. They were on an
island in a sea of trees, and the horizon was veiled.

On the south-eastern side the ground fell very steeply, as if the slopes
of the hill were continued far down under the trees, like island-shores that
really are the sides of a mountain rising out of deep waters. They sat on
the green edge and looked out over the woods below them, while they ate
their mid-day meal. As the sun rose and passed noon they glimpsed far off
in the east the grey-green lines of the Downs that lay beyond the Old Forest
on that side. That cheered them greatly; for it was good to see a sight of
anything beyond the wood's borders, though they did not mean to go that
way, if they could help it: the Barrow-downs had as sinister a reputation
in hobbit-legend as the Forest itself.

At length they made up their minds to go on again. The path that had brought them to the hill reappeared on the northward side; but they had not followed it far before they became aware that it was bending steadily to the right. Soon it began to descend rapidly and they guessed that it must actually be heading towards the Withywindle valley: not at all the direction they wished to take. After some discussion they decided to leave this misleading path and strike northward; for although they had not been able to see it from the hill-top, the Road must lie that way, and it could not be many miles off. Also northward, and to the left of the path, the land seemed to be drier and more open, climbing up to slopes where the trees were thinner, and pines and firs replaced the oaks and ashes and other strange and nameless trees of the denser wood.

At first their choice seemed to be good: they got along at a fair speed, though whenever they got a glimpse of the sun in an open glade they seemed unaccountably to have veered eastwards. But after a time the trees began to close in again, just where they had appeared from a distance to be thinner and less tangled. Then deep folds in the ground were discovered unexpectedly, like the ruts of great giant-wheels or wide moats and sunken roads long disused and choked with brambles. These lay usually right across their line of march, and could only be crossed by scrambling down and out again, which was troublesome and difficult with their ponies. Each time they climbed down they found the hollow filled with thick bushes and matted undergrowth, which somehow would not yield to the left, but only gave way when they turned to the right; and they had to go some distance along the bottom before they could find a way up the further bank. Each time they clambered out, the trees seemed deeper and darker; and always to the left and upwards it was most difficult to find a way, and they were forced to the right and downwards.

After an hour or two they had lost all clear sense of direction, though they knew well enough that they had long ceased to go northward at all. They were being headed off, and were simply following a course chosen for them – eastwards and southwards, into the heart of the Forest and not out of it.

The afternoon was wearing away when they scrambled and stumbled into a fold that was wider and deeper than any they had yet met. It was so steep and overhung that it proved impossible to climb out of it again, either forwards or backwards, without leaving their ponies and their baggage behind. All they could do was to follow the fold – downwards. The ground grew soft, and in places boggy; springs appeared in the banks, and soon they found themselves following a brook that trickled and babbled through a weedy bed. Then the ground began to fall rapidly, and the brook growing strong and noisy, flowed and leaped swiftly downhill. They were in a deep dim-lit gully over-arched by trees high above them.

After stumbling along for some way along the stream, they came quite suddenly out of the gloom. As if through a gate they saw the sunlight before them. Coming to the opening they found that they had made their way down through a cleft in a high steep bank, almost a cliff. At its feet was a wide space of grass and reeds; and in the distance could be glimpsed another bank almost as steep. A golden afternoon of late sunshine lay warm and drowsy upon the hidden land between. In the midst of it there wound lazily a dark river of brown water, bordered with ancient willows, arched over with willows, blocked with fallen willows, and flecked with thousands of faded willow-leaves. The air was thick with them, fluttering yellow from the branches; for there was a warm and gentle breeze blowing softly in the valley, and the reeds were rustling, and the willow-boughs were creaking.

'Well, now I have at least some notion of where we are!' said Merry. 'We have come almost in the opposite direction to which we intended. This is the River Withywindle! I will go on and explore.'

He passed out into the sunshine and disappeared into the long grasses. After a while he reappeared, and reported that there was fairly solid ground between the cliff-foot and the river; in some places firm turf went down to the water's edge. 'What's more,' he said, 'there seems to be something like a footpath winding along on this side of the river. If we turn left and follow it, we shall be bound to come out on the east side of the Forest eventually.'

'I dare say!' said Pippin. 'That is, if the track goes on so far, and does not simply lead us into a bog and leave us there. Who made the track, do you suppose, and why? I am sure it was not for our benefit. I am getting very suspicious of this Forest and everything in it, and I begin to believe all the stories about it. And have you any idea how far eastward we should have to go?'

'No,' said Merry, 'I haven't. I don't know in the least how far down the Withywindle we are, or who could possibly come here often enough to make a path along it. But there is no other way out that I can see or think of.'

There being nothing else for it, they filed out, and Merry led them to the path that he had discovered. Everywhere the reeds and grasses were lush and tall, in places far above their heads; but once found, the path was easy to follow, as it turned and twisted, picking out the sounder ground among the bogs and pools. Here and there it passed over other rills, running down gullies into the Withywindle out of the higher forest-lands, and at these points there were tree-trunks or bundles of brushwood laid carefully across.

The hobbits began to feel very hot. There were armies of flies of all kinds buzzing round their ears, and the afternoon sun was burning on their backs. At last they came suddenly into a thin shade; great grey branches reached across the path. Each step forward became more reluctant than the last. Sleepiness seemed to be creeping out of the ground and up their legs, and falling softly out of the air upon their heads and eyes.

Frodo felt his chin go down and his head nod. Just in front of him Pippin fell forward on to his knees. Frodo halted. 'It's no good,' he heard Merry saying. 'Can't go another step without rest. Must have nap. It's cool under the willows. Less flies!'

Frodo did not like the sound of this. 'Come on!' he cried. 'We can't have a nap yet. We must get clear of the Forest first.' But the others were too far gone to care. Beside them Sam stood yawning and blinking stupidly.

Suddenly Frodo himself felt sleep overwhelming him. His head swam. There now seemed hardly a sound in the air. The flies had stopped buzzing. Only a gentle noise on the edge of hearing, a soft fluttering as of a song half whispered, seemed to stir in the boughs above. He lifted his heavy eyes and saw leaning over him a huge willow-tree, old and hoary. Enormous it looked, its sprawling branches going up like reaching arms with many long-fingered hands, its knotted and twisted trunk gaping in wide fissures that creaked faintly as the boughs moved. The leaves fluttering against the bright sky dazzled him, and he toppled over, lying where he fell upon the grass.

Merry and Pippin dragged themselves forward and lay down with their backs to the willow-trunk. Behind them the great cracks gaped wide to receive them as the tree swayed and creaked. They looked up at the grey and yellow leaves, moving softly against the light, and singing. They shut their eyes, and then it seemed that they could almost hear words, cool words, saying something about water and sleep. They gave themselves up to the spell and fell fast asleep at the foot of the great grey willow.

Frodo lay for a while fighting with the sleep that was overpowering him; then with an effort he struggled to his feet again. He felt a compelling desire for cool water. 'Wait for me, Sam,' he stammered. 'Must bathe feet a minute.'

Half in a dream he wandered forward to the riverward side of the tree, where great winding roots grew out into the stream, like gnarled dragonets straining down to drink. He straddled one of these, and paddled his hot feet in the cool brown water; and there he too suddenly fell asleep with his back against the tree.

Sam sat down and scratched his head, and yawned like a cavern. He was worried. The afternoon was getting late, and he thought this sudden sleepiness uncanny. 'There's more behind this than sun and warm air,' he muttered to himself. 'I don't like this great big tree. I don't trust it. Hark at it singing about sleep now! This won't do at all!'

He pulled himself to his feet, and staggered off to see what had become of the ponies. He found that two had wandered on a good way along the path; and he had just caught them and brought them back towards the others, when he heard two noises; one loud, and the other soft but very clear. One was the splash of something heavy falling into the water; the other was a noise like the snick of a lock when a door quietly closes fast.

He rushed back to the bank. Frodo was in the water close to the edge, and a great tree-root seemed to be over him and holding him down, but he was not struggling. Sam gripped him by the jacket, and dragged him from under the root; and then with difficulty hauled him on to the bank. Almost at once he woke, and coughed and spluttered.

'Do you know, Sam,' he said at length, 'the beastly tree *threw* me in! I felt it. The big root just twisted round and tipped me in!'

'You were dreaming I expect, Mr. Frodo,' said Sam. 'You shouldn't sit in such a place, if you feel sleepy.'

'What about the others?' Frodo asked. 'I wonder what sort of dreams they are having.'

They went round to the other side of the tree, and then Sam understood the click that he had heard. Pippin had vanished. The crack by which he had laid himself had closed together, so that not a chink could be seen. Merry was trapped: another crack had closed about his waist; his legs lay outside, but the rest of him was inside a dark opening, the edges of which gripped like a pair of pincers.

Frodo and Sam beat first upon the tree-trunk where Pippin had lain. They then struggled frantically to pull open the jaws of the crack that held poor Merry. It was quite useless.

'What a foul thing to happen!' cried Frodo wildly. 'Why did we ever come into this dreadful Forest? I wish we were all back at Crickhollow!' He kicked the tree with all his strength, heedless of his own feet. A hardly perceptible shiver ran through the stem and up into the branches; the leaves rustled and whispered, but with a sound now of faint and far-off laughter.

'I suppose we haven't got an axe among our luggage, Mr. Frodo?' asked Sam.

'I brought a little hatchet for chopping firewood,' said Frodo. 'That wouldn't be much use.'

'Wait a minute!' cried Sam, struck by an idea suggested by firewood. 'We might do something with fire!'

'We might,' said Frodo doubtfully. 'We might succeed in roasting Pippin alive inside.'

'We might try to hurt or frighten this tree to begin with,' said Sam fiercely. 'If it don't let them go, I'll have it down, if I have to gnaw it.' He ran to the ponies and before long came back with two tinder-boxes and a hatchet.

Quickly they gathered dry grass and leaves, and bits of bark; and made a pile of broken twigs and chopped sticks. These they heaped against the trunk on the far side of the tree from the prisoners. As soon as Sam had struck a spark into the tinder, it kindled the dry grass and a flurry of flame and smoke went up. The twigs crackled. Little fingers of fire licked against the dry scored rind of the ancient tree and scorched it. A tremor ran through the whole willow. The leaves seemed to hiss above their heads with a sound of pain and anger. A loud scream came from Merry, and from far inside the tree they heard Pippin give a muffled yell.

'Put it out! Put it out!' cried Merry. 'He'll squeeze me in two, if you don't. He says so!'

'Who? What?' shouted Frodo, rushing round to the other side of the tree.

'Put it out! Put it out!' begged Merry. The branches of the willow began to sway violently. There was a sound as of a wind rising and spreading outwards to the branches of all the other trees round about, as though they had dropped a stone into the quiet slumber of the river-valley and set up ripples of anger that ran out over the whole Forest. Sam kicked at the little fire and stamped out the sparks. But Frodo, without any clear idea of why he did so, or what he hoped for, ran along the path crying *help! help! help!* It seemed to him that he could hardly hear the sound of his own shrill voice: it was blown away from him by the willow-wind and drowned in a clamour of leaves, as soon as the words left his mouth. He felt desperate: lost and witless.

Suddenly he stopped. There was an answer, or so he thought; but it seemed to come from behind him, away down the path further back in the Forest. He turned round and listened, and soon there could be no doubt: someone was singing a song; a deep glad voice was singing carelessly and happily, but it was singing nonsense:

> *Hey dol! merry dol! ring a dong dillo!*
> *Ring a dong! hop along! fal lal the willow!*
> *Tom Bom, jolly Tom, Tom Bombadillo!*

Half hopeful and half afraid of some new danger, Frodo and Sam now both stood still. Suddenly out of a long string of nonsense-words (or so they seemed) the voice rose up loud and clear and burst into this song:

Hey! Come merry dol! derry dol! My darling!
Light goes the weather-wind and the feathered starling.
Down along under Hill, shining in the sunlight,
Waiting on the doorstep for the cold starlight,
There my pretty lady is, River-woman's daughter,
Slender as the willow-wand, clearer than the water.
Old.Tom Bombadil water-lilies bringing
Comes hopping home again. Can you hear him singing?
Hey! Come merry dol! derry dol! and merry-o,
Goldberry, Goldberry, merry yellow berry-o!
Poor old Willow-man, you tuck your roots away!
Tom's in a hurry now. Evening will follow day.
Tom's going home again water-lilies bringing.
Hey! Come derry dol! Can you hear me singing?

Frodo and Sam stood as if enchanted. The wind puffed out. The leaves hung silently again on stiff branches. There was another burst of song, and then suddenly, hopping and dancing along the path, there appeared above the reeds an old battered hat with a tall crown and a long blue feather stuck in the band. With another hop and a bound there came into view a man, or so it seemed. At any rate he was too large and heavy for a hobbit, if not quite tall enough for one of the Big People, though he made noise enough for one, stumping along with great yellow boots on his thick legs, and charging through grass and rushes like a cow going down to drink. He had a blue coat and a long brown beard; his eyes were blue and bright, and his face was red as a ripe apple, but creased into a hundred wrinkles of laughter. In his hands he carried on a large leaf as on a tray a small pile of white water-lilies.

'Help!' cried Frodo and Sam running towards him with their hands stretched out.

'Whoa! Whoa! steady there!' cried the old man, holding up one hand, and they stopped short, as if they had been struck stiff. 'Now, my little fellows, where be you a-going to, puffing like a bellows? What's the matter here then? Do you know who I am? I'm Tom Bombadil. Tell me what's your trouble! Tom's in a hurry now. Don't you crush my lilies!'

'My friends are caught in the willow-tree,' cried Frodo breathlessly.

'Master Merry's being squeezed in a crack!' cried Sam.

'What?' shouted Tom Bombadil, leaping up in the air. 'Old Man Willow? Naught worse than that, eh? That can soon be mended. I know the tune for him. Old grey Willow-man! I'll freeze his marrow cold, if he don't behave himself. I'll sing his roots off. I'll sing a wind up and blow leaf and branch away. Old Man Willow!'

Setting down his lilies carefully on the grass, he ran to the tree. There

he saw Merry's feet still sticking out – the rest had already been drawn
further inside. Tom put his mouth to the crack and began singing into it
in a low voice. They could not catch the words, but evidently Merry was
aroused. His legs began to kick. Tom sprang away, and breaking off a
hanging branch smote the side of the willow with it. 'You let them out
again, Old Man Willow!' he said. 'What be you a-thinking of? You should
not be waking. Eat earth! Dig deep! Drink water! Go to sleep! Bombadil
is talking!' He then seized Merry's feet and drew him out of the suddenly
widening crack.

There was a tearing creak and the other crack split open, and out of it
Pippin sprang, as if he had been kicked. Then with a loud snap both cracks
closed fast again. A shudder ran through the tree from root to tip, and
complete silence fell.

'Thank you!' said the hobbits, one after the other.

Tom Bombadil burst out laughing. 'Well, my little fellows!' said he,
stooping so that he peered into their faces. 'You shall come home with me!
The table is all laden with yellow cream, honeycomb, and white bread
and butter. Goldberry is waiting. Time enough for questions around the
supper table. You follow after me as quick as you are able!' With that he
picked up his lilies, and then with a beckoning wave of his hand went
hopping and dancing along the path eastward, still singing loudly and
nonsensically.

Too surprised and too relieved to talk, the hobbits followed after him as
fast as they could. But that was not fast enough. Tom soon disappeared in
front of them, and the noise of his singing got fainter and further away.
Suddenly his voice came floating back to them in a loud halloo!

> Hop along, my little friends, up the Withywindle!
> Tom's going on ahead candles for to kindle.
> Down west sinks the Sun: soon you will be groping.
> When the night-shadows fall, then the door will open,
> Out of the window-panes light will twinkle yellow.
> Fear no alder black! Heed no hoary willow!
> Fear neither root nor bough! Tom goes on before you.
> Hey now! merry dol! We'll be waiting for you!

After that the hobbits heard no more. Almost at once the sun seemed to
sink into the trees behind them. They thought of the slanting light of
evening glittering on the Brandywine River, and the windows of
Bucklebury beginning to gleam with hundreds of lights. Great shadows fell
across them; trunks and branches of trees hung dark and threatening over
the path. White mists began to rise and curl on the surface of the river and

stray about the roots of the trees upon its borders. Out of the very ground at their feet a shadowy steam arose and mingled with the swiftly falling dusk.

It became difficult to follow the path, and they were very tired. Their legs seemed leaden. Strange furtive noises ran among the bushes and reeds on either side of them; and if they looked up to the pale sky, they caught sight of queer gnarled and knobbly faces that gloomed dark against the twilight, and leered down at them from the high bank and the edges of the wood. They began to feel that all this country was unreal, and that they were stumbling through an ominous dream that led to no awakening.

Just as they felt their feet slowing down to a standstill, they noticed that the ground was gently rising. The water began to murmur. In the darkness they caught the white glimmer of foam, where the river flowed over a short fall. Then suddenly the trees came to an end and the mists were left behind. They stepped out from the Forest, and found a wide sweep of grass welling up before them. The river, now small and swift, was leaping merrily down to meet them, glinting here and there in the light of the stars, which were already shining in the sky.

The grass under their feet was smooth and short, as if it had been mown or shaven. The eaves of the Forest behind were clipped, and trim as a hedge. The path was now plain before them, well-tended and bordered with stone. It wound up on to the top of a grassy knoll, now grey under the pale starry night; and there, still high above them on a further slope, they saw the twinkling lights of a house. Down again the path went, and then up again, up a long smooth hillside of turf, towards the light. Suddenly a wide yellow beam flowed out brightly from a door that was opened. There was Tom Bombadil's house before them, up, down, under hill. Behind it a steep shoulder of the land lay grey and bare, and beyond that the dark shapes of the Barrow-downs stalked away into the eastern night.

They all hurried forward, hobbits and ponies. Already half their weariness and all their fears had fallen from them. *Hey! Come merry dol!* rolled out the song to greet them.

> *Hey! Come derry dol! Hop along, my hearties!*
> *Hobbits! Ponies all! We are fond of parties.*
> *Now let the fun begin! Let us sing together!*

Then another clear voice, as young and as ancient as Spring, like the song of a glad water flowing down into the night from a bright morning in the hills, came falling like silver to meet them:

Now let the song begin! Let us sing together
Of sun, stars, moon and mist, rain and cloudy weather,
Light on the budding leaf, dew on the feather,
Wind on the open hill, bells on the heather,
Reeds by the shady pool, lilies on the water:
Old Tom Bombadil and the River-daughter!

And with that song the hobbits stood upon the threshold, and a golden light was all about them.

CHAPTER VII

IN THE HOUSE OF TOM BOMBADIL

The four hobbits stepped over the wide stone threshold, and stood still, blinking. They were in a long low room, filled with the light of lamps swinging from the beams of the roof; and on the table of dark polished wood stood many candles, tall and yellow, burning brightly.

In a chair, at the far side of the room facing the outer door, sat a woman. Her long yellow hair rippled down her shoulders; her gown was green, green as young reeds, shot with silver like beads of dew; and her belt was of gold, shaped like a chain of flag-lilies set with the pale-blue eyes of forget-me-nots. About her feet in wide vessels of green and brown earthenware, white water-lilies were floating, so that she seemed to be enthroned in the midst of a pool.

'Enter, good guests!' she said, and as she spoke they knew that it was her clear voice they had heard singing. They came a few timid steps further into the room, and began to bow low, feeling strangely surprised and awkward, like folk that, knocking at a cottage door to beg for a drink of water, have been answered by a fair young elf-queen clad in living flowers. But before they could say anything, she sprang lightly up and over the lily-bowls, and ran laughing towards them; and as she ran her gown rustled softly like the wind in the flowering borders of a river.

'Come dear folk!' she said, taking Frodo by the hand. 'Laugh and be merry! I am Goldberry, daughter of the River.' Then lightly she passed them and closing the door she turned her back to it, with her white arms spread out across it. 'Let us shut out the night!' she said. 'For you are still afraid, perhaps, of mist and tree-shadows and deep water, and untame things. Fear nothing! For tonight you are under the roof of Tom Bombadil.'

The hobbits looked at her in wonder; and she looked at each of them and smiled. 'Fair lady Goldberry!' said Frodo at last, feeling his heart moved with a joy that he did not understand. He stood as he had at times stood enchanted by fair elven-voices; but the spell that was now laid upon him was different: less keen and lofty was the delight, but deeper and nearer to mortal heart; marvellous and yet not strange. 'Fair lady Goldberry!' he said again. 'Now the joy that was hidden in the songs we heard is made plain to me.

O slender as a willow-wand! O clearer than clear water!
O reed by the living pool! Fair River-daughter!

> *O spring-time and summer-time, and spring again after!*
> *O wind on the waterfall, and the leaves' laughter!'*

Suddenly he stopped and stammered, overcome with surprise to hear himself saying such things. But Goldberry laughed.

'Welcome!' she said. 'I had not heard that folk of the Shire were so sweet-tongued. But I see you are an elf-friend; the light in your eyes and the ring in your voice tells it. This is a merry meeting! Sit now, and wait for the Master of the house! He will not be long. He is tending your tired beasts.'

The hobbits sat down gladly in low rush-seated chairs, while Goldberry busied herself about the table; and their eyes followed her, for the slender grace of her movement filled them with quiet delight. From somewhere behind the house came the sound of singing. Every now and again they caught, among many a *derry dol* and a *merry dol* and a *ring a ding dillo* the repeated words:

> *Old Tom Bombadil is a merry fellow;*
> *Bright blue his jacket is, and his boots are yellow.*

'Fair lady!' said Frodo again after a while. 'Tell me, if my asking does not seem foolish, who is Tom Bombadil?'

'He is,' said Goldberry, staying her swift movements and smiling.

Frodo looked at her questioningly. 'He is, as you have seen him,' she said in answer to his look. 'He is the Master of wood, water, and hill.'

'Then all this strange land belongs to him?'

'No indeed!' she answered, and her smile faded. 'That would indeed be a burden,' she added in a low voice, as if to herself. 'The trees and the grasses and all things growing or living in the land belong each to themselves. Tom Bombadil is the Master. No one has ever caught old Tom walking in the forest, wading in the water, leaping on the hill-tops under light and shadow. He has no fear. Tom Bombadil is master.'

A door opened and in came Tom Bombadil. He had now no hat and his thick brown hair was crowned with autumn leaves. He laughed, and going to Goldberry, took her hand.

'Here's my pretty lady!' he said, bowing to the hobbits. 'Here's my Goldberry clothed all in silver-green with flowers in her girdle! Is the table laden? I see yellow cream and honeycomb, and white bread, and butter; milk, cheese, and green herbs and ripe berries gathered. Is that enough for us? Is the supper ready?'

'It is,' said Goldberry; 'but the guests perhaps are not?'

Tom clapped his hands and cried: 'Tom, Tom! your guests are tired, and you had near forgotten! Come now, my merry friends, and Tom will refresh you! You shall clean grimy hands, and wash your weary faces; cast off your muddy cloaks and comb out your tangles!'

He opened the door, and they followed him down a short passage and round a sharp turn. They came to a low room with a sloping roof (a penthouse, it seemed, built on to the north end of the house). Its walls were of clean stone, but they were mostly covered with green hanging mats and yellow curtains. The floor was flagged, and strewn with fresh green rushes. There were four deep mattresses, each piled with white blankets, laid on the floor along one side. Against the opposite wall was a long bench laden with wide earthenware basins, and beside it stood brown ewers filled with water, some cold, some steaming hot. There were soft green slippers set ready beside each bed.

Before long, washed and refreshed, the hobbits were seated at the table, two on each side, while at either end sat Goldberry and the Master. It was a long and merry meal. Though the hobbits ate, as only famished hobbits can eat, there was no lack. The drink in their drinking-bowls seemed to be clear cold water, yet it went to their hearts like wine and set free their voices. The guests became suddenly aware that they were singing merrily, as if it was easier and more natural than talking.

At last Tom and Goldberry rose and cleared the table swiftly. The guests were commanded to sit quiet, and were set in chairs, each with a footstool to his tired feet. There was a fire in the wide hearth before them, and it was burning with a sweet smell, as if it were built of apple-wood. When everything was set in order, all the lights in the room were put out, except one lamp and a pair of candles at each end of the chimney-shelf. Then Goldberry came and stood before them, holding a candle; and she wished them each a good night and deep sleep.

'Have peace now,' she said, 'until the morning! Heed no nightly noises! For nothing passes door and window here save moonlight and starlight and the wind off the hill-top. Good night!' She passed out of the room with a glimmer and a rustle. The sound of her footsteps was like a stream falling gently away downhill over cool stones in the quiet of night.

Tom sat on a while beside them in silence, while each of them tried to muster the courage to ask one of the many questions he had meant to ask at supper. Sleep gathered on their eyelids. At last Frodo spoke:

'Did you hear me calling, Master, or was it just chance that brought you at that moment?'

Tom stirred like a man shaken out of a pleasant dream. 'Eh, what?' said he. 'Did I hear you calling? Nay, I did not hear: I was busy singing. Just chance brought me then, if chance you call it. It was no plan of mine, though I was waiting for you. We heard news of you, and learned that you were wandering. We guessed you'd come ere long down to the water: all paths lead that way, down to Withywindle. Old grey Willow-man, he's a mighty singer; and it's hard for little folk to escape his cunning mazes. But Tom had an errand there, that he dared not hinder.' Tom nodded as if sleep was taking him again; but he went on in a soft singing voice:

> *I had an errand there: gathering water-lilies,*
> *green leaves and lilies white to please my pretty lady,*
> *the last ere the year's end to keep them from the winter,*
> *to flower by her pretty feet till the snows are melted.*
> *Each year at summer's end I go to find them for her,*
> *in a wide pool, deep and clear, far down Withywindle;*
> *there they open first in spring and there they linger latest.*
> *By that pool long ago I found the River-daughter,*
> *fair young Goldberry sitting in the rushes.*
> *Sweet was her singing then, and her heart was beating!*

He opened his eyes and looked at them with a sudden glint of blue:

> *And that proved well for you – for now I shall no longer*
> *go down deep again along the forest-water,*
> *not while the year is old. Nor shall I be passing*
> *Old Man Willow's house this side of spring-time,*
> *not till the merry spring, when the River-daughter*
> *dances down the withy-path to bathe in the water.*

He fell silent again; but Frodo could not help asking one more question: the one he most desired to have answered. 'Tell us, Master,' he said, 'about the Willow-man. What is he? I have never heard of him before.'

'No, don't!' said Merry and Pippin together, sitting suddenly upright. 'Not now! Not until the morning!'

'That is right!' said the old man. 'Now is the time for resting. Some things are ill to hear when the world's in shadow. Sleep till the morning-light, rest on the pillow! Heed no nightly noise! Fear no grey willow!' And with that he took down the lamp and blew it out, and grasping a candle in either hand he led them out of the room.

Their mattresses and pillows were soft as down, and the blankets were of white wool. They had hardly laid themselves on the deep beds and drawn the light covers over them before they were asleep.

In the dead night, Frodo lay in a dream without light. Then he saw the young moon rising; under its thin light there loomed before him a black wall of rock, pierced by a dark arch like a great gate. It seemed to Frodo that he was lifted up, and passing over he saw that the rock-wall was a circle of hills, and that within it was a plain, and in the midst of the plain stood a pinnacle of stone, like a vast tower but not made by hands. On its top stood the figure of a man. The moon as it rose seemed to hang for a moment above his head and glistened in his white hair as the wind stirred it. Up from the dark plain below came the crying of fell voices, and the howling of many wolves. Suddenly a shadow, like the shape of great wings, passed across the moon. The figure lifted his arms and a light flashed from the staff that he wielded. A mighty eagle swept down and bore him away. The voices wailed and the wolves yammered. There was a noise like a strong wind blowing, and on it was borne the sound of hoofs, galloping, galloping, galloping from the East. 'Black Riders!' thought Frodo as he wakened, with the sound of the hoofs still echoing in his mind. He wondered if he would ever again have the courage to leave the safety of these stone walls. He lay motionless, still listening; but all was now silent, and at last he turned and fell asleep again or wandered into some other unremembered dream.

At his side Pippin lay dreaming pleasantly; but a change came over his dreams and he turned and groaned. Suddenly he woke, or thought he had waked, and yet still heard in the darkness the sound that had disturbed his dream: *tip-tap*, *squeak*: the noise was like branches fretting in the wind, twig-fingers scraping wall and window: *creak, creak, creak*. He wondered if there were willow-trees close to the house; and then suddenly he had a dreadful feeling that he was not in an ordinary house at all, but inside the willow and listening to that horrible dry creaking voice laughing at him again. He sat up, and felt the soft pillows yield to his hands, and he lay down again relieved. He seemed to hear the echo of words in his ears: 'Fear nothing! Have peace until the morning! Heed no nightly noises!' Then he went to sleep again.

It was the sound of water that Merry heard falling into his quiet sleep: water streaming down gently, and then spreading, spreading irresistibly all round the house into a dark shoreless pool. It gurgled under the walls, and was rising slowly but surely. 'I shall be drowned!' he thought. 'It will find its way in, and then I shall drown.' He felt that he was lying in a soft slimy bog, and springing up he set his foot on the corner of a cold hard flagstone. Then he remembered where he was and lay down again. He seemed to hear or remember hearing: 'Nothing passes doors or windows save moonlight and starlight and the wind off the hill-top.' A little breath of sweet air moved the curtain. He breathed deep and fell asleep again.

As far as he could remember, Sam slept through the night in deep content, if logs are contented.

They woke up, all four at once, in the morning light. Tom was moving about the room whistling like a starling. When he heard them stir he clapped his hands, and cried: 'Hey! Come merry dol! derry dol! My hearties!' He drew back the yellow curtains, and the hobbits saw that these had covered the windows, at either end of the room, one looking east and the other looking west.

They leapt up refreshed. Frodo ran to the eastern window, and found himself looking into a kitchen-garden grey with dew. He had half expected to see turf right up to the walls, turf all pocked with hoof-prints. Actually his view was screened by a tall line of beans on poles; but above and far beyond them the grey top of the hill loomed up against the sunrise. It was a pale morning: in the East, behind long clouds like lines of soiled wool stained red at the edges, lay glimmering deeps of yellow. The sky spoke of rain to come; but the light was broadening quickly, and the red flowers on the beans began to glow against the wet green leaves.

Pippin looked out of the western window, down into a pool of mist. The Forest was hidden under a fog. It was like looking down on to a sloping cloud-roof from above. There was a fold or channel where the mist was broken into many plumes and billows; the valley of the Withywindle. The stream ran down the hill on the left and vanished into the white shadows. Near at hand was a flower-garden and a clipped hedge silver-netted, and beyond that grey shaven grass pale with dew-drops. There was no willow-tree to be seen.

'Good morning, merry friends!' cried Tom, opening the eastern window wide. A cool air flowed in; it had a rainy smell. 'Sun won't show her face much today, I'm thinking. I have been walking wide, leaping on the hill-tops, since the grey dawn began, nosing wind and weather, wet grass underfoot, wet sky above me. I wakened Goldberry singing under window; but nought wakes hobbit-folk in the early morning. In the night little folk wake up in the darkness, and sleep after light has come! Ring a ding dillo! Wake now, my merry friends! Forget the nightly noises! Ring a ding dillo del! derry del, my hearties! If you come soon you'll find breakfast on the table. If you come late you'll get grass and rain-water!'

Needless to say – not that Tom's threat sounded very serious – the hobbits came soon, and left the table late and only when it was beginning to look rather empty. Neither Tom nor Goldberry were there. Tom could be heard about the house, clattering in the kitchen, and up and down the stairs, and singing here and there outside. The room looked westward over the mist-clouded valley, and the window was open. Water dripped down from the thatched eaves above. Before they had finished breakfast the clouds had joined into an unbroken roof, and a straight grey rain came softly and steadily down. Behind its deep curtain the Forest was completely veiled.

As they looked out of the window there came falling gently as if it was flowing down the rain out of the sky, the clear voice of Goldberry singing up above them. They could hear few words, but it seemed plain to them that the song was a rain-song, as sweet as showers on dry hills, that told the tale of a river from the spring in the highlands to the Sea far below. The hobbits listened with delight; and Frodo was glad in his heart, and blessed the kindly weather, because it delayed them from departing. The thought of going had been heavy upon him from the moment he awoke; but he guessed now that they would not go further that day.

The upper wind settled in the West and deeper and wetter clouds rolled up to spill their laden rain on the bare heads of the Downs. Nothing could be seen all round the house but falling water. Frodo stood near the open door and watched the white chalky path turn into a little river of milk and go bubbling away down into the valley. Tom Bombadil came trotting round the corner of the house, waving his arms as if he was warding off the rain – and indeed when he sprang over the threshold he seemed quite dry, except for his boots. These he took off and put in the chimney-corner. Then he sat in the largest chair and called the hobbits to gather round him.

'This is Goldberry's washing day,' he said, 'and her autumn-cleaning. Too wet for hobbit-folk – let them rest while they are able! It's a good day for long tales, for questions and for answers, so Tom will start the talking.'

He then told them many remarkable stories, sometimes half as if speaking to himself, sometimes looking at them suddenly with a bright blue eye under his deep brows. Often his voice would turn to song, and he would get out of his chair and dance about. He told them tales of bees and flowers, the ways of trees, and the strange creatures of the Forest, about the evil things and good things, things friendly and things unfriendly, cruel things and kind things, and secrets hidden under brambles.

As they listened, they began to understand the lives of the Forest, apart from themselves, indeed to feel themselves as the strangers where all other things were at home. Moving constantly in and out of his talk was Old Man Willow, and Frodo learned now enough to content him, indeed more than enough, for it was not comfortable lore. Tom's words laid bare the hearts of trees and their thoughts, which were often dark and strange, and filled with a hatred of things that go free upon the earth, gnawing, biting, breaking, hacking, burning: destroyers and usurpers. It was not called the Old Forest without reason, for it was indeed ancient, a survivor of vast forgotten woods; and in it there lived yet, ageing no quicker than the hills, the fathers of the fathers of trees, remembering times when they were lords. The countless years had filled them with pride and rooted wisdom, and with malice. But none were more dangerous than the Great Willow: his heart was rotten, but his strength was green; and he was cunning, and a master of winds, and his song and thought ran through the woods on·both sides of the river. His grey thirsty spirit drew power out of the earth and spread like fine root-threads in the ground, and invisible twig-fingers in the air, till it had under its dominion nearly all the trees of the Forest from the Hedge to the Downs.

Suddenly Tom's talk left the woods and went leaping up the young stream, over bubbling waterfalls, over pebbles and worn rocks, and among small flowers in close grass and wet crannies, wandering at last up on to the Downs. They heard of the Great Barrows, and the green mounds, and the stone-rings upon the hills and in the hollows among the hills. Sheep were bleating in flocks. Green walls and white walls rose. There were fortresses on the heights. Kings of little kingdoms fought together, and the young Sun shone like fire on the red metal of their new and greedy swords. There was victory and defeat; and towers fell, fortresses were burned, and flames went up into the sky. Gold was piled on the biers of dead kings and queens; and mounds covered them, and the stone doors were shut; and the grass grew over all. Sheep walked for a while biting the grass, but soon the hills were empty again. A shadow came out of dark places far away, and the bones were stirred in the mounds. Barrow-wights walked in the hollow places with a clink of rings on cold fingers, and gold chains in the wind. Stone rings grinned out of the ground like broken teeth in the moonlight.

The hobbits shuddered. Even in the Shire the rumour of the Barrow-wights of the Barrow-downs beyond the Forest had been heard. But it was not a tale that any hobbit liked to listen to, even by a comfortable fireside far away. These four now suddenly remembered what the joy of this house had driven from their minds: the house of Tom Bombadil nestled under the very shoulder of those dreaded hills. They lost the thread of his tale and shifted uneasily, looking aside at one another.

When they caught his words again they found that he had now wandered into strange regions beyond their memory and beyond their waking thought, into times when the world was wider, and the seas flowed straight to the western Shore; and still on and back Tom went singing out into ancient starlight, when only the Elf-sires were awake. Then suddenly he stopped, and they saw that he nodded as if he was falling asleep. The hobbits sat still before him, enchanted; and it seemed as if, under the spell of his words, the wind had gone, and the clouds had dried up, and the day had been withdrawn, and darkness had come from East and West, and all the sky was filled with the light of white stars.

Whether the morning and evening of one day or of many days had passed Frodo could not tell. He did not feel either hungry or tired, only filled with wonder. The stars shone through the window and the silence of the heavens seemed to be round him. He spoke at last out of his wonder and a sudden fear of that silence:

'Who are you, Master?' he asked.

'Eh, what?' said Tom sitting up, and his eyes glinting in the gloom. 'Don't you know my name yet? That's the only answer. Tell me, who are you, alone, yourself and nameless? But you are young and I am old. Eldest, that's what I am. Mark my words, my friends: Tom was here before the river and the trees; Tom remembers the first raindrop and the first acorn. He made paths before the Big People, and saw the little People arriving. He was here before the Kings and the graves and the Barrow-wights. When the Elves passed westward, Tom was here already, before the seas were bent. He knew the dark under the stars when it was fearless – before the Dark Lord came from Outside.'

A shadow seemed to pass by the window, and the hobbits glanced hastily through the panes. When they turned again, Goldberry stood in the door behind, framed in light. She held a candle, shielding its flame from the draught with her hand; and the light flowed through it, like sunlight through a white shell.

'The rain has ended,' she said; 'and new waters are running downhill, under the stars. Let us now laugh and be glad!'

'And let us have food and drink!' cried Tom. 'Long tales are thirsty. And long listening's hungry work, morning, noon, and evening!' With that he jumped out of his chair, and with a bound took a candle from the chimney-shelf and lit it in the flame that Goldberry held; then he danced about the table. Suddenly he hopped through the door and disappeared.

Quickly he returned, bearing a large and laden tray. Then Tom and Goldberry set the table; and the hobbits sat half in wonder and half in laughter: so fair was the grace of Goldberry and so merry and odd the caperings of Tom. Yet in some fashion they seemed to weave a single dance, neither hindering the other, in and out of the room, and round about the table; and with great speed food and vessels and lights were set in order. The boards blazed with candles, white and yellow. Tom bowed to his guests. 'Supper is ready,' said Goldberry; and now the hobbits saw that she was clothed all in silver with a white girdle, and her shoes were like fishes' mail. But Tom was all in clean blue, blue as rain-washed forget-me-nots, and he had green stockings.

It was a supper even better than before. The hobbits under the spell of Tom's words may have missed one meal or many, but when the food was before them it seemed at least a week since they had eaten. They did not sing or even speak much for a while, and paid close attention to business. But after a time their hearts and spirit rose high again, and their voices rang out in mirth and laughter.

After they had eaten, Goldberry sang many songs for them, songs that began merrily in the hills and fell softly down into silence; and in the silences they saw in their minds pools and waters wider than any they had known, and looking into them they saw the sky below them and the stars like jewels in the depths. Then once more she wished them each good night and left them by the fireside. But Tom now seemed wide awake and plied them with questions.

He appeared already to know much about them and all their families, and indeed to know much of all the history and doings of the Shire down from days hardly remembered among the hobbits themselves. It no longer surprised them; but he made no secret that he owed his recent knowledge largely to Farmer Maggot, whom he seemed to regard as a person of more importance than they had imagined. 'There's earth under his old feet, and clay on his fingers; wisdom in his bones, and both his eyes are open,' said Tom. It was also clear that Tom had dealings with the Elves, and it seemed that in some fashion, news had reached him from Gildor concerning the flight of Frodo.

Indeed so much did Tom know, and so cunning was his questioning, that Frodo found himself telling him more about Bilbo and his own hopes and fears than he had told before even to Gandalf. Tom wagged his head up and down, and there was a glint in his eyes when he heard of the Riders.

'Show me the precious Ring!' he said suddenly in the midst of the story: and Frodo, to his own astonishment, drew out the chain from his pocket, and unfastening the Ring handed it at once to Tom.

It seemed to grow larger as it lay for a moment on his big brown-skinned hand. Then suddenly he put it to his eye and laughed. For a second the hobbits had a vision, both comical and alarming, of his bright blue eye gleaming through a circle of gold. Then Tom put the Ring round the end of his little finger and held it up to the candlelight. For a moment the hobbits noticed nothing strange about this. Then they gasped. There was no sign of Tom disappearing!

Tom laughed again, and then he spun the Ring in the air – and it vanished with a flash. Frodo gave a cry – and Tom leaned forward and handed it back to him with a smile.

Frodo looked at it closely, and rather suspiciously (like one who has lent a trinket to a juggler). It was the same Ring, or looked the same and weighed the same: for that Ring had always seemed to Frodo to weigh strangely heavy in the hand. But something prompted him to make sure.

He was perhaps a trifle annoyed with Tom for seeming to make so light of what even Gandalf thought so perilously important. He waited for an opportunity, when the talk was going again, and Tom was telling an absurd story about badgers and their queer ways – then he slipped the Ring on.

Merry turned towards him to say something and gave a start, and checked an exclamation. Frodo was delighted (in a way): it was his own ring all right, for Merry was staring blankly at his chair, and obviously could not see him. He got up and crept quietly away from the fireside towards the outer door.

'Hey there!' cried Tom, glancing towards him with a most seeing look in his shining eyes. 'Hey! Come Frodo, there! Where be you a-going? Old Tom Bombadil's not as blind as that yet. Take off your golden ring! Your hand's more fair without it. Come back! Leave your game and sit down beside me! We must talk a while more, and think about the morning. Tom must teach the right road, and keep your feet from wandering.'

Frodo laughed (trying to feel pleased), and taking off the Ring he came and sat down again. Tom now told them that he reckoned the Sun would shine tomorrow, and it would be a glad morning, and setting out would be hopeful. But they would do well to start early; for weather in that country was a thing that even Tom could not be sure of for long, and it would change sometimes quicker than he could change his jacket. 'I am no weather-master,' he said; 'nor is aught that goes on two legs.'

By his advice they decided to make nearly due North from his house, over the western and lower slopes of the Downs: they might hope in that way to strike the East Road in a day's journey, and avoid the Barrows. He told them not to be afraid – but to mind their own business.

'Keep to the green grass. Don't you go a-meddling with old stone or cold Wights or prying in their houses, unless you be strong folk with hearts that never falter!' He said this more than once; and he advised them to pass barrows by on the west-side, if they chanced to stray near one. Then he taught them a rhyme to sing, if they should by ill-luck fall into any danger or difficulty the next day.

> *Ho! Tom Bombadil, Tom Bombadillo!*
> *By water, wood and hill, by the reed and willow,*
> *By fire, sun and moon, harken now and hear us!*
> *Come, Tom Bombadil, for our need is near us!*

When they had sung this altogether after him, he clapped them each on the shoulder with a laugh, and taking candles led them back to their bedroom.

CHAPTER VIII

FOG ON THE BARROW-DOWNS

That night they heard no noises. But either in his dreams or out of them, he could not tell which, Frodo heard a sweet singing running in his mind: a song that seemed to come like a pale light behind a grey rain-curtain, and growing stronger to turn the veil all to glass and silver, until at last it was rolled back, and a far green country opened before him under a swift sunrise.

The vision melted into waking; and there was Tom whistling like a tree-full of birds; and the sun was already slanting down the hill and through the open window. Outside everything was green and pale gold.

After breakfast, which they again ate alone, they made ready to say farewell, as nearly heavy of heart as was possible on such a morning: cool, bright, and clean under a washed autumn sky of thin blue. The air came fresh from the North-west. Their quiet ponies were almost frisky, sniffing and moving restlessly. Tom came out of the house and waved his hat and danced upon the doorstep, bidding the hobbits to get up and be off and go with good speed.

They rode off along a path that wound away from behind the house, and went slanting up towards the north end of the hill-brow under which it sheltered. They had just dismounted to lead their ponies up the last steep slope, when suddenly Frodo stopped.

'Goldberry!' he cried. 'My fair lady, clad all in silver green! We have never said farewell to her, nor seen her since the evening!' He was so distressed that he turned back; but at that moment a clear call came rippling down. There on the hill-brow she stood beckoning to them: her hair was flying loose, and as it caught the sun it shone and shimmered. A light like the glint of water on dewy grass flashed from under her feet as she danced.

They hastened up the last slope, and stood breathless beside her. They bowed, but with a wave of her arm she bade them look round; and they looked out from the hill-top over lands under the morning. It was now as clear and far-seen as it had been veiled and misty when they stood upon the knoll in the Forest, which could now be seen rising pale and green out of the dark trees in the West. In that direction the land rose in wooded ridges, green, yellow, russet under the sun, beyond which lay hidden the valley of the Brandywine. To the South, over the line of the Withywindle, there was a distant glint like pale glass where the Brandywine River made a great loop in the lowlands and flowed away out of the knowledge of the hobbits. Northward beyond the dwindling downs the land ran away in flats and swellings of grey and green and pale earth-colours, until it faded into a featureless and shadowy distance. Eastward the Barrowdowns rose, ridge behind ridge into the morning, and vanished out of eyesight into a guess: it was no more than a guess of blue and a remote white glimmer blending with the hem of the sky, but it spoke to them, out of memory and old tales, of the high and distant mountains.

They took a deep draught of the air, and felt that a skip and a few stout strides would bear them wherever they wished. It seemed fainthearted to go jogging aside over the crumpled skirts of the downs towards the Road, when they should be leaping, as lusty as Tom, over the stepping stones of the hills straight towards the Mountains.

Goldberry spoke to them and recalled their eyes and thoughts. 'Speed now, fair guests!' she said. 'And hold to your purpose! North with the wind in the left eye and a blessing on your footsteps! Make haste while the Sun shines!' And to Frodo she said: 'Farewell, Elf-friend, it was a merry meeting!'

But Frodo found no words to answer. He bowed low, and mounted his pony, and followed by his friends jogged slowly down the gentle slope behind the hill. Tom Bombadil's house and the valley, and the Forest were lost to view. The air grew warmer between the green walls of hillside and hillside, and the scent of turf rose strong and sweet as they breathed. Turning back, when they reached the bottom of the green hollow, they saw Goldberry, now small and slender like a sunlit flower against the sky: she was standing still watching them, and her hands were stretched out towards them. As they looked she gave a clear call, and lifting up her hand she turned and vanished behind the hill.

Their way wound along the floor of the hollow, and round the green feet of a steep hill into another deeper and broader valley, and then over the shoulder of further hills, and down their long limbs, and up their smooth sides again, up on to new hill-tops and down into new valleys. There was no tree nor any visible water: it was a country of grass and short springy turf, silent except for the whisper of the air over the edges of the land, and high lonely cries of strange birds. As they journeyed the sun mounted, and grew hot. Each time they climbed a ridge the breeze seemed to have grown less. When they caught a glimpse of the country westward the distant Forest seemed to be smoking, as if the fallen rain was steaming up again from leaf and root and mould. A shadow now lay round the edge of sight, a dark haze above which the upper sky was like a blue cap, hot and heavy.

About mid-day they came to a hill whose top was wide and flattened, like a shallow saucer with a green mounded rim. Inside there was no air stirring, and the sky seemed near their heads. They rode across and looked northwards. Then their hearts rose, for it seemed plain that they had come further already than they had expected. Certainly the distances had now all become hazy and deceptive, but there could be no doubt that the Downs were coming to an end. A long valley lay below them winding away northwards, until it came to an opening between two steep shoulders. Beyond, there seemed to be no more hills. Due north they faintly glimpsed a long dark line. 'That is a line of trees,' said Merry, 'and that must mark the Road. All along it for many leagues east of the Bridge there are trees growing. Some say they were planted in the old days.'

'Splendid!' said Frodo. 'If we make as good going this afternoon as we have done this morning, we shall have left the Downs before the Sun sets and be jogging on in search of a camping place.' But even as he spoke he turned his glance eastwards, and he saw that on that side the hills were higher and looked down upon them; and all those hills were crowned with green mounds, and on some were standing stones, pointing upwards like jagged teeth out of green gums.

That view was somehow disquieting; so they turned from the sight and went down into the hollow circle. In the midst of it there stood a single stone, standing tall under the sun above, and at this hour casting no shadow. It was shapeless and yet significant: like a landmark, or a guarding finger, or more like a warning. But they were now hungry, and the sun was still at the fearless noon; so they set their backs against the east side of the stone. It was cool, as if the sun had had no power to warm it; but at that time this seemed pleasant. There they took food and drink, and made as good a noon-meal under the open sky as anyone could wish; for the food came from 'down under Hill'. Tom had provided them with plenty for the comfort of the day. Their ponies unburdened strayed upon the grass.

Riding over the hills, and eating their fill, the warm sun and the scent of turf, lying a little too long, stretching out their legs and looking at the sky above their noses: these things are, perhaps, enough to explain what happened. However, that may be: they woke suddenly and uncomfortably from a sleep they had never meant to take. The standing stone was cold, and it cast a long pale shadow that stretched eastward over them. The sun, a pale and watery yellow, was gleaming through the mist just above the west wall of the hollow in which they lay; north, south, and east, beyond the wall the fog was thick, cold and white. The air was silent, heavy and chill. Their ponies were standing crowded together with their heads down.

The hobbits sprang to their feet in alarm, and ran to the western rim. They found that they were upon an island in the fog. Even as they looked out in dismay towards the setting sun, it sank before their eyes into a white sea, and a cold grey shadow sprang up in the East behind. The fog rolled up to the walls and rose above them, and as it mounted it bent over their heads until it became a roof: they were shut in a hall of mist whose central pillar was the standing stone.

They felt as if a trap was closing about them; but they did not quite lose heart. They still remembered the hopeful view they had had of the line of the Road ahead, and they still knew in which direction it lay. In any case, they now had so great a dislike for that hollow place about the stone that no thought of remaining there was in their minds. They packed up as quickly as their chilled fingers would work.

Soon they were leading their ponies in single file over the rim and down the long northward slope of the hill, down into a foggy sea. As they went down the mist became colder and damper, and their hair hung lank and dripping on their foreheads. When they reached the bottom it was so cold that they halted and got out cloaks and hoods, which soon became bedewed with grey drops. Then, mounting their ponies, they went slowly on again, feeling their way by the rise and fall of the ground. They were steering, as well as they could guess, for the gate-like opening at the far northward end of the long valley which they had seen in the morning. Once they were through the gap, they had only to keep on in anything like a straight line and they were bound in the end to strike the Road. Their thoughts did not go beyond that, except for a vague hope that perhaps away beyond the Downs there might be no fog.

Their going was very slow. To prevent their getting separated and wandering in different directions they went in file, with Frodo leading. Sam was behind him, and after him came Pippin, and then Merry. The valley seemed to stretch on endlessly. Suddenly Frodo saw a hopeful sign. On either side ahead a darkness began to loom through the mist; and he guessed that they were at last approaching the gap in the hills, the north-gate of the Barrow-downs. If they could pass that, they would be free.

'Come on! Follow me!' he called back over his shoulder, and he hurried forward. But his hope soon changed to bewilderment and alarm. The dark patches grew darker, but they shrank; and suddenly he saw, towering ominous before him and leaning slightly towards one another like the pillars of a headless door, two huge standing stones. He could not remember having seen any sign of these in the valley, when he looked out from the hill in the morning. He had passed between them almost before he was aware: and even as he did so darkness seemed to fall round him. His pony reared and snorted, and he fell off. When he looked back he found that he was alone: the others had not followed him.

'Sam!' he called. 'Pippin! Merry! Come along! Why don't you keep up?'

There was no answer. Fear took him, and he ran back past the stones shouting wildly: 'Sam! Sam! Merry! Pippin!' The pony bolted into the mist and vanished. From some way off, or so it seemed, he thought he heard a cry: 'Hoy! Frodo! Hoy!' It was away eastward, on his left as he stood under the great stones, staring and straining into the gloom. He plunged off in the direction of the call, and found himself going steeply uphill.

As he struggled on he called again, and kept on calling more and more frantically; but he heard no answer for some time, and then it seemed faint and far ahead and high above him. 'Frodo! Hoy!' came the thin voices out of the mist: and then a cry that sounded like *help*, *help!* often repeated, ending with a last *help!* that trailed off into a long wail suddenly cut short. He stumbled forward with all the speed he could towards the cries; but the light was now gone, and clinging night had closed about him, so that it was impossible to be sure of any direction. He seemed all the time to be climbing up and up.

Only the change in the level of the ground at his feet told him when he at last came to the top of a ridge or hill. He was weary, sweating and yet chilled. It was wholly dark.

'Where are you?' he cried out miserably.

There was no reply. He stood listening. He was suddenly aware that it was getting very cold, and that up here a wind was beginning to blow, an icy wind. A change was coming in the weather. The mist was flowing past him now in shreds and tatters. His breath was smoking, and the darkness was less near and thick. He looked up and saw with surprise that faint stars were appearing overhead amid the strands of hurrying cloud and fog. The wind began to hiss over the grass.

He imagined suddenly that he caught a muffled cry, and he made towards it; and even as he went forward the mist was rolled up and thrust aside, and the starry sky was unveiled. A glance showed him that he was now facing southwards and was on a round hill-top, which he must have climbed from the north. Out of the east the biting wind was blowing. To his right there loomed against the westward stars a dark black shape. A great barrow stood there.

'Where are you?' he cried again, both angry and afraid.

'Here!' said a voice, deep and cold, that seemed to come out of the ground. 'I am waiting for you!'

'No!' said Frodo; but he did not run away. His knees gave, and he fell on the ground. Nothing happened, and there was no sound. Trembling he looked up, in time to see a tall dark figure like a shadow against the stars. It leaned over him. He thought there were two eyes, very cold though lit with a pale light that seemed to come from some remote distance. Then a grip stronger and colder than iron seized him. The icy touch froze his bones, and he remembered no more.

When he came to himself again, for a moment he could recall nothing except a sense of dread. Then suddenly he knew that he was imprisoned, caught hopelessly; he was in a barrow. A Barrow-wight had taken him, and he was probably already under the dreadful spells of the Barrow-wights about which whispered tales spoke. He dared not move, but lay as he found himself: flat on his back upon a cold stone with his hands on his breast.

But though his fear was so great that it seemed to be part of the very darkness that was round him, he found himself as he lay thinking about Bilbo Baggins and his stories, of their jogging along together in the lanes of the Shire and talking about roads and adventures. There is a seed of courage hidden (often deeply, it is true) in the heart of the fattest and most timid hobbit, waiting for some final and desperate danger to make it grow. Frodo was neither very fat nor very timid; indeed, though he did not know it, Bilbo (and Gandalf) had thought him the best hobbit in the Shire. He thought he had come to the end of his adventure, and a terrible end, but the thought hardened him. He found himself stiffening, as if for a final spring; he no longer felt limp like a helpless prey.

As he lay there, thinking and getting a hold of himself, he noticed all at once that the darkness was slowly giving way: a pale greenish light was growing round him. It did not at first show him what kind of a place he was in, for the light seemed to be coming out of himself, and from the floor beside him, and had not yet reached the roof or wall. He turned, and there in the cold glow he saw lying beside him Sam, Pippin, and Merry. They were on their backs, and their faces looked deathly pale; and they were clad in white. About them lay many treasures, of gold maybe, though in that light they looked cold and unlovely. On their heads were circlets, gold chains were about their waists, and on their fingers were many rings. Swords lay by their sides, and shields were at their feet. But across their three necks lay one long naked sword.

Suddenly a song began: a cold murmur, rising and falling. The voice seemed far away and immeasurably dreary, sometimes high in the air and thin, sometimes like a low moan from the ground. Out of the formless stream of sad but horrible sounds, strings of words would now and again shape themselves: grim, hard, cold words, heartless and miserable. The night was railing against the morning of which it was bereaved, and the cold was cursing the warmth for which it hungered. Frodo was chilled to the marrow. After a while the song became clearer, and with dread in his heart he perceived that it had changed into an incantation:

Cold be hand and heart and bone,
and cold be sleep under stone:
never more to wake on stony bed,
never, till the Sun fails and the Moon is dead.
In the black wind the stars shall die,
and still on gold here let them lie,
till the dark lord lifts his hand
over dead sea and withered land.

He heard behind his head a creaking and scraping sound. Raising himself on one arm he looked, and saw now in the pale light that they were in a kind of passage which behind them turned a corner. Round the corner a long arm was groping, walking on its fingers towards Sam, who was lying nearest, and towards the hilt of the sword that lay upon him.

At first Frodo felt as if he had indeed been turned into stone by the incantation. Then a wild thought of escape came to him. He wondered if he put on the Ring, whether the Barrow-wight would miss him, and he might find some way out. He thought of himself running free over the grass, grieving for Merry, and Sam, and Pippin, but free and alive himself. Gandalf would admit that there had been nothing else he could do.

But the courage that had been awakened in him was now too strong: he could not leave his friends so easily. He wavered, groping in his pocket, and then fought with himself again; and as he did so the arm crept nearer. Suddenly resolve hardened in him, and he seized a short sword that lay beside him, and kneeling he stooped low over the bodies of his companions. With what strength he had he hewed at the crawling arm near the wrist, and the hand broke off; but at the same moment the sword splintered up to the hilt. There was a shriek and the light vanished. In the dark there was a snarling noise.

Frodo fell forward over Merry, and Merry's face felt cold. All at once back into his mind, from which it had disappeared with the first coming of the fog, came the memory of the house down under the Hill, and of Tom singing. He remembered the rhyme that Tom had taught them. In a small desperate voice he began: *Ho! Tom Bombadil!* and with that name his voice seemed to grow strong: it had a full and lively sound, and the dark chamber echoed as if to drum and trumpet.

Ho! Tom Bombadil, Tom Bombadillo!
By water, wood and hill, by the reed and willow,
By fire, sun and moon, harken now and hear us!
Come, Tom Bombadil, for our need is near us!

There was a sudden deep silence, in which Frodo could hear his heart beating. After a long slow moment he heard plain, but far away, as if it was coming down through the ground or through thick walls, an answering voice singing:

> Old Tom Bombadil is a merry fellow,
> Bright blue his jacket is, and his boots are yellow.
> None has ever caught him yet, for Tom, he is the master:
> His songs are stronger songs, and his feet are faster.

There was a loud rumbling sound, as of stones rolling and falling, and suddenly light streamed in, real light, the plain light of day. A low door-like opening appeared at the end of the chamber beyond Frodo's feet; and there was Tom's head (hat, feather, and all) framed against the light of the sun rising red behind him. The light fell upon the floor, and upon the faces of the three hobbits lying beside Frodo. They did not stir, but the sickly hue had left them. They looked now as if they were only very deeply asleep.

Tom stooped, removed his hat, and came into the dark chamber, singing:

> Get out, you old Wight! Vanish in the sunlight!
> Shrivel like the cold mist, like the winds go wailing,
> Out into the barren lands far beyond the mountains!
> Come never here again! Leave your barrow empty!
> Lost and forgotten be, darker than the darkness,
> Where gates stand for ever shut, till the world is mended.

At these words there was a cry and part of the inner end of the chamber fell in with a crash. Then there was a long trailing shriek, fading away into an unguessable distance; and after that silence.

'Come, friend Frodo!' said Tom. 'Let us get out on to clean grass! You must help me bear them.'

Together they carried out Merry, Pippin, and Sam. As Frodo left the barrow for the last time he thought he saw a severed hand wriggling still, like a wounded spider, in a heap of fallen earth. Tom went back in again, and there was a sound of much thumping and stamping. When he came out he was bearing in his arms a great load of treasure: things of gold, silver, copper, and bronze; many beads and chains and jewelled ornaments. He climbed the green barrow and laid them all on top in the sunshine.

There he stood, with his hat in his hand and the wind in his hair, and looked down upon the three hobbits, that had been laid on their backs upon the grass at the west side of the mound. Raising his right hand he said in a clear and commanding voice:

Wake now my merry lads! Wake and hear me calling!
Warm now be heart and limb! The cold stone is fallen;
Dark door is standing wide; dead hand is broken.
Night under Night is flown, and the Gate is open!

To Frodo's great joy the hobbits stirred, stretched their arms, rubbed their eyes, and then suddenly sprang up. They looked about in amazement, first at Frodo, and then at Tom standing large as life on the barrow-top above them; and then at themselves in their thin white rags, crowned and belted with pale gold, and jingling with trinkets.

'What in the name of wonder?' began Merry, feeling the golden circlet that had slipped over one eye. Then he stopped, and a shadow came over his face, and he closed his eyes. 'Of course, I remember!' he said. 'The men of Carn Dûm came on us at night, and we were worsted. Ah! the spear in my heart!' He clutched at his breast. 'No! No!' he said, opening his eyes. 'What am I saying? I have been dreaming. Where did you get to, Frodo?'

'I thought that I was lost,' said Frodo; 'but I don't want to speak of it. Let us think of what we are to do now! Let us go on!'

'Dressed up like this, sir?' said Sam. 'Where are my clothes?' He flung his circlet, belt, and rings on the grass, and looked round helplessly, as if he expected to find his cloak, jacket, and breeches, and other hobbit-garments lying somewhere to hand.

'You won't find your clothes again,' said Tom, bounding down from the mound, and laughing as he danced round them in the sunlight. One would have thought that nothing dangerous or dreadful had happened; and indeed the horror faded out of their hearts as they looked at him, and saw the merry glint in his eyes.

'What do you mean?' asked Pippin, looking at him, half puzzled and half amused. 'Why not?'

But Tom shook his head, saying: 'You've found yourselves again, out of the deep water. Clothes are but little loss, if you escape from drowning. Be glad, my merry friends, and let the warm sunlight heat now heart and limb! Cast off these cold rags! Run naked on the grass, while Tom goes a-hunting!'

He sprang away down hill, whistling and calling. Looking down after him Frodo saw him running away southwards along the green hollow between their hill and the next, still whistling and crying:

Hey! now! Come hoy now! Whither do you wander?
Up, down, near or far, here, there or yonder?
Sharp-ears, Wise-nose, Swish-tail and Bumpkin,
White-socks my little lad, and old Fatty Lumpkin!

So he sang, running fast, tossing up his hat and catching it, until he was hidden by a fold of the ground: but for some time his *hey now! hoy now!* came floating back down the wind, which had shifted round towards the south.

The air was growing very warm again. The hobbits ran about for a while on the grass, as he told them. Then they lay basking in the sun with the delight of those that have been wafted suddenly from bitter winter to a friendly clime, or of people that, after being long ill and bedridden, wake one day to find that they are unexpectedly well and the day is again full of promise.

By the time that Tom returned they were feeling strong (and hungry). He reappeared, hat first, over the brow of the hill, and behind him came in an obedient line *six* ponies: their own five and one more. The last was plainly old Fatty Lumpkin: he was larger, stronger, fatter (and older) than their own ponies. Merry, to whom the others belonged, had not, in fact, given them any such names, but they answered to the new names that Tom had given them for the rest of their lives. Tom called them one by one and they climbed over the brow and stood in a line. Then Tom bowed to the hobbits.

'Here are your ponies, now!' he said. 'They've more sense (in some ways) than you wandering hobbits have – more sense in their noses. For they sniff danger ahead which you walk right into; and if they run to save themselves, then they run the right way. You must forgive them all; for though their hearts are faithful, to face fear of Barrow-wights is not what they were made for. See, here they come again, bringing all their burdens!'

Merry, Sam, and Pippin now clothed themselves in spare garments from their packs; and they soon felt too hot, for they were obliged to put on some of the thicker and warmer things that they had brought against the oncoming of winter.

'Where does that other old animal, that Fatty Lumpkin, come from?' asked Frodo.

'He's mine,' said Tom. 'My four-legged friend; though I seldom ride him, and he wanders often far, free upon the hillsides. When your ponies stayed with me, they got to know my Lumpkin; and they smelt him in the night, and quickly ran to meet him. I thought he'd look for them and with his words of wisdom take all their fear away. But now, my jolly Lumpkin, old Tom's going to ride. Hey! he's coming with you, just to set you on the road; so he needs a pony. For you cannot easily talk to hobbits that are riding, when you're on your own legs trying to trot beside them.'

The hobbits were delighted to hear this, and thanked Tom many times; but he laughed, and said that they were so good at losing themselves that he would not feel happy till he had seen them safe over the borders of his land. 'I've got things to do,' he said: 'my making and my singing, my talking and my walking, and my watching of the country. Tom can't be always near to open doors and willow-cracks. Tom has his house to mind, and Goldberry is waiting.'

It was still fairly early by the sun, something between nine and ten, and the hobbits turned their minds to food. Their last meal had been lunch beside the standing stone the day before. They breakfasted now off the remainder of Tom's provisions, meant for their supper, with additions that Tom had brought with him. It was not a large meal (considering hobbits and the circumstances), but they felt much better for it. While they were eating Tom went up to the mound, and looked through the treasures. Most of these he made into a pile that glistened and sparkled on the grass. He bade them lie there 'free to all finders, birds, beasts, Elves or Men, and all kindly creatures'; for so the spell of the mound should be broken and scattered and no Wight ever come back to it. He chose for himself from the pile a brooch set with blue stones, many-shaded like flax-flowers or the wings of blue butterflies. He looked long at it, as if stirred by some memory, shaking his head, and saying at last:

'Here is a pretty toy for Tom and for his lady! Fair was she who long ago wore this on her shoulder. Goldberry shall wear it now, and we will not forget her!'

For each of the hobbits he chose a dagger, long, leaf-shaped, and keen, of marvellous workmanship, damasked with serpent-forms in red and gold. They gleamed as he drew them from their black sheaths, wrought of some strange metal, light and strong, and set with many fiery stones. Whether by some virtue in these sheaths or because of the spell that lay on the mound, the blades seemed untouched by time, unrusted, sharp, glittering in the sun.

'Old knives are long enough as swords for hobbit-people,' he said. 'Sharp blades are good to have, if Shire-folk go walking, east, south, or far away into dark and danger.' Then he told them that these blades were forged many long years ago by Men of Westernesse: they were foes of the Dark Lord, but they were overcome by the evil king of Carn Dûm in the Land of Angmar.

'Few now remember them,' Tom murmured, 'yet still some go wandering, sons of forgotten kings walking in loneliness, guarding from evil things folk that are heedless.'

The hobbits did not understand his words, but as he spoke they had a vision as it were of a great expanse of years behind them, like a vast shadowy plain over which there strode shapes of Men, tall and grim with bright

swords, and last came one with a star on his brow. Then the vision faded,
and they were back in the sunlit world. It was time to start again. They
made ready, packing their bags and lading their ponies. Their new weapons
they hung on their leather belts under their jackets, feeling them very
awkward, and wondering if they would be of any use. Fighting had not
before occurred to any of them as one of the adventures in which their
flight would land them.

At last they set off. They led their ponies down the hill; and then mounting they trotted quickly along the valley. They looked back and saw the
top of the old mound on the hill, and from it the sunlight on the gold went
up like a yellow flame. Then they turned a shoulder of the Downs and it
was hidden from view.

Though Frodo looked about him on every side he saw no sign of the
great stones standing like a gate, and before long they came to the northern
gap and rode swiftly through, and the land fell away before them. It was
a merry journey with Tom Bombadil trotting gaily beside them, or before
them, on Fatty Lumpkin, who could move much faster than his girth
promised. Tom sang most of the time, but it was chiefly nonsense, or else
perhaps a strange language unknown to the hobbits, an ancient language
whose words were mainly those of wonder and delight.

They went forward steadily, but they soon saw that the Road was further
away than they had imagined. Even without a fog, their sleep at mid-day
would have prevented them from reaching it until after nightfall on the
day before. The dark line they had seen was not a line of trees but a line
of bushes growing on the edge of a deep dike with a steep wall on the
further side. Tom said that it had once been the boundary of a kingdom,
but a very long time ago. He seemed to remember something sad about it,
and would not say much.

They climbed down and out of the dike and through a gap in the wall,
and then Tom turned due north, for they had been bearing somewhat to
the west. The land was now open and fairly level, and they quickened their
pace, but the sun was already sinking low when at last they saw a line of
tall trees ahead, and they knew that they had come back to the Road after
many unexpected adventures. They galloped their ponies over the last
furlongs, and halted under the long shadows of the trees. They were on
the top of a sloping bank, and the Road, now dim as evening drew on,
wound away below them. At this point it ran nearly from South-west to
North-east, and on their right it fell quickly down into a wide hollow. It
was rutted and bore many signs of the recent heavy rain; there were pools
and pot-holes full of water.

They rode down the bank and looked up and down. There was nothing to be seen. 'Well, here we are again at last!' said Frodo. 'I suppose we haven't lost more than two days by my short cut through the Forest! But perhaps the delay will prove useful – it may have put them off our trail.'

The others looked at him. The shadow of the fear of the Black Riders came suddenly over them again. Ever since they had entered the Forest they had thought chiefly of getting back to the Road; only now when it lay beneath their feet did they remember the danger which pursued them, and was more than likely to be lying in wait for them upon the Road itself. They looked anxiously back towards the setting sun, but the Road was brown and empty.

'Do you think,' asked Pippin hesitatingly, 'do you think we may be pursued, tonight?'

'No, I hope not tonight,' answered Tom Bombadil; 'nor perhaps the next day. But do not trust my guess; for I cannot tell for certain. Out east my knowledge fails. Tom is not master of Riders from the Black Land far beyond his country.'

All the same the hobbits wished he was coming with them. They felt that he would know how to deal with Black Riders, if anyone did. They would soon now be going forward into lands wholly strange to them, and beyond all but the most vague and distant legends of the Shire, and in the gathering twilight they longed for home. A deep loneliness and sense of loss was on them. They stood silent, reluctant to make the final parting, and only slowly became aware that Tom was wishing them farewell, and telling them to have good heart and to ride on till dark without halting.

'Tom will give you good advice, till this day is over (after that your own luck must go with you and guide you): four miles along the Road you'll come upon a village, Bree under Bree-hill, with doors looking westward. There you'll find an old inn that is called *The Prancing Pony*. Barliman Butterbur is the worthy keeper. There you can stay the night, and afterwards the morning will speed you upon your way. Be bold, but wary! Keep up your merry hearts, and ride to meet your fortune!'

They begged him to come at least as far as the inn and drink once more with them; but he laughed and refused, saying:

> Tom's country ends here: he will not pass the borders.
> Tom has his house to mind, and Goldberry is waiting!

Then he turned, tossed up his hat, leaped on Lumpkin's back, and rode up over the bank and away singing into the dusk.

The hobbits climbed up and watched him until he was out of sight.

'I am sorry to take leave of Master Bombadil,' said Sam. 'He's a caution and no mistake. I reckon we may go a good deal further and see naught better, nor queerer. But I won't deny I'll be glad to see this *Prancing Pony* he spoke of. I hope it'll be like *The Green Dragon* away back home! What sort of folk are they in Bree?'

'There are hobbits in Bree,' said Merry, 'as well as Big Folk. I daresay it will be homelike enough. *The Pony* is a good inn by all accounts. My people ride out there now and again.'

'It may be all we could wish,' said Frodo; 'but it is outside the Shire all the same. Don't make yourselves too much at home! Please remember – all of you – that the name of Baggins must NOT be mentioned. I am Mr. Underhill, if any name must be given.'

They now mounted their ponies and rode off silently into the evening. Darkness came down quickly, as they plodded slowly downhill and up again, until at last they saw lights twinkling some distance ahead.

Before them rose Bree-hill barring the way, a dark mass against misty stars; and under its western flank nestled a large village. Towards it they now hurried desiring only to find a fire, and a door between them and the night.

CHAPTER IX

AT THE SIGN OF THE PRANCING PONY

Bree was the chief village of the Bree-land, a small inhabited region, like an island in the empty lands round about. Besides Bree itself, there was Staddle on the other side of the hill, Combe in a deep valley a little further eastward, and Archet on the edge of the Chetwood. Lying round Bree-hill and the villages was a small country of fields and tamed woodland only a few miles broad.

The Men of Bree were brown-haired, broad, and rather short, cheerful and independent: they belonged to nobody but themselves; but they were more friendly and familiar with Hobbits, Dwarves, Elves, and other inhabitants of the world about them than was (or is) usual with Big People. According to their own tales they were the original inhabitants and were the descendants of the first Men that ever wandered into the West of the middle-world. Few had survived the turmoils of the Elder Days; but when the Kings returned again over the Great Sea they had found the Bree-men still there, and they were still there now, when the memory of the old Kings had faded into the grass.

In those days no other Men had settled dwellings so far west, or within a hundred leagues of the Shire. But in the wild lands beyond Bree there were mysterious wanderers. The Bree-folk called them Rangers, and knew nothing of their origin. They were taller and darker than the Men of Bree and were believed to have strange powers of sight and hearing, and to understand the languages of beasts and birds. They roamed at will southwards, and eastwards even as far as the Misty Mountains; but they were now few and rarely seen. When they appeared they brought news from afar, and told strange forgotten tales which were eagerly listened to; but the Bree-folk did not make friends of them.

There were also many families of hobbits in the Bree-land and *they* claimed to be the oldest settlement of Hobbits in the world, one that was founded long before even the Brandywine was crossed and the Shire colonized. They lived mostly in Staddle though there were some in Bree itself, especially on the higher slopes of the hill, above the houses of the Men. The Big Folk and the Little Folk (as they called one another) were on friendly terms, minding their own affairs in their own ways, but both rightly regarding themselves as necessary parts of the Bree-folk. Nowhere else in the world was this peculiar (but excellent) arrangement to be found.

The Bree-folk, Big and Little, did not themselves travel much; and the affairs of the four villages were their chief concern. Occasionally the Hobbits of Bree went as far as Buckland, or the Eastfarthing; but though their little land was not much further than a day's riding east of the Brandywine Bridge, the Hobbits of the Shire now seldom visited it. An occasional Bucklander or adventurous Took would come out to the Inn for a night or two, but even that was becoming less and less usual. The Shire-hobbits referred to those of Bree, and to any others that lived beyond the borders, as Outsiders, and took very little interest in them, considering them dull and uncouth. There were probably many more Outsiders scattered about in the West of the World in those days than the people of the Shire imagined. Some, doubtless, were no better than tramps, ready to dig a hole in any bank and stay only as long as it suited them. But in the Bree-land, at any rate, the hobbits were decent and prosperous, and no more rustic than most of their distant relatives Inside. It was not yet forgotten that there had been a time when there was much coming and going between the Shire and Bree. There was Bree-blood in the Brandybucks by all accounts.

The village of Bree had some hundred stone houses of the Big Folk, mostly above the Road, nestling on the hillside with windows looking west. On that side, running in more than half a circle from the hill and back to it, there was a deep dike with a thick hedge on the inner side. Over this the Road crossed by a causeway; but where it pierced the hedge it was barred by a great gate. There was another gate in the southern corner where the Road ran out of the village. The gates were closed at nightfall; but just inside them were small lodges for the gatekeepers.

Down on the Road, where it swept to the right to go round the foot of the hill, there was a large inn. It had been built long ago when the traffic on the roads had been far greater. For Bree stood at an old meeting of ways; another ancient road crossed the East Road just outside the dike at the western end of the village, and in former days Men and other folk of various sorts had travelled much on it. *Strange as News from Bree* was still a saying in the Eastfarthing, descending from those days, when news from North, South, and East could be heard in the inn, and when the Shire-hobbits used to go more often to hear it. But the Northern Lands had long been desolate, and the North Road was now seldom used: it was grass-grown, and the Bree-folk called it the Greenway.

The Inn of Bree was still there, however, and the innkeeper was an important person. His house was a meeting place for the idle, talkative, and inquisitive among the inhabitants, large and small, of the four villages; and a resort of Rangers and other wanderers, and for such travellers (mostly dwarves) as still journeyed on the East Road, to and from the Mountains.

It was dark, and white stars were shining, when Frodo and his companions came at last to the Greenway-crossing and drew near the village. They came to the West-gate and found it shut, but at the door of the lodge beyond it, there was a man sitting. He jumped up and fetched a lantern and looked over the gate at them in surprise.

'What do you want, and where do you come from?' he asked gruffly.

'We are making for the inn here,' answered Frodo. 'We are journeying east and cannot go further tonight.'

'Hobbits! Four hobbits! And what's more, out of the Shire by their talk,' said the gatekeeper, softly as if speaking to himself. He stared at them darkly for a moment, and then slowly opened the gate and let them ride through.

'We don't often see Shire-folk riding on the Road at night,' he went on, as they halted a moment by his door. 'You'll pardon my wondering what business takes you away east of Bree! What may your names be, might I ask?'

'Our names and our business are our own, and this does not seem a good place to discuss them,' said Frodo, not liking the look of the man or the tone of his voice.

'Your business is your own, no doubt,' said the man; 'but it's my business to ask questions after nightfall.'

'We are hobbits from Buckland, and we have a fancy to travel and to stay at the inn here,' put in Merry. 'I am Mr. Brandybuck. Is that enough for you? The Bree-folk used to be fair-spoken to travellers, or so I had heard.'

'All right, all right!' said the man. 'I meant no offence. But you'll find maybe that more folk than old Harry at the gate will be asking you questions. There's queer folk about. If you go on to *The Pony*, you'll find you're not the only guests.'

He wished them good night, and they said no more; but Frodo could see in the lantern-light that the man was still eyeing them curiously. He was glad to hear the gate clang to behind them, as they rode forward. He wondered why the man was so suspicious, and whether any one had been asking for news of a party of hobbits. Could it have been Gandalf? He might have arrived, while they were delayed in the Forest and the Downs. But there was something in the look and the voice of the gatekeeper that made him uneasy.

The man stared after the hobbits for a moment, and then he went back to his house. As soon as his back was turned, a dark figure climbed quickly in over the gate and melted into the shadows of the village street.

The hobbits rode on up a gentle slope, passing a few detached houses, and drew up outside the inn. The houses looked large and strange to them. Sam stared up at the inn with its three storeys and many windows, and felt his heart sink. He had imagined himself meeting giants taller than trees, and other creatures even more terrifying, some time or other in the course of his journey; but at the moment he was finding his first sight of Men and their tall houses quite enough, indeed too much for the dark end of a tiring day. He pictured black horses standing all saddled in the shadows of the inn-yard, and Black Riders peering out of dark upper windows.

'We surely aren't going to stay here for the night, are we, sir?' he exclaimed. 'If there are hobbit-folk in these parts, why don't we look for some that would be willing to take us in? It would be more homelike.'

'What's wrong with the inn?' said Frodo. 'Tom Bombadil recommended it. I expect it's homelike enough inside.'

Even from the outside the inn looked a pleasant house to familiar eyes. It had a front on the Road, and two wings running back on land partly cut out of the lower slopes of the hill, so that at the rear the second-floor windows were level with the ground. There was a wide arch leading to a courtyard between the two wings, and on the left under the arch there was a large doorway reached by a few broad steps. The door was open and light streamed out of it. Above the arch there was a lamp, and beneath it swung a large signboard: a fat white pony reared up on its hind legs. Over the door was painted in white letters: THE PRANCING PONY by BARLIMAN BUTTERBUR. Many of the lower windows showed lights behind thick curtains.

As they hesitated outside in the gloom, someone began singing a merry song inside, and many cheerful voices joined loudly in the chorus. They listened to this encouraging sound for a moment and then got off their ponies. The song ended and there was a burst of laughter and clapping.

They led their ponies under the arch, and leaving them standing in the yard they climbed up the steps. Frodo went forward and nearly bumped into a short fat man with a bald head and a red face. He had a white apron on, and was bustling out of one door and in through another, carrying a tray laden with full mugs.

'Can we——' began Frodo.

'Half a minute, if you please!' shouted the man over his shoulder, and vanished into a babel of voices and a cloud of smoke. In a moment he was out again, wiping his hands on his apron.

'Good evening, little master!' he said, bending down. 'What may you be wanting?'

'Beds for four, and stabling for five ponies, if that can be managed. Are you Mr. Butterbur?'

'That's right! Barliman is my name. Barliman Butterbur at your service! You're from the Shire, eh?' he said, and then suddenly he clapped his hand to his forehead, as if trying to remember something. 'Hobbits!' he cried. 'Now what does that remind me of? Might I ask your names, sir?'

'Mr. Took and Mr. Brandybuck,' said Frodo; 'and this is Sam Gamgee. My name is Underhill.'

'There now!' said Mr. Butterbur, snapping his fingers. 'It's gone again! But it'll come back, when I have time to think. I'm run off my feet; but I'll see what I can do for you. We don't often get a party out of the Shire nowadays, and I should be sorry not to make you welcome. But there is such a crowd already in the house tonight as there hasn't been for long enough. It never rains but it pours, we say in Bree.

'Hi! Nob!' he shouted. 'Where are you, you woolly-footed slowcoach? Nob!'

'Coming, sir! Coming!' A cheery-looking hobbit bobbed out of a door, and seeing the travellers, stopped short and stared at them with great interest.

'Where's Bob?' asked the landlord. 'You don't know? Well find him! Double sharp! I haven't got six legs, nor six eyes neither! Tell Bob there's five ponies that have to be stabled. He must find room somehow.' Nob trotted off with a grin and a wink.

'Well, now, what was I going to say?' said Mr. Butterbur, tapping his forehead. 'One thing drives out another, so to speak. I'm that busy tonight, my head is going round. There's a party that came up the Greenway from down South last night – and that was strange enough to begin with. Then there's a travelling company of dwarves going West come in this evening. And now there's you. If you weren't hobbits, I doubt if we could house you. But we've got a room or two in the north wing that were made special for hobbits, when this place was built. On the ground floor as they usually prefer; round windows and all as they like it. I hope you'll be comfortable. You'll be wanting supper, I don't doubt. As soon as may be. This way now!'

He led them a short way down a passage, and opened a door. 'Here is a nice little parlour!' he said. 'I hope it will suit. Excuse me now. I'm that busy. No time for talking. I must be trotting. It's hard work for two legs, but I don't get thinner. I'll look in again later. If you want anything, ring the hand-bell, and Nob will come. If he don't come, ring and shout!'

Off he went at last, and left them feeling rather breathless. He seemed capable of an endless stream of talk, however busy he might be. They found themselves in a small and cosy room. There was a bit of bright fire burning on the hearth, and in front of it were some low and comfortable chairs. There was a round table, already spread with a white cloth, and on it was a large hand-bell. But Nob, the hobbit servant, came bustling in long before they thought of ringing. He brought candles and a tray full of plates.

'Will you be wanting anything to drink, masters?' he asked. 'And shall I show you the bedrooms, while your supper is got ready?'

They were washed and in the middle of good deep mugs of beer when Mr. Butterbur and Nob came in again. In a twinkling the table was laid. There was hot soup, cold meats, a blackberry tart, new loaves, slabs of butter, and half a ripe cheese: good plain food, as good as the Shire could show, and homelike enough to dispel the last of Sam's misgivings (already much relieved by the excellence of the beer).

The landlord hovered round for a little, and then prepared to leave them. 'I don't know whether you would care to join the company, when you have supped,' he said, standing at the door. 'Perhaps you would rather go to your beds. Still the company would be very pleased to welcome you, if you had a mind. We don't get Outsiders – travellers from the Shire, I should say, begging your pardon – often; and we like to hear a bit of news, or any story or song you may have in mind. But as you please! Ring the bell, if you lack anything!'

So refreshed and encouraged did they feel at the end of their supper (about three quarters of an hour's steady going, not hindered by unnecessary talk) that Frodo, Pippin, and Sam decided to join the company. Merry said it would be too stuffy. 'I shall sit here quietly by the fire for a bit, and perhaps go out later for a sniff of the air. Mind your Ps and Qs, and don't forget that you are supposed to be escaping in secret, and are still on the high-road and not very far from the Shire!'

'All right!' said Pippin. 'Mind yourself! Don't get lost, and don't forget that it is safer indoors!'

The company was in the big common-room of the inn. The gathering was large and mixed, as Frodo discovered, when his eyes got used to the light. This came chiefly from a blazing log-fire, for the three lamps hanging from the beams were dim, and half veiled in smoke. Barliman Butterbur was standing near the fire, talking to a couple of dwarves and one or two strange-looking men. On the benches were various folk: men of Bree, a collection of local hobbits (sitting chattering together), a few more dwarves, and other vague figures difficult to make out away in the shadows and corners.

As soon as the Shire-hobbits entered, there was a chorus of welcome from the Bree-landers. The strangers, especially those that had come up the Greenway, stared at them curiously. The landlord introduced the newcomers to the Bree-folk, so quickly that, though they caught many names, they were seldom sure who the names belonged to. The Men of Bree seemed all to have rather botanical (and to the Shire-folk rather odd) names, like Rushlight, Goatleaf, Heathertoes, Appledore, Thistlewool and Ferny (not to mention Butterbur). Some of the hobbits had similar names. The Mugworts, for instance, seemed numerous. But most of them had natural names, such as Banks, Brockhouse, Longholes, Sandheaver, and Tunnelly, many of which were used in the Shire. There were several Underhills from Staddle, and as they could not imagine sharing a name without being related, they took Frodo to their hearts as a long-lost cousin.

The Bree-hobbits were, in fact, friendly and inquisitive, and Frodo soon found that some explanation of what he was doing would have to be given. He gave out that he was interested in history and geography (at which there was much wagging of heads, although neither of these words were much used in the Bree-dialect). He said he was thinking of writing a book (at which there was silent astonishment), and that he and his friends wanted to collect information about hobbits living outside the Shire, especially in the eastern lands.

At this a chorus of voices broke out. If Frodo had really wanted to write a book, and had had many ears, he would have learned enough for several chapters in a few minutes. And if that was not enough, he was given a whole list of names, beginning with 'Old Barliman here', to whom he could go for further information. But after a time, as Frodo did not show any sign of writing a book on the spot, the hobbits returned to their questions about doings in the Shire. Frodo did not prove very communicative, and he soon found himself sitting alone in a corner, listening and looking around.

The Men and Dwarves were mostly talking of distant events and telling news of a kind that was becoming only too familiar. There was trouble away in the South, and it seemed that the Men who had come up the Greenway were on the move, looking for lands where they could find some peace. The Bree-folk were sympathetic, but plainly not very ready to take a large number of strangers into their little land. One of the travellers, a squint-eyed ill-favoured fellow, was foretelling that more and more people would be coming north in the near future. 'If room isn't found for them, they'll find it for themselves. They've a right to live, same as other folk,' he said loudly. The local inhabitants did not look pleased at the prospect.

The hobbits did not pay much attention to all this, and it did not at the moment seem to concern hobbits. Big Folk could hardly beg for lodgings in hobbit-holes. They were more interested in Sam and Pippin, who were now feeling quite at home, and were chatting gaily about events in the Shire. Pippin roused a good deal of laughter with an account of the collapse of the roof of the Town Hole in Michel Delving: Will Whitfoot, the Mayor, and the fattest hobbit in the Westfarthing, had been buried in chalk, and came out like a floured dumpling. But there were several questions asked that made Frodo a little uneasy. One of the Bree-landers, who seemed to have been in the Shire several times, wanted to know where the Underhills lived and who they were related to.

Suddenly Frodo noticed that a strange-looking weather-beaten man, sitting in the shadows near the wall, was also listening intently to the hobbit-talk. He had a tall tankard in front of him, and was smoking a long-stemmed pipe curiously carved. His legs were stretched out before him, showing high boots of supple leather that fitted him well, but had seen much wear and were now caked with mud. A travel-stained cloak of heavy dark-green cloth was drawn close about him, and in spite of the heat of the room he wore a hood that overshadowed his face; but the gleam of his eyes could be seen as he watched the hobbits.

'Who is that?' Frodo asked, when he got a chance to whisper to Mr. Butterbur. 'I don't think you introduced him?'

'Him?' said the landlord in an answering whisper, cocking an eye without turning his head. 'I don't rightly know. He is one of the wandering folk – Rangers we call them. He seldom talks: not but what he can tell a rare tale when he has the mind. He disappears for a month, or a year, and then he pops up again. He was in and out pretty often last spring; but I haven't seen him about lately. What his right name is I've never heard: but he's known round here as Strider. Goes about at a great pace on his long shanks; though he don't tell nobody what cause he has to hurry. But there's no accounting for East and West, as we say in Bree, meaning the Rangers and the Shire-folk, begging your pardon. Funny you should ask about him.' But at that moment Mr. Butterbur was called away by a demand for more ale and his last remark remained unexplained.

Frodo found that Strider was now looking at him, as if he had heard or guessed all that had been said. Presently, with a wave of his hand and a nod, he invited Frodo to come over and sit by him. As Frodo drew near he threw back his hood, showing a shaggy head of dark hair flecked with grey, and in a pale stern face a pair of keen grey eyes.

'I am called Strider,' he said in a low voice. 'I am very pleased to meet you, Master – Underhill, if old Butterbur got your name right.'

'He did,' said Frodo stiffly. He felt far from comfortable under the stare of those keen eyes.

'Well, Master Underhill,' said Strider, 'if I were you, I should stop your young friends from talking too much. Drink, fire, and chance-meeting are pleasant enough, but, well – this isn't the Shire. There are queer folk about. Though I say it as shouldn't, you may think,' he added with a wry smile, seeing Frodo's glance. 'And there have been even stranger travellers through Bree lately,' he went on, watching Frodo's face.

Frodo returned his gaze but said nothing; and Strider made no further sign. His attention seemed suddenly to be fixed on Pippin. To his alarm Frodo became aware that the ridiculous young Took, encouraged by his success with the fat Mayor of Michel Delving, was now actually giving a comic account of Bilbo's farewell party. He was already giving an imitation of the Speech, and was drawing near to the astonishing Disappearance.

Frodo was annoyed. It was a harmless enough tale for most of the local hobbits, no doubt: just a funny story about those funny people away beyond the River; but some (old Butterbur, for instance) knew a thing or two, and had probably heard rumours long ago about Bilbo's vanishing. It would bring the name of Baggins to their minds, especially if there had been inquiries in Bree after that name.

Frodo fidgeted, wondering what to do. Pippin was evidently much enjoying the attention he was getting, and had become quite forgetful of their danger. Frodo had a sudden fear that in his present mood he might even mention the Ring; and that might well be disastrous.

'You had better do something quick!' whispered Strider in his ear.

Frodo jumped up and stood on a table, and began to talk. The attention of Pippin's audience was disturbed. Some of the hobbits looked at Frodo and laughed and clapped, thinking that Mr. Underhill had taken as much ale as was good for him.

Frodo suddenly felt very foolish, and found himself (as was his habit when making a speech) fingering the things in his pocket. He felt the Ring on its chain, and quite unaccountably the desire came over him to slip it on and vanish out of the silly situation. It seemed to him, somehow, as if the suggestion came to him from outside, from someone or something in the room. He resisted the temptation firmly, and clasped the Ring in his hand, as if to keep a hold on it and prevent it from escaping or doing any mischief. At any rate it gave him no inspiration. He spoke 'a few suitable words', as they would have said in the Shire: *We are all very much gratified by the kindness of your reception, and I venture to hope that my brief visit will help to renew the old ties of friendship between the Shire and Bree*; and then he hesitated and coughed.

Everyone in the room was now looking at him. 'A song!' shouted one of the hobbits. 'A song! A song!' shouted all the others. 'Come on now, master, sing us something that we haven't heard before!'

For a moment Frodo stood gaping. Then in desperation he began a ridiculous song that Bilbo had been rather fond of (and indeed rather proud of, for he had made up the words himself). It was about an inn; and that is probably why it came into Frodo's mind just then. Here it is in full. Only a few words of it are now, as a rule, remembered.

There is an inn, a merry old inn
　　beneath an old grey hill,
And there they brew a beer so brown
That the Man in the Moon himself came down
　　one night to drink his fill.

The ostler has a tipsy cat
　　that plays a five-stringed fiddle;
And up and down he runs his bow,
Now squeaking high, now purring low,
　　now sawing in the middle.

The landlord keeps a little dog
　　that is mighty fond of jokes;
When there's good cheer among the guests,
He cocks an ear at all the jests
　　and laughs until he chokes.

They also keep a hornéd cow
　　as proud as any queen;
But music turns her head like ale,
And makes her wave her tufted tail
　　and dance upon the green.

And O! the rows of silver dishes
　　and the store of silver spoons!
For Sunday* there's a special pair,
And these they polish up with care
　　on Saturday afternoons.

The Man in the Moon was drinking deep,
　　and the cat began to wail;
A dish and a spoon on the table danced,
The cow in the garden madly pranced,
　　and the little dog chased his tail.

The Man in the Moon took another mug,
　　and then rolled beneath his chair;
And there he dozed and dreamed of ale,
Till in the sky the stars were pale,
　　and dawn was in the air.

* See note 1, p. 1084

Then the ostler said to his tipsy cat:
'The white horses of the Moon,
They neigh and champ their silver bits;
But their master's been and drowned his wits,
and the Sun'll be rising soon!'

So the cat on his fiddle played hey-diddle-diddle,
a jig that would wake the dead:
He squeaked and sawed and quickened the tune,
While the landlord shook the Man in the Moon:
'It's after three!' he said.

They rolled the Man slowly up the hill
and bundled him into the Moon,
While his horses galloped up in rear,
And the cow came capering like a deer,
and a dish ran up with the spoon.

Now quicker the fiddle went deedle-dum-diddle;
the dog began to roar,
The cow and the horses stood on their heads;
The guests all bounded from their beds
and danced upon the floor.

With a ping and a pong the fiddle-strings broke!
the cow jumped over the Moon,
And the little dog laughed to see such fun,
And the Saturday dish went off at a run
with the silver Sunday spoon.

The round Moon rolled behind the hill
as the Sun raised up her head.
She* hardly believed her fiery eyes;
For though it was day, to her surprise
they all went back to bed!

There was loud and long applause. Frodo had a good voice, and the song tickled their fancy. 'Where's old Barley?' they cried. 'He ought to hear this. Bob ought to learn his cat the fiddle, and then we'd have a dance.' They called for more ale, and began to shout: 'Let's have it again, master! Come on now! Once more!'

---

* Elves (and Hobbits) always refer to the Sun as She.

They made Frodo have another drink, and then begin his song again, while many of them joined in; for the tune was well known, and they were quick at picking up words. It was now Frodo's turn to feel pleased with himself. He capered about on the table; and when he came a second time to *the cow jumped over the Moon*, he leaped in the air. Much too vigorously; for he came down, bang, into a tray full of mugs, and slipped, and rolled off the table with a crash, clatter, and bump! The audience all opened their mouths wide for laughter, and stopped short in gaping silence; for the singer disappeared. He simply vanished, as if he had gone slap through the floor without leaving a hole!

The local hobbits stared in amazement, and then sprang to their feet and shouted for Barliman. All the company drew away from Pippin and Sam, who found themselves left alone in a corner, and eyed darkly and doubtfully from a distance. It was plain that many people regarded them now as the companions of a travelling magician of unknown powers and purpose. But there was one swarthy Bree-lander, who stood looking at them with a knowing and half-mocking expression that made them feel very uncomfortable. Presently he slipped out of the door, followed by the squint-eyed southerner: the two had been whispering together a good deal during the evening. Harry the gatekeeper also went out just behind them.

Frodo felt a fool. Not knowing what else to do, he crawled away under the tables to the dark corner by Strider, who sat unmoved, giving no sign of his thoughts. Frodo leaned back against the wall and took off the Ring. How it came to be on his finger he could not tell. He could only suppose that he had been handling it in his pocket while he sang, and that somehow it had slipped on when he stuck out his hand with a jerk to save his fall. For a moment he wondered if the Ring itself had not played him a trick; perhaps it had tried to reveal itself in response to some wish or command that was felt in the room. He did not like the looks of the men that had gone out.

'Well?' said Strider, when he reappeared. 'Why did you do that? Worse than anything your friends could have said! You have put your foot in it! Or should I say your finger?'

'I don't know what you mean,' said Frodo, annoyed and alarmed.

'Oh yes, you do,' answered Strider; 'but we had better wait until the uproar has died down. Then, if you please, Mr. *Baggins*, I should like a quiet word with you.'

'What about?' asked Frodo, ignoring the sudden use of his proper name.

'A matter of some importance – to us both,' answered Strider, looking Frodo in the eye. 'You may hear something to your advantage.'

'Very well,' said Frodo, trying to appear unconcerned. 'I'll talk to you later.'

Meanwhile an argument was going on by the fireplace. Mr. Butterbur had come trotting in, and he was now trying to listen to several conflicting accounts of the event at the same time.

'I saw him, Mr. Butterbur,' said a hobbit; 'or leastways I didn't see him, if you take my meaning. He just vanished into thin air, in a manner of speaking.'

'You don't say, Mr. Mugwort!' said the landlord, looking puzzled.

'Yes I do!' replied Mugwort. 'And I mean what I say, what's more.'

'There's some mistake somewhere,' said Butterbur, shaking his head. 'There was too much of that Mr. Underhill to go vanishing into thin air; or into thick air, as is more likely in this room.'

'Well, where is he now?' cried several voices.

'How should I know? He's welcome to go where he will, so long as he pays in the morning. There's Mr. Took, now: he's not vanished.'

'Well, I saw what I saw, and I saw what I didn't,' said Mugwort obstinately.

'And I say there's some mistake,' repeated Butterbur, picking up the tray and gathering up the broken crockery.

'Of course there's a mistake!' said Frodo. 'I haven't vanished. Here I am! I've just been having a few words with Strider in the corner.'

He came forward into the firelight; but most of the company backed away, even more perturbed than before. They were not in the least satisfied by his explanation that he had crawled away quickly under the tables after he had fallen. Most of the Hobbits and the Men of Bree went off then and there in a huff, having no fancy for further entertainment that evening. One or two gave Frodo a black look and departed muttering among themselves. The Dwarves and the two or three strange Men that still remained got up and said good night to the landlord, but not to Frodo and his friends. Before long no one was left but Strider, who sat on, unnoticed, by the wall.

Mr. Butterbur did not seem much put out. He reckoned, very probably, that his house would be full again on many future nights, until the present mystery had been thoroughly discussed. 'Now what have you been doing, Mr. Underhill?' he asked. 'Frightening my customers and breaking up my crocks with your acrobatics!'

'I am very sorry to have caused any trouble,' said Frodo. 'It was quite unintentional, I assure you. A most unfortunate accident.'

'All right, Mr. Underhill! But if you're going to do any more tumbling, or conjuring, or whatever it was, you'd best warn folk beforehand – and warn *me*. We're a bit suspicious round here of anything out of the way – uncanny, if you understand me; and we don't take to it all of a sudden.'

'I shan't be doing anything of the sort again, Mr. Butterbur, I promise you. And now I think I'll be getting to bed. We shall be making an early start. Will you see that our ponies are ready by eight o'clock?'

'Very good! But before you go, I should like a word with you in private, Mr. Underhill. Something has just come back to my mind that I ought to tell you. I hope that you'll not take it amiss. When I've seen to a thing or two, I'll come along to your room, if you're willing.'

'Certainly!' said Frodo; but his heart sank. He wondered how many private talks he would have before he got to bed, and what they would reveal. Were these people all in league against him? He began to suspect even old Butterbur's fat face of concealing dark designs.

CHAPTER X

STRIDER

Frodo, Pippin, and Sam made their way back to the parlour. There was no light. Merry was not there, and the fire had burned low. It was not until they had puffed up the embers into a blaze and thrown on a couple of faggots that they discovered Strider had come with them. There he was calmly sitting in a chair by the door!

'Hallo!' said Pippin. 'Who are you, and what do you want?'

'I am called Strider,' he answered: 'and though he may have forgotten it, your friend promised to have a quiet talk with me.'

'You said I might hear something to my advantage, I believe,' said Frodo. 'What have you to say?'

'Several things,' answered Strider. 'But, of course, I have my price.'

'What do you mean?' asked Frodo sharply.

'Don't be alarmed! I mean just this: I will tell you what I know, and give you some good advice – but I shall want a reward.'

'And what will that be, pray?' said Frodo. He suspected now that he had fallen in with a rascal, and he thought uncomfortably that he had brought only a little money with him. All of it would hardly satisfy a rogue, and he could not spare any of it.

'No more than you can afford,' answered Strider with a slow smile, as if he guessed Frodo's thoughts. 'Just this: you must take me along with you, until I wish to leave you.'

'Oh, indeed!' replied Frodo, surprised, but not much relieved. 'Even if I wanted another companion, I should not agree to any such thing, until I knew a good deal more about you, and your business.'

'Excellent!' exclaimed Strider, crossing his legs and sitting back comfortably. 'You seem to be coming to your senses again, and that is all to the good. You have been much too careless so far. Very well! I will tell you what I know, and leave the reward to you. You may be glad to grant it, when you have heard me.'

'Go on then!' said Frodo. 'What do you know?'

'Too much; too many dark things,' said Strider grimly. 'But as for your business——' He got up and went to the door, opened it quickly and looked out. Then he shut it quietly and sat down again. 'I have quick ears,' he went on, lowering his voice, 'and though I cannot disappear, I have hunted many wild and wary things and I can usually avoid being seen, if I wish. Now, I was behind the hedge this evening on the Road west of

Bree, when four hobbits came out of the Downlands. I need not repeat all that they said to old Bombadil or to one another, but one thing interested me. *Please remember*, said one of them, *that the name Baggins must not be mentioned. I am Mr. Underhill, if any name must be given.* That interested me so much that I followed them here. I slipped over the gate just behind them. Maybe Mr. Baggins has an honest reason for leaving his name behind; but if so, I should advise him and his friends to be more careful.'

'I don't see what interest my name has for any one in Bree,' said Frodo angrily, 'and I have still to learn why it interests you. Mr. Strider may have an honest reason for spying and eavesdropping; but if so, I should advise him to explain it.'

'Well answered!' said Strider laughing. 'But the explanation is simple: I was looking for a Hobbit called Frodo Baggins. I wanted to find him quickly. I had learned that he was carrying out of the Shire, well, a secret that concerned me and my friends.

'Now, don't mistake me!' he cried, as Frodo rose from his seat, and Sam jumped up with a scowl. 'I shall take more care of the secret than you do. And care is needed!' He leaned forward and looked at them. 'Watch every shadow!' he said in a low voice. 'Black horsemen have passed through Bree. On Monday one came down the Greenway, they say; and another appeared later, coming up the Greenway from the south.'

There was a silence. At last Frodo spoke to Pippin and Sam: 'I ought to have guessed it from the way the gatekeeper greeted us,' he said. 'And the landlord seems to have heard something. Why did he press us to join the company? And why on earth did we behave so foolishly: we ought to have stayed quiet in here.'

'It would have been better,' said Strider. 'I would have stopped your going into the common-room, if I could; but the innkeeper would not let me in to see you, or take a message.'

'Do you think he——' began Frodo.

'No, I don't think any harm of old Butterbur. Only he does not altogether like mysterious vagabonds of my sort.' Frodo gave him a puzzled look. 'Well, I have rather a rascally look, have I not?' said Strider with a curl of his lip and a queer gleam in his eye. 'But I hope we shall get to know one another better. When we do, I hope you will explain what happened at the end of your song. For that little prank——'

'It was sheer accident!' interrupted Frodo.

'I wonder,' said Strider. 'Accident, then. That accident has made your position dangerous.'

'Hardly more than it was already,' said Frodo. 'I knew these horsemen were pursuing me; but now at any rate they seem to have missed me and to have gone away.'

'You must not count on that!' said Strider sharply. 'They will return. And more are coming. There are others. I know their number. I know these Riders.' He paused, and his eyes were cold and hard. 'And there are some folk in Bree who are not to be trusted,' he went on. 'Bill Ferny, for instance. He has an evil name in the Bree-land, and queer folk call at his house. You must have noticed him among the company: a swarthy sneering fellow. He was very close with one of the Southern strangers, and they slipped out together just after your "accident". Not all of those Southerners mean well; and as for Ferny, he would sell anything to anybody; or make mischief for amusement.'

'What will Ferny sell, and what has my accident got to do with him?' said Frodo, still determined not to understand Strider's hints.

'News of you, of course,' answered Strider. 'An account of your perform-ance would be very interesting to certain people. After that they would hardly need to be told your real name. It seems to me only too likely that they will hear of it before this night is over. Is that enough? You can do as you like about my reward: take me as a guide or not. But I may say that I know all the lands between the Shire and the Misty Mountains, for I have wandered over them for many years. I am older than I look. I might prove useful. You will have to leave the open road after tonight; for the horsemen will watch it night and day. You may escape from Bree, and be allowed to go forward while the Sun is up; but you won't go far. They will come on you in the wild, in some dark place where there is no help. Do you wish them to find you? They are terrible!'

The hobbits looked at him, and saw with surprise that his face was drawn as if with pain, and his hands clenched the arms of his chair. The room was very quiet and still, and the light seemed to have grown dim. For a while he sat with unseeing eyes as if walking in distant memory or listening to sounds in the Night far away.

'There!' he cried after a moment, drawing his hand across his brow. 'Perhaps I know more about these pursuers than you do. You fear them, but you do not fear them enough, yet. Tomorrow you will have to escape, if you can. Strider can take you by paths that are seldom trodden. Will you have him?'

There was a heavy silence. Frodo made no answer, his mind was confused with doubt and fear. Sam frowned, and looked at his master; and at last he broke out:

'With your leave, Mr. Frodo, I'd say no! This Strider here, he warns and he says take care; and I say yes to that, and let's begin with him. He comes out of the Wild, and I never heard no good of such folk. He knows something, that's plain, and more than I like; but it's no reason why we should let him go leading us out into some dark place far from help, as he puts it.'

Pippin fidgeted and looked uncomfortable. Strider did not reply to Sam, but turned his keen eyes on Frodo. Frodo caught his glance and looked away. 'No,' he said slowly. 'I don't agree. I think, I think you are not really as you choose to look. You began to talk to me like the Bree-folk, but your voice has changed. Still Sam seems right in this: I don't see why you should warn us to take care, and yet ask us to take you on trust. Why the disguise? Who are you? What do you really know about – about my business; and how do you know it?'

'The lesson in caution has been well learned,' said Strider with a grim smile. 'But caution is one thing and wavering is another. You will never get to Rivendell now on your own, and to trust me is your only chance. You must make up your mind. I will answer some of your questions, if that will help you to do so. But why should you believe my story, if you do not trust me already? Still here it is——'

At that moment there came a knock at the door. Mr. Butterbur had arrived with candles, and behind him was Nob with cans of hot water. Strider withdrew into a dark corner.

'I've come to bid you good night,' said the landlord, putting the candles on the table. 'Nob! Take the water to the rooms!' He came in and shut the door.

'It's like this,' he began, hesitating and looking troubled. 'If I've done any harm, I'm sorry indeed. But one thing drives out another, as you'll admit; and I'm a busy man. But first one thing and then another this week have jogged my memory, as the saying goes; and not too late I hope. You see, I was asked to look out for hobbits of the Shire, and for one by the name of Baggins in particular.'

'And what has that got to do with me?' asked Frodo.

'Ah! you know best,' said the landlord, knowingly. 'I won't give you away; but I was told that this Baggins would be going by the name of Underhill, and I was given a description that fits you well enough, if I may say so.'

'Indeed! Let's have it then!' said Frodo, unwisely interrupting.

'*A stout little fellow with red cheeks*,' said Mr. Butterbur solemnly. Pippin chuckled, but Sam looked indignant. '*That won't help you much; it goes for most hobbits, Barley*, he says to me,' continued Mr. Butterbur with a glance at Pippin. '*But this one is taller than some and fairer than most, and he has a cleft in his chin: perky chap with a bright eye*. Begging your pardon, but he said it, not me.'

'*He* said it? And who was he?' asked Frodo eagerly.

'Ah! That was Gandalf, if you know who I mean. A wizard they say he is, but he's a good friend of mine, whether or no. But now I don't know what he'll have to say to me, if I see him again: turn all my ale sour or me into a block of wood, I shouldn't wonder. He's a bit hasty. Still what's done can't be undone.'

'Well, what have you done?' said Frodo, getting impatient with the slow unravelling of Butterbur's thoughts.

'Where was I?' said the landlord, pausing and snapping his fingers. 'Ah, yes! Old Gandalf. Three months back he walked right into my room without a knock. *Barley*, he says, *I'm off in the morning. Will you do something for me? You've only to name it*, I said. *I'm in a hurry*, said he, *and I've no time myself, but I want a message took to the Shire. Have you anyone you can send, and trust to go? I can find someone*, I said, *tomorrow, maybe, or the day after. Make it tomorrow*, he says, and then he gave me a letter.

'It's addressed plain enough,' said Mr. Butterbur, producing a letter from his pocket, and reading out the address slowly and proudly (he valued his reputation as a lettered man):

Mr. FRODO BAGGINS, BAG END, HOBBITON in the SHIRE.

'A letter for me from Gandalf!' cried Frodo.

'Ah!' said Mr. Butterbur. 'Then your right name is Baggins?'

'It is,' said Frodo, 'and you had better give me that letter at once, and explain why you never sent it. That's what you came to tell me, I suppose, though you've taken a long time to come to the point.'

Poor Mr. Butterbur looked troubled. 'You're right, master,' he said, 'and I beg your pardon. And I'm mortal afraid of what Gandalf will say, if harm comes of it. But I didn't keep it back a-purpose. I put it by safe. Then I couldn't find nobody willing to go to the Shire next day, nor the day after, and none of my own folk were to spare; and then one thing after another drove it out of my mind. I'm a busy man. I'll do what I can to set matters right, and if there's any help I can give, you've only to name it.

'Leaving the letter aside, I promised Gandalf no less. *Barley*, he says to me, *this friend of mine from the Shire, he may be coming out this way before long, him and another. He'll be calling himself Underhill. Mind that! But you need ask no questions. And if I'm not with him, he may be in trouble, and he may need help. Do whatever you can for him, and I'll be grateful*, he says. And here you are, and trouble is not far off, seemingly.'

'What do you mean?' asked Frodo.

'These black men,' said the landlord lowering his voice. 'They're looking for *Baggins*, and if they mean well, then I'm a hobbit. It was on Monday, and all the dogs were yammering and the geese screaming. Uncanny, I called it. Nob, he came and told me that two black men were at the door asking for a hobbit called Baggins. Nob's hair was all stood on end. I bid the black fellows be off, and slammed the door on them; but they've been asking the same question all the way to Archet, I hear. And that Ranger, Strider, he's been asking questions, too. Tried to get in here to see you, before you'd had bite or sup, he did.'

'He did!' said Strider suddenly, coming forward into the light. 'And much trouble would have been saved, if you had let him in, Barliman.'

The landlord jumped with surprise. 'You!' he cried. 'You're always popping up. What do you want now?'

'He's here with my leave,' said Frodo. 'He came to offer me his help.'

'Well, you know your own business, maybe,' said Mr. Butterbur, looking suspiciously at Strider. 'But if I was in your plight, I wouldn't take up with a Ranger.'

'Then who would you take up with?' asked Strider. 'A fat innkeeper who only remembers his own name because people shout it at him all day? They cannot stay in *The Pony* for ever, and they cannot go home. They have a long road before them. Will you go with them and keep the black men off?'

'Me? Leave Bree! I wouldn't do that for any money,' said Mr. Butterbur, looking really scared. 'But why can't you stay here quiet for a bit, Mr. Underhill? What are all these queer goings on? What are these black men after, and where do they come from, I'd like to know?'

'I'm sorry I can't explain it all,' answered Frodo. 'I am tired and very worried, and it's a long tale. But if you mean to help me, I ought to warn you that you will be in danger as long as I am in your house. These Black Riders: I am not sure, but I think, I fear they come from——'

'They come from Mordor,' said Strider in a low voice. 'From Mordor, Barliman, if that means anything to you.'

'Save us!' cried Mr. Butterbur turning pale; the name evidently was known to him. 'That is the worst news that has come to Bree in my time.'

'It is,' said Frodo. 'Are you still willing to help me?'

'I am,' said Mr. Butterbur. 'More than ever. Though I don't know what the likes of me can do against, against——' he faltered.

'Against the Shadow in the East,' said Strider quietly. 'Not much, Barliman, but every little helps. You can let Mr. Underhill stay here tonight, as Mr. Underhill, and you can forget the name of Baggins, till he is far away.'

'I'll do that,' said Butterbur. 'But they'll find out he's here without help from me, I'm afraid. It's a pity Mr. Baggins drew attention to himself this evening, to say no more. The story of that Mr. Bilbo's going off has been heard before tonight in Bree. Even our Nob has been doing some guessing in his slow pate; and there are others in Bree quicker in the uptake than he is.'

'Well, we can only hope the Riders won't come back yet,' said Frodo.

'I hope not, indeed,' said Butterbur. 'But spooks or no spooks, they won't get in *The Pony* so easy. Don't you worry till the morning. Nob'll say no word. No black man shall pass my doors, while I can stand on my legs. Me and my folk'll keep watch tonight; but you had best get some sleep, if you can.'

'In any case we must be called at dawn,' said Frodo. 'We must get off as early as possible. Breakfast at six-thirty, please.'

'Right! I'll see to the orders,' said the landlord. 'Good night, Mr. Baggins – Underhill, I should say! Good night – now, bless me! Where's your Mr. Brandybuck?'

'I don't know,' said Frodo with sudden anxiety. They had forgotten all about Merry, and it was getting late. 'I am afraid he is out. He said something about going for a breath of air.'

'Well, you do want looking after and no mistake: your party might be on a holiday!' said Butterbur. 'I must go and bar the doors quick, but I'll see your friend is let in when he comes. I'd better send Nob to look for him. Good night to you all!' At last Mr. Butterbur went out, with another doubtful look at Strider and a shake of his head. His footsteps retreated down the passage.

'Well?' said Strider. 'When are you going to open that letter?' Frodo looked carefully at the seal before he broke it. It seemed certainly to be Gandalf's. Inside, written in the wizard's strong but graceful script, was the following message:

THE PRANCING PONY, BREE. Midyear's Day, Shire Year, 1418.

Dear Frodo,

Bad news has reached me here. I must go off at once. You had better leave Bag End soon, and get out of the Shire before the end of July at latest. I will return as soon as I can; and I will follow you, if I find that you are gone. Leave a message for me here, if you pass through Bree. You can trust the landlord (Butterbur). You may meet a friend of mine on the Road: a Man, lean, dark, tall, by some called Strider. He knows our business and will help you. Make for Rivendell. There I hope we may meet again. If I do not come, Elrond will advise you.

Yours in haste
GANDALF.

*PS. Do NOT use It again, not for any reason whatever! Do not travel by
night!*

*PPS. Make sure that it is the real Strider. There are many strange men on
the roads. His true name is Aragorn.*

> *All that is gold does not glitter,*
> *Not all those who wander are lost;*
> *The old that is strong does not wither,*
> *Deep roots are not reached by the frost.*
> *From the ashes a fire shall be woken,*
> *A light from the shadows shall spring;*
> *Renewed shall be blade that was broken,*
> *The crownless again shall be king.*

*PPPS. I hope Butterbur sends this promptly. A worthy man, but his memory
is like a lumber-room:
thing wanted always buried. If he
forgets, I shall roast him.*
> *Fare Well!*

Frodo read the letter to himself, and then passed it to Pippin and Sam.
'Really old Butterbur has made a mess of things!' he said. 'He deserves
roasting. If I had got this at once, we might all have been safe in Rivendell
by now. But what can have happened to Gandalf? He writes as if he was
going into great danger.'

'He has been doing that for many years,' said Strider.

Frodo turned and looked at him thoughtfully, wondering about Gandalf's second postscript. 'Why didn't you tell me that you were Gandalf's
friend at once?' he asked. 'It would have saved time.'

'Would it? Would any of you have believed me till now?' said Strider.
'I knew nothing of this letter. For all I knew I had to persuade you to trust
me without proofs, if I was to help you. In any case, I did not intend to
tell you all about myself at once. I had to study *you* first, and make sure
of you. The Enemy has set traps for me before now. As soon as I had made
up my mind, I was ready to tell you whatever you asked. But I must admit,'
he added with a queer laugh, 'that I hoped you would take to me for
my own sake. A hunted man sometimes wearies of distrust and longs for
friendship. But there, I believe my looks are against me.'

'They are – at first sight at any rate,' laughed Pippin with sudden relief
after reading Gandalf's letter. 'But handsome is as handsome does, as we
say in the Shire; and I daresay we shall all look much the same after lying
for days in hedges and ditches.'

'It would take more than a few days, or weeks, or years, of wandering in the Wild to make you look like Strider,' he answered. 'And you would die first, unless you are made of sterner stuff than you look to be.'

Pippin subsided; but Sam was not daunted, and he still eyed Strider dubiously. 'How do we know you are the Strider that Gandalf speaks about?' he demanded. 'You never mentioned Gandalf, till this letter came out. You might be a play-acting spy, for all I can see, trying to get us to go with you. You might have done in the real Strider and took his clothes. What have you to say to that?'

'That you are a stout fellow,' answered Strider; 'but I am afraid my only answer to you, Sam Gamgee, is this. If I had killed the real Strider, I could kill you. And I should have killed you already without so much talk. If I was after the Ring, I could have it – NOW!'

He stood up, and seemed suddenly to grow taller. In his eyes gleamed a light, keen and commanding. Throwing back his cloak, he laid his hand on the hilt of a sword that had hung concealed by his side. They did not dare to move. Sam sat wide-mouthed staring at him dumbly.

'But I *am* the real Strider, fortunately,' he said, looking down at them with his face softened by a sudden smile. 'I am Aragorn son of Arathorn; and if by life or death I can save you, I will.'

There was a long silence. At last Frodo spoke with hesitation. 'I believed that you were a friend before the letter came,' he said, 'or at least I wished to. You have frightened me several times tonight, but never in the way that servants of the Enemy would, or so I imagine. I think one of his spies would – well, seem fairer and feel fouler, if you understand.'

'I see,' laughed Strider. 'I look foul and feel fair. Is that it? *All that is gold does not glitter, not all those who wander are lost.*'

'Did the verses apply to you then?' asked Frodo. 'I could not make out what they were about. But how did you know that they were in Gandalf's letter, if you have never seen it?'

'I did not know,' he answered. 'But I am Aragorn, and those verses go with that name.' He drew out his sword, and they saw that the blade was indeed broken a foot below the hilt. 'Not much use is it, Sam?' said Strider. 'But the time is near when it shall be forged anew.'

Sam said nothing.

'Well,' said Strider, 'with Sam's permission we will call that settled. Strider shall be your guide. We shall have a rough road tomorrow. Even if we are allowed to leave Bree unhindered, we can hardly hope now to leave it unnoticed. But I shall try to get lost as soon as possible. I know one or two ways out of Bree-land other than the main road. If once we shake off the pursuit, I shall make for Weathertop.'

'Weathertop?' said Sam. 'What's that?'

'It is a hill, just to the north of the Road, about half way from here to Rivendell. It commands a wide view all round; and there we shall have a chance to look about us. Gandalf will make for that point, if he follows us. After Weathertop our journey will become more difficult, and we shall have to choose between various dangers.'

'When did you last see Gandalf?' asked Frodo. 'Do you know where he is, or what he is doing?'

Strider looked grave. 'I do not know,' he said. 'I came west with him in the spring. I have often kept watch on the borders of the Shire in the last few years, when he was busy elsewhere. He seldom left it unguarded. We last met on the first of May: at Sarn Ford down the Brandywine. He told me that his business with you had gone well, and that you would be starting for Rivendell in the last week of September. As I knew he was at your side, I went away on a journey of my own. And that has proved ill; for plainly some news reached him, and I was not at hand to help.

'I am troubled, for the first time since I have known him. We should have had messages, even if he could not come himself. When I returned, many days ago, I heard the ill news. The tidings had gone far and wide that Gandalf was missing and the horsemen had been seen. It was the Elven-folk of Gildor that told me this; and later they told me that you had left your home; but there was no news of your leaving Buckland. I have been watching the East Road anxiously.'

'Do you think the Black Riders have anything to do with it – with Gandalf's absence, I mean?' asked Frodo.

'I do not know of anything else that could have hindered him, except the Enemy himself,' said Strider. 'But do not give up hope! Gandalf is greater than you Shire-folk know – as a rule you can only see his jokes and toys. But this business of ours will be his greatest task.'

Pippin yawned. 'I am sorry,' he said, 'but I am dead tired. In spite of all the danger and worry I must go to bed, or sleep where I sit. Where is that silly fellow, Merry? It would be the last straw, if we had to go out in the dark to look for him.'

At that moment they heard a door slam; then feet came running along the passage. Merry came in with a rush followed by Nob. He shut the door hastily, and leaned against it. He was out of breath. They stared at him in alarm for a moment before he gasped: 'I have seen them, Frodo! I have seen them! Black Riders!'

'Black Riders!' cried Frodo. 'Where?'

'Here. In the village. I stayed indoors for an hour. Then as you did not come back, I went out for a stroll. I had come back again and was standing just outside the light of the lamp looking at the stars. Suddenly I shivered and felt that something horrible was creeping near: there was a sort of deeper shade among the shadows across the road, just beyond the edge of the lamplight. It slid away at once into the dark without a sound. There was no horse.'

'Which way did it go?' asked Strider, suddenly and sharply.

Merry started, noticing the stranger for the first time. 'Go on!' said Frodo. 'This is a friend of Gandalf's. I will explain later.'

'It seemed to make off up the Road, eastward,' continued Merry. 'I tried to follow. Of course, it vanished almost at once; but I went round the corner and on as far as the last house on the Road.'

Strider looked at Merry with wonder. 'You have a stout heart,' he said; 'but it was foolish.'

'I don't know,' said Merry. 'Neither brave nor silly, I think. I could hardly help myself. I seemed to be drawn somehow. Anyway, I went, and suddenly I heard voices by the hedge. One was muttering; and the other was whispering, or hissing. I couldn't hear a word that was said. I did not creep any closer, because I began to tremble all over. Then I felt terrified, and I turned back, and was just going to bolt home, when something came behind me and I . . . I fell over.'

'I found him, sir,' put in Nob. 'Mr. Butterbur sent me out with a lantern. I went down to West-gate, and then back up towards South-gate. Just nigh Bill Ferny's house I thought I could see something in the Road. I couldn't swear to it, but it looked to me as if two men was stooping over something, lifting it. I gave a shout, but when i got up to the spot there was no signs of them, and only Mr. Brandybuck lying by the roadside. He seemed to be asleep. "I thought I had fallen into deep water," he says to me, when I shook him. Very queer he was, and as soon as I had roused him, he got up and ran back here like a hare.'

'I am afraid that's true,' said Merry, 'though I don't know what I said. I had an ugly dream, which I can't remember. I went to pieces. I don't know what came over me.'

'I do,' said Strider. 'The Black Breath. The Riders must have left their horses outside, and passed back through the South-gate in secret. They will know all the news now, for they have visited Bill Ferny; and probably that Southerner was a spy as well. Something may happen in the night, before we leave Bree.'

'What will happen?' said Merry. 'Will they attack the inn?'

'No, I think not,' said Strider. 'They are not all here yet. And in any case that is not their way. In dark and loneliness they are strongest; they will not openly attack a house where there are lights and many people – not until they are desperate, not while all the long leagues of Eriador still lie before us. But their power is in terror, and already some in Bree are in their clutch. They will drive these wretches to some evil work: Ferny, and some of the strangers, and, maybe, the gatekeeper too. They had words with Harry at West-gate on Monday. I was watching them. He was white and shaking when they left him.'

'We seem to have enemies all round,' said Frodo. 'What are we to do?'

'Stay here, and do not go to your rooms! They are sure to have found out which those are. The hobbit-rooms have windows looking north and close to the ground. We will all remain together and bar this window and the door. But first Nob and I will fetch your luggage.'

While Strider was gone, Frodo gave Merry a rapid account of all that had happened since supper. Merry was still reading and pondering Gandalf's letter when Strider and Nob returned.

'Well Masters,' said Nob, 'I've ruffled up the clothes and put in a bolster down the middle of each bed. And I made a nice imitation of your head with a brown woollen mat, Mr. Bag – Underhill, sir,' he added with a grin.

Pippin laughed. 'Very life-like!' he said. 'But what will happen when they have penetrated the disguise?'

'We shall see,' said Strider. 'Let us hope to hold the fort till morning.'

'Good night to you,' said Nob, and went off to take his part in the watch on the doors.

Their bags and gear they piled on the parlour-floor. They pushed a low chair against the door and shut the window. Peering out, Frodo saw that the night was still clear. The Sickle* was swinging bright above the shoulders of Bree-hill. He then closed and barred the heavy inside shutters and drew the curtains together. Strider built up the fire and blew out all the candles.

The hobbits lay down on their blankets with their feet towards the hearth; but Strider settled himself in the chair against the door. They talked for a little, for Merry still had several questions to ask.

'Jumped over the Moon!' chuckled Merry as he rolled himself in his blanket. 'Very ridiculous of you, Frodo! But I wish I had been there to see. The worthies of Bree will be discussing it a hundred years hence.'

'I hope so,' said Strider. Then they all fell silent, and one by one the hobbits dropped off to sleep.

---

* The Hobbits' name for the Plough or Great Bear.

CHAPTER XI

A KNIFE IN THE DARK

As they prepared for sleep in the inn at Bree, darkness lay on Buckland; a mist strayed in the dells and along the river-bank. The house at Crickhollow stood silent. Fatty Bolger opened the door cautiously and peered out. A feeling of fear had been growing on him all day, and he was unable to rest or go to bed: there was a brooding threat in the breathless night-air. As he stared out into the gloom, a black shadow moved under the trees; the gate seemed to open of its own accord and close again without a sound. Terror seized him. He shrank back, and for a moment he stood trembling in the hall. Then he shut and locked the door.

The night deepened. There came the soft sound of horses led with stealth along the lane. Outside the gate they stopped, and three black figures entered, like shades of night creeping across the ground. One went to the door, one to the corner of the house on either side; and there they stood, as still as the shadows of stones, while night went slowly on. The house and the quiet trees seemed to be waiting breathlessly.

There was a faint stir in the leaves, and a cock crowed far away. The cold hour before dawn was passing. The figure by the door moved. In the dark without moon or stars a drawn blade gleamed, as if a chill light had been unsheathed. There was a blow, soft but heavy, and the door shuddered.

'Open, in the name of Mordor!' said a voice thin and menacing.

At a second blow the door yielded and fell back, with timbers burst and lock broken. The black figures passed swiftly in.

At that moment, among the trees nearby, a horn rang out. It rent the night like fire on a hill-top.

AWAKE! FEAR! FIRE! FOES! AWAKE!

Fatty Bolger had not been idle. As soon as he saw the dark shapes creep from the garden, he knew that he must run for it, or perish. And run he did, out of the back door, through the garden, and over the fields. When he reached the nearest house, more than a mile away, he collapsed on the doorstep. 'No, no, no!' he was crying. 'No, not me! I haven't got it!' It was some time before anyone could make out what he was babbling about. At last they got the idea that enemies were in Buckland, some strange invasion from the Old Forest. And then they lost no more time.

FEAR! FIRE! FOES!

The Brandybucks were blowing the Horn-call of Buckland, that had not been sounded for a hundred years, not since the white wolves came in the Fell Winter, when the Brandywine was frozen over.

AWAKE! AWAKE!

Far-away answering horns were heard. The alarm was spreading. The black figures fled from the house. One of them let fall a hobbit-cloak on the step, as he ran. In the lane the noise of hoofs broke out, and gathering to a gallop, went hammering away into the darkness. All about Crickhollow there was the sound of horns blowing, and voices crying and feet running. But the Black Riders rode like a gale to the North-gate. Let the little people blow! Sauron would deal with them later. Meanwhile they had another errand: they knew now that the house was empty and the Ring had gone. They rode down the guards at the gate and vanished from the Shire.

In the early night Frodo woke from deep sleep, suddenly, as if some sound or presence had disturbed him. He saw that Strider was sitting alert in his chair: his eyes gleamed in the light of the fire, which had been tended and was burning brightly; but he made no sign or movement.

Frodo soon went to sleep again; but his dreams were again troubled with the noise of wind and of galloping hoofs. The wind seemed to be curling round the house and shaking it; and far off he heard a horn blowing wildly. He opened his eyes, and heard a cock crowing lustily in the inn-yard. Strider had drawn the curtains and pushed back the shutters with a clang. The first grey light of day was in the room, and a cold air was coming through the open window.

As soon as Strider had roused them all, he led the way to their bedrooms. When they saw them they were glad that they had taken his advice: the windows had been forced open and were swinging, and the curtains were flapping; the beds were tossed about, and the bolsters slashed and flung upon the floor; the brown mat was torn to pieces.

Strider immediately went to fetch the landlord. Poor Mr. Butterbur looked sleepy and frightened. He had hardly closed his eyes all night (so he said), but he had never heard a sound.

'Never has such a thing happened in my time!' he cried, raising his hands in horror. 'Guests unable to sleep in their beds, and good bolsters ruined and all! What are we coming to?'

'Dark times,' said Strider. 'But for the present you may be left in peace, when you have got rid of us. We will leave at once. Never mind about breakfast: a drink and a bite standing will have to do. We shall be packed in a few minutes.'

Mr. Butterbur hurried off to see that their ponies were got ready, and to fetch them a 'bite'. But very soon he came back in dismay. The ponies had vanished! The stable-doors had all been opened in the night, and they were gone: not only Merry's ponies, but every other horse and beast in the place.

Frodo was crushed by the news. How could they hope to reach Rivendell on foot, pursued by mounted enemies? They might as well set out for the Moon. Strider sat silent for a while, looking at the hobbits, as if he was weighing up their strength and courage.

'Ponies would not help us to escape horsemen,' he said at last, thoughtfully, as if he guessed what Frodo had in mind. 'We should not go much slower on foot, not on the roads that I mean to take. I was going to walk in any case. It is the food and stores that trouble me. We cannot count on getting anything to eat between here and Rivendell, except what we take with us; and we ought to take plenty to spare; for we may be delayed, or forced to go round-about, far out of the direct way. How much are you prepared to carry on your backs?'

'As much as we must,' said Pippin with a sinking heart, but trying to show that he was tougher than he looked (or felt).

'I can carry enough for two,' said Sam defiantly.

'Can't anything be done, Mr. Butterbur?' asked Frodo. 'Can't we get a couple of ponies in the village, or even one just for the baggage? I don't suppose we could hire them, but we might be able to buy them,' he added, doubtfully, wondering if he could afford it.

'I doubt it,' said the landlord unhappily. 'The two or three riding-ponies that there were in Bree were stabled in my yard, and they're gone. As for other animals, horses or ponies for draught or what not, there are very few of them in Bree, and they won't be for sale. But I'll do what I can. I'll rout out Bob and send him round as soon as may be.'

'Yes,' said Strider reluctantly, 'you had better do that. I am afraid we shall have to try to get one pony at least. But so ends all hope of starting early, and slipping away quietly! We might as well have blown a horn to announce our departure. That was part of their plan, no doubt.'

'There is one crumb of comfort,' said Merry, 'and more than a crumb, I hope: we can have breakfast while we wait – and sit down to it. Let's get hold of Nob!'

In the end there was more than three hours' delay. Bob came back with the report that no horse or pony was to be got for love or money in the neighbourhood – except one: Bill Ferny had one that he might possibly sell. 'A poor old half-starved creature it is,' said Bob; 'but he won't part with it for less than thrice its worth, seeing how you're placed, not if I knows Bill Ferny.'

'Bill Ferny?' said Frodo. 'Isn't there some trick? Wouldn't the beast bolt back to him with all our stuff, or help in tracking us, or something?'

'I wonder,' said Strider. 'But I cannot imagine any animal running home to him, once it got away. I fancy this is only an afterthought of kind Master Ferny's: just a way of increasing his profits from the affair. The chief danger is that the poor beast is probably at death's door. But there does not seem any choice. What does he want for it?'

Bill Ferny's price was twelve silver pennies; and that was indeed at least three times the pony's value in those parts. It proved to be a bony, underfed, and dispirited animal; but it did not look like dying just yet. Mr. Butterbur paid for it himself, and offered Merry another eighteen pence as some compensation for the lost animals. He was an honest man, and well-off as things were reckoned in Bree; but thirty silver pennies was a sore blow to him, and being cheated by Bill Ferny made it harder to bear.

As a matter of fact he came out on the right side in the end. It turned out later that only one horse had been actually stolen. The others had been driven off, or had bolted in terror, and were found wandering in different corners of the Bree-land. Merry's ponies had escaped altogether, and eventually (having a good deal of sense) they made their way to the Downs in search of Fatty Lumpkin. So they came under the care of Tom Bombadil for a while, and were well-off. But when news of the events at Bree came to Tom's ears, he sent them to Mr. Butterbur, who thus got five good beasts at a very fair price. They had to work harder in Bree, but Bob treated them well; so on the whole they were lucky: they missed a dark and dangerous journey. But they never came to Rivendell.

However, in the meanwhile for all Mr. Butterbur knew his money was gone for good, or for bad. And he had other troubles. For there was a great commotion as soon as the remaining guests were astir and heard news of the raid on the inn. The southern travellers had lost several horses and blamed the innkeeper loudly, until it became known that one of their own number had also disappeared in the night, none other than Bill Ferny's squint-eyed companion. Suspicion fell on him at once.

'If you pick up with a horse-thief, and bring him to my house,' said Butterbur angrily, 'you ought to pay for all the damage yourselves and not come shouting at me. Go and ask Ferny where your handsome friend is!' But it appeared that he was nobody's friend, and nobody could recollect when he had joined their party.

After their breakfast the hobbits had to re-pack, and get together further supplies for the longer journey they were now expecting. It was close on ten o'clock before they at last got off. By that time the whole of Bree was buzzing with excitement. Frodo's vanishing trick; the appearance of the black horsemen; the robbing of the stables; and not least the news that Strider the Ranger had joined the mysterious hobbits, made such a tale as would last for many uneventful years. Most of the inhabitants of Bree and Staddle, and many even from Combe and Archet, were crowded in the road to see the travellers start. The other guests in the inn were at the doors or hanging out of the windows.

Strider had changed his mind, and he decided to leave Bree by the main road. Any attempt to set off across country at once would only make matters worse: half the inhabitants would follow them, to see what they were up to, and to prevent them from trespassing.

They said farewell to Nob and Bob, and took leave of Mr. Butterbur with many thanks. 'I hope we shall meet again some day, when things are merry once more,' said Frodo. 'I should like nothing better than to stay in your house in peace for a while.'

They tramped off, anxious and downhearted, under the eyes of the crowd. Not all the faces were friendly, nor all the words that were shouted. But Strider seemed to be held in awe by most of the Bree-landers, and those that he stared at shut their mouths and drew away. He walked in front with Frodo; next came Merry and Pippin; and last came Sam leading the pony, which was laden with as much of their baggage as they had the heart to give it; but already it looked less dejected, as if it approved of the change in its fortunes. Sam was chewing an apple thoughtfully. He had a pocket full of them: a parting present from Nob and Bob. 'Apples for walking, and a pipe for sitting,' he said. 'But I reckon I'll miss them both before long.'

The hobbits took no notice of the inquisitive heads that peeped out of doors, or popped over walls and fences, as they passed. But as they drew near to the further gate, Frodo saw a dark ill-kept house behind a thick hedge: the last house in the village. In one of the windows he caught a glimpse of a sallow face with sly, slanting eyes; but it vanished at once.

'So that's where that southerner is hiding!' he thought. 'He looks more than half like a goblin.'

Over the hedge another man was staring boldly. He had heavy black brows, and dark scornful eyes; his large mouth curled in a sneer. He was smoking a short black pipe. As they approached he took it out of his mouth and spat.

'Morning, Longshanks!' he said. 'Off early? Found some friends at last?' Strider nodded, but did not answer.

'Morning, my little friends!' he said to the others. 'I suppose you know who you've taken up with? That's Stick-at-naught Strider, that is! Though I've heard other names not so pretty. Watch out tonight! And you, Sammie, don't go ill-treating my poor old pony! Pah!' He spat again.

Sam turned quickly. 'And you, Ferny,' he said, 'put your ugly face out of sight, or it will get hurt.' With a sudden flick, quick as lightning, an apple left his hand and hit Bill square on the nose. He ducked too late, and curses came from behind the hedge. 'Waste of a good apple,' said Sam regretfully, and strode on.

At last they left the village behind. The escort of children and stragglers that had followed them got tired and turned back at the South-gate. Passing through, they kept on along the Road for some miles. It bent to the left, curving back into its eastward line as it rounded the feet of Bree-hill, and then it began to run swiftly downwards into wooded country. To their left they could see some of the houses and hobbit-holes of Staddle on the gentler south-eastern slopes of the hill; down in a deep hollow away north of the Road there were wisps of rising smoke that showed where Combe lay; Archet was hidden in the trees beyond.

After the Road had run down some way, and had left Bree-hill standing tall and brown behind, they came on a narrow track that led off towards the North. 'This is where we leave the open and take to cover,' said Strider.

'Not a "short cut", I hope,' said Pippin. 'Our last short cut through woods nearly ended in disaster.'

'Ah, but you had not got me with you then,' laughed Strider. 'My cuts, short or long, don't go wrong.' He took a look up and down the Road. No one was in sight; and he led the way quickly down towards the wooded valley.

His plan, as far as they could understand it without knowing the country, was to go towards Archet at first, but to bear right and pass it on the east, and then to steer as straight as he could over the wild lands to Weathertop Hill. In that way they would, if all went well, cut off a great loop of the Road, which further on bent southwards to avoid the Midgewater Marshes. But, of course, they would have to pass through the marshes themselves, and Strider's description of them was not encouraging.

However, in the meanwhile, walking was not unpleasant. Indeed, if it had not been for the disturbing events of the night before, they would have enjoyed this part of the journey better than any up to that time. The sun was shining, clear but not too hot. The woods in the valley were still leafy and full of colour, and seemed peaceful and wholesome. Strider guided them confidently among the many crossing paths, although left to themselves they would soon have been at a loss. He was taking a wandering course with many turns and doublings, to put off any pursuit.

'Bill Ferny will have watched where we left the Road, for certain,' he said; 'though I don't think he will follow us himself. He knows the land round here well enough, but he knows he is not a match for me in a wood. It is what he may tell others that I am afraid of. I don't suppose they are far away. If they think we have made for Archet, so much the better.'

Whether because of Strider's skill or for some other reason, they saw no sign and heard no sound of any other living thing all that day: neither two-footed, except birds; nor four-footed, except one fox and a few squirrels. The next day they began to steer a steady course eastwards; and still all was quiet and peaceful. On the third day out from Bree they came out of the Chetwood. The land had been falling steadily, ever since they turned aside from the Road, and they now entered a wide flat expanse of country, much more difficult to manage. They were far beyond the borders of the Bree-land, out in the pathless wilderness, and drawing near to the Midgewater Marshes.

The ground now became damp, and in places boggy and here and there they came upon pools, and wide stretches of reeds and rushes filled with the warbling of little hidden birds. They had to pick their way carefully to keep both dry-footed and on their proper course. At first they made fair progress, but as they went on, their passage became slower and more dangerous. The marshes were bewildering and treacherous, and there was no permanent trail even for Rangers to find through their shifting quagmires. The flies began to torment them, and the air was full of clouds of tiny midges that crept up their sleeves and breeches and into their hair.

'I am being eaten alive!' cried Pippin. 'Midgewater! There are more midges than water!'

'What do they live on when they can't get hobbit?' asked Sam, scratching his neck.

They spent a miserable day in this lonely and unpleasant country. Their camping-place was damp, cold, and uncomfortable; and the biting insects would not let them sleep. There were also abominable creatures haunting the reeds and tussocks that from the sound of them were evil relatives of the cricket. There were thousands of them, and they squeaked all round, *neek-breek, breek-neek*, unceasingly all the night, until the hobbits were nearly frantic.

The next day, the fourth, was little better, and the night almost as comfortless. Though the Neekerbreekers (as Sam called them) had been left behind, the midges still pursued them.

As Frodo lay, tired but unable to close his eyes, it seemed to him that far away there came a light in the eastern sky: it flashed and faded many times. It was not the dawn, for that was still some hours off.

'What is the light?' he said to Strider, who had risen, and was standing, gazing ahead into the night.

'I do not know,' Strider answered. 'It is too distant to make out. It is like lightning that leaps up from the hill-tops.'

Frodo lay down again, but for a long while he could still see the white flashes, and against them the tall dark figure of Strider, standing silent and watchful. At last he passed into uneasy sleep.

They had not gone far on the fifth day when they left the last straggling pools and reed-beds of the marshes behind them. The land before them began steadily to rise again. Away in the distance eastward they could now see a line of hills. The highest of them was at the right of the line and a little separated from the others. It had a conical top, slightly flattened at the summit.

'That is Weathertop,' said Strider. 'The Old Road, which we have left far away on our right, runs to the south of it and passes not far from its foot. We might reach it by noon tomorrow, if we go straight towards it. I suppose we had better do so.'

'What do you mean?' asked Frodo.

'I mean: when we do get there, it is not certain what we shall find. It is close to the Road.'

'But surely we were hoping to find Gandalf there?'

'Yes; but the hope is faint. If he comes this way at all, he may not pass through Bree, and so he may not know what we are doing. And anyway, unless by luck we arrive almost together, we shall miss one another; it will not be safe for him or for us to wait there long. If the Riders fail to find us in the wilderness, they are likely to make for Weathertop themselves. It commands a wide view all round. Indeed, there are many birds and beasts in this country that could see us, as we stand here, from that hill-top. Not all the birds are to be trusted, and there are other spies more evil than they are.'

The hobbits looked anxiously at the distant hills. Sam looked up into the pale sky, fearing to see hawks or eagles hovering over them with bright unfriendly eyes. 'You do make me feel uncomfortable and lonesome, Strider!' he said.

'What do you advise us to do?' asked Frodo.

'I think,' answered Strider slowly, as if he was not quite sure, 'I think the best thing is to go as straight eastward from here as we can, to make for the line of hills, not for Weathertop. There we can strike a path I know that runs at their feet; it will bring us to Weathertop from the north and less openly. Then we shall see what we shall see.'

All that day they plodded along, until the cold and early evening came down. The land became drier and more barren; but mists and vapours lay behind them on the marshes. A few melancholy birds were piping and wailing, until the round red sun sank slowly into the western shadows; then an empty silence fell. The hobbits thought of the soft light of sunset glancing through the cheerful windows of Bag End far away.

At the day's end they came to a stream that wandered down from the hills to lose itself in the stagnant marshland, and they went up along its banks while the light lasted. It was already night when at last they halted and made their camp under some stunted alder-trees by the shores of the stream. Ahead there loomed now against the dusky sky the bleak and treeless backs of the hills. That night they set a watch, and Strider, it seemed, did not sleep at all. The moon was waxing, and in the early night-hours a cold grey light lay on the land.

Next morning they set out again soon after sunrise. There was a frost in the air, and the sky was a pale clear blue. The hobbits felt refreshed, as if they had had a night of unbroken sleep. Already they were getting used to much walking on short commons – shorter at any rate than what in the Shire they would have thought barely enough to keep them on their legs. Pippin declared that Frodo was looking twice the hobbit that he had been.

'Very odd,' said Frodo, tightening his belt, 'considering that there is actually a good deal less of me. I hope the thinning process will not go on indefinitely, or I shall become a wraith.'

'Do not speak of such things!' said Strider quickly, and with surprising earnestness.

The hills drew nearer. They made an undulating ridge, often rising almost to a thousand feet, and here and there falling again to low clefts or passes leading into the eastern land beyond. Along the crest of the ridge the hobbits could see what looked to be the remains of green-grown walls and dikes, and in the clefts there still stood the ruins of old works of stone. By night they had reached the feet of the westward slopes, and there they camped. It was the night of the fifth of October, and they were six days out from Bree.

In the morning they found, for the first time since they had left the Chetwood, a track plain to see. They turned right and followed it south-wards. It ran cunningly, taking a line that seemed chosen so as to keep as much hidden as possible from the view, both of the hill-tops above and of the flats to the west. It dived into dells, and hugged steep banks; and where it passed over flatter and more open ground on either side of it there were lines of large boulders and hewn stones that screened the travellers almost like a hedge.

'I wonder who made this path, and what for,' said Merry, as they walked along one of these avenues, where the stones were unusually large and closely set. 'I am not sure that I like it: it has a – well, rather a barrow-wightish look. Is there any barrow on Weathertop?'

'No. There is no barrow on Weathertop, nor on any of these hills,' answered Strider. 'The Men of the West did not live here; though in their latter days they defended the hills for a while against the evil that came out of Angmar. This path was made to serve the forts along the walls. But long before, in the first days of the North Kingdom, they built a great watch-tower on Weathertop, Amon Sûl they called it. It was burned and broken, and nothing remains of it now but a tumbled ring, like a rough crown on the old hill's head. Yet once it was tall and fair. It is told that Elendil stood there watching for the coming of Gil-galad out of the West, in the days of the Last Alliance.'

The hobbits gazed at Strider. It seemed that he was learned in old lore, as well as in the ways of the wild. 'Who was Gil-galad?' asked Merry; but Strider did not answer, and seemed to be lost in thought. Suddenly a low voice murmured:

> *Gil-galad was an Elven-king.*
> *Of him the harpers sadly sing:*
> *the last whose realm was fair and free*
> *between the Mountains and the Sea.*
>
> *His sword was long, his lance was keen,*
> *his shining helm afar was seen;*
> *the countless stars of heaven's field*
> *were mirrored in his silver shield.*
>
> *But long ago he rode away,*
> *and where he dwelleth none can say;*
> *for into darkness fell his star*
> *in Mordor where the shadows are.*

The others turned in amazement, for the voice was Sam's.

'Don't stop!' said Merry.

'That's all I know,' stammered Sam, blushing. 'I learned it from Mr. Bilbo when I was a lad. He used to tell me tales like that, knowing how I was always one for hearing about Elves. It was Mr. Bilbo as taught me my letters. He was mighty book-learned was dear old Mr. Bilbo. And he wrote *poetry*. He wrote what I have just said.'

'He did not make it up,' said Strider. 'It is part of the lay that is called

The Fall of Gil-galad, which is in an ancient tongue. Bilbo must have translated it. I never knew that.'

'There was a lot more,' said Sam, 'all about Mordor. I didn't learn that part, it gave me the shivers. I never thought I should be going that way myself!'

'Going to Mordor!' cried Pippin. 'I hope it won't come to that!'

'Do not speak that name so loudly!' said Strider.

It was already mid-day when they drew near the southern end of the path, and saw before them, in the pale clear light of the October sun, a grey-green bank, leading up like a bridge on to the northward slope of the hill. They decided to make for the top at once, while the daylight was broad. Concealment was no longer possible, and they could only hope that no enemy or spy was observing them. Nothing was to be seen moving on the hill. If Gandalf was anywhere about, there was no sign of him.

On the western flank of Weathertop they found a sheltered hollow, at the bottom of which there was a bowl-shaped dell with grassy sides. There they left Sam and Pippin with the pony and their packs and luggage. The other three went on. After half an hour's plodding climb Strider reached the crown of the hill; Frodo and Merry followed, tired and breathless. The last slope had been steep and rocky.

On the top they found, as Strider had said, a wide ring of ancient stone-work, now crumbling or covered with age-long grass. But in the centre a cairn of broken stones had been piled. They were blackened as if with fire. About them the turf was burned to the roots and all within the ring the grass was scorched and shrivelled, as if flames had swept the hill-top; but there was no sign of any living thing.

Standing upon the rim of the ruined circle, they saw all round below them a wide prospect, for the most part of lands empty and featureless, except for patches of woodland away to the south, beyond which they caught here and there the glint of distant water. Beneath them on this southern side there ran like a ribbon the Old Road, coming out of the West and winding up and down, until it faded behind a ridge of dark land to the east. Nothing was moving on it. Following its line eastward with their eyes they saw the Mountains: the nearer foothills were brown and sombre; behind them stood taller shapes of grey, and behind those again were high white peaks glimmering among the clouds.

'Well, here we are!' said Merry. 'And very cheerless and uninviting it looks! There is no water and no shelter. And no sign of Gandalf. But I don't blame him for not waiting – if he ever came here.'

'I wonder,' said Strider, looking round thoughtfully. 'Even if he was a day or two behind us at Bree, he could have arrived here first. He can ride very swiftly when need presses.' Suddenly he stooped and looked at the stone on the top of the cairn; it was flatter than the others, and whiter, as if it had escaped the fire. He picked it up and examined it, turning it in his fingers. 'This has been handled recently,' he said. 'What do you think of these marks?'

On the flat under-side Frodo saw some scratches: I⁊·lll· 'There seems to be a stroke, a dot, and three more strokes,' he said.

'The stroke on the left might be a G-rune with thin branches,' said Strider. 'It might be a sign left by Gandalf, though one cannot be sure. The scratches are fine, and they certainly look fresh. But the marks might mean something quite different, and have nothing to do with us. Rangers use runes, and they come here sometimes.'

'What could they mean, even if Gandalf made them?' asked Merry.

'I should say,' answered Strider, 'that they stood for G3, and were a sign that Gandalf was here on October the third: that is three days ago now. It would also show that he was in a hurry and danger was at hand, so that he had no time or did not dare to write anything longer or plainer. If that is so, we must be wary.'

'I wish we could feel sure that he made the marks, whatever they may mean,' said Frodo. 'It would be a great comfort to know that he was on the way, in front of us or behind us.'

'Perhaps,' said Strider. 'For myself, I believe that he was here, and was in danger. There have been scorching flames here; and now the light that we saw three nights ago in the eastern sky comes back to my mind. I guess that he was attacked on this hill-top, but with what result I cannot tell. He is here no longer, and we must now look after ourselves and make our own way to Rivendell, as best we can.'

'How far is Rivendell?' asked Merry, gazing round wearily. The world looked wild and wide from Weathertop.

'I don't know if the Road has ever been measured in miles beyond the *Forsaken Inn*, a day's journey east of Bree,' answered Strider. 'Some say it is so far, and some say otherwise. It is a strange road, and folk are glad to reach their journey's end, whether the time is long or short. But I know how long it would take me on my own feet, with fair weather and no ill fortune: twelve days from here to the Ford of Bruinen, where the Road crosses the Loudwater that runs out of Rivendell. We have at least a fortnight's journey before us, for I do not think we shall be able to use the Road.'

'A fortnight!' said Frodo. 'A lot may happen in that time.'

'It may,' said Strider.

They stood for a while silent on the hill-top, near its southward edge. In that lonely place Frodo for the first time fully realized his homelessness and danger. He wished bitterly that his fortune had left him in the quiet and beloved Shire. He stared down at the hateful Road, leading back westward – to his home. Suddenly he was aware that two black specks were moving slowly along it, going westward; and looking again he saw that three others were creeping eastward to meet them. He gave a cry and clutched Strider's arm.

'Look,' he said, pointing downwards.

At once Strider flung himself on the ground behind the ruined circle, pulling Frodo down beside him. Merry threw himself alongside.

'What is it?' he whispered.

'I do not know, but I fear the worst,' answered Strider.

Slowly they crawled up to the edge of the ring again, and peered through a cleft between two jagged stones. The light was no longer bright, for the clear morning had faded, and clouds creeping out of the East had now overtaken the sun, as it began to go down. They could all see the black specks, but neither Frodo nor Merry could make out their shapes for certain; yet something told them that there, far below, were Black Riders assembling on the Road beyond the foot of the hill.

'Yes,' said Strider, whose keener sight left him in no doubt. 'The enemy is here!'

Hastily they crept away and slipped down the north side of the hill to find their companions.

Sam and Peregrin had not been idle. They had explored the small dell and the surrounding slopes. Not far away they found a spring of clear water in the hillside, and near it footprints not more than a day or two old. In the dell itself they found recent traces of a fire, and other signs of a hasty camp. There were some fallen rocks on the edge of the dell nearest to the hill. Behind them Sam came upon a small store of firewood neatly stacked.

'I wonder if old Gandalf has been here,' he said to Pippin. 'Whoever it was put this stuff here meant to come back it seems.'

Strider was greatly interested in these discoveries. 'I wish I had waited and explored the ground down here myself,' he said, hurrying off to the spring to examine the footprints.

'It is just as I feared,' he said, when he came back. 'Sam and Pippin have trampled the soft ground, and the marks are spoilt or confused. Rangers have been here lately. It is they who left the firewood behind. But there are also several newer tracks that were not made by Rangers. At least one set was made, only a day or two ago, by heavy boots. At least one. I cannot now be certain, but I think there were many booted feet.' He paused and stood in anxious thought.

Each of the hobbits saw in his mind a vision of the cloaked and booted

Riders. If the horsemen had already found the dell, the sooner Strider led them somewhere else the better. Sam viewed the hollow with great dislike, now that he had heard news of their enemies on the Road, only a few miles away.

'Hadn't we better clear out quick, Mr. Strider?' he asked impatiently. 'It is getting late, and I don't like this hole: it makes my heart sink somehow.'

'Yes, we certainly must decide what to do at once,' answered Strider, looking up and considering the time and the weather. 'Well, Sam,' he said at last, 'I do not like this place either; but I cannot think of anywhere better that we could reach before nightfall. At least we are out of sight for the moment, and if we moved we should be much more likely to be seen by spies. All we could do would be to go right out of our way back north on this side of the line of hills, where the land is all much the same as it is here. The Road is watched, but we should have to cross it, if we tried to take cover in the thickets away to the south. On the north side of the Road beyond the hills the country is bare and flat for miles.'

'Can the Riders *see?*' asked Merry. 'I mean, they seem usually to have used their noses rather than their eyes, smelling for us, if smelling is the right word, at least in the daylight. But you made us lie down flat when you saw them down below; and now you talk of being seen, if we move.'

'I was too careless on the hill-top,' answered Strider. 'I was very anxious to find some sign of Gandalf; but it was a mistake for three of us to go up and stand there so long. For the black horses can see, and the Riders can use men and other creatures as spies, as we found at Bree. They themselves do not see the world of light as we do, but our shapes cast shadows in their minds, which only the noon sun destroys; and in the dark they perceive many signs and forms that are hidden from us: then they are most to be feared. And at all times they smell the blood of living things, desiring and hating it. Senses, too, there are other than sight or smell. We can feel their presence – it troubled our hearts, as soon as we came here, and before we saw them; they feel ours more keenly. Also,' he added, and his voice sank to a whisper, 'the Ring draws them.'

'Is there no escape then?' said Frodo, looking round wildly. 'If I move I shall be seen and hunted! If I stay, I shall draw them to me!'

Strider laid his hand on his shoulder. 'There is still hope,' he said. 'You are not alone. Let us take this wood that is set ready for the fire as a sign. There is little shelter or defence here, but fire shall serve for both. Sauron can put fire to his evil uses, as he can all things, but these Riders do not love it, and fear those who wield it. Fire is our friend in the wilderness.'

'Maybe,' muttered Sam. 'It is also as good a way of saying "here we are" as I can think of, bar shouting.'

Down in the lowest and most sheltered corner of the dell they lit a fire, and prepared a meal. The shades of evening began to fall, and it grew cold. They were suddenly aware of great hunger, for they had not eaten anything since breakfast; but they dared not make more than a frugal supper. The lands ahead were empty of all save birds and beasts, unfriendly places deserted by all the races of the world. Rangers passed at times beyond the hills, but they were few and did not stay. Other wanderers were rare, and of evil sort: trolls might stray down at times out of the northern valleys of the Misty Mountains. Only on the Road would travellers be found, most often dwarves, hurrying along on business of their own, and with no help and few words to spare for strangers.

'I don't see how our food can be made to last,' said Frodo. 'We have been careful enough in the last few days, and this supper is no feast; but we have used more than we ought, if we have two weeks still to go, and perhaps more.'

'There is food in the wild,' said Strider; 'berry, root, and herb; and I have some skill as a hunter at need. You need not be afraid of starving before winter comes. But gathering and catching food is long and weary work, and we need haste. So tighten your belts, and think with hope of the tables of Elrond's house!'

The cold increased as darkness came on. Peering out from the edge of the dell they could see nothing but a grey land now vanishing quickly into shadow. The sky above had cleared again and was slowly filled with twinkling stars. Frodo and his companions huddled round the fire, wrapped in every garment and blanket they possessed; but Strider was content with a single cloak, and sat a little apart, drawing thoughtfully at his pipe.

As night fell and the light of the fire began to shine out brightly he began to tell them tales to keep their minds from fear. He knew many histories and legends of long ago, of Elves and Men and the good and evil deeds of the Elder Days. They wondered how old he was, and where he had learned all this lore.

'Tell us of Gil-galad,' said Merry suddenly, when he paused at the end of a story of the Elf-Kingdoms. 'Do you know any more of that old lay that you spoke of?'

'I do indeed,' answered Strider. 'So also does Frodo, for it concerns us closely.' Merry and Pippin looked at Frodo, who was staring into the fire.

'I know only the little that Gandalf has told me,' said Frodo slowly. 'Gil-galad was the last of the great Elf-kings of Middle-earth. Gil-galad is *Starlight* in their tongue. With Elendil, the Elf-friend, he went to the land of———'

'No!' said Strider interrupting, 'I do not think that tale should be told now with the servants of the Enemy at hand. If we win through to the house of Elrond, you may hear it there, told in full.'

'Then tell us some other tale of the old days,' begged Sam; 'a tale about the Elves before the fading time. I would dearly like to hear more about Elves; the dark seems to press round so close.'

'I will tell you the tale of Tinúviel,' said Strider, 'in brief – for it is a long tale of which the end is not known; and there are none now, except Elrond, that remember it aright as it was told of old. It is a fair tale, though it is sad, as are all the tales of Middle-earth, and yet it may lift up your hearts.' He was silent for some time, and then he began not to speak but to chant softly:

> The leaves were long, the grass was green,
> The hemlock-umbels tall and fair,
> And in the glade a light was seen
> Of stars in shadow shimmering.
> Tinúviel was dancing there
> To music of a pipe unseen,
> And light of stars was in her hair,
> And in her raiment glimmering.
>
> There Beren came from mountains cold,
> And lost he wandered under leaves,
> And where the Elven-river rolled
> He walked alone and sorrowing.
> He peered between the hemlock-leaves
> And saw in wonder flowers of gold
> Upon her mantle and her sleeves,
> And her hair like shadow following.
>
> Enchantment healed his weary feet
> That over hills were doomed to roam;
> And forth he hastened, strong and fleet,
> And grasped at moonbeams glistening.
> Through woven woods in Elvenhome
> She lightly fled on dancing feet,
> And left him lonely still to roam
> In the silent forest listening.
>
> He heard there oft the flying sound
> Of feet as light as linden-leaves,
> Or music welling underground,
> In hidden hollows quavering.

Now withered lay the hemlock-sheaves,
*   And one by one with sighing sound*
Whispering fell the beechen leaves
*   In the wintry woodland wavering.*

He sought her ever, wandering far
*   Where leaves of years were thickly strewn,*
By light of moon and ray of star
*   In frosty heavens shivering.*
Her mantle glinted in the moon,
*   As on a hill-top high and far*
She danced, and at her feet was strewn
*   A mist of silver quivering.*

When winter passed, she came again,
*   And her song released the sudden spring,*
Like rising lark, and falling rain,
*   And melting water bubbling.*
He saw the elven-flowers spring
*   About her feet, and healed again*
He longed by her to dance and sing
*   Upon the grass untroubling.*

Again she fled, but swift he came.
*   Tinúviel! Tinúviel!*
He called her by her elvish name;
*   And there she halted listening.*
One moment stood she, and a spell
*   His voice laid on her: Beren came,*
And doom fell on Tinúviel
*   That in his arms lay glistening.*

As Beren looked into her eyes
*   Within the shadows of her hair,*
The trembling starlight of the skies
*   He saw there mirrored shimmering.*
Tinúviel the elven-fair,
*   Immortal maiden elven-wise,*
About him cast her shadowy hair
*   And arms like silver glimmering.*

Long was the way that fate them bore,

O'er stony mountains cold and grey,
Through halls of iron and darkling door,
And woods of nightshade morrowless.
The Sundering Seas between them lay,
And yet at last they met once more,
And long ago they passed away
In the forest singing sorrowless.

Strider sighed and paused before he spoke again. 'That is a song,' he said, 'in the mode that is called *ann-thennath* among the Elves, but is hard to render in our Common Speech, and this is but a rough echo of it. It tells of the meeting of Beren son of Barahir and Lúthien Tinúviel. Beren was a mortal man, but Lúthien was the daughter of Thingol, a King of Elves upon Middle-earth when the world was young; and she was the fairest maiden that has ever been among all the children of this world. As the stars above the mists of the Northern lands was her loveliness, and in her face was a shining light. In those days the Great Enemy, of whom Sauron of Mordor was but a servant, dwelt in Angband in the North, and the Elves of the West coming back to Middle-earth made war upon him to regain the Silmarils which he had stolen; and the fathers of Men aided the Elves. But the Enemy was victorious and Barahir was slain, and Beren escaping through great peril came over the Mountains of Terror into the hidden Kingdom of Thingol in the forest of Neldoreth. There he beheld Lúthien singing and dancing in a glade beside the enchanted river Esgalduin; and he named her Tinúviel, that is Nightingale in the language of old. Many sorrows befell them afterwards, and they were parted long. Tinúviel rescued Beren from the dungeons of Sauron, and together they passed through great dangers, and cast down even the Great Enemy from his throne, and took from his iron crown one of the three Silmarils, brightest of all jewels, to be the bride-price of Lúthien to Thingol her father. Yet at the last Beren was slain by the Wolf that came from the gates of Angband, and he died in the arms of Tinúviel. But she chose mortality, and to die from the world, so that she might follow him; and it is sung that they met again beyond the Sundering Seas, and after a brief time walking alive once more in the green woods, together they passed, long ago, beyond the confines of this world. So it is that Lúthien Tinúviel alone of the Elf-kindred has died indeed and left the world, and they have lost her whom they most loved. But from her the lineage of the Elf-lords of old descended among Men. There live still those of whom Lúthien was the foremother, and it is said that her line shall never fail. Elrond of Rivendell is of that Kin. For of Beren and Lúthien was born Dior Thingol's heir; and of him Elwing the White whom Eärendil wedded, he that sailed his ship out of the mists of the world into the seas of heaven with the Silmaril upon his brow. And of Eärendil came the Kings of Númenor, that is Westernesse.'

As Strider was speaking they watched his strange eager face, dimly lit in the red glow of the wood-fire. His eyes shone, and his voice was rich and deep. Above him was a black starry sky. Suddenly a pale light appeared over the crown of Weathertop behind him. The waxing moon was climbing slowly above the hill that overshadowed them, and the stars above the hill-top faded.

The story ended. The hobbits moved and stretched. 'Look!' said Merry. 'The Moon is rising: it must be getting late.'

The others looked up. Even as they did so, they saw on the top of the hill something small and dark against the glimmer of the moonrise. It was perhaps only a large stone or jutting rock shown up by the pale light.

Sam and Merry got up and walked away from the fire. Frodo and Pippin remained seated in silence. Strider was watching the moonlight on the hill intently. All seemed quiet and still, but Frodo felt a cold dread creeping over his heart, now that Strider was no longer speaking. He huddled closer to the fire. At that moment Sam came running back from the edge of the dell.

'I don't know what it is,' he said, 'but I suddenly felt afraid. I durstn't go outside this dell for any money; I felt that something was creeping up the slope.'

'Did you *see* anything?' asked Frodo, springing to his feet.

'No, sir. I saw nothing, but I didn't stop to look.'

'I saw something,' said Merry; 'or I thought I did – away westwards where the moonlight was falling on the flats beyond the shadow of the hill-tops, I *thought* there were two or three black shapes. They seemed to be moving this way.'

'Keep close to the fire, with your faces outward!' cried Strider. 'Get some of the longer sticks ready in your hands!'

For a breathless time they sat there, silent and alert, with their backs turned to the wood-fire, each gazing into the shadows that encircled them. Nothing happened. There was no sound or movement in the night. Frodo stirred, feeling that he must break the silence: he longed to shout out aloud.

'Hush!' whispered Strider. 'What's that?' gasped Pippin at the same moment.

Over the lip of the little dell, on the side away from the hill, they felt, rather than saw, a shadow rise, one shadow or more than one. They strained their eyes, and the shadows seemed to grow. Soon there could be no doubt: three or four tall black figures were standing there on the slope, looking down on them. So black were they that they seemed like black holes in the deep shade behind them. Frodo thought that he heard a faint hiss as of venomous breath and felt a thin piercing chill. Then the shapes slowly advanced.

Terror overcame Pippin and Merry, and they threw themselves flat on the ground. Sam shrank to Frodo's side. Frodo was hardly less terrified than his companions; he was quaking as if he was bitter cold, but his terror was swallowed up in a sudden temptation to put on the Ring. The desire to do this laid hold of him, and he could think of nothing else. He did not forget the Barrow, nor the message of Gandalf; but something seemed to be compelling him to disregard all warnings, and he longed to yield. Not with the hope of escape, or of doing anything, either good or bad: he simply felt that he must take the Ring and put it on his finger. He could not speak. He felt Sam looking at him, as if he knew that his master was in some great trouble, but he could not turn towards him. He shut his eyes and struggled for a while; but resistance became unbearable, and at last he slowly drew out the chain, and slipped the Ring on the forefinger of his left hand.

Immediately, though everything else remained as before, dim and dark, the shapes became terribly clear. He was able to see beneath their black wrappings. There were five tall figures: two standing on the lip of the dell, three advancing. In their white faces burned keen and merciless eyes; under their mantles were long grey robes; upon their grey hairs were helms of silver; in their haggard hands were swords of steel. Their eyes fell on him and pierced him, as they rushed towards him. Desperate, he drew his own sword, and it seemed to him that it flickered red, as if it was a firebrand. Two of the figures halted. The third was taller than the others: his hair was long and gleaming and on his helm was a crown. In one hand he held a long sword, and in the other a knife; both the knife and the hand that held it glowed with a pale light. He sprang forward and bore down on Frodo.

At that moment Frodo threw himself forward on the ground, and he heard himself crying aloud: _O Elbereth! Gilthoniel!_ At the same time he struck at the feet of his enemy. A shrill cry rang out in the night; and he felt a pain like a dart of poisoned ice pierce his left shoulder. Even as he swooned he caught, as through a swirling mist, a glimpse of Strider leaping out of the darkness with a flaming brand of wood in either hand. With a last effort Frodo, dropping his sword, slipped the Ring from his finger and closed his right hand tight upon it.

CHAPTER XII

FLIGHT TO THE FORD

When Frodo came to himself he was still clutching the Ring desperately. He was lying by the fire, which was now piled high and burning brightly. His three companions were bending over him.

'What has happened? Where is the pale king?' he asked wildly.

They were too overjoyed to hear him speak to answer for a while; nor did they understand his question. At length he gathered from Sam that they had seen nothing but the vague shadowy shapes coming towards them. Suddenly to his horror Sam found that his master had vanished; and at that moment a black shadow rushed past him, and he fell. He heard Frodo's voice, but it seemed to come from a great distance, or from under the earth, crying out strange words. They saw nothing more, until they stumbled over the body of Frodo, lying as if dead, face downwards on the grass with his sword beneath him. Strider ordered them to pick him up and lay him near the fire, and then he disappeared. That was now a good while ago.

Sam plainly was beginning to have doubts again about Strider; but while they were talking he returned, appearing suddenly out of the shadows. They started, and Sam drew his sword and stood over Frodo; but Strider knelt down swiftly at his side.

'I am not a Black Rider, Sam,' he said gently, 'nor in league with them. I have been trying to discover something of their movements; but I have found nothing. I cannot think why they have gone and do not attack again. But there is no feeling of their presence anywhere at hand.'

When he heard what Frodo had to tell, he became full of concern, and shook his head and sighed. Then he ordered Pippin and Merry to heat as much water as they could in their small kettles, and to bathe the wound with it. 'Keep the fire going well, and keep Frodo warm!' he said. Then he got up and walked away, and called Sam to him. 'I think I understand things better now,' he said in a low voice. 'There seem only to have been five of the enemy. Why they were not all here, I don't know; but I don't think they expected to be resisted. They have drawn off for the time being. But not far, I fear. They will come again another night, if we cannot escape. They are only waiting, because they think that their purpose is almost accomplished, and that the Ring cannot fly much further. I fear, Sam, that they believe your master has a deadly wound that will subdue him to their will. We shall see!'

Sam choked with tears. 'Don't despair!' said Strider. 'You must trust

me now. Your Frodo is made of sterner stuff than I had guessed, though
Gandalf hinted that it might prove so. He is not slain, and I think he will
resist the evil power of the wound longer than his enemies expect. I
will do all I can to help and heal him. Guard him well, while I am away!'
He hurried off and disappeared again into the darkness.

Frodo dozed, though the pain of his wound was slowly growing, and a
deadly chill was spreading from his shoulder to his arm and side. His
friends watched over him, warming him, and bathing his wound. The night
passed slowly and wearily. Dawn was growing in the sky, and the dell was
filling with grey light, when Strider at last returned.

'Look!' he cried; and stooping he lifted from the ground a black cloak
that had lain there hidden by the darkness. A foot above the lower hem
there was a slash. 'This was the stroke of Frodo's sword,' he said. 'The
only hurt that it did to his enemy, I fear; for it is unharmed, but all blades
perish that pierce that dreadful King. More deadly to him was the name
of Elbereth.'

'And more deadly to Frodo was this!' He stooped again and lifted up a
long thin knife. There was a cold gleam in it. As Strider raised it they saw
that near the end its edge was notched and the point was broken off. But
even as he held it up in the growing light, they gazed in astonishment, for
the blade seemed to melt, and vanished like a smoke in the air, leaving
only the hilt in Strider's hand. 'Alas!' he cried. 'It was this accursed knife
that gave the wound. Few now have the skill in healing to match such evil
weapons. But I will do what I can.'

He sat down on the ground, and taking the dagger-hilt laid it on his
knees, and he sang over it a slow song in a strange tongue. Then setting
it aside, he turned to Frodo and in a soft tone spoke words the others could
not catch. From the pouch at his belt he drew out the long leaves of a
plant.

'These leaves,' he said, 'I have walked far to find; for this plant does not
grow in the bare hills; but in the thickets away south of the Road I found
it in the dark by the scent of its leaves.' He crushed a leaf in his fingers,
and it gave out a sweet and pungent fragrance. 'It is fortunate that I could
find it, for it is a healing plant that the Men of the West brought to Middle-
earth. *Athelas* they named it, and it grows now sparsely and only near
places where they dwelt or camped of old; and it is not known in the North,
except to some of those who wander in the Wild. It has great virtues, but
over such a wound as this its healing powers may be small.'

He threw the leaves into boiling water and bathed Frodo's shoulder. The
fragrance of the steam was refreshing, and those that were unhurt felt their
minds calmed and cleared. The herb had also some power over the wound,

for Frodo felt the pain and also the sense of frozen cold lessen in his side; but the life did not return to his arm, and he could not raise or use his hand. He bitterly regretted his foolishness, and reproached himself for weakness of will; for he now perceived that in putting on the Ring he obeyed not his own desire but the commanding wish of his enemies. He wondered if he would remain maimed for life, and how they would now manage to continue their journey. He felt too weak to stand.

The others were discussing this very question. They quickly decided to leave Weathertop as soon as possible. 'I think now,' said Strider, 'that the enemy has been watching this place for some days. If Gandalf ever came here, then he must have been forced to ride away, and he will not return. In any case we are in great peril here after dark, since the attack of last night, and we can hardly meet greater danger wherever we go.'

As soon as the daylight was full, they had some hurried food and packed. It was impossible for Frodo to walk, so they divided the greater part of their baggage among the four of them, and put Frodo on the pony. In the last few days the poor beast had improved wonderfully; it already seemed fatter and stronger, and had begun to show an affection for its new masters, especially for Sam. Bill Ferny's treatment must have been very hard for the journey in the wild to seem so much better than its former life.

They started off in a southerly direction. This would mean crossing the Road, but it was the quickest way to more wooded country. And they needed fuel; for Strider said that Frodo must be kept warm, especially at night, while fire would be some protection for them all. It was also his plan to shorten their journey by cutting across another great loop of the Road: east beyond Weathertop it changed its course and took a wide bend northwards.

They made their way slowly and cautiously round the south-western slopes of the hill, and came in a little while to the edge of the Road. There was no sign of the Riders. But even as they were hurrying across they heard far away two cries: a cold voice calling and a cold voice answering. Trembling they sprang forward, and made for the thickets that lay ahead. The land before them sloped away southwards, but it was wild and pathless; bushes and stunted trees grew in dense patches with wide barren spaces in between. The grass was scanty, coarse, and grey; and the leaves in the thickets were faded and falling. It was a cheerless land, and their journey was slow and gloomy. They spoke little as they trudged along. Frodo's heart was grieved as he watched them walking beside him with their heads down, and their backs bowed under their burdens. Even Strider seemed tired and heavy-hearted.

Before the first day's march was over Frodo's pain began to grow again, but he did not speak of it for a long time. Four days passed, without the ground or the scene changing much, except that behind them Weathertop slowly sank, and before them the distant mountains loomed a little nearer. Yet since that far cry they had seen and heard no sign that the enemy had marked their flight or followed them. They dreaded the dark hours, and kept watch in pairs by night, expecting at any time to see black shapes stalking in the grey night, dimly lit by the cloud-veiled moon; but they saw nothing, and heard no sound but the sigh of withered leaves and grass. Not once did they feel the sense of present evil that had assailed them before the attack in the dell. It seemed too much to hope that the Riders had already lost their trail again. Perhaps they were waiting to make some ambush in a narrow place?

At the end of the fifth day the ground began once more to rise slowly out of the wide shallow valley into which they had descended. Strider now turned their course again north-eastwards, and on the sixth day they reached the top of a long slow-climbing slope, and saw far ahead a huddle of wooded hills. Away below them they could see the Road sweeping round the feet of the hills; and to their right a grey river gleamed pale in the thin sunshine. In the distance they glimpsed yet another river in a stony valley half-veiled in mist.

'I am afraid we must go back to the Road here for a while,' said Strider. 'We have now come to the River Hoarwell, that the Elves call Mitheithel. It flows down out of the Ettenmoors, the troll-fells north of Rivendell, and joins the Loudwater away in the South. Some call it the Greyflood after that. It is a great water before it finds the Sea. There is no way over it below its sources in the Ettenmoors, except by the Last Bridge on which the Road crosses.'

'What is that other river we can see far away there?' asked Merry.

'That is Loudwater, the Bruinen of Rivendell,' answered Strider. 'The Road runs along the edge of the hills for many miles from the Bridge to the Ford of Bruinen. But I have not yet thought how we shall cross that water. One river at a time! We shall be fortunate indeed if we do not find the Last Bridge held against us.'

Next day, early in the morning, they came down again to the borders of the Road. Sam and Strider went forward, but they found no sign of any travellers or riders. Here under the shadow of the hills there had been some rain. Strider judged that it had fallen two days before, and had washed away all footprints. No horseman had passed since then, as far as he could see.

They hurried along with all the speed they could make, and after a mile or two they saw the Last Bridge ahead, at the bottom of a short steep slope.

They dreaded to see black figures waiting there, but they saw none. Strider made them take cover in a thicket at the side of the Road, while he went forward to explore.

Before long he came hurrying back. 'I can see no sign of the enemy,' he said, 'and I wonder very much what that means. But I have found something very strange.'

He held out his hand, and showed a single pale-green jewel. 'I found it in the mud in the middle of the Bridge,' he said. 'It is a beryl, an elf-stone. Whether it was set there, or let fall by chance, I cannot say; but it brings hope to me. I will take it as a sign that we may pass the Bridge; but beyond that I dare not keep to the Road, without some clearer token.'

At once they went on again. They crossed the Bridge in safety, hearing no sound but the water swirling against its three great arches. A mile further on they came to a narrow ravine that led away northwards through the steep lands on the left of the Road. Here Strider turned aside, and soon they were lost in a sombre country of dark trees winding among the feet of sullen hills.

The hobbits were glad to leave the cheerless lands and the perilous Road behind them; but this new country seemed threatening and unfriendly. As they went forward the hills about them steadily rose. Here and there upon heights and ridges they caught glimpses of ancient walls of stone, and the ruins of towers: they had an ominous look. Frodo, who was not walking, had time to gaze ahead and to think. He recalled Bilbo's account of his journey and the threatening towers on the hills north of the Road, in the country near the Troll's wood where his first serious adventure had happened. Frodo guessed that they were now in the same region, and wondered if by chance they would pass near the spot.

'Who lives in this land?' he asked. 'And who built these towers? Is this troll-country?'

'No!' said Strider. 'Trolls do not build. No one lives in this land. Men once dwelt here, ages ago; but none remain now. They became an evil people, as legends tell, for they fell under the shadow of Angmar. But all were destroyed in the war that brought the North Kingdom to its end. But that is now so long ago that the hills have forgotten them, though a shadow still lies on the land.'

'Where did you learn such tales, if all the land is empty and forgetful?' asked Peregrin. 'The birds and beasts do not tell tales of that sort.'

'The heirs of Elendil do not forget all things past,' said Strider; 'and many more things than I can tell are remembered in Rivendell.'

'Have you often been to Rivendell?' said Frodo.

'I have,' said Strider. 'I dwelt there once, and still I return when I may.

There my heart is; but it is not my fate to sit in peace, even in the fair house of Elrond.'

The hills now began to shut them in. The Road behind held on its way to the River Bruinen, but both were now hidden from view. The travellers came into a long valley; narrow, deeply cloven, dark and silent. Trees with old and twisted roots hung over cliffs, and piled up behind into mounting slopes of pine-wood.

The hobbits grew very weary. They advanced slowly, for they had to pick their way through a pathless country, encumbered by fallen trees and tumbled rocks. As long as they could they avoided climbing for Frodo's sake, and because it was in fact difficult to find any way up out of the narrow dales. They had been two days in this country when the weather turned wet. The wind began to blow steadily out of the West and pour the water of the distant seas on the dark heads of the hills in fine drenching rain. By nightfall they were all soaked, and their camp was cheerless, for they could not get any fire to burn. The next day the hills rose still higher and steeper before them, and they were forced to turn away northwards out of their course. Strider seemed to be getting anxious: they were nearly ten days out from Weathertop, and their stock of provisions was beginning to run low. It went on raining.

That night they camped on a stony shelf with a rock-wall behind them, in which there was a shallow cave, a mere scoop in the cliff. Frodo was restless. The cold and wet had made his wound more painful than ever, and the ache and sense of deadly chill took away all sleep. He lay tossing and turning and listening fearfully to the stealthy night-noises: wind in chinks of rock, water dripping, a crack, the sudden rattling fall of a loosened stone. He felt that black shapes were advancing to smother him; but when he sat up he saw nothing but the back of Strider sitting hunched up, smoking his pipe, and watching. He lay down again and passed into an uneasy dream, in which he walked on the grass in his garden in the Shire, but it seemed faint and dim, less clear than the tall black shadows that stood looking over the hedge.

In the morning he woke to find that the rain had stopped. The clouds were still thick, but they were breaking, and pale strips of blue appeared between them. The wind was shifting again. They did not start early. Immediately after their cold and comfortless breakfast Strider went off alone, telling the others to remain under the shelter of the cliff, until he came back. He was going to climb up, if he could, and get a look at the lie of the land.

When he returned he was not reassuring. 'We have come too far to the north,' he said, 'and we must find some way to turn back southwards again. If we keep on as we are going we shall get up into the Ettendales far north of Rivendell. That is troll-country, and little known to me. We could perhaps find our way through and come round to Rivendell from the north; but it would take too long, for I do not know the way, and our food would not last. So somehow or other we must find the Ford of Bruinen.'

The rest of that day they spent scrambling over rocky ground. They found a passage between two hills that led them into a valley running south-east, the direction that they wished to take; but towards the end of the day they found their road again barred by a ridge of high land; its dark edge against the sky was broken into many bare points like teeth of a blunted saw. They had a choice between going back or climbing over it.

They decided to attempt the climb, but it proved very difficult. Before long Frodo was obliged to dismount and struggle along on foot. Even so they often despaired of getting their pony up, or indeed of finding a path for themselves, burdened as they were. The light was nearly gone, and they were all exhausted, when at last they reached the top. They had climbed on to a narrow saddle between two higher points, and the land fell steeply away again, only a short distance ahead. Frodo threw himself down, and lay on the ground shivering. His left arm was lifeless, and his side and shoulder felt as if icy claws were laid upon them. The trees and rocks about him seemed shadowy and dim.

'We cannot go any further,' said Merry to Strider. 'I am afraid this has been too much for Frodo. I am dreadfully anxious about him. What are we to do? Do you think they will be able to cure him in Rivendell, if we ever get there?'

'We shall see,' answered Strider. 'There is nothing more that I can do in the wilderness; and it is chiefly because of his wound that I am so anxious to press on. But I agree that we can go no further tonight.'

'What is the matter with my master?' asked Sam in a low voice, looking appealingly at Strider. 'His wound was small, and it is already closed. There's nothing to be seen but a cold white mark on his shoulder.'

'Frodo has been touched by the weapons of the Enemy,' said Strider, 'and there is some poison or evil at work that is beyond my skill to drive out. But do not give up hope, Sam!'

Night was cold up on the high ridge. They lit a small fire down under the gnarled roots of an old pine, that hung over a shallow pit: it looked as if stone had once been quarried there. They sat huddled together. The wind blew chill through the pass, and they heard the tree-tops lower down moaning and sighing. Frodo lay half in a dream, imagining that endless dark wings were sweeping by above him, and that on the wings rode pursuers that sought him in all the hollows of the hills.

The morning dawned bright and fair; the air was clean, and the light pale and clear in a rain-washed sky. Their hearts were encouraged, but they longed for the sun to warm their cold stiff limbs. As soon as it was light, Strider took Merry with him and went to survey the country from the height to the east of the pass. The sun had risen and was shining brightly when he returned with more comforting news. They were now going more or less in the right direction. If they went on, down the further side of the ridge, they would have the Mountains on their left. Some way ahead Strider had caught a glimpse of the Loudwater again, and he knew that, though it was hidden from view, the Road to the Ford was not far from the River and lay on the side nearest to them.

'We must make for the Road again,' he said. 'We cannot hope to find a path through these hills. Whatever danger may beset it, the Road is our only way to the Ford.'

As soon as they had eaten they set out again. They climbed slowly down the southern side of the ridge; but the way was much easier than they had expected, for the slope was far less steep on this side, and before long Frodo was able to ride again. Bill Ferny's poor old pony was developing an unexpected talent for picking out a path, and for sparing its rider as many jolts as possible. The spirits of the party rose again. Even Frodo felt better in the morning light, but every now and again a mist seemed to obscure his sight, and he passed his hands over his eyes.

Pippin was a little ahead of the others. Suddenly he turned round and called to them. 'There is a path here!' he cried.

When they came up with him, they saw that he had made no mistake: there were clearly the beginnings of a path, that climbed with many windings out of the woods below and faded away on the hill-top behind. In places it was now faint and overgrown, or choked with fallen stones and trees; but at one time it seemed to have been much used. It was a path made by strong arms and heavy feet. Here and there old trees had been cut or broken down, and large rocks cloven or heaved aside to make a way.

They followed the track for some while, for it offered much the easiest way down, but they went cautiously, and their anxiety increased as they came into the dark woods, and the path grew plainer and broader. Suddenly coming out of a belt of fir-trees it ran steeply down a slope, and turned sharply to the left round the corner of a rocky shoulder of the hill. When they came to the corner they looked round and saw that the path ran on over a level strip under the face of a low cliff overhung with trees. In the stony wall there was a door hanging crookedly ajar upon one great hinge.

Outside the door they all halted. There was a cave or rock-chamber behind, but in the gloom inside nothing could be seen. Strider, Sam, and Merry pushing with all their strength managed to open the door a little wider, and then Strider and Merry went in. They did not go far, for on the floor lay many old bones, and nothing else was to be seen near the entrance except some great empty jars and broken pots.

'Surely this is a troll-hole, if ever there was one!' said Pippin. 'Come out, you two, and let us get away. Now we know who made the path – and we had better get off it quick.'

'There is no need, I think,' said Strider, coming out. 'It is certainly a troll-hole, but it seems to have been long forsaken. I don't think we need be afraid. But let us go on down warily, and we shall see.'

The path went on again from the door, and turning to the right again across the level space plunged down a thick wooded slope. Pippin, not liking to show Strider that he was still afraid, went on ahead with Merry. Sam and Strider came behind, one on each side of Frodo's pony, for the path was now broad enough for four or five hobbits to walk abreast. But they had not gone very far before Pippin came running back, followed by Merry. They both looked terrified.

'There *are* trolls!' Pippin panted. 'Down in a clearing in the woods not far below. We got a sight of them through the tree-trunks. They are very large!'

'We will come and look at them,' said Strider, picking up a stick. Frodo said nothing, but Sam looked scared.

The sun was now high, and it shone down through the half-stripped branches of the trees, and lit the clearing with bright patches of light. They halted suddenly on the edge, and peered through the tree-trunks, holding their breath. There stood the trolls: three large trolls. One was stooping, and the other two stood staring at him.

Strider walked forward unconcernedly. 'Get up, old stone!' he said, and broke his stick upon the stooping troll.

Nothing happened. There was a gasp of astonishment from the hobbits, and then even Frodo laughed. 'Well!' he said. 'We are forgetting our family history! These must be the very three that were caught by Gandalf, quarrelling over the right way to cook thirteen dwarves and one hobbit.'

'I had no idea we were anywhere near the place!' said Pippin. He knew the story well. Bilbo and Frodo had told it often; but as a matter of fact he had never more than half believed it. Even now he looked at the stone trolls with suspicion, wondering if some magic might not suddenly bring them to life again.

'You are forgetting not only your family history, but all you ever knew about trolls,' said Strider. 'It is broad daylight with a bright sun, and yet you come back trying to scare me with a tale of live trolls waiting for us in this glade! In any case you might have noticed that one of them has an old bird's nest behind his ear. That would be a most unusual ornament for a live troll!'

They all laughed. Frodo felt his spirits reviving: the reminder of Bilbo's first successful adventure was heartening. The sun, too, was warm and comforting, and the mist before his eyes seemed to be lifting a little. They rested for some time in the glade, and took their mid-day meal right under the shadow of the trolls' large legs.

'Won't somebody give us a bit of a song, while the sun is high?' said Merry, when they had finished. 'We haven't had a song or a tale for days.'

'Not since Weathertop,' said Frodo. The others looked at him. 'Don't worry about me!' he added. 'I feel much better, but I don't think I could sing. Perhaps Sam could dig something out of his memory.'

'Come on, Sam!' said Merry. 'There's more stored in your head than you let on about.'

'I don't know about that,' said Sam. 'But how would this suit? It ain't what I call proper poetry, if you understand me: just a bit of nonsense. But these old images here brought it to my mind.' Standing up, with his hands behind his back, as if he was at school, he began to sing to an old tune.

> *Troll sat alone on his seat of stone,*
> *And munched and mumbled a bare old bone;*
> *For many a year he had gnawed it near,*
> *For meat was hard to come by.*
> *Done by! Gum by!*
> *In a cave in the hills he dwelt alone,*
> *And meat was hard to come by.*
>
> *Up came Tom with his big boots on.*
> *Said he to Troll: 'Pray, what is yon?*
> *For it looks like the shin o' my nuncle Tim,*
> *As should be a-lyin' in graveyard.*
> *Caveyard! Paveyard!*
> *This many a year has Tim been gone,*
> *And I thought he were lyin' in graveyard.'*
>
> *'My lad,' said Troll, 'this bone I stole.*
> *But what be bones that lie in a hole?*
> *Thy nuncle was dead as a lump o' lead,*

Afore I found his shinbone.
Tinbone! Thinbone!
He can spare a share for a poor old troll,
For he don't need his shinbone.'

Said Tom: 'I don't see why the likes o' thee
Without axin' leave should go makin' free
With the shank or the shin o' my father's kin;
So hand the old bone over!
Rover! Trover!
Though dead he be, it belongs to he;
So hand the old bone over!'

'For a couple o' pins,' says Troll, and grins,
'I'll eat thee too, and gnaw thy shins.
A bit o' fresh meat will go down sweet!
I'll try my teeth on thee now.
Hee now! See now!
I'm tired o' gnawing old bones and skins;
I've a mind to dine on thee now.'

But just as he thought his dinner was caught,
He found his hands had hold of naught.
Before he could mind, Tom slipped behind
And gave him the boot to larn him.
Warn him! Darn him!
A bump o' the boot on the seat, Tom thought,
Would be the way to larn him.

But harder than stone is the flesh and bone
Of a troll that sits in the hills alone.
As well set your boot to the mountain's root,
For the seat of a troll don't feel it.
Peel it! Heal it!
Old Troll laughed, when he heard Tom groan,
And he knew his toes could feel it.

Tom's leg is game, since home he came,
And his bootless foot is lasting lame;
But Troll don't care, and he's still there
With the bone he boned from its owner.
Doner! Boner!

Troll's old seat is still the same,
And the bone he boned from its owner!

'Well, that's a warning to us all!' laughed Merry. 'It is as well you used a stick, and not your hand, Strider!'

'Where did you come by that, Sam?' asked Pippin. 'I've never heard those words before.'

Sam muttered something inaudible. 'It's out of his own head, of course,' said Frodo. 'I am learning a lot about Sam Gamgee on this journey. First he was a conspirator, now he's a jester. He'll end up by becoming a wizard – or a warrior!'

'I hope not,' said Sam. 'I don't want to be neither!'

In the afternoon they went on down the woods. They were probably following the very track that Gandalf, Bilbo, and the dwarves had used many years before. After a few miles they came out on the top of a high bank above the Road. At this point the Road had left the Hoarwell far behind in its narrow valley, and now clung close to the feet of the hills, rolling and winding eastward among woods and heather-covered slopes towards the Ford and the Mountains. Not far down the bank Strider pointed out a stone in the grass. On it roughly cut and now much weathered could still be seen dwarf-runes and secret marks.

'There!' said Merry. 'That must be the stone that marked the place where the trolls' gold was hidden. How much is left of Bilbo's share, I wonder, Frodo?'

Frodo looked at the stone, and wished that Bilbo had brought home no treasure more perilous, nor less easy to part with. 'None at all,' he said. 'Bilbo gave it all away. He told me he did not feel it was really his, as it came from robbers.'

The Road lay quiet under the long shadows of early evening. There was no sign of any other travellers to be seen. As there was now no other possible course for them to take, they climbed down the bank, and turning left went off as fast as they could. Soon a shoulder of the hills cut off the light of the fast westering sun. A cold wind flowed down to meet them from the mountains ahead.

They were beginning to look out for a place off the Road, where they could camp for the night, when they heard a sound that brought sudden fear back into their hearts: the noise of hoofs behind them. They looked back, but they could not see far because of the many windings and rollings of the Road. As quickly as they could they scrambled off the beaten way and up into the deep heather and bilberry brushwood on the slopes above, until they came to a small patch of thick-growing hazels. As they peered out from among the bushes, they could see the Road, faint and grey in the failing light, some thirty feet below them. The sound of hoofs drew nearer. They were going fast, with a light *clippety-clippety-clip*. Then faintly, as if it was blown away from them by the breeze, they seemed to catch a dim ringing, as of small bells tinkling.

'That does not sound like a Black Rider's horse!' said Frodo, listening intently. The other hobbits agreed hopefully that it did not, but they all remained full of suspicion. They had been in fear of pursuit for so long that any sound from behind seemed ominous and unfriendly. But Strider was now leaning forward, stooped to the ground, with a hand to his ear, and a look of joy on his face.

The light faded, and the leaves on the bushes rustled softly. Clearer and nearer now the bells jingled, and *clippety-clip* came the quick trotting feet. Suddenly into view below came a white horse, gleaming in the shadows, running swiftly. In the dusk its headstall flickered and flashed, as if it were studded with gems like living stars. The rider's cloak streamed behind him, and his hood was thrown back; his golden hair flowed shimmering in the wind of his speed. To Frodo it appeared that a white light was shining through the form and raiment of the rider, as if through a thin veil.

Strider sprang from hiding and dashed down towards the Road, leaping with a cry through the heather; but even before he had moved or called, the rider had reined in his horse and halted, looking up towards the thicket where they stood. When he saw Strider, he dismounted and ran to meet him calling out: *Ai na vedui Dúnadan! Mae govannen!* His speech and clear ringing voice left no doubt in their hearts: the rider was of the Elven-folk. No others that dwelt in the wide world had voices so fair to hear. But there seemed to be a note of haste or fear in his call, and they saw that he was now speaking quickly and urgently to Strider.

Soon Strider beckoned to them, and the hobbits left the bushes and hurried down to the Road. 'This is Glorfindel, who dwells in the house of Elrond,' said Strider.

'Hail, and well met at last!' said the Elf-lord to Frodo. 'I was sent from Rivendell to look for you. We feared that you were in danger upon the road.'

'Then Gandalf has reached Rivendell?' cried Frodo joyfully.

'No. He had not when I departed; but that was nine days ago,' answered Glorfindel. 'Elrond received news that troubled him. Some of my kindred, journeying in your land beyond the Baranduin,* learned that things were

---

* The Brandywine River.

amiss, and sent messages as swiftly as they could. They said that the Nine were abroad, and that you were astray bearing a great burden without guidance, for Gandalf had not returned. There are few even in Rivendell that can ride openly against the Nine; but such as there were, Elrond sent out north, west, and south. It was thought that you might turn far aside to avoid pursuit, and become lost in the Wilderness.

'It was my lot to take the Road, and I came to the Bridge of Mitheithel, and left a token there, nigh on seven days ago. Three of the servants of Sauron were upon the Bridge, but they withdrew and I pursued them westward. I came also upon two others, but they turned away southward. Since then I have searched for your trail. Two days ago I found it, and followed it over the Bridge; and today I marked where you descended from the hills again. But come! There is no time for further news. Since you are here we must risk the peril of the Road and go. There are five behind us, and when they find your trail upon the Road they will ride after us like the wind. And they are not all. Where the other four may be, I do not know. I fear that we may find the Ford is already held against us.'

While Glorfindel was speaking the shades of evening deepened. Frodo felt a great weariness come over him. Ever since the sun began to sink the mist before his eyes had darkened, and he felt that a shadow was coming between him and the faces of his friends. Now pain assailed him, and he felt cold. He swayed, clutching at Sam's arm.

'My master is sick and wounded,' said Sam angrily. 'He can't go on riding after nightfall. He needs rest.'

Glorfindel caught Frodo as he sank to the ground, and taking him gently in his arms he looked in his face with grave anxiety.

Briefly Strider told of the attack on their camp under Weathertop, and of the deadly knife. He drew out the hilt, which he had kept, and handed it to the Elf. Glorfindel shuddered as he took it, but he looked intently at it.

'There are evil things written on this hilt,' he said; 'though maybe your eyes cannot see them. Keep it, Aragorn, till we reach the house of Elrond! But be wary, and handle it as little as you may! Alas! the wounds of this weapon are beyond my skill to heal. I will do what I can – but all the more do I urge you now to go on without rest.'

He searched the wound on Frodo's shoulder with his fingers, and his face grew graver, as if what he learned disquieted him. But Frodo felt the chill lessen in his side and arm; a little warmth crept down from his shoulder to his hand, and the pain grew easier. The dusk of evening seemed to grow lighter about him, as if a cloud had been withdrawn. He saw his friends' faces more clearly again, and a measure of new hope and strength returned.

'You shall ride my horse,' said Glorfindel. 'I will shorten the stirrups up to the saddle-skirts, and you must sit as tight as you can. But you need not fear: my horse will not let any rider fall that I command him to bear. His pace is light and smooth; and if danger presses too near, he will bear you away with a speed that even the black steeds of the enemy cannot rival.'

'No, he will not!' said Frodo. 'I shall not ride him, if I am to be carried off to Rivendell or anywhere else, leaving my friends behind in danger.'

Glorfindel smiled. 'I doubt very much,' he said, 'if your friends would be in danger if you were not with them! The pursuit would follow you and leave us in peace, I think. It is you, Frodo, and that which you bear that brings us all in peril.'

To that Frodo had no answer, and he was persuaded to mount Glorfindel's white horse. The pony was laden instead with a great part of the others' burdens, so that they now marched lighter, and for a time made good speed; but the hobbits began to find it hard to keep up with the swift tireless feet of the Elf. On he led them, into the mouth of darkness, and still on under the deep clouded night. There was neither star nor moon. Not until the grey of dawn did he allow them to halt. Pippin, Merry, and Sam were by that time nearly asleep on their stumbling legs; and even Strider seemed by the sag of his shoulders to be weary. Frodo sat upon the horse in a dark dream.

They cast themselves down in the heather a few yards from the road-side, and fell asleep immediately. They seemed hardly to have closed their eyes when Glorfindel, who had set himself to watch while they slept, awoke them again. The sun had now climbed far into the morning, and the clouds and mists of the night were gone.

'Drink this!' said Glorfindel to them, pouring for each in turn a little liquor from his silver-studded flask of leather. It was clear as spring water and had no taste, and it did not feel either cool or warm in the mouth; but strength and vigour seemed to flow into all their limbs as they drank it. Eaten after that draught the stale bread and dried fruit (which was now all that they had left) seemed to satisfy their hunger better than many a good breakfast in the Shire had done.

They had rested rather less than five hours when they took to the Road again. Glorfindel still urged them on, and only allowed two brief halts during the day's march. In this way they covered almost twenty miles before nightfall, and came to a point where the Road bent right and ran down towards the bottom of the valley, now making straight for the Bruinen. So far there had been no sign or sound of pursuit that the hobbits could see or hear; but often Glorfindel would halt and listen for a moment, if they lagged behind, and a look of anxiety clouded his face. Once or twice he spoke to Strider in the elf-tongue.

But however anxious their guides might be, it was plain that the hobbits could go no further that night. They were stumbling along dizzy with weariness, and unable to think of anything but their feet and legs. Frodo's pain had redoubled, and during the day things about him faded to shadows of ghostly grey. He almost welcomed the coming of night, for then the world seemed less pale and empty.

The hobbits were still weary, when they set out again early next morning. There were many miles yet to go between them and the Ford, and they hobbled forward at the best pace they could manage.

'Our peril will be greatest just ere we reach the river,' said Glorfindel; 'for my heart warns me that the pursuit is now swift behind us, and other danger may be waiting by the Ford.'

The Road was still running steadily downhill, and there was now in places much grass at either side, in which the hobbits walked when they could, to ease their tired feet. In the late afternoon they came to a place where the Road went suddenly under the dark shadow of tall pine-trees, and then plunged into a deep cutting with steep moist walls of red stone. Echoes ran along as they hurried forward; and there seemed to be a sound of many footfalls following their own. All at once, as if through a gate of light, the Road ran out again from the end of the tunnel into the open. There at the bottom of a sharp incline they saw before them a long flat mile, and beyond that the Ford of Rivendell. On the further side was a steep brown bank, threaded by a winding path; and behind that the tall mountains climbed, shoulder above shoulder, and peak beyond peak, into the fading sky.

There was still an echo as of following feet in the cutting behind them; a rushing noise as if a wind were rising and pouring through the branches of the pines. One moment Glorfindel turned and listened, then he sprang forward with a loud cry.

'Fly!' he called. 'Fly! The enemy is upon us!'

The white horse leaped forward. The hobbits ran down the slope. Glorfindel and Strider followed as rear-guard. They were only half way across the flat, when suddenly there was a noise of horses galloping. Out of the gate in the trees that they had just left rode a Black Rider. He reined his horse in, and halted, swaying in his saddle. Another followed him, and then another; then again two more.

'Ride forward! Ride!' cried Glorfindel to Frodo.

He did not obey at once, for a strange reluctance seized him. Checking

the horse to a walk, he turned and looked back. The Riders seemed to sit
upon their great steeds like threatening statues upon a hill, dark and solid,
while all the woods and land about them receded as if into a mist. Suddenly
he knew in his heart that they were silently commanding him to wait. Then
at once fear and hatred awoke in him. His hand left the bridle and gripped
the hilt of his sword, and with a red flash he drew it.

'Ride on! Ride on!' cried Glorfindel, and then loud and clear he called
to the horse in the elf-tongue: *noro lim, noro lim, Asfaloth!*

At once the white horse sprang away and sped like the wind along the
last lap of the Road. At the same moment the black horses leaped down
the hill in pursuit, and from the Riders came a terrible cry, such as Frodo
had heard filling the woods with horror in the Eastfarthing far away. It
was answered; and to the dismay of Frodo and his friends out from the
trees and rocks away on the left four other Riders came flying. Two rode
towards Frodo: two galloped madly towards the Ford to cut off his escape.
They seemed to him to run like the wind and to grow swiftly larger and
darker, as their courses converged with his.

Frodo looked back for a moment over his shoulder. He could no longer
see his friends. The Riders behind were falling back: even their great steeds
were no match in speed for the white elf-horse of Glorfindel. He looked
forward again, and hope faded. There seemed no chance of reaching the
Ford before he was cut off by the others that had lain in ambush. He could
see them clearly now: they appeared to have cast aside their hoods and
black cloaks, and they were robed in white and grey. Swords were naked
in their pale hands; helms were on their heads. Their cold eyes glittered,
and they called to him with fell voices.

Fear now filled all Frodo's mind. He thought no longer of his sword.
No cry came from him. He shut his eyes and clung to the horse's mane.
The wind whistled in his ears, and the bells upon the harness rang wild
and shrill. A breath of deadly cold pierced him like a spear, as with a last
spurt, like a flash of white fire, the elf-horse speeding as if on wings, passed
right before the face of the foremost Rider.

Frodo heard the splash of water. It foamed about his feet. He felt the
quick heave and surge as the horse left the river and struggled up the stony
path. He was climbing the steep bank. He was across the Ford.

But the pursuers were close behind. At the top of the bank the horse
halted and turned about neighing fiercely. There were Nine Riders at the
water's edge below, and Frodo's spirit quailed before the threat of their
uplifted faces. He knew of nothing that would prevent them from crossing
as easily as he had done; and he felt that it was useless to try to escape
over the long uncertain path from the Ford to the edge of Rivendell, if
once the Riders crossed. In any case he felt that he was commanded urgently

to halt. Hatred again stirred in him, but he had no longer the strength to refuse.

Suddenly the foremost Rider spurred his horse forward. It checked at the water and reared up. With a great effort Frodo sat upright and brandished his sword.

'Go back!' he cried. 'Go back to the Land of Mordor, and follow me no more!' His voice sounded thin and shrill in his own ears. The Riders halted, but Frodo had not the power of Bombadil. His enemies laughed at him with a harsh and chilling laughter. 'Come back! Come back!' they called. 'To Mordor we will take you!'

'Go back!' he whispered.

'The Ring! The Ring!' they cried with deadly voices; and immediately their leader urged his horse forward into the water, followed closely by two others.

'By Elbereth and Lúthien the Fair,' said Frodo with a last effort, lifting up his sword, 'you shall have neither the Ring nor me!'

Then the leader, who was now half across the Ford, stood up menacing in his stirrups, and raised up his hand. Frodo was stricken dumb. He felt his tongue cleave to his mouth, and his heart labouring. His sword broke and fell out of his shaking hand. The elf-horse reared and snorted. The foremost of the black horses had almost set foot upon the shore.

At that moment there came a roaring and a rushing: a noise of loud waters rolling many stones. Dimly Frodo saw the river below him rise, and down along its course there came a plumed cavalry of waves. White flames seemed to Frodo to flicker on their crests and he half fancied that he saw amid the water white riders upon white horses with frothing manes. The three Riders that were still in the midst of the Ford were overwhelmed: they disappeared, buried suddenly under angry foam. Those that were behind drew back in dismay.

With his last failing senses Frodo heard cries, and it seemed to him that he saw, beyond the Riders that hesitated on the shore, a shining figure of white light; and behind it ran small shadowy forms waving flames, that flared red in the grey mist that was falling over the world.

The black horses were filled with madness, and leaping forward in terror they bore their riders into the rushing flood. Their piercing cries were drowned in the roaring of the river as it carried them away. Then Frodo felt himself falling, and the roaring and confusion seemed to rise and engulf him together with his enemies. He heard and saw no more.

BOOK TWO

CHAPTER I

MANY MEETINGS

Frodo woke and found himself lying in bed. At first he thought that he had slept late, after a long unpleasant dream that still hovered on the edge of memory. Or perhaps he had been ill? But the ceiling looked strange; it was flat, and it had dark beams richly carved. He lay a little while longer looking at patches of sunlight on the wall, and listening to the sound of a waterfall.

'Where am I, and what is the time?' he said aloud to the ceiling.

'In the House of Elrond, and it is ten o'clock in the morning,' said a voice. 'It is the morning of October the twenty-fourth, if you want to know.'

'Gandalf!' cried Frodo, sitting up. There was the old wizard, sitting in a chair by the open window.

'Yes,' he said, 'I am here. And you are lucky to be here, too, after all the absurd things you have done since you left home.'

Frodo lay down again. He felt too comfortable and peaceful to argue, and in any case he did not think he would get the better of an argument. He was fully awake now, and the memory of his journey was returning: the disastrous 'short cut' through the Old Forest; the 'accident' at *The Prancing Pony*; and his madness in putting on the Ring in the dell under Weathertop. While he was thinking of all these things and trying in vain to bring his memory down to his arriving in Rivendell, there was a long silence, broken only by the soft puffs of Gandalf's pipe, as he blew white smoke-rings out of the window.

'Where's Sam?' Frodo asked at length. 'And are the others all right?'

'Yes, they are all safe and sound,' answered Gandalf. 'Sam was here until I sent him off to get some rest, about half an hour ago.'

'What happened at the Ford?' said Frodo. 'It all seemed so dim, some-how; and it still does.'

'Yes, it would. You were beginning to fade,' answered Gandalf. 'The wound was overcoming you at last. A few more hours and you would have been beyond our aid. But you have some strength in you, my dear hobbit! As you showed in the Barrow. That was touch and go: perhaps the most dangerous moment of all. I wish you could have held out at Weathertop.'

'You seem to know a great deal already,' said Frodo. 'I have not spoken to the others about the Barrow. At first it was too horrible, and afterwards there were other things to think about. How do you know about it?'

'You have talked long in your sleep, Frodo,' said Gandalf gently, 'and it has not been hard for me to read your mind and memory. Do not worry! Though I said "absurd" just now, I did not mean it. I think well of you – and of the others. It is no small feat to have come so far, and through such dangers, still bearing the Ring.'

'We should never have done it without Strider,' said Frodo. 'But we needed you. I did not know what to do without you.'

'I was delayed,' said Gandalf, 'and that nearly proved our ruin. And yet I am not sure: it may have been better so.'

'I wish you would tell me what happened!'

'All in good time! You are not supposed to talk or worry about anything today, by Elrond's orders.'

'But talking would stop me thinking and wondering, which are quite as tiring,' said Frodo. 'I am wide awake now, and I remember so many things that want explaining. Why were you delayed? You ought to tell me that at least.'

'You will soon hear all you wish to know,' said Gandalf. 'We shall have a Council, as soon as you are well enough. At the moment I will only say that I was held captive.'

'You?' cried Frodo.

'Yes, I, Gandalf the Grey,' said the wizard solemnly. 'There are many powers in the world, for good or for evil. Some are greater than I am. Against some I have not yet been measured. But my time is coming. The Morgul-lord and his Black Riders have come forth. War is preparing!'

'Then you knew of the Riders already – before I met them?'

'Yes, I knew of them. Indeed I spoke of them once to you; for the Black Riders are the Ringwraiths, the Nine Servants of the Lord of the Rings. But I did not know that they had arisen again or I should have fled with you at once. I heard news of them only after I left you in June; but that story must wait. For the moment we have been saved from disaster, by Aragorn.'

'Yes,' said Frodo, 'it was Strider that saved us. Yet I was afraid of him at first. Sam never quite trusted him, I think, not at any rate until we met Glorfindel.'

Gandalf smiled. 'I have heard all about Sam,' he said. 'He has no more doubts now.'

'I am glad,' said Frodo. 'For I have become very fond of Strider. Well, fond is not the right word. I mean he is dear to me; though he is strange, and grim at times. In fact, he reminds me often of you. I didn't know that any of the Big People were like that. I thought, well, that they were just big, and rather stupid: kind and stupid like Butterbur; or stupid and wicked like Bill Ferny. But then we don't know much about Men in the Shire, except perhaps the Breelanders.'

'You don't know much even about them, if you think old Barliman is stupid,' said Gandalf. 'He is wise enough on his own ground. He thinks less than he talks, and slower; yet he can see through a brick wall in time (as they say in Bree). But there are few left in Middle-earth like Aragorn son of Arathorn. The race of the Kings from over the Sea is nearly at an end. It may be that this War of the Ring will be their last adventure.'

'Do you really mean that Strider is one of the people of the old Kings?' said Frodo in wonder. 'I thought they had all vanished long ago. I thought he was only a Ranger.'

'Only a Ranger!' cried Gandalf. 'My dear Frodo, that is just what the Rangers are: the last remnant in the North of the great people, the Men of the West. They have helped me before; and I shall need their help in the days to come; for we have reached Rivendell, but the Ring is not yet at rest.'

'I suppose not,' said Frodo. 'But so far my only thought has been to get here; and I hope I shan't have to go any further. It is very pleasant just to rest. I have had a month of exile and adventure, and I find that has been as much as I want.'

He fell silent and shut his eyes. After a while he spoke again. 'I have been reckoning,' he said, 'and I can't bring the total up to October the twenty-fourth. It ought to be the twenty-first. We must have reached the Ford by the twentieth.'

'You have talked and reckoned more than is good for you,' said Gandalf. 'How do the side and shoulder feel now?'

'I don't know,' Frodo answered. 'They don't feel at all: which is an improvement, but' – he made an effort – 'I can move my arm again a little. Yes, it is coming back to life. It is not cold,' he added, touching his left hand with his right.

'Good!' said Gandalf. 'It is mending fast. You will soon be sound again. Elrond has cured you: he has tended you for days, ever since you were brought in.'

'Days?' said Frodo.

'Well, four nights and three days, to be exact. The Elves brought you from the Ford on the night of the twentieth, and that is where you lost count. We have been terribly anxious, and Sam has hardly left your side, day or night, except to run messages. Elrond is a master of healing, but the weapons of our Enemy are deadly. To tell you the truth, I had very little hope; for I suspected that there was some fragment of the blade still in the closed wound. But it could not be found until last night. Then Elrond removed a splinter. It was deeply buried, and it was working inwards.'

Frodo shuddered, remembering the cruel knife with notched blade that had vanished in Strider's hands. 'Don't be alarmed!' said Gandalf. 'It is gone now. It has been melted. And it seems that Hobbits fade very reluctantly. I have known strong warriors of the Big People who would quickly have been overcome by that splinter, which you bore for seventeen days.'

'What would they have done to me?' asked Frodo. 'What were the Riders trying to do?'

'They tried to pierce your heart with a Morgul-knife which remains in the wound. If they had succeeded, you would have become like they are, only weaker and under their command. You would have become a wraith under the dominion of the Dark Lord; and he would have tormented you for trying to keep his Ring, if any greater torment were possible than being robbed of it and seeing it on his hand.'

'Thank goodness I did not realize the horrible danger!' said Frodo faintly. 'I was mortally afraid, of course; but if I had known more, I should not have dared even to move. It is a marvel that I escaped!'

'Yes, fortune or fate have helped you,' said Gandalf, 'not to mention courage. For your heart was not touched, and only your shoulder was pierced; and that was because you resisted to the last. But it was a terribly narrow shave, so to speak. You were in gravest peril while you wore the Ring, for then you were half in the wraith-world yourself, and they might have seized you. You could see them, and they could see you.'

'I know,' said Frodo. 'They were terrible to behold! But why could we all see their horses?'

'Because they are real horses; just as the black robes are real robes that they wear to give shape to their nothingness when they have dealings with the living.'

'Then why do these black horses endure such riders? All other animals are terrified when they draw near, even the elf-horse of Glorfindel. The dogs howl and the geese scream at them.'

'Because these horses are born and bred to the service of the Dark Lord in Mordor. Not all his servants and chattels are wraiths! There are orcs and trolls, there are wargs and werewolves; and there have been and still are many Men, warriors and kings, that walk alive under the Sun, and yet are under his sway. And their number is growing daily.'

'What about Rivendell and the Elves? Is Rivendell safe?'

'Yes, at present, until all else is conquered. The Elves may fear the Dark Lord, and they may fly before him, but never again will they listen to him or serve him. And here in Rivendell there live still some of his chief foes: the Elven-wise, lords of the Eldar from beyond the furthest seas. They do not fear the Ringwraiths, for those who have dwelt in the Blessed Realm live at once in both worlds, and against both the Seen and the Unseen they have great power.'

'I thought that I saw a white figure that shone and did not grow dim like the others. Was that Glorfindel then?'

'Yes, you saw him for a moment as he is upon the other side: one of the mighty of the Firstborn. He is an Elf-lord of a house of princes. Indeed there is a power in Rivendell to withstand the might of Mordor, for a while: and elsewhere other powers still dwell. There is power, too, of another kind in the Shire. But all such places will soon become islands under siege, if things go on as they are going. The Dark Lord is putting forth all his strength.

'Still,' he said, standing suddenly up and sticking out his chin, while his beard went stiff and straight like bristling wire, 'we must keep up our courage. You will soon be well, if I do not talk you to death. You are in Rivendell, and you need not worry about anything for the present.'

'I haven't any courage to keep up,' said Frodo, 'but I am not worried at the moment. Just give me news of my friends, and tell me the end of the affair at the Ford, as I keep on asking, and I shall be content for the present. After that I shall have another sleep, I think; but I shan't be able to close my eyes until you have finished the story for me.'

Gandalf moved his chair to the bedside, and took a good look at Frodo. The colour had come back to his face, and his eyes were clear, and fully awake and aware. He was smiling, and there seemed to be little wrong with him. But to the wizard's eye there was a faint change, just a hint as it were of transparency, about him, and especially about the left hand that lay outside upon the coverlet.

'Still that must be expected,' said Gandalf to himself. 'He is not half through yet, and to what he will come in the end not even Elrond can foretell. Not to evil, I think. He may become like a glass filled with a clear light for eyes to see that can.'

'You look splendid,' he said aloud. 'I will risk a brief tale without consulting Elrond. But quite brief, mind you, and then you must sleep again. This is what happened, as far as I can gather. The Riders made straight for you, as soon as you fled. They did not need the guidance of their horses any longer: you had become visible to them, being already on the threshold of their world. And also the Ring drew them. Your friends sprang aside, off the road, or they would have been ridden down. They knew that nothing could save you, if the white horse could not. The Riders were too swift to overtake, and too many to oppose. On foot even Glorfindel and Aragorn together could not withstand all the Nine at once.

'When the Ringwraiths swept by, your friends ran up behind. Close to the Ford there is a small hollow beside the road masked by a few stunted trees. There they hastily kindled fire; for Glorfindel knew that a flood would come down, if the Riders tried to cross, and then he would have to deal with any that were left on his side of the river. The moment the flood appeared, he rushed out, followed by Aragorn and the others with flaming brands. Caught between fire and water, and seeing an Elf-lord revealed in his wrath, they were dismayed, and their horses were stricken with madness. Three were carried away by the first assault of the flood; the others were now hurled into the water by their horses and overwhelmed.'

'And is that the end of the Black Riders?' asked Frodo.

'No,' said Gandalf. 'Their horses must have perished, and without them they are crippled. But the Ringwraiths themselves cannot be so easily destroyed. However, there is nothing more to fear from them at present. Your friends crossed after the flood had passed and they found you lying on your face at the top of the bank, with a broken sword under you. The horse was standing guard beside you. You were pale and cold, and they feared that you were dead, or worse. Elrond's folk met them, carrying you slowly towards Rivendell.'

'Who made the flood?' asked Frodo.

'Elrond commanded it,' answered Gandalf. 'The river of this valley is under his power, and it will rise in anger when he has great need to bar the Ford. As soon as the captain of the Ringwraiths rode into the water the flood was released. If I may say so, I added a few touches of my own: you may not have noticed, but some of the waves took the form of great white horses with shining white riders; and there were many rolling and grinding boulders. For a moment I was afraid that we had let loose too fierce a wrath, and the flood would get out of hand and wash you all away. There is great vigour in the waters that come down from the snows of the Misty Mountains.'

'Yes, it all comes back to me now,' said Frodo: 'the tremendous roaring. I thought I was drowning, with my friends and enemies and all. But now we are safe!'

Gandalf looked quickly at Frodo, but he had shut his eyes. 'Yes, you are all safe for the present. Soon there will be feasting and merrymaking to celebrate the victory at the Ford of Bruinen, and you will all be there in places of honour.'

'Splendid!' said Frodo. 'It is wonderful that Elrond, and Glorfindel and such great lords, not to mention Strider, should take so much trouble and show me so much kindness.'

'Well, there are many reasons why they should,' said Gandalf, smiling. 'I am one good reason. The Ring is another: you are the Ring-bearer. And you are the heir of Bilbo, the Ring-finder.'

'Dear Bilbo!' said Frodo sleepily. 'I wonder where he is. I wish he was here and could hear all about it. It would have made him laugh. The cow jumped over the Moon! And the poor old troll!' With that he fell fast asleep.

Frodo was now safe in the Last Homely House east of the Sea. That house was, as Bilbo had long ago reported, 'a perfect house, whether you like food or sleep or story-telling or singing, or just sitting and thinking best, or a pleasant mixture of them all'. Merely to be there was a cure for weariness, fear, and sadness.

As the evening drew on, Frodo woke up again, and he found that he no longer felt in need of rest or sleep, but had a mind for food and drink, and probably for singing and story-telling afterwards. He got out of bed and discovered that his arm was already nearly as useful again as it ever had been. He found laid ready clean garments of green cloth that fitted him excellently. Looking in a mirror he was startled to see a much thinner reflection of himself than he remembered: it looked remarkably like the young nephew of Bilbo who used to go tramping with his uncle in the Shire; but the eyes looked out at him thoughtfully.

'Yes, you have seen a thing or two since you last peeped out of a looking-glass,' he said to his reflection. 'But now for a merry meeting!' He stretched out his arms and whistled a tune.

At that moment there was a knock on the door, and Sam came in. He ran to Frodo and took his left hand, awkwardly and shyly. He stroked it gently and then he blushed and turned hastily away.

'Hullo, Sam!' said Frodo.

'It's warm!' said Sam. 'Meaning your hand, Mr. Frodo. It has felt so cold through the long nights. But glory and trumpets!' he cried, turning round again with shining eyes and dancing on the floor. 'It's fine to see you up and yourself again, sir! Gandalf asked me to come and see if you were ready to come down, and I thought he was joking.'

'I am ready,' said Frodo. 'Let's go and look for the rest of the party!'

'I can take you to them, sir,' said Sam. 'It's a big house this, and very peculiar. Always a bit more to discover, and no knowing what you'll find round a corner. And Elves, sir! Elves here, and Elves there! Some like kings, terrible and splendid; and some as merry as children. And the music and the singing – not that I have had the time or the heart for much listening since we got here. But I'm getting to know some of the ways of the place.'

'I know what you have been doing, Sam,' said Frodo, taking his arm. 'But you shall be merry tonight, and listen to your heart's content. Come on, guide me round the corners!'

Sam led him along several passages and down many steps and out into a high garden above the steep bank of the river. He found his friends sitting in a porch on the side of the house looking east. Shadows had fallen in the valley below, but there was still a light on the faces of the mountains far above. The air was warm. The sound of running and falling water was loud, and the evening was filled with a faint scent of trees and flowers, as if summer still lingered in Elrond's gardens.

'Hurray!' cried Pippin, springing up. 'Here is our noble cousin! Make way for Frodo, Lord of the Ring!'

'Hush!' said Gandalf from the shadows at the back of the porch. 'Evil things do not come into this valley; but all the same we should not name them. The Lord of the Ring is not Frodo, but the master of the Dark Tower of Mordor, whose power is again stretching out over the world! We are sitting in a fortress. Outside it is getting dark.'

'Gandalf has been saying many cheerful things like that,' said Pippin. 'He thinks I need keeping in order. But it seems impossible, somehow, to feel gloomy or depressed in this place. I feel I could sing, if I knew the right song for the occasion.'

'I feel like singing myself,' laughed Frodo. 'Though at the moment I feel more like eating and drinking!'

'That will soon be cured,' said Pippin. 'You have shown your usual cunning in getting up just in time for a meal.'

'More than a meal! A feast!' said Merry. 'As soon as Gandalf reported that you were recovered, the preparations began.' He had hardly finished speaking when they were summoned to the hall by the ringing of many bells.

The hall of Elrond's house was filled with folk: Elves for the most part, though there were a few guests of other sorts. Elrond, as was his custom, sat in a great chair at the end of the long table upon the dais; and next to him on the one side sat Glorfindel, on the other side sat Gandalf.

Frodo looked at them in wonder, for he had never before seen Elrond, of whom so many tales spoke; and as they sat upon his right hand and his left, Glorfindel, and even Gandalf, whom he thought he knew so well, were revealed as lords of dignity and power.

Gandalf was shorter in stature than the other two; but his long white hair, his sweeping silver beard, and his broad shoulders, made him look like some wise king of ancient legend. In his aged face under great snowy brows his dark eyes were set like coals that could leap suddenly into fire.

Glorfindel was tall and straight; his hair was of shining gold, his face fair and young and fearless and full of joy; his eyes were bright and keen, and his voice like music; on his brow sat wisdom, and in his hand was strength.

The face of Elrond was ageless, neither old nor young, though in it was written the memory of many things both glad and sorrowful. His hair was dark as the shadows of twilight, and upon it was set a circlet of silver; his eyes were grey as a clear evening, and in them was a light like the light of stars. Venerable he seemed as a king crowned with many winters, and yet hale as a tried warrior in the fulness of his strength. He was the Lord of Rivendell and mighty among both Elves and Men.

In the middle of the table, against the woven cloths upon the wall, there was a chair under a canopy, and there sat a lady fair to look upon, and so like was she in form of womanhood to Elrond that Frodo guessed that she was one of his close kindred. Young she was and yet not so. The braids of her dark hair were touched by no frost; her white arms and clear face were flawless and smooth, and the light of stars was in her bright eyes, grey as a cloudless night; yet queenly she looked, and thought and knowledge were in her glance, as of one who has known many things that the years bring. Above her brow her head was covered with a cap of silver lace netted with small gems, glittering white; but her soft grey raiment had no ornament save a girdle of leaves wrought in silver.

So it was that Frodo saw her whom few mortals had yet seen; Arwen, daughter of Elrond, in whom it was said that the likeness of Lúthien had come on earth again; and she was called Undómiel, for she was the Evenstar of her people. Long she had been in the land of her mother's kin, in Lórien beyond the mountains, and was but lately returned to Rivendell to her father's house. But her brothers, Elladan and Elrohir, were out upon errantry: for they rode often far afield with the Rangers of the North, forgetting never their mother's torment in the dens of the orcs.

Such loveliness in living thing Frodo had never seen before nor imagined in his mind; and he was both surprised and abashed to find that he had a seat at Elrond's table among all these folk so high and fair. Though he had a suitable chair, and was raised upon several cushions, he felt very small, and rather out of place; but that feeling quickly passed. The feast was merry and the food all that his hunger could desire. It was some time before he looked about him again or even turned to his neighbours.

He looked first for his friends. Sam had begged to be allowed to wait on his master, but had been told that for this time he was a guest of honour. Frodo could see him now, sitting with Pippin and Merry at the upper end of one of the side-tables close to the dais. He could see no sign of Strider.

Next to Frodo on his right sat a dwarf of important appearance, richly dressed. His beard, very long and forked, was white, nearly as white as the snow-white cloth of his garments. He wore a silver belt, and round his neck hung a chain of silver and diamonds. Frodo stopped eating to look at him.

'Welcome and well met!' said the dwarf, turning towards him. Then he actually rose from his seat and bowed. 'Glóin at your service,' he said, and bowed still lower.

'Frodo Baggins at your service and your family's,' said Frodo correctly, rising in surprise and scattering his cushions. 'Am I right in guessing that you are *the* Glóin, one of the twelve companions of the great Thorin Oakenshield?'

'Quite right,' answered the dwarf, gathering up the cushions and courteously assisting Frodo back into his seat. 'And I do not ask, for I have already been told that you are the kinsman and adopted heir of our friend Bilbo the renowned. Allow me to congratulate you on your recovery.'

'Thank you very much,' said Frodo.

'You have had some very strange adventures, I hear,' said Glóin. 'I wonder greatly what brings *four* hobbits on so long a journey. Nothing like it has happened since Bilbo came with us. But perhaps I should not inquire too closely, since Elrond and Gandalf do not seem disposed to talk of this?'

'I think we will not speak of it, at least not yet,' said Frodo politely. He guessed that even in Elrond's house the matter of the Ring was not one for casual talk; and in any case he wished to forget his troubles for a time. 'But I am equally curious,' he added, 'to learn what brings so important a dwarf so far from the Lonely Mountain.'

Glóin looked at him. 'If you have not heard, I think we will not speak yet of that either. Master Elrond will summon us all ere long, I believe, and then we shall all hear many things. But there is much else that may be told.'

Throughout the rest of the meal they talked together, but Frodo listened more than he spoke; for the news of the Shire, apart from the Ring, seemed small and far-away and unimportant, while Glóin had much to tell of events in the northern regions of Wilderland. Frodo learned that Grimbeorn the Old, son of Beorn, was now the lord of many sturdy men, and to their land between the Mountains and Mirkwood neither orc nor wolf dared to go.

'Indeed,' said Glóin, 'if it were not for the Beornings, the passage from Dale to Rivendell would long ago have become impossible. They are valiant men and keep open the High Pass and the Ford of Carrock. But their tolls are high,' he added with a shake of his head; 'and like Beorn of old they are not over fond of dwarves. Still, they are trusty, and that is much in these days. Nowhere are there any men so friendly to us as the Men of Dale. They are good folk, the Bardings. The grandson of Bard the Bowman rules them, Brand son of Bain son of Bard. He is a strong king, and his realm now reaches far south and east of Esgaroth.'

'And what of your own people?' asked Frodo.

'There is much to tell, good and bad,' said Glóin; 'yet it is mostly good:

we have so far been fortunate, though we do not escape the shadow of these times. If you really wish to hear of us, I will tell you tidings gladly. But stop me when you are weary! Dwarves' tongues run on when speaking of their handiwork, they say.'

And with that Glóin embarked on a long account of the doings of the Dwarf-kingdom. He was delighted to have found so polite a listener; for Frodo showed no sign of weariness and made no attempt to change the subject, though actually he soon got rather lost among the strange names of people and places that he had never heard of before. He was interested, however, to hear that Dáin was still King under the Mountain, and was now old (having passed his two hundred and fiftieth year), venerable, and fabulously rich. Of the ten companions who had survived the Battle of Five Armies seven were still with him: Dwalin, Glóin, Dori, Nori, Bifur, Bofur, and Bombur. Bombur was now so fat that he could not move himself from his couch to his chair at table, and it took six young dwarves to lift him.

'And what has become of Balin and Ori and Óin?' asked Frodo.

A shadow passed over Glóin's face. 'We do not know,' he answered. 'It is largely on account of Balin that I have come to ask the advice of those that dwell in Rivendell. But tonight let us speak of merrier things!'

Glóin began then to talk of the works of his people, telling Frodo about their great labours in Dale and under the Mountain. 'We have done well,' he said. 'But in metal-work we cannot rival our fathers, many of whose secrets are lost. We make good armour and keen swords, but we cannot again make mail or blade to match those that were made before the dragon came. Only in mining and building have we surpassed the old days. You should see the waterways of Dale, Frodo, and the fountains, and the pools! You should see the stone-paved roads of many colours! And the halls and cavernous streets under the earth with arches carved like trees; and the terraces and towers upon the Mountain's sides! Then you would see that we have not been idle.'

'I will come and see them, if ever I can,' said Frodo. 'How surprised Bilbo would have been to see all the changes in the Desolation of Smaug!'

Glóin looked at Frodo and smiled. 'You were very fond of Bilbo were you not?' he asked.

'Yes,' answered Frodo. 'I would rather see him than all the towers and palaces in the world.'

At length the feast came to an end. Elrond and Arwen rose and went down the hall, and the company followed them in due order. The doors were thrown open, and they went across a wide passage and through other doors, and came into a further hall. In it were no tables, but a bright fire was burning in a great hearth between the carven pillars upon either side.

Frodo found himself walking with Gandalf. 'This is the Hall of Fire,' said the wizard. 'Here you will hear many songs and tales – if you can keep awake. But except on high days it usually stands empty and quiet, and people come here who wish for peace, and thought. There is always a fire here, all the year round, but there is little other light.'

As Elrond entered and went towards the seat prepared for him, elvish minstrels began to make sweet music. Slowly the hall filled, and Frodo looked with delight upon the many fair faces that were gathered together; the golden firelight played upon them and shimmered in their hair. Suddenly he noticed, not far from the further end of the fire, a small dark figure seated on a stool with his back propped against a pillar. Beside him on the ground was a drinking-cup and some bread. Frodo wondered whether he was ill (if people were ever ill in Rivendell), and had been unable to come to the feast. His head seemed sunk in sleep on his breast, and a fold of his dark cloak was drawn over his face.

Elrond went forward and stood beside the silent figure. 'Awake, little master!' he said, with a smile. Then, turning to Frodo, he beckoned to him. 'Now at last the hour has come that you have wished for, Frodo,' he said. 'Here is a friend that you have long missed.'

The dark figure raised its head and uncovered its face.

'Bilbo!' cried Frodo with sudden recognition, and he sprang forward.

'Hullo, Frodo my lad!' said Bilbo. 'So you have got here at last. I hoped you would manage it. Well, well! So all this feasting is in your honour, I hear. I hope you enjoyed yourself?'

'Why weren't you there?' cried Frodo. 'And why haven't I been allowed to see you before?'

'Because you were asleep. I have seen a good deal of *you*. I have sat by your side with Sam each day. But as for the feast, I don't go in for such things much now. And I had something else to do.'

'What were you doing?'

'Why, sitting and thinking. I do a lot of that nowadays, and this is the best place to do it in, as a rule. Wake up, indeed!' he said, cocking an eye at Elrond. There was a bright twinkle in it and no sign of sleepiness that Frodo could see. 'Wake up! I was not asleep, Master Elrond. If you want to know, you have all come out from your feast too soon, and you have disturbed me – in the middle of making up a song. I was stuck over a line or two, and was thinking about them; but now I don't suppose I shall ever get them right. There will be such a deal of singing that the ideas will be driven clean out of my head. I shall have to get my friend the Dúnadan to help me. Where is he?'

Elrond laughed. 'He shall be found,' he said. 'Then you two shall go into a corner and finish your task, and we will hear it and judge it before we end our merrymaking.' Messengers were sent to find Bilbo's friend, though none knew where he was, or why he had not been present at the feast.

In the meanwhile Frodo and Bilbo sat side by side, and Sam came quickly and placed himself near them. They talked together in soft voices, oblivious of the mirth and music in the hall about them. Bilbo had not much to say of himself. When he had left Hobbiton he had wandered off aimlessly, along the Road or in the country on either side; but somehow he had steered all the time towards Rivendell.

'I got here without much adventure,' he said, 'and after a rest I went on with the dwarves to Dale: my last journey. I shan't travel again. Old Balin had gone away. Then I came back here, and here I have been. I have done this and that. I have written some more of my book. And, of course, I make up a few songs. They sing them occasionally: just to please me, I think; for, of course, they aren't really good enough for Rivendell. And I listen and I think. Time doesn't seem to pass here: it just is. A remarkable place altogether.

'I hear all kinds of news, from over the Mountains, and out of the South, but hardly anything from the Shire. I heard about the Ring, of course. Gandalf has been here often. Not that he has told me a great deal, he has become closer than ever these last few years. The Dúnadan has told me more. Fancy that ring of mine causing such a disturbance! It is a pity that Gandalf did not find out more sooner. I could have brought the thing here myself long ago without so much trouble. I have thought several times of going back to Hobbiton for it; but I am getting old, and they would not let me: Gandalf and Elrond, I mean. They seemed to think that the Enemy was looking high and low for me, and would make mincemeat of me, if he caught me tottering about in the Wild.

'And Gandalf said: "The Ring has passed on, Bilbo. It would do no good to you or to others, if you tried to meddle with it again." Odd sort of remark, just like Gandalf. But he said he was looking after you, so I let things be. I am frightfully glad to see you safe and sound.' He paused and looked at Frodo doubtfully.

'Have you got it here?' he asked in a whisper. 'I can't help feeling curious, you know, after all I've heard. I should very much like just to peep at it again.'

'Yes, I've got it,' answered Frodo, feeling a strange reluctance. 'It looks just the same as ever it did.'

'Well, I should just like to see it for a moment,' said Bilbo.

When he had dressed, Frodo found that while he slept the Ring had been hung about his neck on a new chain, light but strong. Slowly he drew it out. Bilbo put out his hand. But Frodo quickly drew back the Ring. To his distress and amazement he found that he was no longer looking at

Bilbo; a shadow seemed to have fallen between them, and through it he found himself eyeing a little wrinkled creature with a hungry face and bony groping hands. He felt a desire to strike him.

The music and singing round them seemed to falter, and a silence fell. Bilbo looked quickly at Frodo's face and passed his hand across his eyes. 'I understand now,' he said. 'Put it away! I am sorry: sorry you have come in for this burden: sorry about everything. Don't adventures ever have an end? I suppose not. Someone else always has to carry on the story. Well, it can't be helped. I wonder if it's any good trying to finish my book? But don't let's worry about it now – let's have some real News! Tell me all about the Shire!'

Frodo hid the Ring away, and the shadow passed leaving hardly a shred of memory. The light and music of Rivendell was about him again. Bilbo smiled and laughed happily. Every item of news from the Shire that Frodo could tell – aided and corrected now and again by Sam – was of the greatest interest to him, from the felling of the least tree to the pranks of the smallest child in Hobbiton. They were so deep in the doings of the Four Farthings that they did not notice the arrival of a man clad in dark green cloth. For many minutes he stood looking down at them with a smile.

Suddenly Bilbo looked up. 'Ah, there you are at last, Dúnadan!' he cried.

'Strider!' said Frodo. 'You seem to have a lot of names.'

'Well, *Strider* is one that I haven't heard before, anyway,' said Bilbo. 'What do you call him that for?'

'They call me that in Bree,' said Strider laughing, 'and that is how I was introduced to him.'

'And why do you call him Dúnadan?' asked Frodo.

'*The* Dúnadan,' said Bilbo. 'He is often called that here. But I thought you knew enough Elvish at least to know *dún-adan*: Man of the West, Númenorean. But this is not the time for lessons!' He turned to Strider. 'Where have you been, my friend? Why weren't you at the feast? The Lady Arwen was there.'

Strider looked down at Bilbo gravely. 'I know,' he said. 'But often I must put mirth aside. Elladan and Elrohir have returned out of the Wild unlooked-for, and they had tidings that I wished to hear at once.'

'Well, my dear fellow,' said Bilbo, 'now you've heard the news, can't you spare me a moment? I want your help in something urgent. Elrond says this song of mine is to be finished before the end of the evening, and I am stuck. Let's go off into a corner and polish it up!'

Strider smiled. 'Come then!' he said. 'Let me hear it!'

Frodo was left to himself for a while, for Sam had fallen asleep. He was alone and felt rather forlorn, although all about him the folk of Rivendell were gathered. But those near him were silent, intent upon the music of the voices and the instruments, and they gave no heed to anything else. Frodo began to listen.

At first the beauty of the melodies and of the interwoven words in elven-tongues, even though he understood them little, held him in a spell, as soon as he began to attend to them. Almost it seemed that the words took shape, and visions of far lands and bright things that he had never yet imagined opened out before him; and the firelit hall became like a golden mist above seas of foam that sighed upon the margins of the world. Then the enchantment became more and more dreamlike, until he felt that an endless river of swelling gold and silver was flowing over him, too multitudinous for its pattern to be comprehended; it became part of the throbbing air about him, and it drenched and drowned him. Swiftly he sank under its shining weight into a deep realm of sleep.

There he wandered long in a dream of music that turned into running water, and then suddenly into a voice. It seemed to be the voice of Bilbo chanting verses. Faint at first and then clearer ran the words.

> *Eärendil was a mariner*
> *that tarried in Arvernien;*
> *he built a boat of timber felled*
> *in Nimbrethil to journey in;*
> *her sails he wove of silver fair,*
> *of silver were her lanterns made,*
> *her prow was fashioned like a swan,*
> *and light upon her banners laid.*
>
> *In panoply of ancient kings,*
> *in chainéd rings he armoured him;*
> *his shining shield was scored with runes*
> *to ward all wounds and harm from him;*
> *his bow was made of dragon-horn,*
> *his arrows shorn of ebony,*
> *of silver was his habergeon,*
> *his scabbard of chalcedony;*
> *his sword of steel was valiant,*
> *of adamant his helmet tall,*
> *an eagle-plume upon his crest,*
> *upon his breast an emerald.*

Beneath the Moon and under star
he wandered far from northern strands,
bewildered on enchanted ways
beyond the days of mortal lands.
From gnashing of the Narrow Ice
where shadow lies on frozen hills,
from nether heats and burning waste
he turned in haste, and roving still
on starless waters far astray
at last he came to Night of Naught,
and passed, and never sight he saw
of shining shore nor light he sought.
The winds of wrath came driving him,
and blindly in the foam he fled
from west to east and errandless,
unheralded he homeward sped.

There flying Elwing came to him,
and flame was in the darkness lit;
more bright than light of diamond
the fire upon her carcanet.
The Silmaril she bound on him
and crowned him with the living light
and dauntless then with burning brow
he turned his prow; and in the night
from Otherworld beyond the Sea
there strong and free a storm arose,
a wind of power in Tarmenel;
by paths that seldom mortal goes
his boat it bore with biting breath
as might of death across the grey
and long-forsaken seas distressed:
from east to west he passed away.

Through Evernight he back was borne
on black and roaring waves that ran
o'er leagues unlit and foundered shores
that drowned before the Days began,
until he heard on strands of pearl
where ends the world the music long,
where ever-foaming billows roll
the yellow gold and jewels wan.

He saw the Mountain silent rise
where twilight lies upon the knees
of Valinor, and Eldamar
beheld afar beyond the seas.
A wanderer escaped from night
to haven white he came at last,
to Elvenhome the green and fair
where keen the air, where pale as glass
beneath the Hill of Ilmarin
a-glimmer in a valley sheer
the lamplit towers of Tirion
are mirrored on the Shadowmere.

He tarried there from errantry,
and melodies they taught to him,
and sages old him marvels told,
and harps of gold they brought to him.
They clothed him then in elven-white,
and seven lights before him sent,
as through the Calacirian
to hidden land forlorn he went.
He came unto the timeless halls
where shining fall the countless years,
and endless reigns the Elder King
in Ilmarin on Mountain sheer;
and words unheard were spoken then
of folk of Men and Elven-kin,
beyond the world were visions showed
forbid to those that dwell therein.

A ship then new they built for him
of mithril and of elven-glass
with shining prow; no shaven oar
nor sail she bore on silver mast:
the Silmaril as lantern light
and banner bright with living flame
to gleam thereon by Elbereth
herself was set, who thither came
and wings immortal made for him,
and laid on him undying doom,
to sail the shoreless skies and come
behind the Sun and light of Moon.

From Evereven's lofty hills
where softly silver fountains fall
his wings him bore, a wandering light,
beyond the mighty Mountain Wall.
From World's End then he turned away,
and yearned again to find afar
his home through shadows journeying,
and burning as an island star
on high above the mists he came,
a distant flame before the Sun,
a wonder ere the waking dawn
where grey the Norland waters run.

And over Middle-earth he passed
and heard at last the weeping sore
of women and of elven-maids
in Elder Days, in years of yore.
But on him mighty doom was laid,
till Moon should fade, an orbéd star
to pass, and tarry never more
on Hither Shores where mortals are;
for ever still a herald on
an errand that should never rest
to bear his shining lamp afar,
the Flammifer of Westernesse.

The chanting ceased. Frodo opened his eyes and saw that Bilbo was seated on his stool in a circle of listeners, who were smiling and applauding.

'Now we had better have it again,' said an Elf.

Bilbo got up and bowed. 'I am flattered, Lindir,' he said. 'But it would be too tiring to repeat it all.'

'Not too tiring for you,' the Elves answered laughing. 'You know you are never tired of reciting your own verses. But really we cannot answer your question at one hearing!'

'What!' cried Bilbo. 'You can't tell which parts were mine, and which were the Dúnadan's?'

'It is not easy for us to tell the difference between two mortals,' said the Elf.

'Nonsense, Lindir,' snorted Bilbo. 'If you can't distinguish between a Man and a Hobbit, your judgement is poorer than I imagined. They're as different as peas and apples.'

'Maybe. To sheep other sheep no doubt appear different,' laughed Lindir. 'Or to shepherds. But Mortals have not been our study. We have other business.'

'I won't argue with you,' said Bilbo. 'I am sleepy after so much music and singing. I'll leave you to guess, if you want to.'

He got up and came towards Frodo. 'Well, that's over,' he said in a low voice. 'It went off better than I expected. I don't often get asked for a second hearing. What did you think of it?'

'I am not going to try and guess,' said Frodo smiling.

'You needn't,' said Bilbo. 'As a matter of fact it was all mine. Except that Aragorn insisted on my putting in a green stone. He seemed to think it important. I don't know why. Otherwise he obviously thought the whole thing rather above my head, and he said that if I had the cheek to make verses about Eärendil in the house of Elrond, it was my affair. I suppose he was right.'

'I don't know,' said Frodo. 'It seemed to me to fit somehow, though I can't explain. I was half asleep when you began, and it seemed to follow on from something that I was dreaming about. I didn't understand that it was really you speaking until near the end.'

'It *is* difficult to keep awake here, until you get used to it,' said Bilbo. 'Not that hobbits would ever acquire quite the elvish appetite for music and poetry and tales. They seem to like them as much as food, or more. They will be going on for a long time yet. What do you say to slipping off for some more quiet talk?'

'Can we?' said Frodo.

'Of course. This is merrymaking not business. Come and go as you like, as long as you don't make a noise.'

They got up and withdrew quietly into the shadows, and made for the doors. Sam they left behind, fast asleep still with a smile on his face. In spite of his delight in Bilbo's company Frodo felt a tug of regret as they passed out of the Hall of Fire. Even as they stepped over the threshold a single clear voice rose in song.

> *A Elbereth Gilthoniel,*
> *silivren penna míriel*
> *o menel aglar elenath!*
> *Na-chaered palan-díriel*
> *o galadhremmin ennorath,*
> *Fanuilos, le linnathon*
> *nef aear, sí nef aearon!*

Frodo halted for a moment, looking back. Elrond was in his chair and the fire was on his face like summer-light upon the trees. Near him sat the Lady Arwen. To his surprise Frodo saw that Aragorn stood beside her; his dark cloak was thrown back, and he seemed to be clad in elven-mail, and a star shone on his breast. They spoke together, and then suddenly it seemed to Frodo that Arwen turned towards him, and the light of her eyes fell on him from afar and pierced his heart.

He stood still enchanted, while the sweet syllables of the elvish song fell like clear jewels of blended word and melody. 'It is a song to Elbereth,' said Bilbo. 'They will sing that, and other songs of the Blessed Realm, many times tonight. Come on!'

He led Frodo back to his own little room. It opened on to the gardens and looked south across the ravine of the Bruinen. There they sat for some while, looking through the window at the bright stars above the steep-climbing woods, and talking softly. They spoke no more of the small news of the Shire far away, nor of the dark shadows and perils that encompassed them, but of the fair things they had seen in the world together, of the Elves, of the stars, of trees, and the gentle fall of the bright year in the woods.

At last there came a knock on the door. 'Begging your pardon,' said Sam, putting in his head, 'but I was just wondering if you would be wanting anything.'

'And begging yours, Sam Gamgee,' replied Bilbo. 'I guess you mean that it is time your master went to bed.'

'Well, sir, there is a Council early tomorrow, I hear, and he only got up today for the first time.'

'Quite right, Sam,' laughed Bilbo. 'You can trot off and tell Gandalf that he has gone to bed. Good night, Frodo! Bless me, but it has been good to see you again! There are no folk like hobbits after all for a real good talk. I am getting very old, and I began to wonder if I should ever live to see your chapters of our story. Good night! I'll take a walk, I think, and look at the stars of Elbereth in the garden. Sleep well!'

CHAPTER II

THE COUNCIL OF ELROND

Next day Frodo woke early, feeling refreshed and well. He walked along the terraces above the loud-flowing Bruinen and watched the pale, cool sun rise above the far mountains, and shine down, slanting through the thin silver mist; the dew upon the yellow leaves was glimmering, and the woven nets of gossamer twinkled on every bush. Sam walked beside him, saying nothing, but sniffing the air, and looking every now and again with wonder in his eyes at the great heights in the East. The snow was white upon their peaks.

On a seat cut in the stone beside a turn in the path they came upon Gandalf and Bilbo deep in talk. 'Hullo! Good morning!' said Bilbo. 'Feel ready for the great council?'

'I feel ready for anything,' answered Frodo. 'But most of all I should like to go walking today and explore the valley. I should like to get into those pine-woods up there.' He pointed away far up the side of Rivendell to the north.

'You may have a chance later,' said Gandalf. 'But we cannot make any plans yet. There is much to hear and decide today.'

Suddenly as they were talking a single clear bell rang out. 'That is the warning bell for the Council of Elrond,' cried Gandalf. 'Come along now! Both you and Bilbo are wanted.'

Frodo and Bilbo followed the wizard quickly along the winding path back to the house; behind them, uninvited and for the moment forgotten, trotted Sam.

Gandalf led them to the porch where Frodo had found his friends the evening before. The light of the clear autumn morning was now glowing in the valley. The noise of bubbling waters came up from the foaming river-bed. Birds were singing, and a wholesome peace lay on the land. To Frodo his dangerous flight, and the rumours of the darkness growing in the world outside, already seemed only the memories of a troubled dream; but the faces that were turned to meet them as they entered were grave.

Elrond was there, and several others were seated in silence about him. Frodo saw Glorfindel and Glóin; and in a corner alone Strider was sitting, clad in his old travel-worn clothes again. Elrond drew Frodo to a seat by his side, and presented him to the company, saying:

'Here, my friends, is the hobbit, Frodo son of Drogo. Few have ever come hither through greater peril or on an errand more urgent.'

He then pointed out and named those whom Frodo had not met before. There was a younger dwarf at Glóin's side: his son Gimli. Beside Glorfindel there were several other counsellors of Elrond's household, of whom Erestor was the chief; and with him was Galdor, an Elf from the Grey Havens who had come on an errand from Círdan the Shipwright. There was also a strange Elf clad in green and brown, Legolas, a messenger from his father, Thranduil, the King of the Elves of Northern Mirkwood. And seated a little apart was a tall man with a fair and noble face, dark-haired and grey-eyed, proud and stern of glance.

He was cloaked and booted as if for a journey on horseback; and indeed though his garments were rich, and his cloak was lined with fur, they were stained with long travel. He had a collar of silver in which a single white stone was set; his locks were shorn about his shoulders. On a baldric he wore a great horn tipped with silver that now was laid upon his knees. He gazed at Frodo and Bilbo with sudden wonder.

'Here,' said Elrond, turning to Gandalf, 'is Boromir, a man from the South. He arrived in the grey morning, and seeks for counsel. I have bidden him to be present, for here his questions will be answered.'

Not all that was spoken and debated in the Council need now be told. Much was said of events in the world outside, especially in the South, and in the wide lands east of the Mountains. Of these things Frodo had already heard many rumours; but the tale of Glóin was new to him, and when the dwarf spoke he listened attentively. It appeared that amid the splendour of their works of hand the hearts of the Dwarves of the Lonely Mountain were troubled.

'It is now many years ago,' said Glóin, 'that a shadow of disquiet fell upon our people. Whence it came we did not at first perceive. Words began to be whispered in secret: it was said that we were hemmed in a narrow place, and that greater wealth and splendour would be found in a wider world. Some spoke of Moria: the mighty works of our fathers that are called in our own tongue Khazad-dûm; and they declared that now at last we had the power and numbers to return.'

Glóin sighed. 'Moria! Moria! Wonder of the Northern world! Too deep we delved there, and woke the nameless fear. Long have its vast mansions lain empty since the children of Durin fled. But now we spoke of it again with longing, and yet with dread; for no dwarf has dared to pass the doors of Khazad-dûm for many lives of kings, save Thrór only, and he perished. At last, however, Balin listened to the whispers, and resolved to go; and though Dáin did not give leave willingly, he took with him Ori and Óin and many of our folk, and they went away south.

'That was nigh on thirty years ago. For a while we had news and it seemed good: messages reported that Moria had been entered and a great work begun there. Then there was silence, and no word has ever come from Moria since.

'Then about a year ago a messenger came to Dáin, but not from Moria – from Mordor: a horseman in the night, who called Dáin to his gate. The Lord Sauron the Great, so he said, wished for our friendship. Rings he would give for it, such as he gave of old. And he asked urgently concerning *hobbits*, of what kind they were, and where they dwelt. "For Sauron knows," said he, "that one of these was known to you on a time."

'At this we were greatly troubled, and we gave no answer. And then his fell voice was lowered, and he would have sweetened it if he could. "As a small token only of your friendship Sauron asks this," he said: "that you should find this thief," such was his word, "and get from him, willing or no, a little ring, the least of rings, that once he stole. It is but a trifle that Sauron fancies, and an earnest of your good will. Find it, and three rings that the Dwarf-sires possessed of old shall be returned to you, and the realm of Moria shall be yours for ever. Find only news of the thief, whether he still lives and where, and you shall have great reward and lasting friendship from the Lord. Refuse, and things will not seem so well. Do you refuse?"

'At that his breath came like the hiss of snakes, and all who stood by shuddered, but Dáin said: "I say neither yea nor nay. I must consider this message and what it means under its fair cloak."

'"Consider well, but not too long," said·he.

'"The time of my thought is my own to spend," answered Dáin.

'"For the present," said he, and rode into the darkness.

'Heavy have the hearts of our chieftains been since that night. We needed not the fell voice of the messenger to warn us that his words held both menace and deceit; for we knew already that the power that has re-entered Mordor has not changed, and ever it betrayed us of old. Twice the messenger has returned, and has gone unanswered. The third and last time, so he says, is soon to come, before the ending of the year.

'And so I have been sent at last by Dáin to warn Bilbo that he is sought by the Enemy, and to learn, if may be, why he desires this ring, this least of rings. Also we crave the advice of Elrond. For the Shadow grows and draws nearer. We discover that messengers have come also to King Brand in Dale, and that he is afraid. We fear that he may yield. Already war is gathering on his eastern borders. If we make no answer, the Enemy may move Men of his rule to assail King Brand, and Dáin also.'

'You have done well to come,' said Elrond. 'You will hear today all that you need in order to understand the purposes of the Enemy. There is naught that you can do, other than to resist, with hope or without it. But you do not stand alone. You will learn that your trouble is but part of the trouble of all the western world. The Ring! What shall we do with the Ring, the least of rings, the trifle that Sauron fancies? That is the doom that we must deem.

'That is the purpose for which you are called hither. Called, I say, though I have not called you to me, strangers from distant lands. You have come and are here met, in this very nick of time, by chance as it may seem. Yet it is not so. Believe rather that it is so ordered that we, who sit here, and none others, must now find counsel for the peril of the world.

'Now, therefore, things shall be openly spoken that have been hidden from all but a few until this day. And first, so that all may understand what is the peril, the Tale of the Ring shall be told from the beginning even to this present. And I will begin that tale, though others shall end it.'

Then all listened while Elrond in his clear voice spoke of Sauron and the Rings of Power, and their forging in the Second Age of the world long ago. A part of his tale was known to some there, but the full tale to none, and many eyes were turned to Elrond in fear and wonder as he told of the Elven-smiths of Eregion and their friendship with Moria, and their eagerness for knowledge, by which Sauron ensnared them. For in that time he was not yet evil to behold, and they received his aid and grew mighty in craft, whereas he learned all their secrets, and betrayed them, and forged secretly in the Mountain of Fire the One Ring to be their master. But Celebrimbor was aware of him, and hid the Three which he had made; and there was war, and the land was laid waste, and the gate of Moria was shut.

Then through all the years that followed he traced the Ring; but since that history is elsewhere recounted, even as Elrond himself set it down in his books of lore, it is not here recalled. For it is a long tale, full of deeds great and terrible, and briefly though Elrond spoke, the sun rode up the sky, and the morning was passing ere he ceased.

Of Númenor he spoke, its glory and its fall, and the return of the Kings of Men to Middle-earth out of the deeps of the Sea, borne upon the wings of storm. Then Elendil the Tall and his mighty sons, Isildur and Anárion, became great lords; and the North-realm they made in Arnor, and the South-realm in Gondor above the mouths of Anduin. But Sauron of Mordor assailed them, and they made the Last Alliance of Elves and Men, and the hosts of Gil-galad and Elendil were mustered in Arnor.

Thereupon Elrond paused a while and sighed. 'I remember well the splendour of their banners,' he said. 'It recalled to me the glory of the Elder Days and the hosts of Beleriand, so many great princes and captains were assembled. And yet not so many, nor so fair, as when Thangorodrim was broken, and the Elves deemed that evil was ended for ever, and it was not so.'

'You remember?' said Frodo, speaking his thought aloud in his astonishment. 'But I thought,' he stammered as Elrond turned towards him, 'I thought that the fall of Gil-galad was a long age ago.'

'So it was indeed,' answered Elrond gravely. 'But my memory reaches back even to the Elder Days. Eärendil was my sire, who was born in Gondolin before its fall; and my mother was Elwing, daughter of Dior, son of Lúthien of Doriath. I have seen three ages in the West of the world, and many defeats, and many fruitless victories.

'I was the herald of Gil-galad and marched with his host. I was at the Battle of Dagorlad before the Black Gate of Mordor, where we had the mastery: for the Spear of Gil-galad and the Sword of Elendil, Aiglos and Narsil, none could withstand. I beheld the last combat on the slopes of Orodruin, where Gil-galad died, and Elendil fell, and Narsil broke beneath him; but Sauron himself was overthrown, and Isildur cut the Ring from his hand with the hilt-shard of his father's sword, and took it for his own.'

At this the stranger, Boromir, broke in. 'So that is what became of the Ring!' he cried. 'If ever such a tale was told in the South, it has long been forgotten. I have heard of the Great Ring of him that we do not name; but we believed that it perished from the world in the ruin of his first realm. Isildur took it! That is tidings indeed.'

'Alas! yes,' said Elrond. 'Isildur took it, as should not have been. It should have been cast then into Orodruin's fire nigh at hand where it was made. But few marked what Isildur did. He alone stood by his father in that last mortal contest; and by Gil-galad only Círdan stood, and I. But Isildur would not listen to our counsel.

'"This I will have as weregild for my father, and my brother," he said; and therefore whether we would or no, he took it to treasure it. But soon he was betrayed by it to his death; and so it is named in the North Isildur's Bane. Yet death maybe was better than what else might have befallen him.

'Only to the North did these tidings come, and only to a few. Small wonder it is that you have not heard them, Boromir. From the ruin of the Gladden Fields, where Isildur perished, three men only came ever back over the mountains after long wandering. One of these was Ohtar, the esquire of Isildur, who bore the shards of the sword of Elendil; and he brought them to Valandil, the heir of Isildur, who being but a child had remained here in Rivendell. But Narsil was broken and its light extinguished, and it has not yet been forged again.

'Fruitless did I call the victory of the Last Alliance? Not wholly so, yet it did not achieve its end. Sauron was diminished, but not destroyed. His Ring was lost but not unmade. The Dark Tower was broken, but its foundations were not removed; for they were made with the power of the Ring, and while it remains they will endure. Many Elves and many mighty Men, and many of their friends, had perished in the war. Anárion was slain, and Isildur was slain; and Gil-galad and Elendil were no more. Never again shall there be any such league of Elves and Men; for Men multiply and the Firstborn decrease, and the two kindreds are estranged. And ever since that day the race of Númenor has decayed, and the span of their years has lessened.

'In the North after the war and the slaughter of the Gladden Fields the Men of Westernesse were diminished, and their city of Annúminas beside Lake Evendim fell into ruin; and the heirs of Valandil removed and dwelt at Fornost on the high North Downs, and that now too is desolate. Men call it Deadmen's Dike, and they fear to tread there. For the folk of Arnor dwindled, and their foes devoured them, and their lordship passed, leaving only green mounds in the grassy hills.

'In the South the realm of Gondor long endured; and for a while its splendour grew, recalling somewhat of the might of Númenor, ere it fell. High towers that people built, and strong places, and havens of many ships; and the winged crown of the Kings of Men was held in awe by folk of many tongues. Their chief city was Osgiliath, Citadel of the Stars, through the midst of which the River flowed. And Minas Ithil they built, Tower of the Rising Moon, eastward upon a shoulder of the Mountains of Shadow; and westward at the feet of the White Mountains Minas Anor they made, Tower of the Setting Sun. There in the courts of the King grew a white tree, from the seed of that tree which Isildur brought over the deep waters, and the seed of that tree before came from Eressëa, and before that out of the Uttermost West in the Day before days when the world was young.

'But in the wearing of the swift years of Middle-earth the line of Meneldil son of Anárion failed, and the Tree withered, and the blood of the Númenoreans became mingled with that of lesser men. Then the watch upon the walls of Mordor slept, and dark things crept back to Gorgoroth. And on a time evil things came forth, and they took Minas Ithil and abode in it, and they made it into a place of dread; and it is called Minas Morgul, the Tower of Sorcery. Then Minas Anor was named anew Minas Tirith, the Tower of Guard; and these two cities were ever at war, but Osgiliath which lay between was deserted and in its ruins shadows walked.

'So it has been for many lives of men. But the Lords of Minas Tirith still fight on, defying our enemies, keeping the passage of the River from Argonath to the Sea. And now that part of the tale that I shall tell is drawn to its close. For in the days of Isildur the Ruling Ring passed out of all knowledge, and the Three were released from its dominion. But now in this latter day they are in peril once more, for to our sorrow the One has been found. Others shall speak of its finding, for in that I played small part.'

He ceased, but at once Boromir stood up, tall and proud, before them. 'Give me leave, Master Elrond,' said he, 'first to say more of Gondor, for verily from the land of Gondor I am come. And it would be well for all to know what passes there. For few, I deem, know of our deeds, and therefore guess little of their peril, if we should fail at last.

'Believe not that in the land of Gondor the blood of Númenor is spent, nor all its pride and dignity forgotten. By our valour the wild folk of the East are still restrained, and the terror of Morgul kept at bay; and thus alone are peace and freedom maintained in the lands behind us, bulwark of the West. But if the passages of the River should be won, what then?

'Yet that hour, maybe, is not now far away. The Nameless Enemy has arisen again. Smoke rises once more from Orodruin that we call Mount Doom. The power of the Black Land grows and we are hard beset. When the Enemy returned our folk were driven from Ithilien, our fair domain east of the River, though we kept a foothold there and strength of arms. But this very year, in the days of June, sudden war came upon us out of Mordor, and we were swept away. We were outnumbered, for Mordor has allied itself with the Easterlings and the cruel Haradrim; but it was not by numbers that we were defeated. A power was there that we have not felt before.

'Some said that it could be seen, like a great black horseman, a dark shadow under the moon. Wherever he came a madness filled our foes, but fear fell on our boldest, so that horse and man gave way and fled. Only a remnant of our eastern force came back, destroying the last bridge that still stood amid the ruins of Osgiliath.

'I was in the company that held the bridge, until it was cast down behind us. Four only were saved by swimming: my brother and myself and two others. But still we fight on, holding all the west shores of Anduin; and those who shelter behind us give us praise, if ever they hear our name: much praise but little help. Only from Rohan now will any men ride to us when we call.

'In this evil hour I have come on an errand over many dangerous leagues to Elrond: a hundred and ten days I have journeyed all alone. But I do not seek allies in war. The might of Elrond is in wisdom not in weapons, it is said. I come to ask for counsel and the unravelling of hard words. For on the eve of the sudden assault a dream came to my brother in a troubled sleep; and afterwards a like dream came oft to him again, and once to me.

'In that dream I thought the eastern sky grew dark and there was a growing thunder, but in the West a pale light lingered, and out of it I heard a voice, remote but clear, crying:

> Seek for the Sword that was broken:
>   In Imladris it dwells;
> There shall be counsels taken
>   Stronger than Morgul-spells.
> There shall be shown a token
>   That Doom is near at hand,
> For Isildur's Bane shall waken,
>   And the Halfling forth shall stand.

Of these words we could understand little, and we spoke to our father, Denethor, Lord of Minas Tirith, wise in the lore of Gondor. This only would he say, that Imladris was of old the name among the Elves of a far northern dale, where Elrond the Halfelven dwelt, greatest of lore-masters. Therefore my brother, seeing how desperate was our need, was eager to heed the dream and seek for Imladris; but since the way was full of doubt and danger, I took the journey upon myself. Loth was my father to give me leave, and long have I wandered by roads forgotten, seeking the house of Elrond, of which many had heard, but few knew where it lay.'

'And here in the house of Elrond more shall be made clear to you,' said Aragorn, standing up. He cast his sword upon the table that stood before Elrond, and the blade was in two pieces. 'Here is the Sword that was Broken!' he said.

'And who are you, and what have you to do with Minas Tirith?' asked Boromir, looking in wonder at the lean face of the Ranger and his weather-stained cloak.

'He is Aragorn son of Arathorn,' said Elrond; 'and he is descended through many fathers from Isildur Elendil's son of Minas Ithil. He is the Chief of the Dúnedain in the North, and few are now left of that folk.'

'Then it belongs to you, and not to me at all!' cried Frodo in amazement, springing to his feet, as if he expected the Ring to be demanded at once.

'It does not belong to either of us,' said Aragorn; 'but it has been ordained that you should hold it for a while.'

'Bring out the Ring, Frodo!' said Gandalf solemnly. 'The time has come. Hold it up, and then Boromir will understand the remainder of his riddle.'

There was a hush, and all turned their eyes on Frodo. He was shaken by a sudden shame and fear; and he felt a great reluctance to reveal the Ring, and a loathing of its touch. He wished he was far away. The Ring gleamed and flickered as he held it up before them in his trembling hand.

'Behold Isildur's Bane!' said Elrond.

Boromir's eyes glinted as he gazed at the golden thing. 'The Halfling!' he muttered. 'Is then the doom of Minas Tirith come at last? But why then should we seek a broken sword?'

'The words were not *the doom of Minas Tirith*,' said Aragorn. 'But doom and great deeds are indeed at hand. For the Sword that was Broken is the Sword of Elendil that broke beneath him when he fell. It has been treasured by his heirs when all other heirlooms were lost; for it was spoken of old among us that it should be made again when the Ring, Isildur's Bane, was found. Now you have seen the sword that you have sought, what would you ask? Do you wish for the House of Elendil to return to the Land of Gondor?'

'I was not sent to beg any boon, but to seek only the meaning of a riddle,' answered Boromir proudly. 'Yet we are hard pressed, and the Sword of Elendil would be a help beyond our hope – if such a thing could indeed return out of the shadows of the past.' He looked again at Aragorn, and doubt was in his eyes.

Frodo felt Bilbo stir impatiently at his side. Evidently he was annoyed on his friend's behalf. Standing suddenly up he burst out:

> *All that is gold does not glitter,*
> *Not all those who wander are lost;*
> *The old that is strong does not wither,*
> *Deep roots are not reached by the frost.*

> *From the ashes a fire shall be woken,*
> *A light from the shadows shall spring;*
> *Renewed shall be blade that was broken:*
> *The crownless again shall be king.*

'Not very good perhaps, but to the point – if you need more beyond the word of Elrond. If that was worth a journey of a hundred and ten days to hear, you had best listen to it.' He sat down with a snort.

'I made that up myself,' he whispered to Frodo, 'for the Dúnadan, a long time ago when he first told me about himself. I almost wish that my adventures were not over, and that I could go with him when his day comes.'

Aragorn smiled at him; then he turned to Boromir again. 'For my part I forgive your doubt,' he said. 'Little do I resemble the figures of Elendil and Isildur as they stand carven in their majesty in the halls of Denethor. I am but the heir of Isildur, not Isildur himself. I have had a hard life and a long; and the leagues that lie between here and Gondor are a small part in the count of my journeys. I have crossed many mountains and many rivers, and trodden many plains, even into the far countries of Rhûn and Harad where the stars are strange.

'But my home, such as I have, is in the North. For here the heirs of Valandil have ever dwelt in long line unbroken from father unto son for many generations. Our days have darkened, and we have dwindled; but ever the Sword has passed to a new keeper. And this I will say to you, Boromir, ere I end. Lonely men are we, Rangers of the wild, hunters – but hunters ever of the servants of the Enemy; for they are found in many places, not in Mordor only.

'If Gondor, Boromir, has been a stalwart tower, we have played another part. Many evil things there are that your strong walls and bright swords do not stay. You know little of the lands beyond your bounds. Peace and freedom, do you say? The North would have known them little but for us. Fear would have destroyed them. But when dark things come from the houseless hills, or creep from sunless woods, they fly from us. What roads would any dare to tread, what safety would there be in quiet lands, or in the homes of simple men at night, if the Dúnedain were asleep, or were all gone into the grave?

'And yet less thanks have we than you. Travellers scowl at us, and countrymen give us scornful names. "Strider" I am to one fat man who lives within a day's march of foes that would freeze his heart, or lay his little town in ruin, if he were not guarded ceaselessly. Yet we would not have it otherwise. If simple folk are free from care and fear, simple they will be, and we must be secret to keep them so. That has been the task of my kindred, while the years have lengthened and the grass has grown.

'But now the world is changing once again. A new hour comes. Isildur's Bane is found. Battle is at hand. The Sword shall be reforged. I will come to Minas Tirith.'

'Isildur's Bane is found, you say,' said Boromir. 'I have seen a bright ring in the Halfling's hand; but Isildur perished ere this age of the world began, they say. How do the Wise know that this ring is his? And how has it passed down the years, until it is brought hither by so strange a messenger?'

'That shall be told,' said Elrond.

'But not yet, I beg, Master!' said Bilbo. 'Already the Sun is climbing to noon, and I feel the need of something to strengthen me.'

'I had not named you,' said Elrond smiling. 'But I do so now. Come! Tell us your tale. And if you have not yet cast your story into verse, you may tell it in plain words. The briefer, the sooner shall you be refreshed.'

'Very well,' said Bilbo. 'I will do as you bid. But I will now tell the true story, and if some here have heard me tell it otherwise' – he looked sidelong at Glóin – 'I ask them to forget it and forgive me. I only wished to claim the treasure as my very own in those days, and to be rid of the name of thief that was put on me. But perhaps I understand things a little better now. Anyway, this is what happened.'

To some there Bilbo's tale was wholly new, and they listened with amazement while the old hobbit, actually not at all displeased, recounted his adventure with Gollum, at full length. He did not omit a single riddle. He would have given also an account of his party and disappearance from the Shire, if he had been allowed; but Elrond raised his hand.

'Well told, my friend,' he said, 'but that is enough at this time. For the moment it suffices to know that the Ring passed to Frodo, your heir. Let him now speak!'

Then, less willingly than Bilbo, Frodo told of all his dealings with the Ring from the day that it passed into his keeping. Every step of his journey from Hobbiton to the Ford of Bruinen was questioned and considered, and everything that he could recall concerning the Black Riders was examined. At last he sat down again.

'Not bad,' Bilbo said to him. 'You would have made a good story of it, if they hadn't kept on interrupting. I tried to make a few notes, but we shall have to go over it all again together some time, if I am to write it up. There are whole chapters of stuff before you ever got here!'

'Yes, it made quite a long tale,' answered Frodo. 'But the story still does not seem complete to me. I still want to know a good deal, especially about Gandalf.'

Galdor of the Havens, who sat near by, overheard him. 'You speak for me also,' he cried, and turning to Elrond he said: 'The Wise may have good reason to believe that the halfling's trove is indeed the Great Ring of long debate, unlikely though that may seem to those who know less. But may we not hear the proofs? And I would ask this also. What of Saruman? He is learned in the lore of the Rings, yet he is not among us. What is his counsel – if he knows the things that we have heard?'

'The questions that you ask, Galdor, are bound together,' said Elrond. 'I had not overlooked them, and they shall be answered. But these things it is the part of Gandalf to make clear; and I call upon him last, for it is the place of honour, and in all this matter he has been the chief.'

'Some, Galdor,' said Gandalf, 'would think the tidings of Glóin, and the pursuit of Frodo, proof enough that the halfling's trove is a thing of great worth to the Enemy. Yet it is a ring. What then? The Nine the Nazgûl keep. The Seven are taken or destroyed.' At this Glóin stirred, but did not speak. 'The Three we know of. What then is this one that he desires so much?

'There is indeed a wide waste of time between the River and the Mountain, between the loss and the finding. But the gap in the knowledge of the Wise has been filled at last. Yet too slowly. For the Enemy has been close behind, closer even than I feared. And well is it that not until this year, this very summer, as it seems, did he learn the full truth.

'Some here will remember that many years ago I myself dared to pass the doors of the Necromancer in Dol Guldur, and secretly explored his ways, and found thus that our fears were true: he was none other than Sauron, our Enemy of old, at length taking shape and power again. Some, too, will remember also that Saruman dissuaded us from open deeds against him, and for long we watched him only. Yet at last, as his shadow grew, Saruman yielded, and the Council put forth its strength and drove the evil out of Mirkwood – and that was in the very year of the finding of this Ring: a strange chance, if chance it was.

'But we were too late, as Elrond foresaw. Sauron also had watched us, and had long prepared against our stroke, governing Mordor from afar through Minas Morgul, where his Nine servants dwelt, until all was ready. Then he gave way before us, but only feigned to flee, and soon after came to the Dark Tower and openly declared himself. Then for the last time the Council met; for now we learned that he was seeking ever more eagerly for the One. We feared then that he had some news of it that we knew nothing of. But Saruman said nay, and repeated what he had said to us before: that the One would never again be found in Middle-earth.

' "At the worst," said he, "our Enemy knows that we have it not, and that it still is lost. But what was lost may yet be found, he thinks. Fear not! His hope will cheat him. Have I not earnestly studied this matter? Into Anduin the Great it fell; and long ago, while Sauron slept, it was rolled down the River to the Sea. There let it lie until the End." '

Gandalf fell silent, gazing eastward from the porch to the far peaks of the Misty Mountains, at whose great roots the peril of the world had so long lain hidden. He sighed.

'There I was at fault,' he said. 'I was lulled by the words of Saruman the Wise; but I should have sought for the truth sooner, and our peril would now be less.'

'We were all at fault,' said Elrond, 'and but for your vigilance the Darkness, maybe, would already be upon us. But say on!'

'From the first my heart misgave me, against all reason that I knew,' said Gandalf, 'and I desired to know how this thing came to Gollum, and how long he had possessed it. So I set a watch for him, guessing that he would ere long come forth from his darkness to seek for his treasure. He came, but he escaped and was not found. And then alas! I let the matter rest, watching and waiting only, as we have too often done.

'Time passed with many cares, until my doubts were awakened again to sudden fear. Whence came the hobbit's ring? What, if my fear was true, should be done with it? Those things I must decide. But I spoke yet of my dread to none, knowing the peril of an untimely whisper, if it went astray. In all the long wars with the Dark Tower treason has ever been our greatest foe.

'That was seventeen years ago. Soon I became aware that spies of many sorts, even beasts and birds, were gathered round the Shire, and my fear grew. I called for the help of the Dúnedain, and their watch was doubled; and I opened my heart to Aragorn, the heir of Isildur.'

'And I,' said Aragorn, 'counselled that we should hunt for Gollum, too late though it may seem. And since it seemed fit that Isildur's heir should labour to repair Isildur's fault, I went with Gandalf on the long and hopeless search.'

Then Gandalf told how they had explored the whole length of Wilderland, down even to the Mountains of Shadow and the fences of Mordor. 'There we had rumour of him, and we guess that he dwelt there long in the dark hills; but we never found him, and at last I despaired. And then in my despair I thought again of a test that might make the finding of Gollum unneeded. The ring itself might tell if it were the One. The memory of words at the Council came back to me: words of Saruman, half-heeded at the time. I heard them now clearly in my heart.

'"The Nine, the Seven, and the Three," he said, "had each their proper gem. Not so the One. It was round and unadorned, as it were one of the lesser rings; but its maker set marks upon it that the skilled, maybe, could still see and read."

'What those marks were he had not said. Who now would know? The maker. And Saruman? But great though his lore may be, it must have a source. What hand save Sauron's ever held this thing, ere it was lost? The hand of Isildur alone.

'With that thought, I forsook the chase, and passed swiftly to Gondor. In former days the members of my order had been well received there, but Saruman most of all. Often he had been for long the guest of the Lords of the City. Less welcome did the Lord Denethor show me then than of old, and grudgingly he permitted me to search among his hoarded scrolls and books.

'"If indeed you look only, as you say, for records of ancient days, and the beginnings of the City, read on!" he said. "For to me what was is less dark than what is to come, and that is my care. But unless you have more skill even than Saruman, who has studied here long, you will find naught that is not well known to me, who am master of the lore of this City."

'So said Denethor. And yet there lie in his hoards many records that few now can read, even of the lore-masters, for their scripts and tongues have become dark to later men. And Boromir, there lies in Minas Tirith still, unread, I guess, by any save Saruman and myself since the kings failed, a scroll that Isildur made himself. For Isildur did not march away straight from the war in Mordor, as some have told the tale.'

'Some in the North, maybe,' Boromir broke in. 'All know in Gondor that he went first to Minas Anor and dwelt a while with his nephew Meneldil, instructing him, before he committed to him the rule of the South Kingdom. In that time he planted there the last sapling of the White Tree in memory of his brother.'

'But in that time also he made this scroll,' said Gandalf; 'and that is not remembered in Gondor, it would seem. For this scroll concerns the Ring, and thus wrote Isildur therein:

The Great Ring shall go now to be an heirloom of the North Kingdom; but records of it shall be left in Gondor, where also dwell the heirs of Elendil, lest a time come when the memory of these great matters shall grow dim.

'And after these words Isildur described the Ring, such as he found it.

It was hot when I first took it, hot as a glede, and my hand was scorched, so that I doubt if ever again I shall be free of the pain of it. Yet even as I write it is cooled, and it seemeth to shrink, though it loseth neither its beauty nor its shape. Already the writing upon it, which at first was as clear as red flame, fadeth and is now only barely to be read. It is fashioned in an elven-script of Eregion, for they have no letters in Mordor for such subtle work; but the language is unknown to me. I deem it to be a tongue of the Black Land, since it is foul and uncouth. What evil it saith I do not know; but I trace here a copy of it, lest it fade beyond recall. The Ring misseth, maybe, the heat of Sauron's hand, which was black and yet burned like fire, and so Gil-galad was destroyed; and maybe were the gold made hot again, the writing would be refreshed. But for my part I will risk no hurt to this thing: of all the works of Sauron the only fair. It is precious to me, though I buy it with great pain.

'When I read these words, my quest was ended. For the traced writing was indeed as Isildur guessed, in the tongue of Mordor and the servants of the Tower. And what was said therein was already known. For in the day that Sauron first put on the One, Celebrimbor, maker of the Three, was aware of him, and from afar he heard him speak these words, and so his evil purposes were revealed.

'At once I took my leave of Denethor, but even as I went northwards, messages came to me out of Lórien that Aragorn had passed that way, and that he had found the creature called Gollum. Therefore I went first to meet him and hear his tale. Into what deadly perils he had gone alone I dared not guess.'

'There is little need to tell of them,' said Aragorn. 'If a man must needs walk in sight of the Black Gate, or tread the deadly flowers of Morgul Vale, then perils he will have. I, too, despaired at last, and I began my homeward journey. And then, by fortune, I came suddenly on what I sought: the marks of soft feet beside a muddy pool. But now the trail was fresh and swift, and it led not to Mordor but away. Along the skirts of the Dead Marshes I followed it, and then I had him. Lurking by a stagnant mere, peering in the water as the dark eve fell, I caught him, Gollum. He was covered with green slime. He will never love me, I fear; for he bit me, and I was not gentle. Nothing more did I ever get from his mouth than the marks of his teeth. I deemed it the worst part of all my journey, the road back, watching him day and night, making him walk before me with a halter on his neck, gagged, until he was tamed by lack of drink and food, driving him ever towards Mirkwood. I brought him there at last and gave him to the Elves, for we had agreed that this should be done; and I was glad to be rid of his company, for he stank. For my part I hope never to look upon him again; but Gandalf came and endured long speech with him.'

'Yes, long and weary,' said Gandalf, 'but not without profit. For one thing, the tale he told of his loss agreed with that which Bilbo has now told openly for the first time; but that mattered little, since I had already guessed it. But I learned then first that Gollum's ring came out of the Great River nigh to the Gladden Fields. And I learned also that he had possessed it long. Many lives of his small kind. The power of the ring had lengthened his years far beyond their span; but that power only the Great Rings wield.

'And if that is not proof enough, Galdor, there is the other test that I spoke of. Upon this very ring which you have here seen held aloft, round and unadorned, the letters that Isildur reported may still be read, if one has the strength of will to set the golden thing in the fire a while. That I have done, and this I have read:

*Ash nazg durbatulûk, ash nazg gimbatul, ash nazg thrakatulûk
agh burzum-ishi krimpatul.*'

The change in the wizard's voice was astounding. Suddenly it became menacing, powerful, harsh as stone. A shadow seemed to pass over the high sun, and the porch for a moment grew dark. All trembled, and the Elves stopped their ears.

'Never before has any voice dared to utter words of that tongue in Imladris, Gandalf the Grey,' said Elrond, as the shadow passed and the company breathed once more.

'And let us hope that none will ever speak it here again,' answered Gandalf. 'Nonetheless I do not ask your pardon, Master Elrond. For if that tongue is not soon to be heard in every corner of the West, then let all put doubt aside that this thing is indeed what the Wise have declared: the treasure of the Enemy, fraught with all his malice; and in it lies a great part of his strength of old. Out of the Black Years come the words that the Smiths of Eregion heard, and knew that they had been betrayed:

> One Ring to rule them all, One Ring to find them, One Ring to
> bring them all and in the Darkness bind them.

'Know also, my friends, that I learned more yet from Gollum. He was loth to speak and his tale was unclear, but it is beyond all doubt that he went to Mordor, and there all that he knew was forced from him. Thus the Enemy knows now that the One is found, that it was long in the Shire; and since his servants have pursued it almost to our door, he soon will know, already he may know, even as I speak, that we have it here.'

All sat silent for a while, until at length Boromir spoke. 'He is a small thing, you say, this Gollum? Small, but great in mischief. What became of him? To what doom did you put him?'

'He is in prison, but no worse,' said Aragorn. 'He had suffered much. There is no doubt that he was tormented, and the fear of Sauron lies black on his heart. Still I for one am glad that he is safely kept by the watchful Elves of Mirkwood. His malice is great and gives him a strength hardly to be believed in one so lean and withered. He could work much mischief still, if he were free. And I do not doubt that he was allowed to leave Mordor on some evil errand.'

'Alas! alas!' cried Legolas, and in his fair elvish face there was great distress. 'The tidings that I was sent to bring must now be told. They are not good, but only here have I learned how evil they may seem to this company. Sméagol, who is now called Gollum, has escaped.'

'Escaped?' cried Aragorn. 'That is ill news indeed. We shall all rue it bitterly, I fear. How came the folk of Thranduil to fail in their trust?'

'Not through lack of watchfulness,' said Legolas; 'but perhaps through over-kindliness. And we fear that the prisoner had aid from others, and that more is known of our doings than we could wish. We guarded this creature day and night, at Gandalf's bidding, much though we wearied of the task. But Gandalf bade us hope still for his cure, and we had not the heart to keep him ever in dungeons under the earth, where he would fall back into his old black thoughts.'

'You were less tender to me,' said Glóin with a flash of his eyes, as old memories were stirred of his imprisonment in the deep places of the Elven-king's halls.

'Now come!' said Gandalf. 'Pray do not interrupt, my good Glóin. That was a regrettable misunderstanding, long set right. If all the grievances that stand between Elves and Dwarves are to be brought up here, we may as well abandon this Council.'

Glóin rose and bowed, and Legolas continued. 'In the days of fair weather we led Gollum through the woods; and there was a high tree standing alone far from the others which he liked to climb. Often we let him mount up to the highest branches, until he felt the free wind; but we set a guard at the tree's foot. One day he refused to come down, and the guards had no mind to climb after him: he had learned the trick of clinging to boughs with his feet as well as with his hands; so they sat by the tree far into the night.

'It was that very night of summer, yet moonless and starless, that Orcs came on us at unawares. We drove them off after some time; they were many and fierce, but they came from over the mountains, and were unused to the woods. When the battle was over, we found that Gollum was gone, and his guards were slain or taken. It then seemed plain to us that the attack had been made for his rescue, and that he knew of it beforehand. How that was contrived we cannot guess; but Gollum is cunning, and the spies of the Enemy are many. The dark things that were driven out in the year of the Dragon's fall have returned in greater numbers, and Mirkwood is again an evil place, save where our realm is maintained.

'We have failed to recapture Gollum. We came on his trail among those of many Orcs, and it plunged deep into the Forest, going south. But ere long it escaped our skill, and we dared not continue the hunt; for we were drawing nigh to Dol Guldur, and that is still a very evil place; we do not go that way.'

'Well, well, he is gone,' said Gandalf. 'We have no time to seek for him again. He must do what he will. But he may play a part yet that neither he nor Sauron have foreseen.

'And now I will answer Galdor's other questions. What of Saruman? What are his counsels to us in this need? This tale I must tell in full, for only Elrond has heard it yet, and that in brief; but it will bear on all that we must resolve. It is the last chapter in the Tale of the Ring, so far as it has yet gone.

'At the end of June I was in the Shire, but a cloud of anxiety was on my mind, and I rode to the southern borders of the little land; for I had a foreboding of some danger, still hidden from me but drawing near. There messages reached me telling me of war and defeat in Gondor, and when I heard of the Black Shadow a chill smote my heart. But I found nothing save a few fugitives from the South; yet it seemed to me that on them sat a fear of which they would not speak. I turned then east and north and journeyed along the Greenway; and not far from Bree I came upon a traveller sitting on a bank beside the road with his grazing horse beside him. It was Radagast the Brown, who at one time dwelt at Rhosgobel, near the borders of Mirkwood. He is one of my order, but I had not seen him for many a year.

'"Gandalf!" he cried. "I was seeking you. But I am a stranger in these parts. All I knew was that you might be found in a wild region with the uncouth name of Shire."

'"Your information was correct," I said. "But do not put it that way, if you meet any of the inhabitants. You are near the borders of the Shire now. And what do you want with me? It must be pressing. You were never a traveller, unless driven by great need."

'"I have an urgent errand," he said. "My news is evil." Then he looked about him, as if the hedges might have ears. "Nazgûl," he whispered. "The Nine are abroad again. They have crossed the River secretly and are moving westward. They have taken the guise of riders in black."

'I knew then what I had dreaded without knowing it.

'"The Enemy must have some great need or purpose," said Radagast; "but what it is that makes him look to these distant and desolate parts, I cannot guess."

'"What do you mean?" said I.

'"I have been told that wherever they go the Riders ask for news of a land called Shire."

'"The Shire," I said; but my heart sank. For even the Wise might fear to withstand the Nine, when they are gathered together under their fell chieftain. A great king and sorcerer he was of old, and now he wields a deadly fear. "Who told you, and who sent you?" I asked.

'"Saruman the White," answered Radagast. "And he told me to say that if you feel the need, he will help; but you must seek his aid at once, or it will be too late."

'And that message brought me hope. For Saruman the White is the greatest of my order. Radagast is, of course, a worthy Wizard, a master of shapes and changes of hue; and he has much lore of herbs and beasts, and birds are especially his friends. But Saruman has long studied the arts of the Enemy himself, and thus we have often been able to forestall him. It was by the devices of Saruman that we drove him from Dol Guldur. It might be that he had found some weapons that would drive back the Nine.

'"I will go to Saruman," I said.

'"Then you must go *now*," said Radagast; "for I have wasted time in looking for you, and the days are running short. I was told to find you before Midsummer, and that is now here. Even if you set out from this spot, you will hardly reach him before the Nine discover the land that they seek. I myself shall turn back at once." And with that he mounted and would have ridden straight off.

'"Stay a moment!" I said. "We shall need your help, and the help of all things that will give it. Send out messages to all the beasts and birds that are your friends. Tell them to bring news of anything that bears on this matter to Saruman and Gandalf. Let messages be sent to Orthanc."

'"I will do that," he said, and rode off as if the Nine were after him.

'I could not follow him then and there. I had ridden very far already that day, and I was as weary as my horse; and I needed to consider matters. I stayed the night in Bree, and decided that I had no time to return to the Shire. Never did I make a greater mistake!

'However, I wrote a message to Frodo, and trusted to my friend the innkeeper to send it to him. I rode away at dawn; and I came at long last to the dwelling of Saruman. That is far south in Isengard, in the end of the Misty Mountains, not far from the Gap of Rohan. And Boromir will tell you that that is a great open vale that lies between the Misty Mountains and the northmost foothills of Ered Nimrais, the White Mountains of his home. But Isengard is a circle of sheer rocks that enclose a valley as with a wall, and in the midst of that valley is a tower of stone called Orthanc. It was not made by Saruman, but by the Men of Númenor long ago; and it is very tall and has many secrets; yet it looks not to be a work of craft. It cannot be reached save by passing the circle of Isengard; and in that circle there is only one gate.

'Late one evening I came to the gate, like a great arch in the wall of rock; and it was strongly guarded. But the keepers of the gate were on the watch for me and told me that Saruman awaited me. I rode under the arch, and the gate closed silently behind me, and suddenly I was afraid, though I knew no reason for it.

'But I rode to the foot of Orthanc, and came to the stair of Saruman; and there he met me and led me up to his high chamber. He wore a ring on his finger.

' "So you have come, Gandalf," he said to me gravely; but in his eyes there seemed to be a white light, as if a cold laughter was in his heart.

' "Yes, I have come," I said. "I have come for your aid, Saruman the White." And that title seemed to anger him.

' "Have you indeed, Gandalf the *Grey*!" he scoffed. "For aid? It has seldom been heard of that Gandalf the Grey sought for aid, one so cunning and so wise, wandering about the lands, and concerning himself in every business, whether it belongs to him or not."

'I looked at him and wondered. "But if I am not deceived," said I, "things are now moving which will require the union of all our strength."

' "That may be so," he said, "but the thought is late in coming to you. How long, I wonder, have you concealed from me, the head of the Council, a matter of greatest import? What brings you now from your lurking-place in the Shire?"

' "The Nine have come forth again," I answered. "They have crossed the River. So Radagast said to me."

' "Radagast the Brown!" laughed Saruman, and he no longer concealed his scorn. "Radagast the Bird-tamer! Radagast the Simple! Radagast the Fool! Yet he had just the wit to play the part that I set him. For you have come, and that was all the purpose of my message. And here you will stay, Gandalf the Grey, and rest from journeys. For I am Saruman the Wise, Saruman Ring-maker, Saruman of Many Colours!"

'I looked then and saw that his robes, which had seemed white, were not so, but were woven of all colours, and if he moved they shimmered and changed hue so that the eye was bewildered.

' "I liked white better," I said.

' "White!" he sneered. "It serves as a beginning. White cloth may be dyed. The white page can be overwritten; and the white light can be broken."

' "In which case it is no longer white," said I. "And he that breaks a thing to find out what it is has left the path of wisdom."

' "You need not speak to me as to one of the fools that you take for friends," said he. "I have not brought you hither to be instructed by you, but to give you a choice."

'He drew himself up then and began to declaim, as if he were making a speech long rehearsed. "The Elder Days are gone. The Middle Days are passing. The Younger Days are beginning. The time of the Elves is over, but our time is at hand: the world of Men, which We must rule. But we must have power, power to order all things as we will, for that good which only the Wise can see.

' "And listen, Gandalf, my old friend and helper!" he said, coming near and speaking now in a softer voice. "I said *we*, for *we* it may be, if you will join with me. A new Power is rising. Against it the old allies and policies will not avail us at all. There is no hope left in Elves or dying Númenor. This then is one choice before you, before us. We may join with that Power. It would be wise, Gandalf. There is hope that way. Its victory is at hand; and there will be rich reward for those that aided it. As the Power grows, its proved friends will also grow; and the Wise, such as you and I, may with patience come at last to direct its courses, to control it. We can bide our time, we can keep our thoughts in our hearts, deploring maybe evils done by the way, but approving the high and ultimate purpose: Knowledge, Rule, Order; all the things that we have so far striven in vain to accomplish, hindered rather than helped by our weak or idle friends. There need not be, there would not be, any real change in our designs, only in our means."

'"Saruman," I said, "I have heard speeches of this kind before, but only in the mouths of emissaries sent from Mordor to deceive the ignorant. I cannot think that you brought me so far only to weary my ears."

'He looked at me sidelong, and paused a while considering. "Well, I see that this wise course does not commend itself to you," he said. "Not yet? Not if some better way can be contrived?"

'He came and laid his long hand on my arm. "And why not, Gandalf?" he whispered. "Why not? The Ruling Ring? If we could command that, then the Power would pass to *us*. That is in truth why I brought you here. For I have many eyes in my service, and I believe that you know where this precious thing now lies. Is it not so? Or why do the Nine ask for the Shire, and what is your business there?" As he said this a lust which he could not conceal shone suddenly in his eyes.

'"Saruman," I said, standing away from him, "only one hand at a time can wield the One, and you know that well, so do not trouble to say *we*! But I would not give it, nay, I would not give even news of it to you, now that I learn your mind. You were head of the Council, but you have unmasked yourself at last. Well, the choices are, it seems, to submit to Sauron, or to yourself. I will take neither. Have you others to offer?"

'He was cold now and perilous. "Yes," he said. "I did not expect you to show wisdom, even in your own behalf; but I gave you the chance of aiding me willingly, and so saving yourself much trouble and pain. The third choice is to stay here, until the end."

'"Until what end?"

'"Until you reveal to me where the One may be found. I may find means to persuade you. Or until it is found in your despite, and the Ruler has time to turn to lighter matters: to devise, say, a fitting reward for the hindrance and insolence of Gandalf the Grey."

' "That may not prove to be one of the lighter matters," said I. He laughed at me, for my words were empty, and he knew it.

'They took me and they set me alone on the pinnacle of Orthanc, in the place where Saruman was accustomed to watch the stars. There is no descent save by a narrow stair of many thousand steps, and the valley below seems far away. I looked on it and saw that, whereas it had once been green and fair, it was now filled with pits and forges. Wolves and orcs were housed in Isengard, for Saruman was mustering a great force on his own account, in rivalry of Sauron and not in his service yet. Over all his works a dark smoke hung and wrapped itself about the sides of Orthanc. I stood alone on an island in the clouds; and I had no chance of escape, and my days were bitter. I was pierced with cold, and I had but little room in which to pace to and fro, brooding on the coming of the Riders to the North.

'That the Nine had indeed arisen I felt assured, apart from the words of Saruman which might be lies. Long ere I came to Isengard I had heard tidings by the way that could not be mistaken. Fear was ever in my heart for my friends in the Shire; but still I had some hope. I hoped that Frodo had set forth at once, as my letter had urged, and that he had reached Rivendell before the deadly pursuit began. And both my fear and my hope proved ill-founded. For my hope was founded on a fat man in Bree; and my fear was founded on the cunning of Sauron. But fat men who sell ale have many calls to answer; and the power of Sauron is still less than fear makes it. But in the circle of Isengard, trapped and alone, it was not easy to think that the hunters before whom all have fled or fallen would falter in the Shire far away.'

'I saw you!' cried Frodo. 'You were walking backwards and forwards. The moon shone in your hair.'

Gandalf paused astonished and looked at him. 'It was only a dream,' said Frodo, 'but it suddenly came back to me. I had quite forgotten it. It came some time ago; after I left the Shire, I think.'

'Then it was late in coming,' said Gandalf, 'as you will see. I was in an evil plight. And those who know me will agree that I have seldom been in such need, and do not bear such misfortune well. Gandalf the Grey caught like a fly in a spider's treacherous web! Yet even the most subtle spiders may leave a weak thread.

'At first I feared, as Saruman no doubt intended, that Radagast had also fallen. Yet I had caught no hint of anything wrong in his voice or in his eye at our meeting. If I had, I should never have gone to Isengard, or I should have gone more warily. So Saruman guessed, and he had concealed his mind and deceived his messenger. It would have been useless in any case to try and win over the honest Radagast to treachery. He sought me in good faith, and so persuaded me.

'That was the undoing of Saruman's plot. For Radagast knew no reason why he should not do as I asked; and he rode away towards Mirkwood where he had many friends of old. And the Eagles of the Mountains went far and wide, and they saw many things: the gathering of wolves and the mustering of Orcs; and the Nine Riders going hither and thither in the lands; and they heard news of the escape of Gollum. And they sent a messenger to bring these tidings to me.

'So it was that when summer waned, there came a night of moon, and Gwaihir the Windlord, swiftest of the Great Eagles, came unlooked-for to Orthanc; and he found me standing on the pinnacle. Then I spoke to him and he bore me away, before Saruman was aware. I was far from Isengard, ere the wolves and orcs issued from the gate to pursue me.

' "How far can you bear me?" I said to Gwaihir.

' "Many leagues," said he, "but not to the ends of the earth. I was sent to bear tidings not burdens."

' "Then I must have a steed on land," I said, "and a steed surpassingly swift, for I have never had such need of haste before."

' "Then I will bear you to Edoras, where the Lord of Rohan sits in his halls," he said; "for that is not very far off." And I was glad, for in the Riddermark of Rohan the Rohirrim, the Horse-lords, dwell, and there are no horses like those that are bred in that great vale between the Misty Mountains and the White.

' "Are the Men of Rohan still to be trusted, do you think?" I said to Gwaihir, for the treason of Saruman had shaken my faith.

' "They pay a tribute of horses," he answered, "and send many yearly to Mordor, or so it is said; but they are not yet under the yoke. But if Saruman has become evil, as you say, then their doom cannot be long delayed."

'He set me down in the land of Rohan ere dawn; and now I have lengthened my tale over long. The rest must be more brief. In Rohan I found evil already at work: the lies of Saruman; and the king of the land would not listen to my warnings. He bade me take a horse and be gone; and I chose one much to my liking, but little to his. I took the best horse in his land, and I have never seen the like of him.'

'Then he must be a noble beast indeed,' said Aragorn; 'and it grieves me more than many tidings that might seem worse to learn that Sauron levies such tribute. It was not so when last I was in that land.'

'Nor is it now, I will swear,' said Boromir. 'It is a lie that comes from the Enemy. I know the Men of Rohan, true and valiant, our allies, dwelling still in the lands that we gave them long ago.'

'The shadow of Mordor lies on distant lands,' answered Aragorn. 'Saruman has fallen under it. Rohan is beset. Who knows what you will find there, if ever you return?'

'Not this at least,' said Boromir, 'that they will buy their lives with horses. They love their horses next to their kin. And not without reason, for the horses of the Riddermark come from the fields of the North, far from the Shadow, and their race, as that of their masters, is descended from the free days of old.'

'True indeed!' said Gandalf. 'And there is one among them that might have been foaled in the morning of the world. The horses of the Nine cannot vie with him; tireless, swift as the flowing wind. Shadowfax they called him. By day his coat glistens like silver; and by night it is like a shade, and he passes unseen. Light is his footfall! Never before had any man mounted him, but I took him and I tamed him, and so speedily he bore me that I reached the Shire when Frodo was on the Barrow-downs, though I set out from Rohan only when he set out from Hobbiton.

'But fear grew in me as I rode. Ever as I came north I heard tidings of the Riders, and though I gained on them day by day, they were ever before me. They had divided their forces, I learned: some remained on the eastern borders, not far from the Greenway, and some invaded the Shire from the south. I came to Hobbiton and Frodo had gone; but I had words with old Gamgee. Many words and few to the point. He had much to say about the shortcomings of the new owners of Bag End.

'"I can't abide changes," said he, "not at my time of life, and least of all changes for the worst." "Changes for the worst," he repeated many times.

'"Worst is a bad word," I said to him, "and I hope you do not live to see it." But amidst his talk I gathered at last that Frodo had left Hobbiton less than a week before, and that a black horseman had come to the Hill the same evening. Then I rode on in fear. I came to Buckland and found it in uproar, as busy as a hive of ants that has been stirred with a stick. I came to the house at Crickhollow, and it was broken open and empty; but on the threshold there lay a cloak that had been Frodo's. Then for a while hope left me, and I did not wait to gather news, or I might have been comforted; but I rode on the trail of the Riders. It was hard to follow, for it went many ways, and I was at a loss. But it seemed to me that one or two had ridden towards Bree; and that way I went, for I thought of words that might be said to the innkeeper.

'"Butterbur they call him," thought I. "If this delay was his fault, I will melt all the butter in him. I will roast the old fool over a slow fire." He expected no less, and when he saw my face he fell down flat and began to melt on the spot.'

'What did you do to him?' cried Frodo in alarm. 'He was really very kind to us and did all that he could.'

Gandalf laughed. 'Don't be afraid!' he said. 'I did not bite, and I barked very little. So overjoyed was I by the news that I got out of him, when he stopped quaking, that I embraced the old fellow. How it happened I could not then guess, but I learned that you had been in Bree the night before, and had gone off that morning with Strider.

' "Strider!" I cried, shouting for joy.

' "Yes, sir, I am afraid so, sir," said Butterbur, mistaking me. "He got at them, in spite of all that I could do, and they took up with him. They behaved very queer all the time they were here: wilful, you might say."

' "Ass! Fool! Thrice worthy and beloved Barliman!" said I. "It's the best news I have had since midsummer: it's worth a gold piece at the least. May your beer be laid under an enchantment of surpassing excellence for seven years!" said I. "Now I can take a night's rest, the first since I have forgotten when."

'So I stayed there that night, wondering much what had become of the Riders; for only of two had there yet been any news in Bree, it seemed. But in the night we heard more. Five at least came from the west, and they threw down the gates and passed through Bree like a howling wind; and the Bree-folk are still shivering and expecting the end of the world. I got up before dawn and went after them.

'I do not know, but it seems clear to me that this is what happened. Their Captain remained in secret away south of Bree, while two rode ahead through the village, and four more invaded the Shire. But when these were foiled in Bree and at Crickhollow, they returned to their Captain with tidings, and so left the Road unguarded for a while, except by their spies. The Captain then sent some eastward straight across country, and he himself with the rest rode along the Road in great wrath.

'I galloped to Weathertop like a gale, and I reached it before sundown on my second day from Bree – and they were there before me. They drew away from me, for they felt the coming of my anger and they dared not face it while the Sun was in the sky. But they closed round at night, and I was besieged on the hill-top, in the old ring of Amon Sûl. I was hard put to it indeed: such light and flame cannot have been seen on Weathertop since the war-beacons of old.

'At sunrise I escaped and fled towards the north. I could not hope to do more. It was impossible to find you, Frodo, in the wilderness, and it would have been folly to try with all the Nine at my heels. So I had to trust to Aragorn. But I hoped to draw some of them off, and yet reach Rivendell ahead of you and send out help. Four Riders did indeed follow me, but they turned back after a while and made for the Ford, it seems. That helped a little, for there were only five, not nine, when your camp was attacked.

'I reached here at last by a long hard road, up the Hoarwell and through the Ettenmoors, and down from the north. It took me nearly fourteen days from Weathertop, for I could not ride among the rocks of the troll-fells, and Shadowfax departed. I sent him back to his master; but a great friendship has grown between us, and if I have need he will come at my call. But so it was that I came to Rivendell only three days before the Ring, and news of its peril had already been brought here – which proved well indeed.

'And that, Frodo, is the end of my account. May Elrond and the others forgive the length of it. But such a thing has not happened before, that Gandalf broke tryst and did not come when he promised. An account to the Ring-bearer of so strange an event was required, I think.

'Well, the Tale is now told, from first to last. Here we all are, and here is the Ring. But we have not yet come any nearer to our purpose. What shall we do with it?'

There was a silence. At last Elrond spoke again.

'This is grievous news concerning Saruman,' he said; 'for we trusted him and he is deep in all our counsels. It is perilous to study too deeply the arts of the Enemy, for good or for ill. But such falls and betrayals, alas, have happened before. Of the tales that we have heard this day the tale of Frodo was most strange to me. I have known few hobbits, save Bilbo here; and it seems to me that he is perhaps not so alone and singular as I had thought him. The world has changed much since I last was on the westward roads.

'The Barrow-wights we know by many names; and of the Old Forest many tales have been told: all that now remains is but an outlier of its northern march. Time was when a squirrel could go from tree to tree from what is now the Shire to Dunland west of Isengard. In those lands I journeyed once, and many things wild and strange I knew. But I had forgotten Bombadil, if indeed this is still the same that walked the woods and hills long ago, and even then was older than the old. That was not then his name. Iarwain Ben-adar we called him, oldest and fatherless. But many another name he has since been given by other folk: Forn by the Dwarves, Orald by Northern Men, and other names beside. He is a strange creature, but maybe I should have summoned him to our Council.'

'He would not have come,' said Gandalf.

'Could we not still send messages to him and obtain his help?' asked Erestor. 'It seems that he has a power even over the Ring.'

'No, I should not put it so,' said Gandalf. 'Say rather that the Ring has no power over him. He is his own master. But he cannot alter the Ring itself, nor break its power over others. And now he is withdrawn into a little land, within bounds that he has set, though none can see them, waiting perhaps for a change of days, and he will not step beyond them.'

'But within those bounds nothing seems to dismay him,' said Erestor. 'Would he not take the Ring and keep it there, for ever harmless?'

'No,' said Gandalf, 'not willingly. He might do so, if all the free folk of the world begged him, but he would not understand the need. And if he were given the Ring, he would soon forget it, or most likely throw it away. Such things have no hold on his mind. He would be a most unsafe guardian; and that alone is answer enough.'

'But in any case,' said Glorfindel, 'to send the Ring to him would only postpone the day of evil. He is far away. We could not now take it back to him, unguessed, unmarked by any spy. And even if we could, soon or late the Lord of the Rings would learn of its hiding place and would bend all his power towards it. Could that power be defied by Bombadil alone? I think not. I think that in the end, if all else is conquered, Bombadil will fall, Last as he was First; and then Night will come.'

'I know little of Iarwain save the name,' said Galdor; 'but Glorfindel, I think, is right. Power to defy our Enemy is not in him, unless such power is in the earth itself. And yet we see that Sauron can torture and destroy the very hills. What power still remains lies with us, here in Imladris, or with Círdan at the Havens, or in Lórien. But have they the strength, have we here the strength to withstand the Enemy, the coming of Sauron at the last, when all else is overthrown?'

'I have not the strength,' said Elrond; 'neither have they.'

'Then if the Ring cannot be kept from him for ever by strength,' said Glorfindel, 'two things only remain for us to attempt: to send it over the Sea, or to destroy it.'

'But Gandalf has revealed to us that we cannot destroy it by any craft that we here possess,' said Elrond. 'And they who dwell beyond the Sea would not receive it: for good or ill it belongs to Middle-earth; it is for us who still dwell here to deal with it.'

'Then,' said Glorfindel, 'let us cast it into the deeps, and so make the lies of Saruman come true. For it is clear now that even at the Council his feet were already on a crooked path. He knew that the Ring was not lost for ever, but wished us to think so; for he began to lust for it for himself. Yet oft in lies truth is hidden: in the Sea it would be safe.'

'Not safe for ever,' said Gandalf. 'There are many things in the deep waters; and seas and lands may change. And it is not our part here to take thought only for a season, or for a few lives of Men, or for a passing age of the world. We should seek a final end of this menace, even if we do not hope to make one.'

'And that we shall not find on the roads to the Sea,' said Galdor. 'If the return to Iarwain be thought too dangerous, then flight to the Sea is now fraught with gravest peril. My heart tells me that Sauron will expect us to take the western way, when he learns what has befallen. He soon will. The Nine have been unhorsed indeed but that is but a respite, ere they find new steeds and swifter. Only the waning might of Gondor stands now between him and a march in power along the coasts into the North; and if he comes, assailing the White Towers and the Havens, hereafter the Elves may have no escape from the lengthening shadows of Middle-earth.'

'Long yet will that march be delayed,' said Boromir. 'Gondor wanes, you say. But Gondor stands, and even the end of its strength is still very strong.'

'And yet its vigilance can no longer keep back the Nine,' said Galdor. 'And other roads he may find that Gondor does not guard.'

'Then,' said Erestor, 'there are but two courses, as Glorfindel already has declared: to hide the Ring for ever; or to unmake it. But both are beyond our power. Who will read this riddle for us?'

'None here can do so,' said Elrond gravely. 'At least none can foretell what will come to pass, if we take this road or that. But it seems to me now clear which is the road that we must take. The westward road seems easiest. Therefore it must be shunned. It will be watched. Too often the Elves have fled that way. Now at this last we must take a hard road, a road unforeseen. There lies our hope, if hope it be. To walk into peril – to Mordor. We must send the Ring to the Fire.'

Silence fell again. Frodo, even in that fair house, looking out upon a sunlit valley filled with the noise of clear waters, felt a dead darkness in his heart. Boromir stirred, and Frodo looked at him. He was fingering his great horn and frowning. At length he spoke.

'I do not understand all this,' he said. 'Saruman is a traitor, but did he not have a glimpse of wisdom? Why do you speak ever of hiding and destroying? Why should we not think that the Great Ring has come into our hands to serve us in the very hour of need? Wielding it the Free Lords of the Free may surely defeat the Enemy. That is what he most fears, I deem.

'The Men of Gondor are valiant, and they will never submit; but they may be beaten down. Valour needs first strength, and then a weapon. Let the Ring be your weapon, if it has such power as you say. Take it and go forth to victory!'

'Alas, no,' said Elrond. 'We cannot use the Ruling Ring. That we now know too well. It belongs to Sauron and was made by him alone, and is altogether evil. Its strength, Boromir, is too great for anyone to wield at will, save only those who have already a great power of their own. But for them it holds an even deadlier peril. The very desire of it corrupts the heart. Consider Saruman. If any of the Wise should with this Ring overthrow the Lord of Mordor, using his own arts, he would then set himself on Sauron's throne, and yet another Dark Lord would appear. And that is another reason why the Ring should be destroyed: as long as it is in the world it will be a danger even to the Wise. For nothing is evil in the beginning. Even Sauron was not so. I fear to take the Ring to hide it. I will not take the Ring to wield it.'

'Nor I,' said Gandalf.

Boromir looked at them doubtfully, but he bowed his head. 'So be it,' he said. 'Then in Gondor we must trust to such weapons as we have. And at the least, while the Wise ones guard this Ring, we will fight on. Mayhap the Sword-that-was-Broken may still stem the tide – if the hand that wields it has inherited not an heirloom only, but the sinews of the Kings of Men.'

'Who can tell?' said Aragorn. 'But we will put it to the test one day.'

'May the day not be too long delayed,' said Boromir. 'For though I do not ask for aid, we need it. It would comfort us to know that others fought also with all the means that they have.'

'Then be comforted,' said Elrond. 'For there are other powers and realms that you know not, and they are hidden from you. Anduin the Great flows past many shores, ere it comes to Argonath and the Gates of Gondor.'

'Still it might be well for all,' said Glóin the Dwarf, 'if all these strengths were joined, and the powers of each were used in league. Other rings there may be, less treacherous, that might be used in our need. The Seven are lost to us – if Balin has not found the ring of Thrór, which was the last; naught has been heard of it since Thrór perished in Moria. Indeed I may now reveal that it was partly in hope to find that ring that Balin went away.'

'Balin will find no ring in Moria,' said Gandalf. 'Thrór gave it to Thráin his son, but not Thráin to Thorin. It was taken with torment from Thráin in the dungeons of Dol Guldur. I came too late.'

'Ah, alas!' cried Glóin. 'When will the day come of our revenge? But still there are the Three. What of the Three Rings of the Elves? Very mighty Rings, it is said. Do not the Elf-lords keep them? Yet they too were made by the Dark Lord long ago. Are they idle? I see Elf-lords here. Will they not say?'

The Elves returned no answer. 'Did you not hear me, Glóin?' said

Elrond. 'The Three were not made by Sauron, nor did he ever touch them. But of them it is not permitted to speak. So much only in this hour of doubt I may now say. They are not idle. But they were not made as weapons of war or conquest: that is not their power. Those who made them did not desire strength or domination or hoarded wealth, but understanding, making, and healing, to preserve all things unstained. These things the Elves of Middle-earth have in some measure gained, though with sorrow. But all that has been wrought by those who wield the Three will turn to their undoing, and their minds and hearts will become revealed to Sauron, if he regains the One. It would be better if the Three had never been. That is his purpose.'

'But what then would happen, if the Ruling Ring were destroyed, as you counsel?' asked Glóin.

'We know not for certain,' answered Elrond sadly. 'Some hope that the Three Rings, which Sauron has never touched, would then become free, and their rulers might heal the hurts of the world that he has wrought. But maybe when the One has gone, the Three will fail, and many fair things will fade and be forgotten. That is my belief.'

'Yet all the Elves are willing to endure this chance,' said Glorfindel, 'if by it the power of Sauron may be broken, and the fear of his dominion be taken away for ever.'

'Thus we return once more to the destroying of the Ring,' said Erestor, 'and yet we come no nearer. What strength have we for the finding of the Fire in which it was made? That is the path of despair. Of folly I would say, if the long wisdom of Elrond did not forbid me.'

'Despair, or folly?' said Gandalf. 'It is not despair, for despair is only for those who see the end beyond all doubt. We do not. It is wisdom to recognize necessity, when all other courses have been weighed, though as folly it may appear to those who cling to false hope. Well, let folly be our cloak, a veil before the eyes of the Enemy! For he is very wise, and weighs all things to a nicety in the scales of his malice. But the only measure that he knows is desire, desire for power; and so he judges all hearts. Into his heart the thought will not enter that any will refuse it, that having the Ring we may seek to destroy it. If we seek this, we shall put him out of reckoning.'

'At least for a while,' said Elrond. 'The road must be trod, but it will be very hard. And neither strength nor wisdom will carry us far upon it. This quest may be attempted by the weak with as much hope as the strong. Yet such is oft the course of deeds that move the wheels of the world: small hands do them because they must, while the eyes of the great are elsewhere.'

'Very well, very well, Master Elrond!' said Bilbo suddenly. 'Say no more! It is plain enough what you are pointing at. Bilbo the silly hobbit started this affair, and Bilbo had better finish it, or himself. I was very comfortable here, and getting on with my book. If you want to know, I am just writing an ending for it. I had thought of putting: *and he lived happily ever afterwards to the end of his days*. It is a good ending, and none the worse for having been used before. Now I shall have to alter that: it does not look like coming true; and anyway there will evidently have to be several more chapters, if I live to write them. It is a frightful nuisance. When ought I to start?'

Boromir looked in surprise at Bilbo, but the laughter died on his lips when he saw that all the others regarded the old hobbit with grave respect. Only Glóin smiled, but his smile came from old memories.

'Of course, my dear Bilbo,' said Gandalf. 'If you had really started this affair, you might be expected to finish it. But you know well enough now that *starting* is too great a claim for any, and that only a small part is played in great deeds by any hero. You need not bow! Though the word was meant, and we do not doubt that under jest you are making a valiant offer. But one beyond your strength, Bilbo. You cannot take this thing back. It has passed on. If you need my advice any longer, I should say that your part is ended, unless as a recorder. Finish your book, and leave the ending unaltered! There is still hope for it. But get ready to write a sequel, when they come back.'

Bilbo laughed. 'I have never known you give me pleasant advice before,' he said. 'As all your unpleasant advice has been good, I wonder if this advice is not bad. Still, I don't suppose I have the strength or luck left to deal with the Ring. It has grown, and I have not. But tell me: what do you mean by *they*?'

'The messengers who are sent with the Ring.'

'Exactly! And who are they to be? That seems to me what this Council has to decide, and all that it has to decide. Elves may thrive on speech alone, and Dwarves endure great weariness; but I am only an old hobbit, and I miss my meal at noon. Can't you think of some names now? Or put it off till after dinner?'

No one answered. The noon-bell rang. Still no one spoke. Frodo glanced at all the faces, but they were not turned to him. All the Council sat with downcast eyes, as if in deep thought. A great dread fell on him, as if he was awaiting the pronouncement of some doom that he had long foreseen and vainly hoped might after all never be spoken. An overwhelming longing to rest and remain at peace by Bilbo's side in Rivendell filled all his heart. At last with an effort he spoke, and wondered to hear his own words, as if some other will was using his small voice.

'I will take the Ring,' he said, 'though I do not know the way.'

Elrond raised his eyes and looked at him, and Frodo felt his heart pierced by the sudden keenness of the glance. 'If I understand aright all that I have heard,' he said, 'I think that this task is appointed for you, Frodo; and that if you do not find a way, no one will. This is the hour of the Shire-folk, when they arise from their quiet fields to shake the towers and counsels of the Great. Who of all the Wise could have foreseen it? Or, if they are wise, why should they expect to know it, until the hour has struck?

'But it is a heavy burden. So heavy that none could lay it on another. I do not lay it on you. But if you take it freely, I will say that your choice is right; and though all the mighty elf-friends of old, Hador, and Húrin, and Túrin, and Beren himself were assembled together, your seat should be among them.'

'But you won't send him off alone surely, Master?' cried Sam, unable to contain himself any longer, and jumping up from the corner where he had been quietly sitting on the floor.

'No indeed!' said Elrond, turning towards him with a smile. 'You at least shall go with him. It is hardly possible to separate you from him, even when he is summoned to a secret council and you are not.'

Sam sat down, blushing and muttering. 'A nice pickle we have landed ourselves in, Mr. Frodo!' he said, shaking his head.

CHAPTER III

THE RING GOES SOUTH

Later that day the hobbits held a meeting of their own in Bilbo's room. Merry and Pippin were indignant when they heard that Sam had crept into the Council, and had been chosen as Frodo's companion.

'It's most unfair,' said Pippin. 'Instead of throwing him out, and clapping him in chains, Elrond goes and *rewards* him for his cheek!'

'Rewards!' said Frodo. 'I can't imagine a more severe punishment. You are not thinking what you are saying: condemned to go on this hopeless journey, a reward? Yesterday I dreamed that my task was done, and I could rest here, a long while, perhaps for good.'

'I don't wonder,' said Merry, 'and I wish you could. But we are envying Sam, not you. If you have to go, then it will be a punishment for any of us to be left behind, even in Rivendell. We have come a long way with you and been through some stiff times. We want to go on.'

'That's what I meant,' said Pippin. 'We hobbits ought to stick together, and we will. I shall go, unless they chain me up. There must be someone with intelligence in the party.'

'Then you certainly will not be chosen, Peregrin Took!' said Gandalf, looking in through the window, which was near the ground. 'But you are all worrying yourselves unnecessarily. Nothing is decided yet.'

'Nothing decided!' cried Pippin. 'Then what were you all doing? You were shut up for hours.'

'Talking,' said Bilbo. 'There was a deal of talk, and everyone had an eye-opener. Even old Gandalf. I think Legolas's bit of news about Gollum caught even him on the hop, though he passed it off.'

'You were wrong,' said Gandalf. 'You were inattentive. I had already heard of it from Gwaihir. If you want to know, the only real eye-openers, as you put it, were you and Frodo; and I was the only one that was not surprised.'

'Well, anyway,' said Bilbo, 'nothing was decided beyond choosing poor Frodo and Sam. I was afraid all the time that it might come to that, if I was let off. But if you ask me, Elrond will send out a fair number, when the reports come in. Have they started yet, Gandalf?'

'Yes,' said the wizard. 'Some of the scouts have been sent out already. More will go tomorrow. Elrond is sending Elves, and they will get in touch with the Rangers, and maybe with Thranduil's folk in Mirkwood. And Aragorn has gone with Elrond's sons. We shall have to scour the lands all round for many long leagues before any move is made. So cheer up, Frodo! You will probably make quite a long stay here.'

'Ah!' said Sam gloomily. 'We'll just wait long enough for winter to come.'

'That can't be helped,' said Bilbo. 'It's your fault partly, Frodo my lad: insisting on waiting for my birthday. A funny way of honouring it, I can't help thinking. *Not* the day I should have chosen for letting the S.-B.s into Bag End. But there it is: you can't wait now till spring; and you can't go till the reports come back.

> *When winter first begins to bite*
> *and stones crack in the frosty night,*
> *when pools are black and trees are bare,*
> *'tis evil in the Wild to fare.*

But that I am afraid will be just your luck.'

'I am afraid it will,' said Gandalf. 'We can't start until we have found out about the Riders.'

'I thought they were all destroyed in the flood,' said Merry.

'You cannot destroy Ringwraiths like that,' said Gandalf. 'The power of their master is in them, and they stand or fall by him. We hope that they were all unhorsed and unmasked, and so made for a while less dangerous; but we must find out for certain. In the meantime you should try and forget your troubles, Frodo. I do not know if I can do anything to help you; but I will whisper this in your ears. Someone said that intelligence would be needed in the party. He was right. I think I shall come with you.'

So great was Frodo's delight at this announcement that Gandalf left the window-sill, where he had been sitting, and took off his hat and bowed. 'I only said *I think I shall come.* Do not count on anything yet. In this matter Elrond will have much to say, and your friend the Strider. Which reminds me, I want to see Elrond. I must be off.'

'How long do you think I shall have here?' said Frodo to Bilbo when Gandalf had gone.

'Oh, I don't know. I can't count days in Rivendell,' said Bilbo. 'But quite long, I should think. We can have many a good talk. What about helping me with my book, and making a start on the next? Have you thought of an ending?'

'Yes, several, and all are dark and unpleasant,' said Frodo.

'Oh, that won't do!' said Bilbo. 'Books ought to have good endings. How would this do: *and they all settled down and lived together happily ever after?*'

'It will do well, if it ever comes to that,' said Frodo.

'Ah!' said Sam. 'And where will they live? That's what I often wonder.'

For a while the hobbits continued to talk and think of the past journey and of the perils that lay ahead; but such was the virtue of the land of Rivendell that soon all fear and anxiety was lifted from their minds. The future, good or ill, was not forgotten, but ceased to have any power over the present. Health and hope grew strong in them, and they were content with each good day as it came, taking pleasure in every meal, and in every word and song.

So the days slipped away, as each morning dawned bright and fair, and each evening followed cool and clear. But autumn was waning fast; slowly the golden light faded to pale silver, and the lingering leaves fell from the naked trees. A wind began to blow chill from the Misty Mountains to the east. The Hunter's Moon waxed round in the night sky, and put to flight all the lesser stars. But low in the South one star shone red. Every night, as the Moon waned again, it shone brighter and brighter. Frodo could see it from his window, deep in the heavens, burning like a watchful eye that glared above the trees on the brink of the valley.

The hobbits had been nearly two months in the House of Elrond, and November had gone by with the last shreds of autumn, and December was passing, when the scouts began to return. Some had gone north beyond the springs of the Hoarwell into the Ettenmoors; and others had gone west, and with the help of Aragorn and the Rangers had searched the lands far down the Greyflood, as far as Tharbad, where the old North Road crossed the river by a ruined town. Many had gone east and south; and some of these had crossed the Mountains and entered Mirkwood, while others had climbed the pass at the source of the Gladden River, and had come down into Wilderland and over the Gladden Fields and so at length had reached the old home of Radagast at Rhosgobel. Radagast was not there; and they had returned over the high pass that was called the Dimrill Stair. The sons of Elrond, Elladan and Elrohir, were the last to return; they had made a great journey, passing down the Silverlode into a strange country, but of their errand they would not speak to any save to Elrond.

In no region had the messengers discovered any signs or tidings of the Riders or other servants of the Enemy. Even from the Eagles of the Misty Mountains they had learned no fresh news. Nothing had been seen or heard of Gollum; but the wild wolves were still gathering, and were hunting again far up the Great River. Three of the black horses had been found at once drowned in the flooded Ford. On the rocks of the rapids below it searchers discovered the bodies of five more, and also a long black cloak, slashed and tattered. Of the Black Riders no other trace was to be seen, and nowhere was their presence to be felt. It seemed that they had vanished from the North.

'Eight out of the Nine are accounted for at least,' said Gandalf. 'It is rash to be too sure, yet I think that we may hope now that the Ringwraiths were scattered, and have been obliged to return as best they could to their Master in Mordor, empty and shapeless.

'If that is so, it will be some time before they can begin the hunt again. Of course the Enemy has other servants, but they will have to journey all the way to the borders of Rivendell before they can pick up our trail. And if we are careful that will be hard to find. But we must delay no longer.'

Elrond summoned the hobbits to him. He looked gravely at Frodo. 'The time has come,' he said. 'If the Ring is to set out, it must go soon. But those who go with it must not count on their errand being aided by war or force. They must pass into the domain of the Enemy far from aid. Do you still hold to your word, Frodo, that you will be the Ring-bearer?'

'I do,' said Frodo. 'I will go with Sam.'

'Then I cannot help you much, not even with counsel,' said Elrond. 'I can foresee very little of your road; and how your task is to be achieved I do not know. The Shadow has crept now to the feet of the Mountains, and draws nigh even to the borders of the Greyflood; and under the Shadow all is dark to me. You will meet many foes, some open, and some disguised; and you may find friends upon your way when you least look for it. I will send out messages, such as I can contrive, to those whom I know in the wide world; but so perilous are the lands now become that some may well miscarry, or come no quicker than you yourself.

'And I will choose you companions to go with you, as far as they will or fortune allows. The number must be few, since your hope is in speed and secrecy. Had I a host of Elves in armour of the Elder Days, it would avail little, save to arouse the power of Mordor.

'The Company of the Ring shall be Nine; and the Nine Walkers shall be set against the Nine Riders that are evil. With you and your faithful servant, Gandalf will go; for this shall be his great task, and maybe the end of his labours.

'For the rest, they shall represent the other Free Peoples of the World: Elves, Dwarves, and Men. Legolas shall be for the Elves; and Gimli son of Glóin for the Dwarves. They are willing to go at least to the passes of the Mountains, and maybe beyond. For men you shall have Aragorn son of Arathorn, for the Ring of Isildur concerns him closely.'

'Strider!' cried Frodo.

'Yes,' he said with a smile. 'I ask leave once again to be your companion, Frodo.'

'I would have begged you to come,' said Frodo, 'only I thought you were going to Minas Tirith with Boromir.'

'I am,' said Aragorn. 'And the Sword-that-was-Broken shall be re-forged ere I set out to war. But your road and our road lie together for many hundreds of miles. Therefore Boromir will also be in the Company. He is a valiant man.'

'There remain two more to be found,' said Elrond. 'These I will consider. Of my household I may find some that it seems good to me to send.'

'But that will leave no place for us!' cried Pippin in dismay. 'We don't want to be left behind. We want to go with Frodo.'

'That is because you do not understand and cannot imagine what lies ahead,' said Elrond.

'Neither does Frodo,' said Gandalf, unexpectedly supporting Pippin. 'Nor do any of us see clearly. It is true that if these hobbits understood the danger, they would not dare to go. But they would still wish to go, or wish that they dared, and be shamed and unhappy. I think, Elrond, that in this matter it would be well to trust rather to their friendship than to great wisdom. Even if you chose for us an elf-lord, such as Glorfindel, he could not storm the Dark Tower, nor open the road to the Fire by the power that is in him.'

'You speak gravely,' said Elrond, 'but I am in doubt. The Shire, I forebode, is not free now from peril; and these two I had thought to send back there as messengers, to do what they could, according to the fashion of their country, to warn the people of their danger. In any case, I judge that the younger of these two, Peregrin Took, should remain. My heart is against his going.'

'Then, Master Elrond, you will have to lock me in prison, or send me home tied in a sack,' said Pippin. 'For otherwise I shall follow the Company.'

'Let it be so then. You shall go,' said Elrond, and he sighed. 'Now the tale of Nine is filled. In seven days the Company must depart.'

The Sword of Elendil was forged anew by Elvish smiths, and on its blade was traced a device of seven stars set between the crescent Moon and the rayed Sun, and about them was written many runes; for Aragorn son of Arathorn was going to war upon the marches of Mordor. Very bright was that sword when it was made whole again; the light of the sun shone redly in it, and the light of the moon shone cold, and its edge was hard and keen. And Aragorn gave it a new name and called it Andúril, Flame of the West.

Aragorn and Gandalf walked together or sat speaking of their road and the perils they would meet; and they pondered the storied and figured maps and books of lore that were in the house of Elrond. Sometimes Frodo was with them; but he was content to lean on their guidance, and he spent as much time as he could with Bilbo.

In those last days the hobbits sat together in the evening in the Hall of Fire, and there among many tales they heard told in full the lay of Beren and Lúthien and the winning of the Great Jewel; but in the day, while Merry and Pippin were out and about, Frodo and Sam were to be found with Bilbo in his own small room. Then Bilbo would read passages from his book (which still seemed very incomplete), or scraps of his verses, or would take notes of Frodo's adventures.

On the morning of the last day Frodo was alone with Bilbo, and the old hobbit pulled out from under his bed a wooden box. He lifted the lid and fumbled inside.

'Here is your sword,' he said. 'But it was broken, you know. I took it to keep it safe but I've forgotten to ask if the smiths could mend it. No time now. So I thought, perhaps, you would care to have this, don't you know?'

He took from the box a small sword in an old shabby leathern scabbard. Then he drew it, and its polished and well-tended blade glittered suddenly, cold and bright. 'This is Sting,' he said, and thrust it with little effort deep into a wooden beam. 'Take it, if you like. I shan't want it again, I expect.'

Frodo accepted it gratefully.

'Also there is this!' said Bilbo, bringing out a parcel which seemed to be rather heavy for its size. He unwound several folds of old cloth, and held up a small shirt of mail. It was close-woven of many rings, as supple almost as linen, cold as ice, and harder than steel. It shone like moonlit silver, and was studded with white gems. With it was a belt of pearl and crystal.

'It's a pretty thing, isn't it?' said Bilbo, moving it in the light. 'And useful. It is my dwarf-mail that Thorin gave me. I got it back from Michel Delving before I started, and packed it with my luggage. I brought all the mementoes of my Journey away with me, except the Ring. But I did not expect to use this, and I don't need it now, except to look at sometimes. You hardly feel any weight when you put it on.'

'I should look – well, I don't think I should look right in it,' said Frodo.

'Just what I said myself,' said Bilbo. 'But never mind about looks. You can wear it under your outer clothes. Come on! You must share this secret with me. Don't tell anybody else! But I should feel happier if I knew you were wearing it. I have a fancy it would turn even the knives of the Black Riders,' he ended in a low voice.

'Very well, I will take it,' said Frodo. Bilbo put it on him, and fastened

Sting upon the glittering belt; and then Frodo put over the top his old weather-stained breeches, tunic, and jacket.

'Just a plain hobbit you look,' said Bilbo. 'But there is more about you now than appears on the surface. Good luck to you!' He turned away and looked out of the window, trying to hum a tune.

'I cannot thank you as I should, Bilbo, for this, and for all your past kindnesses,' said Frodo.

'Don't try!' said the old hobbit, turning round and slapping him on the back. 'Ow!' he cried. 'You are too hard now to slap! But there you are: Hobbits must stick together, and especially Bagginses. All I ask in return is: take as much care of yourself as you can, and bring back all the news you can, and any old songs and tales you can come by. I'll do my best to finish my book before you return. I should like to write the second book, if I am spared.' He broke off and turned to the window again, singing softly.

> *I sit beside the fire and think*
> *of all that I have seen,*
> *of meadow-flowers and butterflies*
> *in summers that have been;*
>
> *Of yellow leaves and gossamer*
> *in autumns that there were,*
> *with morning mist and silver sun*
> *and wind upon my hair.*
>
> *I sit beside the fire and think*
> *of how the world will be*
> *when winter comes without a spring*
> *that I shall ever see.*
>
> *For still there are so many things*
> *that I have never seen:*
> *in every wood in every spring*
> *there is a different green.*
>
> *I sit beside the fire and think*
> *of people long ago,*
> *and people who will see a world*
> *that I shall never know.*

But all the while I sit and think
of times there were before,
I listen for returning feet
and voices at the door.

It was a cold grey day near the end of December. The East Wind was streaming through the bare branches of the trees, and seething in the dark pines on the hills. Ragged clouds were hurrying overhead, dark and low. As the cheerless shadows of the early evening began to fall the Company made ready to set out. They were to start at dusk, for Elrond counselled them to journey under cover of night as often as they could, until they were far from Rivendell.

'You should fear the many eyes of the servants of Sauron,' he said. 'I do not doubt that news of the discomfiture of the Riders has already reached him, and he will be filled with wrath. Soon now his spies on foot and wing will be abroad in the northern lands. Even of the sky above you must beware as you go on your way.'

The Company took little gear of war, for their hope was in secrecy not in battle. Aragorn had Andúril but no other weapon, and he went forth clad only in rusty green and brown, as a Ranger of the wilderness. Boromir had a long sword, in fashion like Andúril but of less lineage, and he bore also a shield and his war-horn.

'Loud and clear it sounds in the valleys of the hills,' he said, 'and then let all the foes of Gondor flee!' Putting it to his lips he blew a blast, and the echoes leapt from rock to rock, and all that heard that voice in Rivendell sprang to their feet.

'Slow should you be to wind that horn again, Boromir,' said Elrond, 'until you stand once more on the borders of your land, and dire need is on you.'

'Maybe,' said Boromir. 'But always I have let my horn cry at setting forth, and though thereafter we may walk in the shadows, I will not go forth as a thief in the night.'

Gimli the dwarf alone wore openly a short shirt of steel-rings, for dwarves make light of burdens; and in his belt was a broad-bladed axe. Legolas had a bow and a quiver, and at his belt a long white knife. The younger hobbits wore the swords that they had taken from the barrow; but Frodo took only Sting; and his mail-coat, as Bilbo wished, remained hidden. Gandalf bore his staff, but girt at his side was the elven-sword Glamdring, the mate of Orcrist that lay now upon the breast of Thorin under the Lonely Mountain.

All were well furnished by Elrond with thick warm clothes, and they had jackets and cloaks lined with fur. Spare food and clothes and blankets and other needs were laden on a pony, none other than the poor beast that they had brought from Bree.

The stay in Rivendell had worked a great wonder of change on him: he was glossy and seemed to have the vigour of youth. It was Sam who had insisted on choosing him, declaring that Bill (as he called him) would pine, if he did not come.

'That animal can nearly talk,' he said, 'and would talk, if he stayed here much longer. He gave me a look as plain as Mr. Pippin could speak it: if you don't let me go with you, Sam, I'll follow on my own.' So Bill was going as the beast of burden, yet he was the only member of the Company that did not seem depressed.

Their farewells had been said in the great hall by the fire, and they were only waiting now for Gandalf, who had not yet come out of the house. A gleam of firelight came from the open doors, and soft lights were glowing in many windows. Bilbo huddled in a cloak stood silent on the doorstep beside Frodo. Aragorn sat with his head bowed to his knees; only Elrond knew fully what this hour meant to him. The others could be seen as grey shapes in the darkness.

Sam was standing by the pony, sucking his teeth, and staring moodily into the gloom where the river roared stonily below; his desire for adventure was at its lowest ebb.

'Bill, my lad,' he said, 'you oughtn't to have took up with us. You could have stayed here and et the best hay till the new grass comes.' Bill swished his tail and said nothing.

Sam eased the pack on his shoulders, and went over anxiously in his mind all the things that he had stowed in it, wondering if he had forgotten anything: his chief treasure, his cooking gear; and the little box of salt that he always carried and refilled when he could; a good supply of pipe-weed (but not near enough, I'll warrant); flint and tinder; woollen hose; linen; various small belongings of his master's that Frodo had forgotten and Sam had stowed to bring them out in triumph when they were called for. He went through them all.

'Rope!' he muttered. 'No rope! And only last night you said to yourself: "Sam, what about a bit of rope? You'll want it, if you haven't got it." Well, I'll want it. I can't get it now.'

At that moment Elrond came out with Gandalf, and he called the Company to him. 'This is my last word,' he said in a low voice. 'The Ring-bearer is setting out on the Quest of Mount Doom. On him alone is any charge laid: neither to cast away the Ring, nor to deliver it to any servant of the Enemy nor indeed to let any handle it, save members of the Company and the Council, and only then in gravest need. The others go with him as free companions, to help him on his way. You may tarry, or come back, or turn aside into other paths, as chance allows. The further you go, the less easy will it be to withdraw; yet no oath or bond is laid on you to go further than you will. For you do not yet know the strength of your hearts, and you cannot foresee what each may meet upon the road.'

'Faithless is he that says farewell when the road darkens,' said Gimli.

'Maybe,' said Elrond, 'but let him not vow to walk in the dark, who has not seen the nightfall.'

'Yet sworn word may strengthen quaking heart,' said Gimli.

'Or break it,' said Elrond. 'Look not too far ahead! But go now with good hearts! Farewell, and may the blessing of Elves and Men and all Free Folk go with you. May the stars shine upon your faces!'

'Good . . . good luck!' cried Bilbo, stuttering with the cold. 'I don't suppose you will be able to keep a diary, Frodo my lad, but I shall expect a full account when you get back. And don't be too long! Farewell!'

Many others of Elrond's household stood in the shadows and watched them go, bidding them farewell with soft voices. There was no laughter, and no song or music. At last they turned away and faded silently into the dusk.

They crossed the bridge and wound slowly up the long steep paths that led out of the cloven vale of Rivendell; and they came at length to the high moor where the wind hissed through the heather. Then with one glance at the Last Homely House twinkling below them they strode away far into the night.

At the Ford of Bruinen they left the Road and turning southwards went on by narrow paths among the folded lands. Their purpose was to hold this course west of the Mountains for many miles and days. The country was much rougher and more barren than in the green vale of the Great River in Wilderland on the other side of the range, and their going would be slow; but they hoped in this way to escape the notice of unfriendly eyes. The spies of Sauron had hitherto seldom been seen in this empty country, and the paths were little known except to the people of Rivendell.

Gandalf walked in front, and with him went Aragorn, who knew this land even in the dark. The others were in file behind, and Legolas whose eyes were keen was the rearguard. The first part of their journey was hard and dreary, and Frodo remembered little of it, save the wind. For many sunless days an icy blast came from the Mountains in the east, and no garment seemed able to keep out its searching fingers. Though the Company was well clad, they seldom felt warm, either moving or at rest. They slept uneasily during the middle of the day, in some hollow of the land, or hidden under the tangled thorn-bushes that grew in thickets in many places. In the late afternoon they were roused by the watch, and took their chief meal: cold and cheerless as a rule, for they could seldom risk the lighting of a fire. In the evening they went on again, always as nearly southward as they could find a way.

At first it seemed to the hobbits that although they walked and stumbled until they were weary, they were creeping forward like snails, and getting nowhere. Each day the land looked much the same as it had the day before. Yet steadily the mountains were drawing nearer. South of Rivendell they rose ever higher, and bent westwards; and about the feet of the main range there was tumbled an ever wider land of bleak hills, and deep valleys filled with turbulent waters. Paths were few and winding, and led them often only to the edge of some sheer fall, or down into treacherous swamps.

They had been a fortnight on the way when the weather changed. The wind suddenly fell and then veered round to the south. The swift-flowing clouds lifted and melted away, and the sun came out, pale and bright. There came a cold clear dawn at the end of a long stumbling night-march. The travellers reached a low ridge crowned with ancient holly-trees whose grey-green trunks seemed to have been built out of the very stone of the hills. Their dark leaves shone and their berries glowed red in the light of the rising sun.

Away in the south Frodo could see the dim shapes of lofty mountains that seemed now to stand across the path that the Company was taking. At the left of this high range rose three peaks; the tallest and nearest stood up like a tooth tipped with snow; its great, bare, northern precipice was still largely in the shadow, but where the sunlight slanted upon it, it glowed red.

Gandalf stood at Frodo's side and looked out under his hand. 'We have done well,' he said. 'We have reached the borders of the country that Men call Hollin; many Elves lived here in happier days, when Eregion was its name. Five-and-forty leagues as the crow flies we have come, though many long miles further our feet have walked. The land and the weather will be milder now, but perhaps all the more dangerous.'

'Dangerous or not, a real sunrise is mighty welcome,' said Frodo, throwing back his hood and letting the morning light fall on his face.

'But the mountains are ahead of us,' said Pippin. 'We must have turned eastwards in the night.'

'No,' said Gandalf. 'But you see further ahead in the clear light. Beyond those peaks the range bends round south-west. There are many maps in Elrond's house, but I suppose you never thought to look at them?'

'Yes I did, sometimes,' said Pippin, 'but I don't remember them. Frodo has a better head for that sort of thing.'

'I need no map,' said Gimli, who had come up with Legolas, and was gazing out before him with a strange light in his deep eyes. 'There is the land where our fathers worked of old, and we have wrought the image of those mountains into many works of metal and of stone, and into many songs and tales. They stand tall in our dreams: Baraz, Zirak, Shathûr.

'Only once before have I sèen them from afar in waking life, but I know them and their names, for under them lies Khazad-dûm, the Dwarrowdelf, that is now called the Black Pit, Moria in the Elvish tongue. Yonder stands Barazinbar, the Redhorn, cruel Caradhras; and beyond him are Silvertine and Cloudyhead: Celebdil the White, and Fanuidhol the Grey, that we call Zirakzigil and Bundushathûr.

'There the Misty Mountains divide, and between their arms lies the deep-shadowed valley which we cannot forget: Azanulbizar, the Dimrill Dale, which the Elves call Nanduhirion.'

'It is for the Dimrill Dale that we are making,' said Gandalf. 'If we climb the pass that is called the Redhorn Gate, under the far side of Caradhras, we shall come down by the Dimrill Stair into the deep vale of the Dwarves. There lies the Mirrormere, and there the River Silverlode rises in its icy springs.'

'Dark is the water of Kheled-zâram,' said Gimli, 'and cold are the springs of Kibil-nâla. My heart trembles at the thought that I may see them soon.'

'May you have joy of the sight, my good dwarf!' said Gandalf. 'But whatever you may do, we at least cannot stay in that valley. We must go down the Silverlode into the secret woods, and so to the Great River, and then——'

He paused.

'Yes, and where then?' asked Merry.

'To the end of the journey – in the end,' said Gandalf. 'We cannot look too far ahead. Let us be glad that the first stage is safely over. I think we will rest here, not only today but tonight as well. There is a wholesome air about Hollin. Much evil must befall a country before it wholly forgets the Elves, if once they dwelt there.'

'That is true,' said Legolas. 'But the Elves of this land were of a race strange to us of the silvan folk, and the trees and the grass do not now remember them. Only I hear the stones lament them: *deep they delved us, fair they wrought us, high they builded us; but they are gone*. They are gone. They sought the Havens long ago.'

That morning they lit a fire in a deep hollow shrouded by great bushes of holly, and their supper-breakfast was merrier than it had been since they set out. They did not hurry to bed afterwards, for they expected to have all the night to sleep in, and they did not mean to go on again until the evening of the next day. Only Aragorn was silent and restless. After a while he left the Company and wandered on to the ridge; there he stood in the shadow of a tree, looking out southwards and westwards, with his head posed as if he was listening. Then he returned to the brink of the dell and looked down at the others laughing and talking.

'What is the matter, Strider?' Merry called up. 'What are you looking for? Do you miss the East Wind?'

'No indeed,' he answered. 'But I miss something. I have been in the country of Hollin in many seasons. No folk dwell here now, but many other creatures live here at all times, especially birds. Yet now all things but you are silent. I can feel it. There is no sound for miles about us, and your voices seem to make the ground echo. I do not understand it.'

Gandalf looked up with sudden interest. 'But what do you guess is the reason?' he asked. 'Is there more in it than surprise at seeing four hobbits, not to mention the rest of us, where people are so seldom seen or heard?'

'I hope that is it,' answered Aragorn. 'But I have a sense of watchfulness, and of fear, that I have never had here before.'

'Then we must be more careful,' said Gandalf. 'If you bring a Ranger with you, it is well to pay attention to him, especially if the Ranger is Aragorn. We must stop talking aloud, rest quietly, and set the watch.'

It was Sam's turn that day to take the first watch, but Aragorn joined him. The others fell asleep. Then the silence grew until even Sam felt it. The breathing of the sleepers could be plainly heard. The swish of the pony's tail and the occasional movements of his feet became loud noises. Sam could hear his own joints creaking, if he stirred. Dead silence was around him, and over all hung a clear blue sky, as the Sun rode up from the East. Away in the South a dark patch appeared, and grew, and drove north like flying smoke in the wind.

'What's that, Strider? It don't look like a cloud,' said Sam in a whisper to Aragorn. He made no answer, he was gazing intently at the sky; but before long Sam could see for himself what was approaching. Flocks of birds, flying at great speed, were wheeling and circling, and traversing all the land as if they were searching for something; and they were steadily drawing nearer.

'Lie flat and still!' hissed Aragorn, pulling Sam down into the shade of a holly-bush; for a whole regiment of birds had broken away suddenly from the main host, and came, flying low, straight towards the ridge. Sam thought they were a kind of crow of large size. As they passed overhead, in so dense a throng that their shadow followed them darkly over the ground below, one harsh croak was heard.

Not until they had dwindled into the distance, north and west, and the sky was again clear would Aragorn rise. Then he sprang up and went and wakened Gandalf.

'Regiments of black crows are flying over all the land between the Mountains and the Greyflood,' he said, 'and they have passed over Hollin. They are not natives here; they are *crebain* out of Fangorn and Dunland. I do not know what they are about: possibly there is some trouble away south from which they are fleeing; but I think they are spying out the land. I have also glimpsed many hawks flying high up in the sky. I think we ought to move again this evening. Hollin is no longer wholesome for us: it is being watched.'

'And in that case so is the Redhorn Gate,' said Gandalf; 'and how we can get over that without being seen, I cannot imagine. But we will think of that when we must. As for moving as soon as it is dark, I am afraid that you are right.'

'Luckily our fire made little smoke, and had burned low before the *crebain* came,' said Aragorn. 'It must be put out and not lit again.'

'Well if that isn't a plague and a nuisance!' said Pippin. The news: no fire, and a move again by night, had been broken to him, as soon as he woke in the late afternoon. 'All because of a pack of crows! I had looked forward to a real good meal tonight: something hot.'

'Well, you can go on looking forward,' said Gandalf. 'There may be many unexpected feasts ahead for you. For myself I should like a pipe to smoke in comfort, and warmer feet. However, we are certain of one thing at any rate: it will get warmer as we get south.'

'Too warm, I shouldn't wonder,' muttered Sam to Frodo. 'But I'm beginning to think it's time we got a sight of that Fiery Mountain, and saw the end of the Road, so to speak. I thought at first that this here Redhorn, or whatever its name is, might be it, till Gimli spoke his piece. A fair jaw-cracker dwarf-language must be!' Maps conveyed nothing to Sam's mind, and all distances in these strange lands seemed so vast that he was quite out of his reckoning.

All that day the Company remained in hiding. The dark birds passed over now and again; but as the westering Sun grew red they disappeared southwards. At dusk the Company set out, and turning now half east they steered their course towards Caradhras, which far away still glowed faintly red in the last light of the vanished Sun. One by one white stars sprang forth as the sky faded.

Guided by Aragorn they struck a good path. It looked to Frodo like the remains of an ancient road, that had once been broad and well planned, from Hollin to the mountain-pass. The Moon, now at the full, rose over the mountains, and cast a pale light in which the shadows of stones were black. Many of them looked to have been worked by hands, though now they lay tumbled and ruinous in a bleak, barren land.

It was the cold chill hour before the first stir of dawn, and the moon was low. Frodo looked up at the sky. Suddenly he saw or felt a shadow pass over the high stars, as if for a moment they faded and then flashed out again. He shivered.

'Did you see anything pass over?' he whispered to Gandalf, who was just ahead.

'No, but I felt it, whatever it was,' he answered. 'It may be nothing, only a wisp of thin cloud.'

'It was moving fast then,' muttered Aragorn, 'and not with the wind.'

Nothing further happened that night. The next morning dawned even brighter than before. But the air was chill again; already the wind was turning back towards the east. For two more nights they marched on, climbing steadily but ever more slowly as their road wound up into the hills, and the mountains towered up, nearer and nearer. On the third morning Caradhras rose before them, a mighty peak, tipped with snow like silver, but with sheer naked sides, dull red as if stained with blood.

There was a black look in the sky, and the sun was wan. The wind had gone now round to the north-east. Gandalf snuffed the air and looked back.

'Winter deepens behind us,' he said quietly to Aragorn. 'The heights away north are whiter than they were; snow is lying far down their shoulders. Tonight we shall be on our way high up towards the Redhorn Gate. We may well be seen by watchers on that narrow path, and waylaid by some evil; but the weather may prove a more deadly enemy than any. What do you think of your course now, Aragorn?'

Frodo overheard these words, and understood that Gandalf and Aragorn were continuing some debate that had begun long before. He listened anxiously.

'I think no good of our course from beginning to end, as you know well, Gandalf,' answered Aragorn. 'And perils known and unknown will grow as we go on. But we must go on; and it is no good our delaying the passage of the mountains. Further south there are no passes, till one comes to the Gap of Rohan. I do not trust that way since your news of Saruman. Who knows which side now the marshals of the Horse-lords serve?'

'Who knows indeed!' said Gandalf. 'But there is another way, and not by the pass of Caradhras: the dark and secret way that we have spoken of.'

'But let us not speak of it again! Not yet. Say nothing to the others, I beg, not until it is plain that there is no other way.'

'We must decide before we go further,' answered Gandalf.

'Then let us weigh the matter in our minds, while the others rest and sleep,' said Aragorn.

In the late afternoon, while the others were finishing their breakfast, Gandalf and Aragorn went aside together and stood looking at Caradhras. Its sides were now dark and sullen, and its head was in grey cloud. Frodo watched them, wondering which way the debate would go. When they returned to the Company Gandalf spoke, and then he knew that it had been decided to face the weather and the high pass. He was relieved. He could not guess what was the other dark and secret way, but the very mention of it had seemed to fill Aragorn with dismay, and Frodo was glad that it had been abandoned.

'From signs that we have seen lately,' said Gandalf, 'I fear that the Redhorn Gate may be watched; and also I have doubts of the weather that is coming up behind. Snow may come. We must go with all the speed that we can. Even so it will take us more than two marches before we reach the top of the pass. Dark will come early this evening. We must leave as soon as you can get ready.'

'I will add a word of advice, if I may,' said Boromir. 'I was born under the shadow of the White Mountains and know something of journeys in the high places. We shall meet bitter cold, if no worse, before we come down on the other side. It will not help us to keep so secret that we are frozen to death. When we leave here, where there are still a few trees and bushes, each of us should carry a faggot of wood, as large as he can bear.'

'And Bill could take a bit more, couldn't you, lad?' said Sam. The pony looked at him mournfully.

'Very well,' said Gandalf. 'But we must not use the wood – not unless it is a choice between fire and death.'

The Company set out again, with good speed at first; but soon their way became steep and difficult. The twisting and climbing road had in many places almost disappeared, and was blocked with many fallen stones. The night grew deadly dark under great clouds. A bitter wind swirled among the rocks. By midnight they had climbed to the knees of the great mountains. The narrow path now wound under a sheer wall of cliffs to the left, above which the grim flanks of Caradhras towered up invisible in the gloom; on the right was a gulf of darkness where the land fell suddenly into a deep ravine.

Laboriously they climbed a sharp slope and halted for a moment at the top. Frodo felt a soft touch on his face. He put out his arm and saw the dim white flakes of snow settling on his sleeve.

They went on. But before long the snow was falling fast, filling all the air, and swirling into Frodo's eyes. The dark bent shapes of Gandalf and Aragorn only a pace or two ahead could hardly be seen.

'I don't like this at all,' panted Sam just behind. 'Snow's all right on a fine morning, but I like to be in bed while it's falling. I wish this lot would go off to Hobbiton! Folk might welcome it there.' Except on the high moors of the Northfarthing a heavy fall was rare in the Shire, and was regarded as a pleasant event and a chance for fun. No living hobbit (save Bilbo) could remember the Fell Winter of 1311, when white wolves invaded the Shire over the frozen Brandywine.

Gandalf halted. Snow was thick on his hood and shoulders; it was already ankle-deep about his boots.

'This is what I feared,' he said. 'What do you say now, Aragorn?'

'That I feared it too,' Aragorn answered, 'but less than other things. I knew the risk of snow, though it seldom falls heavily so far south, save high up in the mountains. But we are not high yet; we are still far down, where the paths are usually open all the winter.'

'I wonder if this is a contrivance of the Enemy,' said Boromir. 'They say in my land that he can govern the storms in the Mountains of Shadow that stand upon the borders of Mordor. He has strange powers and many allies.'

'His arm has grown long indeed,' said Gimli, 'if he can draw snow down from the North to trouble us here three hundred leagues away.'

'His arm has grown long,' said Gandalf.

While they were halted, the wind died down, and the snow slackened until it almost ceased. They tramped on again. But they had not gone more than a furlong when the storm returned with fresh fury. The wind whistled and the snow became a blinding blizzard. Soon even Boromir found it hard to keep going. The hobbits, bent nearly double, toiled along behind the taller folk, but it was plain that they could not go much further, if the snow continued. Frodo's feet felt like lead. Pippin was dragging behind. Even Gimli, as stout as any dwarf could be, was grumbling as he trudged.

The Company halted suddenly, as if they had come to an agreement without any words being spoken. They heard eerie noises in the darkness round them. It may have been only a trick of the wind in the cracks and gullies of the rocky wall, but the sounds were those of shrill cries, and wild howls of laughter. Stones began to fall from the mountain-side, whistling over their heads, or crashing on the path beside them. Every now and again they heard a dull rumble, as a great boulder rolled down from hidden heights above.

'We cannot go further tonight,' said Boromir. 'Let those call it the wind who will; there are fell voices on the air; and these stones are aimed at us.'

'I do call it the wind,' said Aragorn. 'But that does not make what you say untrue. There are many evil and unfriendly things in the world that have little love for those that go on two legs, and yet are not in league with Sauron, but have purposes of their own. Some have been in this world longer than he.'

'Caradhras was called the Cruel, and had an ill name,' said Gimli, 'long years ago, when rumour of Sauron had not been heard in these lands.'

'It matters little who is the enemy, if we cannot beat off his attack,' said Gandalf.

'But what can we do?' cried Pippin miserably. He was leaning on Merry and Frodo, and he was shivering.

'Either stop where we are, or go back,' said Gandalf. 'It is no good going on. Only a little higher, if I remember rightly, this path leaves the cliff and runs into a wide shallow trough at the bottom of a long hard slope. We should have no shelter there from snow, or stones – or anything else.'

'And it is no good going back while the storm holds,' said Aragorn. 'We have passed no place on the way up that offered more shelter than this cliff-wall we are under now.'

'Shelter!' muttered Sam. 'If this is shelter, then one wall and no roof make a house.'

The Company now gathered together as close to the cliff as they could. It faced southwards, and near the bottom it leaned out a little, so that they hoped it would give them some protection from the northerly wind and from the falling stones. But eddying blasts swirled round them from every side, and the snow flowed down in ever denser clouds.

They huddled together with their backs to the wall. Bill the pony stood patiently but dejectedly in front of the hobbits, and screened them a little; but before long the drifting snow was above his hocks, and it went on mounting. If they had had no larger companions the hobbits would soon have been entirely buried.

A great sleepiness came over Frodo; he felt himself sinking fast into a warm and hazy dream. He thought a fire was heating his toes, and out of the shadows on the other side of the hearth he heard Bilbo's voice speaking. *I don't think much of your diary*, he said. *Snowstorms on January the twelfth: there was no need to come back to report that!*

But I wanted rest and sleep, Bilbo, Frodo answered with an effort, when he felt himself shaken, and he came back painfully to wakefulness. Boromir had lifted him off the ground out of a nest of snow.

'This will be the death of the halflings, Gandalf,' said Boromir. 'It is useless to sit here until the snow goes over our heads. We must do something to save ourselves.'

'Give them this,' said Gandalf, searching in his pack and drawing out a leathern flask. 'Just a mouthful each – for all of us. It is very precious. It is *miruvor*, the cordial of Imladris. Elrond gave it to me at our parting. Pass it round!'

As soon as Frodo had swallowed a little of the warm and fragrant liquor he felt a new strength of heart, and the heavy drowsiness left his limbs. The others also revived and found fresh hope and vigour. But the snow did not relent. It whirled about them thicker than ever, and the wind blew louder.

'What do you say to fire?' asked Boromir suddenly. 'The choice seems near now between fire and death, Gandalf. Doubtless we shall be hidden from all unfriendly eyes when the snow has covered us, but that will not help us.'

'You may make a fire, if you can,' answered Gandalf. 'If there are any watchers that can endure this storm, then they can see us, fire or no.'

But though they had brought wood and kindlings by the advice of Boromir, it passed the skill of Elf or even Dwarf to strike a flame that would hold amid the swirling wind or catch in the wet fuel. At last reluctantly Gandalf himself took a hand. Picking up a faggot he held it aloft for a moment, and then with a word of command, *naur an edraith ammen!* he thrust the end of his staff into the midst of it. At once a great spout of green and blue flame sprang out, and the wood flared and sputtered.

'If there are any to see, then I at least am revealed to them,' he said. 'I have written *Gandalf is here* in signs that all can read from Rivendell to the mouths of Anduin.'

But the Company cared no longer for watchers or unfriendly eyes. Their hearts were rejoiced to see the light of the fire. The wood burned merrily; and though all round it the snow hissed, and pools of slush crept under their feet, they warmed their hands gladly at the blaze. There they stood, stooping in a circle round the little dancing and blowing flames. A red light was on their tired and anxious faces; behind them the night was like a black wall.

But the wood was burning fast, and the snow still fell.

The fire burned low, and the last faggot was thrown on.

'The night is getting old,' said Aragorn. 'The dawn is not far off.'

'If any dawn can pierce these clouds,' said Gimli.

Boromir stepped out of the circle and stared up into the blackness. 'The snow is growing less,' he said, 'and the wind is quieter.'

Frodo gazed wearily at the flakes still falling out of the dark to be revealed white for a moment in the light of the dying fire; but for a long time he could see no sign of their slackening. Then suddenly, as sleep was beginning to creep over him again, he was aware that the wind had indeed fallen, and the flakes were becoming larger and fewer. Very slowly a dim light began to grow. At last the snow stopped altogether.

As the light grew stronger it showed a silent shrouded world. Below their refuge were white humps and domes and shapeless deeps beneath which the path that they had trodden was altogether lost; but the heights above were hidden in great clouds still heavy with the threat of snow.

Gimli looked up and shook his head. 'Caradhras has not forgiven us,' he said. 'He has more snow yet to fling at us, if we go on. The sooner we go back and down the better.'

To this all agreed, but their retreat was now difficult. It might well prove impossible. Only a few paces from the ashes of their fire the snow lay many feet deep, higher than the heads of the hobbits; in places it had been scooped and piled by the wind into great drifts against the cliff.

'If Gandalf would go before us with a bright flame, he might melt a path for you,' said Legolas. The storm had troubled him little, and he alone of the Company remained still light of heart.

'If Elves could fly over mountains, they might fetch the Sun to save us,' answered Gandalf. 'But I must have something to work on. I cannot burn snow.'

'Well,' said Boromir, 'when heads are at a loss bodies must serve, as we say in my country. The strongest of us must seek a way. See! Though all is now snow-clad, our path, as we came up, turned about that shoulder of rock down yonder. It was there that the snow first began to burden us. If we could reach that point, maybe it would prove easier beyond. It is no more than a furlong off, I guess.'

'Then let us force a path thither, you and I!' said Aragorn.

Aragorn was the tallest of the Company, but Boromir, little less in height, was broader and heavier in build. He led the way, and Aragorn followed him. Slowly they moved off, and were soon toiling heavily. In places the snow was breast-high, and often Boromir seemed to be swimming or burrowing with his great arms rather than walking.

Legolas watched them for a while with a smile upon his lips, and then he turned to the others. 'The strongest must seek a way, say you? But I say: let a ploughman plough, but choose an otter for swimming, and for running light over grass and leaf, or over snow – an Elf.'

With that he sprang forth nimbly, and then Frodo noticed as if for the first time, though he had long known it, that the Elf had no boots, but wore only light shoes, as he always did, and his feet made little imprint in the snow.

'Farewell!' he said to Gandalf. 'I go to find the Sun!' Then swift as a runner over firm sand he shot away, and quickly overtaking the toiling men, with a wave of his hand he passed them, and sped into the distance, and vanished round the rocky turn.

The others waited huddled together, watching until Boromir and Aragorn dwindled into black specks in the whiteness. At length they too passed from sight. The time dragged on. The clouds lowered, and now a few flakes of snow came curling down again.

An hour, maybe, went by, though it seemed far longer, and then at last they saw Legolas coming back. At the same time Boromir and Aragorn reappeared round the bend far behind him and came labouring up the slope.

'Well,' cried Legolas as he ran up, 'I have not brought the Sun. She is walking in the blue fields of the South, and a little wreath of snow on this Redhorn hillock troubles her not at all. But I have brought back a gleam of good hope for those who are doomed to go on feet. There is the greatest wind-drift of all just beyond the turn, and there our Strong Men were almost buried. They despaired, until I returned and told them that the drift was little wider than a wall. And on the other side the snow suddenly grows less, while further down it is no more than a white coverlet to cool a hobbit's toes.'

'Ah, it is as I said,' growled Gimli. 'It was no ordinary storm. It is the ill will of Caradhras. He does not love Elves and Dwarves, and that drift was laid to cut off our escape.'

'But happily your Caradhras has forgotten that you have Men with you,' said Boromir, who came up at that moment. 'And doughty Men too, if I may say it; though lesser men with spades might have served you better. Still, we have thrust a lane through the drift; and for that all here may be grateful who cannot run as light as Elves.'

'But how are we to get down there, even if you have cut through the drift?' said Pippin, voicing the thought of all the hobbits.

'Have hope!' said Boromir. 'I am weary, but I still have some strength left, and Aragorn too. We will bear the little folk. The others no doubt will make shift to tread the path behind us. Come, Master Peregrin! I will begin with you.'

He lifted up the hobbit. 'Cling to my back! I shall need my arms,' he said and strode forward. Aragorn with Merry came behind. Pippin marvelled at his strength, seeing the passage that he had already forced with no other tool than his great limbs. Even now, burdened as he was, he was widening the track for those who followed, thrusting the snow aside as he went.

They came at length to the great drift. It was flung across the mountain-path like a sheer and sudden wall, and its crest, sharp as if shaped with knives, reared up more than twice the height of Boromir; but through the middle a passage had been beaten, rising and falling like a bridge. On the far side Merry and Pippin were set down, and there they waited with Legolas for the rest of the Company to arrive.

After a while Boromir returned carrying Sam. Behind in the narrow but now well-trodden track came Gandalf, leading Bill with Gimli perched among the baggage. Last came Aragorn carrying Frodo. They passed through the lane; but hardly had Frodo touched the ground when with a deep rumble there rolled down a fall of stones and slithering snow. The spray of it half blinded the Company as they crouched against the cliff, and when the air cleared again they saw that the path was blocked behind them.

'Enough, enough!' cried Gimli. 'We are departing as quickly as we may!' And indeed with that last stroke the malice of the mountain seemed to be expended, as if Caradhras was satisfied that the invaders had been beaten off and would not dare to return. The threat of snow lifted; the clouds began to break and the light grew broader.

As Legolas had reported, they found that the snow became steadily more shallow as they went down, so that even the hobbits could trudge along. Soon they all stood once more on the flat shelf at the head of the steep slope where they had felt the first flakes of snow the night before.

The morning was now far advanced. From the high place they looked back westwards over the lower lands. Far away in the tumble of country that lay at the foot of the mountain was the dell from which they had started to climb the pass.

Frodo's legs ached. He was chilled to the bone and hungry; and his head was dizzy as he thought of the long and painful march downhill. Black specks swam before his eyes. He rubbed them, but the black specks remained. In the distance below him, but still high above the lower foot-hills, dark dots were circling in the air.

'The birds again!' said Aragorn, pointing down.

'That cannot be helped now,' said Gandalf. 'Whether they are good or evil, or have nothing to do with us at all, we must go down at once. Not even on the knees of Caradhras will we wait for another night-fall!'

A cold wind flowed down behind them, as they turned their backs on the Redhorn Gate, and stumbled wearily down the slope. Caradhras had defeated them.

CHAPTER IV

A JOURNEY IN THE DARK

It was evening, and the grey light was again waning fast, when they halted for the night. They were very weary. The mountains were veiled in deepening dusk, and the wind was cold. Gandalf spared them one more mouthful each of the *miruvor* of Rivendell. When they had eaten some food he called a council.

'We cannot, of course, go on again tonight,' he said. 'The attack on the Redhorn Gate has tired us out, and we must rest here for a while.'

'And then where are we to go?' asked Frodo.

'We still have our journey and our errand before us,' answered Gandalf. 'We have no choice but to go on, or to return to Rivendell.'

Pippin's face brightened visibly at the mere mention of return to Rivendell; Merry and Sam looked up hopefully. But Aragorn and Boromir made no sign. Frodo looked troubled.

'I wish I was back there,' he said. 'But how can I return without shame – unless there is indeed no other way, and we are already defeated?'

'You are right, Frodo,' said Gandalf: 'to go back is to admit defeat, and face worse defeat to come. If we go back now, then the Ring must remain there: we shall not be able to set out again. Then sooner or later Rivendell will be besieged, and after a brief and bitter time it will be destroyed. The Ringwraiths are deadly enemies, but they are only shadows yet of the power and terror they would possess if the Ruling Ring was on their master's hand again.'

'Then we must go on, if there is a way,' said Frodo with a sigh. Sam sank back into gloom.

'There is a way that we may attempt,' said Gandalf. 'I thought from the beginning, when first I considered this journey, that we should try it. But it is not a pleasant way, and I have not spoken of it to the Company before. Aragorn was against it, until the pass over the mountains had at least been tried.'

'If it is a worse road than the Redhorn Gate, then it must be evil indeed,' said Merry. 'But you had better tell us about it, and let us know the worst at once.'

'The road that I speak of leads to the Mines of Moria,' said Gandalf. Only Gimli lifted up his head; a smouldering fire was in his eyes. On all the others a dread fell at the mention of that name. Even to the hobbits it was a legend of vague fear.

'The road may lead to Moria, but how can we hope that it will lead through Moria?' said Aragorn darkly.

'It is a name of ill omen,' said Boromir. 'Nor do I see the need to go there. If we cannot cross the mountains, let us journey southwards, until we come to the Gap of Rohan, where men are friendly to my people, taking the road that I followed on my way hither. Or we might pass by and cross the Isen into Langstrand and Lebennin, and so come to Gondor from the regions nigh to the sea.'

'Things have changed since you came north, Boromir,' answered Gandalf. 'Did you not hear what I told you of Saruman? With him I may have business of my own ere all is over. But the Ring must not come near Isengard, if that can by any means be prevented. The Gap of Rohan is closed to us while we go with the Bearer.

'As for the longer road: we cannot afford the time. We might spend a year in such a journey, and we should pass through many lands that are empty and harbourless. Yet they would not be safe. The watchful eyes both of Saruman and of the Enemy are on them. When you came north, Boromir, you were in the Enemy's eyes only one stray wanderer from the South and a matter of small concern to him: his mind was busy with the pursuit of the Ring. But you return now as a member of the Ring's Company, and you are in peril as long as you remain with us. The danger will increase with every league that we go south under the naked sky.

'Since our open attempt on the mountain-pass our plight has become more desperate, I fear. I see now little hope, if we do not soon vanish from sight for a while, and cover our trail. Therefore I advise that we should go neither over the mountains, nor round them, but under them. That is a road at any rate that the Enemy will least expect us to take.'

'We do not know what he expects,' said Boromir. 'He may watch all roads, likely and unlikely. In that case to enter Moria would be to walk into a trap, hardly better than knocking at the gates of the Dark Tower itself. The name of Moria is black.'

'You speak of what you do not know, when you liken Moria to the stronghold of Sauron,' answered Gandalf. 'I alone of you have ever been in the dungeons of the Dark Lord, and only in his older and lesser dwelling in Dol Guldur. Those who pass the gates of Barad-dûr do not return. But I would not lead you into Moria if there were no hope of coming out again. If there are Orcs there, it may prove ill for us, that is true. But most of the Orcs of the Misty Mountains were scattered or destroyed in the Battle of Five Armies. The Eagles report that Orcs are gathering again from afar; but there is a hope that Moria is still free.

'There is even a chance that Dwarves are there, and that in some deep hall of his fathers, Balin son of Fundin may be found. However it may prove, one must tread the path that need chooses!'

'I will tread the path with you, Gandalf!' said Gimli. 'I will go and look on the halls of Durin, whatever may wait there – if you can find the doors that are shut.'

'Good, Gimli!' said Gandalf. 'You encourage me. We will seek the hidden doors together. And we will come through. In the ruins of the Dwarves, a dwarf's head will be less easy to bewilder than Elves or Men or Hobbits. Yet it will not be the first time that I have been to Moria. I sought there long for Thráin son of Thrór after he was lost. I passed through, and I came out again alive!'

'I too once passed the Dimrill Gate,' said Aragorn quietly; 'but though I also came out again, the memory is very evil. I do not wish to enter Moria a second time.'

'And I don't wish to enter it even once,' said Pippin.

'Nor me,' muttered Sam.

'Of course not!' said Gandalf. 'Who would? But the question is: who will follow me, if I lead you there?'

'I will,' said Gimli eagerly.

'I will,' said Aragorn heavily. 'You followed my lead almost to disaster in the snow, and have said no word of blame. I will follow your lead now – if this last warning does not move you. It is not of the Ring, nor of us others that I am thinking now, but of you, Gandalf. And I say to you: if you pass the doors of Moria, beware!'

'I will *not* go,' said Boromir; 'not unless the vote of the whole company is against me. What do Legolas and the little folk say? The Ring-bearer's voice surely should be heard?'

'I do not wish to go to Moria,' said Legolas.

The hobbits said nothing. Sam looked at Frodo. At last Frodo spoke. 'I do not wish to go,' he said; 'but neither do I wish to refuse the advice of Gandalf. I beg that there should be no vote, until we have slept on it. Gandalf will get votes easier in the light of the morning than in this cold gloom. How the wind howls!'

At these words all fell into silent thought. They heard the wind hissing among the rocks and trees, and there was a howling and wailing round them in the empty spaces of the night.

Suddenly Aragorn leapt to his feet. 'How the wind howls!' he cried. 'It is howling with wolf-voices. The Wargs have come west of the Mountains!'

'Need we wait until morning then?' said Gandalf. 'It is as I said. The hunt is up! Even if we live to see the dawn, who now will wish to journey south by night with the wild wolves on his trail?'

'How far is Moria?' asked Boromir.

'There was a door south-west of Caradhras, some fifteen miles as the crow flies, and maybe twenty as the wolf runs,' answered Gandalf grimly.

'Then let us start as soon as it is light tomorrow, if we can,' said Boromir. 'The wolf that one hears is worse than the orc that one fears.'   ·

'True!' said Aragorn, loosening his sword in its sheath. 'But where the warg howls, there also the orc prowls.'

'I wish I had taken Elrond's advice,' muttered Pippin to Sam. 'I am no good after all. There is not enough of the breed of Bandobras the Bullroarer in me: these howls freeze my blood. I don't ever remember feeling so wretched.'

'My heart's right down in my toes, Mr. Pippin,' said Sam. 'But we aren't etten yet, and there are some stout folk here with us. Whatever may be in store for old Gandalf, I'll wager it isn't a wolf's belly.'

For their defence in the night the Company climbed to the top of the small hill under which they had been sheltering. It was crowned with a knot of old and twisted trees, about which lay a broken circle of boulder-stones. In the midst of this they lit a fire, for there was no hope that darkness and silence would keep their trail from discovery by the hunting packs.

Round the fire they sat, and those that were not on guard dozed uneasily. Poor Bill the pony trembled and sweated where he stood. The howling of the wolves was now all round them, sometimes nearer and sometimes further off. In the dead of night many shining eyes were seen peering over the brow of the hill. Some advanced almost to the ring of stones. At a gap in the circle a great dark wolf-shape could be seen halted, gazing at them. A shuddering howl broke from him, as if he were a captain summoning his pack to the assault.

Gandalf stood up and strode forward, holding his staff aloft. 'Listen, Hound of Sauron!' he cried. 'Gandalf is here. Fly, if you value your foul skin! I will shrivel you from tail to snout, if you come within this ring.'

The wolf snarled and sprang towards them with a great leap. At that moment there was a sharp twang. Legolas had loosed his bow. There was a hideous yell, and the leaping shape thudded to the ground; the elvish arrow had pierced its throat. The watching eyes were suddenly ex-tinguished. Gandalf and Aragorn strode forward, but the hill was deserted; the hunting packs had fled. All about them the darkness grew silent, and no cry came on the sighing wind.

The night was old, and westward the waning moon was setting, gleaming fitfully through the breaking clouds. Suddenly Frodo started from sleep.

Without warning a storm of howls broke out fierce and wild all about the camp. A great host of Wargs had gathered silently and was now attacking them from every side at once.

'Fling fuel on the fire!' cried Gandalf to the hobbits. 'Draw your blades, and stand back to back!'

In the leaping light, as the fresh wood blazed up, Frodo saw many grey shapes spring over the ring of stones. More and more followed. Through the throat of one huge leader Aragorn passed his sword with a thrust; with a great sweep Boromir hewed the head off another. Beside them Gimli stood with his stout legs apart, wielding his dwarf-axe. The bow of Legolas was singing.

In the wavering firelight Gandalf seemed suddenly to grow: he rose up, a great menacing shape like the monument of some ancient king of stone set upon a hill. Stooping like a cloud, he lifted a burning branch and strode to meet the wolves. They gave back before him. High in the air he tossed the blazing brand. It flared with a sudden white radiance like lightning; and his voice rolled like thunder.

'*Naur an edraith ammen! Naur dan i ngaurhoth!*' he cried.

There was a roar and a crackle, and the tree above him burst into a leaf and bloom of blinding flame. The fire leapt from tree-top to tree-top. The whole hill was crowned with dazzling light. The swords and knives of the defenders shone and flickered. The last arrow of Legolas kindled in the air as it flew, and plunged burning into the heart of a great wolf-chieftain. All the others fled.

Slowly the fire died till nothing was left but falling ash and sparks; a bitter smoke curled above the burned tree-stumps, and blew darkly from the hill, as the first light of dawn came dimly in the sky. Their enemies were routed and did not return.

'What did I tell you, Mr. Pippin?' said Sam, sheathing his sword. 'Wolves won't get him. That was an eye-opener, and no mistake! Nearly singed the hair off my head!'

When the full light of the morning came no signs of the wolves were to be found, and they looked in vain for the bodies of the dead. No trace of the fight remained but the charred trees and the arrows of Legolas lying on the hill-top. All were undamaged save one of which only the point was left.

'It is as I feared,' said Gandalf. 'These were no ordinary wolves hunting for food in the wilderness. Let us eat quickly and go!'

That day the weather changed again, almost as if it was at the command of some power that had no longer any use for snow, since they had retreated from the pass, a power that wished now to have a clear light in which things that moved in the wild could be seen from far away. The wind had been turning through north to north-west during the night, and now it failed. The clouds vanished southwards and the sky was opened, high and blue. As they stood upon the hillside, ready to depart, a pale sunlight gleamed over the mountain-tops.

'We must reach the doors before sunset,' said Gandalf, 'or I fear we shall not reach them at all. It is not far, but our path may be winding, for here Aragorn cannot guide us; he has seldom walked in this country, and only once have I been under the west wall of Moria, and that was long ago.

'There it lies,' he said, pointing away south-eastwards to where the mountains' sides fell sheer into the shadows at their feet. In the distance could be dimly seen a line of bare cliffs, and in their midst, taller than the rest, one great grey wall. 'When we left the pass I led you southwards, and not back to our starting point, as some of you may have noticed. It is well that I did so, for now we have several miles less to cross, and haste is needed. Let us go!'

'I do not know which to hope,' said Boromir grimly: 'that Gandalf will find what he seeks, or that coming to the cliff we shall find the gates lost for ever. All choices seem ill, and to be caught between wolves and the wall the likeliest chance. Lead on!'

Gimli now walked ahead by the wizard's side, so eager was he to come to Moria. Together they led the Company back towards the mountains. The only road of old to Moria from the west had lain along the course of a stream, the Sirannon, that ran out from the feet of the cliffs near where the doors had stood. But either Gandalf was astray, or else the land had changed in recent years; for he did not strike the stream where he looked to find it, only a few miles southwards from their start.

The morning was passing towards noon, and still the Company wandered and scrambled in a barren country of red stones. Nowhere could they see any gleam of water or hear any sound of it. All was bleak and dry. Their hearts sank. They saw no living thing, and not a bird was in the sky; but what the night would bring, if it caught them in that lost land, none of them cared to think.

Suddenly Gimli, who had pressed on ahead, called back to them. He was standing on a knoll and pointing to the right. Hurrying up they saw below them a deep and narrow channel. It was empty and silent, and hardly a trickle of water flowed among the brown and red-stained stones of its bed; but on the near side there was a path, much broken and decayed, that wound its way among the ruined walls and paving-stones of an ancient highroad.

'Ah! Here it is at last!' said Gandalf. 'This is where the stream ran: Sirannon, the Gate-stream, they used to call it. But what has happened to the water, I cannot guess; it used to be swift and noisy. Come! We must hurry on. We are late.'

The Company were footsore and tired; but they trudged doggedly along the rough and winding track for many miles. The sun turned from the noon and began to go west. After a brief halt and a hasty meal they went on again. Before them the mountains frowned, but their path lay in a deep trough of land and they could see only the higher shoulders and the far eastward peaks.

At length they came to a sharp bend. There the road, which had been veering southwards between the brink of the channel and a steep fall of the land to the left, turned and went due east again. Rounding the corner they saw before them a low cliff, some five fathoms high, with a broken and jagged top. Over it a trickling water dripped, through a wide cleft that seemed to have been carved out by a fall that had once been strong and full.

'Indeed things have changed!' said Gandalf. 'But there is no mistaking the place. There is all that remains of the Stair Falls. If I remember right, there was a flight of steps cut in the rock at their side, but the main road wound away left and climbed with several loops up to the level ground at the top. There used to be a shallow valley beyond the falls right up to the Walls of Moria, and the Sirannon flowed through it with the road beside it. Let us go and see what things are like now!'

They found the stone steps without difficulty, and Gimli sprang swiftly up them, followed by Gandalf and Frodo. When they reached the top they saw that they could go no further that way, and the reason for the drying up of the Gate-stream was revealed. Behind them the sinking Sun filled the cool western sky with glimmering gold. Before them stretched a dark still lake. Neither sky nor sunset was reflected on its sullen surface. The Sirannon had been dammed and had filled all the valley. Beyond the ominous water were reared vast cliffs, their stern faces pallid in the fading light: final and impassable. No sign of gate or entrance, not a fissure or crack could Frodo see in the frowning stone.

'There are the Walls of Moria,' said Gandalf, pointing across the water. 'And there the Gate stood once upon a time, the Elven Door at the end of the road from Hollin by which we have come. But this way is blocked. None of the Company, I guess, will wish to swim this gloomy water at the end of the day. It has an unwholesome look.'

'We must find a way round the northern edge,' said Gimli. 'The first thing for the Company to do is to climb up by the main path and see where that will lead us. Even if there were no lake, we could not get our baggage-pony up this stair.'

'But in any case we cannot take the poor beast into the Mines,' said Gandalf. 'The road under the mountains is a dark road, and there are places narrow and steep which he cannot tread, even if we can.'

'Poor old Bill!' said Frodo. 'I had not thought of that. And poor Sam! I wonder what he will say?'

'I am sorry,' said Gandalf. 'Poor Bill has been a useful companion, and it goes to my heart to turn him adrift now. I would have travelled lighter and brought no animal, least of all this one that Sam is fond of, if I had had my way. I feared all along that we should be obliged to take this road.'

The day was drawing to its end, and cold stars were glinting in the sky high above the sunset, when the Company, with all the speed they could, climbed up the slopes and reached the side of the lake. In breadth it looked to be no more than two or three furlongs at the widest point. How far it stretched away southward they could not see in the failing light; but its northern end was no more than half a mile from where they stood, and between the stony ridges that enclosed the valley and the water's edge there was a rim of open ground. They hurried forward, for they had still a mile or two to go before they could reach the point on the far shore that Gandalf was making for; and then he had still to find the doors.

When they came to the northernmost corner of the lake they found a narrow creek that barred their way. It was green and stagnant, thrust out like a slimy arm towards the enclosing hills. Gimli strode forward undeterred, and found that the water was shallow, no more than ankle-deep at the edge. Behind him they walked in file, threading their way with care, for under the weedy pools were sliding and greasy stones, and footing was treacherous. Frodo shuddered with disgust at the touch of the dark unclean water on his feet.

As Sam, the last of the Company, led Bill up on to the dry ground on the far side, there came a soft sound: a swish, followed by a plop, as if a fish had disturbed the still surface of the water. Turning quickly they saw ripples, black-edged with shadow in the waning light: great rings were widening outwards from a point far out in the lake. There was a bubbling noise, and then silence. The dusk deepened, and the last gleams of the sunset were veiled in cloud.

Gandalf now pressed on at a great pace, and the others followed as quickly as they could. They reached the strip of dry land between the lake and the cliffs: it was narrow, often hardly a dozen yards across, and encumbered with fallen rock and stones; but they found a way, hugging the cliff, and keeping as far from the dark water as they might. A mile southwards along the shore they came upon holly trees. Stumps and dead boughs were rotting in the shallows, the remains it seemed of old thickets, or of a hedge that had once lined the road across the drowned valley. But close under the cliff there stood, still strong and living, two tall trees, larger than any trees of holly that Frodo had ever seen or imagined. Their great roots spread from the wall to the water. Under the looming cliffs they had looked like mere bushes, when seen far off from the top of the Stair; but now they towered overhead, stiff, dark, and silent, throwing deep night-shadows about their feet, standing like sentinel pillars at the end of the road.

'Well, here we are at last!' said Gandalf. 'Here the Elven-way from Hollin ended. Holly was the token of the people of that land, and they planted it here to mark the end of their domain; for the West-door was made chiefly for their use in their traffic with the Lords of Moria. Those were happier days, when there was still close friendship at times between folk of different race, even between Dwarves and Elves.'

'It was not the fault of the Dwarves that the friendship waned,' said Gimli.

'I have not heard that it was the fault of the Elves,' said Legolas.

'I have heard both,' said Gandalf; 'and I will not give judgement now. But I beg you two, Legolas and Gimli, at least to be friends, and to help me. I need you both. The doors are shut and hidden, and the sooner we find them the better. Night is at hand!'

Turning to the others he said: 'While I am searching, will you each make ready to enter the Mines? For here I fear we must say farewell to our good beast of burden. You must lay aside much of the stuff that we brought against bitter weather: you will not need it inside, nor, I hope, when we come through and journey on down into the South. Instead each of us must take a share of what the pony carried, especially the food and the water-skins.'

'But you can't leave poor old Bill behind in this forsaken place, Mr. Gandalf!' cried Sam, angry and distressed. 'I won't have it, and that's flat. After he has come so far and all!'

'I am sorry, Sam,' said the wizard. 'But when the Door opens I do not think you will be able to drag your Bill inside, into the long dark of Moria. You will have to choose between Bill and your master.'

'He'd follow Mr. Frodo into a dragon's den, if I led him,' protested Sam. 'It'd be nothing short of murder to turn him loose with all these wolves about.'

'It will be short of murder, I hope,' said Gandalf. He laid his hand on the pony's head, and spoke in a low voice. 'Go with words of guard and guiding on you,' he said. 'You are a wise beast, and have learned much in Rivendell. Make your ways to places where you can find grass, and so come in time to Elrond's house, or wherever you wish to go.

'There, Sam! He will have quite as much chance of escaping wolves and getting home as we have.'

Sam stood sullenly by the pony and returned no answer. Bill, seeming to understand well what was going on, nuzzled up to him, putting his nose to Sam's ear. Sam burst into tears, and fumbled with the straps, unlading all the pony's packs and throwing them on the ground. The others sorted out the goods, making a pile of all that could be left behind, and dividing up the rest.

When this was done they turned to watch Gandalf. He appeared to have done nothing. He was standing between the two trees gazing at the blank wall of the cliff, as if he would bore a hole into it with his eyes. Gimli was wandering about, tapping the stone here and there with his axe. Legolas was pressed against the rock, as if listening.

'Well, here we are and all ready,' said Merry; 'but where are the Doors? I can't see any sign of them.'

'Dwarf-doors are not made to be seen when shut,' said Gimli. 'They are invisible, and their own masters cannot find them or open them, if their secret is forgotten.'

'But this Door was not made to be a secret known only to Dwarves,' said Gandalf, coming suddenly to life and turning round. 'Unless things are altogether changed, eyes that know what to look for may discover the signs.'

He walked forward to the wall. Right between the shadow of the trees there was a smooth space, and over this he passed his hands to and fro, muttering words under his breath. Then he stepped back.

'Look!' he said. 'Can you see anything now?'

The Moon now shone upon the grey face of the rock; but they could see nothing else for a while. Then slowly on the surface, where the wizard's hands had passed, faint lines appeared, like slender veins of silver running in the stone. At first they were no more than pale gossamer-threads, so fine that they only twinkled fitfully where the Moon caught them, but steadily they grew broader and clearer, until their design could be guessed.

At the top, as high as Gandalf could reach, was an arch of interlacing letters in an Elvish character. Below, though the threads were in places blurred or broken, the outline could be seen of an anvil and a hammer surmounted by a crown with seven stars. Beneath these again were two trees, each bearing crescent moons. More clearly than all else there shone forth in the middle of the door a single star with many rays.

'There are the emblems of Durin!' cried Gimli.

'And there is the Tree of the High Elves!' said Legolas.

'And the Star of the House of Fëanor,' said Gandalf. 'They are wrought of *ithildin* that mirrors only starlight and moonlight, and sleeps until it is touched by one who speaks words now long forgotten in Middle-earth. It is long since I heard them, and I thought deeply before I could recall them to my mind.'

'What does the writing say?' asked Frodo, who was trying to decipher the inscription on the arch. 'I thought I knew the elf-letters, but I cannot read these.'

'The words are in the elven-tongue of the West of Middle-earth in the Elder Days,' answered Gandalf. 'But they do not say anything of importance to us. They say only: *The Doors of Durin, Lord of Moria. Speak, friend, and enter.* And underneath small and faint is written: *I, Narvi, made them. Celebrimbor of Hollin drew these signs.*'

'What does it mean by *speak, friend, and enter?*' asked Merry.

'That is plain enough,' said Gimli. 'If you are a friend, speak the password, and the doors will open, and you can enter.'

'Yes,' said Gandalf, 'these doors are probably governed by words. Some dwarf-gates will open only at special times, or for particular persons; and some have locks and keys that are still needed when all necessary times and words are known. These doors have no key. In the days of Durin they were not secret. They usually stood open and doorwards sat here. But if they were shut, any who knew the opening word could speak it and pass in. At least so it is recorded, is it not, Gimli?'

'It is,' said the dwarf. 'But what the word was is not remembered. Narvi and his craft and all his kindred have vanished from the earth.'

'But do not *you* know the word, Gandalf?' asked Boromir in surprise.

'No!' said the wizard.

The others looked dismayed; only Aragorn, who knew Gandalf well, remained silent and unmoved.

'Then what was the use of bringing us to this accursed spot?' cried Boromir, glancing back with a shudder at the dark water. 'You told us that you had once passed through the Mines. How could that be, if you did not know how to enter?'

'The answer to your first question, Boromir,' said the wizard, 'is that I do not know the word – yet. But we shall soon see. And,' he added, with a glint in his eyes under their bristling brows, 'you may ask what is the use of my deeds when they are proved useless. As for your other question: do you doubt my tale? Or have you no wits left? I did not enter this way. I came from the East.

'If you wish to know, I will tell you that these doors open outwards.

Here is written in the Fëanorian characters according to the mode of Beleriand: Ennyn Durin Aran Moria: pedo mellon a minno. Im Narvi hain echant: Celebrimbor o Eregion teithant i thiw hin.

From the inside you may thrust them open with your hands. From the outside nothing will move them save the spell of command. They cannot be forced inwards.'

'What are you going to do then?' asked Pippin, undaunted by the wizard's bristling brows.

'Knock on the doors with your head, Peregrin Took,' said Gandalf. 'But if that does not shatter them, and I am allowed a little peace from foolish questions, I will seek for the opening words.

'I once knew every spell in all the tongues of Elves or Men or Orcs, that was ever used for such a purpose. I can still remember ten score of them without searching in my mind. But only a few trials, I think, will be needed; and I shall not have to call on Gimli for words of the secret dwarf-tongue that they teach to none. The opening words were Elvish, like the writing on the arch: that seems certain.'

He stepped up to the rock again, and lightly touched with his staff the silver star in the middle beneath the sign of the anvil.

> *Annon edhellen, edro hi ammen!*
> *Fennas nogothrim, lasto beth lammen!*

he said in a commanding voice. The silver lines faded, but the blank grey stone did not stir.

Many times he repeated these words in different order, or varied them. Then he tried other spells, one after another, speaking now faster and louder, now soft and slow. Then he spoke many single words of Elvish speech. Nothing happened. The cliff towered into the night, the countless stars were kindled, the wind blew cold, and the doors stood fast.

Again Gandalf approached the wall, and lifting up his arms he spoke in tones of command and rising wrath. *Edro, edro!* he cried, and struck the rock with his staff. *Open, open!* he shouted, and followed it with the same command in every language that had ever been spoken in the West of Middle-earth. Then he threw his staff on the ground, and sat down in silence.

At that moment from far off the wind bore to their listening ears the howling of wolves. Bill the pony started in fear, and Sam sprang to his side and whispered softly to him.

'Do not let him run away!' said Boromir. 'It seems that we shall need him still, if the wolves do not find us. How I hate this foul pool!' He stooped and picking up a large stone he cast it far into the dark water.

The stone vanished with a soft slap; but at the same instant there was a swish and a bubble. Great rippling rings formed on the surface out beyond where the stone had fallen, and they moved slowly towards the foot of the cliff.

'Why did you do that, Boromir?' said Frodo. 'I hate this place, too, and I am afraid. I don't know of what: not of wolves, or the dark behind the doors, but of something else. I am afraid of the pool. Don't disturb it!'

'I wish we could get away!' said Merry.

'Why doesn't Gandalf do something quick?' said Pippin.

Gandalf took no notice of them. He sat with his head bowed, either in despair or in anxious thought. The mournful howling of the wolves was heard again. The ripples on the water grew and came closer; some were already lapping on the shore.

With a suddenness that startled them all the wizard sprang to his feet. He was laughing! 'I have it!' he cried. 'Of course, of course! Absurdly simple, like most riddles when you see the answer.'

Picking up his staff he stood before the rock and said in a clear voice: *Mellon!*

The star shone out briefly and faded again. Then silently a great doorway was outlined, though not a crack or joint had been visible before. Slowly it divided in the middle and swung outwards inch by inch, until both doors lay back against the wall. Through the opening a shadowy stair could be seen climbing steeply up; but beyond the lower steps the darkness was deeper than the night. The Company stared in wonder.

'I was wrong after all,' said Gandalf, 'and Gimli too. Merry, of all people, was on the right track. The opening word was inscribed on the archway all the time! The translation should have been: *Say "Friend" and enter*. I had only to speak the Elvish word for *friend* and the doors opened. Quite simple. Too simple for a learned lore-master in these suspicious days. Those were happier times. Now let us go!'

He strode forward and set his foot on the lowest step. But at that moment several things happened. Frodo felt something seize him by the ankle, and he fell with a cry. Bill the pony gave a wild neigh of fear, and turned tail and dashed away along the lakeside into the darkness. Sam leaped after him, and then hearing Frodo's cry he ran back again, weeping and cursing. The others swung round and saw the waters of the lake seething, as if a host of snakes were swimming up from the southern end.

Out from the water a long sinuous tentacle had crawled; it was pale-green and luminous and wet. Its fingered end had hold of Frodo's foot, and was dragging him into the water. Sam on his knees was now slashing at it with a knife.

The arm let go of Frodo, and Sam pulled him away, crying out for help.

Twenty other arms came rippling out. The dark water boiled, and there was a hideous stench.

'Into the gateway! Up the stairs! Quick!' shouted Gandalf leaping back. Rousing them from the horror that seemed to have rooted all but Sam to the ground where they stood, he drove them forward.

They were just in time. Sam and Frodo were only a few steps up, and Gandalf had just begun to climb, when the groping tentacles writhed across the narrow shore and fingered the cliff-wall and the doors. One came wriggling over the threshold, glistening in the starlight. Gandalf turned and paused. If he was considering what word would close the gate again from within, there was no need. Many coiling arms seized the doors on either side, and with horrible strength, swung them round. With a shattering echo they slammed, and all light was lost. A noise of rending and crashing came dully through the ponderous stone.

Sam, clinging to Frodo's arm, collapsed on a step in the black darkness. 'Poor old Bill!' he said in a choking voice. 'Poor old Bill! Wolves and snakes! But the snakes were too much for him. I had to choose, Mr. Frodo. I had to come with you.'

They heard Gandalf go back down the steps and thrust his staff against the doors. There was a quiver in the stone and the stairs trembled, but the doors did not open.

'Well, well!' said the wizard. 'The passage is blocked behind us now, and there is only one way out – on the other side of the mountains. I fear from the sounds that boulders have been piled up, and the trees uprooted and thrown across the gate. I am sorry; for the trees were beautiful, and had stood so long.'

'I felt that something horrible was near from the moment that my foot first touched the water,' said Frodo. 'What was the thing, or were there many of them?'

'I do not know,' answered Gandalf; 'but the arms were all guided by one purpose. Something has crept, or has been driven out of dark waters under the mountains. There are older and fouler things than Orcs in the deep places of the world.' He did not speak aloud his thought that whatever it was that dwelt in the lake, it had seized on Frodo first among all the Company.

Boromir muttered under his breath, but the echoing stone magnified the sound to a hoarse whisper that all could hear: 'In the deep places of the world! And thither we are going against my wish. Who will lead us now in this deadly dark?'

'I will,' said Gandalf, 'and Gimli shall walk with me. Follow my staff!'

As the wizard passed on ahead up the great steps, he held his staff aloft, and from its tip there came a faint radiance. The wide stairway was sound and undamaged. Two hundred steps they counted, broad and shallow; and at the top they found an arched passage with a level floor leading on into the dark.

'Let us sit and rest and have something to eat, here on the landing, since we can't find a dining-room!' said Frodo. He had begun to shake off the terror of the clutching arm, and suddenly he felt extremely hungry.

The proposal was welcomed by all; and they sat down on the upper steps, dim figures in the gloom. After they had eaten, Gandalf gave them each a third sip of the *miruvor* of Rivendell.

'It will not last much longer, I am afraid,' he said; 'but I think we need it after that horror at the gate. And unless we have great luck, we shall need all that is left before we see the other side! Go carefully with the water, too! There are many streams and wells in the Mines, but they should not be touched. We may not have a chance of filling our skins and bottles till we come down into Dimrill Dale.'

'How long is that going to take us?' asked Frodo.

'I cannot say,' answered Gandalf. 'It depends on many chances. But going straight, without mishap or losing our way, we shall take three or four marches, I expect. It cannot be less than forty miles from West-door to East-gate in a direct line, and the road may wind much.'

After only a brief rest they started on their way again. All were eager to get the journey over as quickly as possible, and were willing, tired as they were, to go on marching still for several hours. Gandalf walked in front as before. In his left hand he held up his glimmering staff, the light of which just showed the ground before his feet; in his right he held his sword Glamdring. Behind him came Gimli, his eyes glinting in the dim light as he turned his head from side to side. Behind the dwarf walked Frodo, and he had drawn the short sword, Sting. No gleam came from the blades of Sting or of Glamdring; and that was some comfort, for being the work of Elvish smiths in the Elder Days these swords shone with a cold light, if any Orcs were near at hand. Behind Frodo went Sam, and after him Legolas, and the young hobbits, and Boromir. In the dark at the rear, grim and silent, walked Aragorn.

The passage twisted round a few turns, and then began to descend. It went steadily down for a long while before it became level once again. The air grew hot and stifling, but it was not foul, and at times they felt currents of cooler air upon their faces, issuing from half-guessed openings in the walls. There were many of these. In the pale ray of the wizard's staff, Frodo caught glimpses of stairs and arches, and of other passages and tunnels, sloping up, or running steeply down, or opening blankly dark on either side. It was bewildering beyond hope of remembering.

Gimli aided Gandalf very little, except by his stout courage. At least he was not, as were most of the others, troubled by the mere darkness in itself. Often the wizard consulted him at points where the choice of way was doubtful; but it was always Gandalf who had the final word. The Mines of Moria were vast and intricate beyond the imagination of Gimli, Glóin's son, dwarf of the mountain-race though he was. To Gandalf the far-off memories of a journey long before were now of little help, but even in the gloom and despite all windings of the road he knew whither he wished to go, and he did not falter, as long as there was a path that led towards his goal.

'Do not be afraid!' said Aragorn. There was a pause longer than usual, and Gandalf and Gimli were whispering together; the others were crowded behind, waiting anxiously. 'Do not be afraid! I have been with him on many a journey, if never on one so dark; and there are tales of Rivendell of greater deeds of his than any that I have seen. He will not go astray – if there is any path to find. He has led us in here against our fears, but he will lead us out again, at whatever cost to himself. He is surer of finding the way home in a blind night than the cats of Queen Berúthiel.'

It was well for the Company that they had such a guide. They had no fuel nor any means of making torches; in the desperate scramble at the doors many things had been left behind. But without any light they would soon have come to grief. There were not only many roads to choose from, there were also in many places holes and pitfalls, and dark wells beside the path in which their passing feet echoed. There were fissures and chasms in the walls and floor, and every now and then a crack would open right before their feet. The widest was more than seven feet across, and it was long before Pippin could summon enough courage to leap over the dreadful gap. The noise of churning water came up from far below, as if some great mill-wheel was turning in the depths.

'Rope!' muttered Sam. 'I knew I'd want it, if I hadn't got it!'

As these dangers became more frequent their march became slower. Already they seemed to have been tramping on, on, endlessly to the mountains' roots. They were more than weary, and yet there seemed no comfort in the thought of halting anywhere. Frodo's spirits had risen for a while after his escape, and after food and a draught of the cordial; but now a deep uneasiness, growing to dread, crept over him again. Though he had been healed in Rivendell of the knife-stroke, that grim wound had not been without effect. His senses were sharper and more aware of things that could not be seen. One sign of change that he soon had noticed was that he could see more in the dark than any of his companions, save perhaps Gandalf. And he was in any case the bearer of the Ring: it hung upon its chain against his breast, and at whiles it seemed a heavy weight. He felt the certainty of evil ahead and of evil following; but he said nothing. He gripped tighter on the hilt of his sword and went on doggedly.

The Company behind him spoke seldom, and then only in hurried whispers. There was no sound but the sound of their own feet; the dull stump of Gimli's dwarf-boots; the heavy tread of Boromir; the light step of Legolas; the soft, scarce-heard patter of hobbit-feet; and in the rear the slow firm footfalls of Aragorn with his long stride. When they halted for a moment they heard nothing at all, unless it were occasionally a faint trickle and drip of unseen water. Yet Frodo began to hear, or to imagine that he heard, something else: like the faint fall of soft bare feet. It was never loud enough, or near enough, for him to feel certain that he heard it; but once it had started it never stopped, while the Company was moving. But it was not an echo, for when they halted it pattered on for a little all by itself, and then grew still.

It was after nightfall when they had entered the Mines. They had been going for several hours with only brief halts, when Gandalf came to his first serious check. Before him stood a wide dark arch opening into three passages: all led in the same general direction, eastwards; but the left-hand passage plunged down, while the right-hand climbed up, and the middle way seemed to run on, smooth and level but very narrow.

'I have no memory of this place at all!' said Gandalf, standing uncertainly under the arch. He held up his staff in the hope of finding some marks or inscription that might help his choice; but nothing of the kind was to be seen. 'I am too weary to decide,' he said, shaking his head. 'And I expect that you are all as weary as I am, or wearier. We had better halt here for what is left of the night. You know what I mean! In here it is ever dark; but outside the late Moon is riding westward and the middle-night has passed.'

'Poor old Bill!' said Sam. 'I wonder where he is. I hope those wolves haven't got him yet.'

To the left of the great arch they found a stone door: it was half closed, but swung back easily to a gentle thrust. Beyond there seemed to lie a wide chamber cut in the rock.

'Steady! Steady!' cried Gandalf as Merry and Pippin pushed forward, glad to find a place where they could rest with at least more feeling of shelter than in the open passage. 'Steady! You do not know what is inside yet. I will go first.'

He went in cautiously, and the others filed behind. 'There!' he said, pointing with his staff to the middle of the floor. Before his feet they saw a large round hole like the mouth of a well. Broken and rusty chains lay at the edge and trailed down into the black pit. Fragments of stone lay near.

'One of you might have fallen in and still be wondering when you were going to strike the bottom,' said Aragorn to Merry. 'Let the guide go first while you have one.'

'This seems to have been a guardroom, made for the watching of the three passages,' said Gimli. 'That hole was plainly a well for the guards' use, covered with a stone lid. But the lid is broken, and we must all take care in the dark.'

Pippin felt curiously attracted by the well. While the others were unrolling blankets and making beds against the walls of the chamber, as far as possible from the hole in the floor, he crept to the edge and peered over. A chill air seemed to strike his face, rising from invisible depths. Moved by a sudden impulse he groped for a loose stone, and let it drop. He felt his heart beat many times before there was any sound. Then far below, as if the stone had fallen into deep water in some cavernous place, there came a *plunk*, very distant, but magnified and repeated in the hollow shaft.

'What's that?' cried Gandalf. He was relieved when Pippin confessed what he had done; but he was angry, and Pippin could see his eye glinting. 'Fool of a Took!' he growled. 'This is a serious journey, not a hobbit walking-party. Throw yourself in next time, and then you will be no further nuisance. Now be quiet!'

Nothing more was heard for several minutes; but then there came out of the depths faint knocks: *tom-tap, tap-tom*. They stopped, and when the echoes had died away, they were repeated: *tap-tom, tom-tap, tap-tap, tom*. They sounded disquietingly like signals of some sort; but after a while the knocking died away and was not heard again.

'That was the sound of a hammer, or I have never heard one,' said Gimli.

'Yes,' said Gandalf, 'and I do not like it. It may have nothing to do with Peregrin's foolish stone; but probably something has been disturbed that would have been better left quiet. Pray, do nothing of the kind again! Let us hope we shall get some rest without further trouble. You, Pippin, can go on the first watch, as a reward,' he growled, as he rolled himself in a blanket.

Pippin sat miserably by the door in the pitch dark; but he kept on turning round, fearing that some unknown thing would crawl up out of the well. He wished he could cover the hole, if only with a blanket, but he dared not move or go near it, even though Gandalf seemed to be asleep.

Actually Gandalf was awake, though lying still and silent. He was deep in thought, trying to recall every memory of his former journey in the Mines, and considering anxiously the next course that he should take; a false turn now might be disastrous. After an hour he rose up and came over to Pippin.

'Get into a corner and have a sleep, my lad,' he said in a kindly tone. 'You want to sleep, I expect. I cannot get a wink, so I may as well do the watching.'

'I know what is the matter with me,' he muttered, as he sat down by the door. 'I need smoke! I have not tasted it since the morning before the snowstorm.'

The last thing that Pippin saw, as sleep took him, was a dark glimpse of the old wizard huddled on the floor, shielding a glowing chip in his gnarled hands between his knees. The flicker for a moment showed his sharp nose, and the puff of smoke.

It was Gandalf who roused them all from sleep. He had sat and watched all alone for about six hours, and had let the others rest. 'And in the watches I have made up my mind,' he said. 'I do not like the feel of the middle way; and I do not like the smell of the left-hand way: there is foul air down there, or I am no guide. I shall take the right-hand passage. It is time we began to climb up again.'

For eight dark hours, not counting two brief halts, they marched on; and they met no danger, and heard nothing, and saw nothing but the faint gleam of the wizard's light, bobbing like a will-o'-the-wisp in front of them. The passage they had chosen wound steadily upwards. As far as they could judge it went in great mounting curves, and as it rose it grew loftier and wider. There were now no openings to other galleries or tunnels on either side, and the floor was level and sound, without pits or cracks. Evidently they had struck what once had been an important road; and they went forward quicker than they had done on their first march.

In this way they advanced some fifteen miles, measured in a direct line east, though they must have actually walked twenty miles or more. As the road climbed upwards, Frodo's spirits rose a little; but he still felt oppressed, and still at times he heard, or thought he heard, away behind the Company and beyond the fall and patter of their feet, a following footstep that was not an echo.

They had marched as far as the hobbits could endure without a rest, and all were thinking of a place where they could sleep, when suddenly the walls to right and left vanished. They seemed to have passed through some arched doorway into a black and empty space. There was a great draught of warmer air behind them, and before them the darkness was cold on their faces. They halted and crowded anxiously together.

Gandalf seemed pleased. 'I chose the right way,' he said. 'At last we are coming to the habitable parts, and I guess that we are not far now from the eastern side. But we are high up, a good deal higher than the Dimrill Gate, unless I am mistaken. From the feeling of the air we must be in a wide hall. I will now risk a little real light.'

He raised his staff, and for a brief instant there was blaze like a flash of lightning. Great shadows sprang up and fled, and for a second they saw a vast roof far above their heads upheld by many mighty pillars hewn of stone. Before them and on either side stretched a huge empty hall; its black walls, polished and smooth as glass, flashed and glittered. Three other entrances they saw, dark black arches: one straight before them eastwards, and one on either side. Then the light went out.

'That is all that I shall venture on for the present,' said Gandalf. 'There used to be great windows on the mountain-side, and shafts leading out to the light in the upper reaches of the Mines. I think we have reached them now, but it is night outside again, and we cannot tell until morning. If I am right, tomorrow we may actually see the morning peeping in. But in the meanwhile we had better go no further. Let us rest, if we can. Things have gone well so far, and the greater part of the dark road is over. But we are not through yet, and it is a long way down to the Gates that open on the world.'

The Company spent that night in the great cavernous hall, huddled close together in a corner to escape the draught: there seemed to be a steady inflow of chill air through the eastern archway. All about them as they lay hung the darkness, hollow and immense, and they were oppressed by the loneliness and vastness of the dolven halls and endlessly branching stairs and passages. The wildest imaginings that dark rumour had ever suggested to the hobbits fell altogether short of the actual dread and wonder of Moria.

'There must have been a mighty crowd of dwarves here at one time,' said Sam; 'and every one of them busier than badgers for five hundred years to make all this, and most in hard rock too! What did they do it all for? They didn't live in these darksome holes surely?'

'These are not holes,' said Gimli. 'This is the great realm and city of the Dwarrowdelf. And of old it was not darksome, but full of light and splendour, as is still remembered in our songs.'

He rose and standing in the dark he began to chant in a deep voice, while the echoes ran away into the roof.

The world was young, the mountains green,
No stain yet on the Moon was seen,
No words were laid on stream or stone
When Durin woke and walked alone.
He named the nameless hills and dells;
He drank from yet untasted wells;
He stooped and looked in Mirrormere,
And saw a crown of stars appear,
As gems upon a silver thread,
Above the shadow of his head.

The world was fair, the mountains tall,
In Elder Days before the fall
Of mighty kings in Nargothrond
And Gondolin, who now beyond
The Western Seas have passed away:
The world was fair in Durin's Day.

A king he was on carven throne
In many-pillared halls of stone
With golden roof and silver floor,
And runes of power upon the door.
The light of sun and star and moon
In shining lamps of crystal hewn
Undimmed by cloud or shade of night
There shone for ever fair and bright.

There hammer on the anvil smote,
There chisel clove, and graver wrote;
There forged was blade, and bound was hilt;
The delver mined, the mason built.
There beryl, pearl, and opal pale,
And metal wrought like fishes' mail,
Buckler and corslet, axe and sword,
And shining spears were laid in hoard.

Unwearied then were Durin's folk;
Beneath the mountains music woke:
The harpers harped, the minstrels sang,
And at the gates the trumpets rang.

The world is grey, the mountains old,
The forge's fire is ashen-cold;

> *No harp is wrung, no hammer falls:*
> *The darkness dwells in Durin's halls;*
> *The shadow lies upon his tomb*
> *In Moria, in Khazad-dûm.*
> *But still the sunken stars appear*
> *In dark and windless Mirrormere;*
> *There lies his crown in water deep,*
> *Till Durin wakes again from sleep.*

'I like that!' said Sam. 'I should like to learn it. *In Moria, in Khazad-dûm!* But it makes the darkness seem heavier, thinking of all those lamps. Are there piles of jewels and gold lying about here still?'

Gimli was silent. Having sung his song he would say no more.

'Piles of jewels?' said Gandalf. 'No. The Orcs have often plundered Moria; there is nothing left in the upper halls. And since the dwarves fled, no one dares to seek the shafts and treasuries down in the deep places: they are drowned in water – or in a shadow of fear.'

'Then what do the dwarves want to come back for?' asked Sam.

'For *mithril*,' answered Gandalf. 'The wealth of Moria was not in gold and jewels, the toys of the Dwarves; nor in iron, their servant. Such things they found here, it is true, especially iron; but they did not need to delve for them: all things that they desired they could obtain in traffic. For here alone in the world was found Moria-silver, or true-silver as some have called it: *mithril* is the Elvish name. The Dwarves have a name which they do not tell. Its worth was ten times that of gold, and now it is beyond price; for little is left above ground, and even the Orcs dare not delve here for it. The lodes lead away north towards Caradhras, and down to darkness. The Dwarves tell no tale; but even as *mithril* was the foundation of their wealth, so also it was their destruction: they delved too greedily and too deep, and disturbed that from which they fled, Durin's Bane. Of what they brought to light the Orcs have gathered nearly all, and given it in tribute to Sauron, who covets it.

'*Mithril!* All folk desired it. It could be beaten like copper, and polished like glass; and the Dwarves could make of it a metal, light and yet harder than tempered steel. Its beauty was like to that of common silver, but the beauty of *mithril* did not tarnish or grow dim. The Elves dearly loved it, and among many uses they made of it *ithildin*, starmoon, which you saw upon the doors. Bilbo had a corslet of mithril-rings that Thorin gave him. I wonder what has become of it? Gathering dust still in Michel Delving Mathom-house, I suppose.'

'What?' cried Gimli, startled out of his silence. 'A corslet of Moria-silver? That was a kingly gift!'

'Yes,' said Gandalf. 'I never told him, but its worth was greater than the value of the whole Shire and everything in it.'

Frodo said nothing, but he put his hand under his tunic and touched the rings of his mail-shirt. He felt staggered to think that he had been walking about with the price of the Shire under his jacket. Had Bilbo known? He felt no doubt that Bilbo knew quite well. It was indeed a kingly gift. But now his thoughts had been carried away from the dark Mines, to Rivendell, to Bilbo, and to Bag End in the days while Bilbo was still there. He wished with all his heart that he was back there, and in those days, mowing the lawn, or pottering among the flowers, and that he had never heard of Moria, or *mithril* – or the Ring.

A deep silence fell. One by one the others fell asleep. Frodo was on guard. As if it were a breath that came in through unseen doors out of deep places, dread came over him. His hands were cold and his brow damp. He listened. All his mind was given to listening and nothing else for two slow hours; but he heard no sound, not even the imagined echo of a footfall.

His watch was nearly over, when, far off where he guessed that the western archway stood, he fancied that he could see two pale points of light, almost like luminous eyes. He started. His head had nodded. 'I must have nearly fallen asleep on guard,' he thought. 'I was on the edge of a dream.' He stood up and rubbed his eyes, and remained standing, peering into the dark, until he was relieved by Legolas.

When he lay down he quickly went to sleep, but it seemed to him that the dream went on: he heard whispers, and saw the two pale points of light approaching, slowly. He woke and found that the others were speaking softly near him, and that a dim light was falling on his face. High up above the eastern archway through a shaft near the roof came a long pale gleam; and across the hall through the northern arch light also glimmered faint and distantly.

Frodo sat up. 'Good morning!' said Gandalf. 'For morning it is again at last. I was right, you see. We are high up on the east side of Moria. Before today is over we ought to find the Great Gates and see the waters of Mirrormere lying in the Dimrill Dale before us.'

'I shall be glad,' said Gimli. 'I have looked on Moria, and it is very great, but it has become dark and dreadful; and we have found no sign of my kindred. I doubt now that Balin ever came here.'

After they had breakfasted Gandalf decided to go on again at once. 'We are tired, but we shall rest better when we are outside,' he said. 'I think that none of us will wish to spend another night in Moria.'

'No indeed!' said Boromir. 'Which way shall we take? Yonder eastward arch?'

'Maybe,' said Gandalf. 'But I do not know yet exactly where we are. Unless I am quite astray, I guess that we are above and to the north of the Great Gates; and it may not be easy to find the right road down to them. The eastern arch will probably prove to be the way that we must take; but before we make up our minds we ought to look about us. Let us go towards that light in the north door. If we could find a window it would help, but I fear that the light comes only down deep shafts.'

Following his lead the Company passed under the northern arch. They found themselves in a wide corridor. As they went along it the glimmer grew stronger, and they saw that it came through a doorway on their right. It was high and flat-topped, and the stone door was still upon its hinges, standing half open. Beyond it was a large square chamber. It was dimly lit, but to their eyes, after so long a time in the dark, it seemed dazzlingly bright, and they blinked as they entered.

Their feet disturbed a deep dust upon the floor, and stumbled among things lying in the doorway whose shapes they could not at first make out. The chamber was lit by a wide shaft high in the further eastern wall; it slanted upwards and, far above, a small square patch of blue sky could be seen. The light of the shaft fell directly on a table in the middle of the room: a single oblong block, about two feet high, upon which was laid a great slab of white stone.

'It looks like a tomb,' muttered Frodo, and bent forwards with a curious sense of foreboding, to look more closely at it. Gandalf came quickly to his side. On the slab runes were deeply graven:

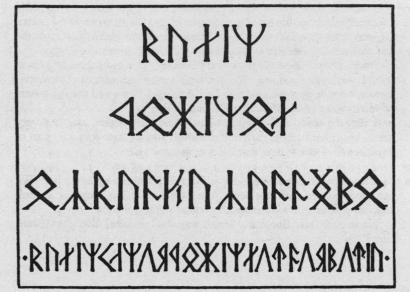

'These are Daeron's Runes, such as were used of old in Moria,' said Gandalf. 'Here is written in the tongues of Men and Dwarves:

BALIN SON OF FUNDIN
LORD OF MORIA.'

'He is dead then,' said Frodo. 'I feared it was so.' Gimli cast his hood over his face.

CHAPTER V

THE BRIDGE OF KHAZAD-DÛM

The Company of the Ring stood silent beside the tomb of Balin. Frodo thought of Bilbo and his long friendship with the dwarf, and of Balin's visit to the Shire long ago. In that dusty chamber in the mountains it seemed a thousand years ago and on the other side of the world.

At length they stirred and looked up, and began to search for anything that would give them tidings of Balin's fate, or show what had become of his folk. There was another smaller door on the other side of the chamber, under the shaft. By both the doors they could now see that many bones were lying, and among them were broken swords and axe-heads, and cloven shields and helms. Some of the swords were crooked: orc-scimitars with blackened blades.

There were many recesses cut in the rock of the walls, and in them were large iron-bound chests of wood. All had been broken and plundered; but beside the shattered lid of one there lay the remains of a book. It had been slashed and stabbed and partly burned, and it was so stained with black and other dark marks like old blood that little of it could be read. Gandalf lifted it carefully, but the leaves crackled and broke as he laid it on the slab. He pored over it for some time without speaking. Frodo and Gimli standing at his side could see, as he gingerly turned the leaves, that they were written by many different hands, in runes, both of Moria and of Dale, and here and there in Elvish script.

At last Gandalf looked up. 'It seems to be a record of the fortunes of Balin's folk,' he said. 'I guess that it began with their coming to Dimrill Dale nigh on thirty years ago: the pages seem to have numbers referring to the years after their arrival. The top page is marked *one – three*, so at least two are missing from the beginning. Listen to this!

'*We drove out orcs from the great gate and guard* – I think; the next word is blurred and burned: probably *room – we slew many in the bright* – I think – *sun in the dale. Flói was killed by an arrow. He slew the great.* Then there is a blur followed by *Flói under grass near Mirror mere.* The next line or two I cannot read. Then comes *We have taken the twentyfirst hall of North end to dwell in. There is* I cannot read what. A *shaft* is mentioned. Then *Balin has set up his seat in the Chamber of Mazarbul.*'

'The Chamber of Records,' said Gimli. 'I guess that is where we now stand.'

'Well, I can read no more for a long way,' said Gandalf, 'except the word *gold*, and *Durin's Axe* and something *helm*. Then *Balin is now lord of Moria*. That seems to end a chapter. After some stars another hand begins, and I can see *we found truesilver*, and later the word *wellforged*, and then something, I have it! *mithril*; and the last two lines *Óin to seek for the upper armouries of Third Deep*, something *go westwards*, a blur, *to Hollin gate*.'

Gandalf paused and set a few leaves aside. 'There are several pages of the same sort, rather hastily written and much damaged,' he said; 'but I can make little of them in this light. Now there must be a number of leaves missing, because they begin to be numbered *five*, the fifth year of the colony, I suppose. Let me see! No, they are too cut and stained; I cannot read them. We might do better in the sunlight. Wait! Here is something: a large bold hand using an Elvish script.'

'That would be Ori's hand,' said Gimli, looking over the wizard's arm. 'He could write well and speedily, and often used the Elvish characters.'

'I fear he had ill tidings to record in a fair hand,' said Gandalf. 'The first clear word is *sorrow*, but the rest of the line is lost, unless it ends in *estre*. Yes, it must be *yestre* followed by *day being the tenth of novembre Balin lord of Moria fell in Dimrill Dale. He went alone to look in Mirror mere. an orc shot him from behind a stone. we slew the orc, but many more . . . up from east up the Silverlode*. The remainder of the page is so blurred that I can hardly make anything out, but I think I can read *we have barred the gates*, and then *can hold them long if*, and then perhaps *horrible* and *suffer*. Poor Balin! He seems to have kept the title that he took for less than five years. I wonder what happened afterwards; but there is no time to puzzle out the last few pages. Here is the last page of all.' He paused and sighed.

'It is grim reading,' he said. 'I fear their end was cruel. Listen! *We cannot get out. We cannot get out. They have taken the Bridge and second hall. Frár and Lóni and Náli fell there*. Then there are four lines smeared so that I can only read *went 5 days ago*. The last lines run *the pool is up to the wall at Westgate. The Watcher in the Water took Óin. We cannot get out. The end comes*, and then *drums, drums in the deep*. I wonder what that means. The last thing written is in a trailing scrawl of elf-letters: *they are coming*. There is nothing more.' Gandalf paused and stood in silent thought.

A sudden dread and a horror of the chamber fell on the Company. '*We cannot get out*,' muttered Gimli. 'It was well for us that the pool had sunk a little, and that the Watcher was sleeping down at the southern end.'

Gandalf raised his head and looked round. 'They seem to have made a last stand by both doors,' he said; 'but there were not many left by that time. So ended the attempt to retake Moria! It was valiant but foolish. The time is not come yet. Now, I fear, we must say farewell to Balin son of Fundin. Here he must lie in the halls of his fathers. We will take this book, the Book of Mazarbul, and look at it more closely later. You had better keep it, Gimli, and take it back to Dáin, if you get a chance. It will interest him, though it will grieve him deeply. Come, let us go! The morning is passing.'

'Which way shall we go?' asked Boromir.

'Back to the hall,' answered Gandalf. 'But our visit to this room has not been in vain. I now know where we are. This must be, as Gimli says, the Chamber of Mazarbul; and the hall must be the twenty-first of the North-end. Therefore we should leave by the eastern arch of the hall, and bear right and south, and go downwards. The Twenty-first Hall should be on the Seventh Level, that is six above the level of the Gates. Come now! Back to the hall!'

Gandalf had hardly spoken these words, when there came a great noise: a rolling *Boom* that seemed to come from depths far below, and to tremble in the stone at their feet. They sprang towards the door in alarm. *Doom, doom* it rolled again, as if huge hands were turning the very caverns of Moria into a vast drum. Then there came an echoing blast: a great horn was blown in the hall, and answering horns and harsh cries were heard further off. There was a hurrying sound of many feet.

'They are coming!' cried Legolas.

'We cannot get out,' said Gimli.

'Trapped!' cried Gandalf. 'Why did I delay? Here we are, caught, just as they were before. But I was not here then. We will see what——'

Doom, doom came the drum-beat and the walls shook.

'Slam the doors and wedge them!' shouted Aragorn. 'And keep your packs on as long as you can: we may get a chance to cut our way out yet.'

'No!' said Gandalf. 'We must not get shut in. Keep the east door ajar! We will go that way, if we get a chance.'

Another harsh horn-call and shrill cries rang out. Feet were coming down the corridor. There was a ring and clatter as the Company drew their swords. Glamdring shone with a pale light, and Sting glinted at the edges. Boromir set his shoulder against the western door.

'Wait a moment! Do not close it yet!' said Gandalf. He sprang forward to Boromir's side and drew himself up to his full height.

'Who comes hither to disturb the rest of Balin Lord of Moria?' he cried in a loud voice.

There was a rush of hoarse laughter, like the fall of sliding stones into a pit; amid the clamour a deep voice was raised in command. *Doom, boom, doom* went the drums in the deep.

With a quick movement Gandalf stepped before the narrow opening of the door and thrust forward his staff. There was a dazzling flash that lit the chamber and the passage outside. For an instant the wizard looked out. Arrows whined and whistled down the corridor as he sprang back.

'There are Orcs, very many of them,' he said. 'And some are large and evil: black Uruks of Mordor. For the moment they are hanging back, but there is something else there. A great cave-troll, I think, or more than one. There is no hope of escape that way.'

'And no hope at all, if they come at the other door as well,' said Boromir.

'There is no sound outside here yet,' said Aragorn, who was standing by the eastern door listening. 'The passage on this side plunges straight down a stair: it plainly does not lead back towards the hall. But it is no good flying blindly this way with the pursuit just behind. We cannot block the door. Its key is gone and the lock is broken, and it opens inwards. We must do something to delay the enemy first. We will make them fear the Chamber of Mazarbul!' he said grimly, feeling the edge of his sword, Andúril.

Heavy feet were heard in the corridor. Boromir flung himself against the door and heaved it to; then he wedged it with broken sword-blades and splinters of wood. The Company retreated to the other side of the chamber. But they had no chance to fly yet. There was a blow on the door that made it quiver; and then it began to grind slowly open, driving back the wedges. A huge arm and shoulder, with a dark skin of greenish scales, was thrust through the widening gap. Then a great, flat, toeless foot was forced through below. There was a dead silence outside.

Boromir leaped forward and hewed at the arm with all his might; but his sword rang, glanced aside, and fell from his shaken hand. The blade was notched.

Suddenly, and to his own surprise, Frodo felt a hot wrath blaze up in his heart. 'The Shire!' he cried, and springing beside Boromir, he stooped, and stabbed with Sting at the hideous foot. There was a bellow, and the foot jerked back, nearly wrenching Sting from Frodo's arm. Black drops dripped from the blade and smoked on the floor. Boromir hurled himself against the door and slammed it again.

'One for the Shire!' cried Aragorn. 'The hobbit's bite is deep! You have a good blade, Frodo son of Drogo!'

There was a crash on the door, followed by crash after crash. Rams and hammers were beating against it. It cracked and staggered back, and the opening grew suddenly wide. Arrows came whistling in, but struck the northern wall, and fell harmlessly to the floor. There was a horn-blast and a rush of feet, and orcs one after another leaped into the chamber.

How many there were the Company could not count. The affray was sharp, but the orcs were dismayed by the fierceness of the defence. Legolas

shot two through the throat. Gimli hewed the legs from under another that
had sprung up on Balin's tomb. Boromir and Aragorn slew many. When
thirteen had fallen the rest fled shrieking, leaving the defenders unharmed,
except for Sam who had a scratch along the scalp. A quick duck had saved
him; and he had felled his orc: a sturdy thrust with his Barrow-blade. A
fire was smouldering in his brown eyes that would have made Ted
Sandyman step backwards, if he had seen it.

'Now is the time!' cried Gandalf. 'Let us go, before the troll returns!'

But even as they retreated, and before Pippin and Merry had reached
the stair outside, a huge orc-chieftain, almost man-high, clad in black mail
from head to foot, leaped into the chamber; behind him his followers
clustered in the doorway. His broad flat face was swart, his eyes were like
coals, and his tongue was red; he wielded a great spear. With a thrust of
his huge hide shield he turned Boromir's sword and bore him backwards,
throwing him to the ground. Diving under Aragorn's blow with the speed
of a striking snake he charged into the Company and thrust with his spear
straight at Frodo. The blow caught him on the right side, and Frodo was
hurled against the wall and pinned. Sam, with a cry, hacked at the spear-
shaft, and it broke. But even as the orc flung down the truncheon and
swept out his scimitar, Andúril came down upon his helm. There was a
flash like flame and the helm burst asunder. The orc fell with cloven head.
His followers fled howling, as Boromir and Aragorn sprang at them.

Doom, doom went the drums in the deep. The great voice rolled out
again.

'Now!' shouted Gandalf. 'Now is the last chance. Run for it!'

Aragorn picked up Frodo where he lay by the wall and made for the
stair, pushing Merry and Pippin in front of him. The others followed; but
Gimli had to be dragged away by Legolas: in spite of the peril he lingered
by Balin's tomb with his head bowed. Boromir hauled the eastern door to,
grinding upon its hinges: it had great iron rings on either side, but could
not be fastened.

'I am all right,' gasped Frodo. 'I can walk. Put me down!'

Aragorn nearly dropped him in his amazement. 'I thought you were
dead!' he cried.

'Not yet!' said Gandalf. 'But there is no time for wonder. Off you go,
all of you, down the stairs! Wait a few minutes for me at the bottom, but
if I do not come soon, go on! Go quickly and choose paths leading right
and downwards.'

'We cannot leave you to hold the door alone!' said Aragorn.

'Do as I say!' said Gandalf fiercely. 'Swords are no more use here. Go!'

The passage was lit by no shaft and was utterly dark. They groped their way down a long flight of steps, and then looked back; but they could see nothing, except high above them the faint glimmer of the wizard's staff. He seemed to be still standing on guard by the closed door. Frodo breathed heavily and leaned against Sam, who put his arms about him. They stood peering up the stairs into the darkness. Frodo thought he could hear the voice of Gandalf above, muttering words that ran down the sloping roof with a sighing echo. He could not catch what was said. The walls seemed to be trembling. Every now and again the drum-beats throbbed and rolled: *doom, doom*.

Suddenly at the top of the stair there was a stab of white light. Then there was a dull rumble and a heavy thud. The drum-beats broke out wildly: *doom-boom, doom-boom*, and then stopped. Gandalf came flying down the steps and fell to the ground in the midst of the Company.

'Well, well! That's over!' said the wizard struggling to his feet. 'I have done all that I could. But I have met my match, and have nearly been destroyed. But don't stand here! Go on! You will have to do without light for a while: I am rather shaken. Go on! Go on! Where are you, Gimli? Come ahead with me! Keep close behind, all of you!'

They stumbled after him wondering what had happened. *Doom, doom* went the drum-beats again: they now sounded muffled and far away, but they were following. There was no other sound of pursuit, neither tramp of feet, nor any voice. Gandalf took no turns, right or left, for the passage seemed to be going in the direction that he desired. Every now and again it descended a flight of steps, fifty or more, to a lower level. At the moment that was their chief danger; for in the dark they could not see a descent, until they came on it and put their feet out into emptiness. Gandalf felt the ground with his staff like a blind man.

At the end of an hour they had gone a mile, or maybe a little more, and had descended many flights of stairs. There was still no sound of pursuit. Almost they began to hope that they would escape. At the bottom of the seventh flight Gandalf halted.

'It is getting hot!' he gasped. 'We ought to be down at least to the level of the Gates now. Soon I think we should look for a left-hand turn to take us east. I hope it is not far. I am very weary. I must rest here a moment, even if all the orcs ever spawned are after us.'

Gimli took his arm and helped him down to a seat on the step. 'What happened away up there at the door?' he asked. 'Did you meet the beater of the drums?'

'I do not know,' answered Gandalf. 'But I found myself suddenly faced by something that I have not met before. I could think of nothing to do but to try and put a shutting-spell on the door. I know many; but to do things of that kind rightly requires time, and even then the door can be broken by strength.

'As I stood there I could hear orc-voices on the other side: at any moment I thought they would burst it open. I could not hear what was said; they seemed to be talking in their own hideous language. All I caught was *ghâsh*: that is "fire". Then something came into the chamber – I felt it through the door, and the orcs themselves were afraid and fell silent. It laid hold of the iron ring, and then it perceived me and my spell.

'What it was I cannot guess, but I have never felt such a challenge. The counter-spell was terrible. It nearly broke me. For an instant the door left my control and began to open! I had to speak a word of Command. That proved too great a strain. The door burst in pieces. Something dark as a cloud was blocking out all the light inside, and I was thrown backwards down the stairs. All the wall gave way, and the roof of the chamber as well, I think.

'I am afraid Balin is buried deep, and maybe something else is buried there too. I cannot say. But at least the passage behind us was completely blocked. Ah! I have never felt so spent, but it is passing. And now what about you, Frodo? There was not time to say so, but I have never been more delighted in my life than when you spoke. I feared that it was a brave but dead hobbit that Aragorn was carrying.'

'What about me?' said Frodo. 'I am alive, and whole I think. I am bruised and in pain, but it is not too bad.'

'Well,' said Aragorn, 'I can only say that hobbits are made of a stuff so tough that I have never met the like of it. Had I known, I would have spoken softer in the Inn at Bree! That spear-thrust would have skewered a wild boar!'

'Well, it did not skewer me, I am glad to say,' said Frodo; 'though I feel as if I had been caught between a hammer and an anvil.' He said no more. He found breathing painful.

'You take after Bilbo,' said Gandalf. 'There is more about you than meets the eye, as I said of him long ago.' Frodo wondered if the remark meant more than it said.

They now went on again. Before long Gimli spoke. He had keen eyes in the dark. 'I think,' he said, 'that there is a light ahead. But it is not daylight. It is red. What can it be?'

'*Ghâsh!*' muttered Gandalf. 'I wonder if that is what they meant: that the lower levels are on fire? Still, we can only go on.'

Soon the light became unmistakable, and could be seen by all. It was flickering and glowing on the walls away down the passage before them.

They could now see their way: in front the road sloped down swiftly, and some way ahead there stood a low archway; through it the growing light came. The air became very hot.

When they came to the arch Gandalf went through, signing to them to wait. As he stood just beyond the opening they saw his face lit by a red glow. Quickly he stepped back.

'There is some new devilry here,' he said, 'devised for our welcome, no doubt. But I know now where we are: we have reached the First Deep, the level immediately below the Gates. This is the Second Hall of Old Moria; and the Gates are near: away beyond the eastern end, on the left, not more than a quarter of a mile. Across the Bridge, up a broad stair, along a wide road, through the First Hall, and out! But come and look!'

They peered out. Before them was another cavernous hall. It was loftier and far longer than the one in which they had slept. They were near its eastern end; westward it ran away into darkness. Down the centre stalked a double line of towering pillars. They were carved like boles of mighty trees whose boughs upheld the roof with a branching tracery of stone. Their stems were smooth and black, but a red glow was darkly mirrored in their sides. Right across the floor, close to the feet of two huge pillars a great fissure had opened. Out of it a fierce red light came, and now and again flames licked at the brink and curled about the bases of the columns. Wisps of dark smoke wavered in the hot air.

'If we had come by the main road down from the upper halls, we should have been trapped here,' said Gandalf. 'Let us hope that the fire now lies between us and pursuit. Come! There is no time to lose.'

Even as he spoke they heard again the pursuing drum-beat: *Doom, doom, doom*. Away beyond the shadows at the western end of the hall there came cries and horn-calls. *Doom, doom*: the pillars seemed to tremble and the flames to quiver.

'Now for the last race!' said Gandalf. 'If the sun is shining outside, we may still escape. After me!'

He turned left and sped across the smooth floor of the hall. The distance was greater than it had looked. As they ran they heard the beat and echo of many hurrying feet behind. A shrill yell went up: they had been seen. There was a ring and clash of steel. An arrow whistled over Frodo's head.

Boromir laughed. 'They did not expect this,' he said. 'The fire has cut them off. We are on the wrong side!'

'Look ahead!' called Gandalf. 'The Bridge is near. It is dangerous and narrow.'

Suddenly Frodo saw before him a black chasm. At the end of the hall the floor vanished and fell to an unknown depth. The outer door could only be reached by a slender bridge of stone, without kerb or rail, that spanned the chasm with one curving spring of fifty feet. It was an ancient defence of the Dwarves against any enemy that might capture the First Hall and the outer passages. They could only pass across it in single file. At the brink Gandalf halted and the others came up in a pack behind.

'Lead the way, Gimli!' he said. 'Pippin and Merry next. Straight on, and up the stair beyond the door!'

Arrows fell among them. One struck Frodo and sprang back. Another pierced Gandalf's hat and stuck there like a black feather. Frodo looked behind. Beyond the fire he saw swarming black figures: there seemed to be hundreds of orcs. They brandished spears and scimitars which shone red as blood in the firelight. *Doom, doom* rolled the drum-beats, growing louder and louder, *doom, doom.*

Legolas turned and set an arrow to the string, though it was a long shot for his small bow. He drew, but his hand fell, and the arrow slipped to the ground. He gave a cry of dismay and fear. Two great trolls appeared; they bore great slabs of stone, and flung them down to serve as gangways over the fire. But it was not the trolls that had filled the Elf with terror. The ranks of the orcs had opened, and they crowded away, as if they themselves were afraid. Something was coming up behind them. What it was could not be seen: it was like a great shadow, in the middle of which was a dark form, of man-shape maybe, yet greater; and a power and terror seemed to be in it and to go before it.

It came to the edge of the fire and the light faded as if a cloud had bent over it. Then with a rush it leaped across the fissure. The flames roared up to greet it, and wreathed about it; and a black smoke swirled in the air. Its streaming mane kindled, and blazed behind it. In its right hand was a blade like a stabbing tongue of fire; in its left it held a whip of many thongs.

'Ai! ai!' wailed Legolas. 'A Balrog! A Balrog is come!'

Gimli stared with wide eyes. 'Durin's Bane!' he cried, and letting his axe fall he covered his face.

'A Balrog,' muttered Gandalf. 'Now I understand.' He faltered and leaned heavily on his staff. 'What an evil fortune! And I am already weary.'

The dark figure streaming with fire raced towards them. The orcs yelled and poured over the stone gangways. Then Boromir raised his horn and blew. Loud the challenge rang and bellowed, like the shout of many throats under the cavernous roof. For a moment the orcs quailed and the fiery shadow halted. Then the echoes died as suddenly as a flame blown out by a dark wind, and the enemy advanced again.

'Over the bridge!' cried Gandalf, recalling his strength. 'Fly! This is a foe beyond any of you. I must hold the narrow way. Fly!' Aragorn and Boromir did not heed the command, but still held their ground, side by side, behind Gandalf at the far end of the bridge. The others halted just within the doorway at the hall's end, and turned, unable to leave their leader to face the enemy alone.

The Balrog reached the bridge. Gandalf stood in the middle of the span, leaning on the staff in his left hand, but in his other hand Glamdring gleamed, cold and white. His enemy halted again, facing him, and the shadow about it reached out like two vast wings. It raised the whip, and the thongs whined and cracked. Fire came from its nostrils. But Gandalf stood firm.

'You cannot pass,' he said. The orcs stood still, and a dead silence fell. 'I am a servant of the Secret Fire, wielder of the flame of Anor. You cannot pass. The dark fire will not avail you, flame of Udûn. Go back to the Shadow! You cannot pass.'

The Balrog made no answer. The fire in it seemed to die, but the darkness grew. It stepped forward slowly on to the bridge, and suddenly it drew itself up to a great height, and its wings were spread from wall to wall; but still Gandalf could be seen, glimmering in the gloom; he seemed small, and altogether alone: grey and bent, like a wizened tree before the onset of a storm.

From out of the shadow a red sword leaped flaming.

Glamdring glittered white in answer.

There was a ringing clash and a stab of white fire. The Balrog fell back and its sword flew up in molten fragments. The wizard swayed on the bridge, stepped back a pace, and then again stood still.

'You cannot pass!' he said.

With a bound the Balrog leaped full upon the bridge. Its whip whirled and hissed.

'He cannot stand alone!' cried Aragorn suddenly and ran back along the bridge. '*Elendil!*' he shouted. 'I am with you, Gandalf!'

'Gondor!' cried Boromir and leaped after him.

At that moment Gandalf lifted his staff, and crying aloud he smote the bridge before him. The staff broke asunder and fell from his hand. A blinding sheet of white flame sprang up. The bridge cracked. Right at the Balrog's feet it broke, and the stone upon which it stood crashed into the gulf, while the rest remained, poised, quivering like a tongue of rock thrust out into emptiness.

With a terrible cry the Balrog fell forward, and its shadow plunged down and vanished. But even as it fell it swung its whip, and the thongs lashed and curled about the wizard's knees, dragging him to the brink. He staggered and fell, grasped vainly at the stone, and slid into the abyss. 'Fly, you fools!' he cried, and was gone.

The fires went out, and blank darkness fell. The Company stood rooted with horror staring into the pit. Even as Aragorn and Boromir came flying back, the rest of the bridge cracked and fell. With a cry Aragorn roused them.

'Come! I will lead you now!' he called. 'We must obey his last command. Follow me!'

They stumbled wildly up the great stairs beyond the door. Aragorn leading, Boromir at the rear. At the top was a wide echoing passage. Along this they fled. Frodo heard Sam at his side weeping, and then he found that he himself was weeping as he ran. *Doom, doom, doom* the drum-beats rolled behind, mournful now and slow; *doom!*

They ran on. The light grew before them; great shafts pierced the roof. They ran swifter. They passed into a hall, bright with daylight from its high windows in the east. They fled across it. Through its huge broken doors they passed, and suddenly before them the Great Gates opened, an arch of blazing light.

There was a guard of orcs crouching in the shadows behind the great door-posts towering on either side, but the gates were shattered and cast down. Aragorn smote to the ground the captain that stood in his path, and the rest fled in terror of his wrath. The Company swept past them and took no heed of them. Out of the Gates they ran and sprang down the huge and age-worn steps, the threshold of Moria.

Thus, at last, they came beyond hope under the sky and felt the wind on their faces.

They did not halt until they were out of bowshot from the walls. Dimrill Dale lay about them. The shadow of the Misty Mountains lay upon it, but eastwards there was a golden light on the land. It was but one hour after noon. The sun was shining; the clouds were white and high.

They looked back. Dark yawned the archway of the Gates under the mountain-shadow. Faint and far beneath the earth rolled the slow drum-beats: *doom*. A thin black smoke trailed out. Nothing else was to be seen; the dale all around was empty. *Doom*. Grief at last wholly overcame them, and they wept long: some standing and silent, some cast upon the ground. *Doom, doom*. The drum-beats faded.

CHAPTER VI

LOTHLÓRIEN

'Alas! I fear we cannot stay here longer,' said Aragorn. He looked towards the mountains and held up his sword. 'Farewell, Gandalf!' he cried. 'Did I not say to you: *if you pass the doors of Moria, beware?* Alas that I spoke true! What hope have we without you?'

He turned to the Company. 'We must do without hope,' he said. 'At least we may yet be avenged. Let us gird ourselves and weep no more! Come! We have a long road, and much to do.'

They rose and looked about them. Northward the dale ran up into a glen of shadows between two great arms of the mountains, above which three white peaks were shining: Celebdil, Fanuidhol, Caradhras, the Mountains of Moria. At the head of the glen a torrent flowed like a white lace over an endless ladder of short falls, and a mist of foam hung in the air about the mountains' feet.

'Yonder is the Dimrill Stair,' said Aragorn, pointing to the falls. 'Down the deep-cloven way that climbs beside the torrent we should have come, if fortune had been kinder.'

'Or Caradhras less cruel,' said Gimli. 'There he stands smiling in the sun!' He shook his fist at the furthest of the snow-capped peaks and turned away.

To the east the outflung arm of the mountains marched to a sudden end, and far lands could be descried beyond them, wide and vague. To the south the Misty Mountains receded endlessly as far as sight could reach. Less than a mile away, and a little below them, for they still stood high up on the west side of the dale, there lay a mere. It was long and oval, shaped like a great spear-head thrust deep into the northern glen; but its southern end was beyond the shadows under the sunlit sky. Yet its waters were dark: a deep blue like clear evening sky seen from a lamp-lit room. Its face was still and unruffled. About it lay a smooth sward, shelving down on all sides to its bare unbroken rim.

'There lies the Mirrormere, deep Kheled-zâram!' said Gimli sadly. 'I remember that he said: "May you have joy of the sight! But we cannot linger there." Now long shall I journey ere I have joy again. It is I that must hasten away, and he that must remain.'

The Company now went down the road from the Gates. It was rough and broken, fading to a winding track between heather and whin that thrust amid the cracking stones. But still it could be seen that once long ago a great paved way had wound upwards from the lowlands of the Dwarf-kingdom. In places there were ruined works of stone beside the path, and mounds of green topped with slender birches, or fir-trees sighing in the wind. An eastward bend led them hard by the sward of Mirrormere, and there not far from the roadside stood a single column broken at the top.

'That is Durin's Stone!' cried Gimli. 'I cannot pass without turning aside for a moment to look at the wonder of the dale!'

'Be swift then!' said Aragorn, looking back towards the Gates. 'The Sun sinks early. The Orcs will not, maybe, come out till after dusk, but we must be far away before nightfall. The Moon is almost spent, and it will be dark tonight.'

'Come with me, Frodo!' cried the dwarf, springing from the road. 'I would not have you go without seeing Kheled-zâram.' He ran down the long green slope. Frodo followed slowly, drawn by the still blue water in spite of hurt and weariness; Sam came up behind.

Beside the standing stone Gimli halted and looked up. It was cracked and weather-worn, and the faint runes upon its side could not be read. 'This pillar marks the spot where Durin first looked in the Mirrormere,' said the dwarf. 'Let us look ourselves once, ere we go!'

They stooped over the dark water. At first they could see nothing. Then slowly they saw the forms of the encircling mountains mirrored in a profound blue, and the peaks were like plumes of white flame above them; beyond there was a space of sky. There like jewels sunk in the deep shone glinting stars, though sunlight was in the sky above. Of their own stooping forms no shadow could be seen.

'O Kheled-zâram fair and wonderful!' said Gimli. 'There lies the Crown of Durin till he wakes. Farewell!' He bowed, and turned away, and hastened back up the green-sward to the road again.

'What did you see?' said Pippin to Sam, but Sam was too deep in thought to answer.

The road now turned south and went quickly downwards, running out from between the arms of the dale. Some way below the mere they came on a deep well of water, clear as crystal, from which a freshet fell over a stone lip and ran glistening and gurgling down a steep rocky channel.

'Here is the spring from which the Silverlode rises,' said Gimli. 'Do not drink of it! It is icy cold.'

'Soon it becomes a swift river, and it gathers water from many other mountain-streams,' said Aragorn. 'Our road leads beside it for many miles. For I shall take you by the road that Gandalf chose, and first I hope to come to the woods where the Silverlode flows into the Great River – out yonder.' They looked as he pointed, and before them they could see the stream leaping down to the trough of the valley, and then running on and away into the lower lands, until it was lost in a golden haze.

'There lie the woods of Lothlórien!' said Legolas. 'That is the fairest of all the dwellings of my people. There are no trees like the trees of that land. For in the autumn their leaves fall not, but turn to gold. Not till the spring comes and the new green opens do they fall, and then the boughs are laden with yellow flowers; and the floor of the wood is golden, and golden is the roof, and its pillars are of silver, for the bark of the trees is smooth and grey. So still our songs in Mirkwood say. My heart would be glad if I were beneath the eaves of that wood, and it were springtime!'

'My heart will be glad, even in the winter,' said Aragorn. 'But it lies many miles away. Let us hasten!'

For some time Frodo and Sam managed to keep up with the others; but Aragorn was leading them at a great pace, and after a while they lagged behind. They had eaten nothing since the early morning. Sam's cut was burning like fire, and his head felt light. In spite of the shining sun the wind seemed chill after the warm darkness of Moria. He shivered. Frodo felt every step more painful and he gasped for breath.

At last Legolas turned, and seeing them now far behind, he spoke to Aragorn. The others halted, and Aragorn ran back, calling to Boromir to come with him.

'I am sorry, Frodo!' he cried, full of concern. 'So much has happened this day and we have such need of haste, that I have forgotten that you were hurt; and Sam too. You should have spoken. We have done nothing to ease you, as we ought, though all the orcs of Moria were after us. Come now! A little further on there is a place where we can rest for a little. There I will do what I can for you. Come, Boromir! We will carry them.'

Soon afterwards they came upon another stream that ran down from the west, and joined its bubbling water with the hurrying Silverlode. Together they plunged over a fall of green-hued stone, and foamed down into a dell. About it stood fir-trees, short and bent, and its sides were steep and clothed with harts-tongue and shrubs of whortle-berry. At the bottom there was a level space through which the stream flowed noisily over shining pebbles. Here they rested. It was now nearly three hours after noon, and they had come only a few miles from the Gates. Already the sun was westering.

While Gimli and the two younger hobbits kindled a fire of brush- and fir-wood, and drew water, Aragorn tended Sam and Frodo. Sam's wound was not deep, but it looked ugly, and Aragorn's face was grave as he examined it. After a moment he looked up with relief.

'Good luck, Sam!' he said. 'Many have received worse than this in payment for the slaying of their first orc. The cut is not poisoned, as the wounds of orc-blades too often are. It should heal well when I have tended it. Bathe it when Gimli has heated water.'

He opened his pouch and drew out some withered leaves. 'They are dry, and some of their virtue has gone,' he said, 'but here I have still some of the leaves of *athelas* that I gathered near Weathertop. Crush one in the water, and wash the wound clean, and I will bind it. Now it is your turn, Frodo!'

'I am all right,' said Frodo, reluctant to have his garments touched. 'All I needed was some food and a little rest.'

'No!' said Aragorn. 'We must have a look and see what the hammer and the anvil have done to you. I still marvel that you are alive at all.' Gently he stripped off Frodo's old jacket and worn tunic, and gave a gasp of wonder. Then he laughed. The silver corslet shimmered before his eyes like the light upon a rippling sea. Carefully he took it off and held it up, and the gems on it glittered like stars, and the sound of the shaken rings was like the tinkle of rain in a pool.

'Look, my friends!' he called. 'Here's a pretty hobbit-skin to wrap an elven-princeling in! If it were known that hobbits had such hides, all the hunters of Middle-earth would be riding to the Shire.'

'And all the arrows of all the hunters in the world would be in vain,' said Gimli, gazing at the mail in wonder. 'It is a mithril-coat. Mithril! I have never seen or heard tell of one so fair. Is this the coat that Gandalf spoke of? Then he undervalued it. But it was well given!'

'I have often wondered what you and Bilbo were doing, so close in his little room,' said Merry. 'Bless the old hobbit! I love him more than ever. I hope we get a chance of telling him about it!'

There was a dark and blackened bruise on Frodo's right side and breast. Under the mail there was a shirt of soft leather, but at one point the rings had been driven through it into the flesh. Frodo's left side also was scored and bruised where he had been hurled against the wall. While the others set the food ready, Aragorn bathed the hurts with water in which *athelas* was steeped. The pungent fragrance filled the dell, and all those who stooped over the steaming water felt refreshed and strengthened. Soon Frodo felt the pain leave him, and his breath grew easy: though he was stiff and sore to the touch for many days. Aragorn bound some soft pads of cloth at his side.

'The mail is marvellously light,' he said. 'Put it on again, if you can bear it. My heart is glad to know that you have such a coat. Do not lay it aside, even in sleep, unless fortune brings you where you are safe for a while; and that will seldom chance while your quest lasts.'

When they had eaten, the Company got ready to go on. They put out the fire and hid all traces of it. Then climbing out of the dell they took to the road again. They had not gone far before the sun sank behind the westward heights and great shadows crept down the mountain-sides. Dusk veiled their feet, and mist rose in the hollows. Away in the east the evening light lay pale upon the dim lands of distant plain and wood. Sam and Frodo now feeling eased and greatly refreshed were able to go at a fair pace, and with only one brief halt Aragorn led the Company on for nearly three more hours.

It was dark. Deep night had fallen. There were many clear stars, but the fast-waning moon would not be seen till late. Gimli and Frodo were at the rear, walking softly and not speaking, listening for any sound upon the road behind. At length Gimli broke the silence.

'Not a sound but the wind,' he said. 'There are no goblins near, or my ears are made of wood. It is to be hoped that the Orcs will be content with driving us from Moria. And maybe that was all their purpose, and they had nothing else to do with us – with the Ring. Though Orcs will often pursue foes for many leagues into the plain, if they have a fallen captain to avenge.'

Frodo did not answer. He looked at Sting, and the blade was dull. Yet he had heard something, or thought he had. As soon as the shadows had fallen about them and the road behind was dim, he had heard again the quick patter of feet. Even now he heard it. He turned swiftly. There were two tiny gleams of light behind, or for a moment he thought he saw them, but at once they slipped aside and vanished.

'What is it?' said the dwarf.

'I don't know,' answered Frodo. 'I thought I heard feet, and I thought I saw a light – like eyes. I have thought so often, since we first entered Moria.'

Gimli halted and stooped to the ground. 'I hear nothing but the night-speech of plant and stone,' he said. 'Come! Let us hurry! The others are out of sight.'

The night-wind blew chill up the valley to meet them. Before them a wide grey shadow loomed, and they heard an endless rustle of leaves like poplars in the breeze.

'Lothlórien!' cried Legolas. 'Lothlórien! We have come to the eaves of the Golden Wood. Alas that it is winter!'

Under the night the trees stood tall before them, arched over the road and stream that ran suddenly beneath their spreading boughs. In the dim light of the stars their stems were grey, and their quivering leaves a hint of fallow gold.

'Lothlórien!' said Aragorn. 'Glad I am to hear again the wind in the trees! We are still little more than five leagues from the Gates, but we can go no further. Here let us hope that the virtue of the Elves will keep us tonight from the peril that comes behind.'

'If Elves indeed still dwell here in the darkening world,' said Gimli.

'It is long since any of my own folk journeyed hither back to the land whence we wandered in ages long ago,' said Legolas, 'but we hear that Lórien is not yet deserted, for there is a secret power here that holds evil from the land. Nevertheless its folk are seldom seen, and maybe they dwell now deep in the woods and far from the northern border.'

'Indeed deep in the wood they dwell,' said Aragorn, and sighed as if some memory stirred in him. 'We must fend for ourselves tonight. We will go forward a short way, until the trees are all about us, and then we will turn aside from the path and seek a place to rest in.'

He stepped forward; but Boromir stood irresolute and did not follow. 'Is there no other way?' he said.

'What other fairer way would you desire?' said Aragorn.

'A plain road, though it led through a hedge of swords,' said Boromir. 'By strange paths has this Company been led, and so far to evil fortune. Against my will we passed under the shades of Moria, to our loss. And now we must enter the Golden Wood, you say. But of that perilous land we have heard in Gondor, and it is said that few come out who once go in; and of that few none have escaped unscathed.'

'Say not *unscathed*, but if you say *unchanged*, then maybe you will speak the truth,' said Aragorn. 'But lore wanes in Gondor, Boromir, if in the city of those who once were wise they now speak evil of Lothlórien. Believe what you will, there is no other way for us – unless you would go back to Moria-gate, or scale the pathless mountains, or swim the Great River all alone.'

'Then lead on!' said Boromir. 'But it is perilous.'

'Perilous indeed,' said Aragorn, 'fair and perilous; but only evil need fear it, or those who bring some evil with them. Follow me!'

They had gone little more than a mile into the forest when they came upon another stream flowing down swiftly from the tree-clad slopes that climbed back westward towards the mountains. They heard it splashing over a fall away among the shadows on their right. Its dark hurrying waters ran across the path before them, and joined the Silverlode in a swirl of dim pools among the roots of trees.

'Here is Nimrodel!' said Legolas. 'Of this stream the Silvan Elves made many songs long ago, and still we sing them in the North, remembering the rainbow on its falls, and the golden flowers that floated in its foam. All

is dark now and the Bridge of Nimrodel is broken down. I will bathe
my feet, for it is said that the water is healing to the weary.' He went
forward and climbed down the deep-cloven bank and stepped into the
stream.

'Follow me!' he cried. 'The water is not deep. Let us wade across! On
the further bank we can rest, and the sound of the falling water may bring
us sleep and forgetfulness of grief.'

One by one they climbed down and followed Legolas. For a moment
Frodo stood near the brink and let the water flow over his tired feet. It
was cold but its touch was clean, and as he went on and it mounted to his
knees, he felt that the stain of travel and all weariness was washed from
his limbs.

When all the Company had crossed, they sat and rested and ate a little
food; and Legolas told them tales of Lothlórien that the Elves of Mirkwood
still kept in their hearts, of sunlight and starlight upon the meadows by
the Great River before the world was grey.

At length a silence fell, and they heard the music of the waterfall running
sweetly in the shadows. Almost Frodo fancied that he could hear a voice
singing, mingled with the sound of the water.

'Do you hear the voice of Nimrodel?' asked Legolas. 'I will sing you a
song of the maiden Nimrodel, who bore the same name as the stream
beside which she lived long ago. It is a fair song in our woodland tongue;
but this is how it runs in the Westron Speech, as some in Rivendell now
sing it.' In a soft voice hardly to be heard amid the rustle of the leaves
above them he began:

> An Elven-maid there was of old,
>   A shining star by day:
> Her mantle white was hemmed with gold,
>   Her shoes of silver-grey.
>
> A star was bound upon her brows,
>   A light was on her hair
> As sun upon the golden boughs
>   In Lórien the fair.
>
> Her hair was long, her limbs were white,
>   And fair she was and free;
> And in the wind she went as light
>   As leaf of linden-tree.

Beside the falls of Nimrodel,
By water clear and cool,
Her voice as falling silver fell
Into the shining pool.

Where now she wanders none can tell,
In sunlight or in shade;
For lost of yore was Nimrodel
And in the mountains strayed.

The elven-ship in haven grey
Beneath the mountain-lee
Awaited her for many a day
Beside the roaring sea.

A wind by night in Northern lands
Arose, and loud it cried,
And drove the ship from elven-strands
Across the streaming tide.

When dawn came dim the land was lost,
The mountains sinking grey
Beyond the heaving waves that tossed
Their plumes of blinding spray.

Amroth beheld the fading shore
Now low beyond the swell,
And cursed the faithless ship that bore
Him far from Nimrodel.

Of old he was an Elven-king,
A lord of tree and glen,
When golden were the boughs in spring
In fair Lothlórien.

From helm to sea they saw him leap,
As arrow from the string,
And dive into the water deep,
As mew upon the wing.

The wind was in his flowing hair,
The foam about him shone;

Afar they saw him strong and fair
Go riding like a swan.

But from the West has come no word,
And on the Hither Shore
No tidings Elven-folk have heard
Of Amroth evermore.

The voice of Legolas faltered, and the song ceased. 'I cannot sing any more,' he said. 'That is but a part, for I have forgotten much. It is long and sad, for it tells how sorrow came upon Lothlórien, Lórien of the Blossom, when the Dwarves awakened evil in the mountains.'

'But the Dwarves did not make the evil,' said Gimli.

'I said not so; yet evil came,' answered Legolas sadly. 'Then many of the Elves of Nimrodel's kindred left their dwellings and departed, and she was lost far in the South, in the passes of the White Mountains; and she came not to the ship where Amroth her lover waited for her. But in the spring when the wind is in the new leaves the echo of her voice may still be heard by the falls that bear her name. And when the wind is in the South the voice of Amroth comes up from the sea; for Nimrodel flows into Silverlode, that Elves call Celebrant, and Celebrant into Anduin the Great, and Anduin flows into the Bay of Belfalas whence the Elves of Lórien set sail. But neither Nimrodel nor Amroth ever came back.

'It is told that she had a house built in the branches of a tree that grew near the falls; for that was the custom of the Elves of Lórien, to dwell in the trees, and maybe it is so still. Therefore they were called the Galadhrim, the Tree-people. Deep in their forest the trees are very great. The people of the woods did not delve in the ground like Dwarves, nor build strong places of stone before the Shadow came.'

'And even in these latter days dwelling in the trees might be thought safer than sitting on the ground,' said Gimli. He looked across the stream to the road that led back to Dimrill Dale, and then up into the roof of dark boughs above.

'Your words bring good counsel, Gimli,' said Aragorn. 'We cannot build a house, but tonight we will do as the Galadhrim and seek refuge in the tree-tops, if we can. We have sat here beside the road already longer than was wise.'

The Company now turned aside from the path, and went into the shadow of the deeper woods, westward along the mountain-stream away from Silverlode. Not far from the falls of Nimrodel they found a cluster of trees, some of which overhung the stream. Their great grey trunks were of mighty girth, but their height could not be guessed.

'I will climb up,' said Legolas. 'I am at home among trees, by root or bough, though these trees are of a kind strange to me, save as a name in song. *Mellyrn* they are called, and are those that bear the yellow blossom, but I have never climbed in one. I will see now what is their shape and way of growth.'

'Whatever it may be,' said Pippin, 'they will be marvellous trees indeed if they can offer any rest at night, except to birds. I cannot sleep on a perch!'

'Then dig a hole in the ground,' said Legolas, 'if that is more after the fashion of your kind. But you must dig swift and deep, if you wish to hide from Orcs.' He sprang lightly up from the ground and caught a branch that grew from the trunk high above his head. But even as he swung there for a moment, a voice spoke suddenly from the tree-shadows above him.

'*Daro!*' it said in commanding tone, and Legolas dropped back to earth in surprise and fear. He shrank against the bole of the tree.

'Stand still!' he whispered to the others. 'Do not move or speak!'

There was a sound of soft laughter over their heads, and then another clear voice spoke in an elven-tongue. Frodo could understand little of what was said, for the speech that the Silvan folk east of the mountains used among themselves was unlike that of the West. Legolas looked up and answered in the same language.*

'Who are they, and what do they say?' asked Merry.

'They're Elves,' said Sam. 'Can't you hear their voices?'

'Yes, they are Elves,' said Legolas; 'and they say that you breathe so loud that they could shoot you in the dark.' Sam hastily put his hand over his mouth. 'But they say also that you need have no fear. They have been aware of us for a long while. They heard my voice across the Nimrodel, and knew that I was one of their Northern kindred, and therefore they did not hinder our crossing; and afterwards they heard my song. Now they bid me climb up with Frodo; for they seem to have had some tidings of him and of our journey. The others they ask to wait a little, and to keep watch at the foot of the tree, until they have decided what is to be done.'

Out of the shadows a ladder was let down: it was made of rope, silver-grey and glimmering in the dark, and though it looked slender it proved strong enough to bear many men. Legolas ran lightly up, and Frodo followed slowly; behind came Sam trying not to breathe loudly. The branches of the mallorn-tree grew out nearly straight from the trunk, and then swept upward; but near the top the main stem divided into a crown of many boughs, and among these they found that there had been built a wooden

* See note in Appendix F: *Of the Elves.*

platform, or *flet* as such things were called in those days: the Elves called it a *talan*. It was reached by a round hole in the centre through which the ladder passed.

When Frodo came at last up on to the flet he found Legolas seated with three other Elves. They were clad in shadowy-grey, and could not be seen among the tree-stems, unless they moved suddenly. They stood up, and one of them uncovered a small lamp that gave out a slender silver beam. He held it up, looking at Frodo's face, and Sam's. Then he shut off the light again, and spoke words of welcome in his elven-tongue. Frodo spoke haltingly in return.

'Welcome!' the Elf then said again in the Common Language, speaking slowly. 'We seldom use any tongue but our own; for we dwell now in the heart of the forest, and do not willingly have dealings with any other folk. Even our own kindred in the North are sundered from us. But there are some of us still who go abroad for the gathering of news and the watching of our enemies, and they speak the languages of other lands. I am one. Haldir is my name. My brothers, Rúmil and Orophin, speak little of your tongue.

'But we have heard rumours of your coming, for the messengers of Elrond passed by Lórien on their way home up the Dimrill Stair. We had not heard of – hobbits, of halflings, for many a long year, and did not know that any yet dwelt in Middle-earth. You do not look evil! And since you come with an Elf of our kindred, we are willing to befriend you, as Elrond asked; though it is not our custom to lead strangers through our land. But you must stay here tonight. How many are you?'

'Eight,' said Legolas. 'Myself, four hobbits; and two men, one of whom, Aragorn, is an Elf-friend of the folk of Westernesse.'

'The name of Aragorn son of Arathorn is known in Lórien,' said Haldir, 'and he has the favour of the Lady. All then is well. But you have yet spoken only of seven.'

'The eighth is a dwarf,' said Legolas.

'A dwarf!' said Haldir. 'That is not well. We have not had dealings with the Dwarves since the Dark Days. They are not permitted in our land. I cannot allow him to pass.'

'But he is from the Lonely Mountain, one of Dáin's trusty people, and friendly to Elrond,' said Frodo. 'Elrond himself chose him to be one of our companions, and he has been brave and faithful.'

The Elves spoke together in soft voices, and questioned Legolas in their own tongue. 'Very good,' said Haldir at last. 'We will do this, though it is against our liking. If Aragorn and Legolas will guard him, and answer for him, he shall pass; but he must go blindfold through Lothlórien.

'But now we must debate no longer. Your folk must not remain on the ground. We have been keeping watch on the rivers, ever since we saw a great troop of Orcs going north toward Moria, along the skirts of the mountains, many days ago. Wolves are howling on the wood's borders. If you have indeed come from Moria, the peril cannot be far behind. Tomorrow early you must go on.

'The four hobbits shall climb up here and stay with us – we do not fear them! There is another *talan* in the next tree. There the others must take refuge. You, Legolas, must answer to us for them. Call us, if anything is amiss! And have an eye on that dwarf!'

Legolas at once went down the ladder to take Haldir's message; and soon afterwards Merry and Pippin clambered up on to the high flet. They were out of breath and seemed rather scared.

'There!' said Merry panting. 'We have lugged up your blankets as well as our own. Strider has hidden all the rest of our baggage in a deep drift of leaves.'

'You had no need of your burdens,' said Haldir. 'It is cold in the tree-tops in winter, though the wind tonight is in the South; but we have food and drink to give you that will drive away the night-chill, and we have skins and cloaks to spare.'

The hobbits accepted this second (and far better) supper very gladly. Then they wrapped themselves warmly, not only in the fur-cloaks of the Elves, but in their own blankets as well, and tried to go to sleep. But weary as they were only Sam found that easy to do. Hobbits do not like heights, and do not sleep upstairs, even when they have any stairs. The flet was not at all to their liking as a bedroom. It had no walls, not even a rail; only on one side was there a light plaited screen, which could be moved and fixed in different places according to the wind.

Pippin went on talking for a while. 'I hope, if I do go to sleep in this bed-loft, that I shan't roll off,' he said.

'Once I do get to sleep,' said Sam, 'I shall go on sleeping, whether I roll off or no. And the less said, the sooner I'll drop off, if you take my meaning.'

Frodo lay for some time awake, and looked up at the stars glinting through the pale roof of quivering leaves. Sam was snoring at his side long before he himself closed his eyes. He could dimly see the grey forms of two elves sitting motionless with their arms about their knees, speaking in whispers. The other had gone down to take up his watch on one of the lower branches. At last lulled by the wind in the boughs above, and the sweet murmur of the falls of Nimrodel below, Frodo fell asleep with the song of Legolas running in his mind.

Late in the night he awoke. The other hobbits were asleep. The Elves were gone. The sickle Moon was gleaming dimly among the leaves. The wind was still. A little way off he heard a harsh laugh and the tread of many feet on the ground below. There was a ring of metal. The sounds died slowly away, and seemed to go southward, on into the wood.

A head appeared suddenly through the hole in the flet. Frodo sat up in alarm and saw that it was a grey-hooded Elf. He looked towards the hobbits.

'What is it?' said Frodo.

'*Yrch!*' said the Elf in a hissing whisper, and cast on to the flet the rope-ladder rolled up.

'Orcs!' said Frodo. 'What are they doing?' But the Elf had gone.

There were no more sounds. Even the leaves were silent, and the very falls seemed to be hushed. Frodo sat and shivered in his wraps. He was thankful that they had not been caught on the ground; but he felt that the trees offered little protection, except concealment. Orcs were as keen as hounds on a scent, it was said, but they could also climb. He drew out Sting: it flashed and glittered like a blue flame; and then slowly faded again and grew dull. In spite of the fading of his sword the feeling of immediate danger did not leave Frodo, rather it grew stronger. He got up and crawled to the opening and peered down. He was almost certain that he could hear stealthy movements at the tree's foot far below.

Not Elves; for the woodland folk were altogether noiseless in their movements. Then he heard faintly a sound like sniffing; and something seemed to be scrabbling on the bark of the tree-trunk. He stared down into the dark, holding his breath.

Something was now climbing slowly, and its breath came like a soft hissing through closed teeth. Then coming up, close to the stem, Frodo saw two pale eyes. They stopped and gazed upward unwinking. Suddenly they turned away, and a shadowy figure slipped round the trunk of the tree and vanished.

Immediately afterwards Haldir came climbing swiftly up through the branches. 'There was something in this tree that I have never seen before,' he said. 'It was not an orc. It fled as soon as I touched the tree-stem. It seemed to be wary, and to have some skill in trees, or I might have thought that it was one of you hobbits.

'I did not shoot, for I dared not arouse any cries: we cannot risk battle. A strong company of Orcs has passed. They crossed the Nimrodel – curse their foul feet in its clean water! – and went on down the old road beside the river. They seemed to pick up some scent, and they searched the ground for a while near the place where you halted. The three of us could not challenge a hundred, so we went ahead and spoke with feigned voices, leading them on into the wood.

'Orophin has now gone in haste back to our dwellings to warn our people. None of the Orcs will ever return out of Lórien. And there will be many

Elves hidden on the northern border before another night falls. But you must take the road south as soon as it is fully light.'

Day came pale from the East. As the light grew it filtered through the yellow leaves of the mallorn, and it seemed to the hobbits that the early sun of a cool summer's morning was shining. Pale-blue sky peeped among the moving branches. Looking through an opening on the south side of the flet Frodo saw all the valley of the Silverlode lying like a sea of fallow gold tossing gently in the breeze.

The morning was still young and cold when the Company set out again, guided now by Haldir and his brother Rúmil. 'Farewell, sweet Nimrodel!' cried Legolas. Frodo looked back and caught a gleam of white foam among the grey tree-stems. 'Farewell,' he said. It seemed to him that he would never hear again a running water so beautiful, for ever blending its innumerable notes in an endless changeful music.

They went back to the path that still went on along the west side of the Silverlode, and for some way they followed it southward. There were the prints of orc-feet in the earth. But soon Haldir turned aside into the trees and halted on the bank of the river under their shadows.

'There is one of my people yonder across the stream,' he said, 'though you may not see him.' He gave a call like the low whistle of a bird, and out of a thicket of young trees an Elf stepped, clad in grey, but with his hood thrown back; his hair glinted like gold in the morning sun. Haldir skilfully cast over the stream a coil of grey rope, and he caught it and bound the end about a tree near the bank.

'Celebrant is already a strong stream here, as you see,' said Haldir, 'and it runs both swift and deep, and is very cold. We do not set foot in it so far north, unless we must. But in these days of watchfulness we do not make bridges. This is how we cross! Follow me!' He made his end of the rope fast about another tree, and then ran lightly along it, over the river and back again, as if he were on a road.

'I can walk this path,' said Legolas; 'but the others have not this skill. Must they swim?'

'No!' said Haldir. 'We have two more ropes. We will fasten them above the other, one shoulder-high, and another half-high, and holding these the strangers should be able to cross with care.'

When this slender bridge had been made, the Company passed over, some cautiously and slowly, others more easily. Of the hobbits Pippin proved the best for he was sure-footed, and he walked over quickly, holding only with one hand; but he kept his eyes on the bank ahead and did not look down. Sam shuffled along, clutching hard, and looking down into the pale eddying water as if it was a chasm in the mountains.

He breathed with relief when he was safely across. 'Live and learn! as my gaffer used to say. Though he was thinking of gardening, not of roosting like a bird, nor of trying to walk like a spider. Not even my uncle Andy ever did a trick like that!'

When at length all the Company was gathered on the east bank of the Silverlode, the Elves untied the ropes and coiled two of them. Rúmil, who had remained on the other side, drew back the last one, slung it on his shoulder, and with a wave of his hand went away, back to Nimrodel to keep watch.

'Now, friends,' said Haldir, 'you have entered the Naith of Lórien, or the Gore, as you would say, for it is the land that lies like a spearhead between the arms of Silverlode and Anduin the Great. We allow no strangers to spy out the secrets of the Naith. Few indeed are permitted even to set foot there.

'As was agreed, I shall here blindfold the eyes of Gimli the Dwarf. The others may walk free for a while, until we come nearer to our dwellings, down in Egladil, in the Angle between the waters.'

This was not at all to the liking of Gimli. 'The agreement was made without my consent,' he said. 'I will not walk blindfold, like a beggar or a prisoner. And I am no spy. My folk have never had dealings with any of the servants of the Enemy. Neither have we done harm to the Elves. I am no more likely to betray you than Legolas, or any other of my companions.'

'I do not doubt you,' said Haldir. 'Yet this is our law. I am not the master of the law, and cannot set it aside. I have done much in letting you set foot over Celebrant.'

Gimli was obstinate. He planted his feet firmly apart, and laid his hand upon the haft of his axe. 'I will go forward free,' he said, 'or I will go back and seek my own land, where I am known to be true of word, though I perish alone in the wilderness.'

'You cannot go back,' said Haldir sternly. 'Now you have come thus far, you must be brought before the Lord and the Lady. They shall judge you, to hold you or to give you leave, as they will. You cannot cross the rivers again, and behind you there are now secret sentinels that you cannot pass. You would be slain before you saw them.'

Gimli drew his axe from his belt. Haldir and his companion bent their bows. 'A plague on Dwarves and their stiff necks!' said Legolas.

'Come!' said Aragorn. 'If I am still to lead this Company, you must do as I bid. It is hard upon the Dwarf to be thus singled out. We will all be blindfold, even Legolas. That will be best, though it will make the journey slow and dull.'

Gimli laughed suddenly. 'A merry troop of fools we shall look! Will

Haldir lead us all on a string, like many blind beggars with one dog? But I will be content, if only Legolas here shares my blindness.'

'I am an Elf and a kinsman here,' said Legolas, becoming angry in his turn.

'Now let us cry: "a plague on the stiff necks of Elves!"' said Aragorn. 'But the Company shall all fare alike. Come, bind our eyes, Haldir!'

'I shall claim full amends for every fall and stubbed toe, if you do not lead us well,' said Gimli as they bound a cloth about his eyes.

'You will have no claim,' said Haldir. 'I shall lead you well, and the paths are smooth and straight.'

'Alas for the folly of these days!' said Legolas. 'Here all are enemies of the one Enemy, and yet I must walk blind, while the sun is merry in the woodland under leaves of gold!'

'Folly it may seem,' said Haldir. 'Indeed in nothing is the power of the Dark Lord more clearly shown than in the estrangement that divides all those who still oppose him. Yet so little faith and trust do we find now in the world beyond Lothlórien, unless maybe in Rivendell, that we dare not by our own trust endanger our land. We live now upon an island amid many perils, and our hands are more often upon the bowstring than upon the harp.

'The rivers long defended us, but they are a sure guard no more; for the Shadow has crept northward all about us. Some speak of departing, yet for that it already seems too late. The mountains to the west are growing evil; to the east the lands are waste, and full of Sauron's creatures; and it is rumoured that we cannot now safely pass southward through Rohan, and the mouths of the Great River are watched by the Enemy. Even if we could come to the shores of the Sea, we should find no longer any shelter there. It is said that there are still havens of the High Elves, but they are far north and west, beyond the land of the Halflings. But where that may be, though the Lord and Lady may know, I do not.'

'You ought at least to guess, since you have seen us,' said Merry. 'There are Elf-havens west of my land, the Shire, where Hobbits live.'

'Happy folk are Hobbits to dwell near the shores of the sea!' said Haldir. 'It is long indeed since any of my folk have looked on it, yet still we remember it in song. Tell me of these havens as we walk.'

'I cannot,' said Merry. 'I have never seen them. I have never been out of my own land before. And if I had known what the world outside was like, I don't think I should have had the heart to leave it.'

'Not even to see fair Lothlórien?' said Haldir. 'The world is indeed full of peril, and in it there are many dark places; but still there is much that is fair, and though in all lands love is now mingled with grief, it grows perhaps the greater.

'Some there are among us who sing that the Shadow will draw back, and peace shall come again. Yet I do not believe that the world about us will ever again be as it was of old, or the light of the Sun as it was aforetime. For the Elves, I fear, it will prove at best a truce, in which they may pass to the Sea unhindered and leave the Middle-earth for ever. Alas for Lothlórien that I love! It would be a poor life in a land where no mallorn grew. But if there are mallorn-trees beyond the Great Sea, none have reported it.'

As they spoke thus, the Company filed slowly along the paths in the wood, led by Haldir, while the other Elf walked behind. They felt the ground beneath their feet smooth and soft, and after a while they walked more freely, without fear of hurt or fall. Being deprived of sight, Frodo found his hearing and other senses sharpened. He could smell the trees and the trodden grass. He could hear many different notes in the rustle of the leaves overhead, the river murmuring away on his right, and the thin clear voices of birds in the sky. He felt the sun upon his face and hands when they passed through an open glade.

As soon as he set foot upon the far bank of Silverlode a strange feeling had come upon him, and it deepened as he walked on into the Naith: it seemed to him that he had stepped over a bridge of time into a corner of the Elder Days, and was now walking in a world that was no more. In Rivendell there was memory of ancient things; in Lórien the ancient things still lived on in the waking world. Evil had been seen and heard there, sorrow had been known; the Elves feared and distrusted the world outside: wolves were howling on the wood's borders: but on the land of Lórien no shadow lay.

All that day the Company marched on, until they felt the cool evening come and heard the early night-wind whispering among many leaves. Then they rested and slept without fear upon the ground; for their guides would not permit them to unbind their eyes, and they could not climb. In the morning they went on again, walking without haste. At noon they halted, and Frodo was aware that they had passed out under the shining Sun. Suddenly he heard the sound of many voices all around him.

A marching host of Elves had come up silently: they were hastening toward the northern borders to guard against any attack from Moria; and they brought news, some of which Haldir reported. The marauding orcs had been waylaid and almost all destroyed; the remnant had fled westward towards the mountains, and were being pursued. A strange creature also had been seen, running with bent back and with hands near the ground, like a beast and yet not of beast-shape. It had eluded capture, and they had not shot it, not knowing whether it was good or ill, and it had vanished down the Silverlode southward.

'Also,' said Haldir, 'they bring me a message from the Lord and Lady of the Galadhrim. You are all to walk free, even the dwarf Gimli. It seems that the Lady knows who and what is each member of your Company. New messages have come from Rivendell perhaps.'

He removed the bandage first from Gimli's eyes. 'Your pardon!' he said, bowing low. 'Look on us now with friendly eyes! Look and be glad, for you are the first dwarf to behold the trees of the Naith of Lórien since Durin's Day!'

When his eyes were in turn uncovered, Frodo looked up and caught his breath. They were standing in an open space. To the left stood a great mound, covered with a sward of grass as green as Springtime in the Elder Days. Upon it, as a double crown, grew two circles of trees: the outer had bark of snowy white, and were leafless but beautiful in their shapely nakedness; the inner were mallorn-trees of great height, still arrayed in pale gold. High amid the branches of a towering tree that stood in the centre of all there gleamed a white flet. At the feet of the trees, and all about the green hillsides the grass was studded with small golden flowers shaped like stars. Among them, nodding on slender stalks, were other flowers, white and palest green: they glimmered as a mist amid the rich hue of the grass. Over all the sky was blue, and the sun of afternoon glowed upon the hill and cast long green shadows beneath the trees.

'Behold! You are come to Cerin Amroth,' said Haldir. 'For this is the heart of the ancient realm as it was long ago, and here is the mound of Amroth, where in happier days his high house was built. Here ever bloom the winter flowers in the unfading grass: the yellow *elanor*, and the pale *niphredil*. Here we will stay awhile, and come to the city of the Galadhrim at dusk.'

The others cast themselves down upon the fragrant grass, but Frodo stood awhile still lost in wonder. It seemed to him that he had stepped through a high window that looked on a vanished world. A light was upon it for which his language had no name. All that he saw was shapely, but the shapes seemed at once clear cut, as if they had been first conceived and drawn at the uncovering of his eyes, and ancient as if they had endured for ever. He saw no colour but those he knew, gold and white and blue and green, but they were fresh and poignant, as if he had at that moment first perceived them and made for them names new and wonderful. In winter here no heart could mourn for summer or for spring. No blemish or sickness or deformity could be seen in anything that grew upon the earth. On the land of Lórien there was no stain.

He turned and saw that Sam was now standing beside him, looking round with a puzzled expression, and rubbing his eyes as if he was not sure that he was awake. 'It's sunlight and bright day, right enough,' he said. 'I thought that Elves were all for moon and stars: but this is more elvish than anything I ever heard tell of. I feel as if I was *inside* a song, if you take my meaning.'

Haldir looked at them, and he seemed indeed to take the meaning of both thought and word. He smiled. 'You feel the power of the Lady of the Galadhrim,' he said. 'Would it please you to climb with me up Cerin Amroth?'

They followed him as he stepped lightly up the grass-clad slopes. Though he walked and breathed, and about him living leaves and flowers were stirred by the same cool wind as fanned his face, Frodo felt that he was in a timeless land that did not fade or change or fall into forgetfulness. When he had gone and passed again into the outer world, still Frodo the wanderer from the Shire would walk there, upon the grass among *elanor* and *niphredil* in fair Lothlórien.

They entered the circle of white trees. As they did so the South Wind blew upon Cerin Amroth and sighed among the branches. Frodo stood still, hearing far off great seas upon beaches that had long ago been washed away, and sea-birds crying whose race had perished from the earth.

Haldir had gone on and was now climbing to the high flet. As Frodo prepared to follow him, he laid his hand upon the tree beside the ladder: never before had he been so suddenly and so keenly aware of the feel and texture of a tree's skin and of the life within it. He felt a delight in wood and the touch of it, neither as forester nor as carpenter; it was the delight of the living tree itself.

As he stepped out at last upon the lofty platform, Haldir took his hand and turned him toward the South. 'Look this way first!' he said.

Frodo looked and saw, still at some distance, a hill of many mighty trees, or a city of green towers: which it was he could not tell. Out of it, it seemed to him that the power and light came that held all the land in sway. He longed suddenly to fly like a bird to rest in the green city. Then he looked eastward and saw all the land of Lórien running down to the pale gleam of Anduin, the Great River. He lifted his eyes across the river and all the light went out, and he was back again in the world he knew. Beyond the river the land appeared flat and empty, formless and vague, until far away it rose again like a wall, dark and drear. The sun that lay on Lothlórien had no power to enlighten the shadow of that distant height.

'There lies the fastness of Southern Mirkwood,' said Haldir. 'It is clad in a forest of dark fir, where the trees strive one against another and their branches rot and wither. In the midst upon a stony height stands Dol

Guldur, where long the hidden Enemy had his dwelling. We fear that now it is inhabited again, and with power sevenfold. A black cloud lies often over it of late. In this high place you may see the two powers that are opposed one to another; and ever they strive now in thought, but whereas the light perceives the very heart of the darkness, its own secret has not been discovered. Not yet.' He turned and climbed swiftly down, and they followed him.

At the hill's foot Frodo found Aragorn, standing still and silent as a tree; but in his hand was a small golden bloom of *elanor*, and a light was in his eyes. He was wrapped in some fair memory: and as Frodo looked at him he knew that he beheld things as they once had been in this same place. For the grim years were removed from the face of Aragorn, and he seemed clothed in white, a young lord tall and fair; and he spoke words in the Elvish tongue to one whom Frodo could not see. *Arwen vanimelda, namarië!* he said, and then he drew a breath, and returning out of his thought he looked at Frodo and smiled.

'Here is the heart of Elvendom on earth,' he said, 'and here my heart dwells ever, unless there be a light beyond the dark roads that we still must tread, you and I. Come with me!' And taking Frodo's hand in his, he left the hill of Cerin Amroth and came there never again as living man.

CHAPTER VII

THE MIRROR OF GALADRIEL

The sun was sinking behind the mountains, and the shadows were deepening in the woods, when they went on again. Their paths now went into thickets where the dusk had already gathered. Night came beneath the trees as they walked, and the Elves uncovered their silver lamps.

Suddenly they came out into the open again and found themselves under a pale evening sky pricked by a few early stars. There was a wide treeless space before them, running in a great circle and bending away on either hand. Beyond it was a deep fosse lost in soft shadow, but the grass upon its brink was green, as if it glowed still in memory of the sun that had gone. Upon the further side there rose to a great height a green wall encircling a green hill thronged with mallorn-trees taller than any they had yet seen in all the land. Their height could not be guessed, but they stood up in the twilight like living towers. In their many-tiered branches and amid their ever-moving leaves countless lights were gleaming, green and gold and silver. Haldir turned towards the Company.

'Welcome to Caras Galadhon!' he said. 'Here is the city of the Galadhrim where dwell the Lord Celeborn and Galadriel the Lady of Lórien. But we cannot enter here, for the gates do not look northward. We must go round to the southern side, and the way is not short, for the city is great.'

There was a road paved with white stone running on the outer brink of the fosse. Along this they went westward, with the city ever climbing up like a green cloud upon their left; and as the night deepened more lights sprang forth, until all the hill seemed afire with stars. They came at last to a white bridge, and crossing found the great gates of the city: they faced south-west, set between the ends of the encircling wall that here overlapped, and they were tall and strong, and hung with many lamps.

Haldir knocked and spoke, and the gates opened soundlessly; but of guards Frodo could see no sign. The travellers passed within, and the gates shut behind them. They were in a deep lane between the ends of the wall, and passing quickly through it they entered the City of the Trees. No folk could they see, nor hear any feet upon the paths; but there were many voices, about them, and in the air above. Far away up on the hill they could hear the sound of singing falling from on high like soft rain upon leaves.

They went along many paths and climbed many stairs, until they came to the high places and saw before them amid a wide lawn a fountain shim-mering. It was lit by silver lamps that swung from the boughs of trees, and it fell into a basin of silver, from which a white stream spilled. Upon the south side of the lawn there stood the mightiest of all the trees; its great smooth bole gleamed like grey silk, and up it towered, until its first branches, far above, opened their huge limbs under shadowy clouds of leaves. Beside it a broad white ladder stood, and at its foot three Elves were seated. They sprang up as the travellers approached, and Frodo saw that they were tall and clad in grey mail, and from their shoulders hung long white cloaks.

'Here dwell Celeborn and Galadriel,' said Haldir. 'It is their wish that you should ascend and speak with them.'

One of the Elf-wardens then blew a clear note on a small horn, and it was answered three times from far above. 'I will go first,' said Haldir. 'Let Frodo come next and with him Legolas. The others may follow as they wish. It is a long climb for those that are not accustomed to such stairs, but you may rest upon the way.'

As he climbed slowly up Frodo passed many flets: some on one side, some on another, and some set about the bole of the tree, so that the ladder passed through them. At a great height above the ground he came to a wide *talan*, like the deck of a great ship. On it was built a house, so large that almost it would have served for a hall of Men upon the earth. He entered behind Haldir, and found that he was in a chamber of oval shape, in the midst of which grew the trunk of the great mallorn, now tapering towards its crown, and yet making still a pillar of wide girth.

The chamber was filled with a soft light; its walls were green and silver and its roof of gold. Many Elves were seated there. On two chairs beneath the bole of the tree and canopied by a living bough there sat, side by side, Celeborn and Galadriel. They stood up to greet their guests, after the manner of Elves, even those who were accounted mighty kings. Very tall they were, and the Lady no less tall than the Lord; and they were grave and beautiful. They were clad wholly in white; and the hair of the Lady was of deep gold, and the hair of the Lord Celeborn was of silver long and bright; but no sign of age was upon them, unless it were in the depths of their eyes; for these were keen as lances in the starlight, and yet profound, the wells of deep memory.

Haldir led Frodo before them, and the Lord welcomed him in his own tongue. The Lady Galadriel said no word but looked long upon his face.

'Sit now beside my chair, Frodo of the Shire!' said Celeborn. 'When all have come we will speak together.'

Each of the companions he greeted courteously by name as they entered.

'Welcome Aragorn son of Arathorn!' he said. 'It is eight and thirty years of the world outside since you came to this land; and those years lie heavy on you. But the end is near, for good or ill. Here lay aside your burden for a while!'

'Welcome son of Thranduil! Too seldom do my kindred journey hither from the North.'

'Welcome Gimli son of Glóin! It is long indeed since we saw one of Durin's folk in Caras Galadhon. But today we have broken our long law. May it be a sign that though the world is now dark better days are at hand, and that friendship shall be renewed between our peoples.' Gimli bowed low.

When all the guests were seated before his chair the Lord looked at them again. 'Here there are eight,' he said. 'Nine were to set out: so said the messages. But maybe there has been some change of counsel that we have not heard. Elrond is far away, and darkness gathers between us, and all this year the shadows have grown longer.'

'Nay, there was no change of counsel,' said the Lady Galadriel, speaking for the first time. Her voice was clear and musical, but deeper than woman's wont. 'Gandalf the Grey set out with the Company, but he did not pass the borders of this land. Now tell us where he is; for I much desired to speak with him again. But I cannot see him from afar, unless he comes within the fences of Lothlórien: a grey mist is about him, and the ways of his feet and of his mind are hidden from me.'

'Alas!' said Aragorn. 'Gandalf the Grey fell into shadow. He remained in Moria and did not escape.'

At these words all the Elves in the hall cried aloud in grief and amazement. 'These are evil tidings,' said Celeborn, 'the most evil that have been spoken here in long years full of grievous deeds.' He turned to Haldir. 'Why has nothing of this been told to me before?' he asked in the Elven-tongue.

'We have not spoken to Haldir of our deeds or our purpose,' said Legolas. 'At first we were weary and danger was too close behind; and afterwards we almost forgot our grief for a time, as we walked in gladness on the fair paths of Lórien.'

'Yet our grief is great and our loss cannot be mended,' said Frodo. 'Gandalf was our guide, and he led us through Moria; and when our escape seemed beyond hope he saved us, and he fell.'

'Tell us now the full tale!' said Celeborn.

Then Aragorn recounted all that had happened upon the pass of Caradhras, and in the days that followed; and he spoke of Balin and his book, and the fight in the Chamber of Mazarbul, and the fire, and the narrow bridge, and the coming of the Terror. 'An evil of the Ancient World it seemed, such as I have never seen before,' said Aragorn. 'It was both a shadow and a flame, strong and terrible.'

'It was a Balrog of Morgoth,' said Legolas; 'of all elf-banes the most deadly, save the One who sits in the Dark Tower.'

'Indeed I saw upon the bridge that which haunts our darkest dreams, I saw Durin's Bane,' said Gimli in a low voice, and dread was in his eyes.

'Alas!' said Celeborn. 'We long have feared that under Caradhras a terror slept. But had I known that the Dwarves had stirred up this evil in Moria again, I would have forbidden you to pass the northern borders, you and all that went with you. And if it were possible, one would say that at the last Gandalf fell from wisdom into folly, going needlessly into the net of Moria.'

'He would be rash indeed that said that thing,' said Galadriel gravely. 'Needless were none of the deeds of Gandalf in life. Those that followed him knew not his mind and cannot report his full purpose. But however it may be with the guide, the followers are blameless. Do not repent of your welcome to the Dwarf. If our folk had been exiled long and far from Lothlórien, who of the Galadhrim, even Celeborn the Wise, would pass nigh and would not wish to look upon their ancient home, though it had become an abode of dragons?

'Dark is the water of Kheled-zâram, and cold are the springs of Kibilnâla, and fair were the many-pillared halls of Khazad-dûm in Elder Days before the fall of mighty kings beneath the stone.' She looked upon Gimli, who sat glowering and sad, and she smiled. And the Dwarf, hearing the names given in his own ancient tongue, looked up and met her eyes; and it seemed to him that he looked suddenly into the heart of an enemy and saw there love and understanding. Wonder came into his face, and then he smiled in answer.

He rose clumsily and bowed in dwarf-fashion, saying: 'Yet more fair is the living land of Lórien, and the Lady Galadriel is above all the jewels that lie beneath the earth!'

There was a silence. At length Celeborn spoke again. 'I did not know that your plight was so evil,' he said. 'Let Gimli forget my harsh words: I spoke in the trouble of my heart. I will do what I can to aid you, each according to his wish and need, but especially that one of the little folk who bears the burden.'

'Your quest is known to us,' said Galadriel, looking at Frodo. 'But we will not here speak of it more openly. Yet not in vain will it prove, maybe, that you came to this land seeking aid, as Gandalf himself plainly purposed. For the Lord of the Galadhrim is accounted the wisest of the Elves of Middle-earth, and a giver of gifts beyond the power of kings. He has dwelt in the West since the days of dawn, and I have dwelt with him years uncounted; for ere the fall of Nargothrond or Gondolin I passed over the mountains, and together through ages of the world we have fought the long defeat.

'I it was who first summoned the White Council. And if my designs had not gone amiss, it would have been governed by Gandalf the Grey, and then mayhap things would have gone otherwise. But even now there is hope left. I will not give you counsel, saying do this, or do that. For not in doing or contriving, nor in choosing between this course and another, can I avail; but only in knowing what was and is, and in part also what shall be. But this I will say to you: your Quest stands upon the edge of a knife. Stray but a little and it will fail, to the ruin of all. Yet hope remains while all the Company is true.'

And with that word she held them with her eyes, and in silence looked searchingly at each of them in turn. None save Legolas and Aragorn could long endure her glance. Sam quickly blushed and hung his head.

At length the Lady Galadriel released them from her eyes, and she smiled. 'Do not let your hearts be troubled,' she said. 'Tonight you shall sleep in peace.' Then they sighed and felt suddenly weary, as those who have been questioned long and deeply, though no words had been spoken openly.

'Go now!' said Celeborn. 'You are worn with sorrow and much toil. Even if your Quest did not concern us closely, you should have refuge in this City, until you were healed and refreshed. Now you shall rest, and we will not speak of your further road for a while.'

That night the Company slept upon the ground, much to the satisfaction of the hobbits. The Elves spread for them a pavilion among the trees near the fountain, and in it they laid soft couches; then speaking words of peace with fair elvish voices they left them. For a little while the travellers talked of their night before in the tree-tops, and of their day's journey, and of the Lord and Lady; for they had not yet the heart to look further back.

'What did you blush for, Sam?' said Pippin. 'You soon broke down. Anyone would have thought you had a guilty conscience. I hope it was nothing worse than a wicked plot to steal one of my blankets.'

'I never thought no such thing,' answered Sam, in no mood for jest. 'If you want to know, I felt as if I hadn't got nothing on, and I didn't like it. She seemed to be looking inside me and asking me what I would do if she gave me the chance of flying back home to the Shire to a nice little hole with – with a bit of garden of my own.'

'That's funny,' said Merry. 'Almost exactly what I felt myself; only, only well, I don't think I'll say any more,' he ended lamely.

All of them, it seemed, had fared alike: each had felt that he was offered a choice between a shadow full of fear that lay ahead, and something that he greatly desired: clear before his mind it lay, and to get it he had only to turn aside from the road and leave the Quest and the war against Sauron to others.

'And it seemed to me, too,' said Gimli, 'that my choice would remain secret and known only to myself.'

'To me it seemed exceedingly strange,' said Boromir. 'Maybe it was only a test, and she thought to read our thoughts for her own good purpose; but almost I should have said that she was tempting us, and offering what she pretended to have the power to give. It need not be said that I refused to listen. The Men of Minas Tirith are true to their word.' But what he thought that the Lady had offered him Boromir did not tell.

And as for Frodo, he would not speak, though Boromir pressed him with questions. 'She held you long in her gaze, Ring-bearer,' he said.

'Yes,' said Frodo; 'but whatever came into my mind then I will keep there.'

'Well, have a care!' said Boromir. 'I do not feel too sure of this Elvish Lady and her purposes.'

'Speak no evil of the Lady Galadriel!' said Aragorn sternly. 'You know not what you say. There is in her and in this land no evil, unless a man bring it hither himself. Then let him beware! But tonight I shall sleep without fear for the first time since I left Rivendell. And may I sleep deep, and forget for a while my grief! I am weary in body and in heart.' He cast himself down upon his couch and fell at once into a long sleep.

The others soon did the same, and no sound or dream disturbed their slumber. When they woke they found that the light of day was broad upon the lawn before the pavilion, and the fountain rose and fell glittering in the sun.

They remained some days in Lothlórien, so far as they could tell or remember. All the while that they dwelt there the sun shone clear, save for a gentle rain that fell at times, and passed away leaving all things fresh and clean. The air was cool and soft, as if it were early spring, yet they felt about them the deep and thoughtful quiet of winter. It seemed to them that they did little but eat and drink and rest, and walk among the trees; and it was enough.

They had not seen the Lord and Lady again, and they had little speech with the Elven-folk; for few of these knew or would use the Westron tongue. Haldir had bidden them farewell and gone back again to the fences of the North, where great watch was now kept since the tidings of Moria that the Company had brought. Legolas was away much among the Galadhrim, and after the first night he did not sleep with the other companions, though he returned to eat and talk with them. Often he took Gimli with him when he went abroad in the land, and the others wondered at this change.

Now as the companions sat or walked together they spoke of Gandalf, and all that each had known and seen of him came clear before their minds. As they were healed of hurt and weariness of body the grief of their loss grew more keen. Often they heard nearby Elvish voices singing, and knew that they were making songs of lamentation for his fall, for they caught his name among the sweet sad words that they could not understand.

Mithrandir, Mithrandir sang the Elves, *O Pilgrim Grey!* For so they loved to call him. But if Legolas was with the Company, he would not interpret the songs for them, saying that he had not the skill, and that for him the grief was still too near, a matter for tears and not yet for song.

It was Frodo who first put something of his sorrow into halting words. He was seldom moved to make song or rhyme; even in Rivendell he had listened and had not sung himself, though his memory was stored with many things that others had made before him. But now as he sat beside the fountain in Lórien and heard about him the voices of the Elves, his thought took shape in a song that seemed fair to him; yet when he tried to repeat it to Sam only snatches remained, faded as a handful of withered leaves.

> *When evening in the Shire was grey*
> *his footsteps on the Hill were heard;*
> *before the dawn he went away*
> *on journey long without a word.*

> *From Wilderland to Western shore,*
> *from northern waste to southern hill,*
> *through dragon-lair and hidden door*
> *and darkling woods he walked at will.*

> *With Dwarf and Hobbit, Elves and Men,*
> *with mortal and immortal folk,*
> *with bird on bough and beast in den,*
> *in their own secret tongues he spoke.*

> *A deadly sword, a healing hand,*
> *a back that bent beneath its load;*
> *a trumpet-voice, a burning brand,*
> *a weary pilgrim on the road.*

A lord of wisdom throned he sat,
swift in anger, quick to laugh;
an old man in a battered hat
who leaned upon a thorny staff.

He stood upon the bridge alone
and Fire and Shadow both defied;
his staff was broken on the stone,
in Khazad-dûm his wisdom died.

'Why, you'll be beating Mr. Bilbo next!' said Sam.

'No, I am afraid not,' said Frodo. 'But that is the best I can do yet.'

'Well, Mr. Frodo, if you do have another go, I hope you'll say a word about his fireworks,' said Sam. 'Something like this:

The finest rockets ever seen:
they burst in stars of blue and green,
or after thunder golden showers
came falling like a rain of flowers.

Though that doesn't do them justice by a long road.'

'No, I'll leave that to you, Sam. Or perhaps to Bilbo. But – well, I can't talk of it any more. I can't bear to think of bringing the news to him.'

One evening Frodo and Sam were walking together in the cool twilight. Both of them felt restless again. On Frodo suddenly the shadow of parting had fallen: he knew somehow that the time was very near when he must leave Lothlórien.

'What do you think of Elves now, Sam?' he said. 'I asked you the same question once before – it seems a very long while ago; but you have seen more of them since then.'

'I have indeed!' said Sam. 'And I reckon there's Elves and Elves. They're all elvish enough, but they're not all the same. Now these folk aren't wanderers or homeless, and seem a bit nearer to the likes of us: they seem to belong here, more even than Hobbits do in the Shire. Whether they've made the land, or the land's made them, it's hard to say, if you take my meaning. It's wonderfully quiet here. Nothing seems to be going on, and nobody seems to want it to. If there's any magic about, it's right down deep, where I can't lay my hands on it, in a manner of speaking.'

'You can see and feel it everywhere,' said Frodo.

'Well,' said Sam, 'you can't see nobody working it. No fireworks like poor Gandalf used to show. I wonder we don't see nothing of the Lord and Lady in all these days. I fancy now that *she* could do some wonderful things, if she had a mind. I'd dearly love to see some Elf-magic, Mr. Frodo!'

'I wouldn't,' said Frodo. 'I am content. And I don't miss Gandalf's fireworks, but his bushy eyebrows, and his quick temper, and his voice.'

'You're right,' said Sam. 'And don't think I'm finding fault. I've often wanted to see a bit of magic like what it tells of in old tales, but I've never heard of a better land than this. It's like being at home and on a holiday at the same time, if you understand me. I don't want to leave. All the same, I'm beginning to feel that if we've got to go on, then we'd best get it over.

'*It's the job that's never started as takes longest to finish*, as my old gaffer used to say. And I don't reckon that these folk can do much more to help us, magic or no. It's when we leave this land that we shall miss Gandalf worse, I'm thinking.'

'I am afraid that's only too true, Sam,' said Frodo. 'Yet I hope very much that before we leave we shall see the Lady of the Elves again.'

Even as he spoke, they saw, as if she came in answer to their words, the Lady Galadriel approaching. Tall and white and fair she walked beneath the trees. She spoke no word, but beckoned to them.

Turning aside, she led them toward the southern slopes of the hill of Caras Galadhon, and passing through a high green hedge they came into an enclosed garden. No trees grew there, and it lay open to the sky. The evening star had risen and was shining with white fire above the western woods. Down a long flight of steps the Lady went into the deep green hollow, through which ran murmuring the silver stream that issued from the fountain on the hill. At the bottom, upon a low pedestal carved like a branching tree, stood a basin of silver, wide and shallow, and beside it stood a silver ewer.

With water from the stream Galadriel filled the basin to the brim, and breathed on it, and when the water was still again she spoke. 'Here is the Mirror of Galadriel,' she said. 'I have brought you here so that you may look in it, if you will.'

The air was very still, and the dell was dark, and the Elf-lady beside him was tall and pale. 'What shall we look for, and what shall we see?' asked Frodo, filled with awe.

'Many things I can command the Mirror to reveal,' she answered, 'and to some I can show what they desire to see. But the Mirror will also show things unbidden, and those are often stranger and more profitable than things which we wish to behold. What you will see, if you leave the Mirror free to work, I cannot tell. For it shows things that were, and things that are, and things that yet may be. But which it is that he sees, even the wisest cannot always tell. Do you wish to look?'

Frodo did not answer.

'And you?' she said, turning to Sam. 'For this is what your folk would call magic, I believe; though I do not understand clearly what they mean; and they seem to use the same word of the deceits of the Enemy. But this, if you will, is the magic of Galadriel. Did you not say that you wished to see Elf-magic?'

'I did,' said Sam, trembling a little between fear and curiosity. 'I'll have a peep, Lady, if you're willing.

'And I'd not mind a glimpse of what's going on at home,' he said in an aside to Frodo. 'It seems a terrible long time that I've been away. But there, like as not I'll only see the stars, or something that I won't understand.'

'Like as not,' said the Lady with a gentle laugh. 'But come, you shall look and see what you may. Do not touch the water!'

Sam climbed up on the foot of the pedestal and leaned over the basin. The water looked hard and dark. Stars were reflected in it.

'There's only stars, as I thought,' he said. Then he gave a low gasp, for the stars went out. As if a dark veil had been withdrawn, the Mirror grew grey, and then clear. There was sun shining, and the branches of trees were waving and tossing in the wind. But before Sam could make up his mind what it was that he saw, the light faded; and now he thought he saw Frodo with a pale face lying fast asleep under a great dark cliff. Then he seemed to see himself going along a dim passage, and climbing an endless winding stair. It came to him suddenly that he was looking urgently for something, but what it was he did not know. Like a dream the vision shifted and went back, and he saw the trees again. But this time they were not so close, and he could see what was going on: they were not waving in the wind, they were falling, crashing to the ground.

'Hi!' cried Sam in an outraged voice. 'There's that Ted Sandyman a-cutting down trees as he shouldn't. They didn't ought to be felled: it's that avenue beyond the Mill that shades the road to Bywater. I wish I could get at Ted, and I'd fell *him*!'

But now Sam noticed that the Old Mill had vanished, and a large red-brick building was being put up where it had stood. Lots of folk were busily at work. There was a tall red chimney nearby. Black smoke seemed to cloud the surface of the Mirror.

'There's some devilry at work in the Shire,' he said. 'Elrond knew what he was about when he wanted to send Mr. Merry back.' Then suddenly Sam gave a cry and sprang away. 'I can't stay here,' he said wildly. 'I must go home. They've dug up Bagshot Row, and there's the poor old gaffer going down the Hill with his bits of things on a barrow. I must go home!'

'You cannot go home alone,' said the Lady. 'You did not wish to go home without your master before you looked in the Mirror, and yet you knew that evil things might well be happening in the Shire. Remember that the Mirror shows many things, and not all have yet come to pass. Some never come to be, unless those that behold the visions turn aside from their path to prevent them. The Mirror is dangerous as a guide of deeds.'

Sam sat on the ground and put his head in his hands. 'I wish I had never come here, and I don't want to see no more magic,' he said and fell silent. After a moment he spoke again thickly, as if struggling with tears. 'No, I'll go home by the long road with Mr. Frodo, or not at all,' he said. 'But I hope I do get back some day. If what I've seen turns out true, somebody's going to catch it hot!'

'Do you now wish to look, Frodo?' said the Lady Galadriel. 'You did not wish to see Elf-magic and were content.'

'Do you advise me to look?' asked Frodo.

'No,' she said. 'I do not counsel you one way or the other. I am not a counsellor. You may learn something, and whether what you see be fair or evil, that may be profitable, and yet it may not. Seeing is both good and perilous. Yet I think, Frodo, that you have courage and wisdom enough for the venture, or I would not have brought you here. Do as you will!'

'I will look,' said Frodo, and he climbed on the pedestal and bent over the dark water. At once the Mirror cleared and he saw a twilit land. Mountains loomed dark in the distance against a pale sky. A long grey road wound back out of sight. Far away a figure came slowly down the road, faint and small at first, but growing larger and clearer as it approached. Suddenly Frodo realized that it reminded him of Gandalf. He almost called aloud the wizard's name, and then he saw that the figure was clothed not in grey but in white, in a white that shone faintly in the dusk; and in its hand there was a white staff. The head was so bowed that he could see no face, and presently the figure turned aside round a bend in the road and went out of the Mirror's view. Doubt came into Frodo's mind: was this a vision of Gandalf on one of his many lonely journeys long ago, or was it Saruman?

The vision now changed. Brief and small but very vivid he caught a glimpse of Bilbo walking restlessly about his room. The table was littered with disordered papers; rain was beating on the windows.

Then there was a pause, and after it many swift scenes followed that Frodo in some way knew to be parts of a great history in which he had become involved. The mist cleared and he saw a sight which he had never seen before but knew at once: the Sea. Darkness fell. The sea rose and raged in a great storm. Then he saw against the Sun, sinking blood-red into a wrack of clouds, the black outline of a tall ship with torn sails riding up out of the West. Then a wide river flowing through a populous city. Then a white fortress with seven towers. And then again a ship with black sails, but now it was morning again, and the water rippled with light, and a banner bearing the emblem of a white tree shone in the sun. A smoke as of fire and battle arose, and again the sun went down in a burning red that faded into a grey mist; and into the mist a small ship passed away, twinkling with lights. It vanished, and Frodo sighed and prepared to draw away.

But suddenly the Mirror went altogether dark, as dark as if a hole had opened in the world of sight, and Frodo looked into emptiness. In the black abyss there appeared a single Eye that slowly grew, until it filled nearly all the Mirror. So terrible was it that Frodo stood rooted, unable to cry out or to withdraw his gaze. The Eye was rimmed with fire, but was itself glazed, yellow as a cat's, watchful and intent, and the black slit of its pupil opened on a pit, a window into nothing.

Then the Eye began to rove, searching this way and that; and Frodo knew with certainty and horror that among the many things that it sought he himself was one. But he also knew that it could not see him – not yet, not unless he willed it. The Ring that hung upon its chain about his neck grew heavy, heavier than a great stone, and his head was dragged downwards. The Mirror seemed to be growing hot and curls of steam were rising from the water. He was slipping forward.

'Do not touch the water!' said the Lady Galadriel softly. The vision faded, and Frodo found that he was looking at the cool stars twinkling in the silver basin. He stepped back shaking all over and looked at the Lady.

'I know what it was that you last saw,' she said; 'for that is also in my mind. Do not be afraid! But do not think that only by singing amid the trees, nor even by the slender arrows of elven-bows, is this land of Lothlórien maintained and defended against its Enemy. I say to you, Frodo, that even as I speak to you, I perceive the Dark Lord and know his mind, or all of his mind that concerns the Elves. And he gropes ever to see me and my thought. But still the door is closed!'

She lifted up her white arms, and spread out her hands towards the East in a gesture of rejection and denial. Eärendil, the Evening Star, most beloved of the Elves, shone clear above. So bright was it that the figure of the Elven-lady cast a dim shadow on the ground. Its rays glanced upon a ring about her finger; it glittered like polished gold overlaid with silver light, and a white stone in it twinkled as if the Even-star had come down to rest upon her hand. Frodo gazed at the ring with awe; for suddenly it seemed to him that he understood.

'Yes,' she said, divining his thought, 'it is not permitted to speak of it, and Elrond could not do so. But it cannot be hidden from the Ring-bearer, and one who has seen the Eye. Verily it is in the land of Lórien upon the finger of Galadriel that one of the Three remains. This is Nenya, the Ring of Adamant, and I am its keeper.

'He suspects, but he does not know – not yet. Do you not see now wherefore your coming is to us as the footstep of Doom? For if you fail, then we are laid bare to the Enemy. Yet if you succeed, then our power is diminished, and Lothlórien will fade, and the tides of Time will sweep it away. We must depart into the West, or dwindle to a rustic folk of dell and cave, slowly to forget and to be forgotten.'

Frodo bent his head. 'And what do you wish?' he said at last.

'That what should be shall be,' she answered. 'The love of the Elves for their land and their works is deeper than the deeps of the Sea, and their regret is undying and cannot ever wholly be assuaged. Yet they will cast all away rather than submit to Sauron: for they know him now. For the fate of Lothlórien you are not answerable, but only for the doing of your own task. Yet I could wish, were it of any avail, that the One Ring had never been wrought, or had remained for ever lost.'

'You are wise and fearless and fair, Lady Galadriel,' said Frodo. 'I will give you the One Ring, if you ask for it. It is too great a matter for me.'

Galadriel laughed with a sudden clear laugh. 'Wise the Lady Galadriel may be,' she said, 'yet here she has met her match in courtesy. Gently are you revenged for my testing of your heart at our first meeting. You begin to see with a keen eye. I do not deny that my heart has greatly desired to ask what you offer. For many long years I had pondered what I might do, should the Great Ring come into my hands, and behold! it was brought within my grasp. The evil that was devised long ago works on in many ways, whether Sauron himself stands or falls. Would not that have been a noble deed to set to the credit of his Ring, if I had taken it by force or fear from my guest?

'And now at last it comes. You will give me the Ring freely! In place of the Dark Lord you will set up a Queen. And I shall not be dark, but beautiful and terrible as the Morning and the Night! Fair as the Sea and the Sun and the Snow upon the Mountain! Dreadful as the Storm and the Lightning! Stronger than the foundations of the earth. All shall love me and despair!'

She lifted up her hand and from the ring that she wore there issued a great light that illumined her alone and left all else dark. She stood before Frodo seeming now tall beyond measurement, and beautiful beyond enduring, terrible and worshipful. Then she let her hand fall, and the light faded, and suddenly she laughed again, and lo! she was shrunken: a slender elf-woman, clad in simple white, whose gentle voice was soft and sad.

'I pass the test,' she said. 'I will diminish, and go into the West, and remain Galadriel.'

They stood for a long while in silence. At length the Lady spoke again. 'Let us return!' she said. 'In the morning you must depart, for now we have chosen, and the tides of fate are flowing.'

'I would ask one thing before we go,' said Frodo, 'a thing which I often meant to ask Gandalf in Rivendell. I am permitted to wear the One Ring: why cannot *I* see all the others and know the thoughts of those that wear them?'

'You have not tried,' she said. 'Only thrice have you set the Ring upon your finger since you knew what you possessed. Do not try! It would destroy you. Did not Gandalf tell you that the rings give power according to the measure of each possessor? Before you could use that power you would need to become far stronger, and to train your will to the domination of others. Yet even so, as Ring-bearer and as one that has borne it on finger and seen that which is hidden, your sight is grown keener. You have perceived my thought more clearly than many that are accounted wise. You saw the Eye of him that holds the Seven and the Nine. And did you not see and recognize the ring upon my finger? Did you see my ring?' she asked turning again to Sam.

'No, Lady,' he answered. 'To tell you the truth, I wondered what you were talking about. I saw a star through your fingers. But if you'll pardon my speaking out, I think my master was right. I wish you'd take his Ring. You'd put things to rights. You'd stop them digging up the gaffer and turning him adrift. You'd make some folk pay for their dirty work.'

'I would,' she said. 'That is how it would begin. But it would not stop with that, alas! We will not speak more of it. Let us go!'

CHAPTER VIII

FAREWELL TO LÓRIEN

That night the Company was again summoned to the chamber of Celeborn, and there the Lord and Lady greeted them with fair words. At length Celeborn spoke of their departure.

'Now is the time,' he said, 'when those who wish to continue the Quest must harden their hearts to leave this land. Those who no longer wish to go forward may remain here, for a while. But whether they stay or go, none can be sure of peace. For we are come now to the edge of doom. Here those who wish may await the oncoming of the hour till either the ways of the world lie open again, or we summon them to the last need of Lórien. Then they may return to their own lands, or else go to the long home of those that fall in battle.'

There was a silence. 'They all resolved to go forward,' said Galadriel looking in their eyes.

'As for me,' said Boromir, 'my way home lies onward and not back.'

'That is true,' said Celeborn, 'but is all this Company going with you to Minas Tirith?'

'We have not decided our course,' said Aragorn. 'Beyond Lothlórien I do not know what Gandalf intended to do. Indeed I do not think that even he had any clear purpose.'

'Maybe not,' said Celeborn, 'yet when you leave this land, you can no longer forget the Great River. As some of you know well, it cannot be crossed by travellers with baggage between Lórien and Gondor, save by boat. And are not the bridges of Osgiliath broken down and all the landings held now by the Enemy?

'On which side will you journey? The way to Minas Tirith lies upon this side, upon the west; but the straight road of the Quest lies east of the River, upon the darker shore. Which shore will you now take?'

'If my advice is heeded, it will be the western shore, and the way to Minas Tirith,' answered Boromir. 'But I am not the leader of the Company.' The others said nothing, and Aragorn looked doubtful and troubled.

'I see that you do not yet know what to do,' said Celeborn. 'It is not my part to choose for you; but I will help you as I may. There are some among you who can handle boats: Legolas, whose folk know the swift Forest River; and Boromir of Gondor; and Aragorn the traveller.'

'And one Hobbit!' cried Merry. 'Not all of us look on boats as wild horses. My people live by the banks of the Brandywine.'

'That is well,' said Celeborn. 'Then I will furnish your Company with boats. They must be small and light, for if you go far by water, there are places where you will be forced to carry them. You will come to the rapids of Sarn Gebir, and maybe at last to the great falls of Rauros where the River thunders down from Nen Hithoe; and there are other perils. Boats may make your journey less toilsome for a while. Yet they will not give you counsel: in the end you must leave them and the River, and turn west – or east.'

Aragorn thanked Celeborn many times. The gift of boats comforted him much, not least because there would now be no need to decide his course for some days. The others, too, looked more hopeful. Whatever perils lay ahead, it seemed better to float down the broad tide of Anduin to meet them than to plod forward with bent backs. Only Sam was doubtful: he at any rate still thought boats as bad as wild horses, or worse, and not all the dangers that he had survived made him think better of them.

'All shall be prepared for you and await you at the haven before noon tomorrow,' said Celeborn. 'I will send my people to you in the morning to help you make ready for the journey. Now we will wish you all a fair night and untroubled sleep.'

'Good night, my friends!' said Galadriel. 'Sleep in peace! Do not trouble your hearts overmuch with thought of the road tonight. Maybe the paths that you each shall tread are already laid before your feet, though you do not see them. Good night!'

The Company now took their leave and returned to their pavilion. Legolas went with them, for this was to be their last night in Lothlórien, and in spite of the words of Galadriel they wished to take counsel together.

For a long time they debated what they should do, and how it would be best to attempt the fulfilling of their purpose with the Ring; but they came to no decision. It was plain that most of them desired to go first to Minas Tirith, and to escape at least for a while from the terror of the Enemy. They would have been willing to follow a leader over the River and into the shadow of Mordor; but Frodo spoke no word, and Aragorn was still divided in his mind.

His own plan, while Gandalf remained with them, had been to go with Boromir, and with his sword help to deliver Gondor. For he believed that the message of the dreams was a summons, and that the hour had come at last when the heir of Elendil should come forth and strive with Sauron for the mastery. But in Moria the burden of Gandalf had been laid on him; and he knew that he could not now forsake the Ring, if Frodo refused in the end to go with Boromir. And yet what help could he or any of the Company give to Frodo, save to walk blindly with him into the darkness?

'I shall go to Minas Tirith, alone if need be, for it is my duty,' said Boromir; and after that he was silent for a while, sitting with his eyes fixed on Frodo, as if he was trying to read the Halfling's thoughts. At length he spoke again, softly, as if he was debating with himself. 'If you wish only to destroy the Ring,' he said, 'then there is little use in war and weapons; and the Men of Minas Tirith cannot help. But if you wish to destroy the armed might of the Dark Lord, then it is folly to go without force into his domain; and folly to throw away.' He paused suddenly, as if he had become aware that he was speaking his thoughts aloud. 'It would be folly to throw lives away, I mean,' he ended. 'It is a choice between defending a strong place and walking openly into the arms of death. At least, that is how I see it.'

Frodo caught something new and strange in Boromir's glance, and he looked hard at him. Plainly Boromir's thought was different from his final words. It would be folly to throw away: what? The Ring of Power? He had said something like this at the Council, but then he had accepted the correction of Elrond. Frodo looked at Aragorn, but he seemed deep in his own thought and made no sign that he had heeded Boromir's words. And so their debate ended. Merry and Pippin were already asleep, and Sam was nodding. The night was growing old.

In the morning, as they were beginning to pack their slender goods, Elves that could speak their tongue came to them and brought them many gifts of food and clothing for the journey. The food was mostly in the form of very thin cakes, made of a meal that was baked a light brown on the outside, and inside was the colour of cream. Gimli took up one of the cakes and looked at it with a doubtful eye.

'*Cram*,' he said under his breath, as he broke off a crisp corner and nibbled at it. His expression quickly changed, and he ate all the rest of the cake with relish.

'No more, no more!' cried the Elves laughing. 'You have eaten enough already for a long day's march.'

'I thought it was only a kind of *cram*, such as the Dale-men make for journeys in the wild,' said the Dwarf.

'So it is,' they answered. 'But we call it *lembas* or waybread, and it is more strengthening than any food made by Men, and it is more pleasant than *cram*, by all accounts.'

'Indeed it is,' said Gimli. 'Why, it is better than the honey-cakes of the Beornings, and that is great praise, for the Beornings are the best bakers that I know of; but they are none too willing to deal out their cakes to travellers in these days. You are kindly hosts!'

'All the same, we bid you spare the food,' they said. 'Eat little at a time, and only at need. For these things are given to serve you when all else fails. The cakes will keep sweet for many many days, if they are unbroken and left in their leaf-wrappings, as we have brought them. One will keep a traveller on his feet for a day of long labour, even if he be one of the tall Men of Minas Tirith.'

The Elves next unwrapped and gave to each of the Company the clothes they had brought. For each they had provided a hood and cloak, made according to his size, of the light but warm silken stuff that the Galadhrim wove. It was hard to say of what colour they were: grey with the hue of twilight under the trees they seemed to be; and yet if they were moved, or set in another light, they were green as shadowed leaves, or brown as fallow fields by night, dusk-silver as water under the stars. Each cloak was fastened about the neck with a brooch like a green leaf veined with silver.

'Are these magic cloaks?' asked Pippin, looking at them with wonder.

'I do not know what you mean by that,' answered the leader of the Elves. 'They are fair garments, and the web is good, for it was made in this land. They are elvish robes certainly, if that is what you mean. Leaf and branch, water and stone: they have the hue and beauty of all these things under the twilight of Lórien that we love; for we put the thought of all that we love into all that we make. Yet they are garments, not armour, and they will not turn shaft or blade. But they should serve you well: they are light to wear, and warm enough or cool enough at need. And you will find them a great aid in keeping out of the sight of unfriendly eyes, whether you walk among the stones or the trees. You are indeed high in the favour of the Lady! For she herself and her maidens wove this stuff; and never before have we clad strangers in the garb of our own people.'

After their morning meal the Company said farewell to the lawn by the fountain. Their hearts were heavy; for it was a fair place, and it had become like home to them, though they could not count the days and nights that they had passed there. As they stood for a moment looking at the white water in the sunlight, Haldir came walking towards them over the green grass of the glade. Frodo greeted him with delight.

'I have returned from the Northern Fences,' said the Elf, 'and I am sent now to be your guide again. The Dimrill Dale is full of vapour and clouds of smoke, and the mountains are troubled. There are noises in the deeps of the earth. If any of you had thought of returning northwards to your homes, you would not have been able to pass that way. But come! Your path now goes south.'

As they walked through Caras Galadhon the green ways were empty; but in the trees above them many voices were murmuring and singing. They themselves went silently. At last Haldir led them down the southward slopes of the hill, and they came again to the great gate hung with lamps, and to the white bridge; and so they passed out and left the city of the Elves. Then they turned away from the paved road and took a path that went off into a deep thicket of mallorn-trees, and passed on, winding through rolling woodlands of silver shadow, leading them ever down, southwards and eastwards, towards the shores of the River.

They had gone some ten miles and noon was at hand when they came on a high green wall. Passing through an opening they came suddenly out of the trees. Before them lay a long lawn of shining grass, studded with golden *elanor* that glinted in the sun. The lawn ran out into a narrow tongue between bright margins: on the right and west the Silverlode flowed glittering; on the left and east the Great River rolled its broad waters, deep and dark. On the further shores the woodlands still marched on southwards as far as the eye could see, but all the banks were bleak and bare. No mallorn lifted its gold-hung boughs beyond the Land of Lórien.

On the bank of the Silverlode, at some distance up from the meeting of the streams, there was a hythe of white stones and white wood. By it were moored many boats and barges. Some were brightly painted, and shone with silver and gold and green, but most were either white or grey. Three small grey boats had been made ready for the travellers, and in these the Elves stowed their goods. And they added also coils of rope, three to each boat. Slender they looked, but strong, silken to the touch, grey of hue like the elven-cloaks.

'What are these?' asked Sam, handling one that lay upon the greensward.

'Ropes indeed!' answered an Elf from the boats. 'Never travel far without a rope! And one that is long and strong and light. Such are these. They may be a help in many needs.'

'You don't need to tell me that!' said Sam. 'I came without any, and I've been worried ever since. But I was wondering what these were made of, knowing a bit about rope-making: it's in the family as you might say.'

'They are made of *hithlain*,' said the Elf, 'but there is no time now to instruct you in the art of their making. Had we known that this craft delighted you, we could have taught you much. But now alas! unless you should at some time return hither, you must be content with our gift. May it serve you well!'

'Come!' said Haldir. 'All is now ready for you. Enter the boats! But take care at first!'

'Heed the words!' said the other Elves. 'These boats are light-built, and they are crafty and unlike the boats of other folk. They will not sink, lade them as you will; but they are wayward if mishandled. It would be wise if you accustomed yourselves to stepping in and out, here where there is a landing-place, before you set off downstream.'

The Company was arranged in this way: Aragorn, Frodo, and Sam were in one boat; Boromir, Merry, and Pippin in another; and in the third were Legolas and Gimli, who had now become fast friends. In this last boat most of the goods and packs were stowed. The boats were moved and steered with short-handled paddles that had broad leaf-shaped blades. When all was ready Aragorn led them on a trial up the Silverlode. The current was swift and they went forward slowly. Sam sat in the bows, clutching the sides, and looking back wistfully to the shore. The sunlight
                                   glittering
on the water dazzled his eyes. As they passed beyond the green field of the Tongue, the trees drew down to the river's brink. Here and there golden leaves tossed and floated on the rippling stream. The air was very bright and still, and there was a silence, except for the high distant song of larks.

They turned a sharp bend in the river, and there, sailing proudly down the stream toward them, they saw a swan of great size. The water rippled on either side of the white breast beneath its curving neck. Its beak shone like burnished gold, and its eyes glinted like jet set in yellow stones; its huge white wings were half lifted. A music came down the river as it drew nearer; and suddenly they perceived that it was a ship, wrought and carved with elven-skill in the likeness of a bird. Two elves clad in white steered it with black paddles. In the midst of the vessel sat Celeborn, and behind him stood Galadriel, tall and white; a circlet of golden flowers was in her hair, and in her hand she held a harp, and she sang. Sad and sweet was the sound of her voice in the cool clear air:

> *I sang of leaves, of leaves of gold, and leaves of gold there grew:*
> *Of wind I sang, a wind there came and in the branches blew.*
> *Beyond the Sun, beyond the Moon, the foam was on the Sea,*
> *And by the strand of Ilmarin there grew a golden Tree.*
> *Beneath the stars of Ever-eve in Eldamar it shone,*
> *In Eldamar beside the walls of Elven Tirion.*
> *There long the golden leaves have grown upon the branching years,*
> *While here beyond the Sundering Seas now fall the Elven-tears.*
> *O Lórien! The Winter comes, the bare and leafless Day;*
> *The leaves are falling in the stream, the River flows away.*
> *O Lórien! Too long I have dwelt upon this Hither Shore*
> *And in a fading crown have twined the golden elanor.*
> *But if of ships I now should sing, what ship would come to me,*
> *What ship would bear me ever back across so wide a Sea?*

Aragorn stayed his boat as the Swan-ship drew alongside. The Lady ended her song and greeted them. 'We have come to bid our last farewell,' she said, 'and to speed you with blessings from our land.'

'Though you have been our guests,' said Celeborn, 'you have not yet eaten with us, and we bid you, therefore, to a parting feast, here between the flowing waters that will bear you far from Lórien.'

The Swan passed on slowly to the hythe, and they turned their boats and followed it. There in the last end of Egladil upon the green grass the parting feast was held; but Frodo ate and drank little, heeding only the beauty of the Lady and her voice. She seemed no longer perilous or terrible, nor filled with hidden power. Already she seemed to him, as by men of later days Elves still at times are seen: present and yet remote, a living vision of that which has already been left far behind by the flowing streams of Time.

After they had eaten and drunk, sitting upon the grass, Celeborn spoke to them again of their journey, and lifting his hand he pointed south to the woods beyond the Tongue.

'As you go down the water,' he said, 'you will find that the trees will fail, and you will come to a barren country. There the River flows in stony vale amid high moors, until at last after many leagues it comes to the tall island of the Tindrock, that we call Tol Brandir. There it casts its arms about the steep shores of the isle, and falls then with a great noise and smoke over the cataracts of Rauros down into the Nindalf, the Wetwang as it is called in your tongue. That is a wide region of sluggish fen where the stream becomes tortuous and much divided. There the Entwash flows in by many mouths from the Forest of Fangorn in the west. About that stream, on this side of the Great River, lies Rohan. On the further side are the bleak hills of the Emyn Muil. The wind blows from the East there, for they look out over the Dead Marshes and the Noman-lands to Cirith Gorgor and the black gates of Mordor.

'Boromir, and any that go with him seeking Minas Tirith, will do well to leave the Great River above Rauros and cross the Entwash before it finds the marshes. Yet they should not go too far up that stream, nor risk becoming entangled in the Forest of Fangorn. That is a strange land, and is now little known. But Boromir and Aragorn doubtless do not need this warning.'

'Indeed we have heard of Fangorn in Minas Tirith,' said Boromir. 'But what I have heard seems to me for the most part old wives' tales, such as we tell to our children. All that lies north of Rohan is now to us so far away that fancy can wander freely there. Of old Fangorn lay upon the borders of our realm; but it is now many lives of men since any of us visited it, to prove or disprove the legends that have come down from distant years.

'I have myself been at whiles in Rohan, but I have never crossed it northwards. When I was sent out as a messenger, I passed through the Gap by the skirts of the White Mountains, and crossed the Isen and the Greyflood into Northerland. A long and wearisome journey. Four hundred leagues I reckoned it, and it took me many months; for I lost my horse at Tharbad, at the fording of the Greyflood. After that journey, and the road I have trodden with this Company, I do not much doubt that I shall find a way through Rohan, and Fangorn too, if need be.'

'Then I need say no more,' said Celeborn. 'But do not despise the lore that has come down from distant years; for oft it may chance that old wives keep in memory word of things that once were needful for the wise to know.'

Now Galadriel rose from the grass, and taking a cup from one of her maidens she filled it with white mead and gave it to Celeborn.

'Now it is time to drink the cup of farewell,' she said. 'Drink, Lord of the Galadhrim! And let not your heart be sad, though night must follow noon, and already our evening draweth nigh.'

Then she brought the cup to each of the Company, and bade them drink and farewell. But when they had drunk she commanded them to sit again on the grass, and chairs were set for her and for Celeborn. Her maidens stood silent about her, and a while she looked upon her guests. At last she spoke again.

'We have drunk the cup of parting,' she said, 'and the shadows fall between us. But before you go, I have brought in my ship gifts which the Lord and Lady of the Galadhrim now offer you in memory of Lothlórien.' Then she called to each in turn.

'Here is the gift of Celeborn and Galadriel to the leader of your Company,' she said to Aragorn, and she gave him a sheath that had been made to fit his sword. It was overlaid with a tracery of flowers and leaves wrought of silver and gold, and on it were set in elven-runes formed of many gems the name Andúril and the lineage of the sword.

'The blade that is drawn from this sheath shall not be stained or broken even in defeat,' she said. 'But is there aught else that you desire of me at our parting? For darkness will flow between us, and it may be that we shall not meet again, unless it be far hence upon a road that has no returning.'

And Aragorn answered: 'Lady, you know all my desire, and long held in keeping the only treasure that I seek. Yet it is not yours to give me, even if you would; and only through darkness shall I come to it.'

'Yet maybe this will lighten your heart,' said Galadriel; 'for it was left in my care to be given to you, should you pass through this land.' Then she lifted from her lap a great stone of a clear green, set in a silver brooch that was wrought in the likeness of an eagle with outspread wings; and as she held it up the gem flashed like the sun shining through the leaves of spring. 'This stone I gave to Celebrían my daughter, and she to hers; and now it comes to you as a token of hope. In this hour take the name that was foretold for you, Elessar, the Elfstone of the house of Elendil!'

Then Aragorn took the stone and pinned the brooch upon his breast, and those who saw him wondered; for they had not marked before how tall and kingly he stood, and it seemed to them that many years of toil had fallen from his shoulders. 'For the gifts that you have given me I thank you,' he said, 'O Lady of Lórien of whom were sprung Celebrían and Arwen Evenstar. What praise could I say more?'

The Lady bowed her head, and she turned then to Boromir, and to him she gave a belt of gold; and to Merry and Pippin she gave small silver belts, each with a clasp wrought like a golden flower. To Legolas she gave a bow such as the Galadhrim used, longer and stouter than the bows of Mirkwood, and strung with a string elf-hair. With it went a quiver of arrows.

'For you little gardener and lover of trees,' she said to Sam, 'I have only a small gift.' She put into his hand a little box of plain grey wood, unadorned save for a single silver rune upon the lid. 'Here is set G for Galadriel,' she said; 'but also it may stand for garden in your tongue. In this box there is earth from my orchard, and such blessing as Galadriel has still to bestow is upon it. It will not keep you on your road, nor defend you against any peril; but if you keep it and see your home again at last, then perhaps it may reward you. Though you should find all barren and laid waste, there will be few gardens in Middle-earth that will bloom like your garden, if you sprinkle this earth there. Then you may remember Galadriel, and catch a glimpse far off of Lórien, that you have seen only in our winter. For our spring and our summer are gone by, and they will never be seen on earth again save in memory.'

Sam went red to the ears and muttered something inaudible, as he clutched the box and bowed as well as he could.

'And what gift would a Dwarf ask of the Elves?' said Galadriel, turning to Gimli.

'None, Lady,' answered Gimli. 'It is enough for me to have seen the Lady of the Galadhrim, and to have heard her gentle words.'

'Hear all ye Elves!' she cried to those about her. 'Let none say again that Dwarves are grasping and ungracious! Yet surely, Gimli son of Glóin, you desire something that I could give? Name it, I bid you! You shall not be the only guest without a gift.'

'There is nothing, Lady Galadriel,' said Gimli, bowing low and stammering. 'Nothing, unless it might be – unless it is permitted to ask, nay, to name a single strand of your hair, which surpasses the gold of the earth as the stars surpass the gems of the mine. I do not ask for such a gift. But you commanded me to name my desire.'

The Elves stirred and murmured with astonishment, and Celeborn gazed at the Dwarf in wonder, but the Lady smiled. 'It is said that the skill of the Dwarves is in their hands rather than in their tongues,' she said; 'yet that is not true of Gimli. For none have ever made to me a request so bold and yet so courteous. And how shall I refuse, since I commanded him to speak? But tell me, what would you do with such a gift?'

'Treasure it, Lady,' he answered, 'in memory of your words to me at our first meeting. And if ever I return to the smithies of my home, it shall be set in imperishable crystal to be an heirloom of my house, and a pledge of good will between the Mountain and the Wood until the end of days.'

Then the Lady unbraided one of her long tresses, and cut off three golden hairs, and laid them in Gimli's hand. 'These words shall go with the gift,' she said. 'I do not foretell, for all foretelling is now vain: on the one hand lies darkness, and on the other only hope. But if hope should not fail, then I say to you, Gimli son of Glóin, that your hands shall flow with gold, and yet over you gold shall have no dominion.

'And you, Ring-bearer,' she said, turning to Frodo. 'I come to you last who are not last in my thoughts. For you I have prepared this.' She held up a small crystal phial: it glittered as she moved it, and rays of white light sprang from her hand. 'In this phial,' she said, 'is caught the light of Eärendil's star, set amid the waters of my fountain. It will shine still brighter when night is about you. May it be a light to you in dark places, when all other lights go out. Remember Galadriel and her Mirror!'

Frodo took the phial, and for a moment as it shone between them, he saw her again standing like a queen, great and beautiful, but no longer terrible. He bowed, but found no words to say.

Now the Lady arose, and Celeborn led them back to the hythe. A yellow noon lay on the green land of the Tongue, and the water glittered with silver. All at last was made ready. The Company took their places in the boats as before. Crying farewell, the Elves of Lórien with long grey poles thrust them out into the flowing stream, and the rippling waters bore them slowly away. The travellers sat still without moving or speaking. On the green bank near to the very point of the Tongue the Lady Galadriel stood alone and silent. As they passed her they turned and their eyes watched her slowly floating away from them. For so it seemed to them: Lórien was slipping backward, like a bright ship masted with enchanted trees, sailing on to forgotten shores, while they sat helpless upon the margin of the grey and leafless world.

Even as they gazed, the Silverlode passed out into the currents of the Great River, and their boats turned and began to speed southward. Soon the white form of the Lady was small and distant. She shone like a window of glass upon a far hill in the westering sun, or as a remote lake seen from a mountain: a crystal fallen in the lap of the land. Then it seemed to Frodo that she lifted her arms in a final farewell, and far but piercing-clear on the following wind came the sound of her voice singing. But now she sang in the ancient tongue of the Elves beyond the Sea, and he did not understand the words: fair was the music, but it did not comfort him.

Yet as is the way of Elvish words, they remained graven in his memory, and long afterwards he interpreted them, as well as he could: the language was that of Elven-song and spoke of things little known on Middle-earth.

Ai! laurië lantar lassi súrinen,
yéni únótimë ve rámar aldaron!
Yéni ve lintë yuldar avánier
mi oromardi lisse-miruvóreva
Andúnë pella, Vardo tellumar
nu luini yassen tintilar i eleni
ómaryo airetári-lírinen.

Sí man i yulma nin enquantuva?

An sí Tintallë Varda Oiolossëo
ve fanyar máryat Elentári ortanë,
ar ilyë tier undulávë lumbulë;
ar sindanóriello caita mornië
i falmalinnar imbë met, ar hísië
untúpa Calaciryo míri oialë.
Sí vanwa ná, Rómello vanwa, Valimar!

Namárië! Nai hiruvalyë Valimar.
Nai elyë hiruva. Namárië!

'Ah! like gold fall the leaves in the wind, long years numberless as the wings of trees! The years have passed like swift draughts of the sweet mead in lofty halls beyond the West, beneath the blue vaults of Varda wherein the stars tremble in the song of her voice, holy and queenly. Who now shall refill the cup for me? For now the Kindler, Varda, the Queen of the Stars, from Mount Everwhite has uplifted her hands like clouds, and all paths are drowned deep in shadow; and out of a grey country darkness lies on the foaming waves between us, and mist covers the jewels of Calacirya for ever. Now lost, lost to those from the East is Valimar! Farewell! Maybe thou shalt find Valimar. Maybe even thou shalt find it. Farewell!' Varda is the name of that Lady whom the Elves in these lands of exile name Elbereth.

Suddenly the River swept round a bend, and the banks rose upon either side, and the light of Lórien was hidden. To that fair land Frodo never came again.

The travellers now turned their faces to the journey; the sun was before them, and their eyes were dazzled, for all were filled with tears. Gimli wept openly.

'I have looked the last upon that which was fairest,' he said to Legolas his companion. 'Henceforward I will call nothing fair, unless it be her gift.' He put his hand to his breast.

'Tell me, Legolas, why did I come on this Quest? Little did I know where the chief peril lay! Truly Elrond spoke, saying that we could not foresee what we might meet upon our road. Torment in the dark was the danger that I feared, and it did not hold me back. But I would not have come, had I known the danger of light and joy. Now I have taken my worst wound in this parting, even if I were to go this night straight to the Dark Lord. Alas for Gimli son of Glóin!'

'Nay!' said Legolas. 'Alas for us all! And for all that walk the world in these after-days. For such is the way of it: to find and lose, as it seems to those whose boat is on the running stream. But I count you blessed, Gimli son of Glóin: for your loss you suffer of your own free will, and you might have chosen otherwise. But you have not forsaken your companions, and the least reward that you shall have is that the memory of Lothlórien shall remain ever clear and unstained in your heart, and shall neither fade nor grow stale.'

'Maybe,' said Gimli; 'and I thank you for your words. True words doubtless; yet all such comfort is cold. Memory is not what the heart desires. That is only a mirror, be it clear as Kheled-zâram. Or so says the heart of Gimli the Dwarf. Elves may see things otherwise. Indeed I have heard that for them memory is more like to the waking world than to a dream. Not so for Dwarves.

'But let us talk no more of it. Look to the boat! She is too low in the water with all this baggage, and the Great River is swift. I do not wish to drown my grief in cold water.' He took up a paddle, and steered towards the western bank, following Aragorn's boat ahead, which had already moved out of the middle stream.

So the Company went on their long way, down the wide hurrying waters, borne ever southwards. Bare woods stalked along either bank, and they could not see any glimpse of the lands behind. The breeze died away and the River flowed without a sound. No voice of bird broke the silence. The sun grew misty as the day grew old, until it gleamed in a pale sky like a high white pearl. Then it faded into the West, and dusk came early, followed by a grey and starless night. Far into the dark quiet hours they floated on, guiding their boats under the overhanging shadows of the western woods. Great trees passed by like ghosts, thrusting their twisted thirsty roots through the mist down into the water. It was dreary and cold. Frodo sat and listened to the faint lap and gurgle of the River fretting among the tree-roots and driftwood near the shore, until his head nodded and he fell into an uneasy sleep.

CHAPTER IX

THE GREAT RIVER

Frodo was roused by Sam. He found that he was lying, well wrapped, under tall grey-skinned trees in a quiet corner of the woodlands on the west bank of the Great River, Anduin. He had slept the night away, and the grey of morning was dim among the bare branches. Gimli was busy with a small fire near at hand.

They started again before the day was broad. Not that most of the Company were eager to hurry southwards: they were content that the decision, which they must make at latest when they came to Rauros and the Tindrock Isle, still lay some days ahead; and they let the River bear them on at its own pace, having no desire to hasten towards the perils that lay beyond, whichever course they took in the end. Aragorn let them drift with the stream as they wished, husbanding their strength against weariness to come. But he insisted that at least they should start early each day and journey on far into the evening; for he felt in his heart that time was pressing, and he feared that the Dark Lord had not been idle while they lingered in Lórien.

Nonetheless they saw no sign of an enemy that day, nor the next. The dull grey hours passed without event. As the third day of their voyage wore on the lands changed slowly: the trees thinned and then failed altogether. On the eastern bank to their left they saw long formless slopes stretching up and away toward the sky; brown and withered they looked, as if fire had passed over them, leaving no living blade of green: an unfriendly waste without even a broken tree or a bold stone to relieve the emptiness. They had come to the Brown Lands that lay, vast and desolate, between Southern Mirkwood and the hills of the Emyn Muil. What pestilence or war or evil deed of the Enemy had so blasted all that region even Aragorn could not tell.

Upon the west to their right the land was treeless also, but it was flat, and in many places green with wide plains of grass. On this side of the River they passed forests of great reeds, so tall that they shut out all view to the west, as the little boats went rustling by along their fluttering borders. Their dark withered plumes bent and tossed in the light cold airs, hissing softly and sadly. Here and there through openings Frodo could catch sudden glimpses of rolling meads, and far beyond them hills in the sunset, and away on the edge of sight a dark line, where marched the southernmost ranks of the Misty Mountains.

There was no sign of living moving things, save birds. Of these there were many: small fowl whistling and piping in the reeds, but they were seldom seen. Once or twice the travellers heard the rush and whine of swan-wings, and looking up they saw a great phalanx streaming along the sky.

'Swans!' said Sam. 'And mighty big ones too!'

'Yes,' said Aragorn, 'and they are black swans.'

'How wide and empty and mournful all this country looks!' said Frodo. 'I always imagined that as one journeyed south it got warmer and merrier, until winter was left behind for ever.'

'But we have not journeyed far south yet,' answered Aragorn. 'It is still winter, and we are far from the sea. Here the world is cold until the sudden spring, and we may yet have snow again. Far away down in the Bay of Belfalas, to which Anduin runs, it is warm and merry, maybe, or would be but for the Enemy. But here we are not above sixty leagues, I guess, south of the Southfarthing away in your Shire, hundreds of long miles yonder. You are looking now south-west across the north plains of the Riddermark, Rohan the land of the Horse-lords. Ere long we shall come to the mouth of the Limlight that runs down from Fangorn to join the Great River. That is the north boundary of Rohan; and of old all that lay between Limlight and the White Mountains belonged to the Rohirrim. It is a rich and pleasant land, and its grass has no rival; but in these evil days folk do not dwell by the River or ride often to its shores. Anduin is wide, yet the orcs can shoot their arrows far across the stream; and of late, it is said, they have dared to cross the water and raid the herds and studs of Rohan.'

Sam looked from bank to bank uneasily. The trees had seemed hostile before, as if they harboured secret eyes and lurking dangers; now he wished that the trees were still there. He felt that the Company was too naked, afloat in little open boats in the midst of shelterless lands, and on a river that was the frontier of war.

In the next day or two, as they went on, borne steadily southwards, this feeling of insecurity grew on all the Company. For a whole day they took to their paddles and hastened forward. The banks slid by. Soon the River broadened and grew more shallow; long stony beaches lay upon the east, and there were gravel-shoals in the water, so that careful steering was needed. The Brown Lands rose into bleak wolds, over which flowed a chill air from the East. On the other side the meads had become rolling downs of withered grass amidst a land of fen and tussock. Frodo shivered, thinking of the lawns and fountains, the clear sun and gentle rains of Lothlórien. There was little speech and no laughter in any of the boats. Each member of the Company was busy with his own thoughts.

The heart of Legolas was running under the stars of a summer night in some northern glade amid the beech-woods; Gimli was fingering gold in his mind, and wondering if it were fit to be wrought into the housing of the Lady's gift. Merry and Pippin in the middle boat were ill at ease, for Boromir sat muttering to himself, sometimes biting his nails, as if some restlessness or doubt consumed him, sometimes seizing a paddle and driving the boat close behind Aragorn's. Then Pippin, who sat in the bow looking back, caught a queer gleam in his eye, as he peered forward gazing at Frodo. Sam had long ago made up his mind that, though boats were maybe not as dangerous as he had been brought up to believe, they were far more uncomfortable than even he had imagined. He was cramped and miserable, having nothing to do but stare at the winter-lands crawling by and the grey water on either side of him. Even when the paddles were in use they did not trust Sam with one.

As dusk drew down on the fourth day, he was looking back over the bowed heads of Frodo and Aragorn and the following boats; he was drowsy and longed for camp and the feel of earth under his toes. Suddenly something caught his sight: at first he stared at it listlessly, then he sat up and rubbed his eyes; but when he looked again he could not see it any more.

That night they camped on a small eyot close to the western bank. Sam lay rolled in blankets beside Frodo. 'I had a funny dream an hour or two before we stopped, Mr. Frodo,' he said. 'Or maybe it wasn't a dream. Funny it was anyway.'

'Well, what was it?' said Frodo, knowing that Sam would not settle down until he had told his tale, whatever it was. 'I haven't seen or thought of anything to make me smile since we left Lothlórien.'

'It wasn't funny that way, Mr. Frodo. It was queer. All wrong, if it wasn't a dream. And you had best hear it. It was like this: I saw a log with eyes!'

'The log's all right,' said Frodo. 'There are many in the River. But leave out the eyes!'

'That I won't,' said Sam. ''Twas the eyes as made me sit up, so to speak. I saw what I took to be a log floating along in the half-light behind Gimli's boat; but I didn't give much heed to it. Then it seemed as if the log was slowly catching us up. And that was peculiar, as you might say, seeing as we were all floating on the stream together. Just then I saw the eyes: two pale sort of points, shiny-like, on a hump at the near end of the log. What's more, it wasn't a log, for it had paddle-feet, like a swan's almost, only they seemed bigger, and kept dipping in and out of the water.

'That's when I sat right up and rubbed my eyes, meaning to give a shout, if it was still there when I had rubbed the drowse out of my head. For the whatever-it-was was coming along fast now and getting close behind Gimli. But whether those two lamps spotted me moving and staring, or whether I came to my senses, I don't know. When I looked again, it wasn't there. Yet I think I caught a glimpse, with the tail of my eye, as the saying is, of something dark shooting under the shadow of the bank. I couldn't see no more eyes, though.

'I said to myself: "dreaming again, Sam Gamgee," I said; and I said no more just then. But I've been thinking since, and now I'm not so sure. What do you make of it, Mr. Frodo?'

'I should make nothing of it but a log and the dusk and sleep in your eyes, Sam,' said Frodo, 'if this was the first time that those eyes had been seen. But it isn't. I saw them away back north before we reached Lórien. And I saw a strange creature with eyes climbing to the flet that night. Haldir saw it too. And do you remember the report of the Elves that went after the orc-band?'

'Ah,' said Sam, 'I do; and I remember more too. I don't like my thoughts; but thinking of one thing and another, and Mr. Bilbo's stories and all, I fancy I could put a name on the creature, at a guess. A nasty name. Gollum, maybe?'

'Yes, that is what I have feared for some time,' said Frodo. 'Ever since the night on the flet. I suppose he was lurking in Moria, and picked up our trail then; but I hoped that our stay in Lórien would throw him off the scent again. The miserable creature must have been hiding in the woods by the Silverlode, watching us start off!'

'That's about it,' said Sam. 'And we'd better be a bit more watchful ourselves, or we'll feel some nasty fingers round our necks one of these nights, if we ever wake up to feel anything. And that's what I was leading up to. No need to trouble Strider or the others tonight. I'll keep watch. I can sleep tomorrow, being no more than luggage in a boat, as you might say.'

'I might,' said Frodo, 'and I might say "luggage with eyes". You shall watch; but only if you promise to wake me half-way towards morning, if nothing happens before then.'

In the dead hours Frodo came out of a deep dark sleep to find Sam shaking him. 'It's a shame to wake you,' whispered Sam, 'but that's what you said. There's nothing to tell, or not much. I thought I heard some soft plashing and a sniffing noise, a while back; but you hear a lot of such queer sounds by a river at night.'

He lay down, and Frodo sat up, huddled in his blankets, and fought off his sleep. Minutes or hours passed slowly, and nothing happened. Frodo was just yielding to the temptation to lie down again when a dark shape, hardly visible, floated close to one of the moored boats. A long whitish hand could be dimly seen as it shot out and grabbed the gunwale; two pale lamplike eyes shone coldly as they peered inside, and then they lifted and gazed up at Frodo on the eyot. They were not more than a yard or two away, and Frodo heard the soft hiss of intaken breath. He stood up, drawing Sting from its sheath, and faced the eyes. Immediately their light was shut off. There was another hiss and a splash, and the dark log-shape shot away downstream into the night. Aragorn stirred in his sleep, turned over, and sat up.

'What is it?' he whispered, springing up and coming to Frodo. 'I felt something in my sleep. Why have you drawn your sword?'

'Gollum,' answered Frodo. 'Or at least, so I guess.'

'Ah!' said Aragorn. 'So you know about our little footpad, do you? He padded after us all through Moria and right down to Nimrodel. Since we took to boats, he has been lying on a log and paddling with hands and feet. I have tried to catch him once or twice at night; but he is slier than a fox, and as slippery as a fish. I hoped the river-voyage would beat him, but he is too clever a waterman.

'We shall have to try going faster tomorrow. You lie down now, and I will keep watch for what is left of the night. I wish I could lay my hands on the wretch. We might make him useful. But if I cannot, we shall have to try and lose him. He is very dangerous. Quite apart from murder by night on his own account, he may put any enemy that is about on our track.'

The night passed without Gollum showing so much as a shadow again. After that the Company kept a sharp look-out, but they saw no more of Gollum while the voyage lasted. If he was still following, he was very wary and cunning. At Aragorn's bidding they paddled now for long spells, and the banks went swiftly by. But they saw little of the country, for they journeyed mostly by night and twilight, resting by day, and lying as hidden as the land allowed. In this way the time passed without event until the seventh day.

The weather was still grey and overcast, with wind from the East, but as evening drew into night the sky away westward cleared, and pools of faint light, yellow and pale green, opened under the grey shores of cloud. There the white rind of the new Moon could be seen glimmering in the remote lakes. Sam looked at it and puckered his brows.

The next day the country on either side began to change rapidly. The banks began to rise and grow stony. Soon they were passing through a hilly rocky land, and on both shores there were steep slopes buried in deep brakes of thorn and sloe, tangled with brambles and creepers. Behind them stood low crumbling cliffs, and chimneys of grey weathered stone dark with ivy; and beyond these again there rose high ridges crowned with wind-writhen firs. They were drawing near to the grey hill-country of the Emyn Muil, the southern march of Wilderland.

There were many birds about the cliffs and the rock-chimneys, and all day high in the air flocks of birds had been circling, black against the pale sky. As they lay in their camp that day Aragorn watched the flights doubt-fully, wondering if Gollum had been doing some mischief and the news of their voyage was now moving in the wilderness. Later as the sun was setting, and the Company was stirring and getting ready to start again, he descried a dark spot against the fading light: a great bird high and far off, now wheeling, now flying on slowly southwards.

'What is that, Legolas?' he asked, pointing to the northern sky. 'Is it, as I think, an eagle?'

'Yes,' said Legolas. 'It is an eagle, a hunting eagle. I wonder what that forebodes. It is far from the mountains.'

'We will not start until it is fully dark,' said Aragorn.

The eighth night of their journey came. It was silent and windless; the grey east wind had passed away. The thin crescent of the Moon had fallen early into the pale sunset, but the sky was clear above, and though far away in the South there were great ranges of cloud that still shone faintly, in the West stars glinted bright.

'Come!' said Aragorn. 'We will venture one more journey by night. We are coming to reaches of the River that I do not know well; for I have never journeyed by water in these parts before, not between here and the rapids of Sarn Gebir. But if I am right in my reckoning, those are still many miles ahead. Still there are dangerous places even before we come there: rocks and stony eyots in the stream. We must keep a sharp watch and not try to paddle swiftly.'

To Sam in the leading boat was given the task of watchman. He lay forward peering into the gloom. The night grew dark, but the stars above were strangely bright, and there was a glimmer on the face of the River. It was close on midnight, and they had been drifting for some while, hardly using the paddles, when suddenly Sam cried out. Only a few yards ahead dark shapes loomed up in the stream and he heard the swirl of racing water. There was a swift current which swung left, towards the eastern shore where the channel was clear. As they were swept aside the travellers could see, now very close, the pale foam of the River lashing against sharp rocks that were thrust out far into the stream like a ridge of teeth. The boats were all huddled together.

'Hoy there, Aragorn!' shouted Boromir, as his boat bumped into the leader. 'This is madness! We cannot dare the Rapids by night! But no boat can live in Sarn Gebir, be it night or day.'

'Back, back!' cried Aragorn. 'Turn! Turn if you can!' He drove his paddle into the water, trying to hold the boat and bring it round.

'I am out of my reckoning,' he said to Frodo. 'I did not know that we had come so far: Anduin flows faster than I thought. Sarn Gebir must be close at hand already.'

With great efforts they checked the boats and slowly brought them about; but at first they could make only small headway against the current, and all the time they were carried nearer and nearer to the eastern bank. Now dark and ominous it loomed up in the night.

'All together, paddle!' shouted Boromir. 'Paddle! Or we shall be driven on the shoals.' Even as he spoke Frodo felt the keel beneath him grate upon stone.

At that moment there was a twang of bowstrings: several arrows whistled over them, and some fell among them. One smote Frodo between the shoulders and he lurched forward with a cry, letting go his paddle: but the arrow fell back, foiled by his hidden coat of mail. Another passed through Aragorn's hood; and a third stood fast in the gunwale of the second boat, close by Merry's hand. Sam thought he could glimpse black figures running to and fro upon the long shingle-banks that lay under the eastern shore. They seemed very near.

'*Yrch!*' said Legolas, falling into his own tongue.

'Orcs!' cried Gimli.

'Gollum's doing, I'll be bound,' said Sam to Frodo. 'And a nice place to choose, too. The River seems set on taking us right into their arms!'

They all leaned forward straining at the paddles: even Sam took a hand. Every moment they expected to feel the bite of black-feathered arrows. Many whined overhead or struck the water nearby; but there were no more hits. It was dark, but not too dark for the night-eyes of Orcs, and in the star-glimmer they must have offered their cunning foes some mark, unless it was that the grey cloaks of Lórien and the grey timber of the elf-wrought boats defeated the malice of the archers of Mordor.

Stroke by stroke they laboured on. In the darkness it was hard to be sure that they were indeed moving at all; but slowly the swirl of the water grew less, and the shadow of the eastern bank faded back into the night. At last, as far as they could judge, they had reached the middle of the stream again and had driven their boats back some distance above the jutting rocks. Then half turning they thrust them with all their strength towards the western shore. Under the shadow of bushes leaning out over the water they halted and drew breath.

Legolas laid down his paddle and took up the bow that he had brought from Lórien. Then he sprang ashore and climbed a few paces up the bank. Stringing the bow and fitting an arrow he turned, peering back over the River into the darkness. Across the water there were shrill cries, but nothing could be seen.

Frodo looked up at the Elf standing tall above him, as he gazed into the night, seeking a mark to shoot at. His head was dark, crowned with sharp white stars that glittered in the black pools of the sky behind. But now rising and sailing up from the South the great clouds advanced, sending out dark outriders into the starry fields. A sudden dread fell on the Company. '*Elbereth Gilthoniel!*' sighed Legolas as he looked up. Even as he did so, a dark shape, like a cloud and yet not a cloud, for it moved far more swiftly, came out of the blackness in the South, and sped towards the Company, blotting out all light as it approached. Soon it appeared as a great winged creature, blacker than the pits in the night. Fierce voices rose up to greet it from across the water. Frodo felt a sudden chill running through him and clutching at his heart; there was a deadly cold, like the memory of an old wound, in his shoulder. He crouched down, as if to hide.

Suddenly the great bow of Lórien sang. Shrill went the arrow from the elven-string. Frodo looked up. Almost above him the winged shape swerved. There was a harsh croaking scream, as it fell out of the air, vanishing down into the gloom of the eastern shore. The sky was clean again. There was a tumult of many voices far away, cursing and wailing in the darkness, and then silence. Neither shaft nor cry came again from the east that night.

After a while Aragorn led the boats back upstream. They felt their way along the water's edge for some distance, until they found a small shallow bay. A few low trees grew there close to the water, and behind them rose a steep rocky bank. Here the Company decided to stay and await the dawn: it was useless to attempt to move further by night. They made no camp and lit no fire, but lay huddled in the boats, moored close together.

'Praised be the bow of Galadriel, and the hand and eye of Legolas!' said Gimli, as he munched a wafer of *lembas*. 'That was a mighty shot in the dark, my friend!'

'But who can say what it hit?' said Legolas.

'I cannot,' said Gimli. 'But I am glad that the shadow came no nearer. I liked it not at all. Too much it reminded me of the shadow in Moria – the shadow of the Balrog,' he ended in a whisper.

'It was not a Balrog,' said Frodo, still shivering with the chill that had come upon him. 'It was something colder. I think it was——' Then he paused and fell silent.

'What do you think?' asked Boromir eagerly, leaning from his boat, as if he was trying to catch a glimpse of Frodo's face.

'I think – No, I will not say,' answered Frodo. 'Whatever it was, its fall has dismayed our enemies.'

'So it seems,' said Aragorn. 'Yet where they are, and how many, and what they will do next, we do not know. This night we must all be sleepless! Dark hides us now. But what the day will show who can tell? Have your weapons close to hand!'

Sam sat tapping the hilt of his sword as if he were counting on his fingers, and looking up at the sky. 'It's very strange,' he murmured. 'The Moon's the same in the Shire and in Wilderland, or it ought to be. But either it's out of its running, or I'm all wrong in my reckoning. You'll remember, Mr. Frodo, the Moon was waning as we lay on the flet up in that tree: a week from the full, I reckon. And we'd been a week on the way last night, when up pops a New Moon as thin as a nail-paring, as if we had never stayed no time in the Elvish country.

'Well, I can remember three nights there for certain, and I seem to remember several more, but I would take my oath it was never a whole month. Anyone would think that time did not count in there!'

'And perhaps that was the way of it,' said Frodo. 'In that land, maybe, we were in a time that has elsewhere long gone by. It was not, I think, until Silverlode bore us back to Anduin that we returned to the time that flows through mortal lands to the Great Sea. And I don't remember any moon, either new or old, in Caras Galadhon: only stars by night and sun by day.'

Legolas stirred in his boat. 'Nay, time does not tarry ever,' he said; 'but change and growth is not in all things and places alike. For the Elves the world moves, and it moves both very swift and very slow. Swift, because they themselves change little, and all else fleets by: it is a grief to them. Slow, because they do not count the running years, not for themselves. The passing seasons are but ripples ever repeated in the long long stream. Yet beneath the Sun all things must wear to an end at last.'

'But the wearing is slow in Lórien,' said Frodo. 'The power of the Lady is on it. Rich are the hours, though short they seem, in Caras Galadhon, where Galadriel wields the Elven-ring.'

'That should not have been said outside Lórien, not even to me,' said Aragorn. 'Speak no more of it! But so it is, Sam: in that land you lost your count. There time flowed swiftly by us, as for the Elves. The old moon passed, and a new moon waxed and waned in the world outside, while we tarried there. And yestereve a new moon came again. Winter is nearly gone. Time flows on to a spring of little hope.'

The night passed silently. No voice or call was heard again across the water. The travellers huddled in their boats felt the changing of the weather. The air grew warm and very still under the great moist clouds that had floated up from the South and the distant seas. The rushing of the River over the rocks of the rapids seemed to grow louder and closer. The twigs of the trees above them began to drip.

When the day came the mood of the world about them had become soft and sad. Slowly the dawn grew to a pale light, diffused and shadowless. There was mist on the River, and white fog swathed the shore; the far bank could not be seen.

'I can't abide fog,' said Sam; 'but this seems to be a lucky one. Now perhaps we can get away without those cursed goblins seeing us.'

'Perhaps so,' said Aragorn. 'But it will be hard to find the path unless the fog lifts a little later on. And we must find the path, if we are to pass Sarn Gebir and come to the Emyn Muil.'

'I do not see why we should pass the Rapids or follow the River any further,' said Boromir. 'If the Emyn Muil lie before us, then we can abandon these cockle-boats, and strike westward and southward, until we come to the Entwash and cross into my own land.'

'We can, if we are making for Minas Tirith,' said Aragorn, 'but that is not yet agreed. And such a course may be more perilous than it sounds. The vale of Entwash is flat and fenny, and fog is a deadly peril there for those on foot and laden. I would not abandon our boats until we must. The River is at least a path that cannot be missed.'

'But the Enemy holds the eastern bank,' objected Boromir. 'And even if you pass the Gates of Argonath and come unmolested to the Tindrock, what will you do then? Leap down the Falls and land in the marshes?'

'No!' answered Aragorn. 'Say rather that we will bear our boats by the ancient way to Rauros-foot, and there take to the water again. Do you not know, Boromir, or do you choose to forget the North Stair, and the high seat upon Amon Hen, that were made in the days of the great kings? I at least have a mind to stand in that high place again, before I decide my further course. There, maybe, we shall see some sign that will guide us.'

Boromir held out long against this choice; but when it became plain that Frodo would follow Aragorn, wherever he went, he gave in. 'It is not the way of the Men of Minas Tirith to desert their friends at need,' he said, 'and you will need my strength, if ever you are to reach the Tindrock. To the tall isle I will go, but no further. There I shall turn to my home, alone if my help has not earned the reward of any companionship.'

The day was now growing, and the fog had lifted a little. It was decided that Aragorn and Legolas should at once go forward along the shore, while the others remained by the boats. Aragorn hoped to find some way by which they could carry both their boats and their baggage to the smoother water beyond the Rapids.

'Boats of the Elves would not sink, maybe,' he said, 'but that does not say that we should come through Sarn Gebir alive. None have ever done so yet. No road was made by the Men of Gondor in this region, for even in their great days their realm did not reach up Anduin beyond the Emyn Muil; but there is a portage-way somewhere on the western shore, if I can find it. It cannot yet have perished; for light boats used to journey out of Wilderland down to Osgiliath, and still did so until a few years ago, when the Orcs of Mordor began to multiply.'

'Seldom in my life has any boat come out of the North, and the Orcs prowl on the east-shore,' said Boromir. 'If you go forward, peril will grow with every mile, even if you find a path.'

'Peril lies ahead on every southward road,' answered Aragorn. 'Wait for us one day. If we do not return in that time, you will know that evil has indeed befallen us. Then you must take a new leader and follow him as best you can.'

It was with a heavy heart that Frodo saw Aragorn and Legolas climb the steep bank and vanish into the mists; but his fears proved groundless. Only two or three hours had passed, and it was barely mid-day, when the shadowy shapes of the explorers appeared again.

'All is well,' said Aragorn, as he clambered down the bank. 'There is a track, and it leads to a good landing that is still serviceable. The distance is not great: the head of the Rapids is but half a mile below us, and they are little more than a mile long. Not far beyond them the stream becomes clear and smooth again, though it runs swiftly. Our hardest task will be to get our boats and baggage to the old portage-way. We have found it, but it lies well back from the water-side here, and runs under the lee of a rock-wall, a furlong or more from the shore. We did not find where the northward landing lies. If it still remains, we must have passed it yesterday night. We might labour far upstream and yet miss it in the fog. I fear we must leave the River now, and make for the portage-way as best we can from here.'

'That would not be easy, even if we were all Men,' said Boromir.

'Yet such as we are we will try it,' said Aragorn.

'Aye, we will,' said Gimli. 'The legs of Men will lag on a rough road, while a Dwarf goes on, be the burden twice his own weight, Master Boromir!'

The task proved hard indeed, yet in the end it was done. The goods were taken out of the boats and brought to the top of the bank, where there was a level space. Then the boats were drawn out of the water and carried up. They were far less heavy than any had expected. Of what tree growing in the elvish country they were made not even Legolas knew; but the wood was tough and yet strangely light. Merry and Pippin alone could carry their boat with ease along the flat. Nonetheless it needed the strength of the two Men to lift and haul them over the ground that the Company now had to cross. It sloped up away from the River, a tumbled waste of grey limestone-boulders, with many hidden holes shrouded with weeds and bushes; there were thickets of brambles, and sheer dells; and here and there boggy pools fed by waters trickling from the terraces further inland.

One by one Boromir and Aragorn carried the boats, while the others toiled and scrambled after them with the baggage. At last all was removed and laid on the portage-way. Then with little further hindrance, save from sprawling briars and many fallen stones, they moved forward all together. Fog still hung in veils upon the crumbling rock-wall, and to their left mist shrouded the River: they could hear it rushing and foaming over the sharp shelves and stony teeth of Sarn Gebir, but they could not see it. Twice they made the journey, before all was brought safe to the southern landing.

There the portage-way, turning back to the water-side, ran gently down to the shallow edge of a little pool. It seemed to have been scooped in the river-side, not by hand, but by the water swirling down from Sarn Gebir against a low pier of rock that jutted out some way into the stream. Beyond it the shore rose sheer into a grey cliff, and there was no further passage for those on foot.

Already the short afternoon was past, and a dim cloudy dusk was closing in. They sat beside the water listening to the confused rush and roar of the Rapids hidden in the mist; they were tired and sleepy, and their hearts were as gloomy as the dying day.

'Well, here we are, and here we must pass another night,' said Boromir. 'We need sleep, and even if Aragorn had a mind to pass the Gates of Argonath by night, we are all too tired – except, no doubt, our sturdy dwarf.'

Gimli made no reply: he was nodding as he sat.

'Let us rest as much as we can now,' said Aragorn. 'Tomorrow we must journey by day again. Unless the weather changes once more and cheats us, we shall have a good chance of slipping through, unseen by any eyes on the eastern shore. But tonight two must watch together in turns: three hours off and one on guard.'

Nothing happened that night worse than a brief drizzle of rain an hour before dawn. As soon as it was fully light they started. Already the fog was thinning. They kept as close as they could to the western side, and they could see the dim shapes of the low cliffs rising ever higher, shadowy walls with their feet in the hurrying river. In the mid-morning the clouds drew down lower, and it began to rain heavily. They drew the skin-covers over their boats to prevent them from being flooded, and drifted on; little could be seen before them or about them through the grey falling curtains.

The rain, however, did not last long. Slowly the sky above grew lighter, and then suddenly the clouds broke, and their draggled fringes trailed away northward up the River. The fogs and mists were gone. Before the travellers lay a wide ravine, with great rocky sides to which clung, upon shelves and in narrow crevices, a few thrawn trees. The channel grew narrower and the River swifter. Now they were speeding along with little hope of stopping or turning, whatever they might meet ahead. Over them was a lane of pale-blue sky, around them the dark overshadowed River, and before them black, shutting out the sun, the hills of Emyn Muil, in which no opening could be seen.

Frodo peering forward saw in the distance two great rocks approaching: like great pinnacles or pillars of stone they seemed. Tall and sheer and ominous they stood upon either side of the stream. A narrow gap appeared between them, and the River swept the boats towards it.

'Behold the Argonath, the Pillars of the Kings!' cried Aragorn. 'We shall pass them soon. Keep the boats in line, and as far apart as you can! Hold the middle of the stream!'

As Frodo was borne towards them the great pillars rose like towers to meet him. Giants they seemed to him, vast grey figures silent but threatening. Then he saw that they were indeed shaped and fashioned: the craft and power of old had wrought upon them, and still they preserved through the suns and rains of forgotten years the mighty likenesses in which they had been hewn. Upon great pedestals founded in the deep waters stood two great kings of stone: still with blurred eyes and crannied brows they frowned upon the North. The left hand of each was raised palm outwards in gesture of warning; in each right hand there was an axe; upon each head there was a crumbling helm and crown. Great power and majesty they still wore, the silent wardens of a long-vanished kingdom. Awe and fear fell upon Frodo, and he cowered down, shutting his eyes and not daring to look up as the boat drew near. Even Boromir bowed his head as the boats whirled by, frail and fleeting as little leaves, under the enduring shadow of the sentinels of Númenor. So they passed into the dark chasm of the Gates.

Sheer rose the dreadful cliffs to unguessed heights on either side. Far off was the dim sky. The black waters roared and echoed, and a wind screamed over them. Frodo crouching over his knees heard Sam in front muttering and groaning: 'What a place! What a horrible place! Just let me get out of this boat, and I'll never wet my toes in a puddle again, let alone a river!'

'Fear not!' said a strange voice behind him. Frodo turned and saw Strider, and yet not Strider; for the weatherworn Ranger was no longer there. In the stern sat Aragorn son of Arathorn, proud and erect, guiding the boat with skilful strokes; his hood was cast back, and his dark hair was blowing in the wind, a light was in his eyes: a king returning from exile to his own land.

'Fear not!' he said. 'Long have I desired to look upon the likenesses of Isildur and Anárion, my sires of old. Under their shadow Elessar, the Elfstone son of Arathorn of the House of Valandil Isildur's son, heir of Elendil, has nought to dread!'

Then the light of his eyes faded, and he spoke to himself: 'Would that Gandalf were here! How my heart yearns for Minas Anor and the walls of my own city! But whither now shall I go?'

The chasm was long and dark, and filled with the noise of wind and rushing water and echoing stone. It bent somewhat towards the west so that at first all was dark ahead; but soon Frodo saw a tall gap of light before him, ever growing. Swiftly it drew near, and suddenly the boats shot through, out into a wide clear light.

The sun, already long fallen from the noon, was shining in a windy sky. The pent waters spread out into a long oval lake, pale Nen Hithoel, fenced by steep grey hills whose sides were clad with trees, but their heads were bare, cold-gleaming in the sunlight. At the far southern end rose three peaks. The midmost stood somewhat forward from the others and sundered from them, an island in the waters, about which the flowing River flung pale shimmering arms. Distant but deep there came up on the wind a roaring sound like the roll of thunder heard far away.

'Behold Tol Brandir!' said Aragorn, pointing south to the tall peak. 'Upon the left stands Amon Lhaw, and upon the right is Amon Hen, the Hills of Hearing and of Sight. In the days of the great kings there were high seats upon them, and watch was kept there. But it is said that no foot of man or beast has ever been set upon Tol Brandir. Ere the shade of night falls we shall come to them. I hear the endless voice of Rauros calling.'

The Company rested now for a while, drifting south on the current that flowed through the middle of the lake. They ate some food, and then they took to their paddles and hastened on their way. The sides of the westward hills fell into shadow, and the Sun grew round and red. Here and there a misty star peered out. The three peaks loomed before them, darkling in the twilight. Rauros was roaring with a great voice. Already night was laid on the flowing waters when the travellers came at last under the shadow of the hills.

The tenth day of their journey was over. Wilderland was behind them. They could go no further without choice between the east-way and the west. The last stage of the Quest was before them.

CHAPTER X

THE BREAKING OF THE FELLOWSHIP

Aragorn led them to the right arm of the River. Here upon its western side under the shadow of Tol Brandir a green lawn ran down to the water from the feet of Amon Hen. Behind it rose the first gentle slopes of the hill clad with trees, and trees marched away westward along the curving shores of the lake. A little spring fell tumbling down and fed the grass.

'Here we will rest tonight,' said Aragorn. 'This is the lawn of Parth Galen: a fair place in the summer days of old. Let us hope that no evil has yet come here.'

They drew up their boats on the green banks, and beside them they made their camp. They set a watch, but had no sight nor sound of their enemies. If Gollum had contrived to follow them, he remained unseen and unheard. Nonetheless as the night wore on Aragorn grew uneasy, tossing often in his sleep and waking. In the small hours he got up and came to Frodo, whose turn it was to watch.

'Why are you waking?' asked Frodo. 'It is not your watch.'

'I do not know,' answered Aragorn; 'but a shadow and a threat has been growing in my sleep. It would be well to draw your sword.'

'Why?' said Frodo. 'Are enemies at hand?'

'Let us see what Sting may show,' answered Aragorn.

Frodo then drew the elf-blade from its sheath. To his dismay the edges gleamed dimly in the night. 'Orcs!' he said. 'Not very near, and yet too near, it seems.'

'I feared as much,' said Aragorn. 'But maybe they are not on this side of the River. The light of Sting is faint, and it may point to no more than spies of Mordor roaming on the slopes of Amon Lhaw. I have never heard before of Orcs upon Amon Hen. Yet who knows what may happen in these evil days, now that Minas Tirith no longer holds secure the passages of Anduin. We must go warily tomorrow.'

The day came like fire and smoke. Low in the East there were black bars of cloud like the fumes of a great burning. The rising sun lit them from beneath with flames of murky red; but soon it climbed above them into a clear sky. The summit of Tol Brandir was tipped with gold. Frodo looked out eastward and gazed at the tall island. Its sides sprang sheer out of the running water. High up above the tall cliffs were steep slopes upon which trees climbed, mounting one head above another; and above them again were grey faces of inaccessible rock, crowned by a great spire of stone. Many birds were circling about it, but no sign of other living things could be seen.

When they had eaten, Aragorn called the Company together. 'The day has come at last,' he said: 'the day of choice which we have long delayed. What shall now become of our Company that has travelled so far in fellowship? Shall we turn west with Boromir and go to the wars of Gondor; or turn east to the Fear and Shadow; or shall we break our fellowship and go this way and that as each may choose? Whatever we do must be done soon. We cannot long halt here. The enemy is on the eastern shore, we know; but I fear that the Orcs may already be on this side of the water.'

There was a long silence in which no one spoke or moved.

'Well, Frodo,' said Aragorn at last. 'I fear that the burden is laid upon you. You are the Bearer appointed by the Council. Your own way you alone can choose. In this matter I cannot advise you. I am not Gandalf, and though I have tried to bear his part, I do not know what design or hope he had for this hour, if indeed he had any. Most likely it seems that if he were here now the choice would still wait on you. Such is your fate.'

Frodo did not answer at once. Then he spoke slowly. 'I know that haste is needed, yet I cannot choose. The burden is heavy. Give me an hour longer, and I will speak. Let me be alone!'

Aragorn looked at him with kindly pity. 'Very well, Frodo son of Drogo,' he said. 'You shall have an hour, and you shall be alone. We will stay here for a while. But do not stray far or out of call.'

Frodo sat for a moment with his head bowed. Sam, who had been watching his master with great concern, shook his head and muttered: 'Plain as a pikestaff it is, but it's no good Sam Gamgee putting in his spoke just now.'

Presently Frodo got up and walked away; and Sam saw that while the others restrained themselves and did not stare at him, the eyes of Boromir followed Frodo intently, until he passed out of sight in the trees at the foot of Amon Hen.

Wandering aimlessly at first in the wood, Frodo found that his feet were leading him up towards the slopes of the hill. He came to a path, the dwindling ruins of a road of long ago. In steep places stairs of stone had been hewn, but now they were cracked and worn, and split by the roots of trees. For some while he climbed, not caring which way he went, until he came to a grassy place. Rowan-trees grew about it, and in the midst was a wide flat stone. The little upland lawn was open upon the East and was filled now with the early sunlight. Frodo halted and looked out over the River, far below him, to Tol Brandir and the birds wheeling in the great gulf of air between him and the untrodden isle. The voice of Rauros was a mighty roaring mingled with a deep throbbing boom.

He sat down upon the stone and cupped his chin in his hands, staring eastwards but seeing little with his eyes. All that had happened since Bilbo left the Shire was passing through his mind, and he recalled and pondered everything that he could remember of Gandalf's words. Time went on, and still he was no nearer to a choice.

Suddenly he awoke from his thoughts: a strange feeling came to him that something was behind him, that unfriendly eyes were upon him. He sprang up and turned; but all that he saw to his surprise was Boromir, and his face was smiling and kind.

'I was afraid for you, Frodo,' he said, coming forward. 'If Aragorn is right and Orcs are near, then none of us should wander alone, and you least of all: so much depends on you. And my heart too is heavy. May I stay now and talk for a while, since I have found you? It would comfort me. Where there are so many, all speech becomes a debate without end. But two together may perhaps find wisdom.'

'You are kind,' answered Frodo. 'But I do not think that any speech will help me. For I know what I should do, but I am afraid of doing it, Boromir: afraid.'

Boromir stood silent. Rauros roared endlessly on. The wind murmured in the branches of the trees. Frodo shivered.

Suddenly Boromir came and sat beside him. 'Are you sure that you do not suffer needlessly?' he said. 'I wish to help you. You need counsel in your hard choice. Will you not take mine?'

'I think I know already what counsel you would give, Boromir,' said Frodo. 'And it would seem like wisdom but for the warning of my heart.'

'Warning? Warning against what?' said Boromir sharply.

'Against delay. Against the way that seems easier. Against refusal of the burden that is laid on me. Against — well, if it must be said, against trust in the strength and truth of Men.'

'Yet that strength has long protected you far away in your little country, though you knew it not.'

'I do not doubt the valour of your people. But the world is changing. The walls of Minas Tirith may be strong, but they are not strong enough. If they fail, what then?'

'We shall fall in battle valiantly. Yet there is still hope that they will not fail.'

'No hope while the Ring lasts,' said Frodo.

'Ah! The Ring!' said Boromir, his eyes lighting. 'The Ring! Is it not a strange fate that we should suffer so much fear and doubt for so small a thing? So small a thing! And I have seen it only for an instant in the House of Elrond. Could I not have a sight of it again?'

Frodo looked up. His heart went suddenly cold. He caught the strange gleam in Boromir's eyes, yet his face was still kind and friendly. 'It is best that it should lie hidden,' he answered.

'As you wish. I care not,' said Boromir. 'Yet may I not even speak of it? For you seem ever to think only of its power in the hands of the Enemy: of its evil uses not of its good. The world is changing, you say. Minas Tirith will fall, if the Ring lasts. But why? Certainly, if the Ring were with the Enemy. But why, if it were with us?'

'Were you not at the Council?' answered Frodo. 'Because we cannot use it, and what is done with it turns to evil.'

Boromir got up and walked about impatiently. 'So you go on,' he cried. 'Gandalf, Elrond – all these folk have taught you to say so. For themselves they may be right. These elves and half-elves and wizards, they would come to grief perhaps. Yet often I doubt if they are wise and not merely timid. But each to his own kind. True-hearted Men, they will not be corrupted. We of Minas Tirith have been staunch through long years of trial. We do not desire the power of wizard-lords, only strength to defend ourselves, strength in a just cause. And behold! in our need chance brings to light the Ring of Power. It is a gift, I say; a gift to the foes of Mordor. It is mad not to use it, to use the power of the Enemy against him. The fearless, the ruthless, these alone will achieve victory. What could not a warrior do in this hour, a great leader? What could not Aragorn do? Or if he refuses, why not Boromir? The Ring would give me power of Command. How I would drive the hosts of Mordor, and all men would flock to my banner!'

Boromir strode up and down, speaking ever more loudly. Almost he seemed to have forgotten Frodo, while his talk dwelt on walls and weapons, and the mustering of men; and he drew plans for great alliances and glorious victories to be; and he cast down Mordor, and became himself a mighty king, benevolent and wise. Suddenly he stopped and waved his arms.

'And they tell us to throw it away!' he cried. 'I do not say *destroy* it. That might be well, if reason could show any hope of doing so. It does not. The only plan that is proposed to us is that a halfling should walk blindly into Mordor and offer the Enemy every chance of recapturing it for himself. Folly!

'Surely you see it, my friend?' he said, turning now suddenly to Frodo again. 'You say that you are afraid. If it is so, the boldest should pardon you. But is it not really your good sense that revolts?'

'No, I am afraid,' said Frodo. 'Simply afraid. But I am glad to have heard you speak so fully. My mind is clearer now.'

'Then you will come to Minas Tirith?' cried Boromir. His eyes were shining and his face eager.

'You misunderstand me,' said Frodo.

'But you will come, at least for a while?' Boromir persisted. 'My city is not far now; and it is little further from there to Mordor than from here. We have been long in the wilderness, and you need news of what the Enemy is doing before you make a move. Come with me, Frodo,' he said. 'You need rest before your venture, if go you must.' He laid his hand on the hobbit's shoulder in friendly fashion; but Frodo felt the hand trembling with suppressed excitement. He stepped quickly away, and eyed with alarm the tall Man, nearly twice his height and many times his match in strength.

'Why are you so unfriendly?' said Boromir. 'I am a true man, neither thief nor tracker. I need your Ring: that you know now; but I give you my word that I do not desire to keep it. Will you not at least let me make trial of my plan? Lend me the Ring!'

'No! no!' cried Frodo. 'The Council laid it upon me to bear it.'

'It is by our own folly that the Enemy will defeat us,' cried Boromir. 'How it angers me! Fool! Obstinate fool! Running wilfully to death and ruining our cause. If any mortals have claim to the Ring, it is the men of Númenor, and not Halflings. It is not yours save by unhappy chance. It might have been mine. It should be mine. Give it to me!'

Frodo did not answer, but moved away till the great flat stone stood between them. 'Come, come, my friend!' said Boromir in a softer voice. 'Why not get rid of it? Why not be free of your doubt and fear? You can lay the blame on me, if you will. You can say that I was too strong and took it by force. For I am too strong for you, halfling,' he cried; and suddenly he sprang over the stone and leaped at Frodo. His fair and pleasant face was hideously changed; a raging fire was in his eyes.

Frodo dodged aside and again put the stone between them. There was only one thing he could do: trembling he pulled out the Ring upon its chain and quickly slipped it on his finger, even as Boromir sprang at him again. The Man gasped, stared for a moment amazed, and then ran wildly about, seeking here and there among the rocks and trees.

'Miserable trickster!' he shouted. 'Let me get my hands on you! Now I see your mind. You will take the Ring to Sauron and sell us all. You have only waited your chance to leave us in the lurch. Curse you and all halflings to death and darkness!' Then, catching his foot on a stone, he fell sprawling and lay upon his face. For a while he was as still as if his own curse had struck him down; then suddenly he wept.

He rose and passed his hand over his eyes, dashing away the tears. 'What have I said?' he cried. 'What have I done? Frodo, Frodo!' he called. 'Come back! A madness took me, but it has passed. Come back!'

There was no answer. Frodo did not even hear his cries. He was already far away, leaping blindly up the path to the hill-top. Terror and grief shook him, seeing in his thought the mad fierce face of Boromir, and his burning eyes.

Soon he came out alone on the summit of Amon Hen, and halted, gasping for breath. He saw as through a mist a wide flat circle, paved with mighty flags, and surrounded with a crumbling battlement; and in the middle, set upon four carven pillars, was a high seat, reached by a stair of many steps. Up he went and sat upon the ancient chair, feeling like a lost child that had clambered upon the throne of mountain-kings.

At first he could see little. He seemed to be in a world of mist in which there were only shadows: the Ring was upon him. Then here and there the mist gave way and he saw many visions: small and clear as if they were under his eyes upon a table, and yet remote. There was no sound, only bright living images. The world seemed to have shrunk and fallen silent. He was sitting upon the Seat of Seeing, on Amon Hen, the Hill of the Eye of the Men of Númenor. Eastward he looked into wide uncharted lands, nameless plains, and forests unexplored. Northward he looked, and the Great River lay like a ribbon beneath him, and the Misty Mountains stood small and hard as broken teeth. Westward he looked and saw the broad pastures of Rohan; and Orthanc, the pinnacle of Isengard, like a black spike. Southward he looked, and below his very feet the Great River curled like a toppling wave and plunged over the falls of Rauros into a foaming pit; a glimmering rainbow played upon the fume. And Ethir Anduin he saw, the mighty delta of the River, and myriads of sea-birds whirling like a white dust in the sun, and beneath them a green and silver sea, rippling in endless lines.

But everywhere he looked he saw the signs of war. The Misty Mountains were crawling like anthills: orcs were issuing out of a thousand holes. Under the boughs of Mirkwood there was deadly strife of Elves and Men and fell beasts. The land of the Beornings was aflame; a cloud was over Moria; smoke rose on the borders of Lórien.

Horsemen were galloping on the grass of Rohan; wolves poured from Isengard. From the havens of Harad ships of war put out to sea; and out of the East Men were moving endlessly: swordsmen, spearmen, bowmen upon horses, chariots of chieftains and laden wains. All the power of the Dark Lord was in motion. Then turning south again he beheld Minas Tirith. Far away it seemed, and beautiful: white-walled, many-towered, proud and fair upon its mountain-seat; its battlements glittered with steel, and its turrets were bright with many banners. Hope leaped in his heart. But against Minas Tirith was set another fortress, greater and more strong. Thither, eastward, unwilling his eye was drawn. It passed the ruined bridges of Osgiliath, the grinning gates of Minas Morgul, and the haunted Mountains, and it looked upon Gorgoroth, the valley of terror in the Land of Mordor. Darkness lay there under the Sun. Fire glowed amid the smoke. Mount Doom was burning, and a great reek rising. Then at last his gaze was held: wall upon wall, battlement upon battlement, black, immeasurably strong, mountain of iron, gate of steel, tower of adamant, he saw it: Barad-dûr, Fortress of Sauron. All hope left him.

And suddenly he felt the Eye. There was an eye in the Dark Tower that did not sleep. He knew that it had become aware of his gaze. A fierce eager will was there. It leaped towards him; almost like a finger he felt it, searching for him. Very soon it would nail him down, know just exactly where he was. Amon Lhaw it touched. It glanced upon Tol Brandir – he threw himself from the seat, crouching, covering his head with his grey hood.

He heard himself crying out: *Never, never!* Or was it: *Verily I come, I come to you?* He could not tell. Then as a flash from some other point of power there came to his mind another thought: *Take it off! Take it off! Fool, take it off! Take off the Ring!*

The two powers strove in him. For a moment, perfectly balanced between their piercing points, he writhed, tormented. Suddenly he was aware of himself again. Frodo, neither the Voice nor the Eye: free to choose, and with one remaining instant in which to do so. He took the Ring off his finger. He was kneeling in clear sunlight before the high seat. A black shadow seemed to pass like an arm above him; it missed Amon Hen and groped out west, and faded. Then all the sky was clean and blue and birds sang in every tree.

Frodo rose to his feet. A great weariness was on him, but his will was firm and his heart lighter. He spoke aloud to himself. 'I will do now what I must,' he said. 'This at least is plain: the evil of the Ring is already at work even in the Company, and the Ring must leave them before it does more harm. I will go alone. Some I cannot trust, and those I can trust are too dear to me: poor old Sam, and Merry and Pippin. Strider, too: his heart yearns for Minas Tirith, and he will be needed there, now Boromir has fallen into evil. I will go alone. At once.'

He went quickly down the path and came back to the lawn where Boromir had found him. Then he halted, listening. He thought he could hear cries and calls from the woods near the shore below.

'They'll be hunting for me,' he said. 'I wonder how long I have been away. Hours, I should think.' He hesitated. 'What can I do?' he muttered. 'I must go now or I shall never go. I shan't get a chance again. I hate leaving them, and like this without any explanation. But surely they will understand. Sam will. And what else can I do?'

Slowly he drew out the Ring and put it on once more. He vanished and passed down the hill, less than a rustle of the wind.

The others remained long by the river-side. For some time they had been silent, moving restlessly about; but now they were sitting in a circle, and they were talking. Every now and again they made efforts to speak of other things, of their long road and many adventures; they questioned Aragorn concerning the realm of Gondor and its ancient history, and the remnants of its great works that could still be seen in this strange borderland of the Emyn Muil: the stone kings and the seats of Lhaw and Hen, and the great Stair beside the falls of Rauros. But always their thoughts and words strayed back to Frodo and the Ring. What would Frodo choose to do? Why was he hesitating?

'He is debating which course is the most desperate, I think,' said Aragorn. 'And well he may. It is now more hopeless than ever for the Company to go east, since we have been tracked by Gollum, and must fear that the secret of our journey is already betrayed. But Minas Tirith is no nearer to the Fire and the destruction of the Burden.

'We may remain there for a while and make a brave stand; but the Lord Denethor and all his men cannot hope to do what even Elrond said was beyond his power: either to keep the Burden secret, or to hold off the full might of the Enemy when he comes to take it. Which way would any of us choose in Frodo's place? I do not know. Now indeed we miss Gandalf most.'

'Grievous is our loss,' said Legolas. 'Yet we must needs make up our minds without his aid. Why cannot we decide, and so help Frodo? Let us call him back and then vote! I should vote for Minas Tirith.'

'And so should I,' said Gimli. 'We, of course, were only sent to help the Bearer along the road, to go no further than we wished; and none of us is under any oath or command to seek Mount Doom. Hard was my parting from Lothlórien. Yet I have come so far, and I say this: now we have reached the last choice, it is clear to me that I cannot leave Frodo. I would choose Minas Tirith, but if he does not, then I follow him.'

'And I too will go with him,' said Legolas. 'It would be faithless now to say farewell.'

'It would indeed be a betrayal, if we all left him,' said Aragorn. 'But if he goes east, then all need not go with him; nor do I think that all should. That venture is desperate: as much so for eight as for three or two, or one alone. If you would let me choose, then I should appoint three companions: Sam, who could not bear it otherwise; and Gimli; and myself. Boromir will return to his own city, where his father and his people need him; and with him the others should go, or at least Meriadoc and Peregrin, if Legolas is not willing to leave us.'

'That won't do at all!' cried Merry. 'We can't leave Frodo! Pippin and I always intended to go wherever he went, and we still do. But we did not realize what that would mean. It seemed different so far away, in the Shire or in Rivendell. It would be mad and cruel to let Frodo go to Mordor. Why can't we stop him?'

'We must stop him,' said Pippin. 'And that is what he is worrying about, I am sure. He knows we shan't agree to his going east. And he doesn't like to ask anyone to go with him, poor old fellow. Imagine it: going off to Mordor alone!' Pippin shuddered. 'But the dear silly old hobbit, he ought to know that he hasn't got to ask. He ought to know that if we can't stop him, we shan't leave him.'

'Begging your pardon,' said Sam. 'I don't think you understand my master at all. He isn't hesitating about which way to go. Of course not! What's the good of Minas Tirith anyway? To him, I mean, begging your pardon, Master Boromir,' he added, and turned. It was then that they discovered that Boromir, who at first had been sitting silent on the outside of the circle, was no longer there.

'Now where's he got to?' cried Sam, looking worried. 'He's been a bit queer lately, to my mind. But anyway he's not in this business. He's off to his home, as he always said; and no blame to him. But Mr. Frodo, he knows he's got to find the Cracks of Doom, if he can. But he's *afraid*. Now it's come to the point, he's just plain terrified. That's what his trouble is. Of course he's had a bit of schooling, so to speak – we all have – since we left home, or he'd be so terrified he'd just fling the Ring in the River and bolt. But he's still too frightened to start. And he isn't worrying about us either: whether we'll go along with him or no. He knows we mean to. That's another thing that's bothering him. If he screws himself up to go, he'll want to go alone. Mark my words! We're going to have trouble when he comes back. For he'll screw himself up all right, as sure as his name's Baggins.'

'I believe you speak more wisely than any of us, Sam,' said Aragorn. 'And what shall we do, if you prove right?'

'Stop him! Don't let him go!' cried Pippin.

'I wonder?' said Aragorn. 'He is the Bearer, and the fate of the Burden is on him. I do not think that it is our part to drive him one way or the other. Nor do I think that we should succeed, if we tried. There are other powers at work far stronger.'

'Well, I wish Frodo would "screw himself up" and come back, and let us get it over,' said Pippin. 'This waiting is horrible! Surely the time is up?'

'Yes,' said Aragorn. 'The hour is long passed. The morning is wearing away. We must call for him.'

At that moment Boromir reappeared. He came out from the trees and walked towards them without speaking. His face looked grim and sad. He paused as if counting those that were present, and then sat down aloof, with his eyes on the ground.

'Where have you been, Boromir?' asked Aragorn. 'Have you seen Frodo?'

Boromir hesitated for a second. 'Yes, and no,' he answered slowly. 'Yes: I found him some way up the hill, and I spoke to him. I urged him to come to Minas Tirith and not to go east. I grew angry and he left me. He vanished. I have never seen such a thing happen before, though I have heard of it in tales. He must have put the Ring on. I could not find him again. I thought he would return to you.'

'Is that all that you have to say?' said Aragorn, looking hard and not too kindly at Boromir.

'Yes,' he answered. 'I will say no more yet.'

'This is bad!' cried Sam, jumping up. 'I don't know what this Man has been up to. Why should Mr. Frodo put the thing on? He didn't ought to have; and if he has, goodness knows what may have happened!'

'But he wouldn't keep it on,' said Merry. 'Not when he had escaped the unwelcome visitor, like Bilbo used to.'

'But where did he go? Where is he?' cried Pippin. 'He's been away ages now.'

'How long is it since you saw Frodo last, Boromir?' asked Aragorn.

'Half an hour, maybe,' he answered. 'Or it might be an hour. I have wandered for some time since. I do not know! I do not know!' He put his head in his hands, and sat as if bowed with grief.

'An hour since he vanished!' shouted Sam. 'We must try and find him at once. Come on!'

'Wait a moment!' cried Aragorn. 'We must divide up into pairs, and arrange – here, hold on! Wait!'

It was no good. They took no notice of him. Sam had dashed off first. Merry and Pippin had followed, and were already disappearing westward into the trees by the shore, shouting: *Frodo! Frodo!* in their clear, high, hobbit-voices. Legolas and Gimli were running. A sudden panic or madness seemed to have fallen on the Company.

'We shall all be scattered and lost,' groaned Aragorn. 'Boromir! I do not know what part you have played in this mischief, but help now! Go after those two young hobbits, and guard them at the least, even if you cannot find Frodo. Come back to this spot, if you find him, or any traces of him. I shall return soon.'

Aragorn sprang swiftly away and went in pursuit of Sam. Just as he reached the little lawn among the rowans he overtook him, toiling uphill, panting and calling, *Frodo!*

'Come with me, Sam!' he said. 'None of us should be alone. There is mischief about. I feel it. I am going to the top, to the Seat of Amon Hen, to see what may be seen. And look! It is as my heart guessed, Frodo went this way. Follow me, and keep your eyes open!' He sped up the path.

Sam did his best, but he could not keep up with Strider the Ranger, and soon fell behind. He had not gone far before Aragorn was out of sight ahead. Sam stopped and puffed. Suddenly he clapped his hand to his head.

'Whoa, Sam Gamgee!' he said aloud. 'Your legs are too short, so use your head! Let me see now! Boromir isn't lying, that's not his way; but he hasn't told us everything. Something scared Mr. Frodo badly. He screwed himself up to the point, sudden. He made up his mind at last – to go. Where to? Off East. Not without Sam? Yes, without even his Sam. That's hard, cruel hard.'

Sam passed his hand over his eyes, brushing away the tears. 'Steady, Gamgee!' he said. 'Think, if you can! He can't fly across rivers, and he can't jump waterfalls. He's got no gear. So he's got to get back to the boats. Back to the boats! Back to the boats, Sam, like lightning!'

Sam turned and bolted back down the path. He fell and cut his knees. Up he got and ran on. He came to the edge of the lawn of Parth Galen by the shore, where the boats were drawn up out of the water. No one was there. There seemed to be cries in the woods behind, but he did not heed them. He stood gazing for a moment, stock-still, gaping. A boat was sliding down the bank all by itself. With a shout Sam raced across the grass. The boat slipped into the water.

'Coming, Mr. Frodo! Coming!' called Sam, and flung himself from the bank, clutching at the departing boat. He missed it by a yard. With a cry and a splash he fell face downward into deep swift water. Gurgling he went under, and the River closed over his curly head.

An exclamation of dismay came from the empty boat. A paddle swirled and the boat put about. Frodo was just in time to grasp Sam by the hair as he came up, bubbling and struggling. Fear was staring in his round brown eyes.

'Up you come, Sam my lad!' said Frodo. 'Now take my hand!'

'Save me, Mr. Frodo!' gasped Sam. 'I'm drownded. I can't see your hand.'

'Here it is. Don't pinch, lad! I won't let you go. Tread water and don't flounder, or you'll upset the boat. There now, get hold of the side, and let me use the paddle!'

With a few strokes Frodo brought the boat back to the bank, and Sam was able to scramble out, wet as a water-rat. Frodo took off the Ring and stepped ashore again.

'Of all the confounded nuisances you are the worst, Sam!' he said.

'Oh, Mr. Frodo, that's hard!' said Sam shivering. 'That's hard, trying to go without me and all. If I hadn't a guessed right, where would you be now?'

'Safely on my way.'

'Safely!' said Sam. 'All alone and without me to help you? I couldn't have a borne it, it'd have been the death of me.'

'It would be the death of you to come with me, Sam,' said Frodo, 'and I could not have borne that.'

'Not as certain as being left behind,' said Sam.

'But I am going to Mordor.'

'I know that well enough, Mr. Frodo. Of course you are. And I'm coming with you.'

'Now, Sam,' said Frodo, 'don't hinder me! The others will be coming back at any minute. If they catch me here, I shall have to argue and explain, and I shall never have the heart or the chance to get off. But I must go at once. It's the only way.'

'Of course it is,' answered Sam. 'But not alone. I'm coming too, or neither of us isn't going. I'll knock holes in all the boats first.'

Frodo actually laughed. A sudden warmth and gladness touched his heart. 'Leave one!' he said. 'We'll need it. But you can't come like this without your gear or food or anything.'

'Just hold on a moment, and I'll get my stuff!' cried Sam eagerly. 'It's all ready. I thought we should be off today.' He rushed to the camping place, fished out his pack from the pile where Frodo had laid it when he emptied the boat of his companions' goods, grabbed a spare blanket, and some extra packages of food, and ran back.

'So all my plan is spoilt!' said Frodo. 'It is no good trying to escape you. But I'm glad, Sam. I cannot tell you how glad. Come along! It is plain that we were meant to go together. We will go, and may the others find a safe road! Strider will look after them. I don't suppose we shall see them again.'

'Yet we may, Mr. Frodo. We may,' said Sam.

So Frodo and Sam set off on the last stage of the Quest together. Frodo paddled away from the shore, and the River bore them swiftly away, down the western arm, and past the frowning cliffs of Tol Brandir. The roar of the great falls drew nearer. Even with such help as Sam could give, it was hard work to pass across the current at the southward end of the island and drive the boat eastward towards the far shore.

At length they came to land again upon the southern slopes of Amon Lhaw. There they found a shelving shore, and they drew the boat out, high above the water, and hid it as well as they could behind a great boulder. Then shouldering their burdens, they set off, seeking a path that would bring them over the grey hills of the Emyn Muil, and down into the Land of Shadow.

THE TWO TOWERS

BEING THE SECOND PART

OF

The Lord of the Rings

BOOK THREE

CHAPTER I

THE DEPARTURE OF BOROMIR

Aragorn sped on up the hill. Every now and again he bent to the ground. Hobbits go light, and their footprints are not easy even for a Ranger to read, but not far from the top a spring crossed the path, and in the wet earth he saw what he was seeking.

'I read the signs aright,' he said to himself. 'Frodo ran to the hill-top. I wonder what he saw there? But he returned by the same way, and went down the hill again.'

Aragorn hesitated. He desired to go to the high seat himself, hoping to see there something that would guide him in his perplexities; but time was pressing. Suddenly he leaped forward, and ran to the summit, across the great flag-stones, and up the steps. Then sitting in the high seat he looked out. But the sun seemed darkened, and the world dim and remote. He turned from the North back again to North, and saw nothing save the distant hills, unless it were that far away he could see again a great bird like an eagle high in the air, descending slowly in wide circles down towards the earth.

Even as he gazed his quick ears caught sounds in the woodlands below, on the west side of the River. He stiffened. There were cries, and among them, to his horror, he could distinguish the harsh voices of Orcs. Then suddenly with a deep-throated call a great horn blew, and the blasts of it smote the hills and echoed in the hollows, rising in a mighty shout above the roaring of the falls.

'The horn of Boromir!' he cried. 'He is in need!' He sprang down the steps and away, leaping down the path. 'Alas! An ill fate is on me this day, and all that I do goes amiss. Where is Sam?'

As he ran the cries came louder, but fainter now and desperately the horn was blowing. Fierce and shrill rose the yells of the Orcs, and suddenly the horn-calls ceased. Aragorn raced down the last slope, but before he could reach the hill's foot, the sounds died away; and as he turned to the left and ran towards them they retreated, until at last he could hear them no more. Drawing his bright sword and crying *Elendil! Elendil!* he crashed through the trees.

A mile, maybe, from Parth Galen in a little glade not far from the lake he found Boromir. He was sitting with his back to a great tree, as if he was resting. But Aragorn saw that he was pierced with many black-feathered arrows; his sword was still in his hand, but it was broken near the hilt; his horn cloven in two was at his side. Many Orcs lay slain, piled all about him and at his feet.

Aragorn knelt beside him. Boromir opened his eyes and strove to speak. At last slow words came. 'I tried to take the Ring from Frodo,' he said. 'I am sorry. I have paid.' His glance strayed to his fallen enemies; twenty at least lay there. 'They have gone: the Halflings: the Orcs have taken them. I think they are not dead. Orcs bound them.' He paused and his eyes closed wearily. After a moment he spoke again.

'Farewell, Aragorn! Go to Minas Tirith and save my people! I have failed.'

'No!' said Aragorn, taking his hand and kissing his brow. 'You have conquered. Few have gained such a victory. Be at peace! Minas Tirith shall not fall!'

Boromir smiled.

'Which way did they go? Was Frodo there?' said Aragorn.

But Boromir did not speak again.

'Alas!' said Aragorn. 'Thus passes the heir of Denethor, Lord of the Tower of Guard! This is a bitter end. Now the Company is all in ruin. It is I that have failed. Vain was Gandalf's trust in me. What shall I do now? Boromir has laid it on me to go to Minas Tirith, and my heart desires it; but where are the Ring and the Bearer? How shall I find them and save the Quest from disaster?'

He knelt for a while, bent with weeping, still clasping Boromir's hand. So it was that Legolas and Gimli found him. They came from the western slopes of the hill, silently, creeping through the trees as if they were hunting. Gimli had his axe in hand, and Legolas his long knife: all his arrows were spent. When they came into the glade they halted in amazement; and then they stood a moment with heads bowed in grief, for it seemed to them plain what had happened.

'Alas!' said Legolas, coming to Aragorn's side. 'We have hunted and slain many Orcs in the woods, but we should have been of more use here. We came when we heard the horn – but too late, it seems. I fear you have taken deadly hurt.'

'Boromir is dead,' said Aragorn. 'I am unscathed, for I was not here with him. He fell defending the hobbits, while I was away upon the hill.'

'The hobbits!' cried Gimli. 'Where are they then? Where is Frodo?'

'I do not know,' answered Aragorn wearily. 'Before he died Boromir told me that the Orcs had bound them; he did not think that they were dead. I sent him to follow Merry and Pippin; but I did not ask him if Frodo or Sam were with him: not until it was too late. All that I have done today has gone amiss. What is to be done now?'

'First we must tend the fallen,' said Legolas. 'We cannot leave him lying like carrion among these foul Orcs.'

'But we must be swift,' said Gimli. 'He would not wish us to linger. We must follow the Orcs, if there is hope that any of our Company are living prisoners.'

'But we do not know whether the Ring-bearer is with them or not,' said Aragorn. 'Are we to abandon him? Must we not seek him first? An evil choice is now before us!'

'Then let us do first what we must do,' said Legolas. 'We have not the time or the tools to bury our comrade fitly, or to raise a mound over him. A cairn we might build.'

'The labour would be hard and long: there are no stones that we could use nearer than the water-side,' said Gimli.

'Then let us lay him in a boat with his weapons, and the weapons of his vanquished foes,' said Aragorn. 'We will send him to the Falls of Rauros and give him to Anduin. The River of Gondor will take care at least that no evil creature dishonours his bones.'

Quickly they searched the bodies of the Orcs, gathering their swords and cloven helms and shields into a heap.

'See!' cried Aragorn. 'Here we find tokens!' He picked out from the pile of grim weapons two knives, leaf-bladed, damasked in gold and red; and searching further he found also the sheaths, black, set with small red gems. 'No orc-tools these!' he said. 'They were borne by the hobbits. Doubtless the Orcs despoiled them, but feared to keep the knives, knowing them for what they are: work of Westernesse, wound about with spells for the bane of Mordor. Well, now, if they still live, our friends are weaponless. I will take these things, hoping against hope, to give them back.'

'And I,' said Legolas, 'will take all the arrows that I can find, for my quiver is empty.' He searched in the pile and on the ground about and found not a few that were undamaged and longer in the shaft than such arrows as the Orcs were accustomed to use. He looked at them closely.

And Aragorn looked on the slain, and he said: 'Here lie many that are not folk of Mordor. Some are from the North, from the Misty Mountains, if I know anything of Orcs and their kinds. And here are others strange to me. Their gear is not after the manner of Orcs at all!'

There were four goblin-soldiers of greater stature, swart, slant-eyed, with thick legs and large hands. They were armed with short broad-bladed swords, not with the curved scimitars usual with Orcs; and they had bows of yew, in length and shape like the bows of Men. Upon their shields they bore a strange device: a small white hand in the centre of a black field; on the front of their iron helms was set an S-rune, wrought of some white metal.

'I have not seen these tokens before,' said Aragorn. 'What do they mean?'

'S is for Sauron,' said Gimli. 'That is easy to read.'

'Nay!' said Legolas. 'Sauron does not use the Elf-runes.'

'Neither does he use his right name, nor permit it to be spelt or spoken,' said Aragorn. 'And he does not use white. The Orcs in the service of Barad-dûr use the sign of the Red Eye.' He stood for a moment in thought. 'S is for Saruman, I guess,' he said at length. 'There is evil afoot in Isengard, and the West is no longer safe. It is as Gandalf feared: by some means the traitor Saruman has had news of our journey. It is likely too that he knows of Gandalf's fall. Pursuers from Moria may have escaped the vigilance of Lórien, or they may have avoided that land and come to Isengard by other paths. Orcs travel fast. But Saruman has many ways of learning news. Do you remember the birds?'

'Well, we have no time to ponder riddles,' said Gimli. 'Let us bear Boromir away!'

'But after that we must guess the riddles, if we are to choose our course rightly,' answered Aragorn.

'Maybe there is no right choice,' said Gimli.

Taking his axe the Dwarf now cut several branches. These they lashed together with bowstrings, and spread their cloaks upon the frame. Upon this rough bier they carried the body of their companion to the shore, together with such trophies of his last battle as they chose to send forth with him. It was only a short way, yet they found it no easy task, for Boromir was a man both tall and strong.

At the water-side Aragorn remained, watching the bier, while Legolas and Gimli hastened back on foot to Parth Galen. It was a mile or more, and it was some time before they came back, paddling two boats swiftly along the shore.

'There is a strange tale to tell!' said Legolas. 'There are only two boats upon the bank. We could find no trace of the other.'

'Have Orcs been there?' asked Aragorn.

'We saw no signs of them,' answered Gimli. 'And Orcs would have taken or destroyed all the boats, and the baggage as well.'

'I will look at the ground when we come there,' said Aragorn.

Now they laid Boromir in the middle of the boat that was to bear him away. The grey hood and elven-cloak they folded and placed beneath his head. They combed his long dark hair and arrayed it upon his shoulders. The golden belt of Lórien gleamed about his waist. His helm they set beside him, and across his lap they laid the cloven horn and the hilts and shards of his sword; beneath his feet they put the swords of his enemies. Then fastening the prow to the stern of the other boat, they drew him out into the water. They rowed sadly along the shore, and turning into the swift-running channel they passed the green sward of Parth Galen. The steep sides of Tol Brandir were glowing: it was now mid-afternoon. As they went south the fume of Rauros rose and shimmered before them, a haze of gold. The rush and thunder of the falls shook the windless air.

Sorrowfully they cast loose the funeral boat: there Boromir lay, restful, peaceful, gliding upon the bosom of the flowing water. The stream took him while they held their own boat back with their paddles. He floated by them, and slowly his boat departed, waning to a dark spot against the golden light; and then suddenly it vanished. Rauros roared on unchanging. The River had taken Boromir son of Denethor, and he was not seen again in Minas Tirith, standing as he used to stand upon the White Tower in the morning. But in Gondor in after-days it long was said that the elven-boat rode the falls and the foaming pool, and bore him down through Osgiliath, and past the many mouths of Anduin, out into the Great Sea at night under the stars.

For a while the three companions remained silent, gazing after him. Then Aragorn spoke. 'They will look for him from the White Tower,' he said, 'but he will not return from mountain or from sea.' Then slowly he began to sing:

Through Rohan over fen and field where the long grass grows
The West Wind comes walking, and about the walls it goes.
'What news from the West, O wandering wind, do you bring to me tonight?
Have you seen Boromir the Tall by moon or by starlight?'
'I saw him ride over seven streams, over waters wide and grey;
I saw him walk in empty lands, until he passed away
Into the shadows of the North. I saw him then no more.
The North Wind may have heard the horn of the son of Denethor.'
'O Boromir! From the high walls westward I looked afar,
But you came not from the empty lands where no men are.'

Then Legolas sang:

From the mouths of the Sea the South Wind flies, from the
  sandhills and the stones;
The wailing of the gulls it bears, and at the gate it moans.
'What news from the South, O sighing wind, do you bring to me at eve?

Where now is Boromir the Fair? He. tarries and I grieve.'
'Ask not of me where he doth dwell – so many bones there lie
On the white shores and the dark shores under the stormy sky;
So many·have passed down Anduin to find the flowing Sea.
Ask of the North Wind news of them the North Wind sends
　　　to me!'
'O Boromir! Beyond the gate the seaward road runs south,
But you came not with the wailing gulls from the grey
　　　sea's mouth.'

Then Aragorn sang again:

From the Gate of Kings the North Wind rides, and past the roaring falls;
And clear and cold about the tower its loud horn calls.
'What news from the North, O mighty wind, do you bring to
　　　me today?
What news of Boromir the Bold? For he is long away.'
'Beneath Amon Hen I heard his cry. There many foes he fought.
His cloven shield, his broken sword, they to the water brought.
His head so proud, his face so fair, his limbs they laid to rest;
And Rauros, golden Rauros-falls, bore him upon its breast.'
'O Boromir! The Tower of Guard shall ever northward gaze
To Rauros, golden Rauros-falls, until the end of days.'

So they ended. Then they turned their boat and drove it with all the speed they could against the stream back to Parth Galen.

'You left the East Wind to me,' said Gimli, 'but I will say naught of it.'

'That is as it should be,' said Aragorn. 'In Minas Tirith they endure the East Wind, but they do not ask it for tidings. But now Boromir has taken his road, and we must make haste to choose our own.'

He surveyed the green lawn, quickly but thoroughly, stooping often to the earth. 'No Orcs have been on this ground,' he said. 'Otherwise nothing can be made out for certain. All our footprints are here, crossing and re-crossing. I cannot tell whether any of the hobbits have come back since the search for Frodo began.' He returned to the bank, close to where the rill from the spring trickled out into the River. 'There are some clear prints here,' he said. 'A hobbit waded out into the water and back; but I cannot say how long ago.'

'How then do you read this riddle?' asked Gimli.

Aragorn did not answer at once, but went back to the camping-place and looked at the baggage. 'Two packs are missing,' he said, 'and one is certainly Sam's: it was rather large and heavy. This then is the answer:

Frodo has gone by boat, and his servant has gone with him. Frodo must have returned while we were all away. I met Sam going up the hill and told him to follow me; but plainly he did not do so. He guessed his master's mind and came back here before Frodo had gone. He did not find it easy to leave Sam behind!'

'But why should he leave us behind, and without a word?' said Gimli. 'That was a strange deed!'

'And a brave deed,' said Aragorn. 'Sam was right, I think. Frodo did not wish to lead any friend to death with him in Mordor. But he knew that he must go himself. Something happened after he left us that overcame his fear and doubt.'

'Maybe hunting Orcs came on him and he fled,' said Legolas.

'He fled, certainly,' said Aragorn, 'but not, I think, from Orcs.' What he thought was the cause of Frodo's sudden resolve and flight Aragorn did not say. The last words of Boromir he long kept secret.

'Well, so much at least is now clear,' said Legolas: 'Frodo is no longer on this side of the River: only he can have taken the boat. And Sam is with him; only he would have taken his pack.'

'Our choice then,' said Gimli, 'is either to take the remaining boat and follow Frodo, or else to follow the Orcs on foot. There is little hope either way. We have already lost precious hours.'

'Let me think!' said Aragorn. 'And now may I make a right choice, and change the evil fate of this unhappy day!' He stood silent for a moment. 'I will follow the Orcs,' he said at last. 'I would have guided Frodo to Mordor and gone with him to the end; but if I seek him now in the wilderness, I must abandon the captives to torment and death. My heart speaks clearly at last: the fate of the Bearer is in my hands no longer. The Company has played its part. Yet we that remain cannot forsake our companions while we have strength left. Come! We will go now. Leave all that can be spared behind! We will press on by day and dark!'

They drew up the last boat and carried it to the trees. They laid beneath it such of their goods as they did not need and could not carry away. Then they left Parth Galen. The afternoon was fading as they came back to the glade where Boromir had fallen. There they picked up the trail of the Orcs. It needed little skill to find.

'No other folk make such a trampling,' said Legolas. 'It seems their delight to slash and beat down growing things that are not even in their way.'

'But they go with a great speed for all that,' said Aragorn, 'and they do not tire. And later we may have to search for our path in hard bare lands.'

'Well, after them!' said Gimli. 'Dwarves too can go swiftly, and they do

not tire sooner than Orcs. But it will be a long chase: they have a long
start.'

'Yes,' said Aragorn, 'we shall all need the endurance of Dwarves. But
come! With hope or without hope we will follow the trail of our enemies.
And woe to them, if we prove the swifter! We will make such a chase as
shall be accounted a marvel among the Three Kindreds: Elves, Dwarves,
and Men. Forth the Three Hunters!'

Like a deer he sprang away. Through the trees he sped. On and on he
led them, tireless and swift, now that his mind was at last made up. The
woods about the lake they left behind. Long slopes they climbed, dark,
hard-edged against the sky already red with sunset. Dusk came. They
passed away, grey shadows in a stony land.

CHAPTER II

THE RIDERS OF ROHAN

Dusk deepened. Mist lay behind them among the trees below, and brooded on the pale margins of the Anduin, but the sky was clear. Stars came out. The waxing moon was riding in the West, and the shadows of the rocks were black. They had come to the feet of stony hills, and their pace was slower, for the trail was no longer easy to follow. Here the highlands of the Emyn Muil ran from North to South in two long tumbled ridges. The western side of each ridge was steep and difficult, but the eastward slopes were gentler, furrowed with many gullies and narrow ravines. All night the three companions scrambled in this bony land, climbing to the crest of the first and tallest ridge, and down again into the darkness of a deep winding valley on the other side.

There in the still cool hour before dawn they rested for a brief space. The moon had long gone down before them, the stars glittered above them; the first light of day had not yet come over the dark hills behind. For the moment Aragorn was at a loss: the orc-trail had descended into the valley, but there it had vanished.

'Which way would they turn, do you think?' said Legolas. 'Northward to take a straighter road to Isengard, or Fangorn, if that is their aim as you guess? Or southward to strike the Entwash?'

'They will not make for the river, whatever mark they aim at,' said Aragorn. 'And unless there is much amiss in Rohan and the power of Saruman is greatly increased, they will take the shortest way that they can find over the fields of the Rohirrim. Let us search northwards!'

The dale ran like a stony trough between the ridged hills, and a trickling stream flowed among the boulders at the bottom. A cliff frowned upon their right; to their left rose grey slopes, dim and shadowy in the late night. They went on for a mile or more northwards. Aragorn was searching, bent towards the ground, among the folds and gullies leading up into the western ridge. Legolas was some way ahead. Suddenly the Elf gave a cry and the others came running towards him.

'We have already overtaken some of those that we are hunting,' he said. 'Look!' He pointed, and they saw that what they had at first taken to be boulders lying at the foot of the slope were huddled bodies. Five dead Orcs lay there. They had been hewn with many cruel strokes, and two had been beheaded. The ground was wet with their dark blood.

'Here is another riddle!' said Gimli. 'But it needs the light of day, and for that we cannot wait.'

'Yet however you read it, it seems not unhopeful,' said Legolas. 'Enemies of the Orcs are likely to be our friends. Do any folk dwell in these hills?'

'No,' said Aragorn. 'The Rohirrim seldom come here, and it is far from Minas Tirith. It might be that some company of Men were hunting here for reasons that we do not know. Yet I think not.'

'What do you think?' said Gimli.

'I think that the enemy brought his own enemy with him,' answered Aragorn. 'These are Northern Orcs from far away. Among the slain are none of the great Orcs with the strange badges. There was a quarrel, I guess: it is no uncommon thing with these foul folk. Maybe there was some dispute about the road.'

'Or about the captives,' said Gimli. 'Let us hope that they, too, did not meet their end here.'

Aragorn searched the ground in a wide circle, but no other traces of the fight could be found. They went on. Already the eastward sky was turning pale; the stars were fading, and a grey light was slowly growing. A little further north they came to a fold in which a tiny stream, falling and winding, had cut a stony path down into the valley. In it some bushes grew, and there were patches of grass upon its sides.

'At last!' said Aragorn. 'Here are the tracks that we seek! Up this water-channel: this is the way that the Orcs went after their debate.'

Swiftly now the pursuers turned and followed the new path. As if fresh from a night's rest they sprang from stone to stone. At last they reached the crest of the grey hill, and a sudden breeze blew in their hair and stirred their cloaks: the chill wind of dawn.

Turning back they saw across the River the far hills kindled. Day leaped into the sky. The red rim of the sun rose over the shoulders of the dark land. Before them in the West the world lay still, formless and grey; but even as they looked, the shadows of night melted, the colours of the waking earth returned: green flowed over the wide meads of Rohan; the white mists shimmered in the water-vales; and far off to the left, thirty leagues or more, blue and purple stood the White Mountains, rising into peaks of jet, tipped with glimmering snows, flushed with the rose of morning.

'Gondor! Gondor!' cried Aragorn. 'Would that I looked on you again in happier hour! Not yet does my road lie southward to your bright streams.

Gondor! Gondor, between the Mountains and the Sea!
West Wind blew there; the light upon the Silver Tree
Fell like bright rain in gardens of the Kings of old.

O proud walls! White towers! O wingéd crown and throne of gold!
O Gondor, Gondor! Shall Men behold the Silver Tree,
Or West Wind blow again between the Mountains and the Sea?

Now let us go!' he said, drawing his eyes away from the South, and looking out west and north to the way that he must tread.

The ridge upon which the companions stood went down steeply before their feet. Below it twenty fathoms or more, there was a wide and rugged shelf which ended suddenly in the brink of a sheer cliff: the East Wall of Rohan. So ended the Emyn Muil, and the green plains of the Rohirrim stretched away before them to the edge of sight.

'Look!' cried Legolas, pointing up into the pale sky above them. 'There is the eagle again! He is very high. He seems to be flying now away, from this land back to the North. He is going with great speed. Look!'

'No, not even my eyes can see him, my good Legolas,' said Aragorn. 'He must be far aloft indeed. I wonder what is his errand, if he is the same bird that I have seen before. But look! I can see something nearer at hand and more urgent; there is something moving over the plain!'

'Many things,' said Legolas. 'It is a great company on foot; but I cannot say more, nor see what kind of folk they may be. They are many leagues away: twelve, I guess; but the flatness of the plain is hard to measure.'

'I think, nonetheless, that we no longer need any trail to tell us which way to go,' said Gimli. 'Let us find a path down to the fields as quick as may be.'

'I doubt if you will find a path quicker than the one that the Orcs chose,' said Aragorn.

They followed their enemies now by the clear light of day. It seemed that the Orcs had pressed on with all possible speed. Every now and again the pursuers found things that had been dropped or cast away: food-bags, the rinds and crusts of hard grey bread, a torn black cloak, a heavy iron-nailed shoe broken on the stones. The trail led them north along the top of the escarpment, and at length they came to a deep cleft carved in the rock by a stream that splashed noisily down. In the narrow ravine a rough path descended like a steep stair into the plain.

At the bottom they came with a strange suddenness on the grass of Rohan. It swelled like a green sea up to the very foot of the Emyn Muil. The falling stream vanished into a deep growth of cresses and water-plants, and they could hear it tinkling away in green tunnels, down long gentle slopes towards the fens of Entwash Vale far away. They seemed to have left winter clinging to the hills behind. Here the air was softer and warmer, and faintly scented, as if spring was already stirring and the sap was flowing again in herb and leaf. Legolas took a deep breath, like one that drinks a great draught after long thirst in barren places.

'Ah! the green smell!' he said. 'It is better than much sleep. Let us run!'

'Light feet may run swiftly here,' said Aragorn. 'More swiftly, maybe, than iron-shod Orcs. Now we have a chance to lessen their lead!'

They went in single file, running like hounds on a strong scent, and an eager light was in their eyes. Nearly due west the broad swath of the marching Orcs tramped its ugly slot; the sweet grass of Rohan had been bruised and blackened as they passed. Presently Aragorn gave a cry and turned aside.

'Stay!' he shouted. 'Do not follow me yet!' He ran quickly to the right, away from the main trail; for he had seen footprints that went that way, branching off from the others, the marks of small unshod feet. These, however, did not go far before they were crossed by orc-prints, also coming out from the main trail behind and in front, and then they curved sharply back again and were lost in the trampling. At the furthest point Aragorn stooped and picked up something from the grass; then he ran back.

'Yes,' he said, 'they are quite plain: a hobbit's footprints. Pippin's, I think. He is smaller than the other. And look at this!' He held up a thing that glittered in the sunlight. It looked like the new-opened leaf of a beech-tree, fair and strange in that treeless plain.

'The brooch of an elven-cloak!' cried Legolas and Gimli together.

'Not idly do the leaves of Lórien fall,' said Aragorn. 'This did not drop by chance: it was cast away as a token to any that might follow. I think Pippin ran away from the trail for that purpose.'

'Then he at least was alive,' said Gimli. 'And he had the use of his wits, and of his legs too. That is heartening. We do not pursue in vain.'

'Let us hope that he did not pay too dearly for his boldness,' said Legolas. 'Come! Let us go on! The thought of those merry young folk driven like cattle burns my heart.'

The sun climbed to the noon and then rode slowly down the sky. Light clouds came up out of the sea in the distant South and were blown away upon the breeze. The sun sank. Shadows rose behind and reached out long arms from the East. Still the hunters held on. One day now had passed since Boromir fell, and the Orcs were yet far ahead. No longer could any sight of them be seen in the level plains.

As nightshade was closing about them Aragorn halted. Only twice in the day's march had they rested for a brief while, and twelve leagues now lay between them and the eastern wall where they had stood at dawn.

'We have come at last to a hard choice,' he said. 'Shall we rest by night, or shall we go on while our will and strength hold?'

'Unless our enemies rest also, they will leave us far behind, if we stay to sleep,' said Legolas.

'Surely even Orcs must pause on the march?' said Gimli.

'Seldom will Orcs journey in the open under the sun, yet these have done so,' said Legolas. 'Certainly they will not rest by night.'

'But if we walk by night, we cannot follow their trail,' said Gimli.

'The trail is straight, and turns neither right nor left, as far as my eyes can see,' said Legolas.

'Maybe, I could lead you at guess in the darkness and hold to the line,' said Aragorn; 'but if we strayed, or they turned aside, then when light came there might be long delay before the trail was found again.'

'And there is this also,' said Gimli: 'only by day can we see if any tracks lead away. If a prisoner should escape, or if one should be carried off, eastward, say, to the Great River, towards Mordor, we might pass the signs and never know it.'

'That is true,' said Aragorn. 'But if I read the signs back yonder rightly, the Orcs of the White Hand prevailed, and the whole company is now bound for Isengard. Their present course bears me out.'

'Yet it would be rash to be sure of their counsels,' said Gimli. 'And what of escape? In the dark we should have passed the signs that led you to the brooch.'

'The Orcs will be doubly on their guard since then, and the prisoners even wearier,' said Legolas. 'There will be no escape again, if we do not contrive it. How that is to be done cannot be guessed, but first we must overtake them.'

'And yet even I, Dwarf of many journeys, and not the least hardy of my folk, cannot run all the way to Isengard without any pause,' said Gimli. 'My heart burns me too, and I would have started sooner; but now I must rest a little to run the better. And if we rest, then the blind night is the time to do so.'

'I said that it was a hard choice,' said Aragorn. 'How shall we end this debate?'

'You are our guide,' said Gimli, 'and you are skilled in the chase. You shall choose.'

'My heart bids me go on,' said Legolas. 'But we must hold together. I will follow your counsel.'

'You give the choice to an ill chooser,' said Aragorn. 'Since we passed through the Argonath my choices have gone amiss.' He fell silent, gazing north and west into the gathering night for a long while.

'We will not walk in the dark,' he said at length. 'The peril of missing the trail or signs of other coming and going seems to me the greater. If the Moon gave enough light, we would use it, but alas! he sets early and is yet young and pale.'

'And tonight he is shrouded anyway,' Gimli murmured. 'Would that the Lady had given us a light, such a gift as she gave to Frodo!'

'It will be more needed where it is bestowed,' said Aragorn. 'With him lies the true Quest. Ours is but a small matter in the great deeds of this time. A vain pursuit from its beginning, maybe, which no choice of mine can mar or mend. Well, I have chosen. So let us use the time as best we may!'

He cast himself on the ground and fell at once into sleep, for he had not slept since their night under the shadow of Tol Brandir. Before dawn was in the sky he woke and rose. Gimli was still deep in slumber, but Legolas was standing, gazing northwards into the darkness, thoughtful and silent as a young tree in a windless night.

'They are far far away,' he said sadly, turning to Aragorn. 'I know in my heart that they have not rested this night. Only an eagle could overtake them now.'

'Nonetheless we will still follow as we may,' said Aragorn. Stooping he roused the Dwarf. 'Come! We must go,' he said. 'The scent is growing cold.'

'But it is still dark,' said Gimli. 'Even Legolas on a hill-top could not see them till the Sun is up.'

'I fear they have passed beyond my sight from hill or plain, under moon or sun,' said Legolas.

'Where sight fails the earth may bring us rumour,' said Aragorn. 'The land must groan under their hated feet.' He stretched himself upon the ground with his ear pressed against the turf. He lay there motionless, for so long a time that Gimli wondered if he had swooned or fallen asleep again. Dawn came glimmering, and slowly a grey light grew about them. At last he rose, and now his friends could see his face: it was pale and drawn, and his look was troubled.

'The rumour of the earth is dim and confused,' he said. 'Nothing walks upon it for many miles about us. Faint and far are the feet of our enemies. But loud are the hoofs of the horses. It comes to my mind that I heard them, even as I lay on the ground in sleep, and they troubled my dreams: horses galloping, passing in the West. But now they are drawing ever further from us, riding northward. I wonder what is happening in this land!'

'Let us go!' said Legolas.

So the third day of their pursuit began. During all its long hours of cloud and fitful sun they hardly paused, now striding, now running, as if no weariness could quench the fire that burned them. They seldom spoke. Over the wide solitude they passed and their elven-cloaks faded against the background of the grey-green fields; even in the cool sunlight of mid-day few but elvish eyes would have marked them, until they were close at hand. Often in their hearts they thanked the Lady of Lórien for the gift of *lembas*, for they could eat of it and find new strength even as they ran.

All day the track of their enemies led straight on, going north-west without a break or turn. As once again the day wore to its end they came to long treeless slopes, where the land rose, swelling up towards a line of low humpbacked downs ahead. The orc-trail grew fainter as it bent north towards them, for the ground became harder and the grass shorter. Far away to the left the river Entwash wound, a silver thread in a green floor. No moving thing could be seen. Often Aragorn wondered that they saw no sign of beast or man. The dwellings of the Rohirrim were for the most part many leagues away to the South, under the wooded eaves of the White Mountains, now hidden in mist and cloud; yet the Horse-lords had formerly kept many herds and studs in the Eastemnet, this easterly region of their realm, and there the herdsmen had wandered much, living in camp and tent, even in winter-time. But now all the land was empty, and there was a silence that did not seem to be the quiet of peace.

At dusk they halted again. Now twice twelve leagues they had passed over the plains of Rohan and the wall of the Emyn Muil was lost in the shadows of the East. The young moon was glimmering in a misty sky, but it gave small light, and the stars were veiled.

'Now do I most grudge a time of rest or any halt in our chase,' said Legolas. 'The Orcs have run before us, as if the very whips of Sauron were behind them. I fear they have already reached the forest and the dark hills, and even now are passing into the shadows of the trees.'

Gimli ground his teeth. 'This is a bitter end to our hope and to all our toil!' he said.

'To hope, maybe, but not to toil,' said Aragorn. 'We shall not turn back here. Yet I am weary.' He gazed back along the way that they had come towards the night gathering in the East. 'There is something strange at work in this land. I distrust the silence. I distrust even the pale Moon. The stars are faint; and I am weary as I have seldom been before, weary as no Ranger should be with a clear trail to follow. There is some will that lends speed to our foes and sets an unseen barrier before us: a weariness that is in the heart more than in the limb.'

'Truly!' said Legolas. 'That I have known since first we came down from the Emyn Muil. For the will is not behind us but before us.' He pointed away over the land of Rohan into the darkling West under the sickle moon.

'Saruman!' muttered Aragorn. 'But he shall not turn us back! Halt we must once more; for, see! even the Moon is falling into gathering cloud. But north lies our road between down and fen when day returns.'

As before Legolas was first afoot, if indeed he had ever slept. 'Awake! Awake!' he cried. 'It is a red dawn. Strange things await us by the eaves of the forest. Good or evil, I do not know; but we are called. Awake!'

The others sprang up, and almost at once they set off again. Slowly the downs drew near. It was still an hour before noon when they reached them: green slopes rising to bare ridges that ran in a line straight towards the North. At their feet the ground was dry and the turf short, but a long strip of sunken land, some ten miles wide, lay between them and the river wandering deep in dim thickets of reed and rush. Just to the West of the southernmost slope there was a great ring, where the turf had been torn and beaten by many trampling feet. From it the orc-trail ran out again, turning north along the dry skirts of the hills. Aragorn halted and examined the tracks closely.

'They rested here a while,' he said, 'but even the outward trail is already old. I fear that your heart spoke truly, Legolas: it is thrice twelve hours, I guess, since the Orcs stood where we now stand. If they held to their pace, then at sundown yesterday they would reach the borders of Fangorn.'

'I can see nothing away north or west but grass dwindling into mist,' said Gimli. 'Could we see the forest, if we climbed the hills?'

'It is still far away,' said Aragorn. 'If I remember rightly, these downs run eight leagues or more to the north, and then north-west to the issuing of the Entwash there lies still a wide land, another fifteen leagues it may be.'

'Well, let us go on,' said Gimli. 'My legs must forget the miles. They would be more willing, if my heart were less heavy.'

The sun was sinking when at last they drew near to the end of the line of downs. For many hours they had marched without rest. They were going slowly now, and Gimli's back was bent. Stone-hard are the Dwarves in labour or journey, but this endless chase began to tell on him, as all hope failed in his heart. Aragorn walked behind him, grim and silent, stooping now and again to scan some print or mark upon the ground. Only Legolas still stepped as lightly as ever, his feet hardly seeming to press the grass, leaving no footprints as he passed; but in the waybread of the Elves he found all the sustenance that he needed, and he could sleep, if sleep it could be called by Men, resting his mind in the strange paths of elvish dreams, even as he walked open-eyed in the light of this world.

'Let us go up on to this green hill!' he said. Wearily they followed him, climbing the long slope, until they came out upon the top. It was a round hill smooth and bare, standing by itself, the most northerly of the downs. The sun sank and the shadows of evening fell like a curtain. They were alone in a grey formless world without mark or measure. Only far away north-west there was a deeper darkness against the dying light: the Mountains of Mist and the forest at their feet.

'Nothing can we see to guide us here,' said Gimli. 'Well,·now we must halt again and wear the night away. It is growing cold!'

'The wind is north from the snows,' said Aragorn.

'And ere morning it will be in the East,' said Legolas. 'But rest, if you must. Yet do not cast all hope away. Tomorrow is unknown. Rede oft is found at the rising of the Sun.'

'Three suns already have risen on our chase and brought no counsel,' said Gimli.

The night grew ever colder. Aragorn and Gimli slept fitfully, and whenever they awoke they saw Legolas standing beside them, or walking to and fro, singing softly to himself in his own tongue, and as he sang the white stars opened in the hard black vault above. So the night passed. Together they watched the dawn grow slowly in the sky, now bare and cloudless, until at last the sunrise came. It was pale and clear. The wind was in the East and all the mists had rolled away; wide lands lay bleak about them in the bitter light.

Ahead and eastward they saw the windy uplands of the Wold of Rohan that they had already glimpsed many days ago from the Great River. Northwestward stalked the dark forest of Fangorn; still ten leagues away stood its shadowy eaves, and its further slopes faded into the distant blue. Beyond there glimmered far away, as if floating on a grey cloud, the white head of tall Methedras, the last peak of the Misty Mountains. Out of the forest the Entwash flowed to meet them, its stream now swift and narrow, and its banks deep-cloven. The orc-trail turned from the downs towards it.

Following with his keen eyes the trail to the river, and then the river back towards the forest, Aragorn saw a shadow on the distant green, a dark swift-moving blur. He cast himself upon the ground and listened again intently. But Legolas stood beside him, shading his bright elven-eyes with his long slender hand, and he saw not a shadow, nor a blur, but the small figures of horsemen, many horsemen, and the glint of morning on the tips of their spears was like the twinkle of minute stars beyond the edge of mortal sight. Far behind them a dark smoke rose in thin curling threads.

There was a silence in the empty fields, and Gimli could hear the air moving in the grass.

'Riders!' cried Aragorn, springing to his feet. 'Many riders on swift steeds are coming towards us!'

'Yes,' said Legolas, 'there are one hundred and five. Yellow is their hair, and bright are their spears. Their leader is very tall.'

Aragorn smiled. 'Keen are the eyes of the Elves,' he said.

'Nay! The riders are little more than five leagues distant,' said Legolas.

'Five leagues or one,' said Gimli, 'we cannot escape them in this bare land. Shall we wait for them here or go on our way?'

'We will wait,' said Aragorn. 'I am weary, and our hunt has failed. Or at least others were before us; for these horsemen are riding back down the orc-trail. We may get news from them.'

'Or spears,' said Gimli.

'There are three empty saddles, but I see no hobbits,' said Legolas.

'I did not say that we should hear good news,' said Aragorn. 'But evil or good we will await it here.'

The three companions now left the hill-top, where they might be an easy mark against the pale sky, and they walked slowly down the northward slope. A little above the hill's foot they halted, and wrapping their cloaks about them, they sat huddled together upon the faded grass. The time passed slowly and heavily. The wind was thin and searching. Gimli was uneasy.

'What do you know of these horsemen, Aragorn?' he said. 'Do we sit here waiting for sudden death?'

'I have been among them,' answered Aragorn. 'They are proud and wilful, but they are true-hearted, generous in thought and deed; bold but not cruel; wise but unlearned, writing no books but singing many songs, after the manner of the children of Men before the Dark Years. But I do not know what has happened here of late, nor in what mind the Rohirrim may now be between the traitor Saruman and the threat of Sauron. They have long been the friends of the people of Gondor, though they are not akin to them. It was in forgotten years long ago that Eorl the Young brought them out of the North, and their kinship is rather with the Bardings of Dale, and with the Beornings of the Wood, among whom may still be seen many men tall and fair, as are the Riders of Rohan. At least they will not love the Orcs.'

'But Gandalf spoke of a rumour that they pay tribute to Mordor,' said Gimli.

'I believe it no more than did Boromir,' answered Aragorn.

'You will soon learn the truth,' said Legolas. 'Already they approach.'

At length even Gimli could hear the distant beat of galloping hoofs. The horsemen, following the trail, had turned from the river, and were drawing near the downs. They were riding like the wind.

Now the cries of clear strong voices came ringing over the fields. Suddenly they swept up with a noise like thunder, and the foremost horseman swerved, passing by the foot of the hill, and leading the host back southward along the western skirts of the downs. After him they rode: a long line of mail-clad men, swift, shining, fell and fair to look upon.

Their horses were of great stature, strong and clean-limbed; their grey coats glistened, their long tails flowed in the wind, their manes were braided on their proud necks. The Men that rode them matched them well: tall and long-limbed; their hair, flaxen-pale, flowed under their light helms, and streamed in long braids behind them; their faces were stern and keen. In their hands were tall spears of ash, painted shields were slung at their backs, long swords were at their belts, their burnished shirts of mail hung down upon their knees.

In pairs they galloped by, and though every now and then one rose in his stirrups and gazed ahead and to either side, they appeared not to perceive the three strangers sitting silently and watching them. The host had almost passed when suddenly Aragorn stood up, and called in a loud voice:

'What news from the North, Riders of Rohan?'

With astonishing speed and skill they checked their steeds, wheeled, and came charging round. Soon the three companions found themselves in a ring of horsemen moving in a running circle, up the hill-slope behind them and down, round and round them, and drawing ever inwards. Aragorn stood silent, and the other two sat without moving, wondering what way things would turn.

Without a word or cry, suddenly, the Riders halted. A thicket of spears were pointed towards the strangers; and some of the horsemen had bows in hand, and their arrows were already fitted to the string. Then one rode forward, a tall man, taller than all the rest; from his helm as a crest a white horsetail flowed. He advanced until the point of his spear was within a foot of Aragorn's breast. Aragorn did not stir.

'Who are you, and what are you doing in this land?' said the Rider, using the Common Speech of the West, in manner and tone like to the speech of Boromir, Man of Gondor.

'I am called Strider,' answered Aragorn. 'I came out of the North. I am hunting Orcs.'

The Rider leaped from his horse. Giving his spear to another who rode up and dismounted at his side, he drew his sword and stood face to face with Aragorn, surveying him keenly, and not without wonder. At length he spoke again.

'At first I thought that you yourselves were Orcs,' he said; 'but now I see that it is not so. Indeed you know little of Orcs, if you go hunting them in this fashion. They were swift and well-armed, and they were many. You would have changed from hunters to prey, if ever you had overtaken them. But there is something strange about you, Strider.' He bent his clear bright eyes again upon the Ranger. 'That is no name for a Man that you give. And strange too is your raiment. Have you sprung out of the grass? How did you escape our sight? Are you elvish folk?'

'No,' said Aragorn. 'One only of us is an Elf, Legolas from the Woodland Realm in distant Mirkwood. But we have passed through Lothlórien, and the gifts and favour of the Lady go with us.'

The Rider looked at them with renewed wonder, but his eyes hardened. 'Then there is a Lady in the Golden Wood, as old tales tell!' he said. 'Few escape her nets, they say. These are strange days! But if you have her favour, then you also are net-weavers and sorcerers, maybe.' He turned a cold glance suddenly upon Legolas and Gimli. 'Why do you not speak, silent ones?' he demanded.

Gimli rose and planted his feet firmly apart: his hand gripped the handle of his axe, and his dark eyes flashed. 'Give me your name, horse-master, and I will give you mine, and more besides,' he said.

'As for that,' said the Rider, staring down at the Dwarf, 'the stranger should declare himself first. Yet I am named Éomer son of Éomund, and am called the Third Marshal of Riddermark.'

'Then Éomer son of Éomund, Third Marshal of Riddermark, let Gimli the Dwarf Glóin's son warn you against foolish words. You speak evil of that which is fair beyond the reach of your thought, and only little wit can excuse you.'

Éomer's eyes blazed, and the Men of Rohan murmured angrily, and closed in, advancing their spears. 'I would cut off your head, beard and all, Master Dwarf, if it stood but a little higher from the ground,' said Éomer.

'He stands not alone,' said Legolas, bending his bow and fitting an arrow with hands that moved quicker than sight. 'You would die before your stroke fell.'

Éomer raised his sword, and things might have gone ill, but Aragorn sprang between them, and raised his hand. 'Your pardon, Éomer!' he cried. 'When you know more you will understand why you have angered my companions. We intend no evil to Rohan, nor to any of its folk, neither to man nor to horse. Will you not hear our tale before you strike?'

'I will,' said Éomer lowering his blade. 'But wanderers in the Riddermark would be wise to be less haughty in these days of doubt. First tell me your right name.'

'First tell me whom you serve,' said Aragorn. 'Are you friend or foe of Sauron, the Dark Lord of Mordor?'

'I serve only the Lord of the Mark, Théoden King son of Thengel,' answered Éomer. 'We do not serve the Power of the Black Land far away, but neither are we yet at open war with him; and if you are fleeing from him, then you had best leave this land. There is trouble now on all our borders, and we are threatened; but we desire only to be free, and to live as we have lived, keeping our own, and serving no foreign lord, good or evil. We welcomed guests kindly in the better days, but in these times the unbidden stranger finds us swift and hard. Come! Who are you? Whom do *you* serve? At whose command do you hunt Orcs in our land?'

'I serve no man,' said Aragorn; 'but the servants of Sauron I pursue into whatever land they may go. There are few among mortal Men who know more of Orcs; and I do not hunt them in this fashion out of choice. The Orcs whom we pursued took captive two of my friends. In such need a man that has no horse will go on foot, and he will not ask for leave to follow the trail. Nor will he count the heads of the enemy save with a sword. I am not weaponless.'

Aragorn threw back his cloak. The elven-sheath glittered as he grasped it, and the bright blade of Andúril shone like a sudden flame as he swept it out. 'Elendil!' he cried. 'I am Aragorn son of Arathorn, and am called Elessar, the Elfstone, Dúnadan, the heir of Isildur Elendil's son of Gondor. Here is the Sword that was Broken and is forged again! Will you aid me or thwart me? Choose swiftly!'

Gimli and Legolas looked at their companion in amazement, for they had not seen him in this mood before. He seemed to have grown in stature while Éomer had shrunk; and in his living face they caught a brief vision of the power and majesty of the kings of stone. For a moment it seemed to the eyes of Legolas that a white flame flickered on the brows of Aragorn like a shining crown.

Éomer stepped back and a look of awe was in his face. He cast down his proud eyes. 'These are indeed strange days,' he muttered. 'Dreams and legends spring to life out of the grass.

'Tell me, lord,' he said, 'what brings you here? And what was the meaning of the dark words? Long has Boromir son of Denethor been gone seeking an answer, and the horse that we lent him came back riderless. What doom do you bring out of the North?'

'The doom of choice,' said Aragorn. 'You may say this to Théoden son of Thengel: open war lies before him, with Sauron or against him. None may live now as they have lived, and few shall keep what they call their own. But of these great matters we will speak later. If chance allows, I will come myself to the king. Now I am in great need, and I ask for help, or at least for tidings. You heard that we are pursuing an orc-host that carried off our friends. What can you tell us?'

'That you need not pursue them further,' said Éomer. 'The Orcs are destroyed.'

'And our friends?'

'We found none but Orcs.'

'But that is strange indeed,' said Aragorn. 'Did you search the slain? Were there no bodies other than those of orc-kind? They would be small, only children to your eyes, unshod but clad in grey.'

'There were no dwarves nor children,' said Éomer. 'We counted all the slain and despoiled them, and then we piled the carcases and burned them, as is our custom. The ashes are smoking still.'

'We do not speak of dwarves or children,' said Gimli. 'Our friends were hobbits.'

'Hobbits?' said Éomer. 'And what may they be? It is a strange name.'

'A strange name for a strange folk,' said Gimli. 'But these were very dear to us. It seems that you have heard in Rohan of the words that troubled Minas Tirith. They spoke of the Halfling. These hobbits are Halflings.'

'Halflings!' laughed the Rider that stood beside Éomer. 'Halflings! But they are only a little people in old songs and children's tales out of the North. Do we walk in legends or on the green earth in the daylight?'

'A man may do both,' said Aragorn. 'For not we but those who come after will make the legends of our time. The green earth, say you? That is a mighty matter of legend, though you tread it under the light of day!'

'Time is pressing,' said the Rider, not heeding Aragorn. 'We must hasten south, lord. Let us leave these wild folk to their fancies. Or let us bind them and take them to the king.'

'Peace, Éothain!' said Éomer in his own tongue. 'Leave me a while. Tell the *éored* to assemble on the path, and make ready to ride to the Entwade.'

Muttering Éothain retired, and spoke to the others. Soon they drew off and left Éomer alone with the three companions.

'All that you say is strange, Aragorn,' he said. 'Yet you speak the truth, that is plain: the Men of the Mark do not lie, and therefore they are not easily deceived. But you have not told all. Will you not now speak more fully of your errand, so that I may judge what to do?'

'I set out from Imladris, as it is named in the rhyme, many weeks ago,' answered Aragorn. 'With me went Boromir of Minas Tirith. My errand was to go to that city with the son of Denethor, to aid his folk in their war against Sauron. But the Company that I journeyed with had other business. Of that I cannot speak now. Gandalf the Grey was our leader.'

'Gandalf!' Éomer exclaimed. 'Gandalf Greyhame is known in the Mark; but his name, I warn you, is no longer a password to the king's favour. He has been a guest in the land many times in the memory of men, coming as he will, after a season, or after many years. He is ever the herald of strange events: a bringer of evil, some now say.

'Indeed since his last coming in the summer all things have gone amiss. At that time our trouble with Saruman began. Until then we counted Saruman our friend, but Gandalf came then and warned us that sudden war was preparing in Isengard. He said that he himself had been a prisoner in Orthanc and had hardly escaped, and he begged for help. But Théoden would not listen to him, and he went away. Speak not the name of Gandalf loudly in Théoden's ears! He is wroth. For Gandalf took the horse that is called Shadowfax, the most precious of all the king's steeds, chief of the *Mearas*, which only the Lord of the Mark may ride. For the sire of their race was the great horse of Eorl that knew the speech of Men. Seven nights ago Shadowfax returned; but the king's anger is not less, for now the horse is wild and will let no man handle him.'

'Then Shadowfax has found his way alone from the far North,' said Aragorn; 'for it was there that he and Gandalf parted. But alas! Gandalf will ride no longer. He fell into darkness in the Mines of Moria and comes not again.'

'That is heavy tidings,' said Éomer. 'At least to me, and to many; though not to all, as you may find, if you come to the king.'

'It is tidings more grievous than any in this land can understand, though it may touch them sorely ere the year is much older,' said Aragorn. 'But when the great fall, the less must lead. My part it has been to guide our Company on the long road from Moria. Through Lórien we came – of which it were well that you should learn the truth ere you speak of it again – and thence down the leagues of the Great River to the falls of Rauros. There Boromir was slain by the same Orcs whom you destroyed.'

'Your news is all of woe!' cried Éomer in dismay. 'Great harm is this death to Minas Tirith, and to us all. That was a worthy man! All spoke his praise. He came seldom to the Mark, for he was ever in the wars on the East-borders; but I have seen him. More like to the swift sons of Eorl than to the grave Men of Gondor he seemed to me, and likely to prove a great captain of his people when his time came. But we have had no word of this grief out of Gondor. When did he fall?'

'It is now the fourth day since he was slain,' answered Aragorn; 'and since the evening of that day we have journeyed from the shadow of Tol Brandir.'

'On foot?' cried Éomer.

'Yes, even as you see us.'

Wide wonder came into Éomer's eyes. 'Strider is too poor a name, son of Arathorn,' he said. 'Wingfoot I name you. This deed of the three friends should be sung in many a hall. Forty leagues and five you have measured ere the fourth day is ended! Hardy is the race of Elendil!

'But now, lord, what would you have me do! I must return in haste to Théoden. I spoke warily before my men. It is true that we are not yet at open war with the Black Land, and there are some, close to the king's ear, that speak craven counsels; but war is coming. We shall not forsake our old alliance with Gondor, and while they fight we shall aid them: so say I and all who hold with me. The East-mark is my charge, the ward of the Third Marshal, and I have removed all our herds and herdfolk, withdrawing them beyond Entwash, and leaving none here but guards and swift scouts.'

'Then you do not pay tribute to Sauron?' said Gimli.

'We do not and we never have,' said Éomer with a flash of his eyes; 'though it comes to my ears that that lie has been told. Some years ago the Lord of the Black Land wished to purchase horses of us at great price, but we refused him, for he puts beasts to evil use. Then he sent plundering Orcs, and they carry off what they can, choosing always the black horses: few of these are now left. For that reason our feud with the Orcs is bitter.

'But at this time our chief concern is with Saruman. He has claimed lordship over all this land, and there has been war between us for many months. He has taken Orcs into his service, and Wolf-riders, and evil Men, and he has closed the Gap against us, so that we are likely to be beset both east and west.

'It is ill dealing with such a foe: he is a wizard both cunning and dwimmer-crafty, having many guises. He walks here and there, they say, as an old man hooded and cloaked, very like to Gandalf, as many now recall. His spies slip through every net, and his birds of ill omen are abroad in the sky. I do not know how it will all end, and my heart misgives me; for it seems to me that his friends do not all dwell in Isengard. But if you come to the king's house, you shall see for yourself. Will you not come? Do I hope in vain that you have been sent to me for a help in doubt and need?'

'I will come when I may,' said Aragorn.

'Come now!' said Éomer. 'The Heir of Elendil would be a strength indeed to the Sons of Eorl in this evil tide. There is battle even now upon the Westemnet, and I fear that it may go ill for us.

'Indeed in this riding north I went without the king's leave, for in my absence his house is left with little guard. But scouts warned me of the orc-host coming down out of the East Wall three nights ago, and among them they reported that some bore the white badges of Saruman. So suspecting what I most fear, a league between Orthanc and the Dark Tower, I led forth my *éored*, men of my own household; and we overtook the Orcs at nightfall two days ago, near to the borders of the Entwood. There we surrounded them, and gave battle yesterday at dawn. Fifteen of my men I lost, and twelve horses alas! For the Orcs were greater in number than we counted on. Others joined them, coming out of the East across the Great River: their trail is plain to see a little north of this spot. And others, too, came out of the forest. Great Orcs, who also bore the White Hand of Isengard: that kind is stronger and more fell than all others.

'Nonetheless we put an end to them. But we have been too long away. We are needed south and west. Will you not come? There are spare horses as you see. There is work for the Sword to do. Yes, and we could find a use for Gimli's axe and the bow of Legolas, if they will pardon my rash words concerning the Lady of the Wood. I spoke only as do all men in my land, and I would gladly learn better.'

'I thank you for your fair words,' said Aragorn, 'and my heart desires to come with you; but I cannot desert my friends while hope remains.'

'Hope does not remain,' said Éomer. 'You will not find your friends on the North-borders.'

'Yet my friends are not behind. We found a clear token not far from the East Wall that one at least of them was still alive there. But between the wall and the downs we have found no other trace of them, and no trail has turned aside, this way or that, unless my skill has wholly left me.'

'Then what do you think has become of them?'

'I do not know. They may have been slain and burned among the Orcs; but that you will say cannot be, and I do not fear it. I can only think that they were carried off into the forest before the battle, even before you encircled your foes, maybe. Can you swear that none escaped your net in such a way?'

'I would swear that no Orc escaped after we sighted them,' said Éomer. 'We reached the forest-eaves before them, and if after that any living thing broke through our ring, then it was no Orc and had some elvish power.'

'Our friends were attired even as we are,' said Aragorn; 'and you passed us by under the full light of day.'

'I had forgotten that,' said Éomer. 'It is hard to be sure of anything among so many marvels. The world is all grown strange. Elf and Dwarf in company walk in our daily fields; and folk speak with the Lady of the Wood and yet live; and the Sword comes back to war that was broken in the long ages ere the fathers of our fathers rode into the Mark! How shall a man judge what to do in such times?'

'As he ever has judged,' said Aragorn. 'Good and ill have not changed since yesteryear; nor are they one thing among Elves and Dwarves and another among Men. It is a man's part to discern them, as much in the Golden Wood as in his own house.'

'True indeed,' said Éomer. 'But I do not doubt you, nor the deed which my heart would do. Yet I am not free to do all as I would. It is against our law to let strangers wander at will in our land, until the king himself shall give them leave, and more strict is the command in these days of peril. I have begged you to come back willingly with me, and you will not. Loth am I to begin a battle of one hundred against three.'

'I do not think your law was made for such a chance,' said Aragorn. 'Nor indeed am I a stranger; for I have been in this land before, more than once, and ridden with the host of the Rohirrim, though under other name and in other guise. You I have not seen before, for you are young, but I have spoken with Éomund your father, and with Théoden son of Thengel. Never in former days would any high lord of this land have constrained a man to abandon such a quest as mine. My duty at least is clear, to go on. Come now, son of Éomund, the choice must be made at last. Aid us, or at the worst let us go free. Or seek to carry out your law. If you do so there will be fewer to return to your war or to your king.'

Éomer was silent for a moment, then he spoke. 'We both have need of haste,' he said. 'My company chafes to be away, and every hour lessens your hope. This is my choice. You may go; and what is more, I will lend you horses. This only I ask: when your quest is achieved, or is proved vain, return with the horses over the Entwade to Meduseld, the high house in Edoras where Théoden now sits. Thus you shall prove to him that I have not misjudged. In this I place myself, and maybe my very life, in the keeping of your good faith. Do not fail.'

'I will not,' said Aragorn.

There was great wonder, and many dark and doubtful glances, among his men, when Éomer gave orders that the spare horses were to be lent to the strangers; but only Éothain dared to speak openly.

'It may be well enough for this lord of the race of Gondor, as he claims,' he said, 'but who has heard of a horse of the Mark being given to a Dwarf?'

'No one,' said Gimli. 'And do not trouble: no one will ever hear of it. I would sooner walk than sit on the back of any beast so great, free or begrudged.'

'But you must ride now, or you will hinder us,' said Aragorn.

'Come, you shall sit behind me, friend Gimli,' said Legolas. 'Then all will be well, and you need neither borrow a horse nor be troubled by one.'

A great dark-grey horse was brought to Aragorn, and he mounted it.

'Hasufel is his name,' said Éomer. 'May he bear you well and to better fortune than Gárulf, his late master!'

A smaller and lighter horse, but restive and fiery, was brought to Legolas. Arod was his name. But Legolas asked them to take off saddle and rein. 'I need them not,' he said, and leaped lightly up, and to their wonder Arod was tame and willing beneath him, moving here and there with but a spoken word: such was the elvish way with all good beasts. Gimli was lifted up behind his friend, and he clung to him, not much more at ease than Sam Gamgee in a boat.

'Farewell, and may you find what you seek!' cried Éomer. 'Return with what speed you may, and let our swords hereafter shine together!'

'I will come,' said Aragorn.

'And I will come, too,' said Gimli. 'The matter of the Lady Galadriel lies still between us. I have yet to teach you gentle speech.'

'We shall see,' said Éomer. 'So many strange things have chanced that to learn the praise of a fair lady under the loving strokes of a Dwarf's axe will seem no great wonder. Farewell!'

With that they parted. Very swift were the horses of Rohan. When after a little Gimli looked back, the company of Éomer were already small and far away. Aragorn did not look back: he was watching the trail as they sped on their way, bending low with his head beside the neck of Hasufel. Before long they came to the borders of the Entwash, and there they met the other trail of which Éomer had spoken, coming down from the East out of the Wold.

Aragorn dismounted and surveyed the ground, then leaping back into the saddle, he rode away for some distance eastward, keeping to one side and taking care not to override the footprints. Then he again dismounted and examined the ground, going backwards and forwards on foot.

'There is little to discover,' he said when he returned. 'The main trail is all confused with the passage of the horsemen as they came back; their outward course must have lain nearer the river. But this eastward trail is fresh and clear. There is no sign there of any feet going the other way, back towards Anduin. Now we must ride slower, and make sure that no trace or footstep branches off on either side. The Orcs must have been aware from this point that they were pursued; they may have made some attempt to get their captives away before they were overtaken.'

As they rode forward the day was overcast. Low grey clouds came over the Wold. A mist shrouded the sun. Ever nearer the tree-clad slopes of Fangorn loomed, slowly darkling as the sun went west. They saw no sign of any trail to right or left, but here and there they passed single Orcs, fallen in their tracks as they ran, with grey-feathered arrows sticking in back or throat.

At last as the afternoon was waning they came to the eaves of the forest, and in an open glade among the first trees they found the place of the great burning: the ashes were still hot and smoking. Beside it was a great pile of helms and mail, cloven shields, and broken swords, bows and darts and other gear of war. Upon a stake in the middle was set a great goblin head; upon its shattered helm the white badge could still be seen. Further away, not far from the river, where it came streaming out from the edge of the wood, there was a mound. It was newly raised: the raw earth was covered with fresh-cut turves: about it were planted fifteen spears.

Aragorn and his companions searched far and wide about the field of battle, but the light faded, and evening soon drew down, dim and misty. By nightfall they had discovered no trace of Merry and Pippin.

'We can do no more,' said Gimli sadly. 'We have been set many riddles since we came to Tol Brandir, but this is the hardest to unravel. I would guess that the burned bones of the hobbits are now mingled with the Orcs'. It will be hard news for Frodo, if he lives to hear it; and hard too for the old hobbit who waits in Rivendell. Elrond was against their coming.'

'But Gandalf was not,' said Legolas.

'But Gandalf chose to come himself, and he was the first to be lost,' answered Gimli. 'His foresight failed him.'

'The counsel of Gandalf was not founded on foreknowledge of safety, for himself or for others,' said Aragorn. 'There are some things that it is better to begin than to refuse, even though the end may be dark. But I shall not depart from this place yet. In any case we must here await the morning-light.'

A little way beyond the battle-field they made their camp under a spreading tree: it looked like a chestnut, and yet it still bore many broad brown leaves of a former year, like dry hands with long splayed fingers; they rattled mournfully in the night-breeze.

Gimli shivered. They had brought only one blanket apiece. 'Let us light a fire,' he said. 'I care no longer for the danger. Let the Orcs come as thick as summer-moths round a candle!'

'If those unhappy hobbits are astray in the woods, it might draw them hither,' said Legolas.

'And it might draw other things, neither Orc nor Hobbit,' said Aragorn. 'We are near to the mountain-marches of the traitor Saruman. Also we are on the very edge of Fangorn, and it is perilous to touch the trees of that wood, it is said.'

'But the Rohirrim made a great burning here yesterday,' said Gimli, 'and they felled trees for the fire, as can be seen. Yet they passed the night after safely here, when their labour was ended.'

'They were many,' said Aragorn, 'and they do not heed the wrath of Fangorn, for they come here seldom, and they do not go under the trees. But our paths are likely to lead us into the very forest itself. So have a care! Cut no living wood!'

'There is no need,' said Gimli. 'The Riders have left chip and bough enough, and there is dead wood lying in plenty.' He went off to gather fuel, and busied himself with building and kindling a fire; but Aragorn sat silent with his back to the great tree, deep in thought; and Legolas stood alone in the open, looking towards the profound shadow of the wood, leaning forward, as one who listens to voices calling from a distance.

When the Dwarf had a small bright blaze going, the three companions drew close to it and sat together, shrouding the light with their hooded forms. Legolas looked up at the boughs of the tree reaching out above them.

'Look!' he said. 'The tree is glad of the fire!'

It may have been that the dancing shadows tricked their eyes, but certainly to each of the companions the boughs appeared to be bending this way and that so as to come above the flames, while the upper branches were stooping down; the brown leaves now stood out stiff, and rubbed together like many cold cracked hands taking comfort in the warmth.

There was a silence, for suddenly the dark and unknown forest, so near at hand, made itself felt as a great brooding presence, full of secret purpose. After a while Legolas spoke again.

'Celeborn warned us not to go far into Fangorn,' he said. 'Do you know why, Aragorn? What are the fables of the forest that Boromir had heard?'

'I have heard many tales in Gondor and elsewhere,' said Aragorn, 'but if it were not for the words of Celeborn I should deem them only fables that Men have made as true knowledge fades. I had thought of asking you what was the truth of the matter. And if an Elf of the wood does not know, how shall a Man answer?'

'You have journeyed further than I,' said Legolas. 'I have heard nothing of this in my own land, save only songs that tell how the Onodrim, that Men call Ents, dwelt there long ago; for Fangorn is old, old even as the Elves would reckon it.'

'Yes, it is old,' said Aragorn, 'as old as the forest by the Barrow-downs, and it is far greater. Elrond says that the two are akin, the last strongholds of the mighty woods of the Elder Days, in which the Firstborn roamed while Men still slept. Yet Fangorn holds some secret of its own. What it is I do not know.'

'And I do not wish to know,' said Gimli. 'Let nothing that dwells in Fangorn be troubled on my account!'

They now drew lots for the watches, and the lot for the first watch fell to Gimli. The others lay down. Almost at once sleep laid hold on them. 'Gimli!' said Aragorn drowsily. 'Remember, it is perilous to cut bough or twig from a living tree in Fangorn. But do not stray far in search of dead wood. Let the fire die rather! Call me at need!'

With that he fell asleep. Legolas already lay motionless, his fair hands folded upon his breast, his eyes unclosed, blending living night and deep dream, as is the way with Elves. Gimli sat hunched by the fire, running his thumb thoughtfully along the edge of his axe. The tree rustled. There was no other sound.

Suddenly Gimli looked up, and there just on the edge of the firelight stood an old bent man, leaning on a staff, and wrapped in a great cloak; his wide-brimmed hat was pulled down over his eyes. Gimli sprang up, too amazed for the moment to cry out, though at once the thought flashed into his mind that Saruman had caught them. Both Aragorn and Legolas, roused by his sudden movement, sat up and stared. The old man did not speak or make a sign.

'Well, father, what can we do for you?' said Aragorn, leaping to his feet. 'Come and be warm, if you are cold!' He strode forward, but the old man was gone. There was no trace of him to be found near at hand, and they did not dare to wander far. The moon had set and the night was very dark. Suddenly Legolas gave a cry. 'The horses! The horses!'

The horses were gone. They had dragged their pickets and disappeared. For some time the three companions stood still and silent, troubled by this new stroke of ill fortune. They were under the eaves of Fangorn, and endless leagues lay between them and the Men of Rohan, their only friends in this wide and dangerous land. As they stood, it seemed to them that they heard, far off in the night, the sound of horses whinnying and neighing. Then all was quiet again, except for the cold rustle of the wind.

'Well, they are gone,' said Aragorn at last. 'We cannot find them or catch them; so that if they do not return of their own will, we must do without. We started on our feet, and we have those still.'

'Feet!' said Gimli. 'But we cannot eat them as well as walk on them.' He threw some fuel on the fire and slumped down beside it.

'Only a few hours ago you were unwilling to sit on a horse of Rohan,' laughed Legolas. 'You will make a rider yet.'

'It seems unlikely that I shall have the chance,' said Gimli.

'If you wish to know what I think,' he began again after a while, 'I think it was Saruman. Who else? Remember the words of Éomer: *he walks about like an old man hooded and cloaked.* Those were the words. He has gone off with our horses, or scared them away, and here we are. There is more trouble coming to us, mark my words!'

'I mark them,' said Aragorn. 'But I marked also that this old man had a hat not a hood. Still I do not doubt that you guess right, and that we are in peril here, by night or day. Yet in the meantime there is nothing that we can do but rest, while we may. I will watch for a while now, Gimli. I have more need of thought than of sleep.'

The night passed slowly. Legolas followed Aragorn, and Gimli followed Legolas, and their watches wore away. But nothing happened. The old man did not appear again, and the horses did not return.

CHAPTER III

THE URUK-HAI

Pippin lay in a dark and troubled dream: it seemed that he could hear his own small voice echoing in black tunnels, calling *Frodo, Frodo!* But instead of Frodo hundreds of hideous orc-faces grinned at him out of the shadows, hundreds of hideous arms grasped at him from every side. Where was Merry?

He woke. Cold air blew on his face. He was lying on his back. Evening was coming and the sky above was growing dim. He turned and found that the dream was little worse than the waking. His wrists, legs, and ankles were tied with cords. Beside him Merry lay, white-faced, with a dirty rag bound across his brows. All about them sat or stood a great company of Orcs.

Slowly in Pippin's aching head memory pieced itself together and became separated from dream-shadows. Of course: he and Merry had run off into the woods. What had come over them? Why had they dashed off like that, taking no notice of old Strider? They had run a long way shouting – he could not remember how far or how long; and then suddenly they had crashed right into a group of Orcs: they were standing listening, and they did not appear to see Merry and Pippin until they were almost in their arms. Then they yelled and dozens of other goblins had sprung out of the trees. Merry and he had drawn their swords, but the Orcs did not wish to fight, and had tried only to lay hold of them, even when Merry had cut off several of their arms and hands. Good old Merry!

Then Boromir had come leaping through the trees. He had made them fight. He slew many of them and the rest fled. But they had not gone far on the way back when they were attacked again, by a hundred Orcs at least, some of them very large, and they shot a rain of arrows: always at Boromir. Boromir had blown his great horn till the woods rang, and at first the Orcs had been dismayed and had drawn back; but when no answer but the echoes came, they had attacked more fiercely than ever. Pippin did not remember much more. His last memory was of Boromir leaning against a tree, plucking out an arrow; then darkness fell suddenly.

'I suppose I was knocked on the head,' he said to himself. 'I wonder if poor Merry is much hurt. What has happened to Boromir? Why didn't the Orcs kill us? Where are we, and where are we going?'

He could not answer the questions. He felt cold and sick. 'I wish Gandalf had never persuaded Elrond to let us come,' he thought. 'What good have

I been? Just a nuisance: a passenger, a piece of luggage. And now I have been stolen and I am just a piece of luggage for the Orcs. I hope Strider or someone will come and claim us! But ought I to hope for it? Won't that throw out all the plans? I wish I could get free!'

He struggled a little, quite uselessly. One of the Orcs sitting near laughed and said something to a companion in their abominable tongue. 'Rest while you can, little fool!' he said then to Pippin, in the Common Speech, which he made almost as hideous as his own language. 'Rest while you can! We'll find a use for your legs before long. You'll wish you had got none before we get home.'

'If I had my way, you'd wish you were dead now,' said the other. 'I'd make you squeak, you miserable rat.' He stooped over Pippin, bringing his yellow fangs close to his face. He had a black knife with a long jagged blade in his hand. 'Lie quiet, or I'll tickle you with this,' he hissed. 'Don't draw attention to yourself, or I may forget my orders. Curse the Isengarders! *Uglúk u bagronk sha pushdug Saruman-glob búbhosh skai*': he passed into a long angry speech in his own tongue that slowly died away into muttering and snarling.

Terrified Pippin lay still, though the pain at his wrists and ankles was growing, and the stones beneath him were boring into his back. To take his mind off himself he listened intently to all that he could hear. There were many voices round about, and though orc-speech sounded at all times full of hate and anger, it seemed plain that something like a quarrel had begun, and was getting hotter.

To Pippin's surprise he found that much of the talk was intelligible; many of the Orcs were using ordinary language. Apparently the members of two or three quite different tribes were present, and they could not understand one another's orc-speech. There was an angry debate concerning what they were to do now: which way they were to take and what should be done with the prisoners.

'There's no time to kill them properly,' said one. 'No time for play on this trip.'

'That can't be helped,' said another. 'But why not kill them quick, kill them now? They're a cursed nuisance, and we're in a hurry. Evening's coming on, and we ought to get a move on.'

'Orders,' said a third voice in a deep growl. '*Kill all but* NOT *the Halflings; they are to be brought back* ALIVE *as quickly as possible.* That's my orders.'

'What are they wanted for?' asked several voices. 'Why alive? Do they give good sport?'

'No! I heard that one of them has got something, something that's wanted for the War, some elvish plot or other. Anyway they'll both be questioned.'

'Is that all you know? Why don't we search them and find out? We might find something that we could use ourselves.'

'That is a very interesting remark,' sneered a voice, softer than the others but more evil. 'I may have to report that. The prisoners are NOT to be searched or plundered: those are *my* orders.'

'And mine too,' said the deep voice. '*Alive and as captured; no spoiling.* That's my orders.'

'Not our orders!' said one of the earlier voices. 'We have come all the way from the Mines to kill, and avenge our folk. I wish to kill, and then go back north.'

'Then you can wish again,' said the growling voice. 'I am Uglúk. I command. I return to Isengard by the shortest road.'

'Is Saruman the master or the Great Eye?' said the evil voice. 'We should go back at once to Lugbúrz.'

'If we could cross the Great River, we might,' said another voice. 'But there are not enough of us to venture down to the bridges.'

'I came across,' said the evil voice. 'A winged Nazgûl awaits us northward on the east-bank.'

'Maybe, maybe! Then you'll fly off with our prisoners, and get all the pay and praise in Lugbúrz, and leave us to foot it as best we can through the Horse-country. No, we must stick together. These lands are dangerous: full of foul rebels and brigands.'

'Aye, we must stick together,' growled Uglúk. 'I don't trust you little swine. You've no guts outside your own sties. But for us you'd all have run away. We are the fighting Uruk-hai! We slew the great warrior. We took the prisoners. We are the servants of Saruman the Wise, the White Hand: the Hand that gives us man's-flesh to eat. We came out of Isengard, and led you here, and we shall lead you back by the way we choose. I am Uglúk. I have spoken.'

'You have spoken more than enough, Uglúk,' sneered the evil voice. 'I wonder how they would like it in Lugbúrz. They might think that Uglúk's shoulders needed relieving of a swollen head. They might ask where his strange ideas came from. Did they come from Saruman, perhaps? Who does *he* think he is, setting up on his own with his filthy white badges? They might agree with me, with Grishnákh their trusted messenger; and I Grishnákh say this: Saruman is a fool, and a dirty treacherous fool. But the Great Eye is on him.

'*Swine* is it? How do you folk like being called *swine* by the muck-rakers of a dirty little wizard? It's orc-flesh they eat, I'll warrant.'

Many loud yells in orc-speech answered him, and the ringing clash of weapons being drawn. Cautiously Pippin rolled over, hoping to see what would happen. His guards had gone to join in the fray. In the twilight he saw a large black Orc, probably Uglúk, standing facing Grishnákh, a short crook-legged creature, very broad and with long arms that hung almost to the ground. Round them were many smaller goblins. Pippin supposed that these were the ones from the North. They had drawn their knives and swords, but hesitated to attack Uglúk.

Uglúk shouted, and a number of other Orcs of nearly his own size ran up. Then suddenly, without warning, Uglúk sprang forwards, and with two swift strokes swept the heads off two of his opponents. Grishnákh stepped aside and vanished into the shadows. The others gave way, and one stepped backwards and fell over Merry's prostrate form with a curse. Yet that probably saved his life, for Uglúk's followers leaped over him and cut down another with their broad-bladed swords. It was the yellow-fanged guard. His body fell right on top of Pippin, still clutching its long saw-edged knife.

'Put up your weapons!' shouted Uglúk. 'And let's have no more nonsense! We go straight west from here, and down the stair. From there straight to the downs, then along the river to the forest. And we march day and night. That clear?'

'Now,' thought Pippin, 'if only it takes that ugly fellow a little while to get his troop under control, I've got a chance.' A gleam of hope had come to him. The edge of the black knife had snicked his arm, and then slid down to his wrist. He felt the blood trickling on to his hand, but he also felt the cold touch of steel against his skin.

The Orcs were getting ready to march again, but some of the Northerners were still unwilling, and the Isengarders slew two more before the rest were cowed. There was much cursing and confusion. For the moment Pippin was unwatched. His legs were securely bound, but his arms were only tied about the wrists, and his hands were in front of him. He could move them both together, though the bonds were cruelly tight. He pushed the dead Orc to one side, then hardly daring to breathe, he drew the knot of the wrist-cord up and down against the blade of the knife. It was sharp and the dead hand held it fast. The cord was cut! Quickly Pippin took it in his fingers and knotted it again into a loose bracelet of two loops and slipped it over his hands. Then he lay very still.

'Pick up those prisoners!' shouted Uglúk. 'Don't play any tricks with them! If they are not alive when we get back, someone else will die too.'

An Orc seized Pippin like a sack, put its head between his tied hands, grabbed his arms and dragged them down, until Pippin's face was crushed against its neck; then it jolted off with him. Another treated Merry in the same way. The Orc's clawlike hand gripped Pippin's arms like iron; the nails bit into him. He shut his eyes and slipped back into evil dreams.

Suddenly he was thrown on to the stony floor again. It was early night, but the slim moon was already falling westward. They were on the edge of a cliff that seemed to look out over a sea of pale mist. There was a sound of water falling nearby.

'The scouts have come back at last,' said an Orc close at hand.

'Well, what did you discover?' growled the voice of Uglúk.

'Only a single horseman, and he made off westwards. All's clear now.'

'Now, I daresay. But how long? You fools! You should have shot him. He'll raise the alarm. The cursed horsebreeders will hear of us by morning. Now we'll have to leg it double quick.'

A shadow bent over Pippin. It was Uglúk. 'Sit up!' said the Orc. 'My lads are tired of lugging you about. We have got to climb down, and you must use your legs. Be helpful now. No crying out, no trying to escape. We have ways of paying for tricks that you won't like, though they won't spoil your usefulness for the Master.'

He cut the thongs round Pippin's legs and ankles, picked him up by his hair and stood him on his feet. Pippin fell down, and Uglúk dragged him up by his hair again. Several Orcs laughed. Uglúk thrust a flask between his teeth and poured some burning liquid down his throat: he felt a hot fierce glow flow through him. The pain in his legs and ankles vanished. He could stand.

'Now for the other!' said Uglúk. Pippin saw him go to Merry, who was lying close by, and kick him. Merry groaned. Seizing him roughly Uglúk pulled him into a sitting position, and tore the bandage off his head. Then he smeared the wound with some dark stuff out of a small wooden box. Merry cried out and struggled wildly.

The Orcs clapped and hooted. 'Can't take his medicine,' they jeered. 'Doesn't know what's good for him. Ai! We shall have some fun later.'

But at the moment Uglúk was not engaged in sport. He needed speed and had to humour unwilling followers. He was healing Merry in orc-fashion; and his treatment worked swiftly. When he had forced a drink from his flask down the hobbit's throat, cut his leg-bonds, and dragged him to his feet, Merry stood up, looking pale but grim and defiant, and very much alive. The gash in his forehead gave him no more trouble, but he bore a brown scar to the end of his days.

'Hullo, Pippin!' he said. 'So you've come on this little expedition, too? Where do we get bed and breakfast?'

'Now then!' said Uglúk. 'None of that! Hold your tongues. No talk to one another. Any trouble will be reported at the other end, and He'll know how to pay you. You'll get bed and breakfast all right: more than you can stomach.'

The orc-band began to descend a narrow ravine leading down into the misty plain below. Merry and Pippin, separated by a dozen Orcs or more, climbed down with them. At the bottom they stepped on to grass, and the hearts of the hobbits rose.

'Now straight on!' shouted Uglúk. 'West and a little north. Follow Lugdush.'

'But what are we going to do at sunrise?' said some of the Northerners.

'Go on running,' said Uglúk. 'What do you think? Sit on the grass and wait for the Whiteskins to join the picnic?'

'But we can't run in the sunlight.'

'You'll run with me behind you,' said Uglúk. 'Run! Or you'll never see your beloved holes again. By the White Hand! What's the use of sending out mountain-maggots on a trip, only half trained. Run, curse you! Run while night lasts!'

Then the whole company began to run with the long loping strides of Orcs. They kept no order, thrusting, jostling, and cursing; yet their speed was very great. Each hobbit had a guard of three. Pippin was far back in the line. He wondered how long he would be able to go on at this pace: he had had no food since the morning. One of his guards had a whip. But at present the orc-liquor was still hot in him. His wits, too, were wide-awake.

Every now and again there came into his mind unbidden a vision of the keen face of Strider bending over a dark trail, and running, running behind. But what could even a Ranger see except a confused trail of orc-feet? His own little prints and Merry's were overwhelmed by the trampling of the iron-shod shoes before them and behind them and about them.

They had gone only a mile or so from the cliff when the land sloped down into a wide shallow depression, where the ground was soft and wet. Mist lay there, pale-glimmering in the last rays of the sickle moon. The dark shapes of the Orcs in front grew dim, and then were swallowed up.

'Ai! Steady now!' shouted Uglúk from the rear.

A sudden thought leaped into Pippin's mind, and he acted on it at once. He swerved aside to the right, and dived out of the reach of his clutching guard, headfirst into the mist; he landed sprawling on the grass.

'Halt!' yelled Uglúk.

There was for a moment turmoil and confusion. Pippin sprang up and ran. But the Orcs were after him. Some suddenly loomed up right in front of him.

'No hope of escape!' thought Pippin. 'But there is a hope that I have left some of my own marks unspoilt on the wet ground.' He groped with his two tied hands at his throat, and unclasped the brooch of his cloak. Just as long arms and hard claws seized him, he let it fall. 'There I suppose it will lie until the end of time,' he thought. 'I don't know why I did it. If the others have escaped, they've probably all gone with Frodo.'

A whip-thong curled round his legs, and he stifled a cry.

'Enough!' shouted Uglúk running up. 'He's still got to run a long way yet. Make 'em both run! Just use the whip as a reminder.'

'But that's not all,' he snarled, turning to Pippin. 'I shan't forget. Payment is only put off. Leg it!'

Neither Pippin nor Merry remembered much of the later part of the journey. Evil dreams and evil waking were blended into a long tunnel of misery, with hope growing ever fainter behind. They ran, and they ran, striving to keep up the pace set by the Orcs, licked every now and again with a cruel thong cunningly handled. If they halted or stumbled, they were seized and dragged for some distance.

The warmth of the orc-draught had gone. Pippin felt cold and sick again. Suddenly he fell face downward on the turf. Hard hands with rending nails gripped and lifted him. He was carried like a sack once more, and darkness grew about him: whether the darkness of another night, or a blindness of his eyes, he could not tell.

Dimly he became aware of voices clamouring: it seemed that many of the Orcs were demanding a halt. Uglúk was shouting. He felt himself flung to the ground, and he lay as he fell, till black dreams took him. But he did not long escape from pain; soon the iron grip of merciless hands was on him again. For a long time he was tossed and shaken, and then slowly the darkness gave way, and he came back to the waking world and found that it was morning. Orders were shouted and he was thrown roughly on the grass.

There he lay for a while, fighting with despair. His head swam, but from the heat in his body he guessed that he had been given another draught. An Orc stooped over him, and flung him some bread and a strip of raw dried flesh. He ate the stale grey bread hungrily, but not the meat. He was famished but not yet so famished as to eat flesh flung to him by an Orc, the flesh of he dared not guess what creature.

He sat up and looked about. Merry was not far away. They were by the banks of a swift narrow river. Ahead mountains loomed: a tall peak was catching the first rays of the sun. A dark smudge of forest lay on the lower slopes before them.

There was much shouting and debating among the Orcs; a quarrel seemed on the point of breaking out again between the Northerners and the Isengarders. Some were pointing back away south, and some were pointing eastward.

'Very well,' said Uglúk. 'Leave them to me then! No killing, as I've told you before; but if you want to throw away what we've come all the way to get, throw it away! I'll look after it. Let the fighting Uruk-hai do the work, as usual. If you're afraid of the Whiteskins, run! Run! There's the forest,' he shouted, pointing ahead. 'Get to it! It's your best hope. Off you go! And quick, before I knock a few more heads off, to put some sense into the others.'

There was some cursing and scuffling, and then most of the Northerners broke away and dashed off, over a hundred of them, running wildly along the river towards the mountains. The hobbits were left with the Isengarders: a grim dark band, four score at least of large, swart, slant-eyed Orcs with great bows and short broad-bladed swords. A few of the larger and bolder Northerners remained with them.

'Now we'll deal with Grishnákh,' said Uglúk; but some even of his own followers were looking uneasily southwards.

'I know,' growled Uglúk. 'The cursed horse-boys have got wind of us. But that's all your fault, Snaga. You and the other scouts ought to have your ears cut off. But we are the fighters. We'll feast on horseflesh yet, or something better.'

At that moment Pippin saw why some of the troop had been pointing eastward. From that direction there now came hoarse cries, and there was Grishnákh again, and at his back a couple of score of others like him: long-armed crook-legged Orcs. They had a red eye painted on their shields. Uglúk stepped forward to meet them.

'So you've come back?' he said. 'Thought better of it, eh?'

'I've returned to see that Orders are carried out and the prisoners safe,' answered Grishnákh.

'Indeed!' said Uglúk. 'Waste of effort. I'll see that orders are carried out in my command. And what else did you come back for? You went in a hurry. Did you leave anything behind?'

'I left a fool,' snarled Grishnákh. 'But there were some stout fellows with him that are too good to lose. I knew you'd lead them into a mess. I've come to help them.'

'Splendid!' laughed Uglúk. 'But unless you've got some guts for fighting, you've taken the wrong way. Lugbúrz was your road. The Whiteskins are coming. What's happened to your precious Nazgûl? Has he had another mount shot under him? Now, if you'd brought him along, that might have been useful – if these Nazgûl are all they make out.'

'Nazgûl, Nazgûl,' said Grishnákh, shivering and licking his lips, as if the word had a foul taste that he savoured painfully. 'You speak of what is deep beyond the reach of your muddy dreams, Uglúk,' he said. 'Nazgûl! Ah! All that they make out! One day you'll wish that you had not said that. Ape!' he snarled fiercely. 'You ought to know that they're the apple of the Great Eye. But the winged Nazgûl: not yet, not yet. He won't let them show themselves across the Great River yet, not too soon. They're for the War – and other purposes.'

'You seem to know a lot,' said Uglúk. 'More than is good for you, I guess. Perhaps those in Lugbúrz might wonder how, and why. But in the meantime the Uruk-hai of Isengard can do the dirty work, as usual. Don't stand slavering there! Get your rabble together! The other swine are legging it to the forest. You'd better follow. You wouldn't get back to the Great River alive. Right off the mark! Now! I'll be on your heels.'

The Isengarders seized Merry and Pippin again and slung them on their backs. Then the troop started off. Hour after hour they ran, pausing now and again only to sling the hobbits to fresh carriers. Either because they were quicker and hardier, or because of some plan of Grishnákh's, the Isengarders gradually passed through the Orcs of Mordor, and Grishnákh's folk closed in behind. Soon they were gaining also on the Northerners ahead. The forest began to draw nearer.

Pippin was bruised and torn, his aching head was grated by the filthy jowl and hairy ear of the Orc that held him. Immediately in front were bowed backs, and tough thick legs going up and down, up and down, unresting, as if they were made of wire and horn, beating out the nightmare seconds of an endless time.

In the afternoon Uglúk's troop overtook the Northerners. They were flagging in the rays of the bright sun, winter sun shining in a pale cool sky though it was; their heads were down and their tongues lolling out.

'Maggots!' jeered the Isengarders. 'You're cooked. The Whiteskins will catch you and eat you. They're coming!'

A cry from Grishnákh showed that this was not mere jest. Horsemen, riding very swiftly, had indeed been sighted: still far behind but gaining on the Orcs, gaining on them like a tide over the flats on folk straying in a quicksand.

The Isengarders began to run with a redoubled pace that astonished Pippin, a terrific spurt it seemed for the end of a race. Then he saw that the sun was sinking, falling behind the Misty Mountains; shadows reached over the land. The soldiers of Mordor lifted their heads and also began to put on speed. The forest was dark and close. Already they had passed a few outlying trees. The land was beginning to slope upwards, ever more steeply; but the Orcs did not halt. Both Uglúk and Grishnákh shouted, spurring them on to a last effort.

'They will make it yet. They will escape,' thought Pippin. And then he managed to twist his neck, so as to glance back with one eye over his shoulder. He saw that riders away eastward were already level with the Orcs, galloping over the plain. The sunset gilded their spears and helmets, and glinted in their pale flowing hair. They were hemming the Orcs in, preventing them from scattering, and driving them along the line of the river.

He wondered very much what kind of folk they were. He wished now that he had learned more in Rivendell, and looked more at maps and things; but in those days the plans for the journey seemed to be in more competent hands, and he had never reckoned with being cut off from Gandalf, or from Strider, and even from Frodo. All that he could remember about Rohan was that Gandalf's horse, Shadowfax, had come from that land. That sounded hopeful, as far as it went.

'But how will they know that we are not Orcs?' he thought. 'I don't suppose they've ever heard of hobbits down here. I suppose I ought to be glad that the beastly Orcs look like being destroyed, but I would rather be saved myself.' The chances were that he and Merry would be killed together with their captors, before ever the Men of Rohan were aware of them.

A few of the riders appeared to be bowmen, skilled at shooting from a running horse. Riding swiftly into range they shot arrows at the Orcs that straggled behind, and several of them fell; then the riders wheeled away out of the range of the answering bows of their enemies, who shot wildly, not daring to halt. This happened many times, and on one occasion arrows fell among the Isengarders. One of them, just in front of Pippin, stumbled and did not get up again.

Night came down without the Riders closing in for battle. Many Orcs had fallen, but fully two hundred remained. In the early darkness the Orcs came to a hillock. The eaves of the forest were very near, probably no more than three furlongs away, but they could gó no further. The horsemen had encircled them. A small band disobeyed Uglúk's command, and ran on towards the forest: only three returned.

'Well, here we are,' sneered Grishnákh. 'Fine leadership! I hope the great Uglúk will lead us out again.'

'Put those Halflings down!' ordered Uglúk, taking no notice of Grishnákh. 'You, Lugdush, get two others and stand guard over them! They're not to be killed, unless the filthy Whiteskins break through. Understand? As long as I'm alive, I want 'em. But they're not to cry out, and they're not to be rescued. Bind their legs!'

The last part of the order was carried out mercilessly. But Pippin found that for the first time he was close to Merry. The Orcs were making a great deal of noise, shouting and clashing their weapons, and the hobbits managed to whisper together for a while.

'I don't think much of this,' said Merry. 'I feel nearly done in. Don't think I could crawl away far, even if I was free.'

'*Lembas!*' whispered Pippin. '*Lembas*: I've got some. Have you? I don't think they've taken anything but our swords.'

'Yes, I had a packet in my pocket,' answered Merry, 'but it must be battered to crumbs. Anyway I can't put my mouth in my pocket!'

'You won't have to. I've——'; but just then a savage kick warned Pippin that the noise had died down, and the guards were watchful.

The night was cold and still. All round the knoll on which the Orcs were gathered little watch-fires sprang up, golden-red in the darkness, a complete ring of them. They were within a long bowshot, but the riders did not show themselves against the light, and the Orcs wasted many arrows shooting at the fires, until Uglúk stopped them. The riders made no sound. Later in the night when the moon came out of the mist, then occasionally they could be seen, shadowy shapes that glinted now and again in the white light, as they moved in ceaseless patrol.

'They'll wait for the Sun, curse them!' growled one of the guards. 'Why don't we get together and charge through? What's old Uglúk think he's doing, I should like to know?'

'I daresay you would,' snarled Uglúk stepping up from behind. 'Meaning I don't think at all, eh? Curse you! You're as bad as the other rabble: the maggots and the apes of Lugbúrz. No good trying to charge with them. They'd just squeal and bolt, and there are more than enough of these filthy horse-boys to mop up our lot on the flat.

'There's only one thing those maggots can do: they can see like gimlets in the dark. But these Whiteskins have better night-eyes than most Men, from all I've heard; and don't forget their horses! They can see the night-breeze, or so it's said. Still there's one thing the fine fellows don't know: Mauhúr and his lads are in the forest, and they should turn up any time now.'

Uglúk's words were enough, apparently, to satisfy the Isengarders; but the other Orcs were both dispirited and rebellious. They posted a few watchers, but most of them lay on the ground, resting in the pleasant darkness. It did indeed become very dark again; for the moon passed westward into thick cloud, and Pippin could not see anything a few feet away. The fires brought no light to the hillock. The riders were not, however, content merely to wait for the dawn and let their enemies rest. A sudden outcry on the east side of the knoll showed that something was wrong. It seemed that some of the Men had ridden in close, slipped off their horses, crawled to the edge of the camp and killed several Orcs, and then had faded away again. Uglúk dashed off to stop a stampede.

Pippin and Merry sat up. Their guards, Isengarders, had gone with Uglúk. But if the hobbits had any thought of escape, it was soon dashed. A long hairy arm took each of them by the neck and drew them close together. Dimly they were aware of Grishnákh's great head and hideous face between them; his foul breath was on their cheeks. He began to paw them and feel them. Pippin shuddered as hard cold fingers groped down his back.

'Well, my little ones!' said Grishnákh in a soft whisper. 'Enjoying your nice rest? Or not? A little awkwardly placed perhaps: swords and whips on one side, and nasty spears on the other! Little people should not meddle in affairs that are too big for them.' His fingers continued to grope. There was a light like a pale but hot fire behind his eyes.

The thought came suddenly into Pippin's mind, as if caught direct from the urgent thought of his enemy: 'Grishnákh knows about the Ring! He's looking for it, while Uglúk is busy: he probably wants it for himself.' Cold fear was in Pippin's heart, yet at the same time he was wondering what use he could make of Grishnákh's desire.

'I don't think you will find it that way,' he whispered. 'It isn't easy to find.'

'*Find it?*' said Grishnákh: his fingers stopped crawling and gripped Pippin's shoulder. 'Find what? What are you talking about, little one?'

For a moment Pippin was silent. Then suddenly in the darkness he made a noise in his throat: *gollum, gollum.* 'Nothing, my precious,' he added.

The hobbits felt Grishnákh's fingers twitch. 'O ho!' hissed the goblin softly. 'That's what he means, is it? O ho! Very ve-ry dangerous, my little ones.'

'Perhaps,' said Merry, now alert and aware of Pippin's guess. 'Perhaps; and not only for us. Still you know your own business best. Do you want it, or not? And what would you give for it?'

'Do I want it? Do I want it?' said Grishnákh, as if puzzled; but his arms were trembling. 'What would I give for it? What do you mean?'

'We mean,' said Pippin, choosing his words carefully, 'that it's no good groping in the dark. We could save you time and trouble. But you must untie our legs first, or we'll do nothing, and say nothing.'

'My dear tender little fools,' hissed Grishnákh, 'everything you have, and everything you know, will be got out of you in due time: everything! You'll wish there was more that you could tell to satisfy the Questioner, indeed you will: quite soon. We shan't hurry the enquiry. Oh dear no! What do you think you've been kept alive for? My dear little fellows, please believe me when I say that it was not out of kindness: that's not even one of Uglúk's faults.'

'I find it quite easy to believe,' said Merry. 'But you haven't got your prey home yet. And it doesn't seem to be going your way, whatever happens. If we come to Isengard, it won't be the great Grishnákh that benefits: Saruman will take all that he can find. If you want anything for yourself, now's the time to do a deal.'

Grishnákh began to lose his temper. The name of Saruman seemed specially to enrage him. Time was passing and the disturbance was dying down. Uglúk or the Isengarders might return at any minute. 'Have you got it – either of you?' he snarled.

'*Gollum, gollum!*' said Pippin.

'Untie our legs!' said Merry.

They felt the Orc's arms trembling violently. 'Curse you, you filthy little vermin!' he hissed. 'Untie your legs? I'll untie every string in your bodies. Do you think I can't search you to the bones? Search you! I'll cut you both to quivering shreds. I don't need the help of your legs to get you away – and have you all to myself!'

Suddenly he seized them. The strength in his long arms and shoulders was terrifying. He tucked them one under each armpit, and crushed them fiercely to his sides; a great stifling hand was clapped over each of their mouths. Then he sprang forward, stooping low. Quickly and silently he went, until he came to the edge of the knoll. There, choosing a gap between the watchers, he passed like an evil shadow out into the night, down the slope and away westward towards the river that flowed out of the forest. In that direction there was a wide open space with only one fire.

After going a dozen yards he halted, peering and listening. Nothing could be seen or heard. He crept slowly on, bent almost double. Then he squatted and listened again. Then he stood up, as if to risk a sudden dash. At that very moment the dark form of a rider loomed up right in front of him. A horse snorted and reared. A man called out.

Grishnákh flung himself on the ground flat, dragging the hobbits under him; then he drew his sword. No doubt he meant to kill his captives, rather than allow them to escape or to be rescued; but it was his undoing. The sword rang faintly, and glinted a little in the light of the fire away to his left. An arrow came whistling out of the gloom: it was aimed with skill, or guided by fate, and it pierced his right hand. He dropped the sword and shrieked. There was a quick beat of hoofs, and even as Grishnákh leaped up and ran, he was ridden down and a spear passed through him. He gave a hideous shivering cry and lay still.

The hobbits remained flat on the ground, as Grishnákh had left them. Another horseman came riding swiftly to his comrade's aid. Whether because of some special keenness of sight, or because of some other sense, the horse lifted and sprang lightly over them; but its rider did not see them, lying covered in their elven-cloaks, too crushed for the moment, and too afraid to move.

At last Merry stirred and whispered softly: 'So far so good; but how are *we* to avoid being spitted?'

The answer came almost immediately. The cries of Grishnákh had roused the Orcs. From the yells and screeches that came from the knoll the hobbits guessed that their disappearance had been discovered: Uglúk was probably knocking off a few more heads. Then suddenly the answering cries of orc-voices came from the right, outside the circle of watch-fires, from the direction of the forest and the mountains. Mauhúr had apparently arrived and was attacking the besiegers. There was the sound of galloping horses. The Riders were drawing in their ring close round the knoll, risking the orc-arrows, so as to prevent any sortie, while a company rode off to deal with the newcomers. Suddenly Merry and Pippin realized that without moving they were now outside the circle: there was nothing between them and escape.

'Now,' said Merry, 'if only we had our legs and hands free, we might get away. But I can't touch the knots, and I can't bite them.'

'No need to try,' said Pippin. 'I was going to tell you: I've managed to free my hands. These loops are only left for show. You'd better have a bit of *lembas* first.'

He slipped the cords off his wrists, and fished out a packet. The cakes were broken, but good, still in their leaf-wrappings. The hobbits each ate two or three pieces. The taste brought back to them the memory of fair faces, and laughter, and wholesome food in quiet days now far away. For a while they ate thoughtfully, sitting in the dark, heedless of the cries and sounds of battle nearby. Pippin was the first to come back to the present.

'We must be off,' he said. 'Half a moment!' Grishnákh's sword was lying close at hand, but it was too heavy and clumsy for him to use; so he crawled forward, and finding the body of the goblin he drew from its sheath a long sharp knife. With this he quickly cut their bonds.

'Now for it!' he said. 'When we've warmed up a bit, perhaps we shall be able to stand again, and walk. But in any case we had better start by crawling.'

They crawled. The turf was deep and yielding, and that helped them; but it seemed a long slow business. They gave the watch-fire a wide berth, and wormed their way forward bit by bit, until they came to the edge of the river, gurgling away in the black shadows under its deep banks. Then they looked back.

The sounds had died away. Evidently Mauhúr and his 'lads' had been killed or driven off. The Riders had returned to their silent ominous vigil.

It would not last very much longer. Already the night was old. In the East, which had remained unclouded, the sky was beginning to grow pale.

'We must get under cover,' said Pippin, 'or we shall be seen. It will not be any comfort to us, if these riders discover that we are not Orcs after we are dead.' He got up and stamped his feet. 'Those cords have cut me like wires; but my feet are getting warm again. I could stagger on now. What about you, Merry?'

Merry got up. 'Yes,' he said, 'I can manage it. *Lembas* does put heart into you ! A more wholesome sort of feeling, too, than the heat of that orc-draught. I wonder what it was made of. Better not to know, I expect. Let's get a drink of water to wash away the thought of it!'

'Not here, the banks are too steep,' said Pippin. 'Forward now!'

They turned and walked side by side slowly along the line of the river. Behind them the light grew in the East. As they walked they compared notes, talking lightly in hobbit-fashion of the things that had happened since their capture. No listener would have guessed from their words that they had suffered cruelly, and been in dire peril, going without hope towards torment and death; or that even now, as they knew well, they had little chance of ever finding friend or safety again.

'You seem to have been doing well, Master Took,' said Merry. 'You will get almost a chapter in old Bilbo's book, if ever I get a chance to report to him. Good work: especially guessing that hairy villain's little game, and playing up to him. But I wonder if anyone will ever pick up your trail and find that brooch. I should hate to lose mine, but I am afraid yours is gone for good.

'I shall have to brush up my toes, if I am to get level with you. Indeed Cousin Brandybuck is going in front now. This is where he comes in. I don't suppose you have much notion where we are; but I spent my time at Rivendell rather better. We are walking west along the Entwash. The butt-end of the Misty Mountains is in front, and Fangorn Forest.'

Even as he spoke the dark edge of the forest loomed up straight before them. Night seemed to have taken refuge under its great trees, creeping away from the coming Dawn.

'Lead on, Master Brandybuck!' said Pippin. 'Or lead back! We have been warned against Fangorn. But one so knowing will not have forgotten that.'

'I have not,' answered Merry; 'but the forest seems better to me, all the same, than turning back into the middle of a battle.'

He led the way in under the huge branches of the trees. Old beyond guessing, they seemed. Great trailing beards of lichen hung from them, blowing and swaying in the breeze. Out of the shadows the hobbits peeped, gazing back down the slope: little furtive figures that in the dim light looked like elf-children in the deeps of time peering out of the Wild Wood in wonder at their first Dawn.

Far over the Great River, and the Brown Lands, leagues upon grey leagues away, the Dawn came, red as flame. Loud rang the hunting-horns to greet it. The Riders of Rohan sprang suddenly to life. Horn answered horn again.

Merry and Pippin heard, clear in the cold air, the neighing of war-horses, and the sudden singing of many men. The Sun's limb was lifted, an arc of fire, above the margin of the world. Then with a great cry the Riders charged from the East; the red light gleamed on mail and spear. The Orcs yelled and shot all the arrows that remained to them. The hobbits saw several horsemen fall; but their line held on up the hill and over it, and wheeled round and charged again. Most of the raiders that were left alive then broke and fled, this way and that, pursued one by one to the death. But one band, holding together in a black wedge, drove forward resolutely in the direction of the forest. Straight up the slope they charged towards the watchers. Now they were drawing near, and it seemed certain that they would escape: they had already hewn down three Riders that barred their way.

'We have watched too long,' said Merry. 'There's Uglúk! I don't want to meet him again.' The hobbits turned and fled deep into the shadows of the wood.

So it was that they did not see the last stand, when Uglúk was overtaken and brought to bay at the very edge of Fangorn. There he was slain at last by Éomer, the Third Marshal of the Mark, who dismounted and fought him sword to sword. And over the wide fields the keen-eyed Riders hunted down the few Orcs that had escaped and still had strength to fly.

Then when they had laid their fallen comrades in a mound and had sung their praises, the Riders made a great fire and scattered the ashes of their enemies. So ended the raid, and no news of it came ever back either to Mordor or to Isengard; but the smoke of the burning rose high to heaven and was seen by many watchful eyes.

CHAPTER IV

TREEBEARD

Meanwhile the·hobbits went with as much speed as the dark and tangled forest allowed, following the line of the running stream, westward and up towards the slopes of the mountains, deeper and deeper into Fangorn. Slowly their fear of the Orcs died away, and their pace slackened. A queer stifling feeling came over them, as if the air were too thin or too scanty for breathing.

At last Merry halted. 'We can't go on like this,' he panted. 'I want some air.'

'Let's have a drink at any rate,' said Pippin. 'I'm parched.' He clambered on to a great tree-root that wound down into the stream, and stooping drew up some water in his cupped hands. It was clear and cold, and he took many draughts. Merry followed him. The water refreshed them and seemed to cheer their hearts; for a while they sat together on the brink of the stream, dabbling their sore feet and legs, and peering round at the trees that stood silently about them, rank upon rank, until they faded away into grey twilight in every direction.

'I suppose you haven't lost us already?' said Pippin, leaning back against a great tree-trunk. 'We can at least follow the course of this stream, the Entwash or whatever you call it, and get out again the way we came.'

'We could, if our legs would do it,' said Merry; 'and if we could breathe properly.'

'Yes, it is all very dim, and stuffy, in here,' said Pippin. 'It reminds me, somehow, of the old room in the Great Place of the Tooks away back in the Smials at Tuckborough: a huge place, where the furniture has never been moved or changed for generations. They say the Old Took lived in it year after year, while he and the room got older and shabbier together – and it has never been changed since he died, a century ago. And Old Gerontius was my great-great-grandfather: that puts it back a bit. But that is nothing to the old feeling of this wood. Look at all those weeping, trailing, beards and whiskers of lichen! And most of the trees seem to be half covered with ragged dry leaves that have never fallen. Untidy. I can't imagine what spring would look like here, if it ever comes; still less a spring-cleaning.'

'But the Sun at any rate must peep in sometimes,' said Merry. 'It does not look or feel at all like Bilbo's description of Mirkwood. That was all dark and black, and the home of dark black things. This is just dim, and frightfully tree-ish. You can't imagine *animals* living here at all, or staying for long.'

'No, nor hobbits,' said Pippin. 'And I don't like the thought of trying to get through it either. Nothing to eat for a hundred miles, I should guess. How are our supplies?'

'Low,' said Merry. 'We ran off with nothing but a couple of spare packets of *lembas*, and left everything else behind.' They looked at what remained of the elven-cakes: broken fragments for about five meagre days, that was all. 'And not a wrap or a blanket,' said Merry. 'We shall be cold tonight, whichever way we go.'

'Well, we'd better decide on the way now,' said Pippin. 'The morning must be getting on.'

Just then they became aware of a yellow light that had appeared, some way further on into the wood: shafts of sunlight seemed suddenly to have pierced the forest-roof.

'Hullo!' said Merry. 'The Sun must have run into a cloud while we've been under these trees, and now she has run out again; or else she has climbed high enough to look down through some opening. It isn't far – let's go and investigate!'

They found it was further than they thought. The ground was rising steeply still, and it was becoming increasingly stony. The light grew broader as they went on, and soon they saw that there was a rock-wall before them: the side of a hill, or the abrupt end of some long root thrust out by the distant mountains. No trees grew on it, and the sun was falling full on its stony face. The twigs of the trees at its foot were stretched out stiff and still, as if reaching out to the warmth. Where all had looked so shabby and grey before, the wood now gleamed with rich browns, and with the smooth black-greys of bark like polished leather. The boles of the trees glowed with a soft green like young grass: early spring or a fleeting vision of it was about them.

In the face of the stony wall there was something like a stair: natural perhaps, and made by the weathering and splitting of the rock, for it was rough and uneven. High up, almost level with the tops of forest-trees, there was a shelf under a cliff. Nothing grew there but a few grasses and weeds at its edge, and one old stump of a tree with only two bent branches left: it looked almost like the figure of some gnarled old man, standing there, blinking in the morning-light.

'Up we go!' said Merry joyfully. 'Now for a breath of air, and a sight of the land!'

They climbed and scrambled up the rock. If the stair had been made it was for bigger feet and longer legs than theirs. They were too eager to be surprised at the remarkable way in which the cuts and sores of their captivity had healed and their vigour had returned. They came at length to the edge of the shelf almost at the feet of the old stump; then they sprang up and turned round with their backs to the hill, breathing deep, and looking out eastward. They saw that they had only come some three or four miles into the forest: the heads of the trees marched down the slopes towards the plain. There, near the fringe of the forest, tall spires of curling black smoke went up, wavering and floating towards them.

'The wind's changing,' said Merry. 'It's turned east again. It feels cool up here.'

'Yes,' said Pippin; 'I'm afraid this is only a passing gleam, and it will all go grey again. What a pity! This shaggy old forest looked so different in the sunlight. I almost felt I liked the place.'

'Almost felt you liked the Forest! That's good! That's uncommonly kind of you,' said a strange voice. 'Turn round and let me have a look at your faces. I almost feel that I dislike you both, but do not let us be hasty. Turn around!' A large knob-knuckled hand was laid on each of their shoulders, and they were twisted round, gently but irresistibly; then two great arms lifted them up.

They found that they were looking at a most extraordinary face. It belonged to a large Man-like, almost Troll-like, figure, at least fourteen foot high, very sturdy, with a tall head, and hardly any neck. Whether it was clad in stuff like green and grey bark, or whether that was its hide, was difficult to say. At any rate the arms, at a short distance from the trunk, were not wrinkled, but covered with a brown smooth skin. The large feet had seven toes each. The lower part of the long face was covered with a sweeping grey beard, bushy, almost twiggy at the roots, thin and mossy at the ends. But at the moment the hobbits noted little but the eyes. These deep eyes were now surveying them, slow and solemn, but very penetrating. They were brown, shot with a green light. Often afterwards Pippin tried to describe his first impression of them.

'One felt as if there was an enormous well behind them, filled up with ages of memory and long, slow, steady thinking; but their surface was sparkling with the present; like sun shimmering on the outer leaves of a vast tree, or on the ripples of a very deep lake. I don't know, but it felt as if something that grew in the ground – asleep, you might say, or just feeling itself as something between root-tip and leaf-tip, between deep earth and sky had suddenly waked up, and was considering you with the same slow care that it had given to its own inside affairs for endless years.'

'*Hrum, Hoom*,' murmured the voice, a deep voice like a very deep woodwind instrument. 'Very odd indeed! Do not be hasty, that is my motto.

But if I had seen you, before I heard your voices – I liked them: nice little voices; they reminded me of something I cannot remember – if I had seen you before I heard you, I should have just trodden on you, taking you for little Orcs, and found out my mistake afterwards. Very odd you are, indeed. Root and twig, very odd!'

Pippin, though still amazed, no longer felt afraid. Under those eyes he felt a curious suspense, but not fear. 'Please,' he said, 'who are you? And what are you?'

A queer look came into the old eyes, a kind of wariness; the deep wells were covered over. '*Hrum*, now,' answered the voice; 'well, I am an Ent, or that's what they call me. Yes, Ent is the word. *The* Ent, I am, you might say, in your manner of speaking. *Fangorn* is my name according to some, *Treebeard* others make it. *Treebeard* will do.'

'An *Ent*?' said Merry. 'What's that? But what do you call yourself? What's your real name?'

'Hoo now!' replied Treebeard. 'Hoo! Now that would be telling! Not so hasty. And *I* am doing the asking. You are in *my* country. What are *you*, I wonder? I cannot place you. You do not seem to come in the old lists that I learned when I was young. But that was a long, long time ago, and they may have made new lists. Let me see! Let me see! How did it go?

> *Learn now the lore of Living Creatures!*
> *First name the four, the free peoples:*
> *Eldest of all, the elf-children;*
> *Dwarf the delver, dark are his houses;*
> *Ent the earthborn, old as mountains;*
> *Man the mortal, master of horses:*

Hm, hm, hm.

> *Beaver the builder, buck the leaper,*
> *Bear bee-hunter, boar the fighter;*
> *Hound is hungry, hare is fearful* . . .

hm, hm.

> *Eagle in eyrie, ox in pasture,*
> *Hart horn-crownéd; hawk is swiftest,*
> *Swan the whitest, serpent coldest* . . .

Hoom, hm; hoom, hm, how did it go? Room tum, room tum, roomty toom tum. It was a long list. But anyway you do not seem to fit in anywhere!'

'We always seem to have got left out of the old lists, and the old stories,' said Merry. 'Yet we've been about for quite a long time. We're *hobbits*.'

'Why not make a new line?' said Pippin.

'Half-grown hobbits, the hole-dwellers.

Put us in amongst the four, next to Man (the Big People) and you've got it.'

'Hm! Not bad, not bad,' said Treebeard. 'That would do. So you live in holes, eh? It sounds very right and proper. Who calls you *hobbits*, though? That does not sound elvish to me. Elves made all the old words: they began it.'

'Nobody else calls us hobbits; we call ourselves that,' said Pippin.

'Hoom, hmm! Come now! Not so hasty! You call *yourselves* hobbits? But you should not go telling just anybody. You'll be letting out your own right names if you're not careful.'

'We aren't careful about that,' said Merry. 'As a matter of fact I'm a Brandybuck, Meriadoc Brandybuck, though most people call me just Merry.'

'And I'm a Took, Peregrin Took, but I'm generally called Pippin, or even Pip.'

'Hm, but you *are* hasty folk, I see,' said Treebeard. 'I am honoured by your confidence; but you should not be too free all at once. There are Ents and Ents, you know; or there are Ents and things that look like Ents but ain't, as you might say. I'll call you Merry-and Pippin, if you please – nice names. For I am not going to tell you *my* name, not yet at any rate.' A queer half-knowing, half-humorous look came with a green flicker into his eyes. 'For one thing it would take a long while: my name is growing all the time, and I've lived a very long, long time; so *my* name is like a story. Real names tell you the story of the things they belong to in my language, in the Old Entish as you might say. It is a lovely language, but it takes a very long time to say anything in it, because we do not say anything in it, unless it is worth taking a long time to say, and to listen to.

'But now,' and the eyes became very bright and 'present', seeming to grow smaller and almost sharp, 'what is going on? What are you doing in it all? I can see and hear (*and* smell *and* feel) a great deal from this, from this, from this *a-lalla-lalla-rumba-kamanda-lind-or-burúmë*. Excuse me: that is a part of my name for it; I do not know what the word is in the outside languages: you know, the thing we are on, where I stand and look out on fine mornings, and think about the Sun, and the grass beyond the wood, and the horses, and the clouds, and the unfolding of the world. What is going on? What is Gandalf up to? And these – *burárum*,' he made a deep rumbling noise like a discord on a great organ – 'these Orcs, and young Saruman down at Isengard? I like news. But not too quick now.'

'There is quite a lot going on,' said Merry; 'and even if we tried to be quick, it would take a long time to tell. But you told us not to be hasty. Ought we to tell you anything so soon? Would you think it rude, if we asked what you are going to do with us, and which side you are on? And did you know Gandalf?'

'Yes, I do know him: the only wizard that really cares about trees,' said Treebeard. 'Do you know him?'

'Yes,' said Pippin sadly, 'we did. He was a great friend, and he was our guide.'

'Then I can answer your other questions,' said Treebeard. 'I am not going to do anything *with* you: not if you mean by that "do something *to* you" without your leave. We might do some things together. I don't know about *sides*. I go my own way; but your way may go along with mine for a while. But you speak of Master Gandalf, as if he was in a story that had come to an end.'

'Yes, we do,' said Pippin sadly. 'The story seems to be going on, but I am afraid Gandalf has fallen out of it.'

'Hoo, come now!' said Treebeard. 'Hoom, hm, ah well.' He paused, looking long at the hobbits. 'Hoom, ah, well I do not know what to say. Come now!'

'If you would like to hear more,' said Merry, 'we will tell you. But it will take some time. Wouldn't you like to put us down? Couldn't we sit here together in the sun, while it lasts? You must be getting tired of holding us up.'

'Hm, *tired*? No, I am not tired. I do not easily get tired. And I do not sit down. I am not very, hm, bendable. But there, the Sun *is* going in. Let us leave this – did you say what you call it?'

'Hill?' suggested Pippin. 'Shelf? Step?' suggested Merry.

Treebeard repeated the words thoughtfully. '*Hill*. Yes, that was it. But it is a hasty word for a thing that has stood here ever since this part of the world was shaped. Never mind. Let us leave it, and go.'

'Where shall we go?' asked Merry.

'To my home, or one of my homes,' answered Treebeard.

'Is it far?'

'I do not know. You might call it far, perhaps. But what does that matter?'

'Well, you see, we have lost all our belongings,' said Merry. 'We have only a little food.'

'O! Hm! You need not trouble about that,' said Treebeard. 'I can give you a drink that will keep you green and growing for a long, long while.

And if we decide to part company, I can set you down outside my country at any point you choose. Let us go!'

Holding the hobbits gently but firmly, one in the crook of each arm, Treebeard lifted up first one large foot and then the other, and moved them to the edge of the shelf. The rootlike toes grasped the rocks. Then carefully and solemnly, he stalked down from step to step, and reached the floor of the Forest.

At once he set off with long deliberate strides through the trees, deeper and deeper into the wood, never far from the stream, climbing steadily up towards the slopes of the mountains. Many of the trees seemed asleep, or as unaware of him as of any other creature that merely passed by; but some quivered, and some raised up their branches above his head as he approached. All the while, as he walked, he talked to himself in a long running stream of musical sounds.

The hobbits were silent for some time. They felt, oddly enough, safe and comfortable, and they had a great deal to think and wonder about. At last Pippin ventured to speak again.

'Please, Treebeard,' he said, 'could I ask you something? Why did Celeborn warn us against your forest? He told us not to risk getting entangled in it.'

'Hmm, did he now?' rumbled Treebeard. 'And I might have said much the same, if you had been going the other way. Do not risk getting entangled in the woods of *Laurelindórenan*! That is what the Elves used to call it, but now they make the name shorter: *Lothlórien* they call it. Perhaps they are right: maybe it is fading, not growing. Land of the Valley of Singing Gold, that was it, once upon a time. Now it is the Dreamflower. Ah well! But it is a queer place, and not for just any one to venture in. I am surprised that you ever got out, but much more surprised that you ever got in: that has not happened to strangers for many a year. It is a queer land.

'And so is this. Folk have come to grief here. Aye, they have, to grief. *Laurelindórenan lindelorendor malinornélion ornemalin*,' he hummed to himself. 'They are falling rather behind the world in there, I guess,' he said. 'Neither this country, nor anything else outside the Golden Wood, is what it was when Celeborn was young. Still:

Taurelilómëa-tumbalemorna Tumbaletaurëa Lómëanor,*

that is what they used to say. Things have changed, but it is still true in places.'

---

* See Appendix F under *Ents*.

'What do you mean?' said Pippin. 'What is true?'

'The trees and the Ents,' said Treebeard. 'I do not understand all that goes on myself, so I cannot explain it to you. Some of us are still true Ents, and lively enough in our fashion, but many are growing sleepy, going tree-ish, as you might say. Most of the trees are just trees, of course; but many are half awake. Some are quite wide awake, and a few are, well, ah, well getting *Entish*. That is going on all the time.

'When that happens to a tree, you find that some have *bad* hearts. Nothing to do with their wood: I do not mean that. Why, I knew some good old willows down the Entwash, gone long ago, alas! They were quite hollow, indeed they were falling all to pieces, but as quiet and sweet-spoken as a young leaf. And then there are some trees in the valleys under the mountains, sound as a bell, and bad right through. That sort of thing seems to spread. There used to be some very dangerous parts in this country. There are still some very black patches.'

'Like the Old Forest away to the north, do you mean?' asked Merry.

'Aye, aye, something like, but much worse. I do not doubt there is some shadow of the Great Darkness lying there still away north; and bad memories are handed down. But there are hollow dales in this land where the Darkness has never been lifted, and the trees are older than I am. Still, we do what we can. We keep off strangers and the foolhardy; and we train and we teach, we walk and we weed.

'We are tree-herds, we old Ents. Few enough of us are left now. Sheep get like shepherd, and shepherds like sheep, it is said; but slowly, and neither have long in the world. It is quicker and closer with trees and Ents, and they walk down the ages together. For Ents are more like Elves: less interested in themselves than Men are, and better at getting inside other things. And yet again Ents are more like Men, more changeable than Elves are, and quicker at taking the colour of the outside, you might say. Or better than both: for they are steadier and keep their minds on things longer.

'Some of my kin look just like trees now, and need something great to rouse them; and they speak only in whispers. But some of my trees are limb-lithe, and many can talk to me. Elves began it, of course, waking trees up and teaching them to speak and learning their tree-talk. They always wished to talk to everything, the old Elves did. But then the Great Darkness came, and they passed away over the Sea, or fled into far valleys, and hid themselves, and made songs about days that would never come again. Never again. Aye, aye, there was all one wood once upon a time from here to the Mountains of Lune, and this was just the East End.

'Those were the broad days! Time was when I could walk and sing all day and hear no more than the echo of my own voice in the hollow hills.

The woods were like the woods of Lothlórien, only thicker, stronger, younger. And the smell of the air! I used to spend a week just breathing.'

Treebeard fell silent, striding along, and yet making hardly a sound with his great feet. Then he began to hum again, and passed into a murmuring chant. Gradually the hobbits became aware that he was chanting to them:

> In the willow-meads of Tasarinan I walked in the Spring.
> Ah! the sight and the smell of the Spring in Nan-tasarion!
> And I said that was good.
> I wandered in Summer in the elm-woods of Ossiriand.
> Ah! the light and the music in the Summer by the Seven Rivers
>   of Ossir!
> And I thought that was best.
> To the beeches of Neldoreth I came in the Autumn.
> Ah! the gold and the red and the sighing of leaves in the
>   Autumn in Taur-na-neldor!
> It was more than my desire.
> To the pine-trees upon the highland of Dorthonion I climbed in
>   the Winter.
> Ah! the wind and the whiteness and the black branches of
>   Winter upon Orod-na-Thôn!
> My voice went up and sang in the sky.
> And now all those lands lie under the wave,
> And I walk in Ambaróna, in Tauremorna, in Aldalómë,
> In my own land, in the country of Fangorn,
> Where the roots are long,
> And the years lie thicker than the leaves
> In Tauremornalómë.

He ended, and strode on silently, and in all the wood, as far as ear could reach, there was not a sound.

The day waned, and dusk was twined about the boles of the trees. At last the hobbits saw, rising dimly before them, a steep dark land: they had come to the feet of the mountains, and to the green roots of tall Methedras. Down the hillside the young Entwash, leaping from its springs high above, ran noisily from step to step to meet them. On the right of the stream there was a long slope, clad with grass, now grey in the twilight. No trees grew there and it was open to the sky; stars were shining already in lakes between shores of cloud.

Treebeard strode up the slope, hardly slackening his pace. Suddenly before them the hobbits saw a wide opening. Two great trees stood there, one on either side, like living gate-posts; but there was no gate save their crossing and interwoven boughs. As the old Ent approached, the trees lifted up their branches, and all their leaves quivered and rustled. For they were evergreen trees, and their leaves were dark and polished, and gleamed in the twilight. Beyond them was a wide level space, as though the floor of a great hall had been cut in the side of the hill. On either hand the walls sloped upwards, until they were fifty feet high or more, and along each wall stood an aisle of trees that also increased in height as they marched inwards.

At the far end the rock-wall was sheer, but at the bottom it had been hollowed back into a shallow bay with an arched roof: the only roof of the hall, save the branches of the trees, which at the inner end overshadowed all the ground leaving only a broad open path in the middle. A little stream escaped from the springs above, and leaving the main water, fell tinkling down the sheer face of the wall, pouring in silver drops, like a fine curtain in front of the arched bay. The water was gathered again into a stone basin in the floor between the trees, and thence it spilled and flowed away beside the open path, out to rejoin the Entwash in its journey through the forest.

'Hm! Here we are!' said Treebeard, breaking his long silence. 'I have brought you about seventy thousand ent-strides, but what that comes to in the measurement of your land I do not know. Anyhow we are near the roots of the Last Mountain. Part of the name of this place might be Wellinghall, if it were turned into your language. I like it. We will stay here tonight.' He set them down on the grass between the aisles of the trees, and they followed him towards the great arch. The hobbits now noticed that as he walked his knees hardly bent, but his legs opened in a great stride. He planted his big toes (and they were indeed big, and very broad) on the ground first, before any other part of his feet.

For a moment Treebeard stood under the rain of the falling spring, and took a deep breath; then he laughed, and passed inside. A great stone table stood there, but no chairs. At the back of the bay it was already quite dark. Treebeard lifted two great vessels and stood them on the table. They seemed to be filled with water; but he held his hands over them, and immediately they began to glow, one with a golden and the other with a rich green light; and the blending of the two lights lit the bay, as if the sun of summer was shining through a roof of young leaves. Looking back, the hobbits saw that the trees in the court had also begun to glow, faintly at first, but steadily quickening, until every leaf was edged with light: some green, some gold, some red as copper; while the tree-trunks looked like pillars moulded out of luminous stone.

'Well, well, now we can talk again,' said Treebeard. 'You are thirsty, I expect. Perhaps you are also tired. Drink this!' He went to the back of the bay, and then they saw that several tall stone jars stood there, with heavy lids. He removed one of the lids, and dipped in a great ladle, and with it filled three bowls, one very large bowl, and two smaller ones.

'This is an ent-house,' he said, 'and there are no seats, I fear. But you may sit on the table.' Picking up the hobbits he set them on the great stone slab, six feet above the ground, and there they sat dangling their legs, and drinking in sips.

The drink was like water, indeed very like the taste of the draughts they had drunk from the Entwash near the borders of the forest, and yet there was some scent or savour in it which they could not describe: it was faint, but it reminded them of the smell of a distant wood borne from afar by a cool breeze at night. The effect of the draught began at the toes, and rose steadily through every limb, bringing refreshment and vigour as it coursed upwards, right to the tips of the hair. Indeed the hobbits felt that the hair on their heads was actually standing up, waving and curling and growing. As for Treebeard, he first laved his feet in the basin beyond the arch, and then he drained his bowl at one draught, one long, slow draught. The hobbits thought he would never stop.

At last he set the bowl down again. 'Ah – ah,' he sighed. 'Hm, hoom, now we can talk easier. You can sit on the floor, and I will lie down; that will prevent this drink from rising to my head and sending me to sleep.'

On the right side of the bay there was a great bed on low legs, not more than a couple of feet high, covered deep in dried grass and bracken. Treebeard lowered himself slowly on to this (with only the slightest sign of bending at his middle), until he lay at full length, with his arms behind his head, looking up at the ceiling, upon which lights were flickering, like the play of leaves in the sunshine. Merry and Pippin sat beside him on pillows of grass.

'Now tell me your tale, and do not hurry!' said Treebeard.

The hobbits began to tell him the story of their adventures ever since they left Hobbiton. They followed no very clear order, for they interrupted one another continually, and Treebeard often stopped the speaker, and went back to some earlier point, or jumped forward asking questions about later events. They said nothing whatever about the Ring, and did not tell him why they set out or where they were going to; and he did not ask for any reasons.

He was immensely interested in everything: in the Black Riders, in Elrond, and Rivendell, in the Old Forest, and Tom Bombadil, in the Mines of Moria, and in Lothlórien and Galadriel. He made them describe the

Shire and its country over and over again. He said an odd thing at this point. 'You never see any, hm, any Ents round there, do you?' he asked. 'Well, not Ents, *Entwives* I should really say.'

'*Entwives?*' said Pippin. 'Are they like you at all?'

'Yes, hm, well no: I do not really know now,' said Treebeard thóughtfully. 'But they would like your country, so I just wondered.'

Treebeard was however especially interested in everything that concerned Gandalf; and most interested of all in Saruman's doings. The hobbits regretted very much that they knew so little about them: only a rather vague report by Sam of what Gandalf had told the Council. But they were clear at any rate that Uglúk and his troop came from Isengard, and spoke of Saruman as their master.

'Hm, hoom!' said Treebeard, when at last their story had wound and wandered down to the battle of the Orcs and the Riders of Rohan. 'Well, well! That is a bundle of news and no mistake. You have not told me all, no indeed, not by a long way. But I do not doubt that you are doing as Gandalf would wish. There is something very big going on, that I can see, and what it is maybe I shall learn in good time, or in bad time. By root and twig, but it is a strange business: up sprout a little folk that are not in the old lists, and behold! the Nine forgotten Riders reappear to hunt them, and Gandalf takes them on a great journey, and Galadriel harbours them in Caras Galadhon, and Orcs pursue them down all the leagues of Wilderland: indeed they seem to be caught up in a great storm. I hope they weather it!'

'And what about yourself?' asked Merry.

'Hoom, hm, I have not troubled about the Great Wars,' said Treebeard; 'they mostly concern Elves and Men. That is the business of Wizards: Wizards are always troubled about the future. I do not like worrying about the future. I am not altogether on anybody's *side*, because nobody is altogether on my *side*, if you understand me: nobody cares for the woods as I care for them, not even Elves nowadays. Still, I take more kindly to Elves than to others: it was the Elves that cured us of dumbness long ago, and that was a great gift that cannot be forgotten, though our ways have parted since. And there are some things, of course, whose side I am altogether *not* on; I am against them altogether: these – *burárum*' (he again made a deep rumble of disgust) '——these Orcs, and their masters.

'I used to be anxious when the shadow lay on Mirkwood, but when it removed to Mordor, I did not trouble for a while: Mordor is a long way away. But it seems that the wind is setting East, and the withering of all woods may be drawing near. There is naught that an old Ent can do to hold back that storm: he must weather it or crack.

'But Saruman now! Saruman is a neighbour: I cannot overlook him. I must do something, I suppose. I have often wondered lately what I should do about Saruman.'

'Who is Saruman?' asked Pippin. 'Do you know anything about his history?'

'Saruman is a Wizard,' answered Treebeard. 'More than that I cannot say. I do not know the history of Wizards. They appeared first after the Great Ships came over the Sea; but if they came with the Ships I never can tell. Saruman was reckoned great among them, I believe. He gave up wandering about and minding the affairs of Men and Elves, some time ago – you would call it a very long time ago; and he settled down at Angrenost, or Isengard as the Men of Rohan call it. He was very quiet to begin with, but his fame began to grow. He was chosen to be the head of the White Council, they say; but that did not turn out too well. I wonder now if even then Saruman was not turning to evil ways. But at any rate he used to give no trouble to his neighbours. I used to talk to him. There was a time when he was always walking about my woods. He was polite in those days, always asking my leave (at least when he met me); and always eager to listen. I told him many things that he would never have found out by himself; but he never repaid me in like kind. I cannot remember that he ever told me anything. And he got more and more like that; his face, as I remember it – I have not seen it for many a day – became like windows in a stone wall: windows with shutters inside.

'I think that I now understand what he is up to. He is plotting to become a Power. He has a mind of metal and wheels; and he does not care for growing things, except as far as they serve him for the moment. And now it is clear that he is a black traitor. He has taken up with foul folk, with the Orcs. Brm, hoom! Worse than that: he has been doing something to them; something dangerous. For these Isengarders are more like wicked Men. It is a mark of evil things that came in the Great Darkness that they cannot abide the Sun; but Saruman's Orcs can endure it, even if they hate it. I wonder what he has done? Are they Men he has ruined, or has he blended the races of Orcs and Men? That would be a black evil!'

Treebeard rumbled for a moment, as if he were pronouncing some deep, subterranean Entish malediction. 'Some time ago I began to wonder how Orcs dared to pass through my woods so freely,' he went on. 'Only lately did I guess that Saruman was to blame, and that long ago he had been spying out all the ways, and discovering my secrets. He and his foul folk are making havoc now. Down on the borders they are felling trees – good trees. Some of the trees they just cut down and leave to rot – orc-mischief that; but most are hewn up and carried off to feed the fires of Orthanc. There is always a smoke rising from Isengard these days.

'Curse him, root and branch! Many of those trees were my friends, creatures I had known from nut and acorn; many had voices of their own that are lost for ever now. And there are wastes of stump and bramble where once there were singing groves. I have been idle. I have let things slip. It must stop!'

Treebeard raised himself from his bed with a jerk, stood up, and thumped his hand on the table. The vessels of light trembled and sent up two jets of flame. There was a flicker like green fire in his eyes, and his beard stood out stiff as a great besom.

'I will stop it!' he boomed. 'And you shall come with me. You may be able to help me. You will be helping your own friends that way, too; for if Saruman is not checked Rohan and Gondor will have an enemy behind as well as in front. Our roads go together – to Isengard!'

'We will come with you,' said Merry. 'We will do what we can.'

'Yes!' said Pippin. 'I should like to see the White Hand overthrown. I should like to be there, even if I could not be of much use: I shall never forget Uglúk and the crossing of Rohan.'

'Good! Good!' said Treebeard. 'But I spoke hastily. We must not be hasty. I have become too hot. I must cool myself and think; for it is easier to shout *stop!* than to do it.'

He strode to the archway and stood for some time under the falling rain of the spring. Then he laughed and shook himself, and wherever the drops of water fell glittering from him to the ground they glinted like red and green sparks. He came back and laid himself on the bed again and was silent.

After some time the hobbits heard him murmuring again. He seemed to be counting on his fingers. 'Fangorn, Finglas, Fladrif, aye, aye,' he sighed. 'The trouble is that there are so few of us left,' he said turning towards the hobbits. 'Only three remain of the first Ents that walked in the woods before the Darkness: only myself, Fangorn, and Finglas and Fladrif – to give them their Elvish names; you may call them Leaflock and Skinbark if you like that better. And of us three, Leaflock and Skinbark are not much use for this business. Leaflock has grown sleepy, almost tree-ish, you might say: he has taken to standing by himself half-asleep all through the summer with the deep grass of the meadows round his knees. Covered with leafy hair he is. He used to rouse up in winter; but of late he has been too drowsy to walk far even then. Skinbark lived on the mountain-slopes west of Isengard. That is where the worst trouble has been. He was wounded by the Orcs, and many of his folk and his tree-herds have been murdered and destroyed. He has gone up into the high places, among the birches that he loves best, and he will not come down. Still, I daresay I could get together a fair company of our younger folks – if I could make them understand the need; if I could rouse them: we are not a hasty folk. What a pity there are so few of us!'

'Why are there so few, when you have lived in this country so long?' asked Pippin. 'Have a great many died?'

'Oh, no!' said Treebeard. 'None have died from inside, as you might say. Some have fallen in the evil chances of the long years, of course; and more have grown tree-ish. But there were never many of us and we have not increased. There have been no Entings – no children, you would say, not for a terrible long count of years. You see, we lost the Entwives.'

'How very sad!' said Pippin. 'How was it that they all died?'

'They did not die!' said Treebeard. 'I never said died. We lost them, I said. We lost them and we cannot find them.' He sighed. 'I thought most folk knew that. There were songs about the hunt of the Ents for the Entwives sung among Elves and Men from Mirkwood to Gondor. They cannot be quite forgotten.'

'Well, I am afraid the songs have not come west over the Mountains to the Shire,' said Merry. 'Won't you tell us some more, or sing us one of the songs?'

'Yes, I will indeed,' said Treebeard, seeming pleased with the request. 'But I cannot tell it properly, only in short; and then we must end our talk: tomorrow we have councils to call, and work to do, and maybe a journey to begin.'

'It is rather a strange and sad story,' he went on after a pause. 'When the world was young, and the woods were wide and wild, the Ents and the Entwives – and there were Entmaidens then: ah! the loveliness of Fimbrethil, of Wandlimb the lightfooted, in the days of our youth! – they walked together and they housed together. But our hearts did not go on growing in the same way: the Ents gave their love to things that they met in the world, and the Entwives gave their thought to other things, for the Ents loved the great trees, and the wild woods, and the slopes of the high hills; and they drank of the mountain-streams, and ate only such fruit as the trees let fall in their path; and they learned of the Elves and spoke with the Trees. But the Entwives gave their minds to the lesser trees, and to the meads in the sunshine beyond the feet of the forests; and they saw the sloe in the thicket, and the wild apple and the cherry blossoming in spring, and the green herbs in the waterlands in summer, and the seeding grasses in the autumn fields. They did not desire to speak with these things; but they wished them to hear and obey what was said to them. The Entwives ordered them to grow according to their wishes, and bear leaf and fruit to their liking; for the Entwives desired order, and plenty, and peace (by which they meant that things should remain where they had set them). So the Entwives made gardens to live in. But we Ents went on wandering, and we only came to the gardens now and again. Then when the Darkness came in the North, the Entwives crossed the Great River, and made new gardens, and tilled new fields, and we saw them more seldom. After the Darkness was overthrown the land of the Entwives blossomed richly, and their fields were full of corn. Many men learned the crafts of the Entwives and honoured them greatly; but we were only a legend to them, a secret in the heart of the forest. Yet here we still are, while all the gardens of the Entwives are wasted: Men call them the Brown Lands now.

'I remember it was long ago – in the time of the war between Sauron and the Men of the Sea – desire came over me to see Fimbrethil again. Very fair she was still in my eyes, when I had last seen her, though little like the Entmaiden of old. For the Entwives were bent and browned by their labour; their hair parched by the sun to the hue of ripe corn and their cheeks like red apples. Yet their eyes were still the eyes of our own people. We crossed over Anduin and came to their land; but we found a desert: it was all burned and uprooted, for war had passed over it. But the Entwives were not there. Long we called, and long we searched; and we asked all folk that we met which way the Entwives had gone. Some said they had never seen them; and some said that they had seen them walking away west, and some said east, and others south. But nowhere that we went could we find them. Our sorrow was very great. Yet the wild wood called, and we returned to it. For many years we used to go out every now and again and look for the Entwives, walking far and wide and calling them by their beautiful names. But as time passed we went more seldom and wandered less far. And now the Entwives are only a memory for us, and our beards are long and grey. The Elves made many songs concerning the Search of the Ents, and some of the songs passed into the tongues of Men. But we made no songs about it, being content to chant their beautiful names when we thought of the Entwives. We believe that we may meet again in a time to come, and perhaps we shall find somewhere a land where we can live together and both be content. But it is foreboded that that will only be when we have both lost all that we now have. And it may well be that that time is drawing near at last. For if Sauron of old destroyed the gardens, the Enemy today seems likely to wither all the woods.

'There was an Elvish song that spoke of this, or at least so I understand it. It used to be sung up and down the Great River. It was never an Entish song, mark you: it would have been a very long song in Entish! But we know it by heart, and hum it now and again. This is how it runs in your tongue:

ENT.   *When Spring unfolds the beechen leaf, and sap is in the bough;*
When light is on the wild-wood stream, and wind is on the brow;
When stride is long, and breath is deep, and keen the
    mountain-air,
Come back to me! Come back to me, and say my land is fair!

ENTWIFE.   *When Spring is come to garth and field, and corn is in the blade;*
When blossom like a shining snow is on the orchard laid;
When shower and Sun upon the Earth with fragrance fill the
    air,
I'll linger here, and will not come, because my land is fair.

ENT.   *When Summer lies upon the world, and in a noon of gold*
Beneath the roof of sleeping leaves the dreams of trees unfold;
When woodland halls are green and cool, and wind is in the
    West,
Come back to me! Come back to me, and say my land is best!

ENTWIFE.   *When Summer warms the hanging fruit and burns the berry*
    brown;
When straw is gold, and ear is white, and harvest comes to
    town;
When honey spills, and apple swells, though wind be in the
    West,
I'll linger here beneath the Sun, because my land is best!

ENT.   *When Winter comes, the winter wild that hill and wood shall*
    slay;
When trees shall fall and starless night devour the sunless day;
When wind is in the deadly East, then in the bitter rain
I'll look for thee, and call to thee; I'll come to thee again!

ENTWIFE.   *When Winter comes, and singing ends; when darkness falls at*
    last;
When broken is the barren bough, and light and labour past;
I'll look for thee, and wait for thee, until we meet again:
Together we will take the road beneath the bitter rain!

BOTH.   *Together we will take the road that leads into the West,*
And far away will find a land where both our hearts may rest.'

Treebeard ended his song. 'That is how it goes,' he said. 'It is Elvish, of course: lighthearted, quickworded, and soon over. I daresay it is fair enough. But the Ents could say more on their side, if they had time! But now I am going to stand up and take a little sleep. Where will you stand?'

'We usually lie down to sleep,' said Merry. 'We shall be all right where we are.'

'Lie down to sleep!' said Treebeard. 'Why of course you do! Hm, hoom:

I was forgetting: singing that song put me in mind of old times; almost thought that I was talking to young Entings, I did. Well, you can lie on the bed. I am going to stand in the rain. Good night!'

Merry and Pippin climbed on to the bed and curled up in the soft grass and fern. It was fresh, and sweet-scented, and warm. The lights died down, and the glow of the trees faded; but outside under the arch they could see old Treebeard standing, motionless, with his arms raised above his head. The bright stars peered out of the sky, and lit the falling water as it spilled on to his fingers and head, and dripped, dripped, in hundreds of silver drops on to his feet. Listening to the tinkling of the drops the hobbits fell asleep.

They woke to find a cool sun shining into the great court, and on to the floor of the bay. Shreds of high cloud were overhead, running on a stiff easterly wind. Treebeard was not to be seen; but while Merry and Pippin were bathing in the basin by the arch, they heard him humming and singing, as he came up the path between the trees.

'Hoo, ho! Good morning, Merry and Pippin!' he boomed, when he saw them. 'You sleep long. I have been many a hundred strides already today. Now we will have a drink, and go to Entmoot.'

He poured them out two full bowls from a stone jar; but from a different jar. The taste was not the same as it had been the night before: it was earthier and richer, more sustaining and food-like, so to speak. While the hobbits drank, sitting on the edge of the bed, and nibbling small pieces of elf-cake (more because they felt that eating was a necessary part of breakfast than because they felt hungry), Treebeard stood, humming in Entish or Elvish or some strange tongue, and looking up at the sky.

'Where is Entmoot?' Pippin ventured to ask.

'Hoo, eh? Entmoot?' said Treebeard, turning round. 'It is not a place, it is a gathering of Ents – which does not often happen nowadays. But I have managed to make a fair number promise to come. We shall meet in the place where we have always met: Derndingle Men call it. It is away south from here. We must be there before noon.'

Before long they set off. Treebeard carried the hobbits in his arms as on the previous day. At the entrance to the court he turned to the right, stepped over the stream, and strode away southwards along the feet of great tumbled slopes where trees were scanty. Above these the hobbits saw thickets of birch and rowan, and beyond them dark climbing pinewoods. Soon Treebeard turned a little away from the hills and plunged into deep groves, where the trees were larger, taller, and thicker than any that the hobbits had ever seen before. For a while they felt faintly the sense of stifling which they had noticed when they first ventured into Fangorn, but it soon passed. Treebeard did not talk to them. He hummed to himself deeply and thoughtfully, but Merry and Pippin caught no proper words: it sounded like *boom, boom, rumboom, boorar, boom boom, dahrar boom boom, dahrar boom,* and so on with a constant change of note and rhythm. Now and again they thought they heard an answer, a hum or a quiver of sound, that seemed to come out of the earth, or from boughs above their heads, or perhaps from the boles of the trees; but Treebeard did not stop or turn his head to either side.

They had been going for a long while – Pippin had tried to keep count of the 'ent-strides' but had failed, getting lost at about three thousand – when Treebeard began to slacken his pace. Suddenly he stopped, put the hobbits down, and raised his curled hands to his mouth so that they made a hollow tube; then he blew or called through them. A great *hoom, hom* rang out like a deep-throated horn in the woods, and seemed to echo from the trees. Far off there came from several directions a similar *hoom, hom, hoom* that was not an echo but an answer.

Treebeard now perched Merry and Pippin on his shoulders and strode on again, every now and then sending out another horn-call, and each time the answers came louder and nearer. In this way they came at last to what looked like an impenetrable wall of dark evergreen trees, trees of a kind that the hobbits had never seen before: they branched out right from the roots, and were densely clad in dark glossy leaves like thornless holly, and they bore many stiff upright flower-spikes with large shining olive-coloured buds.

Turning to the left and skirting this huge hedge Treebeard came in a few strides to a narrow entrance. Through it a worn path passed and dived suddenly down a long steep slope. The hobbits saw that they were descending into a great dingle, almost as round as a bowl, very wide and deep, crowned at the rim with the high dark evergreen hedge. It was smooth and grassclad inside, and there were no trees except three very tall and beautiful silver-birches that stood at the bottom of the bowl. Two other paths led down into the dingle: from the west and from the east.

Several Ents had already arrived. More were coming in down the other paths, and some were now following Treebeard. As they drew near the hobbits gazed at them. They had expected to see a number of creatures as much like Treebeard as one hobbit is like another (at any rate to a stranger's eye); and they were very much surprised to see nothing of the kind. The Ents were as different from one another as trees from trees: some as different as one tree is from another of the same name but quite different growth and history; and some as different as one tree-kind from another, as birch from beech, oak from fir. There were a few older Ents, bearded and gnarled like hale but ancient trees (though none looked as ancient as Treebeard);

and there were tall strong Ents, clean-limbed and smooth-skinned like forest-trees in their prime; but there were no young Ents, no saplings. Altogether there were about two dozen standing on the wide grassy floor of the dingle, and as many more were marching in.

At first Merry and Pippin were struck chiefly by the variety that they saw: the many shapes, and colours, the differences in girth, and height, and length of leg and arm; and in the number of toes and fingers (anything from three to nine). A few seemed more or less related to Treebeard, and reminded them of beech-trees or oaks. But there were other kinds. Some recalled the chestnut: brown-skinned Ents with large splayfingered hands, and short thick legs. Some recalled the ash: tall straight grey Ents with many-fingered hands and long legs; some the fir (the tallest Ents), and others the birch, the rowan, and the linden. But when the Ents all gathered round Treebeard, bowing their heads slightly, murmuring in their slow musical voices, and looking long and intently at the strangers, then the hobbits saw that they were all of the same kindred, and all had the same eyes: not all so old or so deep as Treebeard's, but all with the same slow, steady, thoughtful expression, and the same green flicker.

As soon as the whole company was assembled, standing in a wide circle round Treebeard, a curious and unintelligible conversation began. The Ents began to murmur slowly: first one joined and then another, until they were all chanting together in a long rising and falling rhythm, now louder on one side of the ring, now dying away there and rising to a great boom on the other side. Though he could not catch or understand any of the words – he supposed the language was Entish – Pippin found the sound very pleasant to listen to at first; but gradually his attention wavered. After a long time (and the chant showed no signs of slackening) he found himself wondering, since Entish was such an 'unhasty' language, whether they had yet got further than Good Morning; and if Treebeard was to call the roll, how many days it would take to sing all their names. 'I wonder what the Entish is for yes or no,' he thought. He yawned.

Treebeard was immediately aware of him. 'Hm, ha, hey, my Pippin!' he said, and the other Ents all stopped their chant. 'You are a hasty folk, I was forgetting; and anyway it is wearisome listening to a speech you do not understand. You may get down now. I have told your names to the Entmoot, and they have seen you, and they have agreed that you are not Orcs, and that a new line shall be put in the old lists. We have got no further yet, but that is quick work for an Entmoot. You and Merry can stroll about in the dingle, if you like. There is a well of good water, if you need refreshing, away yonder in the north bank. There are still some words to speak before the Moot really begins. I will come and see you again, and tell you how things are going.'

He put the hobbits down. Before they walked away, they bowed low. This feat seemed to amuse the Ents very much, to judge by the tone of their murmurs, and the flicker of their eyes; but they soon turned back to their own business. Merry and Pippin climbed up the path that came in from the west, and looked through the opening in the great hedge: Long tree-clad slopes rose from the lip of the dingle, and away beyond them, above the fir-trees of the furthest ridge there rose, sharp and white, the peak of a high mountain. Southwards to their left they could see the forest falling away down into the grey distance. There far away there was a pale green glimmer that Merry guessed to be a glimpse of the plains of Rohan.

'I wonder where Isengard is?' said Pippin.

'I don't know quite where we are,' said Merry; 'but that peak is probably Methedras, and as far as I can remember the ring of Isengard lies in a fork or deep cleft at the end of the mountains. It is probably down behind this great ridge. There seems to be a smoke or haze over there, left of the peak, don't you think?'

'What is Isengard like?' said Pippin. 'I wonder what Ents can do about it anyway.'

'So do I,' said Merry. 'Isengard is a sort of ring of rocks or hills, I think, with a flat space inside and an island or pillar of rock in the middle, called Orthanc. Saruman has a tower on it. There is a gate, perhaps more than one, in the encircling wall, and I believe there is a stream running through it; it comes out of the mountains, and flows on across the Gap of Rohan. It does not seem the sort of place for Ents to tackle. But I have an odd feeling about these Ents: somehow I don't think they are quite as safe and, well funny as they seem. They seem slow, queer, and patient, almost sad; and yet I believe they *could* be roused. If that happened, I would rather not be on the other side.'

'Yes!' said Pippin. 'I know what you mean. There might be all the difference between an old cow sitting and thoughtfully chewing, and a bull charging; and the change might come suddenly. I wonder if Treebeard will rouse them. I am sure he means to try. But they don't like being roused. Treebeard got roused himself last night, and then bottled it up again.'

The hobbits turned back. The voices of the Ents were still rising and falling in their conclave. The sun had now risen high enough to look over the high hedge: it gleamed on the tops of the birches and lit the northward side of the dingle with a cool yellow light. There they saw a little glittering fountain. They walked along the rim of the great bowl at the feet of the evergreens – it was pleasant to feel cool grass about their toes again, and not to be in a hurry – and then they climbed down to the gushing water. They drank a little, a clean, cold, sharp draught, and sat down on a mossy stone, watching the patches of sun on the grass and the shadows of the sailing clouds passing over the floor of the dingle. The murmur of the Ents went on. It seemed a very strange and remote place, outside their world, and far from everything that had ever happened to them. A great longing came over them for the faces and voices of their companions, especially for Frodo and Sam, and for Strider.

At last there came a pause in the Ent-voices; and looking up they saw Treebeard coming towards them, with another Ent at his side.

'Hm, hoom, here I am again,' said Treebeard. 'Are you getting weary, or feeling impatient, hmm, eh? Well, I am afraid that you must not get impatient yet. We have finished the first stage now; but I have still got to explain things again to those that live a long way off, far from Isengard, and those that I could not get round to before the Moot, and after that we shall have to decide what to do. However, deciding what to do does not take Ents so long as going over all the facts and events that they have to make up their minds about. Still, it is no use denying, we shall be here a long time yet: a couple of days very likely. So I have brought you a companion. He has an ent-house nearby. Bregalad is his Elvish name. He says he has already made up his mind and does not need to remain at the Moot. Hm, hm, he is the nearest thing among us to a hasty Ent. You ought to get on together. Good-bye!' Treebeard turned and left them.

Bregalad stood for some time surveying the hobbits solemnly; and they looked at him, wondering when he would show any signs of 'hastiness'. He was tall, and seemed to be one of the younger Ents; he had smooth shining skin on his arms and legs; his lips were ruddy, and his hair was grey-green. He could bend and sway like a slender tree in the wind. At last he spoke, and his voice though resonant was higher and clearer than Treebeard's.

'Ha, hmm, my friends, let us go for a walk!' he said. 'I am Bregalad, that is Quickbeam in your language. But it is only a nickname, of course. They have called me that ever since I said *yes* to an elder Ent before he had finished his question. Also I drink quickly, and go out while some are still wetting their beards. Come with me!'

He reached down two shapely arms and gave a long-fingered hand to each of the hobbits. All that day they walked about, in the woods with him, singing, and laughing; for Quickbeam often laughed. He laughed if the sun came out from behind a cloud, he laughed if they came upon a stream or spring: then he stooped and splashed his feet and head with water; he laughed sometimes at some sound or whisper in the trees. Whenever he saw a rowan-tree he halted a while with his arms stretched out, and sang, and swayed as he sang.

At nightfall he brought them to his ent-house: nothing more than a mossy stone set upon turves under a green bank. Rowan-trees grew in a circle about it, and there was water (as in all ent-houses), a spring bubbling out from the bank. They talked for a while as darkness fell on the forest. Not far away the voices of the Entmoot could be heard still going on; but now they seemed deeper and less leisurely, and every now and again one great voice would rise in a high and quickening music, while all the others died away. But beside them Bregalad spoke gently in their own tongue, almost whispering; and they learned that he belonged to Skinbark's people, and the country where they had lived had been ravaged. That seemed to the hobbits quite enough to explain his 'hastiness', at least in the matter of Orcs.

'There were rowan-trees in my home,' said Bregalad, softly and sadly, 'rowan-trees that took root when I was an Enting, many many years ago in the quiet of the world. The oldest were planted by the Ents to try and please the Entwives; but they looked at them and smiled and said that they knew where whiter blossom and richer fruit were growing. Yet there are no trees of all that race, the people of the Rose, that are so beautiful to me. And these trees grew and grew, till the shadow of each was like a green hall, and their red berries in the autumn were a burden, and a beauty and a wonder. Birds used to flock there. I like birds, even when they chatter; and the rowan has enough and to spare. But the birds became unfriendly and greedy and tore at the trees, and threw the fruit down and did not eat it. Then Orcs came with axes and cut down my trees. I came and called them by their long names, but they did not quiver, they did not hear or answer: they lay dead.

> O Orofarnë, Lassemista, Carnimírië!
> O rowan fair, upon your hair how white the blossom lay!
> O rowan mine, I saw you shine upon a summer's day,
> Your rind so bright, your leaves so light, your voice so cool and soft:
> Upon your head how golden-red the crown you bore aloft!
> O rowan dead, upon your head your hair is dry and grey;
> Your crown is spilled, your voice is stilled for ever and a day.
> O Orofarnë, Lassemista, Carnimírië!'

The hobbits fell asleep to the sound of the soft singing of Bregalad, that seemed to lament in many tongues the fall of trees that he had loved.

The next day they spent also in his company, but they did not go far from his 'house'. Most of the time they sat silent under the shelter of the bank; for the wind was colder, and the clouds closer and greyer; there was little sunshine, and in the distance the voices of the Ents at the Moot still rose and fell, sometimes loud and strong, sometimes low and sad, sometimes quickening, sometimes slow and solemn as a dirge. A second night came and still the Ents held conclave under hurrying clouds and fitful stars.

The third day broke, bleak and windy. At sunrise the Ents' voices rose to a great clamour and then died down again. As the morning wore on the wind fell and the air grew heavy with expectancy. The hobbits could see that Bregalad was now listening intently, although to them, down in the dell of his ent-house, the sound of the Moot was faint.

The afternoon came, and the sun, going west towards the mountains, sent out long yellow beams between the cracks and fissures of the clouds. Suddenly they were aware that everything was very quiet; the whole forest stood in listening silence. Of course, the Ent-voices had stopped. What did that mean? Bregalad was standing up erect and tense, looking back northwards towards Derndingle.

Then with a crash came a great ringing shout: *ra-hoom-rah!* The trees quivered and bent as if a gust had struck them. There was another pause, and then a marching music began like solemn drums, and above the rolling beats and booms there welled voices singing high and strong.

> *We come, we come with roll of drum: ta-runda runda*
> *runda rom!*

The Ents were coming: ever nearer and louder rose their song:

> *We come, we come with horn and drum: ta-rūna rūna*
> *rūna rom!*

Bregalad picked up the hobbits and strode from his house.

Before long they saw the marching line approaching: the Ents were swinging along with great strides down the slope towards them. Treebeard was at their head, and some fifty followers were behind him, two abreast, keeping step with their feet and beating time with their hands upon their flanks. As they drew near the flash and flicker of their eyes could be seen.

'Hoom, hom! Here we come with a boom, here we come at last!' called Treebeard when he caught sight of Bregalad and the hobbits. 'Come, join the Moot! We are off. We are off to Isengard!'

'To Isengard!' the Ents cried in many voices.

'To Isengard!'

To Isengard! Though Isengard be ringed and barred with doors
  of stone;
Though Isengard be strong and hard, as cold as stone and bare
  as bone,
We go, we go, we go to war, to hew the stone and break the door;
For bole and bough are burning now, the furnace roars – we go
  to war!
To land of gloom with tramp of doom, with roll of drum, we come, we
  come;
    To Isengard with doom we come!
  With doom we come, with doom we come!

So they sang as they marched southwards.

Bregalad, his eyes shining, swung into the line beside Treebeard. The old Ent now took the hobbits back, and set them on his shoulders again, and so they rode proudly at the head of the singing company with beating hearts and heads held high. Though they had expected something to happen eventually, they were amazed at the change that had come over the Ents. It seemed now as sudden as the bursting of a flood that had long been held back by a dike.

'The Ents made up their minds rather quickly, after all, didn't they?' Pippin ventured to say after some time, when for a moment the singing paused, and only the beating of hands and feet was heard.

'Quickly?' said Treebeard. 'Hoom! Yes, indeed. Quicker than I expected. Indeed I have not seen them roused like this for many an age. We Ents do not like being roused; and we never are roused unless it is clear to us that our trees and our lives are in great danger. That has not happened in this Forest since the wars of Sauron and the Men of the Sea. It is the orc-work, the wanton hewing – *rárum* – without even the bad excuse of feeding the fires, that has so angered us; and the treachery of a neighbour, who should have helped us. Wizards ought to know better: they do know better. There is no curse in Elvish, Entish, or the tongues of Men bad enough for such treachery. Down with Saruman!'

'Will you really break the doors of Isengard?' asked Merry.

'Ho, hm, well, we could, you know! You do not know, perhaps, how strong we are. Maybe you have heard of Trolls? They are mighty strong. But Trolls are only counterfeits, made by the Enemy in the Great Darkness, in mockery of Ents, as Orcs were of Elves. We are stronger than Trolls. We are made of the bones of the earth. We can split stone like the roots of trees, only quicker, far quicker, if our minds are roused! If we are not hewn down, or destroyed by fire or blast of sorcery, we could split Isengard into splinters and crack its walls into rubble.'

'But Saruman will try to stop you, won't he?'

'Hm, ah, yes, that is so. I have not forgotten it. Indeed I have thought long about it. But, you see, many of the Ents are younger than I am, by many lives of trees. They are all roused now, and their mind is all on one thing: breaking Isengard. But they will start thinking again before long; they will cool down a little, when we take our evening drink. What a thirst we shall have! But let them march now and sing! We have a long way to go, and there is time ahead for thought. It is something to have started.'

Treebeard marched on, singing with the others for a while. But after a time his voice died to a murmur and fell silent again. Pippin could see that his old brow was wrinkled and knotted. At last he looked up, and Pippin could see a sad look in his eyes, sad but not unhappy. There was a light in them, as if the green flame had sunk deeper into the dark wells of his thought.

'Of course, it is likely enough, my friends,' he said slowly, 'likely enough that we are going to our doom: the last march of the Ents. But if we stayed at home and did nothing, doom would find us anyway, sooner or later. That thought has long been growing in our hearts; and that is why we are marching now. It was not a hasty resolve. Now at least the last march of the Ents may be worth a song. Aye,' he sighed, 'we may help the other peoples before we pass away. Still, I should have liked to see the songs come true about the Entwives. I should dearly have liked to see Fimbrethil again. But there, my friends, songs like trees bear fruit only in their own time and their own way: and sometimes they are withered untimely.'

The Ents went striding on at a great pace. They had descended into a long fold of the land that fell away southward; now they began to climb up, and up, on to the high western ridge. The woods fell away and they came to scattered groups of birch, and then to bare slopes where only a few gaunt pine-trees grew. The sun sank behind the dark hill-back in front. Grey dusk fell.

Pippin looked behind. The number of the Ents had grown – or what was happening? Where the dim bare slopes that they had crossed should lie, he thought he saw groves of trees. But they were moving! Could it be that the trees of Fangorn were awake, and the forest was rising, marching over the hills to war? He rubbed his eyes wondering if sleep and shadow had deceived him; but the great grey shapes moved steadily onward. There was a noise like wind in many branches. The Ents were drawing near the crest of the ridge now, and all song had ceased. Night fell, and there was silence: nothing was to be heard save a faint quiver of the earth beneath

the feet of the Ents, and a rustle, the shade of a whisper as of many drifting
leaves. At last they stood upon the summit, and looked down into a dark
pit: the great cleft at the end of the mountains: Nan Curunír, the Valley
of Saruman.

'Night lies over Isengard,' said Treebeard.

CHAPTER V

THE WHITE RIDER

'My very bones are chilled,' said Gimli, flapping his arms and stamping his feet. Day had come at last. At dawn the companions had made such breakfast as they could; now in the growing light they were getting ready to search the ground again for signs of the hobbits.

'And do not forget that old man!' said Gimli. 'I should be happier if I could see the print of a boot.'

'Why would that make you happy?' said Legolas.

'Because an old man with feet that leave marks might be no more than he seemed,' answered the Dwarf.

'Maybe,' said the Elf; 'but a heavy boot might leave no print here: the grass is deep and springy.'

'That would not baffle a Ranger,' said Gimli. 'A bent blade is enough for Aragorn to read. But I do not expect him to find any traces. It was an evil phantom of Saruman that we saw last night. I am sure of it, even under the light of morning. His eyes are looking out on us from Fangorn even now, maybe.'

'It is likely enough,' said Aragorn; 'yet I am not sure. I am thinking of the horses. You said last night, Gimli, that they were scared away. But I did not think so. Did you hear them, Legolas? Did they sound to you like beasts in terror?'

'No,' said Legolas. 'I heard them clearly. But for the darkness and our own fear I should have guessed that they were beasts wild with some sudden gladness. They spoke as horses will when they meet a friend that they have long missed.'

'So I thought,' said Aragorn; 'but I cannot read the riddle, unless they return. Come! The light is growing fast. Let us look first and guess later! We should begin here, near to our own camping-ground, searching carefully all about, and working up the slope towards the forest. To find the hobbits is our errand, whatever we may think of our visitor in the night. If they escaped by some chance, then they must have hidden in the trees, or they would have been seen. If we find nothing between here and the eaves of the wood, then we will make a last search upon the battle-field and among the ashes. But there is little hope there: the horsemen of Rohan did their work too well.'

For some time the companions crawled and groped upon the ground.

The tree stood mournfully above them, its dry leaves now hanging limp, and rattling in the chill easterly wind. Aragorn moved slowly away. He came to the ashes of the watch-fire near the river-bank, and then began to retrace the ground back towards the knoll where the battle had been fought. Suddenly he stooped and bent low with his face almost in the grass. Then he called to the others. They came running up.

'Here at last we find news!' said Aragorn. He lifted up a broken leaf for them to see, a large pale leaf of golden hue, now fading and turning brown. 'Here is a mallorn-leaf of Lórien, and there are small crumbs on it, and a few more crumbs in the grass. And see! there are some pieces of cut cord lying nearby!'

'And here is the knife that cut them!' said Gimli. He stooped and drew out of a tussock, into which some heavy foot had trampled it, a short jagged blade. The haft from which it had been snapped was beside it. 'It was an orc-weapon,' he said, holding it gingerly, and looking with disgust at the carved handle: it had been shaped like a hideous head with squinting eyes and leering mouth.

'Well, here is the strangest riddle that we have yet found!' exclaimed Legolas. 'A bound prisoner escapes both from the Orcs and from the surrounding horsemen. He then stops, while still in the open, and cuts his bonds with an orc-knife. But how and why? For if his legs were tied, how did he walk? And if his arms were tied, how did he use the knife? And if neither were tied, why did he cut the cords at all? Being pleased with his skill, he then sat down and quietly ate some waybread! That at least is enough to show that he was a hobbit, without the mallorn-leaf. After that, I suppose, he turned his arms into wings and flew away singing into the trees. It should be easy to find him: we only need wings ourselves!'

'There was sorcery here right enough,' said Gimli. 'What was that old man doing? What have you to say, Aragorn, to the reading of Legolas. Can you better it?'

'Maybe, I could,' said Aragorn, smiling. 'There are some other signs near at hand that you have not considered. I agree that the prisoner was a hobbit and must have had either legs or hands free, before he came here. I guess that it was hands, because the riddle then becomes easier, and also because, as I read the marks, he was *carried* to this point by an Orc. Blood was spilled there, a few paces away, orc-blood. There are deep prints of hoofs all about this spot, and signs that a heavy thing was dragged away. The Orc was slain by horsemen, and later his body was hauled to the fire. But the hobbit was not seen: he was not "in the open", for it was night and he still had his elven-cloak. He was exhausted and hungry, and it is not to be wondered at that, when he had cut his bonds with the knife of his fallen enemy, he rested and ate a little before he crept away. But it is a comfort to know that he had some *lembas* in his pocket, even though he ran away without gear or pack; that, perhaps, is like a hobbit. I say *he*, though I hope and guess that both Merry and Pippin were here together. There is, however, nothing to show that for certain.'

'And how do you suppose that either of our friends came to have a hand free?' asked Gimli.

'I do not know how it happened,' answered Aragorn. 'Nor do I know why an Orc was carrying them away. Not to help them to escape, we may be sure. Nay, rather I think that I now begin to understand a matter that has puzzled me from the beginning: why when Boromir had fallen were the Orcs content with the capture of Merry and Pippin? They did not seek out the rest of us, nor attack our camp; but instead they went with all speed towards Isengard. Did they suppose they had captured the Ring-bearer and his faithful comrade? I think not. Their masters would not dare to give such plain orders to Orcs, even if they knew so much themselves; they would not speak openly to them of the Ring: they are not trusty servants. But I think the Orcs had been commanded to capture *hobbits*, alive, at all costs. An attempt was made to slip out with the precious prisoners before the battle. Treachery perhaps, likely enough with such folk; some large and bold Orc may have been trying to escape with the prize alone, for his own ends. There, that is my tale. Others might be devised. But on this we may count in any case: one at least of our friends escaped. It is our task to find him and help him before we return to Rohan. We must not be daunted by Fangorn, since need drove him into that dark place.'

'I do not know which daunts me more: Fangorn, or the thought of the long road through Rohan on foot,' said Gimli.

'Then let us go to the forest,' said Aragorn.

It was not long before Aragorn found fresh signs. At one point, near the bank of the Entwash, he came upon footprints: hobbit-prints, but too light for much to be made of them. Then again beneath the bole of a great tree on the very edge of the wood more prints were discovered. The earth was bare and dry, and did not reveal much.

'One hobbit at least stood here for a while and looked back; and then he turned away into the forest,' said Aragorn.

'Then we must go in, too,' said Gimli. 'But I do not like the look of this Fangorn; and we were warned against it. I wish the chase had led anywhere else!'

'I do not think the wood feels evil, whatever tales may say,' said Legolas. He stood under the eaves of the forest, stooping forward, as if he were listening, and peering with wide eyes into the shadows. 'No, it is not evil; or what evil is in it is far away. I catch only the faintest echoes of dark places where the hearts of the trees are black. There is no malice near us; but there is watchfulness, and anger.'

'Well, it has no cause to be angry with me,' said Gimli. 'I have done it no harm.'

'That is just as well,' said Legolas. 'But nonetheless it has suffered harm. There is something happening inside, or going to happen. Do you not feel the tenseness? It takes my breath.'

'I feel the air is stuffy,' said the Dwarf. 'This wood is lighter than Mirkwood, but it is musty and shabby.'

'It is old, very old,' said the Elf. 'So old that almost I feel young again, as I have not felt since I journeyed with you children. It is old and full of memory. I could have been happy here, if I had come in days of peace.'

'I dare say you could,' snorted Gimli. 'You are a Wood-elf, anyway, though Elves of any kind are strange folk. Yet you comfort me. Where you go, I will go. But keep your bow ready to hand, and I will keep my axe loose in my belt. Not for use on trees,' he added hastily, looking up at the tree under which they stood. 'I do not wish to meet that old man at unawares without an argument ready to hand, that is all. Let us go!'

With that the three hunters plunged into the forest of Fangorn. Legolas and Gimli left the tracking to Aragorn. There was little for him to see. The floor of the forest was dry and covered with a drift of leaves; but guessing that the fugitives would stay near the water, he returned often to the banks of the stream. So it was that he came upon the place where Merry and Pippin had drunk and bathed their feet. There plain for all to see were the footprints of two hobbits, one somewhat smaller than the other.

'This is good tidings,' said Aragorn. 'Yet the marks are two days old. And it seems that at this point the hobbits left the water-side.'

'Then what shall we do now?' said Gimli. 'We cannot pursue them through the whole fastness of Fangorn. We have come ill supplied. If we do not find them soon, we shall be of no use to them, except to sit down beside them and show our friendship by starving together.'

'If that is indeed all we can do, then we must do that,' said Aragorn. 'Let us go on.'

They came at length to the steep abrupt end of Treebeard's Hill, and looked up at the rock-wall with its rough steps leading to the high shelf. Gleams of sun were striking through the hurrying clouds, and the forest now looked less grey and drear.

'Let us go up and look about us!' said Legolas. 'I still feel my breath short. I should like to taste a freer air for a while.'

The companions climbed up. Aragorn came last, moving slowly: he was scanning the steps and ledges closely.

'I am almost sure that the hobbits have been up here,' he said. 'But there are other marks, very strange marks, which I do not understand. I wonder if we can see anything from this ledge which will help us to guess which way they went next?'

He stood up and looked about, but he saw nothing that was of any use. The shelf faced southward and eastward; but only on the east was the view open. There he could see the heads of the trees descending in ranks towards the plain from which they had come.

'We have journeyed a long way round,' said Legolas. 'We could have all come here safe together, if we had left the Great River on the second or third day and struck west. Few can foresee whither their road will lead them, till they come to its end.'

'But we did not wish to come to Fangorn,' said Gimli.

'Yet here we are – and nicely caught in the net,' said Legolas. 'Look!'

'Look at what?' said Gimli.

'There in the trees.'

'Where? I have not elf-eyes.'

'Hush! Speak more softly! Look!' said Legolas pointing. 'Down in the wood, back in the way that we have just come. It is he. Cannot you see him, passing from tree to tree?'

'I see, I see now!' hissed Gimli. 'Look, Aragorn! Did I not warn you? There is the old man. All in dirty grey rags: that is why I could not see him at first.'

Aragorn looked and beheld a bent figure moving slowly. It was not far away. It looked like an old beggar-man, walking wearily, leaning on a rough staff. His head was bowed, and he did not look towards them. In other lands they would have greeted him with kind words; but now they stood silent, each feeling a strange expectancy: something was approaching that held a hidden power – or menace.

Gimli gazed with wide eyes for a while, as step by step the figure drew nearer. Then suddenly, unable to contain himself longer, he burst out: 'Your bow, Legolas! Bend it! Get ready! It is Saruman. Do not let him speak, or put a spell upon us! Shoot first!'

Legolas took his bow and bent it, slowly and as if some other will resisted him. He held an arrow loosely in his hand but did not fit it to the string. Aragorn stood silent, his face was watchful and intent.

'Why are you waiting? What is the matter with you?' said Gimli in a hissing whisper.

'Legolas is right,' said Aragorn quietly. 'We may not shoot an old man so, at unawares and unchallenged, whatever fear or doubt be on us. Watch and wait!'

At that moment the old man quickened his pace and came with surprising speed to the foot of the rock-wall. Then suddenly he looked up, while they stood motionless looking down. There was no sound.

They could not see his face: he was hooded, and above the hood he wore a wide-brimmed hat, so that all his features were overshadowed, except for the end of his nose and his grey beard. Yet it seemed to Aragorn that he caught the gleam of eyes keen and bright from within the shadow of the hooded brows.

At last the old man broke the silence. 'Well met indeed, my friends,' he said in a soft voice. 'I wish to speak to you. Will you come down, or shall I come up?' Without waiting for an answer he began to climb.

'Now!' cried Gimli. 'Stop him, Legolas!'

'Did I not say that I wished to speak to you?' said the old man. 'Put away that bow, Master Elf!'

The bow and arrow fell from Legolas' hands, and his arms hung loose at his sides.

'And you, Master Dwarf, pray take your hand from your axe-haft, till I am up! You will not need such arguments.'

Gimli started and then stood still as stone, staring, while the old man sprang up the rough steps as nimbly as a goat. All weariness seemed to have left him. As he stepped up on to the shelf there was a gleam, too brief for certainty, a quick glint of white, as if some garment shrouded by the grey rags had been for an instant revealed. The intake of Gimli's breath could be heard as a loud hiss in the silence.

'Well met, I say again!' said the old man, coming towards them. When he was a few feet away, he stood, stooping over his staff, with his head thrust forward, peering at them from under his hood. 'And what may you be doing in these parts? An Elf, a Man, and a Dwarf, all clad in elvish fashion. No doubt there is a tale worth hearing behind it all. Such things are not often seen here.'

'You speak as one that knows Fangorn well,' said Aragorn. 'Is that so?'

'Not well,' said the old man: 'that would be the study of many lives. But I come here now and again.'

'Might we know your name, and then hear what it is that you have to say to us?' said Aragorn. 'The morning passes, and we have an errand that will not wait.'

'As for what I wished to say, I have said it: What may you be doing, and what tale can you tell of yourselves? As for my name!' He broke off, laughing long and softly. Aragorn felt a shudder run through him at the sound, a strange cold thrill; and yet it was not fear or terror that he felt: rather it was like the sudden bite of a keen air, or the slap of a cold rain that wakes an uneasy sleeper.

'My name!' said the old man again. 'Have you not guessed it already? You have heard it before, I think. Yes, you have heard it before. But come now, what of your tale?'

The three companions stood silent and made no answer.

'There are some who would begin to doubt whether your errand is fit to tell,' said the old man. 'Happily I know something of it. You are tracking the footsteps of two young hobbits, I believe. Yes, hobbits. Don't stare, as if you had never heard the strange name before. You have, and so have I. Well, they climbed up here the day before yesterday; and they met someone that they did not expect. Does that comfort you? And now you would like to know where they were taken? Well, well, maybe I can give you some news about that. But why are we standing? Your errand, you see, is no longer as urgent as you thought. Let us sit down and be more at ease.'

The old man turned away and went towards a heap of fallen stones and rock at the foot of the cliff behind. Immediately, as if a spell had been removed, the others relaxed and stirred. Gimli's hand went at once to his axe-haft. Aragorn drew his sword. Legolas picked up his bow.

The old man took no notice, but stooped and sat himself on a low flat stone. Then his grey cloak drew apart, and they saw, beyond doubt, that he was clothed beneath all in white.

'Saruman!' cried Gimli, springing towards him with axe in hand. 'Speak! Tell us where you have hidden our friends! What have you done with them? Speak, or I will make a dint in your hat that even a wizard will find it hard to deal with!'

The old man was too quick for him. He sprang to his feet and leaped to the top of a large rock. There he stood, grown suddenly tall, towering above them. His hood and his grey rags were flung away. His white garments shone. He lifted up his staff, and Gimli's axe leaped from his grasp and fell ringing on the ground. The sword of Aragorn, stiff in his motionless hand, blazed with a sudden fire. Legolas gave a great shout and shot an arrow high into the air: it vanished in a flash of flame.

'Mithrandir!' he cried. 'Mithrandir!'

'Well met, I say to you again, Legolas!' said the old man.

They all gazed at him. His hair was white as snow in the sunshine; and gleaming white was his robe; the eyes under his deep brows were bright, piercing as the rays of the sun; power was in his hand. Between wonder, joy, and fear they stood and found no words to say.

At last Aragorn stirred. 'Gandalf!' he said. 'Beyond all hope you return to us in our need! What veil was over my sight? Gandalf!' Gimli said nothing, but sank to his knees, shading his eyes.

'Gandalf,' the old man repeated, as if recalling from old memory a long disused word. 'Yes, that was the name. I was Gandalf.'

He stepped down from the rock, and picking up his grey cloak wrapped it about him: it seemed as if the sun had been shining, but now was hid in cloud again. 'Yes, you may still call me Gandalf,' he said, and the voice was the voice of their old friend and guide. 'Get up, my good Gimli! No blame to you, and no harm done to me. Indeed my friends, none of you have any weapon that could hurt me. Be merry! We meet again. At the turn of the tide. The great storm is coming, but the tide has turned.'

He laid his hand on Gimli's head, and the Dwarf looked up and laughed suddenly. 'Gandalf!' he said. 'But you are all in white!'

'Yes, I am white now,' said Gandalf. 'Indeed I *am* Saruman, one might almost say, Saruman as he should have been. But come now, tell me of yourselves! I have passed through fire and deep water, since we parted. I have forgotten much that I thought I knew, and learned again much that I had forgotten. I can see many things far off, but many things that are close at hand I cannot see. Tell me of yourselves!'

'What do you wish to know?' said Aragorn. 'All that has happened since we parted on the bridge would be a long tale. Will you not first give us news of the hobbits? Did you find them, and are they safe?'

'No, I did not find them,' said Gandalf. 'There was a darkness over the valleys of the Emyn Muil, and I did not know of their captivity, until the eagle told me.'

'The eagle!' said Legolas. 'I have seen an eagle high and far off: the last time was three days ago, above the Emyn Muil.'

'Yes,' said Gandalf, 'that was Gwaihir the Windlord, who rescued me from Orthanc. I sent him before me to watch the River and gather tidings. His sight is keen, but he cannot see all that passes under hill and tree. Some things he has seen, and others I have seen myself. The Ring now has passed beyond my help, or the help of any of the Company that set out from Rivendell. Very nearly it was revealed to the Enemy, but it escaped. I had some part in that: for I sat in a high place, and I strove with the Dark Tower; and the Shadow passed. Then I was weary, very weary; and I walked long in dark thought.'

'Then you know about Frodo!' said Gimli. 'How do things go with him?'

'I cannot say. He was saved from a great peril, but many lie before him still. He resolved to go alone to Mordor, and he set out: that is all that I can say.'

'Not alone,' said Legolas. 'We think that Sam went with him.'

'Did he!' said Gandalf, and there was a gleam in his eye and a smile on his face. 'Did he indeed? It is news to me, yet it does not surprise me. Good! Very good! You lighten my heart. You must tell me more. Now sit by me and tell me the tale of your journey.'

The companions sat on the ground at his feet, and Aragorn took up the tale. For a long while Gandalf said nothing, and he asked no questions. His hands were spread upon his knees, and his eyes were closed. At last when Aragorn spoke of the death of Boromir and of his last journey upon the Great River, the old man sighed.

'You have not said all that you know or guess, Aragorn my friend,' he said quietly. 'Poor Boromir! I could not see what happened to him. It was a sore trial for such a man: a warrior, and a lord of men. Galadriel told me that he was in peril. But he escaped in the end. I am glad. It was not in vain that the young hobbits came with us, if only for Boromir's sake. But that is not the only part they have to play. They were brought to Fangorn, and their coming was like the falling of small stones that starts an avalanche in the mountains. Even as we talk here, I hear the first rumblings. Saruman had best not be caught away from home when the dam bursts!'

'In one thing you have not changed, dear friend,' said Aragorn: 'you still speak in riddles.'

'What? In riddles?' said Gandalf. 'No! For I was talking aloud to myself. A habit of the old: they choose the wisest person present to speak to; the long explanations needed by the young are wearying.' He laughed, but the sound now seemed warm and kindly as a gleam of sunshine.

'I am no longer young even in the reckoning of Men of the Ancient Houses,' said Aragorn. 'Will you not open your mind more clearly to me?'

'What then shall I say?' said Gandalf, and paused for a while in thought. 'This in brief is how I see things at the moment, if you wish to have a piece of my mind as plain as possible. The Enemy, of course, has long known that the Ring is abroad, and that it is borne by a hobbit. He knows now the number of our Company that set out from Rivendell, and the kind of each of us. But he does not yet perceive our purpose clearly. He supposes that we were all going to Minas Tirith; for that is what he would himself have done in our place. And according to his wisdom it would have been a heavy stroke against his power. Indeed he is in great fear, not knowing what mighty one may suddenly appear, wielding the Ring, and assailing him with war, seeking to cast him down and take his place. That we should wish to cast him down and have *no* one in his place is not a thought that occurs to his mind. That we should try to destroy the Ring itself has not yet entered into his darkest dream. In which no doubt you will see our good fortune and our hope. For imagining war he has let loose war, believing that he has no time to waste; for he that strikes the first blow, if he strikes it hard enough, may need to strike no more. So the forces that he has long been preparing he is now setting in motion, sooner than he intended. Wise fool. For if he had used all his power to guard Mordor, so that none could enter, and bent all his guile to the hunting of the Ring, then indeed hope would have faded: neither Ring nor bearer could have eluded him. But now his eye gazes abroad rather than near at home; and mostly he looks towards Minas Tirith. Very soon now his strength will fall upon it like a storm.

'For already he knows that the messengers that he sent to waylay the Company have failed again. They have not found the Ring. Neither have they brought away any hobbits as hostages. Had they done even so much as that, it would have been a heavy blow to us, and it might have been fatal. But let us not darken our hearts by imagining the trial of their gentle loyalty in the Dark Tower. For the Enemy has failed – so far. Thanks to Saruman.'

'Then is not Saruman a traitor?' said Gimli.

'Indeed yes,' said Gandalf. 'Doubly. And is not that strange? Nothing that we have endured of late has seemed so grievous as the treason of Isengard. Even reckoned as a lord and captain Saruman has grown very strong. He threatens the Men of Rohan and draws off their help from Minas Tirith, even as the main blow is approaching from the East. Yet a treacherous weapon is ever a danger to the hand. Saruman also had a mind to capture the Ring, for himself, or at least to snare some hobbits for his evil purposes. So between them our enemies have contrived only to bring Merry and Pippin with marvellous speed, and in the nick of time, to Fangorn, where otherwise they would never have come at all!

'Also they have filled themselves with new doubts that disturb their plans. No tidings of the battle will come to Mordor, thanks to the horsemen of Rohan; but the Dark Lord knows that two hobbits were taken in the Emyn Muil and borne away towards Isengard against the will of his own servants. He now has Isengard to fear as well as Minas Tirith. If Minas Tirith falls, it will go ill with Saruman.'

'It is a pity that our friends lie in between,' said Gimli. 'If no land divided Isengard and Mordor, then they could fight while we watched and waited.'

'The victor would emerge stronger than either, and free from doubt,' said Gandalf. 'But Isengard cannot fight Mordor, unless Saruman first obtains the Ring. That he will never do now. He does not yet know his peril. There is much that he does not know. He was so eager to lay his hands on his prey that he could not wait at home, and he came forth to meet and to spy on his messengers. But he came too late, for once, and the battle was over and beyond his help before he reached these parts. He did not remain here long. I look into his mind and I see his doubt. He has no woodcraft. He believes that the horsemen slew and burned all upon the field of battle; but he does not know whether the Orcs were bringing any prisoners or not. And he does not know of the quarrel between his servants and the Orcs of Mordor; nor does he know of the Winged Messenger.'

'The Winged Messenger!' cried Legolas. 'I shot at him with the bow of Galadriel above Sarn Gebir, and I felled him from the sky. He filled us all with fear. What new terror is this?'

'One that you cannot slay with arrows,' said Gandalf. 'You only slew his steed. It was a good deed; but the Rider was soon horsed again. For he was a Nazgûl, one of the Nine, who ride now upon winged steeds. Soon their terror will overshadow the last armies of our friends, cutting off the sun. But they have not yet been allowed to cross the River, and Saruman does not know of this new shape in which the Ringwraiths have been clad. His thought is ever on the Ring. Was it present in the battle? Was it found? What if Théoden, Lord of the Mark, should come by it and learn of its power? That is the danger that he sees, and he has fled back to Isengard to double and treble his assault on Rohan. And all the time there is another danger, close at hand, which he does not see, busy with his fiery thoughts. He has forgotten Treebeard.'

'Now you speak to yourself again,' said Aragorn with a smile. 'Treebeard is not known to me. And I have guessed part of Saruman's double treachery; yet I do not see in what way the coming of two hobbits to Fangorn has served, save to give us a long and fruitless chase.'

'Wait a minute!' cried Gimli. 'There is another thing that I should like to know first. Was it you, Gandalf, or Saruman that we saw last night?'

'You certainly did not see me,' answered Gandalf, 'therefore I must guess that you saw Saruman. Evidently we look so much alike that your desire to make an incurable dent in my hat must be excused.'

'Good, good!' said Gimli. 'I am glad that it was not you.'

Gandalf laughed again. 'Yes, my good Dwarf,' he said, 'it is a comfort not to be mistaken at all points. Do I not know it only too well! But, of course, I never blamed you for your welcome of me. How could I do so, who have so often counselled my friends to suspect even their own hands when dealing with the Enemy. Bless you, Gimli, son of Glóin! Maybe you will see us both together one day and judge between us!'

'But the hobbits!' Legolas broke in. 'We have come far to seek them, and you seem to know where they are. Where are they now?'

'With Treebeard and the Ents,' said Gandalf.

'The Ents!' exclaimed Aragorn. 'Then there is truth in the old legends about the dwellers in the deep forests and the giant shepherds of the trees? Are there still Ents in the world? I thought they were only a memory of ancient days, if indeed they were ever more than a legend of Rohan.'

'A legend of Rohan!' cried Legolas. 'Nay, every Elf in Wilderland has sung songs of the old Onodrim and their long sorrow. Yet even among us they are only a memory. If I were to meet one still walking in this world, then indeed I should feel young again! But Treebeard: that is only a rendering of Fangorn into the Common Speech; yet you seem to speak of a person. Who is this Treebeard?'

'Ah! now you are asking much,' said Gandalf. 'The little that I know of his long slow story would make a tale for which we have no time now. Treebeard is Fangorn, the guardian of the forest; he is the oldest of the Ents, the oldest living thing that still walks beneath the Sun upon this Middle-earth. I hope indeed, Legolas, that you may yet meet him. Merry and Pippin have been fortunate: they met him here, even where we sit. For he came here two days ago and bore them away to his dwelling far off by the roots of the mountains. He often comes here, especially when his mind is uneasy, and rumours of the world outside trouble him. I saw him four days ago striding among the trees, and I think he saw me, for he paused; but I did not speak, for I was heavy with thought, and weary after my struggle with the Eye of Mordor; and he did not speak either, nor call my name.'

'Perhaps he also thought that you were Saruman,' said Gimli. 'But you speak of him as if he was a friend. I thought Fangorn was dangerous.

'Dangerous!' cried Gandalf. 'And so am I, very dangerous: more dangerous than anything you will ever meet, unless you are brought alive before the seat of the Dark Lord. And Aragorn is dangerous, and Legolas is dangerous. You are beset with dangers, Gimli son of Glóin; for you are dangerous yourself, in your own fashion. Certainly the forest of Fangorn is perilous – not least to those that are too ready with their axes; and Fangorn himself, he is perilous too; yet he is wise and kindly nonetheless. But now his long slow wrath is brimming over, and all the forest is filled with it. The coming of the hobbits and the tidings that they brought have spilled it: it will soon be running like a flood; but its tide is turned against Saruman and the axes of Isengard. A thing is about to happen which has not happened since the Elder Days: the Ents are going to wake up and find that they are strong.'

'What will they do?' asked Legolas in astonishment.

'I do not know,' said Gandalf. 'I do not think they know themselves. I wonder.' He fell silent, his head bowed in thought.

The others looked at him. A gleam of sun through fleeting clouds fell on his hands, which lay now upturned on his lap: they seemed to be filled with light as a cup is with water. At last he looked up and gazed straight at the sun.

'The morning is wearing away,' he said. 'Soon we must go.'

'Do we go to find our friends and to see Treebeard?' asked Aragorn.

'No,' said Gandalf. 'That is not the road that you must take. I have spoken words of hope. But only of hope. Hope is not victory. War is upon us and all our friends, a war in which only the use of the Ring could give us surety of victory. It fills me with great sorrow and great fear: for much shall be destroyed and all may be lost. I am Gandalf, Gandalf the White, but Black is mightier still.'

He rose and gazed out eastward, shading his eyes, as if he saw things far away that none of them could see. Then he shook his head. 'No,' he said in a soft voice, 'it has gone beyond our reach. Of that at least let us be glad. We can no longer be tempted to use the Ring. We must go down to face a peril near despair, yet that deadly peril is removed.'

He turned. 'Come, Aragorn son of Arathorn!' he said. 'Do not regret your choice in the valley of the Emyn Muil, nor call it a vain pursuit. You chose amid doubts the path that seemed right: the choice was just, and it has been rewarded. For so we have met in time, who otherwise might have met too late. But the quest of your companions is over. Your next journey is marked by your given word. You must go to Edoras and seek out Théoden in his hall. For you are needed. The light of Andúril must now be uncovered in the battle for which it has so long waited. There is war in Rohan, and worse evil: it goes ill with Théoden.'

'Then are we not to see the merry young hobbits again?' said Legolas.

'I did not say so,' said Gandalf. 'Who knows? Have patience. Go where you must go, and hope! To Edoras! I go thither also.'

'It is a long way for a man to walk, young or old,' said Aragorn. 'I fear the battle will be over long ere I come there.'

'We shall see, we shall see,' said Gandalf. 'Will you come now with me?'

'Yes, we will set out together,' said Aragorn. 'But I do not doubt that you will come there before me, if you wish.' He rose and looked long at Gandalf. The others gazed at them in silence as they stood there facing one another. The grey figure of the Man, Aragorn son of Arathorn, was tall, and stern as stone, his hand upon the hilt of his sword; he looked as if some king out of the mists of the sea had stepped upon the shores of lesser men. Before him stooped the old figure, white, shining now as if with some light kindled within, bent, laden with years, but holding a power beyond the strength of kings.

'Do I not say truly, Gandalf,' said Aragorn at last, 'that you could go whithersoever you wished quicker than I? And this I also say: you are our captain and our banner. The Dark Lord has Nine. But we have One, mightier than they: the White Rider. He has passed through the fire and the abyss, and they shall fear him. We will go where he leads.'

'Yes, together we will follow you,' said Legolas. 'But first, it would ease my heart, Gandalf, to hear what befell you in Moria. Will you not tell us? Can you not stay even to tell your friends how you were delivered?'

'I have stayed already too long,' answered Gandalf. 'Time is short. But if there were a year to spend, I would not tell you all.'

'Then tell us what you will, and time allows!' said Gimli. 'Come, Gandalf, tell us how you fared with the Balrog!'

'Name him not!' said Gandalf, and for a moment it seemed that a cloud of pain passed over his face, and he sat silent, looking old as death. 'Long time I fell,' he said at last, slowly, as if thinking back with difficulty. 'Long I fell, and he fell with me. His fire was about me. I was burned. Then we plunged into the deep water and all was dark. Cold it was as the tide of death: almost it froze my heart.'

'Deep is the abyss that is spanned by Durin's Bridge, and none has measured it,' said Gimli.

'Yet it has a bottom, beyond light and knowledge,' said Gandalf. 'Thither I came at last, to the uttermost foundations of stone. He was with me still. His fire was quenched, but now he was a thing of slime, stronger than a strangling snake.

'We fought far under the living earth, where time is not counted. Ever he clutched me, and ever I hewed him, till at last he fled into dark tunnels. They were not made by Durin's folk, Gimli son of Glóin. Far, far below the deepest delvings of the Dwarves, the world is gnawed by nameless things. Even Sauron knows them not. They are older than he. Now I have walked there, but I will bring no report to darken the light of day. In that despair my enemy was my only hope, and I pursued him, clutching at his heel. Thus he brought me back at last to the secret ways of Khazad-dûm: too well he knew them all. Ever up now we went, until we came to the Endless Stair.'

'Long has that been lost,' said Gimli. 'Many have said that it was never made save in legend, but others say that it was destroyed.'

'It was made, and it had not been destroyed,' said Gandalf. 'From the lowest dungeon to the highest peak it climbed, ascending in unbroken spiral in many thousand steps, until it issued at last in Durin's Tower carved in the living rock of Zirakzigil, the pinnacle of the Silvertine.

'There upon Celebdil was a lonely window in the snow, and before it lay a narrow space, a dizzy eyrie above the mists of the world. The sun shone fiercely there, but all below was wrapped in cloud. Out he sprang, and even as I came behind, he burst into new flame. There was none to see, or perhaps in after ages songs would still be sung of the Battle of the Peak.' Suddenly Gandalf laughed. 'But what would they say in song? Those that looked up from afar thought that the mountain was crowned with storm. Thunder they heard, and lightning, they said, smote upon Celebdil, and leaped back broken into tongues of fire. Is not that enough? A great smoke rose about us, vapour and steam. Ice fell like rain. I threw down my enemy, and he fell from the high place and broke the mountain-side where he smote it in his ruin. Then darkness took me, and I strayed out of thought and time, and I wandered far on roads that I will not tell.

'Naked I was sent back – for a brief time, until my task is done. And naked I lay upon the mountain-top. The tower behind was crumbled into dust, the window gone; the ruined stair was choked with burned and broken stone. I was alone, forgotten, without escape upon the hard horn of the world. There I lay staring upward, while the stars wheeled over, and each day was as long as a life-age of the earth. Faint to my ears came the gathered rumour of all lands: the springing and the dying, the song and the weeping, and the slow everlasting groan of overburdened stone. And so at the last Gwaihir the Windlord found me again, and he took me up and bore me away.

'"Ever am I fated to be your burden, friend at need," I said.

'"A burden you have been," he answered, "but not so now. Light as a swan's feather in my claw you are. The Sun shines through you. Indeed I do not think you need me any more: were I to let you fall, you would float upon the wind."

'"Do not let me fall!" I gasped, for I felt life in me again. "Bear me to Lothlórien!"

'"That indeed is the command of the Lady Galadriel who sent me to look for you," he answered.

'Thus it was that I came to Caras Galadhon and found you but lately gone. I tarried there in the ageless time of that land where days bring healing not decay. Healing I found, and I was clothed in white. Counsel I gave and counsel took. Thence by strange roads I came, and messages I bring to some of you. To Aragorn I was bidden to say this:

> *Where now are the Dúnedain, Elessar, Elessar?*
> *Why do thy kinsfolk wander afar?*
> *Near is the hour when the Lost should come forth,*
> *And the Grey Company ride from the North.*
> *But dark is the path appointed for thee:*
> *The Dead watch the road that leads to the Sea.*

To Legolas she sent this word:

> *Legolas Greenleaf long under tree*
> *In joy thou hast lived. Beware of the Sea!*
> *If thou hearest the cry of the gull on the shore,*
> *Thy heart shall then rest in the forest no more.'*

Gandalf fell silent and shut his eyes.

'Then she sent me no message?' said Gimli and bent his head.

'Dark are her words,' said Legolas, 'and little do they mean to those that receive them.'

'That is no comfort,' said Gimli.

'What then?' said Legolas. 'Would you have her speak openly to you of your death?'

'Yes, if she had nought else to say.'

'What is that?' said Gandalf, opening his eyes. 'Yes, I think I can guess what her words may mean. Your pardon, Gimli! I was pondering the messages once again. But indeed she sent words to you, and neither dark nor sad.

'"To Gimli son of Glóin," she said, "give his Lady's greeting. Lock-bearer, wherever thou goest my thought goes with thee. But have a care to lay thine axe to the right tree!"'

'In happy hour you have returned to us, Gandalf,' cried the Dwarf, capering as he sang loudly in the strange dwarf-tongue. 'Come, come!' he shouted, swinging his axe. 'Since Gandalf's head is now sacred, let us find one that it is right to cleave!'

'That will not be far to seek,' said Gandalf, rising from his seat. 'Come! We have spent all the time that is allowed to a meeting of parted friends. Now there is need of haste.'

He wrapped himself again in his old tattered cloak, and led the way. Following him they descended quickly from the high shelf and made their way back through the forest, down the bank of the Entwash. They spoke no more words, until they stood again upon the grass beyond the eaves of Fangorn. There was no sign of their horses to be seen.

'They have not returned,' said Legolas. 'It will be a weary walk!'

'I shall not walk. Time presses,' said Gandalf. Then lifting up his head he gave a long whistle. So clear and piercing was the note that the others stood amazed to hear such a sound come from those old bearded lips. Three times he whistled; and then faint and far off it seemed to them that they heard the whinny of a horse borne up from the plains upon the eastern wind. They waited wondering. Before long there came the sound of hoofs, at first hardly more than a tremor of the ground perceptible only to Aragorn as he lay upon the grass, then growing steadily louder and clearer to a quick beat.

'There is more than one horse coming,' said Aragorn.

'Certainly,' said Gandalf. 'We are too great a burden for one.'

'There are three,' said Legolas, gazing out over the plain. 'See how they run! There is Hasufel, and there is my friend Arod beside him! But there is another that strides ahead: a very great horse. I have not seen his like before.'

'Nor will you again,' said Gandalf. 'That is Shadowfax. He is the chief of the *Mearas*, lords of horses, and not even Théoden, King of Rohan, has ever looked on a better. Does he not shine like silver, and run as smoothly as a swift stream? He has come for me: the horse of the White Rider. We are going to battle together.'

Even as the old wizard spoke, the great horse came striding up the slope towards them; his coat was glistening and his mane flowing in the wind of his speed. The two others followed, now far behind. As soon as Shadowfax saw Gandalf, he checked his pace and whinnied loudly; then trotting gently forward he stooped his proud head and nuzzled his great nostrils against the old man's neck.

Gandalf caressed him. 'It is a long way from Rivendell, my friend,' he said; 'but you are wise and swift and come at need. Far let us ride now together, and part not in this world again!'

Soon the other horses came up and stood quietly by, as if awaiting orders. 'We go at once to Meduseld, the hall of your master, Théoden,' said Gandalf, addressing them gravely. They bowed their heads. 'Time presses, so with your leave, my friends, we will ride. We beg you to use all the speed that you can. Hasufel shall bear Aragorn and Arod Legolas. I will set Gimli before me, and by his leave Shadowfax shall bear us both. We will wait now only to drink a little.'

'Now I understand a part of last night's riddle,' said Legolas as he sprang lightly upon Arod's back. 'Whether they fled at first in fear, or not, our horses met Shadowfax, their chieftain, and greeted him with joy. Did you know that he was at hand, Gandalf?'

'Yes, I knew,' said the wizard. 'I bent my thought upon him, bidding him to make haste; for yesterday he was far away in the south of this land. Swiftly may he bear me back again!'

Gandalf spoke now to Shadowfax, and the horse set off at a good pace, yet not beyond the measure of the others. After a little while he turned suddenly, and choosing a place where the banks were lower, he waded the river, and then led them away due south into a flat land, treeless and wide.

The wind went like grey waves through the endless miles of grass. There was no sign of road or track, but Shadowfax did not stay or falter.

'He is steering a straight course now for the halls of Théoden under the slopes of the White Mountains,' said Gandalf. 'It will be quicker so. The ground is firmer in the Eastemnet, where the chief northward track lies, across the river, but Shadowfax knows the way through every fen and hollow.'

For many hours they rode on through the meads and riverlands. Often the grass was so high that it reached above the knees of the riders, and their steeds seemed to be swimming in a grey-green sea. They came upon many hidden pools, and broad acres of sedge waving above wet and treacherous bogs; but Shadowfax found the way, and the other horses followed in his swath. Slowly the sun fell from the sky down into the West. Looking out over the great plain, far away the riders saw it for a moment like a red fire sinking into the grass. Low upon the edge of sight shoulders of the mountains glinted red upon either side. A smoke seemed to rise up and darken the sun's disc to the hue of blood, as if it had kindled the grass as it passed down under the rim of earth.

'There lies the Gap of Rohan,' said Gandalf. 'It is now almost due west of us. That way lies Isengard.'

'I see a great smoke,' said Legolas. 'What may that be?'

'Battle and war!' said Gandalf. 'Ride on!'

CHAPTER VI

THE KING OF THE GOLDEN HALL

They rode on through sunset, and slow dusk, and gathering night. When at last they halted and dismounted, even Aragorn was stiff and weary. Gandalf only allowed them a few hours' rest. Legolas and Gimli slept, and Aragorn lay flat, stretched upon his back; but Gandalf stood, leaning on his staff, gazing into the darkness, east and west. All was silent, and there was no sign or sound of living thing. The night was barred with long clouds, fleeting on a chill wind, when they arose again. Under the cold moon they went on once more, as swift as by the light of day.

Hours passed and still they rode on. Gimli nodded, and would have fallen from his seat, if Gandalf had not clutched and shaken him. Hasufel and Arod, weary but proud, followed their tireless leader, a grey shadow before them hardly to be seen. The miles went by. The waxing moon sank into the cloudy West.

A bitter chill came into the air. Slowly in the East the dark faded to a cold grey. Red shafts of light leapt above the black walls of the Emyn Muil far away upon their left. Dawn came clear and bright; a wind swept across their path, rushing through the bent grasses. Suddenly Shadowfax stood still and neighed. Gandalf pointed ahead.

'Look!' he cried, and they lifted their tired eyes. Before them stood the mountains of the South: white-tipped and streaked with black. The grass-lands rolled against the hills that clustered at their feet, and flowed up into many valleys still dim and dark, untouched by the light of dawn, winding their way into the heart of the great mountains. Immediately before the travellers the widest of these glens opened like a long gulf among the hills. Far inward they glimpsed a tumbled mountain-mass with one tall peak, at the mouth of the vale there stood like a sentinel a lonely height. About its feet there flowed, as a thread of silver, the stream that issued from the dale; upon its brow they caught, still far away, a glint in the rising sun, a glimmer of gold.

'Speak, Legolas!' said Gandalf. 'Tell us what you see there before us!'

Legolas gazed ahead, shading his eyes from the level shafts of the new-risen sun. 'I see a white stream that comes down from the snows,' he said. 'Where it issues from the shadow of the vale a green hill rises upon the east. A dike and mighty wall and thorny fence encircle it. Within there rise the roofs of houses; and in the midst, set upon a green terrace, there stands aloft a great hall of Men. And it seems to my eyes that it is thatched with gold. The light of it shines far over the land. Golden, too, are the posts of its doors. There men in bright mail stand; but all else within the courts are yet asleep.'

'Edoras those courts are called,' said Gandalf, 'and Meduseld is that golden hall. There dwells Théoden son of Thengel, King of the Mark of Rohan. We are come with the rising of the day. Now the road lies plain to see before us. But we must ride more warily; for war is abroad, and the Rohirrim, the Horse-lords, do not sleep, even if it seem so from afar. Draw no weapon, speak no haughty word, I counsel you all, until we are come before Théoden's seat.'

The morning was bright and clear about them, and birds were singing, when the travellers came to the stream. It ran down swiftly into the plain, and beyond the feet of the hills turned across their path in a wide bend, flowing away east to feed the Entwash far off in its reed-choked beds. The land was green: in the wet meads and along the grassy borders of the stream grew many willow-trees. Already in this southern land they were blushing red at their fingertips, feeling the approach of spring. Over the stream there was a ford between low banks much trampled by the passage of horses. The travellers passed over and came upon a wide rutted track leading towards the uplands.

At the foot of the walled hill the way ran under the shadow of many mounds, high and green. Upon their western sides the grass was white as with a drifted snow: small flowers sprang there like countless stars amid the turf.

'Look!' said Gandalf. 'How fair are the bright eyes in the grass! Evermind they are called, *simbelmynë* in this land of Men, for they blossom in all the seasons of the year, and grow where dead men rest. Behold! we are come to the great barrows where the sires of Théoden sleep.'

'Seven mounds upon the left, and nine upon the right,' said Aragorn. 'Many long lives of men it is since the golden hall was built.'

'Five hundred times have the red leaves fallen in Mirkwood in my home since then,' said Legolas, 'and but a little while does that seem to us.'

'But to the Riders of the Mark it seems so long ago,' said Aragorn, 'that the raising of this house is but a memory of song, and the years before are lost in the mist of time. Now they call this land their home, their own, and their speech is sundered from their northern kin.' Then he began to chant softly in a slow tongue unknown to the Elf and Dwarf; yet they listened, for there was a strong music in it.

'That, I guess, is the language of the Rohirrim,' said Legolas; 'for it is like to this land itself; rich and rolling in part, and else hard and stern as the mountains. But I cannot guess what it means, save that it is laden with the sadness of Mortal Men.'

'It runs thus in the Common Speech,' said Aragorn, 'as near as I can make it.

Where now the horse and the rider? Where is the horn that was blowing?
Where is the helm and the hauberk, and the bright hair flowing?
Where is the hand on the harpstring, and the red fire glowing?
Where is the spring and the harvest and the tall corn growing?
They have passed like rain on the mountain, like a wind in the meadow;
The days have gone down in the West behind the hills into shadow.
Who shall gather the smoke of the dead wood burning,
Or behold the flowing years from the Sea returning?

Thus spoke a forgotten poet long ago in Rohan, recalling how tall and fair was Eorl the Young, who rode down out of the North; and there were wings upon the feet of his steed, Felaróf, father of horses. So men still sing in the evening.'

With these words the travellers passed the silent mounds. Following the winding way up the green shoulders of the hills, they came at last to the wide wind-swept walls and the gates of Edoras.

There sat many men in bright mail, who sprang at once to their feet and barred the way with spears. 'Stay, strangers here unknown!' they cried in the tongue of the Riddermark, demanding the names and errand of the strangers. Wonder was in their eyes but little friendliness; and they looked darkly upon Gandalf.

'Well do I understand your speech,' he answered in the same language; 'yet few strangers do so. Why then do you not speak in the Common Tongue, as is the custom in the West, if you wish to be answered?'

'It is the will of Théoden King that none should enter his gates, save those who know our tongue and are our friends,' replied one of the guards. 'None are welcome here in days of war but our own folk, and those that come from Mundburg in the land of Gondor. Who are you that come heedless over the plain thus strangely clad, riding horses like to our own horses? Long have we kept guard here, and we have watched you from afar. Never have we seen other riders so strange, nor any horse more proud than is one of these that bear you. He is one of the *Mearas*, unless our eyes are cheated by some spell. Say, are you not a wizard, some spy from Saruman, or phantoms of his craft? Speak now and be swift!'

'We are no phantoms,' said Aragorn, 'nor do your eyes cheat you. For indeed these are your own horses that we ride, as you knew well ere you asked, I guess. But seldom does thief ride home to the stable. Here are

Hasufel and Arod, that Éomer, the Third Marshal of the Mark, lent to us, only two days ago. We bring them back now, even as we promised him. Has not Éomer then returned and given warning of our coming?'

A troubled look came into the guard's eyes. 'Of Éomer I have naught to say,' he answered. 'If what you tell me is truth, then doubtless Théoden will have heard of it. Maybe your coming was not wholly unlooked-for. It is but two nights ago that Wormtongue came to us and said that by the will of Théoden no stranger should pass these gates.'

'Wormtongue?' said Gandalf, looking sharply at the guard. 'Say no more! My errand is not to Wormtongue, but to the Lord of the Mark himself. I am in haste. Will you not go or send to say that we are come?' His eyes glinted under his deep brows as he bent his gaze upon the man.

'Yes, I will go,' he answered slowly. 'But what names shall I report? And what shall I say of you? Old and weary you seem now, and yet you are fell and grim beneath, I deem.'

'Well do you see and speak,' said the wizard. 'For I am Gandalf. I have returned. And behold! I too bring back a horse. Here is Shadowfax the Great, whom no other hand can tame. And here beside me is Aragorn son of Arathorn, the heir of Kings, and it is to Mundburg that he goes. Here also are Legolas the Elf and Gimli the Dwarf, our comrades. Go now and say to your master that we are at his gates and would have speech with him, if he will permit us to come into his hall.'

'Strange names you give indeed! But I will report them as you bid, and learn my master's will,' said the guard. 'Wait here a little while, and I will bring you such answer as seems good to him. Do not hope too much! These are dark days.' He went swiftly away, leaving the strangers in the watchful keeping of his comrades.

After some time he returned. 'Follow me!' he said. 'Théoden gives you leave to enter; but any weapon that you bear, be it only a staff, you must leave on the threshold. The doorwardens will keep them.'

The dark gates were swung open. The travellers entered, walking in file behind their guide. They found a broad path, paved with hewn stones, now winding upward, now climbing in short flights of well-laid steps. Many houses built of wood and many dark doors they passed. Beside the way in a stone channel a stream of clear water flowed, sparkling and chattering. At length they came to the crown of the hill. There stood a high platform above a green terrace, at the foot of which a bright spring gushed from a stone carved in the likeness of a horse's head; beneath was a wide basin from which the water spilled and fed the falling stream. Up the green terrace went a stair of stone, high and broad, and on either side of the topmost step were stone-hewn seats. There sat other guards, with drawn swords laid upon their knees. Their golden hair was braided on their shoulders; the sun was blazoned upon their green shields, their long corslets were burnished bright, and when they rose taller they seemed than mortal men.

'There are the doors before you,' said the guide. 'I must return now to my duty at the gate. Farewell! And may the Lord of the Mark be gracious to you!'

He turned and went swiftly back down the road. The others climbed the long stair under the eyes of the tall watchmen. Silent they stood now above and spoke no word, until Gandalf stepped out upon the paved terrace at the stair's head. Then suddenly with clear voices they spoke a courteous greeting in their own tongue.

'Hail, comers from afar!' they said, and they turned the hilts of their swords towards the travellers in token of peace. Green gems flashed in the sunlight. Then one of the guards stepped forward and spoke in the Common Speech.

'I am the Doorward of Théoden,' he said. 'Háma is my name. Here I must bid you lay aside your weapons before you enter.'

Then Legolas gave into his hand his silver-hafted knife, his quiver, and his bow. 'Keep these well,' he said, 'for they come from the Golden Wood and the Lady of Lothlórien gave them to me.'

Wonder came into the man's eyes, and he laid the weapons hastily by the wall, as if he feared to handle them. 'No man will touch them, I promise you,' he said.

Aragorn stood a while hesitating. 'It is not my will,' he said, 'to put aside my sword or to deliver Andúril to the hand of any other man.'

'It is the will of Théoden,' said Háma.

'It is not clear to me that the will of Théoden son of Thengel, even though he be lord of the Mark, should prevail over the will of Aragorn son of Arathorn, Elendil's heir of Gondor.'

'This is the house of Théoden, not of Aragorn, even were he King of Gondor in the seat of Denethor,' said Háma, stepping swiftly before the doors and barring the way. His sword was now in his hand and the point towards the strangers.

'This is idle talk,' said Gandalf. 'Needless is Théoden's demand, but it is useless to refuse. A king will have his way in his own hall, be it folly or wisdom.'

'Truly,' said Aragorn. 'And I would do as the master of the house bade me, were this only a woodman's cot, if I bore now any sword but Andúril.'

'Whatever its name may be,' said Háma, 'here you shall lay it, if you would not fight alone against all the men in Edoras.'

'Not alone!' said Gimli, fingering the blade of his axe, and looking darkly up at the guard, as if he were a young tree that Gimli had a mind to fell. 'Not alone!'

'Come, come!' said Gandalf. 'We are all friends here. Or should be; for the laughter of Mordor will be our only reward, if we quarrel. My errand is pressing. Here at least is *my* sword, goodman Háma. Keep it well. Glamdring it is called, for the Elves made it long ago. Now let me pass. Come, Aragorn!'

Slowly Aragorn unbuckled his belt and himself set his sword upright against the wall. 'Here I set it,' he said; 'but I command you not to touch it, nor to permit any other to lay hand on it. In this elvish sheath dwells the Blade that was Broken and has been made again. Telchar first wrought it in the deeps of time. Death shall come to any man that draws Elendil's sword save Elendil's heir.'

The guard stepped back and looked with amazement on Aragorn. 'It seems that you are come on the wings of song out of the forgotten days,' he said. 'It shall be, lord, as you command.'

'Well,' said Gimli, 'if it has Andúril to keep it company, my axe may stay here, too, without shame'; and he laid it on the floor. 'Now then, if all is as you wish, let us go and speak with your master.'

The guard still hesitated. 'Your staff,' he said to Gandalf. 'Forgive me, but that too must be left at the doors.'

'Foolishness!' said Gandalf. 'Prudence is one thing, but discourtesy is another. I am old. If I may not lean on my stick as I go, then I will sit out here, until it pleases Théoden to hobble out himself to speak with me.'

Aragorn laughed. 'Every man has something too dear to trust to another. But would you part an old man from his support? Come, will you not let us enter?'

'The staff in the hand of a wizard may be more than a prop for age,' said Háma. He looked hard at the ash-staff on which Gandalf leaned. 'Yet in doubt a man of worth will trust to his own wisdom. I believe you are friends and folk worthy of honour, who have no evil purpose. You may go in.'

The guards now lifted the heavy bars of the doors and swung them slowly inwards grumbling on their great hinges. The travellers entered. Inside it seemed dark and warm after the clear air upon the hill. The hall was long and wide and filled with shadows and half lights; mighty pillars upheld its lofty roof. But here and there bright sunbeams fell in glimmering shafts from the eastern windows, high under the deep eaves. Through the louver in the roof, above the thin wisps of issuing smoke, the sky showed pale and blue. As their eyes changed, the travellers perceived that the floor was paved with stones of many hues; branching runes and strange devices intertwined beneath their feet. They saw now that the pillars were richly carved, gleaming dully with gold and half-seen colours. Many woven cloths were hung upon the walls, and over their wide spaces marched figures of ancient legend, some dim with years, some darkling in the shade. But upon one form the sunlight fell: a young man upon a white horse. He was blowing a great horn, and his yellow hair was flying in the wind. The horse's head was lifted, and its nostrils were wide and red as it neighed, smelling battle afar. Foaming water, green and white, rushed and curled about its knees.

'Behold Eorl the Young!' said Aragorn. 'Thus he rode out of the North to the Battle of the Field of Celebrant.'

Now the four companions went forward, past the clear wood-fire burning upon the long hearth in the midst of the hall. Then they halted. At the far end of the house, beyond the hearth and facing north towards the doors, was a dais with three steps; and in the middle of the dais was a great gilded chair. Upon it sat a man so bent with age that he seemed almost a dwarf; but his white hair was long and thick and fell in great braids from beneath a thin golden circlet set upon his brow. In the centre upon his forehead shone a single white diamond. His beard was laid like snow upon his knees; but his eyes still burned with a bright light, glinting as he gazed at the strangers. Behind his chair stood a woman clad in white. At his feet upon the steps sat a wizened figure of a man, with a pale wise face and heavy-lidded eyes.

There was a silence. The old man did not move in his chair. At length Gandalf spoke. 'Hail, Théoden son of Thengel! I have returned. For behold! the storm comes, and now all friends should gather together, lest each singly be destroyed.'

Slowly the old man rose to his feet, leaning heavily upon a short black staff with a handle of white bone; and now the strangers saw that, bent though he was, he was still tall and must in youth have been high and proud indeed.

'I greet you,' he said, 'and maybe you look for welcome. But truth to tell your welcome is doubtful here, Master Gandalf. You have ever been a herald of woe. Troubles follow you like crows, and ever the oftener the worse. I will not deceive you: when I heard that Shadowfax had come back riderless, I rejoiced at the return of the horse, but still more at the lack of the rider; and when Éomer brought the tidings that you had gone at last to your long home, I did not mourn. But news from afar is seldom sooth. Here you come again! And with you come evils worse than before, as might be expected. Why should I welcome you, Gandalf Stormcrow? Tell me that.' Slowly he sat down again in his chair.

'You speak justly, lord,' said the pale man sitting upon the steps of the dais. 'It is not yet five days since the bitter tidings came that Théodred your son was slain upon the West Marches: your right-hand, Second Marshal of the Mark. In Éomer there is little trust. Few men would be left to guard your walls, if he had been allowed to rule. And even now we learn from Gondor that the Dark Lord is stirring in the East. Such is the hour in which this wanderer chooses to return. Why indeed should we welcome you, Master Stormcrow? *Láthspell* I name you, Ill-news; and ill news is an ill guest they say.' He laughed grimly, as he lifted his heavy lids for a moment and gazed on the strangers with dark eyes.

'You are held wise, my friend Wormtongue, and are doubtless a great support to your master,' answered Gandalf in a soft voice. 'Yet in two ways may a man come with evil tidings. He may be a worker of evil; or he may be such as leaves well alone, and comes only to bring aid in time of need.'

'That is so,' said Wormtongue; 'but there is a third kind: pickers of bones, meddlers in other men's sorrows, carrion-fowl that grow fat on war. What aid have you ever brought, Stormcrow? And what aid do you bring now? It was aid from us that you sought last time that you were here. Then my lord bade you choose any horse that you would and be gone; and to the wonder of all you took Shadowfax in your insolence. My lord was sorely grieved; yet to some it seemed that to speed you from the land the price was not too great. I guess that it is likely to turn out the same once more: you will seek aid rather than render it. Do you bring men? Do you bring horses, swords, spears? That I would call aid; that is our present need. But who are these that follow at your tail? Three ragged wanderers in grey, and you yourself the most beggar-like of the four!'

'The courtesy of your hall is somewhat lessened of late, Théoden son of Thengel,' said Gandalf. 'Has not the messenger from your gate reported the names of my companions? Seldom has any lord of Rohan received three such guests. Weapons they have laid at your doors that are worth many a mortal man, even the mightiest. Grey is their raiment, for the Elves clad them, and thus they have passed through the shadow of great perils to your hall.'

'Then it is true, as Éomer reported, that you are in league with the Sorceress of the Golden Wood?' said Wormtongue. 'It is not to be wondered at: webs of deceit were ever woven in Dwimordene.'

Gimli strode a pace forward, but felt suddenly the hand of Gandalf clutch him by the shoulder, and he halted, standing stiff as stone.

> *In Dwimordene, in Lórien*
> *Seldom have walked the feet of Men,*
> *Few mortal eyes have seen the light*

That lies there ever, long and bright.
Galadriel! Galadriel!
Clear is the water of your well;
White is the star in your white hand;
Unmarred, unstained is leaf and land
In Dwimordene, in Lórien
More fair than thoughts of Mortal Men.

Thus Gandalf softly sang, and then suddenly he changed. Casting his tattered cloak aside, he stood up and leaned no longer on his staff; and he spoke in a clear cold voice.

'The wise speak only of what they know, Gríma son of Gálmód. A witless worm have you become. Therefore be silent, and keep your forked tongue behind your teeth. I have not passed through fire and death to bandy crooked words with a serving-man till the lightning falls.'

He raised his staff. There was a roll of thunder. The sunlight was blotted out from the eastern windows; the whole hall became suddenly dark as night. The fire faded to sullen embers. Only Gandalf could be seen, standing white and tall before the blackened hearth.

In the gloom they heard the hiss of Wormtongue's voice: 'Did I not counsel you, lord, to forbid his staff? That fool, Háma, has betrayed us!' There was a flash as if lightning had cloven the roof. Then all was silent. Wormtongue sprawled on his face.

'Now Théoden son of Thengel, will you hearken to me?' said Gandalf. 'Do you ask for help?' He lifted his staff and pointed to a high window. There the darkness seemed to clear, and through the opening could be seen, high and far, a patch of shining sky. 'Not all is dark. Take courage, Lord of the Mark; for better help you will not find. No counsel have I to give to those that despair. Yet counsel I could give, and words I could speak to you. Will you hear them? They are not for all ears. I bid you come out before your doors and look abroad. Too long have you sat in shadows and trusted to twisted tales and crooked promptings.'

Slowly Théoden left his chair. A faint light grew in the hall again. The woman hastened to the king's side, taking his arm, and with faltering steps the old man came down from the dais and paced softly through the hall. Wormtongue remained lying on the floor. They came to the doors and Gandalf knocked.

'Open!' he cried. 'The Lord of the Mark comes forth!'

The doors rolled back and a keen air came whistling in. A wind was blowing on the hill.

'Send your guards down to the stairs' foot,' said Gandalf. 'And you, lady, leave him a while with me. I will care for him.'

'Go, Éowyn sister-daughter!' said the old king. 'The time for fear is past.'

The woman turned and went slowly into the house. As she passed the doors she turned and looked back. Grave and thoughtful was her glance, as she looked on the king with cool pity in her eyes. Very fair was her face, and her long hair was like a river of gold. Slender and tall she was in her white robe girt with silver; but strong she seemed and stern as steel, a daughter of kings. Thus Aragorn for the first time in the full light of day beheld Éowyn, Lady of Rohan, and thought her fair, fair and cold, like a morning of pale spring that is not yet come to womanhood. And she now was suddenly aware of him: tall heir of kings, wise with many winters, greycloaked, hiding a power that yet she felt. For a moment still as stone she stood, then turning swiftly she was gone.

'Now, lord,' said Gandalf, 'look out upon your land! Breathe the free air again!'

From the porch upon the top of the high terrace they could see beyond the stream the green fields of Rohan fading into distant grey. Curtains of wind-blown rain were slanting down. The sky above and to the west was still dark with thunder, and lightning far away flickered among the tops of hidden hills. But the wind had shifted to the north, and already the storm that had come out of the East was receding, rolling away southward to the sea. Suddenly through a rent in the clouds behind them a shaft of sun stabbed down. The falling showers gleamed like silver, and far away the river glittered like a shimmering glass.

'It is not so dark here,' said Théoden.

'No,' said Gandalf. 'Nor does age lie so heavily on your shoulders as some would have you think. Cast aside your prop!'

From the king's hand the black staff fell clattering on the stones. He drew himself up, slowly, as a man that is stiff from long bending over some dull toil. Now tall and straight he stood, and his eyes were blue as he looked into the opening sky.

'Dark have been my dreams of late,' he said, 'but I feel as one new-awakened. I would now that you had come before, Gandalf. For I fear that already you have come too late, only to see the last days of my house. Not long now shall stand the high hall which Brego son of Eorl built. Fire shall devour the high seat. What is to be done?'

'Much,' said Gandalf. 'But first send for Éomer. Do I not guess rightly that you hold him prisoner, by the counsel of Gríma, of him that all save you name the Wormtongue?'

'It is true,' said Théoden. 'He had rebelled against my commands, and threatened death to Gríma in my hall.'

'A man may love you and yet not love Wormtongue or his counsels,' said Gandalf.

'That may be. I will do as you ask. Call Háma to me. Since he proved untrusty as a doorward, let him become an errand-runner. The guilty shall bring the guilty to judgement,' said Théoden, and his voice was grim, yet he looked at Gandalf and smiled and as he did so many lines of care were smoothed away and did not return.

When Háma had been summoned and had gone, Gandalf led Théoden to a stone seat, and then sat himself before the king upon the topmost stair. Aragorn and his companions stood nearby.

'There is no time to tell all that you should hear,' said Gandalf. 'Yet if my hope is not cheated, a time will come ere long when I can speak more fully. Behold! you are come into a peril greater even than the wit of Wormtongue could weave into your dreams. But see! you dream no longer. You live. Gondor and Rohan do not stand alone. The enemy is strong beyond our reckoning, yet we have a hope at which he has not guessed.'

Quickly now Gandalf spoke. His voice was low and secret, and none save the king heard what he said. But ever as he spoke the light shone brighter in Théoden's eye, and at the last he rose from his seat to his full height, and Gandalf beside him, and together they looked out from the high place towards the East.

'Verily,' said Gandalf, now in a loud voice, keen and clear, 'that way lies our hope, where sits our greatest fear. Doom hangs still on a thread. Yet hope there is still, if we can but stand unconquered for a little while.'

The others too now turned their eyes eastward. Over the sundering leagues of land, far away they gazed to the edge of sight, and hope and fear bore their thoughts still on, beyond dark mountains to the Land of Shadow. Where now was the Ring-bearer? How thin indeed was the thread upon which doom still hung! It seemed to Legolas, as he strained his farseeing eyes, that he caught a glint of white: far away perchance the sun twinkled on a pinnacle of the Tower of Guard. And further still, endlessly remote and yet a present threat, there was a tiny tongue of flame.

Slowly Théoden sat down again, as if weariness still struggled to master him against the will of Gandalf. He turned and looked at his great house. 'Alas!' he said, 'that these evil days should be mine, and should come in my old age instead of that peace which I have earned. Alas for Boromir the brave! The young perish and the old linger, withering.' He clutched his knees with his wrinkled hands.

'Your fingers would remember their old strength better, if they grasped a sword-hilt,' said Gandalf.

Théoden rose and put his hand to his side; but no sword hung at his belt. 'Where has Gríma stowed it?' he muttered under his breath.

'Take this, dear lord!' said a clear voice. 'It was ever at your service.' Two men had come softly up the stair and stood now a few steps from the top. Éomer was there. No helm was on his head, no mail was on his breast, but in his hand he held a drawn sword; and as he knelt he offered the hilt to his master.

'How comes this?' said Théoden sternly. He turned towards Éomer, and the men looked in wonder at him, standing now proud and erect. Where was the old man whom they had left crouching in his chair or leaning on his stick?

'It is my doing, lord,' said Háma, trembling. 'I understood that Éomer was to be set free. Such joy was in my heart that maybe I have erred. Yet, since he was free again, and he a Marshal of the Mark, I brought him his sword as he bade me.'

'To lay at your feet, my lord,' said Éomer.

For a moment of silence Théoden stood looking down at Éomer as he knelt still before him. Neither moved.

'Will you not take the sword?' said Gandalf.

Slowly Théoden stretched forth his hand. As his fingers took the hilt, it seemed to the watchers that firmness and strength returned to his thin arm. Suddenly he lifted the blade and swung it shimmering and whistling in the air. Then he gave a great cry. His voice rang clear as he chanted in the tongue of Rohan a call to arms.

> *Arise now, arise, Riders of Théoden!*
> *Dire deeds awake, dark is it eastward.*
> *Let horse be bridled, horn be sounded!*
> *Forth Eorlingas!*

The guards, thinking that they were summoned, sprang up the stair. They looked at their lord in amazement, and then as one man they drew their swords and laid them at his feet. 'Command us!' they said.

'*Westu Théoden hál!*' cried Éomer. 'It is a joy to us to see you return into your own. Never again shall it be said, Gandalf, that you come only with grief!'

'Take back your sword, Éomer, sister-son!' said the king. 'Go, Háma, and seek my own sword! Gríma has it in his keeping. Bring him to me also. Now, Gandalf, you said that you had counsel to give, if I would hear it. What is your counsel?'

'You have yourself already taken it,' answered Gandalf. 'To put your trust in Éomer, rather than in a man of crooked mind. To cast aside regret and fear. To do the deed at hand. Every man that can ride should be sent west at once, as Éomer counselled you: we must first destroy the threat of Saruman, while we have time. If we fail, we fall. If we succeed – then we will face the next task. Meanwhile your people that are left, the women and the children and the old, should fly to the refuges that you have in the mountains. Were they not prepared against just such an evil day as this? Let them take provision, but delay not, nor burden themselves with treasures, great or small. It is their lives that are at stake.'

'This counsel seems good to me now,' said Théoden. 'Let all my folk get ready! But you my guests – truly you said, Gandalf, that the courtesy of my hall is lessened. You have ridden through the night, and the morning wears away. You have had neither sleep nor food. A guest-house shall be made ready: there you shall sleep, when you have eaten.'

'Nay, lord,' said Aragorn. 'There is no rest yet for the weary. The men of Rohan must ride forth today, and we will ride with them, axe, sword, and bow. We did not bring them to rest against your wall, Lord of the Mark. And I promised Éomer that my sword and his should be drawn together.'

'Now indeed there is hope of victory!' said Éomer.

'Hope, yes,' said Gandalf. 'But Isengard is strong. And other perils draw ever nearer. Do not delay, Théoden, when we are gone. Lead your people swiftly to the Hold of Dunharrow in the hills!'

'Nay, Gandalf!' said the king. 'You do not know your own skill in healing. It shall not be so. I myself will go to war, to fall in the front of the battle, if it must be. Thus shall I sleep better.'

'Then even the defeat of Rohan will be glorious in song,' said Aragorn. The armed men that stood near clashed their weapons, crying: 'The Lord of the Mark will ride! Forth Eorlingas!'

'But your people must not be both unarmed and shepherdless,' said Gandalf. 'Who shall guide them and govern them in your place?'

'I will take thought for that ere I go,' answered Théoden. 'Here comes my counsellor.'

At that moment Háma came again from the hall. Behind him cringing between two other men, came Gríma the Wormtongue. His face was very white. His eyes blinked in the sunlight. Háma knelt and presented to Théoden a long sword in a scabbard clasped with gold and set with green gems.

'Here, lord, is Herugrim, your ancient blade,' he said. 'It was found in his chest. Loth was he to render up the keys. Many other things are there which men have missed.'

'You lie,' said Wormtongue. 'And this sword your master himself gave into my keeping.'

'And he now requires it of you again,' said Théoden. 'Does that displease you?'

'Assuredly not, lord,' said Wormtongue. 'I care for you and yours as best I may. But do not weary yourself, or tax too heavily your strength. Let others deal with these irksome guests. Your meat is about to be set on the board. Will you not go to it?'

'I will,' said Théoden. 'And let food for my guests be set on the board beside me. The host rides today. Send the heralds forth! Let them summon all who dwell nigh! Every man and strong lad able to bear arms, all who have horses, let them be ready in the saddle at the gate ere the second hour from noon!'

'Dear lord!' cried Wormtongue. 'It is as I feared. This wizard has bewitched you. Are none to be left to defend the Golden Hall of your fathers, and all your treasure? None to guard the Lord of the Mark?'

'If this is bewitchment,' said Théoden, 'it seems to me more wholesome than your whisperings. Your leechcraft ere long would have had me walking on all fours like a beast. No, not one shall be left, not even Gríma. Gríma shall ride too. Go! You have yet time to clean the rust from your sword.'

'Mercy, lord!' whined Wormtongue, grovelling on the ground. 'Have pity on one worn out in your service. Send me not from your side! I at least will stand by you when all others have gone. Do not send your faithful Gríma away!'

'You have my pity,' said Théoden. 'And I do not send you from my side. I go myself to war with my men. I bid you come with me and prove your faith.'

Wormtongue looked from face to face. In his eyes was the hunted look of a beast seeking some gap in the ring of his enemies. He licked his lips with a long pale tongue. 'Such a resolve might be expected from a lord of the House of Eorl, old though he be,' he said. 'But those who truly love him would spare his failing years. Yet I see that I come too late. Others, whom the death of my lord would perhaps grieve less, have already persuaded him. If I cannot undo their work, hear me at least in this, lord! One who knows your mind and honours your commands should be left in Edoras. Appoint a faithful steward. Let your counsellor Gríma keep all things till your return – and I pray that we may see it, though no wise man will deem it hopeful.'

Éomer laughed. 'And if that plea does not excuse you from war, most noble Wormtongue,' he said, 'what office of less honour would you accept?

To carry a sack of meal up into the mountains – if any man would trust you with it?'

'Nay, Éomer, you do not fully understand the mind of Master Wormtongue,' said Gandalf, turning his piercing glance upon him. 'He is bold and cunning. Even now he plays a game with peril and wins a throw. Hours of my precious time he has wasted already. Down, snake!' he said suddenly in a terrible voice. 'Down on your belly! How long is it since Saruman bought you? What was the promised price? When all the men were dead, you were to pick your share of the treasure, and take the woman you desire? Too long have you watched her under your eyelids and haunted her steps.'

Éomer grasped his sword. 'That I knew already,' he muttered. 'For that reason I would have slain him before, forgetting the law of the hall. But there are other reasons.' He stepped forward, but Gandalf stayed him with his hand.

'Éowyn is safe now,' he said. 'But you, Wormtongue, you have done what you could for your true master. Some reward you have earned at least. Yet Saruman is apt to overlook his bargains. I should advise you to go quickly and remind him, lest he forget your faithful service.'

'You lie,' said Wormtongue.

'That word comes too oft and easy from your lips,' said Gandalf. 'I do not lie. See, Théoden, here is a snake! With safety you cannot take it with you, nor can you leave it behind. To slay it would be just. But it was not always as it now is. Once it was a man, and did you service in its fashion. Give him a horse and let him go at once, wherever he chooses. By his choice you shall judge him.'

'Do you hear this, Wormtongue?' said Théoden. 'This is your choice: to ride with me to war, and let us see in battle whether you are true; or to go now, whither you will. But then, if ever we meet again, I shall not be merciful.'

Slowly Wormtongue rose. He looked at them with half-closed eyes. Last of all he scanned Théoden's face and opened his mouth as if to speak. Then suddenly he drew himself up. His hands worked. His eyes glittered. Such malice was in them that men stepped back from him. He bared his teeth; and then with a hissing breath he spat before the king's feet, and darting to one side, he fled down the stair.

'After him!' said Théoden. 'See that he does no harm to any, but do not hurt him or hinder him. Give him a horse, if he wishes it.'

'And if any will bear him,' said Éomer.

One of the guards ran down the stair. Another went to the well at the foot of the terrace and in his helm drew water. With it he washed clean the stones that Wormtongue had defiled.

'Now my guests, come!' said Théoden. 'Come and take such refreshment as haste allows.'

They passed back into the great house. Already they heard below them in the town the heralds crying and the war-horns blowing. For the king was to ride forth as soon as the men of the town and those dwelling near could be armed and assembled.

At the king's board sat Éomer and the four guests, and there also waiting upon the king was the lady Éowyn. They ate and drank swiftly. The others were silent while Théoden questioned Gandalf concerning Saruman.

'How far back his treachery goes, who can guess?' said Gandalf. 'He was not always evil. Once I do not doubt that he was the friend of Rohan; and even when his heart grew colder, he found you useful still. But for long now he has plotted your ruin, wearing the mask of friendship, until he was ready. In those years Wormtongue's task was easy, and all that you did was swiftly known in Isengard; for your land was open, and strangers came and went. And ever Wormtongue's whispering was in your ears, poisoning your thought, chilling your heart, weakening your limbs, while others watched and could do nothing, for your will was in his keeping.

'But when I escaped and warned you, then the mask was torn, for those who would see. After that Wormtongue played dangerously, always seeking to delay you, to prevent your full strength being gathered. He was crafty: dulling men's wariness, or working on their fears, as served the occasion. Do you not remember how eagerly he urged that no man should be spared on a wildgoose chase northward, when the immediate peril was westward? He persuaded you to forbid Éomer to pursue the raiding Orcs. If Éomer had not defied Wormtongue's voice speaking with your mouth, those Orcs would have reached Isengard by now, bearing a great prize. Not indeed that prize which Saruman desires above all else, but at the least two members of my Company, sharers of a secret hope, of which even to you, lord, I cannot yet speak openly. Dare you think of what they might now be suffering, or what Saruman might now have learned to our destruction?'

'I owe much to Éomer,' said Théoden. 'Faithful heart may have forward tongue.'

'Say also,' said Gandalf, 'that to crooked eyes truth may wear a wry face.'

'Indeed my eyes were almost blind,' said Théoden. 'Most of all I owe to you, my guest. Once again you have come in time. I would give you a gift ere we go, at your own choosing. You have only to name aught that is mine. I reserve now only my sword!'

'Whether I came in time or not is yet to be seen,' said Gandalf. 'But as for your gift, lord, I will choose one that will fit my need: swift and sure. Give me Shadowfax! He was only lent before, if loan we may call it. But now I shall ride him into great hazard, setting silver against black: I would not risk anything that is not my own. And already there is a bond of love between us.'

' 'You choose well,' said Théoden; 'and I give him now gladly. Yet it is a great gift. There is none like to Shadowfax. In him one of the mighty steeds of old has returned. None such shall return again. And to you my other guests I will offer such things as may be found in my armoury. Swords you do not need, but there are helms and coats of mail of cunning work, gifts to my fathers out of Gondor. Choose from these ere we go, and may they serve you well!'

Now men came bearing raiment of war from the king's hoard, and they arrayed Aragorn and Legolas in shining mail. Helms too they chose, and round shields: their bosses were overlaid with gold and set with gems, green and red and white. Gandalf took no armour; and Gimli needed no coat of rings, even if one had been found to match his stature, for there was no hauberk in the hoards of Edoras of better make than his short corslet forged beneath the Mountain in the North. But he chose a cap of iron and leather that fitted well upon his round head; and a small shield he also took. It bore the running horse, white upon green, that was the emblem of the House of Eorl.

'May it keep you well!' said Théoden. 'It was made for me in Thengel's day, while still I was a boy.'

Gimli bowed. 'I am proud, Lord of the Mark, to bear your device,' he said. 'Indeed sooner would I bear a horse than be borne by one. I love my feet better. But, maybe, I shall come yet where I can stand and fight.'

'It may well be so,' said Théoden.

The king now rose, and at once Éowyn came forward bearing wine. '*Ferthu Théoden hál!*' she said. 'Receive now this cup and drink in happy hour. Health be with thee at thy going and coming!'

Théoden drank from the cup, and she then proffered it to the guests. As she stood before Aragorn she paused suddenly and looked upon him, and her eyes were shining. And he looked down upon her fair face and smiled; but as he took the cup, his hand met hers, and he knew that she trembled at the touch. 'Hail Aragorn son of Arathorn!' she said. 'Hail Lady of Rohan!' he answered, but his face now was troubled and he did not smile.

When they had all drunk, the king went down the hall to the doors. There the guards awaited him, and heralds stood, and all the lords and chiefs were gathered together that remained in Edoras or dwelt nearby.

'Behold! I go forth, and it seems like to be my last riding,' said Théoden. 'I have no child. Théodred my son is slain. I name Éomer my sister-son to be my heir. If neither of us return, then choose a new lord as you will.

ut to some one I must now entrust my people that I leave behind, to rule
1em in my place. Which of you will stay?'

No man spoke.

'Is there none whom you would name? In whom do my people trust?'

'In the House of Eorl,' answered Háma.

'But Éomer I cannot spare, nor would he stay,' said the king; 'and he
the last of that House.'

'I said not Éomer,' answered Háma. 'And he is not the last. There is
owyn, daughter of Éomund, his sister. She is fearless and high-hearted.
ll love her. Let her be as lord to the Eorlingas, while we are gone.'

'It shall be so,' said Théoden. 'Let the heralds announce to the folk that
1e Lady Éowyn will lead them!'

Then the king sat upon a seat before his doors, and Éowyn knelt before
1m and received from him a sword and a fair corslet. 'Farewell sister-
1ughter!' he said. 'Dark is the hour, yet maybe we shall return to the
olden Hall. But in Dunharrow the people may long defend themselves,
1d if the battle go ill, thither will come all who escape.'

'Speak not so!' she answered. 'A year shall I endure for every day that
1sses until your return.' But as she spoke her eyes went to Aragorn who
ood nearby.

'The king shall come again,' he said. 'Fear not! Not West but East does
1r doom await us.'

The king now went down the stair with Gandalf beside him. The others
llowed. Aragorn looked back as they passed towards the gate. Alone
owyn stood before the doors of the house at the stair's head; the sword
as set upright before her, and her hands were laid upon the hilt. She was
ad now in mail and shone like silver in the sun.

Gimli walked with Legolas, his axe on his shoulder. 'Well, at last we set
f!' he said. 'Men need many words before deeds. My axe is restless in
y hands. Though I doubt not that these Rohirrim are fell-handed when
ey come to it. Nonetheless this is not the warfare that suits me. How
all I come to the battle? I wish I could walk and not bump like a sack
Gandalf's saddlebow.'

'A safer seat than many, I guess,' said Legolas. 'Yet doubtless Gandalf
ill gladly put you down on your feet when blows begin; or Shadowfax
mself. An axe is no weapon for a rider.'

'And a Dwarf is no horseman. It is orc-necks I would hew, not shave
e scalps of Men,' said Gimli, patting the haft of his axe.

At the gate they found a great host of men, old and young, all ready in
e saddle. More than a thousand were there mustered. Their spears were
ce a springing wood. Loudly and joyously they shouted as Théoden came

forth. Some held in readiness the king's horse, Snowmane, and others held the horses of Aragorn and Legolas. Gimli stood ill at ease, frowning, but Éomer came up to him, leading his horse.

'Hail, Gimli Glóin's son!' he cried. 'I have not had time to learn gentle speech under your rod, as you promised. But shall we not put aside our quarrel? At least I will speak no evil again of the Lady of the Wood.'

'I will forget my wrath for a while, Éomer son of Éomund,' said Gimli; 'but if ever you chance to see the Lady Galadriel with your eyes, then you shall acknowledge her the fairest of ladies, or our friendship will end.'

'So be it!' said Éomer. 'But until that time pardon me, and in token of pardon ride with me, I beg. Gandalf will be at the head with the Lord of the Mark; but Firefoot, my horse, will bear us both, if you will.'

'I thank you indeed,' said Gimli greatly pleased. 'I will gladly go with you, if Legolas, my comrade, may ride beside us.'

'It shall be so,' said Éomer. 'Legolas upon my left, and Aragorn upon my right, and none will dare to stand before us!'

'Where is Shadowfax?' said Gandalf.

'Running wild over the grass,' they answered. 'He will let no man handle him. There he goes, away down by the ford, like a shadow among the willows.'

Gandalf whistled and called aloud the horse's name, and far away he tossed his head and neighed, and turning sped towards the host like an arrow.

'Were the breath of the West Wind to take a body visible, even so would it appear,' said Éomer, as the great horse ran up, until he stood before the wizard.

'The gift seems already to be given,' said Théoden. 'But hearken all! Here now I name my guest, Gandalf Greyhame, wisest of counsellors, most welcome of wanderers, a lord of the Mark, a chieftain of the Eorlingas while our kin shall last; and I give to him Shadowfax, prince of horses.'

'I thank you, Théoden King,' said Gandalf. Then suddenly he threw back his grey cloak, and cast aside his hat, and leaped to horseback. He wore no helm nor mail. His snowy hair flew free in the wind, his white robes shone dazzling in the sun.

'Behold the White Rider!' cried Aragorn, and all took up the words.

'Our King and the White Rider!' they shouted. 'Forth Eorlingas!'

The trumpets sounded. The horses reared and neighed. Spear clashed on shield. Then the king raised his hand, and with a rush like the sudden onset of a great wind the last host of Rohan rode thundering into the West.

Far over the plain Éowyn saw the glitter of their spears, as she stood still, alone before the doors of the silent house.

CHAPTER VII

HELM'S DEEP

The sun was already westering as they rode from Edoras, and the light of it was in their eyes, turning all the rolling fields of Rohan to a golden haze. There was a beaten way, north-westward along the foot-hills of the White Mountains, and this they followed, up and down in a green country, crossing small swift streams by many fords. Far ahead and to their right the Misty Mountains loomed; ever darker and taller they grew as the miles went by. The sun went slowly down before them. Evening came behind.

The host rode on. Need drove them. Fearing to come too late, they rode with all the speed they could, pausing seldom. Swift and enduring were the steeds of Rohan, but there were many leagues to go. Forty leagues and more it was, as a bird flies, from Edoras to the fords of the Isen, where they hoped to find the king's men that held back the hosts of Saruman.

Night closed about them. At last they halted to make their camp. They had ridden for some five hours and were far out upon the western plain, yet more than half their journey lay still before them. In a great circle, under the starry sky and the waxing moon, they now made their bivouac. They lit no fires, for they were uncertain of events; but they set a ring of mounted guards about them, and scouts rode out far ahead, passing like shadows in the folds of the land. The slow night passed without tidings or alarm. At dawn the horns sounded, and within an hour they took the road again.

There were no clouds overhead yet, but a heaviness was in the air; it was hot for the season of the year. The rising sun was hazy, and behind it, following it slowly up the sky, there was a growing darkness, as of a great storm moving out of the East. And away in the North-west there seemed to be another darkness brooding about the feet of the Misty Mountains, a shadow that crept down slowly from the Wizard's Vale.

Gandalf dropped back to where Legolas rode beside Éomer. 'You have the keen eyes of your fair kindred, Legolas,' he said; 'and they can tell a sparrow from a finch a league off. Tell me, can you see anything away yonder towards Isengard?'

'Many miles lie between,' said Legolas, gazing thither and shading his eyes with his long hand. 'I can see a darkness. There are shapes moving in it, great shapes far away upon the bank of the river; but what they are I cannot tell. It is not mist or cloud that defeats my eyes: there is a veiling shadow that some power lays upon the land, and it marches slowly down stream. It is as if the twilight under endless trees were flowing downwards from the hills.'

'And behind us comes a very storm of Mordor,' said Gandalf. 'It will be a black night.'

As the second day of their riding drew on, the heaviness in the air increased. In the afternoon the dark clouds began to overtake them: a sombre canopy with great billowing edges flecked with dazzling light. The sun went down, blood-red in a smoking haze. The spears of the Riders were tipped with fire as the last shafts of light kindled the steep faces of the peaks of Thrihyrne: now very near they stood on the northernmost arm of the White Mountains, three jagged horns staring at the sunset. In the last red glow men in the vanguard saw a black speck, a horseman riding back towards them. They halted awaiting him.

He came, a weary man with dinted helm and cloven shield. Slowly he climbed from his horse and stood there a while gasping. At length he spoke. 'Is Éomer here?' he asked. 'You come at last, but too late, and with too little strength. Things have gone evilly since Théodred fell. We were driven back yesterday over the Isen with great loss; many perished at the crossing. Then at night fresh forces came over the river against our camp. All Isengard must be emptied; and Saruman has armed the wild hillmen and herd-folk of Dunland beyond the rivers, and these also he loosed upon us. We were overmastered. The shield-wall was broken. Erkenbrand of Westfold has drawn off those men he could gather towards his fastness in Helm's Deep. The rest are scattered.

'Where is Éomer? Tell him there is no hope ahead. He should return to Edoras before the wolves of Isengard come there.'

Théoden had sat silent, hidden from the man's sight behind his guards; now he urged his horse forward. 'Come, stand before me, Ceorl!' he said. 'I am here. The last host of the Eorlingas has ridden forth. It will not return without battle.'

The man's face lightened with joy and wonder. He drew himself up. Then he knelt, offering his notched sword to the king. 'Command me, lord!' he cried. 'And pardon me! I thought——'

'You thought I remained in Meduseld bent like an old tree under winter snow. So it was when you rode to war. But a west wind has shaken the boughs,' said Théoden. 'Give this man a fresh horse! Let us ride to the help of Erkenbrand!'

While Théoden was speaking, Gandalf rode a short way ahead, and he sat there alone, gazing north to Isengard and west to the setting sun. Now he came back.

'Ride, Théoden!' he said. 'Ride to Helm's Deep! Go not to the Fords of Isen, and do not tarry in the plain! I must leave you for a while. Shadowfax must bear me now on a swift errand.' Turning to Aragorn and Éomer and the men of the king's household, he cried: 'Keep well the Lord of the Mark, till I return. Await me at Helm's Gate! Farewell!'

He spoke a word to Shadowfax, and like an arrow from the bow the great horse sprang away. Even as they looked he was gone: a flash of silver in the sunset, a wind over the grass, a shadow that fled and passed from sight. Snowmane snorted and reared, eager to follow; but only a swift bird on the wing could have overtaken him.

'What does that mean?' said one of the guard to Háma.

'That Gandalf Greyhame has need of haste,' answered Háma. 'Ever he goes and comes unlooked-for.'

'Wormtongue, were he here, would not find it hard to explain,' said the other.

'True enough,' said Háma; 'but for myself, I will wait until I see Gandalf again.'

'Maybe you will wait long,' said the other.

The host turned away now from the road to the Fords of Isen and bent their course southward. Night fell, and still they rode on. The hills drew near, but the tall peaks of Thrihyrne were already dim against the darkening sky. Still some miles away, on the far side of the Westfold Vale, lay a green coomb, a great bay in the mountains, out of which a gorge opened in the hills. Men of that land called it Helm's Deep, after a hero of old wars who had made his refuge there. Ever steeper and narrower it wound inward from the north under the shadow of the Thrihyrne, till the crowhaunted cliffs rose like mighty towers on either side, shutting out the light.

At Helm's Gate, before the mouth of the Deep, there was a heel of rock thrust outward by the northern cliff. There upon its spur stood high walls of ancient stone, and within them was a lofty tower. Men said that in the far-off days of the glory of Gondor the sea-kings had built here this fastness with the hands of giants. The Hornburg it was called, for a trumpet sounded upon the tower echoed in the Deep behind, as if armies long-forgotten were issuing to war from caves beneath the hills. A wall, too, the men of old had made from the Hornburg to the southern cliff, barring the entrance to the gorge. Beneath it by a wide culvert the Deeping-stream passed out. About the feet of the Hornrock it wound, and flowed then in a gully through the midst of a wide green gore, sloping gently down from Helm's Gate to Helm's Dike. Thence it fell into the Deeping-coomb and out into the Westfold Vale. There in the Hornburg at Helm's Gate Erkenbrand, master of Westfold on the borders of the Mark, now dwelt. As the days darkened with threat of war, being wise, he had repaired the wall and made the fastness strong.

The Riders were still in the low valley before the mouth of the Coomb, when cries and hornblasts were heard from their scouts that went in front. Out of the darkness arrows whistled. Swiftly a scout rode back and reported that wolf-riders were abroad in the valley, and that a host of Orcs and wild men were hurrying southward from the Fords of Isen and seemed to be making for Helm's Deep.

'We have found many of our folk lying slain as they fled thither,' said the scout. 'And we have met scattered companies, going this way and that, leaderless. What has become of Erkenbrand none seem to know. It is likely that he will be overtaken ere he can reach Helm's Gate, if he has not already perished.'

'Has aught been seen of Gandalf?' asked Théoden.

'Yes, lord. Many have seen an old man in white upon a horse, passing hither and thither over the plains like wind in the grass. Some thought he was Saruman. It is said that he went away ere nightfall towards Isengard. Some say also that Wormtongue was seen earlier, going northward with a company of Orcs.'

'It will go ill with Wormtongue, if Gandalf comes upon him,' said Théoden. 'Nonetheless I miss now both my counsellors, the old and the new. But in this need we have no better choice than to go on, as Gandalf said, to Helm's Gate, whether Erkenbrand be there or no. Is it known how great is the host that comes from the North?'

'It is very great,' said the scout. 'He that flies counts every foeman twice, yet I have spoken to stouthearted men, and I do not doubt that the main strength of the enemy is many times as great as all that we have here.'

'Then let us be swift,' said Éomer. 'Let us drive through such foes as are already between us and the fastness. There are caves in Helm's Deep where hundreds may lie hid; and secret ways lead thence up on to the hills.'

'Trust not to secret ways,' said the king. 'Saruman has long spied out this land. Still in that place our defence may last long. Let us go!'

Aragorn and Legolas went now with Éomer in the van. On through the dark night they rode, ever slower as the darkness deepened and their way climbed southward, higher and higher into the dim folds about the mountains' feet. They found few of the enemy before them. Here and there they came upon roving bands of Orcs; but they fled ere the Riders could take or slay them.

'It will not be long I fear,' said Éomer, 'ere the coming of the king's host will be known to the leader of our enemies, Saruman or whatever captain he has sent forth.'

The rumour of war grew behind them. Now they could hear, borne over the dark, the sound of harsh singing. They had climbed far up into the Deeping-coomb when they looked back. Then they saw torches, countless points of fiery light upon the black fields behind, scattered like red flowers, or winding up from the lowlands in long flickering lines. Here and there a larger blaze leapt up.

'It is a great host and follows us hard,' said Aragorn.

'They bring fire,' said Théoden, 'and they are burning as they come, rick, cot, and tree. This was a rich vale and had many homesteads. Alas for my folk!'

'Would that day was ·here and we might ride down upon them like a storm out of the mountains!' said Aragorn. 'It grieves me to fly before them.'

'We need not fly much further,' said Éomer. 'Not far ahead now lies Helm's Dike, an ancient trench and rampart scored across the coomb, two furlongs below Helm's Gate. There we can turn and give battle.'

'Nay, we are too few to defend the Dike,' said Théoden. 'It is a mile long or more, and the breach in it is wide.'

'At the breach our rearguard must stand, if we are pressed,' said Éomer.

There was neither star nor moon when the Riders came to the breach in the Dike, where the stream from above passed out, and the road beside it ran down from the Hornburg. The rampart loomed suddenly before them, a high shadow beyond a dark pit. As they rode up a sentinel challenged them.

'The Lord of the Mark rides to Helm's Gate,' Éomer answered. 'I, Éomer son of Éomund, speak.'

'This is good tidings beyond hope,' said the sentinel. 'Hasten! The enemy is on your heels.'

The host passed through the breach and halted on the sloping sward above. They now learned to their joy that Erkenbrand had left many men to hold Helm's Gate, and more had since escaped thither.

'Maybe, we have a thousand fit to fight on foot,' said Gamling, an old man, the leader of those that watched the Dike. 'But most of them have seen too many winters, as I have, or too few, as my son's son here. What news of Erkenbrand? Word came yesterday that he was retreating hither with all that is left of the best Riders of Westfold. But he has not come.'

'I fear that he will not come now,' said Éomer. 'Our scouts have gained no news of him, and the enemy fills all the valley behind us.'

'I would that he had escaped,' said Théoden. 'He was a mighty man. In him lived again the valour of Helm the Hammerhand. But we cannot await him here. We must draw all our forces now behind the walls. Are you well stored? We bring little provision, for we rode forth to open battle, not to a siege.'

'Behind us in the caves of the Deep are three parts of the folk of Westfold, old and young, children and women,' said Gamling. 'But great store of food, and many beasts and their fodder, have also been gathered there.'

'That is well,' said Éomer. 'They are burning or despoiling all that is left in the vale.'

'If they come to bargain for our goods at Helm's Gate, they will pay a high price,' said Gamling.

The king and his Riders passed on. Before the causeway that crossed the stream they dismounted. In a long file they led their horses up the ramp and passed within the gates of the Hornburg. There they were welcomed again with joy and renewed hope; for now there were men enough to man both the burg and the barrier wall.

Quickly Éomer set his men in readiness. The king and the men of his household were in the Hornburg, and there also were many of the Westfoldmen. But on the Deeping Wall and its tower, and behind it, Éomer arrayed most of the strength that he had, for here the defence seemed more doubtful, if the assault were determined and in great force. The horses were led far up the Deep under such guard as could be spared.

The Deeping Wall was twenty feet high, and so thick that four men could walk abreast along the top, sheltered by a parapet over which only a tall man could look. Here and there were clefts in the stone through which men could shoot. This battlement could be reached by a stair running down from a door in the outer court of the Hornburg; three flights of steps led also up on to the wall from the Deep behind; but in front it was smooth, and the great stones of it were set with such skill that no foothold could be found at their joints, and at the top they hung over like a sea-delved cliff.

Gimli stood leaning against the breastwork upon the wall. Legolas sat above on the parapet, fingering his bow, and peering out into the gloom.

'This is more to my liking,' said the dwarf, stamping on the stones. 'Ever my heart rises as we draw near the mountains. There is good rock here. This country has tough bones. I felt them in my feet as we came up from

the dike. Give me a year and a hundred of my kin and I would make this
a place that armies would break upon like water.'

'I do not doubt it,' said Legolas. 'But you are a dwarf, and dwarves are
strange folk. I do not like this place, and I shall like it no more by the
light of day. But you comfort me, Gimli, and I am glad to have you standing
nigh with your stout legs and your hard axe. I wish there were more of
your kin among us. But even more would I give for a hundred good archers
of Mirkwood. We shall need them. The Rohirrim have good bowmen after
their fashion, but there are too few here, too few.'

'It is dark for archery,' said Gimli. 'Indeed it is time for sleep. Sleep! I
feel the need of it, as never I thought any dwarf could. Riding is tiring
work. Yet my axe is restless in my hand. Give me a row of orc-necks and
room to swing and all weariness will fall from me!'

A slow time passed. Far down in the valley scattered fires still burned.
The hosts of Isengard were advancing in silence now. Their torches could
be seen winding up the coomb in many lines.

Suddenly from the Dike yells and screams, and the fierce battle-cries of
men broke out. Flaming brands appeared over the brink and clustered
thickly at the breach. Then they scattered and vanished. Men came galloping back over the field and up the ramp to the gate of the Hornburg. The
rearguard of the Westfolders had been driven in.

'The enemy is at hand!' they said. 'We loosed every arrow that we had,
and filled the Dike with Orcs. But it will not halt them long. Already they
are scaling the bank at many points, thick as marching ants. But we have
taught them not to carry torches.'

It was now past midnight. The sky was utterly dark, and the stillness of
the heavy air foreboded storm. Suddenly the clouds were seared by a
blinding flash. Branched lightning smote down upon the eastward hills.
For a staring moment the watchers on the walls saw all the space between
them and the Dike lit with white light: it was boiling and crawling with
black shapes, some squat and broad, some tall and grim, with high helms
and sable shields. Hundreds and hundreds more were pouring over the
Dike and through the breach. The dark tide flowed up to the walls from
cliff to cliff. Thunder rolled in the valley. Rain came lashing down.

Arrows thick as the rain came whistling over the battlements, and fell
clinking and glancing on the stones. Some found a mark. The assault on
Helm's Deep had begun, but no sound or challenge was heard within; no
answering arrows came.

The assailing hosts halted, foiled by the silent menace of rock and wall.
Ever and again the lightning tore aside the darkness. Then the Orcs

screamed, waving spear and sword, and shooting a cloud of arrows at any that stood revealed upon the battlements; and the men of the Mark amazed looked out, as it seemed to them, upon a great field of dark corn, tossed by a tempest of war, and every ear glinted with barbed light.

Brazen trumpets sounded. The enemy surged forward, some against the Deeping Wall, others towards the causeway and the ramp that led up to the Hornburg-gates. There the hugest Orcs were mustered, and the wild men of the Dunland fells. A moment they hesitated and then on they came. The lightning flashed, and blazoned upon every helm and shield the ghastly hand of Isengard was seen. They reached the summit of the rock; they drove towards the gates.

Then at last an answer came: a storm of arrows met them, and a hail of stones. They wavered, broke, and fled back; and then charged again, broke and charged again; and each time, like the incoming sea, they halted at a higher point. Again trumpets rang, and a press of roaring men leaped forth. They held their great shields above them like a roof, while in their midst they bore two trunks of mighty trees. Behind them orc-archers crowded, sending a hail of darts against the bowmen on the walls. They gained the gates. The trees, swung by strong arms, smote the timbers with a rending boom. If any man fell, crushed by a stone hurtling from above, two others sprang to take his place. Again and again the great rams swung and crashed.

Éomer and Aragorn stood together on the Deeping Wall. They heard the roar of voices and the thudding of the rams; and then in a sudden flash of light they beheld the peril of the gates.

'Come!' said Aragorn. 'This is the hour when we draw swords together!'

Running like fire, they sped along the wall, and up the steps, and passed into the outer court upon the Rock. As they ran they gathered a handful of stout swordsmen. There was a small postern-door that opened in an angle of the burg-wall on the west, where the cliff stretched out to meet it. On that side a narrow path ran round towards the great gate, between the wall and the sheer brink of the Rock. Together Éomer and Aragorn sprang through the door, their men close behind. The two swords flashed from the sheath as one.

'Gúthwinë!' cried Éomer. 'Gúthwinë for the Mark!'

'Andúril!' cried Aragorn. 'Andúril for the Dúnedain!'

Charging from the side, they hurled themselves upon the wild men. Andúril rose and fell, gleaming with white fire. A shout went up from wall and tower: 'Andúril! Andúril goes to war. The Blade that was Broken shines again!'

Dismayed the rammers let fall the trees and turned to fight; but the wall of their shields was broken as by a lightning-stroke, and they were swept away, hewn down, or cast over the Rock into the stony stream below. The orc-archers shot wildly and then fled.

For a moment Éomer and Aragorn halted before the gates. The thunder was rumbling in the distance now. The lightning flickered still, far off among the mountains in the South. A keen wind was blowing from the North again. The clouds were torn and drifting, and stars peeped out; and above the hills of the Coomb-side the westering moon rode, glimmering yellow in the storm-wrack.

'We did not come too soon,' said Aragorn, looking at the gates. Their great hinges and iron bars were wrenched and bent; many of their timbers were cracked.

'Yet we cannot stay here beyond the walls to defend them,' said Éomer. 'Look!' He pointed to the causeway. Already a great press of Orcs and Men were gathering again beyond the stream. Arrows whined, and skipped on the stones about them. 'Come! We must get back and see what we can do to pile stone and beam across the gates within. Come now!'

They turned and ran. At that moment some dozen Orcs that had lain motionless among the slain leaped to their feet, and came silently and swiftly behind. Two flung themselves to the ground at Éomer's heels, tripped him, and in a moment they were on top of him. But a small dark figure that none had observed sprang out of the shadows and gave a hoarse shout: *Baruk Khazâd! Khazâd ai-mênu!* An axe swung and swept back. Two Orcs fell headless. The rest fled.

Éomer struggled to his feet, even as Aragorn ran back to his aid.

The postern was closed again, the iron door was barred and piled inside with stones. When all were safe within, Éomer turned: 'I thank you, Gimli son of Glóin!' he said. 'I did not know that you were with us in the sortie. But oft the unbidden guest proves the best company. How came you there?'

'I followed you to shake off sleep,' said Gimli; 'but I looked on the hillmen and they seemed over large for me, so I sat beside a stone to see your sword-play.'

'I shall not find it easy to repay you,' said Éomer.

'There may be many a chance ere the night is over,' laughed the Dwarf. 'But I am content. Till now I have hewn naught but wood since I left Moria.'

'Two!' said Gimli, patting his axe. He had returned to his place on the wall.

'Two?' said Legolas. 'I have done better, though now I must grope for

spent arrows; all mine are gone. Yet I make my tale twenty at the least.
But that is only a few leaves in a forest.'

The sky now was quickly clearing and the sinking moon was shining
brightly. But the light brought little hope to the Riders of the Mark. The
enemy before them seemed to have grown rather than diminished, and still
more were pressing up from the valley through the breach. The sortie upon
the Rock gained only a brief respite. The assault on the gates was redoubled.
Against the Deeping Wall the hosts of Isengard roared like a sea. Orcs and
hillmen swarmed about its feet from end to end. Ropes with grappling
hooks were hurled over the parapet faster than men could cut them or fling
them back. Hundreds of long ladders were lifted up. Many were cast down
in ruin, but many more replaced them, and Orcs sprang up them like apes
in the dark forests of the South. Before the wall's foot the dead and broken
were piled like shingle in a storm; ever higher rose the hideous mounds,
and still the enemy came on.

The men of Rohan grew weary. All their arrows were spent, and
every shaft was shot; their swords were notched, and their shields were
riven. Three times Aragorn and Éomer rallied them, and three times
Andúril flamed in a desperate charge that drove the enemy from the
wall.

Then a clamour arose in the Deep behind. Orcs had crept like rats
through the culvert through which the stream flowed out. There they had
gathered in the shadow of the cliffs, until the assault above was hottest and
nearly all the men of the defence had rushed to the wall's top. Then they
sprang out. Already some had passed into the jaws of the Deep and were
among the horses, fighting with the guards.

Down from the wall leapt Gimli with a fierce cry that echoed in the cliffs.
'Khazâd! Khazâd!' He soon had work enough.

'Ai-oi!' he shouted. 'The Orcs are behind the wall. Ai-oi! Come, Legolas!
There are enough for us both. Khazâd ai-mênu!'

Gamling the Old looked down from the Hornburg, hearing the great
voice of the dwarf above all the tumult. 'The Orcs are in the Deep!' he
cried. 'Helm! Helm! Forth Helmingas!' he shouted as he leaped down the
stair from the Rock with many men of Westfold at his back.

Their onset was fierce and sudden, and the Orcs gave way before them.
Ere long they were hemmed in in the narrows of the gorge, and all were
slain or driven shrieking into the chasm of the Deep to fall before the
guardians of the hidden caves.

'Twenty-one!' cried Gimli. He hewed a two-handed stroke and laid the
last Orc before his feet. 'Now my count passes Master Legolas again.'

'We must stop this rat-hole,' said Gamling. 'Dwarves are said to be cunning folk with stone. Lend us your aid, master!'

'We do not shape stone with battle-axes, nor with our finger-nails,' said Gimli. 'But I will help as I may.'

They gathered such small boulders and broken stones as they could find to hand, and under Gimli's direction the Westfold-men blocked up the inner end of the culvert, until only a narrow outlet remained. Then the Deeping-stream, swollen by the rain, churned and fretted in its choked path, and spread slowly in cold pools from cliff to cliff.

'It will be drier above,' said Gimli. 'Come, Gamling, let us see how things go on the wall!'

He climbed up and found Legolas beside Aragorn and Éomer. The elf was whetting his long knife. There was for a while a lull in the assault, since the attempt to break in through the culvert had been foiled.

'Twenty-one!' said Gimli.

'Good!' said Legolas. 'But my count is now two dozen. It has been knife-work up here.'

Éomer and Aragorn leant wearily on their swords. Away on the left the crash and clamour of the battle on the Rock rose loud again. But the Hornburg still held fast, like an island in the sea. Its gates lay in ruin; but over the barricade of beams and stones within no enemy as yet had passed.

Aragorn looked at the pale stars, and at the moon, now sloping behind the western hills that enclosed the valley. 'This is a night as long as years,' he said. 'How long will the day tarry?'

'Dawn is not far off,' said Gamling, who had now climbed up beside him. 'But dawn will not help us, I fear.'

'Yet dawn is ever the hope of men,' said Aragorn.

'But these creatures of Isengard, these half-orcs and goblin-men that the foul craft of Saruman has bred, they will not quail at the sun,' said Gamling. 'And neither will the wild men of the hills. Do you not hear their voices?'

'I hear them,' said Éomer; 'but they are only the scream of birds and the bellowing of beasts to my ears.'

'Yet there are many that cry in the Dunland tongue,' said Gamling. 'I know that tongue. It is an ancient speech of men, and once was spoken in many western valleys of the Mark. Hark! They hate us, and they are glad; for our doom seems certain to them. "The king, the king!" they cry. "We will take their king. Death to the Forgoil! Death to the Strawheads! Death to the robbers of the North!" Such names they have for us. Not in half a thousand years have they forgotten their grievance that the lords of Gondor gave the Mark to Eorl the Young and made alliance with him. That old hatred Saruman has inflamed. They are fierce folk when roused. They will not give way now for dusk or dawn, until Théoden is taken, or they themselves are slain.'

'Nonetheless day will bring hope to me,' said Aragorn. 'Is it not said that no foe has ever taken the Hornburg, if men defended it?'

'So the minstrels say,' said Éomer.

'Then let us defend it, and hope!' said Aragorn.

Even as they spoke there came a blare of trumpets. Then there was a crash and a flash of flame and smoke. The waters of the Deeping-stream poured out hissing and foaming: they were choked no longer, a gaping hole was blasted in the wall. A host of dark shapes poured in.

'Devilry of Saruman!' cried Aragorn. 'They have crept in the culvert again, while we talked, and they have lit the fire of Orthanc beneath our feet. *Elendil, Elendil!*' he shouted, as he leaped down into the breach; but even as he did so a hundred ladders were raised against the battlements. Over the wall and under the wall the last assault came sweeping like a dark wave upon a hill of sand. The defence was swept away. Some of the Riders were driven back, further and further into the Deep, falling and fighting as they gave way, step by step, towards the caves. Others cut their way back towards the citadel.

A broad stairway climbed from the Deep up to the Rock and the rear-gate of the Hornburg. Near the bottom stood Aragorn. In his hand still Andúril gleamed, and the terror of the sword for a while held back the enemy, as one by one all who could gain the stair passed up towards the gate. Behind on the upper steps knelt Legolas. His bow was bent, but one gleaned arrow was all that he had left, and he peered out now, ready to shoot the first Orc that should dare to approach the stair.

'All who can have now got safe within, Aragorn,' he called. 'Come back!'

Aragorn turned and sped up the stair; but as he ran he stumbled in his weariness. At once his enemies leapt forward. Up came the Orcs, yelling, with their long arms stretched out to seize him. The foremost fell with Legolas' last arrow in his throat, but the rest sprang over him. Then a great boulder, cast from the outer wall above, crashed down upon the stair, and hurled them back into the Deep. Aragorn gained the door, and swiftly it clanged to behind him.

'Things go ill, my friends,' he said, wiping the sweat from his brow with his arm.

'Ill enough,' said Legolas, 'but not yet hopeless, while we have you with us. Where is Gimli?'

'I do not know,' said Aragorn. 'I last saw him fighting on the ground behind the wall, but the enemy swept us apart.'

'Alas! That is evil news,' said Legolas.

'He is stout and strong,' said Aragorn. 'Let us hope that he will escape
back to the caves. There he would be safe for a while. Safer than we. Such
a refuge would be to the liking of a dwarf.'

'That must be my hope,' said Legolas. 'But I wish that he had come this
way. I desired to tell Master Gimli that my tale is now thirty-nine.'

'If he wins back to the caves, he will pass your count again,' laughed
Aragorn. 'Never did I see an axe so wielded.'

'I must go and seek some arrows,' said Legolas. 'Would that this night
would end, and I could have better light for shooting.'

Aragorn now passed into the citadel. There to his dismay he learned that
Éomer had not reached the Hornburg.

'Nay, he did not come to the Rock,' said one of the Westfold-men.
'I last saw him gathering men about him and fighting in the mouth of
the Deep. Gamling was with him, and the dwarf; but I could not come to
them.'

Aragorn strode on through the inner court, and mounted to a high
chamber in the tower. There stood the king, dark against a narrow window,
looking out upon the vale.

'What is the news, Aragorn?' he said.

'The Deeping Wall is taken, lord, and all the defence swept away; but
many have escaped hither to the Rock.'

'Is Éomer here?'

'No, lord. But many of your men retreated into the Deep; and some say
that Éomer was amongst them. In the narrows they may hold back the
enemy and come within the caves. What hope they may have then I do
not know.'

'More than we. Good provision, it is said. And the air is wholesome
there because of the outlets through fissures in the rock far above. None
can force an entrance against determined men. They may hold out long.'

'But the Orcs have brought a devilry from Orthanc,' said Aragorn. 'They
have a blasting fire, and with it they took the Wall. If they cannot come
in the caves, they may seal up those that are inside. But now we must turn
all our thought to our own defence.'

'I fret in this prison,' said Théoden. 'If I could have set a spear in rest,
riding before my men upon the field, maybe I could have felt again the joy
of battle, and so ended. But I serve little purpose here.'

'Here at least you are guarded in the strongest fastness of the Mark,'
said Aragorn. 'More hope we have to defend you in the Hornburg than in
Edoras, or even at Dunharrow in the mountains.'

'It is said that the Hornburg has never fallen to assault,' said Théoden;
'but now my heart is doubtful. The world changes, and all that once was

strong now proves unsure. How shall any tower withstand such numbers and such reckless hate? Had I known that the strength of Isengard was grown so great, maybe I should not so rashly have ridden forth to meet it, for all the arts of Gandalf. His counsel seems not now so good as it did under the morning sun.'

'Do not judge the counsel of Gandalf, until all is over, lord,' said Aragorn.

'The end will not be long,' said the king. 'But I will not end here, taken like an old badger in a trap. Snowmane and Hasufel and the horses of my guard are in the inner court. When dawn comes, I will bid men sound Helm's horn, and I will ride forth. Will you ride with me then, son of Arathorn? Maybe we shall cleave a road, or make such an end as will be worth a song – if any be left to sing of us hereafter.'

'I will ride with you,' said Aragorn.

Taking his leave, he returned to the walls, and passed round all their circuit, enheartening the men, and lending aid wherever the assault was hot. Legolas went with him. Blasts of fire leaped up from below shaking the stones. Grappling-hooks were hurled, and ladders raised. Again and again the Orcs gained the summit of the outer wall, and again the defenders cast them down.

At last Aragorn stood above the great gates, heedless of the darts of the enemy. As he looked forth he saw the eastern sky grow pale. Then he raised his empty hand, palm outward in token of parley.

The Orcs yelled and jeered. 'Come down! Come down!' they cried. 'If you wish to speak to us, come down! Bring out your king! We are the fighting Uruk-hai. We will fetch him from his hole, if he does not come. Bring out your skulking king!'

'The king stays or comes at his own will,' said Aragorn.

'Then what are you doing here?' they answered. 'Why do you look out? Do you wish to see the greatness of our army? We are the fighting Uruk-hai.'

'I looked out to see the dawn,' said Aragorn.

'What of the dawn?' they jeered. 'We are the Uruk-hai: we do not stop the fight for night or day, for fair weather or for storm. We come to kill, by sun or moon. What of the dawn?'

'None knows what the new day shall bring him,' said Aragorn. 'Get you gone, ere it turn to your evil.'

'Get down or we will shoot you from the wall,' they cried. 'This is no parley. You have nothing to say.'

'I have still this to say,' answered Aragorn. 'No enemy has yet taken the Hornburg. Depart, or not one of you will be spared. Not one will be left alive to take back tidings to the North. You do not know your peril.'

So great a power and royalty was revealed in Aragorn, as he stood there alone above the ruined gates before the host of his enemies, that many of the wild men paused, and looked back over their shoulders to the valley, and some looked up doubtfully at the sky. But the Orcs laughed with loud voices; and a hail of darts and arrows whistled over the wall, as Aragorn leaped down.

There was a roar and a blast of fire. The archway of the gate above which he had stood a moment before crumbled and crashed in smoke and dust. The barricade was scattered as if by a thunderbolt. Aragorn ran to the king's tower.

But even as the gate fell, and the Orcs about it yelled, preparing to charge, a murmur arose behind them, like a wind in the distance, and it grew to a clamour of many voices crying strange news in the dawn. The Orcs upon the Rock, hearing the rumour of dismay, wavered and looked back. And then, sudden and terrible, from the tower above, the sound of the great horn of Helm rang out.

All that heard that sound trembled. Many of the Orcs cast themselves on their faces and covered their ears with their claws. Back from the Deep the echoes came, blast upon blast, as if on every cliff and hill a mighty herald stood. But on the walls men looked up, listening with wonder; for the echoes did not die. Ever the hornblasts wound on among the hills; nearer now and louder they answered one to another, blowing fierce and free.

'Helm! Helm!' the Riders shouted. 'Helm is arisen and comes back to war. Helm for Théoden King!'

And with that shout the king came. His horse was white as snow, golden was his shield, and his spear was long. At his right hand was Aragorn, Elendil's heir, behind him rode the lords of the House of Eorl the Young. Light sprang in the sky. Night departed.

'Forth Eorlingas!' With a cry and a great noise they charged. Down from the gates they roared, over the causeway they swept, and they drove through the hosts of Isengard as a wind among grass. Behind them from the Deep came the stern cries of men issuing from the caves, driving forth the enemy. Out poured all the men that were left upon the Rock. And ever the sound of blowing horns echoed in the hills.

On they rode, the king and his companions. Captains and champions fell or fled before them. Neither orc nor man withstood them. Their backs were to the swords and spears of the Riders, and their faces to the valley. They cried and wailed, for fear and great wonder had come upon them with the rising of the day.

So King Théoden rode from Helm's Gate and clove his path to the great
Dike. There the company halted. Light grew bright about them. Shafts of
the sun flared above the eastern hills and glimmered on their spears. But
they sat silent on their horses, and they gazed down upon the
Deeping-coomb.

The land had changed. Where before the green dale had lain, its grassy
slopes lapping the ever-mounting hills, there now a forest loomed. Great
trees, bare and silent, stood, rank on rank, with tangled bough and hoary
head; their twisted roots were buried in the long green grass. Darkness
was under them. Between the Dike and the eaves of that nameless wood
only two open furlongs lay. There now cowered the proud hosts of
Saruman, in terror of the king and in terror of the trees. They streamed
down from Helm's Gate until all above the Dike was empty of them, but
below it they were packed like swarming flies. Vainly they crawled and
clambered about the walls of the coomb, seeking to escape. Upon the east
too sheer and stony was the valley's side; upon the left, from the west,
their final doom approached.

There suddenly upon a ridge appeared a rider, clad in white, shining in
the rising sun. Over the low hills the horns were sounding. Behind him,
hastening down the long slopes, were a thousand men on foot; their swords
were in their hands. Amid them strode a man tall and strong. His shield
was red. As he came to the valley's brink, he set to his lips a great black
horn and blew a ringing blast.

'Erkenbrand!' the Riders shouted. 'Erkenbrand!'

'Behold the White Rider!' cried Aragorn. 'Gandalf is come again!'

'Mithrandir, Mithrandir!' said Legolas. 'This is wizardry indeed! Come!
I would look on this forest, ere the spell changes.'

The hosts of Isengard roared, swaying this way and that, turning from
fear to fear. Again the horn sounded from the tower. Down through the
breach of the Dike charged the king's company. Down from the hills leaped
Erkenbrand, lord of Westfold. Down leaped Shadowfax, like a deer that
runs surefooted in the mountains. The White Rider was upon them, and
the terror of his coming filled the enemy with madness. The wild men fell
on their faces before him. The Orcs reeled and screamed and cast aside
both sword and spear. Like a black smoke driven by a mounting wind they
fled. Wailing they passed under the waiting shadow of the trees; and from
that shadow none ever came again.

CHAPTER VIII

THE ROAD TO ISENGARD

So it was that in the light of a fair morning King Théoden and Gandalf the White Rider met again upon the green grass beside the Deeping-stream. There was also Aragorn son of Arathorn, and Legolas the Elf, and Erkenbrand of Westfold, and the lords of the Golden House. About them were gathered the Rohirrim, the Riders of the Mark: wonder overcame their joy in victory, and their eyes were turned towards the wood.

Suddenly there was a great shout, and down from the Dike came those who had been driven back into the Deep. There came Gamling the Old, and Éomer son of Éomund, and beside them walked Gimli the dwarf. He had no helm, and about his head was a linen band stained with blood; but his voice was loud and strong.

'Forty-two, Master Legolas!' he cried. 'Alas! My axe is notched: the forty-second had an iron collar on his neck. How is it with you?'

'You have passed my score by one,' answered Legolas. 'But I do not grudge you the game, so glad am I to see you on your legs!'

'Welcome, Éomer, sister-son!' said Théoden. 'Now that I see you safe, I am glad indeed.'

'Hail, Lord of the Mark!' said Éomer. 'The dark night has passed, and day has come again. But the day has brought strange tidings.' He turned and gazed in wonder, first at the wood and then at Gandalf. 'Once more you come in the hour of need, unlooked-for,' he said.

'Unlooked-for?' said Gandalf. 'I said that I would return and meet you here.'

'But you did not name the hour, nor foretell the manner of your coming. Strange help you bring. You are mighty in wizardry, Gandalf the White!'

'That may be. But if so, I have not shown it yet. I have but given good counsel in peril, and made use of the speed of Shadowfax. Your own valour has done more, and the stout legs of the Westfold-men marching through the night.'

Then they all gazed at Gandalf with still greater wonder. Some glanced darkly at the wood, and passed their hands over their brows, as if they thought their eyes saw otherwise than his.

Gandalf laughed long and merrily. 'The trees?' he said. 'Nay, I see the wood as plainly as do you. But that is no deed of mine. It is a thing beyond the counsel of the wise. Better than my design, and better even than my hope the event has proved.'

'Then if not yours, whose is the wizardry?' said Théoden. 'Not Saruman's, that is plain. Is there some mightier sage, of whom we have yet to learn?'

'It is not wizardry, but a power far older,' said Gandalf: 'a power that walked the earth, ere elf sang or hammer rang.

> *Ere iron was found or tree was hewn,*
> *When young was mountain under moon;*
> *Ere ring was made, or wrought was woe,*
> *It walked the forests long ago.'*

'And what may be the answer to your riddle?' said Théoden.

'If you would learn that, you should come with me to Isengard,' answered Gandalf.

'To Isengard?' they cried.

'Yes,' said Gandalf. 'I shall return to Isengard, and those who will may come with me. There we may see strange things.'

'But there are not men enough in the Mark, not if they were all gathered together and healed of wounds and weariness, to assault the stronghold of Saruman,' said Théoden.

'Nevertheless to Isengard I go,' said Gandalf. 'I shall not stay there long. My way lies now eastward. Look for me in Edoras, ere the waning of the moon!'

'Nay!' said Théoden. 'In the dark hour before dawn I doubted, but we will not part now. I will come with you, if that is your counsel.'

'I wish to speak with Saruman, as soon as may be now,' said Gandalf, 'and since he has done you great injury, it would be fitting if you were there. But how soon and how swiftly will you ride?'

'My men are weary with battle,' said the King; 'and I am weary also. For I have ridden far and slept little. Alas! My old age is not feigned nor due only to the whisperings of Wormtongue. It is an ill that no leech can wholly cure, not even Gandalf.'

'Then let all who are to ride with me rest now,' said Gandalf. 'We will journey under the shadow of evening. It is as well; for it is my counsel that all our comings and goings should be as secret as may be, henceforth. But do not command many men to go with you, Théoden. We go to a parley not to a fight.'

The King then chose men that were unhurt and had swift horses, and he sent them forth with tidings of the victory into every vale of the Mark; and they bore his summons also, bidding all men, young and old, to come in haste to Edoras. There the Lord of the Mark would hold an assembly of all that could bear arms, on the second day after the full moon. To ride with him to Isengard the King chose Éomer and twenty men of his household. With Gandalf would go Aragorn, and Legolas, and Gimli. In spite of his hurt the dwarf would not stay behind.

'It was only a feeble blow and the cap turned it,' he said. 'It would take more than such an orc-scratch to keep me back.'

'I will tend it, while you rest,' said Aragorn.

The king now returned to the Hornburg, and slept, such a sleep of quiet as he had not known for many years, and the remainder of his chosen company rested also. But the others, all that were not hurt or wounded, began a great labour; for many had fallen in the battle and lay dead upon the field or in the Deep.

No Orcs remained alive; their bodies were uncounted. But a great many of the hillmen had given themselves up; and they were afraid, and cried for mercy.

The Men of the Mark took their weapons from them, and set them to work.

'Help now to repair the evil in which you have joined,' said Erkenbrand; 'and afterwards you shall take an oath never again to pass the Fords of Isen in arms, nor to march with the enemies of Men; and then you shall go free back to your land. For you have been deluded by Saruman. Many of you have got death as the reward of your trust in him; but had you conquered, little better would your wages have been.'

The men of Dunland were amazed; for Saruman had told them that the men of Rohan were cruel and burned their captives alive.

In the midst of the field before the Hornburg two mounds were raised, and beneath them were laid all the Riders of the Mark who fell in the defence, those of the East Dales upon one side, and those of Westfold upon the other. In a grave alone under the shadow of the Hornburg lay Háma, captain of the King's guard. He fell before the Gate.

The Orcs were piled in great heaps, away from the mounds of Men, not far from the eaves of the forest. And the people were troubled in their minds; for the heaps of carrion were too great for burial or for burning. They had little wood for firing, and none would have dared to take an axe to the strange trees, even if Gandalf had not warned them to hurt neither bark nor bough at their great peril.

'Let the Orcs lie,' said Gandalf. 'The morning may bring new counsel.'

In the afternoon the King's company prepared to depart. The work of burial was then but beginning; and Théoden mourned for the loss of Háma, his captain, and cast the first earth upon his grave. 'Great injury indeed has Saruman done to me and all this land,' he said; 'and I will remember it, when we meet.'

The sun was already drawing near the hills upon the west of the Coomb, when at last Théoden and Gandalf and their companions rode down from the Dike. Behind them were gathered a great host, both of the Riders and of the people of Westfold, old and young, women and children, who had come out from the caves. A song of victory they sang with clear voices; and then they fell silent, wondering what would chance, for their eyes were on the trees and they feared them.

The Riders came to the wood, and they halted; horse and man, they were unwilling to pass in. The trees were grey and menacing, and a shadow or a mist was about them. The ends of their long sweeping boughs hung down like searching fingers, their roots stood up from the ground like the limbs of strange monsters, and dark caverns opened beneath them. But Gandalf went forward, leading the company, and where the road from the Hornburg met the trees they saw now an opening like an arched gate under mighty boughs; and through it Gandalf passed, and they followed him. Then to their amazement they found that the road ran on, and the Deeping-stream beside it; and the sky was open above and full of golden light. But on either side the great aisles of the wood were already wrapped in dusk, stretching away into impenetrable shadows; and there they heard the creaking and groaning of boughs, and far cries, and a rumour of wordless voices, murmuring angrily. No Orc or other living creature could be seen.

Legolas and Gimli were now riding together upon one horse; and they kept close beside Gandalf, for Gimli was afraid of the wood.

'It is hot in here,' said Legolas to Gandalf. 'I feel a great wrath about me. Do you not feel the air throb in your ears?'

'Yes,' said Gandalf.

'What has become of the miserable Orcs?' said Legolas.

'That, I think, no one will ever know,' said Gandalf.

They rode in silence for a while; but Legolas was ever glancing from side to side, and would often have halted to listen to the sounds of the wood, if Gimli had allowed it.

'These are the strangest trees that ever I saw,' he said; 'and I have seen many an oak grow from acorn to ruinous age. I wish that there were leisure now to walk among them: they have voices, and in time I might come to understand their thought.'

'No, no!' said Gimli. 'Let us leave them! I guess their thought already: hatred of all that go on two legs; and their speech is of crushing and strangling.'

'Not of all that go on two legs,' said Legolas. 'There I think you are wrong. It is Orcs that they hate. For they do not belong here and know little of Elves and Men. Far away are the valleys where they sprang. From the deep dales of Fangorn, Gimli, that is whence they come, I guess.'

'Then that is the most perilous wood in Middle-earth,' said Gimli. 'I should be grateful for the part they have played, but I do not love them. You may think them wonderful, but I have seen a greater wonder in this land, more beautiful than any grove or glade that ever grew: my heart is still full of it.

'Strange are the ways of Men, Legolas! Here they have one of the marvels of the Northern World, and what do they say of it? Caves, they say! Caves! Holes to fly to in time of war, to store fodder in! My good Legolas, do you know that the caverns of Helm's Deep are vast and beautiful? There would be an endless pilgrimage of Dwarves, merely to gaze at them, if such things were known to be. Aye indeed, they would pay pure gold for a brief glance!'

'And I would give gold to be excused,' said Legolas; 'and double to be let out, if I strayed in!'

'You have not seen, so I forgive your jest,' said Gimli. 'But you speak like a fool. Do you think those halls are fair, where your King dwells under the hill in Mirkwood, and Dwarves helped in their making long ago? They are but hovels compared with the caverns I have seen here: immeasurable halls, filled with an everlasting music of water that tinkles into pools, as fair as Kheled-zâram in the starlight.

'And, Legolas, when the torches are kindled and men walk on the sandy floors under the echoing domes, ah! then, Legolas, gems and crystals and veins of precious ore glint in the polished walls; and the light glows through folded marbles, shell-like, translucent as the living hands of Queen Galadriel. There are columns of white and saffron and dawn-rose, Legolas, fluted and twisted into dreamlike forms; they spring up from many-coloured floors to meet the glistening pendants of the roof: wings, ropes, curtains fine as frozen clouds; spears, banners, pinnacles of suspended palaces! Still lakes mirror them: a glimmering world looks up from dark pools covered with clear glass; cities, such as the mind of Durin could scarce have imagined in his sleep, stretch on through avenues and pillared courts, on into the dark recesses where no light can come. And plink! a silver drop falls, and the round wrinkles in the glass make all the towers bend and waver like weeds and corals in a grotto of the sea. Then evening comes: they fade and twinkle out; the torches pass on into another chamber and another dream. There is chamber after chamber, Legolas; hall opening out of hall, dome after dome, stair beyond stair; and still the winding paths lead on into the mountains' heart. Caves! The Caverns of Helm's Deep! Happy was the chance that drove me there! It makes me weep to leave them.'

'Then I will wish you this fortune for your comfort, Gimli,' said the Elf, 'that you may come safe from war and return to see them again. But do not tell all your kindred! There seems little left for them to do, from your account. Maybe the men of this land are wise to say little: one family of busy dwarves with hammer and chisel might mar more than they made.'

'No, you do not understand,' said Gimli. 'No dwarf could be unmoved by such loveliness. None of Durin's race would mine those caves for stones or ore, not if diamonds and gold could be got there. Do you cut down groves of blossoming trees in the springtime for firewood? We would tend these glades of flowering stone, not quarry them. With cautious skill, tap by tap – a small chip of rock and no more, perhaps, in a whole anxious day – so we could work, and as the years went by, we should open up new ways, and display far chambers that are still dark, glimpsed only as a void beyond fissures in the rock. And lights, Legolas! We should make lights, such lamps as once shone in Khazad-dûm; and when we wished we would drive away the night that has lain there since the hills were made; and when we desired rest, we would let the night return.'

'You move me, Gimli,' said Legolas. 'I have never heard you speak like this before. Almost you make me regret that I have not seen these caves. Come! Let us make this bargain – if we both return safe out of the perils that await us, we will journey for a while together. You shall visit Fangorn with me, and then I will come with you to see Helm's Deep.'

'That would not be the way of return that I should choose,' said Gimli. 'But I will endure Fangorn, if I have your promise to come back to the caves and share their wonder with me.'

'You have my promise,' said Legolas. 'But alas! Now we must leave behind both cave and wood for a while. See! We are coming to the end of the trees. How far is it to Isengard, Gandalf?'

'About fifteen leagues, as the crows of Saruman make it,' said Gandalf: 'five from the mouth of Deeping-coomb to the Fords; and ten more from there to the gates of Isengard. But we shall not ride all the way this night.'

'And when we come there, what shall we see?' asked Gimli. 'You may know, but I cannot guess.'

'I do not know myself for certain,' answered the wizard. 'I was there at nightfall yesterday, but much may have happened since. Yet I think that you will not say that the journey was in vain – not though the Glittering Caves of Aglarond be left behind.'

At last the company passed through the trees, and found that they had come to the bottom of the Coomb, where the road from Helm's Deep branched, going one way east to Edoras, and the other north to the Fords of Isen. As they rode from under the eaves of the wood, Legolas halted and looked back with regret. Then he gave a sudden cry.

'There are eyes!' he said. 'Eyes looking out from the shadows of the boughs! I never saw such eyes before.'

The others, surprised by his cry, halted and turned; but Legolas started to ride back.

'No, no!' cried Gimli. 'Do as you please in your madness, but let me first get down from this horse! I wish to see no eyes!'

'Stay, Legolas Greenleaf!' said Gandalf. 'Do not go back into the wood, not yet! Now is not your time.'

Even as he spoke, there came forward out of the trees three strange shapes. As tall as trolls they were, twelve feet or more in height; their strong bodies, stout as young trees, seemed to be clad with raiment or with hide of close-fitting grey and brown. Their limbs were long, and their hands had many fingers; their hair was stiff, and their beards grey-green as moss. They gazed out with solemn eyes, but they were not looking at the riders: their eyes were bent northwards. Suddenly they lifted their long hands to their mouths, and sent forth ringing calls, clear as notes of a horn, but more musical and various. The calls were answered; and turning again, the riders saw other creatures of the same kind approaching, striding through the grass. They came swiftly from the North, walking like wading herons in their gait, but not in their speed; for their legs in their long paces beat quicker than the heron's wings. The riders cried aloud in wonder, and some set their hands upon their sword-hilts.

'You need no weapons,' said Gandalf. 'These are but herdsmen. They are not enemies, indeed they are not concerned with us at all.'

So it seemed to be; for as he spoke the tall creatures, without a glance at the riders, strode into the wood and vanished.

'Herdsmen!' said Théoden. 'Where are their flocks? What are they, Gandalf? For it is plain that to you, at any rate, they are not strange.'

'They are the shepherds of the trees,' answered Gandalf. 'Is it so long since you listened to tales by the fireside? There are children in your land who, out of the twisted threads of story, could pick the answer to your question. You have seen Ents, O King, Ents out of Fangorn Forest, which in your tongue you call the Entwood. Did you think that the name was given only in idle fancy? Nay, Théoden, it is otherwise: to them you are but the passing tale; all the years from Eorl the Young to Théoden the Old are of little count to them; and all the deeds of your house but a small matter.'

The king was silent. 'Ents!' he said at length. 'Out of the shadows of legend I begin a little to understand the marvel of the trees, I think. I have lived to see strange days. Long we have tended our beasts and our fields, built our houses, wrought our tools, or ridden away to help in the wars of Minas Tirith. And that we called the life of Men, the way of the world.

We cared little for what lay beyond the borders of our land. Songs we have that tell of these things, but we are forgetting them, teaching them only to children, as a careless custom. And now the songs have come down among us out of strange places, and walk visible under the Sun.'

'You should be glad, Théoden King,' said Gandalf. 'For not only the little life of Men is now endangered, but the life also of those things which you have deemed the matter of legend. You are not without allies, even if you know them not.'

'Yet also I should be sad,' said Théoden. 'For however the fortune of war shall go, may it not so end that much that was fair and wonderful shall pass for ever out of Middle-earth?'

'It may,' said Gandalf. 'The evil of Sauron cannot be wholly cured, nor made as if it had not been. But to such days we are doomed. Let us now go on with the journey we have begun!'

The company turned then away from the Coomb and from the wood and took the road towards the Fords. Legolas followed reluctantly. The sun had set, already it had sunk behind the rim of the world; but as they rode out from the shadow of the hills and looked west to the Gap of Rohan the sky was still red, and a burning light was under the floating clouds. Dark against it there wheeled and flew many black-winged birds. Some passed overhead with mournful cries, returning to their homes among the rocks.

'The carrion-fowl have been busy about the battle-field,' said Éomer.

They rode now at an easy pace and dark came down upon the plains about them. The slow moon mounted, now waxing towards the full, and in its cold silver light the swelling grass-lands rose and fell like a wide grey sea. They had ridden for some four hours from the branching of the roads when they drew near to the Fords. Long slopes ran swiftly down to where the river spread in stony shoals between high grassy terraces. Borne upon the wind they heard the howling of wolves. Their hearts were heavy, remembering the many men that had fallen in battle in this place.

The road dipped between rising turf-banks, carving its way through the terraces to the river's edge, and up again upon the further side. There were three lines of flat stepping-stones across the stream, and between them fords for horses, that went from either brink to a bare eyot in the midst. The riders looked down upon the crossings, and it seemed strange to them; for the Fords had ever been a place full of the rush and chatter of water upon stones; but now they were silent. The beds of the stream were almost dry, a bare waste of shingles and grey sand.

'This is become a dreary place,' said Éomer. 'What sickness has befallen the river? Many fair things Saruman has destroyed: has he devoured the springs of Isen too?'

'So it would seem,' said Gandalf.

'Alas!' said Théoden. 'Must we pass this way, where the carrion-beasts devour so many good Riders of the Mark?'

'This is our way,' said Gandalf. 'Grievous is the fall of your men; but you shall see that at least the wolves of the mountains do not devour them. It is with their friends, the Orcs, that they hold their feast: such indeed is the friendship of their kind. Come!'

They rode down to the river, and as they came the wolves ceased their howling and slunk away. Fear fell on them seeing Gandalf in the moon, and Shadowfax his horse shining like silver. The riders passed over to the islet, and glittering eyes watched them wanly from the shadows of the banks.

'Look!' said Gandalf. 'Friends have laboured here.'

And they saw that in the midst of the eyot a mound was piled, ringed with stones, and set about with many spears.

'Here lie all the Men of the Mark that fell near this place,' said Gandalf.

'Here let them rest!' said Éomer. 'And when their spears have rotted and rusted, long still may their mound stand and guard the Fords of Isen!'

'Is this your work also, Gandalf, my friend?' said Théoden. 'You accomplished much in an evening and a night!'

'With the help of Shadowfax – and others,' said Gandalf. 'I rode fast and far. But here beside the mound I will say this for your comfort: many fell in the battles of the Fords, but fewer than rumour made them. More were scattered than were slain; I gathered together all that I could find. Some men I sent with Grimbold of Westfold to join Erkenbrand. Some I set to make this burial. They have now followed your marshal, Elfhelm. I sent him with many Riders to Edoras. Saruman I knew had despatched his full strength against you, and his servants had turned aside from all other errands and gone to Helm's Deep: the lands seemed empty of enemies; yet I feared that wolf-riders and plunderers might ride nonetheless to Meduseld, while it was undefended. But now I think you need not fear: you will find your house to welcome your return.'

'And glad shall I be to see it again,' said Théoden, 'though brief now, I doubt not, shall be my abiding there.'

With that the company said farewell to the island and the mound, and passed over the river, and climbed the further bank. Then they rode on, glad to have left the mournful Fords. As they went the howling of the wolves broke out anew.

There was an ancient highway that ran down from Isengard to the crossings. For some way it took its course beside the river, bending with it east and then north; but at the last it turned away and went straight towards the gates of Isengard; and these were under the mountain-side in the west of the valley, sixteen miles or more from its mouth. This road they followed but they did not ride upon it; for the ground beside it was firm and level, covered for many miles about with short springing turf. They rode now more swiftly, and by midnight the Fords were nearly five leagues behind. Then they halted, ending their night's journey, for the King was weary. They were come to the feet of the Misty Mountains, and the long arms of Nan Curunír stretched down to meet them. Dark lay the vale before them, for the moon had passed into the West, and its light was hidden by the hills. But out of the deep shadow of the dale rose a vast spire of smoke and vapour; as it mounted, it caught the rays of the sinking moon, and spread in shimmering billows, black and silver, over the starry sky.

'What do you think of that, Gandalf?' asked Aragorn. 'One would say that all the Wizard's Vale was burning.'

'There is ever a fume above that valley in these days,' said Éomer: 'but I have never seen aught like this before. These are steams rather than smokes. Saruman is brewing some devilry to greet us. Maybe he is boiling all the waters of Isen, and that is why the river runs dry.'

'Maybe he is,' said Gandalf. 'Tomorrow we shall learn what he is doing. Now let us rest for a while, if we can.'

They camped beside the bed of the Isen river; it was still silent and empty. Some of them slept a little. But late in the night the watchmen cried out, and all awoke. The moon was gone. Stars were shining above; but over the ground there crept a darkness blacker than the night. On both sides of the river it rolled towards them, going northward.

'Stay where you are!' said Gandalf. 'Draw no weapons! Wait! and it will pass you by!'

A mist gathered about them. Above them a few stars still glimmered faintly; but on either side there arose walls of impenetrable gloom; they were in a narrow lane between moving towers of shadow. Voices they heard, whisperings and groanings and an endless rustling sigh; the earth shook under them. Long it seemed to them that they sat and were afraid; but at last the darkness and the rumour passed, and vanished between the mountain's arms.

Away south upon the Hornburg, in the middle night men heard a great noise, as a wind in the valley, and the ground trembled; and all were afraid and no one ventured to go forth. But in the morning they went out and were amazed; for the slain Orcs were gone, and the trees also. Far down into the valley of the Deep the grass was crushed and trampled brown, as if giant herdsmen had pastured great droves of cattle there; but a mile below the Dike a huge pit had been delved in the earth, and over it stones were piled into a hill. Men believed that the Orcs whom they had slain were buried there; but whether those who had fled into the wood were with them, none could say, for no man ever set foot upon that hill. The Death Down it was afterwards called, and no grass would grow there. But the strange trees were never seen in Deeping-coomb again; they had returned at night, and had gone far away to the dark dales of Fangorn. Thus they were revenged upon the Orcs.

The king and his company slept no more that night; but they saw and heard no other strange thing, save one: the voice of the river beside them suddenly awoke. There was a rush of water hurrying down among the stones; and when it had passed, the Isen flowed and bubbled in its bed again, as it had ever done.

At dawn they made ready to go on. The light came grey and pale, and they did not see the rising of the sun. The air above was heavy with fog, and a reek lay on the land about them. They went slowly, riding now upon the highway. It was broad and hard, and well-tended. Dimly through the mists they could descry the long arm of the mountains rising on their left. They had passed into Nan Curunír, the Wizard's Vale. That was a sheltered valley, open only to the South. Once it had been fair and green, and through it the Isen flowed, already deep and strong before it found the plains; for it was fed by many springs and lesser streams among the rain-washed hills, and all about it there had lain a pleasant, fertile land.

It was not so now. Beneath the walls of Isengard there still were acres tilled by the slaves of Saruman; but most of the valley had become a wilderness of weeds and thorns. Brambles trailed upon the ground, or clambering over bush and bank, made shaggy caves where small beasts housed. No trees grew there; but among the rank grasses could still be seen the burned and axe-hewn stumps of ancient groves. It was a sad country, silent now but for the stony noise of quick waters. Smokes and steams drifted in sullen clouds and lurked in the hollows. The riders did not speak. Many doubted in their hearts, wondering to what dismal end their journey led.

After they had ridden for some miles, the highway became a wide street, paved with great flat stones, squared and laid with skill; no blade of grass was seen in any joint. Deep gutters, filled with trickling water, ran down on either side. Suddenly a tall pillar loomed up before them. It was black; and set upon it was a great stone, carved and painted in the likeness of a long White Hand. Its finger pointed north. Not far now they knew that the gates of Isengard must stand, and their hearts were heavy; but their eyes could not pierce the mists ahead.

Beneath the mountain's arm within the Wizard's Vale through years uncounted had stood that ancient place that Men called Isengard. Partly it was shaped in the making of the mountains, but mighty works the Men of Westernesse had wrought there of old; and Saruman had dwelt there long and had not been idle.

This was its fashion, while Saruman was at his height, accounted by many the chief of Wizards. A great ring-wall of stone, like towering cliffs, stood out from the shelter of the mountain-side, from which it ran and then returned again. One entrance only was there made in it, a great arch delved in the southern wall. Here through the black rock a long tunnel had been hewn, closed at either end with mighty doors of iron. They were so wrought and poised upon their huge hinges, posts of steel driven into the living stone, that when unbarred they could be moved with a light thrust of the arms, noiselessly. One who passed in and came at length out of the echoing tunnel, beheld a plain, a great circle, somewhat hollowed like a vast shallow bowl: a mile it measured from rim to rim. Once it had been green and filled with avenues, and groves of fruitful trees, watered by streams that flowed from the mountains to a lake. But no green thing grew there in the latter days of Saruman. The roads were paved with stone-flags, dark and hard; and beside their borders instead of trees there marched long lines of pillars, some of marble, some of copper and of iron, joined by heavy chains.

Many houses there were, chambers, halls, and passages, cut and tunnelled back into the walls upon their inner side, so that all the open circle was overlooked by countless windows and dark doors. Thousands could dwell there, workers, servants, slaves, and warriors with great store of arms; wolves were fed and stabled in deep dens beneath. The plain, too, was bored and delved. Shafts were driven deep into the ground; their upper ends were covered by low mounds and domes of stone, so that in the moonlight the Ring of Isengard looked like a graveyard of unquiet dead. For the ground trembled. The shafts ran down by many slopes and spiral stairs to caverns far under; there Saruman had treasuries, store-houses, armouries, smithies, and great furnaces. Iron wheels revolved there endlessly, and hammers thudded. At night plumes of vapour steamed from the vents, lit from beneath with red light, or blue, or venomous green.

To the centre all the roads ran between their chains. There stood a tower of marvellous shape. It was fashioned by the builders of old, who smoothed the Ring of Isengard, and yet it seemed a thing not made by the craft of Men, but riven from the bones of the earth in the ancient torment of the hills. A peak and isle of rock it was, black and gleaming hard: four mighty piers of many-sided stone were welded into one, but near the summit they opened into gaping horns, their pinnacles sharp as the points of spears, keen-edged as knives. Between them was a narrow space, and there upon a floor of polished stone, written with strange signs, a man might stand five hundred feet above the plain. This was Orthanc, the citadel of Saruman, the name of which had (by design or chance) a twofold meaning; for in the Elvish speech *orthanc* signifies Mount Fang, but in the language'of the Mark of old the Cunning Mind.

A strong place and wonderful was Isengard, and long it had been beauti-ful; and there great lords had dwelt, the wardens of Gondor upon the West, and wise men that watched the stars. But Saruman had slowly shaped it to his shifting purposes, and made it better, as he thought, being deceived – for all those arts and subtle devices, for which he forsook his former wisdom, and which fondly he imagined were his own, came but from Mordor; so that what he made was naught, only a little copy, a child's model or a slave's flattery, of that vast fortress, armoury, prison, furnace of great power, Barad-dûr, the Dark Tower, which suffered no rival, and laughed at flattery, biding its time, secure in its pride and its immeasurable strength.

This was the stronghold of Saruman, as fame reported it; for within living memory the men of Rohan had not passed its gates, save perhaps a few, such as Wormtongue, who came in secret and told no man what they saw.

Now Gandalf rode to the great pillar of the Hand, and passed it; and as he did so the Riders saw to their wonder that the Hand appeared no longer white. It was stained as with dried blood; and looking closer they perceived that its nails were red. Unheeding Gandalf rode on into the mist, and reluctantly they followed him. All about them now, as if there had been a sudden flood, wide pools of water lay beside the road, filling the hollows, and rills went trickling down among the stones.

At last Gandalf halted and beckoned to them; and they came, and saw that beyond him the mists had cleared, and a pale sunlight shone. The hour of noon had passed. They were come to the doors of Isengard.

But the doors lay hurled and twisted on the ground. And all about, stone, cracked and splintered into countless jagged shards, was scattered far and wide, or piled in ruinous heaps. The great arch still stood, but it opened now upon a roofless chasm: the tunnel was laid bare, and through the cliff-like walls on either side great rents and breaches had been torn; their towers were beaten into dust. If the Great Sea had risen in wrath and fallen on the hills with storm, it could have worked no greater ruin.

The ring beyond was filled with steaming water: a bubbling cauldron, in which there heaved and floated a wreckage of beams and spars, chests and casks and broken gear. Twisted and leaning pillars reared their splintered stems above the flood, but all the roads were drowned. Far off, it seemed, half veiled in winding cloud, there loomed the island rock. Still dark and tall, unbroken by the storm, the tower of Orthanc stood. Pale waters lapped about its feet.

The king and all his company sat silent on their horses, marvelling, perceiving that the power of Saruman was overthrown; but how they could not guess. And now they turned their eyes towards the archway and the ruined gates. There they saw close beside them a great rubble-heap; and suddenly they were aware of two small figures lying on it at their ease, grey-clad, hardly to be seen among the stones. There were bottles and bowls and platters laid beside them, as if they had just eaten well, and now rested from their labour. One seemed asleep; the other, with crossed legs and arms behind his head, leaned back against a broken rock and sent from his mouth long wisps and little rings of thin blue smoke.

For a moment Théoden and Éomer and all his men stared at them in wonder. Amid all the wreck of Isengard this seemed to them the strangest sight. But before the king could speak, the small smoke-breathing figure became suddenly aware of them, as they sat there silent on the edge of the mist. He sprang to his feet. A young man he looked, or like one, though not much more than half a man in height; his head of brown curling hair was uncovered, but he was clad in a travel-stained cloak of the same hue and shape as the companions of Gandalf had worn when they rode to Edoras. He bowed very low, putting his hand upon his breast. Then, seeming not to observe the wizard and his friends, he turned to Éomer and the king.

'Welcome, my lords, to Isengard!' he said. 'We are the doorwardens. Meriadoc, son of Saradoc is my name; and my companion, who, alas! is overcome with weariness' – here he gave the other a dig with his foot – 'is Peregrin, son of Paladin, of the house of Took. Far in the North is our home. The Lord Saruman is within; but at the moment he is closeted with one Wormtongue, or doubtless he would be here to welcome such honourable guests.'

'Doubtless he would!' laughed Gandalf. 'And was it Saruman that ordered you to guard his damaged doors, and watch for the arrival of guests, when your attention could be spared from plate and bottle?'

'No, good sir, the matter escaped him,' answered Merry gravely. 'He has been much occupied. Our orders came from Treebeard, who has taken over the management of Isengard. He commanded me to welcome the Lord of Rohan with fitting words. I have done my best.'

'And what about your companions? What about Legolas and me?' cried Gimli, unable to contain himself longer. 'You rascals, you woolly-footed and wool-pated truants! A fine hunt you have led us! Two hundred leagues, through fen and forest, battle and death, to rescue you! And here we find you feasting and idling – and smoking! Smoking! Where did you come by the weed, you villains? Hammer and tongs! I am so torn between rage and joy, that if I do not burst, it will be a marvel!'

'You speak for me, Gimli,' laughed Legolas. 'Though I would sooner learn how they came by the wine.'

'One thing you have not found in your hunting, and that's brighter wits,' said Pippin, opening an eye. 'Here you find us sitting on a field of victory, amid the plunder of armies, and you wonder how we came by a few well-earned comforts!'

'Well-earned?' said Gimli. 'I cannot believe that!'

The Riders laughed. 'It cannot be doubted that we witness the meeting of dear friends,' said Théoden. 'So these are the lost ones of your company, Gandalf? The days are fated to be filled with marvels. Already I have seen many since I left my house; and now here before my eyes stand yet another of the folk of legend. Are not these the Halflings, that some among us call the Holbytlan?'

'Hobbits, if you please, lord,' said Pippin.

'Hobbits?' said Théoden. 'Your tongue is strangely changed; but the name sounds not unfitting so. Hobbits! No report that I have heard does justice to the truth.'

Merry bowed; and Pippin got up and bowed low. 'You are gracious, lord; or I hope that I may so take your words,' he said. 'And here is another marvel! I have wandered in many lands, since I left my home, and never till now have I found people that knew any story concerning hobbits.'

'My people came out of the North long ago,' said Théoden. 'But I will not deceive you: we know no tales about hobbits. All that is said among us is that far away, over many hills and rivers, live the halfling folk that dwell in holes in sand-dunes. But there are no legends of their deeds, for it is said that they do little, and avoid the sight of men, being able to vanish in a twinkling; and they can change their voices to resemble the piping of birds. But it seems that more could be said.'

'It could indeed, lord,' said Merry.

'For one thing,' said Théoden, 'I had not heard that they spouted smoke from their mouths.'

'That is not surprising,' answered Merry; 'for it is an art which we have not practised for more than a few generations. It was Tobold Hornblower, of Longbottom in the Southfarthing, who first grew the true pipe-weed in his gardens, about the year 1070 according to our reckoning. How old Toby came by the plant . . .'

'You do not know your danger, Théoden,' interrupted Gandalf. 'These hobbits will sit on the edge of ruin and discuss the pleasures of the table, or the small doings of their fathers, grandfathers, and great-grandfathers, and remoter cousins to the ninth degree, if you encourage them with undue patience. Some other time would be more fitting for the history of smoking. Where is Treebeard, Merry?'

'Away on the north side, I believe. He went to get a drink – of clean water. Most of the other Ents are with him, still busy at their work – over there.' Merry waved his hand towards the steaming lake; and as they looked, they heard a distant rumbling and rattling, as if an avalanche was falling from the mountain-side. Far away came a *hoom-hom*, as of horns blowing triumphantly.

'And is Orthanc then left unguarded?' asked Gandalf.

'There is the water,' said Merry. 'But Quickbeam and some others are watching it. Not all those posts and pillars in the plain are of Saruman's planting. Quickbeam, I think, is by the rock, near the foot of the stair.'

'Yes, a tall grey Ent is there,' said Legolas, 'but his arms are at his sides, and he stands as still as a door-tree.'

'It is past noon,' said Gandalf, 'and we at any rate have not eaten since early morning. Yet I wish to see Treebeard as soon as may be. Did he leave me no message, or has plate and bottle driven it from your mind?'

'He left a message,' said Merry, 'and I was coming to it, but I have been hindered by many other questions. I was to say that, if the Lord of the Mark and Gandalf will ride to the northern wall they will find Treebeard there, and he will welcome them. I may add that they will also find food of the best there, it was discovered and selected by your humble servants.' He bowed.

Gandalf laughed. 'That is better!' he said. 'Well, Théoden, will you ride with me to find Treebeard? We must go round about, but it is not far. When you see Treebeard, you will learn much. For Treebeard is Fangorn, and the eldest and chief of the Ents, and when you speak with him you will hear the speech of the oldest of all living things.'

'I will come with you,' said Théoden. 'Farewell, my hobbits! May we meet again in my house! There you shall sit beside me and tell me all that your hearts desire: the deeds of your grandsires, as far as you can reckon them; and we will speak also of Tobold the Old and his herb-lore. Farewell!'

The hobbits bowed low. 'So that is the King of Rohan!' said Pippin in an undertone. 'A fine old fellow. Very polite.'

CHAPTER IX

FLOTSAM AND JETSAM

Gandalf and the King's company rode away, turning eastward to make the circuit of the ruined walls of Isengard. But Aragorn, Gimli, and Legolas remained behind. Leaving Arod and Hasufel to stray in search of grass, they came and sat beside the hobbits.

'Well, well! The hunt is over, and we meet again at last, where none of us ever thought to come,' said Aragorn.

'And now that the great ones have gone to discuss high matters,' said Legolas, 'the hunters can perhaps learn the answers to their own small riddles. We tracked you as far as the forest, but there are still many things that I should like to know the truth of.'

'And there is a great deal, too, that we want to know about you,' said Merry. 'We have learnt a few things through Treebeard, the Old Ent, but that is not nearly enough.'

'All in good time,' said Legolas. 'We were the hunters, and you should give an account of yourselves to us first.'

'Or second,' said Gimli. 'It would go better after a meal. I have a sore head; and it is past mid-day. You truants might make amends by finding us some of the plunder that you spoke of. Food and drink would pay off some of my score against you.'

'Then you shall have it,' said Pippin. 'Will you have it here, or in more comfort in what's left of Saruman's guard-house – over there under the arch? We had to picnic out here, so as to keep an eye on the road.'

'Less than an eye!' said Gimli. 'But I will not go into any orc-house; nor touch Orcs' meat or anything that they have mauled.'

'We wouldn't ask you to,' said Merry. 'We have had enough of Orcs ourselves to last a life-time. But there were many other folk in Isengard. Saruman kept enough wisdom not to trust his Orcs. He had Men to guard his gates: some of his most faithful servants, I suppose. Anyway they were favoured and got good provisions.'

'And pipe-weed?' asked Gimli.

'No, I don't think so,' Merry laughed. 'But that is another story, which can wait until after lunch.'

'Well let us go and have lunch then!' said the Dwarf.

The hobbits led the way; and they passed under the arch and came to a wide door upon the left, at the top of a stair. It opened direct into a large chamber, with other smaller doors at the far end, and a hearth and chimney at one side. The chamber was hewn out of the stone; and it must once have been dark, for its windows looked out only into the tunnel. But light came in now through the broken roof. On the hearth wood was burning.

'I lit a bit of fire,' said Pippin. 'It cheered us up in the fogs. There were few faggots about, and most of the wood we could find was wet. But there is a great draught in the chimney: it seems to wind away up through the rock, and fortunately it has not been blocked. A fire is handy. I will make you some toast. The bread is three or four days old, I am afraid.'

Aragorn and his companions sat themselves down at one end of a long table, and the hobbits disappeared through one of the inner doors.

'Store-room in there, and above the floods, luckily,' said Pippin, as they came back laden with dishes, bowls, cups, knives, and food of various sorts.

'And you need not turn up your nose at the provender, Master Gimli,' said Merry. 'This is not orc-stuff, but man-food, as Treebeard calls it. Will you have wine or beer? There's a barrel inside there – very passable. And this is first-rate salted pork. Or I can cut you some rashers of bacon and broil them, if you like. I am sorry there is no green stuff: the deliveries have been rather interrupted in the last few days! I cannot offer you anything to follow but butter and honey for your bread. Are you content?'

'Indeed yes,' said Gimli. 'The score is much reduced.'

The three were soon busy with their meal; and the two hobbits, unabashed, set to a second time. 'We must keep our guests company,' they said.

'You are full of courtesy this morning,' laughed Legolas. 'But maybe, if we had not arrived, you would already have been keeping one another company again.'

'Maybe; and why not?' said Pippin. 'We had foul fare with the Orcs, and little enough for days before that. It seems a long while since we could eat to heart's content.'

'It does not seem to have done you any harm,' said Aragorn. 'Indeed you look in the bloom of health.'

'Aye, you do indeed,' said Gimli, looking them up and down over the top of his cup. 'Why, your hair is twice as thick and curly as when we parted; and I would swear that you have both grown somewhat, if that is possible for hobbits of your age. This Treebeard at any rate has not starved you.'

'He has not,' said Merry. 'But Ents only drink, and drink is not enough for content. Treebeard's draughts may be nourishing, but one feels the need of something solid. And even *lembas* is none the worse for a change.'

'You have drunk of the waters of the Ents, have you?' said Legolas. 'Ah, then I think it is likely that Gimli's eyes do not deceive him. Strange songs have been sung of the draughts of Fangorn.'

'Many strange tales have been told about that land,' said Aragorn. 'I have never entered it. Come, tell me more about it, and about the Ents!'

'Ents,' said Pippin, 'Ents are – well Ents are all different for one thing. But their eyes now, their eyes are very odd.' He tried a few fumbling words that trailed off into silence. 'Oh, well,' he went on, 'you have seen some at a distance, already – they saw you at any rate, and reported that you were on the way – and you will see many others, I expect, before you leave here. You must form your own ideas.'

'Now, now!' said Gimli. 'We are beginning the story in the middle. I should like a tale in the right order, starting with that strange day when our fellowship was broken.'

'You shall have it, if there is time,' said Merry. 'But first – if you have finished eating – you shall fill your pipes and light up. And then for a little while we can pretend that we are all back safe at Bree again, or in Rivendell.'

He produced a small leather bag full of tobacco. 'We have heaps of it,' he said; 'and you can all pack as much as you wish, when we go. We did some salvage-work this morning, Pippin and I. There are lots of things floating about. It was Pippin who found two small barrels, washed up out of some cellar or store-house, I suppose. When we opened them, we found they were filled with this: as fine a pipe-weed as you could wish for, and quite unspoilt.'

Gimli took some and rubbed it in his palms and sniffed it. 'It feels good, and it smells good,' he said.

'It is good!' said Merry. 'My dear Gimli, it is Longbottom Leaf! There were the Hornblower brandmarks on the barrels, as plain as plain. How it came here, I can't imagine. For Saruman's private use, I fancy. I never knew that it went so far abroad. But it comes in handy now!'

'It would,' said Gimli, 'if I had a pipe to go with it. Alas, I lost mine in Moria, or before. Is there no pipe in all your plunder?'

'No, I am afraid not,' said Merry. 'We have not found any, not even here in the guardrooms. Saruman kept this dainty to himself, it seems. And I don't think it would be any use knocking on the doors of Orthanc to beg a pipe of him! We shall have to share pipes, as good friends must at a pinch.'

'Half a moment!' said Pippin. Putting his hand inside the breast of his jacket he pulled out a little soft wallet on a string. 'I keep a treasure or two near my skin, as precious as Rings to me. Here's one: my old wooden pipe. And here's another: an unused one. I have carried it a long way, though I don't know why. I never really expected to find any pipe-weed on the journey, when my own ran out. But now it comes in useful after all.' He held up a small pipe with a wide flattened bowl, and handed it to Gimli. 'Does that settle the score between us?' he said.

'Settle it!' cried Gimli. 'Most noble hobbit, it leaves me deep in your debt.'

'Well, I am going back into the open air, to see what the wind and sky are doing!' said Legolas.

'We will come with you,' said Aragorn.

They went out and seated themselves upon the piled stones before the gateway. They could see far down into the valley now; the mists were lifting and floating away upon the breeze.

'Now let us take our ease here for a little!' said Aragorn. 'We will sit on the edge of ruin and talk, as Gandalf says, while he is busy elsewhere. I feel a weariness such as I have seldom felt before.' He wrapped his grey cloak about him, hiding his mail-shirt, and stretched out his long legs. Then he lay back and sent from his lips a thin stream of smoke.

'Look!' said Pippin. 'Strider the Ranger has come back!'

'He has never been away,' said Aragorn. 'I am Strider and Dúnadan too, and I belong both to Gondor and the North.'

They smoked in silence for a while, and the sun shone on them; slanting into the valley from among white clouds high in the West. Legolas lay still, looking up at the sun and sky with steady eyes, and singing softly to himself. At last he sat up. 'Come now!' he said. 'Time wears on, and the mists are blowing away, or would if you strange folk did not wreathe yourselves in smoke. What of the tale?'

'Well, my tale begins with waking up in the dark and finding myself all strung-up in an orc-camp,' said Pippin. 'Let me see, what is today?'

'The fifth of March in the Shire-reckoning,' said Aragorn. Pippin made some calculations on his fingers. 'Only nine days ago!' he said.* 'It seems a year since we were caught. Well, though half of it was like a bad dream, I reckon that three very horrible days followed. Merry will correct me, if I forget anything important: I am not going into details: the whips and the filth and stench and all that; it does not bear remembering.' With that he plunged into an account of Boromir's last fight and the orc-march from Emyn Muil to the Forest. The others nodded as the various points were fitted in with their guesses.

'Here are some treasures that you let fall,' said Aragorn. 'You will be glad to have them back.' He loosened his belt from under his cloak, and took from it the two sheathed knives.

'Well!' said Merry. 'I never expected to see those again! I marked a few

* Every month in the Shire-calendar had 30 days.

orcs with mine; but Uglúk took them from us. How he glared! At first I thought he was going to stab me, but he threw the things away as if they burned him.'

'And here also is your brooch, Pippin,' said Aragorn. 'I have kept it safe, for it is a very precious thing.'

'I know,' said Pippin. 'It was a wrench to let it go; but what else could I do?'

'Nothing else,' answered Aragorn. 'One who cannot cast away a treasure at need is in fetters. You did rightly.'

'The cutting of the bands on your wrists, that was smart work!' said Gimli. 'Luck served you there; but you seized your chance with both hands, one might say.'

'And set us a pretty riddle,' said Legolas. 'I wondered if you had grown wings!'

'Unfortunately not,' said Pippin. 'But you did not know about Grishnákh.' He shuddered and said no more, leaving Merry to tell of those last horrible moments: the pawing hands, the hot breath, and the dreadful strength of Grishnákh's hairy arms.

'All this about the Orcs of Barad-dûr, Lugbúrz as they call it, makes me uneasy,' said Aragorn. 'The Dark Lord already knew too much, and his servants also; and Grishnákh evidently sent some message across the River after the quarrel. The Red Eye will be looking towards Isengard. But Saruman at any rate is in a cleft stick of his own cutting.'

'Yes, whichever side wins, his outlook is poor,' said Merry. 'Things began to go all wrong for him from the moment his Orcs set foot in Rohan.'

'We caught a glimpse of the old villain, or so Gandalf hints,' said Gimli. 'On the edge of the Forest.'

'When was that?' asked Pippin.

'Five nights ago,' said Aragorn.

'Let me see,' said Merry: 'five nights ago – now we come to a part of the story you know nothing about. We met Treebeard that morning after the battle; and that night we were at Wellinghall, one of his ent-houses. The next morning we went to Entmoot, a gathering of Ents, that is, and the queerest thing I have ever seen in my life. It lasted all that day and the next; and we spent the nights with an Ent called Quickbeam. And then late in the afternoon in the third day of their moot, the Ents suddenly blew up. It was amazing. The Forest had felt as tense as if a thunderstorm was brewing inside it: then all at once it exploded. I wish you could have heard their song as they marched.'

'If Saruman had heard it, he would be a hundred miles away by now, even if he had had to run on his own legs,' said Pippin.

*'Though Isengard be strong and hard, as cold as stone and bare
    as bone,
We go, we go, we go to war, to hew the stone and break the
    door!'*

There was very much more. A great deal of the song had no words, and
was like a music of horns and drums. It was very exciting. But I thought
it was only marching music and no more, just a song – until I got here. I
know better now.'

'We came down over the last ridge into Nan Curunír, after night had
fallen,' Merry continued. 'It was then that I first had the feeling that the
Forest itself was moving behind us. I thought I was dreaming an entish
dream, but Pippin had noticed it too. We were both frightened; but we
did not find out more about it until later.

'It was the Huorns, or so the Ents call them in "short language". Treebeard
won't say much about them, but I think they are Ents that have become
almost like trees, at least to look at. They stand here and there in the wood
or under its eaves, silent, watching endlessly over the trees; but deep in the
darkest dales there are hundreds and hundreds of them, I believe.

'There is a great power in them, and they seem able to wrap themselves
in shadow: it is difficult to see them moving. But they do. They can move
very quickly, if they are angry. You stand still looking at the weather,
maybe, or listening to the rustling of the wind, and then suddenly you find
that you are in the middle of a wood with great groping trees all around
you. They still have voices, and can speak with the Ents – that is why they
are called Huorns, Treebeard says – but they have become queer and wild.
Dangerous. I should be terrified of meeting them, if there were no true
Ents about to look after them.

'Well, in the early night we crept down a long ravine into the upper end
of the Wizard's Vale, the Ents with all their rustling Huorns behind. We
could not see them, of course, but the whole air was full of creaking. It
was very dark, a cloudy night. They moved at a great speed as soon as
they had left the hills, and made a noise like a rushing wind. The Moon
did not appear through the clouds, and not long after midnight there was
a tall wood all round the north side of Isengard. There was no sign of
enemies nor of any challenge. There was a light gleaming from a high
window in the tower, that was all.

'Treebeard and a few more Ents crept on, right round to within sight of
the great gates. Pippin and I were with him. We were sitting on Treebeard's
shoulders, and I could feel the quivering tenseness in him. But even when
they are roused, Ents can be very cautious and patient. They stood still as
carved stones, breathing and listening.

'Then all at once there was a tremendous stir. Trumpets blared, and the walls of Isengard echoed. We thought that we had been discovered, and that battle was going to begin. But nothing of the sort. All Saruman's people were marching away. I don't know much about this war, or about the Horsemen of Rohan, but Saruman seems to have meant to finish off the king and all his men with one final blow. He emptied Isengard. I saw the enemy go: endless lines of marching Orcs; and troops of them mounted on great wolves. And there were battalions of Men, too. Many of them carried torches, and in the flare I could see their faces. Most of them were ordinary men, rather tall and dark-haired, and grim but not particularly evil-looking. But there were some others that were horrible: man-high, but with goblin-faces, sallow, leering, squint-eyed. Do you know, they reminded me at once of that Southerner at Bree; only he was not so obviously orc-like as most of these were.'

'I thought of him too,' said Aragorn. 'We had many of these half-orcs to deal with at Helm's Deep. It seems plain now that that Southerner was a spy of Saruman's; but whether he was working with the Black Riders, or for Saruman alone, I do not know. It is difficult with these evil folk to know when they are in league, and when they are cheating one another.'

'Well, of all sorts together, there must have been ten thousand at the very least,' said Merry. 'They took an hour to pass out of the gates. Some went off down the highway to the Fords, and some turned away and went eastward. A bridge has been built down there, about a mile away, where the river runs in a very deep channel. You could see it now, if you stood up. They were all singing with harsh voices, and laughing, making a hideous din. I thought things looked very black for Rohan. But Treebeard did not move. He said: "My business is with Isengard tonight, with rock and stone."

'But, though I could not see what was happening in the dark, I believe that Huorns began to move south, as soon as the gates were shut again. Their business was with Orcs I think. They were far down the valley in the morning; or at any rate there was a shadow there that one couldn't see through.

'As soon as Saruman had sent off all his army, our turn came. Treebeard put us down, and went up to the gates, and began hammering on the doors, and calling for Saruman. There was no answer, except arrows and stones from the walls. But arrows are no use against Ents. They hurt them, of course, and infuriate them: like stinging flies. But an Ent can be stuck as full of orc-arrows as a pin-cushion, and take no serious harm. They cannot be poisoned, for one thing; and their skin seems to be very thick, and tougher than bark. It takes a very heavy axe-stroke to wound them seriously. They don't like axes. But there would have to be a great many axe-men to one Ent: a man that hacks once at an Ent never gets a chance of a second blow. A punch from an Ent-fist crumples up iron like thin tin. 'When Treebeard had got a few arrows in him, he began to warm up, to get positively "hasty", as he would say. He let out a great *hoom-hom*, and a dozen more Ents came striding up. An angry Ent is terrifying. Their fingers, and their toes, just freeze on to rock; and they tear it up like bread-crust. It was like watching the work of great tree-roots in a hundred years, all packed into a few moments.

'They pushed, pulled, tore, shook, and hammered; and *clang-bang, crash-crack*, in five minutes they had these huge gates just lying in ruin; and some were already beginning to eat into the walls, like rabbits in a sand-pit. I don't know what Saruman thought was happening; but anyway he did not know how to deal with it. His wizardry may have been falling off lately, of course; but anyway I think he has not much grit, not much plain courage alone in a tight place without a lot of slaves and machines and things, if you know what I mean. Very different from old Gandalf. I wonder if his fame was not all along mainly due to his cleverness in settling at Isengard.'

'No,' said Aragorn. 'Once he was as great as his fame made him. His knowledge was deep, his thought was subtle, and his hands marvellously skilled; and he had a power over the minds of others. The wise he could persuade, and the smaller folk he could daunt. That power he certainly still keeps. There are not many in Middle-earth that I should say were safe, if they were left alone to talk with him, even now when he has suffered a defeat. Gandalf, Elrond, and Galadriel, perhaps, now that his wickedness has been laid bare, but very few others.'

'The Ents are safe,' said Pippin. 'He seems at one time to have got round them, but never again. And anyway he did not understand them; and he made the great mistake of leaving them out of his calculations. He had no plan for them, and there was no time to make any, once they had set to work. As soon as our attack began, the few remaining rats in Isengard started bolting through every hole that the Ents made. The Ents let the Men go, after they had questioned them, two or three dozen only down at this end. I don't think many orc-folk, of any size, escaped. Not from the Huorns: there was a wood full of them all round Isengard by that time, as well as those that had gone down the valley.

'When the Ents had reduced a large part of the southern walls to rubbish, and what was left of his people had bolted and deserted him, Saruman fled in a panic. He seems to have been at the gates when we arrived: I expect he came to watch his splendid army march out. When the Ents broke their way in, he left in a hurry. They did not spot him at first. But the night had opened out, and there was a great light of stars, quite enough for

Ents to see by, and suddenly Quickbeam gave a cry "The tree-killer, the tree-killer!" Quickbeam is a gentle creature, but he hates Saruman all the more fiercely for that: his people suffered cruelly from orc-axes. He leapt down the path from the inner gate, and he can move like a wind when he is roused. There was a pale figure hurrying away in and out of the shadows of the pillars, and it had nearly reached the stairs to the tower-door. But it was a near thing. Quickbeam was so hot after him, that he was within a step or two of being caught and strangled when he slipped in through the door.

'When Saruman was safe back in Orthanc, it was not long before he set some of his precious machinery to work. By that time there were many Ents inside Isengard: some had followed Quickbeam, and others had burst in from the north and east; they were roaming about and doing a great deal of damage. Suddenly up came fires and foul fumes: the vents and shafts all over the plain began to spout and belch. Several of the Ents got scorched and blistered. One of them, Beechbone I think he was called, a very tall handsome Ent, got caught in a spray of some liquid fire and burned like a torch: a horrible sight.

'That sent them mad. I thought that they had been really roused before; but I was wrong. I saw what it was like at last. It was staggering. They roared and boomed and trumpeted, until stones began to crack and fall at the mere noise of them. Merry and I lay on the ground and stuffed our cloaks into our ears. Round and round the rock of Orthanc the Ents went striding and storming like a howling gale, breaking pillars, hurling avalanches of boulders down the shafts, tossing up huge slabs of stone into the air like leaves. The tower was in the middle of a spinning whirlwind. I saw iron posts and blocks of masonry go rocketing up hundreds of feet, and smash against the windows of Orthanc. But Treebeard kept his head. He had not had any burns, luckily. He did not want his folk to hurt themselves in their fury, and he did not want Saruman to escape out of some hole in the confusion. Many of the Ents were hurling themselves against the Orthanc-rock; but that defeated them. It is very smooth and hard. Some wizardry is in it, perhaps, older and stronger than Saruman's. Anyway they could not get a grip on it, or make a crack in it; and they were bruising and wounding themselves against it.

'So Treebeard went out into the ring and shouted. His enormous voice rose above all the din. There was a dead silence, suddenly. In it we heard a shrill laugh from a high window in the tower. That had a queer effect on the Ents. They had been boiling over; now they became cold, grim as ice, and quiet. They left the plain and gathered round Treebeard, standing quite still. He spoke to them for a little in their own language; I think he was telling them of a plan he had made in his old head long before. Then they just faded silently away in the grey light. Day was dawning by that time.

'They set a watch on the tower, I believe, but the watchers were so well hidden in shadows and kept so still, that I could not see them. The others went away north. All that day they were busy, out of sight. Most of the time we were left alone. It was a dreary day; and we wandered about a bit, though we kept out of the view of the windows of Orthanc, as much as we could: they stared at us so threateningly. A good deal of the time we spent looking for something to eat. And also we sat and talked, wondering what was happening away south in Rohan, and what had become of all the rest of our Company. Every now and then we could hear in the distance the rattle and fall of stone, and thudding noises echoing in the hills.

'In the afternoon we walked round the circle, and went to have a look at what was going on. There was a great shadowy wood of Huorns at the head of the valley, and another round the northern wall. We did not dare to go in. But there was a rending, tearing noise of work going on inside. Ents and Huorns were digging great pits and trenches, and making great pools and dams, gathering all the waters of the Isen and every other spring and stream that they could find. We left them to it.

'At dusk Treebeard came back to the gate. He was humming and booming to himself, and seemed pleased. He stood and stretched his great arms and legs and breathed deep. I asked him if he was tired.

'"Tired?" he said, "tired? Well no, not tired, but stiff. I need a good draught of Entwash. We have worked hard; we have done more stonecracking and earth-gnawing today than we have done in many a long year before. But it is nearly finished. When night falls do not linger near this gate or in the old tunnel! Water may come through – and it will be foul water for a while, until all the filth of Saruman is washed away. Then Isen can run clean again." He began to pull down a bit more of the walls, in a leisurely sort of way, just to amuse himself.

'We were just wondering where it would be safe to lie and get some sleep, when the most amazing thing of all happened. There was the sound of a rider coming swiftly up the road. Merry and I lay quiet, and Treebeard hid himself in the shadows under the arch. Suddenly a great horse came striding up, like a flash of silver. It was already dark, but I could see the rider's face clearly: it seemed to shine, and all his clothes were white. I just sat up, staring, with my mouth open. I tried to call out, and couldn't.

'There was no need. He halted just by us and looked down at us. "Gandalf!" I said at last, but my voice was only a whisper. Did he say: "Hullo, Pippin! This is a pleasant surprise!"? No, indeed! He said: "Get up, you tom-fool of a Took! Where, in the name of wonder, in all this ruin is Treebeard? I want him. Quick!"

'Treebeard heard his voice and came out of the shadows at once; and there was a strange meeting. I was surprised, because neither of them seemed surprised at all. Gandalf obviously expected to find Treebeard here; and Treebeard might almost have been loitering about near the gates on purpose to meet him. Yet we had told the old Ent all about Moria. But then I remembered a queer look he gave us at the time. I can only suppose that he had seen Gandalf or had some news of him, but would not say anything in a hurry. "Don't be hasty" is his motto; but nobody, not even Elves, will say much about Gandalf's movements when he is not there.

'"Hoom! Gandalf!" said Treebeard. "I am glad you have come. Wood and water, stock and stone, I can master; but there is a Wizard to manage here."

'"Treebeard," said Gandalf. "I need your help. You have done much, but I need more. I have about ten thousand Orcs to manage."

'Then those two went off and had a council together in some corner. It must have seemed very hasty to Treebeard, for Gandalf was in a tremendous hurry, and was already talking at a great pace, before they passed out of hearing. They were only away a matter of minutes, perhaps a quarter of an hour. Then Gandalf came back to us, and he seemed relieved, almost merry. He did say he was glad to see us, then.

'"But Gandalf," I cried, "where have you been? And have you seen the others?"

'"Wherever I have been, I am back," he answered in the genuine Gandalf manner. "Yes, I have seen some of the others. But news must wait. This is a perilous night, and I must ride fast. But the dawn may be brighter; and if so, we shall meet again. Take care of yourselves, and keep away from Orthanc! Good-bye!"

'Treebeard was very thoughtful after Gandalf had gone. He had evidently learnt a lot in a short time and was digesting it. He looked at us and said: "Hm, well, I find you are not such hasty folk as I thought. You said much less than you might, and no more than you should. Hm, this is a bundle of news and no mistake! Well, now Treebeard must get busy again."

'Before he went, we got a little news out of him; and it did not cheer us up at all. But for the moment we thought more about you three than about Frodo and Sam, or about poor Boromir. For we gathered that there was a great battle going on, or soon would be, and that you were in it, and might never come out of it.

'"Huorns will help," said Treebeard. Then he went away and we did not see him again until this morning.

'It was deep night. We lay on top of a pile of stone, and could see nothing beyond it. Mist or shadows blotted out everything like a great blanket all round us. The air seemed hot and heavy; and it was full of rustlings, creakings, and a murmur like voices passing. I think that hundreds more of the Huorns must have been passing by to help in the battle. Later there was a great rumble of thunder away south, and flashes of lightning far away across Rohan. Every now and then we could see mountain-peaks, miles and miles away, stab out suddenly, black and white, and then vanish. And behind us there were noises like thunder in hills, but different. At times the whole valley echoed.

'It must have been about midnight when the Ents broke the dams and poured all the gathered waters through a gap in the northern wall, down into Isengard. The Huorn-dark had passed, and the thunder had rolled away. The Moon was sinking behind the western mountains.

'Isengard began to fill up with black creeping streams and pools. They glittered in the last light of the Moon, as they spread over the plain. Every now and then the waters found their way down into some shaft or spouthole. Great white steams hissed up. Smoke rose in billows. There were explosions and gusts of fire. One great coil of vapour went whirling up, twisting round and round Orthanc, until it looked like a tall peak of cloud, fiery underneath and moonlit above. And still more water poured in, until at last Isengard looked like a huge flat saucepan, all steaming and bubbling.'

'We saw a cloud of smoke and steam from the south last night, when we came to the mouth of Nan Curunír,' said Aragorn. 'We feared that Saruman was brewing some new devilry for us.'

'Not he!' said Pippin. 'He was probably choking and not laughing any more. By the morning, yesterday morning, the water had sunk down into all the holes, and there was a dense fog. We took refuge in that guardroom over there; and we had rather a fright. The lake began to overflow and pour out through the old tunnel, and the water was rapidly rising up the steps. We thought we were going to get caught like Orcs in a hole; but we found a winding stair at the back of the store-room that brought us out on top of the arch. It was a squeeze to get out, as the passages had been cracked and half blocked with fallen stone near the top. There we sat high up above the floods and watched the drowning of Isengard. The Ents kept on pouring in more water, till all the fires were quenched and every cave filled. The fogs slowly gathered together and steamed up into a huge umbrella of cloud: it must have been a mile high. In the evening there was a great rainbow over the eastern hills; and then the sunset was blotted out by a thick drizzle on the mountain-sides. It all went very quiet. A few wolves howled mournfully, far away. The Ents stopped the inflow in the night, and sent the Isen back into its old course. And that was the end of it all.

'Since then the water has been sinking again. There must be outlets somewhere from the caves underneath, I think. If Saruman peeps out of any of his windows, it must look an untidy, dreary mess. We felt very lonely. Not even a visible Ent to talk to in all the ruin; and no news. We spent the night up on top there above the arch, and it was cold and damp and we did not sleep. We had a feeling that anything might happen at any minute. Saruman is still in his tower. There was a noise in the night like a wind coming up the valley. I think the Ents and Huorns that had been away came back then; but where they have all gone to now, I don't know. It was a misty, moisty morning when we climbed down and looked round again, and nobody was about. And that is about all there is to tell. It seems almost peaceful now after all the turmoil. And safer too, somehow, since Gandalf came back. I could sleep!'

They all fell silent for a while. Gimli re-filled his pipe. 'There is one thing I wonder about,' he said as he lit it with his flint and tinder: 'Wormtongue. You told Théoden he was with Saruman. How did he get there?'

'Oh yes, I forgot about him,' said Pippin. 'He did not get here till this morning. We had just lit the fire and had some breakfast when Treebeard appeared again. We heard him hooming and calling our names outside.

' "I have just come round to see how you are faring, my lads," he said; "and to give you some news. Huorns have come back. All's well; aye very well indeed!" he laughed, and slapped his thighs. "No more Orcs in Isengard, no more axes! And there will be folk coming up from the South before the day is old; some that you may be glad to see."

'He had hardly said that, when we heard the sound of hoofs on the road. We rushed out before the gates, and I stood and stared, half expecting to see Strider and Gandalf come riding up at the head of an army. But out of the mist there rode a man on an old tired horse; and he looked a queer twisted sort of creature himself. There was no one else. When he came out of the mist and suddenly saw all the ruin and wreckage in front of him, he sat and gaped, and his face went almost green. He was so bewildered that he did not seem to notice us at first. When he did, he gave a cry, and tried to turn his horse round and ride off. But Treebeard took three strides, put out a long arm, and lifted him out of the saddle. His horse bolted in terror, and he grovelled on the ground. He said he was Gríma, friend and counsellor of the king, and had been sent with important messages from Théoden to Saruman.

' "No one else would dare to ride through the open land, so full of foul Orcs," he said, "so I was sent. And I have had a perilous journey, and I am hungry and weary. I fled far north out of my way, pursued by wolves." '

'I caught the sidelong looks he gave to Treebeard, and I said to myself "liar". Treebeard looked at him in his long slow way for several minutes, till the wretched man was squirming on the floor. Then at last he said: "Ha, hm, I was expecting you, Master Wormtongue." The man started at that name. "Gandalf got here first. So I know as much about you as I need, and I know what to do with you. Put all the rats in one trap, said Gandalf; and I will. I am the master of Isengard now, but Saruman is locked in his tower; and you can go there and give him all the messages that you can think of."

'"Let me go, let me go!" said Wormtongue. "I know the way."

'"You knew the way, I don't doubt," said Treebeard. "But things have changed here a little. Go and see!"

'He let Wormtongue go, and he limped off through the arch, with us close behind, until he came inside the ring and could see all the floods that lay between him and Orthanc. Then he turned to us.

'"Let me go away!" he whined. "Let me go away! My messages are useless now."

'"They are indeed," said Treebeard. "But you have only two choices: to stay with me until Gandalf and your master arrive; or to cross the water. Which will you have?"

'The man shivered at the mention of his master, and put a foot into the water; but he drew back. "I cannot swim," he said.

'"The water is not deep," said Treebeard. "It is dirty, but that will not harm you, Master Wormtongue. In you go now!"

'With that the wretch floundered off into the flood. It rose up nearly to his neck before he got too far away for me to see him. The last I saw of him was clinging to some old barrel or piece of wood. But Treebeard waded after him, and watched his progress.

'"Well, he has gone in," he said when he returned. "I saw him crawling up the steps like a draggled rat. There is someone in the tower still: a hand came out and pulled him in. So there he is, and I hope the welcome is to his liking. Now I must go and wash myself clean of the slime. I'll be away up on the north side, if anyone wants to see me. There is no clean water down here fit for an Ent to drink, or to bathe in. So I will ask you two lads to keep a watch at the gate for the folk that are coming. There'll be the Lord of the Fields of Rohan, mark you! You must welcome him as well as you know how: his men have fought a great fight with the Orcs. Maybe, you know the right fashion of Men's words for such a lord, better than Ents. There have been many lords in the green fields in my time, and I have never learned their speech or their names. They will be wanting man-food, and you know all about that, I guess. So find what you think is fit for a king to eat, if you can." And that is the end of the story. Though

I should like to know who this Wormtongue is. Was he really the king's counsellor?'

'He was,' said Aragorn; 'and also Saruman's spy and servant in Rohan. Fate has not been kinder to him than he deserves. The sight of the ruin of all that he thought so strong and magnificent must have been almost punishment enough. But I fear that worse awaits him.'

'Yes, I don't suppose Treebeard sent him to Orthanc out of kindness,' said Merry. 'He seemed rather grimly delighted with the business, and was laughing to himself when he went to get his bathe and drink. We spent a busy time after that, searching the flotsam, and rummaging about. We found two or three store-rooms in different places nearby, above the flood-level. But Treebeard sent some Ents down, and they carried off a great deal of the stuff.

' "We want man-food for twenty-five," the Ents said, so you can see that somebody had counted your company carefully before you arrived. You three were evidently meant to go with the great people. But you would not have fared any better. We kept as good as we sent, I promise you. Better, because we sent no drink.

' "What about drink?" I said to the Ents.

' "There is water of Isen," they said, "and that is good enough for Ents and Men." But I hope that the Ents may have found time to brew some of their draughts from the mountain-springs, and we shall see Gandalf's beard curling when he returns. After the Ents had gone, we felt tired, and hungry. But we did not grumble – our labours had been well rewarded. It was through our search for man-food that Pippin discovered the prize of all the flotsam, those Hornblower barrels. "Pipe-weed is better after food," said Pippin; that is how the situation arose.'

'We understand it all perfectly now,' said Gimli.

'All except one thing,' said Aragorn: 'leaf from the Southfarthing in Isengard. The more I consider it, the more curious I find it. I have never been in Isengard, but I have journeyed in this land, and I know well the empty countries that lie between Rohan and the Shire. Neither goods nor folk have passed that way for many a long year, not openly. Saruman had secret dealings with someone in the Shire, I guess. Wormtongues may be found in other houses than King Théoden's. Was there a date on the barrels?'

'Yes,' said Pippin. 'It was the 1417 crop, that is last year's; no, the year before, of course, now: a good year.'

'Ah well, whatever evil was afoot is over now, I hope; or else it is beyond our reach at present,' said Aragorn. 'Yet I think I shall mention it to Gandalf, small matter though it may seem among his great affairs.'

'I wonder what he is doing,' said Merry. 'The afternoon is getting on. Let us go and look round! You can enter Isengard now at any rate, Strider, if you want to. But it is not a very cheerful sight.'

CHAPTER X

THE VOICE OF SARUMAN

They passed through the ruined tunnel and stood upon a heap of stones, gazing at the dark rock of Orthanc, and its many windows, a menace still in the desolation that lay all about it. The waters had now nearly all subsided. Here and there gloomy pools remained, covered with scum and wreckage; but most of the wide circle was bare again, a wilderness of slime and tumbled rock, pitted with blackened holes, and dotted with posts and pillars leaning drunkenly this way and that. At the rim of the shattered bowl there lay vast mounds and slopes, like the shingles cast up by a great storm; and beyond them the green and tangled valley ran up into the long ravine between the dark arms of the mountains. Across the waste they saw riders picking their way; they were coming from the north side, and already they were drawing near to Orthanc.

'There is Gandalf, and Théoden and his men!' said Legolas. 'Let us go and meet them!'

'Walk warily!' said Merry. 'There are loose slabs that may tilt up and throw you down into a pit, if you don't take care.'

They followed what was left of the road from the gates to Orthanc, going slowly, for the flag-stones were cracked and slimed. The riders, seeing them approach, halted under the shadow of the rock and waited for them. Gandalf rode forward to meet them.

'Well, Treebeard and I have had some interesting discussions, and made a few plans,' he said; 'and we have all had some much-needed rest. Now we must be going on again. I hope you companions have all rested, too, and refreshed yourselves?'

'We have,' said Merry. 'But our discussions began and ended in smoke. Still we feel less ill-disposed towards Saruman than we did.'

'Do you indeed?' said Gandalf. 'Well, I do not. I have now a last task to do before I go: I must pay Saruman a farewell visit. Dangerous, and probably useless; but it must be done. Those of you who wish may come with me – but beware! And do not jest! This is not the time for it.'

'I will come,' said Gimli. 'I wish to see him and learn if he really looks like you.'

'And how will you learn that, Master Dwarf?' said Gandalf. 'Saruman could look like me in your eyes, if it suited his purpose with you. And are you yet wise enough to detect all his counterfeits? Well, we shall see, perhaps. He may be shy of showing himself before many different eyes together. But I have ordered all the Ents to remove themselves from sight, so perhaps we shall persuade him to come out.'

'What's the danger?' asked Pippin. 'Will he shoot at us, and pour fire out of the windows; or can he put a spell on us from a distance?'

'The last is most likely, if you ride to his door with a light heart,' said Gandalf. 'But there is no knowing what he can do, or may choose to try. A wild beast cornered is not safe to approach. And Saruman has powers you do not guess. Beware of his voice!'

They came now to the foot of Orthanc. It was black, and the rock gleamed as if it were wet. The many faces of the stone had sharp edges as though they had been newly chiselled. A few scorings, and small flake-like splinters near the base, were all the marks that it bore of the fury of the Ents.

On the eastern side, in the angle of two piers, there was a great door, high above the ground; and over it was a shuttered window, opening upon a balcony hedged with iron bars. Up to the threshold of the door there mounted a flight of twenty-seven broad stairs, hewn by some unknown art of the same black stone. This was the only entrance to the tower; but many tall windows were cut with deep embrasures in the climbing walls: far up they peered like little eyes in the sheer faces of the horns.

At the foot of the stairs Gandalf and the king dismounted. 'I will go up,' said Gandalf. 'I have been in Orthanc and I know my peril.'

'And I too will go up,' said the king. 'I am old, and fear no peril any more. I wish to speak with the enemy who has done me so much wrong. Éomer shall come with me, and see that my aged feet do not falter.'

'As you will,' said Gandalf. 'Aragorn shall come with me. Let the others await us at the foot of the stairs. They will hear and see enough, if there is anything to hear or see.'

'Nay!' said Gimli. 'Legolas and I wish for a closer view. We alone here represent our kindreds. We also will come behind.'

'Come then!' said Gandalf, and with that he climbed the steps, and Théoden went beside him.

The Riders of Rohan sat uneasily upon their horses, on either side of the stair, and looked up darkly at the great tower, fearing what might befall their lord. Merry and Pippin sat on the bottom step, feeling both unimportant and unsafe.

'Half a sticky mile from here to the gate!' muttered Pippin. 'I wish I could slip off back to the guardroom unnoticed! What did we come for? We are not wanted.'

Gandalf stood before the door of Orthanc and beat on it with his staff.

It rang with a hollow sound. 'Saruman, Saruman!' he cried in a loud commanding voice. 'Saruman come forth!'

For some time there was no answer. At last the window above the door was unbarred, but no figure could be seen at its dark opening.

'Who is it?' said a voice. 'What do you wish?'

Théoden started. 'I know that voice,' he said, 'and I curse the day when I first listened to it.'

'Go and fetch Saruman, since you have become his footman, Gríma Wormtongue!' said Gandalf. 'And do not waste our time!'

The window closed. They waited. Suddenly another voice spoke, low and melodious, its very sound an enchantment. Those who listened unwarily to that voice could seldom report the words that they heard; and if they did, they wondered, for little power remained in them. Mostly they remembered only that it was a delight to hear the voice speaking, all that it said seemed wise and reasonable, and desire awoke in them by swift agreement to seem wise themselves. When others spoke they seemed harsh and uncouth by contrast; and if they gainsaid the voice, anger was kindled in the hearts of those under the spell. For some the spell lasted only while the voice spoke to them, and when it spoke to another they smiled, as men do who see through a juggler's trick while others gape at it. For many the sound of the voice alone was enough to hold them enthralled; but for those whom it conquered the spell endured when they were far away, and ever they heard that soft voice whispering and urging them. But none were unmoved; none rejected its pleas and its commands without an effort of mind and will, so long as its master had control of it.

'Well?' it said now with gentle question. 'Why must you disturb my rest? Will you give me no peace at all by night or day?' Its tone was that of a kindly heart aggrieved by injuries undeserved.

They looked up, astonished, for they had heard no sound of his coming; and they saw a figure standing at the rail, looking down upon them: an old man, swathed in a great cloak, the colour of which was not easy to tell, for it changed if they moved their eyes or if he stirred. His face was long, with a high forehead, he had deep darkling eyes, hard to fathom, though the look that they now bore was grave and benevolent, and a little weary. His hair and beard were white, but strands of black still showed about his lips and ears.

'Like, and yet unlike,' muttered Gimli.

'But come now,' said the soft voice. 'Two at least of you I know by name. Gandalf I know too well to have much hope that he seeks help or counsel here. But you, Théoden Lord of the Mark of Rohan, are declared by your noble devices, and still more by the fair countenance of the House of Eorl. O worthy son of Thengel the Thrice-renowned! Why have you not come before, and as a friend? Much have I desired to see you, mightiest king of western lands, and especially in these latter years, to save you from the unwise and evil counsels that beset you! Is it yet too late? Despite the injuries that have been done to me, in which the men of Rohan, alas! have had some part, still I would save you, and deliver you from the ruin that draws nigh inevitably, if you ride upon this road which you have taken. Indeed I alone can aid you now.'

Théoden opened his mouth as if to speak, but he said nothing. He looked up at the face of Saruman with its dark solemn eyes bent down upon him, and then to Gandalf at his side; and he seemed to hesitate. Gandalf made no sign; but stood silent as stone, as one waiting patiently for some call that has not yet come. The Riders stirred at first, murmuring with approval of the words of Saruman; and then they too were silent, as men spell-bound. It seemed to them that Gandalf had never spoken so fair and fittingly to their lord. Rough and proud now seemed all his dealings with Théoden. And over their hearts crept a shadow, the fear of a great danger: the end of the Mark in a darkness to which Gandalf was driving them, while Saruman stood beside a door of escape, holding it half open so that a ray of light came through. There was a heavy silence.

It was Gimli the dwarf who broke in suddenly. 'The words of this wizard stand on their heads,' he growled, gripping the handle of his axe. 'In the language of Orthanc help means ruin, and saving means slaying, that is plain. But we do not come here to beg.'

'Peace!' said Saruman, and for a fleeting moment his voice was less suave, and a light flickered in his eyes and was gone. 'I do not speak to you yet, Gimli Glóin's son,' he said. 'Far away is your home and small concern of yours are the troubles of this land. But it was not by design of your own that you became embroiled in them, and so I will not blame such part as you have played – a valiant one, I doubt not. But I pray you, allow me first to speak with the King of Rohan, my neighbour, and once my friend.

'What have you to say, Théoden King? Will you have peace with me, and all the aid that my knowledge, founded in long years, can bring? Shall we make our counsels together against evil days, and repair our injuries with such good will that our estates shall both come to fairer flower than ever before?'

Still Théoden did not answer. Whether he strove with anger or doubt none could say. Éomer spoke.

'Lord, hear me!' he said. 'Now we feel the peril that we were warned of. Have we ridden forth to victory, only to stand at last amazed by an old liar with honey on his forked tongue? So would the trapped wolf speak to the hounds, if he could. What aid can he give to you, forsooth? All he desires is to escape from his plight. But will you parley with this dealer in treachery and murder? Remember Théodred at the Fords, and the grave of Háma in Helm's Deep!'

'If we speak of poisoned tongues what shall we say of yours, young serpent?' said Saruman, and the flash of his anger was now plain to see. 'But come, Éomer, Éomund's son!' he went on in his soft voice again. 'To every man his part. Valour in arms is yours, and you win high honour thereby. Slay whom your lord names as enemies, and be content. Meddle not in policies which you do not understand. But maybe, if you become a king, you will find that he must choose his friends with care. The friendship of Saruman and the power of Orthanc cannot be lightly thrown aside, whatever grievances, real or fancied, may lie behind. You have won a battle but not a war – and that with help on which you cannot count again. You may find the Shadow of the Wood at your own door next: it is wayward, and senseless, and has no love for Men.

'But my lord of Rohan, am I to be called a murderer, because valiant men have fallen in battle? If you go to war, needlessly, for I did not desire it, then men will be slain. But if I am a murderer on that account, then all the House of Eorl is stained with murder; for they have fought many wars, and assailed many who defied them. Yet with some they have afterwards made peace, none the worse for being politic. I say, Théoden King: shall we have peace and friendship, you and I? It is ours to command.'

'We will have peace,' said Théoden at last thickly and with an effort. Several of the Riders cried out gladly. Théoden held up his hand. 'Yes, we will have peace,' he said, now in a clear voice, 'we will have peace, when you and all your works have perished – and the works of your dark master to whom you would deliver us. You are a liar, Saruman, and a corrupter of men's hearts. You hold out your hand to me, and I perceive only a finger of the claw of Mordor. Cruel and cold! Even if your war on me was just – as it was not, for were you ten times as wise you would have no right to rule me and mine for your own profit as you desired – even so, what will you say of your torches in Westfold and the children that lie dead there? And they hewed Háma's body before the gates of the Hornburg, after he was dead. When you hang from a gibbet at your window for the sport of your own crows, I will have peace with you and Orthanc. So much for the House of Eorl. A lesser son of great sires am I, but I do not need to lick your fingers. Turn elsewhither. But I fear your voice has lost its charm.'

The Riders gazed up at Théoden like men startled out of a dream. Harsh as an old raven's their master's voice sounded in their ears after the music of Saruman. But Saruman for a while was beside himself with wrath. He leaned over the rail as if he would smite the King with his staff. To some suddenly it seemed that they saw a snake coiling itself to strike.

'Gibbets and crows!' he hissed, and they shuddered at the hideous change. 'Dotard! What is the house of Eorl but a thatched barn where brigands drink in the reek, and their brats roll on the floor among the dcgs? Too long have they escaped the gibbet themselves. But the noose comes, slow in the drawing, tight and hard in the end. Hang if you will!' Now his voice changed, as he slowly mastered himself. 'I know not why I have had the patience to speak to you. For I need you not, nor your little band of gallopers, as swift to fly as to advance, Théoden Horsemaster. Long ago I offered you a state beyond your merit and your wit. I have offered it again, so that those whom you mislead may clearly see the choice of roads. You give me brag and abuse. So be it. Go back to your huts!

'But you, Gandalf! For you at least I am grieved, feeling for your shame. How comes it that you can endure such company? For you are proud, Gandalf – and not without reason, having a noble mind and eyes that look both deep and far. Even now will you not listen to my counsel?'

Gandalf stirred, and looked up. 'What have you to say that you did not say at our last meeting?' he asked. 'Or, perhaps, you have things to unsay?'

Saruman paused. 'Unsay?' he mused, as if puzzled. 'Unsay? I endeavoured to advise you for your own good, but you scarcely listened. You are proud and do not love advice, having indeed a store of your own wisdom. But on that occasion you erred, I think, misconstruing my intentions wilfully. I fear that in my eagerness to persuade you, I lost patience. And indeed I regret it. For I bore you no ill-will; and even now I bear none, though you return to me in the company of the violent and the ignorant. How should I? Are we not both members of a high and ancient order, most excellent in Middle-earth? Our friendship would profit us both alike. Much we could still accomplish together, to heal the disorders of the world. Let us understand one another, and dismiss from thought these lesser folk! Let them wait on our decisions! For the common good I am willing to redress the past, and to receive you. Will you not consult with me? Will you not come up?'

So great was the power that Saruman exerted in this last effort that none that stood within hearing were unmoved. But now the spell was wholly different. They heard the gentle remonstrance of a kindly king with an erring but much-loved minister. But they were shut out, listening at a door to words not meant for them: ill-mannered children or stupid servants overhearing the elusive discourse of their elders, and wondering how it would affect their lot. Of loftier mould these two were made: reverend and wise. It was inevitable that they should make alliance. Gandalf would ascend into the tower, to discuss deep things beyond their comprehension in the high chambers of Orthanc. The door would be closed, and they would be left outside, dismissed to await allotted work or punishment. Even in the mind of Théoden the thought took shape, like a shadow of doubt: 'He will betray us; he will go – we shall be lost.'

Then Gandalf laughed. The fantasy vanished like a puff of smoke.

'Saruman, Saruman!' said Gandalf still laughing. 'Saruman, you missed your path in life. You should have been the king's jester and earned your bread, and stripes too, by mimicking his counsellors. Ah me!' he paused, getting the better of his mirth. 'Understand one another? I fear I am beyond your comprehension. But you, Saruman, I understand now too well. I keep a clearer memory of your arguments, and deeds, than you suppose. When last I visited you, you were the jailor of Mordor, and there I was to be sent. Nay, the guest who has escaped from the roof, will think twice before he comes back in by the door. Nay, I do not think I will come up. But listen, Saruman, for the last time! Will you not come down? Isengard has proved less strong than your hope and fancy made it. So may other things in which you still have trust. Would it not be well to leave it for a while? To turn to new things, perhaps? Think well, Saruman! Will you not come down?'

A shadow passed over Saruman's face; then it went deathly white. Before he could conceal it, they saw through the mask the anguish of a mind in doubt, loathing to stay and dreading to leave its refuge. For a second he hesitated, and no one breathed. Then he spoke, and his voice was shrill and cold. Pride and hate were conquering him.

'Will I come down?' he mocked. 'Does an unarmed man come down to speak with robbers out of doors? I can hear you well enough here. I am no fool, and I do not trust you, Gandalf. They do not stand openly on my stairs, but I know where the wild wood-demons are lurking, at your command.'

'The treacherous are ever distrustful,' answered Gandalf wearily. 'But you need not fear for your skin. I do not wish to kill you, or hurt you, as you would know, if you really understood me. And I have the power to protect you. I am giving you a last chance. You can leave Orthanc, free – if you choose.'

'That sounds well,' sneered Saruman. 'Very much in the manner of Gandalf the Grey: so condescending, and so very kind. I do not doubt that you would find Orthanc commodious, and my departure convenient. But why should I wish to leave? And what do you mean by "free"? There are conditions, I presume?'

'Reasons for leaving you can see from your windows,' answered Gandalf. 'Others will occur to your thought. Your servants are destroyed and scattered; your neighbours you have made your enemies; and you have cheated your new master, or tried to do so. When his eye turns hither, it will be the red eye of wrath. But when I say "free", I mean "free": free from bond, of chain or command: to go where you will, even, even to Mordor, Saruman, if you desire. But you will first surrender to me the Key of Orthanc, and your staff. They shall be pledges of your conduct, to be returned later, if you merit them.'

Saruman's face grew livid, twisted with rage, and a red light was kindled in his eyes. He laughed wildly. 'Later!' he cried, and his voice rose to a scream. 'Later! Yes, when you also have the Keys of Barad-dûr itself, I suppose; and the crowns of seven kings, and the rods of the Five Wizards, and have purchased yourself a pair of boots many sizes larger than those that you wear now. A modest plan. Hardly one in which my help is needed! I have other things to do. Do not be a fool. If you wish to treat with me, while you have a chance, go away, and come back when you are sober! And leave behind these cut-throats and small rag-tag that dangle at your tail! Good day!' He turned and left the balcony.

'Come back, Saruman!' said Gandalf in a commanding voice. To the amazement of the others, Saruman turned again, and as if dragged against his will, he came slowly back to the iron rail, leaning on it, breathing hard. His face was lined and shrunken. His hand clutched his heavy black staff like a claw.

'I did not give you leave to go,' said Gandalf sternly. 'I have not finished. You have become a fool, Saruman, and yet pitiable. You might still have turned away from folly and evil, and have been of service. But you choose to stay and gnaw the ends of your old plots. Stay then! But I warn you you will not easily come out again. Not unless the dark hands of the East stretch out to take you. Saruman!' he cried, and his voice grew in power and authority. 'Behold, I am not Gandalf the Grey, whom you betrayed. I am Gandalf the White, who has returned from death. You have no colour now, and I cast you from the order and from the Council.'

He raised his hand, and spoke slowly in a clear cold voice. 'Saruman, your staff is broken.' There was a crack, and the staff split asunder in Saruman's hand, and the head of it fell down at Gandalf's feet. 'Go!' said Gandalf. With a cry Saruman fell back and crawled away. At that moment a heavy shining thing came hurtling down from above. It glanced off the iron rail, even as Saruman left it, and passing close to Gandalf's head, it smote the stair on which he stood. The rail rang and snapped. The stair cracked and splintered in glittering sparks. But the ball was unharmed: it rolled on down the steps, a globe of crystal, dark, but glowing with a heart of fire. As it bounded away towards a pool Pippin ran after it and picked it up.

'The murderous rogue!' cried Éomer. But Gandalf was unmoved. 'No, that was not thrown by Saruman,' he said; 'nor even at his bidding, I think. It came from a window far above. A parting shot from Master Wormtongue, I fancy, but ill aimed.'

'The aim was poor, maybe, because he could not make up his mind which he hated more, you or Saruman,' said Aragorn.

'That may be so,' said Gandalf. 'Small comfort will those two have in their companionship: they will gnaw one another with words. But the punishment is just. If Wormtongue ever comes out of Orthanc alive, it will be more than he deserves.

'Here, my lad, I'll take that! I did not ask you to handle it,' he cried, turning sharply and seeing Pippin coming up the steps, slowly, as if he were bearing a great weight. He went down to meet him and hastily took the dark globe from the hobbit, wrapping it in the folds of his cloak. 'I will take care of this,' he said. 'It is not a thing, I guess, that Saruman would have chosen to cast away.'

'But he may have other things to cast,' said Gimli. 'If that is the end of the debate, let us go out of stone's throw, at least!'

'It is the end,' said Gandalf. 'Let us go.'

They turned their backs on the doors of Orthanc, and went down. The riders hailed the king with joy, and saluted Gandalf. The spell of Saruman was broken: they had seen him come at call, and crawl away, dismissed.

'Well, that is done,' said Gandalf. 'Now I must find Treebeard and tell him how things have gone.'

'He will have guessed, surely?' said Merry. 'Were they likely to end any other way?'

'Not likely,' answered Gandalf, 'though they came to the balance of a hair. But I had reasons for trying; some merciful and some less so. First Saruman was shown that the power of his voice was waning. He cannot be both tyrant and counsellor. When the plot is ripe it remains no longer secret. Yet he fell into the trap, and tried to deal with his victims piece-meal, while others listened. Then I gave him a last choice and a fair one: to renounce both Mordor and his private schemes, and make amends by helping us in our need. He knows our need, none better. Great service he could have rendered. But he has chosen to withhold it, and keep the power of Orthanc. He will not serve, only command. He lives now in terror of the shadow of Mordor, and yet he still dreams of riding the storm. Unhappy fool! He will be devoured, if the power of the East stretches out its arms to Isengard. We cannot destroy Orthanc from without, but Sauron – who knows what he can do?'

'And what if Sauron does not conquer? What will you do to him?' asked Pippin.

'I? Nothing!' said Gandalf. 'I will do nothing to him. I do not wish for

mastery. What will become of him? I cannot say. I grieve that so much
that was good now festers in the tower. Still for us things have not gone
badly. Strange are the turns of fortune! Often does hatred hurt itself! I
guess that, even if we had entered in, we could have found few treasures
in Orthanc more precious than the thing which Wormtongue threw down
at us.'

A shrill shriek, suddenly cut off, came from an open window high above.
'It seems that Saruman thinks so too,' said Gandalf. 'Let us leave them!'

They returned now to the ruins of the gate. Hardly had they passed out
under the arch, when, from among the shadows of the piled stones
where they had stood, Treebeard and a dozen other Ents came striding
up. Aragorn, Gimli and Legolas gazed at them in wonder.

'Here are three of my companions, Treebeard,' said Gandalf. 'I have
spoken of them, but you have not yet seen them.' He named them one
by one.

The Old Ent looked at them long and searchingly, and spoke to them
in turn. Last he turned to Legolas. 'So you have come all the way from
Mirkwood, my good Elf? A very great forest it used to be!'

'And still is,' said Legolas. 'But not so great that we who dwell there
ever tire of seeing new trees. I should dearly love to journey in Fangorn's
Wood. I scarcely passed beyond the eaves of it, and I did not wish to turn
back.'

Treebeard's eyes gleamed with pleasure. 'I hope you may have your
wish, ere the hills be much older,' he said.

'I will come, if I have the fortune,' said Legolas. 'I have made a bargain
with my friend that, if all goes well, we will visit Fangorn together – by
your leave.'

'Any Elf that comes with you will be welcome,' said Treebeard.

'The friend I speak of is not an Elf,' said Legolas; 'I mean Gimli, Glóin's
son here.' Gimli bowed low, and the axe slipped from his belt and clattered
on the ground.

'Hoom, hm! Ah now,' said Treebeard, looking dark-eyed at him. 'A
dwarf and an axe-bearer! Hoom! I have good will to Elves; but you ask
much. This is a strange friendship!'

'Strange it may seem,' said Legolas; 'but while Gimli lives I shall not
come to Fangorn alone. His axe is not for trees, but for orc-necks,
O Fangorn, Master of Fangorn's Wood. Forty-two he hewed in the
battle.'

'Hoo! Come now!' said Treebeard. 'That is a better story! Well, well,
things will go as they will; and there is no need to hurry to meet them.
But now we must part for a while. Day is drawing to an end, yet Gandalf

says you must go ere nightfall, and the Lord of the Mark is eager for his own house.'

'Yes, we must go, and go now,' said Gandalf. 'I fear that I must take your gatekeepers from you. But you will manage well enough without them.'

'Maybe I shall,' said Treebeard. 'But I shall miss them. We have become friends in so short a while that I think I must be getting hasty – growing backwards towards youth, perhaps. But there, they are the first new thing under Sun or Moon that I have seen for many a long, long day. I shall not forget them. I have put their names into the Long List. Ents will remember it.

> *Ents the earthborn, old as mountains,*
> *the wide-walkers, water drinking;*
> *and hungry as hunters, the Hobbit children,*
> *the laughing-folk, the little people,*

they shall remain friends as long as leaves are renewed. Fare you well! But if you hear news up in your pleasant land, in the Shire, send me word! You know what I mean: word or sight of the Entwives. Come yourselves if you can!'

'We will!' said Merry and Pippin together, and they turned away hastily. Treebeard looked at them, and was silent for a while, shaking his head thoughtfully. Then he turned to Gandalf.

'So Saruman would not leave?' he said. 'I did not think he would. His heart is as rotten as a black Huorn's. Still, if I were overcome and all my trees destroyed, I would not come while I had one dark hole left to hide in.'

'No,' said Gandalf. 'But you have not plotted to cover all the world with your trees and choke all other living things. But there it is, Saruman remains to nurse his hatred and weave again such webs as he can. He has the Key of Orthanc. But he must not be allowed to escape.'

'Indeed no! Ents will see to that,' said Treebeard. 'Saruman shall not set foot beyond the rock, without my leave. Ents will watch over him.'

'Good!' said Gandalf. 'That is what I hoped. Now I can go and turn to other matters with one care the less. But you must be wary. The waters have gone down. It will not be enough to put sentinels round the tower, I fear. I do not doubt that there were deep ways delved under Orthanc, and that Saruman hopes to go and come unmarked, before long. If you will undertake the labour, I beg you to pour in the waters again; and do so, until Isengard remains a standing pool, or you discover the outlets. When

all the underground places are drowned, and the outlets blocked, then
Saruman must stay upstairs and look out of the windows.'

'Leave it to the Ents!' said Treebeard. 'We shall search the valley from
head to foot and peer under every pebble. Trees are coming back to live
here, old trees, wild trees. The Watchwood we will call it. Not a squirrel
will go here, but I shall know of it. Leave it to Ents! Until seven times
the years in which he tormented us have passed, we shall not tire of
watching him.'

CHAPTER XI

THE PALANTÍR

The sun was sinking behind the long western arm of the mountains when Gandalf and his companions, and the king with his Riders, set out again from Isengard. Gandalf took Merry behind him, and Aragorn took Pippin. Two of the king's men went on ahead, riding swiftly, and passed soon out of sight down into the valley. The others followed at an easy pace.

Ents in a solemn row stood like statues at the gate, with their long arms uplifted, but they made no sound. Merry and Pippin looked back, when they had passed some way down the winding road. Sunlight was still shining in the sky, but long shadows reached over Isengard: grey ruins falling into darkness. Treebeard stood alone there now, like the distant stump of an old tree: the hobbits thought of their first meeting, upon the sunny ledge far away on the borders of Fangorn.

They came to the pillar of the White Hand. The pillar was still standing, but the graven hand had been thrown down and broken into small pieces. Right in the middle of the road the long forefinger lay, white in the dusk, its red nail darkening to black.

'The Ents pay attention to every detail!' said Gandalf.

They rode on, and evening deepened in the valley.

'Are we riding far tonight, Gandalf?' asked Merry after a while. 'I don't know how you feel with small rag-tag dangling behind you; but the rag-tag is tired and will be glad to stop dangling and lie down.'

'So you heard that?' said Gandalf. 'Don't let it rankle! Be thankful no longer words were aimed at you. He had his eyes on you. If it is any comfort to your pride, I should say that, at the moment, you and Pippin are more in his thoughts than all the rest of us. Who you are; how you came there, and why; what you know; whether you were captured, and if so, how you escaped when all the Orcs perished – it is with those little riddles that the great mind of Saruman is troubled. A sneer from him, Meriadoc, is a compliment, if you feel honoured by his concern.'

'Thank you!' said Merry. 'But it is a greater honour to dangle at your tail, Gandalf. For one thing, in that position one has a chance of putting a question a second time. Are we riding far tonight?'

Gandalf laughed. 'A most unquenchable hobbit! All Wizards should have a hobbit or two in their care – to teach them the meaning of the word, and to correct them. I beg your pardon. But I have given thought even to these simple matters. We will ride for a few hours, gently, until we come to the end of the valley. Tomorrow we must ride faster.

'When we came, we meant to go straight from Isengard back to the king's house at Edoras over the plains, a ride of some days. But we have taken thought and changed the plan. Messengers have gone ahead to Helm's Deep, to warn them that the king is returning tomorrow. He will ride from there with many men to Dunharrow by paths among the hills. From now on no more than two or three together are to go openly over the land, by day or night, when it can be avoided.'

'Nothing or a double helping is your way!' said Merry. 'I am afraid I was not looking beyond tonight's bed. Where and what are Helm's Deep and all the rest of it? I don't know anything about this country.'

'Then you'd best learn something, if you wish to understand what is happening. But not just now, and not from me: I have too many pressing things to think about.'

'All right, I'll tackle Strider by the camp-fire: he's less testy. But why all this secrecy? I thought we'd won the battle!'

'Yes, we have won, but only the first victory, and that in itself increases our danger. There was some link between Isengard and Mordor, which I have not yet fathomed. How they exchanged news I am not sure; but they did so. The Eye of Barad-dûr will be looking impatiently towards the Wizard's Vale, I think; and towards Rohan. The less it sees the better.'

The road passed slowly, winding down the valley. Now further, and now nearer Isen flowed in its stony bed. Night came down from the mountains. All the mists were gone. A chill wind blew. The moon, now waxing round, filled the eastern sky with a pale cold sheen. The shoulders of the mountain to their right sloped down to bare hills. The wide plains opened grey before them.

At last they halted. Then they turned aside, leaving the highway and taking to the sweet upland turf again. Going westward a mile or so they came to a dale. It opened southward, leaning back into the slope of round Dol Baran, the last hill of the northern ranges, greenfooted, crowned with heather. The sides of the glen were shaggy with last year's bracken, among which the tight-curled fronds of spring were just thrusting through the sweet-scented earth. Thornbushes grew thick upon the low banks, and under them they made their camp, two hours or so before the middle of the night. They lit a fire in a hollow, down among the roots of a spreading hawthorn, tall as a tree, writhen with age, but hale in every limb. Buds were swelling at each twig's tip.

Guards were set, two at a watch. The rest, after they had supped, wrapped themselves in a cloak and blanket and slept. The hobbits lay in a corner by themselves upon a pile of old bracken. Merry was sleepy, but Pippin now seemed curiously restless. The bracken cracked and rustled, as he twisted and turned.

'What's the matter?' asked Merry. 'Are you lying on an ant-hill?'

'No,' said Pippin, 'but I'm not comfortable. I wonder how long it is since I slept in a bed?'

Merry yawned. 'Work it out on your fingers!' he said. 'But you must know how long it is since we left Lórien.'

'Oh, that!' said Pippin. 'I mean a real bed in a bedroom.'

'Well, Rivendell then,' said Merry. 'But I could sleep anywhere tonight.'

'You had the luck, Merry,' said Pippin softly, after a long pause. 'You were riding with Gandalf.'

'Well, what of it?'

'Did you get any news, any information out of him?'

'Yes, a good deal. More than usual. But you heard it all or most of it; you were close by, and we were talking no secrets. But you can go with him tomorrow, if you think you can get more out of him – and if he'll have you.'

'Can I? Good! But he's close, isn't he? Not changed at all.'

'Oh yes, he is!' said Merry, waking up a little, and beginning to wonder what was bothering his companion. 'He has grown, or something. He can be both kinder and more alarming, merrier and more solemn than before, I think. He has changed; but we have not had a chance to see how much, yet. But think of the last part of that business with Saruman! Remember Saruman was once Gandalf's superior: head of the Council, whatever that may be exactly. He was Saruman the White. Gandalf is the White now. Saruman came when he was told, and his rod was taken; and then he was just told to go, and he went!'

'Well, if Gandalf has changed at all, then he's closer than ever that's all,' Pippin argued. 'That – glass ball, now. He seemed mighty pleased with it. He knows or guesses something about it. But does he tell us what? No, not a word. Yet I picked it up, and I saved it from rolling into a pool. *Here, I'll take that, my lad* – that's all. I wonder what it is? It felt so very heavy.' Pippin's voice fell very low, as if he was talking to himself.

'Hullo!' said Merry. 'So that's what is bothering you? Now, Pippin my lad, don't forget Gildor's saying – the one Sam used to quote: *Do not meddle in the affairs of Wizards, for they are subtle and quick to anger.*'

'But our whole life for months has been one long meddling in the affairs of Wizards,' said Pippin. 'I should like a bit of information as well as danger. I should like a look at that ball.'

'Go to sleep!' said Merry. 'You'll get information enough, sooner or later. My dear Pippin, no Took ever beat a Brandybuck for inquisitiveness; but is this the time, I ask you?'

'All right! What's the harm in my telling you what I should like: a look at that stone? I know I can't have it, with old Gandalf sitting on it, like a hen on an egg. But it doesn't help much to get no more from you than a *you-can't-have-it so-go-to-sleep!*'

'Well, what else could I say?' said Merry. 'I'm sorry, Pippin, but you really must wait till the morning. I'll be as curious as you like after breakfast, and I'll help in any way I can at wizard-wheedling. But I can't keep awake any longer. If I yawn any more, I shall split at the ears. Good night!'

Pippin said no more. He lay still now, but sleep remained far away; and it was not encouraged by the sound of Merry breathing softly, asleep in a few minutes after saying good night. The thought of the dark globe seemed to grow stronger as all grew quiet. Pippin felt again its weight in his hands, and saw again the mysterious red depths into which he had looked for a moment. He tossed and turned and tried to think of something else.

At last he could stand it no longer. He got up and looked round. It was chilly, and he wrapped his cloak about him. The moon was shining cold and white, down into the dell, and the shadows of the bushes were black. All about lay sleeping shapes. The two guards were not in view: they were up on the hill, perhaps, or hidden in the bracken. Driven by some impulse that he did not understand, Pippin walked softly to where Gandalf lay. He looked down at him. The wizard seemed asleep, but with lids not fully closed: there was a glitter of eyes under his long lashes. Pippin stepped back hastily. But Gandalf made no sign; and drawn forward once more, half against his will, the hobbit crept up again from behind the wizard's head. He was rolled in a blanket, with his cloak spread over the top; and close beside him, between his right side and his bent arm, there was a hummock, something round wrapped in a dark cloth; his hand seemed only just to have slipped off it to the ground.

Hardly breathing, Pippin crept nearer, foot by foot. At last he knelt down. Then he put his hands out stealthily, and slowly lifted the lump up: it did not seem quite so heavy as he had expected. 'Only some bundle of oddments, perhaps, after all,' he thought with a strange sense of relief; but he did not put the bundle down again. He stood for a moment clasping it. Then an idea came into his mind. He tiptoed away, found a large stone, and came back.

Quickly now he drew off the cloth, wrapped the stone in it and kneeling down, laid it back by the wizard's hand. Then at last he looked at the thing that he had uncovered. There it was: a smooth globe of crystal, now dark and dead, lying bare before his knees. Pippin lifted it, covered it hurriedly in his own cloak, and half turned to go back to his bed. At that moment Gandalf moved in his sleep, and muttered some words: they seemed to be in a strange tongue; his hand groped out and clasped the wrapped stone, then he sighed and did not move again.

'You idiotic fool!' Pippin muttered to himself. 'You're going to get yourself into frightful trouble. Put it back quick!' But he found now that his knees quaked, and he did not dare to go near enough to the wizard to reach the bundle. 'I'll never get it back now without waking him,' he thought, 'not till I'm a bit calmer. So I may as well have a look first. Not just here though!' He stole away, and sat down on a green hillock not far from his bed. The moon looked in over the edge of the dell.

Pippin sat with his knees drawn up and the ball between them. He bent low over it, looking like a greedy child stooping over a bowl of food, in a corner away from others. He drew his cloak aside and gazed at it. The air seemed still and tense about him. At first the globe was dark, black as jet, with the moonlight gleaming on its surface. Then there came a faint glow and stir in the heart of it, and it held his eyes, so that now he could not look away. Soon all the inside seemed on fire; the ball was spinning, or the lights within were revolving. Suddenly the lights went out. He gave a gasp and struggled; but he remained bent, clasping the ball with both hands. Closer and closer he bent, and then became rigid; his lips moved soundlessly for a while. Then with a strangled cry he fell back and lay still.

The cry was piercing. The guards leapt down from the banks. All the camp was soon astir.

'So this is the thief!' said Gandalf. Hastily he cast his cloak over the globe where it lay. 'But you, Pippin! This is a grievous turn to things!' He knelt by Pippin's body: the hobbit was lying on his back, rigid, with unseeing eyes staring up at the sky. 'The devilry! What mischief has he done — to himself, and to all of us?' The wizard's face was drawn and haggard.

He took Pippin's hand and bent over his face, listening for his breath; then he laid his hands on his brow. The hobbit shuddered. His eyes closed. He cried out; and sat up, staring in bewilderment at all the faces round him, pale in the moonlight.

'It is not for you, Saruman!' he cried in a shrill and toneless voice, shrinking away from Gandalf. 'I will send for it at once. Do you understand? Say just that!' Then he struggled to get up and escape, but Gandalf held him gently and firmly.

'Peregrin Took!' he said. 'Come back!'

The hobbit relaxed and fell back, clinging to the wizard's hand. 'Gandalf!' he cried. 'Gandalf! Forgive me!'

'Forgive you?' said the wizard. 'Tell me first what you have done!'

'I, I took the ball and looked at it,' stammered Pippin; 'and I saw things that frightened me. And I wanted to go away, but I couldn't. And then he came and questioned me; and he looked at me, and, and, that is all I remember.'

'That won't do,' said Gandalf sternly. 'What did you see, and what did you say?'

Pippin shut his eyes and shivered, but said nothing. They all stared at him in silence, except Merry who turned away. But Gandalf's face was still hard. 'Speak!' he said.

In a low hesitating voice Pippin began again, and slowly his words grew clearer and stronger. 'I saw a dark sky, and tall battlements,' he said. 'And tiny stars. It seemed very far away and long ago, yet hard and clear. Then the stars went in and out – they were cut off by things with wings. Very big, I think, really; but in the glass they looked like bats wheeling round the tower. I thought there were nine of them. One began to fly straight towards me, getting bigger and bigger. It had a horrible – no, no! I can't say.

'I tried to get away, because I thought it would fly out; but when it had covered all the globe, it disappeared. Then *he* came. He did not speak so that I could hear words. He just looked, and I understood.

' "So you have come back? Why have you neglected to report for so long?"

'I did not answer. He said: "Who are you?" I still did not answer, but it hurt me horribly; and he pressed me, so I said: "A hobbit."

'Then suddenly he seemed to see me, and he laughed at me. It was cruel. It was like being stabbed with knives. I struggled. But he said: "Wait a moment! We shall meet again soon. Tell Saruman that this dainty is not for him. I will send for it at once. Do you understand? Say just that!"

'Then he gloated over me. I felt I was falling to pieces. No, no! I can't say any more. I don't remember anything else.'

'Look at me!' said Gandalf.

Pippin looked up straight into his eyes. The wizard held his gaze for a moment in silence. Then his face grew gentler, and the shadow of a smile appeared. He laid his hand softly on Pippin's head.

'All right!' he said. 'Say no more! You have taken no harm. There is no lie in your eyes, as I feared. But he did not speak long with you. A fool, but an honest fool, you remain, Peregrin Took. Wiser ones might have done worse in such a pass. But mark this! You have been saved, and all your friends too, mainly by good fortune, as it is called. You cannot count on it a second time. If he had questioned you, then and there, almost certainly you would have told all that you know, to the ruin of us all. But he was too eager. He did not want information only: he wanted *you*, quickly, so that he could deal with you in the Dark Tower, slowly. Don't shudder! If you will meddle in the affairs of Wizards, you must be prepared to think of such things. But come! I forgive you. Be comforted! Things have not turned out as evilly as they might.'

He lifted Pippin gently and carried him back to his bed. Merry followed, and sat down beside him. 'Lie there and rest, if you can, Pippin!' said Gandalf. 'Trust me. If you feel an itch in your palms again, tell me of it! Such things can be cured. But anyway, my dear hobbit, don't put a lump of rock under my elbow again! Now, I will leave you two together for a while.'

With that Gandalf returned to the others, who were still standing by the Orthanc-stone in troubled thought. 'Peril comes in the night when least expected,' he said. 'We have had a narrow escape!'

'How is the hobbit, Pippin?' asked Aragorn.

'I think all will be well now,' answered Gandalf. 'He was not held long, and hobbits have an amazing power of recovery. The memory, or the horror of it, will probably fade quickly. Too quickly, perhaps. Will you, Aragorn, take the Orthanc-stone and guard it? It is a dangerous charge.'

'Dangerous indeed, but not to all,' said Aragorn. 'There is one who may claim it by right. For this assuredly is the *palantír* of Orthanc from the treasury of Elendil, set here by the Kings of Gondor. Now my hour draws near. I will take it.'

Gandalf looked at Aragorn, and then, to the surprise of the others, he lifted the covered Stone, and bowed as he presented it.

'Receive it, lord!' he said: 'in earnest of other things that shall be given back. But if I may counsel you in the use of your own, do not use it – yet! Be wary!'

'When have I been hasty or unwary, who have waited and prepared for so many long years?' said Aragorn.

'Never yet. Do not then stumble at the end of the road,' answered Gandalf. 'But at the least keep this thing secret. You, and all others that stand here! The hobbit, Peregrin, above all should not know where it is bestowed. The evil fit may come on him again. For alas! he has handled it and looked in it, as should never have happened. He ought never to have touched it in Isengard, and there I should have been quicker. But my mind was bent on Saruman, and I did not at once guess the nature of the Stone. Then I was weary, and as I lay pondering it, sleep overcame me. Now I know!'

'Yes, there can be no doubt,' said Aragorn. 'At last we know the link between Isengard and Mordor, and how it worked. Much is explained.'

'Strange powers have our enemies, and strange weaknesses!' said Théoden. 'But it has long been said: *oft evil will shall evil mar.*'

'That many times is seen,' said Gandalf. 'But at this time we have been strangely fortunate. Maybe, I have been saved by this hobbit from a grave blunder. I had considered whether or not to probe this Stone myself to find its uses. Had I done so, I should have been revealed to him myself. I am not ready for such a trial, if indeed I shall ever be so. But even if I found the power to withdraw myself, it would be disastrous for him to see me, yet – until the hour comes when secrecy will avail no longer.'

'That hour is now come, I think,' said Aragorn.

'Not yet,' said Gandalf. 'There remains a short while of doubt, which we must use. The Enemy, it is clear, thought that the Stone was in Orthanc – why should he not? And that therefore the hobbit was captive there, driven to look in the glass for his torment by Saruman. That dark mind will be filled now with the voice and face of the hobbit and with expectation: it may take some time before he learns his error. We must snatch that time. We have been too leisurely. We must move. The neighbourhood of Isengard is no place now to linger in. I will ride ahead at once with Peregrin Took. It will be better for him than lying in the dark while others sleep.'

'I will keep Éomer and ten Riders,' said the king. 'They shall ride with me at early day. The rest may go with Aragorn and ride as soon as they have a mind.'

'As you will,' said Gandalf. 'But make all the speed you may to the cover of the hills, to Helm's Deep!'

At that moment a shadow fell over them. The bright moonlight seemed to be suddenly cut off. Several of the Riders cried out, and crouched, holding their arms above their heads, as if to ward off a blow from above: a blind fear and a deadly cold fell on them. Cowering they looked up. A vast winged shape passed over the moon like a black cloud. It wheeled and went north, flying at a speed greater than any wind of Middle-earth. The stars fainted before it. It was gone.

They stood up, rigid as stones. Gandalf was gazing up, his arms out and downwards, stiff, his hands clenched.

'Nazgûl!' he cried. 'The messenger of Mordor. The storm is coming. The Nazgûl have crossed the River! Ride, ride! Wait not for the dawn! Let not the swift wait for the slow! Ride!'

He sprang away, calling Shadowfax as he ran. Aragorn followed him. Going to Pippin, Gandalf picked him up in his arms. 'You shall come with me this time,' he said. 'Shadowfax shall show you his paces.' Then he ran to the place where he had slept. Shadowfax stood there already. Slinging the small bag which was all his luggage across his shoulders, the wizard leapt upon the horse's back. Aragorn lifted Pippin and set him in Gandalf's arms, wrapped in cloak and blanket.

'Farewell! Follow fast!' cried Gandalf. 'Away, Shadowfax!' The great horse tossed his head. His flowing tail flicked in the moonlight. Then he leapt forward, spurning the earth, and was gone like the north wind from the mountains.

'A beautiful, restful night!' said Merry to Aragorn. 'Some folk have wonderful luck. He did not want to sleep, and he wanted to ride with Gandalf – and there he goes! Instead of being turned into a stone himself to stand here for ever as a warning.'

'If you had been the first to lift the Orthanc-stone, and not he, how would it be now?' said Aragorn. 'You might have done worse. Who can say? But now it is your luck to come with me, I fear. At once. Go and get ready, and bring anything that Pippin left behind. Make haste!'

Over the plains Shadowfax was flying, needing no urging and no guidance. Less than an hour had passed, and they had reached the Fords of Isen and crossed them. The Mound of the Riders and its cold spears lay grey behind them.

Pippin was recovering. He was warm, but the wind in his face was keen and refreshing. He was with Gandalf. The horror of the stone and of the hideous shadow over the moon was fading, things left behind in the mists of the mountains or in a passing dream. He drew a deep breath.

'I did not know you rode bare-back, Gandalf,' he said. 'You haven't a saddle or a bridle!'

'I do not ride elf-fashion, except on Shadowfax,' said Gandalf. 'But Shadowfax will have no harness. You do not ride Shadowfax: he is willing to carry you – or not. If he is willing, that is enough. It is then his business to see that you remain on his back, unless you jump off into the air.'

'How fast is he going?' asked Pippin. 'Fast by the wind, but very smooth. And how light his footfalls are!'

'He is running now as fast as the swiftest horse could gallop,' answered Gandalf; 'but that is not fast for him. The land is rising a little here, and is more broken than it was beyond the river. But see how the White Mountains are drawing near under the stars! Yonder are the Thrihyrne peaks like black spears. It will not be long before we reach the branching roads and come to the Deeping-coomb, where the battle was fought two nights ago.'

Pippin was silent again for a while. He heard Gandalf singing softly to himself, murmuring brief snatches of rhyme in many tongues, as the miles ran under them. At last the wizard passed into a song of which the hobbit caught the words: a few lines came clear to his ears through the rushing of the wind:

Tall ships and tall kings
Three times three,
What brought they from the foundered land
Over the flowing sea?
Seven stars and seven stones
And one white tree.

'What are you saying, Gandalf?' asked Pippin.

'I was just running over some of the Rhymes of Lore in my mind,' answered the wizard. 'Hobbits, I suppose, have forgotten them, even those that they ever knew.'

'No, not all,' said Pippin. 'And we have many of our own, which wouldn't interest you, perhaps. But I have never heard this one. What is it about – the seven stars and seven stones?'

'About the *palantíri* of the Kings of Old,' said Gandalf.

'And what are they?'

'The name meant *that which looks far away*. The Orthanc-stone was one.'

'Then it was not made, not made' – Pippin hesitated – 'by the Enemy?'

'No,' said Gandalf. 'Nor by Saruman. It is beyond his art, and beyond Sauron's too. The *palantíri* came from beyond Westernesse, from Eldamar. The Noldor made them. Fëanor himself, maybe, wrought them, in days so long ago that the time cannot be measured in years. But there is nothing that Sauron cannot turn to evil uses. Alas for Saruman! It was his downfall, as I now perceive. Perilous to us all are the devices of an art deeper than we possess ourselves. Yet he must bear the blame. Fool! to keep it secret, for his own profit. No word did he ever speak of it to any of the Council. We had not yet given thought to the fate of the *palantíri* of Gondor in its ruinous wars. By Men they were almost forgotten. Even in Gondor they were a secret known only to a few; in Arnor they were remembered only in a rhyme of lore among the Dúnedain.'

'What did the Men of old use them for?' asked Pippin, delighted and astonished at getting answers to so many questions, and wondering how long it would last.

'To see far off, and to converse in thought with one another,' said Gandalf. 'In that way they long guarded and united the realm of Gondor. They set up Stones at Minas Anor, and at Minas Ithil, and at Orthanc in the ring of Isengard. The chief and master of these was under the Dome of Stars at Osgiliath before its ruin. The three others were far away in the North. In the house of Elrond it is told that they were at Annúminas, and

Amon Sûl, and Elendil's Stone was on the Tower Hills that look towards Mithlond in the Gulf of Lune where the grey ships lie.

'Each *palantír* replied to each, but all those in Gondor were ever open to the view of Osgiliath. Now it appears that, as the rock of Orthanc has withstood the storms of time, so there the *palantír* of that tower has remained. But alone it could do nothing but see small images of things far off and days remote. Very useful, no doubt, that was to Saruman; yet it seems that he was not content. Further and further abroad he gazed, until he cast his gaze upon Barad-dûr. Then he was caught!

'Who knows where the lost Stones of Arnor and Gondor now lie, buried, or drowned deep? But one at least Sauron must have obtained and mastered to his purposes. I guess that it was the Ithil-stone, for he took Minas Ithil long ago and turned it into an evil place: Minas Morgul, it has become.

'Easy it is now to guess how quickly the roving eye of Saruman was trapped and held; and how ever since he has been persuaded from afar, and daunted when persuasion would not serve. The biter bit, the hawk under the eagle's foot, the spider in a steel web! How long, I wonder, has he been constrained to come often to his glass for inspection and instruction, and the Orthanc-stone so bent towards Barad-dûr that, if any save a will of adamant now looks into it, it will bear his mind and sight swiftly thither? And how it draws one to itself! Have I not felt it? Even now my heart desires to test my will upon it, to see if I could not wrench it from him and turn it where I would – to look across the wide seas of water and of time to Tirion the Fair, and perceive the unimaginable hand and mind of Fëanor at their work, while both the White Tree and the Golden were in flower!' He sighed and fell silent.

'I wish I had known all this before,' said Pippin. 'I had no notion of what I was doing.'

'Oh yes, you had,' said Gandalf. 'You knew you were behaving wrongly and foolishly; and you told yourself so, though you did not listen. I did not tell you all this before, because it is only by musing on all that has happened that I have at last understood, even as we ride together. But if I had spoken sooner, it would not have lessened your desire, or made it easier to resist. On the contrary! No, the burned hand teaches best. After that advice about fire goes to the heart.'

'It does,' said Pippin. 'If all the seven stones were laid out before me now, I should shut my eyes and put my hands in my pockets.'

'Good!' said Gandalf. 'That is what I hoped.'

'But I should like to know——' Pippin began.

'Mercy!' cried Gandalf. 'If the giving of information is to be the cure of your inquisitiveness, I shall spend all the rest of my days in answering you. What more do you want to know?'

'The names of all the stars, and of all living things, and the whole history of Middle-earth and Over-heaven and of the Sundering Seas,' laughed Pippin. 'Of course! What less? But I am not in a hurry tonight. At the moment I was just wondering about the black shadow. I heard you shout "messenger of Mordor". What was it? What could it do at Isengard?'

'It was a Black Rider on wings, a Nazgûl,' said Gandalf. 'It could have taken you away to the Dark Tower.'

'But it was not coming for me, was it?' faltered Pippin. 'I mean, it didn't know that I had . . .'

'Of course not,' said Gandalf. 'It is two hundred leagues or more in straight flight from Barad-dûr to Orthanc, and even a Nazgûl would take a few hours to fly between them. But Saruman certainly looked in the Stone since the orc-raid, and more of his secret thought, I do not doubt, has been read than he intended. A messenger has been sent to find out what he is doing. And after what has happened tonight another will come, I think, and swiftly. So Saruman will come to the last pinch of the vice that he has put his hand in. He has no captive to send. He has no Stone to see with, and cannot answer the summons. Sauron will only believe that he is with-holding the captive and refusing to use the Stone. It will not help Saruman to tell the truth to the messenger. For Isengard may be ruined, yet he is still safe in Orthanc. So whether he will or no, he will appear a rebel. Yet he rejected us, so as to avoid that very thing! What he will do in such a plight, I cannot guess. He has power still, I think, while in Orthanc, to resist the Nine Riders. He may try to do so. He may try to trap the Nazgûl, or at least to slay the thing on which it now rides the air. In that case let Rohan look to its horses!

'But I cannot tell how it will fall out, well or ill for us. It may be that the counsels of the Enemy will be confused, or hindered by his wrath with Saruman. It may be that he will learn that I was there and stood upon the stairs of Orthanc – with hobbits at my tail. Or that an heir of Elendil lives and stood beside me. If Wormtongue was not deceived by the armour of Rohan, he would remember Aragorn and the title that he claimed. That is what I fear. And so we fly – not from danger but into greater danger. Every stride of Shadowfax bears you nearer to the Land of Shadow, Peregrin Took.'

Pippin made no answer, but clutched his cloak, as if a sudden chill had struck him. Grey land passed under them.

'See now!' said Gandalf. 'The Westfold dales are opening before us. Here we come back to the eastward road. The dark shadow yonder is the mouth of the Deeping-coomb. That way lies Aglarond and the Glittering Caves. Do not ask me about them. Ask Gimli, if you meet again, and for the first time you may get an answer longer than you wish. You will not see the caves yourself, not on this journey. Soon they will be far behind.'

'I thought you were going to stop at Helm's Deep!' said Pippin. 'Where are you going then?'

'To Minas Tirith, before the seas of war surround it.'

'Oh! And how far is that?'

'Leagues upon leagues,' answered Gandalf. 'Thrice as far as the dwellings of King Théoden, and they are more than a hundred miles east from here, as the messengers of Mordor fly. Shadowfax must run a longer road. Which will prove the swifter?

'We shall ride now till daybreak, and that is some hours away. Then even Shadowfax must rest, in some hollow of the hills: at Edoras, I hope. Sleep, if you can! You may see the first glimmer of dawn upon the golden roof of the house of Eorl. And in two days thence you shall see the purple shadow of Mount Mindolluin and the walls of the tower of Denethor white in the morning.

'Away now, Shadowfax! Run, greatheart, run as you have never run before! Now we are come to the lands where you were foaled, and every stone you know. Run now! Hope is in speed!'

Shadowfax tossed his head and cried aloud, as if a trumpet had summoned him to battle. Then he sprang forward. Fire flew from his feet; night rushed over him.

As he fell slowly into sleep, Pippin had a strange feeling: he and Gandalf were still as stone, seated upon the statue of a running horse, while the world rolled away beneath his feet with a great noise of wind.

BOOK FOUR

CHAPTER I

THE TAMING OF SMÉAGOL

'Well, master, we're in a fix and no mistake,' said Sam Gamgee. He stood despondently with hunched shoulders beside Frodo, and peered out with puckered eyes into the gloom.

It was the third evening since they had fled from the Company, as far as they could tell: they had almost lost count of the hours during which they had climbed and laboured among the barren slopes and stones of the Emyn Muil, sometimes retracing their steps because they could find no way forward, sometimes discovering that they had wandered in a circle back to where they had been hours before. Yet on the whole they had worked steadily eastward, keeping as near as they could find a way to the outer edge of this strange twisted knot of hills. But always they found its outward faces sheer, high and impassable, frowning over the plain below; beyond its tumbled skirts lay livid festering marshes where nothing moved and not even a bird was to be seen.

The hobbits stood now on the brink of a tall cliff, bare and bleak, its feet wrapped in mist; and behind them rose the broken highlands crowned with drifting cloud. A chill wind blew from the East. Night was gathering over the shapeless lands before them; the sickly green of them was fading to a sullen brown. Far away to the right the Anduin, that had gleamed fitfully in sun-breaks during the day, was now hidden in shadow. But their eyes did not look beyond the River, back to Gondor, to their friends, to the lands of Men. South and east they stared to where, at the edge of the oncoming night, a dark line hung, like distant mountains of motionless smoke. Every now and again a tiny red gleam far away flickered upwards on the rim of earth and sky.

'What a fix!' said Sam. 'That's the one place in all the lands we've ever heard of that we don't want to see any closer; and that's the one place we're trying to get to! And that's just where we can't get, nohow. We've come the wrong way altogether, seemingly. We can't get down; and if we did get down, we'd find all that green land a nasty bog, I'll warrant. Phew! Can you smell it?' He sniffed at the wind.

'Yes, I can smell it,' said Frodo, but he did not move, and his eyes remained fixed, staring out towards the dark line and the flickering flame. 'Mordor!' he muttered under his breath. 'If I must go there, I wish I could come there quickly and make an end!' He shuddered. The wind was chilly and yet heavy with an odour of cold decay. 'Well,' he said, at last withdrawing his eyes, 'we cannot stay here all night, fix or no fix. We must find a more sheltered spot, and camp once more; and perhaps another day will show us a path.'

'Or another and another and another,' muttered Sam. 'Or maybe no day. We've come the wrong way.'

'I wonder,' said Frodo. 'It's my doom, I think, to go to that Shadow yonder, so that a way will be found. But will good or evil show it to me? What hope we had was in speed. Delay plays into the Enemy's hands – and here I am: delayed. Is it the will of the Dark Tower that steers us? All my choices have proved ill. I should have left the Company long before, and come down from the North, east of the River and of the Emyn Muil, and so over the hard of Battle Plain to the passes of Mordor. But now it isn't possible for you and me alone to find a way back, and the Orcs are prowling on the east bank. Every day that passes is a precious day lost. I am tired, Sam. I don't know what is to be done. What food have we got left?'

'Only those, what d'you call 'em, *lembas*, Mr. Frodo. A fair supply. But they are better than naught, by a long bite. I never thought, though, when I first set tooth in them, that I should ever come to wish for a change. But I do now: a bit of plain bread, and a mug – aye, half a mug – of beer would go down proper. I've lugged my cooking-gear all the way from the last camp, and what use has it been? Naught to make a fire with, for a start; and naught to cook, not even grass!'

They turned away and went down into a stony hollow. The westering sun was caught into clouds, and night came swiftly. They slept as well as they could for the cold, turn and turn about, in a nook among great jagged pinnacles of weathered rock; at least they were sheltered from the easterly wind.

'Did you see them again, Mr. Frodo?' asked Sam, as they sat, stiff and chilled, munching wafers of *lembas*, in the cold grey of early morning.

'No,' said Frodo. 'I've heard nothing, and seen nothing, for two nights now.'

'Nor me,' said Sam. 'Grrr! Those eyes did give me a turn! But perhaps we've shaken him off at last, the miserable slinker. Gollum! I'll give him *gollum* in his throat, if ever I get my hands on his neck.'

'I hope you'll never need to,' said Frodo. 'I don't know how he followed us; but it may be that he's lost us again, as you say. In this dry bleak land we can't leave many footprints, nor much scent, even for his snuffling nose.'

'I hope that's the way of it,' said Sam. 'I wish we could be rid of him for good!'

'So do I,' said Frodo; 'but he's not my chief trouble. I wish we could get away from these hills! I hate them. I feel all naked on the east side, stuck up here with nothing but the dead flats between me and that Shadow yonder. There's an Eye in it. Come on! We've got to get down today somehow.'

But that day wore on, and when afternoon faded towards evening they were still scrambling along the ridge and had found no way of escape.

Sometimes in the silence of that barren country they fancied that they heard faint sounds behind them, a stone falling, or the imagined step of flapping feet on the rock. But if they halted and stood still listening, they heard no more, nothing but the wind sighing over the edges of the stones – yet even that reminded them of breath softly hissing through sharp teeth.

All that day the outer ridge of the Emyn Muil had been bending gradually northward, as they struggled on. Along its brink there now stretched a wide tumbled flat of scored and weathered rock, cut every now and again by trench-like gullies that sloped steeply down to deep notches in the cliff-face. To find a path in these clefts, which were becoming deeper and more frequent, Frodo and Sam were driven to their left, well away from the edge, and they did not notice that for several miles they had been going slowly but steadily downhill: the cliff-top was sinking towards the level of the lowlands.

At last they were brought to a halt. The ridge took a sharper bend northward and was gashed by a deeper ravine. On the further side it reared up again, many fathoms at a single leap: a great grey cliff loomed before them, cut sheer down as if by a knife stroke. They could go no further forwards, and must turn now either west or east. But west would lead them only into more labour and delay, back towards the heart of the hills; east would take them to the outer precipice.

'There's nothing for it but to scramble down this gully, Sam,' said Frodo. 'Let's see what it leads to!'

'A nasty drop, I'll bet,' said Sam.

The cleft was longer and deeper than it seemed. Some way down they found a few gnarled and stunted trees, the first they had seen for days: twisted birch for the most part, with here and there a fir-tree. Many were dead and gaunt, bitten to the core by the eastern winds. Once in milder days there must have been a fair thicket in the ravine, but now, after some fifty yards, the trees came to an end, though old broken stumps straggled on almost to the cliff's brink. The bottom of the gully, which lay along the edge of a rock-fault, was rough with broken stone and slanted steeply down. When they came at last to the end of it, Frodo stooped and leaned out.

'Look!' he said. 'We must have come down a long way, or else the cliff has sunk. It's much lower here than it was, and it looks easier too.'

Sam knelt beside him and peered reluctantly over the edge. Then he glanced up at the great cliff rising up, away on their left. 'Easier!' he grunted. 'Well, I suppose it's always easier getting down than up. Those as can't fly can jump!'

'It would be a big jump still,' said Frodo. 'About, well' – he stood for a moment measuring it with his eyes – 'about eighteen fathoms, I should guess. Not more.'

'And that's enough!' said Sam. 'Ugh! How I do hate looking down from a height! But looking's better than climbing.'

'All the same,' said Frodo, 'I think we could climb here; and I think we shall have to try. See – the rock is quite different from what it was a few miles back. It has slipped and cracked.'

The outer fall was indeed no longer sheer, but sloped outwards a little. It looked like a great rampart or sea-wall whose foundations had shifted, so that its courses were all twisted and disordered, leaving great fissures and long slanting edges that were in places almost as wide as stairs.

'And if we're going to try and get down, we had better try at once. It's getting dark early. I think there's a storm coming.'

The smoky blur of the mountains in the East was lost in a deeper blackness that was already reaching out westwards with long arms. There was a distant mutter of thunder borne on the rising breeze. Frodo sniffed the air and looked up doubtfully at the sky. He strapped his belt outside his cloak and tightened it, and settled his light pack on his back; then he stepped towards the edge. 'I'm going to try it,' he said.

'Very good!' said Sam gloomily. 'But I'm going first.'

'You?' said Frodo. 'What's made you change your mind about climbing?'

'I haven't changed my mind. But it's only sense: put the one lowest as is most likely to slip. I don't want to come down atop of you and knock you off – no sense in killing two with one fall.'

Before Frodo could stop him, he sat down, swung his legs over the brink, and twisted round, scrabbling with his toes for a foothold. It is doubtful if he ever did anything braver in cold blood, or more unwise.

'No, no! Sam, you old ass!' said Frodo. 'You'll kill yourself for certain, going over like that without even a look to see what to make for. Come back!' He took Sam under the armpits and hauled him up again. 'Now, wait a bit and be patient!' he said. Then he lay on the ground, leaning out and looking down; but the light seemed to be fading quickly, although the sun had not yet set. 'I think we could manage this,' he said presently. 'I could at any rate; and you could too, if you kept your head and followed me carefully.'

'I don't know how you can be so sure,' said Sam. 'Why! You can't see to the bottom in this light. What if you comes to a place where there's nowhere to put your feet or your hands?'

'Climb back, I suppose,' said Frodo.

'Easy said,' objected Sam. 'Better wait till morning and more light.'

'No! Not if I can help it,' said Frodo with a sudden strange vehemence. 'I grudge every hour, every minute. I'm going down to try it out. Don't you follow till I come back or call!'

Gripping the stony lip of the fall with his fingers he let himself gently down, until when his arms were almost at full stretch, his toes found a ledge. 'One step down!' he said. 'And this ledge broadens out to the right. I could stand there without a hold. I'll——' his words were cut short.

The hurrying darkness, now gathering great speed, rushed up from the East and swallowed the sky. There was a dry splitting crack of thunder right overhead. Searing lightning smote down into the hills. Then came a blast of savage wind, and with it, mingling with its roar, there came a high shrill shriek. The hobbits had heard just such a cry far away in the Marish as they fled from Hobbiton, and even there in the woods of the Shire it had frozen their blood. Out here in the waste its terror was far greater: it pierced them with cold blades of horror and despair, stopping heart and breath. Sam fell flat on his face. Involuntarily Frodo loosed his hold and put his hands over his head and ears. He swayed, slipped, and slithered downwards with a wailing cry.

Sam heard him and crawled with an effort to the edge. 'Master, master!' he called. 'Master!'

He heard no answer. He found he was shaking all over, but he gathered his breath, and once again he shouted: 'Master!' The wind seemed to blow his voice back into his throat, but as it passed, roaring up the gully and away over the hills, a faint answering cry came to his ears:

'All right, all right! I'm here. But I can't see.'

Frodo was calling with a weak voice. He was not actually very far away. He had slid and not fallen, and had come up with a jolt to his feet on a wider ledge not many yards lower down. Fortunately the rock-face at this point leaned well back and the wind had pressed him against the cliff, so that he had not toppled over. He steadied himself a little, laying his face against the cold stone, feeling his heart pounding. But either the darkness had grown complete, or else his eyes had lost their sight. All was black about him. He wondered if he had been struck blind. He took a deep breath.

'Come back! Come back!' he heard Sam's voice out of the blackness above.

'I can't,' he said. 'I can't see. I can't find any hold. I can't move yet.'

'What can I do, Mr. Frodo? What can I do?' shouted Sam, leaning out dangerously far. Why could not his master see? It was dim, certainly, but not as dark as all that. He could see Frodo below him, a grey forlorn figure splayed against the cliff. But he was far out of the reach of any helping hand.

There was another crack of thunder; and then the rain came. In a blinding sheet, mingled with hail, it drove against the cliff, bitter cold.

'I'm coming down to you,' shouted Sam, though how he hoped to help in that way he could not have said.

'No, no! wait!' Frodo called back, more strongly now. 'I shall be better soon. I feel better already. Wait! You can't do anything without a rope.'

'Rope!' cried Sam, talking wildly to himself in his excitement and relief. 'Well, if I don't deserve to be hung on the end of one as a warning to numbskulls! You're nowt but a ninnyhammer, Sam Gamgee: that's what the Gaffer said to me often enough, it being a word of his. Rope!'

'Stop chattering!' cried Frodo, now recovered enough to feel both amused and annoyed. 'Never mind your Gaffer! Are you trying to tell yourself you've got some rope in your pocket? If so, out with it!'

'Yes, Mr. Frodo, in my pack and all. Carried it hundreds of miles, and I'd clean forgotten it!'

'Then get busy and let an end down!'

Quickly Sam unslung his pack and rummaged in it. There indeed at the bottom was a coil of the silken-grey rope made by the folk of Lórien. He cast an end to his master. The darkness seemed to lift from Frodo's eyes, or else his sight was returning. He could see the grey line as it came dangling down, and he thought it had a faint silver sheen. Now that he had some point in the darkness to fix his eyes on, he felt less giddy. Leaning his weight forward, he made the end fast round his waist, and then he grasped the line with both hands.

Sam stepped back and braced his feet against a stump a yard or two from the edge. Half hauled, half scrambling, Frodo came up and threw himself on the ground.

Thunder growled and rumbled in the distance, and the rain was still falling heavily. The hobbits crawled away back into the gully; but they did not find much shelter there. Rills of water began to run down; soon they grew to a spate that splashed and fumed on the stones, and spouted out over the cliff like the gutters of a vast roof.

'I should have been half drowned down there, or washed clean off,' said Frodo. 'What a piece of luck you had that rope!'

'Better luck if I'd thought of it sooner,' said Sam. 'Maybe you remember them putting the ropes in the boats, as we started off: in the elvish country.

I took a fancy to it, and I stowed a coil in my pack. Years ago, it seems. "It may be a help in many needs," he said: Haldir, or one of those folk. And he spoke right.'

'A pity I didn't think of bringing another length,' said Frodo; 'but I left the Company in such a hurry and confusion. If only we had enough we could use it to get down. How long is your rope, I wonder?'

Sam paid it out slowly, measuring it with his arms: 'Five, ten, twenty, thirty ells, more or less,' he said.

'Who'd have thought it!' Frodo exclaimed.

'Ah! Who would?' said Sam. 'Elves are wonderful folk. It looks a bit thin, but it's tough; and soft as milk to the hand. Packs close too, and as light as light. Wonderful folk to be sure!'

'Thirty ells!' said Frodo considering. 'I believe it would be enough. If the storm passes before nightfall, I'm going to try it.'

'The rain's nearly given over already,' said Sam; 'but don't you go doing anything risky in the dim again, Mr. Frodo! And I haven't got over that shriek on the wind yet, if you have. Like a Black Rider it sounded – but one up in the air, if they can fly. I'm thinking we'd best lay up in this crack till night's over.'

'And I'm thinking that I won't spend a moment longer than I need, stuck up on this edge with the eyes of the Dark Country looking over the marshes,' said Frodo.

With that he stood up and went down to the bottom of the gully again. He looked out. Clear sky was growing in the East once more. The skirts of the storm were lifting, ragged and wet, and the main battle had passed to spread its great wings over the Emyn Muil, upon which the dark thought of Sauron brooded for a while. Thence it turned, smiting the Vale of Anduin with hail and lightning, and casting its shadow upon Minas Tirith with threat of war. Then, lowering in the mountains, and gathering its great spires, it rolled on slowly over Gondor and the skirts of Rohan, until far away the Riders on the plain saw its black towers moving behind the sun, as they rode into the West. But here, over the desert and the reeking marshes the deep blue sky of evening opened once more, and a few pallid stars appeared, like small white holes in the canopy above the crescent moon.

'It's good to be able to see again,' said Frodo, breathing deep. 'Do you know, I thought for a bit that I had lost my sight? From the lightning or something else worse. I could see nothing, nothing at all, until the grey rope came down. It seemed to shimmer somehow.'

'It does look sort of silver in the dark,' said Sam. 'Never noticed it before, though I can't remember as I've ever had it out since I first stowed it. But if you're so set on climbing, Mr. Frodo, how are you going to use it? Thirty ells, or say, about eighteen fathom: that's no more than your guess at the height of the cliff.'

Frodo thought for a while. 'Make it fast to that stump, Sam!' he said. 'Then I think you shall have your wish this time and go first. I'll lower you, and you need do no more than use your feet and hands to fend yourself off the rock. Though, if you put your weight on some of the ledges and give me a rest, it will help. When you're down, I'll follow. I feel quite myself again now.'

'Very well,' said Sam heavily. 'If it must be, let's get it over!' He took up the rope and made it fast over the stump nearest to the brink; then the other end he tied about his own waist. Reluctantly he turned and prepared to go over the edge a second time.

It did not, however, turn out half as bad as he had expected. The rope seemed to give him confidence, though he shut his eyes more than once when he looked down between his feet. There was one awkward spot, where there was no ledge and the wall was sheer and even undercut for a short space; there he slipped and swung out on the silver line. But Frodo lowered him slowly and steadily, and it was over at last. His chief fear had been that the rope-length would give out while he was still high up, but there was still a good bight in Frodo's hands, when Sam came to the bottom and called up: 'I'm down!' His voice came up clearly from below, but Frodo could not see him; his grey elven-cloak had melted into the twilight.

Frodo took rather more time to follow him. He had the rope about his waist and it was fast above, and he had shortened it so that it would pull him up before he reached the ground; still he did not want to risk a fall, and he had not quite Sam's faith in this slender grey line. He found two places, all the same, where he had to trust wholly to it: smooth surfaces where there was no hold even for his strong hobbit fingers and the ledges were far apart. But at last he too was down.

'Well!' he cried. 'We've done it! We've escaped from the Emyn Muil! And now what next, I wonder? Maybe we shall soon be sighing for good hard rock under foot again.'

But Sam did not answer: he was staring back up the cliff. 'Ninnyhammers!' he said. 'Noodles! My beautiful rope! There it is tied to a stump, and we're at the bottom. Just as nice a little stair for that slinking Gollum as we could leave. Better put up a signpost to say which way we've gone! I thought it seemed a bit too easy.'

'If you can think of any way we could have both used the rope and yet brought it down with us, then you can pass on to me ninnyhammer, or any other name your Gaffer gave you,' said Frodo. 'Climb up and untie it and let yourself down, if you want to!'

Sam scratched his head. 'No, I can't think how, begging your pardon,' he said. 'But I don't like leaving it, and that's a fact.' He stroked the rope's end and shook it gently. 'It goes hard parting with anything I brought out of the Elf-country. Made by Galadriel herself, too, maybe. Galadriel,' he murmured, nodding his head mournfully. He looked up and gave one last pull to the rope as if in farewell.

To the complete surprise of both the hobbits it came loose. Sam fell over, and the long grey coils slithered silently down on top of him. Frodo laughed. 'Who tied the rope?' he said. 'A good thing it held as long as it did! To think that I trusted all my weight to your knot!'

Sam did not laugh. 'I may not be much good at climbing, Mr. Frodo,' he said in injured tones, 'but I do know something about rope and about knots. It's in the family, as you might say. Why, my grand-dad, and my uncle Andy after him, him that was the Gaffer's eldest brother, he had a rope-walk over by Tighfield many a year. And I put as fast a hitch over the stump as any one could have done, in the Shire or out of it.'

'Then the rope must have broken – frayed on the rock-edge, I expect,' said Frodo.

'I bet it didn't!' said Sam in an even more injured voice. He stooped and examined the ends. 'Nor it hasn't neither. Not a strand!'

'Then I'm afraid it must have been the knot,' said Frodo.

Sam shook his head and did not answer. He was passing the rope through his fingers thoughtfully. 'Have it your own way, Mr. Frodo,' he said at last, 'but I think the rope came off itself – when I called.' He coiled it up and stowed it lovingly in his pack.

'It certainly came,' said Frodo, 'and that's the chief thing. But now we've got to think of our next move. Night will be on us soon. How beautiful the stars are, and the Moon!'

'They do cheer the heart, don't they?' said Sam looking up. 'Elvish they are, somehow. And the Moon's growing. We haven't seen him for a night or two in this cloudy weather. He's beginning to give quite a light.'

'Yes,' said Frodo; 'but he won't be full for some days. I don't think we'll try the marshes by the light of half a moon.'

Under the first shadows of night they started out on the next stage of their journey. After a while Sam turned and looked back at the way they had come. The mouth of the gully was a black notch in the dim cliff. 'I'm glad we've got the rope,' he said. 'We've set a little puzzle for that footpad, anyhow. He can try his nasty flappy feet on those ledges!'

They picked their steps away from the skirts of the cliff, among a wilderness of boulders and rough stones, wet and slippery with the heavy rain.

The ground still fell away sharply. They had not gone very far when they came upon a great fissure that yawned suddenly black before their feet. It was not wide, but it was too wide to jump across in the dim light. They thought they could hear water gurgling in its depths. It curved away on their left northward, back towards the hills, and so barred their road in that direction, at any rate while darkness lasted.

'We had better try a way back southwards along the line of the cliff, I think,' said Sam. 'We might find some nook there, or even a cave or something.'

'I suppose so,' said Frodo. 'I'm tired, and I don't think I can scramble among stones much longer tonight – though I grudge the delay. I wish there was a clear path in front of us: then I'd go on till my legs gave way.'

They did not find the going any easier at the broken feet of the Emyn Muil. Nor did Sam find any nook or hollow to shelter in: only bare stony slopes frowned over by the cliff, which now rose again, higher and more sheer as they went back. In the end, worn out, they just cast themselves on the ground under the lee of a boulder lying not far from the foot of the precipice. There for some time they sat huddled mournfully together in the cold stony night, while sleep crept upon them in spite of all they could do to hold it off. The moon now rode high and clear. Its thin white light lit up the faces of the rocks and drenched the cold frowning walls of the cliff, turning all the wide looming darkness into a chill pale grey scored with black shadows.

'Well!' said Frodo, standing up and drawing his cloak more closely round him. 'You sleep for a bit Sam and take my blanket. I'll walk up and down on sentry for a while.' Suddenly he stiffened, and stooping he gripped Sam by the arm. 'What's that?' he whispered. 'Look over there on the cliff!'

Sam looked and breathed in sharply through his teeth. 'Ssss!' he said. 'That's what it is. It's that Gollum! Snakes and adders! And to think that I thought that we'd puzzle him with our bit of a climb! Look at him! Like a nasty crawling spider on a wall.'

Down the face of a precipice, sheer and almost smooth it seemed in the pale moonlight, a small black shape was moving with its thin limbs splayed out. Maybe its soft clinging hands and toes were finding crevices and holds that no hobbit could ever have seen or used, but it looked as if it was just creeping down on sticky pads, like some large prowling thing of insect-kind. And it was coming down head first, as if it was smelling its way. Now and again it lifted its head slowly, turning it right back on its long skinny neck, and the hobbits caught a glimpse of two small pale gleaming lights, its eyes that blinked at the moon for a moment and then were quickly lidded again.

'Do you think he can see us?' said Sam.

'I don't know,' said Frodo quietly, 'but I think not. It is hard even for friendly eyes to see these elven-cloaks: I cannot see you in the shadow even at a few paces. And I've heard that he doesn't like Sun or Moon.'

'Then why is he coming down just here?' asked Sam.

'Quietly, Sam!' said Frodo. 'He can smell us, perhaps. And he can hear as keen as Elves, I believe. I think he has heard something now: our voices probably. We did a lot of shouting away back there; and we were talking far too loudly until a minute ago.'

'Well, I'm sick of him,' said Sam. 'He's come once too often for me, and I'm going to have a word with him, if I can. I don't suppose we could give him the slip now anyway.' Drawing his grey hood well over his face, Sam crept stealthily towards the cliff.

'Careful!' whispered Frodo coming behind. 'Don't alarm him! He's much more dangerous than he looks.'

The black crawling shape was now three-quarters of the way down, and perhaps fifty feet or less above the cliff's foot. Crouching stone-still in the shadow of a large boulder the hobbits watched him. He seemed to have come to a difficult passage or to be troubled about something. They could hear him snuffling, and now and again there was a harsh hiss of breath that sounded like a curse. He lifted his head, and they thought they heard him spit. Then he moved on again. Now they could hear his voice creaking and whistling.

'Ach, sss! Cautious, my precious! More haste less speed. We musstn't rissk our neck, musst we, precious? No, precious – *gollum*!' He lifted his head again, blinked at the moon, and quickly shut his eyes. 'We hate it,' he hissed. 'Nassty, nassty shivery light it is – sss – it spies on us, precious – it hurts our eyes.'

He was getting lower now and the hisses became sharper and clearer. 'Where iss it, where iss it: my Precious, my Precious? It's ours, it is, and we wants it. The thieves, the thieves, the filthy little thieves. Where are they with my Precious? Curse them! We hates them.'

'It doesn't sound as if he knew we were here, does it?' whispered Sam. 'And what's his Precious? Does he mean the——'

'Hsh!' breathed Frodo. 'He's getting near now, near enough to hear a whisper.'

Indeed Gollum had suddenly paused again, and his large head on its scrawny neck was lolling from side to side as if he was listening. His pale eyes were half unlidded. Sam restrained himself, though his fingers were twitching. His eyes, filled with anger and disgust, were fixed on the wretched creature as he now began to move again, still whispering and hissing to himself.

At last he was no more than a dozen feet from the ground, right above their heads. From that point there was a sheer drop, for the cliff was slightly undercut, and even Gollum could not find a hold of any kind. He seemed to be trying to twist round, so as to go legs first, when suddenly with a shrill whistling shriek he fell. As he did so, he curled his legs and arms up round him, like a spider whose descending thread is snapped.

Sam was out of his hiding in a flash and crossed the space between him and the cliff-foot in a couple of leaps. Before Gollum could get up, he was on top of him. But he found Gollum more than he bargained for, even taken like that, suddenly, off his guard after a fall. Before Sam could get a hold, long legs and arms were wound round him pinning his arms, and a clinging grip, soft but horribly strong, was squeezing him like slowly tightening cords; clammy fingers were feeling for his throat. Then sharp teeth bit into his shoulder. All he could do was to butt his hard round head sideways into the creature's face. Gollum hissed and spat, but he did not let go.

Things would have gone ill with Sam, if he had been alone. But Frodo sprang up, and drew Sting from its sheath. With his left hand he drew back Gollum's head by his thin lank hair, stretching his long neck, and forcing his pale venomous eyes to stare up at the sky.

'Let go! Gollum,' he said. 'This is Sting. You have seen it before once upon a time. Let go, or you'll feel it this time! I'll cut your throat.'

Gollum collapsed and went as loose as wet string. Sam got up, fingering his shoulder. His eyes smouldered with anger, but he could not avenge himself: his miserable enemy lay grovelling on the stones whimpering.

'Don't hurt us! Don't let them hurt us, precious! They won't hurt us will they, nice little hobbitses? We didn't mean no harm, but they jumps on us like cats on poor mices, they did, precious. And we're so lonely, *gollum*. We'll be nice to them, very nice, if they'll be nice to us, won't we, yes, yess.'

'Well, what's to be done with it?' said Sam. 'Tie it up, so as it can't come sneaking after us no more, I say.'

'But that would kill us, kill us,' whimpered Gollum. 'Cruel little hobbitses. Tie us up in the cold hard lands and leave us, *gollum*, *gollum*.' Sobs welled up in his gobbling throat.

'No,' said Frodo. 'If we kill him, we must kill him outright. But we can't do that, not as things are. Poor wretch! He has done us no harm.'

'Oh hasn't he!' said Sam rubbing his shoulder. 'Anyway he meant to, *and* he means to, I'll warrant. Throttle us in our sleep, that's his plan.'

'I daresay,' said Frodo. 'But what he means to do is another matter.' He paused for a while in thought. Gollum lay still, but stopped whimpering. Sam stood glowering over him.

It seemed to Frodo then that he heard, quite plainly but far off, voices out of the past:

What a pity Bilbo did not stab the vile creature, when he had a chance!

Pity? It was Pity that stayed his hand. Pity, and Mercy: not to strike without need.

I do not feel any pity for Gollum. He deserves death.

Deserves death! I daresay he does. Many that live deserve death. And some die that deserve life. Can you give that to them? Then be not too eager to deal out death in the name of justice, fearing for your own safety. Even the wise cannot see all ends.

'Very well,' he answered aloud, lowering his sword. 'But still I am afraid. And yet, as you see, I will not touch the creature. For now that I see him, I do pity him.'

Sam stared at his master, who seemed to be speaking to some one who was not there. Gollum lifted his head.

'Yess, wretched we are, precious,' he whined. 'Misery misery! Hobbits won't kill us, nice hobbits.'

'No, we won't,' said Frodo. 'But we won't let you go, either. You're full of wickedness and mischief, Gollum. You will have to come with us, that's all, while we keep an eye on you. But you must help us, if you can. One good turn deserves another.'

'Yess, yes indeed,' said Gollum sitting up. 'Nice hobbits! We will come with them. Find them safe paths in the dark, yes we will. And where are they going in these cold hard lands, we wonders, yes we wonders?' He looked up at them, and a faint light of cunning and eagerness flickered for a second in his pale blinking eyes.

Sam scowled at him, and sucked his teeth; but he seemed to sense that there was something odd about his master's mood and that the matter was beyond argument. All the same he was amazed at Frodo's reply.

Frodo looked straight into Gollum's eyes which flinched and twisted away. 'You know that, or you guess well enough, Sméagol,' he said, quietly and sternly. 'We are going to Mordor, of course. And you know the way there, I believe.'

'Ach! sss!' said Gollum, covering his ears with his hands, as if such frankness, and the open speaking of the names, hurt him. 'We guessed, yes we guessed,' he whispered; 'and we didn't want them to go, did we? No, precious, not the nice hobbits. Ashes, ashes, and dust, and thirst there is; and pits, pits, pits, and Orcs, thousands of Orcses. Nice hobbits mustn't go to – sss – those places.'

'So you have been there?' Frodo insisted. 'And you're being drawn back there, aren't you?'

'Yess. Yess. No!' shrieked Gollum. 'Once, by accident it was, wasn't it, precious? Yes, by accident. But we won't go back, no, no!' Then suddenly his voice and language changed, and he sobbed in his throat, and spoke but not to them. 'Leave me alone, *gollum*! You hurt me. O my poor hands, *gollum*! I, we, I don't want to come back. I can't find it. I am tired. I, we can't find it, *gollum, gollum*, no, nowhere. They're always awake. Dwarves, Men, and Elves, terrible Elves with bright eyes. I can't find it. Ach!' He got up and clenched his long hand into a bony fleshless knot, shaking it towards the East. 'We won't!' he cried. 'Not for you.' Then he collapsed again. '*Gollum, gollum*,' he whimpered with his face to the ground. 'Don't look at us! Go away! Go to sleep!'

'He will not go away or go to sleep at your command, Sméagol,' said Frodo. 'But if you really wish to be free of him again, then you must help me. And that I fear means finding us a path towards him. But you need not go all the way, not beyond the gates of his land.'

Gollum sat up again and looked at him under his eyelids. 'He's over there,' he cackled. 'Always there. Orcs will take you all the way. Easy to find Orcs east of the River. Don't ask Sméagol. Poor, poor Sméagol, he went away long ago. They took his Precious, and he's lost now.'

'Perhaps we'll find him again, if you come with us,' said Frodo.

'No, no, never! He's lost his Precious,' said Gollum.

'Get up!' said Frodo.

Gollum stood up and backed away against the cliff.

'Now!' said Frodo. 'Can you find a path easier by day or by night? We're tired; but if you choose the night, we'll start tonight.'

'The big lights hurt our eyes, they do,' Gollum whined. 'Not under the White Face, not yet. It will go behind the hills soon, yess. Rest a bit first, nice hobbits!'

'Then sit down,' said Frodo, 'and don't move!'

The hobbits seated themselves beside him, one on either side, with their backs to the stony wall, resting their legs. There was no need for any arrangement by word: they knew that they must not sleep for a moment. Slowly the moon went by. Shadows fell down from the hills, and all grew dark before them. The stars grew thick and bright in the sky above. No one stirred. Gollum sat with his legs drawn up, knees under chin, flat hands and feet splayed on the ground, his eyes closed; but he seemed tense, as if thinking or listening.

Frodo looked across at Sam. Their eyes met and they understood. They relaxed, leaning their heads back, and shutting their eyes or seeming to. Soon the sound of their soft breathing could be heard. Gollum's hands twitched a little. Hardly perceptibly his head moved to the left and the

right, and first one eye and then the other opened a slit. The hobbits made
no sign.

Suddenly, with startling agility and speed, straight off the ground with
a jump like a grasshopper or a frog, Gollum bounded forward into the
darkness. But that was just what Frodo and Sam had expected. Sam was
on him before he had gone two paces after his spring. Frodo coming behind
grabbed his leg and threw him.

'Your rope might prove useful again, Sam,' he said.

Sam got out the rope. 'And where were you off to in the cold hard lands,
Mr. Gollum?' he growled. 'We wonders, aye, we wonders. To find some
of your orc-friends, I warrant. You nasty treacherous creature. It's round
your neck this rope ought to go, and a tight noose too.'

Gollum lay quiet and tried no further tricks. He did not answer Sam,
but gave him a swift venomous look.

'All we need is something to keep a hold on him,' said Frodo. 'We want
him to walk, so it's no good tying his legs – or his arms, he seems to use
them nearly as much. Tie one end to his ankle, and keep a grip on the
other end.'

He stood over Gollum, while Sam tied the knot. The result surprised
them both. Gollum began to scream, a thin, tearing sound, very horrible
to hear. He writhed, and tried to get his mouth to his ankle and bite the
rope. He kept on screaming.

At last Frodo was convinced that he really was in pain; but it could not
be from the knot. He examined it and found that it was not too tight,
indeed hardly tight enough. Sam was gentler than his words. 'What's the
matter with you?' he said. 'If you will try to run away, you must be tied;
but we don't wish to hurt you.'

'It hurts us, it hurts us,' hissed Gollum. 'It freezes, it bites! Elves twisted
it, curse them! Nasty cruel hobbits! That's why we tries to escape, of course
it is, precious. We guessed they were cruel hobbits. They visits Elves,
fierce Elves with bright eyes. Take it off us! It hurts us.'

'No, I will not take it off you,' said Frodo, 'not unless' – he paused a
moment in thought – 'not unless there is any promise you can make that
I can trust.'

'We will swear to do what he wants, yes, yess,' said Gollum, still twisting
and grabbling at his ankle. 'It hurts us.'

'Swear?' said Frodo.

'Sméagol,' said Gollum suddenly and clearly, opening his eyes wide and
staring at Frodo with a strange light. 'Sméagol will swear on the Precious.'

Frodo drew himself up, and again Sam was startled by his words and
his stern voice. 'On the Precious? How dare you?' he said. 'Think!

One Ring to rule them all and in the Darkness bind them.

Would you commit your promise to that, Sméagol? It will hold you. But it is more treacherous than you are. It may twist your words. Beware!'

Gollum cowered. 'On the Precious, on the Precious!' he repeated.

'And what would you swear?' asked Frodo.

'To be very very good,' said Gollum. Then crawling to Frodo's feet he grovelled before him, whispering hoarsely: a shudder ran over him, as if the words shook his very bones with fear. 'Sméagol will swear never, never, to let Him have it. Never! Sméagol will save it. But he must swear on the Precious.'

'No! not on it,' said Frodo, looking down at him with stern pity. 'All you wish is to see it and touch it, if you can, though you know it would drive you mad. Not on it. Swear by it, if you will. For you know where it is. Yes, you know, Sméagol. It is before you.'

For a moment it appeared to Sam that his master had grown and Gollum had shrunk: a tall stern shadow, a mighty lord who hid his brightness in grey cloud, and at his feet a little whining dog. Yet the two were in some way akin and not alien: they could reach one another's minds. Gollum raised himself and began pawing at Frodo, fawning at his knees.

'Down! down!' said Frodo. 'Now speak your promise!'

'We promises, yes I promise!' said Gollum. 'I will serve the master of the Precious. Good master, good Sméagol, *gollum, gollum*!' Suddenly he began to weep and bite at his ankle again.

'Take the rope off, Sam!' said Frodo.

Reluctantly Sam obeyed. At once Gollum got up and began prancing about, like a whipped cur whose master has patted it. From that moment a change, which lasted for some time, came over him. He spoke with less hissing and whining, and he spoke to his companions direct, not to his precious self. He would cringe and flinch, if they stepped near him or made any sudden movement, and he avoided the touch of their elven-cloaks; but he was friendly, and indeed pitifully anxious to please. He would cackle with laughter and caper, if any jest was made, or even if Frodo spoke kindly to him, and weep if Frodo rebuked him. Sam said little to him of any sort. He suspected him more deeply than ever, and if possible liked the new Gollum, the Sméagol, less than the old.

'Well, Gollum, or whatever it is we're to call you,' he said, 'now for it! The Moon's gone, and the night's going. We'd better start.'

'Yes, yes,' agreed Gollum, skipping about. 'Off we go! There's only one way across between the North-end and the South-end. I found it, I did. Orcs don't use it, Orcs don't know it. Orcs don't cross the Marshes, they

go round for miles and miles. Very lucky you came this way. Very lucky
you found Sméagol, yes. Follow Sméagol!'

He took a few steps away and looked back inquiringly, like a dog inviting
them for a walk. 'Wait a bit, Gollum!' cried Sam. 'Not too far ahead now!
I'm going to be at your tail, and I've got the rope handy.'

'No, no!' said Gollum. 'Sméagol promised.'

In the deep of night under hard clear stars they set off. Gollum led them
back northward for a while along the way they had come; then he slanted
to the right away from the steep edge of the Emyn Muil, down the broken
stony slopes towards the vast fens below. They faded swiftly and softly into
the darkness. Over all the leagues of waste before the gates of Mordor there
was a black silence.

CHAPTER II

THE PASSAGE OF THE MARSHES

Gollum moved quickly, with his head and neck thrust forward, often using his hands as well as his feet. Frodo and Sam were hard put to it to keep up with him; but he seemed no longer to have any thought of escaping, and if they fell behind, he would turn and wait for them. After a time he brought them to the brink of the narrow gully that they had struck before; but they were now further from the hills.

'Here it is!' he cried. 'There is a way down inside, yes. Now we follows it – out, out away over there.' He pointed south and east towards the marshes. The reek of them came to their nostrils, heavy and foul even in the cool night air.

Gollum cast up and down along the brink, and at length he called to them. 'Here! We can get down here. Sméagol went this way once: I went this way, hiding from Orcs.'

He led the way, and following him the hobbits climbed down into the gloom. It was not difficult, for the rift was at this point only some fifteen feet deep and about a dozen across. There was running water at the bottom: it was in fact the bed of one of the many small rivers that trickled down from the hills to feed the stagnant pools and mires beyond. Gollum turned to the right, southward more or less, and splashed along with his feet in the shallow stony stream. He seemed greatly delighted to feel the water, and chuckled to himself, sometimes even croaking in a sort of song.

> *The cold hard lands*
> *they bites our hands,*
> *they gnaws our feet.*
> *The rocks and stones*
> *are like old bones*
> *all bare of meat.*
> *But stream and pool*
> *is wet and cool:*
> *so nice for feet!*
> *And now we wish——*

'Ha! ha! What does we wish?' he said, looking sidelong at the hobbits. 'We'll tell you,' he croaked. 'He guessed it long ago, Baggins guessed it.'

A glint came into his eyes, and Sam catching the gleam in the darkness thought it far from pleasant.

> *Alive without breath;*
> *as cold as death;*
> *never thirsting, ever drinking;*
> *clad in mail, never clinking.*
> *Drowns on dry land,*
> *thinks an island*
> *is a mountain;*
> *thinks a fountain*
> *is a puff of air.*
> *So sleek, so fair!*
>   *What a joy to meet!*
> *We only wish*
> *to catch a fish,*
>   *so juicy-sweet!*

These words only made more pressing to Sam's mind a problem that had been troubling him from the moment when he understood that his master was going to adopt Gollum as a guide: the problem of food. It did not occur to him that his master might also have thought of it, but he supposed Gollum had. Indeed how had Gollum kept himself in all his lonely wandering? 'Not too well,' thought Sam. 'He looks fair famished. Not too dainty to try what hobbit tastes like, if there ain't no fish, I'll wager – supposing as he could catch us napping. Well, he won't: not Sam Gamgee for one.'

They stumbled along in the dark winding gully for a long time, or so it seemed to the tired feet of Frodo and Sam. The gully turned eastward, and as they went on it broadened and got gradually shallower. At last the sky above grew faint with the first grey of morning. Gollum had shown no signs of tiring, but now he looked up and halted.

'Day is near,' he whispered, as if Day was something that might overhear him and spring on him. 'Sméagol will stay here: I will stay here, and the Yellow Face won't see me.'

'We should be glad to see the Sun,' said Frodo, 'but we will stay here: we are too tired to go any further at present.'

'You are not wise to be glad of the Yellow Face,' said Gollum. 'It shows you up. Nice sensible hobbits stay with Sméagol. Orcs and nasty things are about. They can see a long way. Stay and hide with me!'

The three of them settled down to rest at the foot of the rocky wall of the gully. It was not much more than a tall man's height now, and at its base there were wide flat shelves of dry stone; the water ran in a channel on the other side. Frodo and Sam sat on one of the flats, resting their backs. Gollum paddled and scrabbled in the stream.

'We must take a little food,' said Frodo. 'Are you hungry, Sméagol? We have very little to share, but we will spare you what we can.'

At the word *hungry* a greenish light was kindled in Gollum's pale eyes, and they seemed to protrude further than ever from his thin sickly face. For a moment he relapsed into his old Gollum-manner. 'We are famisshed, yes famisshed we are, precious,' he said. 'What is it they eats? Have they nice fisshes?' His tongue lolled out between his sharp yellow teeth, licking his colourless lips.

'No, we have got no fish,' said Frodo. 'We have only got this' – he held up a wafer of *lembas* – 'and water, if the water here is fit to drink.'

'Yess, yess, nice water,' said Gollum. 'Drink it, drink it, while we can! But what is it they've got, precious? Is it crunchable? Is it tasty?'

Frodo broke off a portion of a wafer and handed it to him on its leaf-wrapping. Gollum sniffed at the leaf and his face changed: a spasm of disgust came over it, and a hint of his old malice. 'Sméagol smells it!' he said. 'Leaves out of the elf-country, gah! They stinks. He climbed in those trees, and he couldn't wash the smell off his hands, my nice hands.' Dropping the leaf, he took a corner of the *lembas* and nibbled it. He spat, and a fit of coughing shook him.

'Ach! No!' he spluttered. 'You try to choke poor Sméagol. Dust and ashes, he can't eat that. He must starve. But Sméagol doesn't mind. Nice hobbits! Sméagol has promised. He will starve. He can't eat hobbits' food. He will starve. Poor thin Sméagol!'

'I'm sorry,' said Frodo; 'but I can't help you, I'm afraid. I think this food would do you good, if you would try. But perhaps you can't even try, not yet anyway.'

The hobbits munched their *lembas* in silence. Sam thought that it tasted far better, somehow, than it had for a good while: Gollum's behaviour had made him attend to its flavour again. But he did not feel comfortable. Gollum watched every morsel from hand to mouth, like an expectant dog by a diner's chair. Only when they had finished and were preparing to rest, was he apparently convinced that they had no hidden dainties that he could share in. Then he went and sat by himself a few paces away and whimpered a little.

'Look here!' Sam whispered to Frodo, not too softly: he did not really care whether Gollum heard him or not. 'We've got to get some sleep; but not both together with that hungry villain nigh, promise or no promise.

Sméagol or Gollum, he won't change his habits in a hurry, I'll warrant. You go to sleep, Mr. Frodo, and I'll call you when I can't keep my eyelids propped up. Turn and about, same as before, while he's loose.'

'Perhaps you're right, Sam,' said Frodo speaking openly. 'There *is* a change in him, but just what kind of a change and how deep, I'm not sure yet. Seriously though, I don't think there is any need for fear – at present. Still watch if you wish. Give me about two hours, not more, and then call me.'

So tired was Frodo that his head fell forward on his breast and he slept, almost as soon as he had spoken the words. Gollum seemed no longer to have any fears. He curled up and went quickly to sleep, quite unconcerned. Presently his breath was hissing softly through his clenched teeth, but he lay still as stone. After a while, fearing that he would drop off himself, if he sat listening to his two companions breathing, Sam got up and gently prodded Gollum. His hands uncurled and twitched, but he made no other movement. Sam bent down and said *fissh* close to his ear, but there was no response, not even a catch in Gollum's breathing.

Sam scratched his head. 'Must really be asleep,' he muttered. 'And if I was like Gollum, he wouldn't wake up never again.' He restrained the thoughts of his sword and the rope that sprang to his mind, and went and sat down by his master.

When he woke up the sky above was dim, not lighter but darker than when they had breakfasted. Sam leapt to his feet. Not least from his own feeling of vigour and hunger, he suddenly understood that he had slept the daylight away, nine hours at least. Frodo was still fast asleep, lying now stretched on his side. Gollum was not to be seen. Various reproachful names for himself came to Sam's mind, drawn from the Gaffer's large paternal word-hoard; then it also occurred to him that his master had been right: there had for the present been nothing to guard against. They were at any rate both alive and unthrottled.

'Poor wretch!' he said half remorsefully. 'Now I wonder where he's got to?'

'Not far, not far!' said a voice above him. He looked up and saw the shape of Gollum's large head and ears against the evening sky.

'Here, what are you doing?' cried Sam, his suspicions coming back as soon as he saw that shape.

'Sméagol is hungry,' said Gollum. 'Be back soon.'

'Come back now!' shouted Sam. 'Hi! Come back!' But Gollum had vanished.

Frodo woke at the sound of Sam's shout and sat up, rubbing his eyes. 'Hullo!' he said. 'Anything wrong? What's the time?'

'I dunno,' said Sam. 'After sundown, I reckon. And he's gone off. Says he's hungry.'

'Don't worry!' said Frodo. 'There's no help for it. But he'll come back, you'll see. The promise will hold yet a while. And he won't leave his Precious, anyway.'

Frodo made light of it when he learned that they had slept soundly for hours with Gollum, and a very hungry Gollum too, loose beside them. 'Don't think of any of your Gaffer's hard names,' he said. 'You were worn out, and it has turned out well: we are now both rested. And we have a hard road ahead, the worst road of all.'

'About the food,' said Sam. 'How long's it going to take us to do this job? And when it's done, what are we going to do then? This waybread keeps you on your legs in a wonderful way, though it doesn't satisfy the innards proper, as you might say: not to my feeling anyhow, meaning no disrespect to them as made it. But you have to eat some of it every day, and it doesn't grow. I reckon we've got enough to last, say, three weeks or so, and that with a tight belt and a light tooth, mind you. We've been a bit free with it so far.'

'I don't know how long we shall take to – to finish,' said Frodo. 'We were miserably delayed in the hills. But Samwise Gamgee, my dear hobbit – indeed, Sam my dearest hobbit, friend of friends – I do not think we need give thought to what comes after that. To *do the job* as you put it – what hope is there that we ever shall? And if we do, who knows what will come of that? If the One goes into the Fire, and we are at hand? I ask you, Sam, are we ever likely to need bread again? I think not. If we can nurse our limbs to bring us to Mount Doom, that is all we can do. More than I can, I begin to feel.'

Sam nodded silently. He took his master's hand and bent over it. He did not kiss it, though his tears fell on it. Then he turned away, drew his sleeve over his nose, and got up, and stamped about, trying to whistle, and saying between the efforts: 'Where's that dratted creature?'

It was actually not long before Gollum returned; but he came so quietly that they did not hear him till he stood before them. His fingers and face were soiled with black mud. He was still chewing and slavering. What he was chewing, they did not ask or like to think.

'Worms or beetles or something slimy out of holes,' thought Sam. 'Brr! The nasty creature; the poor wretch!'

Gollum said nothing to them, until he had drunk deeply and washed himself in the stream. Then he came up to them, licking his lips. 'Better now,' he said. 'Are we rested? Ready to go on? Nice hobbits, they sleep beautifully. Trust Sméagol now? Very, very good.'

The next stage of their journey was much the same as the last. As they went on the gully became ever shallower and the slope of its floor more gradual. Its bottom was less stony and more earthy, and slowly its sides dwindled to mere banks. It began to wind and wander. That night drew to its end, but clouds were now over moon and star, and they knew of the coming of day only by the slow spreading of the thin grey light.

In a chill hour they came to the end of the water-course. The banks became moss-grown mounds. Over the last shelf of rotting stone the stream gurgled and fell down into a brown bog and was lost. Dry reeds hissed and rattled though they could feel no wind.

On either side and in front wide fens and mires now lay, stretching away southward and eastward into the dim half-light. Mists curled and smoked from dark and noisome pools. The reek of them hung stifling in the still air. Far away, now almost due south, the mountain-walls of Mordor loomed, like a black bar of rugged clouds floating above a dangerous fog-bound sea.

The hobbits were now wholly in the hands of Gollum. They did not know, and could not guess in that misty light, that they were in fact only just within the northern borders of the marshes, the main expanse of which lay south of them. They could, if they had known the lands, with some delay have retraced their steps a little, and then turning east have come round over hard roads to the bare plain of Dagorlad: the field of the ancient battle before the gates of Mordor. Not that there was great hope in such a course. On that stony plain there was no cover, and across it ran the highways of the Orcs and the soldiers of the Enemy. Not even the cloaks of Lórien would have concealed them there.

'How do we shape our course now, Sméagol?' asked Frodo. 'Must we cross these evil-smelling fens?'

'No need, no need at all,' said Gollum. 'Not if hobbits want to reach the dark mountains and go to see Him very quick. Back a little, and round a little' – his skinny arm waved north and east – 'and you can come on hard cold roads to the very gates of His country. Lots of His people will be there looking out for guests, very pleased to take them straight to Him, O yes. His Eye watches that way all the time. It caught Sméagol there, long ago.' Gollum shuddered. 'But Sméagol has used his eyes since then, yes, yes: I've used eyes and feet and nose since then. I know other ways. More difficult, not so quick; but better, if we don't want Him to see. Follow Sméagol! He can take you through the marshes, through the mists, nice thick mists. Follow Sméagol very carefully, and you may go a long way, quite a long way, before He catches you, yes perhaps.'

It was already day, a windless and sullen morning, and the marsh-reeks lay in heavy banks. No sun pierced the low clouded sky, and Gollum seemed anxious to continue the journey at once. So after a brief rest they set out again and were soon lost in a shadowy silent world, cut off from all view of the lands about, either the hills that they had left or the mountains that they sought. They went slowly in single file: Gollum, Sam, Frodo.

Frodo seemed the most weary of the three, and slow though they went, he often lagged. The hobbits soon found that what had looked like one vast fen was really an endless network of pools, and soft mires, and winding half-strangled water-courses. Among these a cunning eye and foot could thread a wandering path. Gollum certainly had that cunning, and needed all of it. His head on its long neck was ever turning this way and that, while he sniffed and muttered all the time to himself. Sometimes he would hold up his hand and halt them, while he went forward a little, crouching, testing the ground with fingers or toes, or merely listening with one ear pressed to the earth.

It was dreary and wearisome. Cold clammy winter still held sway in this forsaken country. The only green was the scum of livid weed on the dark greasy surfaces of the sullen waters. Dead grasses and rotting reeds loomed up in the mists like ragged shadows of long-forgotten summers.

As the day wore on the light increased a little, and the mists lifted, growing thinner and more transparent. Far above the rot and vapours of the world the Sun was riding high and golden now in a serene country with floors of dazzling foam, but only a passing ghost of her could they see below, bleared, pale, giving no colour and no warmth. But even at this faint reminder of her presence Gollum scowled and flinched. He halted their journey, and they rested, squatting like little hunted animals, in the borders of a great brown reed-thicket. There was a deep silence, only scraped on its surfaces by the faint quiver of empty seed-plumes, and broken grass-blades trembling in small air-movements that they could not feel.

'Not a bird!' said Sam mournfully.

'No, no birds,' said Gollum. 'Nice birds!' He licked his teeth. 'No birds here. There are snakeses, wormses, things in the pools. Lots of things, lots of nasty things. No birds,' he ended sadly. Sam looked at him with distaste.

So passed the third day of their journey with Gollum. Before the shadows of evening were long in happier lands, they went on again, always on and on with only brief halts. These they made not so much for rest as to help Gollum; for now even he had to go forward with great care, and he was sometimes at a loss for a while. They had come to the very midst of the Dead Marshes, and it was dark.

They walked slowly, stooping, keeping close in line, following attentively every move that Gollum made. The fens grew more wet, opening into wide stagnant meres, among which it grew more and more difficult to find the firmer places where feet could tread without sinking into gurgling mud. The travellers were light, or maybe none of them would ever have found a way through.

Presently it grew altogether dark: the air itself seemed black and heavy to breathe. When lights appeared Sam rubbed his eyes: he thought his head was going queer. He first saw one with the corner of his left eye, a wisp of pale sheen that faded away; but others appeared soon after: some like dimly shining smoke, some like misty flames flickering slowly above unseen candles; here and there they twisted like ghostly sheets unfurled by hidden hands. But neither of his companions spoke a word.

At last Sam could bear it no longer. 'What's all this, Gollum?' he said in a whisper. 'These lights? They're all round us now. Are we trapped? Who are they?'

Gollum looked up. A dark water was before him, and he was crawling on the ground, this way and that, doubtful of the way. 'Yes, they are all round us,' he whispered. 'The tricksy lights. Candles of corpses, yes, yes. Don't you heed them! Don't look! Don't follow them! Where's the master?'

Sam looked back and found that Frodo had lagged again. He could not see him. He went some paces back into the darkness, not daring to move far, or to call in more than a hoarse whisper. Suddenly he stumbled against Frodo, who was standing lost in thought, looking at the pale lights. His hands hung stiff at his sides; water and slime were dripping from them.

'Come, Mr. Frodo!' said Sam. 'Don't look at them! Gollum says we mustn't. Let's keep up with him and get out of this cursed place as quick as we can – if we can!'

'All right,' said Frodo, as if returning out of a dream. 'I'm coming. Go on!'

Hurrying forward again, Sam tripped, catching his foot in some old root or tussock. He fell and came heavily on his hands, which sank deep into sticky ooze, so that his face was brought close to the surface of the dark mere. There was a faint hiss, a noisome smell went up, the lights flickered and danced and swirled. For a moment the water below him looked like some window, glazed with grimy glass, through which he was peering. Wrenching his hands out of the bog, he sprang back with a cry. 'There are dead things, dead faces in the water,' he said with horror. 'Dead faces!'

Gollum laughed. 'The Dead Marshes, yes, yes: that is their name,' he cackled. 'You should not look in when the candles are lit.'

'Who are they? What are they?' asked Sam shuddering, turning to Frodo, who was now behind him.

'I don't know,' said Frodo in a dreamlike voice. 'But I have seen them too. In the pools when the candles were lit. They lie in all the pools, pale faces, deep deep under the dark water. I saw them: grim faces and evil, and noble faces and sad. Many faces proud and fair, and weeds in their silver hair. But all foul, all rotting, all dead. A fell light is in them.' Frodo hid his eyes in his hands. 'I know not who they are; but I thought I saw there Men and Elves, and Orcs beside them.'

'Yes, yes,' said Gollum. 'All dead, all rotten. Elves and Men and Orcs. The Dead Marshes. There was a great battle long ago, yes, so they told him when Sméagol was young, when I was young before the Precious came. It was a great battle. Tall Men with long swords, and terrible Elves, and Orcses shrieking. They fought on the plain for days and months at the Black Gates. But the Marshes have grown since then, swallowed up the graves; always creeping, creeping.'

'But that is an age and more ago,' said Sam. 'The Dead can't be really there! Is it some devilry hatched in the Dark Land?'

'Who knows? Sméagol doesn't know,' answered Gollum. 'You cannot reach them, you cannot touch them. We tried once, yes, precious. I tried once; but you cannot reach them. Only shapes to see, perhaps, not to touch. No precious! All dead.'

Sam looked darkly at him and shuddered again, thinking that he guessed why Sméagol had tried to touch them. 'Well, I don't want to see them,' he said. 'Never again! Can't we get on and get away?'

'Yes, yes,' said Gollum. 'But slowly, very slowly. Very carefully! Or hobbits go down to join the Dead ones and light little candles. Follow Sméagol! Don't look at lights!'

He crawled away to the right, seeking for a path round the mere. They came close behind, stooping, often using their hands even as he did. 'Three precious little Gollums in a row we shall be, if this goes on much longer,' thought Sam.

At last they came to the end of the black mere, and they crossed it, perilously, crawling or hopping from one treacherous island tussock to another. Often they floundered, stepping or falling hands-first into waters as noisome as a cesspool, till they were slimed and fouled almost up to their necks and stank in one another's nostrils.

It was late in the night when at length they reached firmer ground again. Gollum hissed and whispered to himself, but it appeared that he was pleased: in some mysterious way, by some blended sense of feel, and smell, and uncanny memory for shapes in the dark, he seemed to know just where he was again, and to be sure of his road ahead.

'Now on we go!' he said. 'Nice hobbits! Brave hobbits! Very very weary, of course; so we are, my precious, all of us. But we must take master away from the wicked lights, yes, yes, we must.' With these words he started off again, almost at a trot, down what appeared to be a long lane between high reeds, and they stumbled after him as quickly as they could. But in a little while he stopped suddenly and sniffed the air doubtfully, hissing as if he was troubled or displeased again.

'What is it?' growled Sam, misinterpreting the signs. 'What's the need to sniff? The stink nearly knocks me down with my nose held. You stink, and master stinks; the whole place stinks.'

'Yes, yes, and Sam stinks!' answered Gollum. 'Poor Sméagol smells it, but good Sméagol bears it. Helps nice master. But that's no matter. The air's moving, change is coming. Sméagol wonders; he's not happy.'

He went on again, but his uneasiness grew, and every now and again he stood up to his full height, craning his neck eastward and southward. For some time the hobbits could not hear or feel what was troubling him. Then suddenly all three halted, stiffening and listening. To Frodo and Sam it seemed that they heard, far away, a long wailing cry, high and thin and cruel. They shivered. At the same moment the stirring of the air became perceptible to them; and it grew very cold. As they stood straining their ears, they heard a noise like a wind coming in the distance. The misty lights wavered, dimmed, and went out.

Gollum would not move. He stood shaking and gibbering to himself, until with a rush the wind came upon them, hissing and snarling over the marshes. The night became less dark, light enough for them to see, or half see, shapeless drifts of fog, curling and twisting as it rolled over them and passed them. Looking up they saw the clouds breaking and shredding; and then high in the south the moon glimmered out, riding in the flying wrack.

For a moment the sight of it gladdened the hearts of the hobbits; but Gollum cowered down, muttering curses on the White Face. Then Frodo and Sam staring at the sky, breathing deeply of the fresher air, saw it come: a small cloud flying from the accursed hills; a black shadow loosed from Mordor; a vast shape winged and ominous. It scudded across the moon, and with a deadly cry went away westward, outrunning the wind in its fell speed.

They fell forward, grovelling heedlessly on the cold earth. But the shadow of horror wheeled and returned, passing lower now, right above them, sweeping the fen-reek with its ghastly wings. And then it was gone, flying back to Mordor with the speed of the wrath of Sauron; and behind it the wind roared away, leaving the Dead Marshes bare and bleak. The naked waste, as far as the eye could pierce, even to the distant menace of the mountains, was dappled with the fitful moonlight.

Frodo and Sam got up, rubbing their eyes, like children wakened from an evil dream to find the familiar night still over the world. But Gollum lay on the ground as if he had been stunned. They roused him with difficulty, and for some time he would not lift his face, but knelt forward on his elbows, covering the back of his head with his large flat hands.

'Wraiths!' he wailed. 'Wraiths on wings! The Precious is their master. They see everything, everything. Nothing can hide from them. Curse the White Face! And they tell Him everything. He sees, He knows. Ach, gollum, gollum, gollum!' It was not until the moon had sunk, westering far away beyond Tol Brandir, that he would get up or make a move.

From that time on Sam thought that he sensed a change in Gollum again. He was more fawning and would-be friendly; but Sam surprised some strange looks in his eyes at times, especially towards Frodo; and he went back more and more into his old manner of speaking. And Sam had another growing anxiety. Frodo seemed to be weary, weary to the point of exhaustion. He said nothing, indeed he hardly spoke at all; and he did not complain, but he walked like one who carries a load, the weight of which is ever increasing; and he dragged along, slower and slower, so that Sam had often to beg Gollum to wait and not to leave their master behind.

In fact with every step towards the gates of Mordor Frodo felt the Ring on its chain about his neck grow more burdensome. He was now beginning to feel it as an actual weight dragging him earthwards. But far more he was troubled by the Eye: so he called it to himself. It was that more than the drag of the Ring that made him cower and stoop as he walked. The Eye: that horrible growing sense of a hostile will that strove with great power to pierce all shadows of cloud, and earth, and flesh, and to see you: to pin you under its deadly gaze, naked, immovable. So thin, so frail and thin, the veils were become that still warded it off. Frodo knew just where the present habitation and heart of that will now was: as certainly as a man can tell the direction of the sun with his eyes shut. He was facing it, and its potency beat upon his brow.

Gollum probably felt something of the same sort. But what went on in his wretched heart between the pressure of the Eye, and the lust of the Ring that was so near, and his grovelling promise made half in the fear of cold iron, the hobbits did not guess. Frodo gave no thought to it. Sam's mind was occupied mostly with his master, hardly noticing the dark cloud that had fallen on his own heart. He put Frodo in front of him now, and kept a watchful eye on every movement of his, supporting him if he stumbled, and trying to encourage him with clumsy words.

When day came at last the hobbits were surprised to see how much closer the ominous mountains had already drawn. The air was now clearer and colder, and though still far off, the walls of Mordor were no longer a cloudy menace on the edge of sight, but as grim black towers they frowned across a dismal waste. The marshes were at an end, dying away into dead peats and wide flats of dry cracked mud. The land ahead rose in long shallow slopes, barren and pitiless, towards the desert that lay at Sauron's gate.

While the grey light lasted, they cowered under a black stone like worms, shrinking, lest the winged terror should pass and spy them with its cruel eyes. The remainder of that journey was a shadow of growing fear in which memory could find nothing to rest upon. For two more nights they struggled on through the weary pathless land. The air, as it seemed to them, grew harsh, and filled with a bitter reek that caught their breath and parched their mouths.

At last, on the fifth morning since they took the road with Gollum, they halted once more. Before them dark in the dawn the great mountains reached up to roofs of smoke and cloud. Out from their feet were flung huge buttresses and broken hills that were now at the nearest scarce a dozen miles away. Frodo looked round in horror. Dreadful as the Dead Marshes had been, and the arid moors of the Noman-lands, more loathsome far was the country that the crawling day now slowly unveiled to his shrinking eyes. Even to the Mere of Dead Faces some haggard phantom of green spring would come; but here neither spring nor summer would ever come again. Here nothing lived, not even the leprous growths that feed on rottenness. The gasping pools were choked with ash and crawling muds, sickly white and grey, as if the mountains had vomited the filth of their entrails upon the lands about. High mounds of crushed and powdered rock, great cones of earth fire-blasted and poison-stained, stood like an obscene graveyard in endless rows, slowly revealed in the reluctant light.

They had come to the desolation that lay before Mordor: the lasting monument to the dark labour of its slaves that should endure when all their purposes were made void; a land defiled, diseased beyond all healing – unless the Great Sea should enter in and wash it with oblivion. 'I feel sick,' said Sam. Frodo did not speak.

For a while they stood there, like men on the edge of a sleep where nightmare lurks, holding it off, though they know that they can only come to morning through the shadows. The light broadened and hardened. The gasping pits and poisonous mounds grew hideously clear. The sun was up, walking among clouds and long flags of smoke, but even the sunlight was defiled. The hobbits had no welcome for that light; unfriendly it seemed, revealing them in their helplessness – little squeaking ghosts that wandered among the ash-heaps of the Dark Lord.

Too weary to go further they sought for some place where they could rest. For a while they sat without speaking under the shadow of a mound of slag; but foul fumes leaked out of it, catching their throats and choking them. Gollum was the first to get up. Spluttering and cursing he rose, and without a word or a glance at the hobbits he crawled away on all fours. Frodo and Sam crawled after him until they came to a wide almost circular pit, high-banked upon the west. It was cold and dead, and a foul sump of oily many-coloured ooze lay at its bottom. In this evil hole they cowered, hoping in its shadow to escape the attention of the Eye.

The day passed slowly. A great thirst troubled them, but they drank only a few drops from their bottles – last filled in the gully, which now as they looked back in thought seemed to them a place of peace and beauty. The hobbits took it in turn to watch. At first, tired as they were, neither of them could sleep at all; but as the sun far away was climbing down into slow moving cloud, Sam dozed. It was Frodo's turn to be on guard. He lay back on the slope of the pit, but that did not ease the sense of burden that was on him. He looked up at the smoke-streaked sky and saw strange phantoms, dark riding shapes, and faces out of the past. He lost count of time, hovering between sleep and waking, until forgetfulness came over him.

Suddenly Sam woke up thinking that he heard his master calling. It was evening. Frodo could not have called, for he had fallen asleep, and had slid down nearly to the bottom of the pit. Gollum was by him. For a moment Sam thought that he was trying to rouse Frodo; then he saw that it was not so. Gollum was talking to himself. Sméagol was holding a debate with some other thought that used the same voice but made it squeak and hiss. A pale light and a green light alternated in his eyes as he spoke.

'Sméagol promised,' said the first thought.

'Yes, yes, my precious,' came the answer, 'we promised: to save our Precious, not to let Him have it – never. But it's going to Him, yes, nearer every step. What's the hobbit going to do with it, we wonders, yes we wonders.'

'I don't know. I can't help it. Master's got it. Sméagol promised to help the master.'

'Yes, yes, to help the master: the master of the Precious. But if we was master, then we could help ourselfs, yes, and still keep promises.'

'But Sméagol said he would be very very good. Nice hobbit! He took cruel rope off Sméagol's leg. He speaks nicely to me.'

'Very very good, eh, my precious? Let's be good, good as fish, sweet one, but to ourselfs. Not hurt the nice hobbit, of course, no, no.'

'But the Precious holds the promise,' the voice of Sméagol objected.

'Then take it,' said the other, 'and let's hold it ourselfs! Then we shall be master, *gollum*! Make the other hobbit, the nasty suspicious hobbit make him crawl, yes, *gollum*!'

'But not the nice hobbit?'

'Oh no, not if it doesn't please us. Still he's a Baggins, my precious, yes a Baggins. A Baggins stole it. He found it and he said nothing, nothing We hates Bagginses.'

'No, not this Baggins.'

'Yes, every Baggins. All peoples that keep the Precious. We must have it!'

'But He'll see, He'll know. He'll take it from us!'

'He sees. He knows. He heard us make silly promises – against His orders, yes. Must take it. The Wraiths are searching. Must take it.'

'Not for Him!'

'No, sweet one. See, my precious: if we has it, then we can escape, even from Him, eh? Perhaps we grows very strong, stronger than Wraiths. Lord Sméagol? Gollum the Great? *The* Gollum! Eat fish every day, three times a day, fresh from the sea. Most Precious Gollum! Must have it. We want it, we wants it, we wants it!'

'But there's two of them. They'll wake too quick and kill us,' whined Sméagol in a last effort. 'Not now. Not yet.'

'We wants it! But' – and here there was a long pause, as if a new thought had wakened. 'Not yet, eh? Perhaps not. She might help. She might, yes.

'No, no! Not that way!' wailed Sméagol.

'Yes! We wants it! We wants it!'

Each time that the second thought spoke, Gollum's long hand crept out slowly, pawing towards Frodo, and then was drawn back with a jerk as Sméagol spoke again. Finally both arms, with long fingers flexed and twitching, clawed towards his neck.

Sam had lain still, fascinated by this debate, but watching every move that Gollum made from under his half-closed eye-lids. To his simple mind ordinary hunger, the desire to eat hobbits, had seemed the chief danger in Gollum. He realized now that it was not so: Gollum was feeling the terrible call of the Ring. The Dark Lord was *He*, of course; but Sam wondered who *She* was. One of the nasty friends the little wretch had made in his wanderings, he supposed. Then he forgot the point, for things had plainly gone far enough, and were getting dangerous. A great heaviness was in all his limbs, but he roused himself with an effort and sat up. Something warned him to be careful and not to reveal that he had overheard the debate. He let out a loud sigh and gave a huge yawn.

'What's the time?' he said sleepily.

Gollum sent out a long hiss through his teeth. He stood up for a moment, tense and menacing; and then he collapsed, falling forward on to all fours and crawling up the bank of the pit. 'Nice hobbits! Nice Sam!' he said. 'Sleepy heads, yes, sleepy heads! Leave good Sméagol to watch! But it's evening. Dusk is creeping. Time to go.'

'High time!' thought Sam. 'And time we parted, too.' Yet it crossed his mind to wonder if indeed Gollum was not now as dangerous turned loose as kept with them. 'Curse him! I wish he was choked!' he muttered. He stumbled down the bank and roused his master.

Strangely enough, Frodo felt refreshed. He had been dreaming. The dark shadow had passed, and a fair vision had visited him in this land of disease. Nothing remained of it in his memory, yet because of it he felt glad and lighter of heart. His burden was less heavy on him. Gollum welcomed him with dog-like delight. He chuckled and chattered, cracking his long fingers, and pawing at Frodo's knees. Frodo smiled at him.

'Come!' he said. 'You have guided us well and faithfully. This is the last stage. Bring us to the Gate, and then I will not ask you to go further. Bring us to the Gate, and you may go where you wish – only not to our enemies.'

'To the Gate, eh?' Gollum squeaked, seeming surprised and frightened. 'To the Gate, master says! Yes, he says so. And good Sméagol does what he asks, O yes. But when we gets closer, we'll see perhaps, we'll see then. It won't look nice at all. O no! O no!'

'Go on with you!' said Sam. 'Let's get it over!'

In the falling dusk they scrambled out of the pit and slowly threaded their way through the dead land. They had not gone far before they felt once more the fear that had fallen on them when the winged shape swept over the marshes. They halted, cowering on the evil-smelling ground; but they saw nothing in the gloomy evening sky above, and soon the menace passed, high overhead, going maybe on some swift errand from Barad-dûr. After a while Gollum got up and crept forward again, muttering and shaking.

About an hour after midnight the fear fell on them a third time, but it now seemed more remote, as if it were passing far above the clouds, rushing with terrible speed into the West. Gollum, however, was helpless with terror, and was convinced that they were being hunted, that their approach was known.

'Three times!' he whimpered. 'Three times is a threat. They feel us here they feel the Precious. The Precious is their master. We cannot go an; further this way, no. It's no use, no use!'

Pleading and kind words were no longer of any avail. It was not unti Frodo commanded him angrily and laid a hand on his sword-hilt tha Gollum would get up again. Then at last he rose with a snarl, and wen before them like a beaten dog.

So they stumbled on through the weary end of the night, and until th coming of another day of fear they walked in silence with bowed heads seeing nothing, and hearing nothing but the wind hissing in their ears.

CHAPTER III

THE BLACK GATE IS CLOSED

Before the next day dawned their journey to Mordor was over. The marshes and the desert were behind them. Before them, darkling against a pallid sky, the great mountains reared their threatening heads.

Upon the west of Mordor marched the gloomy range of Ephel Dúath, the Mountains of Shadow, and upon the north the broken peaks and barren ridges of Ered Lithui, grey as ash. But as these ranges approached one another, being indeed but parts of one great wall about the mournful plains of Lithlad and of Gorgoroth, and the bitter inland sea of Núrnen amidmost, they swung out long arms northward; and between these arms there was a deep defile. This was Cirith Gorgor, the Haunted Pass, the entrance to the land of the Enemy. High cliffs lowered upon either side, and thrust forward from its mouth were two sheer hills, black-boned and bare. Upon them stood the Teeth of Mordor, two towers strong and tall. In days long past they were built by the Men of Gondor in their pride and power, after the overthrow of Sauron and his flight, lest he should seek to return to his old realm. But the strength of Gondor failed, and men slept, and for long years the towers stood empty. Then Sauron returned. Now the watch-towers, which had fallen into decay, were repaired, and filled with arms, and garrisoned with ceaseless vigilance. Stony-faced they were, with dark window-holes staring north and east and west, and each window was full of sleepless eyes.

Across the mouth of the pass, from cliff to cliff, the Dark Lord had built a rampart of stone. In it there was a single gate of iron, and upon its battlement sentinels paced unceasingly. Beneath the hills on either side the rock was bored into a hundred caves and maggot-holes; there a host of orcs lurked, ready at a signal to issue forth like black ants going to war. None could pass the Teeth of Mordor and not feel their bite, unless they were summoned by Sauron, or knew the secret passwords that would open the Morannon, the black gate of his land.

The two hobbits gazed at the towers and the wall in despair. Even from a distance they could see in the dim light the movement of the black guards upon the wall, and the patrols before the gate. They lay now peering over the edge of a rocky hollow beneath the outstretched shadow of the northmost buttress of Ephel Dúath. Winging the heavy air in a straight flight a crow, maybe, would have flown but a furlong from their hiding-place to the black summit of the nearer tower. A faint smoke curled above it, as if fire smouldered in the hill beneath.

Day came, and the fallow sun blinked over the lifeless ridges of Ered Lithui. Then suddenly the cry of brazen-throated trumpets was heard: from the watch-towers they blared, and far away from hidden holds and outposts in the hills came answering calls; and further still, remote but deep and ominous, there echoed in the hollow land beyond the mighty horns and drums of Barad-dûr. Another dreadful day of fear and toil had come to Mordor; and the night-guards were summoned to their dungeons and deep halls, and the day-guards, evil-eyed and fell, were marching to their posts. Steel gleamed dimly on the battlement.

'Well, here we are!' said Sam. 'Here's the Gate, and it looks to me as if that's about as far as we are ever going to get. My word, but the Gaffer would have a thing or two to say, if he saw me now! Often said I'd come to a bad end, if I didn't watch my step, he did. But now I don't suppose I'll ever see the old fellow again. He'll miss his chance of *I told 'ee so, Sam*: more's the pity. He could go on telling me as long as he'd got breath, if only I could see his old face again. But I'd have to get a wash first, or he wouldn't know me.

'I suppose it's no good asking "what way do we go now?" We can't go no further – unless we want to ask the Orcs for a lift.'

'No, no!' said Gollum. 'No use. We can't go further. Sméagol said so. He said: we'll go to the Gate, and then we'll see. And we do see. O yes, my precious, we do see. Sméagol knew hobbits could not go this way. O yes, Sméagol knew.'

'Then what the plague did you bring us here for?' said Sam, not feeling in the mood to be just or reasonable.

'Master said so. Master says: Bring us to the Gate. So good Sméagol does so. Master said so, wise master.'

'I did,' said Frodo. His face was grim and set, but resolute. He was filthy, haggard, and pinched with weariness, but he cowered no longer, and his eyes were clear. 'I said so, because I purpose to enter Mordor, and I know no other way. Therefore I shall go this way. I do not ask anyone to go with me.'

'No, no, master!' wailed Gollum, pawing at him, and seeming in great distress. 'No use that way! No use! Don't take the Precious to Him! He'll eat us all, if He gets it, eat all the world. Keep it, nice master, and be kind to Sméagol. Don't let Him have it. Or go away, go to nice places, and give it back to little Sméagol. Yes, yes, master give it back, eh? Sméagol will keep it safe; he will do lots of good, especially to nice hobbits. Hobbits go home. Don't go to the Gate!'

'I am commanded to go to the land of Mordor, and therefore I shall go,' said Frodo. 'If there is only one way, then I must take it. What comes after must come.'

Sam said nothing. The look on Frodo's face was enough for him; he knew that words of his were useless. And after all he never had any real hope in the affair from the beginning; but being a cheerful hobbit he had not needed hope, as long as despair could be postponed. Now they were come to the bitter end. But he had stuck to his master all the way; that was what he had chiefly come for, and he would still stick to him. His master would not go to Mordor alone. Sam would go with him – and at any rate they would get rid of Gollum.

Gollum, however, did not intend to be got rid of, yet. He knelt at Frodo's feet, wringing his hands and squeaking. 'Not this way, master!' he pleaded. 'There is another way. O yes indeed there is. Another way, darker, more difficult to find, more secret. But Sméagol knows it. Let Sméagol show you!'

'Another way!' said Frodo doubtfully, looking down at Gollum with searching eyes.

'Yess! Yess indeed! There *was* another way. Sméagol found it. Let's go and see if it's still there!'

'You have not spoken of this before.'

'No. Master did not ask. Master did not say what he meant to do. He does not tell poor Sméagol. He says: Sméagol, take me to the Gate – and then good-bye! Sméagol can run away and be good. But now he says: I purpose to enter Mordor this way. So Sméagol is very afraid. He does not want to lose nice master. And he promised, master made him promise, to save the Precious. But master is going to take it to Him, straight to the Black Hand, if master will go this way. So Sméagol must save them both, and he thinks of another way that there was, once upon a time. Nice master. Sméagol very good, always helps.'

Sam frowned. If he could have bored holes in Gollum with his eyes, he would have done. His mind was full of doubt. To all appearances Gollum was genuinely distressed and anxious to help Frodo. But Sam, remembering the overheard debate, found it hard to believe that the long submerged Sméagol had come out on top: that voice at any rate had not had the last word in the debate. Sam's guess was that the Sméagol and Gollum halves (or what in his own mind he called Slinker and Stinker) had made a truce and a temporary alliance: neither wanted the Enemy to get the Ring; both

wished to keep Frodo from capture, and under their eye, as long as possible
– at any rate as long as Stinker still had a chance of laying hands on
his 'Precious'. Whether there really was another way into Mordor Sam
doubted.

'And it's a good thing neither half of the old villain don't know what
master means to do,' he thought. 'If he knew that Mr. Frodo is trying to
put an end to his Precious for good and all, there'd be trouble pretty quick,
I bet. Anyhow old Stinker is so frightened of the Enemy – and he's under
orders of some kind from him, or was – that he'd give us away rather than
be caught helping us; and rather than let his Precious be melted, maybe.
At least that's my idea. And I hope the master will think it out carefully.
He's as wise as any, but he's soft-hearted, that's what he is. It's beyond
any Gamgee to guess what he'll do next.'

Frodo did not answer Gollum at once. While these doubts were passing
through Sam's slow but shrewd mind, he stood gazing out towards the
dark cliff of Cirith Gorgor. The hollow in which they had taken refuge was
delved in the side of a low hill, at some little height above a long trenchlike
valley that lay between it and the outer buttresses of the mountain-wall. In
the midst of the valley stood the black foundations of the western watch-
tower. By morning-light the roads that converged upon the Gate of Mordor
could now be clearly seen, pale and dusty; one winding back northwards;
another dwindling eastwards into the mists that clung about the feet of
Ered Lithui; and a third that ran towards him. As it bent sharply round
the tower, it entered a narrow defile and passed not far below the hollow
where he stood. Westward, to his right, it turned, skirting the shoulders
of the mountains, and went off southwards into the deep shadows that
mantled all the western sides of Ephel Dúath; beyond his sight it journeyed
on into the narrow land between the mountains and the Great River.

As he gazed Frodo became aware that there was a great stir and movement
on the plain. It seemed as if whole armies were on the march, though for
the most part they were hidden by the reeks and fumes drifting from the
fens and wastes beyond. But here and there he caught the gleam of spears
and helmets; and over the levels beside the roads horsemen could be seen
riding in many companies. He remembered his vision from afar upon Amon
Hen, so few days before, though now it seemed many years ago. Then he
knew that the hope that had for one wild moment stirred in his heart was
vain. The trumpets had not rung in challenge but in greeting. This was
no assault upon the Dark Lord by the men of Gondor, risen like avenging
ghosts from the graves of valour long passed away. These were Men of
other race, out of the wide Eastlands, gathering to the summons of their
Overlord; armies that had encamped before his Gate by night and now
marched in to swell his mounting power. As if suddenly made fully aware

of the peril of their position, alone, in the growing light of day, so near to
this vast menace, Frodo quickly drew his frail grey hood close upon his
head, and stepped down into the dell. Then he turned to Gollum.

'Sméagol,' he said, 'I will trust you once more. Indeed it seems that I
must do so, and that it is my fate to receive help from you, where I least
looked for it, and your fate to help me whom you long pursued with evil
purpose. So far you have deserved well of me and have kept your promise
truly. Truly, I say and mean,' he added with a glance at Sam, 'for twice
now we have been in your power, and you have done no harm to us. Nor
have you tried to take from me what you once sought. May the third time
prove the best! But I warn you, Sméagol, you are in danger.'

'Yes, yes, master!' said Gollum. 'Dreadful danger! Sméagol's bones shake
to think of it, but he doesn't run away. He must help nice master.'

'I did not mean the danger that we all share,' said Frodo. 'I mean a
danger to yourself alone. You swore a promise by what you call the Precious. Remember that! It will hold you to it; but it will seek a way to twist
it to your own undoing. Already you are being twisted. You revealed yourself to me just now, foolishly. *Give it back to Sméagol* you said. Do not say
that again! Do not let that thought grow in you! You will never get it back.
But the desire of it may betray you to a bitter end. You will never get it
back. In the last need, Sméagol, I should put on the Precious; and the
Precious mastered you long ago. If I, wearing it, were to command you,
you would obey, even if it were to leap from a precipice or to cast yourself
into the fire. And such would be my command. So have a care, Sméagol!'

Sam looked at his master with approval, but also with surprise: there
was a look in his face and a tone in his voice that he had not known before.
It had always been a notion of his that the kindness of dear Mr. Frodo was
of such a high degree that it must imply a fair measure of blindness. Of
course, he also firmly held the incompatible belief that Mr. Frodo was the
wisest person in the world (with the possible exception of Old Mr. Bilbo
and of Gandalf). Gollum in his own way, and with much more excuse as
his acquaintance was much briefer, may have made a similar mistake,
confusing kindness and blindness. At any rate this speech abashed and
terrified him. He grovelled on the ground and could speak no clear words
but *nice master*.

Frodo waited patiently for a while, then he spoke again less sternly.
'Come now, Gollum or Sméagol if you wish, tell me of this other way, and
show me, if you can, what hope there is in it, enough to justify me in
turning aside from my plain path. I am in haste.'

But Gollum was in a pitiable state, and Frodo's threat had quite unnerved
him. It was not easy to get any clear account out of him, amid his mum-
blings and squeakings, and the frequent interruptions in which he crawled

on the floor and begged them both to be kind to 'poor little Sméagol'. After a while he grew a little calmer, and Frodo gathered bit by bit that, if a traveller followed the road that turned west of Ephel Dúath, he would come in time to a crossing in a circle of dark trees. On the right a road went down to Osgiliath and the bridges of the Anduin; in the middle the road went on southwards.

'On, on, on,' said Gollum. 'We never went that way, but they say it goes a hundred leagues, until you can see the Great Water that is never still. There are lots of fishes there, and big birds eat fishes: nice birds: but we never went there, alas no! we never had a chance. And further still there are more lands, they say, but the Yellow Face is very hot there, and there are seldom any clouds, and the men are fierce and have dark faces. We do not want to see that land.'

'No!' said Frodo. 'But do not wander from your road. What of the third turning?'

'O yes, O yes, there is a third way,' said Gollum. 'That is the road to the left. At once it begins to climb up, up, winding and climbing back towards the tall shadows. When it turns round the black rock, you'll see it, suddenly you'll see it above you, and you'll want to hide.'

'See it, see it? What will you see?'

'The old fortress, very old, very horrible now. We used to hear tales from the South, when Sméagol was young, long ago. O yes, we used to tell lots of tales in the evening, sitting by the banks of the Great River, in the willow-lands, when the River was younger too, *gollum, gollum.*' He began to weep and mutter. The hobbits waited patiently.

'Tales out of the South,' Gollum went on again, 'about the tall Men with the shining eyes, and their houses like hills of stone, and the silver crown of their King and his White Tree: wonderful tales. They built very tall towers, and one they raised was silver-white, and in it there was a stone like the Moon, and round it were great white walls. O yes, there were many tales about the Tower of the Moon.'

'That would be Minas Ithil that Isildur the son of Elendil built,' said Frodo. 'It was Isildur who cut off the finger of the Enemy.'

'Yes, He has only four on the Black Hand, but they are enough,' said Gollum shuddering. 'And He hated Isildur's city.'

'What does he not hate?' said Frodo. 'But what has the Tower of the Moon to do with us?'

'Well, master, there it was and there it is: the tall tower and the white houses and the wall; but not nice now, not beautiful. He conquered it long ago. It is a very terrible place now. Travellers shiver when they see it, they creep out of sight, they avoid its shadow. But master will have to go that way. That is the only other way. For the mountains are lower there, and the old road goes up and up, until it reaches a dark pass at the top, and then it goes down, down, again – to Gorgoroth.' His voice sank to a whisper and he shuddered.

'But how will that help us?' asked Sam. 'Surely the Enemy knows all about his own mountains, and that road will be guarded as close as this? The tower isn't empty, is it?'

'O no, not empty!' whispered Gollum. 'It seems empty, but it isn't, O no! Very dreadful things live there. Orcs, yes always Orcs; but worse things, worse things live there too. The road climbs right under the shadow of the walls and passes the gate. Nothing moves on the road that they don't know about. The things inside know: the Silent Watchers.'

'So that's your advice is it,' said Sam, 'that we should go another long march south, to find ourselves in the same fix or a worse one, when we get there, if we ever do?'

'No, no indeed,' said Gollum. 'Hobbits must see, must try to understand. He does not expect attack that way. His Eye is all round, but it attends more to some places than to others. He can't see everything all at once, not yet. You see, He has conquered all the country west of the Shadowy Mountains down to the River, and He holds the bridges now. He thinks no one can come to the Moontower without fighting big battle at the bridges, or getting lots of boats which they cannot hide and He will know about.'

'You seem to know a lot about what He's doing and thinking,' said Sam. 'Have you been talking to Him lately? Or just hobnobbing with Orcs?'

'Not nice hobbit, not sensible,' said Gollum, giving Sam an angry glance and turning to Frodo. 'Sméagol has talked to Orcs, yes of course, before he met master, and to many peoples: he has walked very far. And what he says now many peoples are saying. It's here in the North that the big danger is for Him, and for us. He will come out of the Black Gate one day, one day soon. That is the only way big armies can come. But away down west He is not afraid, and there are the Silent Watchers.'

'Just so!' said Sam, not to be put off. 'And so we are to walk up and knock at their gate and ask if we're on the right road for Mordor? Or are they too silent to answer? It's not sense. We might as well do it here, and save ourselves a long tramp.'

'Don't make jokes about it,' hissed Gollum. 'It isn't funny, O no! Not amusing. It's not sense to try and get into Mordor at all. But if master says *I must go* or *I will go*, then he must try some way. But he must not go to the terrible city, O no, of course not. That is where Sméagol helps, nice Sméagol, though no one tells him what it is all about. Sméagol helps again. He found it. He knows it.'

'What did you find?' asked Frodo.

Gollum crouched down and his voice sank to a whisper again. 'A little path leading up into the mountains; and then a stair, a narrow stair, O yes, very long and narrow. And then more stairs. And then' – his voice sank even lower – 'a tunnel, a dark tunnel; and at last a little cleft, and a path high above the main pass. It was that way that Sméagol got out of the darkness. But it was years ago. The path may have vanished now; but perhaps not, perhaps not.'

'I don't like the sound of it at all,' said Sam. 'Sounds too easy at any rate in the telling. If that path is still there, it'll be guarded too. Wasn't it guarded, Gollum?' As he said this, he caught or fancied he caught a green gleam in Gollum's eye. Gollum muttered but did not reply.

'Is it not guarded?' asked Frodo sternly. 'And did you *escape* out of the darkness, Sméagol? Were you not rather permitted to depart, upon an errand? That at least is what Aragorn thought, who found you by the Dead Marshes some years ago.'

'It's a lie!' hissed Gollum, and an evil light came into his eyes at the naming of Aragorn. 'He lied on me, yes he did. I did escape, all by my poor self. Indeed I was told to seek for the Precious; and I have searched and searched, of course I have. But not for the Black One. The Precious was ours, it was mine I tell you. I did escape.'

Frodo felt a strange certainty that in this matter Gollum was for once not so far from the truth as might be suspected; that he had somehow found a way out of Mordor, and at least believed that it was by his own cunning. For one thing, he noted that Gollum used *I*, and that seemed usually to be a sign, on its rare appearances, that some remnants of old truth and sincerity were for the moment on top. But even if Gollum could be trusted on this point, Frodo did not forget the wiles of the Enemy. The 'escape' may have been allowed or arranged, and well known in the Dark Tower. And in any case Gollum was plainly keeping a good deal back.

'I ask you again,' he said: 'is not this secret way guarded?'

But the name of Aragorn had put Gollum into a sullen mood. He had all the injured air of a liar suspected when for once he has told the truth, or part of it. He did not answer.

'Is it not guarded?' Frodo repeated.

'Yes, yes, perhaps. No safe places in this country,' said Gollum sulkily. 'No safe places. But master must try it or go home. No other way.' They could not get him to say more. The name of the perilous place and the high pass he could not tell, or would not.

Its name was Cirith Ungol, a name of dreadful rumour. Aragorn could perhaps have told them that name and its significance; Gandalf would have warned them. But they were alone, and Aragorn was far away, and Gandalf stood amid the ruin of Isengard and strove with Saruman, delayed by treason. Yet even as he spoke his last words to Saruman, and the *palantír* crashed in fire upon the steps of Orthanc, his thought was ever upon Frodo and Samwise, over the long leagues his mind sought for them in hope and pity.

Maybe Frodo felt it, not knowing it, as he had upon Amon Hen, even though he believed that Gandalf was gone, gone for ever into the shadow in Moria far away. He sat upon the ground for a long while, silent, his head bowed, striving to recall all that Gandalf had said to him. But for this choice he could recall no counsel. Indeed Gandalf's guidance had been taken from them too soon, too soon, while the Dark Land was still very far away. How they should enter it at the last Gandalf had not said. Perhaps he could not say. Into the stronghold of the Enemy in the North, into Dol Guldur, he had once ventured. But into Mordor, to the Mountain of Fire and to Barad-dûr, since the Dark Lord rose in power again, had he ever journeyed there? Frodo did not think so. And here he was a little halfling from the Shire, a simple hobbit of the quiet countryside, expected to find a way where the great ones could not go, or dared not go. It was an evil fate. But he had taken it on himself in his own sitting-room in the far-off spring of another year, so remote now that it was like a chapter in a story of the world's youth, when the Trees of Silver and Gold were still in bloom. This was an evil choice. Which way should he choose? And if both led to terror and death, what good lay in choice?

The day drew on. A deep silence fell upon the little grey hollow where they lay, so near to the borders of the land of fear: a silence that could be felt, as if it were a thick veil that cut them off from all the world about them. Above them was a dome of pale sky barred with fleeting smoke, but it seemed high and far away, as if seen through great deeps of air heavy with brooding thought.

Not even an eagle poised against the sun would have marked the hobbits sitting there, under the weight of doom, silent, not moving, shrouded in their thin grey cloaks. For a moment he might have paused to consider Gollum, a tiny figure sprawling on the ground: there perhaps lay the famished skeleton of some child of Men, its ragged garment still clinging to it, its long arms and legs almost bone-white and bone-thin: no flesh worth a peck.

Frodo's head was bowed over his knees, but Sam leaned back, with hands behind his head, staring out of his hood at the empty sky. At least for a long while it was empty. Then presently Sam thought he saw a dark bird-like figure wheel into the circle of his sight, and hover, and then wheel away again. Two more followed, and then a fourth. They were very small to look at, yet he knew, somehow, that they were huge, with a vast stretch of pinion, flying at a great height. He covered his eyes and bent forward, cowering. The same warning fear was on him as he had felt in the presence of the Black Riders, the helpless horror that had come with the cry in the wind and the shadow on the moon, though now it was not so crushing or compelling: the menace was more remote. But menace it was. Frodo felt it too. His thought was broken. He stirred and shivered, but he did not look up. Gollum huddled himself together like a cornered spider. The winged shapes wheeled, and stooped swiftly down, speeding back to Mordor.

Sam took a deep breath. 'The Riders are about again, up in the air,' he said in a hoarse whisper. 'I saw them. Do you think they could see us? They were very high up. And if they are Black Riders, same as before, then they can't see much by daylight, can they?'

'No, perhaps not,' said Frodo. 'But their steeds could see. And these winged creatures that they ride on now, they can probably see more than any other creature. They are like great carrion birds. They are looking for something: the Enemy is on the watch, I fear.'

The feeling of dread passed, but the enfolding silence was broken. For some time they had been cut off from the world, as if in an invisible island; now they were laid bare again, peril had returned. But still Frodo did not speak to Gollum or make his choice. His eyes were closed, as if he were dreaming, or looking inward into his heart and memory. At last he stirred and stood up, and it seemed that he was about to speak and to decide. But 'hark!' he said. 'What is that?'

A new fear was upon them. They heard singing and hoarse shouting. At first it seemed a long way off, but it drew nearer: it was coming towards them. It leaped into all their minds that the Black Wings had spied them and had sent armed soldiers to seize them: no speed seemed too great for these terrible servants of Sauron. They crouched, listening. The voices and the clink of weapons and harness were very close. Frodo and Sam loosened their small swords in their sheaths. Flight was impossible.

Gollum rose slowly and crawled insect-like to the lip of the hollow. Very cautiously he raised himself inch by inch, until he could peer over it between two broken points of stone. He remained there without moving for some time, making no sound. Presently the voices began to recede again, and then they slowly faded away. Far off a horn blew on the ramparts of the Morannon. Then quietly Gollum drew back and slipped down into the hollow.

'More Men going to Mordor,' he said in a low voice. 'Dark faces. We have not seen Men like these before, no, Sméagol has not. They are fierce. They have black eyes, and long black hair, and gold rings in their ears; yes, lots of beautiful gold. And some have red paint on their cheeks, and red cloaks; and their flags are red, and the tips of their spears; and they have round shields, yellow and black with big spikes. Not nice; very cruel wicked Men they look. Almost as bad as Orcs, and much bigger. Sméagol thinks they have come out of the South beyond the Great River's end: they came up that road. They have passed on to the Black Gate; but more may follow. Always more people coming to Mordor. One day all the peoples will be inside.'

'Were there any oliphaunts?' asked Sam, forgetting his fear in his eagerness for news of strange places.

'No, no oliphaunts. What are oliphaunts?' said Gollum.

Sam stood up, putting his hands behind his back (as he always did when 'speaking poetry'), and began:

> Grey as a mouse,
> Big as a house,
> Nose like a snake,
> I make the earth shake,
> As I tramp through the grass;
> Trees crack as I pass.
> With horns in my mouth
> I walk in the South,
> Flapping big ears.
> Beyond count of years
> I stump round and round,
> Never lie on the ground,
> Not even to die.
> Oliphaunt am I,
> Biggest of all,
> Huge, old, and tall.
> If ever you'd met me
> You wouldn't forget me.
> If you never do,
> You won't think I'm true;
> But old Oliphaunt am I,
> And I never lie.

'That,' said Sam, when he had finished reciting, 'that's a rhyme we have in the Shire. Nonsense maybe, and maybe not. But we have our tales too, and news out of the South, you know. In the old days hobbits used to go on their travels now and again. Not that many ever came back, and not that all they said was believed: *news from Bree*, and not *sure as Shiretalk*, as the sayings go. But I've heard tales of the big folk down away in the Sunlands. Swertings we call 'em in our tales; and they ride on oliphaunts, 'tis said, when they fight. They put houses and towers on the oliphauntses backs and all, and the oliphaunts throw rocks and trees at one another. So when you said "Men out of the South, all in red and gold," I said "were there any oliphaunts?" For if there was, I was going to take a look, risk or no. But now I don't suppose I'll ever see an oliphaunt. Maybe there ain't no such a beast.' He sighed.

'No, no oliphaunts,' said Gollum again. 'Sméagol has not heard of them. He does not want to see them. He does not want them to be. Sméagol wants to go away from here and hide somewhere safer. Sméagol wants master to go. Nice master, won't he come with Sméagol?'

Frodo stood up. He had laughed in the midst of all his cares when Sam trotted out the old fireside rhyme of *Oliphaunt*, and the laugh had released him from hesitation. 'I wish we had a thousand oliphaunts with Gandalf on a white one at their head,' he said. 'Then we'd break a way into this evil land, perhaps. But we've not; just our own tired legs, that's all. Well, Sméagol, the third turn may turn the best. I will come with you.'

'Good master, wise master, nice master!' cried Gollum in delight, patting Frodo's knees. 'Good master! Then rest now, nice hobbits, under the shadow of the stones, close under the stones! Rest and lie quiet, till the Yellow Face goes away. Then we can go quickly. Soft and quick as shadows we must be!'

CHAPTER IV

OF HERBS AND STEWED RABBIT

For the few hours of daylight that were left they rested, shifting into the shade as the sun moved, until at last the shadow of the western rim of their dell grew long, and darkness filled all the hollow. Then they ate a little, and drank sparingly. Gollum ate nothing, but he accepted water gladly.

'Soon get more now,' he said, licking his lips. 'Good water runs down in streams to the Great River, nice water in the lands we are going to. Sméagol will get food there too, perhaps. He's very hungry, yes, *gollum!*' He set his two large flat hands on his shrunken belly, and a pale green light came into his eyes.

The dusk was deep when at length they set out, creeping over the westward rim of the dell, and fading like ghosts into the broken country on the borders of the road. The moon was now three nights from the full, but it did not climb over the mountains until nearly midnight, and the early night was very dark. A single red light burned high up in the Towers of the Teeth, but otherwise no sign could be seen or heard of the sleepless watch on the Morannon.

For many miles the red eye seemed to stare at them as they fled, stumbling through a barren stony country. They did not dare to take the road, but they kept it on their left, following its line as well as they could at a little distance. At last, when night was growing old and they were already weary, for they had taken only one short rest, the eye dwindled to a small fiery point and then vanished: they had turned the dark northern shoulder of the lower mountains and were heading southwards.

With hearts strangely lightened they now rested again, but not for long. They were not going quick enough for Gollum. By his reckoning it was nearly thirty leagues from the Morannon to the cross-roads above Osgiliath, and he hoped to cover that distance in four journeys. So soon they struggled on once more, until the dawn began to spread slowly in the wide grey solitude. They had then walked almost eight leagues, and the hobbits could not have gone any further, even if they had dared.

The growing light revealed to them a land already less barren and ruinous. The mountains still loomed up ominously on their left, but near at hand they could see the southward road, now bearing away from the black roots of the hills and slanting westwards. Beyond it were slopes covered with sombre trees like dark clouds, but all about them lay a tumbled heathland, grown with ling and broom and cornel, and other shrubs that they did not know. Here and there they saw knots of tall pine-trees. The hearts of the hobbits rose again a little in spite of weariness: the air was fresh and fragrant, and it reminded them of the uplands of the Northfarthing far away. It seemed good to be reprieved, to walk in a land that had only been for a few years under the dominion of the Dark Lord and was not yet fallen wholly into decay. But they did not forget their danger, nor the Black Gate that was still all too near, hidden though it was behind the gloomy heights. They looked about for a hiding-place where they could shelter from evil eyes while the light lasted.

The day passed uneasily. They lay deep in the heather and counted out the slow hours, in which there seemed little change; for they were still under the shadows of the Ephel Dúath, and the sun was veiled. Frodo slept at times, deeply and peacefully, either trusting Gollum or too tired to trouble about him; but Sam found it difficult to do more than doze, even when Gollum was plainly fast asleep, whiffling and twitching in his secret dreams. Hunger, perhaps, more than mistrust kept him wakeful: he had begun to long for a good homely meal, 'something hot out of the pot'.

As soon as the land faded into a formless grey under coming night, they started out again. In a little while Gollum led them down on to the southward road; and after that they went on more quickly, though the danger was greater. Their ears were strained for the sound of hoof or foot on the road ahead, or following them from behind; but the night passed, and they heard no sound of walker or rider.

The road had been made in a long lost time, and for perhaps thirty miles below the Morannon it had been newly repaired, but as it went south the wild encroached upon it. The handiwork of Men of old could still be seen in its straight sure flight and level course: now and again it cut its way through hillside slopes, or leaped over a stream upon a wide shapely arch of enduring masonry; but at last all signs of stonework faded, save for a broken pillar here and there, peering out of bushes at the side, or old paving-stones still lurking amid weeds and moss. Heather and trees and bracken scrambled down and overhung the banks, or sprawled out over the surface. It dwindled at last to a country cart-road little used; but it did not wind: it held on its own sure course and guided them by the swiftest way.

So they passed into the northern marches of that land that Men once called Ithilien, a fair country of climbing woods and swift-falling streams. The night became fine under star and round moon, and it seemed to the hobbits that the fragrance of the air grew as they went forward; and from the blowing and muttering of Gollum it seemed that he noticed it too, and did not relish it. At the first signs of day they halted again. They had come to the end of a long cutting, deep, and sheer-sided in the middle, by which the road clove its way through a stony ridge. Now they climbed up the westward bank and looked abroad.

Day was opening in the sky, and they saw that the mountains were now much further off, receding eastward in a long curve that was lost in the distance. Before them, as they turned west, gentle slopes ran down into dim hazes far below. All about them were small woods of resinous trees, fir and cedar and cypress, and other kinds unknown in the Shire, with wide glades among them; and everywhere there was a wealth of sweet-smelling herbs and shrubs. The long journey from Rivendell had brought them far south of their own land, but not until now in this more sheltered region had the hobbits felt the change of clime. Here Spring was already busy about them: fronds pierced moss and mould, larches were green-fingered, small flowers were opening in the turf, birds were singing. Ithilien, the garden of Gondor now desolate kept still a dishevelled dryad loveliness.

South and west it looked towards the warm lower vales of Anduin, shielded from the east by the Ephel Dúath and yet not under the mountain-shadow, protected from the north by the Emyn Muil, open to the southern airs and the moist winds from the Sea far away. Many great trees grew there, planted long ago, falling into untended age amid a riot of careless descendants; and groves and thickets there were of tamarisk and pungent terebinth, of olive and of bay; and there were junipers and myrtles; and thymes that grew in bushes, or with their woody creeping stems mantled in deep tapestries the hidden stones; sages of many kinds putting forth blue flowers, or red, or pale green; and marjorams and new-sprouting parsleys, and many herbs of forms and scents beyond the garden-lore of Sam. The grots and rocky walls were already starred with saxifrages and stonecrops. Primeroles and anemones were awake in the filbert-brakes; and asphodel and many lily-flowers nodded their half-opened heads in the grass: deep green grass beside the pools, where falling streams halted in cool hollows on their journey down to Anduin.

The travellers turned their backs on the road and went downhill. As they walked, brushing their way through bush and herb, sweet odours rose about them. Gollum coughed and retched; but the hobbits breathed deep, and suddenly Sam laughed, for heart's ease not for jest. They followed a stream that went quickly down before them. Presently it brought them to a small clear lake in a shallow dell: it lay in the broken ruins of an ancient stone basin, the carven rim of which was almost wholly covered with mosses and rose-brambles; iris-swords stood in ranks about it, and water-lily leaves floated on its dark gently-rippling surface; but it was deep and fresh, and spilled ever softly out over a stony lip at the far end.

Here they washed themselves and drank their fill at the in-falling freshet. Then they sought for a resting-place, and a hiding-place; for this land, fair-seeming still, was nonetheless now territory of the Enemy. They had not come very far from the road, and yet even in so short a space they had seen scars of the old wars, and the newer wounds made by the Orcs and other foul servants of the Dark Lord: a pit of uncovered filth and refuse; trees hewn down wantonly and left to die, with evil runes or the fell sign of the Eye cut in rude strokes on their bark.

Sam scrambling below the outfall of the lake, smelling and touching the unfamiliar plants and trees, forgetful for the moment of Mordor, was reminded suddenly of their ever-present peril. He stumbled on a ring still scorched by fire, and in the midst of it he found a pile of charred and broken bones and skulls. The swift growth of the wild with briar and eglantine and trailing clematis was already drawing a veil over this place of dreadful feast and slaughter; but it was not ancient. He hurried back to his companions, but he said nothing: the bones were best left in peace and not pawed and routed by Gollum.

'Let's find a place to lie up in,' he said. 'Not lower down. Higher up for me.'

A little way back above the lake they found a deep brown bed of last year's fern. Beyond it was a thicket of dark-leaved bay-trees climbing up a steep bank that was crowned with old cedars. Here they decided to rest and pass the day, which already promised to be bright and warm. A good day for strolling on their way along the groves and glades of Ithilien; but though Orcs may shun the sunlight, there were too many places here where they could lie hid and watch; and other evil eyes were abroad: Sauron had many servants. Gollum, in any case, would not move under the Yellow Face. Soon it would look over the dark ridges of the Ephel Dúath, and he would faint and cower in the light and heat.

Sam had been giving earnest thought to food as they marched. Now that the despair of the impassable Gate was behind him, he did not feel so inclined as his master to take no thought for their livelihood beyond the end of their errand; and anyway it seemed wiser to him to save the waybread of the Elves for worse times ahead. Six days or more had passed since he reckoned that they had only a bare supply for three weeks.

'If we reach the Fire in that time, we'll be lucky at this rate!' he thought. 'And we might be wanting to get back. We might!'

Besides, at the end of a long night-march, and after bathing and drinking, he felt even more hungry than usual. A supper, or a breakfast, by the fire in the old kitchen at Bagshot Row was what he really wanted. An idea struck him and he turned to Gollum. Gollum had just begun to sneak off on his own, and he was crawling away on all fours through the fern.

'Hi! Gollum!' said Sam. 'Where are you going? Hunting? Well, see here, old noser, you don't like our food, and I'd not be sorry for a change myself. Your new motto's *always ready to help*. Could you find anything fit for a hungry hobbit?'

'Yes, perhaps, yes,' said Gollum. 'Sméagol always helps, if they asks – if they asks nicely.'

'Right!' said Sam. 'I does ask. And if that isn't nice enough, I begs.'

Gollum disappeared. He was away some time, and Frodo after a few mouthfuls of *lembas* settled deep into the brown fern and went to sleep. Sam looked at him. The early daylight was only just creeping down into the shadows under the trees, but he saw his master's face very clearly, and his hands, too, lying at rest on the ground beside him. He was reminded suddenly of Frodo as he had lain, asleep in the house of Elrond, after his deadly wound. Then as he had kept watch Sam had noticed that at times a light seemed to be shining faintly within; but now the light was even clearer and stronger. Frodo's face was peaceful, the marks of fear and care had left it; but it looked old, old and beautiful, as if the chiselling of the shaping years was now revealed in many fine lines that had before been hidden, though the identity of the face was not changed. Not that Sam Gamgee put it that way to himself. He shook his head, as if finding words useless, and murmured: 'I love him. He's like that, and sometimes it shines through, somehow. But I love him, whether or no.'

Gollum returned quietly and peered over Sam's shoulder. Looking at Frodo, he shut his eyes and crawled away without a sound. Sam came to him a moment later and found him chewing something and muttering to himself. On the ground beside him lay two small rabbits, which he was beginning to eye greedily.

'Sméagol always helps,' he said. 'He has brought rabbits, nice rabbits. But master has gone to sleep, and perhaps Sam wants to sleep. Doesn't want rabbits now? Sméagol tries to help, but he can't catch things all in a minute.'

Sam, however, had no objection to rabbit at all, and said so. At least not to cooked rabbit. All hobbits, of course, can cook, for they begin to learn the art before their letters (which many never reach); but Sam was a good cook, even by hobbit reckoning, and he had done a good deal of the camp-cooking on their travels, when there was a chance. He still hopefully carried some of his gear in his pack: a small tinder-box, two small shallow pans, the smaller fitting into the larger; inside them a wooden spoon, a short two-pronged fork and some skewers were stowed; and hidden at the bottom of the pack in a flat wooden box a dwindling treasure, some salt. But he needed a fire, and other things besides. He thought for a bit, while he took out his knife, cleaned and whetted it, and began to dress the rabbits. He was not going to leave Frodo alone asleep even for a few minutes.

'Now, Gollum,' he said, 'I've another job for you. Go and fill these pans with water, and bring 'em back!'

'Sméagol will fetch water, yes,' said Gollum. 'But what does the hobbit want all that water for? He has drunk, he has washed.'

'Never you mind,' said Sam. 'If you can't guess, you'll soon find out. And the sooner you fetch the water, the sooner you'll learn. Don't you damage one of my pans, or I'll carve you into mincemeat.'

While Gollum was away Sam took another look at Frodo. He was still sleeping quietly, but Sam was now struck most by the leanness of his face and hands. 'Too thin and drawn he is,' he muttered. 'Not right for a hobbit. If I can get these coneys cooked, I'm going to wake him up.'

Sam gathered a pile of the driest fern, and then scrambled up the bank collecting a bundle of twigs and broken wood; the fallen branch of a cedar at the top gave him a good supply. He cut out some turves at the foot of the bank just outside the fern-brake, and made a shallow hole and laid his fuel in it. Being handy with flint and tinder he soon had a small blaze going. It made little or no smoke but gave off an aromatic scent. He was just stooping over his fire, shielding it and building it up with heavier wood, when Gollum returned, carrying the pans carefully and grumbling to himself.

He set the pans down, and then suddenly saw what Sam was doing. He gave a thin hissing shriek, and seemed to be both frightened and angry. 'Ach! Sss – no!' he cried. 'No! Silly hobbits, foolish, yes foolish! They mustn't do it!'

'Mustn't do what?' asked Sam in surprise.

'Not make the nassty red tongues,' hissed Gollum. 'Fire, fire! It's dangerous, yes it is. It burns, it kills. And it will bring enemies, yes it will.'

'I don't think so,' said Sam. 'Don't see why it should, if you don't put wet stuff on it and make a smother. But if it does, it does. I'm going to risk it, anyhow. I'm going to stew these coneys.'

'Stew the rabbits!' squealed Gollum in dismay. 'Spoil beautiful meat Sméagol saved for you, poor hungry Sméagol! What for? What for, silly hobbit? They are young, they are tender, they are nice. Eat them, eat them!' He clawed at the nearest rabbit, already skinned and lying by the fire.

'Now, now!' said Sam. 'Each to his own fashion. Our bread chokes you, and raw coney chokes me. If you give me a coney, the coney's mine, see, to cook, if I have a mind. And I have. You needn't watch me. Go and catch another and eat it as you fancy – somewhere private and out o' my sight. Then you won't see the fire, and I shan't see you, and we'll both be the happier. I'll see the fire don't smoke, if that's any comfort to you.'

Gollum withdrew grumbling, and crawled into the fern. Sam busied himself with his pans. 'What a hobbit needs with coney,' he said to himself, 'is some herbs and roots, especially taters – not to mention bread. Herbs we can manage, seemingly.'

'Gollum!' he called softly. 'Third time pays for all. I want some herbs.' Gollum's head peeped out of the fern, but his looks were neither helpful nor friendly. 'A few bay-leaves, some thyme and sage, will do – before the water boils,' said Sam.

'No!' said Gollum. 'Sméagol is not pleased. And Sméagol doesn't like smelly leaves. He doesn't eat grasses or roots, no precious, not till he's starving or very sick, poor Sméagol.'

'Sméagol'll get into real true hot water, when this water boils, if he don't do as he's asked,' growled Sam. 'Sam'll put his head in it, yes precious. And I'd make him look for turnips and carrots, and taters too, if it was the time o' the year. I'll bet there's all sorts of good things running wild in this country. I'd give a lot for half a dozen taters.'

'Sméagol won't go, O no precious, not this time,' hissed Gollum. 'He's frightened, and he's very tired, and this hobbit's not nice, not nice at all. Sméagol won't grub for roots and carrotses and – taters. What's taters, precious, eh, what's taters?'

'Po – ta – toes,' said Sam. 'The Gaffer's delight, and rare good ballast for an empty belly. But you won't find any, so you needn't look. But be good Sméagol and fetch me the herbs, and I'll think better of you. What's more, if you turn over a new leaf, and keep it turned, I'll cook you some taters one of these days. I will: fried fish and chips served by S. Gamgee. You couldn't say no to that.'

'Yes, yes we could. Spoiling nice fish, scorching it. Give me fish *now*, and keep nassty chips!'

'Oh you're hopeless,' said Sam. 'Go to sleep!'

In the end he had to find what he wanted for himself; but he did not have to go far, not out of sight of the place where his master lay, still sleeping. For a while Sam sat musing, and tending the fire till the water boiled. The daylight grew and the air became warm; the dew faded off turf and leaf. Soon the rabbits cut up lay simmering in their pans with the bunched herbs. Almost Sam fell asleep as the time went by. He let them stew for close on an hour, testing them now and again with his fork, and tasting the broth.

When he thought all was ready he lifted the pans off the fire, and crept along to Frodo. Frodo half opened his eyes as Sam stood over him, and then he wakened from his dreaming: another gentle, unrecoverable dream of peace.

'Hullo, Sam!' he said. 'Not resting? Is anything wrong? What is the time?'

'About a couple of hours after daybreak,' said Sam, 'and nigh on half past eight by Shire clocks, maybe. But nothing's wrong. Though it ain't quite what I'd call right: no stock, no onions, no taters. I've got a bit of a stew for you, and some broth, Mr. Frodo. Do you good. You'll have to sup it in your mug; or straight from the pan, when it's cooled a bit. I haven't brought no bowls, nor nothing proper.'

Frodo yawned and stretched. 'You should have been resting, Sam,' he said. 'And lighting a fire was dangerous in these parts. But I do feel hungry. Hmm! Can I smell it from here? What have you stewed?'

'A present from Sméagol,' said Sam: 'a brace o' young coneys; though I fancy Gollum's regretting them now. But there's nought to go with them but a few herbs.'

Sam and his master sat just within the fern-brake and ate their stew from the pans, sharing the old fork and spoon. They allowed themselves half a piece of the Elvish waybread each. It seemed a feast.

'Wheew! Gollum!' Sam called and whistled softly. 'Come on! Still time to change your mind. There's some left, if you want to try stewed coney.'

There was no answer.

'Oh well, I suppose he's gone off to find something for himself. We'll finish it,' said Sam.

'And then you must take some sleep,' said Frodo.

'Don't you drop off, while I'm nodding, Mr. Frodo. I don't feel too sure of him. There's a good deal of Stinker – the bad Gollum, if you understand me – in him still, and it's getting stronger again. Not but what I think he'd try to throttle me first now. We don't see eye to eye, and he's not pleased with Sam, O no precious, not pleased at all.'

They finished, and Sam went off to the stream to rinse his gear. As he stood up to return, he looked back up the slope. At that moment he saw the sun rise out of the reek, or haze, or dark shadow, or whatever it was, that lay ever to the east, and it sent its golden beams down upon the trees and glades about him. Then he noticed a thin spiral of blue-grey smoke, plain to see as it caught the sunlight, rising from a thicket above him. With a shock he realized that this was the smoke from his little cooking-fire, which he had neglected to put out.

'That won't do! Never thought it would show like that!' he muttered, and he started to hurry back. Suddenly he halted and listened. Had he heard a whistle or not? Or was it the call of some strange bird? If it was a whistle, it did not come from Frodo's direction. There it went again from another place! Sam began to run as well as he could uphill.

He found that a small brand, burning away to its outer end, had kindled some fern at the edge of the fire, and the fern blazing up had set the turves smouldering. Hastily he stamped out what was left of the fire, scattered the ashes, and laid the turves on the hole. Then he crept back to Frodo.

'Did you hear a whistle, and what sounded like an answer?' he asked. 'A few minutes back. I hope it was only a bird, but it didn't sound quite like that: more like somebody mimicking a bird-call, I thought. And I'm afraid my bit of fire's been smoking. Now if I've gone and brought trouble, I'll never forgive myself. Nor won't have a chance, maybe!'

'Hush!' whispered Frodo. 'I thought I heard voices.'

The two hobbits trussed their small packs, put them on ready for flight, and then crawled deeper into the fern. There they crouched listening.

There was no doubt of the voices. They were speaking low and furtively, but they were near, and coming nearer. Then quite suddenly one spoke clearly close at hand.

'Here! Here is where the smoke came from!' it said. ''Twill be nigh at hand. In the fern, no doubt. We shall have it like a coney in a trap. Then we shall learn what kind of thing it is.'

'Aye, and what it knows!' said a second voice.

At once four men came striding through the fern from different directions. Since flight and hiding were no longer possible, Frodo and Sam sprang to their feet, putting back to back and whipping out their small swords.

If they were astonished at what they saw, their captors were even more astonished. Four tall Men stood there. Two had spears in their hands with broad bright heads. Two had great bows, almost of their own height, and great quivers of long green-feathered arrows. All had swords at their sides, and were clad in green and brown of varied hues, as if the better to walk unseen in the glades of Ithilien. Green gauntlets covered their hands, and their faces were hooded and masked with green, except for their eyes, which were very keen and bright. At once Frodo thought of Boromir, for these Men were like him in stature and bearing, and in their manner of speech.

'We have not found what we sought,' said one. 'But what have we found?'

'Not Orcs,' said another, releasing the hilt of his sword, which he had seized when he saw the glitter of Sting in Frodo's hand.

'Elves?' said a third, doubtfully.

'Nay! Not Elves,' said the fourth, the tallest, and as it appeared the chief among them. 'Elves do not walk in Ithilien in these days. And Elves are wondrous fair to look upon, or so 'tis said.'

'Meaning we're not, I take you,' said Sam. 'Thank you kindly. And when you've finished discussing us, perhaps you'll say who *you* are, and why you can't let two tired travellers rest.'

The tall green man laughed grimly. 'I am Faramir, Captain of Gondor,' he said. 'But there are no travellers in this land: only the servants of the Dark Tower, or of the White.'

'But we are neither,' said Frodo. 'And travellers we are, whatever Captain Faramir may say.'

'Then make haste to declare yourselves and your errand,' said Faramir. 'We have a work to do, and this is no time or place for riddling or parleying. Come! Where is the third of your company?'

'The third?'

'Yes, the skulking fellow that we saw with his nose in the pool down yonder. He had an ill-favoured look. Some spying breed of Orc, I guess, or a creature of theirs. But he gave us the slip by some fox-trick.'

'I do not know where he is,' said Frodo. 'He is only a chance companion met upon our road, and I am not answerable for him. If you come on him, spare him. Bring him or send him to us. He is only a wretched gangrel creature, but I have him under my care for a while. But as for us, we are Hobbits of the Shire, far to the North and West, beyond many rivers. Frodo son of Drogo is my name, and with me is Samwise son of Hamfast, a worthy hobbit in my service. We have come by long ways – out of Rivendell, or Imladris as some call it.' Here Faramir started and grew intent. 'Seven companions we had: one we lost at Moria, the others we left at Parth Galen above Rauros: two of my kin; a Dwarf there was also, and an Elf, and two Men. They were Aragorn; and Boromir, who said that he came out of Minas Tirith, a city in the South.'

'Boromir!' all the four men exclaimed.

'Boromir son of the Lord Denethor?' said Faramir, and a strange stern look came into his face. 'You came with him? That is news indeed, if it be true. Know, little strangers, that Boromir son of Denethor was High Warden of the White Tower, and our Captain-General: sorely do we miss him. Who are you then, and what had you to do with him? Be swift, for the Sun is climbing!'

'Are the riddling words known to you that Boromir brought to Rivendell?' Frodo replied.

Seek for the Sword that was Broken.
In Imladris it dwells.

'The words are known indeed,' said Faramir in astonishment. 'It is some token of your truth that you also know them.'

'Aragorn whom I named is the bearer of the Sword that was Broken,' said Frodo. 'And we are the Halflings that the rhyme spoke of.'

'That I see,' said Faramir thoughtfully. 'Or I see that it might be so. And what is Isildur's Bane?'

'That is hidden,' answered Frodo. 'Doubtless it will be made clear in time.'

'We must learn more of this,' said Faramir, 'and know what brings you so far east under the shadow of yonder———,' he pointed and said no name. 'But not now. We have business in hand. You are in peril, and you would not have gone far by field or road this day. There will be hard handstrokes nigh at hand ere the day is full. Then death, or swift flight back to Anduin. I will leave two to guard you, for your good and for mine. Wise man trusts not to chance-meeting on the road in this land. If I return, I will speak more with you.'

'Farewell!' said Frodo, bowing low. 'Think what you will, I am a friend of all enemies of the One Enemy. We would go with you, if we halfling folk could hope to serve you, such doughty men and strong as you seem, and if my errand permitted it. May the light shine on your swords!'

'The Halflings are courteous folk, whatever else they be,' said Faramir. 'Farewell!'

The hobbits sat down again, but they said nothing to one another of their thoughts and doubts. Close by, just under the dappling shadow of the dark bay-trees, two men remained on guard. They took off their masks now and again to cool them, as the day-heat grew, and Frodo saw that they were goodly men, pale-skinned, dark of hair, with grey eyes and faces sad and proud. They spoke together in soft voices, at first using the Common Speech, but after the manner of older days, and then changing to another language of their own. To his amazement, as he listened Frodo became aware that it was the Elven-tongue that they spoke, or one but little different; and he looked at them with wonder, for he knew then that they must be Dúnedain of the South, men of the line of the Lords of Westernesse.

After a while he spoke to them; but they were slow and cautious in answering. They named themselves Mablung and Damrod, soldiers of Gondor, and they were Rangers of Ithilien; for they were descended from folk who lived in Ithilien at one time, before it was overrun. From such men the Lord Denethor chose his forayers, who crossed the Anduin secretly (how or where, they would not say) to harry the Orcs and other enemies that roamed between the Ephel Dúath and the River.

'It is close on ten leagues hence to the east-shore of Anduin,' said Mablung, 'and we seldom come so far afield. But we have a new errand on this journey: we come to ambush the Men of Harad. Curse them!'

'Aye, curse the Southrons!' said Damrod. "'Tis said that there were dealings of old between Gondor and the kingdoms of the Harad in the Far South; though there was never friendship. In those days our bounds were away south beyond the mouths of Anduin, and Umbar, the nearest of their realms, acknowledged our sway. But that is long since. 'Tis many lives of Men since any passed to or fro between us. Now of late we have learned that the Enemy has been among them, and they are gone over to Him, or back to Him – they were ever ready to His will – as have so many also in the East. I doubt not that the days of Gondor are numbered, and the walls of Minas Tirith are doomed, so great is His strength and malice.'

'But still we will not sit idle and let Him do all as He would,' said Mablung. 'These cursed Southrons come now marching up the ancient roads to swell the hosts of the Dark Tower. Yea, up the very roads that craft of Gondor made. And they go ever more heedlessly, we learn, thinking that the power of their new master is great enough, so that the mere shadow of His hills will protect them. We come to teach them another lesson. Great strength of them was reported to us some days ago, marching north. One of their regiments is due by our reckoning to pass by, some time ere noon – up on the road above, where it passes through the cloven way. The road may pass, but they shall not! Not while Faramir is Captain. He leads now in all perilous ventures. But his life is charmed, or fate spares him for some other end.'

Their talk died down into a listening silence. All seemed still and watchful. Sam, crouched by the edge of the fern-brake, peered out. With his keen hobbit-eyes he saw that many more Men were about. He could see them stealing up the slopes, singly or in long files, keeping always to the shade of grove or thicket, or crawling, hardly visible in their brown and green raiment, through grass and brake. All were hooded and masked, and had gauntlets on their hands, and were armed like Faramir and his companions. Before long they had all passed and vanished. The sun rose till it neared the South. The shadows shrank.

'I wonder where that dratted Gollum is?' thought Sam, as he crawled back into deeper shade. 'He stands a fair chance of being spitted for an Orc, or of being roasted by the Yellow Face. But I fancy he'll look after himself.' He lay down beside Frodo and began to doze.

He woke, thinking that he had heard horns blowing. He sat up. It was now high noon. The guards stood alert and tense in the shadow of the trees. Suddenly the horns rang out louder and beyond mistake from above, over the top of the slope. Sam thought that he heard cries and wild shouting also, but the sound was faint, as if it came out of some distant cave. Then presently the noise of fighting broke out near at hand, just above their hiding-place. He could hear plainly the ringing grate of steel on steel, the clang of sword on iron cap, the dull beat of blade on shield; men were yelling and screaming, and one clear loud voice was calling *Gondor! Gondor!*

'It sounds like a hundred blacksmiths all smithying together,' said Sam to Frodo. 'They're as near as I want them now.'

But the noise grew closer. 'They are coming!' cried Damrod. 'See! Some of the Southrons have broken from the trap and are flying from the road. There they go! Our men after them, and the Captain leading.'

Sam, eager to see more, went now and joined the guards. He scrambled a little way up into one of the larger of the bay-trees. For a moment he caught a glimpse of swarthy men in red running down the slope some way off with green-clad warriors leaping after them, hewing them down as they fled. Arrows were thick in the air. Then suddenly straight over the rim of their sheltering bank, a man fell, crashing through the slender trees, nearly on top of them. He came to rest in the fern a few feet away, face downward, green arrow-feathers sticking from his neck below a golden collar. His scarlet robes were tattered, his corslet of overlapping brazen plates was rent and hewn, his black plaits of hair braided with gold were drenched with blood. His brown hand still clutched the hilt of a broken sword.

It was Sam's first view of a battle of Men against Men, and he did not like it much. He was glad that he could not see the dead face. He wondered what the man's name was and where he came from; and if he was really evil of heart, or what lies or threats had led him on the long march from his home; and if he would not really rather have stayed there in peace – all in a flash of thought which was quickly driven from his mind. For just as Mablung stepped towards the fallen body, there was a new noise. Great crying and shouting. Amidst it Sam heard a shrill bellowing or trumpeting. And then a great thudding and bumping, like huge rams dinning on the ground.

'Ware! Ware!' cried Damrod to his companion. 'May the Valar turn him aside! Mûmak! Mûmak!'

To his astonishment and terror, and lasting delight, Sam saw a vast shape crash out of the trees and come careering down the slope. Big as a house, much bigger than a house, it looked to him, a grey-clad moving hill. Fear and wonder, maybe, enlarged him in the hobbit's eyes, but the Mûmak of Harad was indeed a beast of vast bulk, and the like of him does not walk now in Middle-earth; his kin that live still in latter days are but memories of his girth and majesty. On he came, straight towards the watchers, and then swerved aside in the nick of time, passing only a few yards away, rocking the ground beneath their feet: his great legs like trees, enormous sail-like ears spread out, long snout upraised like a huge serpent about to strike, his small red eyes raging. His upturned hornlike tusks were bound with bands of gold and dripped with blood. His trappings of scarlet and gold flapped about him in wild tatters. The ruins of what seemed a very war-tower lay upon his heaving back, smashed in his furious passage through the woods; and high upon his neck still desperately clung a tiny figure – the body of a mighty warrior, a giant among the Swertings.

On the great beast thundered, blundering in blind wrath through pool and thicket. Arrows skipped and snapped harmlessly about the triple hide of his flanks. Men of both sides fled before him, but many he overtook and crushed to the ground. Soon he was lost to view, still trumpeting and stamping far away. What became of him Sam never heard: whether he escaped to roam the wild for a time, until he perished far from his home or was trapped in some deep pit; or whether he raged on until he plunged in the Great River and was swallowed up.

. Sam drew a deep breath. 'An Oliphaunt it was!' he said. 'So there are Oliphaunts, and I have seen one. What a life! But no one at home will ever believe me. Well, if that's over, I'll have a bit of sleep.'

'Sleep while you may,' said Mablung. 'But the Captain will return, if he is unhurt; and when he comes we shall depart swiftly. We shall be pursued as soon as news of our deed reaches the Enemy, and that will not be long.'

'Go quietly when you must!' said Sam. 'No need to disturb my sleep. I was walking all night.'

Mablung laughed. 'I do not think the Captain will leave you here, Master Samwise,' he said. 'But you shall see.'

CHAPTER V

THE WINDOW ON THE WEST

It seemed to Sam that he had only dozed for a few minutes when he awoke to find that it was late afternoon and Faramir had come back. He had brought many men with him; indeed all the survivors of the foray were now gathered on the slope nearby, two or three hundred strong. They sat in a wide semicircle, between the arms of which Faramir was seated on the ground, while Frodo stood before him. It looked strangely like the trial of a prisoner.

Sam crept out from the fern, but no one paid any attention to him, and he placed himself at the end of the rows of men, where he could see and hear all that was going on. He watched and listened intently, ready to dash to his master's aid if needed. He could see Faramir's face, which was now unmasked: it was stern and commanding, and a keen wit lay behind his searching glance. Doubt was in the grey eyes that gazed steadily at Frodo.

Sam soon became aware that the Captain was not satisfied with Frodo's account of himself at several points: what part he had to play in the Company that set out from Rivendell; why he had left Boromir; and where he was now going. In particular he returned often to Isildur's Bane. Plainly he saw that Frodo was concealing from him some matter of great importance.

'But it was at the coming of the Halfling that Isildur's Bane should waken, or so one must read the words,' he insisted. 'If then you are the Halfling that was named, doubtless you brought this thing, whatever it may be, to the Council of which you speak, and there Boromir saw it. Do you deny it?'

Frodo made no answer. 'So!' said Faramir. 'I wish then to learn from you more of it; for what concerns Boromir concerns me. An orc-arrow slew Isildur, so far as old tales tell. But orc-arrows are plenty, and the sight of one would not be taken as a sign of Doom by Boromir of Gondor. Had you this thing in keeping? It is hidden, you say; but is not that because you choose to hide it?'

'No, not because I choose,' answered Frodo. 'It does not belong to me. It does not belong to any mortal, great or small; though if any could claim it, it would be Aragorn son of Arathorn, whom I named, the leader of our Company from Moria to Rauros.'

'Why so, and not Boromir, prince of the City that the sons of Elendil founded?'

'Because Aragorn is descended in direct lineage, father to father, from

Isildur Elendil's son himself. And the sword that he bears was Elendil's sword.'

A murmur of astonishment ran through all the ring of men. Some cried aloud: 'The sword of Elendil! The sword of Elendil comes to Minas Tirith! Great tidings!' But Faramir's face was unmoved.

'Maybe,' he said. 'But so great a claim will need to be established, and clear proofs will be required, should this Aragorn ever come to Minas Tirith. He had not come, nor any of your Company, when I set out six days ago.'

'Boromir was satisfied of that claim,' said Frodo. 'Indeed, if Boromir were here, he would answer all your questions. And since he was already at Rauros many days back, and intended then to go straight to your city, if you return, you may soon learn the answers there. My part in the Company was known to him, as to all the others, for it was appointed to me by Elrond of Imladris himself before the whole Council. On that errand I came into this country, but it is not mine to reveal to any outside the Company. Yet those who claim to oppose the Enemy would do well not to hinder it.'

Frodo's tone was proud, whatever he felt, and Sam approved of it; but it did not appease Faramir.

'So!' he said. 'You bid me mind my own affairs, and get me back home, and let you be. Boromir will tell all, when he comes. When he comes, say you! Were you a friend of Boromir?'

Vividly before Frodo's mind came the memory of Boromir's assault upon him, and for a moment he hesitated. Faramir's eyes watching him grew harder. 'Boromir was a valiant member of our Company,' said Frodo at length. 'Yes, I was his friend, for my part.'

Faramir smiled grimly. 'Then you would grieve to learn that Boromir is dead?'

'I would grieve indeed,' said Frodo. Then catching the look in Faramir's eyes, he faltered. 'Dead?' he said. 'Do you mean that he is dead, and that you knew it? You have been trying to trap me in words, playing with me? Or are you now trying to snare me with a falsehood?'

'I would not snare even an orc with a falsehood,' said Faramir.

'How then did he die, and how do you know of it? Since you say that none of the Company had reached the city when you left.'

'As to the manner of his death, I had hoped that his friend and companion would tell me how it was.'

'But he was alive and strong when we parted. And he lives still for all that I know. Though surely there are many perils in the world.'

'Many indeed,' said Faramir, 'and treachery not the least.'

Sam had been getting more and more impatient and angry at this conversation. These last words were more than he could bear, and bursting into the middle of the ring, he strode up to his master's side.

'Begging your pardon, Mr. Frodo,' he said, 'but this has gone on long enough. He's no right to talk to you so. After all you've gone through, as much for his good and all these great Men as for anyone else.

'See here, Captain!' He planted himself squarely in front of Faramir, his hands on his hips, and a look on his face as if he was addressing a young hobbit who had offered him what he called 'sauce' when questioned about visits to the orchard. There was some murmuring, but also some grins on the faces of the men looking on: the sight of their Captain sitting on the ground and eye to eye with a young hobbit, legs well apart, bristling with wrath, was one beyond their experience. 'See here!' he said. 'What are you driving at? Let's come to the point before all the Orcs of Mordor come down on us! If you think my master murdered this Boromir and then ran away, you've got no sense; but say it, and have done! And then let us know what you mean to do about it. But it's a pity that folk as talk about fighting the Enemy can't let others do their bit in their own way without interfering. He'd be mighty pleased, if he could see you now. Think he'd got a new friend, he would.'

'Patience!' said Faramir, but without anger. 'Do not speak before your master, whose wit is greater than yours. And I do not need any to teach me of our peril. Even so, I spare a brief time, in order to judge justly in a hard matter. Were I as hasty as you, I might have slain you long ago. For I am commanded to slay all whom I find in this land without the leave of the Lord of Gondor. But I do not slay man or beast needlessly, and not gladly even when it is needed. Neither do I talk in vain. So be comforted. Sit by your master, and be silent!'

Sam sat down heavily with a red face. Faramir turned to Frodo again. 'You asked how do I know that the son of Denethor is dead. Tidings of death have many wings. *Night oft brings news to near kindred*, 'tis said. Boromir was my brother.'

A shadow of sorrow passed over his face. 'Do you remember aught of special mark that the Lord Boromir bore with him among his gear?'

Frodo thought for a moment, fearing some further trap, and wondering how this debate would turn in the end. He had hardly saved the Ring from the proud grasp of Boromir, and how he would fare now among so many men, warlike and strong, he did not know. Yet he felt in his heart that Faramir, though he was much like his brother in looks, was a man less self-regarding, both sterner and wiser. 'I remember that Boromir bore a horn,' he said at last.

'You remember well, and as one who has in truth seen him,' said

Faramir. 'Then maybe you can see it in your mind's eye: a great horn of the wild ox of the East, bound with silver, and written with ancient characters. That horn the eldest son of our house has borne for many generations; and it is said that if it be blown at need anywhere within the bounds of Gondor, as the realm was of old, its voice will not pass unheeded.

'Five days ere I set out on this venture, eleven days ago at about this hour of the day, I heard the blowing of that horn: from the northward it seemed, but dim, as if it were but an echo in the mind. A boding of ill we thought it, my father and I, for no tidings had we heard of Boromir since he went away, and no watcher on our borders had seen him pass. And on the third night after another and a stranger thing befell me.

'I sat at night by the waters of Anduin, in the grey dark under the young pale moon, watching the ever-moving stream; and the sad reeds were rustling. So do we ever watch the shores nigh Osgiliath, which our enemies now partly hold, and issue from it to harry our lands. But that night all the world slept at the midnight hour. Then I saw, or it seemed that I saw, a boat floating on the water, glimmering grey, a small boat of a strange fashion with a high prow, and there was none to row or steer it.

'An awe fell on me, for a pale light was round it. But I rose and went to the bank, and began to walk out into the stream, for I was drawn towards it. Then the boat turned towards me, and stayed its pace, and floated slowly by within my hand's reach, yet I durst not handle it. It waded deep, as if it were heavily burdened, and it seemed to me as it passed under my gaze that it was almost filled with clear water, from which came the light; and lapped in the water a warrior lay asleep.

'A broken sword was on his knee. I saw many wounds on him. It was Boromir, my brother, dead. I knew his gear, his sword, his beloved face. One thing only I missed: his horn. One thing only I knew not: a fair belt, as it were of linked golden leaves, about his waist. *Boromir!* I cried. *Where is thy horn? Whither goest thou? O Boromir!* But he was gone. The boat turned into the stream and passed glimmering on into the night. Dreamlike it was, and yet no dream, for there was no waking. And I do not doubt that he is dead and has passed down the River to the Sea.'

'Alas!' said Frodo. 'That was indeed Boromir as I knew him. For the golden belt was given to him in Lothlórien by the Lady Galadriel. She it was that clothed us as you see us, in elven-grey. This brooch is of the same workmanship.' He touched the green and silver leaf that fastened his cloak beneath his throat.

Faramir looked closely at it. 'It is beautiful,' he said. 'Yes, 'tis work of the same craft. So then you passed through the Land of Lórien? Laurelindó-renan it was named of old, but long now it has lain beyond the knowledge of Men,' he added softly, regarding Frodo with a new wonder in his eyes. 'Much that was strange about you I begin now to understand. Will you not tell me more? For it is a bitter thought that Boromir died, within sight of the land of his home.'

'No more can I say than I have said,' answered Frodo. 'Though your tale fills me with foreboding. A vision it was that you saw, I think, and no more, some shadow of evil fortune that has been or will be. Unless indeed it is some lying trick of the Enemy. I have seen the faces of fair warriors of old laid in sleep beneath the pools of the Dead Marshes, or seeming so by his foul arts.'

'Nay, it was not so,' said Faramir. 'For his works fill the heart with loathing; but my heart was filled with grief and pity.'

'Yet how could such a thing have happened in truth?' asked Frodo. 'For no boat could have been carried over the stony hills from Tol Brandir; and Boromir purposed to go home across the Entwash and the fields of Rohan. And yet how could any vessel ride the foam of the great falls and not founder in the boiling pools, though laden with water?'

'I know not,' said Faramir. 'But whence came the boat?'

'From Lórien,' said Frodo. 'In three such boats we rowed down Anduin to the Falls. They also were of elven-work.'

'You passed through the Hidden Land,' said Faramir, 'but it seems that you little understood its power. If Men have dealings with the Mistress of Magic who dwells in the Golden Wood, then they may look for strange things to follow. For it is perilous for mortal man to walk out of the world of this Sun, and few of old came thence unchanged, 'tis said.

'*Boromir, O Boromir!*' he cried. '*What did she say to you, the Lady that dies not? What did she see? What woke in your heart then? Why went you ever to Laurelindórenan, and came not by your own road, upon the horses of Rohan riding home in the morning?*'

Then turning again to Frodo, he spoke in a quiet voice once more. 'To those questions I guess that you could make some answer, Frodo son of Drogo. But not here or now, maybe. But lest you still should think my tale a vision, I will tell you this. The horn of Boromir at least returned in truth, and not in seeming. The horn came, but it was cloven in two, as it were by axe or sword. The shards came severally to shore: one was found among the reeds where watchers of Gondor lay, northwards below the infalls of the Entwash; the other was found spinning on the flood by one who had an errand on the water. Strange chances, but murder will out, 'tis said.

'And now the horn of the elder son lies in two pieces upon the lap of Denethor, sitting in his high chair, waiting for news. And you can tell me nothing of the cleaving of the horn?'

'No, I did not know of it,' said Frodo. 'But the day when you heard it blowing, if your reckoning is true, was the day when we parted, when I and my servant left the Company. And now your tale fills me with dread. For if Boromir was then in peril and was slain, I must fear that all my companions perished too. And they were my kindred and my friends. 'Will you not put aside your doubt of me and let me go? I am weary, and full of grief, and afraid. But I have a deed to do, or to attempt, before I too am slain. And the more need of haste, if we two halflings are all that remain of our fellowship.

'Go back, Faramir, valiant Captain of Gondor, and defend your city while you may, and let me go where my doom takes me.'

'For me there is no comfort in our speech together,' said Faramir; 'but you surely draw from it more dread than need be. Unless the people of Lórien themselves came to him, who arrayed Boromir as for a funeral? Not Orcs or servants of the Nameless. Some of your Company, I guess, live still.

'But whatever befell on the North March, you, Frodo, I doubt no longer. If hard days have made me any judge of Men's words and faces, then I may make a guess at Halflings! Though,' and now he smiled, 'there is something strange about you, Frodo, an elvish air, maybe. But more lies upon our words together than I thought at first. I should now take you back to Minas Tirith to answer there to Denethor, and my life will justly be forfeit, if I now choose a course that proves ill for my city. So I will not decide in haste what is to be done. Yet we must move hence without more delay.'

He sprang to his feet and issued some orders. At once the men who were gathered round him broke up into small groups, and went off this way and that, vanishing quickly into the shadows of the rocks and trees. Soon only Mablung and Damrod remained.

'Now you, Frodo and Samwise, will come with me and my guards,' said Faramir. 'You cannot go along the road southwards, if that was your purpose. It will be unsafe for some days, and always more closely watched after this affray than it has been yet. And you cannot, I think, go far today in any case, for you are weary. And so are we. We are going now to a secret place we have, somewhat less than ten miles from here. The Orcs and spies of the Enemy have not found it yet, and if they did, we could hold it long even against many. There we may lie up and rest for a while, and you with us. In the morning I will decide what is best for me to do, and for you.'

There was nothing for Frodo to do but to fall in with this request, or order. It seemed in any case a wise course for the moment, since this foray of the men of Gondor had made a journey in Ithilien more dangerous than ever.

They set out at once: Mablung and Damrod a little ahead, and Faramir with Frodo and Sam behind. Skirting the hither side of the pool where the hobbits had bathed, they crossed the stream, climbed a long bank, and passed into green-shadowed woodlands that marched ever downwards and westwards. While they walked, as swiftly as the hobbits could go, they talked in hushed voices.

'I broke off our speech together,' said Faramir, 'not only because time pressed, as Master Samwise had reminded me, but also because we were drawing near to matters that were better not debated openly before many men. It was for that reason that I turned rather to the matter of my brother and let be *Isildur's Bane*. You were not wholly frank with me, Frodo.'

'I told no lies, and of the truth all I could,' said Frodo.

'I do not blame you,' said Faramir. 'You spoke with skill in a hard place, and wisely, it seemed to me. But I learned or guessed more from you than your words said. You were not friendly with Boromir, or you did not part in friendship. You, and Master Samwise, too, I guess have some grievance. Now I loved him dearly, and would gladly avenge his death, yet I knew ·him well. *Isildur's Bane* – I would hazard that *Isildur's Bane* lay between you and was a cause of contention in your Company. Clearly it is a mighty heirloom of some sort, and such things do not breed peace among confederates, not if aught may be learned from ancient tales. Do I not hit near the mark?'

'Near,' said Frodo, 'but not in the gold. There was no contention in our Company, though there was doubt: doubt which way we should take from the Emyn Muil. But be that as it may, ancient tales teach us also the peril of rash words concerning such things as – heirlooms.'

'Ah, then it is as I thought: your trouble was with Boromir alone. He wished this thing brought to Minas Tirith. Alas! it is a crooked fate that seals your lips who saw him last, and holds from me that which I long to know: what was in his heart and thought in his latest hours. Whether he erred or no, of this I am sure: he died well, achieving some good thing. His face was more beautiful even than in life.

'But, Frodo, I pressed you hard at first about *Isildur's Bane*. Forgive me! It was unwise in such an hour and place. I had not had time for thought. We had had a hard fight, and there was more than enough to fill my mind. But even as I spoke with you, I drew nearer to the mark, and so deliberately shot wider. For you must know that much is still preserved of ancient lore among the Rulers of the city that is not spread abroad. We of my house are not of the line of Elendil, though the blood of Númenor is in us. For we reckon back our line to Mardil, the good steward, who ruled in the king's stead when he went away to war. And that was King Eärnur, last of the line of Anárion, and childless, and he came never back. And the stewards have governed the city since that day, though it was many generations of Men ago.

'And this I remember of Boromir as a boy, when we together learned the tale of our sires and the history of our city, that always it displeased him that his father was not king. "How many hundreds of years needs it to make a steward a king, if the king returns not?" he asked. "Few years, maybe, in other places of less royalty," my father answered. "In Gondor ten thousand years would not suffice." Alas! poor Boromir. Does that not tell you something of him?'

'It does,' said Frodo. 'Yet always he treated Aragorn with honour.'

'I doubt it not,' said Faramir. 'If he were satisfied of Aragorn's claim, as you say, he would greatly reverence him. But the pinch had not yet come. They had not yet reached Minas Tirith or become rivals in her wars.

'But I stray. We in the house of Denethor know much ancient lore by long tradition, and there are moreover in our treasuries many things preserved: books and tablets writ on withered parchments, yea, and on stone, and on leaves of silver and of gold, in divers characters. Some none can now read; and for the rest, few ever unlock them. I can read a little in them, for I have had teaching. It was these records that brought the Grey Pilgrim to us. I first saw him when I was a child, and he has been twice or thrice since then.'

'The Grey Pilgrim?' said Frodo. 'Had he a name?'

'Mithrandir we called him in elf-fashion,' said Faramir, 'and he was content. *Many are my names in many countries*, he said. *Mithrandir among the Elves, Tharkûn to the Dwarves; Olórin I was in my youth in the West that is forgotten, in the South Incánus, in the North Gandalf; to the East I go not.*'

'Gandalf!' said Frodo. 'I thought it was he. Gandalf the Grey, dearest of counsellors. Leader of our Company. He was lost in Moria.'

'Mithrandir was lost!' said Faramir. 'An evil fate seems to have pursued your fellowship. It is hard indeed to believe that one of so great wisdom, and of power – for many wonderful things he did among us – could perish, and so much lore be taken from the world. Are you sure of this, and that he did not just leave you and depart where he would?'

'Alas! yes,' said Frodo. 'I saw him fall into the abyss.'

'I see that there is some great tale of dread in this,' said Faramir, 'which perhaps you may tell me in the evening-time. This Mithrandir was, I now guess, more than a lore-master: a great mover of the deeds that are done in our time. Had he been among us to consult concerning the hard words of our dream, he could have made them clear to us without need of messenger. Yet, maybe, he would not have done so, and the journey of Boromir was doomed. Mithrandir never spoke to us of what was to be, nor did he reveal his purposes. He got leave of Denethor, how I do not know, to look at the secrets of our treasury, and I learned a little of him, when he would teach (and that was seldom). Ever he would search and would question us above all else concerning the Great Battle that was fought upon Dagorlad in the beginning of Gondor, when He whom we do not name was overthrown. And he was eager for stories of Isildur, though of him we had less to tell; for nothing certain was ever known among us of his end.'

Now Faramir's voice sank to a whisper. 'But this much I learned, or guessed, and I have kept it ever secret in my heart since: that Isildur took somewhat from the hand of the Unnamed, ere he went away from Gondor, never to be seen among mortal men again. Here I thought was the answer to Mithrandir's questioning. But it seemed then a matter that concerned only the seekers after ancient learning. Nor when the riddling words of our dream were debated among us, did I think of *Isildur's Bane* as being this same thing. For Isildur was ambushed and slain by orc-arrows, according to the only legend that we knew, and Mithrandir had never told me more.

'What in truth this Thing is I cannot yet guess; but some heirloom of power and peril it must be. A fell weapon, perchance, devised by the Dark Lord. If it were a thing that gave advantage in battle, I can well believe that Boromir, the proud and fearless, often rash, ever anxious for the victory of Minas Tirith (and his own glory therein), might desire such a thing and be allured by it. Alas that ever he went on that errand! I should have been chosen by my father and the elders, but he put himself forward, as being the older and the hardier (both true), and he would not be stayed.

'But fear no more! I would not take this thing, if it lay by the highway. Not were Minas Tirith falling in ruin and I alone could save her, so, using the weapon of the Dark Lord for her good and my glory. No, I do not wish for such triumphs, Frodo son of Drogo.'

'Neither did the Council,' said Frodo. 'Nor do I. I would have nothing to do with such matters.'

'For myself,' said Faramir, 'I would see the White Tree in flower again in the courts of the kings, and the Silver Crown return, and Minas Tirith in peace: Minas Anor again as of old, full of light, high and fair, beautiful as a queen among other queens: not a mistress of many slaves, nay, not even a kind mistress of willing slaves. War must be, while we defend our lives against a destroyer who would devour all; but I do not love the bright sword for its sharpness, nor the arrow for its swiftness, nor the warrior for his glory. I love only that which they defend: the city of the Men of Númenor; and I would have her loved for her memory, her ancientry, her beauty, and her present wisdom. Not feared, save as men may fear the dignity of a man, old and wise.

'So fear me not! I do not ask you to tell me more. I do not even ask you to tell me whether I now speak nearer the mark. But if you will trust me, it may be that I can advise you in your present quest, whatever that be – yes, and even aid you.'

Frodo made no answer. Almost he yielded to the desire for help and counsel, to tell this grave young man, whose words seemed so wise and fair, all that was in his mind. But something held him back. His heart was heavy with fear and sorrow: if he and Sam were indeed, as seemed likely, all that was now left of the Nine Walkers, then he was in sole command of the secret of their errand. Better mistrust undeserved than rash words. And the memory of Boromir, of the dreadful change that the lure of the Ring had worked in him, was very present to his mind, when he looked at Faramir and listened to his voice: unlike they were, and yet also much akin.

They walked on in silence for a while, passing like grey and green shadows under the old trees, their feet making no sound; above them many birds sang, and the sun glistened on the polished roof of dark leaves in the evergreen woods of Ithilien.

Sam had taken no part in the conversation, though he had listened; and at the same time he had attended with his keen hobbit ears to all the soft woodland noises about them. One thing he had noted, that in all the talk the name of Gollum had not once come up. He was glad, though he felt that it was too much to hope that he would never hear it again. He soon became aware also that though they walked alone, there were many men close at hand: not only Damrod and Mablung flitting in and out of the shadows ahead, but others on either side, all making their swift secret way to some appointed place.

Once, looking suddenly back, as if some prickle of the skin told him that he was watched from behind, he thought he caught a brief glimpse of a small dark shape slipping behind a tree-trunk. He opened his mouth to speak and shut it again. 'I'm not sure of it,' he said to himself, 'and why should I remind them of the old villain, if they choose to forget him? I wish I could!'

So they passed on, until the woodlands grew thinner and the land began to fall more steeply. Then they turned aside again, to the right, and came quickly to a small river in a narrow gorge: it was the same stream that trickled far above out of the round pool, now grown to a swift torrent, leaping down over many stones in a deep-cloven bed, overhung with ilex and dark box-woods. Looking west they could see, below them in a haze of light, lowlands and broad meads, and glinting far off in the westering sun the wide waters of the Anduin.

'Here, alas! I must do you a discourtesy,' said Faramir. 'I hope you will pardon it to one who has so far made his orders give way to courtesy as not to slay you or to bind you. But it is a command that no stranger, not even one of Rohan that fights with us, shall see the path we now go with open eyes. I must blindfold you.'

'As you will,' said Frodo. 'Even the Elves do likewise at need, and blindfolded we crossed the borders of fair Lothlórien. Gimli the dwarf took it ill, but the hobbits endured it.'

'It is to no place so fair that I shall lead you,' said Faramir. 'But I am glad that you will take this willingly and not by force.'

He called softly and immediately Mablung and Damrod stepped out of the trees and came back to him. 'Blindfold these guests,' said Faramir. 'Securely, but not so as to discomfort them. Do not tie their hands. They will give their word not to try and see. I could trust them to shut their eyes of their own accord, but eyes will blink, if the feet stumble. Lead them so that they do not falter.'

With green scarves the two guards now bound up the hobbits' eyes, and drew their hoods down almost to their mouths; then quickly they took each one by the hand and went on their way. All that Frodo and Sam knew of this last mile of the road they learned from guessing in the dark. After a little they found that they were on a path descending steeply; soon it grew so narrow that they went in single file, brushing a stony wall on either side; their guards steered them from behind with hands laid firmly on their shoulders. Now and again they came to rough places and were lifted from their feet for a while, and then set down again. Always the noise of the running water was on their right hand, and it grew nearer and louder. At length they were halted. Quickly Mablung and Damrod turned them about, several times, and they lost all sense of direction. They climbed upwards a little: it seemed cold and the noise of the stream had become faint. Then they were picked up and carried down, down many steps, and round a corner. Suddenly they heard the water again, loud now, rushing and splashing. All round them it seemed, and they felt a fine rain on their hands and cheeks. At last they were set on their feet once more. For a moment they stood so, half fearful, blindfold, not knowing where they were; and no one spoke.

Then came the voice of Faramir close behind. 'Let them see!' he said. The scarves were removed and their hoods drawn back, and they blinked and gasped.

They stood on a wet floor of polished stone, the doorstep, as it were, of a rough-hewn gate of rock opening dark behind them. But in front a thin veil of water was hung, so near that Frodo could have put an outstretched arm into it. It faced westward. The level shafts of the setting sun behind beat upon it, and the red light was broken into many flickering beams of ever-changing colour. It was as if they stood at the window of some elven-tower, curtained with threaded jewels of silver and gold, and ruby, sapphire and amethyst, all kindled with an unconsuming fire.

'At least by good chance we came at the right hour to reward you for your patience,' said Faramir. 'This is the Window of the Sunset, Henneth Annûn, fairest of all the falls of Ithilien, land of many fountains. Few strangers have ever seen it. But there is no kingly hall behind to match it. Enter now and see!'

Even as he spoke the sun sank, and the fire faded in the flowing water. They turned and passed under the low forbidding arch. At once they found themselves in a rock-chamber, wide and rough, with an uneven stooping roof. A few torches were kindled and cast a dim light on the glistening walls. Many men were already there. Others were still coming in by twos and threes through a dark narrow door on one side. As their eyes grew accustomed to the gloom the hobbits saw that the cave was larger than they had guessed and was filled with great store of arms and victuals.

'Well, here is our refuge,' said Faramir. 'Not a place of great ease, but here you may pass the night in peace. It is dry at least, and there is food, though no fire. At one time the water flowed down through this cave and out of the arch, but its course was changed further up the gorge, by workmen of old, and the stream sent down in a fall of doubled height over the rocks far above. All the ways into this grot were then sealed against the entry of water or aught else, all save one. There are now but two ways out: that passage yonder by which you entered blindfold, and through the Window-curtain into a deep bowl filled with knives of stone. Now rest a while, until the evening meal is set.'

The hobbits were taken to a corner and given a low bed to lie on, if they wished. Meanwhile men busied themselves about the cave, quietly and in orderly quickness. Light tables were taken from the walls and set up on trestles and laden with gear. This was plain and unadorned for the most part, but all well and fairly made: round platters, bowls and dishes of glazed brown clay or turned box-wood, smooth and clean. Here and there was a cup or basin of polished bronze; and a goblet of plain silver was set by the Captain's seat in the middle of the inmost table.

Faramir went about among the men, questioning each as he came in, in a soft voice. Some came back from the pursuit of the Southrons; others, left behind as scouts near the road, came in latest. All the Southrons had been accounted for, save only the great mûmak: what happened to him none could say. Of the enemy no movement could be seen; not even an orc-spy was abroad.

'You saw and heard nothing, Anborn?' Faramir asked of the latest comer. 'Well, no, lord,' said the man. 'No Orc at least. But I saw, or thought I saw, something a little strange. It was getting deep dusk, when the eyes make things greater than they should be. So perhaps it may have been no more than a squirrel.' Sam pricked up his ears at this. 'Yet if so, it was a black squirrel, and I saw no tail. 'Twas like a shadow on the ground, and it whisked behind a tree-trunk when I drew nigh and went up aloft as swift as any squirrel could. You will not have us slay wild beasts for no purpose, and it seemed no more, so I tried no arrow. It was too dark for sure shooting anyway, and the creature was gone into the gloom of the leaves in a twinkling. But I stayed for a while, for it seemed strange, and then I hastened back. I thought I heard the thing hiss at me from high above as I turned away. A large squirrel, maybe. Perhaps under the shadow of the Unnamed some of the beasts of Mirkwood are wandering hither to our woods. They have black squirrels there, 'tis said.'

'Perhaps,' said Faramir. 'But that would be an ill omen, if it were so. We do not want the escapes of Mirkwood in Ithilien.' Sam fancied that he gave a swift glance towards the hobbits as he spoke; but Sam said nothing. For a while he and Frodo lay back and watched the torchlight, and the men moving to and fro speaking in hushed voices. Then suddenly Frodo fell asleep.

Sam struggled with himself, arguing this way and that. 'He may be all right,' he thought, 'and then he may not. Fair speech may hide a foul heart.' He yawned. 'I could sleep for a week, and I'd be better for it. And what can I do, if I do keep awake, me all alone, and all these great Men about? Nothing, Sam Gamgee; but you've got to keep awake all the same.' And somehow he managed it. The light faded from the cave door, and the grey veil of falling water grew dim and was lost in gathering shadow. Always the sound of the water went on, never changing its note, morning or evening or night. It murmured and whispered of sleep. Sam stuck his knuckles in his eyes.

Now more torches were being lit. A cask of wine was broached. Storage barrels were being opened. Men were fetching water from the fall. Some were laving their hands in basins. A wide copper bowl and a white cloth were brought to Faramir and he washed.

'Wake our guests,' he said, 'and take them water. It is time to eat.'

Frodo sat up and yawned and stretched. Sam, not used to being waited on, looked with some surprise at the tall man who bowed, holding a basin of water before him.

'Put it on the ground, master, if you please!' he said. 'Easier for me and you.' Then to the astonishment and amusement of the Men he plunged his head into the cold water and splashed his neck and ears.

'Is it the custom in your land to wash the head before supper?' said the man who waited on the hobbits.

'No, before breakfast,' said Sam. 'But if you're short of sleep cold water on the neck's like rain on a wilted lettuce. There! Now I can keep awake long enough to eat a bit.'

They were led then to seats beside Faramir: barrels covered with pelts and high enough above the benches of the Men for their convenience. Before they ate, Faramir and all his men turned and faced west in a moment of silence. Faramir signed to Frodo and Sam that they should do likewise.

'So we always do,' he said, as they sat down: 'we look towards Númenor that was, and beyond to Elvenhome that is, and to that which is beyond Elvenhome and will ever be. Have you no such custom at meat?'

'No,' said Frodo, feeling strangely rustic and untutored. 'But if we are guests, we bow to our host, and after we have eaten we rise and thank him.'

'That we do also,' said Faramir.

After so long journeying and camping, and days spent in the lonely wild, the evening meal seemed a feast to the hobbits: to drink pale yellow wine, cool and fragrant, and eat bread and butter, and salted meats, and dried fruits, and good red cheese, with clean hands and clean knives and plates. Neither Frodo nor Sam refused anything that was offered, nor a second, nor indeed a third helping. The wine coursed in their veins and tired limbs, and they felt glad and easy of heart as they had not done since they left the land of Lórien.

When all was done Faramir led them to a recess at the back of the cave, partly screened by curtains; and a chair and two stools were brought there. A little earthenware lamp burned in a niche.

'You may soon desire to sleep,' he said, 'and especially good Samwise, who would not close his eyes before he ate – whether for fear of blunting the edge of a noble hunger, or for fear of me, I do not know. But it is not good to sleep too soon after meat, and that following a fast. Let us talk a while. On your journey from Rivendell there must have been many things to tell. And you, too, would perhaps wish to learn something of us and the lands where you now are. Tell me of Boromir my brother, and of old Mithrandir, and of the fair people of Lothlórien.'

Frodo no longer felt sleepy and he was willing to talk. But though the food and wine had put him at his ease, he had not lost all his caution. Sam was beaming and humming to himself, but when Frodo spoke he was at first content to listen, only occasionally venturing to make an exclamation of agreement.

Frodo told many tales, yet always he steered the matter away from the quest of the Company and from the Ring, enlarging rather on the valiant part Boromir had played in all their adventures, with the wolves of the wild, in the snows under Caradhras, and in the mines of Moria where Gandalf fell. Faramir was most moved by the story of the fight on the bridge.

'It must have irked Boromir to run from Orcs,' he said, 'or even from the fell thing you name, the Balrog – even though he was the last to leave.'

'He was the last,' said Frodo, 'but Aragorn was forced to lead us. He alone knew the way after Gandalf's fall. But had there not been us lesser folk to care for, I do not think that either he or Boromir would have fled.'

'Maybe, it would have been better had Boromir fallen there with Mithrandir,' said Faramir, 'and not gone on to the fate that waited above the falls of Rauros.'

'Maybe. But tell me now of your own fortunes,' said Frodo, turning the matter aside once again. 'For I would learn more of Minas Ithil and Osgiliath, and Minas Tirith the long-enduring. What hope have you for that city in your long war?'

'What hope have we?' said Faramir. 'It is long since we had any hope. The sword of Elendil, if it returns indeed, may rekindle it, but I do not think that it will do more than put off the evil day, unless other help unlooked-for also comes, from Elves or Men. For the Enemy increases and we decrease. We are a failing people, a springless autumn.

'The Men of Númenor were settled far and wide on the shores and seaward regions of the Great Lands, but for the most part they fell into evils and follies. Many became enamoured of the Darkness and the black arts; some were given over wholly to idleness and ease, and some fought among themselves, until they were conquered in their weakness by the wild men.

'It is not said that evil arts were ever practised in Gondor, or that the Nameless One was ever named in honour there; and the old wisdom and beauty brought out of the West remained long in the realm of the sons of Elendil the Fair, and they linger there still. Yet even so it was Gondor that brought about its own decay, falling by degrees into dotage, and thinking that the Enemy was asleep, who was only banished not destroyed.

'Death was ever present, because the Númenoreans still, as they had in their old kingdom, and so lost it, hungered after endless life unchanging. Kings made tombs more splendid than houses of the living, and counted old names in the rolls of their descent dearer than the names of sons. Childless lords sat in aged halls musing on heraldry; in secret chambers withered men compounded strong elixirs, or in high cold towers asked questions of the stars. And the last king of the line of Anárion had no heir.

'But the stewards were wiser and more fortunate. Wiser, for they recruited the strength of our people from the sturdy folk of the sea-coast, and from the hardy mountaineers of Ered Nimrais. And they made a truce with the proud peoples of the North, who often had assailed us, men of fierce valour, but our kin from afar off, unlike the wild Easterlings or the cruel Haradrim.

'So it came to pass in the days of Cirion the Twelfth Steward (and my father is the six and twentieth) that they rode to our aid and at the great Field of Celebrant they destroyed our enemies that had seized our northern provinces. These are the Rohirrim, as we name them, masters of horses, and we ceded to them the fields of Calenardhon that are since called Rohan; for that province had long been sparsely peopled. And they became our allies, and have ever proved true to us, aiding us at need, and guarding our northern marches and the Gap of Rohan.

'Of our lore and manners they have learned what they would, and their lords speak our speech at need; yet for the most part they hold by the ways of their own fathers and to their own memories, and they speak among themselves their own North tongue. And we love them: tall men and fair women, valiant both alike, golden-haired, bright-eyed, and strong; they remind us of the youth of Men, as they were in the Elder Days. Indeed it is said by our lore-masters that they have from of old this affinity with us that they are come from those same Three Houses of Men as were the Númenoreans in their beginning; not from Hador the Goldenhaired, the Elf-friend, maybe, yet from such of his sons and people as went not over Sea into the West, refusing the call.

'For so we reckon Men in our lore, calling them the High, or Men of the West, which were Númenoreans; and the Middle Peoples, Men of the Twilight, such as are the Rohirrim and their kin that dwell still far in the North; and the Wild, the Men of Darkness.

'Yet now, if the Rohirrim are grown in some ways more like to us, enhanced in arts and gentleness, we too have become more like to them, and can scarce claim any longer the title High. We are become Middle Men, of the Twilight, but with memory of other things. For as the Rohirrim do, we now love war and valour as things good in themselves, both a sport and an end; and though we still hold that a warrior should have more skills and knowledge than only the craft of weapons and slaying, we esteem a warrior, nonetheless, above men of other crafts. Such is the need of our days. So even was my brother, Boromir: a man of prowess, and for that he was accounted the best man in Gondor. And very valiant indeed he was: no heir of Minas Tirith has for long years been so hardy in toil, so onward into battle, or blown a mightier note on the Great Horn.' Faramir sighed and fell silent for a while.

'You don't say much in all your tales about the Elves, sir,' said Sam, suddenly plucking up courage. He had noted that Faramir seemed to refer to Elves with reverence, and this even more than his courtesy, and his food and wine, had won Sam's respect and quieted his suspicions.

'No indeed, Master Samwise,' said Faramir, 'for I am not learned in Elven-lore. But there you touch upon another point in which we have changed, declining from Númenor to Middle-earth. For as you may know, if Mithrandir was your companion and you have spoken with Elrond, the Edain, the Fathers of the Númenoreans, fought beside the Elves in the first wars, and were rewarded by the gift of the kingdom in the midst of the Sea, within sight of Elvenhome. But in Middle-earth Men and Elves became estranged in the days of darkness, by the arts of the Enemy, and by the slow changes of time in which each kind walked further down their sundered roads. Men now fear and misdoubt the Elves, and yet know little of them. And we of Gondor grow like other Men, like the men of Rohan; for even they, who are foes of the Dark Lord, shun the Elves and speak of the Golden Wood with dread.

'Yet there are among us still some who have dealings with the Elves when they may, and ever and anon one will go in secret to Lórien, seldom to return. Not I. For I deem it perilous now for mortal man wilfully to seek out the Elder People. Yet I envy you that have spoken with the White Lady.'

'The Lady of Lórien! Galadriel!' cried Sam. 'You should see her, indeed you should, sir. I am only a hobbit, and gardening's my job at home, sir, if you understand me, and I'm not much good at poetry – not at making it: a bit of a comic rhyme, perhaps, now and again, you know, but not real poetry – so I can't tell you what I mean. It ought to be sung. You'd have to get Strider, Aragorn that is, or old Mr. Bilbo, for that. But I wish I could make a song about her. Beautiful she is, sir! Lovely! Sometimes like a great tree in flower, sometimes like a white daffadowndilly, small and slender like. Hard as di'monds, soft as moonlight. Warm as sunlight, cold as frost in the stars. Proud and far-off as a snow-mountain, and as merry as any lass I ever saw with daisies in her hair in springtime. But that's a lot o' nonsense, and all wide of my mark.'

'Then she must be lovely indeed,' said Faramir. 'Perilously fair.'

'I don't know about *perilous*,' said Sam. 'It strikes me that folk takes their peril with them into Lórien, and finds it there because they've brought it. But perhaps you could call her perilous, because she's so strong in herself. You, you could dash yourself to pieces on her, like a ship on a rock; or drownd yourself, like a hobbit in a river. But neither rock nor river would be to blame. Now Boro———' He stopped and went red in the face.

'Yes? *Now Boromir* you would say?' said Faramir. 'What would you say? He took his peril with him?'

'Yes sir, begging your pardon, and a fine man as your brother was, if I may say so. But you've been warm on the scent all along. Now I watched Boromir and listened to him, from Rivendell all down the road – looking after my master, as you'll understand, and not meaning any harm to Boromir – and it's my opinion that in Lórien he first saw clearly what I guessed sooner: what he wanted. From the moment he first saw it he wanted the Enemy's Ring!'

'Sam!' cried Frodo aghast. He had fallen deep into his own thoughts for a while, and came out of them suddenly and too late.

'Save me!' said Sam turning white, and then flushing scarlet. 'There I go again! *When ever you open your big mouth you put your foot in it* the Gaffer used to say to me, and right enough. O dear, O dear!

'Now look here, sir!' He turned, facing up to Faramir with all the courage that he could muster. 'Don't you go taking advantage of my master because his servant's no better than a fool. You've spoken very handsome all along, put me off my guard, talking of Elves and all. But *handsome is as handsome does* we say. Now's a chance to show your quality.'

'So it seems,' said Faramir, slowly and very softly, with a strange smile. 'So that is the answer to all the riddles! The One Ring that was thought to have perished from the world. And Boromir tried to take it by force? And you escaped? And ran all the way – to me! And here in the wild I have you: two halflings, and a host of men at my call, and the Ring of Rings. A pretty stroke of fortune! A chance for Faramir, Captain of Gondor, to show his quality! Ha!' He stood up, very tall and stern, his grey eyes glinting.

Frodo and Sam sprang from their stools and set themselves side by side with their backs to the wall, fumbling for their sword-hilts. There was a silence. All the men in the cave stopped talking and looked towards them in wonder. But Faramir sat down again in his chair and began to laugh quietly, and then suddenly became grave again.

'Alas for Boromir! It was too sore a trial!' he said. 'How you have increased my sorrow, you two strange wanderers from a far country, bearing the peril of Men! But you are less judges of Men than I of Halflings. We are truth-speakers, we men of Gondor. We boast seldom, and then perform, or die in the attempt. *Not if I found it on the highway would I take it* I said. Even if I were such a man as to desire this thing, and even though I knew not clearly what this thing was when I spoke, still I should take those words as a vow, and be held by them.

'But I am not such a man. Or I am wise enough to know that there are some perils from which a man must flee. Sit at peace! And be comforted, Samwise. If you seem to have stumbled, think that it was fated to be so. Your heart is shrewd as well as faithful, and saw clearer than your eyes. For strange though it may seem, it was safe to declare this to me. It may even help the master that you love. It shall turn to his good, if it is in my power. So be comforted. But do not even name this thing again aloud. Once is enough.'

The hobbits came back to their seats and sat very quiet. Men turned back to their drink and their talk, perceiving that their captain had had some jest or other with the little guests, and that it was over.

'Well, Frodo, now at last we understand one another,' said Faramir. 'If you took this thing on yourself, unwilling, at others' asking, then you have pity and honour from me. And I marvel at you: to keep it hid and not to use it. You are a new people and a new world to me. Are all your kin of like sort? Your land must be a realm of peace and content, and there must gardeners be in high honour.'

'Not all is well there,' said Frodo, 'but certainly gardeners are honoured.'

'But folk must grow weary there, even in their gardens, as do all things under the Sun of this world. And you are far from home and wayworn. No more tonight. Sleep, both of you – in peace, if you can. Fear not! I do not wish to see it, or touch it, or know more of it than I know (which is enough), lest peril perchance waylay me and I fall lower in the test than Frodo son of Drogo. Go now to rest – but first tell me only, if you will, whither you wish to go, and what to do. For I must watch, and wait, and think. Time passes. In the morning we must each go swiftly on the ways appointed to us.'

Frodo had felt himself trembling as the first shock of fear passed. Now a great weariness came down on him like a cloud. He could dissemble and resist no longer.

'I was going to find a way into Mordor,' he said faintly. 'I was going to Gorgoroth. I must find the Mountain of Fire and cast the thing into the gulf of Doom. Gandalf said so. I do not think I shall ever get there.'

Faramir stared at him for a moment in grave astonishment. Then suddenly he caught him as he swayed, and lifting him gently, carried him to the bed and laid him there, and covered him warmly. At once he fell into a deep sleep.

Another bed was set beside him for his servant. Sam hesitated for a moment, then bowing very low: 'Good night, Captain, my lord,' he said. 'You took the chance, sir.'

'Did I so?' said Faramir.

'Yes sir, and showed your quality: the very highest.'

Faramir smiled. 'A pert servant, Master Samwise. But nay: the praise of the praiseworthy is above all rewards. Yet there was naught in this to praise. I had no lure or desire to do other than I have done.'

'Ah well, sir,' said Sam, 'you said my master had an elvish air; and that was good and true. But I can say this: you have an air too, sir, that reminds me of, of – well, Gandalf, of wizards.'

'Maybe,' said Faramir. 'Maybe you discern from far away the air of Númenor. Good night!'

CHAPTER VI

THE FORBIDDEN POOL

Frodo woke to find Faramir bending over him. For a second old fears seized him and he sat up and shrank away.

'There is nothing to fear,' said Faramir.

'Is it morning already?' said Frodo yawning.

'Not yet, but night is drawing to an end, and the full moon is setting. Will you come and see it? Also there is a matter on which I desire your counsel. I am sorry to rouse you from sleep, but will you come?'

'I will,' said Frodo, rising and shivering a little as he left the warm blanket and pelts. It seemed cold in the fireless cave. The noise of the water was loud in the stillness. He put on his cloak and followed Faramir.

Sam, waking suddenly by some instinct of watchfulness, saw first his master's empty bed and leapt to his feet. Then he saw two dark figures, Frodo and a man, framed against the archway, which was now filled with a pale white light. He hurried after them, past rows of men sleeping on mattresses along the wall. As he went by the cave-mouth he saw that the Curtain was now become a dazzling veil of silk and pearls and silver thread: melting icicles of moonlight. But he did not pause to admire it, and turning aside he followed his master through the narrow doorway in the wall of the cave.

They went first along a black passage, then up many wet steps, and so came to a small flat landing cut in the stone and lit by the pale sky, gleaming high above through a long deep shaft. From here two flights of steps led: one going on, as it seemed, up on to the high bank of the stream; the other turning away to the left. This they followed. It wound its way up like a turret-stair.

At last they came out of the stony darkness and looked about. They were on a wide flat rock without rail or parapet. At their right, eastwards, the torrent fell, splashing over many terraces, and then, pouring down a steep race, it filled a smooth-hewn channel with a dark force of water flecked with foam, and curling and rushing almost at their feet it plunged sheer over the edge that yawned upon their left. A man stood there, near the brink, silent, gazing down.

Frodo turned to watch the sleek necks of the water as they curved and dived. Then he lifted his eyes and gazed far away. The world was quiet and cold, as if dawn were near. Far off in the West the full moon was sinking, round and white. Pale mists shimmered in the great vale below: a wide gulf of silver fume, beneath which rolled the cool night-waters of the Anduin. A black darkness loomed beyond, and in it glinted, here and there, cold, sharp, remote, white as the teeth of ghosts, the peaks of Ered Nimrais, the White Mountains of the realm of Gondor, tipped with everlasting snow.

For a while Frodo stood there on the high stone, and a shiver ran through him, wondering if anywhere in the vastness of the nightlands his old companions walked or slept, or lay dead shrouded in mist. Why was he brought here out of forgetful sleep?

Sam was eager for an answer to the same question and could not refrain himself from muttering, for his master's ear alone as he thought: 'It's a fine view, no doubt, Mr. Frodo, but chilly to the heart, not to mention the bones! What's going on?'

Faramir heard and answered. 'Moonset over Gondor. Fair Ithil, as he goes from Middle-earth, glances upon the white locks of old Mindolluin. It is worth a few shivers. But that is not what I brought you to see – though as for you, Samwise, you were not brought, and do but pay the penalty of your watchfulness. A draught of wine shall amend it. Come, look now!'

He stepped up beside the silent sentinel on the dark edge, and Frodo followed. Sam hung back. He already felt insecure enough on this high wet platform. Faramir and Frodo looked down. Far below them they saw the white waters pour into a foaming bowl, and then swirl darkly about a deep oval basin in the rocks, until they found their way out again through a narrow gate, and flowed away, fuming and chattering, into calmer and more level reaches. The moonlight still slanted down to the fall's foot and gleamed on the ripples of the basin. Presently Frodo was aware of a small dark thing on the near bank, but even as he looked at it, it dived and vanished just beyond the boil and bubble of the fall, cleaving the black water as neatly as an arrow or an edgewise stone.

Faramir turned to the man at his side. 'Now what would you say that it is, Anborn? A squirrel, or a kingfisher? Are there black kingfishers in the night-pools of Mirkwood?'

''Tis not a bird, whatever else it be,' answered Anborn. 'It has four limbs and dives manwise; a pretty mastery of the craft it shows, too. What is it at? Seeking a way up behind the Curtain to our hidings? It seems we are discovered at last. I have my bow here, and I have posted other archers, nigh as good marksmen as myself, on either bank. We wait only for your command to shoot, Captain.'

'Shall we shoot?' said Faramir, turning quickly to Frodo.

Frodo did not answer for a moment. Then 'No!' he said. 'No! I beg you not to.' If Sam had dared, he would have said 'Yes,' quicker and louder.

He could not see, but he guessed well enough from their words what they were looking at.

'You know, then, what this thing is?' said Faramir. 'Come, now you have seen, tell me why it should be spared. In all our words together you have not once spoken of your gangrel companion, and I let him be for the time. He could wait till he was caught and brought before me. I sent my keenest huntsmen to seek him, but he slipped them, and they had no sight of him till now, save Anborn here, once at dusk yesterevening. But now he has done worse trespass than only to go coney-snaring in the uplands: he has dared to come to Henneth Annûn, and his life is forfeit. I marvel at the creature: so secret and so sly as he is, to come sporting in the pool before our very window. Does he think that men sleep without watch all night? Why does he so?'

'There are two answers, I think,' said Frodo. 'For one thing, he knows little of Men, and sly though he is, your refuge is so hidden that perhaps he does not know that Men are concealed here. For another, I think he is allured here by a mastering desire, stronger than his caution.'

'He is lured here, you say?' said Faramir in a low voice. 'Can he, does he then know of your burden?'

'Indeed yes. He bore it himself for many years.'

'*He* bore it?' said Faramir, breathing sharply in his wonder. 'This matter winds itself ever in new riddles. Then he is pursuing it?'

'Maybe. It is precious to him. But I did not speak of that.'

'What then does the creature seek?'

'Fish,' said Frodo. 'Look!'

They peered down at the dark pool. A little black head appeared at the far end of the basin, just out of the deep shadow of the rocks. There was a brief silver glint, and a swirl of tiny ripples. It swam to the side, and then with marvellous agility a froglike figure climbed out of the water and up the bank. At once it sat down and began to gnaw at the small silver thing that glittered as it turned: the last rays of the moon were now falling behind the stony wall at the pool's end.

Faramir laughed softly. 'Fish!' he said. 'It is a less perilous hunger. Or maybe not: fish from the pool of Henneth Annûn may cost him all he has to give.'

'Now I have him at the arrow-point,' said Anborn. 'Shall I not shoot, Captain? For coming unbidden to this place death is our law.'

'Wait, Anborn,' said Faramir. 'This is a harder matter than it seems. What have you to say now, Frodo? Why should we spare?'

'The creature is wretched and hungry,' said Frodo, 'and unaware of his danger. And Gandalf, your Mithrandir, he would have bidden you not to slay him for that reason, and for others. He forbade the Elves to do so. I do not know clearly why, and of what I guess I cannot speak openly out here. But this creature is in some way bound up with my errand. Until you found us and took us, he was my guide.'

'Your guide!' said Faramir. 'The matter becomes ever stranger. I would do much for you, Frodo, but this I cannot grant: to let this sly wanderer go free at his own will from here, to join you later if it please him, or to be caught by orcs and tell all he knows under threat of pain. He must be slain or taken. Slain, if he be not taken very swiftly. But how can this slippery thing of many guises be caught, save by a feathered shaft?'

'Let me go down quietly to him,' said Frodo. 'You may keep your bows bent, and shoot me at least, if I fail. I shall not run away.'

'Go then and be swift!' said Faramir. 'If he comes off alive, he should be your faithful servant for the rest of his unhappy days. Lead Frodo down to the bank, Anborn, and go softly. The thing has a nose and ears. Give me your bow.'

Anborn grunted and led the way down the winding stair to the landing, and then up the other stair, until at last they came to a narrow opening shrouded with thick bushes. Passing silently through, Frodo found himself on the top of the southern bank above the pool. It was now dark and the falls were pale and grey, reflecting only the lingering moonlight of the western sky. He could not see Gollum. He went forward a short way and Anborn came softly behind him.

'Go on!' he breathed in Frodo's ear. 'Have a care to your right. If you fall in the pool, then no one but your fishing friend can help you. And forget not that there are bowmen near at hand, though you may not see them.'

Frodo crept forward, using his hands Gollum-like to feel his way and to steady himself. The rocks were for the most part flat and smooth but slippery. He halted listening. At first he could hear no sound but the unceasing rush of the fall behind him. Then presently he heard, not far ahead, a hissing murmur.

'Fissh, nice fissh. White Face has vanished, my precious, at last, yes. Now we can eat fish in peace. No, not in peace, precious. For Precious is lost; yes, lost. Dirty hobbits, nasty hobbits. Gone and left us, *gollum*; and Precious is gone. Only poor Sméagol all alone. No Precious. Nasty Men, they'll take it, steal my Precious. Thieves. We hates them. Fissh, nice fissh. Makes us strong. Makes eyes bright, fingers tight, yes. Throttle them, precious. Throttle them all, yes, if we gets chances. Nice fissh. Nice fissh!'

So it went on, almost as unceasing as the waterfall, only interrupted by a faint noise of slavering and gurgling. Frodo shivered, listening with pity and disgust. He wished it would stop, and that he never need hear that voice again. Anborn was not far behind. He could creep back and ask him to get the huntsmen to shoot. They would probably get close enough, while Gollum was gorging and off his guard. Only one true shot, and Frodo would be rid of the miserable voice for ever. But no, Gollum had a claim on him now. The servant has a claim on the master for service, even service in fear. They would have foundered in the Dead Marshes but for Gollum. Frodo knew, too, somehow, quite clearly that Gandalf would not have wished it.

'Sméagol!' he said softly.

'Fissh, nice fissh,' said the voice.

'Sméagol!' he said, a little louder. The voice stopped.

'Sméagol, Master has come to look for you. Master is here. Come, Sméagol!' There was no answer but a soft hiss, as of intaken breath.

'Come, Sméagol!' said Frodo. 'We are in danger. Men will kill you, if they find you here. Come quickly, if you wish to escape death. Come to Master!'

'No!' said the voice. 'Not nice Master. Leaves poor Sméagol and goes with new friends. Master can wait. Sméagol hasn't finished.'

'There's no time,' said Frodo. 'Bring fish with you. Come!'

'No! Must finish fish.'

'Sméagol!' said Frodo desperately. 'Precious will be angry. I shall take Precious, and I shall say: make him swallow the bones and choke. Never taste fish again. Come, Precious is waiting!'

There was a sharp hiss. Presently out of the darkness Gollum came crawling on all fours, like an erring dog called to heel. He had a half-eaten fish in his mouth and another in his hand. He came close to Frodo, almost nose to nose, and sniffed at him. His pale eyes were shining. Then he took the fish out of his mouth and stood up.

'Nice Master!' he whispered. 'Nice hobbit, come back to poor Sméagol. Good Sméagol comes. Now let's go, go quickly, yes. Through the trees, while the Faces are dark. Yes, come, let's go!'

'Yes, we'll go soon,' said Frodo. 'But not at once. I will go with you as I promised. I promise again. But not now. You are not safe yet. I will save you, but you must trust me.'

'We must trust Master?' said Gollum doubtfully. 'Why? Why not go at once? Where is the other one, the cross rude hobbit? Where is he?'

'Away up there,' said Frodo, pointing to the waterfall. 'I am not going without him. We must go back to him.' His heart sank. This was too much like trickery. He did not really fear that Faramir would allow Gollum to be killed, but he would probably make him prisoner and bind him; and certainly what Frodo did would seem a treachery to the poor treacherous creature. It would probably be impossible ever to make him understand or believe that Frodo had saved his life in the only way he could. What else could he do? – to keep faith, as near as might be, with both sides. 'Come!' he said. 'Or the Precious will be angry. We are going back now, up the stream. Go on, go on, you go in front!'

Gollum crawled along close to the brink for a little way, snuffling and suspicious. Presently he stopped and raised his head. 'Something's there!' he said. 'Not a hobbit.' Suddenly he turned back. A green light was flickering in his bulging eyes. 'Masster, masster!' he hissed. 'Wicked! Tricksy! False!' He spat and stretched out his long arms with white snapping fingers.

At that moment the great black shape of Anborn loomed up behind him and came down on him. A large strong hand took him in the nape of the neck and pinned him. He twisted round like lightning, all wet and slimy as he was, wriggling like an eel, biting and scratching like a cat. But two more men came up out of the shadows.

'Hold still!' said one. 'Or we'll stick you as full of pins as a hedgehog. Hold still!'

Gollum went limp, and began to whine and weep. They tied him, none too gently.

'Easy, easy!' said Frodo. 'He has no strength to match you. Don't hurt him, if you can help it. He'll be quieter, if you don't. Sméagol! They won't hurt you. I'll go with you, and you shall come to no harm. Not unless they kill me too. Trust Master!'

Gollum turned and spat at him. The men picked him up, put a hood over his eyes, and carried him off.

Frodo followed them, feeling very wretched. They went through the opening behind the bushes, and back, down the stairs and passages, into the cave. Two or three torches had been lit. Men were stirring. Sam was there, and he gave a queer look at the limp bundle that the men carried. 'Got him?' he said to Frodo.

'Yes. Well no, I didn't get him. He came to me, because he trusted me at first, I'm afraid. I did not want him tied up like this. I hope it will be all right; but I hate the whole business.'

'So do I,' said Sam. 'And nothing will ever be all right where that piece of misery is.'

A man came and beckoned to the hobbits, and took them to the recess at the back of the cave. Faramir was sitting there in his chair, and the lamp had been rekindled in its niche above his head. He signed to them to sit down on the stools beside him. 'Bring wine for the guests,' he said. 'And bring the prisoner to me.'

The wine was brought, and then Anborn came carrying Gollum. He removed the cover from Gollum's head and set him on his feet, standing

behind him to support him. Gollum blinked, hooding the malice of his
eyes with their heavy pale lids. A very miserable creature he looked, dripping and dank, smelling of fish (he still clutched one in his hand); his
sparse locks were hanging like rank weed over his bony brows, his nose
was snivelling.

'Loose us! Loose us!' he said. 'The cord hurts us, yes it does, it hurts
us, and we've done nothing.'

'Nothing?' said Faramir, looking at the wretched creature with a keen
glance, but without any expression in his face either of anger, or pity, or
wonder. 'Nothing? Have you never done anything worthy of binding or of
worse punishment? However, that is not for me to judge, happily. But
tonight you have come where it is death to come. The fish of this pool are
dearly bought.'

Gollum dropped the fish from his hand. 'Don't want fish,' he said.

'The price is not set on the fish,' said Faramir. 'Only to come here and
look on the pool bears the penalty of death. I have spared you so far at the
prayer of Frodo here, who says that of him at least you have deserved some
thanks. But you must also satisfy me. What is your name? Whence do you
come? And whither do you go? What is your business?'

'We are lost, lost,' said Gollum. 'No name, no business, no Precious,
nothing. Only empty. Only hungry; yes, we are hungry. A few little fishes,
nasty bony little fishes, for a poor creature, and they say death. So wise
they are; so just, so very just.'

'Not very wise,' said Faramir. 'But just: yes perhaps, as just as our little
wisdom allows. Unloose him Frodo!' Faramir took a small nail-knife from
his belt and handed it to Frodo. Gollum misunderstanding the gesture,
squealed and fell down.

'Now, Sméagol!' said Frodo. 'You must trust me. I will not desert you.
Answer truthfully, if you can. It will do you good not harm.' He cut the
cords on Gollum's wrists and ankles and raised him to his feet.

'Come hither!' said Faramir. 'Look at me! Do you know the name of
this place? Have you been here before?'

Slowly Gollum raised his eyes and looked unwillingly into Faramir's.
All light went out of them, and they stared bleak and pale for a moment
into the clear unwavering eyes of the man of Gondor. There was a still
silence. Then Gollum dropped his head and shrank down, until he was
squatting on the floor, shivering. 'We doesn't know and we doesn't want
to know,' he whimpered. 'Never came here; never come again.'

'There are locked doors and closed windows in your mind, and dark
rooms behind them,' said Faramir. 'But in this I judge that you speak the
truth. It is well for you. What oath will you swear never to return; and
never to lead any living creature hither by word or sign?'

'Master knows,' said Gollum with a sidelong glance at Frodo. 'Yes, he knows. We will promise Master, if he saves us. We'll promise to It, yes.' He crawled to Frodo's feet. 'Save us, nice Master!' he whined. 'Sméagol promises to Precious, promises faithfully. Never come again, never speak, no never! No, precious, no!'

'Are you satisfied?' said Faramir.

'Yes,' said Frodo. 'At least, you must either accept this promise or carry out your law. You will get no more. But I promised that if he came to me, he should not be harmed. And I would not be proved faithless.'

Faramir sat for a moment in thought. 'Very good,' he said at last. 'I surrender you to your master, to Frodo son of Drogo. Let him declare what he will do with you!'

'But, Lord Faramir,' said Frodo bowing, 'you have not yet declared your will concerning the said Frodo, and until that is made known, he cannot shape his plans for himself or his companions. Your judgement was postponed until the morning; but that is now at hand.'

'Then I will declare my doom,' said Faramir. 'As for you, Frodo, in so far as lies in me under higher authority, I declare you free in the realm of Gondor to the furthest of its ancient bounds; save only that neither you nor any that go with you have leave to come to this place unbidden. This doom shall stand for a year and a day, and then cease, unless you shall before that term come to Minas Tirith and present yourself to the Lord and Steward of the City. Then I will entreat him to confirm what I have done and to make it lifelong. In the meantime, whomsoever you take under your protection shall be under my protection and under the shield of Gondor. Are you answered?'

Frodo bowed low. 'I am answered,' he said, 'and I place myself at your service, if that is of any worth to one so high and honourable.'

'It is of great worth,' said Faramir. 'And now, do you take this creature, this Sméagol, under your protection?'

'I do take Sméagol under my protection,' said Frodo. Sam sighed audibly; and not at the courtesies, of which, as any hobbit would, he thoroughly approved. Indeed in the Shire such a matter would have required a great many more words and bows.

'Then I say to you,' said Faramir, turning to Gollum, 'you are under doom of death; but while you walk with Frodo you are safe for our part. Yet if ever you be found by any man of Gondor astray without him, the doom shall fall. And may death find you swiftly, within Gondor or without, if you do not well serve him. Now answer me: whither would you go? You were his guide, he says. Whither were you leading him?' Gollum made no reply.

'This I will not have secret,' said Faramir. 'Answer me, or I will reverse my judgement!' Still Gollum did not answer.

'I will answer for him,' said Frodo. 'He brought me to the Black Gate, as I asked; but it was impassable.'

'There is no open gate into the Nameless Land,' said Faramir.

'Seeing this, we turned aside and came by the Southward road,' Frodo continued; 'for he said that there is, or there may be, a path near to Minas Ithil.'

'Minas Morgul,' said Faramir.

'I do not know clearly,' said Frodo; 'but the path climbs, I think, up into the mountains on the northern side of that vale where the old city stands. It goes up to a high cleft and so down to – that which is beyond.'

'Do you know the name of that high pass?' said Faramir.

'No,' said Frodo.

'It is called Cirith Ungol.' Gollum hissed sharply and began muttering to himself. 'Is not that its name?' said Faramir turning to him.

'No!' said Gollum, and then he squealed, as if something had stabbed him. 'Yes, yes, we heard the name once. But what does the name matter to us? Master says he must get in. So we must try some way. There is no other way to try, no.'

'No other way?' said Faramir. 'How do you know that? And who has explored all the confines of that dark realm?' He looked long and thoughtfully at Gollum. Presently he spoke again. 'Take this creature away, Anborn. Treat him gently, but watch him. And do not you, Sméagol, try to dive into the falls. The rocks have such teeth there as would slay you before your time. Leave us now and take your fish!'

Anborn went out and Gollum went cringing before him. The curtain was drawn across the recess.

'Frodo, I think you do very unwisely in this,' said Faramir. 'I do not think you should go with this creature. It is wicked.'

'No, not altogether wicked,' said Frodo.

'Not wholly, perhaps,' said Faramir; 'but malice eats it like a canker, and the evil is growing. He will lead you to no good. If you will part with him, I will give him safe-conduct and guidance to any point on the borders of Gondor that he may name.'

'He would not take it,' said Frodo. 'He would follow after me as he long has done. And I have promised many times to take him under my protection and to go where he led. You would not ask me to break faith with him?'

'No,' said Faramir. 'But my heart would. For it seems less evil to counsel another man to break troth than to do so oneself, especially if one sees a friend bound unwitting to his own harm. But no – if he will go with you, you must now endure him. But I do not think you are holden to go to Cirith Ungol, of which he has told you less than he knows. That much I perceived clearly in his mind. Do not go to Cirith Ungol!'

'Where then shall I go?' said Frodo. 'Back to the Black Gate and deliver myself up to the guard? What do you know against this place that makes its name so dreadful?'

'Nothing certain,' said Faramir. 'We of Gondor do not ever pass east of the Road in these days, and none of us younger men has ever done so, nor has any of us set foot upon the Mountains of Shadow. Of them we know only old report and the rumour of bygone days. But there is some dark terror that dwells in the passes above Minas Morgul. If Cirith Ungol is named, old men and masters of lore will blanch and fall silent.

'The valley of Minas Morgul passed into evil very long ago, and it was a menace and a dread while the banished Enemy dwelt yet far away, and Ithilien was still for the most part in our keeping. As you know, that city was once a strong place, proud and fair, Minas Ithil, the twin sister of our own city. But it was taken by fell men whom the Enemy in his first strength had dominated, and who wandered homeless and masterless after his fall. It is said that their lords were men of Númenor who had fallen into dark wickedness; to them the Enemy had given rings of power, and he had devoured them: living ghosts they were become, terrible and evil. After his going they took Minas Ithil and dwelt there, and they filled it, and all the valley about, with decay: it seemed empty and was not so, for a shapeless fear lived within the ruined walls. Nine Lords there were, and after the return of their Master, which they aided and prepared in secret, they grew strong again. Then the Nine Riders issued forth from the gates of horror, and we could not withstand them. Do not approach their citadel. You will be espied. It is a place of sleepless malice, full of lidless eyes. Do not go that way!'

'But where else will you direct me?' said Frodo. 'You cannot yourself, you say, guide me to the mountains, nor over them. But over the mountains I am bound, by solemn undertaking to the Council, to find a way or perish in the seeking. And if I turn back, refusing the road in its bitter end, where then shall I go among Elves or Men? Would you have me come to Gondor with this Thing, the Thing that drove your brother mad with desire? What spell would it work in Minas Tirith? Shall there be two cities of Minas Morgul, grinning at each other across a dead land filled with rottenness?'

'I would not have it so,' said Faramir.

'Then what would you have me do?'

'I know not. Only I would not have you go to death or to torment. And I do not think that Mithrandir would have chosen this way.'

'Yet since he is gone, I must take such paths as I can find. And there is no time for long searching,' said Frodo.

'It is a hard doom and a hopeless errand,' said Faramir. 'But at the least, remember my warning: beware of this guide, Sméagol. He has done murder before now. I read it in him.' He sighed.

'Well, so we meet and part, Frodo son of Drogo. You have no need of soft words: I do not hope to see you again on any other day under this Sun. But you shall go now with my blessing upon you, and upon all your people. Rest a little while food is prepared for you.

'I would gladly learn how this creeping Sméagol became possessed of the Thing of which we speak, and how he lost it, but I will not trouble you now. If ever beyond hope you return to the lands of the living and we re-tell our tales, sitting by a wall in the sun, laughing at old grief, you shall tell me then. Until that time, or some other time beyond the vision of the Seeing-stones of Númenor, farewell!'

He rose and bowed low to Frodo, and drawing the curtain passed out into the cave.

CHAPTER VII

JOURNEY TO THE CROSS-ROADS

Frodo and Sam returned to their beds and lay there in silence resting for a little, while men bestirred themselves and the business of the day began. After a while water was brought to them, and then they were led to a table where food was set for three. Faramir broke his fast with them. He had not slept since the battle on the day before, yet he did not look weary.

When they had finished they stood up. 'May no hunger trouble you on the road,' said Faramir. 'You have little provision, but some small store of food fit for travellers I have ordered to be stowed in your packs. You will have no lack of water as you walk in Ithilien, but do not drink of any stream that flows from Imlad Morgul, the Valley of Living Death. This also I must tell you. My scouts and watchers have all returned, even some that have crept within sight of the Morannon. They all find a strange thing. The land is empty. Nothing is on the road, and no sound of foot, or horn, or bowstring is anywhere to be heard. A waiting silence broods above the Nameless Land. I do not know what this portends. But the time draws swiftly to some great conclusion. Storm is coming. Hasten while you may! If you are ready, let us go. The Sun will soon rise above the shadow.'

The hobbits' packs were brought to them (a little heavier than they had been), and also two stout staves of polished wood, shod with iron, and with carven heads through which ran plaited leathern thongs.

'I have no fitting gifts to give you at our parting,' said Faramir; 'but take these staves. They may be of service to those who walk or climb in the wild. The men of the White Mountains use them; though these have been cut down to your height and newly shod. They are made of the fair tree *lebethron*, beloved of the woodwrights of Gondor, and a virtue has been set upon them of finding and returning. May that virtue not wholly fail under the Shadow into which you go!'

The hobbits bowed low. 'Most gracious host,' said Frodo, 'it was said to me by Elrond Halfelven that I should find friendship upon the way, secret and unlooked for. Certainly I looked for no such friendship as you have shown. To have found it turns evil to great good.'

Now they made ready to depart. Gollum was brought out of some corner or hiding-hole, and he seemed better pleased with himself than he had been, though he kept close to Frodo and avoided the glance of Faramir.

'Your guide must be blindfolded,' said Faramir, 'but you and your servant Samwise I release from this, if you wish.'

Gollum squealed, and squirmed, and clutched at Frodo, when they came to bind his eyes; and Frodo said: 'Blindfold us all three, and cover up my eyes first, and then perhaps he will see that no harm is meant.' This was done, and they were led from the cave of Henneth Annûn. After they had passed the passages and stairs they felt the cool morning air, fresh and sweet, about them. Still blind they went on for some little time, up and then gently down. At last the voice of Faramir ordered them to be uncovered.

They stood under the boughs of the woods again. No noise of the falls could be heard, for a long southward slope lay now between them and the ravine in which the stream flowed. To the west they could see light through the trees, as if the world came there to a sudden end, at a brink looking out only on to sky.

'Here is the last parting of our ways,' said Faramir. 'If you take my counsel, you will not turn eastward yet. Go straight on, for thus you will have the cover of the woodland for many miles. On your west is an edge where the land falls into the great vales, sometimes suddenly and sheer, sometimes in long hillsides. Keep near to this edge and the skirts of the forest. In the beginning of your journey you may walk under daylight, I think. The land dreams in a false peace, and for a while all evil is withdrawn. Fare you well, while you may!'

He embraced the hobbits then, after the manner of his people, stooping, and placing his hands upon their shoulders, and kissing their foreheads. 'Go with the good will of all good men!' he said.

They bowed to the ground. Then he turned and without looking back he left them and went to his two guards that stood at a little distance away. They marvelled to see with what speed these green-clad men now moved, vanishing almost in the twinkling of an eye. The forest where Faramir had stood seemed empty and drear, as if a dream had passed.

Frodo sighed and turned back southward. As if to mark his disregard of all such courtesy, Gollum was scrabbling in the mould at the foot of a tree. 'Hungry again already?' thought Sam. 'Well, now for it again!'

'Have they gone at last?' said Gollum. 'Nassty wicked Men! Sméagol's neck still hurts him, yes it does. Let's go!'

'Yes, let us go,' said Frodo. 'But if you can only speak ill of those who showed you mercy, keep silent!'

'Nice Master!' said Gollum. 'Sméagol was only joking. Always forgives, he does, yes, yes, even nice Master's little trickses. Oh yes, nice Master, nice Sméagol!'

Frodo and Sam did not answer. Hoisting their packs and taking their staves in hand, they passed on into the woods of Ithilien.

Twice that day they rested and took a little of the food provided by Faramir: dried fruits and salted meat, enough for many days; and bread enough to last while it was still fresh. Gollum ate nothing.

The sun rose and passed overhead unseen, and began to sink, and the light through the trees to the west grew golden; and always they walked in cool green shadow, and all about them was silence. The birds seemed all to have flown away or to have fallen dumb.

Darkness came early to the silent woods, and before the fall of night they halted, weary, for they had walked seven leagues or more from Henneth Annûn. Frodo lay and slept away the night on the deep mould beneath an ancient tree. Sam beside him was more uneasy: he woke many times, but there was never a sign of Gollum, who had slipped off as soon as the others had settled to rest. Whether he had slept by himself in some hole nearby, or had wandered restlessly prowling through the night, he did not say; but he returned with the first glimmer of light, and roused his companions.

'Must get up, yes they must!' he said. 'Long ways to go still, south and east. Hobbits must make haste!'

That day passed much as the day before had gone, except that the silence seemed deeper; the air grew heavy, and it began to be stifling under the trees. It felt as if thunder was brewing. Gollum often paused, sniffing the air, and then he would mutter to himself and urge them to greater speed.

As the third stage of their day's march drew on and afternoon waned, the forest opened out, and the trees became larger and more scattered. Great ilexes of huge girth stood dark and solemn in wide glades with here and there among them hoary ash-trees, and giant oaks just putting out their brown-green buds. About them lay long launds of green grass dappled with celandine and anemones, white and blue, now folded for sleep; and there were acres populous with the leaves of woodland hyacinths: already their sleek bell-stems were thrusting through the mould. No living creature, beast or bird, was to be seen, but in these open places Gollum grew afraid, and they walked now with caution, flitting from one long shadow to another.

Light was fading fast when they came to the forest-end. There they sat under an old gnarled oak that sent its roots twisting like snakes down a steep crumbling bank. A deep dim valley lay before them. On its further side the woods gathered again, blue and grey under the sullen evening, and marched on southwards. To the right the Mountains of Gondor glowed, remote in the West, under a fire-flecked sky. To the left lay darkness: the towering walls of Mordor; and out of that darkness the long valley came, falling steeply in an ever-widening trough towards the Anduin. At its bottom ran a hurrying stream: Frodo could hear its stony voice coming up through the silence; and beside it on the hither side a road went winding down like a pale ribbon, down into chill grey mists that no gleam of sunset touched. There it seemed to Frodo that he descried far off, floating as it were on a shadowy sea, the high dim tops and broken pinnacles of old towers forlorn and dark.

He turned to Gollum. 'Do you know where we are?' he said.

'Yes, Master. Dangerous places. This is the road from the Tower of the Moon, Master, down to the ruined city by the shores of the River. The ruined city, yes, very nasty place, full of enemies. We shouldn't have taken Men's advice. Hobbits have come a long way out of the path. Must go east now, away up there.' He waved his skinny arm towards the darkling mountains. 'And we can't use this road. Oh no! Cruel peoples come this way, down from the Tower.'

Frodo looked down on to the road. At any rate nothing was moving on it now. It appeared lonely and forsaken, running down to empty ruins in the mist. But there was an evil feeling in the air, as if things might indeed be passing up and down that eyes could not see. Frodo shuddered as he looked again at the distant pinnacles now dwindling into night, and the sound of the water seemed cold and cruel: the voice of Morgulduin, the polluted stream that flowed from the Valley of the Wraiths.

'What shall we do?' he said. 'We have walked long and far. Shall we look for some place in the woods behind where we can lie hidden?'

'No good hiding in the dark,' said Gollum. 'It's in day that hobbits must hide now, yes in day.'

'Oh come!' said Sam. 'We must rest for a bit, even if we get up again in the middle of the night. There'll still be hours of dark then, time enough for you to take us a long march, if you know the way.'

Gollum reluctantly agreed to this, and he turned back towards the trees, working eastward for a while along the straggling edges of the wood. He would not rest on the ground so near the evil road, and after some debate they all climbed up into the crotch of a large holm-oak, whose thick branches springing together from the trunk made a good hiding-place and a fairly comfortable refuge. Night fell and it grew altogether dark under the canopy of the tree. Frodo and Sam drank a little water and ate some bread and dried fruit, but Gollum at once curled up and went to sleep. The hobbits did not shut their eyes.

It must have been a little after midnight when Gollum woke up: suddenly they were aware of his pale eyes unlidded gleaming at them. He listened

and sniffed, which seemed, as they had noticed before, his usual method
of discovering the time of night.

'Are we rested? Have we had beautiful sleep?' he said. 'Let's go!'

'We aren't, and we haven't,' growled Sam. 'But we'll go if we must.'

Gollum dropped at once from the branches of the tree on to all fours,
and the hobbits followed more slowly.

As soon as they were down they went on again with Gollum leading,
eastwards, up the dark sloping land. They could see little, for the night
was now so deep that they were hardly aware of the stems of trees before
they stumbled against them. The ground became more broken and walking
was more difficult, but Gollum seemed in no way troubled. He led them
through thickets and wastes of brambles; sometimes round the lip of a deep
cleft or dark pit, sometimes down into black bush-shrouded hollows and
out again; but if ever they went a little downward, always the further slope
was longer and steeper. They were climbing steadily. At their first
halt they looked back, and they could dimly perceive the roofs of the forest
they had left behind, lying like a vast dense shadow, a darker night under
the dark blank sky. There seemed to be a great blackness looming slowly
out of the East, eating up the faint blurred stars. Later the sinking moon
escaped from the pursuing cloud, but it was ringed all about with a sickly
yellow glare.

At last Gollum turned to the hobbits. 'Day soon,' he said. 'Hobbits must
hurry. Not safe to stay in the open in these places. Make haste!'

He quickened his pace, and they followed him wearily. Soon they began
to climb up on to a great hog-back of land. For the most part it was covered
with a thick growth of gorse and whortleberry, and low tough thorns,
though here and there clearings opened, the scars of recent fires. The
gorse-bushes became more frequent as they got nearer the top; very old
and tall they were, gaunt and leggy below but thick above, and already
putting out yellow flowers that glimmered in the gloom and gave a faint
sweet scent. So tall were the spiny thickets that the hobbits could walk
upright under them, passing through long dry aisles carpeted with a deep
prickly mould.

On the further edge of this broad hill-back they stayed their march and
crawled for hiding underneath a tangled knot of thorns. Their twisted
boughs, stooping to the ground, were overridden by a clambering maze of
old briars. Deep inside there was a hollow hall, raftered with dead branch
and bramble, and roofed with the first leaves and shoots of spring. There
they lay for a while, too tired yet to eat; and peering out through the holes
in the covert they watched for the slow growth of day.

But no day came, only a dead brown twilight. In the East there was a
dull red glare under the lowering cloud: it was not the red of dawn. Across

the tumbled lands between, the mountains of the Ephel Dúath frowned at them, black and shapeless below where night lay thick and did not pass away, above with jagged tops and edges outlined hard and menacing against the fiery glow. Away to their right a great shoulder of the mountains stood out, dark and black amid the shadows, thrusting westward.

'Which way do we go from here?' asked Frodo. 'Is that the opening of – of the Morgul Valley, away over there beyond that black mass?'

'Need we think about it yet?' said Sam. 'Surely we're not going to move any more today, if day it is?'

'Perhaps not, perhaps not,' said Gollum. 'But we must go soon, to the Cross-roads. Yes, to the Cross-roads. That's the way over there, yes, Master.'

The red glare over Mordor died away. The twilight deepened as great vapours rose in the East and crawled above them. Frodo and Sam took a little food and then lay down, but Gollum was restless. He would not eat any of their food, but he drank a little water and then crawled about under the bushes, sniffing and muttering. Then suddenly he disappeared.

'Off hunting, I suppose,' said Sam and yawned. It was his turn to sleep first, and he was soon deep in a dream. He thought he was back in the Bag End garden looking for something; but he had a heavy pack on his back, which made him stoop. It all seemed very weedy and rank somehow, and thorns and bracken were invading the beds down near the bottom hedge.

'A job of work for me, I can see; but I'm so tired,' he kept on saying. Presently he remembered what he was looking for. 'My pipe!' he said, and with that he woke up.

'Silly!' he said to himself, as he opened his eyes and wondered why he was lying down under the hedge. 'It's in your pack all the time!' Then he realized, first that the pipe might be in his pack but he had no leaf, and next that he was hundreds of miles from Bag End. He sat up. It seemed to be almost dark. Why had his master let him sleep on out of turn, right on till evening?

'Haven't you had no sleep, Mr. Frodo?' he said. 'What's the time? Seems to be getting late!'

'No it isn't,' said Frodo. 'But the day is getting darker instead of lighter: darker and darker. As far as I can tell, it isn't midday yet, and you've only slept for about three hours.'

'I wonder what's up,' said Sam. 'Is there a storm coming? If so it's going to be the worst there ever was. We shall wish we were down a deep hole, not just stuck under a hedge.' He listened. 'What's that? Thunder, or drums, or what is it?'

'I don't know,' said Frodo. 'It's been going on for a good while now. Sometimes the ground seems to tremble, sometimes it seems to be the heavy air throbbing in your ears.'

Sam looked round. 'Where's Gollum?' he said. 'Hasn't he come back yet?'

'No,' said Frodo. 'There's not been a sign or sound of him.'

'Well, I can't abide him,' said Sam. 'In fact, I've never taken anything on a journey that I'd have been less sorry to lose on the way. But it would be just like him, after coming all these miles, to go and get lost now, just when we shall need him most – that is, if he's ever going to be any use, which I doubt.'

'You forget the Marshes,' said Frodo. 'I hope nothing has happened to him.'

'And I hope he's up to no tricks. And anyway I hope he doesn't fall into other hands, as you might say. Because if he does, we shall soon be in for trouble.'

At that moment a rolling and rumbling noise was heard again, louder now and deeper. The ground seemed to quiver under their feet. 'I think we are in for trouble anyhow,' said Frodo. 'I'm afraid our journey is drawing to an end.'

'Maybe,' said Sam; 'but *where there's life there's hope*, as my Gaffer used to say; *and need of vittles*, as he mostways used to add. You have a bite, Mr. Frodo, and then a bit of sleep.'

The afternoon, as Sam supposed it must be called, wore on. Looking out from the covert he could see only a dun, shadowless world, fading slowly into a featureless, colourless gloom. It felt stifling but not warm. Frodo slept unquietly, turning and tossing, and sometimes murmuring. Twice Sam thought he heard him speaking Gandalf's name. The time seemed to drag interminably. Suddenly Sam heard a hiss behind him, and there was Gollum on all fours, peering at them with gleaming eyes.

'Wake up, wake up! Wake up, sleepies!' he whispered. 'Wake up! No time to lose. We must go, yes, we must go at once. No time to lose!'

Sam stared at him suspiciously: he seemed frightened or excited. 'Go now? What's your little game? It isn't time yet. It can't be tea-time even, leastways not in decent places where there is tea-time.'

'Silly!' hissed Gollum. 'We're not in decent places. Time's running short, yes, running fast. No time to lose. We must go. Wake up, Master, wake up!' He clawed at Frodo; and Frodo, startled out of sleep, sat up suddenly and seized him by the arm. Gollum tore himself loose and backed away.

'They mustn't be silly,' he hissed. 'We must go. No time to lose!' And nothing more could they get out of him. Where he had been, and what he thought was brewing to make him in such a hurry, he would not say. Sam was filled with deep suspicion, and showed it; but Frodo gave no sign of what was passing in his mind. He sighed, hoisted his pack, and prepared to go out into the ever-gathering darkness.

Very stealthily Gollum led them down the hillside, keeping under cover wherever it was possible, and running, almost bent to the ground, across any open space; but the light was now so dim that even a keen-eyed beast of the wild could scarcely have seen the hobbits, hooded, in their grey cloaks, nor heard them, walking as warily as the little people can. Without the crack of a twig or the rustle of a leaf they passed and vanished.

For about an hour they went on, silently, in single file, oppressed by the gloom and by the absolute stillness of the land, broken only now and again by the faint rumbling as of thunder far away or drumbeats in some hollow of the hills. Down from their hiding-place they went, and then turning south they steered as straight a course as Gollum could find across a long broken slope that leaned up towards the mountains. Presently, not far ahead, looming up like a black wall, they saw a belt of trees. As they drew nearer they became aware that these were of vast size, very ancient it seemed, and still towering high, though their tops were gaunt and broken, as if tempest and lightning-blast had swept across them, but had failed to kill them or to shake their fathomless roots.

'The Cross-roads, yes,' whispered Gollum, the first words that had been spoken since they left their hiding-place. 'We must go that way.' Turning eastward now, he led them up the slope; and then suddenly there it was before them: the Southward Road, winding its way about the outer feet of the mountains, until presently it plunged into the great ring of trees.

'This is the only way,' whispered Gollum. 'No paths beyond the road. No paths. We must go to the Cross-roads. But make haste! Be silent!'

As furtively as scouts within the campment of their enemies, they crept down on to the road, and stole along its westward edge under the stony bank, grey as the stones themselves, and soft-footed as hunting cats. At length they reached the trees, and found that they stood in a great roofless ring, open in the middle to the sombre sky; and the spaces between their immense boles were like the great dark arches of some ruined hall. In the very centre four ways met. Behind them lay the road to the Morannon; before them it ran out again upon its long journey south; to their right the road from old Osgiliath came climbing up, and crossing, passed out eastward into darkness: the fourth way, the road they were to take.

Standing there for a moment filled with dread Frodo became aware that a light was shining; he saw it glowing on Sam's face beside him. Turning towards it, he saw, beyond an arch of boughs, the road to Osgiliath running almost as straight as a stretched ribbon down, down, into the West. There, far away, beyond sad Gondor now overwhelmed in shade, the Sun was sinking, finding at last the hem of the great slow-rolling pall of cloud, and falling in an ominous fire towards the yet unsullied Sea. The brief glow fell upon a huge sitting figure, still and solemn as the great stone kings of Argonath. The years had gnawed it, and violent hands had maimed it. Its head was gone, and in its place was set in mockery a round rough-hewn stone, rudely painted by savage hands in the likeness of a grinning face with one large red eye in the midst of its forehead. Upon its knees and mighty chair, and all about the pedestal, were idle scrawls mixed with the foul symbols that the maggot-folk of Mordor used.

Suddenly, caught by the level beams, Frodo saw the old king's head: it was lying rolled away by the roadside. 'Look, Sam!' he cried, startled into speech. 'Look! The king has got a crown again!'

The eyes were hollow and the carven beard was broken, but about the high stern forehead there was a coronal of silver and gold. A trailing plant with flowers like small white stars had bound itself across the brows as if in reverence for the fallen king, and in the crevices of his stony hair yellow stonecrop gleamed.

'They cannot conquer for ever!' said Frodo. And then suddenly the brief glimpse was gone. The Sun dipped and vanished, and as if at the shuttering of a lamp, black night fell.

CHAPTER VIII

THE STAIRS OF CIRITH UNGOL

Gollum was tugging at Frodo's cloak and hissing with fear and impatience. 'We must go,' he said. 'We mustn't stand here. Make haste!'

Reluctantly Frodo turned his back on the West and followed as his guide led him, out into the darkness of the East. They left the ring of trees and crept along the road towards the mountains. This road, too, ran straight for a while, but soon it began to bend away southwards, until it came right under the great shoulder of rock that they had seen from the distance. Black and forbidding it loomed above them, darker than the dark sky behind. Crawling under its shadow the road went on, and rounding it sprang east again and began to climb steeply.

Frodo and Sam were plodding along with heavy hearts, no longer able to care greatly about their peril. Frodo's head was bowed; his burden was dragging him down again. As soon as the great Cross-roads had been passed, the weight of it, almost forgotten in Ithilien, had begun to grow once more. Now, feeling the way become steep before his feet, he looked wearily up; and then he saw it, even as Gollum had said that he would: the city of the Ringwraiths. He cowered against the stony bank.

A long-tilted valley, a deep gulf of shadow, ran back far into the mountains. Upon the further side, some way within the valley's arms, high on a rocky seat upon the black knees of the Ephel Dúath, stood the walls and tower of Minas Morgul. All was dark about it, earth and sky, but it was lit with light. Not the imprisoned moonlight welling through the marble walls of Minas Ithil long ago, Tower of the Moon, fair and radiant in the hollow of the hills. Paler indeed than the moon ailing in some slow eclipse was the light of it now, wavering and blowing like a noisome exhalation of decay, a corpse-light, a light that illuminated nothing. In the walls and tower windows showed, like countless black holes looking inward into emptiness; but the topmost course of the tower revolved slowly, first one way and then another, a huge ghostly head leering into the night. For a moment the three companions stood there, shrinking, staring up with unwilling eyes. Gollum was the first to recover. Again he pulled at their cloaks urgently, but he spoke no word. Almost he dragged them forward. Every step was reluctant, and time seemed to slow its pace, so that between the raising of a foot and the setting of it down minutes of loathing passed.

So they came slowly to the white bridge. Here the road, gleaming faintly, passed over the stream in the midst of the valley, and went on, winding deviously up towards the city's gate: a black mouth opening in the outer circle of the northward walls. Wide flats lay on either bank, shadowy meads filled with pale white flowers. Luminous these were too, beautiful and yet horrible of shape, like the demented forms in an uneasy dream; and they gave forth a faint sickening charnel-smell; an odour of rottenness filled the air. From mead to mead the bridge sprang. Figures stood there at its head, carven with cunning in forms human and bestial, but all corrupt and loathsome. The water flowing beneath was silent, and it steamed, but the vapour that rose from it, curling and twisting about the bridge, was deadly cold. Frodo felt his senses reeling and his mind darkening. Then suddenly, as if some force were at work other than his own will, he began to hurry, tottering forward, his groping hands held out, his head lolling from side to side. Both Sam and Gollum ran after him. Sam caught his master in his arms, as he stumbled and almost fell, right on the threshold of the bridge.

'Not that way! No, not that way!' whispered Gollum, but the breath between his teeth seemed to tear the heavy stillness like a whistle, and he cowered to the ground in terror.

'Hold up, Mr. Frodo!' muttered Sam in Frodo's ear. 'Come back! Not' that way. Gollum says not, and for once I agree with him.'

Frodo passed his hand over his brow and wrenched his eyes away from the city on the hill. The luminous tower fascinated him, and he fought the desire that was on him to run up the gleaming road towards its gate. At last with an effort he turned back, and as he did so, he felt the Ring resisting him, dragging at the chain about his neck; and his eyes too, as he looked away, seemed for the moment to have been blinded. The darkness before him was impenetrable.

Gollum, crawling on the ground like a frightened animal, was already vanishing into the gloom. Sam, supporting and guiding his stumbling master, followed after him as quickly as he could. Not far from the near bank of the stream there was a gap in the stone-wall beside the road. Through this they passed, and Sam saw that they were on a narrow path that gleamed faintly at first, as the main road did, until climbing above the meads of deadly flowers it faded and went dark, winding its crooked way up into the northern sides of the valley.

Along this path the hobbits trudged, side by side, unable to see Gollum in front of them, except when he turned back to beckon them on. Then his eyes shone with a green-white light, reflecting the noisome Morgul-sheen perhaps, or kindled by some answering mood within. Of that deadly gleam and of the dark eyeholes Frodo and Sam were always conscious, ever glancing fearfully over their shoulders, and ever dragging their eyes back to find the darkening path. Slowly they laboured on. As they rose above the stench and vapours of the poisonous stream their breath became easier and their heads clearer; but now their limbs were deadly tired, as if they had walked all night under a burden, or had been swimming long against a heavy tide of water. At last they could go no further without a halt.

Frodo stopped and sat down on a stone. They had now climbed up to the top of a great hump of bare rock. Ahead of them there was a bay in the valley-side, and round the head of this the path went on, no more than a wide ledge with a chasm on the right; across the sheer southward face of the mountain it crawled upwards, until it disappeared into the blackness above.

'I must rest a while, Sam,' whispered Frodo. 'It's heavy on me, Sam lad, very heavy. I wonder how far I can carry it? Anyway I must rest before we venture on to that.' He pointed to the narrow way ahead.

'Sssh! ssh!' hissed Gollum hurrying back to them. 'Sssh!' His fingers were on his lips and he shook his head urgently. Tugging at Frodo's sleeve, he pointed towards the path; but Frodo would not move.

'Not yet,' he said, 'not yet.' Weariness and more than weariness oppressed him; it seemed as if a heavy spell was laid on his mind and body. 'I must rest,' he muttered.

At this Gollum's fear and agitation became so great that he spoke again, hissing behind his hand, as if to keep the sound from unseen listeners in the air. 'Not here, no. Not rest here. Fools! Eyes can see us. When they come to the bridge they will see us. Come away! Climb, climb! Come!'

'Come, Mr. Frodo,' said Sam. 'He's right again. We can't stay here.'

'All right,' said Frodo in a remote voice, as of one speaking half asleep. 'I will try.' Wearily he got to his feet.

But it was too late. At that moment the rock quivered and trembled beneath them. The great rumbling noise, louder than ever before, rolled in the ground and echoed in the mountains. Then with searing suddenness there came a great red flash. Far beyond the eastern mountains it leapt into the sky and splashed the lowering clouds with crimson. In that valley of shadow and cold deathly light it seemed unbearably violent and fierce. Peaks of stone and ridges like notched knives sprang out in staring black against the uprushing flame in Gorgoroth. Then came a great crack of thunder.

And Minas Morgul answered. There was a flare of livid lightnings: forks of blue flame springing up from the tower and from the encircling hills into the sullen clouds. The earth groaned; and out of the city there came a cry. Mingled with harsh high voices as of birds of prey, and the shrill neighing of horses wild with rage and fear, there came a rending screech, shivering, rising swiftly to a piercing pitch beyond the range of hearing.

The hobbits wheeled round towards it, and cast themselves down, holding their hands upon their ears.

As the terrible cry ended, falling back through a long sickening wail to silence, Frodo slowly raised his head. Across the narrow valley, now almost on a level with his eyes, the walls of the evil city stood, and its cavernous gate, shaped like an open mouth with gleaming teeth, was gaping wide. And out of the gate an army came.

All that host was clad in sable, dark as the night. Against the wan walls and the luminous pavement of the road Frodo could see them, small black figures in rank upon rank, marching swiftly and silently, passing outwards in an endless stream. Before them went a great cavalry of horsemen moving like ordered shadows, and at their head was one greater than all the rest: a Rider, all black, save that on his hooded head he had a helm like a crown that flickered with a perilous light. Now he was drawing near the bridge below, and Frodo's staring eyes followed him, unable to wink or to withdraw. Surely there was the Lord of the Nine Riders returned to earth to lead his ghastly host to battle? Here, yes here indeed was the haggard king whose cold hand had smitten down the Ring-bearer with his deadly knife. The old wound throbbed with pain and a great chill spread towards Frodo's heart.

Even as these thoughts pierced him with dread and held him bound as with a spell, the Rider halted suddenly, right before the entrance of the bridge, and behind him all the host stood still. There was a pause, a dead silence. Maybe it was the Ring that called to the Wraith-lord, and for a moment he was troubled, sensing some other power within his valley. This way and that turned the dark head helmed and crowned with fear, sweeping the shadows with its unseen eyes. Frodo waited, like a bird at the approach of a snake, unable to move. And as he waited, he felt, more urgent than ever before, the command that he should put on the Ring. But great as the pressure was, he felt no inclination now to yield to it. He knew that the Ring would only betray him, and that he had not, even if he put it on, the power to face the Morgul-king – not yet. There was no longer any answer to that command in his own will, dismayed by terror though it was, and he felt only the beating upon him of a great power from outside. It took his hand, and as Frodo watched with his mind, not willing it but in suspense (as if he looked on some old story far away), it moved the hand inch by inch towards the chain upon his neck. Then his own will stirred; slowly it forced the hand back and set it to find another thing, a thing lying hidden near his breast. Cold and hard it seemed as his grip closed on it: the phial of Galadriel, so long treasured, and almost forgotten till that hour. As he touched it, for a while all thought of the Ring was banished from his mind. He sighed and bent his head.

At that moment the Wraith-king turned and spurred his horse and rode across the bridge, and all his dark host followed him. Maybe the elven-hoods defied his unseen eyes, and the mind of his small enemy, being strengthened, had turned aside his thought. But he was in haste. Already the hour had struck, and at his great Master's bidding he must march with war into the West.

Soon he had passed, like a shadow into shadow, down the winding road, and behind him still the black ranks crossed the bridge. So great an army had never issued from that vale since the days of Isildur's might; no host so fell and strong in arms had yet assailed the fords of Anduin; and yet it was but one and not the greatest of the hosts that Mordor now sent forth.

Frodo stirred. And suddenly his heart went out to Faramir. 'The storm has burst at last,' he thought. 'This great array of spears and swords is going to Osgiliath. Will Faramir get across in time? He guessed it, but did he know the hour? And who can now hold the fords when the King of the Nine Riders comes? And other armies will come. I am too late. All is lost. I tarried on the way. All is lost. Even if my errand is performed, no one will ever know. There will be no one I can tell. It will be in vain.' Overcome with weakness he wept. And still the host of Morgul crossed the bridge.

Then at a great distance, as if it came out of memories of the Shire, some sunlit early morning, when the day called and doors were opening, he heard Sam's voice speaking. 'Wake up, Mr. Frodo! Wake up!' Had the voice added: 'Your breakfast is ready,' he would hardly have been surprised. Certainly Sam was urgent. 'Wake up, Mr. Frodo! They're gone,' he said.

There was a dull clang. The gates of Minas Morgul had closed. The last rank of spears had vanished down the road. The tower still grinned across the valley, but the light was fading in it. The whole city was falling back into a dark brooding shade, and silence. Yet still it was filled with watchfulness.

'Wake up, Mr. Frodo! They're gone, and we'd better go too. There's something still alive in that place, something with eyes, or a seeing mind, if you take me; and the longer we stay in one spot, the sooner it will get on to us. Come on, Mr. Frodo!'

Frodo raised his head, and then stood up. Despair had not left him, but the weakness had passed. He even smiled grimly, feeling now as clearly as a moment before he had felt the opposite, that what he had to do, he had to do, if he could, and that whether Faramir or Aragorn or Elrond or Galadriel or Gandalf or anyone else ever knew about it was beside the purpose. He took his staff in one hand and the phial in his other. When he saw that the clear light was already welling through his fingers, he thrust it into his bosom and held it against his heart. Then turning from the city of Morgul, now no more than a grey glimmer across a dark gulf, he prepared to take the upward road.

Gollum, it seemed, had crawled off along the ledge into the darkness beyond, when the gates of Minas Morgul opened, leaving the hobbits where they lay. He now came creeping back, his teeth chattering and his fingers snapping. 'Foolish! Silly!' he hissed. 'Make haste! They mustn't think danger has passed. It hasn't. Make haste!'

They did not answer, but they followed him on to the climbing ledge. It was little to the liking of either of them, not even after facing so many other perils; but it did not last long. Soon the path reached a rounded angle where the mountain-side swelled out again, and there it suddenly entered a narrow opening in the rock. They had come to the first stair that Gollum had spoken of. The darkness was almost complete, and they could see nothing much beyond their hands' stretch; but Gollum's eyes shone pale, several feet above, as he turned back towards them.

'Careful!' he whispered. 'Steps. Lots of steps. Must be careful!'

Care was certainly needed. Frodo and Sam at first felt easier, having now a wall on either side, but the stairway was almost as steep as a ladder, and as they climbed up and up, they became more and more aware of the long black fall behind them. And the steps were narrow, spaced unevenly, and often treacherous: they were worn and smooth at the edges, and some were broken, and some cracked as foot was set upon them. The hobbits struggled on, until at last they were clinging with desperate fingers to the steps ahead, and forcing their aching knees to bend and straighten; and ever as the stair cut its way deeper into the sheer mountain the rocky walls rose higher and higher above their heads.

At length, just as they felt that they could endure no more, they saw Gollum's eyes peering down at them again. 'We're up,' he whispered. 'First stair's past. Clever hobbits to climb so high, very clever hobbits. Just a few more little steps and that's all, yes.'

Dizzy and very tired Sam, and Frodo following him, crawled up the last step, and sat down rubbing their legs and knees. They were in a deep dark passage that seemed still to go up before them, though at a gentler slope and without steps. Gollum did not let them rest long.

'There's another stair still,' he said. 'Much longer stair. Rest when we get to the top of next stair. Not yet.'

Sam groaned. 'Longer, did you say?' he asked.

'Yes, yess, longer,' said Gollum. 'But not so difficult. Hobbits have climbed the Straight Stair. Next comes the Winding Stair.'

'And what after that?' said Sam.

'We shall see,' said Gollum softly. 'O yes, we shall see!'

'I thought you said there was a tunnel,' said Sam. 'Isn't there a tunnel or something to go through?'

'O yes, there's a tunnel,' said Gollum. 'But hobbits can rest before they try that. If they get through that, they'll be nearly at the top. Very nearly, if they get through. O yes!'

Frodo shivered. The climb had made him sweat, but now he felt cold and clammy, and there was a chill draught in the dark passage, blowing down from the invisible heights above. He got up and shook himself. 'Well, let's go on!' he said. 'This is no place to sit in.'

The passage seemed to go on for miles, and always the chill air flowed over them, rising as they went on to a bitter wind. The mountains seemed to be trying with their deadly breath to daunt them, to turn them back from the secrets of the high places, or to blow them away into the darkness behind. They only knew that they had come to the end, when suddenly they felt no wall at their right hand. They could see very little. Great black shapeless masses and deep grey shadows loomed above them and about them, but now and again a dull red light flickered up under the lowering clouds, and for a moment they were aware of tall peaks, in front and on either side, like pillars holding up a vast sagging roof. They seemed to have climbed up many hundreds of feet, on to a wide shelf. A cliff was on their left and a chasm on their right.

Gollum led the way close under the cliff. For the present they were no longer climbing, but the ground was now more broken and dangerous in the dark, and there were blocks and lumps of fallen stone in the way. Their going was slow and cautious. How many hours had passed since they had entered the Morgul Vale neither Sam nor Frodo could any longer guess. The night seemed endless.

At length they were once more aware of a wall looming up, and once more a stairway opened before them. Again they halted, and again they began to climb. It was a long and weary ascent; but this stairway did not delve into the mountain-side. Here the huge cliff-face sloped backwards, and the path like a snake wound to and fro across it. At one point it crawled sideways right to the edge of the dark chasm, and Frodo glancing down saw below him as a vast deep pit the great ravine at the head of the Morgul Valley. Down in its depths glimmered like a glow-worm thread the wraith-road from the dead city to the Nameless Pass. He turned hastily away.

Still on and up the stairway bent and crawled, until at last with a final flight, short and straight, it climbed out again on to another level. The path had veered away from the main pass in the great ravine, and it now followed its own perilous course at the bottom of a lesser cleft among the higher regions of the Ephel Dúath. Dimly the hobbits could discern tall piers and jagged pinnacles of stone on either side, between which were great crevices and fissures blacker than the night, where forgotten winters had gnawed and carved the sunless stone. And now the red light in the sky seemed stronger; though they could not tell whether a dreadful morning were indeed coming to this place of shadow, or whether they saw only the flame of some great violence of Sauron in the torment of Gorgoroth beyond. Still far ahead, and still high above, Frodo, looking up, saw, as he guessed, the very crown of this bitter road. Against the sullen redness of the eastern sky a cleft was outlined in the topmost ridge, narrow, deep-cloven between two black shoulders; and on either shoulder was a horn of stone.

He paused and looked more attentively. The horn upon the left was tall and slender; and in it burned a red light, or else the red light in the land beyond was shining through a hole. He saw now: it was a black tower poised above the outer pass. He touched Sam's arm and pointed.

'I don't like the look of that!' said Sam. 'So this secret way of yours is guarded after all,' he growled, turning to Gollum. 'As you knew all along, I suppose?'

'All ways are watched, yes,' said Gollum. 'Of course they are. But hobbits must try some way. This may be least watched. Perhaps they've all gone away to big battle, perhaps!'

'Perhaps,' grunted Sam. 'Well, it still seems a long way off, and a long way up before we get there. And there's still the tunnel. I think you ought to rest now, Mr. Frodo. I don't know what time of day or night it is, but we've kept going for hours and hours.'

'Yes, we must rest,' said Frodo. 'Let us find some corner out of the wind, and gather our strength – for the last lap.' For so he felt it to be. The terrors of the land beyond, and the deed to be done there, seemed remote, too far off yet to trouble him. All his mind was bent on getting through or over this impenetrable wall and guard. If once he could do that impossible thing, then somehow the errand would be accomplished, or so it seemed to him in that dark hour of weariness, still labouring in the stony shadows under Cirith Ungol.

In a dark crevice between two great piers of rock they sat down: Frodo and Sam a little way within, and Gollum crouched upon the ground near the opening. There the hobbits took what they expected would be their last meal before they went down into the Nameless Land, maybe the last meal they would ever eat together. Some of the food of Gondor they ate, and wafers of the waybread of the Elves, and they drank a little. But of their water they were sparing and took only enough to moisten their dry mouths.

'I wonder when we'll find water again?' said Sam. 'But I suppose even over there they drink? Orcs drink, don't they?'

'Yes, they drink,' said Frodo. 'But do not let us speak of that. Such drink is not for us.'

'Then all the more need to fill our bottles,' said Sam. 'But there isn't any water up here: not a sound or a trickle have I heard. And anyway Faramir said we were not to drink any water in Morgul.'

'No water flowing out of Imlad Morgul, were his words,' said Frodo. 'We are not in that valley now, and if we came on a spring it would be flowing into it and not out of it.'

'I wouldn't trust it,' said Sam, 'not till I was dying of thirst. There's a wicked feeling about this place.' He sniffed. 'And a smell, I fancy. Do you notice it? A queer kind of a smell, stuffy. I don't like it.'

'I don't like anything here at all,' said Frodo, 'step or stone, breath or bone. Earth, air and water all seem accursed. But so our path is laid.'

'Yes, that's so,' said Sam. 'And we shouldn't be here at all, if we'd known more about it before we started. But I suppose it's often that way. The brave things in the old tales and songs, Mr. Frodo: adventures, as I used to call them. I used to think that they were things the wonderful folk of the stories went out and looked for, because they wanted them, because they were exciting and life was a bit dull, a kind of a sport, as you might say. But that's not the way of it with the tales that really mattered, or the ones that stay in the mind. Folk seem to have been just landed in them, usually – their paths were laid that way, as you put it. But I expect they had lots of chances, like us, of turning back, only they didn't. And if they had, we shouldn't know, because they'd have been forgotten. We hear about those as just went on – and not all to a good end, mind you; at least not to what folk inside a story and not outside it call a good end. You know, coming home, and finding things all right, though not quite the same – like old Mr. Bilbo. But those aren't always the best tales to hear, though they may be the best tales to get landed in! I wonder what sort of a tale we've fallen into?'

'I wonder,' said Frodo. 'But I don't know. And that's the way of a real tale. Take any one that you're fond of. You may know, or guess, what kind of a tale it is, happy-ending or sad-ending, but the people in it don't know. And you don't want them to.'

'No, sir, of course not. Beren now, he never thought he was going to get that Silmaril from the Iron Crown in Thangorodrim, and yet he did, and that was a worse place and a blacker danger than ours. But that's a long tale, of course, and goes on past the happiness and into grief and beyond it – and the Silmaril went on and came to Eärendil. And why, sir, I never thought of that before! We've got – you've got some of the light of it in that star-glass that the Lady gave you! Why, to think of it, we're in the same tale still! It's going on. Don't the great tales never end?'

'No, they never end as tales,' said Frodo. 'But the people in them come, and go when their part's ended. Our part will end later – or sooner.'

'And then we can have some rest and some sleep,' said Sam. He laughed grimly. 'And I mean just that, Mr. Frodo. I mean plain ordinary rest, and sleep, and waking up to a morning's work in the garden. I'm afraid that's all I'm hoping for all the time. All the big important plans are not for my sort. Still, I wonder if we shall ever be put into songs or tales. We're in one, of course; but I mean: put into words, you know, told by the fireside, or read out of a great big book with red and black letters, years and years afterwards. And people will say: "Let's hear about Frodo and the Ring!" And they'll say: "Yes, that's one of my favourite stories. Frodo was very brave, wasn't he, dad?" "Yes, my boy, the famousest of the hobbits, and that's saying a lot."'

'It's saying a lot too much,' said Frodo, and he laughed, a long clear laugh from his heart. Such a sound had not been heard in those places since Sauron came to Middle-earth. To Sam suddenly it seemed as if all the stones were listening and the tall rocks leaning over them. But Frodo did not heed them; he laughed again. 'Why, Sam,' he said, 'to hear you somehow makes me as merry as if the story was already written. But you've left out one of the chief characters: Samwise the stouthearted. "I want to hear more about Sam, dad. Why didn't they put in more of his talk, dad? That's what I like, it makes me laugh. And Frodo wouldn't have got far without Sam, would he, dad?"'

'Now, Mr. Frodo,' said Sam, 'you shouldn't make fun. I was serious.'

'So was I,' said Frodo, 'and so I am. We're going on a bit too fast. You and I, Sam, are still stuck in the worst places of the story, and it is all too likely that some will say at this point: "Shut the book now, dad; we don't want to read any more."'

'Maybe,' said Sam, 'but I wouldn't be one to say that. Things done and over and made into part of the great tales are different. Why, even Gollum might be good in a tale, better than he is to have by you, anyway. And he used to like tales himself once, by his own account. I wonder if he thinks he's the hero or the villain?

'Gollum!' he called. 'Would you like to be the hero – now where's he got to again?'

There was no sign of him at the mouth of their shelter nor in the shadows near. He had refused their food, though he had, as usual, accepted a mouthful of water; and then he had seemed to curl up for a sleep. They had supposed that one at any rate of his objects in his long absence the day before had been to hunt for food to his own liking; and now he had evidently slipped off again while they talked. But what for this time?

'I don't like his sneaking off without saying,' said Sam. 'And least of all now. He can't be looking for food up here, not unless there's some kind of rock he fancies. Why, there isn't even a bit of moss!'

'It's no good worrying about him now,' said Frodo. 'We couldn't have got so far, not even within sight of the pass, without him, and so we'll have to put up with his ways. If he's false, he's false.'

'All the same, I'd rather have him under my eye,' said Sam. 'All the more so, if he's false. Do you remember he never would say if this pass was guarded or no? And now we see a tower there – and it may be deserted, and it may not. Do you think he's gone to fetch them, Orcs or whatever they are?'

'No, I don't think so,' answered Frodo. 'Even if he's up to some wickedness, and I suppose that's not unlikely. I don't think it's that: not to fetch Orcs, or any servants of the Enemy. Why wait till now, and go through all the labour of the climb, and come so near the land he fears? He could probably have betrayed us to Orcs many times since we met him. No, if it's anything, it will be some little private trick of his own that he thinks is quite secret.'

'Well, I suppose you're right, Mr. Frodo,' said Sam. 'Not that it comforts me mightily. I don't make no mistake: I don't doubt he'd hand *me* over to Orcs as gladly as kiss his hand. But I was forgetting – his Precious. No, I suppose the whole time it's been *The Precious for poor Sméagol.* That's the one idea in all his little schemes, if he has any. But how bringing us up here will help him in that is more than I can guess.'

'Very likely he can't guess himself,' said Frodo. 'And I don't think he's got just one plain scheme in his muddled head. I think he really is in part trying to save the Precious from the Enemy, as long as he can. For that would be the last disaster for himself too, if the Enemy got it. And in the other part, perhaps, he's just biding his time and waiting on chance.'

'Yes, Slinker and Stinker, as I've said before,' said Sam. 'But the nearer they get to the Enemy's land the more like Stinker Slinker will get. Mark my words: if ever we get to the pass, he won't let us really take the precious thing over the border without making some kind of trouble.'

'We haven't got there yet,' said Frodo.

'No, but we'd better keep our eyes skinned till we do. If we're caught napping, Stinker will come out on top pretty quick. Not but what it would be safe for you to have a wink now, master. Safe, if you lay close to me. I'd be dearly glad to see you have a sleep. I'd keep watch over you; and anyway, if you lay near, with my arm round you, no one could come pawing you without your Sam knowing it.'

'Sleep!' said Frodo and sighed, as if out of a desert he had seen a mirage of cool green. 'Yes, even here I could sleep.'

'Sleep then, master! Lay your head in my lap.'

And so Gollum found them hours later, when he returned, crawling and creeping down the path out of the gloom ahead. Sam sat propped against the stone, his head dropping sideways and his breathing heavy. In his lap lay Frodo's head, drowned deep in sleep; upon his white forehead lay one of Sam's brown hands, and the other lay softly upon his master's breast. Peace was in both their faces.

Gollum looked at them. A strange expression passed over his lean hungry face. The gleam faded from his eyes, and they went dim and grey, old and tired. A spasm of pain seemed to twist him, and he turned away, peering back up towards the pass, shaking his head, as if engaged in some interior debate. Then he came back, and slowly putting out a trembling hand, very cautiously he touched Frodo's knee – but almost the touch was a caress. For a fleeting moment, could one of the sleepers have seen him, they would have thought that they beheld an old weary hobbit, shrunken by the years that had carried him far beyond his time, beyond friends and kin, and the fields and streams of youth, an old starved pitiable thing.

But at that touch Frodo stirred and cried out softly in his sleep, and immediately Sam was wide awake. The first thing he saw was Gollum – 'pawing at master,' as he thought.

'Hey you!' he said roughly. 'What are you up to?'

'Nothing, nothing,' said Gollum softly. 'Nice Master!'

'I daresay,' said Sam. 'But where have you been to – sneaking off and sneaking back, you old villain?'

Gollum withdrew himself, and a green glint flickered under his heavy lids. Almost spider-like he looked now, crouched back on his bent limbs, with his protruding eyes. The fleeting moment had passed, beyond recall. 'Sneaking, sneaking!' he hissed. 'Hobbits always so polite, yes. O nice hobbits! Sméagol brings them up secret ways that nobody else could find. Tired he is, thirsty he is, yes thirsty; and he guides them and he searches for paths, and they say *sneak, sneak*. Very nice friends, O yes my precious, very nice.'

Sam felt a bit remorseful, though not more trustful. 'Sorry,' he said. 'I'm sorry, but you startled me out of my sleep. And I shouldn't have been sleeping, and that made me a bit sharp. But Mr. Frodo, he's that tired, I asked him to have a wink; and well, that's how it is. Sorry. But where *have* you been to?'

'Sneaking,' said Gollum, and the green glint did not leave his eyes.

'O very well,' said Sam, 'have it your own way! I don't suppose it's so far from the truth. And now we'd better all be sneaking along together. What's the time? Is it today or tomorrow?'

'It's tomorrow,' said Gollum, 'or this was tomorrow when hobbits went to sleep. Very foolish, very dangerous – if poor Sméagol wasn't sneaking about to watch.'

'I think we shall get tired of that word soon,' said Sam. 'But never mind. I'll wake master up.' Gently he smoothed the hair back from Frodo's brow, and bending down spoke softly to him.

'Wake up, Mr. Frodo! Wake up!'

Frodo stirred and opened his eyes, and smiled, seeing Sam's face bending over him. 'Calling me early aren't you, Sam?' he said. 'It's dark still!'

'Yes it's always dark here,' said Sam. 'But Gollum's come back, Mr. Frodo, and he says it's tomorrow. So we must be walking on. The last lap.'

Frodo drew a deep breath and sat up. 'The last lap!' he said. 'Hullo, Sméagol! Found any food? Have you had any rest?'

'No food, no rest, nothing for Sméagol,' said Gollum. 'He's a sneak.'

Sam clicked his tongue, but restrained himself.

'Don't take names to yourself, Sméagol,' said Frodo. 'It's unwise, whether they are true or false.'

'Sméagol has to take what's given him,' answered Gollum. 'He was given that name by kind Master Samwise, the hobbit that knows so much.'

Frodo looked at Sam. 'Yes sir,' he said. 'I did use the word, waking up out of my sleep sudden and all and finding him at hand. I said I was sorry, but I soon shan't be.'

'Come, let it pass then,' said Frodo. 'But now we seem to have come to the point, you and I, Sméagol. Tell me. Can we find the rest of the way by ourselves? We're in sight of the pass, of a way in, and if we can find it now, then I suppose our agreement can be said to be over. You have done what you promised, and you're free: free to go back to food and rest, wherever you wish to go, except to servants of the Enemy. And one day I may reward you, I or those that remember me.'

'No, no, not yet,' Gollum whined. 'O no! They can't find the way themselves, can they? O no indeed. There's the tunnel coming. Sméagol must go on. No rest. No food. Not yet.'

CHAPTER IX

SHELOB'S LAIR

It may indeed have been daytime now, as Gollum said, but the hobbits could see little difference, unless, perhaps, the heavy sky above was less utterly black, more like a great roof of smoke; while instead of the darkness of deep night, which lingered still in cracks and holes, a grey blurring shadow shrouded the stony world about them. They passed on, Gollum in front and the hobbits now side by side, up the long ravine between the piers and columns of torn and weathered rock, standing like huge unshapen statues on either hand. There was no sound. Some way ahead, a mile or so, perhaps, was a great grey wall, a last huge upthrusting mass of mountain-stone. Darker it loomed, and steadily it rose as they approached, until it towered up high above them, shutting out the view of all that lay beyond. Deep shadow lay before its feet. Sam sniffed the air.

'Ugh! That smell!' he said. 'It's getting stronger and stronger.'

Presently they were under the shadow, and there in the midst of it they saw the opening of a cave. 'This is the way in,' said Gollum softly. 'This is the entrance to the tunnel.' He did not speak its name: Torech Ungol, Shelob's Lair. Out of it came a stench, not the sickly odour of decay in the meads of Morgul, but a foul reek, as if filth unnameable were piled and hoarded in the dark within.

'Is this the only way, Sméagol?' said Frodo.

'Yes, yes,' he answered. 'Yes, we must go this way now.'

'D'you mean to say you've been through this hole?' said Sam. 'Phew! But perhaps you don't mind bad smells.'

Gollum's eyes glinted. 'He doesn't know what we minds, does he, precious? No, he doesn't. But Sméagol can bear things. Yes. He's been through. O yes, right through. It's the only way.'

'And what makes the smell, I wonder,' said Sam. 'It's like – well, I wouldn't like to say. Some beastly hole of the Orcs, I'll warrant, with a hundred years of their filth in it.'

'Well,' said Frodo, 'Orcs or no, if it's the only way, we must take it.'

Drawing a deep breath they passed inside. In a few steps they were in utter and impenetrable dark. Not since the lightless passages of Moria had Frodo or Sam known such darkness, and if possible here it was deeper and denser. There, there were airs moving, and echoes, and a sense of space. Here the air was still, stagnant, heavy, and sound fell dead. They walked

as it were in a black vapour wrought of veritable darkness itself that, as it
was breathed, brought blindness not only to the eyes but to the mind, so
that even the memory of colours and of forms and of any light faded out
of thought. Night always had been, and always would be, and night
was all.

But for a while they could still feel, and indeed the senses of their feet
and fingers at first seemed sharpened almost painfully. The walls felt, to
their surprise, smooth, and the floor, save for a step now and again, was
straight and even, going ever up at the same stiff slope. The tunnel was
high and wide, so wide that, though the hobbits walked abreast, only
touching the side-walls with their outstretched hands, they were separated,
cut off alone in the darkness.

Gollum had gone in first and seemed to be only a few steps ahead. While
they were still able to give heed to such things, they could hear his breath
hissing and gasping just in front of them. But after a time their senses
became duller, both touch and hearing seemed to grow numb, and they
kept on, groping, walking, on and on, mainly by the force of the will with
which they had entered, will to go through and desire to come at last to
the high gate beyond.

Before they had gone very far, perhaps, but time and distance soon
passed out of his reckoning, Sam on the right, feeling the wall, was aware
that there was an opening at the side: for a moment he caught a faint breath
of some air less heavy, and then they passed it by.

'There's more than one passage here,' he whispered with an effort: it
seemed hard to make his breath give any sound. 'It's as orc-like a place as
ever there could be!'

After that, first he on the right, and then Frodo on the left, passed three
or four such openings, some wider, some smaller; but there was as yet no
doubt of the main way, for it was straight, and did not turn, and still went
steadily up. But how long was it, how much more of this would they have
to endure, or could they endure? The breathlessness of the air was growing
as they climbed; and now they seemed often in the blind dark to sense
some resistance thicker than the foul air. As they thrust forward they felt
things brush against their heads, or against their hands, long tentacles, or
hanging growths perhaps: they could not tell what they were. And still the
stench grew. It grew, until almost it seemed to them that smell was the
only clear sense left to them, and that was for their torment. One hour,
two hours, three hours: how many had they passed in this lightless
hole? Hours – days, weeks rather. Sam left the tunnel-side and shrank
towards Frodo, and their hands met and clasped, and so together they
still went on.

At length Frodo, groping along the left-hand wall, came suddenly to a void. Almost he fell sideways into the emptiness. Here was some opening in the rock far wider than any they had yet passed; and out of it came a reek so foul, and a sense of lurking malice so intense, that Frodo reeled. And at that moment Sam too lurched and fell forwards.

Fighting off both the sickness and the fear, Frodo gripped Sam's hand. 'Up!' he said in a hoarse breath without voice. 'It all comes from here, the stench and the peril. Now for it! Quick!'

Calling up his remaining strength and resolution, he dragged Sam to his feet, and forced his own limbs to move. Sam stumbled beside him. One step, two steps, three steps – at last six steps. Maybe they had passed the dreadful unseen opening, but whether that was so or not, suddenly it was easier to move, as if some hostile will for the moment had released them. They struggled on, still hand in hand.

But almost at once they came to a new difficulty. The tunnel forked, or so it seemed, and in the dark they could not tell which was the wider way, or which kept nearer to the straight. Which should they take, the left, or the right? They knew of nothing to guide them, yet a false choice would almost certainly be fatal.

'Which way has Gollum gone?' panted Sam. 'And why didn't he wait?'

'Sméagol!' said Frodo, trying to call. 'Sméagol!' But his voice croaked, and the name fell dead almost as it left his lips. There was no answer, not an echo, not even a tremor of the air.

'He's really gone this time, I fancy,' muttered Sam. 'I guess this is just exactly where he meant to bring us. Gollum! If ever I lay hands on you again, you'll be sorry for it.'

Presently, groping and fumbling in the dark, they found that the opening on the left was blocked: either it was a blind, or else some great stone had fallen in the passage. 'This can't be the way,' Frodo whispered. 'Right or wrong, we must take the other.'

'And quick!' Sam panted. 'There's something worse than Gollum about. I can feel something looking at us.'

They had not gone more than a few yards when from behind them came a sound, startling and horrible in the heavy padded silence: a gurgling, bubbling noise, and a long venomous hiss. They wheeled round, but nothing could be seen. Still as stones they stood, staring, waiting for they did not know what.

'It's a trap!' said Sam, and he laid his hand upon the hilt of his sword; and as he did so, he thought of the darkness of the barrow whence it came. 'I wish old Tom was near us now!' he thought. Then, as he stood, darkness about him and a blackness of despair and anger in his heart, it seemed to him that he saw a light: a light in his mind, almost unbearably bright at first, as a sun-ray to the eyes of one long hidden in a windowless pit. Then the light became colour: green, gold, silver, white. Far off, as in a little picture drawn by elven-fingers, he saw the Lady Galadriel standing on the grass in Lórien, and gifts were in her hands. *And you, Ring-bearer*, he heard her say, remote but clear, *for you I have prepared this.*

The bubbling hiss drew nearer, and there was a creaking as of some great jointed thing that moved with slow purpose in the dark. A reek came on before it. 'Master, master!' cried Sam, and life and urgency came back into his voice. 'The Lady's gift! The star-glass! A light to you in dark places, she said it was to be. The star-glass!'

'The star-glass?' muttered Frodo, as one answering out of sleep, hardly comprehending. 'Why yes! Why had I forgotten it? *A light when all other lights go out!* And now indeed light alone can help us.'

Slowly his hand went to his bosom, and slowly he held aloft the Phial of Galadriel. For a moment it glimmered, faint as a rising star struggling in heavy earthward mists, and then as its power waxed, and hope grew in Frodo's mind, it began to burn, and kindled to a silver flame, a minute heart of dazzling light, as though Eärendil had himself come down from the high sunset paths with the last Silmaril upon his brow. The darkness receded from it, until it seemed to shine in the centre of a globe of airy crystal, and the hand that held it sparkled with white fire.

Frodo gazed in wonder at this marvellous gift that he had so long carried, not guessing its full worth and potency. Seldom had he remembered it on the road, until they came to Morgul Vale, and never had he used it for fear of its revealing light. *Aiya Eärendil Elenion Ancalima!* he cried, and knew not what he had spoken; for it seemed that another voice spoke through his, clear, untroubled by the foul air of the pit.

But other potencies there are in Middle-earth, powers of night, and they are old and strong. And She that walked in the darkness had heard the Elves cry that cry far back in the deeps of time, and she had not heeded it, and it did not daunt her now. Even as Frodo spoke he felt a great malice bent upon him, and a deadly regard considering him. Not far down the tunnel, between them and the opening where they had reeled and stumbled, he was aware of eyes growing visible, two great clusters of many-windowed eyes – the coming menace was unmasked at last. The radiance of the star-glass was broken and thrown back from their thousand facets, but behind the glitter a pale deadly fire began steadily to glow within, a flame kindled in some deep pit of evil thought. Monstrous and abominable eyes they were, bestial and yet filled with purpose and with hideous delight, gloating over their prey trapped beyond all hope of escape.

Frodo and Sam, horror-stricken, began slowly to back away, their own gaze held by the dreadful stare of those baleful eyes; but as they backed so the eyes advanced. Frodo's hand wavered, and slowly the Phial drooped. Then suddenly, released from the holding spell to run a little while in vain panic for the amusement of the eyes, they both turned and fled together; but even as they ran Frodo looked back and saw with terror that at once the eyes came leaping up behind. The stench of death was like a cloud about him.

'Stand! stand!' he cried desperately. 'Running is no use.'

Slowly the eyes crept nearer.

'Galadriel!' he called, and gathering his courage he lifted up the Phial once more. The eyes halted. For a moment their regard relaxed, as if some hint of doubt troubled them. Then Frodo's heart flamed within him, and without thinking what he did, whether it was folly or despair or courage, he took the Phial in his left hand, and with his right hand drew his sword. Sting flashed out, and the sharp elven-blade sparkled in the silver light, but at its edges a blue fire flicked. Then holding the star aloft and the bright sword advanced, Frodo, hobbit of the Shire, walked steadily down to meet the eyes.

They wavered. Doubt came into them as the light approached. One by one they dimmed, and slowly they drew back. No brightness so deadly had ever afflicted them before. From sun and moon and star they had been safe underground, but now a star had descended into the very earth. Still it approached, and the eyes began to quail. One by one they all went dark; they turned away, and a great bulk, beyond the light's reach, heaved its huge shadow in between. They were gone.

'Master, master!' cried Sam. He was close behind, his own sword drawn and ready. 'Stars and glory! But the Elves would make a song of that, if ever they heard of it! And may I live to tell them and hear them sing. But don't go on, master! Don't go down to that den! Now's our only chance. Now let's get out of this foul hole!'

And so back they turned once more, first walking and then running; for as they went the floor of the tunnel rose steeply, and with every stride they climbed higher above the stenches of the unseen lair, and strength returned to limb and heart. But still the hatred of the Watcher lurked behind them, blind for a while, perhaps, but undefeated, still bent on death. And now there came a flow of air to meet them, cold and thin. The opening, the tunnel's end, at last it was before them. Panting, yearning for a roofless place, they flung themselves forward; and then in amazement they staggered, tumbling back. The outlet was blocked with some barrier, but not of stone: soft and a little yielding it seemed, and yet strong and impervious;

air filtered through, but not a glimmer of any light. Once more they charged and were hurled back.

Holding aloft the Phial Frodo looked and before him he saw a greyness which the radiance of the star-glass did not pierce and did not illuminate, as if it were a shadow that being cast by no light, no light could dissipate. Across the width and height of the tunnel a vast web was spun, orderly as the web of some huge spider, but denser-woven and far greater, and each thread was as thick as rope.

Sam laughed grimly. 'Cobwebs!' he said. 'Is that all? Cobwebs! But what a spider! Have at 'em, down with 'em!'

In a fury he hewed at them with his sword, but the thread that he struck did not break. It gave a little and then sprang back like a plucked bowstring, turning the blade and tossing up both sword and arm. Three times Sam struck with all his force, and at last one single cord of all the countless cords snapped and twisted, curling and whipping through the air. One end of it lashed Sam's hand, and he cried out in pain, starting back and drawing his hand across his mouth.

'It will take days to clear the road like this,' he said. 'What's to be done? Have those eyes come back?'

'No, not to be seen,' said Frodo. 'But I still feel that they are looking at me, or thinking about me: making some other plan, perhaps. If this light were lowered, or if it failed, they would quickly come again.'

'Trapped in the end!' said Sam bitterly, his anger rising again above weariness and despair. 'Gnats in a net. May the curse of Faramir bite that Gollum and bite him quick!'

'That would not help us now,' said Frodo. 'Come! Let us see what Sting can do. It is an elven-blade. There were webs of horror in the dark ravines of Beleriand where it was forged. But you must be the guard and hold back the eyes. Here, take the star-glass. Do not be afraid. Hold it up and watch!'

Then Frodo stepped up to the great grey net, and hewed it with a wide sweeping stroke, drawing the bitter edge swiftly across a ladder of close-strung cords, and at once springing away. The blue-gleaming blade shore through them like a scythe through grass, and they leaped and writhed and then hung loose. A great rent was made.

Stroke after stroke he dealt, until at last all the web within his reach was shattered, and the upper portion blew and swayed like a loose veil in the incoming wind. The trap was broken.

'Come!' cried Frodo. 'On! On!' Wild joy at their escape from the very mouth of despair suddenly filled all his mind. His head whirled as with a draught of potent wine. He sprang out, shouting as he came.

It seemed light in that dark land to his eyes that had passed through the den of night. The great smokes had risen and grown thinner, and the last hours of a sombre day were passing; the red glare of Mordor had died away in sullen gloom. Yet it seemed to Frodo that he looked upon a morning of sudden hope. Almost he had reached the summit of the wall. Only a little higher now. The Cleft, Cirith Ungol, was before him, a dim notch in the black ridge, and the horns of rock darkling in the sky on either side. A short race, a sprinter's course, and he would be through!

'The pass, Sam!' he cried, not heeding the shrillness of his voice, that released from the choking airs of the tunnel rang out now high and wild. 'The pass! Run, run, and we'll be through – through before any one can stop us!'

Sam came up behind as fast as he could urge his legs; but glad as he was to be free, he was uneasy, and as he ran, he kept on glancing back at the dark arch of the tunnel, fearing to see eyes, or some shape beyond his imagining, spring out in pursuit. Too little did he or his master know of the craft of Shelob. She had many exits from her lair.

There agelong she had dwelt, an evil thing in spider-form, even such as once of old had lived in the Land of the Elves in the West that is now under the Sea, such as Beren fought in the Mountains of Terror in Doriath, and so came to Lúthien upon the green sward amid the hemlocks in the moonlight long ago. How Shelob came there, flying from ruin, no tale tells, for out of the Dark Years few tales have come. But still she was there, who was there before Sauron, and before the first stone of Barad-dûr; and she served none but herself, drinking the blood of Elves and Men, bloated and grown fat with endless brooding on her feasts, weaving webs of shadow; for all living things were her food, and her vomit darkness. Far and wide her lesser broods, bastards of the miserable mates, her own offspring, that she slew, spread from glen to glen, from the Ephel Dúath to the eastern hills, to Dol Guldur and the fastnesses of Mirkwood. But none could rival her, Shelob the Great, last child of Ungoliant to trouble the unhappy world.

Already, years before, Gollum had beheld her, Sméagol who pried into all dark holes, and in past days he had bowed and worshipped her, and the darkness of her evil will walked through all the ways of his weariness beside him, cutting him off from light and from regret. And he had promised to bring her food. But her lust was not his lust. Little she knew of or cared for towers, or rings, or anything devised by mind or hand, who only desired death for all others, mind and body, and for herself a glut of life, alone, swollen till the mountains could no longer hold her up and the darkness could not contain her.

But that desire was yet far away, and long now had she been hungry, lurking in her den, while the power of Sauron grew, and light and living things forsook his borders; and the city in the valley was dead, and no Elf or Man came near, only the unhappy Orcs. Poor food and wary. But she must eat, and however busily they delved new winding passages from the pass and from their tower, ever she found some way to snare them. But she lusted for sweeter meat. And Gollum had brought it to her.

'We'll see, we'll see,' he said often to himself, when the evil mood was on him, as he walked the dangerous road from Emyn Muil to Morgul Vale, 'we'll see. It may well be, O yes, it may well be that when She throws away the bones and the empty garments, we shall find it, we shall get it, the Precious, a reward for poor Sméagol who brings nice food. And we'll save the Precious, as we promised. O yes. And when we've got it safe, then She'll know it, O yes, then we'll pay Her back, my precious. Then we'll pay everyone back!'

So he thought in an inner chamber of his cunning, which he still hoped to hide from her, even when he had come to her again and had bowed low before her while his companions slept.

And as for Sauron: he knew where she lurked. It pleased him that she should dwell there hungry but unabated in malice, a more sure watch upon that ancient path into his land than any other that his skill could have devised. And Orcs, they were useful slaves, but he had them in plenty. If now and again Shelob caught them to stay her appetite, she was welcome: he could spare them. And sometimes as a man may cast a dainty to his cat (*his cat* he calls her, but she owns him not) Sauron would send her prisoners that he had no better uses for: he would have them driven to her hole, and report brought back to him of the play she made.

So they both lived, delighting in their own devices, and feared no assault, nor wrath, nor any end of their wickedness. Never yet had any fly escaped from Shelob's webs, and the greater now was her rage and hunger.

But nothing of this evil which they had stirred up against them did poor Sam know, except that a fear was growing on him, a menace which he could not see; and such a weight did it become that it was a burden to him to run, and his feet seemed leaden.

Dread was round him, and enemies before him in the pass, and his master was in a fey mood running heedlessly to meet them. Turning his eyes away from the shadow behind and the deep gloom beneath the cliff upon his left, he looked ahead, and he saw two things that increased his dismay. He saw that the sword which Frodo still held unsheathed was glittering with blue flame; and he saw that though the sky behind was now dark, still the window in the tower was glowing red.

'Orcs!' he muttered. 'We'll never rush it like this. There's Orcs about, and worse than Orcs.' Then returning quickly to his long habit of secrecy, he closed his hand about the precious Phial which he still bore. Red with his own living blood his hand shone for a moment, and then he thrust the revealing light deep into a pocket near his breast and drew his elven-cloak about him. Now he tried to quicken his pace. His master was gaining on him; already he was some twenty strides ahead, flitting on like a shadow; soon he would be lost to sight in that grey world.

Hardly had Sam hidden the light of the star-glass when she came. A little way ahead and to his left he saw suddenly, issuing from a black hole of shadow under the cliff, the most loathly shape that he had ever beheld, horrible beyond the horror of an evil dream. Most like a spider she was, but huger than the great hunting beasts, and more terrible than they because of the evil purpose in her remorseless eyes. Those same eyes that he had thought daunted and defeated, there they were lit with a fell light again, clustering in her out-thrust head. Great horns she had, and behind her short stalk-like neck was her huge swollen body, a vast bloated bag, swaying and sagging between her legs; its great bulk was black, blotched with livid marks, but the belly underneath was pale and luminous and gave forth a stench. Her legs were bent, with great knobbed joints high above her back, and hairs that stuck out like steel spines, and at each leg's end there was a claw.

As soon as she had squeezed her soft squelching body and its folded limbs out of the upper exit from her lair, she moved with a horrible speed, now running on her creaking legs, now making a sudden bound. She was between Sam and his master. Either she did not see Sam, or she avoided him for the moment as the bearer of the light, and fixed all her intent upon one prey, upon Frodo, bereft of his Phial, running heedless up the path, unaware yet of his peril. Swiftly he ran, but Shelob was swifter; in a few leaps she would have him.

Sam gasped and gathered all his remaining breath to shout. 'Look out behind!' he yelled. 'Look out, master! I'm' – but suddenly his cry was stifled.

A long clammy hand went over his mouth and another caught him by the neck, while something wrapped itself about his leg. Taken off his guard he toppled backwards into the arms of his attacker.

'Got him!' hissed Gollum in his ear. 'At last, my precious, we've got him, yes, the nassty hobbit. We takes this one. She'll get the other. O yes, Shelob will get him, not Sméagol: he promised; he won't hurt Master at all. But he's got you, you nassty filthy little sneak!' He spat on Sam's neck.

Fury at the treachery, and desperation at the delay when his master was in deadly peril, gave to Sam a sudden violence and strength that was far beyond anything that Gollum had expected from this slow stupid hobbit, as he thought him. Not Gollum himself could have twisted more quickly or more fiercely. His hold on Sam's mouth slipped, and Sam ducked and lunged forward again, trying to tear away from the grip on his neck. His sword was still in his hand, and on his left arm, hanging by its thong, was Faramir's staff. Desperately he tried to turn and stab his enemy. But Gollum was too quick. His long right arm shot out, and he grabbed Sam's wrist: his fingers were like a vice; slowly and relentlessly he bent the hand down and forward, till with a cry of pain Sam released the sword and it fell to the ground; and all the while Gollum's other hand was tightening on Sam's throat.

Then Sam played his last trick. With all his strength he pulled away and got his feet firmly planted; then suddenly he drove his legs against the ground and with his whole force hurled himself backwards.

Not expecting even this simple trick from Sam, Gollum fell over with Sam on top, and he received the weight of the sturdy hobbit in his stomach. A sharp hiss came out of him, and for a second his hand upon Sam's throat loosened; but his fingers still gripped the sword-hand. Sam tore himself forward and away, and stood up, and then quickly he wheeled away to his right, pivoted on the wrist held by Gollum. Laying hold of the staff with his left hand, Sam swung it up, and down it came with a whistling crack on Gollum's outstretched arm, just below the elbow.

With a squeal Gollum let go. Then Sam waded in; not waiting to change the staff from left to right he dealt another savage blow. Quick as a snake Gollum slithered aside, and the stroke aimed at his head fell across his back. The staff cracked and broke. That was enough for him. Grabbing from behind was an old game of his, and seldom had he failed in it. But this time, misled by spite, he had made the mistake of speaking and gloating before he had both hands on his victim's neck. Everything had gone wrong with his beautiful plan, since that horrible light had so unexpectedly appeared in the darkness. And now he was face to face with a furious enemy, little less than his own size. This fight was not for him. Sam swept up his sword from the ground and raised it. Gollum squealed, and springing aside on to all fours, he jumped away in one big bound like a frog. Before Sam could reach him, he was off, running with amazing speed back towards the tunnel.

Sword in hand Sam went after him. For the moment he had forgotten everything else but the red fury in his brain and the desire to kill Gollum. But before he could overtake him, Gollum was gone. Then as the dark hole stood before him and the stench came out to meet him, like a clap of thunder the thought of Frodo and the monster smote upon Sam's mind. He spun round, and rushed wildly up the path, calling and calling his master's name. He was too late. So far Gollum's plot had succeeded.

CHAPTER X

THE CHOICES OF MASTER SAMWISE

Frodo was lying face upward on the ground and the monster was bending over him, so intent upon her victim that she took no heed of Sam and his cries, until he was close at hand. As he rushed up he saw that Frodo was already bound in cords, wound about him from ankle to shoulder, and the monster with her great forelegs was beginning half to lift, half to drag his body away.

On the near side of him lay, gleaming on the ground, his elven-blade, where it had fallen useless from his grasp. Sam did not wait to wonder what was to be done, or whether he was brave, or loyal, or filled with rage. He sprang forward with a yell, and seized his master's sword in his left hand. Then he charged. No onslaught more fierce was ever seen in the savage world of beasts, where some desperate small creature armed with little teeth, alone, will spring upon a tower of horn and hide that stands above its fallen mate.

Disturbed as if out of some gloating dream by his small yell she turned slowly the dreadful malice of her glance upon him. But almost before she was aware that a fury was upon her greater than any she had known in countless years, the shining sword bit upon her foot and shore away the claw. Sam sprang in, inside the arches of her legs, and with a quick upthrust of his other hand stabbed at the clustered eyes upon her lowered head. One great eye went dark.

Now the miserable creature was right under her, for the moment out of the reach of her sting and of her claws. Her vast belly was above him with its putrid light, and the stench of it almost smote him down. Still his fury held for one more blow, and before she could sink upon him, smothering him and all his little impudence of courage, he slashed the bright elven-blade across her with desperate strength.

But Shelob was not as dragons are, no softer spot had she save only her eyes. Knobbed and pitted with corruption was her age-old hide, but ever thickened from within with layer on layer of evil growth. The blade scored it with a dreadful gash, but those hideous folds could not be pierced by any strength of men, not though Elf or Dwarf should forge the steel or the hand of Beren or of Túrin wield it. She yielded to the stroke, and then heaved up the great bag of her belly high above Sam's head. Poison frothed and bubbled from the wound. Now splaying her legs she drove her huge bulk down on him again. Too soon. For Sam still stood upon his feet, and dropping his own sword, with both hands he held the elven-blade point upwards, fending off that ghastly roof; and so Shelob, with the driving force of her own cruel will, with strength greater than any warrior's hand, thrust herself upon a bitter spike. Deep, deep it pricked, as Sam was crushed slowly to the ground.

No such anguish had Shelob ever known, or dreamed of knowing, in all her long world of wickedness. Not the doughtiest soldier of old Gondor, nor the most savage Orc entrapped, had ever thus endured her, or set blade to her beloved flesh. A shudder went through her. Heaving up again, wrenching away from the pain, she bent her writhing limbs beneath her and sprang backwards in a convulsive leap.

Sam had fallen to his knees by Frodo's head, his senses reeling in the foul stench, his two hands still gripping the hilt of the sword. Through the mist before his eyes he was aware dimly of Frodo's face, and stubbornly he fought to master himself and to drag himself out of the swoon that was upon him. Slowly he raised his head and saw her, only a few paces away, eyeing him, her beak drabbling a spittle of venom, and a green ooze trickling from below her wounded eye. There she crouched, her shuddering belly splayed upon the ground, the great bows of her legs quivering, as she gathered herself for another spring – this time to crush and sting to death: no little bite of poison to still the struggling of her meat; this time to slay and then to rend.

Even as Sam himself crouched, looking at her, seeing his death in her eyes, a thought came to him, as if some remote voice had spoken, and he fumbled in his breast with his left hand, and found what he sought: cold and hard and solid it seemed to his touch in a phantom world of horror, the Phial of Galadriel.

'Galadriel!' he said faintly, and then he heard voices far off but clear: the crying of the Elves as they walked under the stars in the beloved shadows of the Shire, and the music of the Elves as it came through his sleep in the Hall of Fire in the house of Elrond.

Gilthoniel A Elbereth!

And then his tongue was loosed and his voice cried in a language which he did not know:

A Elbereth Gilthoniel
o menel palan-diriel,
le nallon sí di'nguruthos!
A tiro nin, Fanuilos!

And with that he staggered to his feet and was Samwise the hobbit, Hamfast's son, again.

'Now come, you filth!' he cried. 'You've hurt my master, you brute, and you'll pay for it. We're going on; but we'll settle with you first. Come on, and taste it again!'

As if his indomitable spirit had set its potency in motion, the glass blazed suddenly like a white torch in his hand. It flamed like a star that leaping from the firmament sears the dark air with intolerable light. No such terror out of heaven had ever burned in Shelob's face before. The beams of it entered into her wounded head and scored it with unbearable pain, and the dreadful infection of light spread from eye to eye. She fell back beating the air with her forelegs, her sight blasted by inner lightnings, her mind in agony. Then turning her maimed head away, she rolled aside and began to crawl, claw by claw, towards the opening in the dark cliff behind.

Sam came on. He was reeling like a drunken man, but he came on. And Shelob cowed at last, shrunken in defeat, jerked and quivered as she tried to hasten from him. She reached the hole, and squeezing down, leaving a trail of green-yellow slime, she slipped in, even as Sam hewed a last stroke at her dragging legs. Then he fell to the ground.

Shelob was gone; and whether she lay long in her lair, nursing her malice and her misery, and in slow years of darkness healed herself from within, rebuilding her clustered eyes, until with hunger like death she spun once more her dreadful snares in the glens of the Mountains of Shadow, this tale does not tell.

Sam was left alone. Wearily, as the evening of the Nameless Land fell upon the place of battle, he crawled back to his master.

'Master, dear master,' he said, but Frodo did not speak. As he had run forward, eager, rejoicing to be free, Shelob with hideous speed had come behind and with one swift stroke had stung him in the neck. He lay now pale, and heard no voice, and did not move.

'Master, dear master!' said Sam, and through a long silence waited, listening in vain.

Then as quickly as he could he cut away the binding cords and laid his head upon Frodo's breast and to his mouth, but no stir of life could he find, nor feel the faintest flutter of the heart. Often he chafed his master's hands and feet, and touched his brow, but all were cold.

'Frodo, Mr. Frodo!' he called. 'Don't leave me here alone! It's your Sam calling. Don't go where I can't follow! Wake up, Mr. Frodo! O wake up, Frodo, me dear, me dear. Wake up!'

Then anger surged over him, and he ran about his master's body in a rage, stabbing the air, and smiting the stones, and shouting challenges. Presently he came back, and bending looked at Frodo's face, pale beneath him in the dusk. And suddenly he saw that he was in the picture that was revealed to him in the mirror of Galadriel in Lórien: Frodo with a pale face lying fast asleep under a great dark cliff. Or fast asleep he had thought then. 'He's dead!' he said. 'Not asleep, dead!' And as he said it, as if the words had set the venom to its work again, it seemed to him that the hue of the face grew livid green.

And then black despair came down on him, and Sam bowed to the ground, and drew his grey hood over his head, and night came into his heart, and he knew no more.

When at last the blackness passed, Sam looked up and shadows were about him; but for how many minutes or hours the world had gone dragging on he could not tell. He was still in the same place, and still his master lay beside him dead. The mountains had not crumbled nor the earth fallen into ruin.

'What shall I do, what shall I do?' he said. 'Did I come all this way with him for nothing?' And then he remembered his own voice speaking words that at the time he did not understand himself, at the beginning of their journey: *I have something to do before the end. I must see it through, sir, if you understand.*

'But what can I do? Not leave Mr. Frodo dead, unburied on the top of the mountains, and go home? Or go on? Go on?' he repeated, and for a moment doubt and fear shook him. 'Go on? Is that what I've got to do? And leave him?'

Then at last he began to weep; and going to Frodo he composed his body, and folded his cold hands upon his breast, and wrapped his cloak about him; and he laid his own sword at one side, and the staff that Faramir had given at the other.

'If I'm to go on,' he said, 'then I must take your sword, by your leave, Mr. Frodo, but I'll put this one to lie by you, as it lay by the old king in the barrow; and you've got your beautiful mithril coat from old Mr. Bilbo. And your star-glass, Mr. Frodo, you did lend it to me and I'll need it, for I'll be always in the dark now. It's too good for me, and the Lady gave it to you, but maybe she'd understand. Do *you* understand, Mr. Frodo? I've got to go on.'

But he could not go, not yet. He knelt and held Frodo's hand and could not release it. And time went by and still he knelt, holding his master's hand, and in his heart keeping a debate.

Now he tried to find strength to tear himself away and go on a lonely journey – for vengeance. If once he could go, his anger would bear him down all the roads of the world, pursuing, until he had him at last: Gollum. Then Gollum would die in a corner. But that was not what he had set out to do. It would not be worth while to leave his master for that. It would not bring him back. Nothing would. They had better both be dead together. And that too would be a lonely journey.

He looked on the bright point of the sword. He thought of the places behind where there was a black brink and an empty fall into nothingness. There was no escape that way. That was to do nothing, not even to grieve. That was not what he had set out to do. 'What am I to do then?' he cried again, and now he seemed plainly to know the hard answer: *see it through*. Another lonely journey, and the worst.

'What? Me, alone, go to the Crack of Doom and all?' He quailed still, but the resolve grew. 'What? *Me* take the Ring from *him*? The Council gave it to him.'

But the answer came at once: 'And the Council gave him companions, so that the errand should not fail. And you are the last of all the Company. The errand must not fail.'

'I wish I wasn't the last,' he groaned. 'I wish old Gandalf was here, or somebody. Why am I left all alone to make up my mind? I'm sure to go wrong. And it's not for me to go taking the Ring, putting myself forward.'

'But you haven't put yourself forward; you've been put forward. And as for not being the right and proper person, why, Mr. Frodo wasn't, as you might say, nor Mr. Bilbo. They didn't choose themselves.'

'Ah well, I must make up my own mind. I will make it up. But I'll be sure to go wrong: that'd be Sam Gamgee all over.

'Let me see now: if we're found here, or Mr. Frodo's found, and that Thing's on him, well, the Enemy will get it. And that's the end of all of us, of Lórien, and Rivendell, and the Shire and all. And there's no time to lose, or it'll be the end anyway. The war's begun, and more than likely things are all going the Enemy's way already. No chance to go back with It and get advice or permission. No, it's sit here till they come and kill me over master's body, and gets It; or take It and go.' He drew a deep breath. 'Then take It, it is!'

He stooped. Very gently he undid the clasp at the neck and slipped his hand inside Frodo's tunic; then with his other hand raising the head, he kissed the cold forehead, and softly drew the chain over it. And then the head lay quietly back again in rest. No change came over the still face, and by that more than by all other tokens Sam was convinced at last that Frodo had died and laid aside the Quest.

'Good-bye, master, my dear!' he murmured. 'Forgive your Sam. He'll come back to this spot when the job's done – if he manages it. And then he'll not leave you again. Rest you quiet till I come; and may no foul creature come anigh you! And if the Lady could hear me and give me one wish, I would wish to come back and find you again. Good-bye!'

And then he bent his own neck and put the chain upon it, and at once his head was bowed to the ground with the weight of the Ring, as if a great stone had been strung on him. But slowly, as if the weight became less, or new strength grew in him, he raised his head, and then with a great effort got to his feet and found that he could walk and bear his burden. And for a moment he lifted up the Phial and looked down at his master, and the light burned gently now with the soft radiance of the evening-star in summer, and in that light Frodo's face was fair of hue again, pale but beautiful with an elvish beauty, as of one who has long passed the shadows. And with the bitter comfort of that last sight Sam turned and hid the light and stumbled on into the growing dark.

He had not far to go. The tunnel was some way behind; the Cleft a couple of hundred yards ahead, or less. The path was visible in the dusk, a deep rut worn in ages of passage, running now gently up in a long trough with cliffs on either side. The trough narrowed rapidly. Soon Sam came to a long flight of broad shallow steps. Now the orc-tower was right above him, frowning black, and in it the red eye glowed. Now he was hidden in the dark shadow under it. He was coming to the top of the steps and was in the Cleft at last.

'I've made up my mind,' he kept saying to himself. But he had not. Though he had done his best to think it out, what he was doing was altogether against the grain of his nature. 'Have I got it wrong?' he muttered. 'What ought I to have done?'

As the sheer sides of the Cleft closed about him, before he reached the actual summit, before he looked at last on the path descending into the Nameless Land, he turned. For a moment, motionless in intolerable doubt, he looked back. He could still see, like a small blot in the gathering gloom, the mouth of the tunnel; and he thought he could see or guess where Frodo lay. He fancied there was a glimmer on the ground down there, or perhaps it was some trick of his tears, as he peered out at that high stony place where all his life had fallen in ruin.

'If only I could have my wish, my one wish,' he sighed, 'to go back and find him!' Then at last he turned to the road in front and took a few steps: the heaviest and the most reluctant he had ever taken.

Only a few steps; and now only a few more and he would be going down and would never see that high place again. And then suddenly he heard cries and voices. He stood still as stone. Orc-voices. They were behind him and before him. A noise of tramping feet and harsh shouts: Orcs were coming up to the Cleft from the far side, from some entry to the tower, perhaps. Tramping feet and shouts behind. He wheeled round. He saw small red lights, torches, winking away below there as they issued from the tunnel. At last the hunt was up. The red eye of the tower had not been blind. He was caught.

Now the flicker of approaching torches and the clink of steel ahead was very near. In a minute they would reach the top and be on him. He had taken too long in making up his mind, and now it was no good. How could he escape, or save himself, or save the Ring? The Ring. He was not aware of any thought or decision. He simply found himself drawing out the chain and taking the Ring in his hand. The head of the orc-company appeared in the Cleft right before him. Then he put it on.

The world changed, and a single moment of time was filled with an hour of thought. At once he was aware that hearing was sharpened while sight was dimmed, but otherwise than in Shelob's lair. All things about him now were not dark but vague; while he himself was there in a grey hazy world, alone, like a small black solid rock, and the Ring, weighing down his left hand, was like an orb of hot gold. He did not feel invisible at all, but horribly and uniquely visible; and he knew that somewhere an Eye was searching for him.

He heard the crack of stone, and the murmur of water far off in Morgul Vale; and down away under the rock the bubbling misery of Shelob, groping, lost in some blind passage; and voices in the dungeons of the tower; and the cries of the Orcs as they came out of the tunnel; and deafening, roaring in his ears, the crash of the feet and the rending clamour of the Orcs before him. He shrank against the cliff. But they marched up like a phantom company, grey distorted figures in a mist, only dreams of fear with pale flames in their hands. And they passed him by. He cowered, trying to creep away into some cranny and to hide.

He listened. The Orcs from the tunnel and the others marching down had sighted one another, and both parties were now hurrying and shouting. He heard them both clearly, and he understood what they said. Perhaps the Ring gave understanding of tongues, or simply understanding, especially of the servants of Sauron its maker, so that if he gave heed, he understood and translated the thought to himself. Certainly the Ring had grown greatly in power as it approached the places of its forging; but one thing it did not confer, and that was courage. At present Sam still thought only of hiding, of lying low till all was quiet again; and he listened anxiously. He could not tell how near the voices were, the words seemed almost in his ears.

'Hola! Gorbag! What are you doing up here? Had enough of war already?'
'Orders, you lubber. And what are you doing, Shagrat? Tired of lurking up there? Thinking of coming down to fight?'
'Orders to you. I'm in command of this pass. So speak civil. What's your report?'
'Nothing.'
'Hai! hai! yoi!' A yell broke into the exchanges of the leaders. The Orcs lower down had suddenly seen something. They began to run. So did the others.
'Hai! Hola! Here's something! Lying right in the road. A spy, a spy!' There was a hoot of snarling horns and a babel of baying voices.

With a dreadful stroke Sam was wakened from his cowering mood. They had seen his master. What would they do? He had heard tales of the Orcs to make the blood run cold. It could not be borne. He sprang up. He flung the Quest and all his decisions away, and fear and doubt with them. He knew now where his place was and had been: at his master's side, though what he could do there was not clear. Back he ran down the steps, down the path towards Frodo.

'How many are there?' he thought. 'Thirty or forty from the tower at least, and a lot more than that from down below, I guess. How many can I kill before they get me? They'll see the flame of the sword, as soon as I draw it, and they'll get me sooner or later. I wonder if any song will ever mention it: How Samwise fell in the High Pass and made a wall of bodies round his master. No, no song. Of course not, for the Ring'll be found, and there'll be no more songs. I can't help it. My place is by Mr. Frodo. They must understand that – Elrond and the Council, and the great Lords and Ladies with all their wisdom. Their plans have gone wrong. I can't be their Ring-bearer. Not without Mr. Frodo.'

But the Orcs were out of his dim sight now. He had had no time to consider himself, but now he realized that he was weary, weary almost to exhaustion: his legs would not carry him as he wished. He was too slow. The path seemed miles long. Where had they all got to in the mist?

There they were again! A good way ahead still. A cluster of figures round something lying on the ground; a few seemed to be darting this way and that, bent like dogs on a trail. He tried to make a spurt.

'Come on, Sam!' he said, 'or you'll be too late again.' He loosened the sword in its sheath. In a minute he would draw it, and then——

There was a wild clamour, hooting and laughing, as something was lifted from the ground. 'Ya hoi! Ya harri hoi! Up! Up!'

Then a voice shouted: 'Now off! The quick way. Back to the Undergate! She'll not trouble us tonight by all the signs.' The whole band of orc-figures began to move. Four in the middle were carrying a body high on their shoulders. 'Ya hoi!'

They had taken Frodo's body. They were off. He could not catch them up. Still he laboured on. The Orcs reached the tunnel and were passing in. Those with the burden went first, and behind them there was a good deal of struggling and jostling. Sam came on. He drew the sword, a flicker of blue in his wavering hand, but they did not see it. Even as he came panting up, the last of them vanished into the black hole.

For a moment he stood, gasping, clutching his breast. Then he drew his sleeve across his face, wiping away the grime, and sweat, and tears. 'Curse the filth!' he said, and sprang after them into the darkness.

It no longer seemed very dark to him in the tunnel, rather it was as if he had stepped out of a thin mist into a heavier fog. His weariness was growing but his will hardened all the more. He thought he could see the light of torches a little way ahead, but try as he would, he could not catch them up. Orcs go fast in tunnels, and this tunnel they knew well; for in spite of Shelob they were forced to use it often as the swiftest way from the Dead City over the mountains. In what far-off time the main tunnel and the great round pit had been made, where Shelob had taken up her abode in ages past, they did not know; but many byways they had themselves delved about it on either side, so as to escape the lair in their goings to and fro on the business of their masters. Tonight they did not intend to go far down, but were hastening to find a side-passage that led back to their watch-tower on the cliff. Most of them were gleeful, delighted with what they had found and seen, and as they ran they gabbled and yammered after the fashion of their kind. Sam heard the noise of their harsh voices, flat and hard in the dead air, and he could distinguish two voices from among all the rest: they were louder, and nearer to him. The captains of the two parties seemed to be bringing up the rear, debating as they went.

'Can't you stop your rabble making such a racket, Shagrat?' grunted the one. 'We don't want Shelob on us.'

'Go on, Gorbag! Yours are making more than half the noise,' said the other. 'But let the lads play! No need to worry about Shelob for a bit, I reckon. She's sat on a nail, it seems, and we shan't cry about that. Didn't you see: a nasty mess all the way back to that cursed crack of hers? If we've stopped it once, we've stopped it a hundred times. So let 'em laugh. And we've struck a bit of luck at last: got something that Lugbúrz wants.'

'Lugbúrz wants it, eh? What is it, d'you think? Elvish it looked to me, but undersized. What's the danger in a thing like that?'

'Don't know till we've had a look.'

'Oho! So they haven't told you what to expect? They don't tell us all they know, do.they? Not by half. But they can make mistakes, even the Top Ones can.'

'Sh, Gorbag!' Shagrat's voice was lowered, so that even with his strangely sharpened hearing Sam could only just catch what was said. 'They may, but they've got eyes and ears everywhere; some among my lot, as like as not. But there's no doubt about it, they're troubled about something. The Nazgûl down below are, by your account; and Lugbúrz is too. Something nearly slipped.'

'Nearly, you say!' said Gorbag.

'All right,' said Shagrat, 'but we'll talk of that later. Wait till we get to the Under-way. There's a place there where we can talk a bit, while the lads go on.'

Shortly afterwards Sam saw the torches disappear. Then there was a rumbling noise, and just as he hurried up, a bump. As far as he could guess the Orcs had turned and gone into the very opening which Frodo and he had tried and found blocked. It was still blocked.

There seemed to be a great stone in the way, but the Orcs had got through somehow, for he could hear their voices on the other side. They were still running along, deeper and deeper into the mountain, back towards the tower. Sam felt desperate. They were carrying off his master's body for some foul purpose and he could not follow. He thrust and pushed at the block, and he threw himself against it, but it did not yield. Then not far inside, or so he thought, he heard the two captains' voices talking again. He stood still listening for a little, hoping perhaps to learn something useful. Perhaps Gorbag, who seemed to belong to Minas Morgul, would come out, and he could then slip in.

'No, I don't know,' said Gorbag's voice. 'The messages go through quicker than anything could fly, as a rule. But I don't enquire how it's done. Safest not to. Grr! Those Nazgûl give me the creeps. And they skin the body off you as soon as look at you, and leave you all cold in the dark on the other side. But He likes 'em; they're His favourites nowadays, so it's no use grumbling. I tell you, it's no game serving down in the city.'

'You should trý being up here with Shelob for company,' said Shagrat.

'I'd like to try somewhere where there's none of 'em. But the war's on now, and when that's over things may be easier.'

'It's going well, they say.'

'They would,' grunted Gorbag. 'We'll see. But anyway, if it does go well, there should be a lot more room. What d'you say? – if we get a chance, you and me'll slip off and set up somewhere on our own with a few trusty lads, somewhere where there's good loot nice and handy, and no big bosses.'

'Ah!' said Shagrat. 'Like old times.'

'Yes,' said Gorbag. 'But don't count on it. I'm not easy in my mind. As I said, the Big Bosses, ay,' his voice sank almost to a whisper, 'ay, even the Biggest, can make mistakes. Something nearly slipped, you say. I say, something *has* slipped. And we've got to look out. Always the poor Uruks to put slips right, and small thanks. But don't forget: the enemies don't love us any more than they love Him, and if they get topsides on Him, we're done too. But see here: when were you ordered out?'

'About an hour ago, just before you saw us. A message came: *Nazgûl uneasy. Spies feared on Stairs. Double vigilance. Patrol to head of Stairs.* I came at once.'

'Bad business,' said Gorbag. 'See here – our Silent Watchers were uneasy more than two days ago, that I know. But my patrol wasn't ordered out for another day, nor any message sent to Lugbúrz either: owing to the Great Signal going up, and the High Nazgûl going off to the war, and all that. And then they couldn't get Lugbúrz to pay attention for a good while, I'm told.'

'The Eye was busy elsewhere, I suppose,' said Shagrat. 'Big things going on away west, they say.'

'I daresay,' growled Gorbag. 'But in the meantime enemies have got up the Stairs. And what were you up to? You're supposed to keep watch, aren't you, special orders or no? What are you for?'

'That's enough! Don't try and teach me my job. We were awake all right. We knew there were funny things going on.'

'Very funny!'

'Yes, very funny: lights and shouting and all. But Shelob was on the go. My lads saw her and her Sneak.'

'Her Sneak? What's that?'

'You must have seen him: little thin black fellow; like a spider himself, or perhaps more like a starved frog. He's been here before. Came *out* of Lugbúrz the first time, years ago, and we had word from High Up to let him pass. He's been up the Stairs once or twice since then, but we've left him alone: seems to have some understanding with Her Ladyship. I suppose he's no good to eat: she wouldn't worry about words from High Up. But a fine guard you keep in the valley: he was up here a day before all this racket. Early last night we saw him. Anyway my lads reported that Her Ladyship was having some fun, and that seemed good enough for me, until the message came. I thought her Sneak had brought her a toy, or that you'd perhaps sent her a present, a prisoner of war or something. I don't interfere when she's playing. Nothing gets by Shelob when she's on the hunt.'

'Nothing, say you! Didn't you use your eyes back there? I tell you I'm not easy in my mind. Whatever came up the Stairs, *did* get by. It cut her web and got clean out of the hole. That's something to think about!'

'Ah well, but she got him in the end, didn't she?'

'*Got* him? Got *who*? This little fellow? But if he was the only one, then she'd have had him off to her larder long before, and there he'd be now. And if Lugbúrz wanted him, *you'd* have to go and get him. Nice for you. But there was more than one.'

At this point Sam began to listen more attentively and pressed his ear against the stone.

'Who cut the cords she'd put round him, Shagrat? Same one as cut the web. Didn't you see that? And who stuck a pin into Her Ladyship? Same one, I reckon. And where is he? Where is he, Shagrat?'

Shagrat made no reply.

'You may well put your thinking cap on, if you've got one. It's no laughing matter. No one, *no* one has ever stuck a pin in Shelob before, as you should know well enough. There's no grief in that; but think – there's someone loose hereabouts as is more dangerous than any other damned rebel that ever walked since the bad old times, since the Great Siege. Something *has* slipped.'

'And what is it then?' growled Shagrat.

'By all the signs, Captain Shagrat, I'd say there's a large warrior loose, Elf most likely, with an elf-sword anyway, and an axe as well maybe; and he's loose in your bounds, too, and you've never spotted him. Very funny indeed!' Gorbag spat. Sam smiled grimly at this description of himself.

'Ah well, you always did take a gloomy view,' said Shagrat. 'You can read the signs how you like, but there may be other ways to explain them. Anyhow, I've got watchers at every point, and I'm going to deal with one thing at a time. When I've had a look at the fellow we *have* caught, then I'll begin to worry about something else.'

'It's my guess you won't find much in that little fellow,' said Gorbag. 'He may have had nothing to do with the real mischief. The big fellow with the sharp sword doesn't seem to have thought him worth much anyhow – just left him lying: regular elvish trick.'

'We'll see. Come on now! We've talked enough. Let's go and have a look at the prisoner!'

'What are you going to do with him? Don't forget I spotted him first. If there's any game, me and my lads must be in it.'

'Now, now,' growled Shagrat, 'I have my orders. And it's more than my belly's worth, or yours, to break 'em. *Any* trespasser found by the guard is to be held at the tower. Prisoner is to be stripped. Full description of every article, garment, weapon, letter, ring, or trinket is to be sent to Lugbúrz at once, and to Lugbúrz *only*. And the prisoner is to be kept safe and intact, under pain of death for every member of the guard, until He sends or comes Himself. That's plain enough, and that's what I'm going to do.'

'Stripped, eh?' said Gorbag. 'What, teeth, nails, hair, and all?'

'No, none of that. He's for Lugbúrz, I tell you. He's wanted safe and whole.'

'You'll find that difficult,' laughed Gorbag. 'He's nothing but carrion now. What Lugbúrz will do with such stuff I can't guess. He might as well go in the pot.'

'You fool,' snarled Shagrat. 'You've been talking very clever, but there's a lot you don't know, though most other folk do. You'll be for the pot or for Shelob, if you don't take care. Carrion! Is that all you know of Her Ladyship? When she binds with cords, she's after meat. She doesn't eat dead meat, nor suck cold blood. This fellow isn't dead!'

Sam reeled, clutching at the stone. He felt as if the whole dark world was turning upside down. So great was the shock that he almost swooned, but even as he fought to keep a hold on his senses, deep inside him he was aware of the comment: 'You fool, he isn't dead, and your heart knew it. Don't trust your head, Samwise, it is not the best part of you. The trouble with you is that you never really had any hope. Now what is to be done?' For the moment nothing, but to prop himself against the unmoving stone and listen, listen to the vile orc-voices.

'Garn!' said Shagrat. 'She's got more than one poison. When she's hunting, she just gives 'em a dab in the neck and they go as limp as boned fish, and then she has her way with them. D'you remember old Ufthak? We lost him for days. Then we found him in a corner; hanging up he was, but he was wide awake and glaring. How we laughed! She'd forgotten him, maybe, but we didn't touch him – no good interfering with Her. Nar – this little filth, he'll wake up, in a few hours; and beyond feeling a bit sick for a bit, he'll be all right. Or would be, if Lugbúrz would let him alone. And of course, beyond wondering where he is and what's happened to him.'

'And what's going to happen to him,' laughed Gorbag. 'We can tell him a few stories at any rate, if we can't do anything else. I don't suppose he's ever been in lovely Lugbúrz, so he may like to know what to expect. This is going to be more funny than I thought. Let's go!'

'There's going to be no fun, I tell you,' said Shagrat. 'And he's got to be kept safe, or we're all as good as dead.'

'All right! But if I were you, I'd catch the big one that's loose, before you send in any report to Lugbúrz. It won't sound too pretty to say you've caught the kitten and let the cat escape.'

The voices began to move away. Sam heard the sound of feet receding. He was recovering from his shock, and now a wild fury was on him. 'I got it all wrong!' he cried. 'I knew I would. Now they've got him, the devils! the filth! Never leave your master, never, never: that was my right rule. And I knew it in my heart. May I be forgiven! Now I've got to get back to him. Somehow, somehow!'

He drew his sword again and beat on the stone with the hilt, but it only gave out a dull sound. The sword, however, blazed so brightly now that he could see dimly in its light. To his surprise he noticed that the great block was shaped like a heavy door, and was less than twice his own height. Above it was a dark blank space between the top and the low arch of the opening. It was probably only meant to be a stop against the intrusion of Shelob, fastened on the inside with some latch or bolt beyond the reach of her cunning. With his remaining strength Sam leaped and caught the top, scrambled up, and dropped; and then he ran madly, sword blazing in hand, round a bend and up a winding tunnel.

The news that his master was still alive roused him to a last effort beyond thought of weariness. He could not see anything ahead, for this new passage twisted and turned constantly; but he thought he was catching the two Orcs up: their voices were growing nearer again. Now they seemed quite close.

'That's what I'm going to do,' said Shagrat in angry tones. 'Put him right up in the top chamber.'

'What for?' growled Gorbag. 'Haven't you any lock-ups down below?'

'He's going out of harm's way, I tell you,' answered Shagrat. 'See? He's precious. I don't trust all my lads, and none of yours; nor you neither, when you're mad for fun. He's going where I want him, and where you won't come, if you don't keep civil. Up to the top, I say. He'll be safe there.'

'Will he?' said Sam. 'You're forgetting the great big elvish warrior that's loose!' And with that he raced round the last corner, only to find that by some trick of the tunnel, or of the hearing which the Ring gave him, he had misjudged the distance.

The two orc-figures were still some way ahead. He could see them now, black and squat against a red glare. The passage ran straight at last, up an incline; and at the end, wide open, were great double doors, leading probably to deep chambers far below the high horn of the tower. Already the Orcs with their burden had passed inside. Gorbag and Shagrat were drawing near the gate.

Sam heard a burst of hoarse singing, blaring of horns and banging of gongs, a hideous clamour. Gorbag and Shagrat were already on the threshold.

Sam yelled and brandished Sting, but his little voice was drowned in the tumult. No one heeded him.

The great doors slammed to. Boom. The bars of iron fell into place inside. Clang. The gate was shut. Sam hurled himself against the bolted brazen plates and fell senseless to the ground. He was out in the darkness. Frodo was alive but taken by the Enemy.

THE RETURN OF
THE KING

BEING THE THIRD PART

OF

The Lord of the Rings

BOOK FIVE

CHAPTER I

MINAS TIRITH

Pippin looked out from the shelter of Gandalf's cloak. He wondered if he was awake or still sleeping, still in the swift-moving dream in which he had been wrapped so long since the great ride began. The dark world was rushing by and the wind sang loudly in his ears. He could see nothing but the wheeling stars, and away to his right vast shadows against the sky where the mountains of the South marched past. Sleepily he tried to reckon the times and stages of their journey, but his memory was drowsy and uncertain.

There had been the first ride at terrible speed without a halt, and then in the dawn he had seen a pale gleam of gold, and they had come to the silent town and the great empty house on the hill. And hardly had they reached its shelter when the winged shadow had passed over once again, and men wilted with fear. But Gandalf had spoken soft words to him, and he had slept in a corner, tired but uneasy, dimly aware of comings and goings and of men talking and Gandalf giving orders. And then again riding, riding in the night. This was the second, no, the third night since he had looked in the Stone. And with that hideous memory he woke fully, and shivered, and the noise of the wind became filled with menacing voices.

A light kindled in the sky, a blaze of yellow fire behind dark barriers. Pippin cowered back, afraid for a moment, wondering into what dreadful country Gandalf was bearing him. He rubbed his eyes, and then he saw that it was the moon rising above the eastern shadows, now almost at the full. So the night was not yet old and for hours the dark journey would go on. He stirred and spoke.

'Where are we, Gandalf?' he asked.

'In the realm of Gondor,' the wizard answered. 'The land of Anórien is still passing by.'

There was a silence again for a while. Then, 'What is that?' cried Pippin suddenly, clutching at Gandalf's cloak. 'Look! Fire, red fire! Are there dragons in this land? Look, there is another!'

For answer Gandalf cried aloud to his horse. 'On, Shadowfax! We must hasten. Time is short. See! The beacons of Gondor are alight, calling for aid. War is kindled. See, there is the fire on Amon Dîn, and flame on Eilenach; and there they go speeding west: Nardol, Erelas, Min-Rimmon, Calenhad, and the Halifirien on the borders of Rohan.'

But Shadowfax paused in his stride, slowing to a walk, and then he lifted up his head and neighed. And out of the darkness the answering neigh of other horses came; and presently the thudding of hoofs was heard, and three riders swept up and passed like flying ghosts in the moon and vanished into the West. Then Shadowfax gathered himself together and sprang away, and the night flowed over him like a roaring wind.

Pippin became drowsy again and paid little attention to Gandalf telling him of the customs of Gondor, and how the Lord of the City had beacons built on the tops of outlying hills along both borders of the great range, and maintained posts at these points where fresh horses were always in readiness to bear his errand-riders to Rohan in the North, or to Belfalas in the South. 'It is long since the beacons of the North were lit,' he said; 'and in the ancient days of Gondor they were not needed, for they had the Seven Stones.' Pippin stirred uneasily.

'Sleep again, and do not be afraid!' said Gandalf. 'For you are not going like Frodo to Mordor, but to Minas Tirith, and there you will be as safe as you can be anywhere in these days. If Gondor falls, or the Ring is taken, then the Shire will be no refuge.'

'You do not comfort me,' said Pippin, but nonetheless sleep crept over him. The last thing that he remembered before he fell into deep dream was a glimpse of high white peaks, glimmering like floating isles above the clouds as they caught the light of the westering moon. He wondered where Frodo was, and if he was already in Mordor, or if he was dead; and he did not know that Frodo from far away looked on that same moon as it set beyond Gondor ere the coming of the day.

Pippin woke to the sound of voices. Another day of hiding and a night of journey had fleeted by. It was twilight: the cold dawn was at hand again, and chill grey mists were about them. Shadowfax stood steaming with sweat, but he held his neck proudly and showed no sign of weariness. Many tall men heavily cloaked stood beside him, and behind them in the mist loomed a wall of stone. Partly ruinous it seemed, but already before the night was passed the sound of hurried labour could be heard: beat of hammers, clink of trowels, and the creak of wheels. Torches and flares glowed dully here and there in the fog. Gandalf was speaking to the men that barred his way, and as he listened Pippin became aware that he himself was being discussed.

'Yea truly, we know you, Mithrandir,' said the leader of the men, 'and you know the pass-words of the Seven Gates and are free to go forward. But we do not know your companion. What is he? A dwarf out of the mountains in the North? We wish for no strangers in the land at this time, unless they be mighty men of arms in whose faith and help we can trust.'

'I will vouch for him before the seat of Denethor,' said Gandalf. 'And as for valour, that cannot be computed by stature. He has passed through more battles and perils than you have, Ingold, though you be twice his height; and he comes now from the storming of Isengard, of which we bear tidings, and great weariness is on him, or I would wake him. His name is Peregrin, a very valiant man.'

'Man?' said Ingold dubiously, and the others laughed.

'Man!' cried Pippin, now thoroughly roused. 'Man! Indeed not! I am a hobbit and no more valiant than I am a man, save perhaps now and again by necessity. Do not let Gandalf deceive you!'

'Many a doer of great deeds might say no more,' said Ingold. 'But what is a hobbit?'

'A Halfling,' answered Gandalf. 'Nay, not the one that was spoken of,' he added seeing the wonder in the men's faces. 'Not he, yet one of his kindred.'

'Yes, and one who journeyed with him,' said Pippin. 'And Boromir of your City was with us, and he saved me in the snows of the North, and at the last he was slain defending me from many foes.'

'Peace!' said Gandalf. 'The news of that grief should have been told first to the father.'

'It has been guessed already,' said Ingold; 'for there have been strange portents here of late. But pass on now quickly! For the Lord of Minas Tirith will be eager to see any that bear the latest tidings of his son, be he man or——'

'Hobbit,' said Pippin. 'Little service can I offer to your lord, but what I can do, I would do, remembering Boromir the brave.'

'Fare you well!' said Ingold; and the men made way for Shadowfax, and he passed through a narrow gate in the wall. 'May you bring good counsel to Denethor in his need, and to us all, Mithrandir!' Ingold cried. 'But you come with tidings of grief and danger, as is your wont, they say.'

'Because I come seldom but when my help is needed,' answered Gandalf. 'And as for counsel, to you I would say that you are over-late in repairing the wall of the Pelennor. Courage will now be your best defence against the storm that is at hand – that and such hope as I bring. For not all the tidings that I bring are evil. But leave your trowels and sharpen your swords!'

'The work will be finished ere evening,' said Ingold. 'This is the last portion of the wall to be put in defence: the least open to attack, for it looks towards our friends of Rohan. Do you know aught of them? Will they answer the summons, think you?'

'Yes, they will come. But they have fought many battles at your back. This road and no road looks towards safety any longer. Be vigilant! But for Gandalf Stormcrow you would have seen a host of foes coming out of Anórien and no Riders of Rohan. And you may yet. Fare you well, and sleep not!'

Gandalf passed now into the wide land beyond the Rammas Echor. So the men of Gondor called the out-wall that they had built with great labour, after Ithilien fell under the shadow of their Enemy. For ten leagues or more it ran from the mountains' feet and so back again, enclosing in its fence the fields of the Pelennor: fair and fertile townlands on the long slopes and terraces falling to the deep levels of the Anduin. At its furthest point from the Great Gate of the City, north-eastward, the wall was four leagues distant, and there from a frowning bank it overlooked the long flats beside the river, and men had made it high and strong; for at that point, upon a walled causeway, the road came in from the fords and bridges of Osgiliath and passed through a guarded gate between embattled towers. At its nearest point the wall was little more than one league from the City, and that was south-eastward. There Anduin, going in a wide knee about the hills of Emyn Arnen in South Ithilien, bent sharply west, and the out-wall rose upon its very brink; and beneath it lay the quays and landings of the Harlond for craft that came upstream from the southern fiefs.

The townlands were rich, with wide tilth and many orchards, and homesteads there were with oast and garner, fold and byre, and many rills rippling through the green from the highlands down to Anduin. Yet the herdsmen and husbandmen that dwelt there were not many, and the most part of the people of Gondor lived in the seven circles of the City, or in the high vales of the mountain-borders, in Lossarnach, or further south in fair Lebennin with its five swift streams. There dwelt a hardy folk between the mountains and the sea. They were reckoned men of Gondor, yet their blood was mingled, and there were short and swarthy folk among them whose sires came more from the forgotten men who housed in the shadow of the hills in the Dark Years ere the coming of the kings. But beyond, in the great fief of Belfalas, dwelt Prince Imrahil in his castle of Dol Amroth by the sea, and he was of high blood, and his folk also, tall men and proud with sea-grey eyes.

Now after Gandalf had ridden for some time the light of day grew in the sky, and Pippin roused himself and looked up. To his left lay a sea of mist, rising to a bleak shadow in the East; but to his right great mountains reared their heads, ranging from the West to a steep and sudden end, as if in the making of the land the River had burst through a great barrier, carving out a mighty valley to be a land of battle and debate in times to come. And there where the White Mountains of Ered Nimrais came to their end he saw, as Gandalf had promised, the dark mass of Mount Mindolluin, the deep purple shadows of its high glens, and its tall face whitening in the rising day. And upon its out-thrust knee was the Guarded City, with its seven walls of stone so strong and old that it seemed to have been not builded but carven by giants out of the bones of the earth.

Even as Pippin gazed in wonder the walls passed from looming grey to white, blushing faintly in the dawn; and suddenly the sun climbed over the eastern shadow and sent forth a shaft that smote the face of the City. Then Pippin cried aloud, for the Tower of Ecthelion, standing high within the topmost wall, shone out against the sky, glimmering like a spike of pearl and silver, tall and fair and shapely, and its pinnacle glittered as if it were wrought of crystals; and white banners broke and fluttered from the battlements in the morning breeze, and high and far he heard a clear ringing as of silver trumpets.

So Gandalf and Peregrin rode to the Great Gate of the Men of Gondor at the rising of the sun, and its iron doors rolled back before them.

'Mithrandir! Mithrandir!' men cried. 'Now we know that the storm is indeed nigh!'

'It is upon you,' said Gandalf. 'I have ridden on its wings. Let me pass! I must come to your Lord Denethor, while his stewardship lasts. Whatever betide, you have come to the end of the Gondor that you have known. Let me pass!'

Then men fell back before the command of his voice and questioned him no further, though they gazed in wonder at the hobbit that sat before him and at the horse that bore him. For the people of the City used horses very little and they were seldom seen in their streets, save only those ridden by the errand-riders of their lord. And they said: 'Surely that is one of the great steeds of the King of Rohan? Maybe the Rohirrim will come soon to strengthen us.' But Shadowfax walked proudly up the long winding road.

For the fashion of Minas Tirith was such that it was built on seven levels, each delved into the hill, and about each was set a wall, and in each wall was a gate. But the gates were not set in a line: the Great Gate in the City Wall was at the east point of the circuit, but the next faced half south, and the third half north, and so to and fro upwards; so that the paved way that climbed towards the Citadel turned first this way and then that across the face of the hill. And each time that it passed the line of the Great Gate it went through an arched tunnel, piercing a vast pier of rock whose huge out-thrust bulk divided in two all the circles of the City save the first. For partly in the primeval shaping of the hill, partly by the mighty craft and labour of old, there stood up from the rear of the wide court behind the Gate a towering bastion of stone, its edge sharp as a ship-keel facing east. Up it rose, even to the level of the topmost circle, and there was crowned by a battlement; so that those in the Citadel might, like mariners in a mountainous ship, look from its peak sheer down upon the Gate seven hundred feet below. The entrance to the Citadel also looked eastward, but was delved in the heart of the rock; thence a long lamp-lit slope ran up to the seventh gate. Thus men reached at last the High Court, and the Place of the Fountain before the feet of the White Tower: tall and shapely, fifty fathoms from its base to the pinnacle, where the banner of the Stewards floated a thousand feet above the plain.

A strong citadel it was indeed, and not to be taken by a host of enemies, if there were any within that could hold weapons; unless some foe could come behind and scale the lower skirts of Mindolluin, and so come upon the narrow shoulder that joined the Hill of Guard to the mountain mass. But that shoulder, which rose to the height of the fifth wall, was hedged with great ramparts right up to the precipice that overhung its western end; and in that space stood the houses and domed tombs of bygone kings and lords, for ever silent between the mountain and the tower.

Pippin gazed in growing wonder at the great stone city, vaster and more splendid than anything that he had dreamed of; greater and stronger than Isengard, and far more beautiful. Yet it was in truth falling year by year into decay; and already it lacked half the men that could have dwelt at ease there. In every street they passed some great house or court over whose doors and arched gates were carved many fair letters of strange and ancient shapes: names Pippin guessed of great men and kindreds that had once dwelt there; and yet now they were silent, and no footsteps rang on their wide pavements, nor voice was heard in their halls, nor any face looked out from door or empty window.

At last they came out of shadow to the seventh gate, and the warm sun that shone down beyond the river, as Frodo walked in the glades of Ithilien, glowed here on the smooth walls and rooted pillars, and the great arch with keystone carven in the likeness of a crowned and kingly head. Gandalf dismounted, for no horse was allowed in the Citadel, and Shadowfax suffered himself to be led away at the soft word of his master.

The Guards of the gate were robed in black, and their helms were of strange shape, high-crowned, with long cheek-guards close-fitting to the face, and above the cheek-guards were set the white wings of sea-birds; but the helms gleamed with a flame of silver, for they were indeed wrought of *mithril*, heirlooms from the glory of old days. Upon the black surcoats were embroidered in white a tree blossoming like snow beneath a silver crown and many-pointed stars. This was the livery of the heirs of Elendil, and none wore it now in all Gondor, save the Guards of the Citadel before the Court of the Fountain where the White Tree once had grown.

Already it seemed that word of their coming had gone before them; and at once they were admitted, silently, and without question. Quickly Gandalf strode across the white-paved court. A sweet fountain played there in the morning sun, and a sward of bright green lay about it; but in the midst, drooping over the pool, stood a dead tree, and the falling drops dripped sadly from its barren and broken branches back into the clear water.

Pippin glanced at it as he hurried after Gandalf. It looked mournful, he thought, and he wondered why the dead tree was left in this place where everything else was well tended.

Seven stars and seven stones and one white tree.

The words that Gandalf had murmured came back into his mind. And then he found himself at the doors of the great hall beneath the gleaming tower; and behind the wizard he passed the tall silent door-wardens and entered the cool echoing shadows of the house of stone.

They walked down a paved passage, long and empty, and as they went Gandalf spoke softly to Pippin. 'Be careful of your words, Master Peregrin! This is no time for hobbit pertness. Théoden is a kindly old man. Denethor is of another sort, proud and subtle, a man of far greater lineage and power, though he is not called a king. But he will speak most to you, and question you much, since you can tell him of his son Boromir. He loved him greatly: too much perhaps; and the more so because they were unlike. But under cover of this love he will think it easier to learn what he wishes from you rather than from me. Do not tell him more than you need, and leave quiet the matter of Frodo's errand. I will deal with that in due time. And say nothing about Aragorn either, unless you must.'

'Why not? What is wrong with Strider?' Pippin whispered. 'He meant to come here, didn't he? And he'll be arriving soon himself, anyway.'

'Maybe, maybe,' said Gandalf. 'Though if he comes, it is likely to be in some way that no one expects, not even Denethor. It will be better so. At least he should come unheralded by us.'

Gandalf halted before a tall door of polished metal. 'See, Master Pippin, there is no time to instruct you now in the history of Gondor; though it might have been better, if you had learned something of it, when you were still birds-nesting and playing truant in the woods of the Shire. Do as I bid! It is scarcely wise when bringing the news of the death of his heir to a mighty lord to speak over much of the coming of one who will, if he comes, claim the kingship. Is that enough?'

'Kingship?' said Pippin amazed.

'Yes,' said Gandalf. 'If you have walked all these days with closed ears and mind asleep, wake up now!' He knocked on the door.

The door opened, but no one could be seen to open it. Pippin looked into a great hall. It was lit by deep windows in the wide aisles at either side, beyond the rows of tall pillars that upheld the roof. Monoliths of black marble, they rose to great capitals carved in many strange figures of beasts and leaves; and far above in shadow the wide vaulting gleamed with dull gold, inset with flowing traceries of many colours. No hangings nor storied webs, nor any things of woven stuff or of wood, were to be seen in that long solemn hall;

but between the pillars there stood a silent company of tall images graven in cold stone.

Suddenly Pippin was reminded of the hewn rocks of Argonath, and awe fell on him, as he looked down that avenue of kings long dead. At the far end upon a dais of many steps was set a high throne under a canopy of marble shaped like a crowned helm; behind it was carved upon the wall and set with gems an image of a tree in flower. But the throne was empty. At the foot of the dais, upon the lowest step which was broad and deep, there was a stone chair, black and unadorned, and on it sat an old man gazing at his lap. In his hand was a white rod with a golden knob. He did not look up. Solemnly they paced the long floor towards him, until they stood three paces from his footstool. Then Gandalf spoke.

'Hail, Lord and Steward of Minas Tirith, Denethor son of Ecthelion! I am come with counsel and tidings in this dark hour.'

Then the old man looked up. Pippin saw his carven face with its proud bones and skin like ivory, and the long curved nose between the dark deep eyes; and he was reminded not so much of Boromir as of Aragorn. 'Dark indeed is the hour,' said the old man, 'and at such times you are wont to come, Mithrandir. But though all the signs forebode that the doom of Gondor is drawing nigh, less now to me is that darkness than my own darkness. It has been told to me that you bring with you one who saw my son die. Is this he?'

'It is,' said Gandalf. 'One of the twain. The other is with Théoden of Rohan and may come hereafter. Halflings they are, as you see, yet this is not he of whom the omens spoke.'

'Yet a Halfling still,' said Denethor grimly, 'and little love do I bear the name, since those accursed words came to trouble our counsels and drew away my son on the wild errand to his death. My Boromir! Now we have need of you. Faramir should have gone in his stead.'

'He would have gone,' said Gandalf. 'Be not unjust in your grief! Boromir claimed the errand and would not suffer any other to have it. He was a masterful man, and one to take what he desired. I journeyed far with him and learned much of his mood. But you speak of his death. You have had news of that ere we came?'

'I have received this,' said Denethor, and laying down his rod he lifted from his lap the thing that he had been gazing at. In each hand he held up one half of a great horn cloven through the middle: a wild-ox horn bound with silver.

'That is the horn that Boromir always wore!' cried Pippin.

'Verily,' said Denethor. 'And in my turn I bore it, and so did each eldest son of our house, far back into the vanished years before the failing of the kings, since Vorondil father of Mardil hunted the wild kine of Araw in the far fields of Rhûn. I heard it blowing dim upon the northern marches thirteen days ago, and the River brought it to me, broken: it will wind no more.' He paused and there was a heavy silence. Suddenly he turned his black glance upon Pippin. 'What say you to that, Halfling?'

'Thirteen, thirteen days,' faltered Pippin. 'Yes, I think that would be so. Yes, I stood beside him, as he blew the horn. But no help came. Only more orcs.'

'So,' said Denethor, looking keenly at Pippin's face. 'You were there? Tell me more! Why did no help come? And how did you escape, and yet he did not, so mighty a man as he was, and only orcs to withstand him?'

Pippin flushed and forgot his fear. 'The mightiest man may be slain by one arrow,' he said; 'and Boromir was pierced by many. When last I saw him he sank beside a tree and plucked a black-feathered shaft from his side. Then I swooned and was made captive. I saw him no more, and know no more. But I honour his memory, for he was very valiant. He died to save us, my kinsman Meriadoc and myself, waylaid in the woods by the soldiery of the Dark Lord; and though he fell and failed, my gratitude is none the less.'

Then Pippin looked the old man in the eye, for pride stirred strangely within him, still stung by the scorn and suspicion in that cold voice. 'Little service, no doubt, will so great a lord of Men think to find in a hobbit, a halfling from the northern Shire; yet such as it is, I will offer it, in payment of my debt.' Twitching aside his grey cloak, Pippin drew forth his small sword and laid it at Denethor's feet.

A pale smile, like a gleam of cold sun on a winter's evening, passed over the old man's face; but he bent his head and held out his hand, laying the shards of the horn aside. 'Give me the weapon!' he said.

Pippin lifted it and presented the hilt to him. 'Whence came this?' said Denethor. 'Many, many years lie on it. Surely this is a blade wrought by our own kindred in the North in the deep past?'

'It came out of the mounds that lie on the borders of my country,' said Pippin. 'But only evil wights dwell there now, and I will not willingly tell more of them.'

'I see that strange tales are woven about you,' said Denethor, 'and once again it is shown that looks may belie the man – or the halfling. I accept your service. For you are not daunted by words; and you have courteous speech, strange though the sound of it may be to us in the South. And we shall have need of all folk of courtesy, be they great or small, in the days to come. Swear to me now!'

'Take the hilt,' said Gandalf, 'and speak after the Lord, if you are resolved on this.'

'I am,' said Pippin.

The old man laid the sword along his lap, and Pippin put his hand to the hilt, and said slowly after Denethor:

'Here do I swear fealty and service to Gondor, and to the Lord and Steward of the realm, to speak and to be silent, to do and to let be, to come and to go, in need or plenty, in peace or war, in living or dying, from this hour henceforth, until my lord release me, or death take me, or the world end. So say I, Peregrin son of Paladin of the Shire of the Halflings.'

'And this do I hear, Denethor son of Ecthelion, Lord of Gondor, Steward of the High King, and I will not forget it, nor fail to reward that which is given: fealty with love, valour with honour, oath-breaking with vengeance.' Then Pippin received back his sword and put it in its sheath.

'And now,' said Denethor, 'my first command to you: speak and be not silent! Tell me your full tale, and see that you recall all that you can of Boromir, my son. Sit now and begin!' As he spoke he struck a small silver gong that stood near his footstool, and at once servants came forward. Pippin saw then that they had been standing in alcoves on either side of the door, unseen as he and Gandalf entered.

'Bring wine and food and seats for the guests,' said Denethor, 'and see that none trouble us for one hour.'

'It is all that I have to spare, for there is much else to heed,' he said to Gandalf. 'Much of more import, it may seem, and yet to me less pressing. But maybe we can speak again at the end of the day.'

'And earlier, it is to be hoped,' said Gandalf. 'For I have not ridden hither from Isengard, one hundred and fifty leagues, with the speed of wind, only to bring you one small warrior, however courteous. Is it naught to you that Théoden has fought a great battle, and that Isengard is overthrown, and that I have broken the staff of Saruman?'

'It is much to me. But I know already sufficient of these deeds for my own counsel against the menace of the East.' He turned his dark eyes on Gandalf, and now Pippin saw a likeness between the two, and he felt the strain between them, almost as if he saw a line of smouldering fire, drawn from eye to eye, that might suddenly burst into flame.

Denethor looked indeed much more like a great wizard than Gandalf did, more kingly, beautiful, and powerful; and older. Yet by a sense other than sight Pippin perceived that Gandalf had the greater power and the deeper wisdom, and a majesty that was veiled. And he was older, far older. 'How much older?' he wondered, and then he thought how odd it was that he had never thought about it before. Treebeard had said something about wizards, but even then he had not thought of Gandalf as one of them. What was Gandalf? In what far time and place did he come into the world, and when would he leave it? And then his musings broke off, and he saw that Denethor and Gandalf still looked each other in the eye, as if reading the other's mind. But it was Denethor who first withdrew his gaze.

'Yea,' he said; 'for though the Stones be lost, they say, still the lords of

Gondor have keener sight than lesser men, and many messages come to them. But sit now!'

Then men came bearing a chair and a low stool, and one brought a salver with a silver flagon and cups, and white cakes. Pippin sat down, but he could not take his eyes from the old lord. Was it so, or had he only imagined it, that as he spoke of the Stones a sudden gleam of his eye had glanced upon Pippin's face?

'Now tell me your tale, my liege,' said Denethor, half kindly, half mockingly. 'For the words of one whom my son so befriended will be welcome indeed.'

Pippin never forgot that hour in the great hall under the piercing eye of the Lord of Gondor, stabbed ever and anon by his shrewd questions, and all the while conscious of Gandalf at his side, watching and listening, and (so Pippin felt) holding in check a rising wrath and impatience. When the hour was over and Denethor again rang the gong, Pippin felt worn out. 'It cannot be more than nine o'clock,' he thought. 'I could now eat three breakfasts on end.'

'Lead the Lord Mithrandir to the housing prepared for him,' said Denethor, 'and his companion may lodge with him for the present, if he will. But be it known that I have now sworn him to my service, and he shall be known as Peregrin son of Paladin and taught the lesser pass-words. Send word to the Captains that they shall wait on me here, as soon as may be after the third hour has rung.

'And you, my Lord Mithrandir, shall come too, as and when you will. None shall hinder your coming to me at any time, save only in my brief hours of sleep. Let your wrath at an old man's folly run off, and then return to my comfort!'

'Folly?' said Gandalf. 'Nay, my lord, when you are a dotard you will die. You can use even your grief as a cloak. Do you think that I do not understand your purpose in questioning for an hour one who knows the least, while I sit by?'

'If you understand it, then be content,' returned Denethor. 'Pride would be folly that disdained help and counsel at need; but you deal out such gifts according to your own designs. Yet the Lord of Gondor is not to be made the tool of other men's purposes, however worthy. And to him there is no purpose higher in the world as it now stands than the good of Gondor; and the rule of Gondor, my lord, is mine and no other man's, unless the king should come again.'

'Unless the king should come again?' said Gandalf. 'Well, my lord Steward, it is your task to keep some kingdom still against that event, which few now look to see. In that task you shall have all the aid that you are pleased to ask for. But I will say this: the rule of no realm is mine, neither of Gondor nor any other, great or small. But all worthy things that are in peril as the world now stands, those are my care. And for my part, I shall not wholly fail of my task, though Gondor should perish, if anything passes through this night that can still grow fair or bear fruit and flower again in days to come. For I also am a steward. Did you not know?' And with that he turned and strode from the hall with Pippin running at his side.

Gandalf did not look at Pippin or speak a word to him as they went. Their guide brought them from the doors of the hall, and then led them across the Court of the Fountain into a lane between tall buildings of stone. After several turns they came to a house close to the wall of the citadel upon the north side, not far from the shoulder that linked the hill with the mountain. Within, upon the first floor above the street, up a wide carven stair, he showed them to a fair room, light and airy, with goodly hangings of dull gold sheen unfigured. It was sparely furnished, having but a small table, two chairs and a bench; but at either side there were curtained alcoves and well-clad beds within with vessels and basins for washing. There were three high narrow windows that looked northward over the great curve of Anduin, still shrouded in mists, towards the Emyn Muil and Rauros far away. Pippin had to climb on the bench to look out over the deep stone sill.

'Are you angry with me, Gandalf?' he said, as their guide went out and closed the door. 'I did the best I could.'

'You did indeed!' said Gandalf, laughing suddenly; and he came and stood beside Pippin, putting his arm about the hobbit's shoulders, and gazing out of the window. Pippin glanced in some wonder at the face now close beside his own, for the sound of that laugh had been gay and merry. Yet in the wizard's face he saw at first only lines of care and sorrow; though as he looked more intently he perceived that under all there was a great joy: a fountain of mirth enough to set a kingdom laughing, were it to gush forth.

'Indeed you did your best,' said the wizard; 'and I hope that it may be long before you find yourself in such a tight corner again between two such terrible old men. Still the Lord of Gondor learned more from you than you may have guessed, Pippin. You could not hide the fact that Boromir did not lead the Company from Moria, and that there was one among you of high honour who was coming to Minas Tirith; and that he had a famous sword. Men think much about the stories of old days in Gondor; and Denethor has given long thought to the rhyme and to the words *Isildur's Bane*, since Boromir went away.

'He is not as other men of this time, Pippin, and whatever be his descent from father to son, by some chance the blood of Westernesse runs nearly true in him; as it does in his other son, Faramir, and yet did not in Boromir whom he loved best. He has long sight. He can perceive, if he bends his will thither, much of what is passing in the minds of men, even of those that dwell far off. It is difficult to deceive him, and dangerous to try.

'Remember that! For you are now sworn to his service. I do not know what put it into your head, or your heart, to do that. But it was well done. I did not hinder it, for generous deed should not be checked by cold counsel. It touched his heart, as well (may I say it) as pleasing his humour. And at least you are free now to move about as you will in Minas Tirith – when you are not on duty. For there is another side to it. You are at his command; and he will not forget. Be wary still!'

He fell silent and sighed. 'Well, no need to brood on what tomorrow may bring. For one thing, tomorrow will be certain to bring worse than today, for many days to come. And there is nothing more that I can do to help it. The board is set, and the pieces are moving. One piece that I greatly desire to find is Faramir, now the heir of Denethor. I do not think that he is in the City; but I have had no time to gather news. I must go, Pippin. I must go to this lords' council and learn what I can. But the Enemy has the move, and he is about to open his full game. And pawns are likely to see as much of it as any, Peregrin son of Paladin, soldier of Gondor. Sharpen your blade!'

Gandalf went to the door, and there he turned. 'I am in haste, Pippin,' he said. 'Do me a favour when you go out. Even before you rest, if you are not too weary. Go and find Shadowfax and see how he is housed. These people are kindly to beasts, for they are a good and wise folk, but they have less skill with horses than some.'

With that Gandalf went out; and as he did so, there came the note of a clear sweet bell ringing in a tower of the citadel. Three strokes it rang, like silver in the air, and ceased: the third hour from the rising of the sun.

After a minute Pippin went to the door and down the stair and looked about the street. The sun was now shining warm and bright, and the towers and tall houses cast long clear-cut shadows westward. High in the blue air Mount Mindolluin lifted its white helm and snowy cloak. Armed men went to and fro in the ways of the City, as if going at the striking of the hour to changes of post and duty.

'Nine o'clock we'd call it in the Shire,' said Pippin aloud to himself. 'Just the time for a nice breakfast by the open window in spring sunshine. And how I should like breakfast! Do these people ever have it, or is it over? And when do they have dinner, and where?'

Presently he noticed a man, clad in black and white, coming along the narrow street from the centre of the citadel towards him. Pippin felt lonely and made up his mind to speak as the man passed; but he had no need. The man came straight up to him.

'You are Peregrin the Halfling?' he said. 'I am told that you have been sworn to the service of the Lord and of the City. Welcome!' He held out his hand and Pippin took it.

'I am named Beregond son of Baranor. I have no duty this morning, and I have been sent to you to teach you the pass-words, and to tell you some of the many things that no doubt you will wish to know. And for my part, I would learn of you also. For never before have we seen a halfling in this land and though we have heard rumour of them, little is said of them in any tale that we know. Moreover you are a friend of Mithrandir. Do you know him well?'

'Well,' said Pippin. 'I have known *of* him all my short life, as you might say; and lately I have travelled far with him. But there is much to read in that book, and I cannot claim to have seen more than a page or two. Yet perhaps I know him as well as any but a few. Aragorn was the only one of our Company, I think, who really knew him.'

'Aragorn?' said Beregond. 'Who is he?'

'Oh,' stammered Pippin, 'he was a man who went about with us. I think he is in Rohan now.'

'You have been in Rohan, I hear. There is much that I would ask you of that land also; for we put much of what little hope we have in its people. But I am forgetting my errand, which was first to answer what you would ask. What would you know, Master Peregrin?'

'Er well,' said Pippin, 'if I may venture to say so, rather a burning question in my mind at present is, well, what about breakfast and all that? I mean, what are the meal-times, if you understand me, and where is the dining-room, if there is one? And the inns? I looked, but never a one could I see as we rode up, though I had been borne up by the hope of a draught of ale as soon as we came to the homes of wise and courtly men.'

Beregond looked at him gravely. 'An old campaigner, I see,' he said. 'They say that men who go warring afield look ever to the next hope of food and of drink; though I am not a travelled man myself. Then you have not yet eaten today?'

'Well, yes, to speak in courtesy, yes,' said Pippin. 'But no more than a cup of wine and a white cake or two by the kindness of your lord; but he racked me for it with an hour of questions, and that is hungry work.'

Beregond laughed. 'At the table small men may do the greater deeds, we say. But you have broken your fast as well as any man in the Citadel, and with greater honour. This is a fortress and a tower of guard and is now in posture of war. We rise ere the Sun, and take a morsel in the grey light, and go to our duties at the opening hour. But do not despair!' He laughed again, seeing the dismay in Pippin's face. 'Those who have had *heavy* duty take somewhat to refresh their strength in the mid-morning. Then there is the nuncheon, at noon or after as duties allow; and men gather for the daymeal, and such mirth as there still may be, about the hour of sunset.

'Come! We will walk a little and then go find us some refreshment, and eat and drink on the battlement, and survey the fair morning.'

'One moment!' said Pippin blushing. 'Greed, or hunger by your courtesy, put it out of my mind. But Gandalf, Mithrandir as you call him, asked me to see to his horse — Shadowfax, a great steed of Rohan, and the apple of the king's eye, I am told, though he has given him to Mithrandir for his services. I think his new master loves the beast better than he loves many men, and if his good will is of any value to this city, you will treat Shadowfax with all honour: with greater kindness than you have treated this hobbit, if it is possible.'

'Hobbit?' said Beregond.

'That is what we call ourselves,' said Pippin.

'I am glad to learn it,' said Beregond, 'for now I may say that strange accents do not mar fair speech, and hobbits are a fair-spoken folk. But come! You shall make me acquainted with this good horse. I love beasts, and we see them seldom in this stony city; for my people came from the mountain-vales, and before that from Ithilien. But fear not! The visit shall be short, a mere call of courtesy, and we will go thence to the butteries.'

Pippin found that Shadowfax had been well housed and tended. For in the sixth circle, outside the walls of the citadel, there were some fair stables where a few swift horses were kept, hard by the lodgings of the errand-riders of the Lord: messengers always ready to go at the urgent command of Denethor or his chief captains. But now all the horses and the riders were out and away.

Shadowfax whinnied as Pippin entered the stable and turned his head. 'Good morning!' said Pippin. 'Gandalf will come as soon as he may. He is busy, but he sends greetings, and I am to see that all is well with you; and you resting, I hope, after your long labours.'

Shadowfax tossed his head and stamped. But he allowed Beregond to handle his head gently and stroke his great flanks.

'He looks as if he were spoiling for a race, and not newly come from a great journey,' said Beregond. 'How strong and proud he is! Where is his harness? It should be rich and fair.'

'None is rich and fair enough for him,' said Pippin. 'He will have none. If he will consent to bear you, bear you he does; and if not, well, no bit, bridle, whip, or thong will tame him. Farewell, Shadowfax! Have patience. Battle is coming.'

Shadowfax lifted up his head and neighed, so that the stable shook, and they covered their ears. Then they took their leave, seeing that the manger was well filled.

'And now for our manger,' said Beregond, and he led Pippin back to the citadel, and so to a door in the north side of the great tower. There they went down a long cool stair into a wide alley lit with lamps. There were hatches in the walls at the side, and one of these was open.

'This is the storehouse and buttery of my company of the Guard,' said Beregond. 'Greetings, Targon!' he called through the hatch. 'It is early yet, but here is a newcomer that the Lord has taken into his service. He has ridden long and far with a tight belt, and has had sore labour this morning, and he is hungry. Give us what you have!'

They got there bread, and butter, and cheese and apples: the last of the winter store, wrinkled but sound and sweet; and a leather flagon of new-drawn ale, and wooden platters and cups. They put all into a wicker basket and climbed back into the sun; and Beregond brought Pippin to a place at the east end of the great out-thrust battlement where there was an embrasure in the walls with a stone seat beneath the sill. From there they could look out on the morning over the world.

They ate and drank; and they talked now of Gondor and its ways and customs, now of the Shire and the strange countries that Pippin had seen. And ever as they talked Beregond was more amazed, and looked with greater wonder at the hobbit, swinging his short legs as he sat on the seat, or standing tiptoe upon it to peer over the sill at the lands below.

'I will not hide from you, Master Peregrin,' said Beregond, 'that to us you look almost as one of our children, a lad of nine summers or so; and yet you have endured perils and seen marvels that few of our greybeards could boast of. I thought it was the whim of our Lord to take him a noble page, after the manner of the kings of old, they say. But I see that it is not so, and you must pardon my foolishness.'

'I do,' said Pippin. 'Though you are not far wrong. I am still little more than a boy in the reckoning of my own people, and it will be four years yet before I "come of age", as we say in the Shire. But do not bother about me. Come and look and tell me what I can see.'

The sun was now climbing, and the mists in the vale below had been drawn up. The last of them were floating away, just overhead, as wisps of white cloud borne on the stiffening breeze from the East, that was now flapping and tugging the flags and white standards of the citadel. Away down in the valley-bottom, five leagues or so as the eye leaps, the Great River could now be seen grey and glittering, coming out of the north-west, and bending in a mighty sweep south and west again, till it was lost to view in a haze and shimmer, far beyond which lay the Sea fifty leagues away.

Pippin could see all the Pelennor laid out before him, dotted into the distance with farmsteads and little walls, barns and byres, but nowhere could he see any kine or other beasts. Many roads and tracks crossed the green fields, and there was much coming and going: wains moving in lines towards the Great Gate, and others passing out. Now and again a horseman would ride up, and leap from the saddle and hasten into the City. But most of the traffic went out along the chief highway, and that turned south, and then bending swifter than the River skirted the hills and passed soon from sight. It was wide and well-paved, and along its eastern edge ran a broad green riding-track, and beyond that a wall. On the ride horsemen galloped to and fro, but all the street seemed to be choked with great covered wains going south. But soon Pippin saw that all was in fact well-ordered: the wains were moving in three lines, one swifter drawn by horses; another slower, great waggons with fair housings of many colours, drawn by oxen; and along the west rim of the road many smaller carts hauled by trudging men.

'That is the road to the vales of Tumladen and Lossarnach, and the mountain-villages, and then on to Lebennin,' said Beregond. 'There go the last of the wains that bear away to refuge the aged, the children, and the women that must go with them. They must all be gone from the Gate and the road clear for a league before noon: that was the order. It is a sad necessity.' He sighed. 'Few, maybe, of those now sundered will meet again. And there were always too few children in this city; but now there are none – save some young lads that will not depart, and may find some task to do: my own son is one of them.'

They fell silent for a while. Pippin gazed anxiously eastward, as if at any moment he might see thousands of orcs pouring over the fields. 'What can I see there?' he asked, pointing down to the middle of the great curve of the Anduin. 'Is that another city, or what is it?'

'It was a city,' said Beregond, 'the chief city of Gondor, of which this was only a fortress. For that is the ruin of Osgiliath on either side of Anduin, which our enemies took and burned long ago. Yet we won it back in the days of the youth of Denethor: not to dwell in, but to hold as an outpost, and to rebuild the bridge for the passage of our arms. And then came the Fell Riders out of Minas Morgul.'

'The Black Riders?' said Pippin, opening his eyes, and they were wide and dark with an old fear re-awakened.

'Yes, they were black,' said Beregond, 'and I see that you know something of them, though you have not spoken of them in any of your tales.'

'I know of them,' said Pippin softly, 'but I will not speak of them now, so near, so near.' He broke off and lifted his eyes above the River, and it seemed to him that all he could see was a vast and threatening shadow. Perhaps it was mountains looming on the verge of sight, their jagged edges softened by wellnigh twenty leagues of misty air; perhaps it was but a cloud-wall, and beyond that again a yet deeper gloom. But even as he looked it seemed to his eyes that the gloom was growing and gathering, very slowly, slowly rising to smother the regions of the sun.

'So near to Mordor?' said Beregond quietly. 'Yes, there it lies. We seldom name it; but we have dwelt ever in sight of that shadow: sometimes it seems fainter and more distant; sometimes nearer and darker. It is growing and darkening now; and therefore our fear and disquiet grow too. And the Fell Riders, less than a year ago they won back the crossings, and many of our best men were slain. Boromir it was that drove the enemy at last back from this western shore, and we hold still the near half of Osgiliath. For a little while. But we await now a new onslaught there. Maybe the chief onslaught of the war that comes.'

'When?' said Pippin. 'Have you a guess? For I saw the beacons last night and the errand-riders; and Gandalf said that it was a sign that war had begun. He seemed in a desperate hurry. But now everything seems to have slowed up again.'

'Only because everything is now ready,' said Beregond. 'It is but the deep breath before the plunge.'

'But why were the beacons lit last night?'

'It is over-late to send for aid when you are already besieged,' answered Beregond. 'But I do not know the counsel of the Lord and his captains. They have many ways of gathering news. And the Lord Denethor is unlike other men: he sees far. Some say that as he sits alone in his high chamber in the Tower at night, and bends his thought this way and that, he can read somewhat of the future; and that he will at times search even the mind of the Enemy, wrestling with him. And so it is that he is old, worn before his time. But however that may be, my lord Faramir is abroad, beyond the River on some perilous errand, and he may have sent tidings.

'But if you would know what I think set the beacons ablaze, it was the news that came yestereve out of Lebennin. There is a great fleet drawing near to the mouths of Anduin, manned by the corsairs of Umbar in the South. They have long ceased to fear the might of Gondor, and they have allied them with the Enemy, and now make a heavy stroke in his cause. For this attack will draw off much of the help that we looked to have from Lebennin and Belfalas, where folk are hardy and numerous. All the more do our thoughts go north to Rohan; and the more glad are we for these tidings of victory that you bring.

'And yet' – he paused and stood up, and looked round, north, east, and south – 'the doings at Isengard should warn us that we are caught now in a great net and strategy. This is no longer a bickering at the fords, raiding from Ithilien and from Anórien, ambushing and pillaging. This is a great war long-planned, and we are but one piece in it, whatever pride may say. Things move in the far East beyond the Inland Sea, it is reported; and north in Mirkwood and beyond; and south in Harad. And now all realms shall be put to the test, to stand, or fall – under the Shadow.

'Yet, Master Peregrin, we have this honour: ever we bear the brunt of the chief hatred of the Dark Lord, for that hatred comes down out of the depths of time and over the deeps of the Sea. Here will the hammer-stroke fall hardest. And for that reason Mithrandir came hither in such haste. For if we fall, who shall stand? And, Master Peregrin, do you see any hope that we shall stand?'

Pippin did not answer. He looked at the great walls, and the towers and brave banners, and the sun in the high sky, and then at the gathering gloom in the East; and he thought of the long fingers of that Shadow: of the orcs in the woods and the mountains, the treason of Isengard, the birds of evil eye, and the Black Riders even in the lanes of the Shire – and of the winged terror, the Nazgûl. He shuddered, and hope seemed to wither. And even at that moment the sun for a second faltered and was obscured, as though a dark wing had passed across it. Almost beyond hearing he thought he caught, high and far up in the heavens, a cry: faint, but heart-quelling, cruel and cold. He blanched and cowered against the wall.

'What was that?' asked Beregond. 'You also felt something?'

'Yes,' muttered Pippin. 'It is the sign of our fall, and the shadow of doom, a Fell Rider of the air.'

'Yes, the shadow of doom,' said Beregond. 'I fear that Minas Tirith shall fall. Night comes. The very warmth of my blood seems stolen away.'

For a time they sat together with bowed heads and did not speak. Then suddenly Pippin looked up and saw that the sun was still shining and the banners still streaming in the breeze. He shook himself. 'It is passed,' he said. 'No, my heart will not yet despair. Gandalf fell and has returned and is with us. We may stand, if only on one leg, or at least be left still upon our knees.'

'Rightly said!' cried Beregond, rising and striding to and fro. 'Nay, though all things must come utterly to an end in time, Gondor shall not perish yet. Not though the walls be taken by a reckless foe that will build a hill of carrion before them. There are still other fastnesses, and secret ways of escape into the mountains. Hope and memory shall live still in some hidden valley where the grass is green.'

'All the same, I wish it was over for good or ill,' said Pippin. 'I am no warrior at all and dislike any thought of battle; but waiting on the edge of one that I can't escape is worst of all. What a long day it seems already! I should be happier, if we were not obliged to stand and watch, making no move, striking nowhere first. No stroke would have been struck in Rohan, I think, but for Gandalf.'

'Ah, there you lay your finger on the sore that many feel!' said Beregond.

'But things may change when Faramir returns. He is bold, more bold than many deem; for in these days men are slow to believe that a captain can be wise and learned in the scrolls of lore and song, as he is, and yet a man of hardihood and swift judgement in the field. But such is Faramir. Less reckless and eager than Boromir, but not less resolute. Yet what indeed can he do? We cannot assault the mountains of – of yonder realm. Our reach is shortened, and we cannot strike till some foe comes within it. Then our hand must be heavy!' He smote the hilt of his sword.

Pippin looked at him: tall and proud and noble, as all the men that he had yet seen in that land; and with a glitter in his eye as he thought of the battle. 'Alas! my own hand feels as light as a feather,' he thought, but he said nothing. 'A pawn did Gandalf say? Perhaps; but on the wrong chessboard.'

So they talked until the sun reached its height, and suddenly the noon-bells were rung, and there was a stir in the citadel; for all save the watchmen were going to their meal.

'Will you come with me?' said Beregond. 'You may join my mess for this day. I do not know to what company you will be assigned; or the Lord may hold you at his own command. But you will be welcome. And it will be well to meet as many men as you may, while there is yet time.'

'I shall be glad to come,' said Pippin. 'I am lonely, to tell you the truth. I left my best friend behind in Rohan, and I have had no one to talk to or jest with. Perhaps I could really join your company? Are you the captain? If so, you could take me on, or speak for me?'

'Nay, nay,' Beregond laughed, 'I am no captain. Neither office nor rank nor lordship have I, being but a plain man of arms of the Third Company of the Citadel. Yet, Master Peregrin, to be only a man of arms of the Guard of the Tower of Gondor is held worthy in the City, and such men have honour in the land.'

'Then it is far beyond me,' said Pippin. 'Take me back to our room, and if Gandalf is not there, I will go where you like – as your guest.'

Gandalf was not in the lodging and had sent no message; so Pippin went with Beregond and was made known to the men of the Third Company. And it seemed that Beregond got as much honour from it as his guest, for Pippin was very welcome. There had already been much talk in the citadel about Mithrandir's companion and his long closeting with the Lord; and rumour declared that a Prince of the Halflings had come out of the North to offer allegiance to Gondor and five thousand swords. And some said that when the Riders came from Rohan each would bring behind him a halfling warrior, small maybe, but doughty.

Though Pippin had regretfully to destroy this hopeful tale, he could not be rid of his new rank, only fitting, men thought, to one befriended by Boromir and honoured by the Lord Denethor; and they thanked him for coming among them, and hung on his words and stories of the outlands, and gave him as much food and ale as he could wish. Indeed his only trouble was to be 'wary' according to the counsel of Gandalf, and not to let his tongue wag freely after the manner of a hobbit among friends.

At length Beregond rose. 'Farewell for this time!' he said. 'I have duty now till sundown, as have all the others here, I think. But if you are lonely, as you say, maybe you would like a merry guide about the City. My son would go with you gladly. A good lad, I may say. If that pleases you, go down to the lowest circle and ask for the Old Guesthouse in the Rath Celerdain, the Lampwrights' Street. You will find him there with other lads that are remaining in the City. There may be things worth seeing down at the Great Gate ere the closing.'

He went out, and soon after all the others followed. The day was still fine, though it was growing hazy, and it was hot for March, even so far southwards. Pippin felt sleepy, but the lodging seemed cheerless, and he decided to go down and explore the City. He took a few morsels that he had saved to Shadowfax, and they were graciously accepted, though the horse seemed to have no lack. Then he walked on down many winding ways.

People stared much as he passed. To his face men were gravely courteous, saluting him after the manner of Gondor with bowed head and hands upon the breast; but behind him he heard many calls, as those out of doors cried to others within to come and see the Prince of the Halflings, the companion of Mithrandir. Many used some other tongue than the Common Speech, but it was not long before he learned at least what was meant by *Ernil i Pheriannath* and knew that his title had gone down before him into the City.

He came at last by arched streets and many fair alleys and pavements to the lowest and widest circle, and there he was directed to the Lampwrights' Street, a broad way running towards the Great Gate. In it he found the Old Guesthouse, a large building of grey weathered stone with two wings running back from the street, and between them a narrow greensward, behind which was the many-windowed house, fronted along its whole width by a pillared porch and a flight of steps down on to the grass. Boys were playing among the pillars, the only children that Pippin had seen in Minas Tirith, and he stopped to look at them. Presently one of them caught sight of him, and with a shout he sprang across the grass and came into the street, followed by several others. There he stood in front of Pippin, looking him up and down.

'Greetings!' said the lad. 'Where do you come from? You are a stranger in the City.'

'I was,' said Pippin; 'but they say I have become a man of Gondor.'

'Oh come!' said the lad. 'Then we are all men here. But how old are you, and what is your name? I am ten years already, and shall soon be five feet. I am taller than you. But then my father is a Guard, one of the tallest. What is your father?'

'Which question shall I answer first?' said Pippin. 'My father farms the lands round Whitwell near Tuckborough in the Shire. I am nearly twenty-nine, so I pass you there; though I am but four feet, and not likely to grow any more, save sideways.'

'Twenty-nine!' said the lad and whistled. 'Why, you are quite old! As old as my uncle Iorlas. Still,' he added hopefully, 'I wager I could stand you on your head or lay you on your back.'

'Maybe you could, if I let you,' said Pippin with a laugh. 'And maybe I could do the same to you: we know some wrestling tricks in my little country. Where, let me tell you, I am considered uncommonly large and strong; and I have never allowed anyone to stand me on my head. So if it came to a trial and nothing else would serve, I might have to kill you. For when you are older, you will learn that folk are not always what they seem; and though you may have taken me for a soft stranger-lad and easy prey, let me warn you: I am not, I am a halfling, hard, bold, and wicked!' Pippin pulled such a grim face that the boy stepped back a pace, but at once he returned with clenched fists and the light of battle in his eye.

'No!' Pippin laughed. 'Don't believe what strangers say of themselves either! I am not a fighter. But it would be politer in any case for the challenger to say who he is.'

The boy drew himself up proudly. 'I am Bergil son of Beregond of the Guards,' he said.

'So I thought,' said Pippin, 'for you look like your father. I know him and he sent me to find you.'

'Then why did you not say so at once?' said Bergil, and suddenly a look of dismay came over his face. 'Do not tell me that he has changed his mind, and will send me away with the maidens! But no, the last wains have gone.'

'His message is less bad than that, if not good,' said Pippin. 'He says that if you would prefer it to standing me on my head, you might show me round the City for a while and cheer my loneliness. I can tell you some tales of far countries in return.'

Bergil clapped his hands, and laughed with relief. 'All is well,' he cried. 'Come then! We were soon going to the Gate to look on. We will go now.'

'What is happening there?'

'The Captains of the Outlands are expected up the South Road ere sundown. Come with us and you will see.'

Bergil proved a good comrade, the best company Pippin had had since he parted from Merry, and soon they were laughing and talking gaily as they went about the streets, heedless of the many glances that men gave them. Before long they found themselves in a throng going towards the Great Gate. There Pippin went up much in the esteem of Bergil, for when he spoke his name and the pass-word the guard saluted him and let him pass through; and what was more, he allowed him to take his companion with him.

'That is good!' said Bergil. 'We boys are no longer allowed to pass the Gate without an elder. Now we shall see better.'

Beyond the Gate there was a crowd of men along the verge of the road and of the great paved space into which all the ways to Minas Tirith ran. All eyes were turned southwards, and soon a murmur rose: 'There is dust away there! They are coming!'

Pippin and Bergil edged their way forward to the front of the crowd, and waited. Horns sounded at some distance, and the noise of cheering rolled towards them like a gathering wind. Then there was a loud trumpet-blast, and all about them people were shouting.

'Forlong! Forlong!' Pippin heard men calling. 'What do they say?' he asked.

'Forlong has come,' Bergil answered; 'old Forlong the Fat, the Lord of Lossarnach. That is where my grandsire lives. Hurrah! Here he is. Good old Forlong!'

Leading the line there came walking a big thick-limbed horse, and on it sat a man of wide shoulders and huge girth, but old and grey-bearded, yet mail-clad and black-helmed and bearing a long heavy spear. Behind him marched proudly a dusty line of men, well-armed and bearing great battle-axes; grim-faced they were, and shorter and somewhat swarthier than any men that Pippin had yet seen in Gondor.

'Forlong!' men shouted. 'True heart, true friend! Forlong!' But when the men of Lossarnach had passed they muttered: 'So few! Two hundreds, what are they? We hoped for ten times the number. That will be the new tidings of the black fleet. They are sparing only a tithe of their strength. Still every little is a gain.'

And so the companies came and were hailed and cheered and passed through the Gate, men of the Outlands marching to defend the City of Gondor in a dark hour; but always too few, always less than hope looked for or need asked. The men of Ringló Vale behind the son of their lord, Dervorin striding on foot: three hundreds. From the uplands of Morthond, the great Blackroot Vale, tall Duinhir with his sons, Duilin and Derufin, and five hundred bowmen. From the Anfalas, the Langstrand far away, a long line of men of many sorts, hunters and herdsmen and men of little villages, scantily equipped save for the household of Golasgil their lord. From Lamedon, a few grim hillmen without a captain. Fisher-folk of the Ethir, some hundred or more spared from the ships. Hirluin the Fair of the Green Hills from Pinnath Gelin with three hundreds of gallant green-clad men. And last and proudest, Imrahil, Prince of Dol Amroth, kinsman of the Lord, with gilded banners bearing his token of the Ship and the Silver Swan, and a company of knights in full harness riding grey horses; and behind them seven hundreds of men at arms, tall as lords, grey-eyed, dark-haired, singing as they came.

And that was all, less than three thousands full told. No more would come. Their cries and the tramp of their feet passed into the City and died away. The onlookers stood silent for a while. Dust hung in the air, for the wind had died and the evening was heavy. Already the closing hour was drawing nigh, and the red sun had gone behind Mindolluin. Shadow came down on the City.

Pippin looked up, and it seemed to him that the sky had grown ashen-grey, as if a vast dust and smoke hung above them, and light came dully through it. But in the West the dying sun had set all the fume on fire, and now Mindolluin stood black against a burning smoulder flecked with embers. 'So ends a fair day in wrath!' he said, forgetful of the lad at his side.

'So it will, if I have not returned before the sundown-bells,' said Bergil. 'Come! There goes the trumpet for the closing of the Gate.'

Hand in hand they went back into the City, the last to pass the Gate before it was shut; and as they reached the Lampwrights' Street all the bells in the towers tolled solemnly. Lights sprang in many windows, and from the houses and wards of the men at arms along the walls there came the sound of song.

'Farewell for this time,' said Bergil. 'Take my greetings to my father, and thank him for the company that he sent. Come again soon, I beg. Almost I wish now that there was no war, for we might have had some merry times. We might have journeyed to Lossarnach, to my grandsire's house; it is good to be there in Spring, the woods and fields are full of flowers. But maybe we will go thither together yet. They will never overcome our Lord, and my father is very valiant. Farewell and return!'

They parted and Pippin hurried back towards the citadel. It seemed a long way, and he grew hot and very hungry; and night closed down swift and dark. Not a star pricked the sky. He was late for the daymeal in the mess, and Beregond greeted him gladly, and sat him at his side to hear news of his son. After the meal Pippin stayed a while, and then took his leave, for a strange gloom was on him, and now he desired very much to see Gandalf again.

'Can you find your way?' said Beregond at the door of the small hall, on the north side of the citadel, where they had sat. 'It is a black night, and all the blacker since orders came that lights are to be dimmed within the City, and none are to shine out from the walls. And I can give you news of another order: you will be summoned to the Lord Denethor early tomorrow. I fear you will not be for the Third Company. Still we may hope to meet again. Farewell and sleep in peace!'

The lodging was dark, save for a little lantern set on the table. Gandalf was not there. Gloom settled still more heavily on Pippin. He climbed on the bench and tried to peer out of a window, but it was like looking into a pool of ink. He got down and closed the shutter and went to bed. For a while he lay and listened for sounds of Gandalf's return, and then he fell into an uneasy sleep.

In the night he was wakened by a light, and he saw that Gandalf had come and was pacing to and fro in the room beyond the curtain of the alcove. There were candles on the table and rolls of parchment. He heard the wizard sigh, and mutter: 'When will Faramir return?'

'Hullo!' said Pippin, poking his head round the curtain. 'I thought you had forgotten all about me. I am glad to see you back. It has been a long day.'

'But the night will be too short,' said Gandalf. 'I have come back here, for I must have a little peace, alone. You should sleep, in a bed while you still may. At the sunrise I shall take you to the Lord Denethor again. No, when the summons comes, not at sunrise. The Darkness has begun. There will be no dawn.'

CHAPTER II

THE PASSING OF THE GREY COMPANY

Gandalf was gone, and the thudding hoofs of Shadowfax were lost in the night, when Merry came back to Aragorn. He had only a light bundle, for he had lost his pack at Parth Galen, and all he had was a few useful things he had picked up among the wreckage of Isengard. Hasufel was already saddled. Legolas and Gimli with their horse stood close by.

'So four of the Company still remain,' said Aragorn. 'We will ride on together. But we shall not go alone, as I thought. The king is now determined to set out at once. Since the coming of the winged shadow, he desires to return to the hills under cover of night.'

'And then whither?' said Legolas.

'I cannot say yet,' Aragorn answered. 'As for the king, he will go to the muster that he commanded at Edoras, four nights from now. And there, I think, he will hear tidings of war, and the Riders of Rohan will go down to Minas Tirith. But for myself, and any that will go with me . . .'

'I for one!' cried Legolas. 'And Gimli with him!' said the Dwarf.

'Well, for myself,' said Aragorn, 'it is dark before me. I must go down also to Minas Tirith, but I do not yet see the road. An hour long prepared approaches.'

'Don't leave me behind!' said Merry. 'I have not been of much use yet; but I don't want to be laid aside, like baggage to be called for when all is over. I don't think the Riders will want to be bothered with me now. Though, of course, the king did say that I was to sit by him when he came to his house and tell him all about the Shire.'

'Yes,' said Aragorn, 'and your road lies with him, I think, Merry. But do not look for mirth at the ending. It will be long, I fear, ere Théoden sits at ease again in Meduseld. Many hopes will wither in this bitter Spring.'

Soon all were ready to depart: twenty-four horses, with Gimli behind Legolas, and Merry in front of Aragorn. Presently they were riding swiftly through the night. They had not long passed the mounds at the Fords of Isen, when a Rider galloped up from the rear of their line.

'My lord,' he said to the king, 'there are horsemen behind us. As we crossed the fords I thought that I heard them. Now we are sure. They are overtaking us, riding hard.'

Théoden at once called a halt. The Riders turned about and seized their spears. Aragorn dismounted and set Merry on the ground, and drawing his sword he stood by the king's stirrup. Éomer and his esquire rode back to the rear. Merry felt more like unneeded baggage than ever, and he wondered, if there was a fight, what he should do. Supposing the king's small escort was trapped and overcome, but he escaped into the darkness – alone in the wild fields of Rohan with no idea of where he was in all the endless miles? 'No good!' he thought. He drew his sword and tightened his belt.

The sinking moon was obscured by a great sailing cloud, but suddenly it rode out clear again. Then they all heard the sound of hoofs, and at the same moment they saw dark shapes coming swiftly on the path from the fords. The moonlight glinted here and there on the points of spears. The number of the pursuers could not be told, but they seemed no fewer than the king's escort, at the least.

When they were some fifty paces off, Éomer cried in a loud voice: 'Halt! Halt! Who rides in Rohan?'

The pursuers brought their steeds to a sudden stand. A silence followed; and then in the moonlight, a horseman could be seen dismounting and walking slowly forward. His hand showed white as he held it up, palm outward, in token of peace; but the king's men gripped their weapons. At ten paces the man stopped. He was tall, a dark standing shadow. Then his clear voice rang out.

'Rohan? Rohan did you say? That is a glad word. We seek that land in haste from long afar.'

'You have found it,' said Éomer. 'When you crossed the fords yonder you entered it. But it is the realm of Théoden the King. None ride here save by his leave. Who are you? And what is your haste?'

'Halbarad Dúnadan, Ranger of the North I am,' cried the man. 'We seek one Aragorn son of Arathorn, and we heard that he was in Rohan.'

'And you have found him also!' cried Aragorn. Giving his reins to Merry, he ran forward and embraced the newcomer. 'Halbarad!' he said. 'Of all joys this is the least expected!'

Merry breathed a sigh of relief. He had thought that this was some last trick of Saruman's, to waylay the king while he had only a few men about him; but it seemed that there would be no need to die in Théoden's defence, not yet at any rate. He sheathed his sword.

'All is well,' said Aragorn, turning back. 'Here are some of my own kin from the far land where I dwelt. But why they come, and how many they be, Halbarad shall tell us.'

'I have thirty with me,' said Halbarad. 'That is all of our kindred that could be gathered in haste; but the brethren Elladan and Elrohir have ridden with us, desiring to go to the war. We rode as swiftly as we might when your summons came.'

'But I did not summon you,' said Aragorn, 'save only in wish. My thoughts have often turned to you, and seldom more than tonight; yet I have sent no word. But come! All such matters must wait. You find us riding in haste and danger. Ride with us now, if the king will give his leave.'

Théoden was indeed glad of the news. 'It is well!' he said. 'If these kinsmen be in any way like to yourself, my lord Aragorn, thirty such knights will be a strength that cannot be counted by heads.'

Then the Riders set out again, and Aragorn for a while rode with the Dúnedain; and when they had spoken of tidings in the North and in the South, Elrohir said to him:

'I bring word to you from my father: *The days are short. If thou art in haste, remember the Paths of the Dead.*'

'Always my days have seemed to me too short to achieve my desire,' answered Aragorn. 'But great indeed will be my haste ere I take that road.'

'That will soon be seen,' said Elrohir. 'But let us speak no more of these things upon the open road!'

And Aragorn said to Halbarad: 'What is that that you bear, kinsman?' For he saw that instead of a spear he bore a tall staff, as it were a standard, but it was close-furled in a black cloth bound about with many thongs.

'It is a gift that I bring you from the Lady of Rivendell,' answered Halbarad. 'She wrought it in secret, and long was the making. But she also sends word to you: *The days now are short. Either our hope cometh, or all hopes end. Therefore I send thee what I have made for thee. Fare well, Elfstone!*'

And Aragorn said: 'Now I know what you bear. Bear it still for me a while!' And he turned and looked away to the North under the great stars, and then he fell silent and spoke no more while the night's journey lasted.

The night was old and the East grey when they rode up at last from Deeping-coomb and came back to the Hornburg. There they were to lie and rest for a brief while and take counsel.

Merry slept until he was roused by Legolas and Gimli. 'The Sun is high,' said Legolas. 'All others are up and doing. Come, Master Sluggard, and look at this place while you may!'

'There was a battle here three nights ago,' said Gimli, 'and here Legolas and I played a game that I won only by a single orc. Come and see how it was! And there are caves, Merry, caves of wonder! Shall we visit them, Legolas, do you think?'

'Nay! There is no time,' said the Elf. 'Do not spoil the wonder with haste! I have given you my word to return hither with you, if a day of peace and freedom comes again. But it is now near to noon, and at that hour we eat, and then set out again, I hear.'

Merry got up and yawned. His few hours' sleep had not been nearly enough; he was tired and rather dismal. He missed Pippin, and felt that he was only a burden, while everybody was making plans for speed in a business that he did not fully understand. 'Where is Aragorn?' he asked.

'In a high chamber of the Burg,' said Legolas. 'He has neither rested nor slept, I think. He went thither some hours ago, saying that he must take thought, and only his kinsman, Halbarad, went with him; but some dark doubt or care sits on him.'

'They are a strange company, these newcomers,' said Gimli. 'Stout men and lordly they are, and the Riders of Rohan look almost as boys beside them; for they are grim men of face, worn like weathered rocks for the most part, even as Aragorn himself; and they are silent.'

'But even as Aragorn they are courteous, if they break their silence,' said Legolas. 'And have you marked the brethren Elladan and Elrohir? Less sombre is their gear than the others', and they are fair and gallant as Elven-lords; and that is not to be wondered at in the sons of Elrond of Rivendell.'

'Why have they come? Have you heard?' asked Merry. He had now dressed, and he flung his grey cloak about his shoulders; and the three passed out together towards the ruined gate of the Burg.

'They answered a summons, as you heard,' said Gimli. 'Word came to Rivendell, they say: *Aragorn has need of his kindred. Let the Dúnedain ride to him in Rohan!* But whence this message came they are now in doubt. Gandalf sent it, I would guess.'

'Nay, Galadriel,' said Legolas. 'Did she not speak through Gandalf of the ride of the Grey Company from the North?'

'Yes, you have it,' said Gimli. 'The Lady of the Wood! She read many hearts and desires. Now why did not we wish for some of our own kinsfolk, Legolas?'

Legolas stood before the gate and turned his bright eyes away north and east, and his fair face was troubled. 'I do not think that any would come,' he answered. 'They have no need to ride to war; war already marches on their own lands.'

For a while the three companions walked together, speaking of this and that turn of the battle, and they went down from the broken gate, and passed the mounds of the fallen on the greensward beside the road, until they stood on Helm's Dike and looked into the Coomb. The Death Down already stood there, black and tall and stony, and the great trampling and scoring of the grass by the Huorns could be plainly seen. The Dunlendings and many men of the garrison of the Burg were at work on the Dike or in the fields and about the battered walls behind; yet all seemed strangely quiet: a weary valley resting after a great storm. Soon they turned back and went to the midday meal in the hall of the Burg.

The king was already there, and as soon as they entered he called for Merry and had a seat set for him at his side. 'It is not as I would have it,' said Théoden; 'for this is little like my fair house in Edoras. And your friend is gone, who should also be here. But it may be long ere we sit, you and I, at the high table in Meduseld; there will be no time for feasting when I return thither. But come now! Eat and drink, and let us speak together while we may. And then you shall ride with me.'

'May I?' said Merry, surprised and delighted. 'That would be splendid!' He had never felt more grateful for any kindness in words. 'I am afraid I am only in everybody's way,' he stammered; 'but I should like to do anything I could, you know.'

'I doubt it not,' said the king. 'I have had a good hill-pony made ready for you. He will bear you as swift as any horse by the roads that we shall take. For I will ride from the Burg by mountain paths, not by the plain, and so come to Edoras by way of Dunharrow where the Lady Éowyn awaits me. You shall be my esquire, if you will. Is there gear of war in this place, Éomer, that my sword-thain could use?'

'There are no great weapon-hoards here, lord,' answered Éomer. 'Maybe a light helm might be found to fit him; but we have no mail or sword for one of his stature.'

'I have a sword,' said Merry, climbing from his seat, and drawing from its black sheath his small bright blade. Filled suddenly with love for this old man, he knelt on one knee, and took his hand and kissed it. 'May I lay the sword of Meriadoc of the Shire on your lap, Théoden King?' he cried. 'Receive my service, if you will!'

'Gladly will I take it,' said the king; and laying his long old hands upon the brown hair of the hobbit, he blessed him. 'Rise now, Meriadoc, esquire of Rohan of the household of Meduseld!' he said. 'Take your sword and bear it unto good fortune!'

'As a father you shall be to me,' said Merry.

'For a little while,' said Théoden.

They talked then together as they ate, until presently Éomer spoke. 'It is near the hour that we set for our going, lord,' he said. 'Shall I bid men sound the horns? But where is Aragorn? His place is empty and he has not eaten.'

'We will make ready to ride,' said Théoden; 'but let word be sent to the Lord Aragorn that the hour is nigh.'

The king with his guard and Merry at his side passed down from the gate of the Burg to where the Riders were assembling on the green. Many were already mounted. It would be a great company; for the king was leaving only a small garrison in the Burg, and all who could be spared were riding to the weapontake at Edoras. A thousand spears had indeed already ridden away at night; but still there would be some five hundred more to go with the king, for the most part men from the fields and dales of Westfold.

A little apart the Rangers sat, silent, in an ordered company, armed with spear and bow and sword. They were clad in cloaks of dark grey, and their hoods were cast now over helm and head. Their horses were strong and of proud bearing, but rough-haired; and one stood there without a rider, Aragorn's own horse that they had brought from the North; Roheryn was his name. There was no gleam of stone or gold, nor any fair thing in all their gear and harness; nor did their riders bear any badge or token, save only that each cloak was pinned upon the left shoulder by a brooch of silver shaped like a rayed star.

The king mounted his horse, Snowmane, and Merry sat beside him on his pony: Stybba was his name. Presently Éomer came out from the gate, and with him was Aragorn, and Halbarad bearing the great staff close-furled in black, and two tall men, neither young nor old. So much alike were they, the sons of Elrond, that few could tell them apart: dark-haired, grey-eyed, and their faces elven-fair, clad alike in bright mail beneath cloaks of silver-grey. Behind them walked Legolas and Gimli. But Merry had eyes only for Aragorn, so startling was the change that he saw in him. as if in one night many years had fallen on his head. Grim was his face, grey-hued and weary.

'I am troubled in mind, lord,' he said, standing by the king's horse. 'I have heard strange words, and I see new perils far off. I have laboured long in thought, and now I fear that I must change my purpose. Tell me, Théoden, you ride now to Dunharrow, how long will it be ere you come there?'

'It is now a full hour past noon,' said Éomer. 'Before the night of the third day from now we should come to the Hold. The Moon will then be one night past his full, and the muster that the king commanded will be held the day after. More speed we cannot make, if the strength of Rohan is to be gathered.'

Aragorn was silent for a moment. 'Three days,' he murmured, 'and the muster of Rohan will only be begun. But I see that it cannot now be hastened.' He looked up, and it seemed that he had made some decision; his face was less troubled. 'Then, by your leave, lord, I must take new counsel for myself and my kindred. We must ride our own road, and no longer in secret. For me the time of stealth has passed. I will ride east by the swiftest way, and I will take the Paths of the Dead.'

'The Paths of the Dead!' said Théoden, and trembled. 'Why do you speak of them?' Éomer turned and gazed at Aragorn, and it seemed to Merry that the faces of the Riders that sat within hearing turned pale at the words. 'If there be in truth such paths,' said Théoden, 'their gate is in Dunharrow; but no living man may pass it.'

'Alas! Aragorn my friend!' said Éomer. 'I had hoped that we should ride to war together; but if you seek the Paths of the Dead, then our parting is come, and it is little likely that we shall ever meet again under the Sun.'

'That road I will take, nonetheless,' said Aragorn. 'But I say to you, Éomer, that in battle we may yet meet again, though all the hosts of Mordor should stand between.'

'You will do as you will, my lord Aragorn,' said Théoden. 'It is your doom, maybe, to tread strange paths that others dare not. This parting grieves me, and my strength is lessened by it; but now I must take the mountain-roads and delay no longer. Farewell!'

'Farewell, lord!' said Aragorn. 'Ride unto great renown! Farewell, Merry! I leave you in good hands, better than we hoped when we hunted the orcs to Fangorn. Legolas and Gimli will still hunt with me, I hope; but we shall not forget you.'

'Good-bye!' said Merry. He could find no more to say. He felt very small, and he was puzzled and depressed by all these gloomy words. More than ever he missed the unquenchable cheerfulness of Pippin. The Riders were ready, and their horses were fidgeting; he wished they would start and get it over.

Now Théoden spoke to Éomer, and he lifted up his hand and cried aloud, and with that word the Riders set forth. They rode over the Dike and down the Coomb, and then, turning swiftly eastwards, they took a path that skirted the foothills for a mile or so, until bending south it passed back among the hills and disappeared from view. Aragorn rode to the Dike and watched till the king's men were far down the Coomb. Then he turned to Halbarad.

'There go three that I love, and the smallest not the least,' he said. 'He knows not to what end he rides; yet if he knew, he still would go on.'

'A little people, but of great worth are the Shire-folk,' said Halbarad. 'Little do they know of our long labour for the safekeeping of their borders, and yet I grudge it not.'

'And now our fates are woven together,' said Aragorn. 'And yet, alas! here we must part. Well, I must eat a little, and then we also must hasten away. Come, Legolas and Gimli! I must speak with you as I eat.'

Together they went back into the Burg; yet for some time Aragorn sat

silent at the table in the hall, and the others waited for him to speak.
'Come!' said Legolas at last. 'Speak and be comforted, and shake off the
shadow! What has happened since we came back to this grim place in the
grey morning?'

'A struggle somewhat grimmer for my part than the battle of the Hornburg,' answered Aragorn. 'I have looked in the Stone of Orthanc, my
friends.'

'You have looked in that accursed stone of wizardry!' exclaimed Gimli
with fear and astonishment in his face. 'Did you say aught to – him? Even
Gandalf feared that encounter.'

'You forget to whom you speak,' said Aragorn sternly, and his eyes
glinted. 'What do you fear that I should say to him? Did I not openly
proclaim my title before the doors of Edoras? Nay, Gimli,' he said in a
softer voice, and the grimness left his face, and he looked like one who has
laboured in sleepless pain for many nights. 'Nay, my friends, I am the
lawful master of the Stone, and I had both the right and the strength to
use it, or so I judged. The right cannot be doubted. The strength was
enough – barely.'

He drew a deep breath. 'It was a bitter struggle, and the weariness is
slow to pass. I spoke no word to him, and in the end I wrenched the Stone
to my own will. That alone he will find hard to endure. And he beheld
me. Yes, Master Gimli, he saw me, but in other guise than you see me
here. If that will aid him, then I have done ill. But I do not think so. To
know that I lived and walked the earth was a blow to his heart, I deem;
for he knew it not till now. The eyes in Orthanc did not see through the
armour of Théoden; but Sauron has not forgotten Isildur and the sword
of Elendil. Now in the very hour of his great designs the heir of Isildur
and the Sword are revealed; for I showed the blade re-forged to him. He
is not so mighty yet that he is above fear; nay, doubt ever gnaws him.'

'But he wields great dominion, nonetheless,' said Gimli; 'and now he
will strike more swiftly.'

'The hasty stroke goes oft astray,' said Aragorn. 'We must press our
Enemy, and no longer wait upon him for the move. See my friends, when
I had mastered the Stone, I learned many things. A grave peril I saw
coming unlooked-for upon Gondor from the South that will draw off great
strength from the defence of Minas Tirith. If it is not countered swiftly, I
deem that the City will be lost ere ten days be gone.'

'Then lost it must be,' said Gimli. 'For what help is there to send thither,
and how could it come there in time?'

'I have no help to send, therefore I must go myself,' said Aragorn. 'But
there is only one way through the mountains that will bring me to the
coastlands before all is lost. That is the Paths of the Dead.'

'The Paths of the Dead!' said Gimli. 'It is a fell name; and little to the liking to the Men of Rohan, as I saw. Can the living use such a road and not perish? And even if you pass that way, what will so few avail to counter the strokes of Mordor?'

'The living have never used that road since the coming of the Rohirrim,' said Aragorn, 'for it is closed to them. But in this dark hour the heir of Isildur may use it, if he dare. Listen! This is the word that the sons of Elrond bring to me from their father in Rivendell, wisest in lore: *Bid Aragorn remember the words of the seer, and the Paths of the Dead.*'

'And what may be the words of the seer?' said Legolas.

'Thus spoke Malbeth the Seer, in the days of Arvedui, last king at Fornost,' said Aragorn:

> *Over the land there lies a long shadow,*
> *westward reaching wings of darkness.*
> *The Tower trembles; to the tombs of kings*
> *doom approaches. The Dead awaken;*
> *for the hour is come for the oathbreakers:*
> *at the Stone of Erech they shall stand again*
> *and hear there a horn in the hills ringing.*
> *Whose shall the horn be? Who shall call them*
> *from the grey twilight, the forgotten people?*
> *The heir of him to whom the oath they swore.*
> *From the North shall he come, need shall drive him:*
> *he shall pass the Door to the Paths of the Dead.*

'Dark ways, doubtless,' said Gimli, 'but no darker than these staves are to me.'

'If you would understand them better, then I bid you come with me,' said Aragorn; 'for that way I now shall take. But I do not go gladly; only need drives me. Therefore, only of your free will would I have you come, for you will find both toil and great fear, and maybe worse.'

'I will go with you even on the Paths of the Dead, and to whatever end they may lead,' said Gimli.

'I also will come,' said Legolas, 'for I do not fear the Dead.'

'I hope that the forgotten people will not have forgotten how to fight,' said Gimli; 'for otherwise I see not why we should trouble them.'

'That we shall know if ever we come to Erech,' said Aragorn. 'But the oath that they broke was to fight against Sauron, and they must fight therefore, if they are to fulfil it. For at Erech there stands yet a black stone that was brought, it was said, from Númenor by Isildur; and it was set upon a hill, and upon it the King of the Mountains swore allegiance to him in the beginning of the realm of Gondor. But when Sauron returned and grew in might again, Isildur summoned the Men of the Mountains to fulfil their oath, and they would not: for they had worshipped Sauron in the Dark Years.

'Then Isildur said to their king: "Thou shalt be the last king. And if the West prove mightier than thy Black Master, this curse I lay upon thee and thy folk: to rest never until your oath is fulfilled. For this war will last through years uncounted, and you shall be summoned once again ere the end." And they fled before the wrath of Isildur, and did not dare to go forth to war on Sauron's part; and they hid themselves in secret places in the mountains and had no dealings with other men, but slowly dwindled in the barren hills. And the terror of the Sleepless Dead lies about the Hill of Erech and all places where that people lingered. But that way I must go, since there are none living to help me.'

He stood up. 'Come!' he cried, and drew his sword, and it flashed in the twilit hall of the Burg. 'To the Stone of Erech! I seek the Paths of the Dead. Come with me who will!'

Legolas and Gimli made no answer, but they rose and followed Aragorn from the hall. On the green there waited, still and silent, the hooded Rangers. Legolas and Gimli mounted. Aragorn sprang upon Roheryn. Then Halbarad lifted a great horn, and the blast of it echoed in Helm's Deep: and with that they leapt away, riding down the Coomb like thunder, while all the men that were left on Dike or Burg stared in amaze.

And while Théoden went by slow paths in the hills, the Grey Company passed swiftly over the plain, and on the next day in the afternoon they came to Edoras; and there they halted only briefly, ere they passed up the valley, and so came to Dunharrow as darkness fell.

The Lady Éowyn greeted them and was glad of their coming; for no mightier men had she seen than the Dúnedain and the fair sons of Elrond; but on Aragorn most of all her eyes rested. And when they sat at supper with her, they talked together, and she heard of all that had passed since Théoden rode away, concerning which only hasty tidings had yet reached her; and when she heard of the battle in Helm's Deep and the great slaughter of their foes, and of the charge of Théoden and his knights, then her eyes shone.

But at last she said: 'Lords, you are weary and shall now go to your beds with such ease as can be contrived in haste. But tomorrow fairer housing shall be found for you.'

But Aragorn said: 'Nay, lady, be not troubled for us! If we may lie here tonight and break our fast tomorrow, it will be enough. For I ride on an errand most urgent, and with the first light of morning we must go.'

She smiled on him and said: 'Then it was kindly done, lord, to ride so many miles out of your way to bring tidings to Éowyn, and to speak with her in her exile.'

'Indeed no man would count such a journey wasted,' said Aragorn; 'and yet, lady, I could not have come hither, if it were not that the road which I must take leads me to Dunharrow.'

And she answered as one that likes not what is said: 'Then, lord, you are astray; for out of Harrowdale no road runs east or south; and you had best return as you came.'

'Nay, lady,' said he, 'I am not astray; for I walked in this land ere you were born to grace it. There is a road out of this valley, and that road I shall take. Tomorrow I shall ride by the Paths of the Dead.'

Then she stared at him as one that is stricken, and her face blanched, and for long she spoke no more, while all sat silent. 'But, Aragorn,' she said at last, 'is it then your errand to seek death? For that is all that you will find on that road. They do not suffer the living to pass.'

'They may suffer me to pass,' said Aragorn; 'but at the least I will adventure it. No other road will serve.'

'But this is madness,' she said. 'For here are men of renown and prowess, whom you should not take into the shadows, but should lead to war, where men are needed. I beg you to remain and ride with my brother; for then all our hearts will be gladdened, and our hope be the brighter.'

'It is not madness, lady,' he answered; 'for I go on a path appointed. But those who follow me do so of their free will; and if they wish now to remain and ride with the Rohirrim, they may do so. But I shall take the Paths of the Dead, alone, if needs be.'

Then they said no more, and they ate in silence; but her eyes were ever upon Aragorn, and the others saw that she was in great torment of mind. At length they arose, and took their leave of the Lady, and thanked her for her care, and went to their rest.

But as Aragorn came to the booth where he was to lodge with Legolas and Gimli, and his companions had gone in, there came the Lady Éowyn after him and called to him. He turned and saw her as a glimmer in the night, for she was clad in white; but her eyes were on fire.

'Aragorn,' she said, 'why will you go on this deadly road?'

'Because I must,' he said. 'Only so can I see any hope of doing my part in the war against Sauron. I do not choose paths of peril, Éowyn. Were I to go where my heart dwells, far in the North I would now be wandering in the fair valley of Rivendell.'

For a while she was silent, as if pondering what this might mean. Then suddenly she laid her hand on his arm. 'You are a stern lord and resolute,' she said; 'and thus do men win renown.' She paused. 'Lord,' she said, 'if you must go, then let me ride in your following. For I am weary of skulking in the hills, and wish to face peril and battle.'

'Your duty is with your people,' he answered.

'Too often have I heard of duty,' she cried. 'But am I not of the House of Eorl, a shieldmaiden and not a dry-nurse? I have waited on faltering feet long enough. Since they falter no longer, it seems, may I not now spend my life as I will?'

'Few may do that with honour,' he answered. 'But as for you, lady: did you not accept the charge to govern the people until their lord's return? If you had not been chosen, then some marshal or captain would have been set in the same place, and he could not ride away from his charge, were he weary of it or no.'

'Shall I always be chosen?' she said bitterly. 'Shall I always be left behind when the Riders depart, to mind the house while they win renown, and find food and beds when they return?'

'A time may come soon,' said he, 'when none will return. Then there will be need of valour without renown, for none shall remember the deeds that are done in the last defence of your homes. Yet the deeds will not be less valiant because they are unpraised.'

And she answered: 'All your words are but to say: you are a woman, and your part is in the house. But when the men have died in battle and honour, you have leave to be burned in the house, for the men will need it no more. But I am of the House of Eorl and not a serving-woman. I can ride and wield blade, and I do not fear either pain or death.'

'What do you fear, lady?' he asked.

'A cage,' she said. 'To stay behind bars, until use and old age accept them, and all chance of doing great deeds is gone beyond recall or desire.'

'And yet you counselled me not to adventure on the road that I had chosen, because it is perilous?'

'So may one counsel another,' she said. 'Yet I do not bid you flee from peril, but to ride to battle where your sword may win renown and victory. I would not see a thing that is high and excellent cast away needlessly.'

'Nor would I,' he said. 'Therefore I say to you, lady: Stay! For you have no errand to the South.'

'Neither have those others who go with thee. They go only because they would not be parted from thee – because they love thee.' Then she turned and vanished into the night.

When the light of day was come into the sky but the sun was not yet risen above the high ridges in the East, Aragorn made ready to depart. His company was all mounted, and he was about to leap into the saddle, when the Lady Éowyn came to bid them farewell. She was clad as a Rider and girt with a sword. In her hand she bore a cup, and she set it to her lips and drank a little, wishing them good speed; and then she gave the cup to Aragorn, and he drank, and he said: 'Farewell, Lady of Rohan! I drink to the fortunes of your House, and of you, and of all your people. Say to your brother: beyond the shadows we may meet again!'

Then it seemed to Gimli and Legolas who were nearby that she wept, and in one so stern and proud that seemed the more grievous. But she said: 'Aragorn, wilt thou go?'

'I will,' he said.

'Then wilt thou not let me ride with this company, as I have asked?'

'I will not, lady,' he said. 'For that I could not grant without leave of the king and of your brother; and they will not return until tomorrow. But I count now every hour, indeed every minute. Farewell!'

Then she fell on her knees, saying: 'I beg thee!'

'Nay, lady,' he said, and taking her by the hand he raised her. Then he kissed her hand, and sprang into the saddle, and rode away, and did not look back; and only those who knew him well and were near to him saw the pain that he bore.

But Éowyn stood still as a figure carven in stone, her hands clenched at her sides, and she watched them until they passed into the shadows under the black Dwimorberg, the Haunted Mountain, in which was the Door of the Dead. When they were lost to view, she turned, stumbling as one that is blind, and went back to her lodging. But none of her folk saw this parting, for they hid themselves in fear and would not come forth until the day was up, and the reckless strangers were gone.

And some said: 'They are Elvish wights. Let them go where they belong, into the dark places, and never return. The times are evil enough.'

The light was still grey as they rode, for the sun had not yet climbed over the black ridges of the Haunted Mountain before them. A dread fell on them, even as they passed between the lines of ancient stones and so came to the Dimholt. There under the gloom of black trees that not even Legolas could long endure they found a hollow place opening at the mountain's root, and right in their path stood a single mighty stone like a finger of doom.

'My blood runs chill,' said Gimli, but the others were silent, and his voice fell dead on the dank fir-needles at his feet. The horses would not pass the threatening stone, until the riders dismounted and led them about. And so they came at last deep into the glen; and there stood a sheer wall of rock, and in the wall the Dark Door gaped before them like the mouth of night. Signs and figures were carved above its wide arch too dim to read, and fear flowed from it like a grey vapour.

The company halted, and there was not a heart among them that did not quail, unless it were the heart of Legolas of the Elves, for whom the ghosts of Men have no terror.

'This is an evil door,' said Halbarad, 'and my death lies beyond it. I will dare to pass it nonetheless; but no horse will enter.'

'But we must go in, and therefore the horses must go too,' said Aragorn. 'For if ever we come through this darkness, many leagues lie beyond, and every hour that is lost there will bring the triumph of Sauron nearer. Follow me!'

Then Aragorn led the way, and such was the strength of his will in that hour that all the Dúnedain and their horses followed him. And indeed the love that the horses of the Rangers bore for their riders was so great that they were willing to face even the terror of the Door, if their masters' hearts were steady as they walked beside them. But Arod, the horse of Rohan, refused the way, and he stood sweating and trembling in a fear that was grievous to see. Then Legolas laid his hands on his eyes and sang some words that went soft in the gloom, until he suffered himself to be led, and Legolas passed in. And there stood Gimli the Dwarf left all alone.

His knees shook, and he was wroth with himself. 'Here is a thing unheard of!' he said. 'An Elf will go underground and a Dwarf dare not!' With that he plunged in. But it seemed to him that he dragged his feet like lead over the threshold; and at once a blindness came upon him, even upon Gimli Glóin's son who had walked unafraid in many deep places of the world.

Aragorn had brought torches from Dunharrow, and now he went ahead bearing one aloft; and Elladan with another went at the rear, and Gimli, stumbling behind, strove to overtake him. He could see nothing but the dim flame of the torches; but if the company halted, there seemed an endless whisper of voices all about him, a murmur of words in no tongue that he had ever heard before.

Nothing assailed the company nor withstood their passage, and yet steadily fear grew on the Dwarf as he went on: most of all because he knew now that there could be no turning back; all the paths behind were thronged by an unseen host that followed in the dark.

So time unreckoned passed, until Gimli saw a sight that he was ever afterwards loth to recall. The road was wide, as far as he could judge, but now the company came suddenly into a great empty space, and there were no longer any walls upon either side. The dread was so heavy on him that he could hardly walk. Away to the left something glittered in the gloom as Aragorn's torch drew near. Then Aragorn halted and went to look what it might be.

'Does he feel no fear?' muttered the Dwarf. 'In any other cave Gimli

Glóin's son would have been the first to run to the gleam of gold. But not here! Let it lie!'

Nonetheless he drew near, and saw Aragorn kneeling, while Elladan held aloft both torches. Before him were the bones of a mighty man. He had been clad in mail, and still his harness lay there whole; for the cavern's air was as dry as dust, and his hauberk was gilded. His belt was of gold and garnets, and rich with gold was the helm upon his bony head face downward on the floor. He had fallen near the far wall of the cave, as now could be seen, and before him stood a stony door closed fast: his finger-bones were still clawing at the cracks. A notched and broken sword lay by him, as if he had hewn at the rock in his last despair.

Aragorn did not touch him, but after gazing silently for a while he rose and sighed. 'Hither shall the flowers of *simbelmynë* come never unto world's end,' he murmured. 'Nine mounds and seven there are now green with grass, and through all the long years he has lain at the door that he could not unlock. Whither does it lead? Why would he pass? None shall ever know!

'For that is not my errand!' he cried, turning back and speaking to the whispering darkness behind. 'Keep your hoards and your secrets hidden in the Accursed Years! Speed only we ask. Let us pass, and then come! I summon you to the Stone of Erech!'

There was no answer, unless it were an utter silence more dreadful than the whispers before; and then a chill blast came in which the torches flickered and went out, and could not be rekindled. Of the time that followed, one hour or many, Gimli remembered little. The others pressed on, but he was ever hindmost, pursued by a groping horror that seemed always just about to seize him; and a rumour came after him like the shadow-sound of many feet. He stumbled on until he was crawling like a beast on the ground and felt that he could endure no more: he must either find an ending and escape or run back in madness to meet the following fear.

Suddenly he heard the tinkle of water, a sound hard and clear as a stone falling into a dream of dark shadow. Light grew, and lo! the company passed through another gateway, high-arched and broad, and a rill ran out beside them; and beyond, going steeply down, was a road between sheer cliffs, knife-edged against the sky far above. So deep and narrow was that chasm that the sky was dark, and in it small stars glinted. Yet as Gimli after learned it was still two hours ere sunset of the day on which they had set out from Dunharrow; though for all that he could then tell it might have been twilight in some later year, or in some other world.

The Company now mounted again, and Gimli returned to Legolas. They rode in file, and evening came on and a deep blue dusk; and still fear pursued them. Legolas turning to speak to Gimli looked back and the Dwarf saw before his face the glitter in the Elf's bright eyes. Behind them rode Elladan, last of the Company, but not the last of those that took the downward road.

'The Dead are following,' said Legolas. 'I see shapes of Men and of horses, and pale banners like shreds of cloud, and spears like winter-thickets on a misty night. The Dead are following.'

'Yes, the Dead ride behind. They have been summoned,' said Elladan.

The Company came at last out of the ravine, as suddenly as if they had issued from a crack in a wall; and there lay the uplands of a great vale before them, and the stream beside them went down with a cold voice over many falls.

'Where in Middle-earth are we?' said Gimli; and Elladan answered: 'We have descended from the uprising of the Morthond, the long chill river that flows at last to the sea that washes the walls of Dol Amroth. You will not need to ask hereafter how comes its name: Blackroot men call it.'

The Morthond Vale made a great bay that beat up against the sheer southern faces of the mountains. Its steep slopes were grass-grown; but all was grey in that hour, for the sun had gone, and far below lights twinkled in the homes of Men. The vale was rich and many folk dwelt there.

Then without turning Aragorn cried aloud so that all could hear: 'Friends, forget your weariness! Ride now, ride! We must come to the Stone of Erech ere this day passes, and long still is the way.' So without looking back they rode the mountain-fields, until they came to a bridge over the growing torrent and found a road that went down into the land.

Lights went out in house and hamlet as they came, and doors were shut, and folk that were afield cried in terror and ran wild like hunted deer. Ever there rose the same cry in the gathering night: 'The King of the Dead ! The King of the Dead is come upon us!'

Bells were ringing far below, and all men fled before the face of Aragorn; but the Grey Company in their haste rode like hunters, until their horses were stumbling with weariness. And thus, just ere midnight, and in a darkness as black as the caverns in the mountains, they came at last to the Hill of Erech.

Long had the terror of the Dead lain upon that hill and upon the empty fields about it. For upon the top stood a black stone, round as a great globe, the height of a man, though its half was buried in the ground. Unearthly it looked, as though it had fallen from the sky, as some believed; but those who remembered still the lore of Westernesse told that it had been brought out of the ruin of Númenor and there set by Isildur at his landing. None of the people of the valley dared to approach it, nor would they dwell near; for they said that it was a trysting-place of the Shadow-men and there they would gather in times of fear, thronging round the Stone and whispering.

To that Stone the Company came and halted in the dead of night. Then Elrohir gave to Aragorn a silver horn, and he blew upon it; and it seemed to those that stood near that they heard a sound of answering horns, as if it was an echo in deep caves far away. No other sound they heard, and yet they were aware of a great host gathered all about the hill on which they stood; and a chill wind like the breath of ghosts came down from the mountains. But Aragorn dismounted, and standing by the Stone he cried in a great voice:

'Oathbreakers, why have ye come?'

And a voice was heard out of the night that answered him, as if from far away:

'To fulfil our oath and have peace.'

Then Aragorn said: 'The hour is come at last. Now I go to Pelargir upon Anduin, and ye shall come after me. And when all this land is clean of the servants of Sauron, I will hold the oath fulfilled, and ye shall have peace and depart for ever. For I am Elessar, Isildur's heir of Gondor.'

And with that he bade Halbarad unfurl the great standard which he had brought; and behold! it was black, and if there was any device upon it, it was hidden in the darkness. Then there was silence, and not a whisper nor a sigh was heard again all the long night. The Company camped beside the Stone, but they slept little, because of the dread of the Shadows that hedged them round.

But when the dawn came, cold and pale, Aragorn rose at once, and he led the Company forth upon the journey of greatest haste and weariness that any among them had known, save he alone, and only his will held them to go on. No other mortal Men could have endured it, none but the Dúnedain of the North, and with them Gimli the Dwarf and Legolas of the Elves.

They passed Tarlang's Neck and came into Lamedon; and the Shadow Host pressed behind and fear went on before them, until they came to Calembel upon Ciril, and the sun went down like blood behind Pinnath Gelin away in the West behind them. The township and the fords of Ciril they found deserted, for many men had gone away to war, and all that were left fled to the hills at the rumour of the coming of the King of the

Dead. But the next day there came no dawn, and the Grey Company passed on into the darkness of the Storm of Mordor and were lost to mortal sight; but the Dead followed them.

CHAPTER III

THE MUSTER OF ROHAN

Now all roads were running together to the East to meet the coming of war and the onset of the Shadow. And even as Pippin stood at the Great Gate of the City and saw the Prince of Dol Amroth ride in with his banners, the King of Rohan came down out of the hills.

Day was waning. In the last rays of the sun the Riders cast long pointed shadows that went on before them. Darkness had already crept beneath the murmuring fir-woods that clothed the steep mountain-sides. The king rode now slowly at the end of the day. Presently the path turned round a huge bare shoulder of rock and plunged into the gloom of soft-sighing trees. Down, down they went in a long winding file. When at last they came to the bottom of the gorge they found that evening had fallen in the deep places. The sun was gone. Twilight lay upon the waterfalls.

All day far below them a leaping stream had run down from the high pass behind, cleaving its narrow way between pine-clad walls; and now through a stony gate it flowed out and passed into a wider vale. The Riders followed it, and suddenly Harrowdale lay before them, loud with the noise of waters in the evening. There the white Snowbourn, joined by the lesser stream, went rushing, fuming on the stones, down to Edoras and the green hills and the plains. Away to the right at the head of the great dale the mighty Starkhorn loomed up above its vast buttresses swathed in cloud; but its jagged peak, clothed in everlasting snow, gleamed far above the world, blue-shadowed upon the East, red-stained by the sunset in the West.

Merry looked out in wonder upon this strange country, of which he had heard many tales upon their long road. It was a skyless world, in which his eye, through dim gulfs of shadowy air, saw only ever-mounting slopes, great walls of stone behind great walls, and frowning precipices wreathed with mist. He sat for a moment half dreaming, listening to the noise of water, the whisper of dark trees, the crack of stone, and the vast waiting silence that brooded behind all sound. He loved mountains, or he had loved the thought of them marching on the edge of stories brought from far away; but now he was borne down by the insupportable weight of Middle-earth. He longed to shut out the immensity in a quiet room by a fire.

He was very tired, for though they had ridden slowly, they had ridden with very little rest. Hour after hour for nearly three weary days he had jogged up and down, over passes, and through long dales, and across many

THE MUSTER OF ROHAN

streams. Sometimes where the way was broader he had ridden at the king's side, not noticing that many of the Riders smiled to see the two together: the hobbit on his little shaggy grey pony, and the Lord of Rohan on his great white horse. Then he had talked to Théoden, telling him about his home and the doings of the Shire-folk, or listening in turn to tales of the Mark and its mighty men of old. But most of the time, especially on this last day, Merry had ridden by himself just behind the king, saying nothing, and trying to understand the slow sonorous speech of Rohan that he heard the men behind him using. It was a language in which there seemed to be many words that he knew, though spoken more richly and strongly than in the Shire, yet he could not piece the words together. At times some Rider would lift up his clear voice in stirring song, and Merry felt his heart leap, though he did not know what it was about.

All the same he had been lonely, and never more so than now at the day's end. He wondered where in all this strange world Pippin had got to; and what would become of Aragorn and Legolas and Gimli. Then suddenly like a cold touch on his heart he thought of Frodo and Sam. 'I am forgetting them!' he said to himself reproachfully. 'And yet they are more important than all the rest of us. And I came to help them; but now they must be hundreds of miles away, if they are still alive.' He shivered.

'Harrowdale at last!' said Éomer. 'Our journey is almost at an end.' They halted. The paths out of the narrow gorge fell steeply. Only a glimpse, as through a tall window, could be seen of the great valley in the gloaming below. A single small light could be seen twinkling by the river.

'This journey is over, maybe,' said Théoden, 'but I have far yet to go. Last night the moon was full, and in the morning I shall ride to Edoras to the gathering of the Mark.'

'But if you would take my counsel,' said Éomer in a low voice, 'you would then return hither, until the war is over, lost or won.'

Théoden smiled. 'Nay, my son, for so I will call you, speak not the soft words of Wormtongue in my old ears!' He drew himself up and looked back at the long line of his men fading into the dusk behind. 'Long years in the space of days it seems since I rode west; but never will I lean on a staff again. If the war is lost, what good will be my hiding in the hills? And if it is won, what grief will it be, even if I fall, spending my last strength? But we will leave this now. Tonight I will lie in the Hold of Dunharrow. One evening of peace at least is left us. Let us ride on!'

In the deepening dusk they came down into the valley. Here the Snowbourn flowed near to the western walls of the dale, and soon the path led them to a ford where the shallow waters murmured loudly on the stones.

The ford was guarded. As the king approached many men sprang up out of the shadow of the rocks; and when they saw the king they cried with glad voices: 'Théoden King! Théoden King! The King of the Mark returns!'

Then one blew a long call on a horn. It echoed in the valley. Other horns answered it, and lights shone out across the river.

And suddenly there rose a great chorus of trumpets from high above, sounding from some hollow place, as it seemed, that gathered their notes into one voice and sent it rolling and beating on the walls of stone.

So the King of the Mark came back victorious out of the West to Dunharrow beneath the feet of the White Mountains. There he found the remaining strength of his people already assembled; for as soon as his coming was known captains rode to meet him at the ford, bearing messages from Gandalf. Dúnhere, chieftain of the folk of Harrowdale, was at their head.

'At dawn three days ago, lord,' he said, 'Shadowfax came like a wind out of the West to Edoras, and Gandalf brought tidings of your victory to gladden our hearts. But he brought also word from you to hasten the gathering of the Riders. And then came the winged Shadow.'

'The winged Shadow?' said Théoden. 'We saw it also, but that was in the dead of night before Gandalf left us.'

'Maybe, lord,' said Dúnhere. 'Yet the same, or another like to it, a flying darkness in the shape of a monstrous bird, passed over Edoras that morning, and all men were shaken with fear. For it stooped upon Meduseld, and as it came low, almost to the gable, there came a cry that stopped our hearts. Then it was that Gandalf counselled us not to assemble in the fields, but to meet you here in the valley under the mountains. And he bade us to kindle no more lights or fires than barest need asked. So it has been done. Gandalf spoke with great authority. We trust that it is as you would wish. Naught has been seen in Harrowdale of these evil things.'

'It is well,' said Théoden. 'I will ride now to the Hold, and there before I go to rest I will meet the marshals and captains. Let them come to me as soon as may be!'

The road now led eastward straight across the valley, which was at that point little more than half a mile in width. Flats and meads of rough grass, grey now in the falling night, lay all about, but in front on the far side of the dale Merry saw a frowning wall, a last outlier of the great roots of the Starkhorn, cloven by the river in ages past.

On all the level spaces there was great concourse of men. Some thronged to the roadside, hailing the king and the riders from the West with glad cries; but stretching away into the distance behind there were ordered rows of tents and booths, and lines of picketed horses, and great store of arms, and piled spears bristling like thickets of new-planted trees. Now all the great assembly was falling into shadow, and yet, though the night-chill blew cold from the heights, no lanterns glowed, no fires were lit. Watchmen heavily cloaked paced to and fro.

Merry wondered how many Riders there were. He could not guess their number in the gathering gloom, but it looked to him like a great army, many thousands strong. While he was peering from side to side the king's party came up under the looming cliff on the eastern side of the valley; and there suddenly the path began to climb, and Merry looked up in amazement. He was on a road the like of which he had never seen before, a great work of men's hands in years beyond the reach of song. Upwards it wound, coiling like a snake, boring its way across the sheer slope of rock. Steep as a stair, it looped backwards and forwards as it climbed. Up it horses could walk, and wains could be slowly hauled; but no enemy could come that way, except out of the air, if it was defended from above. At each turn of the road there were great standing stones that had been carved in the likeness of men, huge and clumsy-limbed, squatting cross-legged with their stumpy arms folded on fat bellies. Some in the wearing of the years had lost all features save the dark holes of their eyes that still stared sadly at the passers-by. The Riders hardly glanced at them. The Púkel-men they called them, and heeded them little: no power or terror was left in them; but Merry gazed at them with wonder and a feeling almost of pity, as they loomed up mournfully in the dusk.

After a while he looked back and found that he had already climbed some hundreds of feet above the valley, but still far below he could dimly see a winding line of Riders crossing the ford and filing along the road towards the camp prepared for them. Only the king and his guard were going up into the Hold.

At last the king's company came to a sharp brink, and the climbing road passed into a cutting between walls of rock, and so went up a short slope and out on to a wide upland. The Firienfeld men called it, a green mountain-field of grass and heath, high above the deep-delved courses of the Snowbourn, laid upon the lap of the great mountains behind: the Starkhorn southwards, and northwards the saw-toothed mass of Írensaga, between which there faced the riders, the grim black wall of the Dwimorberg, the Haunted Mountain rising out of steep slopes of sombre pines. Dividing the upland into two there marched a double line of unshaped standing stones that dwindled into the dusk and vanished in the trees. Those who dared to follow that road came soon to the black Dimholt under Dwimorberg, and the menace of the pillar of stone, and the yawning shadow of the forbidden door.

Such was the dark Dunharrow, the work of long-forgotten men. Their name was lost and no song or legend remembered it. For what purpose they had made this place, as a town or secret temple or a tomb of kings, none in Rohan could say. Here they laboured in the Dark Years, before ever a ship came to the western shores, or Gondor of the Dúnedain was built; and now they had vanished, and only the old Púkel-men were left, still sitting at the turnings of the road.

Merry stared at the lines of marching stones: they were worn and black; some were leaning, some were fallen, some cracked or broken; they looked like rows of old and hungry teeth. He wondered what they could be, and he hoped that the king was not going to follow them into the darkness beyond. Then he saw that there were clusters of tents and booths on either side of the stony way; but these were not set near the trees, and seemed rather to huddle away from them towards the brink of the cliff. The greater number were on the right, where the Firienfeld was wider; and on the left there was a smaller camp, in the midst of which stood a tall pavilion. From this side a rider now came out to meet them, and they turned from the road.

As they drew near Merry saw that the rider was a woman with long braided hair gleaming in the twilight, yet she wore a helm and was clad to the waist like a warrior and girded with a sword.

'Hail, Lord of the Mark!' she cried. 'My heart is glad at your returning.'

'And you, Éowyn,' said Théoden, 'is all well with you?'

'All is well,' she answered; yet it seemed to Merry that her voice belied her, and he would have thought that she had been weeping, if that could be believed of one so stern of face. 'All is well. It was a weary road for the people to take, torn suddenly from their homes. There were hard words, for it is long since war has driven us from the green fields; but there have been no evil deeds. All is now ordered, as you see. And your lodging is prepared for you; for I have had full tidings of you and knew the hour of your coming.'

'So Aragorn has come then,' said Éomer. 'Is he still here?'

'No, he is gone,' said Éowyn turning away and looking at the mountains dark against the East and South.

'Whither did he go?' asked Éomer.

'I do not know,' she answered. 'He came at night, and rode away yester-morn, ere the Sun had climbed over the mountain-tops. He is gone.'

'You are grieved, daughter,' said Théoden. 'What has happened? Tell me, did he speak of that road?' He pointed away along the darkening lines of stones towards the Dwimorberg. 'Of the Paths of the Dead?'

'Yes, lord,' said Éowyn. 'And he has passed into the shadow from which none have returned. I could not dissuade him. He is gone.'

'Then our paths are sundered,' said Éomer. 'He is lost. We must ride without him, and our hope dwindles.'

Slowly they passed through the short heath and upland grass, speaking no more, until they came to the king's pavilion. There Merry found that everything was made ready, and that he himself was not forgotten. A little tent had been pitched for him beside the king's lodging; and there he sat alone, while men passed to and fro, going in to the king and taking counsel with him. Night came on and the half-seen heads of the mountains westward were crowned with stars, but the East was dark and blank. The marching stones faded slowly from sight, but still beyond them, blacker than the gloom, brooded the vast crouching shadow of the Dwimorberg.

'The Paths of the Dead,' he muttered to himself. 'The Paths of the Dead? What does all this mean? They have all left me now. They have all gone to some doom: Gandalf and Pippin to war in the East; and Sam and Frodo to Mordor; and Strider and Legolas and Gimli to the Paths of the Dead. But my turn will come soon enough, I suppose. I wonder what they are all talking about, and what the king means to do. For I must go where he goes now.'

In the midst of these gloomy thoughts he suddenly remembered that he was very hungry, and he got up to go and see if anyone else in this strange camp felt the same. But at that very moment a trumpet sounded, and a man came summoning him, the king's esquire, to wait at the king's board.

In the inner part of the pavilion was a small space, curtained off with broidered hangings, and strewn with skins; and there at a small table sat Théoden with Éomer and Éowyn, and Dúnhere, lord of Harrowdale. Merry stood beside the king's stool and waited on him, till presently the old man, coming out of deep thought, turned to him and smiled.

'Come, Master Meriadoc!' he said. 'You shall not stand. You shall sit beside me, as long as I remain in my own lands, and lighten my heart with tales.'

Room was made for the hobbit at the king's left hand, but no one called for any tale. There was indeed little speech, and they ate and drank for the most part in silence, until at last, plucking up courage, Merry asked the question that was tormenting him.

'Twice now, lord, I have heard of the Paths of the Dead,' he said. 'What are they? And where has Strider, I mean the Lord Aragorn, where has he gone?'

The king sighed, but no one answered, until at last Éomer spoke. 'We do not know, and our hearts are heavy,' he said. 'But as for the Paths of the Dead, you have yourself walked on their first steps. Nay, I speak no words of ill omen! The road that we have climbed is the approach to the Door, yonder in the Dimholt. But what lies beyond no man knows.'

'No man knows,' said Théoden: 'yet ancient legend, now seldom spoken, has somewhat to report. If these old tales speak true that have come down from father to son in the House of Eorl, then the Door under Dwimorberg leads to a secret way that goes beneath the mountain to some forgotten end. But none have ever ventured in to search its secrets, since Baldor, son of Brego, passed the Door and was never seen among men again. A rash vow he spoke, as he drained the horn at that feast which Brego made to hallow new-built Meduseld, and he came never to the high seat of which he was the heir.

'Folk say that Dead Men out of the Dark Years guard the way and will suffer no living man to come to their hidden halls; but at whiles they may themselves be seen passing out of the door like shadows and down the stony road. Then the people of Harrowdale shut fast their doors and shroud their windows and are afraid. But the Dead come seldom forth and only at times of great unquiet and coming death.'

'Yet it is said in Harrowdale,' said Éowyn in a low voice, 'that in the moonless nights but little while ago a great host in strange array passed by. Whence they came none knew, but they went up the stony road and vanished into the hill, as if they went to keep a tryst.'

'Then why has Aragorn gone that way?' asked Merry. 'Don't you know anything that would explain it?'

'Unless he has spoken words to you as his friend that we have not heard,' said Éomer, 'none now in the land of the living can tell his purpose.'

'Greatly changed he seemed to me since I saw him first in the king's house,' said Éowyn: 'grimmer, older. Fey I thought him, and like one whom the Dead call.'

'Maybe he was called,' said Théoden; 'and my heart tells me that I shall not see him again. Yet he is a kingly man of high destiny. And take comfort in this, daughter, since comfort you seem to need in your grief for this guest. It is said that when the Eorlingas came out of the North and passed at length up the Snowbourn, seeking strong places of refuge in time of need, Brego and his son Baldor climbed the Stair of the Hold and so came before the Door. On the threshold sat an old man, aged beyond guess of years; tall and kingly he had been, but now he was withered as an old stone. Indeed for stone they took him, for he moved not, and he said no word, until they sought to pass him by and enter. And then a voice came out of him, as it were out of the ground, and to their amaze it spoke in the western tongue: *The way is shut.*

'Then they halted and looked at him and saw that he lived still; but he did not look at them. *The way is shut*, his voice said again. *It was made by those who are Dead, and the Dead keep it, until the time comes. The way is shut.*

'*And when will that time be?*' said Baldor. But no answer did he ever get. For the old man died in that hour and fell upon his face; and no other tidings of the ancient dwellers in the mountains have our folk ever learned. Yet maybe at last the time foretold has come, and Aragorn may pass.'

'But how shall a man discover whether that time be come or no, save by daring the Door?' said Éomer. 'And that way I would not go though all the hosts of Mordor stood before me, and I were alone and had no other refuge. Alas that a fey mood should fall on a man so greathearted in this hour of need! Are there not evil things enough abroad without seeking them under the earth? War is at hand.'

He paused, for at that moment there was a noise outside, a man's voice crying the name of Théoden, and the challenge of the guard.

Presently the captain of the Guard thrust aside the curtain. 'A man is here, lord,' he said, 'an errand-rider of Gondor. He wishes to come before you at once.'

'Let him come!' said Théoden.

A tall man entered, and Merry choked back a cry; for a moment it seemed to him that Boromir was alive again and had returned. Then he saw that it was not so; the man was a stranger, though as like to Boromir as if he were one of his kin, tall and grey-eyed and proud. He was clad as a rider with a cloak of dark green over a coat of fine mail; on the front of his helm was wrought a small silver star. In his hand he bore a single arrow, black-feathered and barbed with steel, but the point was painted red.

He sank on one knee and presented the arrow to Théoden. 'Hail, Lord of the Rohirrim, friend of Gondor!' he said. 'Hirgon I am, errand-rider of Denethor, who bring you this token of war. Gondor is in great need. Often the Rohirrim have aided us, but now the Lord Denethor asks for all your strength and all your speed, lest Gondor fall at last.'

'The Red Arrow!' said Théoden, holding it, as one who receives a summons long expected and yet dreadful when it comes. His hand trembled. 'The Red Arrow has not been seen in the Mark in all my years! Has it indeed come to that? And what does the Lord Denethor reckon that all my strength and all my speed may be?'

'That is best known to yourself, lord,' said Hirgon. 'But ere long it may well come to pass that Minas Tirith is surrounded, and unless you have the strength to break a siege of many powers, the Lord Denethor bids me say that he judges that the strong arms of the Rohirrim would be better within his walls than without.'

'But he knows that we are a people who fight rather upon horseback and in the open, and that we are also a scattered people and time is needed for the gathering of our Riders. Is it not true, Hirgon, that the Lord of Minas Tirith knows more than he sets in his message? For we are already at war, as you may have seen, and you do not find us all unprepared. Gandalf the Grey has been among us, and even now we are mustering for battle in the East.'

'What the Lord Denethor may know or guess of all these things I cannot say,' answered Hirgon. 'But indeed our case is desperate. My lord does not issue any command to you, he begs you only to remember old friendship and oaths long spoken, and for your own good to do all that you may. It is reported to us that many kings have ridden in from the East to the service of Mordor. From the North to the field of Dagorlad there is skirmish and rumour of war. In the South the Haradrim are moving, and fear has fallen on all our coastlands, so that little help will come to us thence. Make haste! For it is before the walls of Minas Tirith that the doom of our time will be decided, and if the tide be not stemmed there, then it will flow over all the fair fields of Rohan, and even in this Hold among the hills there shall be no refuge.'

'Dark tidings,' said Théoden, 'yet not all unguessed. But say to Denethor that even if Rohan itself felt no peril, still we would come to his aid. But we have suffered much loss in our battles with Saruman the traitor, and we must still think of our frontier to the north and east, as his own tidings make clear. So great a power as the Dark Lord seems now to wield might well contain us in battle before the City and yet strike with great force across the River away beyond the Gate of Kings.

'But we will speak no longer counsels of prudence. We will come. The weapontake was set for the morrow. When all is ordered we will set out. Ten thousand spears I might have sent riding over the plain to the dismay of your foes. It will be less now, I fear; for I will not leave my strongholds all unguarded. Yet six thousands at the least shall ride behind me. For say to Denethor that in this hour the King of the Mark himself will come down to the land of Gondor, though maybe he will not ride back. But it is a long road, and man and beast must reach the end with strength to fight. A week it may be from tomorrow's morn ere you hear the cry of the Sons of Eorl coming from the North.'

'A week!' said Hirgon. 'If it must be so, it must. But you are like to find only ruined walls in seven days from now, unless other help unlooked-for comes. Still, you may at the least disturb the Orcs and Swarthy Men from their feasting in the White Tower.'

'At the least we will do that,' said Théoden. 'But I myself am new-come from battle and long journey, and I will now go to rest. Tarry here this night. Then you shall look on the muster of Rohan and ride away the gladder for the sight, and the swifter for the rest. In the morning counsels are best, and night changes many thoughts.'

With that the king stood up, and they all rose. 'Go now each to your rest,' he said, 'and sleep well. And you, Master Meriadoc, I need no more tonight. But be ready to my call as soon as the Sun is risen.'

'I will be ready,' said Merry, 'even if you bid me ride with you on the Paths of the Dead.'

'Speak not words of omen!' said the king. 'For there may be more roads than one that could bear that name. But I did not say that I would bid you ride with me on any road. Good night!'

'I won't be left behind, to be called for on return!' said Merry. 'I won't be left, I won't.' And repeating this over and over again to himself he fell asleep at last in his tent.

He was wakened by a man shaking him. 'Wake up, wake up, Master Holbytla!' he cried; and at length Merry came out of deep dreams and sat up with a start. It still seemed very dark, he thought.

'What is the matter?' he asked.

'The king calls for you.'

'But the Sun has not risen, yet,' said Merry.

'No, and will not rise today, Master Holbytla. Nor ever again, one would think under this cloud. But time does not stand still, though the Sun be lost. Make haste!'

Flinging on some clothes, Merry looked outside. The world was darkling. The very air seemed brown, and all things about were black and grey and shadowless; there was a great stillness. No shape of cloud could be seen, unless it were far away westward, where the furthest groping fingers of the great gloom still crawled onwards and a little light leaked through them. Overhead there hung a heavy roof, sombre and featureless, and light seemed rather to be failing than growing.

Merry saw many folk standing, looking up and muttering; all their faces were grey and sad, and some were afraid. With a sinking heart he made his way to the king. Hirgon the rider of Gondor was there before him, and beside him stood now another man, like him and dressed alike, but shorter and broader. As Merry entered he was speaking to the king.

'It comes from Mordor, lord,' he said. 'It began last night at sunset. From the hills in the Eastfold of your realm I saw it rise and creep across the sky, and all night as I rode it came behind eating up the stars. Now the great cloud hangs over all the land between here and the Mountains of Shadow; and it is deepening. War has already begun.'

For a while the king sat silent. At last he spoke. 'So we come to it in the end,' he said: 'the great battle of our time, in which many things shall pass away. But at least there is no longer need for hiding. We will ride the straight way and the open road and with all our speed. The muster shall begin at once, and wait for none that tarry. Have you good store in Minas Tirith? For if we must ride now in all haste, then we must ride light, with but meal and water enough to last us into battle.'

'We have very great store long prepared,' answered Hirgon. 'Ride now as light and as swift as you may!'

'Then call the heralds, Éomer,' said Théoden. 'Let the Riders be marshalled!'

Éomer went out, and presently the trumpets rang in the Hold and were answered by many others from below; but their voices no longer sounded clear and brave as they had seemed to Merry the night before. Dull they seemed and harsh in the heavy air, braying ominously.

The king turned to Merry. 'I am going to war, Master Meriadoc,' he said. 'In a little while I shall take the road. I release you from my service, but not from my friendship. You shall abide here, and if you will, you shall serve the Lady Éowyn, who will govern the folk in my stead.'

'But, but, lord,' Merry stammered, 'I offered you my sword. I do not want to be parted from you like this, Théoden King. And as all my friends have gone to the battle, I should be ashamed to stay behind.'

'But we ride on horses tall and swift,' said Théoden; 'and great though your heart be, you cannot ride on such beasts.'

'Then tie me on to the back of one, or let me hang on a stirrup, or something,' said Merry. 'It is a long way to run; but run I shall, if I cannot ride, even if I wear my feet off and arrive weeks too late.'

Théoden smiled. 'Rather than that I would bear you with me on Snowmane,' he said. 'But at the least you shall ride with me to Edoras and look on Meduseld; for that way I shall go. So far Stybba can bear you: the great race will not begin till we reach the plains.'

Then Éowyn rose up. 'Come now, Meriadoc!' she said. 'I will show you the gear that I have prepared for you.' They went out together. 'This request only did Aragorn make to me,' said Éowyn, as they passed among the tents, 'that you should be armed for battle. I have granted it, as I could. For my heart tells me that you will need such gear ere the end.'

Now she led Merry to a booth among the lodges of the king's guard; and there an armourer brought out to her a small helm, and a round shield, and other gear.

'No mail have we to fit you,' said Éowyn, 'nor any time for the forging of such a hauberk; but here is also a stout jerkin of leather, a belt, and a knife. A sword you have.'

Merry bowed, and the lady showed him the shield, which was like the shield that had been given to Gimli, and it bore on it the device of the white horse. 'Take all these things,' she said, 'and bear them to good fortune! Farewell now, Master Meriadoc! Yet maybe we shall meet again, you and I.'

So it was that amid a gathering gloom the King of the Mark made ready to lead all his Riders on the eastward road. Hearts were heavy and many quailed in the shadow. But they were a stern people, loyal to their lord, and little weeping or murmuring was heard, even in the camp in the Hold where the exiles from Edoras were housed, women and children and old men. Doom hung over them, but they faced it silently.

Two swift hours passed, and now the king sat upon his white horse, glimmering in the half-light. Proud and tall he seemed, though the hair that flowed beneath his high helm was like snow; and many marvelled at him and took heart to see him unbent and unafraid.

There on the wide flats beside the noisy river were marshalled in many companies well nigh five and fifty hundreds of Riders fully armed, and many hundreds of other men with spare horses lightly burdened. A single trumpet sounded. The king raised his hand, and then silently the host of the Mark began to move. Foremost went twelve of the king's household-men, Riders of renown. Then the king followed with Éomer on his right. He had said farewell to Éowyn above in the Hold, and the memory was grievous; but now he turned his mind to the road that lay ahead. Behind him Merry rode on Stybba with the errand riders of Gondor, and behind them again twelve more of the king's household. They passed down the long ranks of waiting men with stern and unmoved faces. But when they had come almost to the end of the line one looked up glancing keenly at the hobbit. A young man, Merry thought as he returned the glance, less in height and girth than most. He caught the glint of clear grey eyes; and then he shivered, for it came suddenly to him that it was the face of one without hope who goes in search of death.

On down the grey road they went beside the Snowbourn rushing on its stones; through the hamlets of Underharrow and Upbourn, where many sad faces of women looked out from dark doors; and so without horn or harp or music of men's voices the great ride into the East began with which the songs of Rohan were busy for many long lives of men thereafter.

From dark Dunharrow in the dim morning
with thane and captain rode Thengel's son:
to Edoras he came, the ancient halls
of the Mark-wardens mist-enshrouded;
golden timbers were in gloom mantled.
Farewell he bade to his free people,
hearth and high-seat, and the hallowed places,
where long he had feasted ere the light faded.
Forth rode the king, fear behind him,
fate before him. Fealty kept he;
oaths he had taken, all fulfilled them.
Forth rode Théoden. Five nights and days
east and onward rode the Eorlingas
through Folde and Fenmarch and the Firienwood,
six thousand spears to Sunlending,
Mundburg the mighty under Mindolluin,
Sea-kings' city in the South-kingdom
foe-beleaguered, fire-encircled.
Doom drove them on. Darkness took them,
horse and horseman; hoofbeats afar
sank into silence: so the songs tell us.

It was indeed in deepening gloom that the king came to Edoras, although it was then but noon by the hour. There he halted only a short while and strengthened his host by some three score of Riders that came late to the weapontake. Now having eaten he made ready to set out again, and he wished his esquire a kindly farewell. But Merry begged for the last time not to be parted from him.

'This is no journey for such steeds as Stybba, as I have told you,' said Théoden. 'And in such a battle as we think to make on the fields of Gondor what would you do, Master Meriadoc, swordthain though you be, and greater of heart than of stature?'

'As for that, who can tell?' answered Merry. 'But why, lord, did you receive me as swordthain, if not to stay by your side? And I would not have it said of me in song only that I was always left behind!'

'I received you for your safe-keeping,' answered Théoden; 'and also to do as I might bid. None of my Riders can bear you as burden. If the battle were before my gates, maybe your deeds would be remembered by the minstrels; but it is a hundred leagues and two to Mundburg where Denethor is lord. I will say no more.'

Merry bowed and went away unhappily, and stared at the lines of horsemen. Already the companies were preparing to start: men were tightening girths, looking to saddles, caressing their horses; some gazed uneasily at the lowering sky. Unnoticed a Rider came up and spoke softly in the hobbit's ear.

'*Where will wants not, a way opens*, so we say,' he whispered; 'and so I have found myself.' Merry looked up and saw that it was the young Rider whom he had noticed in the morning. 'You wish to go whither the Lord of the Mark goes: I see it in your face.'

'I do,' said Merry.

'Then you shall go with me,' said the Rider. 'I will bear you before me, under my cloak until we are far afield, and this darkness is yet darker. Such good will should not be denied. Say no more to any man, but come!'

'Thank you indeed!' said Merry. 'Thank you, sir, though I do not know your name.'

'Do you not?' said the Rider softly. 'Then call me Dernhelm.'

Thus it came to pass that when the king set out, before Dernhelm sat Meriadoc the hobbit, and the great grey steed Windfola made little of the burden; for Dernhelm was less in weight than many men, though lithe and well-knit in frame.

On into the shadow they rode. In the willow-thickets where Snowbourn flowed into Entwash, twelve leagues east of Edoras, they camped that night. And then on again through the Folde; and through the Fenmarch, where to their right great oakwoods climbed on the skirts of the hills under the shades of dark Halifirien by the borders of Gondor; but away to their left the mists lay on the marshes fed by the mouths of Entwash. And as they rode rumour came of war in the North. Lone men, riding wild, brought word of foes assailing their east-borders, of orc-hosts marching in the Wold of Rohan.

'Ride on! Ride on!' cried Éomer. 'Too late now to turn aside. The fens of Entwash must guard our flank. Haste now we need. Ride on!'

And so King Théoden departed from his own realm, and mile by mile the long road wound away, and the beacon hills marched past: Calenhad, Min-Rimmon, Erelas, Nardol. But their fires were quenched. All the lands were grey and still; and ever the shadow deepened before them, and hope waned in every heart.

CHAPTER IV

THE SIEGE OF GONDOR

Pippin was roused by Gandalf. Candles were lit in their chamber, for only a dim twilight came through the windows; the air was heavy as with approaching thunder.

'What is the time?' said Pippin yawning.

'Past the second hour,' said Gandalf. 'Time to get up and make yourself presentable. You are summoned to the Lord of the City to learn your new duties.'

'And will he provide breakfast?'

'No! I have provided it: all that you will get till noon. Food is now doled out by order.'

Pippin looked ruefully at the small loaf and (he thought) very inadequate pat of butter which was set out for him, beside a cup of thin milk. 'Why did you bring me here?' he said.

'You know quite well,' said Gandalf. 'To keep you out of mischief; and if you do not like being here, you can remember that you brought it on yourself.' Pippin said no more.

Before long he was walking with Gandalf once more down the cold corridor to the door of the Tower Hall. There Denethor sat in a grey gloom, like an old patient spider, Pippin thought; he did not seem to have moved since the day before. He beckoned Gandalf to a seat, but Pippin was left for a while standing unheeded. Presently the old man turned to him:

'Well, Master Peregrin, I hope that you used yesterday to your profit, and to your liking? Though I fear that the board is barer in this city than you could wish.'

Pippin had an uncomfortable feeling that most of what he had said or done was somehow known to the Lord of the City, and much was guessed of what he thought as well. He did not answer.

'What would you do in my service?'

'I thought, sir, that you would tell me my duties.'

'I will, when I learn what you are fit for,' said Denethor. 'But that I shall learn soonest, maybe, if I keep you beside me. The esquire of my chamber has begged leave to go to the out-garrison, so you shall take his place for a while. You shall wait on me, bear errands, and talk to me, if war and council leave me any leisure. Can you sing?'

'Yes,' said Pippin. 'Well, yes, well enough for my own people. But we have no songs fit for great halls and evil times, lord. We seldom sing of anything more terrible than wind or rain. And most of my songs are about things that make us laugh; or about food and drink, of course.'

'And why should such songs be unfit for my halls, or for such hours as these? We who have lived long under the Shadow may surely listen to echoes from a land untroubled by it? Then we may feel that our vigil was not fruitless, though it may have been thankless.'

Pippin's heart sank. He did not relish the idea of singing any song of the Shire to the Lord of Minas Tirith, certainly not the comic ones that he knew best; they were too, well, rustic for such an occasion. He was however spared the ordeal for the present. He was not commanded to sing. Denethor turned to Gandalf, asking questions about the Rohirrim and their policies, and the position of Éomer, the king's nephew. Pippin marvelled at the amount that the Lord seemed to know about a people that lived far away, though it must, he thought, be many years since Denethor himself had ridden abroad.

Presently Denethor waved to Pippin and dismissed him again for a while. 'Go to the armouries of the Citadel,' he said, 'and get you there the livery and gear of the Tower. It will be ready. It was commanded yesterday. Return when you are clad!'

It was as he said; and Pippin soon found himself arrayed in strange garments, all of black and silver. He had a small hauberk, its rings forged of steel, maybe, yet black as jet; and a high-crowned helm with small raven-wings on either side, set with a silver star in the centre of the circlet. Above the mail was a short surcoat of black, but broidered on the breast in silver with the token of the Tree. His old clothes were folded and put away, but he was permitted to keep the grey cloak of Lórien, though not to wear it when on duty. He looked now, had he known it, verily *Ernil i Pheriannath*, the Prince of the Halflings, that folk had called him; but he felt uncomfortable. And the gloom began to weigh on his spirits.

It was dark and dim all day. From the sunless dawn until evening the heavy shadow had deepened, and all hearts in the City were oppressed. Far above a great cloud streamed slowly westward from the Black Land, devouring light, borne upon a wind of war; but below the air was still and breathless, as if all the Vale of Anduin waited for the onset of a ruinous storm.

About the eleventh hour, released at last for a while from service, Pippin came out and went in search of food and drink to cheer his heavy heart and make his task of waiting more supportable. In the messes he met Beregond again, who had just come from an errand over the Pelennor out to the Guard-towers upon the Causeway. Together they strolled out to the walls; for Pippin felt imprisoned indoors, and stifled even in the lofty citadel. Now they sat side by side again in the embrasure looking eastward, where they had eaten and talked the day before.

It was the sunset-hour, but the great pall had now stretched far into the West, and only as it sank at last into the Sea did the Sun escape to send out a brief farewell gleam before the night, even as Frodo saw it at the Cross-roads touching the head of the fallen king. But to the fields of the Pelennor, under the shadow of Mindolluin, there came no gleam: they were brown and drear.

Already it seemed years to Pippin since he had sat there before, in some half-forgotten time when he had still been a hobbit, a light-hearted wanderer touched little by the perils he had passed through. Now he was one small soldier in a city preparing for a great assault, clad in the proud but sombre manner of the Tower of Guard.

In some other time and place Pippin might have been pleased with his new array, but he knew now that he was taking part in no play; he was in deadly earnest the servant of a grim master in the greatest peril. The hauberk was burdensome, and the helm weighed upon his head. His cloak he had cast aside upon the seat. He turned his tired gaze away from the darkling fields below and yawned, and then he sighed.

'You are weary of this day?' said Beregond.

'Yes,' said Pippin, 'very: tired out with idleness and waiting. I have kicked my heels at the door of my master's chamber for many slow hours, while he has debated with Gandalf and the Prince and other great persons. And I'm not used, Master Beregond, to waiting hungry on others while they eat. It is a sore trial for a hobbit, that. No doubt you will think I should feel the honour more deeply. But what is the good of such honour? Indeed what is the good even of food and drink under this creeping shadow? What does it mean? The very air seems thick and brown! Do you often have such glooms when the wind is in the East?'

'Nay,' said Beregond, 'this is no weather of the world. This is some device of his malice; some broil of fume from the Mountain of Fire that he sends to darken hearts and counsel. And so it doth indeed. I wish the Lord Faramir would return. He would not be dismayed. But now, who knows if he will ever come back across the River out of the Darkness?'

'Yes,' said Pippin, 'Gandalf, too, is anxious. He was disappointed, I think, not to find Faramir here. And where has he got to himself? He left the Lord's council before the noon-meal, and in no good mood either, I thought. Perhaps he has some foreboding of bad news.'

Suddenly as they talked they were stricken dumb, frozen as it were to listening stones. Pippin cowered down with his hands pressed to his ears;

but Beregond, who had been looking out from the battlement as he spoke of Faramir, remained there, stiffened, staring out with starting eyes. Pippin knew the shuddering cry that he had heard: it was the same that he had heard long ago in the Marish of the Shire, but now it was grown in power and hatred, piercing the heart with a poisonous despair.

At last Beregond spoke with an effort. 'They have come!' he said. 'Take courage and look! There are fell things below.'

Reluctantly Pippin climbed on to the seat and looked out over the wall. The Pelennor lay dim beneath him, fading away to the scarce guessed line of the Great River. But now wheeling swiftly across it, like shadows of untimely night, he saw in the middle airs below him five birdlike forms, horrible as carrion-fowl yet greater than eagles, cruel as death. Now they swooped near, venturing almost within bowshot of the walls, now they circled away.

'Black Riders!' muttered Pippin. 'Black Riders of the air! But see, Beregond!' he cried. 'They are looking for something, surely? See how they wheel and swoop, always down to that point over there! And can you see something moving on the ground? Dark little things. Yes, men on horses: four or five. Ah! I cannot stand it! Gandalf! Gandalf save us!'

Another long screech rose and fell, and he threw himself back again from the wall, panting like a hunted animal. Faint and seemingly remote through that shuddering cry he heard winding up from below the sound of a trumpet ending on a long high note.

'Faramir! The Lord Faramir! It is his call!' cried Beregond. 'Brave heart! But how can he win to the Gate, if these foul hell-hawks have other weapons than fear? But look! They hold on. They will make the Gate. No! the horses are running mad. Look! the men are thrown; they are running on foot. No, one is still up, but he rides back to the others. That will be the Captain: he can master both beasts and men. Ah! there one of the foul things is stooping on him. Help! help! Will no one go out to him? Faramir!'

With that Beregond sprang away and ran off into the gloom. Ashamed of his terror, while Beregond of the Guard thought first of the captain whom he loved, Pippin got up and peered out. At that moment he caught a flash of white and silver coming from the North, like a small star down on the dusky fields. It moved with the speed of an arrow and grew as it came, converging swiftly with the flight of the four men towards the Gate. It seemed to Pippin that a pale light was spread about it and the heavy shadows gave way before it; and then as it drew near he thought that he heard, like an echo in the walls, a great voice calling.

'Gandalf!' he cried. 'Gandalf! He always turns up when things are darkest. Go on! Go on, White Rider! Gandalf, Gandalf!' he shouted wildly, like an onlooker at a great race urging on a runner who is far beyond encouragement.

But now the dark swooping shadows were aware of the newcomer. One wheeled towards him; but it seemed to Pippin that he raised his hand, and from it a shaft of white light stabbed upwards. The Nazgûl gave a long wailing cry and swerved away; and with that the four others wavered, and then rising in swift spirals they passed away eastward vanishing into the lowering cloud above; and down on the Pelennor it seemed for a while less dark.

Pippin watched, and he saw the horseman and the White Rider meet and halt, waiting for those on foot. Men now hurried out to them from the City; and soon they all passed from sight under the outer walls, and he knew that they were entering the Gate. Guessing that they would come at once to the Tower and the Steward, he hurried to the entrance of the citadel. There he was joined by many others who had watched the race and the rescue from the high walls.

It was not long before a clamour was heard in the streets leading up from the outer circles, and there was much cheering and crying of the names of Faramir and Mithrandir. Presently Pippin saw torches, and followed by a press of people two horsemen riding slowly: one was in white but shining no longer, pale in the twilight as if his fire was spent or veiled; the other was dark and his head was bowed. They dismounted, and as grooms took Shadowfax and the other horse, they walked forward to the sentinel at the gate: Gandalf steadily, his grey cloak flung back, and a fire still smouldering in his eyes; the other, clad all in green, slowly, swaying a little as a weary or a wounded man.

Pippin pressed forward as they passed under the lamp beneath the gate-arch, and when he saw the pale face of Faramir he caught his breath. It was the face of one who has been assailed by a great fear or anguish, but has mastered it and now is quiet. Proud and grave he stood for a moment as he spoke to the guard, and Pippin gazing at him saw how closely he resembled his brother Boromir – whom Pippin had liked from the first, admiring the great man's lordly but kindly manner. Yet suddenly for Faramir his heart was strangely moved with a feeling that he had not known before. Here was one with an air of high nobility such as Aragorn at times revealed, less high perhaps, yet also less incalculable and remote: one of the Kings of Men born into a later time, but touched with the wisdom and sadness of the Elder Race. He knew now why Beregond spoke his name with love. He was a captain that men would follow, that he would follow, even under the shadow of the black wings.

'Faramir!' he cried aloud with the others. 'Faramir!' And Faramir, catching his strange voice among the clamour of the men of the City, turned and looked down at him and was amazed.

'Whence come you?' he said. 'A halfling, and in the livery of the Tower! Whence . . . ?'

But with that Gandalf stepped to his side and spoke. 'He came with me from the land of the Halflings,' he said. 'He came with me. But let us not tarry here. There is much to say and to do, and you are weary. He shall come with us. Indeed he must, for if he does not forget his new duties more easily than I do, he must attend on his lord again within this hour. Come, Pippin, follow us!'

So at length they came to the private chamber of the Lord of the City. There deep seats were set about a brazier of charcoal; and wine was brought; and there Pippin, hardly noticed, stood behind the chair of Denethor and felt his weariness little, so eagerly did he listen to all that was said.

When Faramir had taken white bread and drunk a draught of wine, he sat upon a low chair at his father's left hand. Removed a little upon the other side sat Gandalf in a chair of carven wood; and he seemed at first to be asleep. For at the beginning Faramir spoke only of the errand upon which he had been sent out ten days before, and he brought tidings of Ithilien and of movements of the Enemy and his allies; and he told of the fight on the road when the men of Harad and their great beast were overthrown: a captain reporting to his master such matters as had often been heard before, small things of border-war that now seemed useless and petty, shorn of their renown.

Then suddenly Faramir looked at Pippin. 'But now we come to strange matters,' he said. 'For this is not the first halfling that I have seen walking out of northern legends into the Southlands.'

At that Gandalf sat up and gripped the arms of his chair; but he said nothing, and with a look stopped the exclamation on Pippin's lips. Denethor looked at their faces and nodded his head, as though in sign that he had read much there before it was spoken. Slowly, while the others sat silent and still, Faramir told his tale, with his eyes for the most part on Gandalf, though now and again his glance strayed to Pippin, as if to refresh his memory of others that he had seen.

As his story was unfolded of his meeting with Frodo and his servant and of the events at Henneth Annûn, Pippin became aware that Gandalf's hands were trembling as they clutched the carven wood. White they seemed now and very old, and as he looked at them, suddenly with a thrill of fear Pippin knew that Gandalf, Gandalf himself, was troubled, even afraid. The air of the room was close and still. At last when Faramir spoke of his parting with the travellers, and of their resolve to go to Cirith Ungol, his voice fell, and he shook his head and sighed. Then Gandalf sprang up.

'Cirith Ungol? Morgul Vale?' he said. 'The time, Faramir, the time? When did you part with them? When would they reach that accursed valley?'

'I parted with them in the morning two days ago,' said Faramir. 'It is fifteen leagues thence to the vale of the Morgulduin, if they went straight south; and then they would be still five leagues westward of the accursed Tower. At swiftest they could not come there before today, and maybe they have not come there yet. Indeed I see what you fear. But the darkness is not due to their venture. It began yestereve, and all Ithilien was under shadow last night. It is clear to me that the Enemy has long planned an assault on us, and its hour had already been determined before ever the travellers left my keeping.'

Gandalf paced the floor. 'The morning of two days ago, nigh on three days of journey! How far is the place where you parted?'

'Some twenty-five leagues as a bird flies,' answered Faramir. 'But I could not come more swiftly. Yestereve I lay at Cair Andros, the long isle in the River northward which we hold in defence; and horses are kept on the hither bank. As the dark drew on I knew that haste was needed, so I rode thence with three others that could also be horsed. The rest of my company I sent south to strengthen the garrison at the fords of Osgiliath. I hope that I have not done ill?' He looked at his father.

'Ill?' cried Denethor, and his eyes flashed suddenly. 'Why do you ask? The men were under your command. Or do you ask for my judgement on all your deeds? Your bearing is lowly in my presence, yet it is long now since you turned from your own way at my counsel. See, you have spoken skilfully, as ever; but I, have I not seen your eye fixed on Mithrandir, seeking whether you said well or too much? He has long had your heart in his keeping.

'My son, your father is old but not yet dotard. I can see and hear, as was my wont; and little of what you have half said or left unsaid is now hidden from me. I know the answer to many riddles. Alas, alas for Boromir!'

'If what I have done displeases you, my father,' said Faramir quietly, 'I wish I had known your counsel before the burden of so weighty a judgement was thrust on me.'

'Would that have availed to change your judgement?' said Denethor. 'You would still have done just so, I deem. I know you well. Ever your desire is to appear lordly and generous as a king of old, gracious, gentle. That may well befit one of high race, if he sits in power and peace. But in desperate hours gentleness may be repaid with death.'

'So be it,' said Faramir.

'So be it!' cried Denethor. 'But not with your death only, Lord Faramir: with the death also of your father, and of all your people, whom it is your part to protect now that Boromir is gone.'

'Do you wish then,' said Faramir, 'that our places had been exchanged?'

'Yes, I wish that indeed,' said Denethor. 'For Boromir was loyal to me and no wizard's pupil. He would have remembered his father's need, and would not have squandered what fortune gave. He would have brought me a mighty gift.'

For a moment Faramir's restraint gave way. 'I would ask you, my father, to remember why it was that I, not he, was in Ithilien. On one occasion at least your counsel has prevailed, not long ago. It was the Lord of the City that gave the errand to him.'

'Stir not the bitterness in the cup that I mixed for myself,' said Denethor. 'Have I not tasted it now many nights upon my tongue, foreboding that worse yet lay in the dregs? As now indeed I find. Would it were not so! Would that this thing had come to me!'

'Comfort yourself!' said Gandalf. 'In no case would Boromir have brought it to you. He is dead, and died well; may he sleep in peace! Yet you deceive yourself. He would have stretched out his hand to this thing, and taking it he would have fallen. He would have kept it for his own, and when he returned you would not have known your son.'

The face of Denethor set hard and cold. 'You found Boromir less apt to your hand, did you not?' he said softly. 'But I who was his father say that he would have brought it to me. You are wise, maybe, Mithrandir, yet with all your subtleties you have not all wisdom. Counsels may be found that are neither the webs of wizards nor the haste of fools. I have in this matter more lore and wisdom than you deem.'

'What then is your wisdom?' said Gandalf.

'Enough to perceive that there are two follies to avoid. To use this thing is perilous. At this hour, to send it in the hands of a witless halfling into the land of the Enemy himself, as you have done, and this son of mine, that is madness.'

'And the Lord Denethor what would he have done?'

'Neither. But most surely not for any argument would he have set this thing at a hazard beyond all but a fool's hope, risking our utter ruin, if the Enemy should recover what he lost. Nay, it should have been kept, hidden, hidden dark and deep. Not used, I say, unless at the uttermost end of need, but set beyond his grasp, save by a victory so final that what then befell would not trouble us, being dead.'

'You think, as is your wont, my lord, of Gondor only,' said Gandalf. 'Yet there are other men and other lives, and time still to be. And for me, I pity even his slaves.'

'And where will other men look for help, if Gondor falls?' answered Denethor. 'If I had this thing now in the deep vaults of this citadel, we should not then shake with dread under this gloom, fearing the worst, and our counsels would be undisturbed. If you do not trust me to endure the test, you do not know me yet.'

'Nonetheless I do not trust you,' said Gandalf. 'Had I done so, I could have sent this thing hither to your keeping and spared myself and others much anguish. And now hearing you speak I trust you less, no more than Boromir. Nay, stay your wrath! I do not trust myself in this, and I refused this thing, even as a freely given gift. You are strong and can still in some matters govern yourself, Denethor; yet if you had received this thing, it would have overthrown you. Were it buried beneath the roots of Mindolluin, still it would burn your mind away, as the darkness grows, and the yet worse things follow that soon shall come upon us.'

For a moment the eyes of Denethor glowed again as he faced Gandalf, and Pippin felt once more the strain between their wills; but now almost it seemed as if their glances were like blades from eye to eye, flickering as they fenced. Pippin trembled fearing some dreadful stroke. But suddenly Denethor relaxed and grew cold again. He shrugged his shoulders.

'If I had! If you had!' he said. 'Such words and ifs are vain. It has gone into the Shadow, and only time will show what doom awaits it, and us. The time will not be long. In what is left, let all who fight the Enemy in their fashion be at one, and keep hope while they may, and after hope still the hardihood to die free.' He turned to Faramir. 'What think you of the garrison at Osgiliath?'

'It is not strong,' said Faramir. 'I have sent the company of Ithilien to strengthen it, as I have said.'

'Not enough, I deem,' said Denethor. 'It is there that the first blow will fall. They will have need of some stout captain there.'

'There and elsewhere in many places,' said Faramir, and sighed. 'Alas for my brother, whom I too loved!' He rose. 'May I have your leave, father?' And then he swayed and leaned upon his father's chair.

'You are weary, I see,' said Denethor. 'You have ridden fast and far, and under shadows of evil in the air, I am told.'

'Let us not speak of that!' said Faramir.

'Then we will not,' said Denethor. 'Go now and rest as you may. Tomorrow's need will be sterner.'

All now took leave of the Lord of the City and went to rest while they still could. Outside there was a starless blackness as Gandalf, with Pippin beside him bearing a small torch, made his way to their lodging. They did not speak until they were behind closed doors. Then at last Pippin took Gandalf's hand.

'Tell me,' he said, 'is there any hope? For Frodo, I mean; or at least mostly for Frodo.'

Gandalf put his hand on Pippin's head. 'There never was much hope,' he answered. 'Just a fool's hope, as I have been told. And when I heard of Cirith Ungol——' He broke off and strode to the window, as if his eyes could pierce the night in the East. 'Cirith Ungol!' he muttered. 'Why that way, I wonder?' He turned. 'Just now, Pippin, my heart almost failed me, hearing that name. And yet in truth I believe that the news that Faramir brings has some hope in it. For it seems clear that our Enemy has opened his war at last and made the first move while Frodo was still free. So now for many days he will have his eye turned this way and that, away from his own land. And yet, Pippin, I feel from afar his haste and fear. He has begun sooner than he would. Something has happened to stir him.'

Gandalf stood for a moment in thought. 'Maybe,' he muttered. 'Maybe even your foolishness helped, my lad. Let me see: some five days ago now he would discover that we had thrown down Saruman, and had taken the Stone. Still what of that? We could not use it to much purpose, or without his knowing. Ah! I wonder. Aragorn? His time draws near. And he is strong and stern underneath, Pippin; bold, determined, able to take his own counsel and dare great risks at need. That may be it. He may have used the Stone and shown himself to the Enemy, challenging him, for this very purpose. I wonder. Well, we shall not know the answer till the Riders of Rohan come, if they do not come too late. There are evil days ahead. To sleep while we may!'

'But,' said Pippin.

'But what?' said Gandalf. 'Only one *but* will I allow tonight.'

'Gollum,' said Pippin. 'How on earth could they be going about *with* him, even following him? And I could see that Faramir did not like the place he was taking them to any more than you do. What is wrong?'

'I cannot answer that now,' said Gandalf. 'Yet my heart guessed that Frodo and Gollum would meet before the end. For good, or for evil. But of Cirith Ungol I will not speak tonight. Treachery, treachery I fear; treachery of that miserable creature. But so it must be. Let us remember that a traitor may betray himself and do good that he does not intend. It can be so, sometimes. Good night!'

The next day came with a morning like a brown dusk, and the hearts of men, lifted for a while by the return of Faramir, sank low again. The winged Shadows were not seen again that day, yet ever and anon, high above the city, a faint cry would come, and many who heard it would stand stricken with a passing dread, while the less stout-hearted quailed and wept.

And now Faramir was gone again. 'They give him no rest,' some murmured. 'The Lord drives his son too hard, and now he must do the duty of two, for himself and for the one that will not return.' And ever men looked northward, asking: 'Where are the Riders of Rohan?'

In truth Faramir did not go by his own choosing. But the Lord of the City was master of his Council, and he was in no mood that day to bow to others. Early in the morning the Council had been summoned. There all the captains judged that because of the threat in the South their force was too weak to make any stroke of war on their own part, unless perchance the Riders of Rohan yet should come. Meanwhile they must man the walls and wait.

'Yet,' said Denethor, 'we should not lightly abandon the outer defences, the Rammas made with so great a labour. And the Enemy must pay dearly for the crossing of the River. That he cannot do, in force to assail the City, either north of Cair Andros because of the marshes, or southwards towards Lebennin because of the breadth of the River, that needs many boats. It is at Osgiliath that he will put his weight, as before when Boromir denied him the passage.'

'That was but a trial,' said Faramir. 'Today we may make the Enemy pay ten times our loss at the passage and yet rue the exchange. For he can afford to lose a host better than we to lose a company. And the retreat of those that we put out far afield will be perilous, if he wins across in force.'

'And what of Cair Andros?' said the Prince. 'That, too, must be held, if Osgiliath is defended. Let us not forget the danger on our left. The Rohirrim may come, and they may not. But Faramir has told us of great strength drawing ever to the Black Gate. More than one host may issue from it, and strike for more than one passage.'

'Much must be risked in war,' said Denethor. 'Cair Andros is manned, and no more can be sent so far. But I will not yield the River and the Pelennor unfought – not if there is a captain here who has still the courage to do his lord's will.'

Then all were silent. But at length Faramir said: 'I do not oppose your will, sire. Since you are robbed of Boromir, I will go and do what I can in his stead – if you command it.'

'I do so,' said Denethor.

'Then farewell!' said Faramir. 'But if I should return, think better of me!'

'That depends on the manner of your return,' said Denethor.

Gandalf it was that last spoke to Faramir ere he rode east. 'Do not throw your life away rashly or in bitterness,' he said. 'You will be needed here, for other things than war. Your father loves you, Faramir, and will remember it ere the end. Farewell!'

So now the Lord Faramir had gone forth again, and had taken with him such strength of men as were willing to go or could be spared. On the walls some gazed through the gloom towards the ruined city, and they wondered what chanced there, for nothing could be seen. And others, as ever, looked north and counted the leagues to Théoden in Rohan. 'Will he come? Will he remember our old alliance?' they said.

'Yes, he will come,' said Gandalf, 'even if he comes too late. But think! At best the Red Arrow cannot have reached him more than two days ago, and the miles are long from Edoras.'

It was night again ere news came. A man rode in haste from the fords, saying that a host had issued from Minas Morgul and was already drawing nigh to Osgiliath; and it had been joined by regiments from the South, Haradrim, cruel and tall. 'And we have learned,' said the messenger, 'that the Black Captain leads them once again, and the fear of him has passed before him over the River.'

With those ill-boding words the third day closed since Pippin came to Minas Tirith. Few went to rest, for small hope had any now that even Faramir could hold the fords for long.

The next day, though the darkness had reached its full and grew no deeper, it weighed heavier on men's hearts, and a great dread was on them. Ill news came soon again. The passage of Anduin was won by the Enemy. Faramir was retreating to the wall of the Pelennor, rallying his men to the Causeway Forts; but he was ten times outnumbered.

'If he wins back at all across the Pelennor, his enemies will be on his heels,' said the messenger. 'They have paid dear for the crossing, but less dearly than we hoped. The plan has been well laid. It is now seen that in secret they have long been building floats and barges in great number in East Osgiliath. They swarmed across like beetles. But it is the Black Captain that defeats us. Few will stand and abide even the rumour of his coming. His own folk quail at him, and they would slay themselves at his bidding.'

'Then I am needed there more than here,' said Gandalf, and rode off at once, and the glimmer of him faded soon from sight. And all that night Pippin alone and sleepless stood upon the wall and gazed eastward.

The bells of day had scarcely rung out again, a mockery in the unlightened dark, when far away he saw fires spring up, across in the dim spaces where the walls of the Pelennor stood. The watchmen cried aloud, and all men in the City stood to arms. Now ever and anon there was a red flash, and slowly through the heavy air dull rumbles could be heard.

'They have taken the wall!' men cried. 'They are blasting breaches in it. They are coming!'

'Where is Faramir?' cried Beregond in dismay. 'Say not that he has fallen!'

It was Gandalf that brought the first tidings. With a handful of horsemen he came in the middle morning, riding as escort to a line of wains. They were filled with wounded men, all that could be saved from the wreck of the Causeway Forts. At once he went to Denethor. The Lord of the City sat now in a high chamber above the Hall of the White Tower with Pippin at his side; and through the dim windows, north and south and east, he bent his dark eyes, as if to pierce the shadows of doom that ringed him round. Most to the North he looked, and would pause at whiles to listen as if by some ancient art his ears might hear the thunder of hoofs on the plains far away.

'Is Faramir come?' he asked.

'No,' said Gandalf. 'But he still lived when I left him. Yet he is resolved to stay with the rearguard, lest the retreat over the Pelennor become a rout. He may, perhaps, hold his men together long enough, but I doubt it. He is pitted against a foe too great. For one has come that I feared.'

'Not – the Dark Lord?' cried Pippin, forgetting his place in his terror.

Denethor laughed bitterly. 'Nay, not yet, Master Peregrin! He will not come save only to triumph over me when all is won. He uses others as his weapons. So do all great lords, if they are wise, Master Halfling. Or why should I sit here in my tower and think, and watch, and wait, spending even my sons? For I can still wield a brand.'

He stood up and cast open his long black cloak, and behold! he was clad in mail beneath, and girt with a long sword, great-hilted in a sheath of black and silver. 'Thus have I walked, and thus now for many years have I slept,' he said, 'lest with age the body should grow soft and timid.'

'Yet now under the Lord of Barad-dûr the most fell of all his captains is already master of your outer walls,' said Gandalf. 'King of Angmar long ago, Sorcerer, Ringwraith, Lord of the Nazgûl, a spear of terror in the hand of Sauron, shadow of despair.'

'Then, Mithrandir, you had a foe to match you,' said Denethor. 'For myself, I have long known who is the chief captain of the hosts of the Dark Tower. Is this all that you have returned to say? Or can it be that you have withdrawn because you are overmatched?'

Pippin trembled, fearing that Gandalf would be stung to sudden wrath, but his fear was needless. 'It might be so,' Gandalf answered softly. 'But our trial of strength is not yet come. And if words spoken of old be true, not by the hand of man shall he fall, and hidden from the Wise is the doom that awaits him. However that may be, the Captain of Despair does not press forward, yet. He rules rather according to the wisdom that you have just spoken, from the rear, driving his slaves in madness on before.

'Nay, I came rather to guard the hurt men that can yet be healed; for the Rammas is breached far and wide, and soon the host of Morgul will enter in at many points. And I came chiefly to say this. Soon there will be battle on the fields. A sortie must be made ready. Let it be of mounted men. In them lies our brief hope, for in one thing only is the enemy still poorly provided: he has few horsemen.'

'And we also have few. Now would the coming of Rohan be in the nick of time,' said Denethor.

'We are likely to see other newcomers first,' said Gandalf. 'Fugitives from Cair Andros have already reached us. The isle has fallen. Another army is come from the Black Gate, crossing from the north-east.'

'Some have accused you, Mithrandir, of delighting to bear ill news,' said Denethor, 'but to me this is no longer news: it was known to me ere nightfall yesterday. As for the sortie, I had already given thought to it. Let us go down.'

Time passed. At length watchers on the walls could see the retreat of the out-companies. Small bands of weary and often wounded men came first with little order; some were running wildly as if pursued. Away to the eastward the distant fires flickered, and now it seemed that here and there they crept across the plain. Houses and barns were burning. Then from many points little rivers of red flame came hurrying on, winding through the gloom, converging towards the line of the broad road that led from the City-gate to Osgiliath.

'The enemy,' men murmured. 'The dike is down. Here they come pouring through the breaches! And they carry torches, it seems. Where are our own folk?'

It drew now to evening by the hour, and the light was so dim that even far-sighted men upon the Citadel could discern little clearly out upon the fields, save only the burnings that ever multiplied, and the lines of fire that grew in length and speed. At last, less than a mile from the City, a more ordered mass of men came into view, marching not running, still holding together.

The watchers held their breath. 'Faramir must be there,' they said. 'He can govern man and beast. He will make it yet.'

Now the main retreat was scarcely two furlongs distant. Out of the gloom behind a small company of horsemen galloped, all that was left of the rearguard. Once again they turned at bay, facing the oncoming lines of fire. Then suddenly there was a tumult of fierce cries. Horsemen of the enemy swept up. The lines of fire became flowing torrents, file upon file of Orcs bearing flames, and wild Southron men with red banners, shouting with harsh tongues, surging up, overtaking the retreat. And with a piercing cry out of the dim sky fell the winged shadows, the Nazgûl stooping to the kill.

The retreat became a rout. Already men were breaking away, flying wild and witless here and there, flinging away their weapons, crying out in fear, falling to the ground.

And then a trumpet rang from the Citadel, and Denethor at last released the sortie. Drawn up within the shadow of the Gate and under the looming walls outside they had waited for his signal: all the mounted men that were left in the City. Now they sprang forward, formed, quickened to a gallop, and charged with a great shout. And from the walls an answering shout went up; for foremost on the field rode the swan-knights of Dol Amroth with their Prince and his blue banner at their head.

'Amroth for Gondor!' they cried. 'Amroth to Faramir!'

Like thunder they broke upon the enemy on either flank of the retreat; but one rider outran them all, swift as the wind in the grass: Shadowfax bore him, shining, unveiled once more, a light starting from his upraised hand.

The Nazgûl screeched and swept away, for their Captain was not yet come to challenge the white fire of his foe. The hosts of Morgul intent on their prey, taken at unawares in wild career, broke, scattering like sparks in a gale. The out-companies with a great cheer turned and smote their pursuers. Hunters became the hunted. The retreat became an onslaught. The field was strewn with stricken orcs and men, and a reek arose of torches cast away, sputtering out in swirling smoke. The cavalry rode on.

But Denethor did not permit them to go far. Though the enemy was checked, and for the moment driven back, great forces were flowing in from the East. Again the trumpet rang, sounding the retreat. The cavalry of Gondor halted. Behind their screen the out-companies re-formed. Now steadily they came marching back. They reached the Gate of the City and entered, stepping proudly; and proudly the people of the City looked on them and cried their praise, and yet they were troubled in heart. For the companies were grievously reduced. Faramir had lost a third of his men. And where was he?

Last of all he came. His men passed in. The mounted knights returned, and at their rear the banner of Dol Amroth, and the Prince. And in his arms before him on his horse he bore the body of his kinsman, Faramir son of Denethor, found upon the stricken field.

'Faramir! Faramir!' men cried, weeping in the streets. But he did not answer, and they bore him away up the winding road to the Citadel and his father. Even as the Nazgûl had swerved aside from the onset of the White Rider, there came flying a deadly dart, and Faramir, as he held at bay a mounted champion of Harad, had fallen to the earth. Only the charge of Dol Amroth had saved him from the red southland swords that would have hewed him as he lay.

The Prince Imrahil brought Faramir to the White Tower, and he said: 'Your son has returned, lord, after great deeds,' and he told all that he had seen. But Denethor rose and looked on the face of his son and was silent. Then he bade them make a bed in the chamber and lay Faramir upon it and depart. But he himself went up alone into the secret room under the summit of the Tower; and many who looked up thither at that time saw a pale light that gleamed and flickered from the narrow windows for a while, and then flashed and went out. And when Denethor descended again he went to Faramir and sat beside him without speaking, but the face of the Lord was grey, more deathlike than his son's.

So now at last the City was besieged, enclosed in a ring of foes. The Rammas was broken, and all the Pelennor abandoned to the Enemy. The last word to come from outside the walls was brought by men flying down the northward road ere the Gate was shut. They were the remnant of the guard that was kept at that point where the way from Anórien and Rohan ran into the townlands. Ingold led them, the same who had admitted Gandalf and Pippin less than five days before, while the sun still rose and there was hope in the morning.

'There is no news of the Rohirrim,' he said. 'Rohan will not come now. Or if they come, it will not avail us. The new host that we had tidings of has come first, from over the River by way of Andros, it is said. They are strong: battalions of Orcs of the Eye, and countless companies of Men of a new sort that we have not met before. Not tall, but broad and grim, bearded like dwarves, wielding great axes. Out of some savage land in the wide East they come, we deem. They hold the northward road; and many have passed on into Anórien. The Rohirrim cannot come.'

The Gate was shut. All night watchmen on the walls heard the rumour of the enemy that roamed outside, burning field and tree, and hewing any man that they found abroad, living or dead. The numbers that had already passed over the River could not be guessed in the darkness, but when morning, or its dim shadow, stole over the plain, it was seen that even fear by night had scarcely over-counted them. The plain was dark with their marching companies, and as far as eyes could strain in the mirk there sprouted, like a foul fungus-growth, all about the beleaguered city great camps of tents, black or sombre red.

Busy as ants hurrying orcs were digging, digging lines of deep trenches in a huge ring, just out of bowshot from the walls; and as the trenches were made each was filled with fire, though how it was kindled or fed, by art or devilry, none could see. All day the labour went forward, while the men of Minas Tirith looked on, unable to hinder it. And as each length of trench was completed, they could see great wains approaching; and soon yet more companies of the enemy were swiftly setting up, each behind the cover of a trench, great engines for the casting of missiles. There were none upon the City walls large enough to reach so far or to stay the work.

At first men laughed and did not greatly fear such devices. For the main wall of the City was of great height and marvellous thickness, built ere the power and craft of Númenor waned in exile; and its outward face was like to the Tower of Orthanc, hard and dark and smooth, unconquerable by steel or fire, unbreakable except by some convulsion that would rend the very earth on which it stood.

'Nay,' they said, 'not if the Nameless One himself should come, not even he could enter here while we yet live.' But some answered: 'While we yet live? How long? He has a weapon that has brought low many strong places since the world began. Hunger. The roads are cut. Rohan will not come.'

But the engines did not waste shot upon the indomitable wall. It was no brigand or orc-chieftain that ordered the assault upon the Lord of Mordor's greatest foe. A power and mind of malice guided it. As soon as the great catapults were set, with many yells and the creaking of rope and winch, they began to throw missiles marvellously high, so that they passed right above the battlement and fell thudding within the first circle of the City; and many of them by some secret art burst into flame as they came toppling down.

Soon there was great peril of fire behind the wall, and all who could be spared were busy quelling the flames that sprang up in many places. Then among the greater casts there fell another hail, less ruinous but more horrible. All about the streets and lanes behind the Gate it tumbled down, small round shot that did not burn. But when men ran to learn what it might be, they cried aloud or wept. For the enemy was flinging into the City all the heads of those who had fallen fighting at Osgiliath, or on the Rammas, or in the fields. They were grim to look on; for though some were crushed and shapeless, and some had been cruelly hewn, yet many had features that could be told, and it seemed that they had died in pain; and all were branded with the foul token of the Lidless Eye. But marred and dishonoured as they were, it often chanced that thus a man would see again the face of someone that he had known, who had walked proudly once in arms, or tilled the fields, or ridden in upon a holiday from the green vales in the hills.

In vain men shook their fists at the pitiless foes that swarmed before the Gate. Curses they heeded not, nor understood the tongues of western men, crying with harsh voices like beasts and carrion-birds. But soon there were few left in Minas Tirith who had the heart to stand up and defy the hosts of Mordor. For yet another weapon, swifter than hunger, the Lord of the Dark Tower had: dread and despair.

The Nazgûl came again, and as their Dark Lord now grew and put forth his strength, so their voices, which uttered only his will and his malice, were filled with evil and horror. Ever they circled above the City, like vultures that expect their fill of doomed men's flesh. Out of sight and shot they flew, and yet were ever present, and their deadly voices rent the air. More unbearable they became, not less, at each new cry. At length even the stout-hearted would fling themselves to the ground as the hidden menace passed over them, or they would stand, letting their weapons fall from nerveless hands while into their minds a blackness came, and they thought no more of war; but only of hiding and of crawling, and of death.

During all this black day Faramir lay upon his bed in the chamber of the White Tower, wandering in a desperate fever; dying someone said, and soon 'dying' all men were saying upon the walls and in the streets. And by him his father sat, and said nothing, but watched, and gave no longer any heed to the defence.

No hours so dark had Pippin known, not even in the clutches of the Uruk-hai. It was his duty to wait upon the Lord, and wait he did, forgotten it seemed, standing by the door of the unlit chamber, mastering his own fears as best he could. And as he watched, it seemed to him that Denethor grew old before his eyes, as if something had snapped in his proud will, and his stern mind was overthrown. Grief maybe had wrought it, and remorse. He saw tears on that once tearless face, more unbearable than wrath.

'Do not weep, lord,' he stammered. 'Perhaps he will get well. Have you asked Gandalf?'

'Comfort me not with wizards!' said Denethor. 'The fool's hope has failed. The Enemy has found it, and now his power waxes; he sees our very thoughts, and all we do is ruinous.

'I sent my son forth, unthanked, unblessed, out into needless peril, and here he lies with poison in his veins. Nay, nay, whatever may now betide in war, my line too is ending, even the House of the Stewards has failed.

Mean folk shall rule the last remnant of the Kings of Men, lurking in the hills until all are hounded out.'

Men came to the door crying for the Lord of the City. 'Nay, I will not come down,' he said. 'I must stay beside my son. He might still speak before the end. But that is near. Follow whom you will, even the Grey Fool, though his hope has failed. Here I stay.'

So it was that Gandalf took command of the last defence of the City of Gondor. Wherever he came men's hearts would lift again, and the winged shadows pass from memory. Tirelessly he strode from Citadel to Gate, from north to south about the wall; and with him went the Prince of Dol Amroth in his shining mail. For he and his knights still held themselves like lords in whom the race of Númenor ran true. Men that saw them whispered saying: 'Belike the old tales speak well; there is Elvish blood in the veins of that folk, for the people of Nimrodel dwelt in that land once long ago.' And then one would sing amid the gloom some staves of the Lay of Nimrodel, or other songs of the Vale of Anduin out of vanished years.

And yet – when they had gone, the shadows closed on men again, and their hearts went cold, and the valour of Gondor withered into ash. And so slowly they passed out of a dim day of fears into the darkness of a desperate night. Fires now raged unchecked in the first circle of the City, and the garrison upon the outer wall was already in many places cut off from retreat. But the faithful who remained there at their posts were few; most had fled beyond the second gate.

Far behind the battle the River had been swiftly bridged, and all day more force and gear of war had poured across. Now at last in the middle night the assault was loosed. The vanguard passed through the trenches of fire by many devious paths that had been left between them. On they came, reckless of their loss as they approached, still bunched and herded, within the range of bowmen on the wall. But indeed there were too few now left there to do them great damage, though the light of the fires showed up many a mark for archers of such skill as Gondor once had boasted. Then perceiving that the valour of the City was already beaten down, the hidden Captain put forth his strength. Slowly the great siege-towers built in Osgiliath rolled forward through the dark.

Messengers came again to the chamber in the White Tower, and Pippin let them enter, for they were urgent. Denethor turned his head slowly from Faramir's face, and looked at them silently.

'The first circle of the City is burning, lord,' they said. 'What are your commands? You are still the Lord and Steward. Not all will follow Mithrandir. Men are flying from the walls and leaving them unmanned.'

'Why? Why do the fools fly?' said Denethor. 'Better to burn sooner than late, for burn we must. Go back to your bonfire! And I? I will go now to my pyre. To my pyre! No tomb for Denethor and Faramir. No tomb! No long slow sleep of death embalmed. We will burn like heathen kings before ever a ship sailed hither from the West. The West has failed. Go back and burn!'

The messengers without bow or answer turned and fled.

Now Denethor stood up and released the fevered hand of Faramir that he had held. 'He is burning, already burning,' he said sadly. 'The house of his spirit crumbles.' Then stepping softly towards Pippin he looked down at him.

'Farewell!' he said. 'Farewell, Peregrin son of Paladin! Your service has been short, and now it is drawing to an end. I release you from the little that remains. Go now, and die in what way seems best to you. And with whom you will, even that friend whose folly brought you to this death. Send for my servants and then go. Farewell!'

'I will not say farewell, my lord,' said Pippin kneeling. And then suddenly hobbit-like once more, he stood up and looked the old man in the eyes. 'I will take your leave, sir,' he said; 'for I want to see Gandalf very much indeed. But he is no fool; and I will not think of dying until he despairs of life. But from my word and your service I do not wish to be released while you live. And if they come at last to the Citadel, I hope to be here and stand beside you and earn perhaps the arms that you have given me.'

'Do as you will, Master Halfling,' said Denethor. 'But my life is broken. Send for my servants!' He turned back to Faramir.

Pippin left him and called for the servants, and they came: six men of the household, strong and fair; yet they trembled at the summons. But in a quiet voice Denethor bade them lay warm coverlets on Faramir's bed and take it up. And they did so, and lifting up the bed they bore it from the chamber. Slowly they paced to trouble the fevered man as little as might be, and Denethor, now bending on a staff, followed them; and last came Pippin.

Out from the White Tower they walked, as if to a funeral, out into the darkness, where the overhanging cloud was lit beneath with flickers of dull red. Softly they paced the great courtyard, and at a word from Denethor halted beside the Withered Tree.

All was silent, save for the rumour of war in the City down below, and they heard the water dripping sadly from the dead branches into the dark pool. Then they went on through the Citadel gate, where the sentinel stared at them in wonder and dismay as they passed by. Turning westward they came at length to a door in the rearward wall of the sixth circle. Fen Hollen it was called, for it was kept ever shut save at times of funeral, and only the Lord of the City might use that way, or those who bore the token of the tombs and tended the houses of the dead. Beyond it went a winding road that descended in many curves down to the narrow land under the shadow of Mindolluin's precipice where stood the mansions of the dead Kings and of their Stewards.

A porter sat in a little house beside the way, and with fear in his eyes he came forth bearing a lantern in his hand. At the Lord's command he unlocked the door, and silently it swung back; and they passed through, taking the lantern from his hand. It was dark on the climbing road between ancient walls and many-pillared balusters looming in the swaying lantern-beam. Their slow feet echoed as they walked down, down, until at last they came to the Silent Street, Rath Dínen, between pale domes and empty halls and images of men long dead; and they entered into the House of the Stewards and set down their burden.

There Pippin, staring uneasily about him, saw that he was in a wide vaulted chamber, draped as it were with the great shadows that the little lantern threw upon its shrouded walls. And dimly to be seen were many rows of tables, carved of marble; and upon each table lay a sleeping form, hands folded, head pillowed upon stone. But one table near at hand stood broad and bare. Upon it at a sign from Denethor they laid Faramir and his father side by side, and covered them with one covering, and stood then with bowed heads as mourners beside a bed of death. Then Denethor spoke in a low voice.

'Here we will wait,' he said. 'But send not for the embalmers. Bring us wood quick to burn, and lay it all about us, and beneath; and pour oil upon it. And when I bid you thrust in a torch. Do this and speak no more to me. Farewell!'

'By your leave, lord!' said Pippin and turned and fled in terror from the deathly house. 'Poor Faramir!' he thought. 'I must find Gandalf. Poor Faramir! Quite likely he needs medicine more than tears. Oh, where can I find Gandalf? In the thick of things, I suppose; and he will have no time to spare for dying men or madmen.'

At the door he turned to one of the servants who had remained on guard there. 'Your master is not himself,' he said. 'Go slow! Bring no fire to this place while Faramir lives! Do nothing until Gandalf comes!'

'Who is the master of Minas Tirith?' the man answered. 'The Lord Denethor or the Grey Wanderer?'

'The Grey Wanderer or no one, it would seem,' said Pippin, and he sped back and up the winding way as swiftly as his feet would carry him, past the astonished porter, out through the door, and on, till he came near the gate of the Citadel. The sentinel hailed him as he went by, and he recognized the voice of Beregond.

'Whither do you run, Master Peregrin?' he cried.

'To find Mithrandir,' Pippin answered.

'The Lord's errands are urgent and should not be hindered by me,' said Beregond; 'but tell me quickly, if you may: what goes forward? Whither has my Lord gone? I have just come on duty, but I heard that he passed towards the Closed Door, and men were bearing Faramir before him.'

'Yes,' said Pippin, 'to the Silent Street.'

Beregond bowed his head to hide his tears. 'They said that he was dying,' he sighed, 'and now he is dead.'

'No,' said Pippin, 'not yet. And even now his death might be prevented, I think. But the Lord of the City, Beregond, has fallen before his city is taken. He is fey and dangerous.' Quickly he told of Denethor's strange words and deeds. 'I must find Gandalf at once.'

'Then you must go down to the battle.'

'I know. The Lord has given me leave. But, Beregond, if you can, do something to stop any dreadful thing happening.'

'The Lord does not permit those who wear the black and silver to leave their post for any cause, save at his own command.'

'Well, you must choose between orders and the life of Faramir,' said Pippin. 'And as for orders, I think you have a madman to deal with, not a lord. I must run. I will return if I can.'

He ran on, down, down towards the outer city. Men flying back from the burning passed him, and some seeing his livery turned and shouted, but he paid no heed. At last he was through the Second Gate, beyond which great fires leaped up between the walls. Yet it seemed strangely silent. No noise or shouts of battle or din of arms could be heard. Then suddenly there was a dreadful cry and a great shock, and a deep echoing boom. Forcing himself on against a gust of fear and horror that shook him almost to his knees, Pippin turned a corner opening on the wide place behind the City Gate. He stopped dead. He had found Gandalf; but he shrank back, cowering into a shadow.

Ever since the middle night the great assault had gone on. The drums rolled. To the north and to the south company upon company of the enemy pressed to the walls. There came great beasts, like moving houses in the red and fitful light, the *mûmakil* of the Harad dragging through the lanes amid the fires huge towers and engines. Yet their Captain cared not greatly

what they did or how many might be slain: their purpose was only to test
the strength of the defence and to keep the men of Gondor busy in many
places. It was against the Gate that he would throw his heaviest weight.
Very strong it might be, wrought of steel and iron, and guarded with towers
and bastions of indomitable stone, yet it was the key, the weakest point in
all that high and impenetrable wall.

The drums rolled louder. Fires leaped up. Great engines crawled across
the field; and in the midst was a huge ram, great as a forest-tree a hundred
feet in length, swinging on mighty chains. Long had it been forging in the
dark smithies of Mordor, and its hideous head, founded of black steel, was
shaped in the likeness of a ravening wolf; on it spells of ruin lay. Grond
they named it, in memory of the Hammer of the Underworld of old. Great
beasts drew it, orcs surrounded it, and behind walked mountain-trolls to
wield it.

But about the Gate resistance still was stout, and there the knights of
Dol Amroth and the hardiest of the garrison stood at bay. Shot and dart
fell thick; siege-towers crashed or blazed suddenly like torches. All before
the walls on either side of the Gate the ground was choked with wreck and
with bodies of the slain; yet still driven as by a madness more and more
came up.

Grond crawled on. Upon its housing no fire would catch; and though
now and again some great beast that hauled it would go mad and spread
stamping ruin among the orcs innumerable that guarded it, their bodies
were cast aside from its path and others took their place.

Grond crawled on. The drums rolled wildly. Over the hills of slain a
hideous shape appeared: a horseman, tall, hooded, cloaked in black.
Slowly, trampling the fallen, he rode forth, heeding no longer any dart.
He halted and held up a long pale sword. And as he did so a great fear
fell on all, defender and foe alike; and the hands of men drooped to their
sides, and no bow sang. For a moment all was still.

The drums rolled and rattled. With a vast rush Grond was hurled forward
by huge hands. It reached the Gate. It swung. A deep boom rumbled
through the City like thunder running in the clouds. But the doors of iron
and posts of steel withstood the stroke.

Then the Black Captain rose in his stirrups and cried aloud in a dreadful
voice, speaking in some forgotten tongue words of power and terror to
rend both heart and stone.

Thrice he cried. Thrice the great ram boomed. And suddenly upon the
last stroke the Gate of Gondor broke. As if stricken by some blasting spell
it burst asunder: there was a flash of searing lightning, and the doors
tumbled in riven fragments to the ground.

In rode the Lord of the Nazgûl. A great black shape against the fires beyond he loomed up, grown to a vast menace of despair. In rode the Lord of the Nazgûl, under the archway that no enemy ever yet had passed, and all fled before his face.

All save one. There waiting, silent and still in the space before the Gate, sat Gandalf upon Shadowfax: Shadowfax who alone among the free horses of the earth endured the terror, unmoving, steadfast as a graven image in Rath Dínen.

'You cannot enter here,' said Gandalf, and the huge shadow halted. 'Go back to the abyss prepared for you! Go back! Fall into the nothingness that awaits you and your Master. Go!'

The Black Rider flung back his hood, and behold! he had a kingly crown; and yet upon no head visible was it set. The red fires shone between it and the mantled shoulders vast and dark. From a mouth unseen there came a deadly laughter.

'Old fool!' he said. 'Old fool! This is my hour. Do you not know Death when you see it? Die now and curse in vain!' And with that he lifted high his sword and flames ran down the blade.

Gandalf did not move. And in that very moment, away behind in some courtyard of the City, a cock crowed. Shrill and clear he crowed, recking nothing of wizardry or war, welcoming only the morning that in the sky far above the shadows of death was coming with the dawn.

And as if in answer there came from far away another note. Horns, horns, horns. In dark Mindolluin's sides they dimly echoed. Great horns of the North wildly blowing. Rohan had come at last.

CHAPTER V

THE RIDE OF THE ROHIRRIM

It was dark and Merry could see nothing as he lay on the ground rolled in a blanket; yet though the night was airless and windless, all about him hidden trees were sighing softly. He lifted his head. Then he heard it again: a sound like faint drums in the wooded hills and mountain-steps. The throb would cease suddenly and then be taken up again at some other point, now nearer, now further off. He wondered if the watchmen had heard it.

He could not see them, but he knew that all round him were the companies of the Rohirrim. He could smell the horses in the dark, and could hear their shiftings and their soft stamping on the needle-covered ground. The host was bivouacked in the pine-woods that clustered about Eilenach Beacon, a tall hill standing up from the long ridges of the Druadan Forest that lay beside the great road in East Anórien.

Tired as he was Merry could not sleep. He had ridden now for four days on end, and the ever-deepening gloom had slowly weighed down his heart. He began to wonder why he had been so eager to come, when he had been given every excuse, even his lord's command, to stay behind. He wondered, too, if the old King knew that he had been disobeyed and was angry. Perhaps not. There seemed to be some understanding between Dernhelm and Elfhelm, the Marshal who commanded the *éored* in which they were riding. He and all his men ignored Merry and pretended not to hear if he spoke. He might have been just another bag that Dernhelm was carrying. Dernhelm was no comfort: he never spoke to anyone. Merry felt small, unwanted, and lonely. Now the time was anxious, and the host was in peril. They were less than a day's ride from the out-walls of Minas Tirith that encircled the townlands. Scouts had been sent ahead. Some had not returned. Others hastening back had reported that the road was held in force against them. A host of the enemy was encamped upon it, three miles west of Amon Dîn, and some strength of men was already thrusting along the road and was no more than three leagues away. Orcs were roving in the hills and woods along the roadside. The king and Éomer held council in the watches of the night.

Merry wanted somebody to talk to, and he thought of Pippin. But that only increased his restlessness. Poor Pippin, shut up in the great city of stone, lonely and afraid. Merry wished he was a tall Rider like Éomer and could blow a horn or something and go galloping to his rescue. He sat up, listening to the drums that were beating again, now nearer at hand. Presently he heard voices speaking low, and he saw dim half-shrouded lanterns passing through the trees. Men nearby began to move uncertainly in the dark.

A tall figure loomed up and stumbled over him, cursing the tree-roots. He recognized the voice of Elfhelm the Marshal.

'I am not a tree-root, Sir,' he said, 'nor a bag, but a bruised hobbit. The least you can do in amends is to tell me what is afoot.'

'Anything that can keep so in this devil's mirk,' answered Elfhelm. 'But my lord sends word that we must set ourselves in readiness: orders may come for a sudden move.'

'Is the enemy coming then?' asked Merry anxiously. 'Are those their drums? I began to think I was imagining them, as no one else seemed to take any notice of them.'

'Nay, nay,' said Elfhelm, 'the enemy is on the road not in the hills. You hear the Woses, the Wild Men of the Woods: thus they talk together from afar. They still haunt Druadan Forest, it is said. Remnants of an older time they be, living few and secretly, wild and wary as the beasts. They go not to war with Gondor or the Mark; but now they are troubled by the darkness and the coming of the orcs: they fear lest the Dark Years be returning, as seems likely enough. Let us be thankful that they are not hunting us: for they use poisoned arrows, it is said, and they are woodcrafty beyond compare. But they have offered their services to Théoden. Even now one of their headmen is being taken to the king. Yonder go the lights. So much I have heard but no more. And now I must busy myself with my lord's commands. Pack yourself up, Master Bag!' He vanished into the shadows.

Merry did not like this talk of wild men and poisoned darts, but quite apart from that a great weight of dread was on him. Waiting was unbearable. He longed to know what was going to happen. He got up and soon was walking warily in pursuit of the last lantern before it disappeared among the trees.

Presently he came to an open space where a small tent had been set up for the king under a great tree. A large lantern, covered above, was hanging from a bough and cast a pale circle of light below. There sat Théoden and Éomer, and before them on the ground sat a strange squat shape of a man, gnarled as an old stone, and the hairs of his scanty beard straggled on his lumpy chin like dry moss. He was short-legged and fat-armed, thick and stumpy, and clad only with grass about his waist. Merry felt that he had seen him before somewhere, and suddenly he remembered the Púkel-men of Dunharrow. Here was one of those old images brought to life, or maybe a creature descended in true line through endless years from the models used by the forgotten craftsmen long ago.

There was a silence as Merry crept nearer, and then the Wild Man began to speak, in answer to some question, it seemed. His voice was deep and guttural, yet to Merry's surprise he spoke the Common Speech, though in a halting fashion, and uncouth words were mingled with it. 'No, father of Horse-men,' he said, 'we fight not. Hunt only. Kill *gorgûn* in woods, hate orc-folk. You hate *gorgûn* too. We help as we can. Wild Men have long ears and long eyes; know all paths. Wild Men live here before Stone-houses; before Tall Men come up out of Water.'

'But our need is for aid in battle,' said Éomer. 'How will you and your folk help us?'

'Bring news,' said the Wild Man. 'We look out from hills. We climb big mountain and look down. Stone-city is shut. Fire burns there outside; now inside too. You wish to come there? Then you must be quick. But *gorgûn* and men out of far-away,' he waved a short gnarled arm eastward, 'sit on horse-road. Very many, more than Horse-men.'

'How do you know that?' said Éomer.

The old man's flat face and dark eyes showed nothing, but his voice was sullen with displeasure. 'Wild Men are wild, free, but not children,' he answered. 'I am great headman, Ghân-buri-Ghân. I count many things: stars in sky, leaves on trees, men in the dark. You have a score of scores counted ten times and five. They have more. Big fight, and who will win? And many more walk round walls of Stone-houses.'

'Alas! he speaks all too shrewdly,' said Théoden. 'And our scouts say that they have cast trenches and stakes across the road. We cannot sweep them away in sudden onset.'

'And yet we need great haste,' said Éomer. 'Mundburg is on fire!'

'Let Ghân-buri-Ghân finish!' said the Wild Man. 'More than one road he knows. He will lead you by road where no pits are, no *gorgûn* walk, only Wild Men and beasts. Many paths were made when Stonehouse-folk were stronger. They carved hills as hunters carve beast-flesh. Wild Men think they ate stone for food. They went through Drúadan to Rimmon with great wains. They go no longer. Road is forgotten, but not by Wild Men. Over hill and behind hill it lies still under grass and tree, there behind Rimmon and down to Dîn, and back at the end to Horse-men's road. Wild Men will show you that road. Then you will kill *gorgûn* and drive away bad dark with bright iron, and Wild Men can go back to sleep in the wild woods.'

Éomer and the king spoke together in their own tongue. At length Théoden turned to the Wild Man. 'We will receive your offer,' he said. 'For though we leave a host of foes behind, what matter? If the Stone-city falls, then we shall have no returning. If it is saved, then the orc-host itself will be cut off. If you are faithful, Ghân-buri-Ghân, then we will give you rich reward, and you shall have the friendship of the Mark for ever.'

'Dead men are not friends to living men, and give them no gifts,' said the Wild Man. 'But if you live after the Darkness, then leave Wild Men alone in the woods and do not hunt them like beasts any more. Ghân-buri-Ghân will not lead you into trap. He will go himself with father of Horsemen, and if he leads you wrong, you will kill him.'

'So be it!' said Théoden.

'How long will it take to pass by the enemy and come back to the road?' asked Éomer. 'We must go at foot-pace, if you guide us; and I doubt not the way is narrow.'

'Wild Men go quick on feet,' said Ghân. 'Way is wide for four horses in Stonewain Valley yonder,' he waved his hand southwards; 'but narrow at beginning and at end. Wild Man could walk from here to Dîn between sunrise and noon.'

'Then we must allow at least seven hours for the leaders,' said Éomer; 'but we must reckon rather on some ten hours for all. Things unforeseen may hinder us, and if our host is all strung out, it will be long ere it can be set in order when we issue from the hills. What is the hour now?'

'Who knows?' said Théoden. 'All is night now.'

'It is all dark, but it is not all night,' said Ghân. 'When Sun comes we feel her, even when she is hidden. Already she climbs over East-mountains. It is the opening of day in the sky-fields.'

'Then we must set out as soon as may be,' said Éomer. 'Even so we cannot hope to come to Gondor's aid today.'

Merry waited to hear no more, but slipped away to get ready for the summons to the march. This was the last stage before the battle. It did not seem likely to him that many of them would survive it. But he thought of Pippin and the flames in Minas Tirith and thrust down his own dread.

All went well that day, and no sight or sound had they of the enemy waiting to waylay them. The Wild Men had put out a screen of wary hunters, so that no orc or roving spy should learn of the movements in the hills. The light was more dim than ever as they drew nearer to the beleaguered city, and the Riders passed in long files like dark shadows of men and horses. Each company was guided by a wild woodman; but old Ghân walked beside the king. The start had been slower than was hoped, for it had taken time for the Riders, walking and leading their horses, to find paths over the thickly wooded ridges behind their camp and down into the hidden Stonewain Valley. It was late in the afternoon when the leaders came to wide grey thickets stretching beyond the eastward side of Amon Dîn, and masking a great gap in the line of hills that from Nardol to Dîn ran east and west. Through the gap the forgotten wain-road long ago had run down, back into the main horse-way from the City through Anórien; but now for many lives of men trees had had their way with it, and it had vanished, broken and buried under the leaves of uncounted years. But the thickets offered to the Riders their last hope of cover before they went into open battle; for beyond them lay the road and the plains of Anduin, while east and southwards the slopes were bare and rocky, as the writhen hills gathered themselves together and climbed up, bastion upon bastion, into the great mass and shoulders of Mindolluin.

The leading company was halted, and as those behind filed up out of the trough of the Stonewain Valley they spread out and passed to camping-places under the grey trees. The king summoned the captains to council. Éomer sent out scouts to spy upon the road; but old Ghân shook his head.

'No good to send Horse-men,' he said. 'Wild Men have already seen all that can be seen in the bad air. They will come soon and speak to me here.'

The captains came; and then out of the trees crept warily other púkel-shapes so like old Ghân that Merry could hardly tell them apart. They spoke to Ghân in a strange throaty language.

Presently Ghân turned to the king. 'Wild Men say many things,' he said. 'First, be wary! Still many men in camp beyond Dîn, an hour's walk yonder,' he waved his arm west towards the black beacon. 'But none to see between here and Stone-folk's new walls. Many busy there. Walls stand up no longer: gorgûn knock them down with earth-thunder and with clubs of black iron. They are unwary and do not look about them. They think their friends watch all roads!' At that old Ghân made a curious gurgling noise, and it seemed that he was laughing.

'Good tidings!' cried Éomer. 'Even in this gloom hope gleams again. Our Enemy's devices oft serve us in his despite. The accursed darkness itself has been a cloak to us. And now, lusting to destroy Gondor and throw it down stone from stone, his orcs have taken away my greatest fear. The out-wall could have been held long against us. Now we can sweep through – if once we win so far.'

'Once again I thank you, Ghân-buri-Ghân of the woods,' said Théoden. 'Good fortune go with you for tidings and for guidance!'

'Kill gorgûn! Kill orc-folk! No other words please Wild Men,' answered Ghân. 'Drive away bad air and darkness with bright iron!'

'To do these things we have ridden far,' said the king, 'and we shall attempt them. But what we shall achieve only tomorrow will show.'

Ghân-buri-Ghân squatted down and touched the earth with his horny brow in token of farewell. Then he got up as if to depart. But suddenly he

stood looking up like some startled woodland animal snuffling a strange
air. A light came in his eyes.

'Wind is changing!' he cried, and with that, in a twinkling as it seemed,
he and his fellows had vanished into the glooms, never to be seen by any
Rider of Rohan again. Not long after far away eastward the faint drums
throbbed again. Yet to no heart in all the host came any fear that the Wild
Men were unfaithful, strange and unlovely though they might appear.

'We need no further guidance,' said Elfhelm; 'for there are riders in the
host who have ridden down to Mundburg in days of peace. I for one. When
we come to the road it will veer south, and there will lie before us still
seven leagues ere we reach the wall of the townlands. Along most of that
way there is much grass on either side of the road. On that stretch the
errand-riders of Gondor reckoned to make their greatest speed. We may
ride it swiftly and without great rumour.'

'Then since we must look for fell deeds and the need of all our strength,'
said Éomer, 'I counsel that we rest now, and set out hence by night, and
so time our going that we come upon the fields when tomorrow is as light
as it will be, or when our lord give the signal.'

To this the king assented, and the captains departed. But soon Elfhelm
returned. 'The scouts have found naught to report beyond the grey wood,
lord,' he said, 'save two men only: two dead men and two dead horses.'

'Well?' said Éomer. 'What of it?'

'This, lord: they were errand-riders of Gondor; Hirgon was one maybe.
At least his hand still clasped the Red Arrow, but his head was hewn off.
And this also: it would seem by the signs that they were fleeing *westward*
when they fell. As I read it, they found the enemy already on the out-wall,
or assailing it, when they returned – and that would be two nights ago, if
they used fresh horses from the posts, as is their wont. They could not
reach the City and turned back.'

'Alas!' said Théoden. 'Then Denethor has heard no news of our riding
and will despair of our coming.'

'*Need brooks no delay, yet late is better than never,*' said Éomer. 'And
mayhap in this time shall the old saw be proved truer than ever before
since men spoke with mouth.'

It was night. On either side of the road the host of Rohan was moving
silently. Now the road passing about the skirts of Mindolluin turned southward. Far away and almost straight ahead there was a red glow under the
black sky and the sides of the great mountain loomed dark against it. They
were drawing near the Rammas of the Pelennor; but the day was not yet
come.

The king rode in the midst of the leading company, his household-men about him. Elfhelm's *éored* came next; and now Merry noticed that Dernhelm had left his place and in the darkness was moving steadily forward, until at last he was riding just in rear of the king's guard. There came a check. Merry heard voices in front speaking softly. Out-riders had come back who had ventured forward almost to the wall. They came to the king.

'There are great fires, lord,' said one. 'The City is all set about with flame, and the field is full of foes. But all seem drawn off to the assault. As well as we could guess, there are few left upon the out-wall, and they are heedless, busy in destruction.'

'Do you remember the Wild Man's words, lord?' said another. 'I live upon the open Wold in days of peace; Wídfara is my name, and to me also the air brings messages. Already the wind is turning. There comes a breath out of the South; there is a sea-tang in it, faint though it be. The morning will bring new things. Above the reek it will be dawn when you pass the wall.'

'If you speak truly, Wídfara, then may you live beyond this day in years of blessedness!' said Théoden. He turned to the men of his household who were near, and he spoke now in a clear voice so that many also of the riders of the first *éored* heard him:

'Now is the hour come, Riders of the Mark, sons of Eorl! Foes and fire are before you, and your homes far behind. Yet, though you fight upon an alien field, the glory that you reap there shall be your own for ever. Oaths ye have taken: now fulfil them all, to lord and land and league of friendship!'

Men clashed spear upon shield.

'Éomer, my son! You lead the first *éored*,' said Théoden; 'and it shall go behind the king's banner in the centre. Elfhelm, lead your company to the right when we pass the wall. And Grimbold shall lead his towards the left. Let the other companies behind follow these three that lead, as they have chance. Strike wherever the enemy gathers. Other plans we cannot make, for we know not yet how things stand upon the field. Forth now, and fear no darkness!'

The leading company rode off as swiftly as they could, for it was still deep dark, whatever change Wídfara might forebode. Merry was riding behind Dernhelm, clutching with the left hand while with the other he tried to loosen his sword in its sheath. He felt now bitterly the truth of the old king's words: *in such a battle what would you do, Meriadoc?* Just this,' he thought: 'encumber a rider, and hope at best to stay in my seat and not be pounded to death by galloping hoofs!'

It was no more than a league to where the out-walls had stood. They soon reached them; too soon for Merry. 'Wild cries broke out, and there was some clash of arms, but it was brief. The orcs busy about the walls were few and amazed, and they were quickly slain or driven off. Before the ruin of the north-gate in the Rammas the king halted again. The first éored drew up behind him and about him on either side. Dernhelm kept close to the king, though Elfhelm's company was away on the right. Grimbold's men turned aside and passed round to a great gap in the wall further eastward.

Merry peered from behind Dernhelm's back. Far away, maybe ten miles or more, there was a great burning, but between it and the Riders lines of fire blazed in a vast crescent, at the nearest point less than a league distant. He could make out little more on the dark plain, and as yet he neither saw any hope of morning, nor felt any wind, changed or unchanged.

Now silently the host of Rohan moved forward into the field of Gondor, pouring in slowly but steadily, like the rising tide through breaches in a dike that men have thought secure. But the mind and will of the Black Captain were bent wholly on the falling city, and as yet no tidings came to him warning that his designs held any flaw.

After a while the king led his men away somewhat eastward, to come between the fires of the siege and the outer fields. Still they were unchallenged, and still Théoden gave no signal. At last he halted once again. The City was now nearer. A smell of burning was in the air and a very shadow of death. The horses were uneasy. But the king sat upon Snowmane, motionless, gazing upon the agony of Minas Tirith, as if stricken suddenly by anguish, or by dread. He seemed to shrink down, cowed by age. Merry himself felt as if a great weight of horror and doubt had settled on him. His heart beat slowly. Time seemed poised in uncertainty. They were too late! Too late was worse than never! Perhaps Théoden would quail, bow his old head, turn, slink away to hide in the hills.

Then suddenly Merry felt it at last, beyond doubt: a change. Wind was in his face! Light was glimmering. Far, far away, in the South the clouds could be dimly seen as remote grey shapes, rolling up, drifting: morning lay beyond them.

But at that same moment there was a flash, as if lightning had sprung from the earth beneath the City. For a searing second it stood dazzling far off in black and white, its topmost tower like a glittering needle; and then as the darkness closed again there came rolling over the fields a great *boom*.

At that sound the bent shape of the king sprang suddenly erect. Tall and proud he seemed again; and rising in his stirrups he cried in a loud voice, more clear than any there had ever heard a mortal man achieve before:

Arise, arise, Riders of Théoden!
Fell deeds awake: fire and slaughter!
spear shall be shaken, shield be splintered,
a sword-day, a red day, ere the sun rises!
Ride now, ride now! Ride to Gondor!

With that he seized a great horn from Guthláf his banner-bearer, and he blew such a blast upon it that it burst asunder. And straightway all the horns in the host were lifted up in music, and the blowing of the horns of Rohan in that hour was like a storm upon the plain and a thunder in the mountains.

Ride now, ride now! Ride to Gondor!

Suddenly the king cried to Snowmane and the horse sprang away. Behind him his banner blew in the wind, white horse upon a field of green, but he outpaced it. After him thundered the knights of his house, but he was ever before them. Éomer rode there, the white horsetail on his helm floating in his speed, and the front of the first *éored* roared like a breaker foaming to the shore, but Théoden could not be overtaken. Fey he seemed, or the battle-fury of his fathers ran like new fire in his veins, and he was borne up on Snowmane like a god of old, even as Oromë the Great in the battle of the Valar when the world was young. His golden shield was uncovered, and lo! it shone like an image of the Sun, and the grass flamed into green about the white feet of his steed. For morning came, morning and a wind from the sea; and darkness was removed, and the hosts of Mordor wailed, and terror took them, and they fled, and died, and the hoofs of wrath rode over them. And then all the host of Rohan burst into song, and they sang as they slew, for the joy of battle was on them, and the sound of their singing that was fair and terrible came even to the City.

CHAPTER VI

THE BATTLE OF THE PELENNOR FIELDS

But it was no orc-chieftain or brigand that led the assault upon Gondor. The darkness was breaking too soon, before the date that his Master had set for it: fortune had betrayed him for the moment, and the world had turned against him; victory was slipping from his grasp even as he stretched out his hand to seize it. But his arm was long. He was still in command, wielding great powers. King, Ringwraith, Lord of the Nazgûl, he had many weapons. He left the Gate and vanished.

Théoden King of the Mark had reached the road from the Gate to the River, and he turned towards the City that was now less than a mile distant. He slackened his speed a little, seeking new foes, and his knights came about him, and Dernhelm was with them. Ahead nearer the walls Elfhelm's men were among the siege-engines, hewing, slaying, driving their foes into the fire-pits. Well nigh all the northern half of the Pelennor was overrun, and there camps were blazing, orcs were flying towards the River like herds before the hunters; and the Rohirrim went hither and thither at their will. But they had not yet overthrown the siege, nor won the Gate. Many foes stood before it, and on the further half of the plain were other hosts still unfought. Southward beyond the road lay the main force of the Haradrim, and there their horsemen were gathered about the standard of their chieftain. And he looked out, and in the growing light he saw the banner of the king, and that it was far ahead of the battle with few men about it. Then he was filled with a red wrath and shouted aloud, and displaying his standard, black serpent upon scarlet, he came against the white horse and the green with great press of men; and the drawing of the scimitars of the Southrons was like a glitter of stars.

Then Théoden was aware of him, and would not wait for his onset, but crying to Snowmane he charged headlong to greet him. Great was the clash of their meeting. But the white fury of the Northmen burned the hotter, and more skilled was their knighthood with long spears and bitter. Fewer were they but they clove through the Southrons like a fire-bolt in a forest. Right through the press drove Théoden Thengel's son, and his spear was shivered as he threw down their chieftain. Out swept his sword, and he spurred to the standard, hewed staff and bearer; and the black serpent foundered. Then all that was left unslain of their cavalry turned and fled far away.

But lo! suddenly in the midst of the glory of the king his golden shield was dimmed. The new morning was blotted from the sky. Dark fell about him. Horses reared and screamed. Men cast from the saddle lay grovelling on the ground.

'To me! To me!' cried Théoden. 'Up Eorlingas! Fear no darkness!' But Snowmane wild with terror stood up on high, fighting with the air, and then with a great scream he crashed upon his side: a black dart had pierced him. The king fell beneath him.

The great shadow descended like a falling cloud. And behold! it was a winged creature: if bird, then greater than all other birds, and it was naked, and neither quill nor feather did it bear, and its vast pinions were as webs of hide between horned fingers; and it stank. A creature of an older world maybe it was, whose kind, lingering in forgotten mountains cold beneath the Moon, outstayed their day, and in hideous eyrie bred this last untimely brood, apt to evil. And the Dark Lord took it, and nursed it with fell meats, until it grew beyond the measure of all other things that fly; and he gave it to his servant to be his steed. Down, down it came, and then, folding its fingered webs, it gave a croaking cry, and settled upon the body of Snowmane, digging in its claws, stooping its long naked neck.

Upon it sat a shape, black-mantled, huge and threatening. A crown of steel he bore, but between rim and robe naught was there to see, save only a deadly gleam of eyes: the Lord of the Nazgûl. To the air he had returned, summoning his steed ere the darkness failed, and now he was come again, bringing ruin, turning hope to despair, and victory to death. A great black mace he wielded.

But Théoden was not utterly forsaken. The knights of his house lay slain about him, or else mastered by the madness of their steeds were borne far away. Yet one stood there still: Dernhelm the young, faithful beyond fear; and he wept, for he had loved his lord as a father. Right through the charge Merry had been borne unharmed behind him, until the Shadow came; and then Windfola had thrown them in his terror, and now ran wild upon the plain. Merry crawled on all fours like a dazed beast, and such a horror was on him that he was blind and sick.

'King's man! King's man!' his heart cried within him. 'You must stay by him. As a father you shall be to me, you said.' But his will made no answer, and his body shook. He dared not open his eyes or look up.

Then out of the blackness in his mind he thought that he heard Dernhelm speaking; yet now the voice seemed strange, recalling some other voice that he had known.

'Begone, foul dwimmerlaik, lord of carrion! Leave the dead in peace!'

A cold voice answered: 'Come not between the Nazgûl and his prey! Or he will not slay thee in thy turn. He will bear thee away to the houses of lamentation, beyond all darkness, where thy flesh shall be devoured, and thy shrivelled mind be left naked to the Lidless Eye.'

A sword rang as it was drawn. 'Do what you will; but I will hinder it, if I may.'

'Hinder me? Thou fool. No living man may hinder me!'

Then Merry heard of all sounds in that hour the strangest. It seemed that Dernhelm laughed, and the clear voice was like the ring of steel. 'But no living man am I! You look upon a woman. Éowyn I am, Éomund's daughter. You stand between me and my lord and kin. Begone, if you be not deathless! For living or dark undead, I will smite you, if you touch him.'

The winged creature screamed at her, but the Ringwraith made no answer, and was silent, as if in sudden doubt. Very amazement for a moment conquered Merry's fear. He opened his eyes and the blackness was lifted from them. There some paces from him sat the great beast, and all seemed dark about it, and above it loomed the Nazgûl Lord like a shadow of despair. A little to the left facing them stood she whom he had called Dernhelm. But the helm of her secrecy had fallen from her, and her bright hair, released from its bonds, gleamed with pale gold upon her shoulders. Her eyes grey as the sea were hard and fell, and yet tears were on her cheek. A sword was in her hand, and she raised her shield against the horror of her enemy's eyes.

Éowyn it was, and Dernhelm also. For into Merry's mind flashed the memory of the face that he saw at the riding from Dunharrow: the face of one that goes seeking death, having no hope. Pity filled his heart and great wonder, and suddenly the slow-kindled courage of his race awoke. He clenched his hand. She should not die, so fair, so desperate! At least she should not die alone, unaided.

The face of their enemy was not turned towards him, but still he hardly dared to move, dreading lest the deadly eyes should fall on him. Slowly, slowly he began to crawl aside; but the Black Captain, in doubt and malice intent upon the woman before him, heeded him no more than a worm in the mud.

Suddenly the great beast beat its hideous wings, and the wind of them was foul. Again it leaped into the air, and then swiftly fell down upon Éowyn, shrieking, striking with beak and claw.

Still she did not blench: maiden of the Rohirrim, child of kings, slender but as a steel-blade, fair yet terrible. A swift stroke she dealt, skilled and deadly. The outstretched neck she clove asunder, and the hewn head fell like a stone. Backward she sprang as the huge shape crashed to ruin, vast wings outspread, crumpled on the earth; and with its fall the shadow passed away. A light fell about her, and her hair shone in the sunrise.

Out of the wreck rose the Black Rider, tall and threatening, towering above her. With a cry of hatred that stung the very ears like venom he let fall his mace. Her shield was shivered in many pieces, and her arm was broken; she stumbled to her knees. He bent over her like a cloud, and his eyes glittered; he raised his mace to kill.

But suddenly he too stumbled forward with a cry of bitter pain, and his stroke went wide, driving into the ground. Merry's sword had stabbed him from behind, shearing through the black mantle, and passing up beneath the hauberk had pierced the sinew behind his mighty knee.

'Éowyn! Éowyn!' cried Merry. Then tottering, struggling up, with her last strength she drove her sword between crown and mantle, as the great shoulders bowed before her. The sword broke sparkling into many shards. The crown rolled away with a clang. Éowyn fell forward upon her fallen foe. But lo! the mantle and hauberk were empty. Shapeless they lay now on the ground, torn and tumbled; and a cry went up into the shuddering air, and faded to a shrill wailing, passing with the wind, a voice bodiless and thin that died, and was swallowed up, and was never heard again in that age of this world.

And there stood Meriadoc the hobbit in the midst of the slain, blinking like an owl in the daylight, for tears blinded him; and through a mist he looked on Éowyn's fair head, as she lay and did not move; and he looked on the face of the king, fallen in the midst of his glory. For Snowmane in his agony had rolled away from him again; yet he was the bane of his master.

Then Merry stooped and lifted his hand to kiss it, and lo! Théoden opened his eyes, and they were clear, and he spoke in a quiet voice though laboured.

'Farewell, Master Holbytla!' he said. 'My body is broken. I go to my fathers. And even in their mighty company I shall not now be ashamed. I felled the black serpent. A grim morn, and a glad day, and a golden sunset!'

Merry could not speak, but wept anew. 'Forgive me, lord,' he said at last, 'if I broke your command, and yet have done no more in your service than to weep at our parting.'

The old king smiled. 'Grieve not! It is forgiven. Great heart will not be denied. Live now in blessedness; and when you sit in peace with your pipe, think of me! For never now shall I sit with you in Meduseld, as I promised, or listen to your herb-lore.' He closed his eyes, and Merry bowed beside him. Presently he spoke again. 'Where is Éomer? For my eyes darken, and I would see him ere I go. He must be king after me. And I would send word to Éowyn. She, she would not have me leave her, and now I shall not see her again, dearer than daughter.'

'Lord, lord,' began Merry brokenly, 'she is——'; but at that moment there was a great clamour, and all about them horns and trumpets were blowing. Merry looked round: he had forgotten the war, and all the world beside, and many hours it seemed since the king rode to his fall, though in truth it was only a little while. But now he saw that they were in danger of being caught in the very midst of the great battle that would soon be joined.

New forces of the enemy were hastening up the road from the River; and from under the walls came the legions of Morgul; and from the southward fields came footmen of Harad with horsemen before them, and behind them rose the huge backs of the *mûmakil* with war-towers upon them. But northward the white crest of Éomer led the great front of the Rohirrim which he had again gathered and marshalled; and out of the City came all the strength of men that was in it, and the silver swan of Dol Amroth was borne in the van, driving the enemy from the Gate.

For a moment the thought flitted through Merry's mind: 'Where is Gandalf? Is he not here? Could he not have saved the king and Éowyn?' But thereupon Éomer rode up in haste, and with him came the knights of the household that still lived and had now mastered their horses. They looked in wonder at the carcase of the fell beast that lay there; and their steeds would not go near. But Éomer leaped from the saddle, and grief and dismay fell upon him as he came to the king's side and stood there in silence.

Then one of the knights took the king's banner from the hand of Guthláf the banner-bearer who lay dead, and he lifted it up. Slowly Théoden opened his eyes. Seeing the banner he made a sign that it should be given to Éomer. 'Hail, King of the Mark!' he said. 'Ride now to victory! Bid Éowyn farewell!' And so he died, and knew not that Éowyn lay near him. And those who stood by wept, crying: 'Théoden King! Théoden King!'

But Éomer said to them:

> *Mourn not overmuch! Mighty was the fallen,*
> *meet was his ending. When his mound is raised,*
> *women then shall weep. War now calls us!*

Yet he himself wept as he spoke. 'Let his knights remain here,' he said, 'and bear his body in honour from the field, lest the battle ride over it! Yea, and all these other of the king's men that lie here.' And he looked at the slain, recalling their names. Then suddenly he beheld his sister Éowyn as she lay, and he knew her. He stood a moment as a man who is pierced in the midst of a cry by an arrow through the heart; and then his face went deathly white, and a cold fury rose in him, so that all speech failed him for a while. A fey mood took him.

'Éowyn, Éowyn!' he cried at last. 'Éowyn, how come you here? What madness or devilry is this? Death, death, death! Death take us all!'

Then without taking counsel or waiting for the approach of the men of the City, he spurred headlong back to the front of the great host, and blew a horn, and cried aloud for the onset. Over the field rang his clear voice calling: 'Death! Ride, ride to ruin and the world's ending!'

And with that the host began to move. But the Rohirrim sang no more. *Death* they cried with one voice loud and terrible, and gathering speed like a great tide their battle swept about their fallen king and passed, roaring away southwards.

And still Meriadoc the hobbit stood there blinking through his tears, and no one spoke to him, indeed none seemed to heed him. He brushed away the tears, and stooped to pick up the green shield that Éowyn had given him, and he slung it at his back. Then he looked for his sword that he had let fall; for even as he struck his blow his arm was numbed, and now he could only use his left hand. And behold! there lay his weapon, but the blade was smoking like a dry branch that has been thrust in a fire; and as he watched it, it writhed and withered and was consumed.

So passed the sword of the Barrow-downs, work of Westernesse. But glad would he have been to know its fate who wrought it slowly long ago in the North-kingdom when the Dúnedain were young, and chief among their foes was the dread realm of Angmar and its sorcerer king. No other blade, not though mightier hands had wielded it, would have dealt that foe a wound so bitter, cleaving the undead flesh, breaking the spell that knit his unseen sinews to his will.

Men now raised the king, and laying cloaks upon spear-truncheons they made shift to bear him away towards the City; and others lifted Éowyn gently up and bore her after him. But the men of the king's household they could not yet bring from the field; for seven of the king's knights had fallen there, and Déorwine their chief was among them. So they laid them apart from their foes and the fell beast and set spears about them. And afterwards when all was over men returned and made a fire there and burned the carcase of the beast; but for Snowmane they dug a grave and set up a stone upon which was carved in the tongues of Gondor and the Mark:

Faithful servant yet master's bane,
Lightfoot's foal, swift Snowmane.

Green and long grew the grass on Snowmane's Howe, but ever black and bare was the ground where the beast was burned.

Now slowly and sadly Merry walked beside the bearers, and he gave no more heed to the battle. He was weary and full of pain, and his limbs trembled as with a chill. A great rain came out of the Sea, and it seemed that all things wept for Théoden and Éowyn, quenching the fires in the City with grey tears. It was through a mist that presently he saw the van of the men of Gondor approaching. Imrahil, Prince of Dol Amroth, rode up and drew rein before them.

'What burden do you bear, Men of Rohan?' he cried.

'Théoden King,' they answered. 'He is dead. But Éomer King now rides in the battle: he with the white crest in the wind.'

Then the prince went from his horse, and knelt by the bier in honour of the king and his great onset; and he wept. And rising he looked then on Éowyn and was amazed. 'Surely, here is a woman?' he said. 'Have even the women of the Rohirrim come to war in our need?'

'Nay! One only,' they answered. 'The Lady Éowyn is she, sister of Éomer; and we knew naught of her riding until this hour, and greatly we rue it.'

Then the prince seeing her beauty, though her face was pale and cold, touched her hand as he bent to look more closely on her. 'Men of Rohan!' he cried. 'Are there no leeches among you? She is hurt, to the death maybe, but I deem that she yet lives.' And he held the bright-burnished vambrace that was upon his arm before her cold lips, and behold! a little mist was laid on it hardly to be seen.

'Haste now is needed,' he said, and he sent one riding back swiftly to the City to bring aid. But he bowing low to the fallen, bade them farewell, and mounting rode away into battle.

And now the fighting waxed furious on the fields of the Pelennor; and the din of arms rose upon high, with the crying of men and the neighing of horses. Horns were blown and trumpets were braying, and the *mûmakil* were bellowing as they were goaded to war. Under the south walls of the City the footmen of Gondor now drove against the legions of Morgul that were still gathered there in strength. But the horsemen rode eastward to the succour of Éomer: Húrin the Tall, Warden of the Keys, and the Lord of Lossarnach, and Hirluin of the Green Hills, and Prince Imrahil the fair with his knights all about him.

Not too soon came their aid to the Rohirrim; for fortune had turned against Éomer, and his fury had betrayed him. The great wrath of his onset had utterly overthrown the front of his enemies, and great wedges of his Riders had passed clear through the ranks of the Southrons, discomfiting their horsemen and riding their footmen to ruin. But wherever the *mûmakil* came there the horses would not go, but blenched and swerved away; and the great monsters were unfought, and stood like towers of defence, and the Haradrim rallied about them. And if the Rohirrim at their onset were thrice outnumbered by the Haradrim alone, soon their case became worse; for new strength came now streaming to the field out of Osgiliath. There they had been mustered for the sack of the City and the rape of Gondor, waiting on the call of their Captain. He now was destroyed; but Gothmog the lieutenant of Morgul had flung them into the fray; Easterlings with axes, and Variags of Khand, Southrons in scarlet, and out of Far Harad black men like half-trolls with white eyes and red tongues. Some now hastened up behind the Rohirrim, others held westward to hold off the forces of Gondor and prevent their joining with Rohan.

It was even as the day thus began to turn against Gondor and their hope wavered that a new cry went up in the City, it being then mid-morning, and a great wind blowing, and the rain flying north, and the sun shining. In that clear air watchmen on the walls saw afar a new sight of fear, and their last hope left them.

For Anduin, from the bend at the Harlond, so flowed that from the City men could look down it lengthwise for some leagues, and the far-sighted could see any ships that approached. And looking thither they cried in dismay; for black against the glittering stream they beheld a fleet borne up on the wind: dromunds, and ships of great draught with many oars, and with black sails bellying in the breeze.

'The Corsairs of Umbar!' men shouted. 'The Corsairs of Umbar! Look! The Corsairs of Umbar are coming! So Belfalas is taken, and the Ethir, and Lebennin is gone. The Corsairs are upon us! It is the last stroke of doom!'

And some without order, for none could be found to command them in the City, ran to the bells and tolled the alarm; and some blew the trumpets sounding the retreat. 'Back to the walls!' they cried. 'Back to the walls! Come back to the City before all are overwhelmed!' But the wind that sped the ships blew all their clamour away.

The Rohirrim indeed had no need of news or alarm. All too well they could see for themselves the black sails. For Éomer was now scarcely a mile from the Harlond, and a great press of his first foes was between him and the haven there, while new foes came swirling behind, cutting him off from the Prince. Now he looked to the River, and hope died in his heart, and the wind that he had blessed he now called accursed. But the hosts of

Mordor were enheartened, and filled with a new lust and fury they came yelling to the onset.

Stern now was Éomer's mood, and his mind clear again. He let blow the horns to rally all men to his banner that could come thither; for he thought to make a great shield-wall at the last, and stand, and fight there on foot till all fell, and do deeds of song on the fields of Pelennor, though no man should be left in the West to remember the last King of the Mark. So he rode to a green hillock and there set his banner, and the White Horse ran rippling in the wind.

> Out of doubt, out of dark to the day's rising
> I came singing in the sun, sword unsheathing.
> To hope's end I rode and to heart's breaking:
> Now for wrath, now for ruin and a red nightfall!

These staves he spoke, yet he laughed as he said them. For once more lust of battle was on him; and he was still unscathed, and he was young, and he was king: the lord of a fell people. And lo! even as he laughed at despair he looked out again on the black ships, and he lifted up his sword to defy them.

And then wonder took him, and a great joy; and he cast his sword up in the sunlight and sang as he caught it. And all eyes followed his gaze, and behold! upon the foremost ship a great standard broke, and the wind displayed it as she turned towards the Harlond. There flowered a White Tree, and that was for Gondor; but Seven Stars were about it, and a high crown above it, the signs of Elendil that no lord had borne for years beyond count. And the stars flamed in the sunlight, for they were wrought of gems by Arwen daughter of Elrond; and the crown was bright in the morning, for it was wrought of mithril and gold.

Thus came Aragorn son of Arathorn, Elessar, Isildur's heir, out of the Paths of the Dead, borne upon a wind from the Sea to the kingdom of Gondor; and the mirth of the Rohirrim was a torrent of laughter and a flashing of swords, and the joy and wonder of the City was a music of trumpets and a ringing of bells. But the hosts of Mordor were seized with bewilderment, and a great wizardry it seemed to them that their own ships should be filled with their foes; and a black dread fell on them, knowing that the tides of fate had turned against them and their doom was at hand.

East rode the knights of Dol Amroth driving the enemy before them: troll-men and Variags and orcs that hated the sunlight. South strode Éomer and men fled before his face, and they were caught between the hammer and the anvil. For now men leaped from the ships to the quays of the Harlond and swept north like a storm. There came Legolas, and Gimli wielding his axe, and Halbarad with the standard, and Elladan and Elrohir with stars on their brow, and the dour-handed Dúnedain, Rangers of the North, leading a great valour of the folk of Lebennin and Lamedon and the fiefs of the South. But before all went Aragorn with the Flame of the West, Andúril like a new fire kindled, Narsil re-forged as deadly as of old; and upon his brow was the Star of Elendil.

And so at length Éomer and Aragorn met in the midst of the battle, and they leaned on their swords and looked on one another and were glad.

'Thus we meet again, though all the hosts of Mordor lay between us,' said Aragorn. 'Did I not say so at the Hornburg?'

'So you spoke,' said Éomer, 'but hope oft deceives, and I knew not then that you were a man foresighted. Yet twice blessed is help unlooked for, and never was a meeting of friends more joyful.' And they clasped hand in hand. 'Nor indeed more timely,' said Éomer. 'You come none too soon, my friend. Much loss and sorrow has befallen us.'

'Then let us avenge it, ere we speak of it!' said Aragorn, and they rode back to battle together.

Hard fighting and long labour they had still; for the Southrons were bold men and grim, and fierce in despair; and the Easterlings were strong and war-hardened and asked for no quarter. And so in this place and that, by burned homestead or barn, upon hillock or mound, under wall or on field, still they gathered and rallied and fought until the day wore away.

Then the Sun went at last behind Mindolluin and filled all the sky with a great burning, so that the hills and the mountains were dyed as with blood; fire glowed in the River, and the grass of the Pelennor lay red in the nightfall. And in that hour the great Battle of the field of Gondor was over; and not one living foe was left within the circuit of the Rammas. All were slain save those who fled to die, or to drown in the red foam of the River. Few ever came eastward to Morgul or Mordor; and to the land of the Haradrim came only a tale from far off: a rumour of the wrath and terror of Gondor.

Aragorn and Éomer and Imrahil rode back towards the Gate of the City, and they were now weary beyond joy or sorrow. These three were unscathed, for such was their fortune and the skill and might of their arms, and few indeed had dared to abide them or look on their faces in the hour of their wrath. But many others were hurt or maimed or dead upon the field. The axes hewed Forlong as he fought alone and unhorsed; and both Duilin of Morthond and his brother were trampled to death when they assailed the *mûmakil*, leading their bowmen close to shoot at the eyes of the monsters. Neither Hirluin the fair would return to Pinnath Gelin, nor

Grimbold to Grimslade, nor Halbarad to the Northlands, dour-handed Ranger. No few had fallen, renowned or nameless, captain or soldier; for it was a great battle and the full count of it no tale has told. So long afterward a maker in Rohan said in his song of the Mounds of Mundburg:

> *We heard of the horns in the hills ringing,*
> *the swords shining in the South-kingdom.*
> *Steeds went striding to the Stoningland*
> *as wind in the morning. War was kindled.*
> *There Théoden fell, Thengling mighty,*
> *to his golden halls and green pastures*
> *in the Northern fields never returning,*
> *high lord of the host. Harding and Guthláf,*
> *Dúnhere and Déorwine, doughty Grimbold,*
> *Herefara and Herubrand, Horn and Fastred,*
> *fought and fell there in a far country:*
> *in the Mounds of Mundburg under mould they lie*
> *with their league-fellows, lords of Gondor.*
> *Neither Hirluin the Fair to the hills by the sea,*
> *nor Forlong the old to the flowering vales*
> *ever, to Arnach, to his own country*
> *returned in triumph; nor the tall bowmen,*
> *Derufin and Duilin, to their dark waters,*
> *meres of Morthond under mountain-shadows.*
> *Death in the morning and at day's ending*
> *lords took and lowly. Long now they sleep*
> *under grass in Gondor by the Great River.*
> *Grey now as tears, gleaming silver,*
> *red then it rolled, roaring water:*
> *foam dyed with blood flamed at sunset;*
> *as beacons mountains burned at evening;*
> *red fell the dew in Rammas Echor.*

CHAPTER VII

THE PYRE OF DENETHOR

When the dark shadow at the Gate withdrew Gandalf still sat motionless. But Pippin rose to his feet, as if a great weight had been lifted from him; and he stood listening to the horns, and it seemed to him that they would break his heart with joy. And never in after years could he hear a horn blown in the distance without tears starting in his eyes. But now suddenly his errand returned to his memory, and he ran forward. At that moment Gandalf stirred and spoke to Shadowfax, and was about to ride through the Gate.

'Gandalf, Gandalf!' cried Pippin, and Shadowfax halted.

'What are you doing here?' said Gandalf. 'Is it not a law in the City that those who wear the black and silver must stay in the Citadel, unless their lord gives them leave?'

'He has,' said Pippin. 'He sent me away. But I am frightened. Something terrible may happen up there. The Lord is out of his mind, I think. I am afraid he will kill himself, and kill Faramir too. Can't you do something?'

Gandalf looked through the gaping Gate, and already on the fields he heard the gathering sound of battle. He clenched his hand. 'I must go,' he said. 'The Black Rider is abroad, and he will yet bring ruin on us. I have no time.'

'But Faramir!' cried Pippin. 'He is not dead, and they will burn him alive, if someone does not stop them.'

'Burn him alive?' said Gandalf. 'What is this tale? Be quick!'

'Denethor has gone to the Tombs,' said Pippin, 'and he has taken Faramir, and he says we are all to burn, and he will not wait, and they are to make a pyre and burn him on it, and Faramir as well. And he has sent men to fetch wood and oil. And I have told Beregond, but I'm afraid he won't dare to leave his post: he is on guard. And what can he do anyway?' So Pippin poured out his tale, reaching up and touching Gandalf's knee with trembling hands. 'Can't you save Faramir?'

'Maybe I can,' said Gandalf; 'but if I do, then others will die, I fear. Well, I must come, since no other help can reach him. But evil and sorrow will come of this. Even in the heart of our stronghold the Enemy has power to strike us: for his will it is that is at work.'

Then having made up his mind he acted swiftly; and catching up Pippin and setting him before him, he turned Shadowfax with a word. Up the climbing streets of Minas Tirith they clattered, while the noise of war rose behind them. Everywhere men were rising from their despair and dread, seizing their weapons, crying one to another: 'Rohan has come!' Captains were shouting, companies were mustering; many already were marching down to the Gate.

They met the Prince Imrahil, and he called to them: 'Whither now, Mithrandir? The Rohirrim are fighting on the fields of Gondor! We must gather all the strength that we can find.'

'You will need every man and more,' said Gandalf. 'Make all haste. I will come when I can. But I have an errand to the Lord Denethor that will not wait. Take command in the Lord's absence!'

They passed on; and as they climbed and drew near to the Citadel they felt the wind blowing in their faces, and they caught the glimmer of morning far away, a light growing in the southern sky. But it brought little hope to them, not knowing what evil lay before them, fearing to come too late.

'Darkness is passing,' said Gandalf, 'but it still lies heavy on this City.'

At the gate of the Citadel they found no guard. 'Then Beregond has gone,' said Pippin more hopefully. They turned away and hastened along the road to the Closed Door. It stood wide open, and the porter lay before it. He was slain and his key had been taken.

'Work of the Enemy!' said Gandalf. 'Such deeds he loves: friend at war with friend; loyalty divided in confusion of hearts.' Now he dismounted and bade Shadowfax return to his stable. 'For, my friend,' he said, 'you and I should have ridden to the fields long ago, but other matters delay me. Yet come swiftly if I call!'

They passed the Door and walked on down the steep winding road. Light was growing, and the tall columns and carven figures beside the way went slowly by like grey ghosts.

Suddenly the silence was broken, and they heard below them cries and the ringing of swords: such sounds as had not been heard in the hallowed places since the building of the City. At last they came to Rath Dínen and hastened towards the House of the Stewards, looming in the twilight under its great dome.

'Stay! Stay!' cried Gandalf, springing forward to the stone stair before the door. 'Stay this madness!'

For there were the servants of Denethor with swords and torches in their hands; but alone in the porch upon the topmost step stood Beregond, clad in the black and silver of the Guard; and he held the door against them. Two of them had already fallen to his sword, staining the hallows with their blood; and the others cursed him, calling him outlaw and traitor to his master.

Even as Gandalf and Pippin ran forward, they heard from within the house of the dead the voice of Denethor crying: 'Haste, haste! Do as I have bidden! Slay me this renegade! Or must I do so myself?' Thereupon the door which Beregond held shut with his left hand was wrenched open, and there behind him stood the Lord of the City, tall and fell; a light like flame was in his eyes, and he held a drawn sword.

But Gandalf sprang up the steps, and the men fell back from him and covered their eyes; for his coming was like the incoming of a white light into a dark place, and he came with great anger. He lifted up his hand, and in the very stroke, the sword of Denethor flew up and left his grasp and fell behind him in the shadows of the house; and Denethor stepped backward before Gandalf as one amazed.

'What is this, my lord?' said the wizard. 'The houses of the dead are no places for the living. And why do men fight here in the Hallows when there is war enough before the Gate? Or has our Enemy come even to Rath Dínen?'

'Since when has the Lord of Gondor been answerable to thee?' said Denethor. 'Or may I not command my own servants?'

'You may,' said Gandalf. 'But others may contest your will, when it is turned to madness and evil. Where is your son, Faramir?'

'He lies within,' said Denethor, 'burning, already burning. They have set a fire in his flesh. But soon all shall be burned. The West has failed. It shall all go up in a great fire, and all shall be ended. Ash! Ash and smoke blown away on the wind!'

Then Gandalf seeing the madness that was on him feared that he had already done some evil deed, and he thrust forward, with Beregond and Pippin behind him, while Denethor gave back until he stood beside the table within. But there they found Faramir, still dreaming in his fever, lying upon the table. Wood was piled under it, and high all about it, and all was drenched with oil, even the garments of Faramir and the coverlets; but as yet no fire had been set to the fuel. Then Gandalf revealed the strength that lay hid in him, even as the light of his power was hidden under his grey mantle. He leaped up on to the faggots, and raising the sick man lightly he sprang down again, and bore him towards the door. But as he did so Faramir moaned and called on his father in his dream.

Denethor started as one waking from a trance, and the flame died in his eyes, and he wept; and he said: 'Do not take my son from me! He calls for me.'

'He calls,' said Gandalf, 'but you cannot come to him yet. For he must seek healing on the threshold of death, and maybe find it not. Whereas your part is to go out to the battle of your City, where maybe death awaits you. This you know in your heart.'

'He will not wake again,' said Denethor. 'Battle is vain. Why should we wish to live longer? Why should we not go to death side by side?'

'Authority is not given to you, Steward of Gondor, to order the hour of your death,' answered Gandalf. 'And only the heathen kings, under the domination of the Dark Power, did thus, slaying themselves in pride and despair, murdering their kin to ease their own death.' Then passing through the door he took Faramir from the deadly house and laid him on the bier on which he had been brought, and which had now been set in the porch. Denethor followed him, and stood trembling, looking with longing on the face of his son. And for a moment, while all were silent and still, watching the Lord in his throes, he wavered.

'Come!' said Gandalf. 'We are needed. There is much that you can yet do.'

Then suddenly Denethor laughed. He stood up tall and proud again, and stepping swiftly back to the table he lifted from it the pillow on which his head had lain. Then coming to the doorway he drew aside the covering, and lo! he had between his hands a *palantír*. And as he held it up, it seemed to those that looked on that the globe began to glow with an inner flame, so that the lean face of the Lord was lit as with a red fire, and it seemed cut out of hard stone, sharp with black shadows, noble, proud, and terrible. His eyes glittered.

'Pride and despair!' he cried. 'Didst thou think that the eyes of the White Tower were blind? Nay, I have seen more than thou knowest, Grey Fool. For thy hope is but ignorance. Go then and labour in healing! Go forth and fight! Vanity. For a little space you may triumph on the field, for a day. But against the Power that now arises there is no victory. To this City only the first finger of its hand has yet been stretched. All the East is moving. And even now the wind of thy hope cheats thee and wafts up Anduin a fleet with black sails. The West has failed. It is time for all to depart who would not be slaves.'

'Such counsels will make the Enemy's victory certain indeed,' said Gandalf.

'Hope on then!' laughed Denethor. 'Do I not know thee, Mithrandir? Thy hope is to rule in my stead, to stand behind every throne, north, south, or west. I have read thy mind and its policies. Do I not know that you commanded this halfling here to keep silence? That you brought him hither to be a spy within my very chamber? And yet in our speech together I have learned the names and purpose of all thy companions. So! With the left hand thou wouldst use me for a little while as a shield against Mordor, and with the right bring up this Ranger of the North to supplant me.

'But I say to thee, Gandalf Mithrandir, I will not be thy tool! I am Steward of the House of Anárion. I will not step down to be the dotard chamberlain of an upstart. Even were his claim proved to me, still he comes but of the line of Isildur. I will not bow to such a one, last of a ragged house long bereft of lordship and dignity.'

'What then would you have,' said Gandalf, 'if your will could have its way?'

'I would have things as they were in all the days of my life,' answered Denethor, 'and in the days of my longfathers before me: to be the Lord of this City in peace, and leave my chair to a son after me, who would be his own master and no wizard's pupil. But if doom denies this to me, then I will have *naught*: neither life diminished, nor love halved, nor honour abated.'

'To me it would not seem that a Steward who faithfully surrenders his charge is diminished in love or in honour,' said Gandalf. 'And at the least you shall not rob your son of his choice while his death is still in doubt.'

At those words Denethor's eyes flamed again, and taking the Stone under his arm he drew a knife and strode towards the bier. But Beregond sprang forward and set himself before Faramir.

'So!' cried Denethor. 'Thou hadst already stolen half my son's love. Now thou stealest the hearts of my knights also, so that they rob me wholly of my son at the last. But in this at least thou shalt not defy my will: to rule my own end.'

'Come hither!' he cried to his servants. 'Come, if you are not all recreant!' Then two of them ran up the steps to him. Swiftly he snatched a torch from the hand of one and sprang back into the house. Before Gandalf could hinder him he thrust the brand amid the fuel, and at once it crackled and roared into flame.

Then Denethor leaped upon the table, and standing there wreathed in fire and smoke he took up the staff of his stewardship that lay at his feet and broke it on his knee. Casting the pieces into the blaze he bowed and laid himself on the table, clasping the *palantír* with both hands upon his breast. And it was said that ever after, if any man looked in that Stone, unless he had a great strength of will to turn it to other purpose, he saw only two aged hands withering in flame.

Gandalf in grief and horror turned his face away and closed the door. For a while he stood in thought, silent upon the threshold, while those outside heard the greedy roaring of the fire within. And then Denethor gave a great cry, and afterwards spoke no more, nor was ever again seen by mortal men.

'So passes Denethor, son of Ecthelion,' said Gandalf. Then he turned to Beregond and the Lord's servants that stood there aghast. 'And so pass also the days of Gondor that you have known; for good or evil they are ended. Ill deeds have been done here; but let now all enmity that lies between you be put away, for it was contrived by the Enemy and works his will. You have been caught in a net of warring duties that you did not weave. But think, you servants of the Lord, blind in your obedience, that but for the treason of Beregond Faramir, Captain of the White Tower, would now also be burned.

'Bear away from this unhappy place your comrades who have fallen. And we will bear Faramir, Steward of Gondor, to a place where he can sleep in peace, or die if that be his doom.'

Then Gandalf and Beregond taking up the bier bore it away towards the Houses of Healing, while behind them walked Pippin with downcast head. But the servants of the Lord stood gazing as stricken men at the house of the dead; and even as Gandalf came to the end of Rath Dínen there was a great noise. Looking back they saw the dome of the house crack and smokes issue forth; and then with a rush and rumble of stone it fell in a flurry of fire; but still unabated the flames danced and flickered among the ruins. Then in terror the servants fled and followed Gandalf.

At length they came back to the Steward's Door, and Beregond looked with grief at the porter. 'This deed I shall ever rue,' he said; 'but a madness of haste was on me, and he would not listen, but drew sword against me.' Then taking the key that he had wrested from the slain man he closed the door and locked it. 'This should now be given to the Lord Faramir,' he said.

'The Prince of Dol Amroth is in command in the absence of the Lord,' said Gandalf; 'but since he is not here, I must take this on myself. I bid you keep the key and guard it, until the City is set in order again.'

Now at last they passed into the high circles of the City, and in the light of morning they went their way towards the Houses of Healing; and these were fair houses set apart for the care of those who were grievously sick, but now they were prepared for the tending of men hurt in battle or dying. They stood not far from the Citadel-gate, in the sixth circle, nigh to its southward wall, and about them was a garden and a greensward with trees, the only such place in the City. There dwelt the few women that had been permitted to remain in Minas Tirith, since they were skilled in healing or in the service of the healers.

But even as Gandalf and his companions came carrying the bier to the main door of the Houses, they heard a great cry that went up from the field before the Gate and rising shrill and piercing into the sky passed, and died away on the wind. So terrible was the cry that for a moment all stood still, and yet when it had passed, suddenly their hearts were lifted up in such a hope as they had not known since the darkness came out of the

East; and it seemed to them that the light grew clear and the sun broke through the clouds.

But Gandalf's face was grave and sad, and bidding Beregond and Pippin to take Faramir into the Houses of Healing, he went up on to the walls nearby; and there like a figure carven in white he stood in the new sun and looked out. And he beheld with the sight that was given to him all that had befallen; and when Éomer rode out from the forefront of his battle and stood beside those who lay upon the field, he sighed, and he cast his cloak about him again, and went from the walls. And Beregond and Pippin found him standing in thought before the door of the Houses when they came out.

They looked at him, and for a while he was silent. At last he spoke. 'My friends,' he said, 'and all you people of this city and of the Western lands! Things of great sorrow and renown have come to pass. Shall we weep or be glad? Beyond hope the Captain of our foes has been destroyed, and you have heard the echo of his last despair. But he has not gone without woe and bitter loss. And that I might have averted but for the madness of Denethor. So long has the reach of our Enemy become! Alas! but now I perceive how his will was able to enter into the very heart of the City.

'Though the Stewards deemed that it was a secret kept only by themselves, long ago I guessed that here in the White Tower, one at least of the Seven Seeing Stones was preserved. In the days of his wisdom Denethor would not presume to use it to challenge Sauron, knowing the limits of his own strength. But his wisdom failed; and I fear that as the peril of his realm grew he looked in the Stone and was deceived: far too often, I guess, since Boromir departed. He was too great to be subdued to the will of the Dark Power, he saw nonetheless only those things which that Power permitted him to see. The knowledge which he obtained was, doubtless, often of service to him; yet the vision of the great might of Mordor that was shown to him fed the despair of his heart until it overthrew his mind.'

'Now I understand what seemed so strange to me!' said Pippin, shuddering at his memories as he spoke. 'The Lord went away from the room where Faramir lay; and it was only when he returned that I first thought he was changed, old and broken.'

'It was in the very hour that Faramir was brought to the Tower that many of us saw a strange light in the topmost chamber,' said Beregond. 'But we have seen that light before, and it has long been rumoured in the City that the Lord would at times wrestle in thought with his Enemy.'

'Alas! then I have guessed rightly,' said Gandalf. 'Thus the will of Sauron entered into Minas Tirith; and thus I have been delayed here. And here I shall still be forced to remain, for I shall soon have other charges, not Faramir only.

'Now I must go down to meet those who come. I have seen a sight upon the field that is very grievous to my heart, and greater sorrow may yet come to pass. Come with me, Pippin! But you, Beregond, should return to the Citadel and tell the chief of the Guard there what has befallen. It will be his duty, I fear, to withdraw you from the Guard; but say to him that, if I may give him counsel, you should be sent to the Houses of Healing, to be the guard and servant of your captain, and to be at his side when he awakes – if that shall ever be again. For by you he was saved from the fire. Go now! I shall return soon.'

With that he turned away and went with Pippin down towards the lower city. And even as they hastened on their way the wind brought a grey rain, and all the fires sank, and there arose a great smoke before them.

CHAPTER VIII

THE HOUSES OF HEALING

A mist was in Merry's eyes of tears and weariness when they drew near the ruined Gate of Minas Tirith. He gave little heed to the wreck and slaughter that lay about all. Fire and smoke and stench was in the air; for many engines had been burned or cast into the fire-pits, and many of the slain also, while here and there lay many carcases of the great Southron monsters, half-burned, or broken by stone-cast, or shot through the eyes by the valiant archers of Morthond. The flying rain had ceased for a time, and the sun gleamed up above; but all the lower city was still wrapped in a smouldering reek.

Already men were labouring to clear a way through the jetsam of battle; and now out from the Gate came some bearing litters. Gently they laid Éowyn upon soft pillows; but the king's body they covered with a great cloth of gold, and they bore torches about him, and their flames, pale in the sunlight, were fluttered by the wind.

So Théoden and Éowyn came to the City of Gondor, and all who saw them bared their heads and bowed; and they passed through the ash and fume of the burned circle, and went on and up along the streets of stone. To Merry the ascent seemed agelong, a meaningless journey in a hateful dream, going on and on to some dim ending that memory cannot seize.

Slowly the lights of the torches in front of him flickered and went out, and he was walking in a darkness; and he thought: 'This is a tunnel leading to a tomb; there we shall stay forever.' But suddenly into his dream there fell a living voice.

'Well, Merry! Thank goodness I have found you!'

He looked up and the mist before his eyes cleared a little. There was Pippin! They were face to face in a narrow lane, and but for themselves it was empty. He rubbed his eyes.

'Where is the king?' he said. 'And Éowyn?' Then he stumbled and sat down on a doorstep and began to weep again.

'They have gone up into the Citadel,' said Pippin. 'I think you must have fallen asleep on your feet and taken the wrong turning. When we found that you were not with them, Gandalf sent me to look for you. Poor old Merry! How glad I am to see you again! But you are worn out, and I won't bother you with any talk. But tell me, are you hurt, or wounded?'

'No,' said Merry. 'Well, no, I don't think so. But I can't use my right arm, Pippin, not since I stabbed him. And my sword burned all away like a piece of wood.'

Pippin's face was anxious. 'Well, you had better come with me as quick as you can,' he said. 'I wish I could carry you. You aren't fit to walk any further. They shouldn't have let you walk at all; but you must forgive them. So many dreadful things have happened in the City, Merry, that one poor hobbit coming in from the battle is easily overlooked.'

'It's not always a misfortune being overlooked,' said Merry. 'I was overlooked just now by – no, no, I can't speak of it. Help me, Pippin! It's all going dark again, and my arm is so cold.'

'Lean on me, Merry lad!' said Pippin. 'Come now! Foot by foot. It's not far.'

'Are you going to bury me?' said Merry.

'No, indeed!' said Pippin, trying to sound cheerful, though his heart was wrung with fear and pity. 'No, we are going to the Houses of Healing.'

They turned out of the lane that ran between tall houses and the outer wall of the fourth circle, and they regained the main street climbing up to the Citadel. Step by step they went, while Merry swayed and murmured as one in sleep.

'I'll never get him there,' thought Pippin. 'Is there no one to help me? I can't leave him here.' Just then to his surprise a boy came running up behind, and as he passed he recognized Bergil Beregond's son.

'Hullo, Bergil!' he called. 'Where are you going? Glad to see you again, and still alive!'

'I am running errands for the Healers,' said Bergil. 'I cannot stay.'

'Don't!' said Pippin. 'But tell them up there that I have a sick hobbit, a *perian* mind you, come from the battle-field. I don't think he can walk so far. If Mithrandir is there, he will be glad of the message.' Bergil ran on.

'I'd better wait here,' thought Pippin. So he let Merry sink gently down on to the pavement in a patch of sunlight, and then he sat down beside him, laying Merry's head in his lap. He felt his body and limbs gently, and took his friend's hands in his own. The right hand felt icy to the touch.

It was not long before Gandalf himself came in search of them. He stooped over Merry and caressed his brow; then he lifted him carefully. 'He should have been borne in honour into this city,' he said. 'He has well repaid my trust; for if Elrond had not yielded to me, neither of you would have set out; and then far more grievous would the evils of this day have been.' He sighed. 'And yet here is another charge on my hands, while all the time the battle hangs in the balance.'

So at last Faramir and Éowyn and Meriadoc were laid in beds in the Houses of Healing; and there they were tended well. For though all lore was in these latter days fallen from its fullness of old, the leechcraft of Gondor was still wise, and skilled in the healing of wound and hurt, and all such sickness as east of the Sea mortal men were subject to. Save old age only. For that they had found no cure; and indeed the span of their lives had now waned to little more than that of other men, and those among them who passed the tale of five score years with vigour were grown few, save in some houses of purer blood. But now their art and knowledge were baffled; for there were many sick of a malady that would not be healed; and they called it the Black Shadow, for it came from the Nazgûl. And those who were stricken with it fell slowly into an ever deeper dream, and then passed to silence and a deadly cold, and so died. And it seemed to the tenders of the sick that on the Halfling and on the Lady of Rohan this malady lay heavily. Still at whiles as the morning wore away they would speak, murmuring in their dreams; and the watchers listened to all that they said, hoping perhaps to learn something that would help them to understand their hurts. But soon they began to fall down into the darkness, and as the sun turned west a grey shadow crept over their faces. But Faramir burned with a fever that would not abate.

Gandalf went from one to the other full of care, and he was told all that the watchers could hear. And so the day passed, while the great battle outside went on with shifting hopes and strange tidings; and still Gandalf waited and watched and did not go forth; till at last the red sunset filled all the sky, and the light through the windows fell on the grey faces of the sick. Then it seemed to those who stood by that in the glow the faces flushed softly as with health returning, but it was only a mockery of hope.

Then an old wife, Ioreth, the eldest of the women who served in that house, looking on the fair face of Faramir, wept, for all the people loved him. And she said: 'Alas! if he should die. Would that there were kings in Gondor, as there were once upon a time, they say! For it is said in old lore: *The hands of the king are the hands of a healer*. And so the rightful king could ever be known.'

And Gandalf, who stood by, said: 'Men may long remember your words, Ioreth! For there is hope in them. Maybe a king has indeed returned to Gondor; or have you not heard the strange tidings that have come to the City?'

'I have been too busy with this and that to heed all the crying and shouting,' she answered. 'All I hope is that those murdering devils do not come to this House and trouble the sick.'

Then Gandalf went out in haste, and already the fire in the sky was burning out, and the smouldering hills were fading, while ash-grey evening crept over the fields.

Now as the sun went down Aragorn and Éomer and Imrahil drew near the City with their captains and knights; and when they came before the Gate Aragorn said:

'Behold the Sun setting in a great fire! It is a sign of the end and fall of many things, and a change in the tides of the world. But this City and realm has rested in the charge of the Stewards for many long years, and I fear that if I enter it unbidden, then doubt and debate may arise, which should not be while this war is fought. I will not enter in, nor make any claim, until it be seen whether we or Mordor shall prevail. Men shall pitch my tents upon the field, and here I will await the welcome of the Lord of the City.'

But Éomer said: 'Already you have raised the banner of the Kings and displayed the tokens of Elendil's House. Will you suffer these to be challenged?'

'No,' said Aragorn. 'But I deem the time unripe; and I have no mind for strife except with our Enemy and his servants.'

And the Prince Imrahil said: 'Your words, lord, are wise, if one who is a kinsman of the Lord Denethor may counsel you in this matter. He is strong-willed and proud, but old; and his mood has been strange since his son was stricken down. Yet I would not have you remain like a beggar at the door.'

'Not a beggar,' said Aragorn. 'Say a captain of the Rangers, who are unused to cities and houses of stone.' And he commanded that his banner should be furled; and he did off the Star of the North Kingdom and gave it to the keeping of the sons of Elrond.

Then the Prince Imrahil and Éomer of Rohan left him and passed through the City and the tumult of the people, and mounted to the Citadel; and they came to the Hall of the Tower, seeking the Steward. But they found his chair empty, and before the dais lay Théoden King of the Mark upon a bed of state; and twelve torches stood about it, and twelve guards, knights both of Rohan and Gondor. And the hangings of the bed were of green and white, but upon the king was laid the great cloth of gold up to his breast, and upon that his unsheathed sword, and at his feet his shield. The light of the torches shimmered in his white hair like sun in the spray of a fountain, but his face was fair and young, save that a peace lay on it beyond the reach of youth; and it seemed that he slept.

When they had stood silent for a time beside the king, Imrahil said: 'Where is the Steward? And where also is Mithrandir?'

And one of the guards answered: 'The Steward of Gondor is in the Houses of Healing.'

But Éomer said: 'Where is the Lady Éowyn, my sister; for surely she should be lying beside the king, and in no less honour? Where have they bestowed her?'

And Imrahil said: 'But the Lady Éowyn was yet living when they bore her hither. Did you not know?'

Then hope unlooked-for came so suddenly to Éomer's heart, and with it the bite of care and fear renewed, that he said no more, but turned and went swiftly from the hall; and the Prince followed him. And when they came forth evening had fallen and many stars were in the sky. And there came Gandalf on foot and with him one cloaked in grey; and they met before the doors of the Houses of Healing. And they greeted Gandalf and said: 'We seek the Steward, and men say that he is in this House. Has any hurt befallen him? And the Lady Éowyn, where is she?'

And Gandalf answered: 'She lies within and is not dead, but is near death. But the Lord Faramir was wounded by an evil dart, as you have heard, and he is now the Steward; for Denethor has departed, and his house is in ashes.' And they were filled with grief and wonder at the tale that he told.

But Imrahil said: 'So victory is shorn of gladness, and it is bitter bought, if both Gondor and Rohan are in one day bereft of their lords. Éomer rules the Rohirrim. Who shall rule the City meanwhile? Shall we not send now for the Lord Aragorn?'

And the cloaked man spoke and said: 'He is come.' And they saw as he stepped into the light of the lantern by the door that it was Aragorn, wrapped in the grey cloak of Lórien above his mail, and bearing no other token than the green stone of Galadriel. 'I have come because Gandalf begs me to do so,' he said. 'But for the present I am but the Captain of the Dúnedain of Arnor; and the Lord of Dol Amroth shall rule the City until Faramir awakes. But it is my counsel that Gandalf should rule us all in the days that follow and in our dealings with the Enemy.' And they agreed upon that.

Then Gandalf said: 'Let us not stay at the door, for the time is urgent. Let us enter! For it is only in the coming of Aragorn that any hope remains for the sick that lie in the House. Thus spake Ioreth, wise-woman of Gondor: *The hands of the king are the hands of a healer, and so shall the rightful king be known.*'

Then Aragorn entered first and the others followed. And there at the door were two guards in the livery of the Citadel: one tall, but the other scarce the height of a boy; and when he saw them he cried aloud in surprise and joy.

'Strider! How splendid! Do you know, I guessed it was you in the black ships. But they were all shouting *corsairs* and wouldn't listen to me. How did you do it?'

Aragorn laughed, and took the hobbit by the hand. 'Well met indeed!' he said. 'But there is not time yet for travellers' tales.'

But Imrahil said to Éomer: 'Is it thus that we speak to our kings? Yet maybe he will wear his crown in some other name!'

And Aragorn hearing him, turned and said: 'Verily, for in the high tongue of old I am *Elessar*, the Elfstone, and *Envinyatar*, the Renewer': and he lifted from his breast the green stone that lay there. 'But Strider shall be the name of my house, if that be ever established. In the high tongue it will not sound so ill, and *Telcontar* I will be and all the heirs of my body.'

And with that they passed into the House; and as they went towards the rooms where the sick were tended Gandalf told of the deeds of Éowyn and Meriadoc. 'For,' he said, 'long have I stood by them, and at first they spoke much in their dreaming, before they sank into the deadly darkness. Also it is given to me to see many things far off.'

Aragorn went first to Faramir, and then to the Lady Éowyn, and last to Merry. When he had looked on the faces of the sick and seen their hurts he sighed. 'Here I must put forth all such power and skill as is given to me,' he said. 'Would that Elrond were here, for he is the eldest of all our race, and has the greater power.'

And Éomer seeing that he was both sorrowful and weary said: 'First you must rest, surely, and at the least eat a little?'

But Aragorn answered: 'Nay, for these three, and most soon for Faramir, time is running out. All speed is needed.'

Then he called to Ioreth and he said: 'You have store in this House of the herbs of healing?'

'Yes, lord,' she answered; 'but not enough, I reckon, for all that will need them. But I am sure I do not know where we shall find more; for all things are amiss in these dreadful days, what with fires and burnings, and the lads that run errands so few, and all the roads blocked. Why, it is days out of count since ever a carrier came in from Lossarnach to the market! But we do our best in this House with what we have, as I am sure your lordship will know.'

'I will judge that when I see,' said Aragorn. 'One thing also is short, time for speech. Have you *athelas*?'

'I do not know, I am sure, lord,' she answered, 'at least not by that name. I will go and ask of the herb-master; he knows all the old names.'

'It is also called *kingsfoil*,' said Aragorn; 'and maybe you know it by that name, for so the country-folk call it in these latter days.'

'Oh that!' said Ioreth. 'Well, if your lordship had named it at first I could have told you. No, we have none of it, I am sure. Why, I have never heard that it had any great virtue; and indeed I have often said to my sisters when we came upon it growing in the woods: "kingsfoil", I said, "'tis a strange name, and I wonder why 'tis called so; for if I were a king, I would have plants more bright in my garden". Still it smells sweet when bruised, does it not? If sweet is the right word: wholesome, maybe, is nearer.'

'Wholesome verily,' said Aragorn. 'And now, dame, if you love the Lord Faramir, run as quick as your tongue and get me kingsfoil, if there is a leaf in the City.'

'And if not,' said Gandalf, 'I will ride to Lossarnach with Ioreth behind me, and she shall take me to the woods, but not to her sisters. And Shadowfax shall show her the meaning of haste.'

When Ioreth was gone, Aragorn bade the other women to make water hot. Then he took Faramir's hand in his, and laid the other hand upon the sick man's brow. It was drenched with sweat; but Faramir did not move or make any sign, and seemed hardly to breathe.

'He is nearly spent,' said Aragorn turning to Gandalf. 'But this comes not from the wound. See! that is healing. Had he been smitten by some dart of the Nazgûl, as you thought, he would have died that night. This hurt was given by some Southron arrow, I would guess. Who drew it forth? Was it kept?'

'I drew it forth,' said Imrahil, 'and staunched the wound. But I did not keep the arrow, for we had much to do. It was, as I remember, just such a dart as the Southrons use. Yet I believed that it came from the Shadows above, for else his fever and sickness were not to be understood; since the wound was not deep or vital. How then do you read the matter?'

'Weariness, grief for his father's mood, a wound, and over all the Black Breath,' said Aragorn. 'He is a man of staunch will, for already he had come close under the Shadow before ever he rode to battle on the out-walls. Slowly the dark must have crept on him, even as he fought and strove to hold his outpost. Would that I could have been here sooner!'

Thereupon the herb-master entered. 'Your lordship asked for *kingsfoil*, as the rustics name it,' he said; 'or *athelas* in the noble tongue, or to those who know somewhat of the Valinorean . . .'

'I do so,' said Aragorn, 'and I care not whether you say now *asëa aranion* or *kingsfoil*, so long as you have some.'

'Your pardon lord!' said the man. 'I see you are a lore-master, not merely a captain of war. But alas! sir, we do not keep this thing in the Houses of Healing, where only the gravely hurt or sick are tended. For it has no virtue that we know of, save perhaps to sweeten a fouled air, or to drive away some passing heaviness. Unless, of course, you give heed to rhymes of old days which women such as our good Ioreth still repeat without understanding.

> *When the black breath blows*
> *and death's shadow grows*
> *and all lights pass,*
> *come athelas! come athelas!*
> *Life to the dying*
> *In the king's hand lying!*

It is but a doggrel, I fear, garbled in the memory of old wives. Its meaning I leave to your judgement, if indeed it has any. But old folk still use an infusion of the herb for headaches.'

'Then in the name of the king, go and find some old man of less lore and more wisdom who keeps some in his house!' cried Gandalf.

Now Aragorn knelt beside Faramir, and held a hand upon his brow. And those that watched felt that some great struggle was going on. For Aragorn's face grew grey with weariness; and ever and anon he called the name of Faramir, but each time more faintly to their hearing, as if Aragorn himself was removed from them, and walked afar in some dark vale, calling for one that was lost.

And at last Bergil came running in, and he bore six leaves in a cloth. 'It is kingsfoil, Sir,' he said; 'but not fresh, I fear. It must have been culled two weeks ago at the least. I hope it will serve, Sir?' Then looking at Faramir he burst into tears.

But Aragorn smiled. 'It will serve,' he said. 'The worst is now over. Stay and be comforted!' Then taking two leaves, he laid them on his hands and breathed on them, and then he crushed them, and straightway a living freshness filled the room, as if the air itself awoke and tingled, sparkling with joy. And then he cast the leaves into the bowls of steaming water that were brought to him, and at once all hearts were lightened. For the fragrance that came to each was like a memory of dewy mornings of unshadowed sun in some land of which the fair world in Spring is itself but a fleeting memory. But Aragorn stood up as one refreshed, and his eyes smiled as he held a bowl before Faramir's dreaming face.

'Well now! Who would have believed it?' said Ioreth to a woman that stood beside her. 'The weed is better than I thought. It reminds me of the roses of Imloth Melui when I was a lass, and no king could ask for better.'

Suddenly Faramir stirred, and he opened his eyes, and he looked on Aragorn who bent over him; and a light of knowledge and love was kindled in his eyes, and he spoke softly. 'My lord, you called me. I come. What does the king command?'

'Walk no more in the shadows, but awake!' said Aragorn. 'You are weary. Rest a while, and take food, and be ready when I return.'

'I will, lord,' said Faramir. 'For who would lie idle when the king has returned?'

'Farewell then for a while!' said Aragorn. 'I must go to others who need me.' And he left the chamber with Gandalf and Imrahil; but Beregond and his son remained behind, unable to contain their joy. As he followed Gandalf and shut the door Pippin heard Ioreth exclaim:

'King! Did you hear that? What did I say? The hands of a healer, I said.' And soon the word had gone out from the House that the king was indeed come among them, and after war he brought healing; and the news ran through the City.

But Aragorn came to Éowyn, and he said: 'Here there is a grievous hurt and a heavy blow. The arm that was broken has been tended with due skill, and it will mend in time, if she has the strength to live. It is the shield-arm that is maimed; but the chief evil comes through the sword-arm. In that there now seems no life, although it is unbroken.

'Alas! For she was pitted against a foe beyond the strength of her mind or body. And those who will take a weapon to such an enemy must be sterner than steel, if the very shock shall not destroy them. It was an evil doom that set her in his path. For she is a fair maiden, fairest lady of a house of queens. And yet I know not how I should speak of her. When I first looked on her and perceived her unhappiness, it seemed to me that I saw a white flower standing straight and proud, shapely as a lily, and yet knew that it was hard, as if wrought by elf-wrights out of steel. Or was it, maybe, a frost that had turned its sap to ice, and so it stood, bitter-sweet, still fair to see, but stricken, soon to fall and die? Her malady begins far back before this day, does it not, Éomer?'

'I marvel that you should ask me, lord,' he answered. 'For I hold you blameless in this matter, as in all else; yet I knew not that Éowyn, my sister, was touched by any frost, until she first looked on you. Care and dread she had, and shared with me, in the days of Wormtongue and the king's bewitchment; and she tended the king in growing fear. But that did not bring her to this pass!'

'My friend,' said Gandalf, 'you had horses, and deeds of arms, and the free fields; but she, born in the body of a maid, had a spirit and courage at least the match of yours. Yet she was doomed to wait upon an old man, whom she loved as a father, and watch him falling into a mean dishonoured dotage; and her part seemed to her more ignoble than that of the staff he leaned on.

'Think you that Wormtongue had poison only for Théoden's ears? *Dotard! What is the house of Eorl but a thatched barn where brigands drink in the reek, and their brats roll on the floor among their dogs?* Have you not heard those words before? Saruman spoke them, the teacher of Wormtongue. Though I do not doubt that Wormtongue at home wrapped their meaning in terms more cunning. My lord, if your sister's love for you, and her will still bent to her duty, had not restrained her lips, you might have heard even such things as these escape them. But who knows what she spoke to the darkness, alone, in the bitter watches of the night, when all her life seemed shrinking, and the walls of her bower closing in about her, a hutch to trammel some wild thing in?'

Then Éomer was silent, and looked on his sister, as if pondering anew all the days of their past life together. But Aragorn said: 'I saw also what you saw, Éomer. Few other griefs amid the ill chances of this world have more bitterness and shame for a man's heart than to behold the love of a lady so fair and brave that cannot be returned. Sorrow and pity have followed me ever since I left her desperate in Dunharrow and rode to the Paths of the Dead; and no fear upon that way was so present as the fear for what might befall her. And yet, Éomer, I say to you that she loves you more truly than me; for you she loves and knows; but in me she loves only a shadow and a thought: a hope of glory and great deeds, and lands far from the fields of Rohan.

'I have, maybe, the power to heal her body, and to recall her from the dark valley. But to what she will awake: hope, or forgetfulness, or despair, I do not know. And if to despair, then she will die, unless other healing comes which I cannot bring. Alas! for her deeds have set her among the queens of great renown.'

Then Aragorn stooped and looked in her face, and it was indeed white as a lily, cold as frost, and hard as graven stone. But he bent and kissed her on the brow, and called her softly, saying:

'Éowyn Éomund's daughter, awake! For your enemy has passed away!'

She did not stir, but now she began again to breathe deeply, so that her breast rose and fell beneath the white linen of the sheet. Once more Aragorn bruised two leaves of *athelas* and cast them into steaming water; and he laved her brow with it, and her right arm lying cold and nerveless on the coverlet.

Then, whether Aragorn had indeed some forgotten power of Westernesse, or whether it was but his words of the Lady Éowyn that wrought on them, as the sweet influence of the herb stole about the chamber it seemed to those who stood by that a keen wind blew through the window, and it bore no scent, but was an air wholly fresh and clean and young, as if it had not before been breathed by any living thing and came new-made from snowy mountains high beneath a dome of stars, or from shores of silver far away washed by seas of foam.

'Awake, Éowyn, Lady of Rohan!' said Aragorn again, and he took her right hand in his and felt it warm with life returning. 'Awake! The shadow is gone and all darkness is washed clean!' Then he laid her hand in Éomer's and stepped away. 'Call her!' he said, and he passed silently from the chamber.

'Éowyn, Éowyn!' cried Éomer amid his tears. But she opened her eyes and said: 'Éomer! What joy is this? For they said that you were slain. Nay, but that was only the dark voices in my dream. How long have I been dreaming?'

'Not long, my sister,' said Éomer. 'But think no more on it!'

'I am strangely weary,' she said. 'I must rest a little. But tell me, what of the Lord of the Mark? Alas! Do not tell me that that was a dream; for I know that it was not. He is dead as he foresaw.'

'He is dead,' said Éomer, 'but he bade me say farewell to Éowyn, dearer than daughter. He lies now in great honour in the Citadel of Gondor.'

'That is grievous,' she said. 'And yet it is good beyond all that I dared hope in the dark days, when it seemed that the House of Eorl was sunk in honour less than any shepherd's cot. And what of the king's esquire, the Halfling? Éomer, you shall make him a knight of the Riddermark, for he is valiant!'

'He lies nearby in this House, and I will go to him,' said Gandalf. 'Éomer shall stay here for a while. But do not speak yet of war or woe, until you are made whole again. Great gladness it is to see you wake again to health and hope, so valiant a lady!'

'To health?' said Éowyn. 'It may be so. At least while there is an empty saddle of some fallen Rider that I can fill, and there are deeds to do. But to hope? I do not know.'

Gandalf and Pippin came to Merry's room, and there they found Aragorn standing by the bed. 'Poor old Merry!' cried Pippin, and he ran to the bedside, for it seemed to him that his friend looked worse and a greyness was in his face, as if a weight of years of sorrow lay on him; and suddenly a fear seized Pippin that Merry would die.

'Do not be afraid,' said Aragorn. 'I came in time, and I have called him back. He is weary now, and grieved, and he has taken a hurt like the Lady Éowyn, daring to smite that deadly thing. But these evils can be amended, so strong and gay a spirit is in him. His grief he will not forget; but it will not darken his heart, it will teach him wisdom.'

Then Aragorn laid his hand on Merry's head, and passing his hand gently through the brown curls, he touched the eyelids, and called him by name. And when the fragrance of *athelas* stole through the room, like the scent of orchards, and of heather in the sunshine full of bees, suddenly Merry awoke, and he said:

'I am hungry. What is the time?'

'Past supper-time now,' said Pippin; 'though I daresay I could bring you something, if they will let me.'

'They will indeed,' said Gandalf. 'And anything else that this Rider of Rohan may desire, if it can be found in Minas Tirith, where his name is in honour.'

'Good!' said Merry. 'Then I would like supper first, and after that a pipe.' At that his face clouded. 'No, not a pipe. I don't think I'll smoke again.'

'Why not?' said Pippin.

'Well,' answered Merry slowly. 'He is dead. It has brought it all back to me. He said he was sorry he had never had a chance of talking herb-lore with me. Almost the last thing he ever said. I shan't ever be able to smoke again without thinking of him, and that day, Pippin, when he rode up to Isengard and was so polite.'

'Smoke then, and think of him!' said Aragorn. 'For he was a gentle heart and a great king and kept his oaths; and he rose out of the shadows to a last fair morning. Though your service to him was brief, it should be a memory glad and honourable to the end of your days.'

Merry smiled. 'Well then,' he said, 'if Strider will provide what is needed, I will smoke and think. I had some of Saruman's best in my pack, but what became of it in the battle, I am sure I don't know.'

'Master Meriadoc,' said Aragorn, 'if you think that I have passed through the mountains and the realm of Gondor with fire and sword to bring herbs to a careless soldier who throws away his gear, you are mistaken. If your pack has not been found, then you must send for the herb-master of this House. And he will tell you that he did not know that the herb you desire had any virtues, but that it is called *westmansweed* by the vulgar, and *galenas* by the noble, and other names in other tongues more learned, and after adding a few half-forgotten rhymes that he does not understand, he will regretfully inform you that there is none in the House, and he will leave you to reflect on the history of tongues. And so now must I. For I have not slept in such a bed as this, since I rode from Dunharrow, nor eaten since the dark before dawn.'

Merry seized his hand and kissed it. 'I am frightfully sorry,' he said.

'Go at once! Ever since that night at Bree we have been a nuisance to you. But it is the way of my people to use light words at such times and say less than they mean. We fear to say too much. It robs us of the right words when a jest is out of place.'

'I know that well, or I would not deal with you in the same way,' said Aragorn. 'May the Shire live for ever unwithered!' And kissing Merry he went out, and Gandalf went with him.

Pippin remained behind. 'Was there ever any one like him?' he said. 'Except Gandalf, of course. I think they must be related. My dear ass, your pack is lying by your bed, and you had it on your back when I met you. He saw it all the time, of course. And anyway I have some stuff of my own. Come on now! Longbottom Leaf it is. Fill up while I run and see about some food. And then let's be easy for a bit. Dear me! We Tooks and Brandybucks, we can't live long on the heights.'

'No,' said Merry. 'I can't. Not yet, at any rate. But at least, Pippin, we can now see them, and honour them. It is best to love first what you are fitted to love, I suppose: you must start somewhere and have some roots, and the soil of the Shire is deep. Still there are things deeper and higher; and not a gaffer could tend his garden in what he calls peace but for them, whether he knows about them or not. I am glad that I know about them, a little. But I don't know why I am talking like this. Where is that leaf? And get my pipe out of my pack, if it isn't broken.'

Aragorn and Gandalf went now to the Warden of the Houses of Healing, and they counselled him that Faramir and Éowyn should remain there and still be tended with care for many days.

'The Lady Éowyn,' said Aragorn, 'will wish soon to rise and depart; but she should not be permitted to do so, if you can in any way restrain her, until at least ten days be passed.'

'As for Faramir,' said Gandalf, 'he must soon learn that his father is dead. But the full tale of the madness of Denethor should not be told to him, until he is quite healed and has duties to do. See that Beregond and the *perian* who were present do not speak to him of these things yet!'

'And the other *perian*, Meriadoc, who is under my care, what of him?' said the Warden.

'It is likely that he will be fit to arise tomorrow, for a short while,' said Aragorn. 'Let him do so, if he wishes. He may walk a little in the care of his friends.'

'They are a remarkable race,' said the Warden, nodding his head. 'Very tough in the fibre, I deem.'

At the doors of the Houses many were already gathered to see Aragorn, and they followed after him; and when at last he had supped, men came and prayed that he would heal their kinsmen or their friends whose lives were in peril through hurt or wound, or who lay under the Black Shadow. And Aragorn arose and went out, and he sent for the sons of Elrond, and together they laboured far into the night. And word went through the City: 'The King is come again indeed.' And they named him Elfstone, because of the green stone that he wore, and so the name which it was foretold at his birth that he should bear was chosen for him by his own people.

And when he could labour no more, he cast his cloak about him, and slipped out of the City, and went to his tent just ere dawn and slept for a little. And in the morning the banner of Dol Amroth, a white ship like a swan upon blue water, floated from the Tower, and men looked up and wondered if the coming of the King had been but a dream.

CHAPTER IX

THE LAST DEBATE

The morning came after the day of battle, and it was fair with light clouds and the wind turning westward. Legolas and Gimli were early abroad, and they begged leave to go up into the City; for they were eager to see Merry and Pippin.

'It is good to learn that they are still alive,' said Gimli; 'for they cost us great pains in our march over Rohan, and I would not have such pains all wasted.'

Together the Elf and the Dwarf entered Minas Tirith, and folk that saw them pass marvelled to see such companions; for Legolas was fair of face beyond the measure of Men, and he sang an elven-song in a clear voice as he walked in the morning; but Gimli stalked beside him, stroking his beard and staring about him.

'There is some good stone-work here,' he said as he looked at the walls; 'but also some that is less good, and the streets could be better contrived. When Aragorn comes into his own, I shall offer him the service of stonewrights of the Mountain, and we will make this a town to be proud of.'

'They need more gardens,' said Legolas. 'The houses are dead, and there is too little here that grows and is glad. If Aragorn comes into his own, the people of the Wood shall bring him birds that sing and trees that do not die.'

At length they came to the Prince Imrahil, and Legolas looked at him and bowed low; for he saw that here indeed was one who had elven-blood in his veins. 'Hail, lord!' he said. 'It is long since the people of Nimrodel left the woodlands of Lórien, and yet still one may see that not all sailed from Amroth's haven west over water.'

'So it is said in the lore of my land,' said the Prince; 'yet never has one of the fair folk been seen there for years beyond count. And I marvel to see one here now in the midst of sorrow and war. What do you seek?'

'I am one of the Nine Companions who set out with Mithrandir from Imladris,' said Legolas; 'and with this Dwarf, my friend, I came with the Lord Aragorn. But now we wish to see our friends, Meriadoc and Peregrin, who are in your keeping, we are told.'

'You will find them in the Houses of Healing, and I will lead you thither,' said Imrahil.

'It will be enough if you send one to guide us, lord,' said Legolas. 'For Aragorn sends this message to you. He does not wish to enter the City again at this time. Yet there is need for the captains to hold council at once, and he prays that you and Éomer of Rohan will come down to his tents, as soon as may be. Mithrandir is already there.'

'We will come,' said Imrahil; and they parted with courteous words.

'That is a fair lord and a great captain of men,' said Legolas. 'If Gondor has such men still in these days of fading, great must have been its glory in the days of its rising.'

'And doubtless the good stone-work is the older and was wrought in the first building,' said Gimli. 'It is ever so with the things that Men begin: there is a frost in Spring, or a blight in Summer, and they fail of their promise.'

'Yet seldom do they fail of their seed,' said Legolas. 'And that will lie in the dust and rot to spring up again in times and places unlooked-for. The deeds of Men will outlast us, Gimli.'

'And yet come to naught in the end but might-have-beens, I guess,' said the Dwarf.

'To that the Elves know not the answer,' said Legolas.

With that the servant of the Prince came and led them to the Houses of Healing; and there they found their friends in the garden, and their meeting was a merry one. For a while they walked and talked, rejoicing for a brief space in peace and rest under the morning high up in the windy circles of the City. Then when Merry became weary, they went and sat upon the wall with the greensward of the Houses of Healing behind them; and away southward before them was the Anduin glittering in the sun, as it flowed away, out of the sight even of Legolas, into the wide flats and green haze of Lebennin and South Ithilien.

And now Legolas fell silent, while the others talked, and he looked out against the sun, and as he gazed he saw white sea-birds beating up the River.

'Look!' he cried. 'Gulls! They are flying far inland. A wonder they are to me and a trouble to my heart. Never in all my life had I met them, until we came to Pelargir, and there I heard them crying in the air as we rode to the battle of the ships. Then I stood still, forgetting war in Middle-earth; for their wailing voices spoke to me of the Sea. The Sea! Alas! I have not yet beheld it. But deep in the hearts of all my kindred lies the sea-longing, which it is perilous to stir. Alas! for the gulls. No peace shall I have again under beech or under elm.'

'Say not so!' said Gimli. 'There are countless things still to see in

Middle-earth, and great works to do. But if all the fair folk take to the Havens, it will be a duller world for those who are doomed to stay.'

'Dull and dreary indeed!' said Merry. 'You must not go to the Havens, Legolas. There will always be some folk, big or little, and even a few wise dwarves like Gimli, who need you. At least I hope so. Though I feel somehow that the worst of this war is still to come. How I wish it was all over, and well over!'

'Don't be so gloomy!' cried Pippin. 'The Sun is shining, and here we are together for a day or two at least. I want to hear more about you all. Come, Gimli! You and Legolas have mentioned your strange journey with Strider about a dozen times already this morning. But you haven't told me anything about it.'

'The Sun may shine here,' said Gimli, 'but there are memories of that road that I do not wish to recall out of the darkness. Had I known what was before me, I think that not for any friendship would I have taken the Paths of the Dead.'

'The Paths of the Dead?' said Pippin. 'I heard Aragorn say that, and I wondered what he could mean. Won't you tell us some more?'

'Not willingly,' said Gimli. 'For upon that road I was put to shame: Gimli Glóin's son, who had deemed himself more tough than Men, and hardier under earth than any Elf. But neither did I prove; and I was held to the road only by the will of Aragorn.'

'And by the love of him also,' said Legolas. 'For all those who come to know him come to love him after his own fashion, even the cold maiden of the Rohirrim. It was at early morn of the day ere you came there, Merry, that we left Dunharrow, and such a fear was on all the folk that none would look on our going, save the Lady Éowyn, who lies now hurt in the House below. There was grief at that parting, and I was grieved to behold it.'

'Alas! I had heart only for myself,' said Gimli. 'Nay! I will not speak of that journey.'

He fell silent; but Pippin and Merry were so eager for news that at last Legolas said: 'I will tell you enough for your peace; for I felt not the horror, and I feared not the shadows of Men, powerless and frail as I deemed them.'

Swiftly then he told of the haunted road under the mountains, and the dark tryst at Erech, and the great ride thence, ninety leagues and three, to Pelargir on Anduin. 'Four days and nights, and on into a fifth, we rode from the Black Stone,' he said. 'And lo! in the darkness of Mordor my hope rose; for in that gloom the Shadow Host seemed to grow stronger and more terrible to look upon. Some I saw riding, some striding, yet all moving with the same great speed. Silent they were, but there was a gleam in their eyes. In the uplands of Lamedon they overtook our horses, and swept round us, and would have passed us by, if Aragorn had not forbidden them.

'At his command they fell back. "Even the shades of Men are obedient to his will," I thought. "They may serve his needs yet!"

'One day of light we rode, and then came the day without dawn, and still we rode on, and Ciril and Ringló we crossed; and on the third day we came to Linhir above the mouth of Gilrain. And there men of Lamedon contested the fords with fell folk of Umbar and Harad who had sailed up the river. But defenders and foes alike gave up the battle and fled when we came, crying out that the King of the Dead was upon them. Only Angbor, Lord of Lamedon, had the heart to abide us; and Aragorn bade him gather his folk and come behind, if they dared, when the Grey Host had passed.

' "At Pelargir the Heir of Isildur will have need of you," he said.

'Thus we crossed over Gilrain, driving the allies of Mordor in rout before us; and then we rested a while. But soon Aragorn arose, saying: "Lo! already Minas Tirith is assailed. I fear that it will fall ere we come to its aid." So we mounted again before night had passed and went on with all the speed that our horses could endure over the plains of Lebennin.'

Legolas paused and sighed, and turning his eyes southward softly he sang:

> *Silver flow the streams from Celos to Erui*
> *In the green fields of Lebennin!*
> *Tall grows the grass there. In the wind from the Sea*
> *The white lilies sway,*
> *And the golden bells are shaken of mallos and alfirin*
> *In the green fields of Lebennin,*
> *In the wind from the Sea!*

'Green are those fields in the songs of my people; but they were dark then, grey wastes in the blackness before us. And over the wide land, trampling unheeded the grass and the flowers, we hunted our foes through a day and a night, until we came at the bitter end to the Great River at last.

'Then I thought in my heart that we drew near to the Sea; for wide was the water in the darkness, and sea-birds innumerable cried on its shores. Alas for the wailing of the gulls! Did not the Lady tell me to beware of them? And now I cannot forget them.'

'For my part I heeded them not,' said Gimli; 'for we came then at last upon battle in earnest. There at Pelargir lay the main fleet of Umbar, fifty great ships and smaller vessels beyond count. Many of those that we pursued had reached the havens before us, and brought their fear with them; and some of the ships had put off, seeking to escape down the River or to reach the far shore; and many of the smaller craft were ablaze. But the Haradrim, being now driven to the brink, turned at bay, and they were fierce in despair; and they laughed when they looked on us, for they were a great army still.

'But Aragorn halted and cried with a great voice: "Now come! By the Black Stone I call you!" And suddenly the Shadow Host that had hung back at the last came up like a grey tide, sweeping all away before it. Faint cries I heard, and dim horns blowing, and a murmur as of countless far voices: it was like the echo of some forgotten battle in the Dark Years long ago. Pale swords were drawn; but I know not whether their blades would still bite, for the Dead needed no longer any weapon but fear. None would withstand them.

'To every ship they came that was drawn up, and then they passed over the water to those that were anchored; and all the mariners were filled with a madness of terror and leaped overboard, save the slaves chained to the oars. Reckless we rode among our fleeing foes, driving them like leaves, until we came to the shore. And then to each of the great ships that remained Aragorn sent one of the Dúnedain, and they comforted the captives that were aboard, and bade them put aside fear and be free.

'Ere that dark day ended none of the enemy were left to resist us; all were drowned, or were flying south in the hope to find their own lands upon foot. Strange and wonderful I thought it that the designs of Mordor should be overthrown by such wraiths of fear and darkness. With its own weapons was it worsted!'

'Strange indeed,' said Legolas. 'In that hour I looked on Aragorn and thought how great and terrible a Lord he might have become in the strength of his will, had he taken the Ring to himself. Not for naught does Mordor fear him. But nobler is his spirit than the understanding of Sauron; for is he not of the children of Lúthien? Never shall that line fail, though the years may lengthen beyond count.'

'Beyond the eyes of the Dwarves are such foretellings,' said Gimli. 'But mighty indeed was Aragorn that day. Lo! all the black fleet was in his hands; and he chose the greatest ship to be his own, and he went up into it. Then he let sound a great concourse of trumpets taken from the enemy; and the Shadow Host withdrew to the shore. There they stood silent, hardly to be seen, save for a red gleam in their eyes that caught the glare of the ships that were burning. And Aragorn spoke in a loud voice to the Dead Men, crying:

'"Hear now the words of the Heir of Isildur! Your oath is fulfilled. Go back and trouble not the valleys ever again! Depart and be at rest!"

'And thereupon the King of the Dead stood out before the host and broke his spear and cast it down. Then he bowed low and turned away; and swiftly the whole grey host drew on and vanished like a mist that is driven back by a sudden wind; and it seemed to me that I awoke from a dream.

'That night we rested while others laboured. For there were many captives set free, and many slaves released who had been folk of Gondor taken in raids; and soon also there was a great gathering of men out of Lebennin and the Ethir, and Angbor of Lamedon came up with all the horsemen that he could muster. Now that the fear of the Dead was removed they came to aid us and to look on the Heir of Isildur; for the rumour of that name had run like fire in the dark.

'And that is near the end of our tale. For during that evening and night many ships were made ready and manned; and in the morning the fleet set forth. Long past it now seems, yet it was but the morn of the day ere yesterday, the sixth since we rode from Dunharrow. But still Aragorn was driven by fear that time was too short.

'"It is forty leagues and two from Pelargir to the landings at the Harlond," he said. "Yet to the Harlond we must come tomorrow or fail utterly."

'The oars were now wielded by free men, and manfully they laboured; yet slowly we passed up the Great River, for we strove against its stream, and though that is not swift down in the South, we had no help of wind. Heavy would my heart have been, for all our victory at the havens, if Legolas had not laughed suddenly.

'"Up with your beard, Durin's son!" he said. "For thus is it spoken: *Oft hope is born, when all is forlorn.*" But what hope he saw from afar he would not tell. When night came it did but deepen the darkness, and our hearts were hot, for away in the North we saw a red glow under the cloud, and Aragorn said: "Minas Tirith is burning."

'But at midnight hope was indeed born anew. Sea-crafty men of the Ethir gazing southward spoke of a change coming with a fresh wind from the Sea. Long ere day the masted ships hoisted sail, and our speed grew, until dawn whitened the foam at our prows. And so it was, as you know, that we came in the third hour of the morning with a fair wind and the Sun unveiled, and we unfurled the great standard in battle. It was a great day and a great hour, whatever may come after.'

'Follow what may, great deeds are not lessened in worth,' said Legolas. 'Great deed was the riding of the Paths of the Dead, and great it shall remain, though none be left in Gondor to sing of it in the days that are to come.'

'And that may well befall,' said Gimli. 'For the faces of Aragorn and

Gandalf are grave. Much I wonder what counsels they are taking in the tents there below. For my part, like Merry, I wish that with our victory the war was now over. Yet whatever is still to do, I hope to have a part in it, for the honour of the folk of the Lonely Mountain.'

'And I for the folk of the Great Wood,' said Legolas, 'and for the love of the Lord of the White Tree.'

Then the companions fell silent, but a while they sat there in the high place, each busy with his own thoughts, while the Captains debated.

When the Prince Imrahil had parted from Legolas and Gimli, at once he sent for Éomer; and he went down with him from the City, and they came to the tents of Aragorn that were set up on the field not far from the place where King Théoden had fallen. And there they took counsel together with Gandalf and Aragorn and the sons of Elrond.

'My lords,' said Gandalf, 'listen to the words of the Steward of Gondor before he died: *You may triumph on the fields of the Pelennor for a day, but against the Power that has now arisen there is no victory*. I do not bid you despair, as he did, but to ponder the truth in these words.

'The Stones of Seeing do not lie, and not even the Lord of Barad-dûr can make them do so. He can, maybe, by his will choose what things shall be seen by weaker minds, or cause them to mistake the meaning of what they see. Nonetheless it cannot be doubted that when Denethor saw great forces arrayed against him in Mordor, and more still being gathered, he saw that which truly is.

'Hardly has our strength sufficed to beat off the first great assault. The next will be greater. This war then is without final hope, as Denethor perceived. Victory cannot be achieved by arms, whether you sit here to endure siege after siege, or march out to be overwhelmed beyond the River. You have only a choice of evils; and prudence would counsel you to strengthen such strong places as you have, and there await the onset; for so shall the time before your end be made a little longer.'

'Then you would have us retreat to Minas Tirith, or Dol Amroth, or to Dunharrow, and there sit like children on sand-castles when the tide is flowing?' said Imrahil.

'That would be no new counsel,' said Gandalf. 'Have you not done this and little more in all the days of Denethor? But no! I said this would be prudent. I do not counsel prudence. I said victory could not be achieved by arms. I still hope for victory, but not by arms. For into the midst of all these policies comes the Ring of Power, the foundation of Barad-dûr, and the hope of Sauron.

'Concerning this thing, my lords, you now all know enough for the understanding of our plight, and of Sauron's. If he regains it, your valour is vain, and his victory will be swift and complete: so complete that none can foresee the end of it while this world lasts. If it is destroyed, then he will fall; and his fall will be so low that none can foresee his arising ever again. For he will lose the best part of the strength that was native to him in his beginning, and all that was made or begun with that power will crumble, and he will be maimed for ever, becoming a mere spirit of malice that gnaws itself in the shadows, but cannot again grow or take shape. And so a great evil of this world will be removed.

'Other evils there are that may come; for Sauron is himself but a servant or emissary. Yet it is not our part to master all the tides of the world, but to do what is in us for the succour of those years wherein we are set, uprooting the evil in the fields that we know, so that those who live after may have clean earth to till. What weather they shall have is not ours to rule.

'Now Sauron knows all this, and he knows that this precious thing which he lost has been found again; but he does not yet know where it is, or so we hope. And therefore he is now in great doubt. For if we have found this thing, there are some among us with strength enough to wield it. That too he knows. For do I not guess rightly, Aragorn, that you have shown yourself to him in the Stone of Orthanc?'

'I did so ere I rode from the Hornburg,' answered Aragorn. 'I deemed that the time was ripe, and that the Stone had come to me for just such a purpose. It was then ten days since the Ring-bearer went east from Rauros, and the Eye of Sauron, I thought, should be drawn out from his own land. Too seldom has he been challenged since he returned to his Tower. Though if I had foreseen how swift would be his onset in answer, maybe I should not have dared to show myself. Bare time was given me to come to your aid.'

'But how is this?' asked Éomer. 'All is vain, you say, if he has the Ring. Why should he think it not vain to assail us, if we have it?'

'He is not yet sure,' said Gandalf, 'and he has not built up his power by waiting until his enemies are secure, as we have done. Also we could not learn how to wield the full power all in a day. Indeed it can be used only by one master alone, not by many; and he will look for a time of strife, ere one of the great among us makes himself master and puts down the others. In that time the Ring might aid him, if he were sudden.

'He is watching. He sees much and hears much. His Nazgûl are still abroad. They passed over this field ere the sunrise, though few of the weary and sleeping were aware of them. He studies the signs: the Sword that robbed him of his treasure re-made; the winds of fortune turning in our favour, and the defeat unlooked-for of his first assault; the fall of his great Captain.

'His doubt will be growing, even as we speak here. His Eye is now straining towards us, blind almost to all else that is moving. So we must keep it. Therein lies all our hope. This, then, is my counsel. We have not the Ring. In wisdom or great folly it has been sent away to be destroyed, lest it destroy us. Without it we cannot by force defeat his force. But we must at all costs keep his Eye from his true peril. We cannot achieve victory by arms, but by arms we can give the Ring-bearer his only chance, frail though it be.

'As Aragorn has begun, so we must go on. We must push Sauron to his last throw. We must call out his hidden strength, so that he shall empty his land. We must march out to meet him at once. We must make ourselves the bait, though his jaws should close on us. He will take that bait, in hope and in greed, for he will think that in such rashness he sees the pride of the new Ringlord: and he will say: "So! he pushes out his neck too soon and too far. Let him come on, and behold I will have him in a trap from which he cannot escape. There I will crush him, and what he has taken in his insolence shall be mine again for ever."

'We must walk open-eyed into that trap, with courage, but small hope for ourselves. For, my lords, it may well prove that we ourselves shall perish utterly in a black battle far from the living lands; so that even if Barad-dûr be thrown down, we shall not live to see a new age. But this, I deem, is our duty. And better so than to perish nonetheless – as we surely shall, if we sit here – and know as we die that no new age shall be.'

They were silent for a while. At length Aragorn spoke. 'As I have begun, so I will go on. We come now to the very brink, where hope and despair are akin. To waver is to fall. Let none now reject the counsels of Gandalf, whose long labours against Sauron come at last to their test. But for him all would long ago have been lost. Nonetheless I do not yet claim to command any man. Let others choose as they will.'

Then said Elrohir: 'From the North we came with this purpose, and from Elrond our father we brought this very counsel. We will not turn back.'

'As for myself,' said Éomer, 'I have little knowledge of these deep matters; but I need it not. This I know, and it is enough, that as my friend Aragorn succoured me and my people, so I will aid him when he calls. I will go.'

'As for me,' said Imrahil, 'the Lord Aragorn I hold to be my liege-lord, whether he claim it or no. His wish is to me a command. I will go also. Yet for a while I stand in the place of the Steward of Gondor, and it is mine to think first of its people. To prudence some heed must still be given. For we must prepare against all chances, good as well as evil. Now, it may be that we shall triumph, and while there is any hope of this, Gondor must be protected. I would not have us return with victory to a City in ruins and a land ravaged behind us. And yet we learn from the Rohirrim that there is an army still unfought upon our northern flank.'

'That is true,' said Gandalf. 'I do not counsel you to leave the City all unmanned. Indeed the force that we lead east need not be great enough for any assault in earnest upon Mordor, so long as it be great enough to challenge battle. And it must move soon. Therefore I ask the Captains: what force could we muster and lead out in two days' time at the latest? And they must be hardy men that go willingly, knowing their peril.'

'All are weary, and very many have wounds light or grievous,' said Éomer, 'and we have suffered much loss of our horses, and that is ill to bear. If we must ride soon, then I cannot hope to lead even two thousands, and yet leave as many for the defence of the City.'

'We have not only to reckon with those who fought on this field,' said Aragorn. 'New strength is on the way from the southern fiefs, now that the coasts have been rid. Four thousands I sent marching from Pelargir through Lossarnach two days ago; and Angbor the fearless rides before them. If we set out in two days more, they will draw nigh ere we depart. Moreover many were bidden to follow me up the River in any craft they could gather; and with this wind they will soon be at hand, indeed several ships have already come to the Harlond. I judge that we could lead out seven thousands of horse and foot, and yet leave the City in better defence than it was when the assault began.'

'The Gate is destroyed,' said Imrahil, 'and where now is the skill to rebuild it and set it up anew?'

'In Erebor in the Kingdom of Dáin there is such skill,' said Aragorn; 'and if all our hopes do not perish, then in time I will send Gimli Glóin's son to ask for wrights of the Mountain. But men are better than gates, and no gate will endure against our Enemy if men desert it.'

This then was the end of the debate of the lords: that they should set forth on the second morning from that day with seven thousands, if these might be found; and the great part of this force should be on foot, because of the evil lands into which they would go. Aragorn should find some two thousands of those that he had gathered to him in the South; but Imrahil should find three and a half thousands; and Éomer five hundreds of the Rohirrim who were unhorsed but themselves warworthy, and he himself should lead five hundreds of his best Riders on horse; and another company of five hundred horse there should be, among which should ride the sons of Elrond with the Dúnedain and the knights of Dol Amroth: all told six thousand foot and a thousand horse. But the main strength of the Rohirrim that remained horsed and able to fight, some three thousand under the command of Elfhelm, should waylay the West Road against the enemy that was in Anórien. And at once swift riders were sent out to gather what news they could northwards; and eastwards from Osgiliath and the road to Minas Morgul.

And when they had reckoned up all their strength and taken thought for the journeys they should make and the roads they should choose, Imrahil suddenly laughed aloud.

'Surely,' he cried, 'this is the greatest jest in all the history of Gondor: that we should ride with seven thousands, scarce as many as the vanguard of its army in the days of its power, to assail the mountains and the impenetrable gate of the Black Land! So might a child threaten a mail-clad knight with a bow of string and green willow! If the Dark Lord knows so much as you say, Mithrandir, will he not rather smile than fear, and with his little finger crush us like a fly that tries to sting him?'

'No, he will try to trap the fly and take the sting,' said Gandalf. 'And there are names among us that are worth more than a thousand mail-clad knights apiece. No, he will not smile.'

'Neither shall we,' said Aragorn. 'If this be jest, then it is too bitter for laughter. Nay, it is the last move in a great jeopardy, and for one side or the other it will bring the end of the game.' Then he drew Andúril and held it up glittering in the sun. 'You shall not be sheathed again until the last battle is fought,' he said.

CHAPTER X

THE BLACK GATE OPENS

Two days later the army of the West was all assembled on the Pelennor. The host of Orcs and Easterlings had turned back out of Anórien, but harried and scattered by the Rohirrim they had broken and fled with little fighting towards Cair Andros; and with that threat destroyed and new strength arriving out of the South the City was as well manned as might be. Scouts reported that no enemies remained upon the roads east as far as the Cross-roads of the Fallen King. All now was ready for the last throw.

Legolas and Gimli were to ride again together in the company of Aragorn and Gandalf, who went in the van with the Dúnedain and the sons of Elrond. But Merry to his shame was not to go with them.

'You are not fit for such a journey,' said Aragorn. 'But do not be ashamed. If you do no more in this war, you have already earned great honour. Peregrin shall go and represent the Shirefolk; and do not grudge him his chance of peril, for though he has done as well as his fortune allowed him, he has yet to match your deed. But in truth all now are in like danger. Though it may be our part to find a bitter end before the Gate of Mordor, if we do so, then you will come also to a last stand, either here or wherever the black tide overtakes you. Farewell!'

And so despondently Merry now stood and watched the mustering of the army. Bergil was with him, and he also was downcast; for his father was to march leading a company of the Men of the City: he could not rejoin the Guard until his case was judged. In that same company Pippin was also to go, as a soldier of Gondor. Merry could see him not far off, a small but upright figure among the tall men of Minas Tirith.

At last the trumpets rang and the army began to move. Troop by troop, and company by company, they wheeled and went off eastward. And long after they had passed away out of sight down the great road to the Causeway, Merry stood there. The last glint of the morning sun on spear and helm twinkled and was lost, and still he remained with bowed head and heavy heart, feeling friendless and alone. Everyone that he cared for had gone away into the gloom that hung over the distant eastern sky; and little hope at all was left in his heart that he would ever see any of them again.

As if recalled by his mood of despair, the pain in his arm returned, and he felt weak and old, and the sunlight seemed thin. He was roused by the touch of Bergil's hand.

'Come, Master Perian!' said the lad. 'You are still in pain, I see. I will help you back to the Healers. But do not fear! They will come back. The Men of Minas Tirith will never be overcome. And now they have the Lord Elfstone, and Beregond of the Guard too.'

Ere noon the army came to Osgiliath. There all the workers and craftsmen that could be spared were busy. Some were strengthening the ferries and boat-bridges that the enemy had made and in part destroyed when they fled; some gathered stores and booty; and others on the eastern side across the River were throwing up hasty works of defence.

The vanguard passed on through the ruins of Old Gondor, and over the wide River, and on up the long straight road that in the high days had been made to run from the fair Tower of the Sun to the tall Tower of the Moon, which now was Minas Morgul in its accursed vale. Five miles beyond Osgiliath they halted, ending their first day's march.

But the horsemen pressed on and ere evening they came to the Cross-roads and the great ring of trees, and all was silent. No sign of any enemy had they seen, no cry or call had been heard, no shaft had sped from rock or thicket by the way, yet ever as they went forward they felt the watchfulness of the land increase. Tree and stone, blade and leaf were listening. The darkness had been dispelled, and far away westward sunset was on the Vale of Anduin, and the white peaks of the mountains blushed in the blue air; but a shadow and a gloom brooded upon the Ephel Dúath.

Then Aragorn set trumpeters at each of the four roads that ran into the ring of trees, and they blew a great fanfare, and the heralds cried aloud: 'The Lords of Gondor have returned and all this land that is theirs they take back.' The hideous orc-head that was set upon the carven figure was cast down and broken in pieces, and the old king's head was raised and set in its place once more, still crowned with white and golden flowers; and men laboured to wash and pare away all the foul scrawls that orcs had put upon the stone.

Now in their debate some had counselled that Minas Morgul should first be assailed, and if they might take it, it should be utterly destroyed. 'And, maybe,' said Imrahil, 'the road that leads thence to the pass above will prove an easier way of assault upon the Dark Lord than his northern gate.'

But against this Gandalf had spoken urgently, because of the evil that dwelt in the valley, where the minds of living men would turn to madness and horror, and because also of the news that Faramir had brought. For if the Ring-bearer had indeed attempted that way, then above all they should not draw the Eye of Mordor thither. So the next day when the main host came up, they set a strong guard upon the Cross-roads to make some defence, if Mordor should send a force over the Morgul Pass, or should bring more men up from the South. For that guard they chose mostly archers who knew the ways of Ithilien and would lie hid in the woods and slopes about the meeting of the ways. But Gandalf and Aragorn rode with the vanguard to the entrance of Morgul Vale and looked on the evil city.

It was dark and lifeless; for the Orcs and lesser creatures of Mordor that had dwelt there had been destroyed in battle, and the Nazgûl were abroad. Yet the air of the valley was heavy with fear and enmity. Then they broke the evil bridge and set red flames in the noisome fields and departed.

The day after, being the third day since they set out from Minas Tirith, the army began its northward march along the road. It was some hundred miles by that way from the Cross-roads to the Morannon, and what might befall them before they came so far none knew. They went openly but heedfully, with mounted scouts before them on the road, and others on foot upon either side, especially on the eastward flank; for there lay dark thickets, and a tumbled land of rocky ghylls and crags, behind which the long grim slopes of the Ephel Dúath clambered up. The weather of the world remained fair, and the wind held in the west, but nothing could waft away the glooms and the sad mists that clung about the Mountains of Shadow; and behind them at whiles great smokes would arise and hover in the upper winds.

Ever and anon Gandalf let blow the trumpets, and the heralds would cry: 'The Lords of Gondor are come! Let all leave this land or yield them up!' But Imrahil said: 'Say not *The Lords of Gondor*. Say *The King Elessar*. For that is true, even though he has not yet sat upon the throne; and it will give the Enemy more thought, if the heralds use that name.' And thereafter thrice a day the heralds proclaimed the coming of the King Elessar. But none answered the challenge.

Nonetheless, though they marched in seeming peace, the hearts of all the army, from the highest to the lowest, were downcast, and with every mile that they went north foreboding of evil grew heavier on them. It was near the end of the second day of their march from the Cross-roads that they first met any offer of battle. For a strong force of Orcs and Easterlings attempted to take their leading companies in an ambush; and that was in the very place where Faramir had waylaid the men of Harad, and the road went in a deep cutting through an out-thrust of the eastward hills. But the Captains of the West were well warned by their scouts, skilled men from Henneth Annûn led by Mablung; and so the ambush was itself trapped. For horsemen went wide about westward and came up on the flank of the enemy and from behind, and they were destroyed or driven east into the hills.

But the victory did little to enhearten the captains. 'It is but a feint,' said Aragorn; 'and its chief purpose, I deem, was rather to draw us on by a false guess of our Enemy's weakness than to do us much hurt, yet.' And from that evening onward the Nazgûl came and followed every move of the army. They still flew high and out of sight of all save Legolas, and yet their presence could be felt, as a deepening of shadow and a dimming of the sun; and though the Ringwraiths did not yet stoop low upon their foes and were silent, uttering no cry, the dread of them could not be shaken off.

So time and the hopeless journey wore away. Upon the fourth day from the Cross-roads and the sixth from Minas Tirith they came at last to the end of the living lands, and began to pass into the desolation that lay before the gates of the Pass of Cirith Gorgor; and they could descry the marshes and the desert that stretched north and west to the Emyn Muil. So desolate were those places and so deep the horror that lay on them that some of the host were unmanned, and they could neither walk nor ride further north.

Aragorn looked at them, and there was pity in his eyes rather than wrath; for these were young men from Rohan, from Westfold far away, or husbandmen from Lossarnach, and to them Mordor had been from childhood a name of evil, and yet unreal, a legend that had no part in their simple life; and now they walked like men in a hideous dream made true, and they understood not this war nor why fate should lead them to such a pass.

'Go!' said Aragorn. 'But keep what honour you may, and do not run! And there is a task which you may attempt and so be not wholly shamed. Take your way south-west till you come to Cair Andros, and if that is still held by enemies, as I think, then re-take it, if you can; and hold it to the last in defence of Gondor and Rohan!'

Then some being shamed by his mercy overcame their fear and went on, and the others took new hope, hearing of a manful deed within their measure that they could turn to, and they departed. And so, since many men had already been left at the Cross-roads, it was with less than six thousands that the Captains of the West came at last to challenge the Black Gate and the might of Mordor.

They advanced now slowly, expecting at every hour some answer to their challenge, and they drew together, since it was but waste of men to send out scouts or small parties from the main host. At nightfall of the fifth day of the march from Morgul Vale they made their last camp, and set fires about it of such dead wood and heath as they could find. They passed the hours of night in wakefulness and they were aware of many things half-seen that walked and prowled all about them, and they heard the howling of wolves. The wind had died and all the air seemed still. They could see little, for though it was cloudless and the waxing moon was four nights old, there were smokes and fumes that rose out of the earth and the white crescent was shrouded in the mists of Mordor.

It grew cold. As morning came the wind began to stir again, but now it came from the North, and soon it freshened to a rising breeze. All the night-walkers were gone, and the land seemed empty. North amid their noisome pits lay the first of the great heaps and hills of slag and broken rock and blasted earth, the vomit of the maggot-folk of Mordor; but south and now near loomed the great rampart of Cirith Gorgor, and the Black Gate amidmost, and the two Towers of the Teeth tall and dark upon either side. For in their last march the Captains had turned away from the old road as it bent east, and avoided the peril of the lurking hills, and so now they were approaching the Morannon from the north-west, even as Frodo had done.

The two vast iron doors of the Black Gate under its frowning arch were fast closed. Upon the battlement nothing could be seen. All was silent but watchful. They were come to the last end of their folly, and stood forlorn and chill in the grey light of early day before towers and walls which their army could not assault with hope, not even if it had brought thither engines of great power, and the Enemy had no more force than would suffice for the manning of the gate and wall alone. Yet they knew that all the hills and rocks about the Morannon were filled with hidden foes, and the shadowy defile beyond was bored and tunnelled by teeming broods of evil things. And as they stood they saw all the Nazgûl gathered together, hovering above the Towers of the Teeth like vultures; and they knew that they were watched. But still the Enemy made no sign.

No choice was left them but to play their part to its end. Therefore Aragorn now set the host in such array as could best be contrived; and they were drawn up on two great hills of blasted stone and earth that orcs had piled in years of labour. Before them towards Mordor lay like a moat a great mire of reeking mud and foul-smelling pools. When all was ordered, the Captains rode forth towards the Black Gate with a great guard of horsemen and the banner and heralds and trumpeters. There was Gandalf as chief herald, and Aragorn with the sons of Elrond, and Éomer of Rohan, and Imrahil; and Legolas and Gimli and Peregrin were bidden to go also, so that all the enemies of Mordor should have a witness.

They came within cry of the Morannon, and unfurled the banner, and blew upon their trumpets; and the heralds stood out and sent their voices up over the battlement of Mordor.

'Come forth!' they cried. 'Let the Lord of the Black Land come forth!

Justice shall be done upon him. For wrongfully he has made war upon Gondor and wrested its lands. Therefore the King of Gondor demands that he should atone for his evils, and depart then for ever. Come forth!'

There was a long silence, and from wall and gate no cry or sound was heard in answer. But Sauron had already laid his plans, and he had a mind first to play these mice cruelly before he struck to kill. So it was that, even as the Captains were about to turn away, the silence was broken suddenly. There came a long rolling of great drums like thunder in the mountains, and then a braying of horns that shook the very stones and stunned men's ears. And thereupon the door of the Black Gate was thrown open with a great clang, and out of it there came an embassy from the Dark Tower.

At its head there rode a tall and evil shape, mounted upon a black horse, if horse it was; for it was huge and hideous, and its face was a frightful mask, more like a skull than a living head, and in the sockets of its eyes and in its nostrils there burned a flame. The rider was robed all in black, and black was his lofty helm; yet this was no Ringwraith but a living man. The Lieutenant of the Tower of Barad-dûr he was, and his name is remembered in no tale; for he himself had forgotten it, and he said: 'I am the Mouth of Sauron.' But it is told that he was a renegade, who came of the race of those that are named the Black Númenoreans; for they established their dwellings in Middle-earth during the years of Sauron's domi-nation, and they worshipped him, being enamoured of evil knowledge. And he entered the service of the Dark Tower when it first rose again, and because of his cunning he grew ever higher in the Lord's favour; and he learned great sorcery, and knew much of the mind of Sauron; and he was more cruel than any orc.

He it was that now rode out, and with him came only a small company of black-harnessed soldiery, and a single banner, black but bearing on it in red the Evil Eye. Now halting a few paces before the Captains of the West he looked them up and down and laughed.

'Is there anyone in this rout with authority to treat with me?' he asked. 'Or indeed with wit to understand me? Not thou at least!' he mocked, turning to Aragorn with scorn. 'It needs more to make a king than a piece of elvish glass, or a rabble such as this. Why, any brigand of the hills can show as good a following!'

Aragorn said naught in answer, but he took the other's eye and held it, and for a moment they strove thus; but soon, though Aragorn did not stir nor move hand to weapon, the other quailed and gave back as if menaced with a blow. 'I am a herald and ambassador, and may not be assailed!' he cried.

'Where such laws hold,' said Gandalf, 'it is also the custom for ambassadors to use less insolence. But no one has threatened you. You have naught to fear from us, until your errand is done. But unless your master has come to new wisdom, then with all his servants you will be in great peril.'

'So!' said the Messenger. 'Then thou art the spokesman, old greybeard? Have we not heard of thee at whiles, and of thy wanderings, ever hatching plots and mischief at a safe distance? But this time thou hast stuck out thy nose too far, Master Gandalf; and thou shalt see what comes to him who sets his foolish webs before the feet of Sauron the Great. I have tokens that I was bidden to show to thee – to thee in especial, if thou shouldst dare to come.' He signed to one of his guards, and he came forward bearing a bundle swathed in black cloths.

The Messenger put these aside, and there to the wonder and dismay of all the Captains he held up first the short sword that Sam had carried, and next a grey cloak with an elven-brooch, and last the coat of mithril-mail that Frodo had worn wrapped in his tattered garments. A blackness came before their eyes, and it seemed to them in a moment of silence that the world stood still, but their hearts were dead and their last hope gone. Pippin who stood behind Prince Imrahil sprang forward with a cry of grief.

'Silence!' said Gandalf sternly, thrusting him back; but the Messenger laughed aloud.

'So you have yet another of these imps with you!' he cried. 'What use you find in them I cannot guess; but to send them as spies into Mordor is beyond even your accustomed folly. Still, I thank him, for it is plain that this brat at least has seen these tokens before, and it would be vain for you to deny them now.'

'I do not wish to deny them,' said Gandalf. 'Indeed, I know them all and all their history, and despite your scorn, foul Mouth of Sauron, you cannot say as much. But why do you bring them here?'

'Dwarf-coat, elf-cloak, blade of the downfallen West, and spy from the little rat-land of the Shire – nay, do not start! We know it well – here are the marks of a conspiracy. Now, maybe he that bore these things was a creature that you would not grieve to lose, and maybe otherwise: one dear to you, perhaps? If so, take swift counsel with what little wit is left to you. For Sauron does not love spies, and what his fate shall be depends now on your choice.'

No one answered him; but he saw their faces grey with fear and the horror in their eyes, and he laughed again, for it seemed to him that his sport went well. 'Good, good!' he said. 'He was dear to you, I see. Or else his errand was one that you did not wish to fail? It has. And now he shall endure the slow torment of years, as long and slow as our arts in the Great Tower can contrive, and never be released, unless maybe when he is changed and broken, so that he may come to you, and you shall see what you have done. This shall surely be unless you accept my Lord's terms.'

'Name the terms,' said Gandalf steadily, but those nearby saw the anguish in his face, and now he seemed an old and wizened man, crushed, defeated at last. They did not doubt that he would accept.

'These are the terms,' said the Messenger, and smiled as he eyed them one by one. 'The rabble of Gondor and its deluded allies shall withdraw at once beyond the Anduin, first taking oaths never again to assail Sauron the Great in arms, open or secret. All lands east of the Anduin shall be Sauron's for ever, solely. West of the Anduin as far as the Misty Mountains and the Gap of Rohan shall be tributary to Mordor, and men there shall bear no weapons, but shall have leave to govern their own affairs. But they shall help to rebuild Isengard which they have wantonly destroyed, and that shall be Sauron's, and there his lieutenant shall dwell: not Saruman, but one more worthy of trust.'

Looking in the Messenger's eyes they read his thought. He was to be that lieutenant, and gather all that remained of the West under his sway; he would be their tyrant and they his slaves.

But Gandalf said: 'This is much to demand for the delivery of one servant: that your Master should receive in exchange what he must else fight many a war to gain! Or has the field of Gondor destroyed his hope in war, so that he falls to haggling? And if indeed we rated this prisoner so high, what surety have we that Sauron, the Base Master of Treachery, will keep his part? Where is this prisoner? Let him be brought forth and yielded to us, and then we will consider these demands.'

It seemed then to Gandalf, intent, watching him as a man engaged in fencing with a deadly foe, that for the taking of a breath the Messenger was at a loss; yet swiftly he laughed again.

'Do not bandy words in your insolence with the Mouth of Sauron!' he cried. 'Surety you crave! Sauron gives none. If you sue for his clemency you must first do his bidding. These are his terms. Take them or leave them!'

'These we will take!' said Gandalf suddenly. He cast aside his cloak and a white light shone forth like a sword in that black place. Before his upraised hand the foul Messenger recoiled, and Gandalf coming seized and took from him the tokens: coat, cloak, and sword. 'These we will take in memory of our friend,' he cried. 'But as for your terms, we reject them utterly. Get you gone, for your embassy is over and death is near to you. We did not come here to waste words in treating with Sauron, faithless and accursed; still less with one of his slaves. Begone!'

Then the Messenger of Mordor laughed no more. His face was twisted with amazement and anger to the likeness of some wild beast that, as it crouches on its prey, is smitten on the muzzle with a stinging rod. Rage filled him and his mouth slavered, and shapeless sounds of fury came strangling from his throat. But he looked at the fell faces of the Captains and their deadly eyes, and fear overcame his wrath. He gave a great cry, and turned, leaped upon his steed, and with his company galloped madly back to Cirith Gorgor. But as they went his soldiers blew their horns in signal long arranged; and even before they came to the gate Sauron sprang his trap.

Drums rolled and fires leaped up. The great doors of the Black Gate swung back wide. Out of it streamed a great host as swiftly as swirling waters when a sluice is lifted.

The Captains mounted again and rode back, and from the host of Mordor there went up a jeering yell. Dust rose smothering the air, as from near-by there marched up an army of Easterlings that had waited for the signal in the shadows of Ered Lithui beyond the further Tower. Down from the hills on either side of the Morannon poured Orcs innumerable. The men of the West were trapped, and soon, all about the grey mounds where they stood, forces ten times and more than ten times their match would ring them in a sea of enemies. Sauron had taken the proffered bait in jaws of steel.

Little time was left to Aragorn for the ordering of his battle. Upon the one hill he stood with Gandalf, and there fair and desperate was raised the banner of the Tree and Stars. Upon the other hill hard by stood the banners of Rohan and Dol Amroth, White Horse and Silver Swan. And about each hill a ring was made facing all ways, bristling with spear and sword. But in the front towards Mordor where the first bitter assault would come there stood the sons of Elrond on the left with the Dúnedain about them, and on the right the Prince Imrahil with the men of Dol Amroth tall and fair, and picked men of the Tower of Guard.

The wind blew, and the trumpets sang, and arrows whined; but the sun now climbing towards the South was veiled in the reeks of Mordor, and through a threatening haze it gleamed, remote, a sullen red, as if it were the ending of the day, or the end maybe of all the world of light. And out of the gathering mirk the Nazgûl came with their cold voices crying words of death; and then all hope was quenched.

Pippin had bowed crushed with horror when he heard Gandalf reject the terms and doom Frodo to the torment of the Tower; but he had mastered himself, and now he stood beside Beregond in the front rank of Gondor with Imrahil's men. For it seemed best to him to die soon and leave the bitter story of his life, since all was in ruin.

'I wish Merry was here,' he heard himself saying, and quick thoughts raced through his mind, even as he watched the enemy come charging to the assault. 'Well, well, now at any rate I understand poor Denethor a little better. We might die together, Merry and I, and since die we must, why not? Well, as he is not here, I hope he'll find an easier end. But now I must do my best.'

He drew his sword and looked at it, and the intertwining shapes of red and gold; and the flowing characters of Númenor glinted like fire upon the blade. 'This was made for just such an hour,' he thought. 'If only I could smite that foul Messenger with it, then almost I should draw level with old Merry. Well, I'll smite some of this beastly brood before the end. I wish I could see cool sunlight and green grass again!'

Then even as he thought these things the first assault crashed into them. The orcs hindered by the mires that lay before the hills halted and poured their arrows into the defending ranks. But through them there came striding up, roaring like beasts, a great company of hill-trolls out of Gorgoroth. Taller and broader than Men they were, and they were clad only in close-fitting mesh of horny scales, or maybe that was their hideous hide; but they bore round bucklers huge and black and wielded heavy hammers in their knotted hands. Reckless they sprang into the pools and waded across, bellowing as they came. Like a storm they broke upon the line of the men of Gondor, and beat upon helm and head, and arm and shield, as smiths hewing the hot bending iron. At Pippin's side Beregond was stunned and overborne, and he fell; and the great troll-chief that smote him down bent over him, reaching out a clutching claw; for these fell creatures would bite the throats of those that they threw down.

Then Pippin stabbed upwards, and the written blade of Westernesse pierced through the hide and went deep into the vitals of the troll, and his black blood came gushing out. He toppled forward and came crashing down like a falling rock, burying those beneath him. Blackness and stench and crushing pain came upon Pippin, and his mind fell away into a great darkness.

'So it ends as I guessed it would,' his thought said, even as it fluttered away; and it laughed a little within him ere it fled, almost gay it seemed to be casting off at last all doubt and care and fear. And then even as it winged away into forgetfulness it heard voices, and they seemed to be crying in some forgotten world far above:

'The Eagles are coming! The Eagles are coming!'

For one moment more Pippin's thought hovered. 'Bilbo!' it said. 'But no! That came in his tale, long long ago. This is my tale, and it is ended now. Good-bye!' And his thought fled far away and his eyes saw no more.

BOOK SIX

CHAPTER I

THE TOWER OF CIRITH UNGOL

Sam roused himself painfully from the ground. For a moment he wondered where he was, and then all the misery and despair returned to him. He was in the deep dark outside the under-gate of the orcs' stronghold; its brazen doors were shut. He must have fallen stunned when he hurled himself against them; but how long he had lain there he did not know. Then he had been on fire, desperate and furious; now he was shivering and cold. He crept to the doors and pressed his ears against them.

Far within he could hear faintly the voices of orcs clamouring, but soon they stopped or passed out of hearing, and all was still. His head ached and his eyes saw phantom lights in the darkness, but he struggled to steady himself and think. It was clear at any rate that he had no hope of getting into the orc-hold by that gate; he might wait there for days before it was opened, and he could not wait: time was desperately precious. He no longer had any doubt about his duty: he must rescue his master or perish in the attempt.

'The perishing is more likely, and will be a lot easier anyway,' he said grimly to himself, as he sheathed Sting and turned from the brazen doors. Slowly he groped his way back in the dark along the tunnel, not daring to use the elven-light; and as he went he tried to fit together the events since Frodo and he had left the Cross-roads. He wondered what the time was. Somewhere between one day and the next, he supposed; but even of the days he had quite lost count. He was in a land of darkness where the days of the world seemed forgotten, and where all who entered were forgotten too.

'I wonder if they think of us at all,' he said, 'and what is happening to them all away there.' He waved his hand vaguely in the air before him; but he was in fact now facing southwards, as he came back to Shelob's tunnel, not west. Out westward in the world it was drawing to noon upon the fourteenth day of March in the Shire-reckoning, and even now Aragorn was leading the black fleet from Pelargir, and Merry was riding with the Rohirrim down the Stonewain Valley, while in Minas Tirith flames were rising and Pippin watched the madness growing in the eyes of Denethor. Yet amid all their cares and fear the thoughts of their friends turned constantly to Frodo and Sam. They were not forgotten. But they were far beyond aid, and no thought could yet bring any help to Samwise Hamfast's son; he was utterly alone.

He came back at last to the stone door of the orc-passage, and still unable to discover the catch or bolt that held it, he scrambled over as before and dropped softly to the ground. Then he made his way stealthily to the outlet of Shelob's tunnel, where the rags of her great web were still blowing and swaying in the cold airs. For cold they seemed to Sam after the noisome darkness behind; but the breath of them revived him. He crept cautiously out.

All was ominously quiet. The light was no more than that of dusk at a dark day's end. The vast vapours that arose in Mordor and went streaming westward passed low overhead, a great welter of cloud and smoke now lit again beneath with a sullen glow of red.

Sam looked up towards the orc-tower, and suddenly from its narrow windows lights stared out like small red eyes. He wondered if they were some signal. His fear of the orcs, forgotten for a while in his wrath and desperation, now returned. As far as he could see, there was only one possible course for him to take: he must go on and try to find the main entrance to the dreadful tower; but his knees felt weak, and he found that he was trembling. Drawing his eyes down from the tower and the horns of the Cleft before him, he forced his unwilling feet to obey him, and slowly, listening with all his ears, peering into the dense shadows of the rocks beside the way, he retraced his steps, past the place where Frodo fell, and still the stench of Shelob lingered, and then on and up, until he stood again in the very cleft where he had put on the Ring and seen Shagrat's company go by.

There he halted and sat down. For the moment he could drive himself no further. He felt that if once he went beyond the crown of the pass and took one step veritably down into the land of Mordor, that step would be irrevocable. He could never come back. Without any clear purpose he drew out the Ring and put it on again. Immediately he felt the great burden of its weight, and felt afresh, but now more strong and urgent than ever, the malice of the Eye of Mordor, searching, trying to pierce the shadows that it had made for its own defence, but which now hindered it in its unquiet and doubt.

As before, Sam found that his hearing was sharpened, but that to his sight the things of this world seemed thin and vague. The rocky walls of the path were pale, as if seen through a mist, but still at a distance he heard the bubbling of Shelob in her misery; and harsh and clear, and very close it seemed, he heard cries and the clash of metal. He sprang to his feet, and pressed himself against the wall beside the road. He was glad of the Ring, for here was yet another company of orcs on the march. Or so at first he thought. Then suddenly he realized that it was not so, his hearing had deceived him: the orc-cries came from the tower, whose topmost horn was now right above him, on the left hand of the Cleft.

Sam shuddered and tried to force himself to move. There was plainly some devilry going on. Perhaps in spite of all orders the cruelty of the orcs had mastered them, and they were tormenting Frodo, or even savagely hacking him to pieces. He listened; and as he did a gleam of hope came to him. There could not be much doubt: there was fighting in the tower, the orcs must be at war among themselves, Shagrat and Gorbag had come to blows. Faint as was the hope that his guess brought him, it was enough to rouse him. There might be just a chance. His love for Frodo rose above all other thoughts, and forgetting his peril he cried aloud: 'I'm coming Mr. Frodo!'

He ran forward to the climbing path, and over it. At once the road turned left and plunged steeply down. Sam had crossed into Mordor.

He took off the Ring, moved it may be by some deep premonition of danger, though to himself he thought only that he wished to see more clearly. 'Better have a look at the worst,' he muttered. 'No good blundering about in a fog!'

Hard and cruel and bitter was the land that met his gaze. Before his feet the highest ridge of the Ephel Dúath fell steeply in great cliffs down into a dark trough, on the further side of which there rose another ridge, much lower, its edge notched and jagged with crags like fangs that stood out black against the red light behind them: it was the grim Morgai, the inner ring of the fences of the land. Far beyond it, but almost straight ahead, across a wide lake of darkness dotted with tiny fires, there was a great burning glow; and from it rose in huge columns a swirling smoke, dusty red at the roots, black above where it merged into the billowing canopy that roofed in all the accursed land.

Sam was looking at Orodruin, the Mountain of Fire. Ever and anon the furnaces far below its ashen cone would grow hot and with a great surging and throbbing pour forth rivers of molten rock from chasms in its sides. Some would flow blazing towards Barad-dûr down great channels; some would wind their way into the stony plain, until they cooled and lay like twisted dragon-shapes vomited from the tormented earth. In such an hour of labour Sam beheld Mount Doom, and the light of it, cut off by the high screen of the Ephel Dúath from those who climbed up the path from the West, now glared against the stark rock faces, so that they seemed to be drenched with blood.

In that dreadful light Sam stood aghast, for now, looking to his left, he could see the Tower of Cirith Ungol in all its strength. The horn that he had seen from the other side was only its topmost turret. Its eastern face stood up in three great tiers from a shelf in the mountain-wall far below; its back was to a great cliff behind, from which it jutted out in pointed bastions, one above the other, diminishing as they rose, with sheer sides of cunning masonry that looked north-east and south-east. About the lowest tier, two hundred feet below where Sam now stood, there was a battlemented wall enclosing a narrow court. Its gate, upon the near south-eastern side, opened on a broad road, the outer parapet of which ran upon the brink of a precipice, until it turned southward and went winding down into the darkness to join the road that came over the Morgul Pass. Then on it went through a jagged rift in the Morgai out into the valley of Gorgoroth and away to Barad-dûr. The narrow upper way on which Sam stood leapt swiftly down by stair and steep path to meet the main road under the frowning walls close to the Tower-gate.

As he gazed at it suddenly Sam understood, almost with a shock, that this stronghold had been built not to keep enemies out of Mordor, but to keep them in. It was indeed one of the works of Gondor long ago, an eastern outpost of the defences of Ithilien, made when, after the Last Alliance, Men of Westernesse kept watch on the evil land of Sauron where his creatures still lurked. But as with Narchost and Carchost, the Towers of the Teeth, so here too the vigilance had failed, and treachery had yielded up the Tower to the Lord of the Ringwraiths, and now for long years it had been held by evil things. Since his return to Mordor, Sauron had found it useful; for he had few servants but many slaves of fear, and still its chief purpose as of old was to prevent escape from Mordor. Though if an enemy were so rash as to try to enter that land secretly, then it was also a last unsleeping guard against any that might pass the vigilance of Morgul and of Shelob.

Only too clearly Sam saw how hopeless it would be for him to creep down under those many-eyed walls and pass the watchful gate. And even if he did so, he could not go far on the guarded road beyond: not even the black shadows, lying deep where the red glow could not reach, would shield him long from the night-eyed orcs. But desperate as that road might be, his task was now far worse: not to avoid the gate and escape, but to enter it, alone.

His thought turned to the Ring, but there was no comfort there, only dread and danger. No sooner had he come in sight of Mount Doom, burning far away, than he was aware of a change in his burden. As it drew near the great furnaces where, in the deeps of time, it had been shaped and forged, the Ring's power grew, and it became more fell, untameable save by some mighty will. As Sam stood there, even though the Ring was not on him but hanging by its chain about his neck, he felt himself enlarged, as if he were robed in a huge distorted shadow of himself, a vast and ominous threat halted upon the walls of Mordor. He felt that he had from now on only two choices: to forbear the Ring, though it would torment him; or to claim it, and challenge the Power that sat in its dark hold beyond the valley of shadows. Already the Ring tempted him, gnawing at his will and reason. Wild fantasies arose in his mind; and he saw Samwise the Strong, Hero of the Age, striding with a flaming sword across the darkened land, and armies flocking to his call as he marched to the overthrow of Barad-dûr. And then all the clouds rolled away, and the white sun shone, and at his command the vale of Gorgoroth became a garden of flowers and trees and brought forth fruit. He had only to put on the Ring and claim it for his own, and all this could be.

In that hour of trial it was the love of his master that helped most to hold him firm; but also deep down in him lived still unconquered his plain hobbit-sense: he knew in the core of his heart that he was not large enough to bear such a burden, even if such visions were not a mere cheat to betray him. The one small garden of a free gardener was all his need and due, not a garden swollen to a realm; his own hands to use, not the hands of others to command.

'And anyway all these notions are only a trick,' he said to himself. 'He'd spot me and cow me, before I could so much as shout out. He'd spot me, pretty quick, if I put the Ring on now, in Mordor. Well, all I can say is: things look as hopeless as a frost in spring. Just when being invisible would be really useful, I can't use the Ring! And if ever I get any further, it's going to be nothing but a drag and a burden every step. So what's to be done?'

He was not really in any doubt. He knew that he must go down to the gate and not linger any more. With a shrug of his shoulders, as if to shake off the shadow and dismiss the phantoms, he began slowly to descend. With each step he seemed to diminish. He had not gone far before he had shrunk again to a very small and frightened hobbit. He was now passing under the very walls of the Tower, and the cries and sounds of fighting could be heard with his unaided ears. At the moment the noise seemed to be coming from the court behind the outer wall.

Sam was about half way down the path when out of the dark gateway into the red glow there came two orcs running. They did not turn towards him. They were making for the main road; but even as they ran they stumbled and fell to the ground and lay still. Sam had seen no arrows, but he guessed that the orcs had been shot down by others on the battlements or hidden in the shadow of the gate. He went on, hugging the wall on his left. One look upward had shown him that there was no hope of climbing it. The stone-work rose thirty feet, without a crack or ledge, to overhanging courses like inverted steps. The gate was the only way.

He crept on; and as he went he wondered how many orcs lived in the Tower with Shagrat, and how many Gorbag had, and what they were quarrelling about, if that was what was happening. Shagrat's company had seemed to be about forty, and Gorbag's more than twice as large; but of course Shagrat's patrol had only been a part of his garrison. Almost certainly they were quarrelling about Frodo, and the spoil. For a second Sam halted, for suddenly things seemed clear to him, almost as if he had seen them with his eyes. The mithril coat! Of course, Frodo was wearing it, and they would find it. And from what Sam had heard Gorbag would covet it. But the orders of the Dark

Tower were at present Frodo's only protection, and if they were set aside, Frodo might be killed out of hand at any moment.

'Come on, you miserable sluggard!' Sam cried to himself. 'Now for it!' He drew Sting and ran towards the open gate. But just as he was about to pass under its great arch he felt a shock: as if he had run into some web like Shelob's, only invisible. He could see no obstacle, but something too strong for his will to overcome barred the way. He looked about, and then within the shadow of the gate he saw the Two Watchers.

They were like great figures seated upon thrones. Each had three joined bodies, and three heads facing outward, and inward, and across the gateway. The heads had vulture-faces, and on their great knees were laid clawlike hands. They seemed to be carved out of huge blocks of stone, immovable, and yet they were aware: some dreadful spirit of evil vigilance abode in them. They knew an enemy. Visible or invisible none could pass unheeded. They would forbid his entry, or his escape.

Hardening his will Sam thrust forward once again, and halted with a jerk, staggering as if from a blow upon his breast and head. Then greatly daring, because he could think of nothing else to do, answering a sudden thought that came to him, he drew slowly out the phial of Galadriel and held it up. Its white light quickened swiftly, and the shadows under the dark arch fled. The monstrous Watchers sat there cold and still, revealed in all their hideous shape. For a moment Sam caught a glitter in the black stones of their eyes, the very malice of which made him quail; but slowly he felt their will waver and crumble into fear.

He sprang past them; but even as he did so, thrusting the phial back into his bosom, he was aware, as plainly as if a bar of steel had snapped to behind him, that their vigilance was renewed. And from those evil heads there came a high shrill cry that echoed in the towering walls before him. Far up above, like an answering signal, a harsh bell clanged a single stroke.

'That's done it!' said Sam. 'Now I've rung the front-door bell! Well, come on somebody!' he cried. 'Tell Captain Shagrat that the great Elf-warrior has called, with his elf-sword too!'

There was no answer. Sam strode forward. Sting glittered blue in his hand. The courtyard lay in deep shadow, but he could see that the pavement was strewn with bodies. Right at his feet were two orc-archers with knives sticking in their backs. Beyond lay many more shapes; some singly as they had been hewn down or shot; others in pairs, still grappling one another, dead in the very throes of stabbing, throttling, biting. The stones were slippery with dark blood.

Two liveries Sam noticed, one marked by the Red Eye, the other by a Moon disfigured with a ghastly face of death; but he did not stop to look more closely. Across the court a great door at the foot of the Tower stood half open, and a red light came through; a large orc lay dead upon the threshold. Sam sprang over the body and went in; and then he peered about at a loss.

A wide and echoing passage led back from the door towards the mountain-side. It was dimly lit with torches flaring in brackets on the walls but its distant end was lost in gloom. Many doors and openings could be seen on this side and that; but it was empty save for two or three more bodies sprawling on the floor. From what he had heard of the captains' talk Sam knew that, dead or alive, Frodo would most likely be found in a chamber high up in the turret far above; but he might search for a day before he found the way.

'It'll be near the back, I guess,' Sam muttered. 'The whole Tower climbs backwards-like. And anyway I'd better follow these lights.'

He advanced down the passage, but slowly now, each step more reluctant. Terror was beginning to grip him again. There was no sound save the rap of his feet, which seemed to grow to an echoing noise, like the slapping of great hands upon the stones. The dead bodies; the emptiness; the dank black walls that in the torchlight seemed to drip with blood; the fear of sudden death lurking in doorway or shadow; and behind all his mind the waiting watchful malice at the gate: it was almost more than he could screw himself to face. He would have welcomed a fight – with not too many enemies at a time – rather than this hideous brooding uncertainty. He forced himself to think of Frodo, lying bound or in pain or dead somewhere in this dreadful place. He went on.

He had passed beyond the torchlight, almost to a great arched door at the end of the passage, the inner side of the under-gate, as he rightly guessed, when there came from high above a dreadful choking shriek. He stopped short. Then he heard feet coming. Someone was running in great haste down an echoing stairway overhead.

His will was too weak and slow to restrain his hand. It dragged at the chain and clutched the Ring. But Sam did not put it on; for even as he clasped it to his breast, an orc came clattering down. Leaping out of a dark opening at the right, it ran towards him. It was no more than six paces from him when, lifting its head, it saw him; and Sam could hear its gasping breath and see the glare in its bloodshot eyes. It stopped short aghast. For what it saw was not a small frightened hobbit trying to hold a steady sword: it saw a great silent shape, cloaked in a grey shadow, looming against the wavering light behind; in one hand it held a sword, the very light of which was a bitter pain, the other was clutched at its breast, but held concealed some nameless menace of power and doom.

For a moment the orc crouched, and then with a hideous yelp of fear it turned and fled back as it had come. Never was any dog more heartened when its enemy turned tail than Sam at this unexpected flight. With a shout he gave chase.

'Yes! The Elf-warrior is loose!' he cried. 'I'm coming. Just you show me the way up, or I'll skin you!'

But the orc was in its own haunts, nimble and well-fed. Sam was a stranger, hungry and weary. The stairs were high and steep and winding. Sam's breath began to come in gasps. The orc had soon passed out of sight, and now only faintly could be heard the slapping of its feet as it went on and up. Every now and again it gave a yell, and the echo ran along the walls. But slowly all sound of it died away.

Sam plodded on. He felt that he was on the right road, and his spirits had risen a good deal. He thrust the Ring away and tightened his belt. 'Well, well!' he said. 'If only they all take such a dislike to me and my Sting, this may turn out better than I hoped. And anyway it looks as if Shagrat, Gorbag, and company have done nearly all my job for me. Except for that little frightened rat, I do believe there's nobody left alive in the place!'

And with that he stopped, brought up hard, as if he had hit his head against the stone wall. The full meaning of what he had said struck him like a blow. Nobody left alive! Whose had been that horrible dying shriek? 'Frodo, Frodo! Master!' he cried half sobbing. 'If they've killed you, what shall I do? Well, I'm coming at last, right to the top, to see what I must.'

Up, up he went. It was dark save for an occasional torch flaring at a turn, or beside some opening that led into the higher levels of the Tower. Sam tried to count the steps, but after two hundred he lost his reckoning. He was moving quietly now; for he thought that he could hear the sound of voices talking, still some way above. More than one rat remained alive it seemed.

All at once, when he felt that he could pump out no more breath, nor force his knees to bend again, the stair ended. He stood still. The voices were now loud and near. Sam peered about. He had climbed right to the flat roof of the third and highest tier of the Tower: an open space, about twenty yards across, with a low parapet. There the stair was covered by a small domed chamber in the midst of the roof, with low doors facing east and west. Eastward Sam could see the plain of Mordor vast and dark below, and the burning mountain far away. A fresh turmoil was surging in its deep wells, and the rivers of fire blazed so fiercely that even at this distance of many miles the light of them lit the tower-top with a red glare. Westward the view was blocked by the base of the great turret that stood at the back of this upper court and reared its horn high above the crest of the encircling hills. Light gleamed in a window-slit. Its door was not ten yards from where Sam stood. It was open but dark, and from just within its shadow the voices came.

At first Sam did not listen; he took a pace out of the eastward door and looked about. At once he saw that up here the fighting had been fiercest. All the court was choked with dead orcs, or their severed and scattered heads and limbs. The place stank of death. A snarl followed by a blow and a cry sent him darting back into hiding. An orc-voice rose in anger, and he knew it again at once, harsh, brutal, cold. It was Shagrat speaking, Captain of the Tower.

'You won't go again, you say? Curse you, Snaga, you little maggot! If you think I'm so damaged that it's safe to flout me, you're mistaken. Come here, and I'll squeeze your eyes out, like I did to Radbug just now. And when some new lads come, I'll deal with you: I'll send you to Shelob.'

'They won't come, not before you're dead anyway,' answered Snaga surlily. 'I've told you twice that Gorbag's swine got to the gate first, and none of ours got out. Lagduf and Muzgash ran through, but they were shot. I saw it from a window, I tell you. And they were the last.'

'Then you must go. I must stay here anyway. But I'm hurt. The Black Pits take that filthy rebel Gorbag!' Shagrat's voice trailed off into a string of foul names and curses. 'I gave him better than I got, but he knifed me, the dung, before I throttled him. You must go, or I'll eat you. News must get through to Lugbúrz, or we'll both be for the Black Pits. Yes, you too. You won't escape by skulking here.'

'I'm not going down those stairs again,' growled Snaga, 'be you captain or no. Nar! Keep your hands off your knife, or I'll put an arrow in your guts. You won't be a captain long when They hear about all these goings-on. I've fought for the Tower against those stinking Morgul-rats, but a nice mess you two precious captains have made of things, fighting over the swag.'

'That's enough from you,' snarled Shagrat. 'I had my orders. It was Gorbag started it, trying to pinch that pretty shirt.'

'Well, you put his back up, being so high and mighty. And he had more sense than you anyway. He told you more than once that the most dangerous of these spies was still loose, and you wouldn't listen. And you won't listen now. Gorbag was right, I tell you. There's a great fighter about, one of those bloody-handed Elves, or one of the filthy *tarks*.* He's coming here, I tell you. You heard the bell. He's got past the Watchers, and that's *tark's* work. He's on the stairs. And until he's off them, I'm not going down. Not if you were a Nazgûl, I wouldn't.'

'So that's it, is it?' yelled Shagrat. 'You'll do this, and you'll not do that? And when he does come, you'll bolt and leave me? No, you won't! I'll put red maggot-holes in your belly first.'

Out of the turret-door the smaller orc came flying. Behind him came Shagrat, a large orc with long arms that, as he ran crouching, reached to the

---

* See Appendix F, p. 1105.

ground. But one arm hung limp and seemed to be bleeding; the other hugged a large black bundle. In the red glare Sam, cowering behind the stair-door, caught a glimpse of his evil face as it passed: it was scored as if by rending claws and smeared with blood; slaver dripped from its protruding fangs; the mouth snarled like an animal.

As far as Sam could see, Shagrat hunted Snaga round the roof, until ducking and eluding him the smaller orc with a yelp darted back into the turret and disappeared. Then Shagrat halted. Out of the eastward door Sam could see him now by the parapet, panting, his left claw clenching and unclenching feebly. He put the bundle on the floor and with his right claw drew out a long red knife and spat on it. Going to the parapet he leaned over, looking down into the outer court far below. Twice he shouted but no answer came.

Suddenly, as Shagrat was stooped over the battlement, his back to the rooftop, Sam to his amazement saw that one of the sprawling bodies was moving. It was crawling. It put out a claw and clutched the bundle. It staggered up. In its other hand it held a broad-headed spear with a short broken haft. It was poised for a stabbing thrust. But at that very moment a hiss escaped its teeth, a gasp of pain or hate. Quick as a snake Shagrat slipped aside, twisted round, and drove his knife into his enemy's throat.

'Got you, Gorbag!' he cried. 'Not quite dead, eh? Well, I'll finish my job now.' He sprang on to the fallen body, and stamped and trampled it in his fury, stooping now and again to stab and slash it with his knife. Satisfied at last, he threw back his head and let out a horrible gurgling yell of triumph. Then he licked his knife, and put it between his teeth, and catching up the bundle he came loping towards the near door of the stairs.

Sam had no time to think. He might have slipped out of the other door, but hardly without being seen; and he could not have played hide-and-seek with this hideous orc for long. He did what was probably the best thing he could have done. He sprang out to meet Shagrat with a shout. He was no longer holding the Ring, but it was there, a hidden power, a cowing menace to the slaves of Mordor; and in his hand was Sting, and its light smote the eyes of the orc like the glitter of cruel stars in the terrible elf-countries, the dream of which was a cold fear to all his kind. And Shagrat could not both fight and keep hold of his treasure. He stopped, growling, baring his fangs. Then once more, orc-fashion, he leapt aside, and as Sam sprang at him, using the heavy bundle as both shield and weapon, he thrust it hard into his enemy's face. Sam staggered, and before he could recover, Shagrat darted past and down the stairs.

Sam ran after him, cursing, but he did not go far. Soon the thought of Frodo returned to him, and he remembered that the other orc had gone back into the turret. Here was another dreadful choice, and he had no time to ponder it. If Shagrat got away, he would soon get help and come back. But if

Sam pursued him, the other orc might do some horrible deed up there. And anyway Sam might miss Shagrat or be killed by him. He turned quickly and ran back up the stairs. 'Wrong again, I expect,' he sighed. 'But it's my job to go right up to the top first, whatever happens afterwards.'

Away below Shagrat went leaping down the stairs and out over the court and through the gate, bearing his precious burden. If Sam could have seen him and known the grief that his escape would bring, he might have quailed. But now his mind was set on the last stage of his search. He came cautiously to the turret-door and stepped inside. It opened into darkness. But soon his staring eyes were aware of a dim light at his right hand. It came from an opening that led to another stairway, dark and narrow: it appeared to go winding up the turret along the inside of its round outer wall. A torch was glimmering from somewhere up above.

Softly Sam began to climb. He came to the guttering torch, fixed above a door on his left that faced a window-slit looking out westward: one of the red eyes that he and Frodo had seen from down below by the tunnel's mouth. Quickly Sam passed the door and hurried on to the second storey, dreading at any moment to be attacked and to feel throttling fingers seize his throat from behind. He came next to a window looking east and another torch above the door to a passage through the middle of the turret. The door was open, the passage dark save for the glimmer of the torch and the red glare from outside filtering through the window-slit. But here the stair stopped and climbed no further. Sam crept into the passage. On either side there was a low door; both were closed and locked. There was no sound at all.

'A dead end,' muttered Sam; 'and after all my climb! This can't be the top of the tower. But what can I do now?'

He ran back to the lower storey and tried the door. It would not move. He ran up again, and sweat began to trickle down his face. He felt that even minutes were precious, but one by one they escaped; and he could do nothing. He cared no longer for Shagrat or Snaga or any other orc that was ever spawned. He longed only for his master, for one sight of his face or one touch of his hand.

At last, weary and feeling finally defeated, he sat on a step below the level of the passage-floor and bowed his head into his hands. It was quiet, horribly quiet. The torch, that was already burning low when he arrived, sputtered and went out; and he felt the darkness cover him like a tide. And then softly, to his own surprise, there at the vain end of his long journey and his grief, moved by what thought in his heart he could not tell, Sam began to sing.

His voice sounded thin and quavering in the cold dark tower: the voice of a forlorn and weary hobbit that no listening orc could possibly mistake for the clear song of an Elven-lord. He murmured old childish tunes out of the Shire, and snatches of Mr. Bilbo's rhymes that came into his mind like fleeting glimpses of the country of his home. And then suddenly new strength rose in him, and his voice rang out, while words of his own came unbidden to fit the simple tune.

> *In western lands beneath the Sun*
> *the flowers may rise in Spring,*
> *the trees may bud, the waters run,*
> *the merry finches sing.*
> *Or there maybe 'tis cloudless night*
> *and swaying beeches bear*
> *the Elven-stars as jewels white*
> *amid their branching hair.*
>
> *Though here at journey's end I lie*
> *in darkness buried deep,*
> *beyond all towers strong and high,*
> *beyond all mountains steep,*
> *above all shadows rides the Sun*
> *and Stars for ever dwell:*
> *I will not say the Day is done,*
> *nor bid the Stars farewell.*

'Beyond all towers strong and high,' he began again, and then he stopped short. He thought that he had heard a faint voice answering him. But now he could hear nothing. Yes, he could hear something, but not a voice. Footsteps were approaching. Now a door was being opened quietly in the passage above; the hinges creaked. Sam crouched down listening. The door closed with a dull thud; and then a snarling orc-voice rang out.

'Ho la! You up there, you dunghill rat! Stop your squeaking, or I'll come and deal with you. D'you hear?'

There was no answer.

'All right,' growled Snaga. 'But I'll come and have a look at you all the same, and see what you're up to.'

The hinges creaked again, and Sam, now peering over the corner of the passage-threshold, saw a flicker of light in an open doorway, and the dim shape of an orc coming out. He seemed to be carrying a ladder. Suddenly the answer dawned on Sam: the topmost chamber was reached by a trap-door in the roof of the passage. Snaga thrust the ladder upwards, steadied it, and then clambered out of sight. Sam heard a bolt drawn back. Then he heard the hideous voice speaking again.

'You lie quiet, or you'll pay for it! You've not got long to live in peace, I guess; but if you don't want the fun to begin right now, keep your trap shut, see? There's a reminder for you!' There was a sound like the crack of a whip. At that rage blazed in Sam's heart to a sudden fury. He sprang up, ran, and went up the ladder like a cat. His head came out in the middle of the floor of a large round chamber. A red lamp hung from its roof; the westward window-slit was high and dark. Something was lying on the floor by the wall under the window, but over it a black orc-shape was straddled. It raised a whip a second time, but the blow never fell.

With a cry Sam leapt across the floor, Sting in hand. The orc wheeled round, but before it could make a move Sam slashed its whip-hand from its arm. Howling with pain and fear but desperate the orc charged head-down at him. Sam's next blow went wide, and thrown off his balance he fell backwards, clutching at the orc as it stumbled over him. Before he could scramble up he heard a cry and a thud. The orc in its wild haste had tripped on the ladder-head and fallen through the open trap-door. Sam gave no more thought to it. He ran to the figure huddled on the floor. It was Frodo.

He was naked, lying as if in a swoon on a heap of filthy rags: his arm was flung up, shielding his head, and across his side there ran an ugly whip-weal. 'Frodo! Mr. Frodo, my dear!' cried Sam, tears almost blinding him. 'It's Sam, I've come!' He half lifted his master and hugged him to his breast. Frodo opened his eyes.

'Am I still dreaming?' he muttered. 'But the other dreams were horrible.'

'You're not dreaming at all, Master,' said Sam. 'It's real. It's me. I've come.'

'I can hardly believe it,' said Frodo, clutching him. 'There was an orc with a whip, and then it turns into Sam! Then I wasn't dreaming after all when I heard that singing down below, and I tried to answer? Was it you?'

'It was indeed, Mr. Frodo. I'd given up hope, almost. I couldn't find you.'

'Well, you have now, Sam, dear Sam,' said Frodo, and he lay back in Sam's gentle arms, closing his eyes, like a child at rest when night-fears are driven away by some loved voice or hand.

Sam felt that he could sit like that in endless happiness; but it was not allowed. It was not enough for him to find his master, he had still to try and save him. He kissed Frodo's forehead. 'Come! Wake up, Mr. Frodo!' he said, trying to sound as cheerful as he had when he drew back the curtains at Bag End on a summer's morning.

Frodo sighed and sat up. 'Where are we? How did I get here?' he asked.

'There's no time for tales till we get somewhere else, Mr. Frodo,' said Sam. 'But you're in the top of that tower you and me saw from away down by the tunnel before the orcs got you. How long ago that was I don't know. More than a day, I guess.'

'Only that?' said Frodo. 'It seems weeks. You must tell me all about it, if we get a chance. Something hit me, didn't it? And I fell into darkness and foul dreams, and woke and found that waking was worse. Orcs were all round me. I think they had just been pouring some horrible burning drink down my throat. My head grew clear, but I was aching and weary. They stripped me of everything; and then two great brutes came and questioned me, questioned me until I thought I should go mad, standing over me, gloating, fingering their knives. I'll never forget their claws and eyes.'

'You won't, if you talk about them, Mr. Frodo,' said Sam. 'And if we don't want to see them again, the sooner we get going the better. Can you walk?'

'Yes, I can walk,' said Frodo, getting up slowly. 'I am not hurt, Sam. Only I feel very tired, and I've a pain here.' He put his hand to the back of his neck above his left shoulder. He stood up, and it looked to Sam as if he was clothed in flame: his naked skin was scarlet in the light of the lamp above. Twice he paced across the floor.

'That's better!' he said, his spirits rising a little. 'I didn't dare to move when I was left alone, or one of the guards came. Until the yelling and fighting began. The two big brutes: they quarrelled, I think. Over me and my things. I lay here terrified. And then all went deadly quiet, and that was worse.'

'Yes, they quarrelled, seemingly,' said Sam. 'There must have been a couple of hundred of the dirty creatures in this place. A bit of a tall order for Sam Gamgee, as you might say. But they've done all the killing of themselves. That's lucky, but it's too long to make a song about, till we're out of here. Now what's to be done? You can't go walking in the Black Land in naught but your skin, Mr. Frodo.'

'They've taken everything, Sam,' said Frodo. 'Everything I had. Do you understand? *Everything!*' He cowered on the floor again with bowed head, as his own words brought home to him the fullness of the disaster, and despair overwhelmed him. 'The quest has failed, Sam. Even if we get out of here, we can't escape. Only Elves can escape. Away, away out of Middle-earth, far away over the Sea. If even that is wide enough to keep the Shadow out.'

'No, *not* everything, Mr. Frodo. And it hasn't failed, not yet. I took it, Mr. Frodo, begging your pardon. And I've kept it safe. It's round my neck now, and a terrible burden it is, too.' Sam fumbled for the Ring and its chain. 'But I suppose you must take it back.' Now it had come to it, Sam felt reluctant to give up the Ring and burden his master with it again.

'You've got it?' gasped Frodo. 'You've got it here? Sam, you're a marvel!' Then quickly and strangely his tone changed. 'Give it to me!' he cried, standing up, holding out a trembling hand. 'Give it me at once! You can't have it!'

'All right, Mr. Frodo,' said Sam, rather startled. 'Here it is!' Slowly he drew the Ring out and passed the chain over his head. 'But you're in the land of Mordor now, sir; and when you get out, you'll see the Fiery Mountain and all. You'll find the Ring very dangerous now, and very hard to bear. If it's too hard a job, I could share it with you, maybe?'

'No, no!' cried Frodo, snatching the Ring and chain from Sam's hands. 'No you won't, you thief!' He panted, staring at Sam with eyes wide with fear and enmity. Then suddenly, clasping the Ring in one clenched fist, he stood aghast. A mist seemed to clear from his eyes, and he passed a hand over his aching brow. The hideous vision had seemed so real to him, half bemused as he was still with wound and fear. Sam had changed before his very eyes into an orc again, leering and pawing at his treasure, a foul little creature with greedy eyes and slobbering mouth. But now the vision had passed. There was Sam kneeling before him, his face wrung with pain, as if he had been stabbed in the heart; tears welled from his eyes.

'O Sam!' cried Frodo. 'What have I said? What have I done? Forgive me! After all you have done. It is the horrible power of the Ring. I wish it had never, never, been found. But don't mind me, Sam. I must carry the burden to the end. It can't be altered. You can't come between me and this doom.'

'That's all right, Mr. Frodo,' said Sam, rubbing his sleeve across his eyes. 'I understand. But I can still help, can't I? I've got to get you out of here. At once, see! But first you want some clothes and gear, and then some food. The clothes will be the easiest part. As we're in Mordor, we'd best dress up Mordor-fashion; and anyway there isn't no choice. It'll have to be orc-stuff for you, Mr. Frodo, I'm afraid. And for me too. If we go together, we'd best match. Now put this round you!'

Sam unclasped his grey cloak and cast it about Frodo's shoulders. Then unslinging his pack he laid it on the floor. He drew Sting from its sheath. Hardly a flicker was to be seen upon its blade. 'I was forgetting this, Mr. Frodo,' he said. 'No, they didn't get everything! You lent me Sting, if you remember, and the Lady's glass. I've got them both still. But lend them to me a little longer, Mr. Frodo. I must go and see what I can find. You stay here. Walk about a bit and ease your legs. I shan't be long. I shan't have to go far.'

'Take care, Sam!' said Frodo. 'And be quick! There may be orcs still alive, lurking in wait.'

'I've got to chance it,' said Sam. He stepped to the trap-door and slipped down the ladder. In a minute his head reappeared. He threw a long knife on the floor.

'There's something that might be useful,' he said. 'He's dead: the one that whipped you. Broke his neck, it seems, in his hurry. Now you draw up the ladder, if you can, Mr. Frodo; and don't you let it down till you hear me call the pass-word. *Elbereth* I'll call. What the Elves say. No orc would say that.'

Frodo sat for a while and shivered, dreadful fears chasing one another through his mind. Then he got up, drew the grey elven-cloak about him, and to keep his mind occupied, began to walk to and fro, prying and peering into every corner of his prison.

It was not very long, though fear made it seem an hour at least, before he heard Sam's voice calling softly from below: *Elbereth, Elbereth.* Frodo let down the light ladder. Up came Sam, puffing, heaving a great bundle on his head. He let it fall with a thud.

'Quick now, Mr. Frodo!' he said. 'I've had a bit of a search to find anything small enough for the likes of us. We'll have to make do. But we must hurry. I've met nothing alive, and I've seen nothing, but I'm not easy. I think this place is being watched. I can't explain it, but well: it feels to me as if one of those foul flying Riders was about, up in the blackness where he can't be seen.'

He opened the bundle. Frodo looked in disgust at the contents, but there was nothing for it: he had to put the things on, or go naked. There were long hairy breeches of some unclean beast-fell, and a tunic of dirty leather. He drew them on. Over the tunic went a coat of stout ring-mail, short for a full-sized orc, too long for Frodo and heavy. About it he clasped a belt, at which there hung a short sheath holding a broad-bladed stabbing-sword. Sam had brought several orc-helmets. One of them fitted Frodo well enough, a black cap with iron rim, and iron hoops covered with leather upon which the Evil Eye was painted in red above the beaklike nose-guard.

'The Morgul-stuff, Gorbag's gear, was a better fit and better made,' said Sam; 'but it wouldn't do, I guess, to go carrying his tokens into Mordor, not after this business here. Well, there you are, Mr. Frodo. A perfect little orc, if I may make so bold – at least you would be, if we could cover your face with a mask, give you longer arms, and make you bow-legged. This will hide some of the tell-tales.' He put a large black cloak round Frodo's shoulders. 'Now you're ready! You can pick up a shield as we go.'

'What about you, Sam?' said Frodo. 'Aren't we going to match?'

'Well, Mr. Frodo, I've been thinking,' said Sam. 'I'd best not leave any of my stuff behind, and we can't destroy it. And I can't wear orc-mail over all my clothes, can I? I'll just have to cover up.'

He knelt down and carefully folded his elven-cloak. It went into a surprisingly small roll. This he put into his pack that lay on the floor. Standing up, he slung it behind his back, put an orc-helm on his head, and cast another black cloak about his shoulders. 'There!' he said. 'Now we match, near enough. And now we must be off!'

'I can't go all the way at a run, Sam,' said Frodo with a wry smile. 'I hope you've made inquiries about inns along the road? Or have you forgotten about food and drink?'

'Save me, but so I had!' said Sam. He whistled in dismay. 'Bless me, Mr.

Frodo, but you've gone and made me that hungry and thirsty! I don't know when drop or morsel last passed my lips. I'd forgotten it, trying to find you. But let me think! Last time I looked I'd got about enough of that waybread, and of what Captain Faramir gave us, to keep me on my legs for a couple of weeks at a pinch. But if there's a drop left in my bottle, there's no more. That's not going to be enough for two, nohow. Don't orcs eat, and don't they drink? Or do they just live on foul air and poison?'

'No, they eat and drink, Sam. The Shadow that bred them can only mock, it cannot make: not real new things of its own. I don't think it gave life to the orcs, it only ruined them and twisted them; and if they are to live at all, they have to live like other living creatures. Foul waters and foul meats they'll take, if they can get no better, but not poison. They've fed me, and so I'm better off than you. There must be food and water somewhere in this place.'

'But there's no time to look for them,' said Sam.

'Well, things are a bit better than you think,' said Frodo. 'I have had a bit of luck while you were away. Indeed they did not take everything. I've found my food-bag among some rags on the floor. They've rummaged it, of course. But I guess they disliked the very look and smell of the *lembas*, worse than Gollum did. It's scattered about and some of it is trampled and broken, but I've gathered it together. It's not far short of what you've got. But they've taken Faramir's food, and they've slashed up my water-bottle.'

'Well, there's no more to be said,' said Sam. 'We've got enough to start on. But the water's going to be a bad business. But come, Mr. Frodo! Off we go, or a whole lake of it won't do us any good!'

'Not till you've had a mouthful, Sam,' said Frodo. 'I won't budge. Here, take this elven-cake, and drink that last drop in your bottle! The whole thing is quite hopeless, so it's no good worrying about tomorrow. It probably won't come.'

At last they started. Down the ladder they climbed, and then Sam took it and laid it in the passage beside the huddled body of the fallen orc. The stair was dark, but on the roof-top the glare of the Mountain could still be seen, though it was dying down now to a sullen red. They picked up two shields to complete their disguise and then went on.

Down the great stairway they plodded. The high chamber of the turret behind, where they had met again, seemed almost homely: they were out in the open again now, and terror ran along the walls. All might be dead in the Tower of Cirith Ungol, but it was steeped in fear and evil still.

At length they came to the door upon the outer court, and they halted. Even from where they stood they felt the malice of the Watchers beating on them, black silent shapes on either side of the gate through which the glare of Mordor dimly showed. As they threaded their way among the hideous bodies of the orcs each step became more difficult. Before they even reached the archway they were brought to a stand. To move an inch further was a pain and weariness to will and limb.

Frodo had no strength for such a battle. He sank to the ground. 'I can't go on, Sam,' he murmured. 'I'm going to faint. I don't know what's come over me.'

'I do, Mr. Frodo. Hold up now! It's the gate. There's some devilry there. But I got through, and I'm going to get out. It can't be more dangerous than before. Now for it!'

Sam drew out the elven-glass of Galadriel again. As if to do honour to his hardihood, and to grace with splendour his faithful brown hobbit-hand that had done such deeds, the phial blazed forth suddenly, so that all the shadowy court was lit with a dazzling radiance like lightning; but it remained steady and did not pass.

'*Gilthoniel, A Elbereth!*' Sam cried. For, why he did not know, his thought sprang back suddenly to the Elves in the Shire, and the song that drove away the Black Rider in the trees.

'*Aiya elenion ancalima!*' cried Frodo once again behind him.

The will of the Watchers was broken with a suddenness like the snapping of a cord, and Frodo and Sam stumbled forward. Then they ran. Through the gate and past the great seated figures with their glittering eyes. There was a crack. The keystone of the arch crashed almost on their heels, and the wall above crumbled, and fell in ruin. Only by a hair did they escape. A bell clanged; and from the Watchers there went up a high and dreadful wail. Far up above in the darkness it was answered. Out of the black sky there came dropping like a bolt a winged shape, rending the clouds with a ghastly shriek.

CHAPTER II

THE LAND OF SHADOW

Sam had just wits enough left to thrust the phial back into his breast. 'Run, Mr. Frodo!' he cried. 'No, not that way! There's a sheer drop over the wall. Follow me!'

Down the road from the gate they fled. In fifty paces, with a swift bend round a jutting bastion of the cliff, it took them out of sight from the Tower. They had escaped for the moment. Cowering back against the rock they drew breath, and then they clutched at their hearts. Perching now on the wall beside the ruined gate the Nazgûl sent out its deadly cries. All the cliffs echoed.

In terror they stumbled on. Soon the road bent sharply eastward again and exposed them for a dreadful moment to view from the Tower. As they flitted across they glanced back and saw the great black shape upon the battlement; then they plunged down between high rock-walls in a cutting that fell steeply to join the Morgul-road. They came to the way-meeting. There was still no sign of orcs, nor of an answer to the cry of the Nazgûl; but they knew that the silence would not last long. At any moment now the hunt would begin.

'This won't do, Sam,' said Frodo. 'If we were real orcs, we ought to be dashing back to the Tower, not running away. The first enemy we meet will know us. We must get off this road somehow.'

'But we can't,' said Sam, 'not without wings.'

The eastern faces of the Ephel Dúath were sheer, falling in cliff and precipice to the black trough that lay between them and the inner ridge. A short way beyond the way-meeting, after another steep incline, a flying bridge of stone leapt over the chasm and bore the road across into the tumbled slopes and glens of the Morgai. With a desperate spurt Frodo and Sam dashed along the bridge; but they had hardly reached its further end when they heard the hue and cry begin. Away behind them, now high above on the mountain-side, loomed the Tower of Cirith Ungol, its stones glowing dully. Suddenly its harsh bell clanged again, and then broke into a shattering peal. Horns sounded. And now from beyond the bridge-end came answering cries. Down in the dark trough, cut off from the dying glare of Orodruin, Frodo and Sam could not see ahead, but already they heard the tramp of iron-shod feet, and upon the road there rang the swift clatter of hoofs.

'Quick, Sam! Over we go!' cried Frodo. They scrambled on to the low parapet of the bridge. Fortunately there was no longer any dreadful drop into the gulf, for the slopes of the Morgai had already risen almost to the level of the road; but it was too dark for them to guess the depth of the fall.

'Well, here goes, Mr. Frodo,' said Sam. 'Good-bye!'

He let go. Frodo followed. And even as they fell they heard the rush of horsemen sweeping over the bridge and the rattle of orc-feet running up behind. But Sam would have laughed, if he had dared. Half fearing a breaking plunge down on to unseen rocks the hobbits landed, in a drop of no more than a dozen feet, with a thud and a crunch into the last thing that they had expected: a tangle of thorny bushes. There Sam lay still, softly sucking a scratched hand.

When the sound of hoof and foot had passed he ventured a whisper. 'Bless me, Mr. Frodo, but I didn't know as anything grew in Mordor! But if I had a'known, this is just what I'd have looked for. These thorns must be a foot long by the feel of them; they've stuck through everything I've got on. Wish I'd a'put that mailshirt on!'

'Orc-mail doesn't keep these thorns out,' said Frodo. 'Not even a leather jerkin is any good.'

They had a struggle to get out of the thicket. The thorns and briars were as tough as wire and as clinging as claws. Their cloaks were rent and tattered before they broke free at last.

'Now down we go, Sam,' Frodo whispered. 'Down into the valley quick, and then turn northward, as soon as ever we can.'

Day was coming again in the world outside, and far beyond the glooms of Mordor the Sun was climbing over the eastern rim of Middle-earth; but here all was still dark as night. The Mountain smouldered and its fires went out. The glare faded from the cliffs. The easterly wind that had been blowing ever since they left Ithilien now seemed dead. Slowly and painfully they clambered down, groping, stumbling, scrambling among rock and briar and dead wood in the blind shadows, down and down until they could go no further.

At length they stopped, and sat side by side, their backs against a boulder. Both were sweating. 'If Shagrat himself was to offer me a glass of water, I'd shake his hand,' said Sam.

'Don't say such things!' said Frodo. 'It only makes it worse.' Then he stretched himself out, dizzy and weary, and he spoke no more for a while. At last with a struggle he got up again. To his amazement he found that Sam was asleep. 'Wake up, Sam!' he said. 'Come on! It's time we made another effort.'

Sam scrambled to his feet. 'Well I never!' he said. 'I must have dropped off. It's a long time, Mr. Frodo, since I had a proper sleep, and my eyes just closed down on their own.'

Frodo now led the way, northward as near as he could guess, among the stones and boulders lying thick at the bottom of the great ravine. But presently he stopped again.

'It's no good, Sam,' he said. 'I can't manage it. This mail-shirt, I mean. Not in my present state. Even my mithril-coat seemed heavy when I was tired. This is far heavier. And what's the use of it? We shan't win through by fighting.'

'But we may have some to do,' said Sam. 'And there's knives and stray arrows. That Gollum isn't dead, for one thing. I don't like to think of you with naught but a bit of leather between you and a stab in the dark.'

'Look here, Sam dear lad,' said Frodo: 'I am tired, weary, I haven't a hope left. But I have to go on trying to get to the Mountain, as long as I can move. The Ring is enough. This extra weight is killing me. It must go. But don't think I'm ungrateful. I hate to think of the foul work you must have had among the bodies to find it for me.'

'Don't talk about it, Mr. Frodo. Bless you! I'd carry you on my back, if I could. Let it go then!'

Frodo laid aside his cloak and took off the orc-mail and flung it away. He shivered a little. 'What I really need is something warm,' he said. 'It's gone cold, or else I've caught a chill.'

'You can have my cloak, Mr. Frodo,' said Sam. He unslung his pack and took out the elven-cloak. 'How's this, Mr. Frodo?' he said. 'You wrap that orc-rag close round you, and put the belt outside it. Then this can go over all. It don't look quite orc-fashion, but it'll keep you warmer; and I daresay it'll keep you from harm better than any other gear. It was made by the Lady.'

Frodo took the cloak and fastened the brooch. 'That's better!' he said. 'I feel much lighter. I can go on now. But this blind dark seems to be getting into my heart. As I lay in prison, Sam, I tried to remember the Brandywine, and Woody End, and The Water running through the mill at Hobbiton. But I can't see them now.'

'There now, Mr. Frodo, it's you that's talking of water this time!' said Sam. 'If only the Lady could see us or hear us, I'd say to her: "Your Ladyship, all we want is light and water: just clean water and plain daylight, better than any jewels, begging your pardon." But it's a long way to Lórien.' Sam sighed and waved his hand towards the heights of the Ephel Dúath, now only to be guessed as a deeper blackness against the black sky.

They started off again. They had not gone far when Frodo paused. 'There's a Black Rider over us,' he said. 'I can feel it. We had better keep still for a while.'

Crouched under a great boulder they sat facing back westward and did not speak for some time. Then Frodo breathed a sigh of relief. 'It's passed,' he said. They stood up, and then they both stared in wonder. Away to their left, southward, against a sky that was turning grey, the peaks and high ridges of the great range began to appear dark and black, visible shapes. Light was growing behind them. Slowly it crept towards the North. There was battle far above in the high spaces of the air. The billowing clouds of Mordor were being driven back, their edges tattering as a wind out of the living world came up and swept the fumes and smokes towards the dark land of their home. Under the lifting skirts of the dreary canopy dim light leaked into Mordor like pale morning through the grimed window of a prison.

'Look at it, Mr. Frodo!' said Sam. 'Look at it! The wind's changed. Something's happening. He's not having it all his own way. His darkness is breaking up out in the world there. I wish I could see what is going on!'

It was the morning of the fifteenth of March, and over the Vale of Anduin the Sun was rising above the eastern shadow, and the south-west wind was blowing. Théoden lay dying on the Pelennor Fields.

As Frodo and Sam stood and gazed, the rim of light spread all along the line of the Ephel Dúath, and then they saw a shape, moving at a great speed out of the West, at first only a black speck against the glimmering strip above the mountain-tops, but growing, until it plunged like a bolt into the dark canopy and passed high above them. As it went it sent out a long shrill cry, the voice of a Nazgûl; but this cry no longer held any terror for them: it was a cry of woe and dismay, ill tidings for the Dark Tower. The Lord of the Ringwraiths had met his doom.

'What did I tell you? Something's happening!' cried Sam. '"The war's going well," said Shagrat; but Gorbag he wasn't so sure. And he was right there too. Things are looking up, Mr. Frodo. Haven't you got some hope now?'

'Well no, not much, Sam,' Frodo sighed. 'That's away beyond the mountains. We're going east not west. And I'm so tired. And the Ring is so heavy, Sam. And I begin to see it in my mind all the time, like a great wheel of fire.'

Sam's quick spirits sank again at once. He looked at his master anxiously, and he took his hand. 'Come, Mr. Frodo!' he said. 'I've got one thing I wanted: a bit of light. Enough to help us, and yet I guess it's dangerous too. Try a bit further, and then we'll lie close and have a rest. But take a morsel to eat now, a bit of the Elves' food; it may hearten you.'

Sharing a wafer of *lembas*, and munching it as best they could with their parched mouths, Frodo and Sam plodded on. The light, though no more than a grey dusk, was now enough for them to see-that they were deep in the valley between the mountains. It sloped up gently northward, and at its bottom went the bed of a now dry and withered stream. Beyond its stony course they saw a beaten path that wound its way under the feet of the westward cliffs. Had they known, they could have reached it quicker, for it was a track that left the main Morgul-road at the western bridge-end and went down by a long stair cut in the rock to the valley's bottom. It was used by patrols or by messengers going swiftly to lesser posts and strongholds north-away, between Cirith Ungol and the narrows of Isenmouthe, the iron jaws of Carach Angren.

It was perilous for the hobbits to use such a path, but they needed speed, and Frodo felt that he could not face the toil of scrambling among the boulders or in the trackless glens of the Morgai. And he judged that northward was, maybe, the way that their hunters would least expect them to take. The road east to the plain, or the pass back westward, those they would first search most thoroughly. Only when he was well north of the Tower did he mean to turn and seek for some way to take him east, east on the last desperate stage of his journey. So now they crossed the stony bed and took to the orc-path, and for some time they marched along it. The cliffs at their left were overhung, and they could not be seen from above; but the path made many bends, and at each bend they gripped their sword-hilts and went forward cautiously.

The light grew no stronger, for Orodruin was still belching forth a great fume that, beaten upwards by the opposing airs, mounted higher and higher, until it reached a region above the wind and spread in an immeasurable roof, whose central pillar rose out of the shadows beyond their view. They had trudged for more than an hour when they heard a sound that brought them to a halt. Unbelievable, but unmistakable. Water trickling. Out of a gully on the left, so sharp and narrow that it looked as if the black cliff had been cloven by some huge axe, water came dripping down: the last remains, maybe, of some sweet rain gathered from sunlit seas, but ill-fated to fall at last upon the walls of the Black Land and wander fruitless down into the dust. Here it came out of the rock in a little falling streamlet, and flowed across the path, and turning south ran away swiftly to be lost among the dead stones.

Sam sprang towards it. 'If ever I see the Lady again, I will tell her!' he cried. 'Light and now water!' Then he stopped. 'Let me drink first, Mr. Frodo,' he said.

'All right, but there's room enough for two.'

'I didn't mean that,' said Sam. 'I mean: if it's poisonous, or something that will show its badness quick, well, better me than you, master, if you understand me.'

'I do. But I think we'll trust our luck together, Sam; or our blessing. Still, be careful now, if it's very cold!'

The water was cool but not icy, and it had an unpleasant taste, at once bitter and oily, or so they would have said at home. Here it seemed beyond all praise, and beyond fear or prudence. They drank their fill, and Sam replenished his water-bottle. After that Frodo felt easier, and they went on for several miles, until the broadening of the road and the beginnings of a rough wall along its edge warned them that they were drawing near to another orc-hold.

'This is where we turn aside, Sam,' said Frodo. 'And we must turn east.' He sighed as he looked at the gloomy ridges across the valley. 'I have just about enough strength left to find some hole away up there. And then I must rest a little.'

The river-bed was now some way below the path. They scrambled down to it, and began to cross it. To their surprise they came upon dark pools fed by threads of water trickling down from some source higher up the valley. Upon its outer marges under the westward mountains Mordor was a dying land, but it was not yet dead. And here things still grew, harsh, twisted, bitter, struggling for life. In the glens of the Morgai on the other side of the valley low scrubby trees lurked and clung, coarse grey grass-tussocks fought with the stones, and withered mosses crawled on them; and everywhere great writhing, tangled brambles sprawled. Some had long stabbing thorns, some hooked barbs that rent like knives. The sullen shrivelled leaves of a past year hung on them, grating and rattling in the sad airs, but their maggot-ridden buds were only just opening. Flies, dun or grey, or black, marked like orcs with a red eye-shaped blotch, buzzed and stung; and above the briar-thickets clouds of hungry midges danced and reeled.

'Orc-gear's no good,' said Sam waving his arms. 'I wish I'd got an orc's hide!'

At last Frodo could go no further. They had climbed up a narrow shelving ravine, but they still had a long way to go before they could even come in sight of the last craggy ridge. 'I must rest now, Sam, and sleep if I can,' said Frodo. He looked about, but there seemed nowhere even for an animal to crawl into in this dismal country. At length, tired out, they slunk under a curtain of brambles that hung down like a mat over a low rock-face.

There they sat and made such a meal as they could. Keeping back the precious *lembas* for the evil days ahead, they ate the half of what remained in Sam's bag of Faramir's provision: some dried fruit, and a small slip of cured meat; and they sipped some water. They had drunk again from the pools in the valley, but they were very thirsty again. There was a bitter tang in the air of Mordor that dried the mouth. When Sam thought of water even his hopeful spirit quailed. Beyond the Morgai there was the dreadful plain of Gorgoroth to cross.

'Now you go to sleep first, Mr. Frodo,' he said. 'It's getting dark again. I reckon this day is nearly over.'

Frodo sighed and was asleep almost before the words were spoken. Sam struggled with his own weariness, and he took Frodo's hand; and there he sat silent till deep night fell. Then at last, to keep himself awake, he crawled from the hiding-place and looked out. The land seemed full of creaking and cracking and sly noises, but there was no sound of voice or of foot. Far above the Ephel Dúath in the West the night-sky was still dim and pale. There, peeping among the cloud-wrack above a dark tor high up in the mountains, Sam saw a white star twinkle for a while. The beauty of it smote his heart, as he looked up out of the forsaken land, and hope returned to him. For like a shaft, clear and cold, the thought pierced him that in the end the Shadow was only a small and passing thing: there was light and high beauty for ever beyond its reach. His song in the Tower had been defiance rather than hope; for then he was thinking of himself. Now, for a moment, his own fate, and even his master's, ceased to trouble him. He crawled back into the brambles and laid himself by Frodo's side, and putting away all fear he cast himself into a deep untroubled sleep.

They woke together, hand in hand. Sam was almost fresh, ready for another day; but Frodo sighed. His sleep had been uneasy, full of dreams of fire, and waking brought him no comfort. Still his sleep had not been without all healing virtue: he was stronger, more able to bear his burden one stage further. They did not know the time, nor how long they had slept; but after a morsel of food and a sip of water they went on up the ravine, until it ended in a sharp slope of screes and sliding stones. There the last living things gave up their struggle; the tops of the Morgai were grassless, bare, jagged, barren as a slate.

After much wandering and search they found a way that they could climb, and with a last hundred feet of clawing scramble they were up. They came to a cleft between two dark crags, and passing through found themselves on the very edge of the last fence of Mordor. Below them, at the bottom of a fall of some fifteen hundred feet, lay the inner plain stretching away into a formless gloom beyond their sight. The wind of the world blew now from the West, and the great clouds were lifted high, floating away eastward; but still only a grey light came to the dreary fields of

Gorgoroth. There smokes trailed on the ground and lurked in hollows, and fumes leaked from fissures in the earth.

Still far away, forty miles at least, they saw Mount Doom, its feet founded in ashen ruin, its huge cone rising to a great height, where its reeking head was swathed in cloud. Its fires were now dimmed, and it stood in smouldering slumber, as threatening and dangerous as a sleeping beast. Behind it there hung a vast shadow, ominous as a thunder-cloud, the veils of Barad-dûr that was reared far away upon a long spur of the Ashen Mountains thrust down from the North. The Dark Power was deep in thought, and the Eye turned inward, pondering tidings of doubt and danger: a bright sword, and a stern and kingly face it saw, and for a while it gave little thought to other things; and all its great stronghold, gate on gate, and tower on tower, was wrapped in a brooding gloom.

Frodo and Sam gazed out in mingled loathing and wonder on this hateful land. Between them and the smoking mountain, and about it north and south, all seemed ruinous and dead, a desert burned and choked. They wondered how the Lord of this realm maintained and fed his slaves and his armies. Yet armies he had. As far as their eyes could reach, along the skirts of the Morgai and away southward, there were camps, some of tents, some ordered like small towns. One of the largest of these was right below them. Barely a mile out into the plain it clustered like some huge nest of insects, with straight dreary streets of huts and long low drab buildings. About it the ground was busy with folk going to and fro; a wide road ran from it south-east to join the Morgul-way, and along it many lines of small black shapes were hurrying.

'I don't like the look of things at all,' said Sam. 'Pretty hopeless, I call it – saving that where there's such a lot of folk there must be wells or water, not to mention food. And these are Men not Orcs, or my eyes are all wrong.'

Neither he nor Frodo knew anything of the great slave-worked fields away south in this wide realm, beyond the fumes of the Mountain by the dark sad waters of Lake Núrnen; nor of the great roads that ran away east and south to tributary lands, from which the soldiers of the Tower brought long waggon-trains of goods and booty and fresh slaves. Here in the northward regions were the mines and forges, and the musterings of long-planned war; and here the Dark Power, moving its armies like pieces on the board, was gathering them together. Its first moves, the first feelers of its strength, had been checked upon its western line, southward and northward. For the moment it withdrew them, and brought up new forces, massing them about Cirith Gorgor for an avenging stroke. And if it had also been its purpose to defend the Mountain against all approach, it could scarcely have done more.

'Well!' Sam went on. 'Whatever they have to eat and drink, we can't get it. There's no way down that I can see. And we couldn't cross all that open country crawling with enemies, even if we did get down.'

'Still we shall have to try,' said Frodo. 'It's no worse than I expected. I never hoped to get across. I can't see any hope of it now. But I've still got to do the best I can. At present that is to avoid being captured as long as possible. So we must still go northwards, I think, and see what it is like where the open plain is narrower.'

'I guess what it'll be like,' said Sam. 'Where it's narrower the Orcs and Men will just be packed closer. You'll see, Mr. Frodo.'

'I dare say I shall, if we ever get so far,' said Frodo and turned away.

They soon found that it was impossible to make their way along the crest of the Morgai, or anywhere along its higher levels, pathless as they were and scored with deep ghylls. In the end they were forced to go back down the ravine that they had climbed and seek for a way along the valley. It was rough going, for they dared not cross over to the path on the westward side. After a mile or more they saw, huddled in a hollow at the cliff's foot, the orc-hold that they had guessed was near at hand: a wall and a cluster of stone huts set about the dark mouth of a cave. There was no movement to be seen, but the hobbits crept by cautiously, keeping as much as they could to the thorn-brakes that grew thickly at this point along both sides of the old water-course.

They went two or three miles further, and the orc-hold was hidden from sight behind them; but they had hardly begun to breathe more freely again when harsh and loud they heard orc-voices. Quickly they slunk out of sight behind a brown and stunted bush. The voices drew nearer. Presently two orcs came into view. One was clad in ragged brown and was armed with a bow of horn; it was of a small breed, black-skinned, with wide and snuffling nostrils: evidently a tracker of some kind. The other was a big fighting-orc, like those of Shagrat's company, bearing the token of the Eye. He also had a bow at his back and carried a short broad-headed spear. As usual they were quarrelling, and being of different breeds they used the Common Speech after their fashion.

Hardly twenty paces from where the hobbits lurked the small orc stopped. 'Nar!' it snarled. 'I'm going home.' It pointed across the valley to the orc-hold. 'No good wearing my nose out on stones any more. There's not a trace left, I say. I've lost the scent through giving way to you. It went up into the hills, not along the valley, I tell you.'

'Not much use are you, you little snufflers?' said the big orc. 'I reckon eyes are better than your snotty noses.'

'Then what have you seen with them?' snarled the other. 'Garn! You don't even know what you're looking for.'

'Whose blame's that?' said the soldier. 'Not mine. That comes from Higher Up. First they say it's a great Elf in bright armour, then it's a sort of small dwarf-man, then it must be a pack of rebel Uruk-hai; or maybe it's all the lot together.'

'Ar!' said the tracker. 'They've lost their heads, that's what it is. And some of the bosses are going to lose their skins too, I guess, if what I hear is true: Tower raided and all, and hundreds of your lads done in, and prisoner got away. If that's the way you fighters go on, small wonder there's bad news from the battles.'

'Who says there's bad news?' shouted the soldier.

'Ar! Who says there isn't?'

'That's cursed rebel-talk, and I'll stick you, if you don't shut it down, see?'

'All right, all right!' said the tracker. 'I'll say no more and go on thinking. But what's the black sneak got to do with it all? That gobbler with the flapping hands?'

'I don't know. Nothing, maybe. But he's up to no good, nosing around, I'll wager. Curse him! No sooner had he slipped us and run off than word came he's wanted alive, wanted quick.'

'Well, I hope they get him and put him through it,' growled the tracker. 'He messed up the scent back there, pinching that cast-off mail-shirt that he found, and paddling all round the place before I could get there.'

'It saved his life anyhow,' said the soldier. 'Why, before I knew he was wanted I shot him, as neat as neat, at fifty paces right in the back; but he ran on.'

'Garn! You missed him,' said the tracker. 'First you shoot wild, then you run too slow, and then you send for the poor trackers. I've had enough of you.' He loped off.

'You come back,' shouted the soldier, 'or I'll report you!'

'Who to? Not to your precious Shagrat. He won't be captain any more.'

'I'll give your name and number to the Nazgûl,' said the soldier lowering his voice to a hiss. 'One of *them*'s in charge at the Tower now.'

The other halted, and his voice was full of fear and rage. 'You cursed peaching sneakthief!' he yelled. 'You can't do your job, and you can't even stick by your own folk. Go to your filthy Shriekers, and may they freeze the flesh off you! If the enemy doesn't get them first. They've done in Number One, I've heard, and I hope it's true!'

The big orc, spear in hand, leapt after him. But the tracker, springing behind a stone, put an arrow in his eye as he ran up, and he fell with a crash. The other ran off across the valley and disappeared.

For a while the hobbits sat in silence. At length Sam stirred. 'Well, I call that neat as neat,' he said. 'If this nice friendliness would spread about in Mordor, half our trouble would be over.'

'Quietly, Sam,' Frodo whispered. 'There may be others about. We have evidently had a very narrow escape, and the hunt was hotter on our tracks than we guessed. But that *is* the spirit of Mordor, Sam; and it has spread to every corner of it. Orcs have always behaved like that, or so all tales say, when they are on their own. But you can't get much hope out of it. They hate us far more, altogether and all the time. If those two had seen us, they would have dropped all their quarrel until we were dead.'

There was another long silence. Sam broke it again, but with a whisper this time. 'Did you hear what they said about *that gobbler*, Mr. Frodo? I told you Gollum wasn't dead yet, didn't I?'

'Yes, I remember. And I wondered how you knew,' said Frodo. 'Well, come now! I think we had better not move out from here again, until it has gone quite dark. So you shall tell me how you know, and all about what happened. If you can do it quietly.'

'I'll try,' said Sam, 'but when I think of that Stinker I get so hot I could shout.'

There the hobbits sat under the cover of the thorny bush, while the drear light of Mordor faded slowly into a deep and starless night; and Sam spoke into Frodo's ear all that he could find words for of Gollum's treacherous attack, the horror of Shelob, and his own adventures with the orcs. When he had finished, Frodo said nothing but took Sam's hand and pressed it. At length he stirred.

'Well, I suppose we must be going on again,' he said. 'I wonder how long it will be before we really are caught and all the toiling and the slinking will be over, and in vain.' He stood up. 'It's dark, and we cannot use the Lady's glass. Keep it safe for me, Sam. I have nowhere to keep it now, except in my hand, and I shall need both hands in the blind night. But Sting I give to you. I have got an orc-blade, but I do not think it will be my part to strike any blow again.'

It was difficult and dangerous moving in the night in the pathless land; but slowly and with much stumbling the two hobbits toiled on hour by hour northward along the eastern edge of the stony valley. When a grey light crept back over the western heights, long after day had opened in the lands beyond, they went into hiding again and slept a little, turn by turn. In his times of waking Sam was busy with thoughts of food. At last when Frodo roused himself and spoke of eating and making ready for yet another effort, he asked the question that was troubling him most.

'Begging your pardon, Mr. Frodo,' he said, 'but have you any notion how far there is still to go?'

'No, not any clear notion, Sam,' Frodo answered. 'In Rivendell before I set out I was shown a map of Mordor that was made before the Enemy came back here; but I only remember it vaguely. I remember clearest that there was a place in the north where the western range and the northern range send out spurs that nearly meet. That must be twenty leagues at least from the bridge back by the Tower. It might be a good point at which to cross. But of course, if we get there, we shall be further than we were from the Mountain, sixty miles from it, I should think. I guess that we have gone about twelve leagues north from the bridge now. Even if all goes well, I could hardly reach the Mountain in a week. I am afraid, Sam, that the burden will get very heavy, and I shall go still slower as we get nearer.'

Sam sighed. 'That's just as I feared,' he said. 'Well, to say nothing of water, we've got to eat less, Mr. Frodo, or else move a bit quicker, at any rate while we're still in this valley. One more bite and all the food's ended, save the Elves' waybread.'

'I'll try and be a bit quicker, Sam,' said Frodo, drawing a deep breath. 'Come on then! Let's start another march!'

It was not yet quite dark again. They plodded along, on into the night. The hours passed in a weary stumbling trudge with a few brief halts. At the first hint of grey light under the skirts of the canopy of shadow they hid themselves again in a dark hollow under an overhanging stone.

Slowly the light grew, until it was clearer than it yet had been. A strong wind from the West was now driving the fumes of Mordor from the upper airs. Before long the hobbits could make out the shape of the land for some miles about them. The trough between the mountains and the Morgai had steadily dwindled as it climbed upwards, and the inner ridge was now no more than a shelf in the steep faces of the Ephel Dúath; but to the east it fell as sheerly as ever down into Gorgoroth. Ahead the water-course came to an end in broken steps of rock; for out from the main range there sprang a high barren spur, thrusting eastward like a wall. To meet it there stretched out from the grey and misty northern range of Ered Lithui a long jutting arm; and between the ends there was a narrow gap: Carach Angren, the Isenmouthe, beyond which lay the deep dale of Udûn. In that dale behind the Morannon were the tunnels and deep armouries that the servants of Mordor had made for the defence of the Black Gate of their land; and there now their Lord was gathering in haste great forces to meet the onslaught of the Captains of the West. Upon the out-thrust spurs forts and towers were built, and watch-fires burned; and all across the gap an earth-wall had been raised, and a deep trench delved that could be crossed only by a single bridge.

A few miles north, high up in the angle where the western spur branched away from the main range, stood the old castle of Durthang, now one of the many orc-holds that clustered about the dale of Udûn. A road, already visible in the growing light, came winding down from it, until only a mile or two from where the hobbits lay it turned east and ran along a shelf cut in the side of the spur, and so went down into the plain, and on to the Isenmouthe.

To the hobbits as they looked out it seemed that all their journey north had been useless. The plain to their right was dim and smoky, and they could see there neither camps nor troops moving; but all that region was under the vigilance of the forts of Carach Angren.

'We have come to a dead end, Sam,' said Frodo. 'If we go on, we shall only come up to that orc-tower, but the only road to take is that road that comes down from it – unless we go back. We can't climb up westward, or climb down eastward.'

'Then we must take the road, Mr. Frodo,' said Sam. 'We must take it and chance our luck, if there is any luck in Mordor. We might as well give ourselves up as wander about any more, or try to go back. Our food won't last. We've got to make a dash for it!'

'All right, Sam,' said Frodo. 'Lead me! As long as you've got any hope left. Mine is gone. But I can't dash, Sam. I'll just plod along after you.'

'Before you start any more plodding, you need sleep and food, Mr. Frodo. Come and take what you can get of them!'

He gave Frodo water and an additional wafer of the waybread, and he made a pillow of his cloak for his master's head. Frodo was too weary to debate the matter, and Sam did not tell him that he had drunk the last drop of their water, and eaten Sam's share of the food as well as his own. When Frodo was asleep Sam bent over him and listened to his breathing and scanned his face. It was lined and thin, and yet in sleep it looked content and unafraid. 'Well, here goes, Master!' Sam muttered to himself. 'I'll have to leave you for a bit and trust to luck. Water we must have, or we'll get no further.'

Sam crept out, and flitting from stone to stone with more than hobbit-care, he went down to the water-course, and then followed it for some way as it climbed north, until he came to the rock-steps where long ago, no doubt, its spring had come gushing down in a little waterfall. All now seemed dry and silent; but refusing to despair Sam stooped and listened, and to his delight he caught the sound of trickling. Clambering a few steps up he found a tiny stream of dark water that came out from the hill-side and filled a little bare pool, from which again it spilled, and vanished then under the barren stones.

Sam tasted the water, and it seemed good enough. Then he drank deeply, refilled the bottle, and turned to go back. At that moment he caught a glimpse of a black form or shadow flitting among the rocks away near Frodo's hiding-place. Biting back a cry, he leapt down from the spring and ran, jumping from stone to stone. It was a wary creature, difficult to see, but Sam had little doubt about it: he longed to get his hands on its neck. But it heard him coming and slipped quickly away. Sam thought he saw a last fleeting glimpse of it, peering back over the edge of the eastward precipice, before it ducked and disappeared.

'Well, luck did not let me down,' muttered Sam, 'but that was a near thing! Isn't it enough to have orcs by the thousand without that stinking villain coming nosing round? I wish he had been shot!' He sat down by Frodo and did not rouse him; but he did not dare to go to sleep himself. At last when he felt his eyes closing and knew that his struggle to keep awake could not go on much longer, he wakened Frodo gently.

'That Gollum's about again, I'm afraid, Mr. Frodo,' he said. 'Leastways, if it wasn't him, then there's two of him. I went away to find some water and spied him nosing round just as I turned back. I reckon it isn't safe for us both to sleep together, and begging your pardon, but I can't hold up my lids much longer.'

'Bless you, Sam!' said Frodo. 'Lie down and take your proper turn! But I'd rather have Gollum than orcs. At any rate he won't give us away to them – not unless he's caught himself.'

'But he might do a bit of robbery and murder on his own,' growled Sam. 'Keep your eyes open, Mr. Frodo! There's a bottle full of water. Drink up. We can fill it again when we go on.' With that Sam plunged into sleep.

Light was fading again when he woke. Frodo sat propped against the rock behind, but he had fallen asleep. The water-bottle was empty. There was no sign of Gollum.

Mordor-dark had returned, and the watch-fires on the heights burned fierce and red, when the hobbits set out again on the most dangerous stage of all their journey. They went first to the little spring, and then climbing warily up they came to the road at the point where it swung east towards the Isenmouthe twenty miles away. It was not a broad road, and it had no wall or parapet along the edge, and as it ran on the sheer drop from its brink became deeper and deeper. The hobbits could hear no movements, and after listening for a while they set off eastward at a steady pace.

After doing some twelve miles, they halted. A short way back the road had bent a little northward and the stretch that they had passed over was now screened from sight. This proved disastrous. They rested for some minutes and then went on; but they had not taken many steps when suddenly in the stillness of the night they heard the sound that all along they had secretly dreaded: the noise of marching feet. It was still some way behind them, but looking back they could see the twinkle of torches coming round the bend less than a mile away, and they were moving fast: too fast for Frodo to escape by flight along the road ahead.

'I feared it, Sam,' said Frodo. 'We've trusted to luck, and it has failed us. We're trapped.' He looked wildly up at the frowning wall, where the road-builders of old had cut the rock sheer for many fathoms above their heads. He ran to the other side and looked over the brink into a dark pit of gloom. 'We're trapped at last!' he said. He sank to the ground beneath the wall of rock and bowed his head.

'Seems so,' said Sam. 'Well, we can but wait and see.' And with that he sat down beside Frodo under the shadow of the cliff.

They did not have to wait long. The orcs were going at a great pace. Those in the foremost files bore torches. On they came, red flames in the dark, swiftly growing. Now Sam too bowed his head, hoping that it would hide his face when the torches reached them; and he set their shields before their knees to hide their feet.

'If only they are in a hurry and will let a couple of tired soldiers alone and pass on!' he thought.

And so it seemed that they would. The leading orcs came loping along, panting, holding their heads down. They were a gang of the smaller breeds being driven unwilling to their Dark Lord's wars; all they cared for was to get the march over and escape the whip. Beside them, running up and down the line, went two of the large fierce *uruks*, cracking lashes and shouting. File after file passed, and the tell-tale torchlight was already some way ahead. Sam held his breath. Now more than half the line had gone by. Then suddenly one of the slave-drivers spied the two figures by the road-side. He flicked a whip at them and yelled: 'Hi, you! Get up!' They did not answer, and with a shout he halted the whole company.

'Come on, you slugs!' he cried. 'This is no time for slouching.' He took a step towards them, and even in the gloom he recognized the devices on their shields. 'Deserting, eh?' he snarled. 'Or thinking of it? All your folk should have been inside Udûn before yesterday evening. You know that. Up you get and fall in, or I'll have your numbers and report you.'

They struggled to their feet, and keeping bent, limping like footsore soldiers, they shuffled back towards the rear of the line. 'No, not at the rear!' the slave-driver shouted. 'Three files up. And stay there, or you'll know it, when I come down the line!' He sent his long whip-lash cracking over their heads; then with another crack and a yell he started the company off again at a brisk trot.

It was hard enough for poor Sam, tired as he was; but for Frodo it was a torment, and soon a nightmare. He set his teeth and tried to stop his mind from thinking, and he struggled on. The stench of the sweating orcs about him was stifling, and he began to gasp with thirst. On, on they went, and he bent all his will to draw his breath and to make his legs keep going; and yet to what evil end he toiled and endured he did not dare to think. There was no hope of falling out unseen. Now and again the orc-driver fell back and jeered at them.

'There now!' he laughed, flicking at their legs. 'Where there's a whip there's a will, my slugs. Hold up! I'd give you a nice freshener now, only you'll get as much lash as your skins will carry when you come in late to your camp. Do you good. Don't you know we're at war?'

They had gone some miles, and the road was at last running down a long slope into the plain, when Frodo's strength began to give out and his will wavered. He lurched and stumbled. Desperately Sam tried to help him and hold him up, though he felt that he could himself hardly stay the pace much longer. At any moment now he knew that the end would come: his master would faint or fall, and all would be discovered, and their bitter efforts be in vain. 'I'll have that big slave-driving devil anyway,' he thought.

Then just as he was putting his hand to the hilt of his sword, there came an unexpected relief. They were out on the plain now and drawing near the entrance to Udûn. Some way in front of it, before the gate at the bridge-end, the road from the west converged with others coming from the south, and from Barad-dûr. Along all the roads troops were moving; for the Captains of the West were advancing and the Dark Lord was speeding his forces north. So it chanced that several companies came together at the road-meeting, in the dark beyond the light of the watch-fires on the wall. At once there was great jostling and cursing as each troop tried to get first to the gate and the ending of their march. Though the drivers yelled and plied their whips, scuffles broke out and some blades were drawn. A troop of heavy-armed *uruks* from Barad-dûr charged into the Durthang line and threw them into confusion.

Dazed as he was with pain and weariness, Sam woke up, grasped quickly at his chance, and threw himself to the ground, dragging Frodo down with him. Orcs fell over them, snarling and cursing. Slowly on hand and knee the hobbits crawled away out of the turmoil, until at last unnoticed they dropped over the further edge of the road. It had a high kerb by which troop-leaders could guide themselves in black night or fog, and it was banked up some feet above the level of the open land.

They lay still for a while. It was too dark to seek for cover, if indeed there was any to find; but Sam felt that they ought at least to get further away from the highways and out of the range of torchlight.

'Come on, Mr. Frodo!' he whispered. 'One more crawl, and then you can lie still.'

With a last despairing effort Frodo raised himself on his hands, and struggled on for maybe twenty yards. Then he pitched down into a shallow pit that opened unexpectedly before them, and there he lay like a dead thing.

CHAPTER III

MOUNT DOOM

Sam put his ragged orc-cloak under his master's head, and covered them both with the grey robe of Lórien; and as he did so his thoughts went out to that fair land, and to the Elves, and he hoped that the cloth woven by their hands might have some virtue to keep them hidden beyond all hope in this wilderness of fear. He heard the scuffling and cries die down as the troops passed on through the Isenmouthe. It seemed that in the confusion and the mingling of many companies of various kinds they had not been missed, not yet at any rate.

Sam took a sip of water, but pressed Frodo to drink, and when his master had recovered a little he gave him a whole wafer of their precious waybread and made him eat it. Then, too worn out even to feel much fear, they stretched themselves out. They slept a little in uneasy fits; for their sweat grew chill on them, and the hard stones bit them, and they shivered. Out of the north from the Black Gate through Cirith Gorgor there flowed whispering along the ground a thin cold air.

In the morning a grey light came again, for in the high regions the West Wind still blew, but down on the stones behind the fences of the Black Land the air seemed almost dead, chill and yet stifling. Sam looked up out of the hollow. The land all about was dreary, flat and drab-hued. On the roads nearby nothing was moving now; but Sam feared the watchful eyes on the wall of the Isenmouthe, no more than a furlong away northward. South-eastward, far off like a dark standing shadow, loomed the Mountain. Smokes were pouring from it, and while those that rose into the upper air trailed away eastward, great rolling clouds floated down its sides and spread over the land. A few miles to the north-east the foothills of the Ashen Mountains stood like sombre grey ghosts, behind which the misty northern heights rose like a line of distant cloud hardly darker than the lowering sky.

Sam tried to guess the distances and to decide what way they ought to take. 'It looks every step of fifty miles,' he muttered gloomily, staring at the threatening mountain, 'and that'll take a week, if it takes a day, with Mr. Frodo as he is.' He shook his head, and as he worked things out, slowly a new dark thought grew in his mind. Never for long had hope died in his staunch heart, and always until now he had taken some thought for their return. But the bitter truth came home to him at last: at best their provision would take them to their goal; and when the task was done, there they would come to an end, alone, houseless, foodless in the midst of a terrible desert. There could be no return.

'So that was the job I felt I had to do when I started,' thought Sam: 'to help Mr. Frodo to the last step and then die with him? Well, if that is the job then I must do it. But I would dearly like to see Bywater again, and Rosie Cotton and her brothers, and the Gaffer and Marigold and all. I can't think somehow that Gandalf would have sent Mr. Frodo on this errand, if there hadn't a' been any hope of his ever coming back at all. Things all went wrong when he went down in Moria. I wish he hadn't. He would have done something.'

But even as hope died in Sam, or seemed to die, it was turned to a new strength. Sam's plain hobbit-face grew stern, almost grim, as the will hardened in him, and he felt through all his limbs a thrill, as if he was turning into some creature of stone and steel that neither despair nor weariness nor endless barren miles could subdue.

With a new sense of responsibility he brought his eyes back to the ground near at hand, studying the next move. As the light grew a little he saw to his surprise that what from a distance had seemed wide and featureless flats were in fact all broken and tumbled. Indeed the whole surface of the plains of Gorgoroth was pocked with great holes, as if, while it was still a waste of soft mud, it had been smitten with a shower of bolts and huge slingstones. The largest of these holes were rimmed with ridges of broken rock, and broad fissures ran out from them in all directions. It was a land in which it would be possible to creep from hiding to hiding, unseen by all but the most watchful eyes: possible at least for one who was strong and had no need for speed. For the hungry and worn, who had far to go before life failed, it had an evil look.

Thinking of all these things Sam went back to his master. He had no need to rouse him. Frodo was lying on his back with eyes open, staring at the cloudy sky. 'Well, Mr. Frodo,' said Sam, 'I've been having a look round and thinking a bit. There's nothing on the roads, and we'd best be getting away while there's a chance. Can you manage it?'

'I can manage it,' said Frodo. 'I must.'

Once more they started, crawling from hollow to hollow, flitting behind such cover as they could find, but moving always in a slant towards the foothills of the northern range. But as they went the most easterly of the roads followed them, until it ran off, hugging the skirts of the mountains, away into a wall of black shadow far ahead. Neither man nor orc now moved along its flat grey stretches; for the Dark Lord had almost completed the movement of his forces, and even in the fastness of his own realm he sought the secrecy of night, fearing the winds of the world that had turned against him, tearing aside his veils, and troubled with tidings of bold spies that had passed through his fences.

The hobbits had gone a few weary miles when they halted. Frodo seemed nearly spent. Sam saw that he could not go much further in this fashion, crawling, stooping, now picking a doubtful way very slowly, now hurrying at a stumbling run.

'I'm going back on to the road while the light lasts, Mr. Frodo,' he said. 'Trust to luck again! It nearly failed us last time, but it didn't quite. A steady pace for a few more miles, and then a rest.'

He was taking a far greater risk than he knew; but Frodo was too much occupied with his burden and with the struggle in his mind to debate, and almost too hopeless to care. They climbed on to the causeway and trudged along, down the hard cruel road that led to the Dark Tower itself. But their luck held, and for the rest of that day they met no living or moving thing; and when night fell they vanished into the darkness of Mordor. All the land now brooded as at the coming of a great storm: for the Captains of the West had passed the Cross-roads and set flames in the deadly fields of Imlad Morgul.

So the desperate journey went on, as the Ring went south and the banners of the kings rode north. For the hobbits each day, each mile, was more bitter than the one before, as their strength lessened and the land became more evil. They met no enemies by day. At times by night, as they cowered or drowsed uneasily in some hiding beside the road, they heard cries and the noise of many feet or the swift passing of some cruelly ridden steed. But far worse than all such perils was the ever-approaching threat that beat upon them as they went: the dreadful menace of the Power that waited, brooding in deep thought and sleepless malice behind the dark veil about its Throne. Nearer and nearer it drew, looming blacker, like the oncoming of a wall of night at the last end of the world.

There came at last a dreadful nightfall; and even as the Captains of the West drew near to the end of the living lands, the two wanderers came to an hour of blank despair. Four days had passed since they had escaped from the orcs, but the time lay behind them like an ever-darkening dream. All this last day Frodo had not spoken, but had walked half-bowed, often stumbling, as if his eyes no longer saw the way before his feet. Sam guessed that among all their pains he bore the worst, the growing weight of the Ring, a burden on the body and a torment to his mind. Anxiously Sam had noted how his master's left hand would often be raised as if to ward off a blow, or to screen his shrinking eyes from a dreadful Eye that sought to look in them. And sometimes his right hand would creep to his breast, clutching, and then slowly, as the will recovered mastery, it would be withdrawn.

Now as the blackness of night returned Frodo sat, his head between his knees, his arms hanging wearily to the ground where his hands lay feebly twitching. Sam watched him, till night covered them both and hid them from one another. He could no longer find any words to say; and he turned to his own dark thoughts. As for himself, though weary and under a shadow of fear, he still had some strength left. The *lembas* had a virtue without which they would long ago have lain down to die. It did not satisfy desire, and at times Sam's mind was filled with the memories of food, and the longing for simple bread and meats. And yet this waybread of the Elves had a potency that increased as travellers relied on it alone and did not mingle it with other foods. It fed the will, and it gave strength to endure, and to master sinew and limb beyond the measure of mortal kind. But now a new decision must be made. They could not follow this road any longer; for it went on eastward into the great Shadow, but the Mountain now loomed upon their right, almost due south, and they must turn towards it. Yet still before it there stretched a wide region of fuming, barren, ash-ridden land.

'Water, water!' muttered Sam. He had stinted himself, and in his parched mouth his tongue seemed thick and swollen; but for all his care they now had very little left, perhaps half his bottle, and maybe there were still days to go. All would long ago have been spent, if they had not dared to follow the orc-road. For at long intervals on that highway cisterns had been built for the use of troops sent in haste through the waterless regions. In one Sam had found some water left, stale, muddied by the orcs, but still sufficient for their desperate case. Yet that was now a day ago. There was no hope of any more.

At last wearied with his cares Sam drowsed, leaving the morrow till it came; he could do no more. Dream and waking mingled uneasily. He saw lights like gloating eyes, and dark creeping shapes, and he heard noises as of wild beasts or the dreadful cries of tortured things; and he would start up to find the world all dark and only empty blackness all about him. Once only, as he stood and stared wildly round, did it seem that, though now awake, he could still see pale lights like eyes; but soon they flickered and vanished.

The hateful night passed slowly and reluctantly. Such daylight as followed was dim; for here as the Mountain drew near the air was ever mirky, while out from the Dark Tower there crept the veils of Shadow that Sauron wove about himself. Frodo was lying on his back not moving. Sam stood beside him, reluctant to speak, and yet knowing that the word now lay with him: he must set his master's will to work for another effort. At length, stooping and caressing Frodo's brow, he spoke in his ear.

'Wake up, Master!' he said. 'Time for another start.'

As if roused by a sudden bell, Frodo rose quickly, and stood up and looked away southwards; but when his eyes beheld the Mountain and the desert he quailed again.

'I can't manage it, Sam,' he said. 'It is such a weight to carry, such a weight.'

Sam knew before he spoke, that it was vain, and that such words might do more harm than good, but in his pity he could not keep silent. 'Then let me carry it a bit for you, Master,' he said. 'You know I would, and gladly, as long as I have any strength.'

A wild light came into Frodo's eyes. 'Stand away! Don't touch me!' he cried. 'It is mine, I say. Be off!' His hand strayed to his sword-hilt. But then quickly his voice changed. 'No, no, Sam,' he said sadly. 'But you must understand. It is my burden, and no one else can bear it. It is too late now, Sam dear. You can't help me in that way again. I am almost in its power now. I could not give it up, and if you tried to take it I should go mad.'

Sam nodded. 'I understand,' he said. 'But I've been thinking, Mr. Frodo, there's other things we might do without. Why not lighten the load a bit? We're going that way now, as straight as we can make it.' He pointed to the Mountain. 'It's no good taking anything we're not sure to need.'

Frodo looked again towards the Mountain. 'No,' he said, 'we shan't need much on that road. And at its end nothing.' Picking up his orc-shield he flung it away and threw his helmet after it. Then pulling off the grey cloak he undid the heavy belt and let it fall to the ground, and the sheathed sword with it. The shreds of the black cloak he tore off and scattered.

'There, I'll be an orc no more,' he cried, 'and I'll bear no weapon, fair or foul. Let them take me, if they will!'

Sam did likewise, and put aside his orc-gear; and he took out all the things in his pack. Somehow each of them had become dear to him, if only because he had borne them so far with so much toil. Hardest of all it was to part with his cooking-gear. Tears welled in his eyes at the thought of casting it away.

'Do you remember that bit of rabbit, Mr. Frodo?' he said. 'And our place under the warm bank in Captain Faramir's country, the day I saw an oliphaunt?'

'No, I am afraid not, Sam,' said Frodo. 'At least, I know that such things happened, but I cannot see them. No taste of food, no feel of water, no sound of wind, no memory of tree or grass or flower, no image of moon or star are left to me. I am naked in the dark, Sam, and there is no veil between me and the wheel of fire. I begin to see it even with my waking eyes, and all else fades.'

Sam went to him and kissed his hand. 'Then the sooner we're rid of it, the sooner to rest,' he said haltingly, finding no better words to say. 'Talking won't mend nothing,' he muttered to himself, as he gathered up all the things that they had chosen to cast away. He was not willing to leave them lying open in the wilderness for any eyes to see. 'Stinker picked up that orc-shirt, seemingly, and he isn't going to add a sword to it. His hands are bad enough when empty. And he isn't going to mess with my pans!' With that he carried all the gear away to one of the many gaping fissures that scored the land and threw them in. The clatter of his precious pans as they fell down into the dark was like a death-knell to his heart.

He came back to Frodo, and then of his elven-rope he cut a short piece to serve his master as a girdle and bind the grey cloak close about his waist. The rest he carefully coiled and put back in his pack. Beside that he kept only the remnants of their waybread and the water-bottle, and Sting still hanging by his belt; and hidden away in a pocket of his tunic next his breast the phial of Galadriel and the little box that she gave him for his own.

Now at last they turned their faces to the Mountain and set out, thinking no more of concealment, bending their weariness and failing wills only to the one task of going on. In the dimness of its dreary day few things even in that land of vigilance could have espied them, save from close at hand. Of all the slaves of the Dark Lord, only the Nazgûl could have warned him of the peril that crept, small but indomitable, into the very heart of his guarded realm. But the Nazgûl and their black wings were abroad on other errand: they were gathered far away, shadowing the march of the Captains of the West, and thither the thought of the Dark Tower was turned.

That day it seemed to Sam that his master had found some new strength, more than could be explained by the small lightening of the load that he had to carry. In the first marches they went further and faster than he had hoped. The land was rough and hostile, and yet they made much progress, and ever the Mountain drew nearer. But as the day wore on and all too soon the dim light began to fail, Frodo stooped again, and began to stagger, as if the renewed effort had squandered his remaining strength.

At their last halt he sank down and said: 'I'm thirsty, Sam,' and did not speak again. Sam gave him a mouthful of water; only one more mouthful remained. He went without himself; and now as once more the night of Mordor closed over them, through all his thoughts there came the memory of water; and every brook or stream or fount that he had ever seen, under green willow-shades or twinkling in the sun, danced and rippled for his torment behind the blindness of his eyes. He felt the cool mud about his toes as he paddled in the Pool at Bywater with Jolly Cotton and Tom and Nibs, and their sister Rosie. 'But that was years ago,' he sighed, 'and far away. The way back, if there is one, goes past the Mountain.'

He could not sleep and he held a debate with himself. 'Well, come now, we've done better than you hoped,' he said sturdily. 'Began well anyway. I reckon we crossed half the distance before we stopped. One more day will do it.' And then he paused.

'Don't be a fool, Sam Gamgee,' came an answer in his own voice. 'He won't go another day like that, if he moves at all. And you can't go on much longer giving him all the water and most of the food.'

'I can go on a good way though, and I will.'

'Where to?'

'To the Mountain, of course.'

'But what then, Sam Gamgee, what then? When you get there, what are you going to do? He won't be able to do anything for himself.'

To his dismay Sam realized that he had not got an answer to this. He had no clear idea at all. Frodo had not spoken much to him of his errand, and Sam only knew vaguely that the Ring had somehow to be put into the fire. 'The Cracks of Doom,' he muttered, the old name rising to his mind. 'Well, if Master knows how to find them, I don't.'

'There you are!' came the answer. 'It's all quite useless. He said so himself. You are the fool, going on hoping and toiling. You could have lain down and gone to sleep together days ago, if you hadn't been so dogged. But you'll die just the same, or worse. You might just as well lie down now and give it up. You'll never get to the top anyway.'

'I'll get there, if I leave everything but my bones behind,' said Sam. 'And I'll carry Mr. Frodo up myself, if it breaks my back and heart. So stop arguing!'

At that moment Sam felt a tremor in the ground beneath him, and he heard or sensed a deep remote rumble as of thunder imprisoned under the earth. There was a brief red flame that flickered under the clouds and died away. The Mountain too slept uneasily.

The last stage of their journey to Orodruin came, and it was a torment greater than Sam had ever thought that he could bear. He was in pain, and so parched that he could no longer swallow even a mouthful of food. It remained dark, not only because of the smokes of the Mountain: there seemed to be a storm coming up, and away to the south-east there was a shimmer of lightnings under the black skies. Worst of all, the air was full of fumes; breathing was painful and difficult, and a dizziness came on them, so that they staggered and often fell. And yet their wills did not yield, and they struggled on.

The Mountain crept up ever nearer, until, if they lifted their heavy heads, it filled all their sight, looming vast before them: a huge mass of ash and slag and burned stone, out of which a sheer-sided cone was raised into the clouds. Before the daylong dusk ended and true night came again they had crawled and stumbled to its very feet.

With a gasp Frodo cast himself on the ground. Sam sat by him. To his surprise he felt tired but lighter, and his head seemed clear again. No more debates disturbed his mind. He knew all the arguments of despair and would not listen to them. His will was set, and only death would break it. He felt no longer either desire or need of sleep, but rather of watchfulness. He knew that all the hazards and perils were now drawing together to a point: the next day would be a day of doom, the day of final effort or disaster, the last gasp.

But when would it come? The night seemed endless and timeless, minute after minute falling dead and adding up to no passing hour, bringing no change. Sam began to wonder if a second darkness had begun and no day would ever reappear. At last he groped for Frodo's hand. It was cold and· trembling. His master was shivering.

'I didn't ought to have left my blanket behind,' muttered Sam; and lying down he tried to comfort Frodo with his arms and body. Then sleep took him, and the dim light of the last day of their quest found them side by side. The wind had fallen the day before as it shifted from the West, and now it came from the North and began to rise; and slowly the light of the unseen Sun filtered down into the shadows where the hobbits lay.

'Now for it! Now for the last gasp!' said Sam as he struggled to his feet. He bent over Frodo, rousing him gently. Frodo groaned; but with a great effort of will he staggered up; and then he fell upon his knees again. He raised his eyes with difficulty to the dark slopes of Mount Doom towering above him, and then pitifully he began to crawl forward on his hands.

Sam looked at him and wept in his heart, but no tears came to his dry and stinging eyes. 'I said I'd carry him, if it broke my back,' he muttered, 'and I will!'

'Come, Mr. Frodo!' he cried. 'I can't carry it for you, but I can carry you and it as well. So up you get! Come on, Mr. Frodo dear! Sam will give you a ride. Just tell him where to go, and he'll go.'

As Frodo clung upon his back, arms loosely about his neck, legs clasped firmly under his arms, Sam staggered to his feet; and then to his amazement he felt the burden light. He had feared that he would have barely strength to lift his master alone, and beyond that he had expected to share in the dreadful dragging weight of the accursed Ring. But it was not so. Whether because Frodo was so worn by his long pains, wound of knife, and venomous sting, and sorrow, fear, and homeless wandering, or because some gift of final strength was given to him, Sam lifted Frodo with no more difficulty than if he were carrying a hobbit-child pig-a-back in some romp on the lawns or hayfields of the Shire. He took a deep breath and started off.

They had reached the Mountain's foot on its northern side, and a little to the westward; there its long grey slopes, though broken, were not sheer. Frodo did not speak, and so Sam struggled on as best he could, having no guidance but the will to climb as high as might be before his strength gave out and his will broke. On he toiled, up and up, turning this way and that to lessen the slope, often stumbling forward, and at the last crawling like a snail with a heavy burden on its back. When his will could drive him no further, and his limbs gave way, he stopped and laid his master gently down.

Frodo opened his eyes and drew a breath. It was easier to breathe up here above the reeks that coiled and drifted down below. 'Thank you, Sam,' he said in a cracked whisper. 'How far is there to go?'

'I don't know,' said Sam, 'because I don't know where we're going.'

He looked back, and then he looked up; and he was amazed to see how far his last effort had brought him. The Mountain standing ominous and alone had looked taller than it was. Sam saw now that it was less lofty than the high passes of the Ephel Dúath which he and Frodo had scaled. The confused and tumbled shoulders of its great base rose for maybe three thousand feet above the plain, and above them was reared half as high again its tall central cone, like a vast oast or chimney capped with a jagged crater. But already Sam was more than half way up the base, and the plain of Gorgoroth was dim below him, wrapped in fume and shadow. As he looked up he would have given a shout, if his parched throat had allowed him; for amid the rugged humps and shoulders above him he saw plainly a path or road. It climbed like a rising girdle from the west and wound snakelike about the Mountain, until before it went round out of view it reached the foot of the cone upon its eastern side.

Sam could not see the course immediately above him, where it was lowest, for a steep slope went up from where he stood; but he guessed that if he could only struggle on just a little way further up, they would strike this path. A gleam of hope returned to him. They might conquer the Mountain yet. 'Why, it might have been put there a-purpose!' he said to himself. 'If it wasn't there, I'd have to say I was beaten in the end.'

The path was not put there for the purposes of Sam. He did not know it, but he was looking at Sauron's Road from Barad-dûr to the Sammath Naur, the Chambers of Fire. Out from the Dark Tower's huge western gate it came over a deep abyss by a vast bridge of iron, and then passing into the plain it ran for a league between two smoking chasms, and so reached a long sloping causeway that led up on to the Mountain's eastern side. Thence, turning and encircling all its wide girth from south to north, it climbed at last, high in the upper cone, but still far from the reeking summit, to a dark entrance that gazed back east straight to the Window of the Eye in Sauron's shadow-mantled fortress. Often blocked or destroyed by the tumults of the Mountain's furnaces, always that road was repaired and cleared again by the labours of countless orcs.

Sam drew a deep breath. There was a path, but how he was to get up the slope to it he did not know. First he must ease his aching back. He lay flat beside Frodo for a while. Neither spoke. Slowly the light grew. Suddenly a sense of urgency which he did not understand came to Sam. It was almost as if he had been called: 'Now, now, or it will be too late!' He braced himself and got up. Frodo also seemed to have felt the call. He struggled to his knees.

'I'll crawl, Sam,' he gasped.

So foot by foot, like small grey insects, they crept up the slope. They came to the path and found that it was broad, paved with broken rubble and beaten ash. Frodo clambered on to it, and then moved as if by some compulsion he turned slowly to face the East. Far off the shadows of Sauron hung; but torn by some gust of wind out of the world, or else moved by some great disquiet within, the mantling clouds swirled, and for a moment drew aside; and then he saw, rising black, blacker and darker than the vast shades amid which it stood, the cruel pinnacles and iron crown of the topmost tower of Barad-dûr. One moment only it stared out, but as from some great window immeasurably high there stabbed northward a flame of red, the flicker of a piercing Eye; and then the shadows were furled again and the terrible vision was removed. The Eye was not turned to them: it was gazing north to where the Captains of the West stood at bay, and thither all its malice was now bent, as the Power moved to strike its deadly blow; but Frodo at that dreadful glimpse fell as one stricken mortally. His hand sought the chain about his neck.

Sam knelt by him. Faint, almost inaudibly, he heard Frodo whispering: 'Help me, Sam! Help me, Sam! Hold my hand! I can't stop it.' Sam took his master's hands and laid them together, palm to palm, and kissed them; and then he held them gently between his own. The thought came suddenly to him: 'He's spotted us! It's all up, or it soon will be. Now, Sam Gamgee, this is the end of ends.'

Again he lifted Frodo and drew his hands down to his own breast, letting his master's legs dangle. Then he bowed his head and struggled off along the climbing road. It was not as easy a way to take as it had looked at first. By fortune the fires that had poured forth in the great turmoils when Sam stood upon Cirith Ungol had flowed down mainly on the southern and western slopes, and the road on this side was not blocked. Yet in many places it had crumbled away or was crossed by gaping rents. After climbing eastward for some time it bent back upon itself at a sharp angle and went westward for a space. There at the bend it was cut deep through a crag of old weathered stone once long ago vomited from the Mountain's furnaces. Panting under his load Sam turned the bend; and even as he did so, out of the corner of his eye, he had a glimpse of something falling from the crag, like a small piece of black stone that had toppled off as he passed.

A sudden weight smote him and he crashed forward, tearing the backs of his hands that still clasped his master's. Then he knew what had happened, for above him as he lay he heard a hated voice.

'Wicked masster!' it hissed. 'Wicked masster cheats us; cheats Sméagol, *gollum*. He musstn't go that way. He musstn't hurt Preciouss. Give it to Sméagol, yess, give it to us! Give it to uss!'

With a violent heave Sam rose up. At once he drew his sword; but he could do nothing. Gollum and Frodo were locked together. Gollum was tearing at his master, trying to get at the chain and the Ring. This was probably the only thing that could have roused the dying embers of Frodo's heart and will: an attack, an attempt to wrest his treasure from him by force. He fought back with a sudden fury that amazed Sam, and Gollum also. Even so things might have gone far otherwise, if Gollum himself had remained unchanged; but whatever dreadful paths, lonely and hungry and waterless, he had trodden, driven by a devouring desire and a terrible fear, they had left grievous marks on him. He was a lean, starved, haggard thing, all bones and tight-drawn sallow skin. A wild light flamed in his eyes, but his malice was no longer matched by his old griping strength. Frodo flung him off and rose up quivering.

'Down, down!' he gasped, clutching his hand to his breast, so that beneath the cover of his leather shirt he clasped the Ring. 'Down, you creeping thing, and out of my path! Your time is at an end. You cannot betray me or slay me now.'

Then suddenly, as before under the eaves of the Emyn Muil, Sam saw these two rivals with other vision. A crouching shape, scarcely more than the shadow of a living thing, a creature now wholly ruined and defeated, yet filled with a hideous lust and rage; and before it stood stern, untouchable now by pity, a figure robed in white, but at its breast it held a wheel of fire. Out of the fire there spoke a commanding voice.

'Begone, and trouble me no more! If you touch me ever again, you shall be cast yourself into the Fire of Doom.'

The crouching shape backed away, terror in its blinking eyes, and yet at the same time insatiable desire.

Then the vision passed and Sam saw Frodo standing, hand on breast, his breath coming in great gasps, and Gollum at his feet, resting on his knees with his wide-splayed hands upon the ground.

'Look out!' cried Sam. 'He'll spring!' He stepped forward, brandishing his sword. 'Quick, Master!' he gasped. 'Go on! Go on! No time to lose. I'll deal with him. Go on!'

Frodo looked at him as if at one now far away. 'Yes, I must go on,' he said. 'Farewell, Sam! This is the end at last. On Mount Doom doom shall fall. Farewell!' He turned and went on, walking slowly but erect, up the climbing path.

'Now!' said Sam. 'At last I can deal with you!' He leaped forward with drawn blade ready for battle. But Gollum did not spring. He fell flat upon the ground and whimpered.

'Don't kill us,' he wept. 'Don't hurt us with nassty cruel steel! Let us live, yes, live just a little longer. Lost lost! We're lost. And when Precious goes we'll die, yes, die into the dust.' He clawed up the ashes of the path with his long fleshless fingers. 'Dusst!' he hissed.

Sam's hand wavered. His mind was hot with wrath and the memory of evil. It would be just to slay this treacherous, murderous creature, just and many times deserved; and also it seemed the only safe thing to do. But deep in his heart there was something that restrained him: he could not strike this thing lying in the dust, forlorn, ruinous, utterly wretched. He himself, though only for a little while, had borne the Ring, and now dimly he guessed the agony of Gollum's shrivelled mind and body, enslaved to that Ring, unable to find peace or relief ever in life again. But Sam had no words to express what he felt.

'Oh, curse you, you stinking thing!' he said. 'Go away! Be off! I don't trust you, not as far as I could kick you; but be off. Or I *shall* hurt you, yes, with nasty cruel steel.'

Gollum got up on all fours, and backed away for several paces, and then he turned, and as Sam aimed a kick at him he fled away down the path. Sam gave no more heed to him. He suddenly remembered his master. He looked up the path and could not see him. As fast as he could he trudged up the road. If he had looked back, he might have seen not far below Gollum turn again, and then with a wild light of madness glaring in his eyes come, swiftly but warily, creeping on behind, a slinking shadow among the stones.

The path climbed on. Soon it bent again and with a last eastward course passed in a cutting along the face of the cone and came to the dark door in the Mountain's side, the door of the Sammath Naur. Far away now rising towards the South the sun, piercing the smokes and haze, burned ominous, a dull bleared disc of red; but all Mordor lay about the Mountain like a dead land, silent, shadow-folded, waiting for some dreadful stroke.

Sam came to the gaping mouth and peered in. It was dark and hot, and a deep rumbling shook the air. 'Frodo! Master!' he called. There was no answer. For a moment he stood, his heart beating with wild fears, and then he plunged in. A shadow followed him.

At first he could see nothing. In his great need he drew out once more the phial of Galadriel, but it was pale and cold in his trembling hand and threw no light into that stifling dark. He was come to the heart of the realm of Sauron and the forges of his ancient might, greatest in Middle-earth; all other powers were here subdued. Fearfully he took a few uncertain steps in the dark, and then all at once there came a flash of red that leaped upward, and smote the high black roof. Then Sam saw that he was in a long cave or tunnel that bored into the Mountain's smoking cone. But only a short way ahead its floor and the walls on either side were cloven by a great fissure, out of which the red glare came, now leaping up, now dying down into darkness; and all the while far below there was a rumour and a trouble as of great engines throbbing and labouring.

The light sprang up again, and there on the brink of the chasm, at the very Crack of Doom, stood Frodo, black against the glare, tense, erect, but still as if he had been turned to stone.

'Master!' cried Sam.

Then Frodo stirred and spoke with a clear voice, indeed with a voice clearer and more powerful than Sam had ever heard him use, and it rose above the throb and turmoil of Mount Doom, ringing in the roof and walls.

'I have come,' he said. 'But I do not choose now to do what I came to do. I will not do this deed. The Ring is mine!' And suddenly, as he set it on his finger, he vanished from Sam's sight. Sam gasped, but he had no chance to cry out, for at that moment many things happened.

Something struck Sam violently in the back, his legs were knocked from under him and he was flung aside, striking his head against the stony floor, as a dark shape sprang over him. He lay still and for a moment all went black.

And far away, as Frodo put on the Ring and claimed it for his own, even in Sammath Naur the very heart of his realm, the Power in Barad-dûr was shaken, and the Tower trembled from its foundations to its proud and bitter crown. The Dark Lord was suddenly aware of him, and his Eye piercing all shadows looked across the plain to the door that he had made; and the magnitude of his own folly was revealed to him in a blinding flash, and all the devices of his enemies were at last laid bare. Then his wrath blazed in consuming flame, but his fear rose like a vast black smoke to

choke him. For he knew his deadly peril and the thread upon which his
doom now hung.

From all his policies and webs of fear and treachery, from all his strat-
agems and wars his mind shook free; and throughout his realm a tremor
ran, his slaves quailed, and his armies halted, and his captains suddenly
steerless, bereft of will, wavered and despaired. For they were forgotten.
The whole mind and purpose of the Power that wielded them was now
bent with overwhelming force upon the Mountain. At his summons, wheeling with a rending cry, in a last desperate race there flew, faster than the
winds, the Nazgûl, the Ringwraiths, and with a storm of wings they hurtled
southwards to Mount Doom.

Sam got up. He was dazed, and blood streaming from his head dripped
in his eyes. He groped forward, and then he saw a strange and terrible
thing. Gollum on the edge of the abyss was fighting like a mad thing with
an unseen foe. To and fro he swayed, now so near the brink that almost
he tumbled in, now dragging back, falling to the ground, rising, and falling
again. And all the while he hissed but spoke no words.

The fires below awoke in anger, the red light blazed, and all the cavern
was filled with a great glare and heat. Suddenly Sam saw Gollum's long
hands draw upwards to his mouth; his white fangs gleamed, and then
snapped as they bit. Frodo gave a cry, and there he was, fallen upon his
knees at the chasm's edge. But Gollum, dancing like a mad thing, held
aloft the ring, a finger still thrust within its circle. It shone now as if verily
it was wrought of living fire.

'Precious, precious, precious!' Gollum cried. 'My Precious! O my Precious!' And with that, even as his eyes were lifted up to gloat on his prize,
he stepped too far, toppled, wavered for a moment on the brink, and then
with a shriek he fell. Out of the depths came his last wail *Precious*, and he
was gone.

There was a roar and a great confusion of noise. Fires leaped up and
licked the roof. The throbbing grew to a great tumult, and the Mountain
shook. Sam ran to Frodo and picked him up and carried him out to the
door. And there upon the dark threshold of the Sammath Naur, high above
the plains of Mordor, such wonder and terror came on him that he stood
still forgetting all else, and gazed as one turned to stone.

A brief vision he had of swirling cloud, and in the midst of it towers
and battlements, tall as hills, founded upon a mighty mountain-throne
above immeasurable pits; great courts and dungeons, eyeless prisons sheer
as cliffs, and gaping gates of steel and adamant: and then all passed. Towers
fell and mountains slid; walls crumbled and melted, crashing down; vast
spires of smoke and spouting steams went billowing up, up, until they

toppled like an overwhelming wave, and its wild crest curled and came foaming down upon the land. And then at last over the miles between there came a rumble, rising to a deafening crash and roar; the earth shook, the plain heaved and cracked, and Orodruin reeled. Fire belched from its riven summit. The skies burst into thunder seared with lightning. Down like lashing whips fell a torrent of black rain. And into the heart of the storm, with a cry that pierced all other sounds, tearing the clouds asunder, the Nazgûl came, shooting like flaming bolts, as caught in the fiery ruin of hill and sky they crackled, withered, and went out.

'Well, this is the end, Sam Gamgee,' said a voice by his side. And there was Frodo, pale and worn, and yet himself again; and in his eyes there was peace now, neither strain of will, nor madness, nor any fear. His burden was taken away. There was the dear master of the sweet days in the Shire.

'Master!' cried Sam, and fell upon his knees. In all that ruin of the world for the moment he felt only joy, great joy. The burden was gone. His master had been saved; he was himself again, he was free. And then Sam caught sight of the maimed and bleeding hand.

'Your poor hand!' he said. 'And I have nothing to bind it with, or comfort it. I would have spared him a whole hand of mine rather. But he's gone now beyond recall, gone for ever.'

'Yes,' said Frodo. 'But do you remember Gandalf's words: *Even Gollum may have something yet to do?* But for him, Sam, I could not have destroyed the Ring. The Quest would have been in vain, even at the bitter end. So let us forgive him! For the Quest is achieved, and now all is over. I am glad you are here with me. Here at the end of all things, Sam.'

CHAPTER IV

THE FIELD OF CORMALLEN

All about the hills the hosts of Mordor raged. The Captains of the West were foundering in a gathering sea. The sun gleamed red, and under the wings of the Nazgûl the shadows of death fell dark upon the earth. Aragorn stood beneath his banner, silent and stern, as one lost in thought of things long past or far away; but his eyes gleamed like stars that shine the brighter as the night deepens. Upon the hill-top stood Gandalf, and he was white and cold and no shadow fell on him. The onslaught of Mordor broke like a wave on the beleaguered hills, voices roaring like a tide amid the wreck and crash of arms.

As if to his eyes some sudden vision had been given, Gandalf stirred; and he turned, looking back north where the skies were pale and clear. Then he lifted up his hands and cried in a loud voice ringing above the din: *The Eagles are coming!* And many voices answered crying: *The Eagles are coming! The Eagles are coming!* The hosts of Mordor looked up and wondered what this sign might mean.

There came Gwaihir the Windlord, and Landroval his brother, greatest of all the Eagles of the North, mightiest of the descendants of old Thorondor, who built his eyries in the inaccessible peaks of the Encircling Mountains when Middle-earth was young. Behind them in long swift lines came all their vassals from the northern mountains, speeding on a gathering wind. Straight down upon the Nazgûl they bore, stooping suddenly out of the high airs, and the rush of their wide wings as they passed over was like a gale.

But the Nazgûl turned and fled, and vanished into Mordor's shadows, hearing a sudden terrible call out of the Dark Tower; and even at that moment all the hosts of Mordor trembled, doubt clutched their hearts, their laughter failed, their hands shook and their limbs were loosed. The Power that drove them on and filled them with hate and fury was wavering, its will was removed from them; and now looking in the eyes of their enemies they saw a deadly light and were afraid.

Then all the Captains of the West cried aloud, for their hearts were filled with a new hope in the midst of darkness. Out from the beleaguered hills knights of Gondor, Riders of Rohan, Dúnedain of the North, close-serried companies, drove against their wavering foes, piercing the press with the thrust of bitter spears. But Gandalf lifted up his arms and called once more in a clear voice:

'Stand, Men of the West! Stand and wait! This is the hour of doom.'

And even as he spoke the earth rocked beneath their feet. Then rising swiftly up, far above the Towers of the Black Gate, high above the mountains, a vast soaring darkness sprang into the sky, flickering with fire. The earth groaned and quaked. The Towers of the Teeth swayed, tottered, and fell down; the mighty rampart crumbled; the Black Gate was hurled in ruin; and from far away, now dim, now growing, now mounting to the clouds, there came a drumming rumble, a roar, a long echoing roll of ruinous noise.

'The realm of Sauron is ended!' said Gandalf. 'The Ring-bearer has fulfilled his Quest.' And as the Captains gazed south to the Land of Mordor, it seemed to them that, black against the pall of cloud, there rose a huge shape of shadow, impenetrable, lightning-crowned, filling all the sky. Enormous it reared above the world, and stretched out towards them a vast threatening hand, terrible but impotent: for even as it leaned over them, a great wind took it, and it was all blown away, and passed; and then a hush fell.

The Captains bowed their heads; and when they looked up again, behold! their enemies were flying and the power of Mordor was scattering like dust in the wind. As when death smites the swollen brooding thing that inhabits their crawling hill and holds them all in sway, ants will wander witless and purposeless and then feebly die, so the creatures of Sauron, orc or troll or beast spell-enslaved, ran hither and thither mindless; and some slew themselves, or cast themselves in pits, or fled wailing back to hide in holes and dark lightless places far from hope. But the Men of Rhûn and of Harad, Easterling and Southron, saw the ruin of their war and the great majesty and glory of the Captains of the West. And those that were deepest and longest in evil servitude, hating the West, and yet were men proud and bold, in their turn now gathered themselves for a last stand of desperate battle. But the most part fled eastward as they could; and some cast their weapons down and sued for mercy.

Then Gandalf, leaving all such matters of battle and command to Aragorn and the other lords, stood upon the hill-top and called; and down to him came the great eagle, Gwaihir the Windlord, and stood before him.

'Twice you have borne me, Gwaihir my friend,' said Gandalf. 'Thrice shall pay for all, if you are willing. You will not find me a burden much greater than when you bore me from Zirakzigil, where my old life burned away.'

'I would bear you,' answered Gwaihir, 'whither you will, even were you made of stone.'

'Then come, and let your brother go with us, and some other of your folk who is most swift! For we have need of speed greater than any wind, outmatching the wings of the Nazgûl.'

'The North Wind blows, but we shall outfly it,' said Gwaihir. And he lifted up Gandalf and sped away south, and with him went Landroval, and Meneldor young and swift. And they passed over Udûn and Gorgoroth and saw all the land in ruin and tumult beneath them, and before them Mount Doom blazing, pouring out its fire.

'I am glad that you are here with me,' said Frodo. 'Here at the end of all things, Sam.'

'Yes, I am with you, Master,' said Sam, laying Frodo's wounded hand gently to his breast. 'And you're with me. And the journey's finished. But after coming all that way I don't want to give up yet. It's not like me, somehow, if you understand.'

'Maybe not, Sam,' said Frodo; 'but it's like things are in the world. Hopes fail. An end comes. We have only a little time to wait now. We are lost in ruin and downfall, and there is no escape.'

'Well, Master, we could at least go further from this dangerous place here, from this Crack of Doom, if that's its name. Now couldn't we? Come, Mr. Frodo, let's go down the path at any rate!'

· 'Very well, Sam. If you wish to go, I'll come,' said Frodo; and they rose and went slowly down the winding road; and even as they passed towards the Mountain's quaking feet, a great smoke and steam belched from the Sammath Naur, and the side of the cone was riven open, and a huge fiery vomit rolled in slow thunderous cascade down the eastern mountain-side.

Frodo and Sam could go no further. Their last strength of mind and body was swiftly ebbing. They had reached a low ashen hill piled at the Mountain's foot; but from it there was no more escape. It was an island now, not long to endure, amid the torment of Orodruin. All about it the earth gaped, and from deep rifts and pits smoke and fumes leaped up. Behind them the Mountain was convulsed. Great rents opened in its side. Slow rivers of fire came down the long slopes towards them. Soon they would be engulfed. A rain of hot ash was falling.

They stood now; and Sam still holding his master's hand caressed it. He sighed. 'What a tale we have been in, Mr. Frodo, haven't we?' he said. 'I wish I could hear it told! Do you think they'll say: *Now comes the story of Nine-fingered Frodo and the Ring of Doom*? And then everyone will hush, like we did, when in Rivendell they told us the tale of Beren One-hand and the Great Jewel. I wish I could hear it! And I wonder how it will go on after our part.'

But even while he spoke so, to keep fear away until the very last, his eyes still strayed north, north into the eye of the wind, to where the sky far off was clear, as the cold blast, rising to a gale, drove back the darkness and the ruin of the clouds.

And so it was that Gwaihir saw them with his keen far-seeing eyes, as down the wild wind he came, and daring the great peril of the skies he circled in the air: two small dark figures, forlorn, hand in hand upon a little hill, while the world shook under them, and gasped, and rivers of fire drew near. And even as he espied them and came swooping down, he saw them fall, worn out, or choked with fumes and heat, or stricken down by despair at last, hiding their eyes from death.

Side by side they lay; and down swept Gwaihir, and down came Landroval and Meneldor the swift; and in a dream, not knowing what fate had befallen them, the wanderers were lifted up and borne far away out of the darkness and the fire.

When Sam awoke, he found that he was lying on some soft bed, but over him gently swayed wide beechen boughs, and through their young leaves sunlight glimmered, green and gold. All the air was full of a sweet mingled scent.

He remembered that smell: the fragrance of Ithilien. 'Bless me!' he .mused. 'How long have I been asleep?' For the scent had borne him back to the day when he had lit his little fire under the sunny bank; and for the moment all else between was out of waking memory. He stretched and drew a deep breath. 'Why, what a dream I've had!' he muttered. 'I am glad to wake!' He sat up and then he saw that Frodo was lying beside him, and slept peacefully, one hand behind his head, and the other resting upon the coverlet. It was the right hand, and the third finger was missing.

Full memory flooded back, and Sam cried aloud: 'It wasn't a dream! Then where are we?'

And a voice spoke softly behind him: 'In the land of Ithilien, and in the keeping of the King; and he awaits you.' With that Gandalf stood before him, robed in white, his beard now gleaming like pure snow in the twinkling of the leafy sunlight. 'Well, Master Samwise, how do you feel?' he said.

But Sam lay back, and stared with open mouth, and for a moment, between bewilderment and great joy, he could not answer. At last he gasped: 'Gandalf! I thought you were dead! But then I thought I was dead myself. Is everything sad going to come untrue? What's happened to the world?'

'A great Shadow has departed,' said Gandalf, and then he laughed, and the sound was like music, or like water in a parched land; and as he listened the thought came to Sam that he had not heard laughter, the pure sound of merriment, for days upon days without count. It fell upon his ears like the echo of all the joys he had ever known. But he himself burst into tears. Then, as a sweet rain will pass down a wind of spring and the sun will shine out the clearer, his tears ceased, and his laughter welled up, and laughing he sprang from his bed.

'How do I feel?' he cried. 'Well, I don't know how to say it. I feel, I feel' – he waved his arms in the air – 'I feel like spring after winter, and sun on the leaves; and like trumpets and harps and all the songs I have ever heard!' He stopped and he turned towards his master. 'But how's Mr. Frodo?' he said. 'Isn't it a shame about his poor hand? But I hope he's all right otherwise. He's had a cruel time.'

'Yes, I am all right otherwise,' said Frodo, sitting up and laughing in his turn. 'I fell asleep again waiting for you, Sam, you sleepyhead. I was awake early this morning, and now it must be nearly noon.'

'Noon?' said Sam, trying to calculate. 'Noon of what day?'

'The fourteenth of the New Year,' said Gandalf; 'or if you like, the eighth day of April in the Shire reckoning.* But in Gondor the New Year will always now begin upon the twenty-fifth of March when Sauron fell, and when you were brought out of the fire to the King. He has tended you, and now he awaits you. You shall eat and drink with him. When you are ready I will lead you to him.'

'The King?' said Sam. 'What king, and who is he?'

'The King of Gondor and Lord of the Western Lands,' said Gandalf; 'and he has taken back all his ancient realm. He will ride soon to his crowning, but he waits for you.'

'What shall we wear?' said Sam; for all he could see was the old and tattered clothes that they had journeyed in, lying folded on the ground beside their beds.

'The clothes that you wore on your way to Mordor,' said Gandalf. 'Even the orc-rags that you bore in the black land, Frodo, shall be preserved. No silks and linens, nor any armour or heraldry could be more honourable. But later I will find some other clothes, perhaps.'

Then he held out his hands to them, and they saw that one shone with light. 'What have you got there?' Frodo cried. 'Can it be – ?'

'Yes, I have brought your two treasures. They were found on Sam when you were rescued; the Lady Galadriel's gifts: your glass, Frodo; and your box, Sam. You will be glad to have these safe again.'

When they were washed and clad, and had eaten a light meal, the Hobbits followed Gandalf. They stepped out of the beech-grove in which they had

---

* There were thirty days in March (or Rethe) in the Shire calendar.

lain, and passed on to a long green lawn, glowing in sunshine, bordered by stately dark-leaved trees laden with scarlet blossom. Behind them they could hear the sound of falling water, and a stream ran down before them between flowering banks, until it came to a greenwood at the lawn's foot and passed then on under an archway of trees, through which they saw the shimmer of water far away.

As they came to the opening in the wood, they were surprised to see knights in bright mail and tall guards in silver and black standing there, who greeted them with honour and bowed before them. And then one blew a long trumpet, and they went on through the aisle of trees beside the singing stream. So they came to a wide green land, and beyond it was a broad river in a silver haze, out of which rose a long wooded isle, and many ships lay by its shores. But on the field where they now stood a great host was drawn up, in ranks and companies glittering in the sun. And as the Hobbits approached swords were unsheathed, and spears were shaken, and horns and trumpets sang, and men cried with many voices and in many tongues:

> *'Long live the Halflings! Praise them with great praise!*
> *Cuio i Pheriain anann! Aglar'ni Pheriannath!*
> *Praise them with great praise, Frodo and Samwise!*
> *Daur a Berhael, Conin en Annûn! Eglerio!*
> *Praise them!*
> *Eglerio!*
> *A laita te, laita te! Andave laituvalmet!*
> *Praise them!*
> *Cormacolindor, a laita tárienna!*
> *Praise them! The Ring-bearers, praise them with great praise!'*

And so the red blood blushing in their faces and their eyes shining with wonder, Frodo and Sam went forward and saw that amidst the clamorous host were set three high-seats built of green turves. Behind the seat upon the right floated, white on green, a great horse running free; upon the left was a banner, silver upon blue, a ship swan-prowed faring on the sea; but behind the highest throne in the midst of all a great standard was spread in the breeze, and there a white tree flowered upon a sable field beneath a shining crown and seven glittering stars. On the throne sat a mail-clad man, a great sword was laid across his knees, but he wore no helm. As they drew near he rose. And then they knew him, changed as he was, so high and glad of face, kingly, lord of Men, dark-haired with eyes of grey.

Frodo ran to meet him, and Sam followed close behind. 'Well, if this isn't the crown of all!' he said. 'Strider, or I'm still asleep!'

'Yes, Sam, Strider,' said Aragorn. 'It is a long way, is it not, from Bree, where you did not like the look of me? A long way for us all, but yours has been the darkest road.'

. And then to Sam's surprise and utter confusion he bowed his knee before them; and taking them by the hand, Frodo upon his right and Sam upon his left, he led them to the throne, and setting them upon it, he turned to the men and captains who stood by and spoke, so that his voice rang over all the host, crying:

'Praise them with great praise!'

And when the glad shout had swelled up and died away again, to Sam's final and complete satisfaction and pure joy, a minstrel of Gondor stood forth, and knelt, and begged leave to sing. And behold! he said:

'Lo! lords and knights and men of valour unashamed, kings and princes, and fair people of Gondor, and Riders of Rohan, and ye sons of Elrond, and Dúnedain of the North, and Elf and Dwarf, and greathearts of the Shire, and all free folk of the West, now listen to my lay. For I will sing to you of Frodo of the Nine Fingers and the Ring of Doom.'

And when Sam heard that he laughed aloud for sheer delight, and he stood up and cried: 'O great glory and splendour! And all my wishes have come true!' And then he wept.

And all the host laughed and wept, and in the midst of their merriment and tears the clear voice of the minstrel rose like silver and gold, and all men were hushed. And he sang to them, now in the Elven-tongue, now in the speech of the West, until their hearts, wounded with sweet words, overflowed, and their joy was like swords, and they passed in thought out to regions where pain and delight flow together and tears are the very wine of blessedness.

And at the last, as the Sun fell from the noon and the shadows of the trees lengthened, he ended. 'Praise them with great praise!' he said and knelt. And then Aragorn stood up, and all the host arose, and they passed to pavilions made ready, to eat and drink and make merry while the day lasted.

Frodo and Sam were led apart and brought to a tent, and there their old raiment was taken off, but folded and set aside with honour; and clean linen was given to them. Then Gandalf came and in his arms, to the wonder of Frodo, he bore the sword and the elven-cloak and the mithril-coat that had been taken from him in Mordor. For Sam he brought a coat of gilded mail, and his elven-cloak all healed of the soils and hurts that it had suffered; and then he laid before them two swords.

'I do not wish for any sword,' said Frodo.

'Tonight at least you should wear one,' said Gandalf.

Then Frodo took the small sword that had belonged to Sam, and had been laid at his side in Cirith Ungol. 'Sting I gave to you Sam,' he said.

'No, master! Mr. Bilbo gave it to you, and it goes with his silver coat; he would not wish anyone else to wear it now.'

Frodo gave way; and Gandalf, as if he were their esquire, knelt and girt the sword-belts about them, and then rising he set circlets of silver upon their heads. And when they were arrayed they went to the great feast; and they sat at the King's table with Gandalf, and King Éomer of Rohan, and the Prince Imrahil and all the chief captains; and there also were Gimli and Legolas.

But when, after the Standing Silence, wine was brought there came in two esquires to serve the kings; or so they seemed to be: one was clad in the silver and sable of the Guards of Minas Tirith, and the other in white and green. But Sam wondered what such young boys were doing in an army of mighty men. Then suddenly as they drew near and he could see them plainly, he exclaimed:

'Why, look Mr. Frodo! Look here! Well, if it isn't Pippin. Mr. Peregrin Took I should say, and Mr. Merry! How they have grown! Bless me! But I can see there's more tales to tell than ours.'

'There are indeed,' said Pippin turning towards him. 'And we'll begin telling them, as soon as this feast is ended. In the meantime you can try Gandalf. He's not so close as he used to be, though he laughs now more than he talks. For the present Merry and I are busy. We are knights of the City and of the Mark, as I hope you observe.'

At last the glad day ended; and when the Sun was gone and the round Moon rode slowly above the mists of Anduin and flickered through the fluttering leaves, Frodo and Sam sat under the whispering trees amid the fragrance of fair Ithilien; and they talked deep into the night with Merry and Pippin and Gandalf, and after a while Legolas and Gimli joined them. There Frodo and Sam learned much of all that had happened to the Company after their fellowship was broken on the evil day at Parth Galen by Rauros Falls; and still there was always more to ask and more to tell.

Orcs, and talking trees, and leagues of grass, and galloping riders, and glittering caves, and white towers and golden halls, and battles, and tall ships sailing, all these passed before Sam's mind until he felt bewildered. But amidst all these wonders he returned always to his astonishment at the size of Merry and Pippin; and he made them stand back to back with Frodo and himself. He scratched his head. 'Can't understand it at your age!' he said. 'But there it is: you're three inches taller than you ought to be, or I'm a dwarf.'

'That you certainly are not,' said Gimli. 'But what did I say? Mortals cannot go drinking ent-draughts and expect no more to come of them than of a pot of beer.'

'Ent-draughts?' said Sam. 'There you go about Ents again; but what they are beats me. Why, it will take weeks before we get all these things sized up!'

'Weeks indeed,' said Pippin. 'And then Frodo will have to be locked up in a tower in Minas Tirith and write it all down. Otherwise he will forget half of it, and poor old Bilbo will be dreadfully disappointed.'

At length Gandalf rose. 'The hands of the King are hands of healing, dear friends,' he said. 'But you went to the very brink of death ere he recalled you, putting forth all his power, and sent you into the sweet forgetfulness of sleep. And though you have indeed slept long and blessedly, still it is now time to sleep again.'

'And not only Sam and Frodo here,' said Gimli, 'but you too, Pippin. I love you, if only because of the pains you have cost me, which I shall never forget. Nor shall I forget finding you on the hill of the last battle. But for Gimli the Dwarf you would have been lost then. But at least I know now the look of a hobbit's foot, though it be all that can be seen under a heap of bodies. And when I heaved that great carcase off you, I made sure you were dead. I could have torn out my beard. And it is only a day yet since you were first up and abroad again. To bed now you go. And so shall I.'

'And I,' said Legolas, 'shall walk in the woods of this fair land, which is rest enough. In days to come, if my Elven-lord allows, some of our folk shall remove hither; and when we come it shall be blessed, for a while. For a while: a month, a life, a hundred years of Men. But Anduin is near, and Anduin leads down to the Sea. To the Sea!

> To the Sea, to the Sea! The white gulls are crying,
> The wind is blowing, and the white foam is flying.
> West, west away, the round sun is falling.
> Grey ship, grey ship, do you hear them calling,
> The voices of my people that have gone before me?
> I will leave, I will leave the woods that bore me;
> For our days are ending and our years failing.
> I will pass the wide waters lonely sailing.
> Long are the waves on the Last Shore falling,
> Sweet are the voices in the Lost Isle calling,
> In Eressëa, in Elvenhome that no man can discover,
> Where the leaves fall not: land of my people for ever!'

And so singing Legolas went away down the hill.

Then the others also departed, and Frodo and Sam went to their beds and slept. And in the morning they rose again in hope and peace; and they spent many days in Ithilien. For the Field of Cormallen, where the host was now encamped, was near to Henneth Annûn, and the stream that flowed from its falls could be heard in the night as it rushed down through its rocky gate, and passed through the flowery meads into the tides of Anduin by the Isle of Cair Andros. The hobbits wandered here and there visiting again the places that they had passed before; and Sam hoped always in some shadow of the woods or secret glade to catch, maybe, a glimpse of the great Oliphaunt. And when he learned that at the siege of Gondor there had been a great number of these beasts but that they were all destroyed, he thought it a sad loss.

'Well, one can't be everywhere at once, I suppose,' he said. 'But I missed a lot, seemingly.'

In the meanwhile the host made ready for the return to Minas Tirith. The weary rested and the hurt were healed. For some had laboured and fought much with the remnants of the Easterlings and Southrons, until all were subdued. And, latest of all, those returned who had passed into Mordor and destroyed the fortresses in the north of the land.

But at the last when the month of May was drawing near the Captains of the West set out again; and they went aboard ship with all their men, and they sailed from Cair Andros down Anduin to Osgiliath; and there they remained for one day; and the day after they came to the green fields of the Pelennor and saw again the white towers under tall Mindolluin, the City of the Men of Gondor, last memory of Westernesse, that had passed through the darkness and fire to a new day.

And there in the midst of the fields they set up their pavilions and awaited the morning; for it was the Eve of May, and the King would enter his gates with the rising of the Sun.

CHAPTER V

THE STEWARD AND THE KING

Over the city of Gondor doubt and great dread had hung. Fair weather and clear sun had seemed but a mockery to men whose days held little hope, and who looked each morning for news of doom. Their lord was dead and burned, dead lay the King of Rohan in their citadel, and the new king that had come to them in the night was gone again to a war with powers too dark and terrible for any might or valour to conquer. And no news came. After the host left Morgul Vale and took the northward road beneath the shadow of the mountains no messenger had returned nor any rumour of what was passing in the brooding East.

When the Captains were but two days gone, the Lady Éowyn bade the women who tended her to bring her raiment, and she would not be gainsaid, but rose; and when they had clothed her and set her arm in a sling of linen, she went to the Warden of the Houses of Healing.

'Sir,' she said, 'I am in great unrest, and I cannot lie longer in sloth.'

'Lady,' he answered, 'you are not yet healed, and I was commanded to tend you with especial care. You should not have risen from your bed for seven days yet, or so I was bidden. I beg you to go back.'

'I am healed,' she said, 'healed at least in body, save my left arm only, and that is at ease. But I shall sicken anew, if there is naught that I can do. Are there no tidings of war? The women can tell me nothing.'

'There are no tidings,' said the Warden, 'save that the Lords have ridden to Morgul Vale; and men say that the new captain out of the North is their chief. A great lord is that, and a healer; and it is a thing passing strange to me that the healing hand should also wield the sword. It is not thus in Gondor now, though once it was so, if old tales be true. But for long years we healers have only sought to patch the rents made by the men of swords. Though we should still have enough to do without them: the world is full enough of hurts and mischances without wars to multiply them.'

'It needs but one foe to breed a war, not two, Master Warden,' answered Éowyn. 'And those who have not swords can still die upon them. Would you have the folk of Gondor gather you herbs only, when the Dark Lord gathers armies? And it is not always good to be healed in body. Nor is it always evil to die in battle, even in bitter pain. Were I permitted, in this dark hour I would choose the latter.'

The Warden looked at her. Tall she stood there, her eyes bright in her white face, her hand clenched as she turned and gazed out of his window that opened to the East. He sighed and shook his head. After a pause she turned to him again.

'Is there no deed to do?' she said. 'Who commands in this City?'

'I do not rightly know,' he answered. 'Such things are not my care. There is a marshal over the Riders of Rohan; and the Lord Húrin, I am told, commands the men of Gondor. But the Lord Faramir is by right the Steward of the City.'

'Where can I find him?'

'In this house, lady. He was sorely hurt, but is now set again on the way to health. But I do not know——'

'Will you not bring me to him? Then you will know.'

The Lord Faramir was walking alone in the garden of the Houses of Healing, and the sunlight warmed him, and he felt life run new in his veins; but his heart was heavy, and he looked out over the walls eastward. And coming, the Warden spoke his name, and he turned and saw the Lady Éowyn of Rohan; and he was moved with pity, for he saw that she was hurt, and his clear sight perceived her sorrow and unrest.

'My lord,' said the Warden, 'here is the Lady Éowyn of Rohan. She rode with the king and was sorely hurt, and dwells now in my keeping. But she is not content, and she wishes to speak to the Steward of the City.'

'Do not misunderstand him, lord,' said Éowyn. 'It is not lack of care that grieves me. No houses could be fairer, for those who desire to be healed. But I cannot lie in sloth, idle, caged. I looked for death in battle. But I have not died, and battle still goes on.'

At a sign from Faramir, the Warden bowed and departed. 'What would you have me do, lady?' said Faramir. 'I also am a prisoner of the healers.' He looked at her, and being a man whom pity deeply stirred, it seemed to him that her loveliness amid her grief would pierce his heart. And she looked at him and saw the grave tenderness in his eyes, and yet knew, for she was bred among men of war, that here was one whom no Rider of the Mark would outmatch in battle.

'What do you wish?' he said again. 'If it lies in my power, I will do it.'

'I would have you command this Warden, and bid him let me go,' she said; but though her words were still proud, her heart faltered, and for the first time she doubted herself. She guessed that this tall man, both stern and gentle, might think her merely wayward, like a child that has not the firmness of mind to go on with a dull task to the end.

'I myself am in the Warden's keeping,' answered Faramir. 'Nor have I yet taken up my authority in the City. But had I done so, I should still listen to his counsel, and should not cross his will in matters of his craft, unless in some great need.'

'But I do not desire healing,' she said. 'I wish to ride to war like my brother Éomer, or better like Théoden the king, for he died and has both honour and peace.'

'It is too late, lady, to follow the Captains, even if you had the strength,' said Faramir. 'But death in battle may come to us all yet, willing or unwilling. You will be better prepared to face it in your own manner, if while there is still time you do as the Healer commanded. You and I, we must endure with patience the hours of waiting.'

She did not answer, but as he looked at her it seemed to him that something in her softened, as though a bitter frost were yielding at the first faint presage of Spring. A tear sprang in her eye and fell down her cheek, like a glistening rain-drop. Her proud head drooped a little. Then quietly, more as if speaking to herself than to him: 'But the healers would have me lie abed seven days yet,' she said. 'And my window does not look eastward.' Her voice was now that of a maiden young and sad.

Faramir smiled, though his heart was filled with pity. 'Your window does not look eastward?' he said. 'That can be amended. In this I will command the Warden. If you will stay in this house in our care, lady, and take your rest, then you shall walk in this garden in the sun, as you will; and you shall look east, whither all our hopes have gone. And here you will find me, walking and waiting, and also looking east. It would ease my care, if you would speak to me, or walk at whiles with me.'

Then she raised her head and looked him in the eyes again; and a colour came in her pale face. 'How should I ease your care, my lord?' she said. 'And I do not desire the speech of living men.'

'Would you have my plain answer?' he said.

'I would.'

'Then, Éowyn of Rohan, I say to you that you are beautiful. In the valleys of our hills there are flowers fair and bright, and maidens fairer still; but neither flower nor lady have I seen till now in Gondor so lovely, and so sorrowful. It may be that only a few days are left ere darkness falls upon our world, and when it comes I hope to face it steadily; but it would ease my heart, if while the Sun yet shines, I could see you still. For you and I have both passed under the wings of the Shadow, and the same hand drew us back.'

'Alas, not me, lord!' she said. 'Shadow lies on me still. Look not to me for healing! I am a shieldmaiden and my hand is ungentle. But I thank you for this at least, that I need not keep to my chamber. I will walk abroad by the grace of the Steward of the City.' And she did him a courtesy and walked back to the house. But Faramir for a long while walked alone in the garden, and his glance now strayed rather to the house than to the eastward walls.

When he returned to his chamber he called for the Warden, and heard all that he could tell of the Lady of Rohan.

'But I doubt not, lord,' said the Warden, 'that you would learn more from the Halfling that is with us; for he was in the riding of the king, and with the Lady at the end, they say.'

And so Merry was sent to Faramir, and while that day lasted they talked long together, and Faramir learned much, more even than Merry put into words; and he thought that he understood now something of the grief and unrest of Éowyn of Rohan. And in the fair evening Faramir and Merry walked in the garden, but she did not come.

But in the morning, as Faramir came from the Houses, he saw her, as she stood upon the walls; and she was clad all in white, and gleamed in the sun. And he called to her, and she came down, and they walked on the grass or sat under a green tree together, now in silence, now in speech. And each day after they did likewise. And the Warden looking from his window was glad in heart, for he was a healer, and his care was lightened; and certain it was that, heavy as was the dread and foreboding of those days upon the hearts of men, still these two of his charges prospered and grew daily in strength.

And so the fifth day came since the Lady Éowyn went first to Faramir; and they stood now together once more upon the walls of the City and looked out. No tidings had yet come, and all hearts were darkened. The weather, too, was bright no longer. It was cold. A wind that had sprung up in the night was blowing now keenly from the North, and it was rising; but the lands about looked grey and drear.

They were clad in warm raiment and heavy cloaks, and over all the Lady Éowyn wore a great blue mantle of the colour of deep summer-night, and it was set with silver stars about hem and throat. Faramir had sent for this robe and had wrapped it about her; and he thought that she looked fair and queenly indeed as she stood there at his side. The mantle was wrought for his mother, Finduilas of Amroth, who died untimely, and was to him but a memory of loveliness in far days and of his first grief; and her robe seemed to him raiment fitting for the beauty and sadness of Éowyn.

But she now shivered beneath the starry mantle, and she looked northward, above the grey hither lands, into the eye of the cold wind where far away the sky was hard and clear.

'What do you look for, Éowyn?' said Faramir.

'Does not the Black Gate lie yonder?' said she. 'And must he not now be come thither? It is seven days since he rode away.'

'Seven days,' said Faramir. 'But think not ill of me, if I say to you: they have brought me both a joy and a pain that I never thought to know. Joy to see you; but pain, because now the fear and doubt of this evil time are grown dark indeed. Éowyn, I would not have this world end now, or lose so soon what I have found.'

'Lose what you have found, lord?' she answered; but she looked at him gravely and her eyes were kind. 'I know not what in these days you have found that you could lose. But come, my friend, let us not speak of it! Let us not speak at all! I stand upon some dreadful brink, and it is utterly dark in the abyss before my feet, but whether there is any light behind me I cannot tell. For I cannot turn yet. I wait for some stroke of doom.'

'Yes, we wait for the stroke of doom,' said Faramir. And they said no more; and it seemed to them as they stood upon the wall that the wind died, and the light failed, and the Sun was bleared, and all sounds in the City or in the lands about were hushed: neither wind, nor voice, nor bird-call, nor rustle of leaf, nor their own breath could be heard; the very beating of their hearts was stilled. Time halted.

And as they stood so, their hands met and clasped, though they did not know it. And still they waited for they knew not what. Then presently it seemed to them that above the ridges of the distant mountains another vast mountain of darkness rose, towering up like a wave that should engulf the world, and about it lightnings flickered; and then a tremor ran through the earth, and they felt the walls of the City quiver. A sound like a sigh went up from all the lands about them; and their hearts beat suddenly again.

'It reminds me of Númenor,' said Faramir, and wondered to hear himself speak.

'Of Númenor?' said Éowyn.

'Yes,' said Faramir, 'of the land of Westernesse that foundered, and of the great dark wave climbing over the green lands and above the hills, and coming on, darkness unescapable. I often dream of it.'

'Then you think that the Darkness is coming?' said Éowyn. 'Darkness Unescapable?' And suddenly she drew close to him.

'No,' said Faramir, looking into her face. 'It was but a picture in the mind. I do not know what is happening. The reason of my waking mind tells me that great evil has befallen and we stand at the end of days. But my heart says nay; and all my limbs are light, and a hope and joy are come to me that no reason can deny. Éowyn, Éowyn, White Lady of Rohan, in this hour I do not believe that any darkness will endure!' And he stooped and kissed her brow.

And so they stood on the walls of the City of Gondor, and a great wind rose and blew, and their hair, raven and golden, streamed out mingling in the air. And the Shadow departed, and the Sun was unveiled, and light leaped forth; and the waters of Anduin shone like silver, and in all the houses of the City men sang for the joy that welled up in their hearts from what source they could not tell.

And before the Sun had fallen far from the noon out of the East there came a great Eagle flying, and he bore tidings beyond hope from the Lords of the West, crying:

> *Sing now, ye people of the Tower of Anor,*
> *for the Realm of Sauron is ended for ever,*
> *   and the Dark Tower is thrown down.*
>
> *Sing and rejoice, ye people of the Tower of Guard,*
> *for your watch hath not been in vain,*
> *and the Black Gate is broken,*
> *and your King hath passed through,*
> *   and he is victorious.*
>
> *Sing and be glad, all ye children of the West,*
> *for your King shall come again,*
> *and he shall dwell among you*
> *   all the days of your life.*
>
> *And the Tree that was withered shall be renewed,*
> *and he shall plant it in the high places,*
> *   and the City shall be blessed.*
>
> *Sing all ye people!*

And the people sang in all the ways of the City.

The days that followed were golden, and Spring and Summer joined and made revel together in the fields of Gondor. And tidings now came by swift riders from Cair Andros of all that was done, and the City made ready for the coming of the King. Merry was summoned and rode away with the wains that took store of goods to Osgiliath and thence by ship to Cair Andros; but Faramir did not go, for now being healed he took upon him his authority and the Stewardship, although it was only for a little while, and his duty was to prepare for one who should replace him.

And Éowyn did not go, though her brother sent word begging her to come to the field of Cormallen. And Faramir wondered at this, but he saw her seldom, being busy with many matters; and she dwelt still in the Houses of Healing and walked alone in the garden, and her face grew pale again, and it seemed that in all the City she only was ailing and sorrowful.

And the Warden of the Houses was troubled, and he spoke to Faramir.

Then Faramir came and sought her, and once more they stood on the walls together; and he said to her: 'Éowyn, why do you tarry here, and do not go to the rejoicing in Cormallen beyond Cair Andros, where your brother awaits you?'

And she said: 'Do you not know?'

But he answered: 'Two reasons there may be, but which is true, I do not know.'

And she said: 'I do not wish to play at riddles. Speak plainer!'

'Then if you will have it so, lady,' he said: 'you do not go, because only your brother called for you, and to look on the Lord Aragorn, Elendil's heir, in his triumph would now bring you no joy. Or because I do not go, and you desire still to be near me. And maybe for both these reasons, and you yourself cannot choose between them. Éowyn, do you not love me, or will you not?'

'I wished to be loved by another,' she answered. 'But I desire no man's pity.'

'That I know,' he said. 'You desired to have the love of the Lord Aragorn. Because he was high and puissant, and you wished to have renown and glory and to be lifted far above the mean things that crawl on the earth. And as a great captain may to a young soldier he seemed to you admirable. For so he is, a lord among men, the greatest that now is. But when he gave you only understanding and pity, then you desired to have nothing, unless a brave death in battle. Look at me, Éowyn!'

And Éowyn looked at Faramir long and steadily; and Faramir said: 'Do not scorn pity that is the gift of a gentle heart, Éowyn! But I do not offer you my pity. For you are a lady high and valiant and have yourself won renown that shall not be forgotten; and you are a lady beautiful, I deem, beyond even the words of the Elven-tongue to tell. And I love you. Once I pitied your sorrow. But now, were you sorrowless, without fear or any lack, were you the blissful Queen of Gondor, still I would love you. Éowyn, do you not love me?'

Then the heart of Éowyn changed, or else at last she understood it. And suddenly her winter passed, and the sun shone on her.

'I stand in Minas Anor, the Tower of the Sun,' she said; 'and behold! the Shadow has departed! I will be a shieldmaiden no longer, nor vie with the great Riders, nor take joy only in the songs of slaying. I will be a healer, and love all things that grow and are not barren.' And again she looked at Faramir. 'No longer do I desire to be a queen,' she said.

Then Faramir laughed merrily. 'That is well,' he said; 'for I am not a king. Yet I will wed with the White Lady of Rohan, if it be her will. And if she will, then let us cross the River and in happier days let us dwell in fair Ithilien and there make a garden. All things will grow with joy there, if the White Lady comes.'

'Then must I leave my own people, man of Gondor?' she said. 'And would you have your proud folk say of you: "There goes a lord who tamed a wild shieldmaiden of the North! Was there no woman of the race of Númenor to choose?"'

'I would,' said Faramir. And he took her in his arms and kissed her under the sunlit sky, and he cared not that they stood high upon the walls in the sight of many. And many indeed saw them and the light that shone about them as they came down from the walls and went hand in hand to the Houses of Healing.

And to the Warden of the Houses Faramir said: 'Here is the Lady Éowyn of Rohan, and now she is healed.'

And the Warden said: 'Then I release her from my charge and bid her farewell, and may she suffer never hurt nor sickness again. I commend her to the care of the Steward of the City, until her brother returns.'

But Éowyn said: 'Yet now that I have leave to depart, I would remain. For this House has become to me of all dwellings the most blessed.' And she remained there until King Éomer came.

All things were now made ready in the City; and there was great concourse of people, for the tidings had gone out into all parts of Gondor, from Min-Rimmon even to Pinnath Gelin and the far coasts of the sea; and all that could come to the City made haste to come. And the City was filled again with women and fair children that returned to their homes laden with flowers; and from Dol Amroth came the harpers that harped most skilfully in all the land; and there were players upon viols and upon flutes and upon horns of silver, and clear-voiced singers from the vales of Lebennin.

At last an evening came when from the walls the pavilions could be seen upon the field, and all night lights were burning as men watched for the dawn. And when the sun rose in the clear morning above the mountains in the East, upon which shadows lay no more, then all the bells rang, and all the banners broke and flowed in the wind; and upon the White Tower of the citadel the standard of the Stewards, bright argent like snow in the sun, bearing no charge nor device, was raised over Gondor for the last time.

Now the Captains of the West led their host towards the City, and folk saw them advance in line upon line, flashing and glinting in the sunrise and rippling like silver. And so they came before the Gateway and halted a furlong from the walls. As yet no gates had been set up again, but a barrier was laid across the entrance to the City, and there stood men at arms in silver and black with long swords drawn. Before the barrier stood

Faramir the Steward, and Húrin Warden of the Keys, and other captains of Gondor, and the Lady Éowyn of Rohan with Elfhelm the Marshal and many knights of the Mark; and upon either side of the Gate was a great press of fair people in raiment of many colours and garlands of flowers.

So now there was a wide space before the walls of Minas Tirith, and it was hemmed in upon all sides by the knights and the soldiers of Gondor and of Rohan, and by the people of the City and of all parts of the land. A hush fell upon all as out from the host stepped the Dúnedain in silver and grey; and before them came walking slow the Lord Aragorn. He was clad in black mail girt with silver, and he wore a long mantle of pure white clasped at the throat with a great jewel of green that shone from afar; but his head was bare save for a star upon his forehead bound by a slender fillet of silver. With him were Éomer of Rohan, and the Prince Imrahil, and Gandalf robed all in white, and four small figures that many men marvelled to see.

'Nay, cousin! they are not boys,' said Ioreth to her kinswoman from Imloth Melui, who stood beside her. 'Those are Periain, out of the far country of the Halflings, where they are princes of great fame, it is said. I should know, for I had one to tend in the Houses. They are small, but they are valiant. Why, cousin, one of them went with only his esquire into the Black Country and fought with the Dark Lord all by himself, and set fire to his Tower, if you can believe it. At least that is the tale in the City. That will be the one that walks with our Elfstone. They are dear friends, I hear. Now he is a marvel, the Lord Elfstone: not too soft in his speech, mind you, but he has a golden heart, as the saying is; and he has the healing hands. "The hands of the king are the hands of a healer", I said; and that was how it was all discovered. And Mithrandir, he said to me: "Ioreth, men will long remember your words", and——'

But Ioreth was not permitted to continue the instruction of her kinswoman from the country, for a single trumpet rang, and a dead silence followed. Then forth from the Gate went Faramir with Húrin of the Keys, and no others, save that behind them walked four men in the high helms and armour of the Citadel, and they bore a great casket of black *lebethron* bound with silver.

Faramir met Aragorn in the midst of those there assembled, and he knelt, and said: 'The last Steward of Gondor begs leave to surrender his office.' And he held out a white rod; but Aragorn took the rod and gave it back, saying: 'That office is not ended, and it shall be thine and thy heirs' as long as my line shall last. Do now thy office!'

Then Faramir stood up and spoke in a clear voice: 'Men of Gondor, hear now the Steward of this Realm! Behold! one has come to claim the kingship again at last. Here is Aragorn son of Arathorn, chieftain of the

Dúnedain of Arnor, Captain of the Host of the West, bearer of the Star of the North, wielder of the Sword Reforged, victorious in battle, whose hands bring healing, the Elfstone, Elessar of the line of Valandil, Isildur's son, Elendil's son of Númenor. Shall he be king and enter into the City and dwell there?'

And all the host and all the people cried *yea* with one voice.

And Ioreth said to her kinswoman: 'This is just a ceremony such as we have in the City, cousin; for he has already entered, as I was telling you; and he said to me———' And then again she was obliged to silence, for Faramir spoke again.

'Men of Gondor, the loremasters tell that it was the custom of old that the king should receive the crown from his father ere he died; or if that might not be, that he should go alone and take it from the hands of his father in the tomb where he was laid. But since things must now be done otherwise, using the authority of the Steward, I have today brought hither from Rath Dínen the crown of Eärnur the last king, whose days passed in the time of our longfathers of old.'

Then the guards stepped forward, and Faramir opened the casket, and he held up an ancient crown. It was shaped like the helms of the Guards of the Citadel, save that it was loftier, and it was all white, and the wings at either side were wrought of pearl and silver in the likeness of the wings of a sea-bird, for it was the emblem of kings who came over the Sea; and seven gems of adamant were set in the circlet, and upon its summit was set a single jewel the light of which went up like a flame.

Then Aragorn took the crown and held it up and said:

Et Eärello Endorenna utúlien. Sinome maruvan ar Hildinyar tenn' Ambar-metta!

And those were the words that Elendil spoke when he came up out of the Sea on the wings of the wind: 'Out of the Great Sea to Middle-earth I am come. In this place will I abide, and my heirs, unto the ending of the world.'

Then to the wonder of many Aragorn did not put the crown upon his head, but gave it back to Faramir, and said: 'By the labour and valour of many I have come into my inheritance. In token of this I would have the Ring-bearer bring the crown to me, and let Mithrandir set it upon my head, if he will; for he has been the mover of all that has been accomplished, and this is his victory.'

Then Frodo came forward and took the crown from Faramir and bore it to Gandalf; and Aragorn knelt, and Gandalf set the White Crown upon his head, and said:

'Now come the days of the King, and may they be blessed while the thrones of the Valar endure!'

But when Aragorn arose all that beheld him gazed in silence, for it seemed to them that he was revealed to them now for the first time. Tall as the sea-kings of old, he stood above all that were near; ancient of days he seemed and yet in the flower of manhood; and wisdom sat upon his brow, and strength and healing were in his hands, and a light was about him. And then Faramir cried:

'Behold the King!'

And in that moment all the trumpets were blown, and the King Elessar went forth and came to the barrier, and Húrin of the Keys thrust it back; and amid the music of harp and of viol and of flute and the singing of clear voices the King passed through the flower-laden streets, and came to the Citadel, and entered in; and the banner of the Tree and the Stars was unfurled upon the topmost tower, and the reign of King Elessar began, of which many songs have told.

In his time the City was made more fair than it had ever been, even in the days of its first glory; and it was filled with trees and with fountains, and its gates were wrought of mithril and steel, and its streets were paved with white marble; and the Folk of the Mountain laboured in it, and the Folk of the Wood rejoiced to come there; and all was healed and made good, and the houses were filled with men and women and the laughter of children, and no window was blind nor any courtyard empty; and after the ending of the Third Age of the world into the new age it preserved the memory and the glory of the years that were gone.

In the days that followed his crowning the King sat on his throne in the Hall of the Kings and pronounced his judgements. And embassies came from many lands and peoples, from the East and the South, and from the borders of Mirkwood, and from Dunland in the west. And the King pardoned the Easterlings that had given themselves up, and sent them away free, and he made peace with the peoples of Harad; and the slaves of Mordor he released and gave to them all the lands about Lake Núrnen to be their own. And there were brought before him many to receive his praise and reward for their valour; and last the captain of the Guard brought to him Beregond to be judged.

And the King said to Beregond: 'Beregond, by your sword blood was spilled in the Hallows, where that is forbidden. Also you left your post without leave of Lord or of Captain. For these things, of old, death was the penalty. Now therefore I must pronounce your doom.

'All penalty is remitted for your valour in battle, and still more because all that you did was for the love of the Lord Faramir. Nonetheless you must leave the Guard of the Citadel, and you must go forth from the City of Minas Tirith.'

Then the blood left Beregond's face, and he was stricken to the heart and bowed his head. But the King said:

'So it must be, for you are appointed to the White Company, the Guard of Faramir, Prince of Ithilien, and you shall be its captain and dwell in Emyn Arnen in honour and peace, and in the service of him for whom you risked all, to save him from death.'

And then Beregond, perceiving the mercy and justice of the King, was glad, and kneeling kissed his hand, and departed in joy and content. And Aragorn gave to Faramir Ithilien to be his princedom, and bade him dwell in the hills of Emyn Arnen within sight of the City.

'For,' said he, 'Minas Ithil in Morgul Vale shall be utterly destroyed, and though it may in time to come be made clean, no man may dwell there for many long years.'

And last of all Aragorn greeted Éomer of Rohan, and they embraced, and Aragorn said: 'Between us there can be no word of giving or taking, nor of reward; for we are brethren. In happy hour did Eorl ride from the North, and never has any league of peoples been more blessed, so that neither has ever failed the other, nor shall fail. Now, as you know, we have laid Théoden the Renowned in a tomb in the Hallows, and there he shall lie for ever among the Kings of Gondor, if you will. Or if you desire it, we will come to Rohan and bring him back to rest with his own people.'

And Éomer answered: 'Since the day when you rose before me out of the green grass of the downs I have loved you, and that love shall not fail. But now I must depart for a while to my own realm, where there is much to heal and set in order. But as for the Fallen, when all is made ready we will return for him; but here let him sleep a while.'

And Éowyn said to Faramir: 'Now I must go back to my own land and look on it once again, and help my brother in his labour; but when one whom I long loved as father is laid at last to rest, I will return.'

So the glad days passed; and on the eighth day of May the Riders of Rohan made ready, and rode off by the North-way, and with them went the sons of Elrond. All the road was lined with people to do them honour and praise them, from the Gate of the City to the walls of the Pelennor. Then all others that dwelt afar went back to their homes rejoicing; but in the City there was labour of many willing hands to rebuild and renew and to remove all the scars of war and the memory of the darkness.

The hobbits still remained in Minas Tirith, with Legolas and Gimli; for Aragorn was loth for the fellowship to be dissolved. 'At last all such things must end,' he said, 'but I would have you wait a little while longer: for the end of the deeds that you have shared in has not yet come. A day draws near that I have looked for in all the years of my manhood, and when it comes I would have my friends beside me.' But of that day he would say no more.

In those days the Companions of the Ring dwelt together in a fair house with Gandalf, and they went to and fro as they wished. And Frodo said to Gandalf: 'Do you know what this day is that Aragorn speaks of? For we are happy here, and I don't wish to go; but the days are running away, and Bilbo is waiting; and the Shire is my home.'

'As for Bilbo,' said Gandalf, 'he is waiting for the same day, and he knows what keeps you. And as for the passing of the days, it is now only May and high summer is not yet in; and though all things may seem changed, as if an age of the world had gone by, yet to the trees and the grass it is less than a year since you set out.'

'Pippin,' said Frodo, 'didn't you say that Gandalf was less close than of old? He was weary of his labours then, I think. Now he is recovering.'

And Gandalf said: 'Many folk like to know beforehand what is to be set on the table; but those who have laboured to prepare the feast like to keep their secret; for wonder makes the words of praise louder. And Aragorn himself waits for a sign.'

There came a day when Gandalf could not be found, and the Companions wondered what was going forward. But Gandalf took Aragorn out from the City by night, and he brought him to the southern feet of Mount Mindolluin; and there they found a path made in ages past that few now dared to tread. For it led up on to the mountain to a high hallow where only the kings had been wont to go. And they went up by steep ways, until they came to a high field below the snows that clad the lofty peaks, and it looked down over the precipice that stood behind the City. And standing there they surveyed the lands, for the morning was come; and they saw the towers of the City far below them like white pencils touched by the sunlight, and all the Vale of Anduin was like a garden, and the Mountains of Shadow were veiled in a golden mist. Upon the one side their sight reached to the grey Emyn Muil, and the glint of Rauros was like a star twinkling far off; and upon the other side they saw the River like a ribbon laid down to Pelargir, and beyond that was a light on the hem of the sky that spoke of the Sea.

And Gandalf said: 'This is your realm, and the heart of the greater realm that shall be. The Third Age of the world is ended, and the new age is begun; and it is your task to order its beginning and to preserve what may be preserved. For though much has been saved, much must now pass away; and the power of the Three Rings also is ended. And all the lands that you see, and those that lie round about them, shall be dwellings of

Men. For the time comes of the Dominion of Men, and the Elder Kindred shall fade or depart.'

'I know it well, dear friend,' said Aragorn; 'but I would still have your counsel.'

'Not for long now,' said Gandalf. 'The Third Age was my age. I was the Enemy of Sauron; and my work is finished. I shall go soon. The burden must lie now upon you and your kindred.'

'But I shall die,' said Aragorn. 'For I am a mortal man, and though being what I am and of the race of the West unmingled, I shall have life far longer than other men, yet that is but a little while; and when those who are now in the wombs of women are born and have grown old, I too shall grow old. And who then shall govern Gondor and those who look to this City as to their queen, if my desire be not granted? The Tree in the Court of the Fountain is still withered and barren. When shall I see a sign that it will ever be otherwise?'

'Turn your face from the green world, and look where all seems barren and cold!' said Gandalf.

Then Aragorn turned, and there was a stony slope behind him running down from the skirts of the snow; and as he looked he was aware that alone there in the waste a growing thing stood. And he climbed to it, and saw that out of the very edge of the snow there sprang a sapling tree no more than three foot high. Already it had put forth young leaves long and shapely, dark above and silver beneath, and upon its slender crown it bore one small cluster of flowers whose white petals shone like the sunlit snow.

Then Aragorn cried: '*Yé! utúvienyes!* I have found it! Lo! here is a scion of the Eldest of Trees! But how comes it here? For it is not itself yet seven years old.'

And Gandalf coming looked at it, and said: 'Verily this is a sapling of the line of Nimloth the fair; and that was a seedling of Galathilion, and that a fruit of Telperion of many names, Eldest of Trees. Who shall say how it comes here in the appointed hour? But this is an ancient hallow, and ere the kings failed or the Tree withered in the court, a fruit must have been set here. For it is said that, though the fruit of the Tree comes seldom to ripeness, yet the life within may then lie sleeping through many long years, and none can foretell the time in which it will awake. Remember this. For if ever a fruit ripens, it should be planted, lest the line die out of the world. Here it has lain hidden on the mountain, even as the race of Elendil lay hidden in the wastes of the North. Yet the line of Nimloth is older far than your line, King Elessar.'

Then Aragorn laid his hand gently to the sapling, and lo! it seemed to hold only lightly to the earth, and it was removed without hurt; and Aragorn bore it back to the Citadel. Then the withered tree was uprooted, but with reverence; and they did not burn it, but laid it to rest in the silence of Rath Dínen. And Aragorn planted the new tree in the court by the fountain, and swiftly and gladly it began to grow; and when the month of June entered in it was laden with blossom.

'The sign has been given,' said Aragorn, 'and the day is not far off.' And he set watchmen upon the walls.

It was the day before Midsummer when messengers came from Amon Dîn to the City, and they said that there was a riding of fair folk out of the North, and they drew near now to the walls of the Pelennor. And the King said: 'At last they have come. Let all the City be made ready!'

Upon the very Eve of Midsummer, when the sky was blue as sapphire and white stars opened in the East, but the West was still golden, and the air was cool and fragrant, the riders came down the North-way to the gates of Minas Tirith. First rode Elrohir and Elladan with a banner of silver, and then came Glorfindel and Erestor and all the household of Rivendell, and after them came the Lady Galadriel and Celeborn, Lord of Lothlórien, riding upon white steeds and with them many fair folk of their land, grey-cloaked with white gems in their hair; and last came Master Elrond, mighty among Elves and Men, bearing the sceptre of Annúminas, and beside him upon a grey palfrey rode Arwen his daughter, Evenstar of her people.

And Frodo when he saw her come glimmering in the evening, with stars on her brow and a sweet fragrance about her, was moved with great wonder, and he said to Gandalf: 'At last I understand why we have waited! This is the ending. Now not day only shall be beloved, but night too shall be beautiful and blessed and all its fear pass away!'

Then the King welcomed his guests, and they alighted; and Elrond surrendered the sceptre, and laid the hand of his daughter in the hand of the King, and together they went up into the High City, and all the stars flowered in the sky. And Aragorn the King Elessar wedded Arwen Undómiel in the City of the Kings upon the day of Midsummer, and the tale of their long waiting and labours was come to fulfilment.

CHAPTER VI

MANY PARTINGS

When the days of rejoicing were over at last the Companions thought of returning to their own homes. And Frodo went to the King as he was sitting with the Queen Arwen by the fountain, and she sang a song of Valinor, while the Tree grew and blossomed. They welcomed Frodo and rose to greet him; and Aragorn said:

'I know what you have come to say, Frodo: you wish to return to your own home. Well, dearest friend, the tree grows best in the land of its sires; but for you in all the lands of the West there will ever be a welcome. And though your people have had little fame in the legends of the great, they will now have more renown than any wide realms that are no more.'

'It is true that I wish to go back to the Shire,' said Frodo. 'But first I must go to Rivendell. For if there could be anything wanting in a time so blessed, I missed Bilbo; and I was grieved when among all the household of Elrond I saw that he was not come.'

'Do you wonder at that, Ring-bearer?' said Arwen. 'For you know the power of that thing which is now destroyed; and all that was done by that power is now passing away. But your kinsman possessed this thing longer than you. He is ancient in years now, according to his kind; and he awaits you, for he will not again make any long journey save one.'

'Then I beg leave to depart soon,' said Frodo.

'In seven days we will go,' said Aragorn. 'For we shall ride with you far on the road, even as far as the country of Rohan. In three days now Éomer will return hither to bear Théoden back to rest in the Mark, and we shall ride with him to honour the fallen. But now before you go I will confirm the words that Faramir spoke to you, and you are made free for ever of the realm of Gondor; and all your companions likewise. And if there were any gifts that I could give to match with your deeds you should have them; but whatever you desire you shall take with you, and you shall ride in honour and arrayed as princes of the land.'

But the Queen Arwen said: 'A gift I will give you. For I am the daughter of Elrond. I shall not go with him now when he departs to the Havens; for mine is the choice of Lúthien, and as she so have I chosen, both the sweet and the bitter. But in my stead you shall go, Ring-bearer, when the time comes, and if you then desire it. If your hurts grieve you still and the memory of your burden is heavy, then you may pass into the West, until all your wounds and weariness are healed. But wear this now in memory of Elfstone and Evenstar with whom your life has been woven!'

And she took a white gem like a star that lay upon her breast hanging upon a silver chain, and she set the chain about Frodo's neck. 'When the memory of the fear and the darkness troubles you,' she said, 'this will bring you aid.'

In three days, as the King had said, Éomer of Rohan came riding to the City, and with him came an *éored* of the fairest knights of the Mark. He was welcomed; and when they sat all at table in Merethrond, the Great Hall of Feasts, he beheld the beauty of the ladies that he saw and was filled with great wonder. And before he went to his rest he sent for Gimli the Dwarf, and he said to him: 'Gimli Glóin's son, have you your axe ready?'

'Nay, lord,' said Gimli, 'but I can speedily fetch it, if there be need.'

'You shall judge,' said Éomer. 'For there are certain rash words concerning the Lady in the Golden Wood that lie still between us. And now I have seen her with my eyes.'

'Well, lord,' said Gimli, 'and what say you now?'

'Alas!' said Éomer. 'I will not say that she is the fairest lady that lives.'

'Then I must go for my axe,' said Gimli.

'But first I will plead this excuse,' said Éomer. 'Had I seen her in other company, I would have said all that you could wish. But now I will put Queen Arwen Evenstar first, and I am ready to do battle on my own part with any who deny me. Shall I call for my sword?'

Then Gimli bowed low. 'Nay, you are excused for my part, lord,' he said. 'You have chosen the Evening; but my love is given to the Morning. And my heart forebodes that soon it will pass away for ever.'

At last the day of departure came, and a great and fair company made ready to ride north from the City. Then the kings of Gondor and Rohan went to the Hallows and they came to the tombs in Rath Dínen, and they bore away King Théoden upon a golden bier, and passed through the City in silence. Then they laid the bier upon a great wain with Riders of Rohan all about it and his banner borne before; and Merry being Théoden's esquire rode upon the wain and kept the arms of the king.

For the other Companions steeds were furnished according to their stature; and Frodo and Samwise rode at Aragorn's side, and Gandalf rode upon Shadowfax, and Pippin rode with the knights of Gondor; and Legolas and Gimli as ever rode together upon Arod.

In that riding went also Queen Arwen, and Celeborn and Galadriel with their folk, and Elrond and his sons; and the princes of Dol Amroth and of Ithilien, and many captains and knights. Never had any king of the Mark such company upon the road as went with Théoden Thengel's son to the land of his home.

Without haste and at peace they passed into Anórien, and they came to the Grey Wood under Amon Dîn; and there they heard a sound as of drums beating in the hills, though no living thing could be seen. Then Aragorn let the trumpets be blown; and heralds cried:

'Behold, the King Elessar is come! The Forest of Drúadan he gives to Ghân-buri-ghân and to his folk, to be their own for ever; and hereafter let no man enter it without their leave!'

Then the drums rolled loudly, and were silent.

At length after fifteen days of journey the wain of King Théoden passed through the green fields of Rohan and came to Edoras; and there they all rested. The Golden Hall was arrayed with fair hangings and it was filled with light, and there was held the highest feast that it had known since the days of its building. For after three days the Men of the Mark prepared the funeral of Théoden; and he was laid in a house of stone with his arms and many other fair things that he had possessed, and over him was raised a great mound, covered with green turves of grass and of white evermind. And now there were eight mounds on the east-side of the Barrowfield.

Then the Riders of the King's House upon white horses rode round about the barrow and sang together a song of Théoden Thengel's son that Gléowine his minstrel made, and he made no other song after. The slow voices of the Riders stirred the hearts even of those who did not know the speech of that people; but the words of the song brought a light to the eyes of the folk of the Mark as they heard again afar the thunder of the hooves of the North and the voice of Eorl crying above the battle upon the Field of Celebrant; and the tale of the kings rolled on, and the horn of Helm was loud in the mountains, until the Darkness came and King Théoden arose and rode through the Shadow to the fire, and died in splendour, even as the Sun, returning beyond hope, gleamed upon Mindolluin in the morning.

> *Out of doubt, out of dark, to the day's rising*
> *he rode singing in the sun, sword unsheathing.*
> *Hope he rekindled, and in hope ended;*
> *over death, over dread, over doom lifted*
> *out of loss, out of life, unto long glory.*

But Merry stood at the foot of the green mound, and he wept, and when the song was ended he arose and cried:

'Théoden King, Théoden King! Farewell! As a father you were to me, for a little while. Farewell!'

When the burial was over and the weeping of women was stilled, and Théoden was left at last alone in his barrow, then folk gathered to the Golden Hall for the great feast and put away sorrow; for Théoden had lived to full years and ended in honour no less than the greatest of his sires. And when the time came that in the custom of the Mark they should drink to the memory of the kings, Éowyn Lady of Rohan came forth, golden as the sun and white as snow, and she bore a filled cup to Éomer.

Then a minstrel and loremaster stood up and named all the names of the Lords of the Mark in their order: Eorl the Young; and Brego builder of the Hall; and Aldor brother of Baldor the hapless; and Fréa, and Fréawine, and Goldwine, and Déor, and Gram; and Helm who lay hid in Helm's Deep when the Mark was overrun; and so ended the nine mounds of the west-side, for in that time the line was broken, and after came the mounds of the east-side: Fréalaf, Helm's sister-son, and Léofa, and Walda, and Folca, and Folcwine, and Fengel, and Thengel, and Théoden the latest. And when Théoden was named Éomer drained the cup. Then Éowyn bade those that served to fill the cups, and all there assembled rose and drank to the new king, crying: 'Hail, Éomer, King of the Mark!'

At the last when the feast drew to an end Éomer arose and said: 'Now this is the funeral feast of Théoden the King; but I will speak ere we go of tidings of joy, for he would not grudge that I should do so, since he was ever a father to Éowyn my sister. Hear then all my guests, fair folk of many realms, such as have never before been gathered in this hall! Faramir, Steward of Gondor, and Prince of Ithilien, asks that Éowyn Lady of Rohan should be his wife, and she grants it full willing. Therefore they shall be trothplighted before you all.'

And Faramir and Éowyn stood forth and set hand in hand; and all there drank to them and were glad. 'Thus,' said Éomer, 'is the friendship of the Mark and of Gondor bound with a new bond, and the more do I rejoice.'

'No niggard are you, Éomer,' said Aragorn, 'to give thus to Gondor the fairest thing in your realm!'

Then Éowyn looked in the eyes of Aragorn, and she said: 'Wish me joy, my liege-lord and healer!'

And he answered: 'I have wished thee joy ever since first I saw thee. It heals my heart to see thee now in bliss.'

When the feast was over, those who were to go took leave of King Éomer. Aragorn and his knights, and the people of Lórien and of Rivendell, made ready to ride; but Faramir and Imrahil remained at Edoras; and Arwen

Evenstar remained also, and she said farewell to her brethren. None saw her last meeting with Elrond her father, for they went up into the hills and there spoke long together, and bitter was their parting that should endure beyond the ends of the world.

At the last before the guests set out Éomer and Éowyn came to Merry, and they said: 'Farewell now, Meriadoc of the Shire and Holdwine of the Mark! Ride to good fortune, and ride back soon to our welcome!'

And Éomer said: 'Kings of old would have laden you with gifts that a wain could not bear for your deeds upon the fields of Mundburg; and yet you will take naught, you say, but the arms that were given to you. This I suffer, for indeed I have no gift that is worthy; but my sister begs you to receive this small thing, as a memorial of Dernhelm and of the horns of the Mark at the coming of the morning.'

Then Éowyn gave to Merry an ancient horn, small but cunningly wrought all of fair silver with a baldric of green; and wrights had engraven upon it swift horsemen riding in a line that wound about it from the tip to the mouth; and there were set runes of great virtue.

'This is an heirloom of our house,' said Éowyn. 'It was made by the Dwarves, and came from the hoard of Scatha the Worm. Eorl the Young brought it from the North. He that blows it at need shall set fear in the hearts of his enemies and joy in the hearts of his friends, and they shall hear him and come to him.'

Then Merry took the horn, for it could not be refused, and he kissed Éowyn's hand; and they embraced him, and so they parted for that time.

Now the guests were ready, and they drank the stirrup-cup, and with great praise and friendship they departed, and came at length to Helm's Deep, and there they rested two days. Then Legolas repaid his promise to Gimli and went with him to the Glittering Caves; and when they returned he was silent, and would say only that Gimli alone could find fit words to speak of them. 'And never before has a Dwarf claimed a victory over an Elf in a contest of words,' said he. 'Now therefore let us go to Fangorn and set the score right!'

From Deeping-coomb they rode to Isengard, and saw how the Ents had busied themselves. All the stone-circle had been thrown down and removed, and the land within was made into a garden filled with orchards and trees, and a stream ran through it; but in the midst of all there was a lake of clear water, and out of it the Tower of Orthanc rose still, tall and impregnable, and its black rock was mirrored in the pool.

For a while the travellers sat where once the old gates of Isengard had stood, and there were now two tall trees like sentinels at the beginning of a green-bordered path that ran towards Orthanc; and they looked in wonder at the work that had been done, but no living thing could they see far or near. But presently they heard a voice calling *hoom-hom, hoom-hom*; and there came Tree-beard striding down the path to greet them with Quick-beam at his side.

'Welcome to the Treegarth of Orthanc!' he said. 'I knew that you were coming, but I was at work up the valley; there is much still to be done. But you have not been idle either away in the south and the east, I hear; and all that I hear is good, very good.' Then Treebeard praised all their deeds, of which he seemed to have full knowledge; and at last he stopped and looked long at Gandalf.

'Well, come now!' he said. 'You have proved mightiest, and all your labours have gone well. Where now would you be going? And why do you come here?'

'To see how your work goes, my friend,' said Gandalf, 'and to thank you for your aid in all that has been achieved.'

'*Hoom*, well, that is fair enough,' said Treebeard; 'for to be sure Ents have played their part. And not only in dealing with that, *hoom*, that accursed tree-slayer that dwelt here. For there was a great inrush of those, *burárum*, those evileyed-blackhanded-bowlegged-flinthearted-clawfing-ered-foulbellied-bloodthirsty, *morimaitesincahonda*, *hoom*, well, since you are hasty folk and their full name is as long as years of torment, those vermin of orcs; and they came over the River and down from the North and all round the wood of Laurelindórenan, which they could not get into, thanks to the Great ones who are here.' He bowed to the Lord and Lady of Lórien.

'And these same foul creatures were more than surprised to meet us out on the Wold, for they had not heard of us before; though that might be said also of better folk. And not many will remember us, for not many escaped us alive, and the River had most of those. But it was well for you, for if they had not met us, then the king of the grassland would not have ridden far, and if he had there would have been no home to return to.'

'We know it well,' said Aragorn, 'and never shall it be forgotten in Minas Tirith or in Edoras.'

'*Never* is too long a word even for me,' said Treebeard. 'Not while your kingdoms last, you mean; but they will have to last long indeed to seem long to Ents.'

'The New Age begins,' said Gandalf, 'and in this age it may well prove that the kingdoms of Men shall outlast you, Fangorn my friend. But now come tell me: what of the task that I set you? How is Saruman? Is he not weary of Orthanc yet? For I do not suppose that he will think you have improved the view from his windows.'

Treebeard gave Gandalf a long look, almost a cunning look, Merry thought. 'Ah!' he said. 'I thought you would come to that. Weary of Orthanc? Very weary at last; but not so weary of his tower as he was weary of my voice. *Hoom!* I gave him some long tales, or at least what might be thought long in your speech.'

'Then why did he stay to listen? Did you go into Orthanc?' asked Gandalf.

'*Hoom*, no, not into Orthanc!' said Treebeard. 'But he came to his window and listened, because he could not get news in any other way, and though he hated the news, he was greedy to have it; and I saw that he heard it all. But I added a great many things to the news that it was good for him to think of. He grew very weary. He always was hasty. That was his ruin.'

'I observe, my good Fangorn,' said Gandalf, 'that with great care you say *dwelt, was, grew*. What about *is*? Is he dead?'

'No, not dead, so far as I know,' said Treebeard. 'But he is gone. Yes, he is gone seven days. I let him go. There was little left of him when he crawled out, and as for that worm-creature of his, he was like a pale shadow. Now do not tell me, Gandalf, that I promised to keep him safe; for I know it. But things have changed since then. And I kept him until he was safe, safe from doing any more harm. You should know that above all I hate the caging of live things, and I will not keep even such creatures as these caged beyond great need. A snake without fangs may crawl where he will.'

'You may be right,' said Gandalf; 'but this snake had still one tooth left, I think. He had the poison of his voice, and I guess that he persuaded you, even you Treebeard, knowing the soft spot in your heart. Well, he is gone, and there is no more to be said. But the Tower of Orthanc now goes back to the King, to whom it belongs. Though maybe he will not need it.'

'That will be seen later,' said Aragorn. 'But I will give to Ents all this valley to do with as they will, so long as they keep a watch upon Orthanc and see that none enter it without my leave.'

'It is locked,' said Treebeard. 'I made Saruman lock it and give me the keys. Quickbeam has them.'

Quickbeam bowed like a tree bending in the wind and handed to Aragorn two great black keys of intricate shape, joined by a ring of steel. 'Now I thank you once more,' said Aragorn, 'and I bid you farewell. May your forest grow again in peace. When this valley is filled there is room and to spare west of the mountains, where once you walked long ago.'

Treebeard's face became sad. 'Forests may grow,' he said. 'Woods may spread. But not Ents. There are no Entings.'

'Yet maybe there is now more hope in your search,' said Aragorn. 'Lands will lie open to you eastward that have long been closed.'

But Treebeard shook his head and said: 'It is far to go. And there are too many Men there in these days. But I am forgetting my manners! Will you stay here and rest a while? And maybe there are some that would be pleased to pass through Fangorn Forest and so shorten their road home?' He looked at Celeborn and Galadriel.

But all save Legolas said that they must now take their leave and depart either south or west. 'Come, Gimli!' said Legolas. 'Now by Fangorn's leave I will visit the deep places of the Entwood and see such trees as are nowhere else to be found in Middle-earth. You shall come with me and keep your word; and thus we will journey on together to our own lands in Mirkwood and beyond.' To this Gimli agreed, though with no great delight, it seemed.

'Here then at last comes the ending of the Fellowship of the Ring,' said Aragorn. 'Yet I hope that ere long you will return to my land with the help that you promised.'

'We will come, if our own lords allow it,' said Gimli. 'Well, farewell, my hobbits! You should come safe to your own homes now, and I shall not be kept awake for fear of your peril. We will send word when we may, and some of us may yet meet at times; but I fear that we shall not all be gathered together ever again.'

Then Treebeard said farewell to each of them in turn, and he bowed three times slowly and with great reverence to Celeborn and Galadriel. 'It is long, long since we met by stock or by stone, *A vanimar, vanimálion nostari!*' he said. 'It is sad that we should meet only thus at the ending. For the world is changing: I feel it in the water, I feel it in the earth, and I smell it in the air. I do not think we shall meet again.'

And Celeborn said: 'I do not know, Eldest.' But Galadriel said: 'Not in Middle-earth, nor until the lands that lie under the wave are lifted up again. Then in the willow-meads of Tasarinan we may meet in the Spring. Farewell!'

Last of all Merry and Pippin said good-bye to the old Ent, and he grew gayer as he looked at them. 'Well, my merry folk,' he said, 'will you drink another draught with me before you go?'

'Indeed we will,' they said, and he took them aside into the shade of one of the trees, and there they saw that a great stone jar had been set. And Treebeard filled three bowls, and they drank; and they saw his strange eyes looking at them over the rim of his bowl. 'Take care, take care!' he said. 'For you have already grown since I saw you last.' And they laughed and drained their bowls.

'Well, good-bye!' he said. 'And don't forget that if you hear any news of the Entwives in your land, you will send word to me.' Then he waved his great hands to all the company and went off into the trees.

The travellers now rode with more speed, and they made their way towards the Gap of Rohan; and Aragorn took leave of them at last close to that very place where Pippin had looked into the Stone of Orthanc. The Hobbits were grieved at this parting; for Aragorn had never failed them and he had been their guide through many perils.

'I wish we could have a Stone that we could see all our friends in,' said Pippin, 'and that we could speak to them from far away!'

'Only one now remains that you could use,' answered Aragorn; 'for you would not wish to see what the Stone of Minas Tirith would show you. But the Palantír of Orthanc the King will keep, to see what is passing in his realm, and what his servants are doing. For do not forget, Peregrin Took, that you are a knight of Gondor, and I do not release you from your service. You are going now on leave, but I may recall you. And remember, dear friends of the Shire, that my realm lies also in the North, and I shall come there one day.'

Then Aragorn took leave of Celeborn and Galadriel; and the Lady said to him: 'Elfstone, through darkness you have come to your hope, and have now all your desire. Use well the days!'

But Celeborn said: 'Kinsman, farewell! May your doom be other than mine, and your treasure remain with you to the end!'

With that they parted, and it was then the time of sunset; and when after a while they turned and looked back, they saw the King of the West sitting upon his horse with his knights about him; and the falling Sun shone upon them and made all their harness to gleam like red gold, and the white mantle of Aragorn was turned to a flame. Then Aragorn took the green stone and held it up, and there came a green fire from his hand.

Soon the dwindling company, following the Isen, turned west and rode through the Gap into the waste lands beyond, and then they turned northwards, and passed over the borders of Dunland. The Dunlendings fled and hid themselves, for they were afraid of Elvish folk, though few indeed ever came to their country; but the travellers did not heed them, for they were still a great company and were well provided with all that they needed; and they went on their way at their leisure, setting up their tents when they would.

On the sixth day since their parting from the King they journeyed through a wood climbing down from the hills at the feet of the Misty Mountains that now marched on their right hand. As they came out again into the open country at sundown they overtook an old man leaning on a staff, and he was clothed in rags of grey or dirty white, and at his heels went another beggar, slouching and whining.

'Well Saruman!' said Gandalf. 'Where are you going?'

'What is that to you?' he answered. 'Will you still order my goings, and are you not content with my ruin?'

'You know the answers,' said Gandalf: 'no and no. But in any case the time of my labours now draws to an end. The King has taken on the burden. If you had waited at Orthanc, you would have seen him, and he would have shown you wisdom and mercy.'

'Then all the more reason to have left sooner,' said Saruman; 'for I desire neither of him. Indeed if you wish for an answer to your first question, I am seeking a way out of his realm.'

'Then once more you are going the wrong way,' said Gandalf, 'and I see no hope in your journey. But will you scorn our help? For we offer it to you.'

'To me?' said Saruman. 'Nay, pray do not smile at me! I prefer your frowns. And as for the Lady here, I do not trust her: she always hated me, and schemed for your part. I do not doubt that she has brought you this way to have the pleasure of gloating over my poverty. Had I been warned of your pursuit, I would have denied you the pleasure.'

'Saruman,' said Galadriel, 'we have other errands and other cares that seem to us more urgent than hunting for you. Say rather that you are overtaken by good fortune; for now you have a last chance.'

'If it be truly the last, I am glad,' said Saruman; 'for I shall be spared the trouble of refusing it again. All my hopes are ruined, but I would not share yours. If you have any.'

For a moment his eyes kindled. 'Go!' he said. 'I did not spend long study on these matters for naught. You have doomed yourselves, and you know it. And it will afford me some comfort as I wander to think that you pulled down your own house when you destroyed mine. And now, what ship will bear you back across so wide a sea?' he mocked. 'It will be a grey ship, and full of ghosts.' He laughed, but his voice was cracked and hideous.

'Get up, you idiot!' he shouted to the other beggar, who had sat down on the ground; and he struck him with his staff. 'Turn about! If these fine folk are going our way, then we will take another. Get on, or I'll give you no crust for your supper!'

The beggar turned and slouched past whimpering: 'Poor old Gríma! Poor old Gríma! Always beaten and cursed. How I hate him! I wish I could leave him!'

'Then leave him!' said Gandalf.

But Wormtongue only shot a glance of his bleared eyes full of terror at Gandalf, and then shuffled quickly past behind Saruman. As the wretched pair passed by the company they came to the hobbits, and Saruman stopped and stared at them; but they looked at him with pity.

'So you have come to gloat too, have you, my urchins?' he said. 'You don't care what a beggar lacks, do you? For you have all you want, food and fine clothes, and the best weed for your pipes. Oh yes, I know! I know where it comes from. You would not give a pipeful to a beggar, would you?'

'I would, if I had any,' said Frodo.

'You can have what I have got left,' said Merry, 'if you will wait a moment.' He got down and searched in the bag at his saddle. Then he handed to Saruman a leather pouch. 'Take what there is,' he said. 'You are welcome to it; it came from the flotsam of Isengard.'

'Mine, mine, yes and dearly bought!' cried Saruman, clutching at the pouch. 'This is only a repayment in token; for you took more, I'll be bound. Still, a beggar must be grateful, if a thief returns him even a morsel of his own. Well, it will serve you right when you come home, if you find things less good in the Southfarthing than you would like. Long may your land be short of leaf!'

'Thank you!' said Merry. 'In that case I will have my pouch back, which is not yours and has journeyed far with me. Wrap the weed in a rag of your own.'

'One thief deserves another,' said Saruman, and turned his back on Merry, and kicked Wormtongue, and went away towards the wood.

'Well, I like that!' said Pippin. 'Thief indeed! What of our claim for waylaying, wounding, and orc-dragging us through Rohan?'

'Ah!' said Sam. 'And *bought* he said. How, I wonder? And I didn't like the sound of what he said about the Southfarthing. It's time we got back.'

'I'm sure it is,' said Frodo. 'But we can't go any quicker, if we are to see Bilbo. I am going to Rivendell first, whatever happens.'

'Yes, I think you had better do that,' said Gandalf. 'But alas for Saruman! I fear nothing more can be made of him. He has withered altogether. All the same, I am not sure that Treebeard is right: I fancy he could do some mischief still in a small mean way.'

Next day they went on into northern Dunland, where no men now dwelt, though it was a green and pleasant country. September came in with golden days and silver nights, and they rode at ease until they reached the Swanfleet river, and found the old ford, east of the falls where it went down suddenly into the lowlands. Far to the west in a haze lay the meres and eyots through which it wound its way to the Greyflood: there countless swans housed in a land of reeds.

So they passed into Eregion, and at last a fair morning dawned, shimmering above gleaming mists; and looking from their camp on a low hill the travellers saw away in the east the Sun catching three peaks that thrust up into the sky through floating clouds: Caradhras, Celebdil, and Fanuid-hol. They were near to the Gates of Moria.

Here now for seven days they tarried, for the time was at hand for another parting which they were loth to make. Soon Celeborn and Galadriel and their folk would turn eastward, and so pass by the Redhorn Gate and down the Dimrill Stair to the Silverlode and to their own country. They had journeyed thus far by the west-ways, for they had much to speak of with Elrond and with Gandalf, and here they lingered still in converse with their friends. Often long after the hobbits were wrapped in sleep they would sit together under the stars, recalling the ages that were gone and all their joys and labours in the world, or holding council, concerning the days to come. If any wanderer had chanced to pass, little would he have seen or heard, and it would have seemed to him only that he saw grey figures, carved in stone, memorials of forgotten things now lost in unpeopled lands. For they did not move or speak with mouth, looking from mind to mind; and only their shining eyes stirred and kindled as their thoughts went to and fro.

But at length all was said, and they parted again for a while, until it was time for the Three Rings to pass away. Quickly fading into the stones and the shadows the grey-cloaked people of Lórien rode towards the mountains; and those who were going to Rivendell sat on the hill and watched, until there came out of the gathering mist a flash; and then they saw no more. Frodo knew that Galadriel had held aloft her ring in token of farewell.

Sam turned away and sighed: 'I wish I was going back to Lórien!'

At last one evening they came over the high moors, suddenly as to travellers it always seemed, to the brink of the deep valley of Rivendell and saw far below the lamps shining in Elrond's house. And they went down and crossed the bridge and came to the doors, and all the house was filled with light and song for joy at Elrond's homecoming.

First of all, before they had eaten or washed or even shed their cloaks, the hobbits went in search of Bilbo. They found him all alone in his little room. It was littered with papers and pens and pencils; but Bilbo was sitting in a chair before a small bright fire. He looked very old, but peaceful, and sleepy.

He opened his eyes and looked up as they came in. 'Hullo, hullo!' he said. 'So you've come back? And tomorrow's my birthday, too. How clever of you! Do you know, I shall be one hundred and twenty-nine? And in one year more, if I am spared, I shall equal the Old Took. I should like to beat him; but we shall see.'

After the celebration of Bilbo's birthday the four hobbits stayed in Riven-dell for some days, and they sat much with their old friend, who spent most of his time now in his room, except at meals. For these he was still very punctual as a rule, and he seldom failed to wake up in time for them. Sitting round the fire they told him in turn all that they could remember of their journeys and adventures. At first he pretended to take some notes; but he often fell asleep; and when he woke he would say: 'How splendid! How wonderful! But where were we?' Then they went on with the story from the point where he had begun to nod.

The only part that seemed really to rouse him and hold his attention was the account of the crowning and marriage of Aragorn. 'I was invited to the wedding, of course,' he said. 'And I have waited for it long enough. But somehow, when it came to it, I found I had so much to do here; and packing is such a bother.'

When nearly a fortnight had passed Frodo looked out of his window and saw that there had been a frost in the night, and the cobwebs were like white nets. Then suddenly he knew that he must go, and say good-bye to Bilbo. The weather was still calm and fair, after one of the most lovely summers that people could remember; but October had come, and it must break soon and begin to rain and blow again. And there was still a very long way to go. Yet it was not really the thought of the weather that stirred him. He had a feeling that it was time he went back to the Shire. Sam shared it. Only the night before he had said:

'Well, Mr. Frodo, we've been far and seen a deal, and yet I don't think we've found a better place than this. There's something of everything here, if you understand me: the Shire and the Golden Wood and Gondor and kings' houses and inns and meadows and mountains all mixed. And yet, somehow, I feel we ought to be going soon. I'm worried about my gaffer, to tell you the truth.'

'Yes, something of everything, Sam, except the Sea,' Frodo had answered; and he repeated it now to himself: 'Except the Sea.'

That day Frodo spoke to Elrond, and it was agreed that they should leave the next morning. To their delight Gandalf said: 'I think I shall come too. At least as far as Bree. I want to see Butterbur.'

In the evening they went to say good-bye to Bilbo. 'Well, if you must go, you must,' he said. 'I am sorry. I shall miss you. It is nice just to know that you are about the place. But I am getting very sleepy.' Then he gave Frodo his mithril-coat and Sting, forgetting that he had already done so; and he gave him also three books of lore that he had made at various times, written in his spidery hand, and labelled on their red backs: *Translations from the Elvish, by B.B.*

To Sam he gave a little bag of gold. 'Almost the last drop of the Smaug vintage,' he said. 'May come in useful, if you think of getting married, Sam.' Sam blushed.

'I have nothing much to give to you young fellows,' he said to Merry and Pippin, 'except good advice.' And when he had given them a fair sample of this, he added a last item in Shire-fashion: 'Don't let your heads get too big for your hats! But if you don't finish growing up soon, you are going to find hats and clothes expensive.'

'But if you want to beat the Old Took,' said Pippin, 'I don't see why we shouldn't try and beat the Bullroarer.'

Bilbo laughed, and he produced out of a pocket two beautiful pipes with pearl mouth-pieces and bound with fine-wrought silver. 'Think of me when you smoke them!' he said. 'The Elves made them for me, but I don't smoke now.' And then suddenly he nodded and went to sleep for a little; and when he woke up again he said: 'Now where were we? Yes, of course, giving presents. Which reminds me: what's become of my ring, Frodo, that you took away?'

'I have lost it, Bilbo dear,' said Frodo. 'I got rid of it, you know.'

'What a pity!' said Bilbo. 'I should have liked to see it again. But no, how silly of me! That's what you went for, wasn't it: to get rid of it? But it is all so confusing, for such a lot of other things seem to have got mixed up with it: Aragorn's affairs, and the White Council, and Gondor, and the Horsemen, and Southrons, and oliphaunts – did you really see one, Sam? – and caves and towers and golden trees, and goodness knows what besides.

'I evidently came back by much too straight a road from my trip. I think Gandalf might have shown me round a bit. But then the auction would have been over before I got back, and I should have had even more trouble than I did. Anyway it's too late now; and really I think it's much more comfortable to sit here and hear about it all. The fire's very cosy here, and the food's *very* good, and there are Elves when you want them. What more could one want?

> The Road goes ever on and on
> Out from the door where it began.
> Now far ahead the Road has gone,
> Let others follow it who can!
> Let them a journey new begin,
> But I at last with weary feet
> Will turn towards the lighted inn,
> My evening-rest and sleep to meet.'

And as Bilbo murmured the last words his head dropped on his chest and he slept soundly.

The evening deepened in the room, and the firelight burned brighter; and they looked at Bilbo as he slept and saw that his face was smiling. For some time they sat in silence; and then Sam looking round at the room and the shadows flickering on the walls, said softly:

'I don't think, Mr. Frodo, that he's done much writing while we've been away. He won't ever write our story now.'

At that Bilbo opened an eye, almost as if he had heard. Then he roused himself. 'You see, I am getting so sleepy,' he said. 'And when I have time to write, I only really like writing poetry. I wonder, Frodo my dear fellow, if you would very much mind tidying things up a bit before you go? Collect all my notes and papers, and my diary too, and take them with you, if you will. You see, I haven't much time for the selection and the arrangement and all that. Get Sam to help, and when you've knocked things into shape, come back, and I'll run over it. I won't be too critical.'

'Of course I'll do it!' said Frodo. 'And of course I'll come back soon: it won't be dangerous any more. There is a real king now, and he will soon put the roads in order.'

'Thank you, my dear fellow!' said Bilbo. 'That really is a very great relief to my mind.' And with that he fell asleep again.

The next day Gandalf and the hobbits took leave of Bilbo in his room, for it was cold out of doors; and then they said farewell to Elrond and all his household.

As Frodo stood upon the threshold, Elrond wished him a fair journey, and blessed him, and he said:

'I think, Frodo, that maybe you will not need to come back, unless you come very soon. For about this time of the year, when the leaves are gold before they fall, look for Bilbo in the woods of the Shire. I shall be with him.'

These words no one else heard, and Frodo kept them to himself.

CHAPTER VII

HOMEWARD BOUND

At last the hobbits had their faces turned towards home. They were eager now to see the Shire again; but at first they rode only slowly, for Frodo had been ill at ease. When they came to the Ford of Bruinen, he had halted, and seemed loth to ride into the stream; and they noted that for a while his eyes appeared not to see them or things about him. All that day he was silent. It was the sixth of October.

'Are you in pain, Frodo?' said Gandalf quietly as he rode by Frodo's side.

'Well, yes I am,' said Frodo. 'It is my shoulder. The wound aches, and the memory of darkness is heavy on me. It was a year ago today.'

'Alas! there are some wounds that cannot be wholly cured,' said Gandalf.

'I fear it may be so with mine,' said Frodo. 'There is no real going back. Though I may come to the Shire, it will not seem the same; for I shall not be the same. I am wounded with knife, sting, and tooth, and a long burden. Where shall I find rest?'

Gandalf did not answer.

By the end of the next day the pain and unease had passed, and Frodo was merry again, as merry as if he did not remember the blackness of the day before. After that the journey went well, and the days went quickly by; for they rode at leisure, and often they lingered in the fair woodlands where the leaves were red and yellow in the autumn sun. At length they came to Weathertop; and it was then drawing towards evening and the shadow of the hill lay dark on the road. Then Frodo begged them to hasten, and he would not look towards the hill, but rode through its shadow with head bowed and cloak drawn close about him. That night the weather changed, and a wind came from the West laden with rain, and it blew loud and chill, and the yellow leaves whirled like birds in the air. When they came to the Chetwood already the boughs were almost bare, and a great curtain of rain veiled Bree Hill from their sight.

So it was that near the end of a wild and wet evening in the last days of October the five travellers rode up the climbing road and came to the South-gate of Bree. It was locked fast; and the rain blew in their faces, and in the darkening sky low clouds went hurrying by, and their hearts sank a little, for they had expected more welcome.

When they had called many times, at last the Gate-keeper came out, and they saw that he carried a great cudgel. He looked at them with fear and suspicion; but when he saw that Gandalf was there, and that his companions were hobbits, in spite of their strange gear, then he brightened and wished them welcome.

'Come in!' he said, unlocking the gate. 'We won't stay for news out here in the cold and the wet, a ruffianly evening. But old Barley will no doubt give you a welcome at *The Pony*, and there you'll hear all there is to hear.'

'And there you'll hear later all that we say, and more,' laughed Gandalf. 'How is Harry?'

The Gate-keeper scowled. 'Gone,' he said. 'But you'd best ask Barliman. Good evening!'

'Good evening to you!' they said, and passed through; and then they noticed that behind the hedge at the road-side a long low hut had been built, and a number of men had come out and were staring at them over the fence. When they came to Bill Ferny's house they saw that the hedge there was tattered and unkempt, and the windows were all boarded up.

'Do you think you killed him with that apple, Sam?' said Pippin.

'I'm not so hopeful, Mr. Pippin,' said Sam. 'But I'd like to know what became of that poor pony. He's been on my mind many a time, and the wolves howling and all.'

At last they came to *The Prancing Pony*, and that at least looked outwardly unchanged; and there were lights behind the red curtains in the lower windows. They rang the bell, and Nob came to the door, and opened it a crack and peeped through; and when he saw them standing under the lamp he gave a cry of surprise.

'Mr. Butterbur! Master!' he shouted. 'They've come back!'

'Oh have they? I'll learn them,' came Butterbur's voice, and out he came with a rush, and he had a club in his hand. But when he saw who they were he stopped short, and the black scowl on his face changed to wonder and delight.

'Nob, you woolly-pated ninny!' he cried. 'Can't you give old friends their names? You shouldn't go scaring me like that, with times as they are. Well, well! And where have you come from? I never expected to see any of you folk again, and that's a fact: going off into the Wild with that Strider, and all those Black Men about. But I'm right glad to see you, and none more than Gandalf. Come in! Come in! The same rooms as before? They're free. Indeed most rooms are empty these days, as I'll not hide from you, for you'll find it out soon enough. And I'll see what can be done about supper, as soon as may be; but I'm short-handed at present. Hey, Nob you slowcoach! Tell Bob! Ah, but there I'm forgetting, Bob's gone: goes home to his folk at nightfall now. Well, take the guests' ponies to the stables, Nob! And you'll be taking your horse to his stable yourself, Gandalf, I don't doubt. A fine beast, as I said when I first set eyes on him. Well, come in! Make yourselves at home!'

Mr. Butterbur had at any rate not changed his manner of talking, and still seemed to live in his old breathless bustle. And yet there was hardly anybody about, and all was quiet; from the Common Room there came a low murmur of no more than two or three voices. And seen closer in the light of two candles that he lit and carried before them the landlord's face looked rather wrinkled and careworn.

He led them down the passage to the parlour that they had used on that strange night more than a year ago; and they followed him, a little disquieted, for it seemed plain to them that old Barliman was putting a brave face on some trouble. Things were not what they had been. But they said nothing, and waited.

As they expected Mr. Butterbur came to the parlour after supper to see if all had been to their liking. As indeed it had: no change for the worse had yet come upon the beer or the victuals at *The Pony*, at any rate. 'Now I won't make so bold as to suggest you should come to the Common Room tonight,' said Butterbur. 'You'll be tired; and there isn't many folk there this evening, anyway. But if you could spare me half an hour before you go to your beds, I would dearly like to have some talk with you, quiet-like by ourselves.'

'That is just what we should like, too,' said Gandalf. 'We are not tired. We have been taking things easy. We were wet, cold and hungry, but all that you have cured. Come, sit down! And if you have any pipe-weed, we'll bless you.'

'Well, if you'd called for anything else, I'd have been happier,' said Butterbur. 'That's just a thing that we're short of, seeing how we've only got what we grow ourselves, and that's not enough. There's none to be had from the Shire these days. But I'll do what I can.'

When he came back he brought them enough to last them for a day or two, a wad of uncut leaf. 'Southlinch,' he said, 'and the best we have; but not the match of Southfarthing, as I've always said, though I'm all for Bree in most matters, begging your pardon.'

They put him in a large chair by the wood-fire, and Gandalf sat on the other side of the hearth, and the hobbits in low chairs between them; and then they talked for many times half an hour, and exchanged all such news as Mr. Butterbur wished to hear or give. Most of the things which they had to tell were a mere wonder and bewilderment to their host, and far beyond his vision; and they brought forth few comments other than: 'You don't say,' often repeated in defiance of the evidence of Mr. Butterbur's own ears. 'You don't say, Mr. Baggins, or is it Mr. Underhill? I'm getting so mixed up. You don't say, Master Gandalf! Well I never! Who'd have thought it in our times!'

But he did say much on his own account. Things were far from well, he would say. Business was not even fair, it was downright bad. 'No one comes nigh Bree now from Outside,' he said. 'And the inside folks, they stay at home mostly and keep their doors barred. It all comes of those newcomers and gangrels that began coming up the Greenway last year, as you may remember; but more came later. Some were just poor bodies running away from trouble; but most were bad men, full o' thievery and mischief. And there was trouble right here in Bree, bad trouble. Why, we had a real set-to, and there were some folk killed, killed dead! If you'll believe me.'

'I will indeed,' said Gandalf. 'How many?'

'Three and two,' said Butterbur, referring to the big folk and the little. 'There was poor Mat Heathertoes, and Rowlie Appledore, and little Tom Pickthorn from over the Hill; and Willie Banks from up-away, and one of the Underhills from Staddle: all good fellows, and they're missed. And Harry Goatleaf that used to be on the West-gate, and that Bill Ferny, they came in on the strangers' side, and they've gone off with them; and it's my belief they let them in. On the night of the fight, I mean. And that was after we showed them the gates and pushed them out: before the year's end, that was; and the fight was early in the New Year, after the heavy snow we had.

'And now they're gone for robbers and live outside, hiding in the woods beyond Archet, and out in the wilds north-away. It's like a bit of the bad old times tales tell of, I say. It isn't safe on the road and nobody goes far, and folk lock up early. We have to keep watchers all round the fence and put a lot of men on the gates at nights.'

'Well, no one troubled us,' said Pippin, 'and we came along slowly, and kept no watch. We thought we'd left all trouble behind us.'

'Ah, that you haven't, Master, more's the pity,' said Butterbur. 'But it's no wonder they left you alone. They wouldn't go for armed folk, with swords and helmets and shields and all. Make them think twice, that would. And I must say it put me aback a bit when I saw you.'

Then the hobbits suddenly realized that people had looked at them with amazement not out of surprise at their return so much as in wonder at their gear. They themselves had become so used to warfare and to riding in well-arrayed companies that they had quite forgotten that the bright mail peeping from under their cloaks, and the helms of Gondor and the Mark, and the fair devices on their shields, would seem outlandish in their own country. And Gandalf, too, was now riding on his tall grey horse, all clad

in white with a great mantle of blue and silver over all, and the long sword
Glamdring at his side.

Gandalf laughed. 'Well, well;' he said, 'if they are afraid of just five of
us, then we have met worse enemies on our travels. But at any rate they
will give you peace at night while we stay.'

'How long will that be?' said Butterbur. 'I'll not deny we should be glad
to have you about for a bit. You see, we're not used to such troubles; and
the Rangers have all gone away, folk tell me. I don't think we've rightly
understood till now what they did for us. For there's been worse than
robbers about. Wolves were howling round the fences last winter. And
there's dark shapes in the woods, dreadful things that it makes the blood
run cold to think of. It's been very disturbing, if you understand me.'

'I expect it has,' said Gandalf. 'Nearly all lands have been disturbed
these days, very disturbed. But cheer up, Barliman! You have been on the
edge of very great troubles, and I am only glad to hear that you have not
been deeper in. But better times are coming. Maybe, better than any you
remember. The Rangers have returned. We came back with them. And
there is a king again, Barliman. He will soon be turning his mind this way.

'Then the Greenway will be opened again, and his messengers will come
north, and there will be comings and goings, and the evil things will be
driven out of the waste-lands. Indeed the waste in time will be waste no
longer, and there will be people and fields where once there was wilderness.'

Mr. Butterbur shook his head. 'If there's a few decent respectable folk
on the roads, that won't do no harm,' he said. 'But we don't want no more
rabble and ruffians. And we don't want no outsiders at Bree, nor near Bree
at all. We want to be let alone. I don't want a whole crowd o' strangers
camping here and settling there and tearing up the wild country.'

'You will be let alone, Barliman,' said Gandalf. 'There is room enough
for realms between Isen and Greyflood, or along the shore-lands south of
the Brandywine, without any one living within many days' ride of Bree.
And many folk used to dwell away north, a hundred miles or more from
here, at the far end of the Greenway: on the North Downs or by Lake
Evendim.'

'Up away by Deadmen's Dike?' said Butterbur, looking even more dubi-
ous. 'That's haunted land, they say. None but a robber would go there.'

'The Rangers go there,' said Gandalf. 'Deadmen's Dike, you say. So it
has been called for long years; but its right name, Barliman, is Fornost
Erain, Norbury of the Kings. And the King will come there again one day;
and then you'll have some fair folk riding through.'

'Well, that sounds more hopeful, I'll allow,' said Butterbur. 'And it will
be good for business, no doubt. So long as he lets Bree alone.'

'He will,' said Gandalf. 'He knows it and loves it.'

'Does he now?' said Butterbur looking puzzled. 'Though I'm sure I don't know why he should, sitting in his big chair up in his great castle, hundreds of miles away. And drinking wine out of a golden cup, I shouldn't wonder. What's *The Pony* to him, or mugs o' beer? Not but what my beer's good, Gandalf. It's been uncommon good, since you came in the autumn of last year and put a good word on it. And that's been a comfort in trouble, I will say.'

'Ah!' said Sam. 'But he says your beer is always good.'

'He says?'

'Of course he does. He's Strider. The chief of the Rangers. Haven't you got that into your head yet?'

It went in at last, and Butterbur's face was a study in wonder. The eyes in his broad face grew round, and his mouth opened wide, and he gasped. 'Strider!' he exclaimed when he got back his breath. 'Him with a crown and all and a golden cup! Well, what are we coming to?'

'Better times, for Bree at any rate,' said Gandalf.

'I hope so, I'm sure,' said Butterbur. 'Well, this has been the nicest chat I've had in a month of Mondays. And I'll not deny that I'll sleep easier tonight and with a lighter heart. You've given me a powerful lot to think over, but I'll put that off until tomorrow. I'm for bed, and I've no doubt you'll be glad of your beds too. Hey, Nob!' he called, going to the door. 'Nob, you slowcoach!'

'Nob!' he said to himself, slapping his forehead. 'Now what does that remind me of?'

'Not another letter you've forgotten, I hope, Mr. Butterbur?' said Merry.

'Now, now, Mr. Brandybuck, don't go reminding me of that! But there, you've broken my thought. Now where was I? Nob, stables, ah! that was it. I've something that belongs to you. If you recollect Bill Ferny and the horsethieving: his pony as you bought, well, it's here. Come back all of itself, it did. But where it had been to you know better than me. It was as shaggy as an old dog and as lean as a clothes-rail, but it was alive. Nob's looked after it.'

'What! My Bill?' cried Sam. 'Well, I was born lucky, whatever my gaffer may say. There's another wish come true! Where is he?' Sam would not go to bed until he had visited Bill in his stable.

The travellers stayed in Bree all the next day, and Mr. Butterbur could not complain of his business next evening at any rate. Curiosity overcame all fears, and his house was crowded. For a while out of politeness the hobbits visited the Common Room in the evening and answered a good many questions. Bree memories being retentive, Frodo was asked many times if he had written his book.

'Not yet,' he answered. 'I am going home now to put my notes in order.' He promised to deal with the amazing events at Bree, and so give a bit of interest to a book that appeared likely to treat mostly of the remote and less important affairs 'away south'.

Then one of the younger folk called for a song. But at that a hush fell, and he was frowned down, and the call was not repeated. Evidently there was no wish for any uncanny events in the Common Room again.

No trouble by day, nor any sound by night, disturbed the peace of Bree while the travellers remained there; but the next morning they got up early, for as the weather was still rainy they wished to reach the Shire before night, and it was a long ride. The Bree folk were all out to see them off, and were in merrier mood than they had been for a year; and those who had not seen the strangers in all their gear before gaped with wonder at them: at Gandalf with his white beard, and the light that seemed to gleam from him, as if his blue mantle was only a cloud over sunshine; and at the four hobbits like riders upon errantry out of almost forgotten tales. Even those who had laughed at all the talk about the King began to think there might be some truth in it.

'Well, good luck on your road, and good luck to your homecoming!' said Mr. Butterbur. 'I should have warned you before that all's not well in the Shire neither, if what we hear is true. Funny goings on, they say. But one thing drives out another, and I was full of my own troubles. But if I may be so bold, you've come back changed from your travels, and you look now like folk as can deal with troubles out of hand. I don't doubt you'll soon set all to rights. Good luck to you! And the oftener you come back the better I'll be pleased.'

They wished him farewell and rode away, and passed through the West-gate and on towards the Shire. Bill the pony was with them, and as before he had a good deal of baggage, but he trotted along beside Sam and seemed well content.

'I wonder what old Barliman was hinting at,' said Frodo.

'I can guess some of it,' said Sam gloomily. 'What I saw in the Mirror: trees cut down and all, and my old gaffer turned out of the Row. I ought to have hurried back quicker.'

'And something's wrong with the Southfarthing evidently,' said Merry. 'There's a general shortage of pipe-weed.'

'Whatever it is,' said Pippin, 'Lotho will be at the bottom of it: you can be sure of that.'

'Deep in, but not at the bottom,' said Gandalf. 'You have forgotten Saruman. He began to take an interest in the Shire before Mordor did.'

'Well, we've got you with us,' said Merry, 'so things will soon be cleared up.'

'I am with you at present,' said Gandalf, 'but soon I shall not be. I am not coming to the Shire. You must settle its affairs yourselves; that is what you have been trained for. Do you not yet understand? My time is over: it is no longer my task to set things to rights, nor to help folk to do so. And as for you, my dear friends, you will need no help. You are grown up now. Grown indeed very high; among the great you are, and I have no longer any fear at all for any of you.

'But if you would know, I am turning aside soon. I am going to have a long talk with Bombadil: such a talk as I have not had in all my time. He is a moss-gatherer, and I have been a stone doomed to rolling. But my rolling days are ending, and now we shall have much to say to one another.'

In a little while they came to the point on the East Road where they had taken leave of Bombadil; and they hoped and half expected to see him standing there to greet them as they went by. But there was no sign of him; and there was a grey mist on the Barrow-downs southwards, and a deep veil over the Old Forest far away.

They halted and Frodo looked south wistfully. 'I should dearly like to see the old fellow again,' he said. 'I wonder how he is getting on?'

'As well as ever, you may be sure,' said Gandalf. 'Quite untroubled; and I should guess, not much interested in anything that we have done or seen, unless perhaps in our visits to the Ents. There may be a time later for you to go and see him. But if I were you, I should press on now for home, or you will not come to the Brandywine Bridge before the gates are locked.'

'But there aren't any gates,' said Merry, 'not on the Road; you know that quite well. There's the Buckland Gate, of course; but they'll let me through that at any time.'

'There weren't any gates, you mean,' said Gandalf. 'I think you will find some now. And you might have more trouble even at the Buckland Gate than you think. But you'll manage all right. Good-bye, dear friends! Not for the last time, not yet. Good-bye!'

He turned Shadowfax off the Road, and the great horse leaped the green dike that here ran beside it; and then at a cry from Gandalf he was gone, racing towards the Barrow-downs like a wind from the North.

'Well here we are, just the four of us that started out together,' said Merry. 'We have left all the rest behind, one after another. It seems almost like a dream that has slowly faded.'

'Not to me,' said Frodo. 'To me it feels more like falling asleep again.'

CHAPTER VIII

THE SCOURING OF THE SHIRE

It was after nightfall when, wet and tired, the travellers came at last to the Brandywine, and they found the way barred. At either end of the Bridge there was a great spiked gate; and on the further side of the river they could see that some new houses had been built: two-storeyed with narrow straight-sided windows, bare and dimly lit, all very gloomy and un-Shirelike.

They hammered on the outer gate and called, but there was at first no answer; and then to their surprise someone blew a horn, and the lights in the windows went out. A voice shouted in the dark:

'Who's that? Be off! You can't come in. Can't you read the notice: *No admittance between sundown and sunrise?*'

'Of course we can't read the notice in the dark,' Sam shouted back. 'And if hobbits of the Shire are to be kept out in the wet on a night like this, I'll tear down your notice when I find it.'

At that a window slammed, and a crowd of hobbits with lanterns poured out of the house on the left. They opened the further gate, and some came over the bridge. When they saw the travellers they seemed frightened.

'Come along!' said Merry, recognizing one of the hobbits. 'If you don't know me, Hob Hayward, you ought to. I am Merry Brandybuck, and I should like to know what all this is about, and what a Bucklander like you is doing here. You used to be on the Hay Gate.'

'Bless me! It's Master Merry, to be sure, and all dressed up for fighting!' said old Hob. 'Why, they said you was dead! Lost in the Old Forest by all accounts. I'm pleased to see you alive after all!'

'Then stop gaping at me through the bars, and open the gate!' said Merry.

'I'm sorry, Master Merry, but we have orders.'

'Whose orders?'

'The Chief's up at Bag End.'

'Chief? Chief? Do you mean Mr. Lotho?' said Frodo.

'I suppose so, Mr. Baggins; but we have to say just "the Chief" nowadays.'

'Do you indeed!' said Frodo. 'Well, I am glad he has dropped the Baggins at any rate. But it is evidently high time that the family dealt with him and put him in his place.'

A hush fell on the hobbits beyond the gate. 'It won't do no good talking that way,' said one. 'He'll get to hear of it. And if you make so much noise, you'll wake the Chief's Big Man.'

'We shall wake him up in a way that will surprise him,' said Merry. 'If you mean that your precious Chief has been hiring ruffians out of the wild, then we've not come back too soon.' He sprang from his pony, and seeing the notice in the light of the lanterns, he tore it down and threw it over the gate. The hobbits backed away and made no move to open it. 'Come on, Pippin!' said Merry. 'Two is enough.'

Merry and Pippin climbed the gate, and the hobbits fled. Another horn sounded. Out of the bigger house on the right a large heavy figure appeared against a light in the doorway.

'What's all this,' he snarled as he came forward. 'Gate-breaking? You clear out, or I'll break your filthy little necks!' Then he stopped, for he had caught the gleam of swords.

'Bill Ferny,' said Merry, 'if you don't open that gate in ten seconds, you'll regret it. I shall set steel to you, if you don't obey. And when you have opened the gates you will go through them and never return. You are a ruffian and a highway-robber.'

Bill Ferny flinched and shuffled to the gate and unlocked it. 'Give me the key!' said Merry. But the ruffian flung it at his head and then darted out into the darkness. As he passed the ponies one of them let fly with his heels and just caught him as he ran. He went off with a yelp into the night and was never heard of again.

'Neat work, Bill,' said Sam, meaning the pony.

'So much for your Big Man,' said Merry. 'We'll see the Chief later. In the meantime we want a lodging for the night, and as you seem to have pulled down the Bridge Inn and built this dismal place instead, you'll have to put us up.'

'I am sorry, Mr. Merry,' said Hob, 'but it isn't allowed.'

'What isn't allowed?'

'Taking in folk off-hand like, and eating extra food, and all that,' said Hob.

'What's the matter with the place?' said Merry. 'Has it been a bad year, or what? I thought it had been a fine summer and harvest.'

'Well no, the year's been good enough,' said Hob. 'We grows a lot of food, but we don't rightly know what becomes of it. It's all these "gatherers" and "sharers", I reckon, going round counting and measuring and taking off to storage. They do more gathering than sharing, and we never see most of the stuff again.'

'Oh come!' said Pippin yawning. 'This is all too tiresome for me tonight. We've got food in our bags. Just give us a room to lie down in. It'll be better than many places I have seen.'

The hobbits at the gate still seemed ill at ease, evidently some rule or other was being broken; but there was no gainsaying four such masterful travellers, all armed, and two of them uncommonly large and strong-looking. Frodo ordered the gates to be locked again. There was some sense at any rate in keeping a guard, while ruffians were still about. Then the four companions went into the hobbit guard-house and made themselves as comfortable as they could. It was a bare and ugly place, with a mean little grate that would not allow a good fire. In the upper rooms were little rows of hard beds, and on every wall there was a notice and a list of Rules. Pippin tore them down. There was no beer and very little food, but with what the travellers brought and shared out they all made a fair meal; and Pippin broke Rule 4 by putting most of next day's allowance of wood on the fire.

'Well now, what about a smoke, while you tell us what has been happening in the Shire?' he said.

'There isn't no pipe-weed now,' said Hob; 'at least only for the Chief's men. All the stocks seem to have gone. We do hear that waggon-loads of it went away down the old road out of the Southfarthing, over Sarn Ford way. That would be the end o' last year, after you left. But it had been going away quietly before that, in a small way. That Lotho——'

'Now you shut up, Hob Hayward!' cried several of the others. 'You know talk o' that sort isn't allowed. The Chief will hear of it, and we'll all be in trouble.'

'He wouldn't hear naught, if some of you here weren't sneaks,' rejoined Hob hotly.

'All right, all right!' said Sam. 'That's quite enough. I don't want to hear no more. No welcome, no beer, no smoke, and a lot of rules and orc-talk instead. I hoped to have a rest, but I can see there's work and trouble ahead. Let's sleep and forget it till morning!'

The new 'Chief' evidently had means of getting news. It was a good forty miles from the Bridge to Bag End, but someone made the journey in a hurry. So Frodo and his friends soon discovered.

They had not made any definite plans, but had vaguely thought of going down to Crickhollow together first, and resting there a bit. But now, seeing what things were like, they decided to go straight to Hobbiton. So the next day they set out along the Road and jogged along steadily. The wind had dropped but the sky was grey. The land looked rather sad and forlorn; but it was after all the first of November and the fag-end of Autumn. Still there seemed an unusual amount of burning going on, and smoke rose from many points round about. A great cloud of it was going up far away in the direction of the Woody End.

As evening fell they were drawing near to Frogmorton, a village right on the Road, about twenty-two miles from the Bridge. There they meant to stay the night; *The Floating Log* at Frogmorton was a good inn. But as they came to the east end of the village they met a barrier with a large board saying NO ROAD; and behind it stood a large band of Shirriffs with staves in their hands and feathers in their caps, looking both important and rather scared.

'What's all this?' said Frodo, feeling inclined to laugh.

'This is what it is, Mr. Baggins,' said the leader of the Shirriffs, a two-feather hobbit: 'You're arrested for Gate-breaking, and Tearing up of Rules, and Assaulting Gate-keepers, and Trespassing, and Sleeping in Shire-buildings without Leave, and Bribing Guards with Food.'

'And what else?' said Frodo.

'That'll do to go on with,' said the Shirriff-leader.

'I can add some more, if you'd like it,' said Sam. 'Calling your Chief Names, Wishing to punch his Pimply Face, and Thinking you Shirriffs look a lot of Tom-fools.'

'There now, Mister, that'll do. It's the Chief's orders that you're to come along quiet. We're going to take you to Bywater and hand you over to the Chief's Men; and when he deals with your case you can have your say. But if you don't want to stay in the Lockholes any longer than you need, I should cut the say short, if I was you.'

To the discomfiture of the Shirriffs Frodo and his companions all roared with laughter. 'Don't be absurd!' said Frodo. 'I am going where I please, and in my own time. I happen to be going to Bag End on business, but if you insist on going too, well that is your affair.'

'Very well, Mr. Baggins,' said the leader, pushing the barrier aside. 'But don't forget I've arrested you.'

'I won't,' said Frodo. 'Never. But I may forgive you. Now I am not going any further today, so if you'll kindly escort me to *The Floating Log*, I'll be obliged.'

'I can't do that, Mr. Baggins. The inn's closed. There's a Shirriff-house at the far end of the village. I'll take you there.'

'All right,' said Frodo. 'Go on and we'll follow.'

Sam had been looking the Shirriffs up and down and had spotted one that he knew. 'Hey, come here Robin Smallburrow!' he called. 'I want a word with you.'

With a sheepish glance at his leader, who looked wrathful but did not dare to interfere, Shirriff Smallburrow fell back and walked beside Sam, who got down off his pony.

'Look here, Cock-robin!' said Sam. 'You're Hobbiton-bred and ought to have more sense, coming a-waylaying Mr. Frodo and all. And what's all this about the inn being closed?'

'They're all closed,' said Robin. 'The Chief doesn't hold with beer. Leastways that is how it started. But now I reckon it's his Men that has it all. And he doesn't hold with folk moving about; so if they will or they must, then they has to go to the Shirriff-house and explain their business.'

'You ought to be ashamed of yourself having anything to do with such nonsense,' said Sam. 'You used to like the inside of an inn better than the outside yourself. You were always popping in, on duty or off.'

'And so I would be still, Sam, if I could. But don't be hard on me. What can I do? You know how I went for a Shirriff seven years ago, before any of this began. Gave me a chance of walking round the country and seeing folk, and hearing the news, and knowing where the good beer was. But now it's different.'

'But you can give it up, stop Shirriffing, if it has stopped being a respectable job,' said Sam.

'We're not allowed to,' said Robin.

'If I hear *not allowed* much oftener,' said Sam, 'I'm going to get angry.'

'Can't say as I'd be sorry to see it,' said Robin lowering his voice. 'If we all got angry together something might be done. But it's these Men, Sam, the Chief's Men. He sends them round everywhere, and if any of us small folk stand up for our rights, they drag him off to the Lockholes. They took old Flourdumpling, old Will Whitfoot the Mayor, first, and they've taken a lot more. Lately it's been getting worse. Often they beat 'em now.'

'Then why do you do their work for them?' said Sam angrily. 'Who sent you to Frogmorton?'

'No one did. We stay here in the big Shirriff-house. We're the First Eastfarthing Troop now. There's hundreds of Shirriffs all told, and they want more, with all these new rules. Most of them are in it against their will, but not all. Even in the Shire there are some as like minding other folk's business and talking big. And there's worse than that: there's a few as do spy-work for the Chief and his Men.'

'Ah! So that's how you had news of us, is it?'

'That's right. We aren't allowed to send by it now, but they use the old Quick Post service, and keep special runners at different points. One came in from Whitfurrows last night with a "secret message", and another took it on from here. And a message came back this afternoon saying you was to be arrested and taken to Bywater, not direct to the Lockholes. The Chief wants to see you at once, evidently.'

'He won't be so eager when Mr. Frodo has finished with him,' said Sam.

The Shirriff-house at Frogmorton was as bad as the Bridge-house. It had only one storey, but it had the same narrow windows, and it was built of ugly pale bricks, badly laid. Inside it was damp and cheerless, and supper was served on a long bare table that had not been scrubbed for weeks. The food deserved no better setting. The travellers were glad to leave the place. It was about eighteen miles to Bywater, and they set off at ten o'clock in the morning. They would have started earlier, only the delay so plainly annoyed the Shirriff-leader. The west wind had shifted northward and it was turning colder, but the rain was gone.

It was rather a comic cavalcade that left the village, though the few folk that came out to stare at the 'get-up' of the travellers did not seem quite sure whether laughing was allowed. A dozen Shirriffs had been told off as escort to the 'prisoners'; but Merry made them march in front, while Frodo and his friends rode behind. Merry, Pippin, and Sam sat at their ease laughing and talking and singing, while the Shirriffs stumped along trying to look stern and important. Frodo, however, was silent and looked rather sad and thoughtful.

The last person they passed was a sturdy old gaffer clipping a hedge. 'Hullo, hullo!' he jeered. 'Now who's arrested who?'

Two of the Shirriffs immediately left the party and went towards him. 'Leader!' said Merry. 'Order your fellows back to their places at once, if you don't want me to deal with them!'

The two hobbits at a sharp word from the leader came back sulkily. 'Now get on!' said Merry, and after that the travellers saw to it that their ponies' pace was quick enough to push the Shirriffs along as fast as they could go. The sun came out, and in spite of the chilly wind they were soon puffing and sweating.

At the Three-Farthing Stone they gave it up. They had done nearly fourteen miles with only one rest at noon. It was now three o'clock. They were hungry and very footsore and they could not stand the pace.

'Well, come along in your own time!' said Merry. 'We are going on.'

'Good-bye, Cock-robin!' said Sam. 'I'll wait for you outside *The Green Dragon*, if you haven't forgotten where that is. Don't dawdle on the way!'

'You're breaking arrest, that's what you're doing,' said the leader ruefully, 'and I can't be answerable.'

'We shall break a good many things yet, and not ask you to answer,' said Pippin. 'Good luck to you!'

The travellers trotted on, and as the sun began to sink towards the White Downs far away on the western horizon they came to Bywater by its wide pool; and there they had their first really painful shock. This was Frodo and Sam's own country, and they found out now that they cared about it more than any other place in the world. Many of the houses that they had known were missing. Some seemed to have been burned down. The pleasant row of old hobbit-holes in the bank on the north side of the Pool were deserted, and their little gardens that used to run down bright to the water's edge were rank with weeds. Worse, there was a whole line of the ugly new houses all along Pool Side, where the Hobbiton Road ran close to the bank. An avenue of trees had stood there. They were all gone. And looking with dismay up the road towards Bag End they saw a tall chimney of brick in the distance. It was pouring out black smoke into the evening air.

Sam was beside himself. 'I'm going right on, Mr. Frodo!' he cried. 'I'm going to see what's up. I want to find my gaffer.'

'We ought to find out first what we're in for, Sam,' said Merry. 'I guess that the "Chief" will have a gang of ruffians handy. We had better find someone who will tell us how things are round here.'

But in the village of Bywater all the houses and holes were shut, and no one greeted them. They wondered at this, but they soon discovered the reason of it. When they reached *The Green Dragon*, the last house on the Hobbiton side, now lifeless and with broken windows, they were disturbed to see half a dozen large ill-favoured Men lounging against the inn-wall; they were squint-eyed and sallow-faced.

'Like that friend of Bill Ferny's at Bree,' said Sam.

'Like many that I saw at Isengard,' muttered Merry.

The ruffians had clubs in their hands and horns by their belts, but they had no other weapons, as far as could be seen. As the travellers rode up they left the wall and walked into the road, blocking the way.

'Where d'you think you're going?' said one, the largest and most evil-looking of the crew. 'There's no road for you any further. And where are those precious Shirriffs?'

'Coming along nicely,' said Merry. 'A little footsore, perhaps. We promised to wait for them here.'

'Garn, what did I say?' said the ruffian to his mates. 'I told Sharkey it was no good trusting those little fools. Some of our chaps ought to have been sent.'

'And what difference would that have made, pray?' said Merry. 'We are not used to footpads in this country, but we know how to deal with them.'

'Footpads, eh?' said the man. 'So that's your tone, is it? Change it, or we'll change it for you. You little folk are getting too uppish. Don't you trust too much in the Boss's kind heart. Sharkey's come now, and he'll do what Sharkey says.'

'And what may that be?' said Frodo quietly.

'This country wants waking up and setting to rights,' said the ruffian, 'and Sharkey's going to do it; and make it hard, if you drive him to it. You need a bigger Boss. And you'll get one before the year is out, if there's any more trouble. Then you'll learn a thing or two, you little rat-folk.'

'Indeed. I am glad to hear of your plans,' said Frodo. 'I am on my way to call on Mr. Lotho, and he may be interested to hear of them too.'

The ruffian laughed. 'Lotho! He knows all right. Don't you worry. He'll do what Sharkey says. Because if a Boss gives trouble, we can change him. See? And if little folks try to push in where they're not wanted, we can put them out of mischief. See?'

'Yes, I see,' said Frodo. 'For one thing, I see that you're behind the times and the news here. Much has happened since you left the South. Your day is over, and all other ruffians'. The Dark Tower has fallen, and there is a King in Gondor. And Isengard has been destroyed, and your precious master is a beggar in the wilderness. I passed him on the road. The King's messengers will ride up the Greenway now, not bullies from Isengard.'

The man stared at him and smiled. 'A beggar in the wilderness!' he mocked. 'Oh, is he indeed? Swagger it, swagger it, my little cock-a-whoop. But that won't stop us living in this fat little country where you have lazed long enough. And' – he snapped his fingers in Frodo's face – 'King's messengers! That for them! When I see one, I'll take notice, perhaps.'

This was too much for Pippin. His thoughts went back to the Field of Cormallen, and here was a squint-eyed rascal calling the Ring-bearer 'little cock-a-whoop'. He cast back his cloak, flashed out his sword, and the silver and sable of Gondor gleamed on him as he rode forward.

'I am a messenger of the King,' he said. 'You are speaking to the King's friend, and one of the most renowned in all the lands of the West. You are a ruffian and a fool. Down on your knees in the road and ask pardon, or I will set this troll's bane in you!'

The sword glinted in the westering sun. Merry and Sam drew their swords also and rode up to support Pippin; but Frodo did not move. The ruffians gave back. Scaring Breeland peasants, and bullying bewildered hobbits, had been their work. Fearless hobbits with bright swords and grim faces were a great surprise. And there was a note in the voices of these newcomers that they had not heard before. It chilled them with fear.

'Go!' said Merry. 'If you trouble this village again, you will regret it.' The three hobbits came on, and then the ruffians turned and fled, running away up the Hobbiton Road; but they blew their horns as they ran.

'Well, we've come back none too soon,' said Merry.

'Not a day too soon. Perhaps too late, at any rate to save Lotho,' said Frodo. 'Miserable fool, but I am sorry for him.'

'Save Lotho? Whatever do you mean?' said Pippin. 'Destroy him, I should say.'

'I don't think you quite understand things, Pippin,' said Frodo. 'Lotho never meant things to come to this pass. He has been a wicked fool, but he's caught now. The ruffians are on top, gathering, robbing and bullying, and running or ruining things as they like, in his name. And not in his name even for much longer. He's a prisoner in Bag End now, I expect, and very frightened. We ought to try and rescue him.'

'Well I am staggered!' said Pippin. 'Of all the ends to our journey that is the very last I should have thought of: to have to fight half-orcs and ruffians in the Shire itself – to rescue Lotho Pimple!'

'Fight?' said Frodo. 'Well, I suppose it may come to that. But remember: there is to be no slaying of hobbits, not even if they have gone over to the other side. Really gone over, I mean; not just obeying ruffians' orders because they are frightened. No hobbit has ever killed another on purpose in the Shire, and it is not to begin now. And nobody is to be killed at all, if it can be helped. Keep your tempers and hold your hands to the last possible moment!'

'But if there are many of these ruffians,' said Merry, 'it will certainly mean fighting. You won't rescue Lotho, or the Shire, just by being shocked and sad, my dear Frodo.'

'No,' said Pippin. 'It won't be so easy scaring them a second time. They were taken by surprise. You heard that horn-blowing? Evidently there are other ruffians near at hand. They'll be much bolder when there's more of them together. We ought to think of taking cover somewhere for the night. After all we're only four, even if we are armed.'

'I've an idea,' said Sam. 'Let's go to old Tom Cotton's down South Lane! He always was a stout fellow. And he has a lot of lads that were all friends of mine.'

'No!' said Merry. 'It's no good "getting under cover". That is just what people have been doing, and just what these ruffians like. They will simply come down on us in force, corner us, and then drive us out, or burn us in. No, we have got to do something at once.'

'Do what?' said Pippin.

'Raise the Shire!' said Merry. 'Now! Wake all our people! They hate all this, you can see: all of them except perhaps one or two rascals, and a few fools that want to be important, but don't at all understand what is really going on. But Shire-folk have been so comfortable so long they don't know what to do. They just want a match, though, and they'll go up in fire. The

Chief's Men must know that. They'll try to stamp on us and put us out quick. We've only got a very short time.

'Sam, you can make a dash for Cotton's farm, if you like. He's the chief person round here, and the sturdiest. Come on! I am going to blow the horn of Rohan, and give them all some music they have never heard before.'

They rode back to the middle of the village. There Sam turned aside and galloped off down the lane that led south to Cotton's. He had not gone far when he heard a sudden clear horn-call go up ringing into the sky. Far over hill and field it echoed; and so compelling was that call that Sam himself almost turned and dashed back. His pony reared and neighed.

'On, lad! On!' he cried. 'We'll be going back soon.'

Then he heard Merry change the note, and up went the Horn-cry of Buckland, shaking the air.

> Awake! Awake! Fear, Fire, Foes! Awake!
> Fire, Foes! Awake!

Behind him Sam heard a hubbub of voices and a great din and slamming of doors. In front of him lights sprang out in the gloaming; dogs barked; feet came running. Before he got to the lane's end there was Farmer Cotton with three of his lads, Young Tom, Jolly, and Nick, hurrying towards him. They had axes in their hands, and barred the way.

'Nay! It's not one of them ruffians,' Sam heard the farmer say. 'It's a hobbit by the size of it, but all dressed up queer. Hey!' he cried. 'Who are you, and what's all this to-do?'

'It's Sam, Sam Gamgee. I've come back.'

Farmer Cotton came up close and stared at him in the twilight. 'Well!' he exclaimed. 'The voice is right, and your face is no worse than it was, Sam. But I should a' passed you in the street in that gear. You've been in foreign parts, seemingly. We feared you were dead.'

'That I ain't!' said Sam. 'Nor Mr. Frodo. He's here and his friends. And that's the to-do. They're raising the Shire. We're going to clear out these ruffians, and their Chief too. We're starting now.'

'Good, good!' cried Farmer Cotton. 'So it's begun at last! I've been itching for trouble all this year, but folks wouldn't help. And I've had the wife and Rosie to think of. These ruffians don't stick at nothing. But come on now, lads! Bywater is up! We must be in it!'

'What about Mrs. Cotton and Rosie?' said Sam. 'It isn't safe yet for them to be left all alone.'

'My Nibs is with them. But you can go and help him, if you have a mind,' said Farmer Cotton with a grin. Then he and his sons ran off towards the village.

Sam hurried to the house. By the large round door at the top of the steps from the wide yard stood Mrs. Cotton and Rosie, and Nibs in front of them grasping a hay-fork.

'It's me!' shouted Sam as he trotted up. 'Sam Gamgee! So don't try prodding me, Nibs. Anyway, I've a mail-shirt on me.'

He jumped down from his pony and went up the steps. They stared at him in silence. 'Good evening, Mrs. Cotton!' he said. 'Hullo, Rosie!'

'Hullo, Sam!' said Rosie. 'Where've you been? They said you were dead; but I've been expecting you since the Spring. You haven't hurried, have you?'

'Perhaps not,' said Sam abashed. 'But I'm hurrying now. We're setting about the ruffians, and I've got to get back to Mr. Frodo. But I thought I'd have a look and see how Mrs. Cotton was keeping, and you, Rosie.'

'We're keeping nicely, thank you,' said Mrs. Cotton. 'Or should be, if it weren't for these thieving ruffians.'

'Well, be off with you!' said Rosie. 'If you've been looking after Mr. Frodo all this while, what d'you want to leave him for, as soon as things look dangerous?'

This was too much for Sam. It needed a week's answer, or none. He turned away and mounted his pony. But as he started off, Rosie ran down the steps.

'I think you look fine, Sam,' she said. 'Go on now! But take care of yourself, and come straight back as soon as you have settled the ruffians!'

When Sam got back he found the whole village roused. Already, apart from many younger lads, more than a hundred sturdy hobbits were assembled with axes, and heavy hammers, and long knives, and stout staves; and a few had hunting-bows. More were still coming in from outlying farms.

Some of the village-folk had lit a large fire, just to enliven things, and also because it was one of the things forbidden by the Chief. It burned bright as night came on. Others at Merry's orders were setting up barriers across the road at each end of the village. When the Shirriffs came up to the lower one they were dumbfounded; but as soon as they saw how things were, most of them took off their feathers and joined in the revolt. The others slunk away.

Sam found Frodo and his friends by the fire talking to old Tom Cotton, while an admiring crowd of Bywater folk stood round and stared.

'Well, what's the next move?' said Farmer Cotton.

'I can't say,' said Frodo, 'until I know more. How many of these ruffians are there?'

'That's hard to tell,' said Cotton. 'They moves about and comes and goes. There's sometimes fifty of them in their sheds up Hobbiton way; but they go out from there roving round, thieving or "gathering" as they call it. Still there's seldom less than a score round the Boss, as they names him. He's at Bag End, or was; but he don't go outside the grounds now. No one's seen him at all, in fact, for a week or two; but the Men don't let no one go near.'

'Hobbiton's not their only place, is it?' said Pippin.

'No, more's the pity,' said Cotton. 'There's a good few down south in Longbottom and by Sarn Ford, I hear; and some more lurking in the Woody End; and they've sheds at Waymeet. And then there's the Lock-holes, as they call 'em: the old storage-tunnels at Michel Delving that they've made into prisons for those as stand up to them. Still I reckon there's not above three hundred of them in the Shire all told, and maybe less. We can master them, if we stick together.'

'Have they got any weapons?' asked Merry.

'Whips, knives, and clubs, enough for their dirty work: that's all they've showed so far,' said Cotton. 'But I dare say they've got other gear, if it comes to fighting. Some have bows, anyway. They've shot one or two of our folk.'

'There you are, Frodo!' said Merry. 'I knew we should have to fight. Well, they started the killing.'

'Not exactly,' said Cotton. 'Leastways not the shooting. Tooks started that. You see, your dad, Mr. Peregrin, he's never had no truck with this Lotho, not from the beginning: said that if anyone was going to play the chief at this time of day, it would be the right Thain of the Shire and no upstart. And when Lotho sent his Men they got no change out of him. Tooks are lucky, they've got those deep holes in the Green Hills, the Great Smials and all, and the ruffians can't come at 'em; and they won't let the ruffians come on their land. If they do, Tooks hunt 'em. Tooks shot three for prowling and robbing. After that the ruffians turned nastier. And they keep a pretty close watch on Tookland. No one gets in nor out of it now.'

'Good for the Tooks!' cried Pippin. 'But someone is going to get in again, now. I am off to the Smials. Anyone coming with me to Tuckborough?'

Pippin rode off with half a dozen lads on ponies. 'See you soon!' he cried. 'It's only fourteen miles or so over the fields. I'll bring you back an army of Tooks in the morning.' Merry blew a horn-call after them as they rode off into the gathering night. The people cheered.

'All the same,' said Frodo to all those who stood near, 'I wish for no killing; not even of the ruffians, unless it must be done, to prevent them from hurting hobbits.'

'All right!' said Merry. 'But we shall be having a visit from the Hobbiton gang any time now, I think. They won't come just to talk things over. We'll try to deal with them neatly, but we must be prepared for the worst. Now I've got a plan.'

'Very good,' said Frodo. 'You make the arrangements.'

Just then some hobbits, who had been sent out towards Hobbiton, came running in. 'They're coming!' they said. 'A score or more. But two have gone off west across country.'

'To Waymeet, that'll be,' said Cotton, 'to fetch more of the gang. Well, it's fifteen mile each way. We needn't trouble about them just yet.'

Merry hurried off to give orders. Farmer Cotton cleared the street, sending everyone indoors, except the older hobbits who had weapons of some sort. They had not long to wait. Soon they could hear loud voices, and then the tramping of heavy feet. Presently a whole squad of the ruffians came down the road. They saw the barrier and laughed. They did not imagine that there was anything in this little land that would stand up to twenty of their kind together.

The hobbits opened the barrier and stood aside. 'Thank you!' the Men jeered. 'Now run home to bed before you're whipped.' Then they marched along the street shouting: 'Put those lights out! Get indoors and stay there! Or we'll take fifty of you to the Lockholes for a year. Get in! The Boss is losing his temper.'

No one paid any heed to their orders; but as the ruffians passed, they closed in quietly behind and followed them. When the Men reached the fire there was Farmer Cotton standing all alone warming his hands.

'Who are you, and what d'you think you're doing?' said the ruffian-leader.

Farmer Cotton looked at him slowly. 'I was just going to ask you that,' he said. 'This isn't your country, and you're not wanted.'

'Well, you're wanted anyhow,' said the leader. 'We want you. Take him lads! Lockholes for him, and give him something to keep him quiet!'

The Men took one step forward and stopped short. There rose a roar of voices all round them, and suddenly they were aware that Farmer Cotton was not all alone. They were surrounded. In the dark on the edge of the firelight stood a ring of hobbits that had crept up out of the shadows. There was nearly two hundred of them, all holding some weapon.

Merry stepped forward. 'We have met before,' he said to the leader, 'and I warned you not to come back here. I warn you again: you are standing in the light and you are covered by archers. If you lay a finger on this farmer, or on anyone else, you will be shot at once. Lay down any weapons that you have!'

The leader looked round. He was trapped. But he was not scared, not now with a score of his fellows to back him. He knew too little of hobbits to understand his peril. Foolishly he decided to fight. It would be easy to break out.

'At 'em, lads!' he cried. 'Let 'em have it!'

With a long knife in his left hand and a club in the other he made a rush at the ring, trying to burst out back towards Hobbiton. He aimed a savage blow at Merry who stood in his way. He fell dead with four arrows in him.

That was enough for the others. They gave in. Their weapons were taken from them, and they were roped together, and marched off to an empty hut that they had built themselves, and there they were tied hand and foot, and locked up under guard. The dead leader was dragged off and buried.

'Seems almost too easy after all, don't it?' said Cotton. 'I said we could master them. But we needed a call. You came back in the nick o' time, Mr. Merry.'

'There's more to be done still,' said Merry. 'If you're right in your reckoning, we haven't dealt with a tithe of them yet. But it's dark now. I think the next stroke must wait until morning. Then we must call on the Chief.'

'Why not now?' said Sam. 'It's not much more than six o'clock. And I want to see my gaffer. D'you know what's come of him, Mr. Cotton?'

'He's not too well, and not too bad, Sam,' said the farmer. 'They dug up Bagshot Row, and that was a sad blow to him. He's in one of them new houses that the Chief's Men used to build while they still did any work other than burning and thieving: not above a mile from the end of Bywater. But he comes around to me, when he gets a chance, and I see he's better fed than some of the poor bodies. All against *The Rules*, of course. I'd have had him with me, but that wasn't allowed.'

'Thank'ee indeed, Mr. Cotton, and I'll never forget it,' said Sam. 'But I want to see him. That Boss and that Sharkey, as they spoke of, they might do a mischief up there before the morning.'

'All right, Sam,' said Cotton. 'Choose a lad or two, and go and fetch him to my house. You'll not have need to go near the old Hobbiton village over Water. My Jolly here will show you.'

Sam went off. Merry arranged for look-outs round the village and guards at the barriers during the night. Then he and Frodo went off with Farmer Cotton. They sat with the family in the warm kitchen, and the Cottons asked a few polite questions about their travels, but hardly listened to the answers: they were far more concerned with events in the Shire.

'It all began with Pimple, as we call him,' said Farmer Cotton; 'and it began as soon as you'd gone off, Mr. Frodo. He'd funny ideas, had Pimple. Seems he wanted to own everything himself, and then order other folk about. It soon came out that he already did own a sight more than was good for him; and he was always grabbing more, though where he got the money was a mystery: mills and malt-houses and inns, and farms, and leaf-plantations. He'd already bought Sandyman's mill before he came to Bag End, seemingly.

'Of course he started with a lot of property in the Southfarthing which he had from his dad; and it seems he'd been selling a lot o' the best leaf, and sending it away quietly for a year or two. But at the end o' last year he began sending away loads of stuff, not only leaf. Things began to get short, and winter coming on, too. Folk got angry, but he had his answer. A lot of Men, ruffians mostly, came with great waggons, some to carry off the goods south-away, and others to stay. And more came. And before we knew where we were they were planted here and there all over the Shire, and were felling trees and digging and building themselves sheds and houses just as they liked. At first goods and damage was paid for by Pimple; but soon they began lording it around and taking what they wanted.

'Then there was a bit of trouble, but not enough. Old Will the Mayor set off for Bag End to protest, but he never got there. Ruffians laid hands on him and took and locked him up in a hole in Michel Delving, and there he is now. And after that, it would be soon after New Year, there wasn't no more Mayor, and Pimple called himself Chief Shirriff, or just Chief, and did as he liked; and if anyone got "uppish" as they called it, they followed Will. So things went from bad to worse. There wasn't no smoke left, save for the Men; and the Chief didn't hold with beer, save for his Men, and closed all the inns; and everything except Rules got shorter and shorter, unless one could hide a bit of one's own when the ruffians went round gathering stuff up "for fair distribution": which meant they got it and we didn't, except for the leavings which you could have at the Shirriff-houses, if you could stomach them. All very bad. But since Sharkey came it's been plain ruination.'

'Who is this Sharkey?' said Merry. 'I heard one of the ruffians speak of him.'

'The biggest ruffian o' the lot, seemingly,' answered Cotton. 'It was about last harvest, end o' September maybe, that we first heard of him. We've never seen him, but he's up at Bag End; and he's the real Chief now, I guess. All the ruffians do what he says; and what he says is mostly: hack, burn, and ruin; and now it's come to killing. There's no longer even any bad sense in it. They cut down trees and let 'em lie, they burn houses and build no more.

'Take Sandyman's mill now. Pimple knocked it down almost as soon as he came to Bag End. Then he brought in a lot o' dirty-looking Men to build a bigger one and fill it full o' wheels and outlandish contraptions. Only that fool Ted was pleased by that, and he works there cleaning wheels for the Men, where his dad was the Miller and his own master. Pimple's idea was to grind more and faster, or so he said. He's got other mills like it. But you've got to have grist before you can grind; and there was no more for the new mill to do than for the old. But since Sharkey came they don't grind no more corn at all. They're always a-hammering and a-letting out a smoke and a stench, and there isn't no peace even at night in Hobbiton. And they pour out filth a purpose; they've fouled all the lower Water, and it's getting down into Brandywine. If they want to make the Shire into a desert, they're going the right way about it. I don't believe that fool of a Pimple's behind all this. It's Sharkey, I say.'

'That's right!' put in Young Tom. 'Why, they even took Pimple's old ma, that Lobelia, and he was fond of her, if no one else was. Some of the Hobbiton folk, they saw it. She comes down the lane with her old umberella. Some of the ruffians were going up with a big cart.

' "Where be you a-going?" says she.

' "To Bag End," says they.

' "What for?" says she.

' "To put up some sheds for Sharkey," says they.

' "Who said you could?" says she.

' "Sharkey," says they. "So get out o' the road, old hagling!"

' "I'll give you Sharkey, you dirty thieving ruffians!" says she, and ups with her umberella and goes for the leader, near twice her size. So they took her. Dragged her off to the Lockholes, at her age too. They've took others we miss more, but there's no denying she showed more spirit than most.'

Into the middle of this talk came Sam, bursting in with his gaffer. Old Gamgee did not look much older, but he was a little deafer.

'Good evening, Mr. Baggins!' he said. 'Glad indeed I am to see you safe back. But I've a bone to pick with you, in a manner o' speaking, if I may make so bold. You didn't never ought to have a' sold Bag End, as I always said. That's what started all the mischief. And while you've been trapessing in foreign parts, chasing Black Men up mountains from what my Sam says, though what for he don't make clear, they've been and dug up Bagshot Row and ruined my taters!'

'I am very sorry, Mr. Gamgee,' said Frodo. 'But now I've come back, I'll do my best to make amends.'

'Well, you can't say fairer than that,' said the gaffer. 'Mr. *Frodo* Baggins is a real gentlehobbit, I always have said, whatever you may think of some others of the name, begging your pardon. And I hope my Sam's behaved hisself and given satisfaction?'

'Perfect satisfaction, Mr. Gamgee,' said Frodo. 'Indeed, if you will believe it, he's now one of the most famous people in all the lands, and they are making songs about his deeds from here to the Sea and beyond the Great River.' Sam blushed, but he looked gratefully at Frodo, for Rosie's eyes were shining and she was smiling at him.

'It takes a lot o' believing,' said the gaffer, 'though I can see he's been mixing in strange company. What's come of his weskit? I don't hold with wearing ironmongery, whether it wears well or no.'

Farmer Cotton's household and all his guests were up early next morning. Nothing had been heard in the night, but more trouble would certainly come before the day was old. 'Seems as if none o' the ruffians were left up at Bag End,' said Cotton; 'but the gang from Waymeet will be along any time now.'

After breakfast a messenger from the Tookland rode in. He was in high spirits. 'The Thain has raised all our country,' he said, 'and the news is going like fire all ways. The ruffians that were watching our land have fled off south, those that escaped alive. The Thain has gone after them, to hold off the big gang down that way; but he's sent Mr. Peregrin back with all the other folk he can spare.'

The next news was less good. Merry, who had been out all night, came riding in about ten o'clock. 'There's a big band about four miles away,' he said. 'They're coming along the road from Waymeet, but a good many stray ruffians have joined up with them. There must be close on a hundred of them; and they're fire-raising as they come. Curse them!'

'Ah! This lot won't stay to talk, they'll kill, if they can,' said Farmer Cotton. 'If Tooks don't come sooner, we'd best get behind cover and shoot without arguing. There's got to be some fighting before this is settled, Mr. Frodo.'

The Tooks did come sooner. Before long they marched in, a hundred strong, from Tuckborough and the Green Hills with Pippin at their head. Merry now had enough sturdy hobbitry to deal with the ruffians. Scouts reported that they were keeping close together. They knew that the countryside had risen against them, and plainly meant to deal with the rebellion ruthlessly, at its centre in Bywater. But however grim they might be, they seemed to have no leader among them who understood warfare. They came on without any precautions. Merry laid his plans quickly.

The ruffians came tramping along the East Road, and without halting turned up the Bywater Road, which ran for some way sloping up between high banks with low hedges on top. Round a bend, about a furlong from the main road, they met a stout barrier of old farm-carts upturned. That halted them. At the same moment they became aware that the hedges on both sides, just above their heads, were all lined with hobbits. Behind them other hobbits now pushed out some more waggons that had been hidden in a field, and so blocked the way back. A voice spoke to them from above.

'Well, you have walked into a trap,' said Merry. 'Your fellows from Hobbiton did the same, and one is dead and the rest are prisoners. Lay down your weapons! Then go back twenty paces and sit down. Any who try to break out will be shot.'

But the ruffians could not now be cowed so easily. A few of them obeyed, but were immediately set on by their fellows. A score or more broke back and charged the waggons. Six were shot, but the remainder burst out, killing two hobbits, and then scattering across country in the direction of the Woody End. Two more fell as they ran. Merry blew a loud horn-call, and there were answering calls from a distance.

'They won't get far,' said Pippin. 'All that country is alive with our hunters now.'

Behind, the trapped Men in the lane, still about four score, tried to climb the barrier and the banks, and the hobbits were obliged to shoot many of them or hew them with axes. But many of the strongest and most desperate got out on the west side, and attacked their enemies fiercely, being now more bent on killing than escaping. Several hobbits fell, and the rest were wavering, when Merry and Pippin, who were on the east side, came across and charged the ruffians. Merry himself slew the leader, a great squint-eyed brute like a huge orc. Then he drew his forces off, encircling the last remnant of the Men in a wide ring of archers.

At last all was over. Nearly seventy of the ruffians lay dead on the field, and a dozen were prisoners. Nineteen hobbits were killed, and some thirty were wounded. The dead ruffians were laden on waggons and hauled off to an old sand-pit nearby and there buried: in the Battle Pit, as it was afterwards called. The fallen hobbits were laid together in a grave on the hill-side, where later a great stone was set up with a garden about it. So ended the Battle of Bywater, 1419, the last battle fought in the Shire, and the only battle since the Greenfields, 1147, away up in the Northfarthing. In consequence, though it happily cost very few lives, it has a chapter to itself in the Red Book, and the names of all those who took part were made into a Roll, and learned by heart by Shire-historians. The very considerable rise in the fame and fortune of the Cottons dates from this time; but at the top of the Roll in all accounts stand the names of Captains Meriadoc and Peregrin.

Frodo had been in the battle, but he had not drawn sword, and his chief part had been to prevent the hobbits in their wrath at their losses, from slaying those of their enemies who threw down their weapons. When the fighting was over, and the later labours were ordered, Merry, Pippin, and Sam joined him, and they rode back with the Cottons. They ate a late midday meal, and then Frodo said with a sigh: 'Well, I suppose it is time now that we dealt with the "Chief".'

'Yes indeed; the sooner the better,' said Merry. 'And don't be too gentle! He's responsible for bringing in these ruffians, and for all the evil they have done.'

Farmer Cotton collected an escort of some two dozen sturdy hobbits. 'For it's only a guess that there is no ruffians left at Bag End,' he said. 'We don't know.' Then they set out on foot. Frodo, Sam, Merry, and Pippin led the way.

It was one of the saddest hours in their lives. The great chimney rose up before them; and as they drew near the old village across the Water, through rows of new mean houses along each side of the road, they saw the new mill in all its frowning and dirty ugliness: a great brick building straddling the stream, which it fouled with a steaming and stinking outflow. All along the Bywater Road every tree had been felled.

As they crossed the bridge and looked up the Hill they gasped. Even Sam's vision in the Mirror had not prepared him for what they saw. The Old Grange on the west side had been knocked down, and its place taken by rows of tarred sheds. All the chestnuts were gone. The banks and hedgerows were broken. Great waggons were standing in disorder in a field beaten bare of grass. Bagshot Row was a yawning sand and gravel quarry. Bag End up beyond could not be seen for a clutter of large huts.

'They've cut it down!' cried Sam. 'They've cut down the Party Tree!' He pointed to where the tree had stood under which Bilbo had made his Farewell Speech. It was lying lopped and dead in the field. As if this was the last straw Sam burst into tears.

A laugh put an end to them. There was a surly hobbit lounging over the low wall of the mill-yard. He was grimy-faced and black-handed. 'Don't 'ee like it, Sam?' he sneered. 'But you always was soft. I thought you'd gone off in one o' them ships you used to prattle about, sailing, sailing. What d'you want to come back for? We've work to do in the Shire now.'

'So I see,' said Sam. 'No time for washing, but time for wall-propping. But see here, Master Sandyman, I've a score to pay in this village, and don't you make it any longer with your jeering, or you'll foot a bill too big for your purse.'

Ted Sandyman spat over the wall. 'Garn!' he said. 'You can't touch me.

I'm a friend o' the Boss's. But he'll touch you all right, if I have any more of your mouth.'

'Don't waste any more words on the fool, Sam!' said Frodo. 'I hope there are not many more hobbits that have become like this. It would be a worse trouble than all the damage the Men have done.'

'You are dirty and insolent, Sandyman,' said Merry. 'And also very much out of your reckoning. We are just going up the Hill to remove your precious Boss. We have dealt with his Men.'

Ted gaped, for at that moment he first caught sight of the escort that at a sign from Merry now marched over the bridge. Dashing back into the mill he ran out with a horn and blew it loudly.

'Save your breath!' laughed Merry. 'I've a better.' Then lifting up his silver horn he winded it, and its clear call rang over the Hill; and out of the holes and sheds and shabby houses of Hobbiton the hobbits answered, and came pouring out, and with cheers and loud cries they followed the company up the road to Bag End.

At the top of the lane the party halted, and Frodo and his friends went on; and they came at last to the once beloved place. The garden was full of huts and sheds, some so near the old westward windows that they cut off all their light. There were piles of refuse everywhere. The door was scarred; the bell-chain was dangling loose, and the bell would not ring. Knocking brought no answer. At length they pushed and the door yielded. They went in. The place stank and was full of filth and disorder: it did not appear to have been used for some time.

'Where is that miserable Lotho hiding?' said Merry. They had searched every room and found no living thing save rats and mice. 'Shall we turn on the others to search the sheds?'

'This is worse than Mordor!' said Sam. 'Much worse in a way. It comes home to you, as they say; because it is home, and you remember it before it was all ruined.'

'Yes, this is Mordor,' said Frodo. 'Just one of its works. Saruman was doing its work all the time, even when he thought he was working for himself. And the same with those that Saruman tricked, like Lotho.'

Merry looked round in dismay and disgust. 'Let's get out!' he said. 'If I had known all the mischief he had caused, I should have stuffed my pouch down Saruman's throat.'

'No doubt, no doubt! But you did not, and so I am able to welcome you home.' There standing at the door was Saruman himself, looking well-fed and well-pleased; his eyes gleamed with malice and amusement.

A sudden light broke on Frodo. 'Sharkey!' he cried.

Saruman laughed. 'So you have heard the name, have you? All my people

used to call me that in Isengard, I believe. A sign of affection, possibly.*
But evidently you did not expect to see me here.'

'I did not,' said Frodo. 'But I might have guessed. A little mischief in
a mean way: Gandalf warned me that you were still capable of it.'

'Quite capable,' said Saruman, 'and more than a little. You made me
laugh, you hobbit-lordlings, riding along with all those great people, so
secure and so pleased with your little selves. You thought you had done
very well out of it all, and could now just amble back and have a nice quiet
time in the country. Saruman's home could be all wrecked, and he could
be turned out, but no one could touch yours. Oh no! Gandalf would look
after your affairs.'

Saruman laughed again. 'Not he! When his tools have done their task
he drops them. But you must go dangling after him, dawdling and talking,
and riding round twice as far as you needed. "Well," thought I, "if they're
such fools, I will get ahead of them and teach them a lesson. One ill turn
deserves another." It would have been a sharper lesson, if only you had
given me a little more time and more Men. Still I have already done much
that you will find it hard to mend or undo in your lives. And it will be
pleasant to think of that and set it against my injuries.'

'Well, if that is what you find pleasure in,' said Frodo, 'I pity you. It
will be a pleasure of memory only, I fear. Go at once and never return!'

The hobbits of the villages had seen Saruman come out of one of the
huts, and at once they came crowding up to the door of Bag End. When
they heard Frodo's command, they murmured angrily:

'Don't let him go! Kill him! He's a villain and a murderer. Kill him!'

Saruman looked round at their hostile faces and smiled. 'Kill him!' he
mocked. 'Kill him, if you think there are enough of you, my brave hobbits!'
He drew himself up and stared at them darkly with his black eyes. 'But
do not think that when I lost all my goods I lost all my power! Whoever
strikes me shall be accursed. And if my blood stains the Shire, it shall
wither and never again be healed.'

The hobbits recoiled. But Frodo said: 'Do not believe him! He has lost
all power, save his voice that can still daunt you and deceive you, if you
let it. But I will not have him slain. It is useless to meet revenge with
revenge: it will heal nothing. Go, Saruman, by the speediest way!'

'Worm! Worm!' Saruman called; and out of a nearby hut came Worm-
tongue, crawling, almost like a dog. 'To the road again, Worm!' said
Saruman. 'These fine fellows and lordlings are turning us adrift again.
Come along!'

Saruman turned to go, and Wormtongue shuffled after him. But even

* It was probably Orkish in origin: *sharkû*, 'old man'.

as Saruman passed close to Frodo a knife flashed in his hand, and he stabbed swiftly. The blade turned on the hidden mail-coat and snapped. A dozen hobbits, led by Sam, leaped forward with a cry and flung the villain to the ground. Sam drew his sword.

'No, Sam!' said Frodo. 'Do not kill him even now. For he has not hurt me. And in any case I do not wish him to be slain in this evil mood. He was great once, of a noble kind that we should not dare to raise our hands against. He is fallen, and his cure is beyond us; but I would still spare him, in the hope that he may find it.'

Saruman rose to his feet, and stared at Frodo. There was a strange look in his eyes of mingled wonder and respect and hatred. 'You have grown, Halfling,' he said. 'Yes, you have grown very much. You are wise, and cruel. You have robbed my revenge of sweetness, and now I must go hence in bitterness, in debt to your mercy. I hate it and you! Well, I go and I will trouble you no more. But do not expect me to wish you health and long life. You will have neither. But that is not my doing. I merely foretell.'

He walked away, and the hobbits made a lane for him to pass; but their knuckles whitened as they gripped on their weapons. Wormtongue hesitated, and then followed his master.

'Wormtongue!' called Frodo. 'You need not follow him. I know of no evil you have done to me. You can have rest and food here for a while, until you are stronger and can go your own ways.'

Wormtongue halted and looked back at him, half prepared to stay. Saruman turned. 'No evil?' he cackled. 'Oh no! Even when he sneaks out at night it is only to look at the stars. But did I hear someone ask where poor Lotho is hiding? You know, don't you, Worm? Will you tell them?'

Wormtongue cowered down and whimpered: 'No, no!'

'Then I will,' said Saruman. 'Worm killed your Chief, poor little fellow, your nice little Boss. Didn't you, Worm? Stabbed him in his sleep, I believe. Buried him, I hope; though Worm has been very hungry lately. No, Worm is not really nice. You had better leave him to me.'

A look of wild hatred came into Wormtongue's red eyes. 'You told me to; you made me do it,' he hissed.

Saruman laughed. 'You do what Sharkey says, always, don't you, Worm? Well, now he says: follow!' He kicked Wormtongue in the face as he grovelled, and turned and made off. But at that something snapped: suddenly Wormtongue rose up, drawing a hidden knife, and then with a snarl like a dog he sprang on Saruman's back, jerked his head back, cut his throat, and with a yell ran off down the lane. Before Frodo could recover or speak a word, three hobbit-bows twanged and Wormtongue fell dead.

To the dismay of those that stood by, about the body of Saruman a grey mist gathered, and rising slowly to a great height like smoke from a fire, as a pale shrouded figure it loomed over the Hill. For a moment it wavered, looking to the West; but out of the West came a cold wind, and it bent away, and with a sigh dissolved into nothing.

Frodo looked down at the body with pity and horror, for as he looked it seemed that long years of death were suddenly revealed in it, and it shrank, and the shrivelled face became rags of skin upon a hideous skull. Lifting up the skirt of the dirty cloak that sprawled beside it, he covered it over, and turned away.

'And that's the end of that,' said Sam. 'A nasty end, and I wish I needn't have seen it; but it's a good riddance.'

'And the very last end of the War, I hope,' said Merry.

'I hope so,' said Frodo and sighed. 'The very last stroke. But to think that it should fall here, at the very door of Bag End! Among all my hopes and fears at least I never expected that.'

'I shan't call it the end, till we've cleared up the mess,' said Sam gloomily. 'And that'll take a lot of time and work.'

CHAPTER IX

THE GREY HAVENS

The clearing up certainly needed a lot of work, but it took less time than Sam had feared. The day after the battle Frodo rode to Michel Delving and released the prisoners from the Lockholes. One of the first that they found was poor Fredegar Bolger, Fatty no longer. He had been taken when the ruffians smoked out a band of rebels that he led from their hidings up in the Brockenbores by the hills of Scary.

'You would have done better to come with us after all, poor old Fredegar!' said Pippin, as they carried him out too weak to walk.

He opened an eye and tried gallantly to smile. 'Who's this young giant with the loud voice?' he whispered. 'Not little Pippin! What's your size in hats now?'

Then there was Lobelia. Poor thing, she looked very old and thin when they rescued her from a dark and narrow cell. She insisted on hobbling out on her own feet; and she had such a welcome, and there was such clapping and cheering when she appeared, leaning on Frodo's arm but still clutching her umbrella, that she was quite touched, and drove away in tears. She had never in her life been popular before. But she was crushed by the news of Lotho's murder, and she would not return to Bag End. She gave it back to Frodo, and went to her own people, the Bracegirdles of Hardbottle.

When the poor creature died next Spring – she was after all more than a hundred years old – Frodo was surprised and much moved: she had left all that remained of her money and of Lotho's for him to use in helping hobbits made homeless by the troubles. So that feud was ended.

Old Will Whitfoot had been in the Lockholes longer than any, and though he had perhaps been treated less harshly than some, he needed a lot of feeding up before he could look the part of Mayor; so Frodo agreed to act as his Deputy, until Mr. Whitfoot was in shape again. The only thing that he did as Deputy Mayor was to reduce the Shirriffs to their proper functions and numbers. The task of hunting out the last remnant of the ruffians was left to Merry and Pippin, and it was soon done. The southern gangs, after hearing the news of the Battle of Bywater, fled out of the land and offered little resistance to the Thain. Before the Year's End the few survivors were rounded up in the woods, and those that surrendered were shown to the borders.

Meanwhile the labour of repair went on apace, and Sam was kept very busy. Hobbits can work like bees when the mood and the need comes on them. Now there were thousands of willing hands of all ages, from the small but nimble ones of the hobbit lads and lasses to the well-worn and horny ones of the gaffers and gammers. Before Yule not a brick was left standing of the new Shirriff-houses or of anything that had been built by 'Sharkey's Men'; but the bricks were used to repair many an old hole, to make it snugger and drier. Great stores of goods and food, and beer, were found that had been hidden away by the ruffians in sheds and barns and deserted holes, and especially in the tunnels at Michel Delving and in the old quarries at Scary; so that there was a great deal better cheer that Yule than anyone had hoped for.

One of the first things done in Hobbiton, before even the removal of the new mill, was the clearing of the Hill and Bag End, and the restoration of Bagshot Row. The front of the new sand-pit was all levelled and made into a large sheltered garden, and new holes were dug in the southward face, back into the Hill, and they were lined with brick. The Gaffer was restored to Number Three; and he said often and did not care who heard it:

'It's an ill wind as blows nobody no good, as I always say. And All's well as ends Better!'

There was some discussion of the name that the new row should be given. *Battle Gardens* was thought of, or *Better Smials*. But after a while in sensible hobbit-fashion it was just called *New Row*. It was a purely Bywater joke to refer to it as Sharkey's End.

The trees were the worst loss and damage, for at Sharkey's bidding they had been cut down recklessly far and wide over the Shire; and Sam grieved over this more than anything else. For one thing, this hurt would take long to heal, and only his great-grandchildren, he thought, would see the Shire as it ought to be.

Then suddenly one day, for he had been too busy for weeks to give a thought to his adventures, he remembered the gift of Galadriel. He brought the box out and showed it to the other Travellers (for so they were now called by everyone), and asked their advice.

'I wondered when you would think of it,' said Frodo. 'Open it!'

Inside it was filled with a grey dust, soft and fine, in the middle of which was a seed, like a small nut with a silver shale. 'What can I do with this?' said Sam.

'Throw it in the air on a breezy day and let it do its work!' said Pippin.

'On what?' said Sam.

'Choose one spot as a nursery, and see what happens to the plants there,' said Merry.

'But I'm sure the Lady would not like me to keep it all for my own garden, now so many folk have suffered,' said Sam.

'Use all the wits and knowledge you have of your own, Sam,' said Frodo, 'and then use the gift to help your work and better it. And use it sparingly. There is not much here, and I expect every grain has a value.'

So Sam planted saplings in all the places where specially beautiful or beloved trees had been destroyed, and he put a grain of the precious dust in the soil at the root of each. He went up and down the Shire in this labour; but if he paid special attention to Hobbiton and Bywater no one blamed him. And at the end he found that he still had a little of the dust left; so he went to the Three-Farthing Stone, which is as near the centre of the Shire as no matter, and cast it in the air with his blessing. The little silver nut he planted in the Party Field where the tree had once been; and he wondered what would come of it. All through the winter he remained as patient as he could, and tried to restrain himself from going round constantly to see if anything was happening.

Spring surpassed his wildest hopes. His trees began to sprout and grow, as if time was in a hurry and wished to make one year do for twenty. In the Party Field a beautiful young sapling leaped up: it had silver bark and long leaves and burst into golden flowers in April. It was indeed a *mallorn*, and it was the wonder of the neighbourhood. In after years, as it grew in grace and beauty, it was known far and wide and people would come long journeys to see it: the only *mallorn* west of the Mountains and east of the Sea, and one of the finest in the world.

Altogether 1420 in the Shire was a marvellous year. Not only was there wonderful sunshine and delicious rain, in due times and perfect measure, but there seemed something more: an air of richness and growth, and a gleam of a beauty beyond that of mortal summers that flicker and pass upon this Middle-earth. All the children born or begotten in that year, and there were many, were fair to see and strong, and most of them had a rich golden hair that had before been rare among hobbits. The fruit was so plentiful that young hobbits very nearly bathed in strawberries and cream; and later they sat on the lawns under the plum-trees and ate, until they had made piles of stones like small pyramids or the heaped skulls of a conqueror, and then they moved on. And no one was ill, and everyone was pleased, except those who had to mow the grass.

In the Southfarthing the vines were laden, and the yield of 'leaf' was astonishing; and everywhere there was so much corn that at Harvest every barn was stuffed. The Northfarthing barley was so fine that the beer of

1420 malt was long remembered and became a byword. Indeed a generation later one might hear an old gaffer in an inn, after a good pint of well-earned ale, put down his mug with a sigh: 'Ah! that was proper fourteen-twenty, that was!'

Sam stayed at first at the Cottons' with Frodo; but when the New Row was ready he went with the Gaffer. In addition to all his other labours he was busy directing the cleaning up and restoring of Bag End; but he was often away in the Shire on his forestry work. So he was not at home in early March and did not know that Frodo had been ill. On the thirteenth of that month Farmer Cotton found Frodo lying on his bed; he was clutching a white gem that hung on a chain about his neck and he seemed half in a dream.

'It is gone for ever,' he said, 'and now all is dark and empty.'

But the fit passed, and when Sam got back on the twenty-fifth, Frodo had recovered, and he said nothing about himself. In the meanwhile Bag End had been set in order, and Merry and Pippin came over from Crick-hollow bringing back all the old furniture and gear, so that the old hole soon looked very much as it always had done.

When all was at last ready Frodo said: 'When are you going to move in and join me, Sam?'

Sam looked a bit awkward.

'There is no need to come yet, if you don't want to,' said Frodo. 'But you know the Gaffer is close at hand, and he will be very well looked after by Widow Rumble.'

'It's not that, Mr. Frodo,' said Sam, and he went very red.

'Well, what is it?'

'It's Rosie, Rose Cotton,' said Sam. 'It seems she didn't like my going abroad at all, poor lass; but as I hadn't spoken, she couldn't say so. And I didn't speak, because I had a job to do first. But now I have spoken, and she says: "Well, you've wasted a year, so why wait longer?" "Wasted?" I says. "I wouldn't call it that." Still I see what she means. I feel torn in two, as you might say.'

'I see,' said Frodo: 'you want to get married, and yet you want to live with me in Bag End too? But my dear Sam, how easy! Get married as soon as you can, and then move in with Rosie. There's room enough in Bag End for as big a family as you could wish for.'

And so it was settled. Sam Gamgee married Rose Cotton in the Spring of 1420 (which was also famous for its weddings), and they came and lived at Bag End. And if Sam thought himself lucky, Frodo knew that he was more lucky himself; for there was not a hobbit in the Shire that was looked after with such care. When the labours of repair had all been planned and set going he took to a quiet life, writing a great deal and going through all his notes. He resigned the office of Deputy Mayor at the Free Fair that mid-summer, and dear old Will Whitfoot had another seven years of presiding at Banquets.

Merry and Pippin lived together for some time at Crickhollow, and there was much coming and going between Buckland and Bag End. The two young Travellers cut a great dash in the Shire with their songs and their tales and their finery, and their wonderful parties. 'Lordly' folk called them, meaning nothing but good; for it warmed all hearts to see them go riding by with their mail-shirts so bright and their shields so splendid, laughing and singing songs of far away; and if they were now large and magnificent, they were unchanged otherwise, unless they were indeed more fairspoken and more jovial and full of merriment than ever before.

Frodo and Sam, however, went back to ordinary attire, except that when there was need they both wore long grey cloaks, finely woven and clasped at the throat with beautiful brooches; and Mr. Frodo wore always a white jewel on a chain that he often would finger.

All things now went well, with hope always of becoming still better; and Sam was as busy and as full of delight as even a hobbit could wish. Nothing for him marred that whole year, except for some vague anxiety about his master. Frodo dropped quietly out of all the doings of the Shire, and Sam was pained to notice how little honour he had in his own country. Few people knew or wanted to know about his deeds and adventures; their admiration and respect were given mostly to Mr. Meriadoc and Mr. Peregrin and (if Sam had known it) to himself. Also in the autumn there appeared a shadow of old troubles.

One evening Sam came into the study and found his master looking very strange. He was very pale and his eyes seemed to see things far away.

'What's the matter, Mr. Frodo?' said Sam.

'I am wounded,' he answered, 'wounded; it will never really heal.'

But then he got up, and the turn seemed to pass, and he was quite himself the next day. It was not until afterwards that Sam recalled that the date was October the sixth. Two years before on that day it was dark in the dell under Weathertop.

Time went on, and 1421 came in. Frodo was ill again in March, but with a great effort he concealed it, for Sam had other things to think about. The first of Sam and Rosie's children was born on the twenty-fifth of March, a date that Sam noted.

'Well, Mr. Frodo,' he said. 'I'm in a bit of a fix. Rose and me had settled to call him Frodo, with your leave; but it's not *him*, it's *her*. Though as pretty a maidchild as any one could hope for, taking after Rose more than me, luckily. So we don't know what to do.'

'Well, Sam,' said Frodo, 'what's wrong with the old customs? Choose a flower name like Rose. Half the maidchildren in the Shire are called by such names, and what could be better?'

'I suppose you're right, Mr. Frodo,' said Sam. 'I've heard some beautiful names on my travels, but I suppose they're a bit too grand for daily wear and tear, as you might say. The Gaffer, he says: "Make it short, and then you won't have to cut it short before you can use it." But if it's to be a flower-name, then I don't trouble about the length: it must be a beautiful flower, because, you see, I think she is very beautiful, and is going to be beautifuller still.'

Frodo thought for a moment. 'Well, Sam, what about *elanor*, the sun-star, you remember the little golden flower in the grass of Lothlórien?'

'You're right again, Mr. Frodo!' said Sam delighted. 'That's what I wanted.'

Little Elanor was nearly six months old, and 1421 had passed to its autumn, when Frodo called Sam into the study.

'It will be Bilbo's Birthday on Thursday, Sam,' he said. 'And he will pass the Old Took. He will be a hundred and thirty-one!'

'So he will!' said Sam. 'He's a marvel!'

'Well, Sam,' said Frodo, 'I want you to see Rose and find out if she can spare you, so that you and I can go off together. You can't go far or for a long time now, of course,' he said a little wistfully.

'Well, not very well, Mr. Frodo.'

'Of course not. But never mind. You can see me on my way. Tell Rose that you won't be away very long, not more than a fortnight; and you'll come back quite safe.'

'I wish I could go all the way with you to Rivendell, Mr. Frodo, and see Mr. Bilbo,' said Sam. 'And yet the only place I really want to be in is here. I am that torn in two.'

'Poor Sam! It will feel like that, I am afraid,' said Frodo. 'But you will be healed. You were meant to be solid and whole, and you will be.'

In the next day or two Frodo went through his papers and his writings with Sam, and he handed over his keys. There was a big book with plain red leather covers; its tall pages were now almost filled. At the beginning there were many leaves covered with Bilbo's thin wandering hand; but most of it was written in Frodo's firm flowing script. It was divided into chapters but Chapter 80 was unfinished, and after that were some blank leaves. The title page had many titles on it, crossed out one after another, so:

My Diary. My Unexpected Journey. There and Back Again. And What Happened After.

Adventures of Five Hobbits. The Tale of the Great Ring, compiled by Bilbo Baggins from his own observations and the accounts of his friends. What we did in the War of the Ring.

Here Bilbo's hand ended and Frodo had written:

THE DOWNFALL
OF THE
LORD OF THE RINGS
AND THE
RETURN OF THE KING

(as seen by the Little People; being the memoirs of Bilbo and Frodo of the Shire, supplemented by the accounts of their friends and the learning of the Wise.)

Together with extracts from Books of Lore translated by Bilbo in Rivendell.

'Why, you have nearly finished it, Mr. Frodo!' Sam exclaimed. 'Well, you have kept at it, I must say.'

'I have quite finished, Sam,' said Frodo. 'The last pages are for you.'

On September the twenty-first they set out together, Frodo on the pony that had borne him all the way from Minas Tirith, and was now called Strider; and Sam on his beloved Bill. It was a fair golden morning, and Sam did not ask where they were going: he thought he could guess.

They took the Stock Road over the hills and went towards the Woody End, and they let their ponies walk at their leisure. They camped in the Green Hills, and on September the twenty-second they rode gently down into the beginning of the trees as afternoon was wearing away.

'If that isn't the very tree you hid behind when the Black Rider first showed up, Mr. Frodo!' said Sam pointing to the left. 'It seems like a dream now.'

It was evening, and the stars were glimmering in the eastern sky as they passed the ruined oak and turned and went on down the hill between the hazel-thickets. Sam was silent, deep in his memories. Presently he became aware that Frodo was singing softly to himself, singing the old walking-song, but the words were not quite the same.

> Still round the corner there may wait
> A new road or a secret gate;
> And though I oft have passed them by,
> A day will come at last when I
> Shall take the hidden paths that run
> West of the Moon, East of the Sun.

And as if in answer, from down below, coming up the road out of the valley, voices sang:

> A! Elbereth Gilthoniel!
> silivren penna míriel
> o menel aglar elenath,
> Gilthoniel, A! Elbereth!
> We still remember, we who dwell
> In this far land beneath the trees
> The starlight on the Western Seas.

Frodo and Sam halted and sat silent in the soft shadows, until they saw a shimmer as the travellers came towards them.

There was Gildor and many fair Elven folk; and there to Sam's wonder rode Elrond and Galadriel. Elrond wore a mantle of grey and had a star upon his forehead, and a silver harp was in his hand, and upon his finger was a ring of gold with a great blue stone, Vilya, mightiest of the Three. But Galadriel sat upon a white palfrey and was robed all in glimmering white, like clouds about the Moon; for she herself seemed to shine with a soft light. On her finger was Nenya, the ring wrought of *mithril*, that bore a single white stone flickering like a frosty star. Riding slowly behind on a small grey pony, and seeming to nod in his sleep, was Bilbo himself.

Elrond greeted them gravely and graciously, and Galadriel smiled upon them. 'Well, Master Samwise,' she said. 'I hear and see that you have used my gift well. The Shire shall now be more than ever blessed and beloved.' Sam bowed, but found nothing to say. He had forgotten how beautiful the Lady was.

Then Bilbo woke up and opened his eyes. 'Hullo, Frodo!' he said. 'Well,

I have passed the Old Took today! So that's settled. And now I think I am quite ready to go on another journey. Are you coming?'

'Yes, I am coming,' said Frodo. 'The Ring-bearers should go together.'

'Where are you going, Master?' cried Sam, though at last he understood what was happening.

'To the Havens, Sam,' said Frodo.

'And I can't come.'

'No, Sam. Not yet anyway, not further than the Havens. Though you too were a Ring-bearer, if only for a little while. Your time may come. Do not be too sad, Sam. You cannot be always torn in two. You will have to be one and whole, for many years. You have so much to enjoy and to be, and to do.'

'But,' said Sam, and tears started in his eyes, 'I thought you were going to enjoy the Shire, too, for years and years, after all you have done.'

'So I thought too, once. But I have been too deeply hurt, Sam. I tried to save the Shire, and it has been saved, but not for me. It must often be so, Sam, when things are in danger: some one has to give them up, lose them, so that others may keep them. But you are my heir: all that I had and might have had I leave to you. And also you have Rose, and Elanor; and Frodo-lad will come, and Rosie-lass, and Merry, and Goldilocks, and Pippin; and perhaps more that I cannot see. Your hands and your wits will be needed everywhere. You will be the Mayor, of course, as long as you want to be, and the most famous gardener in history; and you will read things out of the Red Book, and keep alive the memory of the age that is gone, so that people will remember the Great Danger and so love their beloved land all the more. And that will keep you as busy and as happy as anyone can be, as long as your part of the Story goes on.

'Come now, ride with me!'

Then Elrond and Galadriel rode on; for the Third Age was over, and the Days of the Rings were passed, and an end was come of the story and song of those times. With them went many Elves of the High Kindred who would no longer stay in Middle-earth; and among them, filled with a sadness that was yet blessed and without bitterness, rode Sam, and Frodo, and Bilbo, and the Elves delighted to honour them.

Though they rode through the midst of the Shire all the evening and all the night, none saw them pass, save the wild creatures; or here and there some wanderer in the dark who saw a swift shimmer under the trees, or a light and shadow flowing through the grass as the Moon went westward. And when they had passed from the Shire, going about the south skirts of the White Downs, they came to the Far Downs, and to the Towers, and looked on the distant Sea; and so they rode down at last to Mithlond, to the Grey Havens in the long firth of Lune.

As they came to the gates Círdan the Shipwright came forth to greet them. Very tall he was, and his beard was long, and he was grey and old, save that his eyes were keen as stars; and he looked at them and bowed, and said: 'All is now ready.'

Then Círdan led them to the Havens, and there was a white ship lying, and upon the quay beside a great grey horse stood a figure robed all in white awaiting them. As he turned and came towards them Frodo saw that Gandalf now wore openly on his hand the Third Ring, Narya the Great, and the stone upon it was red as fire. Then those who were to go were glad, for they knew that Gandalf also would take ship with them.

But Sam was now sorrowful at heart, and it seemed to him that if the parting would be bitter, more grievous still would be the long road home alone. But even as they stood there, and the Elves were going aboard, and all was being made ready to depart, up rode Merry and Pippin in great haste. And amid his tears Pippin laughed.

'You tried to give us the slip once before and failed, Frodo,' he said. 'This time you have nearly succeeded, but you have failed again. It was not Sam, though, that gave you away this time, but Gandalf himself!'

'Yes,' said Gandalf; 'for it will be better to ride back three together than one alone. Well, here at last, dear friends, on the shores of the Sea comes the end of our fellowship in Middle-earth. Go in peace! I will not say: do not weep; for not all tears are an evil.'

Then Frodo kissed Merry and Pippin, and last of all Sam, and went aboard; and the sails were drawn up, and the wind blew, and slowly the ship slipped away down the long grey firth; and the light of the glass of Galadriel that Frodo bore glimmered and was lost. And the ship went out into the High Sea and passed on into the West, until at last on a night of rain Frodo smelled a sweet fragrance on the air and heard the sound of singing that came over the water. And then it seemed to him that as in his dream in the house of Bombadil, the grey rain-curtain turned all to silver glass and was rolled back, and he beheld white shores and beyond them a far green country under a swift sunrise.

But to Sam the evening deepened to darkness as he stood at the Haven; and as he looked at the grey sea he saw only a shadow on the waters that was soon lost in the West. There still he stood far into the night, hearing only the sigh and murmur of the waves on the shores of Middle-earth, and the sound of them sank deep into his heart. Beside him stood Merry and Pippin, and they were silent.

At last the three companions turned away, and never again looking back they rode slowly homewards; and they spoke no word to one another until they came back to the Shire, but each had great comfort in his friends on the long grey road.

At last they rode over the downs and took the East Road, and then Merry and Pippin rode on to Buckland; and already they were singing again as they went. But Sam turned to Bywater, and so came back up the Hill, as day was ending once more. And he went on, and there was yellow light, and fire within; and the evening meal was ready, and he was expected. And Rose drew him in, and set him in his chair, and put little Elanor upon his lap.

He drew a deep breath. 'Well, I'm back,' he said.

APPENDIX A

ANNALS OF THE KINGS AND RULERS

Concerning the sources for most of the matter contained in the following Appendices, especially A to D, see the note at the end of the Prologue. The section A III, *Durin's Folk*, was probably derived from Gimli the Dwarf, who maintained his friendship with Peregrin and Meriadoc and met them again many times in Gondor and Rohan.

The legends, histories, and lore to be found in the sources are very extensive. Only selections from them, in most places much abridged, are here presented. Their principal purpose is to illustrate the War of the Ring and its origins, and to fill up some of the gaps in the main story. The ancient legends of the First Age, in which Bilbo's chief interest lay, are very briefly referred to, since they concern the ancestry of Elrond and the Númenorean kings and chieftains. Actual extracts from longer annals and tales are placed within quotation marks. Insertions of later date are enclosed in brackets. Notes within quotation marks are found in the sources. Others are editorial.[1]

The dates given are those of the Third Age, unless they are marked S.A. (Second Age) or F.A. (Fourth Age). The Third Age was held to have ended when the Three Rings passed away in September 3021, but for the purposes of records in Gondor F.A.I began on March 25, 3021. On the equation of the dating of Gondor and Shire Reckoning see pp. 4 and 1136. In lists the dates following the names of kings and rulers are the dates of their deaths, if only one date is given. The sign † indicates a premature death, in battle or otherwise, though an annal of the event is not always included.

I

THE NÚMENOREAN KINGS

(i)

NÚMENOR

Fëanor was the greatest of the Eldar in arts and lore, but also the proudest and most selfwilled. He wrought the Three Jewels, the *Silmarilli*, and filled them with the radiance of the Two Trees, Telperion and Laurelin,[2] that gave light to the land of the Valar. The Jewels were coveted by Morgoth the Enemy, who stole them and, after destroying the Trees, took them to Middle-earth, and guarded them in his

---

[1] A few references are given by page to this edition of *The Lord of the Rings*, and to the hardback 3rd edition of *The Hobbit*.

[2] Cf. pp. 238, 584, 950: no likeness remained in Middle-earth of Laurelin the Golden.

great fortress of Thangorodrim.[1] Against the will of the Valar Fëanor forsook the Blessed Realm and went in exile to Middle-earth, leading with him a great part of his people; for in his pride he purposed to recover the Jewels from Morgoth by force. Thereafter followed the hopeless war of the Eldar and the Edain against Thangorodrim, in which they were at last utterly defeated. The Edain (*Atani*) were three peoples of Men who, coming first to the West of Middle-earth and the shores of the Great Sea, became allies of the Eldar against the Enemy.

There were three unions of the Eldar and the Edain: Lúthien and Beren; Idril and Tuor; Arwen and Aragorn. By the last the long-sundered branches of the Half-elven were reunited and their line was restored.

Lúthien Tinúviel was the daughter of King Thingol Grey-cloak of Doriath in the First Age, but her mother was Melian of the people of the Valar. Beren was the son of Barahir of the First House of the Edain. Together they wrested a *silmaril* from the Iron Crown of Morgoth.[2] Lúthien became mortal and was lost to Elven-kind. Dior was her son. Elwing was his daughter and had in her keeping the *silmaril*.

Idril Celebrindal was the daughter of Turgon, king of the hidden city of Gondolin.[3] Tuor was the son of Huor of the House of Hador, the Third House of the Edain and the most renowned in the wars with Morgoth. Eärendil the Mariner was their son.

Eärendil wedded Elwing, and with the power of the *silmaril* passed the Shadows[4] and came to the Uttermost West, and speaking as ambassador of both Elves and Men obtained the help by which Morgoth was overthrown. Eärendil was not permitted to return to mortal lands, and his ship bearing the *silmaril* was set to sail in the heavens as a star, and a sign of hope to the dwellers in Middle-earth oppressed by the Great Enemy or his servants.[5] The *silmarilli* alone preserved the ancient light of the Two Trees of Valinor before Morgoth poisoned them; but the other two were lost at the end of the First Age. Of these things the full tale, and much else concerning Elves and Men, is told in *The Silmarillion*.

The sons of Eärendil were Elros and Elrond, the *Peredhil* or Half-elven. In them alone the line of the heroic chieftains of the Edain in the First Age was preserved; and after the fall of Gil-galad[6] the lineage of the High-elven Kings was also in Middle-earth only represented by their descendants.

At the end of the First Age the Valar gave to the Half-elven an irrevocable choice to which kindred they would belong. Elrond chose to be of Elven-kind, and became a master of wisdom. To him therefore was granted the same grace as to those of the High Elves that still lingered in Middle-earth: that when weary at last of the mortal lands they could take ship from the Grey Havens and pass into the Uttermost West; and this grace continued after the change of the world. But to the children

[1] pp. 236–7, 696.
[2] p. 189, 696.
[3] *The Hobbit*, p. 51; *The Lord of the Rings*, pp. 308–9.
[4] pp. 227–30.
[5] p. 352–6, 696, 704, 894, 901.
[6] pp. 51, 181.

of Elrond a choice was also appointed: to pass with him from the circles of the world; or if they remained to become mortal and die in Middle-earth. For Elrond, therefore, all chances of the War of the Ring were fraught with sorrow.[1]

Elros chose to be of Man-kind and remain with the Edain; but a great life-span was granted to him many times that of lesser men.

As a reward for their sufferings in the cause against Morgoth, the Valar, the Guardians of the World, granted to the Edain a land to dwell in, removed from the dangers of Middle-earth. Most of them, therefore, set sail over Sea, and guided by the Star of Eärendil came to the great Isle of Elenna, westernmost of all Mortal lands. There they founded the realm of Númenor.

There was a tall mountain in the midst of the land, the Meneltarma, and from its summit the farsighted could descry the white tower of the Haven of the Eldar in Eressëa. Thence the Eldar came to the Edain and enriched them with knowledge and many gifts; but one command had been laid upon the Númenoreans, the 'Ban of the Valar': they were forbidden to sail west out of sight of their own shores or to attempt to set foot on the Undying Lands. For though a long span of life had been granted to them, in the beginning thrice that of lesser Men, they must remain mortal, since the Valar were not permitted to take from them the Gift of Men (or the Doom of Men, as it was afterwards called).

Elros was the first King of Númenor, and was afterwards known by the High-elven name Tar-Minyatur. His descendants were long-lived but mortal. Later when they became powerful they begrudged the choice of their forefather, desiring the immortality within the life of the world that was the fate of the Eldar, and murmuring against the Ban. In this way began their rebellion which, under the evil teaching of Sauron, brought about the Downfall of Númenor and the ruin of the ancient world, as is told in the *Akallabêth*.

These are the names of the Kings and Queens of Númenor: Elros-Tar-Minyatur, Vardamir, Tar-Amandil, Tar-Elendil, Tar-Meneldur, Tar-Aldarion, Tar-Ancalimë (the first Ruling Queen), Tar-Anárion, Tar-Súrion, Tar-Telperiën (the second Queen), Tar-Minastir, Tar-Ciryatan, Tar-Atanamir the Great, Tar-Ancalimon, Tar-Telemmaitë, Tar-Vanimeldë (the third Queen), Tar-Alcarin, Tar-Calmacil.

After Calmacil the Kings took the sceptre in names of the Númenorean (or Adûnaic) tongue: Ar-Adûnakhôr, Ar-Zimrathôn, Ar-Sakalthôr, Ar-Gimilzôr, Ar-Inziladûn. Inziladûn repented of the ways of the Kings and changed his name to Tar-Palantir 'The Farsighted'. His daughter should have been the fourth Queen, Tar-Míriel, but the King's nephew usurped the sceptre and became Ar-Pharazôn the Golden, last King of the Númenoreans.

In the days of Tar-Elendil the first ships of the Númenoreans came back to Middle-earth. His elder child was a daughter, Silmariën. Her son was Valandil, first of the Lords of Andúnië in the west of the land, renowned for their friendship with the Eldar. From him were descended Amandil, the last lord, and his son Elendil the Tall.

---

[1] See pp. 952, 956.

The sixth King left only one child, a daughter. She became the first Queen; for it was then made a law of the royal house that the eldest child of the King, whether man or woman, should receive the sceptre.

The realm of Númenor endured to the end of the Second Age and increased ever in power and splendour; and until half the Age had passed the Númenoreans grew also in wisdom and joy. The first sign of the shadow that was to fall upon them appeared in the days of Tar-Minastir, eleventh King. He it was that sent a great force to the aid of Gil-galad. He loved the Eldar but envied them. The Númenoreans had now become great mariners, exploring all the seas eastward, and they began to yearn for the West and the forbidden waters; and the more joyful was their life, the more they began to long for the immortality of the Eldar.

Moreover, after Minastir the Kings became greedy of wealth and power. At first the Númenoreans had come to Middle-earth as teachers and friends of lesser Men afflicted by Sauron; but now their havens became fortresses, holding wide coastlands in subjection. Atanamir and his successors levied heavy tribute, and the ships of the Númenoreans returned laden with spoil.

It was Tar-Atanamir who first spoke openly against the Ban and declared that the life of the Eldar was his by right. Thus the shadow deepened, and the thought of death darkened the hearts of the people. Then the Númenoreans became divided: on the one hand were the Kings and those who followed them, and were estranged from the Eldar and the Valar; on the other were the few who called themselves the Faithful. They lived mostly in the west of the land.

The Kings and their followers little by little abandoned the use of the Eldarin tongues; and at last the twentieth King took his royal name, in Númenorean form, calling himself Ar-Adûnakhôr, 'Lord of the West'. This seemed ill-omened to the Faithful, for hitherto they had given that title only to one of the Valar, or to the Elder King himself.[1] And indeed Ar-Adûnakhôr began to persecute the Faithful and punished those who used the Elven-tongues openly; and the Eldar came no more to Númenor.

The power and wealth of the Númenoreans nonetheless continued to increase; but their years lessened as their fear of death grew, and their joy departed. Tar-Palantir attempted to amend the evil; but it was too late, and there was rebellion and strife in Númenor. When he died, his nephew, leader of the rebellion, seized the sceptre, and became King Ar-Pharazôn. Ar-Pharazôn the Golden was the proudest and most powerful of all the Kings, and no less than the kingship of the world was his desire.

He resolved to challenge Sauron the Great for the supremacy in Middle-earth, and at length he himself set sail with a great navy, and he landed at Umbar. So great was the might and splendour of the Númenoreans that Sauron's own servants deserted him; and Sauron humbled himself, doing homage, and craving pardon. Then Ar-Pharazôn in the folly of his pride carried him back as a prisoner to Númenor. It was not long before he had bewitched the King and was master of his

[1] p. 229.

counsel; and soon he had turned the hearts of all the Númenoreans, except the remnant of the Faithful, back towards the darkness.

And Sauron lied to the King, declaring that everlasting life would be his who possessed the Undying Lands, and that the Ban was imposed only to prevent the Kings of Men from surpassing the Valar. 'But great Kings take what is their right,' he said.

At length Ar-Pharazôn listened to this counsel, for he felt the waning of his days and was besotted by the fear of Death. He prepared then the greatest armament that the world had seen, and when all was ready he sounded his trumpets and set sail; and he broke the Ban of the Valar, going up with war to wrest everlasting life from the Lords of the West. But when Ar-Pharazôn set foot upon the shores of Aman the Blessed, the Valar laid down their Guardianship and called upon the One, and the world was changed. Númenor was thrown down and swallowed in the Sea, and the Undying Lands were removed for ever from the circles of the world. So ended the glory of Númenor.

The last leaders of the Faithful, Elendil and his sons, escaped from the Downfall with nine ships, bearing a seedling of Nimloth, and the Seven Seeing-stones (gifts of the Eldar to their House);[1] and they were borne on the wind of a great storm and cast upon the shores of Middle-earth. There they established in the North-west the Númenorean realms in exile, Arnor and Gondor.[2] Elendil was the High King and dwelt in the North at Annúminas; and the rule in the South was committed to his sons, Isildur and Anárion. They founded there Osgiliath, between Minas Ithil and Minas Anor,[3] not far from the confines of Mordor. For this good at least they believed had come out of ruin, that Sauron also had perished.

But it was not so. Sauron was indeed caught in the wreck of Númenor, so that the bodily form in which he long had walked perished; but he fled back to Middle-earth, a spirit of hatred borne upon a dark wind. He was unable ever again to assume a form that seemed fair to men, but became black and hideous, and his power thereafter was through terror alone. He re-entered Mordor, and hid there for a time in silence. But his anger was great when he learned that Elendil, whom he most hated, had escaped him, and was now ordering a realm upon his borders.

Therefore, after a time he made war upon the Exiles, before they should take root. Orodruin burst once more into flame, and was named anew in Gondor *Amon Amarth*, Mount Doom. But Sauron struck too soon, before his own power was rebuilt, whereas the power of Gil-galad had increased in his absence; and in the Last Alliance that was made against him Sauron was overthrown and the One Ring was taken from him.[4] So ended the Second Age.

---

[1] pp. 583, 950.
[2] p. 236.
[3] p. 238.
[4] p. 237.

(ii)

THE REALMS IN EXILE

The Northern Line
Heirs of Isildur

Arnor. Elendil †S.A. 3441, Isildur †2, Valandil 249,[1] Eldacar 339, Arantar 435, Tarcil 515, Tarondor 602, Valandur †652, Elendur 777, Eärendur 861.

Arthedain. Amlaith of Fornost[2] (eldest son of Eärendur) 946, Beleg 1029, Mallor 1110, Celepharn 1191, Celebrindor 1272, Malvegil 1349,[3] Argeleb I †1356, Arveleg I 1409, Araphor 1589, Argeleb II 1670, Arvegil 1743, Arveleg II 1813, Araval 1891, Araphant 1964, Arvedui Last-king †1975. End of the North-kingdom.

Chieftains. Aranarth (elder son of Arvedui) 2106, Arahael 2177, Aranuir 2247, Aravir 2319, Aragorn I †2327. Araglas 2455, Arahad I 2523, Aragost 2588, Aravorn 2654, Arahad II 2719, Arassuil 2784, Arathorn I †2848, Argonui 2912, Arador †2930, Arathorn II †2933, Aragorn II F.A. 120.

The Southern Line
Heirs of Anárion

Kings of Gondor. Elendil (Isildur and) Anárion †S.A. 3440, Meneldil son of Anárion 158, Cemendur 238, Eärendil 324, Anardil 411, Ostoher 492, Rómendacil I (Tarostar) †541, Turambar 667, Atanatar I 748, Siriondil 830. Here followed the four 'Ship-kings':

Tarannon Falastur 913. He was the first childless king, and was succeeded by the son of his brother Tarciryan. Eärnil I †936, Ciryandil †1015, Hyarmendacil I (Ciryaher) 1149. Gondor now reached the height of its power.

Atanatar II Alcarin 'the Glorious' 1226, Narmacil I 1294. He was the second childless king and was succeeded by his younger brother. Calmacil 1304, Minalcar (regent 1240–1304), crowned as Rómendacil II 1304, died 1366, Valacar. In his time the first disaster of Gondor began, the Kin-strife.

Eldacar son of Valacar (at first called Vinitharya) deposed 1437. Castamir the Usurper †1447. Eldacar restored, died 1490.

Aldamir (second son of Eldacar) †1540. Hyarmendacil II (Vinyarion) 1621, Minardil †1634, Telemnar †1636. Telemnar and all his children perished in the plague; he was succeeded by his nephew, the son of Minastan, second son of Minardil. Tarondor 1798, Telumehtar Umbardacil 1850, Narmacil II †1856, Calimehtar 1936, Ondoher †1944. Ondoher and his two sons were slain in battle. After a year in 1945 the crown was given to the victorious general Eärnil, a descendant of Telumehtar Umbardacil, Eärnil II 2043, Eärnur †2050. Here the line of the Kings came to an end, until it was restored by Elessar Telcontar in 3019. The realm was then ruled by the Stewards.

---

[1] He was the fourth son of Isildur, born in Imladris. His brothers were slain in the Gladden Fields.

[2] After Eärendur the Kings no longer took names in High-elven form.

[3] After Malvegil, the Kings at Fornost again claimed lordship over the whole of Arnor, and took names with the prefix *ar(a)* in token of this.

Stewards of Gondor. The House of Húrin: Pelendur 1998. He ruled for a year after the fall of Ondoher, and advised Gondor to reject Arvedui's claim to the crown. Vorondil the Hunter 2029.[1] Mardil Voronwë 'the Steadfast', the first of the Ruling Stewards. His successors ceased to use High-elven names.

Ruling Stewards. Mardil 2080, Eradan 2116, Herion 2148, Belegorn 2204, Húrin I 2244, Túrin I 2278, Hador 2395, Barahir 2412, Dior 2435, Denethor I 2477, Boromir 2489, Cirion 2567. In his time the Rohirrim came to Calenardhon.

Hallas 2605, Húrin II 2628, Belecthor I 2655, Orodreth 2685, Ecthelion I 2698, Egalmoth 2743, Beren 2763, Beregond 2811, Belecthor II 2872, Thorondir 2882, Túrin II 2914, Turgon 2953, Ecthelion II 2984, Denethor II. He was the last of the Ruling Stewards, and was followed by his second son Faramir, Lord of Emyn Arnen, Steward to King Elessar, F.A. 82.

(iii)

ERIADOR, ARNOR, AND THE HEIRS OF ISILDUR

'Eriador was of old the name of all the lands between the Misty Mountains and the Blue; in the South it was bounded by the Greyflood and the Glanduin that flows into it above Tharbad.

'At its greatest Arnor included all Eriador, except the regions beyond the Lune, and the lands east of Greyflood and Loudwater, in which lay Rivendell and Hollin. Beyond the Lune was Elvish country, green and quiet, where no Men went; but Dwarves dwelt, and still dwell, in the east side of the Blue Mountains, especially in those parts south of the Gulf of Lune, where they have mines that are still in use. For this reason they were accustomed to pass east along the Great Road, as they had done for long years before we came to the Shire. At the Grey Havens dwelt Círdan the Shipwright, and some say he dwells there still, until the Last Ship sets sail into the West. In the days of the Kings most of the High Elves that still lingered in Middle-earth dwelt with Círdan or in the seaward lands of Lindon. If any now remain they are few.'

The North-kingdom and the Dúnedain

After Elendil and Isildur there were eight High Kings of Arnor. After Eärendur, owing to dissensions among his sons their realm was divided into three: Arthedain, Rhudaur, and Cardolan. Arthedain was in the North-west and included the land between Brandywine and Lune, and also the land north of the Great Road as far as the Weather Hills. Rhudaur was in the North-east and lay between the Ettenmoors, the Weather Hills, and the Misty Mountains, but included also the Angle between the Hoarwell and the Loudwater. Cardolan was in the South, its bounds being the Brandywine, the Greyflood, and the Great Road.

---

[1] See p. 738. The wild kine that were still to be found near the Sea of Rhûn were said in legend to be descended from the Kine of Araw, the huntsman of the Valar, who alone of the Valar came often to Middle-earth in the Elder Days. *Oromë* is the High-elven form of his name (p. 820).

In Arthedain the line of Isildur was maintained and endured, but the line soon perished in Cardolan and Rhudaur. There was often strife between the kingdoms, which hastened the waning of the Dúnedain. The chief matter of debate was the possession of the Weather Hills and the land westward towards Bree. Both Rhudaur and Cardolan desired to possess Amon Sûl (Weathertop), which stood on the borders of their realms; for the Tower of Amon Sûl held the chief *Palantír* of the North, and the other two were both in the keeping of Arthedain.

'It was in the beginning of the reign of Malvegil of Arthedain that evil came to Arnor. For at that time the realm of Angmar arose in the North beyond the Ettenmoors. Its lands lay on both sides of the Mountains, and there were gathered many evil men, and Orcs, and other fell creatures. [The lord of that land was known as the Witch-king, but it was not known until later that he was indeed the chief of the Ringwraiths, who came north with the purpose of destroying the Dúnedain in Arnor, seeing hope in their disunion, while Gondor was strong.]'

In the days of Argeleb son of Malvegil, since no descendants of Isildur remained in the other kingdoms, the kings of Arthedain again claimed the lordship of all Arnor. The claim was resisted by Rhudaur. There the Dúnedain were few, and power had been seized by an evil lord of the Hillmen, who was in secret league with Angmar. Argeleb therefore fortified the Weather Hills;[1] but he was slain in battle with Rhudaur and Angmar.

Arveleg son of Argeleb, with the help of Cardolan and Lindon, drove back his enemies from the Hills; and for many years Arthedain and Cardolan held in force a frontier along the Weather Hills, the Great Road, and the lower Hoarwell. It is said that at this time Rivendell was besieged.

A great host came out of Angmar in 1409, and crossing the river entered Cardolan and surrounded Weathertop. The Dúnedain were defeated and Arveleg was slain. The Tower of Amon Sûl was burned and razed; but the *palantír* was saved and carried back in retreat to Fornost. Rhudaur was occupied by evil Men subject to Angmar,[2] and the Dúnedain that remained there were slain or fled west. Cardolan was ravaged. Araphor son of Arveleg was not yet full-grown, but he was valiant, and with aid from Círdan he repelled the enemy from Fornost and the North Downs. A remnant of the faithful among the Dúnedain of Cardolan also held out in Tyrn Gorthad (the Barrowdowns), or took refuge in the Forest behind.

It is said that Angmar was for a time subdued by the Elvenfolk coming from Lindon; and from Rivendell, for Elrond brought help over the Mountains out of Lórien. It was at this time that the Stoors that had dwelt in the Angle (between Hoarwell and Loudwater) fled west and south, because of the wars, and the dread of Angmar, and because the land and clime of Eriador, especially in the east, worsened and became unfriendly. Some returned to Wilderland, and dwelt beside the Gladden, becoming a riverside people of fishers.

[1] p. 181.
[2] p. 196.

In the days of Argeleb II the plague came into Eriador from the South-east, and most of the people of Cardolan perished, especially in Minhiriath. The Hobbits and all other peoples suffered greatly, but the plague lessened as it passed northwards, and the northern parts of Arthedain were little affected. It was at this time that an end came of the Dúnedain of Cardolan, and evil spirits out of Angmar and Rhudaur entered into the deserted mounds and dwelt there.

'It is said that the mounds of Tyrn Gorthad, as the Barrowdowns were called of old, are very ancient, and that many were built in the days of the old world of the First Age by the forefathers of the Edain, before they crossed the Blue Mountains into Beleriand, of which Lindon is all that now remains. Those hills were therefore revered by the Dúnedain after their return; and there many of their lords and kings were buried. [Some say that the mound in which the Ring-bearer was imprisoned had been the grave of the last prince of Cardolan, who fell in the war of 1409.]'

'In 1974 the power of Angmar arose again, and the Witch-king came down upon Arthedain before winter was ended. He captured Fornost, and drove most of the remaining Dúnedain over the Lune; among them were the sons of the king. But King Arvedui held out upon the North Downs until the last, and then fled north with some of his guard; and they escaped by the swiftness of their horses.

'For a while Arvedui hid in the tunnels of the old dwarf-mines near the far end of the Mountains, but he was driven at last by hunger to seek the help of the Lossoth, the Snowmen of Forochel.[1] Some of these he found in camp by the seashore; but they did not help the king willingly, for he had nothing to offer them, save a few jewels which they did not value; and they were afraid of the Witch-king, who (they said) could make frost or thaw at his will. But partly out of pity for the gaunt king and his men, and partly out of fear of their weapons, they gave them a little food and built for them snow-huts. There Arvedui was forced to wait, hoping for help from the south; for his horses had perished.

'When Círdan heard from Aranarth son of Arvedui of the king's flight to the north, he at once sent a ship to Forochel to seek for him. The ship came there at last after many days, because of contrary winds, and the mariners saw from afar the little fire of drift-wood which the lost men contrived to keep alight. But the winter was long in loosing its grip that year; and though it was then March, the ice was only beginning to break, and lay far out from the shore.

'When the Snowmen saw the ship they were amazed and afraid, for they had seen no such ship on the sea within their memories; but they had become now more friendly, and they drew the king and those that survived of his company out over the ice in their sliding carts, as far as they dared. In this way a boat from the ship was able to reach them.

---

[1] These are a strange, unfriendly people, remnant of the Forodwaith, Men of far-off days, accustomed to the bitter colds of the realm of Morgoth. Indeed those colds linger still in that region, though they lie hardly more than a hundred leagues north of the Shire. The Lossoth house in the snow, and it is said that they can run on the ice with bones on their feet, and have carts without wheels. They live mostly, inaccessible to their enemies, on the great Cape of Forochel that shuts off to the north-west the immense bay of that name; but they often camp on the south shores of the bay at the feet of the Mountains.

'But the Snowmen were uneasy: for they said that they smelled danger in the wind. And the chief of the Lossoth said to Arvedui: "Do not mount on this sea-monster! If they have them, let the seamen bring us food and other things that we need, and you may stay here till the Witch-king goes home. For in summer his power wanes; but now his breath is deadly, and his cold arm is long."

'But Arvedui did not take his counsel. He thanked him, and at parting gave him his ring, saying: "This is a thing of worth beyond your reckoning. For its ancientry alone. It has no power, save the esteem in which those hold it who love my house. It will not help you, but if ever you are in need, my kin will ransom it with great store of all that you desire."[1]

'Yet the counsel of the Lossoth was good, by chance or by foresight; for the ship had not reached the open sea when a great storm of wind arose, and came with blinding snow out of the North; and it drove the ship back upon the ice and piled ice up against it. Even the mariners of Círdan were helpless, and in the night the ice crushed the hull, and the ship foundered. So perished Arvedui Last-king, and with him the *palantíri* were buried in the sea.[2] It was long afterwards that news of the shipwreck of Forochel was learned from the Snowmen.'

The Shire-folk survived, though war swept over them and most of them fled into hiding. To the help of the king they sent some archers who never returned; and others went also to the battle in which Angmar was overthrown (of which more is said in the annals of the South). Afterwards in the peace that followed the Shire-folk ruled themselves and prospered. They chose a Thain to take the place of the King, and were content; though for a long time many still looked for the return of the King. But at last that hope was forgotten, and remained only in the saying *When the King comes back*, used of some good that could not be achieved, or of some evil that could not be amended. The first Shire-thain was one Bucca of the Marish, from whom the Oldbucks claimed descent. He became Thain in 379 of our reckoning (1979).

After Arvedui the North-kingdom ended, for the Dúnedain were now few and all the peoples of Eriador diminished. Yet the line of the kings was continued by the Chieftains of the Dúnedain, of whom Aranarth son of Arvedui was the first. Arahael his son was fostered in tbRivendell, and so were all the sons of the chieftains after him; and there also were kept the heirlooms of their house: the ring of Barahir, the shards of Narsil, the star of Elendil, and the sceptre of Annúminas.[3]

---

[1] In this way the ring of the House of Isildur was saved; for it was afterwards ransomed by the Dúnedain. It is said that it was none other than the ring which Felagund of Nargothrond gave to Barahir, and Beren recovered at great peril.

[2] These were the Stones of Annúminas and Amon Sûl. The only Stone left in the North was the one in the Tower on Emyn Beraid that looks towards the Gulf of Lune. That was guarded by the Elves, and though we never knew it, it remained there, until Círdan put it aboard Elrond's ship when he left (pp. 44, 106). But we are told that is was unlike the others and not in accord with them; it looked only to the Sea. Elendil set it there so that he could look back with 'straight sight' and see Eressëa in the vanished West; but the bent seas below covered Númenor for ever.

[3] The sceptre was the chief mark of royalty in Númenor, the King tells us; and that was also so in Arnor, whose kings wore no crown, but bore a single white gem, the Elendilmir,

'When the kingdom ended the Dúnedain passed into the shadows and became a secret and wandering people, and their deeds and labours were seldom sung or recorded. Little now is remembered of them since Elrond departed. Although even before the Watchful Peace ended evil things again began to attack Eriador or to invade it secretly, the Chieftains for the most part lived out their long lives. Aragorn I, it is said, was slain by wolves, which ever after remained a peril in Eriador, and are not yet ended. In the days of Arahad I the Orcs, who had, as later appeared, long been secretly occupying strongholds in the Misty Mountains, so as to bar all the passes into Eriador, suddenly revealed themselves. In 2509 Celebrían wife of Elrond was journeying to Lórien when she was waylaid in the Redhorn Pass, and her escort being scattered by the sudden assault of the Orcs, she was seized and carried off. She was pursued and rescued by Elladan and Elrohir, but not before she had suffered torment and had received a poisoned wound.[1] She was brought back to Imladris, and though healed in body by Elrond, lost all delight in Middle-earth, and the next year went to the Havens and passed over Sea. And later in the days of Arassuil, Orcs, multiplying again in the Misty Mountains, began to ravage the lands, and the Dúnedain and the sons of Elrond fought with them. It was at this time that a large band came so far west as to enter the Shire, and were driven off by Bandobras Took.[2]

There were fifteen Chieftains, before the sixteenth and last was born, Aragorn II, who became again King of both Gondor and Arnor. 'Our King, we call him; and when he comes north to his house in Annúminas restored and stays for a while by Lake Evendim, then everyone in the Shire is glad. But he does not enter this land and binds himself by the law that he has made, that none of the Big People shall pass its borders. But he rides often with many fair people to the Great Bridge, and there he welcomes his friends, and any others who wish to see him; and some ride away with him and stay in his house as long as they have a mind. Thain Peregrin has been there many times; and so has Master Samwise the Mayor. His daughter Elanor the Fair is one of the maids of Queen Evenstar.'

It was the pride and wonder of the Northern Line that, though their power departed and their people dwindled, through all the many generations the succession was unbroken from father to son. Also, though the length of lives of the Dúnedain grew ever less in Middle-earth, after the ending of their kings the waning was swifter in Gondor; and many of the Chieftains of the North still lived to twice the age of

---

Star of Elendil, bound on their brows with a silver fillet (pp. 142, 829, 843, 946). In speaking of a crown (pp. 167, 241) Bilbo no doubt referred to Gondor; he seems to have become well acquainted with matters concerning Aragorn's line. The sceptre of Númenor is said to have perished with Ar-Pharazôn. That of Annúminas was the silver rod of the Lords of Andúnië, and is now perhaps the most ancient work of Men's hands preserved in Middle-earth. It was already more than five thousand years old when Elrond surrendered it to Aragorn (p. 951). The crown of Gondor was derived from the form of a Númenorean war-helm. In the beginning it was indeed a plain helm; and it is said to have been the one that Isildur wore in the Battle of Dagorlad (for the helm of Anárion was crushed by the stone-cast from Barad-dûr that slew him). But in the days of Atanatar Alcarin this was replaced by the jewelled helm that was used in the crowning of Aragorn.

[1] p. 221.
[2] p. 5, 992.

Men, and far beyond the days of even the oldest amongst us. Aragorn indeed lived to be two hundred and ten years old, longer than any of his line since King Arvegil; but in Aragorn Elessar the dignity of the kings of old was renewed.

(iv)
GONDOR AND THE HEIRS OF ANÁRION

There were thirty-one kings in Gondor after Anárion who was slain before the Barad-dûr. Though war never ceased on their borders, for more than a thousand years the Dúnedain of the South grew in wealth and power by land and sea, until the reign of Atanatar II, who was called Alcarin, the Glorious. Yet the signs of decay had then already appeared; for the high men of the South married late, and their children were few. The first childless king was Falastur, and the second Narmacil I, the son of Atanatar Alcarin.

It was Ostoher the seventh king who rebuilt Minas Anor, where afterwards the kings dwelt in summer rather than in Osgiliath. In his time Gondor was first attacked by wild men out of the East. But Tarostar, his son, defeated them and drove them out, and took the name of Rómendacil 'East-victor'. He was, however, later slain in battle with fresh hordes of Easterlings. Turambar his son avenged him, and won much territory eastwards.

With Tarannon, the twelfth king, began the line of the Ship-kings, who built navies and extended the sway of Gondor along the coasts west and south of the Mouths of Anduin. To commemorate his victories as Captain of the Hosts, Tarannon took the crown in the name of Falastur 'Lord of the Coasts'.

Eärnil I, his nephew, who succeeded him, repaired the ancient haven of Pelargir, and built a great navy. He laid siege by sea and land to Umbar, and took it, and it became a great harbour and fortress of the power of Gondor.[1] But Eärnil did not long survive his triumph. He was lost with many ships and men in a great storm off Umbar. Ciryandil his son continued the building of ships; but the Men of the Harad, led by the lords that had been driven from Umbar, came up with great power against that stronghold, and Ciryandil fell in battle in Haradwaith.

For many years Umbar was invested, but could not be taken because of the sea-power of Gondor. Ciryaher son of Ciryandil bided his time, and at last when he had gathered strength he came down from the north by sea and by land, and crossing the River Harnen his armies utterly defeated the Men of the Harad, and their kings were compelled to acknowledge the overlordship of Gondor (1050). Ciryaher then took the name of Hyarmendacil 'South-victor'.

The might of Hyarmendacil no enemy dared to contest during the remainder of his long reign. He was king for one hundred and thirty-four years, the longest reign

[1] The great cape and land-locked firth of Umbar had been Númenorean land since days of old; but it was a stronghold of the King's Men, who were afterwards called the Black Númenoreans, corrupted by Sauron, and who hated above all the followers of Elendil. After the fall of Sauron their race swiftly dwindled or became merged with the Men of Middle-earth, but they inherited without lessening their hatred of Gondor. Umbar, therefore, was only taken at great cost.

but one of all the Line of Anárion. In his day Gondor reached the summit of its power. The realm then extended north to Celebrant and the southern eaves of Mirkwood; west to the Greyflood; east to the inland Sea of Rhûn; south to the River Harnen, and thence along the coast to the peninsula and haven of Umbar. The Men of the Vales of Anduin acknowledged its authority; and the kings of the Harad did homage to Gondor, and their sons lived as hostages in the court of its King. Mordor was desolate, but was watched over by great fortresses that guarded the passes.

So ended the line of the Ship-kings. Atanatar Alcarin son of Hyarmendacil lived in great splendour, so that men said *precious stones are pebbles in Gondor for children to play with*. But Atanatar loved ease and did nothing to maintain the power that he had inherited, and his two sons were of like temper. The waning of Gondor had already begun before he died, and was doubtless observed by its enemies. The watch upon Mordor was neglected. Nonetheless it was not until the days of Valacar that the first great evil came upon Gondor: the civil war of the Kin-strife, in which great loss and ruin was caused and never fully repaired.

Minalcar, son of Calmacil, was a man of great vigour, and in 1240 Narmacil, to rid himself of all cares, made him Regent of the realm. From that time onwards he governed Gondor in the name of the kings until he succeeded his father. His chief concern was with the Northmen.

These had increased greatly in the peace brought by the power of Gondor. The kings showed them favour, since they were the nearest in kin of lesser Men to the Dúnedain (being for the most part descendants of those peoples from whom the Edain of old had come); and they gave them wide lands beyond Anduin south of Greenwood the Great, to be a defence against men of the East. For in the past the attacks of the Easterlings had come mostly over the plain between the Inland Sea and the Ash Mountains.

In the days of Narmacil I their attacks began again, though at first with little force; but it was learned by the regent that the Northmen did not always remain true to Gondor, and some would join forces with the Easterlings, either out of greed for spoil, or in the furtherance of feuds among their princes. Minalcar therefore in 1248 led out a great force, and between Rhovanion and the Inland Sea he defeated a large army of the Easterlings and destroyed all their camps and settlements east of the Sea. He then took the name of Rómendacil.

On his return Rómendacil fortified the west shore of Anduin as far as the inflow of the Limlight, and forbade any stranger to pass down the River beyond the Emyn Muil. He it was that built the pillars of the Argonath at the entrance to Nen Hithoel. But since he needed men, and desired to strengthen the bond between Gondor and the Northmen, he took many of them into his service and gave to some high rank in his armies.

Rómendacil showed especial favour to Vidugavia, who had aided him in the war. He called himself King of Rhovanion, and was indeed the most powerful of the Northern princes, though his own realm lay between Greenwood and the River Celduin.[1] In 1250 Rómendacil sent his son Valacar as an ambassador to dwell for

[1] The River Running.

a while with Vidugavia and make himself acquainted with the language, manners, and policies of the Northmen. But Valacar far exceeded his father's designs. He grew to love the Northern lands and people, and he married Vidumavi, daughter of Vidugavia. It was some years before he returned. From this marriage came later the war of the Kin-strife.

'For the high men of Gondor already looked askance at the Northmen among them; and it was a thing unheard of before that the heir of the crown, or any son of the King, should wed one of lesser and alien race. There was already rebellion in the southern provinces when King Valacar grew old. His queen had been a fair and noble lady, but short-lived according to the fate of lesser Men, and the Dúnedain feared that her descendants would prove the same and fall from the majesty of the Kings of Men. Also they were unwilling to accept as lord her son, who though he was now called Eldacar, had been born in an alien country and was named in his youth Vinitharya, a name of his mother's people.

'Therefore when Eldacar succeeded his father there was war in Gondor. But Eldacar did not prove easy to thrust from his heritage. To the lineage of Gondor he added the fearless spirit of the Northmen. He was handsome and valiant, and showed no sign of ageing more swiftly than his father. When the confederates led by descendants of the kings rose against him, he opposed them to the end of his strength. At last he was besieged in Osgiliath, and held it long, until hunger and the greater forces of the rebels drove him out, leaving the city in flames. In that siege and burning the Dome of Osgiliath was destroyed, and the *palantír* was lost in the waters.

'But Eldacar eluded his enemies, and came to the North, to his kinsfolk in Rhovanion. Many gathered to him there, both of the Northmen in the service of Gondor, and of the Dúnedain of the northern parts of the realm. For many of the latter had learned to esteem him, and many more came to hate his usurper. This was Castamir, grandson of Calimehtar, younger brother of Rómendacil II. He was not only one of those nearest by blood to the crown, but he had the greatest following of all the rebels; for he was the Captain of Ships, and was supported by the people of the coasts and of the great havens of Pelargir and Umbar.

'Castamir had not long sat upon the throne before he proved himself haughty and ungenerous. He was a cruel man, as he had first shown in the taking of Osgiliath. He caused Ornendil son of Eldacar, who was captured, to be put to death; and the slaughter and destruction done in the city at his bidding far exceeded the needs of war. This was remembered in Minas Anor and in Ithilien; and there love for Castamir was further lessened when it became seen that he cared little for the land, and thought only of the fleets, and purposed to remove the king's seat to Pelargir.

'Thus he had been king only ten years, when Eldacar, seeing his time, came with a great army out of the north, and folk flocked to him from Calenardhon and Anórien and Ithilien. There was a great battle in Lebennin at the Crossings of Erui, in which much of the best blood in Gondor was shed. Eldacar himself slew Castamir in combat, and so was avenged for Ornendil; but Castamir's sons escaped, and with others of their kin and many people of the fleets they held out long at Pelargir.

'When they had gathered there all the force that they could (for Eldacar had no ships to beset them by sea) they sailed away, and established themselves at Umbar.

There they made a refuge for all the enemies of the king, and a lordship independent of his crown. Umbar remained at war with Gondor for many lives of men, a threat to its coastlands and to all traffic on the sea. It was never again completely subdued until the days of Elessar; and the region of South Gondor became a debatable land between the Corsairs and the Kings.'

'The loss of Umbar was grievous to Gondor, not only because the realm was diminished in the south and its hold upon the Men of the Harad was loosened, but because it was there that Ar-Pharazôn the Golden, last King of Númenor, had landed and humbled the might of Sauron. Though great evil had come after, even the followers of Elendil remembered with pride the coming of the great host of Ar-Pharazôn out of the deeps of the Sea; and on the highest hill of the headland above the Haven they had set a great white pillar as a monument. It was crowned with a globe of crystal that took the rays of the Sun and of the Moon and shone like a bright star that could be seen in clear weather even on the coasts of Gondor or far out upon the western sea. So it stood, until after the second arising of Sauron, which now approached, Umbar fell under the domination of his servants, and the memorial of his humiliation was thrown down.'

After the return of Eldacar the blood of the kingly house and other houses of the Dúnedain became more mingled with that of lesser Men. For many of the great had been slain in the Kin-strife; while Eldacar showed favour to the Northmen, by whose help he had regained the crown, and the people of Gondor were replenished by great numbers that came from Rhovanion.

This mingling did not at first hasten the waning of the Dúnedain, as had been feared; but the waning still proceeded, little by little, as it had before. For no doubt it was due above all to Middle-earth itself, and to the slow withdrawing of the gifts of the Númenoreans after the downfall of the Land of the Star. Eldacar lived to his two hundred and thirty-fifth year, and was king for fifty-eight years, of which ten were spent in exile.

The second and greatest evil came upon Gondor in the reign of Telemnar, the twenty-six king, whose father Minardil, son of Eldacar, was slain at Pelargir by the Corsairs of Umbar. (They were led by Angamaitë and Sangahyando, the great-grandsons of Castamir.) Soon after a deadly plague came with dark winds out of the East. The King and all his children died, and great numbers of the people of Gondor, especially those that lived in Osgiliath. Then for weariness and fewness of men the watch on the borders of Mordor ceased and the fortresses that guarded the passes were unmanned.

Later it was noted that these things happened even as the Shadow grew deep in Greenwood, and many evil things reappeared, signs of the arising of Sauron. It is true that the enemies of Gondor also suffered, or they might have overwhelmed it in its weakness; but Sauron could wait, and it may well be that the opening of Mordor was what he chiefly desired.

When King Telemnar died the White Trees of Minas Anor also withered and died. But Tarondor, his nephew, who succeeded him, replanted a seedling in the citadel. He it was who removed the King's house permanently to Minas Anor, for Osgiliath was now partly deserted, and began to fall into ruin. Few of those who had fled from the plague into Ithilien or to the western dales were willing to return.

Tarondor, coming young to the throne, had the longest reign of all the Kings of Gondor; but he could achieve little more than the reordering of his realm within, and the slow nursing of its strength. But Telumehtar his son, remembering the death of Minardil, and being troubled by the insolence of the Corsairs, who raided his coasts even as far as the Anfalas, gathered his forces and in 1810 took Umbar by storm. In that war the last descendants of Castamir perished, and Umbar was again held for a while by the kings. Telumehtar added to his name the title Umbardacil. But in the new evils that soon befell Gondor Umbar was again lost, and fell into the hands of the Men of the Harad.

The third evil was the invasion of the Wainriders, which sapped the waning strength of Gondor in wars that lasted for almost a hundred years. The Wainriders were a people, or a confederacy of many peoples, that came from the East; but they were stronger and better armed than any that had appeared before. They journeyed in great wains, and their chieftains fought in chariots. Stirred up, as was afterwards seen, by the emissaries of Sauron, they made a sudden assault upon Gondor, and King Narmacil II was slain in battle with them beyond Anduin in 1856. The people of eastern and southern Rhovanion were enslaved; and the frontiers of Gondor were for that time withdrawn to the Anduin and the Emyn Muil. [At this time it is thought that the Ringwraiths re-entered Mordor.]

Calimehtar, son of Narmacil II, helped by a revolt in Rhovanion, avenged his father with a great victory over the Easterlings upon Dagorlad in 1899, and for a while the peril was averted. It was in the reign of Araphant in the North and of Ondoher son of Calimehtar in the South that the two kingdoms again took counsel together after long silence and estrangement. For at last they perceived that some single power and will was directing the assault from many quarters upon the survivors of Númenor. It was at that time that Arvedui heir of Araphant wedded Fíriel daughter of Ondoher (1940). But neither kingdom was able to send help to the other; for Angmar renewed its attack upon Arthedain at the same time as the Wainriders reappeared in great force.

Many of the Wainriders now passed south of Mordor and made alliance with men of Khand and of Near Harad; and in this great assault from north and south, Gondor came near to destruction. In 1944 King Ondoher and both his sons, Artamir and Faramir, fell in battle north of the Morannon, and the enemy poured into Ithilien. But Eärnil, Captain of the Southern Army, won a great victory in South Ithilien and destroyed the army of Harad that had crossed the River Poros. Hastening north, he gathered to him all that he could of the retreating Northern Army and came up against the main camp of the Wainriders, while they were feasting and revelling, believing that Gondor was overthrown and that nothing remained but to take the spoil. Eärnil stormed the camp and set fire to the wains, and drove the enemy in a great rout out of Ithilien. A great part of those who fled before him perished in the Dead Marshes.

'On the death of Ondoher and his sons, Arvedui of the North-kingdom claimed the crown of Gondor, as the direct descendant of Isildur, and as the husband of Fíriel, only surviving child of Ondoher. The claim was rejected. In this Pelendur, the Steward of King Ondoher, played the chief part.

'The Council of Gondor answered: "The crown and royalty of Gondor belongs solely to the heirs of Meneldil, son of Anárion, to whom Isildur relinquished this realm. In Gondor this heritage is reckoned through the sons only; and we have not heard that the law is otherwise in Arnor."

'To this Arvedui replied: "Elendil had two sons, of whom Isildur was the elder and the heir of his father. We have heard that the name of Elendil stands to this day at the head of the line of the Kings of Gondor, since he was accounted the high king of all lands of the Dúnedain. While Elendil still lived, the conjoint rule in the South was committed to his sons; but when Elendil fell, Isildur departed to take up the high kingship of his father, and committed the rule in the South in like manner to the son of his brother. He did not relinquish his royalty in Gondor, nor intend that the realm of Elendil should be divided for ever.

'"Moreover, in Númenor of old the sceptre descended to the eldest child of the king, whether man or woman. It is true that the law has not been observed in the lands of exile ever troubled by war; but such was the law of our people, to which we now refer, seeing that the sons of Ondoher died childless."[1]

'To this Gondor made no answer. The crown was claimed by Eärnil, the victorious captain; and it was granted to him with the approval of all the Dúnedain in Gondor, since he was of the royal house. He was the son of Siriondil, son of Calimmacil, son of Arciryas brother of Narmacil II. Arvedui did not press his claim; for he had neither the power nor the will to oppose the choice of the Dúnedain of Gondor; yet the claim was never forgotten by his descendants even when their kingship had passed away. For the time was now drawing near when the North-kingdom would come to an end.

'Arvedui was indeed the last king, as his name signifies. It is said that this name was given to him at his birth by Malbeth the Seer, who said to his father: "*Arvedui* you shall call him, for he will be the last in Arthedain. Though a choice will come to the Dúnedain, and if they take the one that seems less hopeful, then your son will change his name and become king of a great realm. If not, then much sorrow and many lives of men shall pass, until the Dúnedain arise and are united again."

'In Gondor also one king only followed Eärnil. It may be that if the crown and the sceptre had been united, then the kingship would have been maintained and much evil averted. But Eärnil was a wise man, and not arrogant, even if, as to most men in Gondor, the realm in Arthedain seemed a small thing, for all the lineage of its lords.

'He sent messages to Arvedui announcing that he received the crown of Gondor,

---

[1] That law was made in Númenor (as we have learned from the King) when Tar-Aldarion, the sixth king, left only one child, a daughter. She became the first Ruling Queen, Tar-Ancalimë. But the law was otherwise before her time. Tar-Elendil, the fourth king, was succeeded by his son Tar-Meneldur, though his daughter Silmariën was the elder. It was, however, from Silmariën that Elendil was descended.

according to the laws and the needs of the South-kingdom, "but I do not forget the royalty of Arnor, nor deny our kinship, nor wish that the realms of Elendil should be estranged. I will send to your aid when you have need, so far as I am able."

'It was, however, long before Eärnil felt himself sufficiently secure to do as he promised. King Araphant continued with dwindling strength to hold off the assaults of Angmar, and Arvedui when he succeeded did likewise; but at last in the autumn of 1973 messages came to Gondor that Arthedain was in great straits, and that the Witch-king was preparing a last stroke against it. Then Eärnil sent his son Eärnur north with a fleet, as swiftly as he could, and with as great strength as he could spare. Too late. Before Eärnur reached the havens of Lindon, the Witch-king had conquered Arthedain and Arvedui had perished.

'But when Eärnur came to the Grey Havens there was joy and great wonder among both Elves and Men. So great in draught and so many were his ships that they could scarcely find harbourage, though both the Harlond and the Forlond also were filled; and from them descended an army of power, with munition and provision for a war of great kings. Or so it seemed to the people of the North, though this was but a small sending-force of the whole might of Gondor. Most of all, the horses were praised, for many of them came from the Vales of Anduin and with them were riders tall and fair, and proud princes of Rhovanion.

'Then Círdan summoned all who would come to him, from Lindon or Arnor, and when all was ready the host crossed the Lune and marched north to challenge the Witch-king of Angmar. He was now dwelling, it is said, in Fornost, which he had filled with evil folk, usurping the house and rule of the kings. In his pride he did not await the onset of his enemies in his stronghold, but went out to meet them, thinking to sweep them, as others before, into the Lune.

'But the Host of the West came down on him out of the Hills of Evendim, and there was a great battle on the plain between Nenuial and the North Downs. The forces of Angmar were already giving way and retreating towards Fornost when the main body of the horsemen that had passed round the hills came down from the north and scattered them in a great rout. Then the Witch-king, with all that he could gather from the wreck, fled northwards, seeking his own land of Angmar. Before he could gain the shelter of Carn Dûm the cavalry of Gondor overtook him with Eärnur riding at their head. At the same time a force under Glorfindel the Elf-lord came up out of Rivendell. Then so utterly was Angmar defeated that not a man nor an orc of that realm remained west of the Mountains.

'But it is said that when all was lost suddenly the Witch-king himself appeared, black-robed and black-masked upon a black horse. Fear fell upon all who beheld him; but he singled out the Captain of Gondor for the fullness of his hatred, and with a terrible cry he rode straight upon him. Eärnur would have withstood him; but his horse could not endure that onset, and it swerved and bore him far away before he could master it.

'Then the Witch-king laughed, and none that heard it ever forgot the horror of that cry. But Glorfindel rode up then on his white horse, and in the midst of his laughter the Witch-king turned to flight and passed into the shadows. For night came down on the battlefield, and he was lost, and none saw whither he went.

'Eärnur now rode back, but Glorfindel, looking into the gathering dark, said:

"Do not pursue him! He will not return to this land. Far off yet is his doom, and not by the hand of man will he fall." These words many remembered; but Eärnur was angry, desiring only to be avenged for his disgrace.

'So ended the evil realm of Angmar; and so did Eärnur, Captain of Gondor, earn the chief hatred of the Witch-king; but many years were still to pass before that was revealed.'

It was thus in the reign of King Eärnil, as later became clear, that the Witch-king escaping from the North came to Mordor, and there gathered the other Ringwraiths, of whom he was the chief. But it was not until 2000 that they issued from Mordor by the Pass of Cirith Ungol and laid siege to Minas Ithil. This they took in 2002, and captured the *palantír* of the tower. They were not expelled while the Third Age lasted; and Minas Ithil became a place of fear, and was renamed Minas Morgul. Many of the people that still remained in Ithilien deserted it.

'Eärnur was a man like his father in valour, but not in wisdom. He was a man of strong body and hot mood; but he would take no wife, for his only pleasure was in fighting, or in the exercise of arms. His prowess was such that none in Gondor could stand against him in those weapon-sports in which he delighted, seeming rather a champion than a captain or king, and retaining his vigour and skill to a later age than was then usual.'

When Eärnur received the crown in 2043 the King of Minas Morgul challenged him to single combat, taunting him that he had not dared to stand before him in battle in the North. For that time Mardil the Steward restrained the wrath of the king. Minas Anor, which had become the chief city of the realm since the days of King Telemnar, and the residence of the kings, was now renamed Minas Tirith, as the city ever on guard against the evil of Morgul.

Eärnur had held the crown only seven years when the Lord of Morgul repeated his challenge, taunting the king that to the faint heart of his youth he had now added the weakness of age. Then Mardil could no longer restrain him, and he rode with a small escort of knights to the gate of Minas Morgul. None of that riding were ever heard of again. It was believed in Gondor that the faithless enemy had trapped the king, and that he had died in torment in Minas Morgul; but since there were no witnesses of his death, Mardil the Good Steward ruled Gondor in his name for many years.

Now the descendants of the kings had become few. Their numbers had been greatly diminished in the Kin-strife; whereas since that time the kings had become jealous and watchful of those near akin. Often those on whom suspicion fell had fled to Umbar and there joined the rebels; while others had renounced their lineage and taken wives not of Númenorean blood.

So it was that no claimant to the crown could be found who was of pure blood, or whose claim all would allow; and all feared the memory of the Kin-strife, knowing that if any such dissension arose again, then Gondor would perish. Therefore, though the years lengthened, the Steward continued to rule Gondor, and the crown of Elendil lay in the lap of King Eärnil in the Houses of the Dead, where Eärnur had left it.

The Stewards

The House of the Stewards was called the House of Húrin, for they were descendants of the Steward of King Minardil (1621–34), Húrin of Emyn Arnen, a man of high Númenorean race. After his day the kings had always chosen their stewards from among his descendants; and after the days of Pelendur the Stewardship became hereditary as a kingship, from father to son or nearest kin.

Each new Steward indeed took office with the oath 'to hold rod and rule in the name of the king, until he shall return'. But these soon became words of ritual little heeded, for the Stewards exercised all the power of the kings. Yet many in Gondor still believed that a king would indeed return in some time to come; and some remembered the ancient line of the North, which it was rumoured still lived on in the shadows. But against such thoughts the Ruling Stewards hardened their hearts.

Nonetheless the Stewards never sat on the ancient throne; and they wore no crown, and held no sceptre. They bore a white rod only as the token of their office; and their banner was white without charge; but the royal banner had been sable, upon which was displayed a white tree in blossom beneath seven stars.

After Mardil Voronwë, who was reckoned the first of the line, there followed twenty-four Ruling Stewards of Gondor, until the time of Denethor II, the twenty-sixth and last. At first they had quiet, for those were the days of the Watchful Peace, during which Sauron withdrew before the power of the White Council and the Ringwraiths remained hidden in Morgul Vale. But from the time of Denethor I, there was never full peace again, and even when Gondor had no great or open war its borders were under constant threat.

In the last years of Denethor I the race of uruks, black orcs of great strength, first appeared out of Mordor, and in 2475 they swept across Ithilien and took Osgiliath. Boromir son of Denethor (after whom Boromir of the Nine Walkers was later named) defeated them and regained Ithilien; but Osgiliath was finally ruined, and its great stone-bridge was broken. No people dwelt there afterwards. Boromir was a great captain, and even the Witch-king feared him. He was noble and fair of face, a man strong in body and in will, but he received a Morgul-wound in that war which shortened his days, and he became shrunken with pain and died twelve years after his father.

After him began the long rule of Cirion. He was watchful and wary, but the reach of Gondor had grown short, and he could do little more than defend his borders, while his enemies (or the power that moved them) prepared strokes against him that he could not hinder. The Corsairs harried his coasts, but it was in the north that his chief peril lay. In the wide lands of Rhovanion, between Mirkwood and the River Running, a fierce people now dwelt, wholly under the shadow of Dol Guldur. Often they made raids through the forest, until the vale of Anduin south of the Gladden was largely deserted. These Balchoth were constantly increased by others of like kind that came in from the east, whereas the people of Calenardhon had dwindled. Cirion was hard put to it to hold the line of the Anduin.

'Foreseeing the storm, Cirion sent north for aid, but over-late; for in that year (2510) the Balchoth, having built many great boats and rafts on the east shores of

Anduin, swarmed over the River and swept away the defenders. An army marching up from the south was cut off and driven north over the Limlight, and there it was suddenly attacked by a horde of Orcs from the Mountains and pressed towards the Anduin. Then out of the North there came help beyond hope, and the horns of the Rohirrim were first heard in Gondor. Eorl the Young came with his riders and swept away the enemy, and pursued the Balchoth to the death over the fields of Calenardhon. Cirion granted to Eorl that land to dwell in, and he swore to Cirion the Oath of Eorl, of friendship at need or at call to the Lords of Gondor.'

In the days of Beren, the nineteenth Steward, an even greater peril came upon Gondor. Three great fleets, long prepared, came up from Umbar and the Harad, and assailed the coasts of Gondor in great force; and the enemy made many landings, even as far north as the mouth of the Isen. At the same time the Rohirrim were assailed from the west and the east, and their land was overrun, and they were driven into the dales of the White Mountains. In that year (2758) the Long Winter began with cold and great snows out of the North and the East which lasted for almost five months. Helm of Rohan and both his sons perished in that war; and there was misery and death in Eriador and in Rohan. But in Gondor south of the mountains things were less evil, and before spring came Beregond son of Beren had overcome the invaders. At once he sent aid to Rohan. He was the greatest captain that had arisen in Gondor since Boromir; and when he succeeded his father (2763) Gondor began to recover its strength. But Rohan was slower to be healed of the hurts that it had received. It was for this reason that Beren welcomed Saruman, and gave to him the keys of Orthanc; and from that year on (2759) Saruman dwelt in Isengard.

It was in the days of Beregond that the War of the Dwarves and Orcs was fought in the Misty Mountains (2793-9), of which only rumour came south, until the Orcs fleeing from Nanduhirion attempted to cross Rohan and establish themselves in the White Mountains. There was fighting for many years in the dales before that danger was ended.

When Belecthor II, the twenty-first Steward, died, the White Tree died also in Minas Tirith; but it was left standing 'until the King returns', for no seedling could be found.

In the days of Túrin II the enemies of Gondor began to move again; for Sauron was grown again to power and the day of his arising was drawing near. All but the hardiest of its people deserted Ithilien and removed west over Anduin, for the land was infested by Mordor-orcs. It was Túrin that built secret refuges for his soldiers in Ithilien, of which Henneth Annûn was the longest guarded and manned. He also fortified again the isle of Cair Andros[1] to defend Anórien. But his chief peril lay in the south, where the Haradrim had occupied South Gondor, and there was much fighting along the Poros. When Ithilien was invaded in great strength, King Folcwine of Rohan fulfilled the Oath of Eorl and repaid his debt for the aid brought

---

[1] This name means 'Ship of Long-foam'; for the isle was shaped like a great ship, with a high prow pointing north, against which the white foam of Anduin broke on sharp rocks.

by Beregond, sending many men to Gondor. With their aid Túrin won a victory at the crossing of the Poros; but the sons of Folcwine both fell in the battle. The Riders buried them after the fashion of their people, and they were laid in one mound, for they were twin brothers. Long it stood, *Haudh in Gwanur*, high upon the shore of the river, and the enemies of Gondor feared to pass it.

Turgon followed Túrin, but of his time it is chiefly remembered that two years ere his death, Sauron arose again, and declared himself openly; and he re-entered Mordor long prepared for him. Then the Barad-dûr was raised once more, and Mount Doom burst into flame, and the last of the folk of Ithilien fled far away. When Turgon died Saruman took Isengard for his own, and fortified it.

'Ecthelion II, son of Turgon, was a man of wisdom. With what power was left to him he began to strengthen his realm against the assault of Mordor. He encouraged all men of worth from near or far to enter his service, and to those who proved trustworthy he gave rank and reward. In much that he did he had the aid and advice of a great captain whom he loved above all. Thorongil men called him in Gondor, the Eagle of the Star, for he was swift and keen-eyed, and wore a silver star upon his cloak; but no one knew his true name nor in what land he was born. He came to Ecthelion from Rohan, where he had served the King Thengel, but he was not one of the Rohirrim. He was a great leader of men, by land or by sea, but he departed into the shadows whence he came, before the days of Ecthelion were ended.

'Thorongil often counselled Ecthelion that the strength of the rebels in Umbar was a great peril to Gondor, and a threat to the fiefs of the south that would prove deadly, if Sauron moved to open war. At last he got leave of the Steward and gathered a small fleet, and he came to Umbar unlooked for by night, and there burned a great part of the ships of the Corsairs. He himself overthrew the Captain of the Haven in battle upon the quays, and then he withdrew his fleet with small loss. But when they came back to Pelargir, to men's grief and wonder, he would not return to Minas Tirith, where great honour awaited him.

'He sent a message of farewell to Ecthelion, saying: "Other tasks now call me, lord, and much time and many perils must pass, ere I come again to Gondor, if that be my fate." Though none could guess what those tasks might be, nor what summons he had received, it was known whither he went. For he took boat and crossed over Anduin, and there he said farewell to his companions and went on alone; and when he was last seen his face was towards the Mountains of Shadow.

'There was dismay in the City at the departure of Thorongil, and to all men it seemed a great loss, unless it were to Denethor, the son of Ecthelion, a man now ripe for the Stewardship, to which after four years he succeeded on the death of his father.

'Denethor II was a proud man, tall, valiant, and more kingly than any man that had appeared in Gondor for many lives of men; and he was wise also, and far-sighted, and learned in lore. Indeed he was as like to Thorongil as to one of nearest kin, and yet was ever placed second to the stranger in the hearts of men and the esteem of his father. At the time many thought that Thorongil had departed before his rival became his master; though indeed Thorongil had never himself vied with Denethor, nor held himself higher than the servant of his father. And in one matter only were their counsels to the Steward at variance: Thorongil often warned Ecthelion not to put trust in Saruman the White in Isengard, but to welcome rather Gandalf the Grey. But there was little love between Denethor and Gandalf; and after the days of Ecthelion there was less welcome for the Grey Pilgrim in Minas Tirith. Therefore later, when all was made clear, many believed that Denethor, who was subtle in mind and looked further and deeper than other men of his day, had discovered who this stranger Thorongil in truth was, and suspected that he and Mithrandir designed to supplant him.

'When Denethor became Steward (2984) he proved a masterful lord, holding the rule of all things in his own hand. He said little. He listened to counsel, and then followed his own mind. He had married late (2976), taking as wife Finduilas, daughter of Adrahil of Dol Amroth. She was a lady of great beauty and gentle heart, but before twelve years had passed she died. Denethor loved her, in his fashion, more dearly than any other, unless it were the elder of the sons that she bore him. But it seemed to men that she withered in the guarded city, as a flower of the seaward vales set upon a barren rock. The shadow in the east filled her with horror, and she turned her eyes ever south to the sea that she missed.

'After her death Denethor became more grim and silent than before, and would sit long alone in his tower deep in thought, foreseeing that the assault of Mordor would come in his time. It was afterwards believed that needing knowledge, but being proud, and trusting in his own strength of will, he dared to look in the *palantír* of the White Tower. None of the Stewards had dared to do this, nor even the kings Eärnil and Eärnur, after the fall of Minas Ithil when the *palantír* of Isildur came into the hands of the Enemy; for the Stone of Minas Tirith was the *palantír* of Anárion, most close in accord with the one that Sauron possessed.

'In this way Denethor gained his great knowledge of things that passed in his realm, and far beyond his borders, at which men marvelled; but he bought the knowledge dearly, being aged before his time by his contest with the will of Sauron. Thus pride increased in Denethor together with despair, until he saw in all the deeds of that time only a single combat between the Lord of the White Tower and the Lord of the Barad-dûr, and mistrusted all others who resisted Sauron, unless they served himself alone.

'So time drew on to the War of the Ring, and the sons of Denethor grew to manhood. Boromir, five years the elder, beloved by his father, was like him in face and pride, but in little else. Rather he was a man after the sort of King Eärnur of old, taking no wife and delighting chiefly in arms; fearless and strong, but caring little for lore, save the tales of old battles. Faramir the younger was like him in looks but otherwise in mind. He read the hearts of men as shrewdly as his father, but what he read moved him sooner to pity than to scorn. He was gentle in bearing, and a lover of lore and of music, and therefore by many in those days his courage was judged less than his brother's. But it was not so, except that he did not seek glory in danger without a purpose. He welcomed Gandalf at such times as he came to the City, and he learned what he could from his wisdom; and in this as in many other matters he displeased his father.

'Yet between the brothers there was great love, and had been since childhood, when Boromir was the helper and protector of Faramir. No jealousy or rivalry had arisen between them since, for their father's favour or for the praise of men. It did not seem possible to Faramir that any one in Gondor could rival Boromir, heir of Denethor, Captain of the White Tower; and of like mind was Boromir. Yet it proved otherwise at the test. But of all that befell these three in the War of the Ring much is said elsewhere. And after the War the days of the Ruling Stewards came to an end; for the heir of Isildur and Anárion returned and the kingship was renewed, and the standard of the White Tree flew once more from the Tower of Ecthelion.'

(v)
HERE FOLLOWS A PART OF THE TALE OF
ARAGORN AND ARWEN

'Arador was the grandfather of the King. His son Arathorn sought in marriage Gilraen the Fair, daughter of Dírhael, who was himself a descendant of Aranarth. To this marriage Dírhael was opposed; for Gilraen was young and had not reached the age at which the women of the Dúnedain were accustomed to marry.

'"Moreover," he said, "Arathorn is a stern man of full age, and will be chieftain sooner than men looked for; yet my heart forebodes that he will be short-lived."

'But Ivorwen, his wife, who was also foresighted, answered: "The more need of haste! The days are darkening before the storm, and great things are to come. If these two wed now, hope may be born for our people; but if they delay, it will not come while this age lasts."

'And it happened that when Arathorn and Gilraen had been married only one year, Arador was taken by hill-trolls in the Coldfells north of Rivendell and was slain; and Arathorn became Chieftain of the Dúnedain. The next year Gilraen bore him a son, and he was called Aragorn. But Aragorn was only two years old when Arathorn went riding against the Orcs with the sons of Elrond, and he was slain by an orc-arrow that pierced his eye; and so he proved indeed short-lived for one of his race, being but sixty years old when he fell.

'Then Aragorn, being now the Heir of Isildur, was taken with his mother to dwell in the house of Elrond; and Elrond took the place of his father and came to love him as a son of his own. But he was called Estel, that is "Hope", and his true name and lineage were kept secret at the bidding of Elrond; for the Wise then knew that the Enemy was seeking to discover the Heir of Isildur, if any remained upon earth.

'But when Estel was only twenty years of age, it chanced that he returned to Rivendell after great deeds in the company of the sons of Elrond; and Elrond looked at him and was pleased, for he saw that he was fair and noble and was early come to manhood, though he would yet become greater in body and in mind. That day therefore Elrond called him by his true name, and told him who he was and whose son; and he delivered to him the heirlooms of his house.

'"Here is the ring of Barahir," he said, "the token of our kinship from afar; and here also are the shards of Narsil. With these you may yet do great deeds; for I foretell that the span of your life shall be greater than the measure of Men, unless evil befalls you or you fail at the test. But the test will be hard and long. The Sceptre of Annúminas I withhold, for you have yet to earn it."

'The next day at the hour of sunset Aragorn walked alone in the woods, and his heart was high within him; and he sang, for he was full of hope and the world was fair. And suddenly even as he sang he saw a maiden walking on a greensward among the white stems of the birches; and he halted amazed, thinking that he had strayed into a dream, or else that he had received the gift of the Elf-minstrels, who can make the things of which they sing appear before the eyes of those that listen.

'For Aragorn had been singing a part of the Lay of Lúthien which tells of the meeting of Lúthien and Beren in the forest of Neldoreth. And behold! there Lúthien walked before his eyes in Rivendell, clad in a mantle of silver and blue, fair as the twilight in Elven-home; her dark hair strayed in a sudden wind, and her brows were bound with gems like stars.

'For a moment Aragorn gazed in silence, but fearing that she would pass away and never be seen again, he called to her crying, *Tinúviel, Tinúviel!* even as Beren had done in the Elder Days long ago.

'Then the maiden turned to him and smiled, and she said: "Who are you? And why do you call me by that name?"

'And he answered: "Because I believed you to be indeed Lúthien Tinúviel, of whom I was singing. But if you are not she, then you walk in her likeness."

'"So many have said," she answered gravely. "Yet her name is not mine. Though maybe my doom will be not unlike hers. But who are you?"

'"Estel I was called," he said; "but I am Aragorn, Arathorn's son, Isildur's Heir, Lord of the Dúnedain"; yet even in the saying he felt that this high lineage, in which his heart had rejoiced, was now of little worth, and as nothing compared to her dignity and loveliness.

'But she laughed merrily and said: "Then we are akin from afar. For I am Arwen Elrond's daughter, and am named also Undómiel."

'"Often is it seen," said Aragorn, "that in dangerous days men hide their chief treasure. Yet I marvel at Elrond and your brothers; for though I have dwelt in this house from childhood, I have heard no word of you. How comes it that we have never met before? Surely your father has not kept you locked in his hoard?"

'"No," she said, and looked up at the Mountains that rose in the east. "I have dwelt for a time in the land of my mother's kin, in far Lothlórien. I have but lately returned to visit my father again. It is many years since I walked in Imladris."

'Then Aragorn wondered, for she had seemed of no greater age than he, who had lived yet no more than a score of years in Middle-earth. But Arwen looked in his eyes and said: "Do not wonder! For the children of Elrond have the life of the Eldar."

'Then Aragorn was abashed, for he saw the elven-light in her eyes and the wisdom of many days; yet from that hour he loved Arwen Undómiel daughter of Elrond.

'In the days that followed Aragorn fell silent, and his mother perceived that some strange thing had befallen him; and at last he yielded to her questions and told her of the meeting in the twilight of the trees.

'"My son," said Gilraen, "your aim is high, even for the descendant of many kings. For this lady is the noblest and fairest that now walks the earth. And it is not fit that mortal should wed with the Elf-kin."

'"Yet we have some part in that kinship," said Aragorn, "if the tale of my forefathers is true that I have learned."

'"It is true," said Gilraen, "but that was long ago and in another age of this world, before our race was diminished. Therefore I am afraid; for without the good will of Master Elrond the Heirs of Isildur will soon come to an end. But I do not think that you will have the good will of Elrond in this matter."

'"Then bitter will my days be, and I will walk in the wild alone," said Aragorn.

'"That will indeed be your fate," said Gilraen; but though she had in a measure the foresight of her people, she said no more to him of her foreboding, nor did she speak to any one of what her son had told her.

'But Elrond saw many things and read many hearts. One day, therefore, before the fall of the year he called Aragorn to his chamber, and he said: "Aragorn, Arathorn's son, Lord of the Dúnedain, listen to me! A great doom awaits you, either to rise above the height of all your fathers since the days of Elendil, or to fall into darkness with all that is left of your kin. Many years of trial lie before you. You shall neither have wife, nor bind any woman to you in troth, until your time comes and you are found worthy of it."

'Then Aragorn was troubled, and he said: "Can it be that my mother has spoken of this?"

'"No indeed," said Elrond. "Your own eyes have betrayed you. But I do not speak of my daughter alone. You shall be betrothed to no man's child as yet. But as for Arwen the Fair, Lady of Imladris and of Lórien, Evenstar of her people, she is of lineage greater than yours, and she has lived in the world already so long that to her you are but as a yearling shoot beside a young birch of many summers. She is too far above you. And so, I think, it may well seem to her. But even if it were not so, and her heart turned towards you, I should still be grieved because of the doom that is laid on us."

'"What is that doom?" said Aragorn.

'"That so long as I abide here, she shall live with the youth of the Eldar," answered Elrond, "and when I depart, she shall go with me, if she so chooses."

'"I see," said Aragorn, "that I have turned my eyes to a treasure no less dear than the treasure of Thingol that Beren once desired. Such is my fate." Then suddenly the foresight of his kindred came to him, and he said: "But lo! Master Elrond, the years of your abiding run short at last, and the choice must soon be laid on your children, to part either with you or with Middle-earth."

'"Truly," said Elrond. "Soon, as we account it, though many years of Men must still pass. But there will be no choice before Arwen, my beloved, unless you, Aragorn Arathorn's son, come between us and bring one of us, you or me, to a bitter parting beyond the end of the world. You do not know yet what you desire of me." He sighed, and after a while, looking gravely upon the young man, he said again: "The years will bring what they will. We will speak no more of this until many have passed. The days darken, and much evil is to come."

'Then Aragorn took leave lovingly of Elrond; and the next day he said farewell to his mother, and to the house of Elrond, and to Arwen, and he went out into the wild. For nearly thirty years he laboured in the cause against Sauron; and he became a friend of Gandalf the Wise, from whom he gained much wisdom. With him he made many perilous journeys, but as the years wore on he went more often alone. His ways were hard and long, and he became somewhat grim to look upon, unless he chanced to smile; and yet he seemed to Men worthy of honour, as a king that is in exile, when he did not hide his true shape. For he went in many guises, and won renown under many names. He rode in the host of the Rohirrim, and fought for the Lord of Gondor by land and by sea; and then in the hour of victory he passed out of the knowledge of Men of the West, and went alone far into the East and deep into the South, exploring the hearts of Men, both evil and good, and uncovering the plots and devices of the servants of Sauron.

'Thus he became at last the most hardy of living Men, skilled in their crafts and lore, and was yet more than they; for he was elven-wise, and there was a light in his eyes that when they were kindled few could endure. His face was sad and stern because of the doom that was laid on him, and yet hope dwelt ever in the depths of his heart, from which mirth would arise at times like a spring from the rock.

'It came to pass that when Aragorn was nine and forty years of age he returned from perils on the dark confines of Mordor, where Sauron now dwelt again and was busy with evil. He was weary and he wished to go back to Rivendell and rest there for a while ere he journeyed into the far countries; and on his way he came to the borders of Lórien and was admitted to the hidden land by the Lady Galadriel.

'He did not know it, but Arwen Undómiel was also there, dwelling again for a time with the kin of her mother. She was little changed, for the mortal years had passed her by; yet her face was more grave, and her laughter now seldom was heard. But Aragorn was grown to full stature of body and mind, and Galadriel bade him cast aside his wayworn raiment, and she clothed him in silver and white, with a cloak of elven-grey and bright gem on his brow. Then more than any kind of Men he appeared, and seemed rather an Elf-lord from the Isles of the West. And thus it was that Arwen first beheld him again after their long parting; and as he came walking towards her under the trees of Caras Galadhon laden with flowers of gold, her choice was made and her doom appointed.

'Then for a season they wandered together in the glades of Lothlórien, until it was time for him to depart. And on the evening of Midsummer Aragorn Arathorn's son, and Arwen daughter of Elrond went to the fair hill, Cerin Amroth, in the midst of the land, and they walked unshod on the undying grass with elanor and niphredil about their feet. And there upon that hill they looked east to the Shadow and west to the Twilight, and they plighted their troth and were glad.

'And Arwen said: "Dark is the Shadow, and yet my heart rejoices; for you, Estel, shall be among the great whose valour will destroy it."

'But Aragorn answered: "Alas! I cannot foresee it, and how it may come to pass is hidden from me. Yet with your hope I will hope. And the Shadow I utterly reject. But neither, lady, is the Twilight for me; for I a mortal, and if you will cleave to me, Evenstar, then the Twilight you must also renounce."

'And she stood then as still as a white tree, looking into the West, and at last she said: "I will cleave to you, Dúnadan, and turn from the Twilight. Yet there lies the land of my people and the long home of all my kin." She loved her father dearly.

'When Elrond learned the choice of his daughter, he was silent, though his heart was grieved and found the doom long feared none the easier to endure. But when Aragorn came again to Rivendell he called him to him, and he said:

' "My son, years come when hope will fade, and beyond them little is clear to me. And now a shadow lies between us. Maybe, it has been appointed so, that by my loss the kingship of Men may be restored. Therefore, though I love you, I say to you: Arwen Undómiel shall not diminish her life's grace for less cause. She shall not be the bride of any Man less than the King of both Gondor and Arnor. To me then even our victory can bring only sorrow and parting – but to you hope of joy for a while. Alas, my son! I fear that to Arwen the Doom of Men may seem hard at the ending."

'So it stood afterwards between Elrond and Aragorn, and they spoke no more of this matter; but Aragorn went forth again to danger and toil. And while the world darkened and fear fell on Middle-earth, as the power of Sauron grew and the Barad-dûr rose ever taller and stronger, Arwen remained in Rivendell, and when Aragorn was abroad, from afar she watched over him in thought; and in hope she made for him a great and kingly standard, such as only one might display who claimed the lordship of the Númenoreans and the inheritance of Elendil.

'After a few years Gilraen took leave of Elrond and returned to her own people in Eriador, and lived alone; and she seldom saw her son again, for he spent many years in far countries. But on a time, when Aragorn had returned to the North, he came to her, and she said to him before he went:

' "This is our last parting, Estel, my son. I am aged by care, even as one of lesser Men; and now that it draws near I cannot face the darkness of our time that gathers upon Middle-earth. I shall leave it soon."

'Aragorn tried to comfort her, saying: "Yet there may be a light beyond the darkness; and if so, I would have you see it and be glad."

'But she answered only with this *linnod*:

Onen i-Estel Edain, ú-chebin estel anim,[1]

and Aragorn went away heavy of heart. Gilraen died before the next spring.

'Thus the years drew on to the War of the Ring; of which more is told elsewhere: how the means unforeseen was revealed whereby Sauron might be overthrown, and how hope beyond hope was fulfilled. And it came to pass that in the hour of defeat Aragorn came up from the sea and unfurled the standard of Arwen in the battle of the Fields of Pelennor, and in that day he was first hailed as king. And at last when all was done he entered into the inheritance of his fathers and received the crown of Gondor and sceptre of Arnor; and at Midsummer in the year of the Fall of Sauron

---

[1] 'I gave Hope to the Dúnedain, I have kept no hope for myself.'

he took the hand of Arwen Undómiel, and they were wedded in the city of the Kings.

'The Third Age ended thus in victory and hope; and yet grievous among the sorrows of that Age was the parting of Elrond and Arwen, for they were sundered by the Sea and by a doom beyond the end of the world. When the Great Ring was unmade and the Three were shorn of their power, then Elrond grew weary at last and forsook Middle-earth, never to return. But Arwen became as a mortal woman, and yet it was not her lot to die until all that she had gained was lost.

'As Queen of Elves and Men she dwelt with Aragorn for six-score years in great glory and bliss; yet at last he felt the approach of old age and knew that the span of his life-days was drawing to an end, long though it had been. Then Aragorn said to Arwen:

'"At last, Lady Evenstar, fairest in this world, and most beloved, my world is fading. Lo! we have gathered, and we have spent, and now the time of payment draws near."

'Arwen knew well what he intended, and long had foreseen it; nonetheless she was overborne by her grief. "Would you then, lord, before your time leave your people that live by your word?" she said.

'"Not before my time," he answered. "For if I will not go now, then I must soon go perforce. And Eldarion our son is a man full-ripe for kingship."

'Then going to the House of the Kings in the Silent Street, Aragorn laid him down on the long bed that had been prepared for him. There he said farewell to Eldarion, and gave into his hands the winged crown of Gondor and the sceptre of Arnor; and then all left him save Arwen, and she stood alone by his bed. And for all her wisdom and lineage she could not forbear to plead with him to stay yet for a while. She was not yet weary of her days, and thus she tasted the bitterness of the mortality that she had taken upon her.

'"Lady Undómiel," said Aragorn, "the hour is indeed hard, yet it was made even in that day when we met under the white birches in the garden of Elrond where none now walk. And on the hill of Cerin Amroth when we forsook both the Shadow and the Twilight this doom we accepted. Take counsel with yourself, beloved, and ask whether you would indeed have me wait until I wither and fall from my high seat unmanned and witless. Nay, lady, I am the last of the Númenoreans and the latest King of the Elder Days; and to me has been given not only a span thrice that of Men of Middle-earth, but also the grace to go at my will, and give back the gift. Now, therefore, I will sleep.

'"I speak no comfort to you, for there is no comfort for such pain within the circles of the world. The uttermost choice is before you: to repent and go to the Havens and bear away into the West the memory of our days together that shall there be evergreen but never more than memory; or else to abide the Doom of Men."

'"Nay, dear lord," she said, "that choice is long over. There is now no ship that would bear me hence, and I must indeed abide the Doom of Men, whether I will or I nill: the loss and the silence. But I say to you, King of the Númenoreans, not till now have I understood the tale of your people and their fall. As wicked fools I scorned them, but I pity them at last. For if this is indeed, as the Eldar say, the gift of the One to Men, it is bitter to receive."

' "So it seems," he said. "But let us not be overthrown at the final test, who of old renounced the Shadow and the Ring. In sorrow we must go, but not in despair. Behold! we are not bound for ever to the circles of the world, and beyond them is more than memory. Farewell!"

' "Estel, Estel!" she cried, and with that even as he took her hand and kissed it, he fell into sleep. Then a great beauty was revealed in him, so that all who after came there looked on him in wonder; for they saw that the grace of his youth, and the valour of his manhood, and the wisdom and majesty of his age were blended together. And long there he lay, an image of the splendour of the Kings of Men in glory undimmed before the breaking of the world.

'But Arwen went forth from the House, and the light of her eyes was quenched, and it seemed to her people that she had become cold and grey as nightfall in winter that comes without a star. Then she said farewell to Eldarion, and to her daughters, and to all whom she had loved; and she went out from the city of Minas Tirith and passed away to the land of Lórien, and dwelt there alone under the fading trees until winter came. Galadriel had passed away and Celeborn also was gone, and the land was silent.

'There at last when the mallorn-leaves were falling, but spring had not yet come,[1] she laid herself to rest upon Cerin Amroth; and there is her green grave, until the world is changed, and all the days of her life are utterly forgotten by men that come after, and elanor and niphredil bloom no more east of the Sea.

'Here ends this tale, as it has come to us from the South; and with the passing of Evenstar no more is said in this book of the days of old.'

II

THE HOUSE OF EORL

'Eorl the Young was lord of the Men of Éothéod. That land lay near the sources of Anduin, between the furthest ranges of the Misty Mountains and the northernmost parts of Mirkwood. The Éothéod had moved to those regions in the days of King Eärnil II from lands in the vales of Anduin between the Carrock and the Gladden, and they were in origin close akin to the Beornings and the men of the west-eaves of the forest. The forefathers of Eorl claimed descent from kings of Rhovanion, whose realm lay beyond Mirkwood before the invasions of the Wainriders, and thus they accounted themselves kinsmen of the kings of Gondor descended from Eldacar. They loved best the plains, and delighted in horses and in all feats of horsemanship, but there were many men in the middle vales of Anduin in those days, and moreover the shadow of Dol Guldur was lengthening; when therefore they heard of the overthrow of the Witch-king, they sought more room in the North, and drove away the remnants of the people of Angmar on the east side of the Mountains. But in the days of Léod, father of Eorl, they had grown to be a numerous people and were again somewhat straitened in the land of their home.

[1] p. 326.

'In the two thousand five hundred and tenth year of the Third Age a new peril threatened Gondor. A great host of wild men from the North-east swept over Rhovanion and coming down out of the Brown-lands crossed the Anduin on rafts. At the same time by chance or design the Orcs (who at that time before their war with the Dwarves were in great strength) made a descent from the Mountains. The invaders overran Calenardhon, and Cirion, Steward of Gondor, sent north for help; for there had been long friendship between the Men of Anduin's Vale and the people of Gondor. But in the valley of the River men were now few and scattered, and slow to render such aid as they could. At last tidings came to Eorl of the need of Gondor, and late though it seemed, he set out with a great host of riders.

'Thus he came to the battle of the Field of Celebrant, for that was the name of the green land that lay between Silverlode and Limlight. There the northern army of Gondor was in peril. Defeated in the Wold and cut off from the south, it had been driven across the Limlight, and was then suddenly assailed by the Orc-host that pressed it towards the Anduin. All hope was lost when, unlooked for, the Riders came out of the North and broke upon the rear of the enemy. Then the fortunes of battle were reversed, and the enemy was driven with slaughter over Limlight. Eorl led his men in pursuit, and so great was the fear that went before horsemen of the North that the invaders of the Wold were also thrown into panic, and the Riders hunted them over the plains of Calenardhon.'

The people of that region had become few since the Plague, and most of those that remained had been slaughtered by the savage Easterlings. Cirion, therefore, in reward for his aid, gave Calenardhon between Anduin and Isen to Eorl and his people; and they sent north for their wives and children and their goods and settled in that land. They named it anew the Mark of the Riders, and they called themselves the Eorlingas; but in Gondor their land was called Rohan, and its people the Rohirrim (that is, the Horse-lords). Thus Eorl became the first King of the Mark, and he chose for his dwelling a green hill before the feet of the White Mountains that were the south-wall of his land. There the Rohirrim lived afterwards as free men under their own kings and laws, but in perpetual alliance with Gondor.

'Many lords and warriors, and many fair and valiant women, are named in the songs of Rohan that still remember the North. Frumgar, they say, was the name of the chieftain who led his people to Éothéod. Of his son, Fram, they tell that he slew Scatha, the great dragon of Ered Mithrin, and the land had peace from the long-worms afterwards. Thus Fram won great wealth, but was at feud with the Dwarves, who claimed the hoard of Scatha. Fram would not yield them a penny, and sent to them instead the teeth of Scatha made into a necklace, saying: "Jewels such as these you will not match in your treasuries, for they are hard to come by." Some say that the Dwarves slew Fram for this insult. There was no great love between Éothéod and the Dwarves.

'Léod was the name of Eorl's father. He was a tamer of wild horses; for there were many at that time in the land. He captured a white foal and it grew quickly to a horse strong, and fair, and proud. No man could tame it. When Léod dared tó mount it, it bore him away, and at last threw him, and Léod's head struck a rock, and so he died. He was then only two and forty years old, and his son a youth of sixteen.

'Eorl vowed that he would avenge his father. He hunted long for the horse, and at last he caught sight of him; and his companions expected that he would try to come within bowshot and kill him. But when they drew near, Eorl stood up and called in a loud voice: "Come hither, Mansbane, and get a new name!" To their wonder the horse looked towards Eorl, and came and stood before him, and Eorl said: "Felaróf I name you. You loved your freedom, and I do not blame you for that. But now you owe me a great weregild, and you shall surrender your freedom to me until your life's end."

'Then Eorl mounted him, and Felaróf submitted; and Eorl rode him home without bit or bridle; and he rode him in like fashion ever after. The horse understood all that men said, though he would allow no man but Eorl to mount him. It was upon Felaróf that Eorl rode to the Field of Celebrant; for that horse proved as long lived as Men, and so were his descendants. These were the *mearas*, who would bear no one but the King of the Mark or his sons, until the time of Shadowfax. Men said of them that Béma (whom the Eldar call Oromë) must have brought their sire from West over Sea.

'Of the Kings of the Mark between Eorl and Théoden most is said of Helm Hammerhand. He was a grim man of great strength. There was at that time a man named Freca, who claimed descent from King Fréawine, though he had, men said, much Dunlendish blood, and was dark-haired. He grew rich and powerful, having wide lands on either side of the Adorn.[1] Near its source he made himself a stronghold and paid little heed to the king. Helm mistrusted him, but called him to his councils; and he came when it pleased him.

'To one of these councils Freca rode with many men, and he asked the hand of Helm's daughter for his son Wulf. But Helm said: "You have grown big since you were last here; but it is mostly fat, I guess"; and men laughed at that, for Freca was wide in the belt.

'Then Freca fell in a rage and reviled the king, and said this at the last: "Old kings that refuse a proffered staff may fall on their knees." Helm answered: "Come! The marriage of your son is a trifle. Let Helm and Freca deal with it later. Meanwhile the king and his council have matters of moment to consider."

'When the council was over, Helm stood up and laid his great hand on Freca's shoulder, saying: "The king does not permit brawls in his house, but men are freer outside"; and he forced Freca to walk before him out from Edoras into the field. To Freca's men that came up he said: "Be off! We need no hearers. We are going to speak of a private matter alone. Go and talk to my men!" And they looked and saw that the king's men and his friends far outnumbered them, and they drew back.

'"Now, Dunlending," said the king, "you have only Helm to deal with, alone and unarmed. But you have said much already, and it is my turn to speak. Freca, your folly has grown with your belly. You talk of a staff! If Helm dislikes a crooked staff that is thrust on him, he breaks it. So!" With that he smote Freca such a blow with his fist that he fell back stunned, and died soon after.

---

[1] It flows into Isen from the west of Ered Nimrais.

'Helm then proclaimed Freca's son and near kin the king's enemies; and they fled, for at once Helm sent many men riding to the west marches.'

Four years later (2758) great troubles came to Rohan, and no help could be sent from Gondor, for three fleets of the Corsairs attacked it and there was war on all its coasts. At the same time Rohan was again invaded from the East, and the Dunlendings seeing their chance came over the Isen and down from Isengard. It was soon known that Wulf was their leader. The were in great force, for they were joined by enemies of Gondor that landed in the mouths of Lefnui and Isen.

The Rohirrim were defeated and their land was overrun; and those who were not slain or enslaved fled to the dales of the mountains. Helm was driven back with great loss from the Crossings of Isen and took refuge in the Hornburg and the ravine behind (which was after known as Helm's Deep). There he was besieged. Wulf took Edoras and sat in Meduseld and called himself king. There Haleth Helm's son fell, last of all, defending the doors.

'Soon afterwards the Long Winter began, and Rohan lay under snow for nearly five months (November to March, 2758–9). Both the Rohirrim and their foes suffered grievously in the cold, and in the dearth that lasted longer. In Helm's Deep there was a great hunger after Yule; and being in despair, against the king's counsel, Háma his younger son led men out on a sortie and foray, but they were lost in the snow. Helm grew fierce and gaunt for famine and grief; and the dread of him alone was worth many men in the defence of the Burg. He would go out by himself, clad in white, and stalk like a snow-troll into the camps of his enemies, and slay many men with his hands. It was believed that if he bore no weapon no weapon would bite on him. The Dunlendings said that if he could find no food he ate men. That tale lasted long in Dunland. Helm had a great horn, and soon it was marked that before he sallied forth he would blow a blast upon it that echoed in the Deep; and then so great a fear fell on his enemies that instead of gathering to take him or kill him they fled away down the Coomb.

'One night men heard the horn blowing, but Helm did not return. In the morning there came a sun-gleam, the first for long days, and they saw a white figure standing still on the Dike, alone, for none of the Dunlendings dared come near. There stood Helm, dead as a stone, but his knees were unbent. Yet men said that the horn was still heard at times in the Deep and the wraith of Helm would walk among the foes of Rohan and kill men with fear.

'Soon after the winter broke. Then Fréaláf, son of Hild, Helm's sister, came down out of Dunharrow, to which many had fled; and with a small company of desperate men he surprised Wulf in Meduseld and slew him, and regained Edoras. There were great floods after the snows, and the vale of Entwash became a vast fen. The Eastern invaders perished or withdrew; and there came help at last from Gondor, by the roads both east and west of the mountains. Before the year (2759) was ended the Dunlendings were driven out, even from Isengard; and then Fréaláf became king.

'Helm was brought from the Hornburg and laid in the ninth mound. Ever after the white *simbelmynë* grew there most thickly, so that the mound seemed to be snow-clad. When Fréaláf died a new line of mounds was begun.'

The Rohirrim were grievously reduced by war and dearth and loss of cattle and horses; and it was well that no great danger threatened them again for many years, for it was not until the time of King Folcwine that they recovered their former strength.

It was at the crowning of Fréaláf that Saruman appeared, bringing gifts, and speaking great praise of the valour of the Rohirrim. All thought him a welcome guest. Soon after he took up his abode in Isengard. For this, Beren, Steward of Gondor, gave him leave, for Gondor still claimed Isengard as a fortress of its realm, and not part of Rohan. Beren also gave into Saruman's keeping the keys of Orthanc. That tower no enemy had been able to harm or to enter.

In this way Saruman began to behave as a lord of Men; for at first he held Isengard as a lieutenant of the Steward and warden of the tower. But Fréaláf was as glad as Beren to have this so, and to know that Isengard was in the hands of a strong friend. A friend he long seemed, and maybe in the beginning he was one in truth. Though afterwards there was little doubt in men's minds that Saruman went to Isengard in hope to find the Stone still there, and with the purpose of building up a power of his own. Certainly after the last White Council (2953) his designs towards Rohan, though he hid them, were evil. He then took Isengard for his own and began to make it a place of guarded strength and fear, as though to rival the Barad-dûr. His friends and servants he drew then from all who hated Gondor and Rohan, whether Men or other creatures more evil.

THE KINGS OF THE MARK

Year[1]   *First Line*

2485–2545   1. *Eorl the Young.* He was so named because he succeeded his father in youth and remained yellow-haired and ruddy to the end of his days. These were shortened by a renewed attack of the Easterlings. Eorl fell in battle in the Wold, and the first mound was raised. Felaróf was laid there also.

2512–70   2. *Brego.* He drove the enemy out of the Wold, and Rohan was not attacked again for many years. In 2569 he completed the great hall of Meduseld. At the feast his son Baldor vowed that he would tread 'the Paths of the Dead' and did not return.[2] Brego died of grief the next year.

2544–2645   3. *Aldor the Old.* He was Brego's second son. He became known as the Old, since he lived to a great age, and was king for 75 years. In his time the Rohirrim increased, and drove out or subdued the last of the Dunlendish people that lingered east of Isen. Harrowdale and other mountain-valleys were settled. Of the next three kings little is said, for Rohan had peace and prospered in their time.

---

[1] The dates are given according to the reckoning of Gondor (Third Age). Those in the margin are of birth and death.

[2] pp. 770, 780.

2570–2659 4. *Fréa*. Eldest son, but fourth child of Aldor; he was already old when he became king.

2594–2680 5. *Frëawine*.

2619–99 6. *Goldwine*.

2644–2718 7. *Déor*. In his time the Dunlendings raided often over the Isen. In 2710 they occupied the deserted ring of Isengard, and could not be dislodged.

2668–2741 8. *Gram*.

2691–2759 9. *Helm Hammerhand*. At the end of his reign Rohan suffered great loss, by invasion and the Long Winter. Helm and his sons Haleth and Háma perished. Fréaláf, Helm's sister's son, became king.

Year	*Second Line*

2726–2798 10. *Fréaláf Hildeson*. In his time Saruman came to Isengard, from which the Dunlendings had been driven. The Rohirrim at first profited by his friendship in the days of dearth and weakness that followed.

2752–2842 11. *Brytta*. He was called by his people *Léofa*, for he was loved by all; he was openhanded and a help to all the needy. In his time there was war with Orcs that, driven from the North, sought refuges in the White Mountains.[1] When he died it was thought that they had all been hunted out; but it was not so.

2780–2851 12. *Walda*. He was king only nine years. He was slain with all his companions when they were trapped by Orcs, as they rode by mountain-paths from Dunharrow.

2804–64 13. *Folca*. He was a great hunter, but he vowed to chase no wild beast while there was an Orc left in Rohan. When the last orc-hold was found and destroyed, he went to hunt the great boar of Everholt in the Firien Wood. He slew the boar but died of the tusk-wounds that it gave him.

2830–2903 14. *Folcwine*. When he became king the Rohirrim had recovered their strength. He reconquered the west-march (between Adorn and Isen) that Dunlendings had occupied. Rohan had received great help from Gondor in the evil days. When, therefore, he heard that the Haradrim were assailing Gondor with great strength, he sent many men to the help of the Steward. He wished to lead them himself, but was dissuaded, and his twin sons Folcred and Fastred (born 2858) went in his stead. They fell side by side in battle in Ithilien (2885). Túrin II of Gondor sent to Folcwine a rich weregild of gold.

2870–2953 15. *Fengel*. He was the third son and fourth child of Folcwine. He is not remembered with praise. He was greedy of food and of gold, and at strife with his marshals, and with his children. Thengel, his third child and only son, left Rohan when he came to manhood and lived long in Gondor, and won honour in the service of Turgon.

[1] p. 1029.

2905-80   16. *Thengel*. He took no wife until late, but in 2943 he wedded Morwen
of Lossarnach in Gondor, though she was seventeen years the younger.
She bore him three children in Gondor, of whom Théoden, the second,
was his only son. When Fengel died the Rohirrim recalled him, and he
returned unwillingly. But he proved a good and wise king; though the
speech of Gondor was used in his house, and not all men thought that
good. Morwen bore him two more daughters in Rohan; and the last,
Théodwyn, was the fairest, though she came late (2963), the child of
his age. Her brother loved her dearly.

It was soon after Thengel's return that Saruman declared himself
Lord of Isengard and began to give trouble to Rohan, encroaching
on its borders and supporting its enemies.

2948-3019 17. *Théoden*. He is called Théoden Ednew in the lore of Rohan, for
he fell into a decline under the spells of Saruman, but was healed by
Gandalf, and in the last year of his life arose and led his men to
victory at the Hornburg, and soon after to the Fields of Pelennor,
the greatest battle of the Age. He fell before the gates of Mundburg.
For a while he rested in the land of his birth, among the dead Kings
of Gondor, but was brought back and laid in the eighth mound of
his line at Edoras. Then a new line was begun.

Third Line

In 2989 Théodwyn married Éomund of Eastfold, the chief Marshal of the Mark.
Her son Éomer was born in 2991, and her daughter Éowyn in 2995. At that time
Sauron had arisen again, and the shadow of Mordor reached out to Rohan. Orcs
began to raid in the eastern regions and slay or steal horses. Others also came down
from the Misty Mountains, many being great uruks in the service of Saruman,
though it was long before that was suspected. Éomund's chief charge lay in the east
marches; and he was a great lover of horses and hater of Orcs. If news came of a
raid he would often ride against them in hot anger, unwarily and with few men.
Thus it came about that he was slain in 3002; for he pursued a small band to the
borders of the Emyn Muil, and was there surprised by a strong force that lay in
wait in the rocks.

Not long after Théodwyn took sick and died to the great grief of the king. Her
children he took into his house, calling them son and daughter. He had only one
child of his own, Théodred his son, then twenty-four years old; for the queen Elfhild
had died in childbirth, and Théoden did not wed again. Éomer and Éowyn grew
up at Edoras and saw the dark shadow fall on the halls of Théoden. Éomer was like
his fathers before him; but Éowyn was slender and tall, with a grace and pride that
came her out of the South from Morwen of Lossarnach, whom the Rohirrim had
called Steelsheen.

2991-F.A. 63 (3084) *Éomer Éadig*. When still young he became a Marshal of the
Mark (3017) and was given his father's charge in the east marches.
In the War of the Ring Théodred fell in battle with Saruman at the

Crossings of Isen. Therefore before he died on the Fields of the Pelennor Théoden named Éomer his heir and called him king. In that day Éowyn also won renown, for she fought in that battle, riding in disguise; and was known after in the Mark as the Lady of the Shield-arm.[1]

Éomer became a great king, and being young when he succeeded Théoden he reigned for sixty-five years, longer than all their kings before him save Aldor the Old. In the War of the Ring he made the friendship of King Elessar, and of Imrahil of Dol Amroth; and he rode often to Gondor. In the last year of the Third Age he wedded Lothíriel, daughter of Imrahil. Their son Elfwine the Fair ruled after him.

In Éomer's day in the Mark men had peace who wished for it, and the people increased both in the dales and the plains, and their horses multiplied. In Gondor the King Elessar now ruled, and in Arnor also. In all the lands of those realms of old he was king, save in Rohan only; for he renewed to Éomer the gift of Cirion, and Éomer took again the Oath of Eorl. Often he fulfilled it. For though Sauron had passed, the hatreds and evils that he bred had not died, and the King of the West had many enemies to subdue before the White Tree could grow in peace. And wherever King Elessar went with war King Éomer went with him; and beyond the Sea of Rhûn and on the far fields of the South the thunder of the cavalry of the Mark was heard, and the White Horse upon Green flew in many winds until Éomer grew old.

III

DURIN'S FOLK

Concerning the beginning of the Dwarves strange tales are told both by the Eldar and by the Dwarves themselves; but since these things lie far back beyond our days little is said of them here. Durin is the name that the Dwarves used for the eldest of the Seven Fathers of their race, and the ancestor of all the kings of the Longbeards.[2] He slept alone, until in the deeps of time and the awakening of that people he came to Azanulbizar, and in the caves above Kheled-zâram in the east of the Misty Mountains he made his dwelling, where afterwards were the Mines of Moria renowned in song.

There he lived so long that he was known far and wide as Durin the Deathless. Yet in the end he died before the Elder Days had passed, and his tomb was in

---

[1] For her shield-arm was broken by the mace of the Witch-king; but he was brought to nothing, and thus the words of Glorfindel long before to King Eärnur were fulfilled, that the Witch-king would not fall by the hand of man. For it is said in the songs of the Mark that in this deed Éowyn had the aid of Théoden's esquire, and that he also was not a Man but a Halfling out of a far country, though Éomer gave him honour in the Mark and the name of Holdwine.

[This Holdwine was none other than Meriadoc the Magnificent who was Master of Buckland.]

[2] *The Hobbit*, p. 52.

Khazad-dûm; but his line never failed, and five times an heir was born in his House so like to his Forefather that he received the name of Durin. He was indeed held by the Dwarves to be the Deathless that returned; for they have many strange tales and beliefs concerning themselves and their fate in the world.

After the end of the First Age the power and wealth of Khazad-dûm was much increased; for it was enriched by many people and much lore and craft when the ancient cities of Nogrod and Belegost in the Blue Mountains were ruined at the breaking of Thangorodrim. The power of Moria endured throughout the Dark Years and the dominion of Sauron, for though Eregion was destroyed and the gates of Moria were shut, the halls of Khazad-dûm were too deep and strong and filled with a people too numerous and valiant for Sauron to conquer from without. Thus its wealth remained long unravished, though its people began to dwindle.

It came to pass that in the middle of the Third Age Durin was again its king, being the sixth of that name. The power of Sauron, servant of Morgoth, was then again growing in the world, though the Shadow in the Forest that looked towards Moria was not yet known for what it was. All evil things were stirring. The Dwarves delved deep at that time, seeking beneath Barazinbar for *mithril*, the metal beyond price that was becoming yearly ever harder to win.[1] Thus they roused from sleep[2] a thing of terror that, flying from Thangorodrim, had lain hidden at the foundations of the earth since the coming of the Host of the West: a Balrog of Morgoth. Durin was slain by it, and the year after Náin I, his son; and then the glory of Moria passed, and its people were destroyed or fled far away.

Most of these that escaped made their way into the North, and Thráin I, Náin's son, came to Erebor, the Lonely Mountain, near the eastern eaves of Mirkwood, and there he began new works, and became King under the Mountain. In Erebor he found the great jewel, the Arkenstone, Heart of the Mountain.[3] But Thorin I his son removed and went into the far North to the Grey Mountains, where most of Durin's folk were now gathering; for those mountains were rich and little explored. But there were dragons in the wastes beyond; and after many years they became strong again and multiplied, and they made war on the Dwarves, and plundered their works. At last Dáin I, together with Frór his second son, was slain at the door of his hall by a great cold-drake.

Not long after most of Durin's Folk abandoned the Grey Mountains. Grór, Dáin's son, went away with many followers to the Iron Hills; but Thrór, Dáin's heir, with Borin his father's brother and the remainder of the people returned to Erebor. To the Great Hall of Thráin, Thrór brought back the Arkenstone, and he and his folk prospered and became rich, and they had the friendship of all Men that dwelt near. For they made not only things of wonder and beauty but weapons and armour of great worth; and there was great traffic of ore between them and their kin in the Iron Hills. Thus the Northmen who lived between Celduin (River Running) and

[1] p. 309.
[2] Or released from prison; it may well be that it had already been awakened by the malice of Sauron.
[3] *The Hobbit*, p. 229.

Carnen (Redwater) became strong and drove back all enemies from the East; and the Dwarves lived in plenty, and there was feasting and song in the Halls of Erebor.[1]

So the rumour of the wealth of Erebor spread abroad and reached the ears of the dragons, and at last Smaug the Golden, greatest of the dragons of his day, arose and without warning came against King Thrór and descended on the Mountain in flames. It was not long before all that realm was destroyed, and the town of Dale near by was ruined and deserted; but Smaug entered into the Great Hall and lay there upon a bed of gold.

From the sack and the burning many of Thrór's kin escaped; and last of all from the halls by a secret door came Thrór himself and his son Thráin II. They went away south with their family[2] into long and homeless wandering. With them went also a small company of their kinsmen and faithful followers.

Years afterwards Thrór, now old, poor, and desperate, gave to his son Thráin the one great treasure he still possessed, the last of the Seven Rings, and then he went away with one old companion only, called Nár. Of the Ring he said to Thráin at their parting:

'This may prove the foundation of new fortune for you yet, though that seems unlikely. But it needs gold to breed gold.'

'Surely you do not think of returning to Erebor?' said Thráin.

'Not at my age,' said Thrór. 'Our vengeance on Smaug I bequeath to you and your sons. But I am tired of poverty and the scorn of Men. I go to see what I can find.' He did not say where.

He was a little crazed perhaps with age and misfortune and long brooding on the splendour of Moria in his forefathers' days; or the Ring, it may be, was turning to evil now that its master was awake, driving him to folly and destruction. From Dunland, where he was then dwelling, he went north with Nár, and they crossed the Redhorn Pass and came down into Azanulbizar.

When Thrór came to Moria the Gate was open. Nár begged him to beware, but he took no heed of him, and walked proudly in as an heir that returns. But he did not come back. Nár stayed near by for many days in hiding. One day he heard a loud shout and the blare of a horn, and a body was flung out on the steps. Fearing that it was Thrór, he began to creep near, but there came a voice from within the gate:

'Come on, beardling! We can see you. But there is no need to be afraid today. We need you as a messenger.'

Then Nár came up, and found that it was indeed the body of Thrór, but the head was severed and lay face downwards. As he knelt there, he heard orc-laughter in the shadows, and the voice said:

'If beggars will not wait at the door, but sneak in to try thieving, that is what we

---

[1] *The Hobbit*, p. 28.
[2] Among whom were the children of Thráin II: Thorin (Oakenshield), Frerin, and Dís. Thorin was then a youngster in the reckoning of the Dwarves. It was afterwards learned that more of the Folk under the Mountain had escaped than was at first hoped; but most of these went to the Iron Hills.

do to them. If any of your people poke their foul beards in here again, they will fare the same. Go and tell them so! But if his family wish to know who is now king here, the name is written on his face. I wrote it! I killed him! I am the master!'

Then Nár turned the head and saw branded on the brow in Dwarfrunes so that he could read it the name A Z O G. That name was branded in his heart and in the hearts of all the Dwarves afterwards. Nár stooped to take the head, but the voice of Azog[1] said:

'Drop it! Be off! Here's your fee, beggar-beard.' A small bag struck him. It held a few coins of little worth.

Weeping, Nár fled down the Silverlode; but he looked back once and saw that Orcs had come from the gate and were hacking up the body and flinging the pieces to the black crows.

Such was the tale that Nár brought back to Thráin; and when he had wept and torn his beard he fell silent. Seven days he sat and said no word. Then he stood up and . said: 'This cannot be borne!' That was the beginning of the War of the Dwarves and the Orcs, which was long and deadly, and fought for the most part in deep places beneath the earth.

Thráin at once sent messengers bearing the tale, north, east, and west; but it was three years before the Dwarves had mustered their strength. Durin's Folk gathered all their host, and they were joined by great forces sent from the Houses of other Fathers; for this dishonour to the heir of the Eldest of their race filled them with wrath. When all was ready they assailed and sacked one by one all the strongholds of the Orcs that they could from Gundabad to the Gladden. Both sides were pitiless, and there was death and cruel deeds by dark and by light. But the Dwarves had the victory through their strength, and their matchless weapons, and the fire of their anger, as they hunted for Azog in every den under mountain.

At last all the Orcs that fled before them were gathered in Moria, and the Dwarf-host in pursuit came to Azanulbizar. That was a great vale that lay between the arms of the mountains about the lake of Kheled-zâram and had been of old part of the kingdom of Khazad-dûm. When the Dwarves saw the gate of their ancient mansions upon the hill-side they sent up a great shout like thunder in the valley. But a great host of foes was arrayed on the slopes above them, and out of the gates poured a multitude of Orcs that had been held back by Azog for the last need.

At first fortune was against the Dwarves; for it was a dark day of winter without sun, and the Orcs did not waver, and they outnumbered their enemies, and had the higher ground. So began the Battle of Azanulbizar (or Nanduhirion in the Elvish tongue), at the memory of which the Orcs still shudder and the Dwarves weep. The first assault of the vanguard led by Thráin was thrown back with loss, and Thráin was driven into a wood of great trees that then still grew not far from Kheled-zâram. There Frerin his son fell, and Fundin his kinsman, and many others, and both Thráin and Thorin were wounded.[2] Elsewhere the battle swayed to and fro with

---

[1] Azog was the father of Bolg; see *The Hobbit*, p. 30.
[2] It is said that Thorin's shield was cloven and he cast it away and he hewed off with his axe a branch of an oak and held it in his left hand to ward off the strokes of his foes, or to wield as a club. In this way he got his name.

great slaughter, until at last the people of the Iron Hills turned the day. Coming late and fresh to the field the mailed warriors of Náin, Grór's son, drove through the Orcs to the very threshold of Moria, crying 'Azog! Azog!' as they hewed down with their mattocks all who stood in their way.

Then Náin stood before the Gate and cried with a great voice: 'Azog! If you are in come out! Or is the play in the valley too rough?'

Thereupon Azog came forth, and he was a great Orc with a huge iron-clad head, and yet agile and strong. With him came many like him, the fighters of his guard, and as they engaged Náin's company he turned to Náin, and said:

'What? Yet another beggar at my doors? Must I brand you too?' With that he rushed at Náin and they fought. But Náin was half blind with rage, and also very weary with battle, whereas Azog was fresh and fell and full of guile. Soon Náin made a great stroke with all his strength that remained, but Azog darted aside and kicked Náin's leg, so that the mattock splintered on the stone where he had stood, but Náin stumbled forward. Then Azog with a swift swing hewed his neck. His mail-collar withstood the edge, but so heavy was the blow that Náin's neck was broken and he fell.

Then Azog laughed, and he lifted up his head to let forth a great yell of triumph; but the cry died in his throat. For he saw that all his host in the valley was in a rout, and the Dwarves went this way and that slaying as they would, and those that could escape from them were flying south, shrieking as they ran. And hard by all the soldiers of his guard lay dead. He turned and fled back towards the Gate.

Up the steps after him leaped a Dwarf with a red axe. It was Dáin Ironfoot, Náin's son. Right before the doors he caught Azog, and there he slew him, and hewed off his head. That was held a great feat, for Dáin was then only a stripling in the reckoning of the Dwarves. But long life and many battles lay before him, until old but unbowed he fell at last in the War of the Ring. Yet hardy and full of wrath as he was, it is said that when he came down from the Gate he looked grey in the face, as one who has felt great fear.

When at last the battle was won the Dwarves that were left gathered in Azanulbizar. They took the head of Azog and thrust into its mouth the purse of small money, and then they set it on a stake. But no feast nor song was there that night; for their dead were beyond the count of grief. Barely half of their number, it is said, could still stand or had hope of healing.

None the less in the morning Thráin stood before them. He had one eye blinded beyond cure, and he was halt with a leg-wound; but he said: 'Good! We have the victory. Khazad-dûm is ours!'

But they answered: 'Durin's Heir you may be, but even with one eye you should see clearer. We fought this war for vengeance, and vengeance we have taken. But it is not sweet. If this is victory, then our hands are too small to hold it.'

And those who were not of Durin's Folk said also: 'Khazad-dûm was not our Fathers' house. What is it to us, unless a hope of treasure? But now, if we must go without the rewards and the weregilds that are owed to us, the sooner we return to our own lands the better pleased we shall be.'

Then Thráin turned to Dáin, and said: 'But surely my own kin will not desert me?' 'No,' said Dáin. 'You are the father of our Folk, and we have bled for you, and will again. But we will not enter Khazad-dûm. You will not enter Khazad-dûm. Only I have looked through the shadow of the Gate. Beyond the shadow it waits for you still: Durin's Bane. The world must change and some other power than ours must come before Durin's Folk walk again in Moria.'

So it was that after Azanulbizar the Dwarves dispersed again. But first with great labour they stripped all their dead, so that Orcs should not come and win there a store of weapons and mail. It is said that every Dwarf that went from that battlefield was bowed under a heavy burden. Then they built many pyres and burned all the bodies of their kin. There was a great felling of trees in the valley, which remained bare ever after, and the reek of the burning was seen in Lórien.[1]

When the dreadful fires were in ashes the allies went away to their own countries, and Dáin Ironfoot led his father's people back to the Iron Hills. Then standing by the great stake, Thráin said to Thorin Oakenshield: 'Some would think this head dearly bought! At least we have given our kingdom for it. Will you come with me back to the anvil? Or will you beg your bread at proud doors?'

'To the anvil,' answered Thorin. 'The hammer will at least keep the arms strong, until they can wield sharper tools again.'

So Thráin and Thorin with what remained of their following (among whom were Balin and Glóin) returned to Dunland, and soon afterwards they removed and wandered in Eriador, until at last they made a home in exile in the east of the Ered Luin beyond the Lune. Of iron were most of the things that they forged in those days, but they prospered after a fashion, and their numbers slowly increased.[2] But, as Thrór had said, the Ring needed gold to breed gold, and of that or any other precious metal they had little or none.

Of this Ring something may be said here. It was believed by the Dwarves of Durin's Folk to be the first of the Seven that was forged; and they say that it was given to the King of Khazad-dûm, Durin III, by the Elven-smiths themselves and not by Sauron, though doubtless his evil power was on it, since he had aided in the forging of all the Seven. But the possessors of the Ring did not display it or speak of it, and they seldom surrendered it until near death, so that others did not know for certain where it was bestowed. Some thought that it had remained in Khazad-dûm, in the secret tombs of the kings, if they had not been discovered and plundered; but among the kindred of Durin's Heir it was believed (wrongly) that Thrór had worn it when he rashly returned there. What then had become of it they did not know. It was not found on the body of Azog.[3]

---

[1] Such dealings with their dead seemed grievous to the Dwarves, for it was against their use; but to make such tombs as they were accustomed to build (since they will lay their dead only in stone not in earth) would have taken many years. To fire therefore they turned, rather than leave their kin to beast or bird or carrion-orc. But those who fell in Azanulbizar were honoured in memory, and to this day a Dwarf will say proudly of one of his sires: 'he was a burned Dwarf', and that is enough.

[2] They had very few women-folk. Dís Thráin's daughter was there. She was the mother of Fíli and Kíli, who were born in the Ered Luin. Thorin had no wife.

[3] pp. 261–2.

None the less it may well be, as the Dwarves now believe, that Sauron by his arts had discovered who had this Ring, the last to remain free, and that the singular misfortunes of the heirs of Durin were largely due to his malice. For the Dwarves had proved untameable by this means. The only power over them that the Rings wielded was to inflame their hearts with a greed of gold and precious things, so that if they lacked them all other good things seemed profitless, and they were filled with wrath and desire for vengeance on all who deprived them. But they were made from their beginning of a kind to resist most steadfastly any domination. Though they could be slain or broken, they could not be reduced to shadows enslaved to another will; and for the same reason their lives were not affected by any Ring, to live either longer or shorter because of it. All the more did Sauron hate the possessors and desire to dispossess them.

It was therefore perhaps partly by the malice of the Ring that Thráin after some years became restless and discontented. The lust for gold was ever in his mind. At last, when he could endure it no longer, he turned his thoughts to Erebor, and resolved to go back there. He said nothing to Thorin of what was in his heart; but with Balin and Dwalin and a few others, he arose and said farewell and departed.

Little is known of what happened to him afterwards. It would now seem that as soon as he was abroad with few companions he was hunted by the emissaries of Sauron. Wolves pursued him, Orcs waylaid him, evil birds shadowed his path, and the more he strove to go north the more misfortunes opposed him. There came a dark night when he and his companions were wandering in the land beyond Anduin, and they were driven by a black rain to take shelter under the eaves of Mirkwood. In the morning he was gone from the camp, and his companions called him in vain. They searched for him many days, until at last giving up hope they departed and came at length back to Thorin. Only long after was it learned that Thráin had been taken alive and brought to the pits of Dol Guldur. There he was tormented and the Ring taken from him, and there at last he died.

So Thorin Oakenshield became the Heir of Durin, but an heir without hope. When Thráin was lost he was ninety-five, a great dwarf of proud bearing; but he seemed content to remain in Eriador. There he laboured long, and trafficked, and gained such wealth as he could; and his people were increased by many of the wandering Folk of Durin who heard of his dwelling in the west and came to him. Now they had fair halls in the mountains, and store of goods, and their days did not seem so hard, though in their songs they spoke ever of the Lonely Mountain far away.

The years lengthened. The embers in the heart of Thorin grew hot again, as he brooded on the wrongs of his House and the vengeance upon the Dragon that he had inherited. He thought of weapons and armies and alliances, as his great hammer rang in his forge; but the armies were dispersed and the alliances broken and the axes of his people were few; and a great anger without hope burned him as he smote the red iron on the anvil.

But at last there came about by chance a meeting between Gandalf and Thorin that changed all the fortunes of the House of Durin, and led to other and greater ends beside. On a time[1] Thorin, returning west from a journey, stayed at Bree for the night. There Gandalf was also. He was on his way to the Shire, which he had not visited for some twenty years. He was weary, and thought to rest there for a while.

Among many cares he was troubled in mind by the perilous state of the North; because he knew then already that Sauron was plotting war, and intended, as soon as he felt strong enough, to attack Rivendell. But to resist any attempt from the East to regain the lands of Angmar and the northern passes in the mountains there were now only the Dwarves of the Iron Hills. And beyond them lay the desolation of the Dragon. The Dragon Sauron might use with terrible effect. How then could the end of Smaug be achieved?

It was even as Gandalf sat and pondered this that Thorin stood before him, and said: 'Master Gandalf, I know you only by sight, but now I should be glad to speak with you. For you have often come into my thoughts of late, as if I were bidden to seek you. Indeed I should have done so, if I had known where to find you.'

Gandalf looked at him with wonder. 'That is strange, Thorin Oakenshield,' he said. 'For I have thought of you also; and though I am on my way to the Shire, it was in my mind that is the way also to your halls.'

'Call them so, if you will,' said Thorin. 'They are only poor lodgings in exile. But you would be welcome there, if you would come. For they say that you are wise and know more than any other of what goes on in the world; and I have much on my mind and would be glad of your counsel.'

'I will come,' said Gandalf; 'for I guess that we share one trouble at least. The Dragon of Erebor is on my mind, and I do not think that he will be forgotten by the grandson of Thrór.'

The story is told elsewhere of what came of that meeting: of the strange plan that Gandalf made for the help of Thorin, and how Thorin and his companions set out from the Shire on the quest of the Lonely Mountain that came to great ends unforeseen. Here only those things are recalled that directly concern Durin's Folk.

The Dragon was slain by Bard of Esgaroth, but there was battle in Dale. For the Orcs came down upon Erebor as soon as they heard of the return of the Dwarves; and they were led by Bolg, son of that Azog whom Dáin slew in his youth. In that first Battle of Dale, Thorin Oakenshield was mortally wounded; and he died and was laid in a tomb under the Mountain with the Arkenstone upon his breast. There fell also Fíli and Kíli, his sister-sons. But Dáin Ironfoot, his cousin, who came from the Iron Hills to his aid and was also his rightful heir, became then King Dáin II, and the Kingdom under the Mountain was restored, even as Gandalf had desired. Dáin proved a great and wise king, and the Dwarves prospered and grew strong again in his day.

In the late summer of that same year (2941) Gandalf had at last prevailed upon Saruman and the White Council to attack Dol Guldur, and Sauron retreated and went to Mordor, there to be secure, as he thought, from all his enemies. So it was that when the War came at last the main assault was turned southwards; yet even so with his far-stretched right hand Sauron might have done great evil in the North,

[1] March 15, 2941.

if King Dáin and King Brand had not stood in his path. Even as Gandalf said afterwards to Frodo and Gimli, when they dwelt together for a time in Minas Tirith. Not long before news had come to Gondor of events far away.

'I grieved at the fall of Thorin,' said Gandalf; 'and now we hear that Dáin has fallen, fighting in Dale again, even while we fought here. I should call that a heavy loss, if it was not a wonder rather that in his great age he could still wield his axe as mightily as they say that he did, standing over the body of King Brand before the Gate of Erebor until the darkness fell.

'Yet things might have gone far otherwise and far worse. When you think of the great Battle of the Pelennor, do not forget the battles in Dale and the valour of Durin's Folk. Think of what might have been. Dragon-fire and savage swords in Eriador, night in Rivendell. There might be no Queen in Gondor. We might now hope to return from the victory here only to ruin and ash. But that has been averted – because I met Thorin Oakenshield one evening on the edge of spring in Bree. A chance-meeting, as we say in Middle-earth.'

Dís was the daughter of Thráin II. She is the only dwarf-woman named in these histories. It was said by Gimli that there are few dwarf-women, probably no more than a third of the whole people. They seldom walk abroad except at great need. They are in voice and appearance, and in garb if they must go on a journey, so like to the dwarf-men that the eyes and ears of other peoples cannot tell them apart. This has given rise to the foolish opinion among Men that there are no dwarf-women, and that the Dwarves 'grow out of stone'.

It is because of the fewness of women among them that the kind of the Dwarves increases slowly, and is in peril when they have no secure dwellings. For Dwarves take only one wife or husband each in their lives, and are jealous, as in all matters of their rights. The number of dwarf-men that marry is actually less than one-third. For not all the women take husbands: some desire none; some desire one that they cannot get, and so will have no other. As for the men, very many also do not desire marriage, being engrossed in their crafts.

Gimli Glóin's son is renowned, for he was one of the Nine Walkers that set out with the Ring; and he remained in the company of King Elessar throughout the War. He was named Elf-friend because of the great love that grew between him and Legolas, son of King Thranduil, and because of his reverence for the Lady Galadriel.

After the fall of Sauron, Gimli brought south a part of the Dwarf-folk of Erebor, and he became Lord of the Glittering Caves. He and his people did great works in Gondor and Rohan. For Minas Tirith they forged gates of *mithril* and steel to replace those broken by the Witch-king. Legolas his friend also brought south Elves out of Greenwood, and they dwelt in Ithilien, and it became once again the fairest country in all the westlands.

But when King Elessar gave up his life Legolas followed at last the desire of his heart and sailed over Sea.

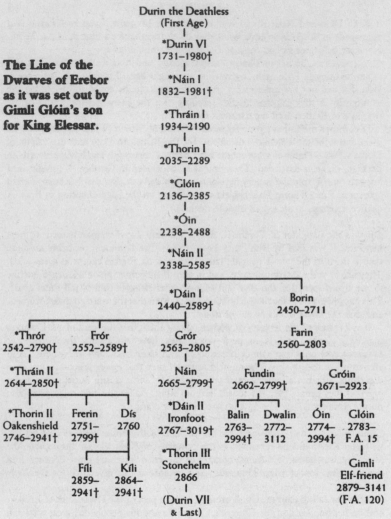

The Line of the Dwarves of Erebor as it was set out by Gimli Glóin's son for King Elessar.

Durin the Deathless
(First Age)
|
*Durin VI
1731–1980†
|
*Náin I
1832–1981†
|
*Thráin I
1934–2190
|
*Thorin I
2035–2289
|
*Glóin
2136–2385
|
*Óin
2238–2488
|
*Náin II
2338–2585
|
*Dáin I
2440–2589†

Borin
2450–2711
|
Farin
2560–2803

*Thrór
2542–2790†
|
*Thráin II
2644–2850†

Frór
2552–2589†

Grór
2563–2805
|
Náin
2665–2799†
|
*Dáin II
Ironfoot
2767–3019†
|
*Thorin III
Stonehelm
2866
|
(Durin VII
& Last)

*Thorin II
Oakenshield
2746–2941†

Frerin
2751–
2799†

Dís
2760

Fíli
2859–
2941†

Kíli
2864–
2941†

Fundin
2662–2799†

Balin
2763–
2994†

Dwalin
2772–
3112

Gróin
2671–2923

Óin
2774–
2994†

Glóin
2783–
F.A. 15
|
Gimli
Elf-friend
2879–3141
(F.A. 120)

Foundation of Erebor, 1999.
Dáin I slain by a dragon, 2589
Return to Erebor, 2590.
Sack of Erebor, 2770.
Murder of Thrór, 2790.
Mustering of the Dwarves, 2790–3.
War of the Dwarves and Orcs, 2793–9.

Battle of Nanduhirion, 2799.
Thráin goes wandering, 2841.
Death of Thráin and loss of his Ring, 2850.
Battle of Five Armies and death of Thorin II, 2941.
Balin goes to Moria, 2989.

* The names of those who were held to be kings of Durin's Folk, whether in exile or not, are marked so. Of the other companions of Thorin Oakenshield in the journey to Erebor Ori, Nori, and Dori were also of the House of Durin, and more remote kinsmen of Thorin: Bifur, Bofur, and Bombur were descended from Dwarves of Moria but were not of Durin's line. For † see p. 1009.

Here follows one of the last notes in the Red Book

We have heard tell that Legolas took Gimli Glóin's son with him because of their great friendship, greater than any that has been between Elf and Dwarf. If this is true, then it is strange indeed: that a Dwarf should be willing to leave Middle-earth for any love, or that the Eldar should receive him, or that the Lords of the West should permit it. But it is said that Gimli went also out of desire to see again the beauty of Galadriel; and it may be that she, being mighty among the Eldar, obtained this grace for him. More cannot be said of this matter.

APPENDIX B

THE TALE OF YEARS

(CHRONOLOGY OF THE WESTLANDS)

The *First Age* ended with the Great Battle, in which the Host of Valinor broke Thangorodrim[1] and overthrew Morgoth. Then most of the Noldor returned into the Far West[2] and dwelt in Eressëa within sight of Valinor; and many of the Sindar went over Sea also.

The *Second Age* ended with the first overthrow of Sauron, servant of Morgoth, and the taking of the One Ring.

The *Third Age* came to its end in the War of the Ring; but the *Fourth Age* was not held to have begun until Master Elrond departed, and the time was come for the dominion of Men and the decline of all other 'speaking-peoples' in Middle-earth.[3]

In the Fourth Age the earlier ages were often called the *Elder Days*; but that name was properly given only to the days before the casting out of Morgoth. The histories of that time are not recorded here.

The Second Age

These were the dark years for Men of Middle-earth, but the years of the glory of Númenor. Of events in Middle-earth the records are few and brief, and their dates are often uncertain.

In the beginning of this age many of the High Elves still remained. Most of these dwelt in Lindon west of the Ered Luin; but before the building of the Barad-dûr many of the Sindar passed eastward, and some established realms in the forests far away, where their people were mostly Silvan Elves. Thranduil, king in the north of Greenwood the Great, was one of these. In Lindon north of the Lune dwelt Gil-galad, last heir of the kings of the Noldor in exile. He was acknowledged as High King of the Elves of the West. In Lindon south of the Lune dwelt for a time Celeborn, kinsman of Thingol; his wife was Galadriel, greatest of Elven women. She was sister of Finrod Felagund, Friend-of-Men, once king of Nargothrond, who gave his life to save Beren son of Barahir.

Later some of the Noldor went to Eregion, upon the west of the Misty Mountains, and near to the West-gate of Moria. This they did because they learned that *mithril* had been discovered in Moria.[4] The Noldor were great craftsmen and less unfriendly to the Dwarves than the Sindar; but the friendship that grew up between the people of Durin and the Elven-smiths of Eregion was the closest that there has ever been between the two races. Celebrimbor was Lord of Eregion and the greatest of their craftsmen; he was descended from Fëanor.

---

[1] p. 236–7.
[2] p. 583, *The Hobbit*, p. 144.
[3] p. 949–50.
[4] p. 309.

Year

1   Foundation of the Grey Havens, and of Lindon.

32   The Edain reach Númenor.

c. 40   Many Dwarves leaving their old cities in Ered Luin go to Moria and swell its numbers.

442   Death of Elros Tar-Minyatur.

c. 500   Sauron begins to stir again in Middle-earth.

548   Birth in Númenor of Silmariën.

600   The first ships of the Númenoreans appear off the coasts.

750   Eregion founded by the Noldor.

c. 1000   Sauron, alarmed by the growing power of the Númenoreans, chooses Mordor as a land to make into a stronghold. He begins the building of Barad-dûr.

1075   Tar-Ancalimë becomes the first Ruling Queen of Númenor.

1200   Sauron endeavours to seduce the Eldar. Gil-galad refuses to treat with him; but the smiths of Eregion are won over. The Númenoreans begin to make permanent havens.

c. 1500   The Elven-smiths instructed by Sauron reach the height of their skill. They begin the forging of the Rings of Power.

c. 1590   The Three Rings are completed in Eregion.

c. 1600   Sauron forges the One Ring in Orodruin. He completes the Barad-dûr. Celebrimbor perceives the designs of Sauron.

1693   War of the Elves and Sauron begins. The Three Rings are hidden.

1695   Sauron's forces invade Eriador. Gil-galad sends Elrond to Eregion.

1697   Eregion laid waste. Death of Celebrimbor. The gates of Moria are shut. Elrond retreats with remnant of the Noldor and founds the refuge of Imladris.

1699   Sauron overruns Eriador.

1700   Tar-Minastir sends a great navy from Númenor to Lindon. Sauron is defeated.

1701   Sauron is driven out of Eriador: The Westlands have peace for a long while.

c. 1800   From about this time onward the Númenoreans begin to establish dominions on the coasts. Sauron extends his power eastwards. The shadow falls on Númenor.

2251   Tar-Atanamir takes the sceptre. Rebellion and division of the Númenoreans begins. About this time the Nazgûl or Ringwraiths, slaves of the Nine Rings, first appear.

2280   Umbar is made into a great fortress of Númenor.

2350   Pelargir is built. It becomes the chief haven of the Faithful Númenoreans.

2899   Ar-Adûnakhôr takes the sceptre.

3175   Repentance of Tar-Palantir. Civil war in Númenor.

3255   Ar-Pharazôn the Golden seizes the sceptre.

3261   Ar-Pharazôn sets sail and lands at Umbar.

3262   Sauron is taken as prisoner to Númenor; 3262–3310 Sauron seduces the King and corrupts the Númenoreans.

3310 Ar-Pharazôn begins the building of the Great Armament.

3319 Ar-Pharazôn assails Valinor. Downfall of Númenor. Elendil and his sons escape.

3320 Foundations of the Realms in Exile: Arnor and Gondor. The Stones are divided (p. 607). Sauron returns to Mordor.

3429 Sauron attacks Gondor, takes Minas Ithil and burns the White Tree. Isildur escapes down Anduin and goes to Elendil in the North. Anárion defends Minas Anor and Osgiliath.

3430 The Last Alliance of Elves and Men is formed.

3431 Gil-galad and Elendil march east to Imladris.

3434 The host of the Alliance crosses the Misty Mountains. Battle of Dagorlad and defeat of Sauron. Siege of Barad-dûr begins.

3440 Anárion slain.

3441 Sauron overthrown by Elendil and Gil-galad, who perish. Isildur takes the One Ring. Sauron passes away and the Ringwraiths go into the shadows. The Second Age ends.

The Third Age

These were the fading years of the Eldar. For long they were at peace, wielding the Three Rings while Sauron slept and the One Ring was lost; but they attempted nothing new, living in memory of the past. The Dwarves hid themselves in deep places, guarding their hoards; but when evil began to stir again and dragons reappeared, one by one their ancient treasures were plundered, and they became a wandering people. Moria for long remained secure, but its numbers dwindled until many of its vast mansions became dark and empty. The wisdom and the life-span of Númenoreans also waned as they became mingled with lesser Men.

When maybe a thousand years had passed, and the first shadow had fallen on Greenwood the Great, the *Istari* or Wizards appeared in Middle-earth. It was afterwards said that they came out of the Far West and were messengers sent to contest the power of Sauron, and to unite all those who had the will to resist him; but they were forbidden to match his power with power, or to seek to dominate Elves or Men by force and fear.

They came therefore in the shape of Men, though they were never young and aged only slowly, and they had many powers of mind and hand. They revealed their true names to few,[1] but used such names as were given to them. The two highest of this order (of whom it is said there were five) were called by the Eldar Curunír, 'the Man of Skill', and Mithrandir, 'the Grey Pilgrim', but by Men in the North Saruman and Gandalf. Curunír journeyed often into the East, but dwelt at last in Isengard. Mithrandir was closest in friendship with the Eldar, and wandered mostly in the West and never made for himself any lasting abode.

Throughout the Third Age the guardianship of the Three Rings was known only to those who possessed them. But at the end it became known that they had been held at first by the three greatest of the Eldar: Gil-galad, Galadriel and Círdan.

[1] p. 655.

Gil-galad before he died gave his ring to Elrond; Círdan later surrendered his to Mithrandir. For Círdan saw further and deeper than any other in Middle-earth, and he welcomed Mithrandir at the Grey Havens, knowing whence he came and whither he would return.

'Take this ring, Master,' he said, 'for your labours will be heavy; but it will support you in the weariness that you have taken upon yourself. For this is the Ring of Fire, and with it you may rekindle hearts in a world that grows chill. But as for me, my heart is with the Sea, and I will dwell by the grey shores until the last ship sails. I will await you.'

Year

2 Isildur plants a seedling of the White Tree in Minas Anor. He delivers the South-kingdom to Meneldil. Disaster of the Gladden Fields; Isildur and his three elder sons are slain.

3 Ohtar brings the shards of Narsil to Imladris.

10 Valandil becomes King of Arnor.

109 Elrond weds Celebrían, daughter of Celeborn.

130 Birth of Elladan and Elrohir, sons of Elrond.

241 Birth of Arwen Undómiel.

420 King Ostoher rebuilds Minas Anor.

490 First invasion of Easterlings.

500 Rómendacil I defeats the Easterlings.

541 Rómendacil slain in battle.

830 Falastur begins the line of the Ship-kings of Gondor.

861 Death of Eärendur, and division of Arnor.

933 King Eärnil I takes Umbar, which becomes a fortress of Gondor.

936 Eärnil lost at sea.

1015 King Ciryandil slain in the siege of Umbar.

1050 Hyarmendacil conquers the Harad. Gondor reaches the height of its power. About this time a shadow falls on Greenwood, and men begin to call it Mirkwood. The Periannath are first mentioned in records, with the coming of the Harfoots to Eriador.

c. 1100 The Wise (the Istari and the chief Eldar) discover that an evil power has made a stronghold at Dol Guldur. It is thought to be one of the Nazgûl.

1149 Reign of Atanatar Alcarin begins.

c. 1150 The Fallohides enter Eriador. The Stoors come over the Redhorn Pass and move to the Angle, or to Dunland.

c. 1300 Evil things begin to multiply again. Orcs increase in the Misty Mountains and attack the Dwarves. The Nazgûl reappear. The chief of these comes north to Angmar. The Periannath migrate westward; many settle at Bree.

1356 King Argeleb I slain in battle with Rhudaur. About this time the Stoors leave the Angle, and some return to Wilderland.

1409 The Witch-king of Angmar invades Arnor. King Arvaleg I slain. Fornost and Tyrn Gorthad are defended. The Tower of Amon Sûl destroyed.

1432 King Valacar of Gondor dies, and the civil war of the Kin-strife begins.

1437 Burning of Osgiliath and loss of the *palantír*. Eldacar flees to Rhovanion; his son Ornendil is murdered.

1447 Eldacar returns and drives out the usurper Castamir. Battle of the Crossings of Erui. Siege of Pelargir.

1448 Rebels escape and seize Umbar.

1540 King Aldamir slain in war with the Harad and Corsairs of Umbar.

1551 Hyarmendacil II defeats the Men of Harad.

1601 Many Periannath migrate from Bree, and are granted land beyond Baranduin by Argeleb II.

c. 1630 They are joined by Stoors coming up from Dunland.

1634 The Corsairs ravage Pelargir and slay King Minardil.

1636 The Great Plague devastates Gondor. Death of King Telemnar and his children. The White Tree dies in Minas Anor. The plague spreads north and west, and many parts of Eriador become desolate. Beyond the Baranduin the Periannath survive, but suffer great loss.

1640 King Tarondor removes the King's House to Minas Anor, plants a seedling of the White Tree. Osgiliath begins to fall into ruin. Mordor is left unguarded.

1810 King Telumehtar Umbardacil retakes Umbar and drives out the Corsairs.

1851 The attacks of the Wainriders upon Gondor begin.

1856 Gondor loses its eastern territories, and Narmacil II falls in battle.

1899 King Calimehtar defeats the Wainriders on Dagorlad.

1900 Calimehtar builds the White Tower in Minas Anor.

1940 Gondor and Arnor renew communications and form an alliance. Arvedui weds Fíriel daughter of Ondoher of Gondor.

1944 Ondoher falls in battle. Eärnil defeats the enemy in South Ithilien. He then wins the Battle of the Camp, and drives Wainriders into the Dead Marshes. Arvedui claims the crown of Gondor.

1945 Eärnil II receives the crown.

1974 End of the North-kingdom. The Witch-king overruns Arthedain and takes Fornost.

1975 Arvedui drowned in the Bay of Forochel. The *palantíri* of Annúminas and Amon Sûl are lost. Eärnur brings a fleet to Lindon. The Witch-king defeated at the Battle of Fornost, and pursued to the Ettenmoors. He vanishes from the North.

1976 Aranarth takes the title of Chieftain of the Dúnedain. The heirlooms of Arnor are given into the keeping of Elrond.

1977 Frumgar leads the Éothéod into the North.

1979 Bucca of the Marish becomes first Thain of the Shire.

1980 The Witch-king comes to Mordor and there gathers the Nazgûl. A Balrog appears in Moria, and slays Durin VI.

1981 Náin I slain. The Dwarves flee from Moria. Many of the Silvan Elves of Lórien flee south. Amroth and Nimrodel are lost.

1999 Thráin I comes to Erebor and founds a dwarf-kingdom 'under the Mountain'.

2000 The Nazgûl issue from Mordor and besiege Minas Ithil.

2002 Fall of Minas Ithil, afterwards known as Minas Morgul. The *palantír* is captured.

2043 Eärnur becomes King of Gondor. He is challenged by the Witch-king.

2050 The challenge is renewed. Eärnur rides to Minas Morgul and is lost. Mardil becomes the first Ruling Steward.

2060 The power of Dol Guldur grows. The Wise fear that it may be Sauron taking shape again.

2063 Gandalf goes to Dol Guldur. Sauron retreats and hides in the East. The Watchful Peace begins. The Nazgûl remain quiet in Minas Morgul.

2210 Thorin I leaves Erebor, and goes north to the Grey Mountains, where most of the remnants of Durin's Folk are now gathering.

2340 Isumbras I becomes thirteenth Thain, and first of the Took line. The Oldbucks occupy the Buckland.

2460 The Watchful Peace ends. Sauron returns with increased strength to Dol Guldur.

2463 The White Council is formed. About this time Déagol the Stoor finds the One Ring, and is murdered by Sméagol.

2470 About this time Sméagol-Gollum hides in the Misty Mountains.

2475 Attack on Gondor renewed. Osgiliath finally ruined, and its stone-bridge broken.

c. 2480 Orcs begin to make secret strongholds in the Misty Mountains so as to bar all the passes into Eriador. Sauron begins to people Moria with his creatures.

2509 Celebrían, journeying to Lórien, is waylaid in the Redhorn Pass, and receives a poisoned wound.

2510 Celebrían departs over Sea. Orcs and Easterlings overrun Calenardhon. Eorl the Young wins the victory of the Field of Celebrant. The Rohirrim settle in Calenardhon.

2545 Eorl falls in battle in the Wold.

2569 Brego son of Eorl completes the Golden Hall.

2570 Baldor son of Brego enters the Forbidden Door and is lost. About this time Dragons reappear in the far North and begin to afflict the Dwarves.

2589 Dáin I slain by a Dragon.

2590 Thrór returns to Erebor. Grór his brother goes to the Iron Hills.

c. 2670 Tobold plants 'pipe-weed' in the Southfarthing.

2683 Isengrim II becomes tenth Thain and begins the excavation of Great Smials.

2698 Ecthelion I rebuilds the White Tower in Minas Tirith.

2740 Orcs renew their invasions of Eriador.

2747 Bandobras Took defeats an Orc-band in the Northfarthing.

2758 Rohan attacked from west and east and overrun. Gondor attacked by fleets of the Corsairs. Helm of Rohan takes refuge in Helm's Deep. Wulf seizes Edoras. 2758–9: The Long Winter follows. Great suffering and loss of life in Eriador and Rohan. Gandalf comes to the aid of the Shire-folk.

2759 Death of Helm. Fréaláf drives out Wulf, and begins second line of Kings of the Mark. Saruman takes up his abode in Isengard.

2770 Smaug the Dragon descends on Erebor. Dale destroyed. Thrór escapes with Thráin II and Thorin II.

2790 Thrór slain by an Orc in Moria. The Dwarves gather for a war of vengeance. Birth of Gerontius, later known as the Old Took.

2793 The War of the Dwarves and Orcs begins.

2799 Battle of Nanduhirion before the East-gate of Moria. Dáin Ironfoot returns to the Iron Hills. Thráin II and his son Thorin wander westwards. They settle in the South of Ered Luin beyond the Shire (2802).

2800-64 Orcs from the North trouble Rohan. King Walda slain by them (2861).

2841 Thráin II sets out to revisit Erebor, but is pursued by the servants of Sauron.

2845 Thráin the Dwarf is imprisoned in Dol Guldur; the last of the Seven Rings is taken from him.

2850 Gandalf again enters Dol Guldur, and discovers that its master is indeed Sauron, who is gathering all the Rings and seeking for news of the One, and of Isildur's Heir. He finds Thráin and receives the key of Erebor. Thráin dies in Dol Guldur.

2851 The White Council meets. Gandalf urges an attack on Dol Guldur. Saruman overrules him.[1] Saruman begins to search near the Gladden Fields.

2852 Belecthor II of Gondor dies. The White Tree dies, and no seedling can be found. The Dead Tree is left standing.

2885 Stirred up by emissaries of Sauron the Haradrim cross the Poros and attack Gondor. The sons of Folcwine of Rohan are slain in the service of Gondor.

2890 Bilbo born in the Shire.

2901 Most of the remaining inhabitants of Ithilien desert it owing to the attacks of Uruks of Mordor. The secret refuge of Henneth Annûn is built.

2907 Birth of Gilraen mother of Aragorn II.

2911 The Fell Winter. The Baranduin and other rivers are frozen. White Wolves invade Eriador from the North.

2912 Great floods devastate Enedwaith and Minhiriath. Tharbad is ruined and deserted.

2920 Death of the Old Took.

2929 Arathorn son of Arador of the Dúnedain weds Gilraen.

2930 Arador slain by Trolls. Birth of Denethor II son of Ecthelion II in Minas Tirith.

2931 Aragorn son of Arathorn II born on March 1st.

2933 Arathorn II slain. Gilraen takes Aragorn to Imladris. Elrond receives

[1] It afterwards became clear that Saruman had then begun to desire to possess the One Ring himself, and he hoped that it might reveal itself, seeking its master, if Sauron were let be for a time.

him as foster-son and gives him the name Estel (Hope); his ancestry is
concealed.

2939   Saruman discovers that Sauron's servants are searching the Anduin near
Gladden Fields, and that Sauron therefore has learned of Isildur's end.
He is alarmed, but says nothing to the Council.

2941   Thorin Oakenshield and Gandalf visit Bilbo in the Shire. Bilbo meets
Sméagol-Gollum and finds the Ring. The White Council meets;
Saruman agrees to an attack on Dol Guldur, since he now wishes to
prevent Sauron from searching the River. Sauron having made his plans
abandons Dol Guldur. The Battle of the Five Armies in Dale. Death of
Thorin II. Bard of Esgaroth slays Smaug. Dáin of the Iron Hills becomes
King under the Mountain (Dáin II).

2942   Bilbo returns to the Shire with the Ring. Sauron returns in secret to
Mordor.

2944   Bard rebuilds Dale and becomes King. Gollum leaves the Mountains
and begins his search for the 'thief' of the Ring.

2948   Théoden son of Thengel, King of Rohan, born.

2949   Gandalf and Balin visit Bilbo in the Shire.

2950   Finduilas, daughter of Adrahil of Dol Amroth, born.

2951   Sauron declares himself openly and gathers power in Mordor. He begins
the rebuilding of Barad-dûr. Gollum turns towards Mordor. Sauron
sends three of the Nazgûl to reoccupy Dol Guldur.

      Elrond reveals to 'Estel' his true name and ancestry, and delivers to
him the shards of Narsil. Arwen, newly returned from Lórien, meets
Aragorn in the woods of Imladris. Aragorn goes out into the Wild.

2953   Last meeting of the White Council. They debate the Rings. Saruman
feigns that he has discovered that the One Ring has passed down Anduin
to the Sea. Saruman withdraws to Isengard, which he takes as his own,
and fortifies it. Being jealous and afraid of Gandalf he sets spies to watch
all his movements; and notes his interest in the Shire. He soon begins
to keep agents in Bree and the Southfarthing.

2954   Mount Doom bursts into flame again. The last inhabitants of Ithilien
flee over Anduin.

2956   Aragorn meets Gandalf and their friendship begins.

2957–80 Aragorn undertakes his great journeys and errantries. As Thorongil he
serves in disguise both Thengel of Rohan and Ecthelion II of Gondor.

2968   Birth of Frodo.

2976   Denethor weds Finduilas of Dol Amroth.

2977   Bain son of Bard becomes King of Dale.

2978   Birth of Boromir son of Denethor II.

2980   Aragorn enters Lórien, and there meets again Arwen Undómiel. Aragorn
gives her the ring of Barahir, and they plight their troth upon the hill
of Cerin Amroth. About this time Gollum reaches the confines of Mordor
and becomes acquainted with Shelob. Théoden becomes King of Rohan.

2983   Faramir son of Denethor born. Birth of Samwise.

2984   Death of Ecthelion II. Denethor II becomes Steward of Gondor.

2988 Finduilas dies young.

2989 Balin leaves Erebor and enters Moria.

2991 Éomer Éomund's son born in Rohan.

2994 Balin perishes, and the dwarf-colony is destroyed.

2995 Éowyn sister of Éomer born.

c. 3000 The shadow of Mordor lengthens. Saruman dares to use the *palantír* of Orthanc, but becomes ensnared by Sauron, who has the Ithil Stone. He becomes a traitor to the Council. His spies report that the Shire is being closely guarded by the Rangers.

3001 Bilbo's farewell feast. Gandalf suspects his ring to be the One Ring. The guard on the Shire is doubled. Gandalf seeks for news of Gollum and calls on the help of Aragorn.

3002 Bilbo becomes a guest of Elrond, and settles in Rivendell.

3004 Gandalf visits Frodo in the Shire, and does so at intervals during the next four years.

3007 Brand son of Bain becomes King in Dale. Death of Gilraen.

3008 In the autumn Gandalf pays his last visit to Frodo.

3009 Gandalf and Aragorn renew their hunt for Gollum at intervals during the next eight years, searching in the vales of Anduin, Mirkwood, and Rhovanion to the confines of Mordor. At some time during these years Gollum himself ventured into Mordor, and was captured by Sauron. Elrond sends for Arwen, and she returns to Imladris; the Mountains and all lands eastward are becoming dangerous.

3017 Gollum is released from Mordor. He is taken by Aragorn in the Dead Marshes, and brought to Thranduil in Mirkwood. Gandalf visits Minas Tirith and reads the scroll of Isildur.

THE GREAT YEARS
3018

April

12 Gandalf reaches Hobbiton.

June

20 Sauron attacks Osgiliath. About the same time Thranduil is attacked, and Gollum escapes.

July

4 Boromir sets out from Minas Tirith.

10 Gandalf imprisoned in Orthanc.

August

All trace of Gollum is lost. It is thought that at about this time, being hunted

both by the Elves and Sauron's servants, he took refuge in Moria; but when
he had at last discovered the way to the West-gate he could not get out.

September

18 Gandalf escapes from Orthanc in the early hours. The Black Riders cross
    the Fords of Isen.
19 Gandalf comes to Edoras as a beggar, and is refused admittance.
20 Gandalf gains entrance to Edoras. Théoden commands him to go: 'Take
    any horse, only be gone ere tomorrow is old!'
21 Gandalf meets Shadowfax, but the horse will not allow him to come near.
    He follows Shadowfax far over the fields.
22 The Black Riders reach Sarn Ford at evening; they drive off the guard of
    Rangers. Gandalf overtakes Shadowfax.
23 Four Riders enter the Shire before dawn. The others pursue the Rangers
    eastward, and then return to watch the Greenway. A Black Rider comes to
    Hobbiton at nightfall. Frodo leaves Bag End. Gandalf having tamed
    Shadowfax rides from Rohan.
24 Gandalf crosses the Isen.
26 The Old Forest. Frodo comes to Bombadil.
27 Gandalf crosses Greyflood. Second night with Bombadil.
28 The Hobbits captured by a Barrow-wight. Gandalf reaches Sarn Ford.
29 Frodo reaches Bree at night. Gandalf visits the Gaffer.
30 Crickhollow and the Inn at Bree are raided in the early hours. Frodo leaves
    Bree. Gandalf comes to Crickhollow, and reaches Bree at night.

October

 1 Gandalf leaves Bree.
 3 He is attacked at night on Weathertop.
 6 The camp under Weathertop attacked at night. Frodo wounded.
 9 Glorfindel leaves Rivendell.
11 He drives the Riders off the Bridge of Mitheithel.
13 Frodo crosses the Bridge.
18 Glorfindel finds Frodo at dusk. Gandalf reaches Rivendell.
20 Escape across the Ford of Bruinen.
24 Frodo recovers and wakes. Boromir arrives in Rivendell at night.
25 Council of Elrond.

December

25 The Company of the Ring leaves Rivendell at dusk.

3019
January

 8 The Company reach Hollin.

11, 12 Snow on Caradhras.
13 Attack by Wolves in the early hours. The Company reaches West-gate of Moria at nightfall. Gollum begins to trail the Ringbearer.
14 Night in Hall Twenty-one.
15 The Bridge of Khazad-dûm, and fall of Gandalf. The Comp reaches Nimro-del late at night.
17 The Company comes to Caras Galadhon at evening.
23 Gandalf pursues the Balrog to the peak of Zirakzigil.
25 He casts down the Balrog, and passes away. His body lies on the peak.

February

14 The Mirror of Galadriel. Gandalf returns to life, and lies in a trance.
16 Farewell to Lórien. Gollum in hiding on the west bank observes the departure.
17 Gwaihir bears Gandalf to Lórien.
23 The boats are attacked at night near Sarn Gebir.
25 The Company pass the Argonath and camp at Parth Galen. First Battle of the Fords of Isen; Théodred son of Théoden slain.
26 Breaking of the Fellowship. Death of Boromir; his horn is heard in Minas Tirith. Meriadoc and Peregrin captured. Frodo and Samwise enter the eastern Emyn Muil. Aragorn sets out in pursuit of the Orcs at evening. Éomer hears of the descent of the Orc-band from Emyn Muil.
27 Aragorn reaches the west-cliff at sunrise. Éomer against Théoden's orders sets out from Eastfold about midnight to pursue the Orcs.
28 Éomer overtakes the Orcs just outside Fangorn Forest.
29 Meriadoc and Pippin escape and meet Treebeard. The Rohirrim attack at sunrise and destroy the Orcs. Frodo descends from the Emyn Muil and meets Gollum. Faramir sees the funeral boat of Boromir.
30 Entmoot begins. Éomer returning to Edoras meets Aragorn.

March

1 Frodo begins the passage of the Dead Marshes at dawn. Entmoot continues. Aragorn meets Gandalf the White. They set out for Edoras. Faramir leaves Minas Tirith on an errand to Ithilien.
2 Frodo comes to the end of the Marshes. Gandalf comes to Edoras and heals Théoden. The Rohirrim ride west against Saruman. Second Battle of Fords of Isen. Erkenbrand defeated. Entmoot ends in afternoon. The Ents march on Isengard and reach it at night.
3 Théoden retreats to Helm's Deep. Battle of the Hornburg begins. Ents complete the destruction of Isengard.
4 Théoden and Gandalf set out from Helm's Deep for Isengard. Frodo reaches the slag-mounds on the edge of the Desolation of the Morannon.
5 Théoden reaches Isengard at noon. Parley with Saruman in Orthanc. Winged Nazgûl passes over the camp at Dol Baran. Gandalf sets out with

Peregrin for Minas Tirith. Frodo hides in sight of the Morannon, and leaves at dusk.

6 Aragorn overtaken by the Dúnedain in the early hours. Théoden sets out from the Hornburg for Harrowdale. Aragorn sets out later.

7 Frodo taken by Faramir to Henneth Annûn. Aragorn comes to Dunharrow at nightfall.

8 Aragorn takes the 'Paths of the Dead' at daybreak; he reaches Erech at midnight. Frodo leaves Henneth Annûn.

9 Gandalf reaches Minas Tirith. Faramir leaves Henneth Annûn. Aragorn sets out from Erech and comes to Calembel. At dusk Frodo reaches the Morgul-road. Théoden comes to Dunharrow. Darkness begins to flow out of Mordor.

10 The Dawnless Day. The Muster of Rohan: the Rohirrim ride from Harrowdale. Faramir rescued by Gandalf outside the gates of the City. Aragorn crosses Ringló. An army from the Morannon takes Cair Andros and passes into Anórien. Frodo passes the Cross Roads, and sees the Morgul-host set forth.

11 Gollum visits Shelob, but seeing Frodo asleep nearly repents. Denethor sends Faramir to Osgiliath. Aragorn reaches Linhir and crosses into Lebennin. Eastern Rohan is invaded from the north. First assault on Lórien.

12 Gollum leads Frodo into Shelob's lair. Faramir retreats to the Causeway Forts. Théoden camps under Minrimmon. Aragorn drives the enemy towards Pelargir. The Ents defeat the invaders of Rohan.

13 Frodo captured by the Orcs of Cirith Ungol. The Pelennor is overrun. Faramir is wounded. Aragorn reaches Pelargir and captures the fleet. Théoden in Drúadan Forest.

14 Samwise finds Frodo in the Tower. Minas Tirith is besieged. The Rohirrim led by the Wild Men come to the Grey Wood.

15 In the early hours the Witch-king breaks the Gates of the City. Denethor burns himself on a pyre. The horns of the Rohirrim are heard at cockcrow. Battle of the Pelennor. Théoden is slain. Aragorn raises the standard of Arwen. Frodo and Samwise escape and begin their journey north along the Morgai. Battle under the trees in Mirkwood; Thranduil repels the forces of Dol Guldur. Second assault on Lórien.

16 Debate of the commanders. Frodo from the Morgai looks out over the camp to Mount Doom.

17 Battle of Dale. King Brand and King Dáin Ironfoot fall. Many Dwarves and Men take refuge in Erebor and are besieged. Shagrat brings Frodo's cloak, mail-shirt, and sword to Barad-dûr.

18 The Host of the West marches from Minas Tirith. Frodo comes in sight of the Isenmouthe; he is overtaken by Orcs on the road from Durthang to Udûn.

19 The Host comes to Morgul-vale. Frodo and Samwise escape and begin their journey along the road to the Barad-dûr.

22 The dreadful nightfall. Frodo and Samwise leave the road and turn south to Mount Doom. Third assault on Lórien.

23 The Host passes out of Ithilien. Aragorn dismisses the faint-hearted. Frodo and Samwise cast away their arms and gear.

24 Frodo and Samwise make their last journey to the feet of Mount Doom. The Host camps in the Desolation of the Morannon.

25 The Host is surrounded on the Slag-hills. Frodo and Samwise reach the Sammath Naur. Gollum seizes the Ring and falls in the Cracks of Doom. Downfall of Barad-dûr and passing of Sauron.

After the fall of the Dark Tower and the passing of Sauron the Shadow was lifted from the hearts of all who opposed him, but fear and despair fell upon his servants and allies. Three times Lórien had been assailed from Dol Guldur, but besides the valour of the elven people of that land, the power that dwelt there was too great for any to overcome, unless Sauron had come there himself. Though grievous harm was done to the fair woods on the borders, the assaults were driven back; and when the Shadow passed, Celeborn came forth and led the host of Lórien over Anduin in many boats. They took Dol Guldur, and Galadriel threw down its walls and laid bare its pits, and the forest was cleansed.

In the North also there had been war and evil. The realm of Thranduil was invaded, and there was long battle under the trees and great ruin of fire; but in the end Thranduil had the victory. And on the day of the New Year of the Elves, Celeborn and Thranduil met in the midst of the forest; and they renamed Mirkwood *Eryn Lasgalen*, The Wood of Greenleaves. Thranduil took all the northern region as far as the mountains that rise in the forest for his realm; and Celeborn took all the southern wood below the Narrows, and named it East Lórien; all the wide forest between was given to the Beornings and the Woodmen. But after the passing of Galadriel in a few years Celeborn grew weary of his realm and went to Imladris to dwell with the sons of Elrond. In the Greenwood the Silvan Elves remained untroubled, but in Lórien there lingered sadly only a few of its former people, and there was no longer light or song in Caras Galadhon.

At the same time as the great armies besieged Minas Tirith a host of the allies of Sauron that had long threatened the borders of King Brand crossed the River Carnen, and Brand was driven back to Dale. There he had the aid of the Dwarves of Erebor; and there was a great battle at the Mountain's feet. It lasted three days, but in the end both King Brand and King Dáin Ironfoot were slain, and the Easterlings had the victory. But they could not take the Gate, and many, both Dwarves and Men, took refuge in Erebor, and there withstood a siege.

When news came of the great victories in the South, then Sauron's northern army was filled with dismay; and the besieged came forth and routed them, and the remnant fled into the East and troubled Dale no more. Then Bard II, Brand's son, became King in Dale, and Thorin III Stonehelm, Dáin's son, became King under the Mountain. They sent their ambassadors to the crowning of King Elessar; and their realms remained ever after, as long as they lasted, in friendship with Gondor; and they were under the crown and protection of the King of the West.

APPENDIX B
THE CHIEF DAYS
FROM THE FALL OF BARAD-DÛR TO THE END
OF THE THIRD AGE[1]

3019
S.R. 1419

March 27. Bard II and Thorin III Stonehelm drive the enemy from Dale.

28. Celeborn crosses Anduin; destruction of Dol Guldur begun.

April 6. Meeting of Celeborn and Thranduil.

8. The Ring-bearers are honoured on the Field of Cormallen.

May 1. Crowning of King Elessar; Elrond and Arwen set out from Rivendell.

8. Éomer and Éowyn depart from Rohan with the sons of Elrond.

20. Elrond and Arwen come to Lórien.

27. The escort of Arwen leaves Lórien.

June 14. The sons of Elrond meet the escort and bring Arwen to Edoras.

16. They set out for Gondor.

25. King Elessar finds the sapling of the White Tree.

1 Lithe. Arwen comes to the City.

Mid-year's Day. Wedding of Elessar and Arwen.

July 18. Éomer returns to Minas Tirith.

19. The funeral escort of King Théoden sets out.

August 7. The escort comes to Edoras.

10. Funeral of King Théoden.

14. The guests take leave of King Éomer.

18. They come to Helm's Deep.

22. They come to Isengard; they take leave of the King of the West at sunset.

28. They overtake Saruman; Saruman turns towards the Shire.

September 6. They halt in sight of the Mountains of Moria.

13. Celeborn and Galadriel depart, the others set out for Rivendell.

21. They return to Rivendell.

22. The hundred and twenty-ninth birthday of Bilbo. Saruman comes to the Shire.

October 5. Gandalf and the Hobbits leave Rivendell.

6. They cross the Ford of Bruinen; Frodo feels the first return of pain.

28. They reach Bree at nightfall.

30. They leave Bree. The 'Travellers' come to the Brandywine Bridge at dark.

November 1. They are arrested at Frogmorton.

2. They come to Bywater and rouse the Shire-folk.

3. Battle of Bywater, and Passing of Saruman. End of the War of the Ring.

[1] Months and days are given according to the Shire Calendar.

3020
S.R. 1420: The Great Year of Plenty

March 13. Frodo is taken ill (on the anniversary of his poisoning by Shelob).
April 6. The mallorn flowers in the Party Field.
May 1. Samwise marries Rose.
Mid-year's Day. Frodo resigns office of mayor, and Will Whitfoot is restored.
September 22. Bilbo's hundred and thirtieth birthday.
October 6. Frodo is again ill.

3021
S.R. 1421: The Last of the Third Age

March 13. Frodo is again ill.
25. Birth of Elanor the Fair,[1] daughter of Samwise. On this day the Fourth Age began in the reckoning of Gondor.
September 21. Frodo and Samwise set out from Hobbiton.
22. They meet the Last Riding of the Keepers of the Rings in Woody End.
29. They come to the Grey Havens. Frodo and Bilbo depart over Sea with the Three Keepers. The end of the Third Age.
October 6. Samwise returns to Bag End.

LATER EVENTS CONCERNING THE MEMBERS OF THE FELLOWSHIP OF THE RING

S.R.

1422 With the beginning of this year the Fourth Age began in the count of years in the Shire; but the numbers of the years of Shire Reckoning were continued.

1427 Will Whitfoot resigns. Samwise is elected Mayor of the Shire. Peregrin Took marries Diamond of Long Cleeve. King Elessar issues an edict that Men are not to enter the Shire, and he makes it a Free Land under the protection of the Northern Sceptre.

1430 Faramir, son of Peregrin, born.

1431 Goldilocks, daughter of Samwise, born.

1432 Meriadoc, called the Magnificent, becomes Master of Buckland. Great gifts are sent to him by King Éomer and the Lady Éowyn of Ithilien.

1434 Peregrin becomes the Took and Thain. King Elessar makes the Thain, the Master, and the Mayor Counsellors of the North-kingdom. Master Samwise is elected Mayor for the second time.

1436 King Elessar rides north, and dwells for a while by Lake Evendim. He

---

[1] She became known as 'the Fair' because of her beauty; many said that she looked more like an elf-maid than a hobbit. She had golden hair, which had been very rare in the Shire; but two others of Samwise's daughters were also golden-haired, and so were many of the children born at this time.

comes to the Brandywine Bridge, and there greets his friends. He gives the Star of the Dúnedain to Master Samwise, and Elanor is made a maid of honour to Queen Arwen.

1441 Master Samwise becomes Mayor for the third time.

1442 Master Samwise and his wife and Elanor ride to Gondor and stay there for a year. Master Tolman Cotton acts as deputy Mayor.

1448 Master Samwise becomes Mayor for the fourth time.

1451 Elanor the Fair marries Fastred of Greenholm on the Far Downs.

1452 The Westmarch, from the Far Downs to the Tower Hills (*Emyn Beraid*),[1] is added to the Shire by the gift of the King. Many hobbits remove to it.

1454 Elfstan Fairbairn, son of Fastred and Elanor, is born.

1455 Master Samwise becomes Mayor for the fifth time. At his request the Thain makes Fastred Warden of Westmarch. Fastred and Elanor make their dwelling at Undertowers on the Tower Hills, where their descendants, the Fairbairns of the Towers, dwelt for many generations.

1462 Master Samwise becomes Mayor for the sixth time.

1463 Faramir Took marries Goldilocks, daughter of Samwise.

1469 Master Samwise becomes Mayor for the seventh and last time, being in 1476, at the end of his office, ninety-six years old.

1482 Death of Mistress Rose, wife of Master Samwise, on Mid-year's Day. On September 22 Master Samwise rides out from Bag End. He comes to the Tower Hills, and is last seen by Elanor, to whom he gives the Red Book afterwards kept by the Fairbairns. Among them the tradition is handed down from Elanor that Samwise passed the Towers, and went to the Grey Havens, and passed over Sea, last of the Ring-bearers.

1484 In the spring of the year a message came from Rohan to Buckland that King Éomer wished to see Master Holdwine once again. Meriadoc was then old (102) but still hale. He took counsel with his friend the Thain, and soon after they handed over their goods and offices to their sons and rode away over the Sarn Ford, and they were not seen again in the Shire. It was heard after that Master Meriadoc came to Edoras and was with King Éomer before he died in that autumn. Then he and Thain Peregrin went to Gondor and passed what short years were left to them in that realm, until they died and were laid in Rath Dínen among the great of Gondor.

1541 In this year[2] on March 1st came at last the Passing of King Elessar. It is said that the beds of Meriadoc and Peregrin were set beside the bed of the great king. Then Legolas built a grey ship in Ithilien, and sailed down Anduin and so over Sea; and with him, it is said, went Gimli the Dwarf. And when that ship passed an end was come in Middle-earth of the Fellowship of the Ring.

---

[1] pp. 6–7, 1018, note 2.
[2] Fourth Age (Gondor) 120.

APPENDIX C

FAMILY TREES

The names given in these Trees are only a selection from many. Most of them are either guests at Bilbo's Farewell Party, or their direct ancestors. The guests at the Party are underlined. A few other names of persons concerned in the events recounted are also given. In addition some genealogical information is provided concerning Samwise the founder of the family of *Gardner*, later famous and influential.

The figures after the names are those of birth (and death where that is recorded). All dates are given according to the Shire-reckoning, calculated from the crossing of the Brandywine by the brothers Marcho and Blanco in the Year 1 of the Shire (Third Age 1601).

BAGGINS OF HOBBITON

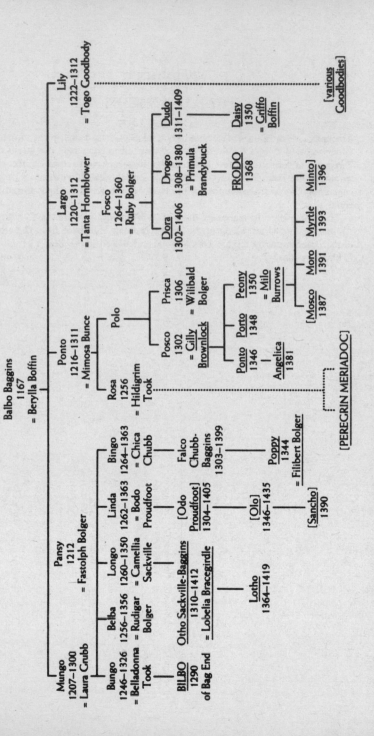

TOOK OF GREAT SMIALS

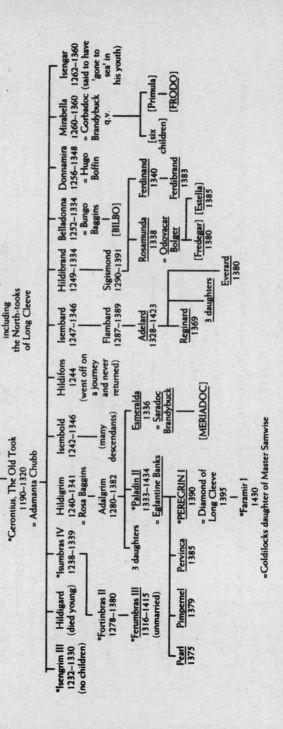

BRANDYBUCK OF BUCKLAND

Gorhendad Oldbuck of the Marish, c. 740 began the building of *Brandy Hall* and changed the family name to *Brandybuck*.

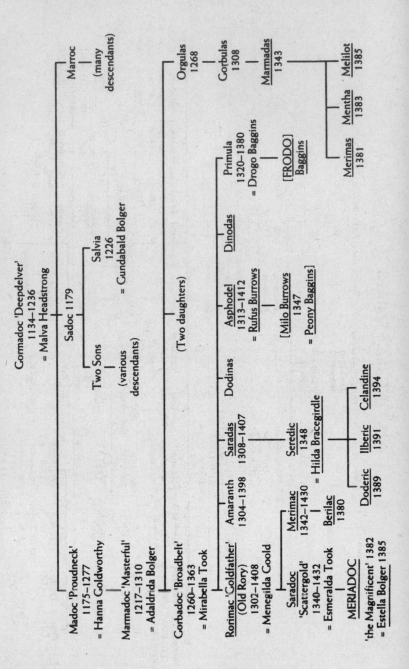

THE LONGFATHER-TREE OF MASTER SAMWISE

(showing also the rise of the families of Gardner of the Hill and of Fairbairn of the Towers.)

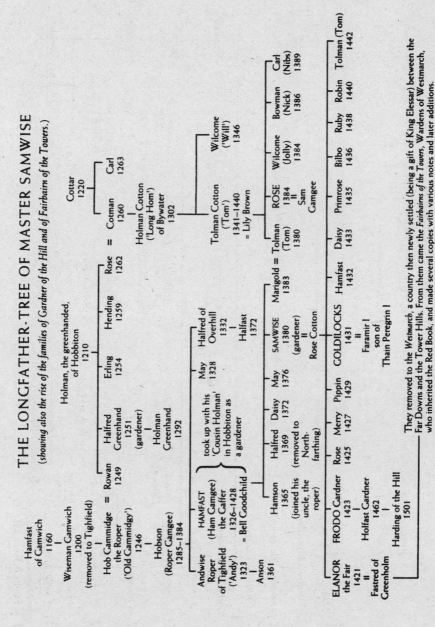

They removed to the *Westmarch*, a country then newly settled (being a gift of King Elessar) between the Far Downs and the Tower Hills. From them came the *Fairbairns of the Towers*, Wardens of *Westmarch*, who inherited the Red Book, and made several copies with various notes and later additions.

SHIRE CALENDAR

FOR USE IN ALL YEARS

(1) *Afteryule*	(4) *Astron*	(7) *Afterlithe*	(10) *Winterfilth*
ʏᴜʟᴇ 7 14 21 28	1 8 15 22 29	ʟɪᴛʜᴇ 7 14 21 28	1 8 15 22 29
1 8 15 22 29	2 9 16 23 30	1 8 15 22 29	2 9 16 23 30
2 9 16 23 30	3 10 17 24 –	2 9 16 23 30	3 10 17 24 –
3 10 17 24 –	4 11 18 25 –	3 10 17 24 –	4 11 18 25 –
4 11 18 25 –	5 12 19 26 –	4 11 18 25 –	5 12 19 26 –
5 12 19 26 –	6 13 20 27 –	5 12 19 26 –	6 13 20 27 –
6 13 20 27 –	7 14 21 28 –	6 13 20 27 –	7 14 21 28 –

(2) *Solmath*	(5) *Thrimidge*	(8) *Wedmath*	(11) *Blotmath*
– 5 12 19 26	– 6 13 20 27	– 5 12 19 26	– 6 13 20 27
– 6 13 20 27	– 7 14 21 28	– 6 13 20 27	– 7 14 21 28
– 7 14 21 28	1 8 15 22 29	– 7 14 21 28	1 8 15 22 29
1 8 15 22 29	2 9 16 23 30	1 8 15 22 29	2 9 16 23 30
2 9 16 23 30	3 10 17 24 –	2 9 16 23 30	3 10 17 24 –
3 10 17 24 –	4 11 18 25 –	3 10 17 24 –	4 11 18 25 –
4 11 18 25 –	5 12 19 26 –	4 11 18 25 –	5 12 19 26 –

(3) *Rethe*	(6) *Forelithe*	(9) *Halimath*	(12) *Foreyule*
– 3 10 17 24	– 4 11 18 25	– 3 10 17 24	– 4 11 18 25
– 4 11 18 25	– 5 12 19 26	– 4 11 18 25	– 5 12 19 26
– 5 12 19 26	– 6 13 20 27	– 5 12 19 26	– 6 13 20 27
– 6 13 20 27	– 7 14 21 28	– 6 13 20 27	– 7 14 21 28
– 7 14 21 28	1 8 15 22 29	– 7 14 21 28	1 8 15 22 29
1 8 15 22 29	2 9 16 23 30	1 8 15 22 29	2 9 16 23 30
2 9 16 23 30	3 10 17 24 ʟɪᴛʜᴇ	2 9 16 23 30	3 10 17 24 ʏᴜʟᴇ
	Midyear's Day		
	(Overlithe)		

Every year began on the first day of the week, Saturday, and ended on the last day of the week, Friday. The Mid-year's Day, and in Leap-years the Overlithe, had no weekday name. The Lithe before Mid-year's Day was called 1 Lithe, and the one after was called 2 Lithe. The Yule at the end of the year was 1 Yule, and that at the beginning was 2 Yule. The Overlithe was a day of special holiday, but it did not occur in any of the years important to the history of the Great Ring. It occurred in 1420, the year of the famous harvest and wonderful summer, and the merrymaking in that year is said to have been the greatest in memory or record.

THE CALENDARS

The Calendar in the Shire differed in several features from ours. The year no doubt was of the same length,[1] for long ago as those times are now reckoned in years and lives of men, they were not very remote according to the memory of the Earth. It is recorded by the Hobbits that they had no 'week' when they were still a wandering people, and though they had 'months', governed more or less by the Moon, their keeping of dates and calculations of time were vague and inaccurate. In the westlands of Eriador, when they had begun to settle down, they adopted the King's reckoning of the Dúnedain, which was ultimately of Eldarin origin; but the Hobbits of the Shire introduced several minor alterations. This calendar, or 'Shire Reckoning' as it was called, was eventually adopted also in Bree, except for the Shire usage of counting as Year 1 the year of the colonization of the Shire.

It is often difficult to discover from old tales and traditions precise information about things which people knew well and took for granted in their own day (such as the names of letters, or of the days of the week, or the names and lengths of months). But owing to their general interest in genealogy, and to the interest in ancient history which the learned amongst them developed after the War of the Ring, the Shire-hobbits seem to have concerned themselves a good deal with dates; and they even drew up complicated tables showing the relations of their own system with others. I am not skilled in these matters, and may have made many errors; but at any rate the chronology of the crucial years S.R. 1418, 1419 is so carefully set out in the Red Book that there cannot be much doubt about days and times at that point.

It seems clear that the Eldar in Middle-earth, who had, as Samwise remarked, more time at their disposal, reckoned in long periods, and the Quenya word *yén*, often translated 'year' (p. 368), really means 144 of our years. The Eldar preferred to reckon in sixes and twelves as far as possible. A 'day' of the sun they called *ré* and reckoned from sunset to sunset. The *yén* contained 52,596 days. For ritual rather than practical purposes the Eldar observed a week or *enquië* of six days; and the *yén* contained 8,766 of these *enquier*, reckoned continuously throughout the period.

In Middle-earth the Eldar also observed a short period or solar year, called a *coranar* or 'sun-round' when considered more or less astronomically, but usually called *loa* 'growth' (especially in the north-western lands) when the seasonal changes in vegetation were primarily considered, as was usual with the Elves generally. The *loa* was broken up into periods that might be regarded either as long months or short seasons. These no doubt varied in different regions; but the Hobbits only provide information concerning the Calendar of Imladris. In that calendar there were six of these 'seasons', of which the Quenya names were *tuilë, lairë, yávië, quellë, hrívë, coirë*, which may be translated 'spring, summer, autumn, fading, winter, stirring'. The Sindarin names were *ethuil, laer, iavas, firith, rhîw, echuir*. 'Fading' was also called *lasse-lanta* 'leaf-fall', or in Sindarin *narbeleth* 'sun-waning'.

Lairë and *hrívë* each contained 72 days, and the remainder 54 each. The *loa* began

[1] 365 days, 5 hours, 48 minutes, 46 seconds.

with *yestarë*, the day immediately before *tuilë*, and ended with *mettarë*, the day immediately after *coirë*. Between *yávië* and *quellë* were inserted three *enderi* or 'middle-days'. This provided a year of 365 days which was supplemented by doubling the *enderi* (adding 3 days) in every twelfth year.

How any resulting inaccuracy was dealt with is uncertain. If the year was then of the same length as now, the *yén* would have been more than a day too long. That there was an inaccuracy is shown by a note in the Calendars of the Red Book to the effect that in the 'Reckoning of Rivendell' the last year of every third *yén* was shortened by three days: the doubling of the three *enderi* due in that year was omitted; 'but that has not happened in our time'. Of the adjustment of any remaining inaccuracy there is no record.

The Númenoreans altered these arrangements. They divided the *loa* into shorter periods of more regular length; and they adhered to the custom of beginning the year in mid-winter, which had been used by Men of the North-west from whom they were derived in the First Age. Later they also made their week one of 7 days, and they reckoned the day from sunrise (out of the eastern sea) to sunrise.

The Númenorean system, as used in Númenor, and in Arnor and Gondor until the end of the kings, was called King's Reckoning. The normal year had 365 days. It was divided into twelve *astar* or months, of which ten had 30 days and two had 31. The long *astar* were those on either side of the Mid-year, approximately our June and July. The first day of the year was called *yestarë*, the middle day (183rd) was called *loëndë*, and the last day *mettarë*; these 3 days belonged to no month. In every fourth year, except the last of a century (*haranyë*), two *enderi* or 'middle-days' were substituted for the *loëndë*.

In Númenor calculation started with S.A. 1. The *Deficit* caused by deducting 1 day from the last year of a century was not adjusted until the last year of a millennium, leaving a *millennial deficit* of 4 hours, 46 minutes, 40 seconds. This addition was made in Númenor in S.A. 1000, 2000, 3000. After the Downfall in S.A. 3319 the system was maintained by the exiles, but it was much dislocated by the beginning of the Third Age with a new numeration: S.A. 3442 became T.A. 1. By making T.A. 4 a leap year instead of T.A. 3 (S.A. 3444) 1 more short year of only 365 days was intruded causing a deficit of 5 hours, 48 minutes, 46 seconds. The millennial additions were made 441 years late: in T.A. 1000 (S.A. 4441) and 2000 (S.A. 5441). To reduce the errors so caused, and the accumulation of the millennial deficits, Mardil the Steward issued a revised calendar to take effect in T.A. 2060, after a special addition of 2 days to 2059 (S.A. 5500), which concluded 5½ millennia since the beginning of the Númenorean system. But this still left about 8 hours deficit. Hador to 2360 added 1 day though this deficiency had not quite reached that amount. After that no more adjustments were made. (In T.A. 3000 with the threat of imminent war such matters were neglected.) By the end of the Third Age, after 660 more years, the Deficit had not yet amounted to 1 day.

The Revised Calendar introduced by Mardil was called Stewards' Reckoning and was adopted eventually by most of the users of the Westron language, except the Hobbits. The months were all of 30 days, and 2 days outside the months were introduced: 1 between the third and four months (March, April), and 1 between the ninth and tenth (September, October). These 5 days outside the months, *yestarë, tuilérë, loëndë, yáviérë*, and *mettarë*, were holidays.

The Hobbits were conservative and continued to use a form of Kings' Reckoning adapted to fit their own customs. Their months were all equal and had 30 days each; but they had 3 Summerdays, called in the Shire the Lithe or the Lithedays, between June and July. The last day of the year and the first of the next year were called the Yuledays. The Yuledays and the Lithedays remained outside the months, so that January 1 was the second and not the first day of the year. Every fourth year, except in the last year of the century,[1] there were four Lithedays. The Lithedays and the Yuledays were the chief holidays and times of feasting. The additional Litheday was added after Mid-year's Day, and so the 184th day of the Leap-years was called Overlithe and was a day of special merrymaking. In full Yuletide was six days long, including the last three and first three days of each year.

The Shire-folk introduced one small innovation of their own (eventually also adopted in Bree), which they called Shire-reform. They found the shifting of the weekday names in relation to dates from year to year untidy and inconvenient. So in the time of Isengrim II they arranged that the odd day which put the succession out, should have no weekday name. After that Mid-year's Day (and the Overlithe) was known only by its name and belonged to no week (p. 174). In consequence of this reform the year always began on the First Day of the week and ended on the Last Day; and the same date in any one year had the same weekday name in all other years, so that Shire-folk no longer bothered to put the weekday in their letters or diaries.[2] They found this quite convenient at home, but not so convenient if they ever travelled further than Bree.

In the above notes, as in the narrative, I have used our modern names for both months and weekdays, though of course neither the Eldar nor the Dúnedain nor the Hobbits actually did so. Translation of the Westron names seemed to be essential to avoid confusion, while the seasonal implications of our names are more or less the same, at any rate in the Shire. It appears, however, that Mid-year's Day was intended to correspond as nearly as possible to the summer solstice. In that case the Shire dates were actually in advance of ours by some ten days, and our New Year's Day corresponded more or less to the Shire January 9.

In the Westron the Quenya names of the months were usually retained as the Latin names are now widely used in alien languages. They were: *Narvinyë, Nénimë, Súlimë, Víressë, Lótessë, Nárië, Cermië, Urimë, Yavannië, Narquelië, Hísimë, Ringarë*. The Sindarin names (used only by the Dúnedain) were: *Narwain, Nínui, Gwaeron, Gwirith, Lothron, Nórui, Cerveth, Urui, Ivanneth, Narbeleth, Hithui, Girithron*.

[1] In the Shire, in which Year 1 corresponded with T.A. 1601. In Bree in which Year 1 corresponded with T.A. 1300 it was the first year of the century.

[2] It will be noted if one glances at a Shire Calendar, that the only weekday on which no month began was Friday. It thus became a jesting idiom in the Shire to speak of 'on Friday the first' when referring to a day that did not exist, or to a day on which very unlikely events such as the flying of pigs or (in the Shire) the walking of trees might occur. In full the expression was 'on Friday the first of Summerfilth'.

In this nomenclature the Hobbits, however, both of the Shire and of Bree, diverged from the Westron usage, and adhered to old-fashioned local names of their own, which they seem to have picked up in antiquity from the Men of the vales of Anduin; at any rate similar names were found in Dale and Rohan (cf. the notes on the languages, pp. 1162–3). The meanings of these names, devised by Men, had as a rule long been forgotten by the Hobbits, even in cases where they had originally known what their significance was; and the forms of the names were much obscured in consequence: *math*, for instance, at the end of some of them is a reduction of *month*.

The Shire names are set out in the Calendar. It may be noted that *Solmath* was usually pronounced, and sometimes written, *Somath*; *Thrimidge* was often written *Thrimich* (archaically *Thrimilch*); and *Blotmath* was pronounced *Blodmath* or *Blommath*. In Bree the names differed, being *Frery*, *Solmath*, *Rethe*, *Chithing*, *Thrimidge*, *Lithe*, *The Summerdays*, *Mede*, *Wedmath*, *Harvestmath*, *Wintring*, *Blooting*, and *Yulemath*. *Frery*, *Chithing* and *Yulemath* were also used in the Eastfarthing.[1]

The Hobbit week was taken from the Dúnedain, and the names were translations of those given to the days in the old North-kingdom, which in their turn were derived from the Eldar. The six-day week of the Eldar had days dedicated to, or named after, the Stars, the Sun, the Moon, the Two Trees, the Heavens, and the Valar or Powers, in that order, the last day being the chief day of the week. Their names in Quenya were *Elenya*, *Anarya*, *Isilya*, *Aldúya*, *Menelya*, *Valanya* (or *Tárion*); the Sindarin names were *Orgilion*, *Oranor*, *Orithil*, *Orgaladhad*, *Ormenel*, *Orbelain* (or *Rodyn*).

The Númenoreans retained the dedications and order, but altered the fourth day to *Aldëa* (*Orgaladh*) with reference to the White Tree only, of which Nimloth that grew in the King's Court in Númenor was believed to be a descendant. Also desiring a seventh day, and being great mariners, they inserted a 'Sea-day', *Eärenya* (*Oraearon*), after the Heavens' Day.

The Hobbits took over this arrangement, but the meanings of their translated names were soon forgotten, or no longer attended to, and the forms were much reduced, especially in everyday pronunciation. The first translation of the Númenorean names was probably made two thousand years or more before the end of the Third Age, when the week of Dúnedain (the feature of their reckoning earliest adopted by alien peoples) was taken up by Men in the North. As with their names of months, the Hobbits adhered to these translations, although elsewhere in the Westron area the Quenya names were used.

Not many ancient documents were preserved in the Shire. At the end of the Third Age far the most notable survival was Yellowskin, or the Yearbook of Tuckborough.[2] Its earliest entries seem to have begun at least nine hundred years before

---

[1] It was a jest in Bree to speak of 'Winterfilth in the (muddy) Shire', but according to the Shire-folk Wintring was a Bree alteration of the older name, which had originally referred to the filling or completion of the year before Winter, and descended from times before the full adoption of Kings' Reckoning when their new year began after harvest.

[2] Recording births, marriages, and deaths in the Took families, as well as matters, such as land-sales, and various Shire events.

Frodo's time; and many are cited in the Red Book annals and genealogies. In these the weekday names appear in archaic forms, of which the following are the oldest: (1) *Sterrendei*, (2) *Sunnendei*, (3) *Monendei*, (4) *Trewesdei*, (5) *Hevenesdei*, (6) *Meresdei*, (7) *Highdei*. In the language of the time of the War of the Ring these had become *Sterday*, *Sunday*, *Monday*, *Trewsday*, *Hevensday* (or *Hensday*), *Mersday*, *Highday*.

I have translated these names also into our own names, naturally beginning with Sunday and Monday, which occur in the Shire week with the same names as ours, and re-naming the others in order. It must be noted, however, that the associations of the names were quite different in the Shire. The last day of the week, Friday (Highday), was the chief days, and one of holiday (after noon) and evening feasts. Saturday thus corresponds more nearly to our Monday, and Thursday to our Saturday.[1]

A few other names may be mentioned that have a reference to time, though not used in precise reckonings. The seasons usually named were *tuilë* spring, *lairë* summer, *yávië* autumn (or harvest), *hrívë* winter; but these had no exact definitions, and *quellë* (or *lasselanta*) was also used for the latter part of autumn and the beginning of winter.

The Eldar paid special attention to the 'twilight' (in the northerly regions), chiefly as the times of star-fading and star-opening. They had many names for these periods, of which the most usual were *tindómë* and *undómë*; the former most often referred to the time near dawn, and *undómë* to the evening. The Sindarin name was *uial*, which could be defined as *minuial* and *aduial*. These were often called in the Shire *morrowdim* and *evendim*. Cf. Lake Evendim as a translation of Nenuial.

The Shire Reckoning and dates are the only ones of importance for the narrative of the War of the Ring. All the days, months, and dates are in the Red Book translated into Shire terms, or equated with them in notes. The months and days, therefore, throughout *The Lord of the Rings* refer to the Shire Calendar. The only points in which the differences between this and our calendar are important to the story at the crucial period, the end of 3018 and the beginning of 3019 (S.R. 1418, 1419), are these: October 1418 has only 30 days, January 1 is the second day of 1419, and February has 30 days; so that March 25, the date of the downfall of the Barad-dûr, would correspond to our March 27, if our years began at the same seasonal point. The date was, however, March 25 in both Kings' and Stewards' Reckoning.

The New Reckoning was begun in the restored Kingdom in T.A. 3019. It represented a return to Kings' Reckoning adapted to fit a spring-beginning as in the Eldarin *loa*.[2]

In the New Reckoning the year began on March 25 old style, in commemoration of the fall of Sauron and the deeds of the Ring-bearers. The months retained their

---

[1] I have therefore in Bilbo's song (pp. 155–6) used Saturday and Sunday instead of Thursday and Friday.

[2] Though actually the *yestarë* of New Reckoning occurred earlier than in the Calendar of Imladris, in which it corresponded more or less with Shire April 6.

former names, beginning now with *Víressë* (April), but referred to periods beginning generally five days earlier than previously. All the months had 30 days. There were 3 *Enderi* or Middle-days (of which the second was called *Loëndë*), between *Yavannië* (September) and *Narquelië* (October), that corresponded with September 23, 24, 25 old style. But in honour of Frodo *Yavannië* 30, which corresponded with former September 22, his birthday, was made a festival, and the leap-year was provided for by doubling this feast, called *Cormarë* or Ringday.

The Fourth Age was held to have begun with the departure of Master Elrond, which took place in September 3021; but for purposes of record in the Kingdom Fourth Age 1 was the year that began according to the New Reckoning in March 25, 3021, old style.

This reckoning was in the course of the reign of King Elessar adopted in all his lands except the Shire, where the old calendar was retained and Shire Reckoning was continued. Fourth Age 1 was thus called 1422; and in so far as the Hobbits took any account of the change of Age, they maintained that it began with 2 Yule 1422, and not in the previous March.

There is no record of the Shire-folk commemorating either March 25 or September 22; but in the Westfarthing, especially in the country round Hobbiton Hill, there grew up a custom of making holiday and dancing in the Party Field, when weather permitted, on April 6. Some said that it was old Sam Gardner's birthday, some that it was the day on which the Golden Tree first flowered in 1420, and some that it was the Elves' New Year. In the Buckland the Horn of the Mark was blown at sundown every November 2 and bonfires and feastings followed.[1]

---

[1] Anniversary of its first blowing in the Shire in 3019.

APPENDIX E

WRITING AND SPELLING

I
PRONUNCIATION OF WORDS AND NAMES

The Westron or Common Speech has been entirely translated into English equivalents. All Hobbit names and special words are intended to be pronounced accordingly: for example, *Bolger* has g as in *bulge*, and *mathom* rhymes with *fathom*.

In transcribing the ancient scripts I have tried to represent the original sounds (so far as they can be determined) with fair accuracy, and at the same time to produce words and names that do not look uncouth in modern letters. The High-elven Quenya has been spelt as much like Latin as its sounds allowed. For this reason *c* has been preferred to *k* in both Eldarin languages.

The following points may be observed by those who are interested in such details.

CONSONANTS

C has always the value of *k* even before *e* and *i*: *celeb* 'silver' should be pronounced as *keleb*.

CH is only used to represent the sound heard in *bach* (in German or Welsh), not that in English *church*. Except at the end of words and before *t* this sound was weakened to *h* in the speech of Gondor, and that change has been recognized in a few names, such as *Rohan*, *Rohirrim*. (*Imrahil* is a Númenorean name.)

DH represents the voiced (soft) *th* of English *these clothes*. It is usually related to *d*, as in S. *galadh* 'tree' compared with Q. *alda*; but is sometimes derived from *n* + *r*, as in *Caradhras* 'Redhorn' from *caran-rass*.

F represents *f*, except at the end of words, where it is used to represent the sound of *v* (as in English *of*): *Nindalf*, *Fladrif*.

G has only the sound of g in *give*, *get*: *gil* 'star', in *Gildor*, *Gilraen*, *Osgiliath*, begins as in English *gild*.

H standing alone with no other consonant has the sound of *h* in *house*, *behold*. The Quenya combination *ht* has the sound of *cht*, as in German *echt*, *acht*: e.g. in the name *Telumehtar* 'Orion'.[1] See also CH, DH, L, R, TH, W, Y.

I   initially before another vowel has the consonantal sound of *y* in *you*, *yore* in Sindarin only: as in *Ioreth*, *Iarwain*. See Y.

K is used in names drawn from other than Elvish languages, with the same value as *c*; *kh* thus represents the same sound as *ch* in Orkish *Grishnákh*, or Adûnaic (Númenorean) *Adunakhor*. On Dwarvish (Khuzdul) see note below.

---

[1] Usually called in Sindarin *Menelvagor* (p. 80), Q. *Menelmacar*.

L   represents more or less the sound of English initial *l*, as in *let*. It was, however, to some degree 'palatalized' between *e*, *i* and a consonant, or finally after *e*, *i*. (The Eldar would probably have transcribed English *bell*, *fill* as *beol*, *fiol*.) LH represents this sound when voiceless (usually derived from initial *sl-*). In (archaic) Quenya this is written *hl*, but was in the Third Age usually pronounced as *l*.

NG   represents *ng* in *finger*, except finally where it was sounded as in English *sing*. The latter sound also occurred initially in Quenya, but has been transcribed *n* (as in *Noldo*), according to the pronunciation of the Third Age.

PH   has the same sound as *f*. It is used *(a)* where the *f*-sound occurs at the end of a word, as in *alph* 'swan'; *(b)* where the *f*-sound is related to or derived from a *p*, as in *i-Pheriannath* 'the Halflings' (*perian*); *(c)* in the middle of a few words where it represents a long *ff* (from *pp*) as in *Ephel* 'outer fence'; and *(d)* in Adûnaic and Westron, as in *Ar-Pharazôn* (*pharaz* 'gold').

QU   has been used for *cw*, a combination very frequent in Quenya, though it did not occur in Sindarin.

R   represents a trilled *r* in all positions; the sound was not lost before consonants (as in English *part*). The Orcs, and some Dwarves, are said to have used a back or uvular *r*, a sound which the Eldar found distasteful. RH represents a voiceless *r* (usually derived from older initial *sr-*). It was written *hr* in Quenya. Cf. L.

S   is always voiceless, as in English *so*, *geese*; the *z*-sound did not occur in contemporary Quenya or Sindarin. SH, occurring in Westron, Dwarvish and Orkish, represents sounds similar to *sh* in English.

TH   represents the voiceless *th* of English in *thin cloth*. This had become *s* in spoken Quenya, though still written with a different letter; as in Q. *Isil*, S. *Ithil*, 'Moon'.

TY   represents a sound probably similar to the *t* in English *tune*. It was derived mainly from *c* or *t* + *y*. The sound of English *ch*, which was frequent in Westron, was usually substituted for it by speakers of that language. Cf. HY under Y.

V   has the sound of English *v*, but is not used finally. See F.

W   has the sound of English *w*. HW is a voiceless *w*, as in English *white* (in northern pronunciation). It was not an uncommon initial sound in Quenya, though examples seem not to occur in this book. Both *v* and *w* are used in the transcription of Quenya, in spite of the assimilation of its spelling to Latin, since the two sounds, distinct in origin, both occurred in the language.

Y   is used in Quenya for the consonant *y*, as in English *you*. In Sindarin *y* is a vowel (see below). HY has the same relation to *y* as HW to *w*, and represents a sound like that often heard in English *hew*, *huge*; *h* in Quenya *eht*, *iht* had the same sound. The sound of English *sh*, which was common in Westron, was often substituted by speakers of that language. Cf. TY above. HY was usually derived from *sy-* and *khy-*; in both cases related Sindarin words show initial *h*, as in Q. *Hyarmen* 'south', S. *Harad*.

Note that consonants written twice, as *tt*, *ll*, *ss*, *nn*, represent long, 'double' consonants. At the end of words of more than one syllable these were usually shortened: as in *Rohan* from *Rochann* (archaic *Rochand*).

In Sindarin the combinations *ng*, *nd*, *mb*, which were specially favoured in the Eldarin languages at an earlier stage, suffered various changes. *mb* became *m* in all cases, but still counted as a long consonant for purposes of stress (see below), and is thus written *mm* in cases where otherwise the stress might be in doubt.[1] *ng* remained unchanged except initially and finally where it became the simple nasal (as in English *sing*). *nd* became *nn* usually, as *Ennor* 'Middle-earth', Q. *Endóre*; but remained *nd* at the end of fully accented monosyllables such as *thond* 'root' (cf. *Morthond* 'Blackroot'), and also before *r*, as *Andros* 'long-foam'. This *nd* is also seen in some ancient names derived from an older period, such as *Nargothrond*, *Gondolin*, *Beleriand*. In the Third Age final *nd* in long words had become *n* from *nn*, as in *Ithilien*, *Rohan*, *Anórien*.

VOWELS

For vowels the letters *i*, *e*, *a*, *o*, *u* are used, and (in Sindarin only) *y*. As far as can be determined the sounds represented by these letters (other than *y*) were of normal kind, though doubtless many local varieties escape detection. That is, the sounds were approximately those represented by *i*, *e*, *a*, *o*, *u* in English *machine*, *were*, *father*, *for*, *brute*, irrespective of quantity.

In Sindarin long *e*, *a*, *o* had the same quality as the short vowels, being derived in comparatively recent times from them (older *é*, *á*, *ó* had been changed). In Quenya long *é* and *ó* were, when correctly[2] pronounced, as by the Eldar, tenser and 'closer' than the short vowels.

Sindarin alone among contemporary languages possessed the 'modified' or fronted *u*, more or less as *u* in French *lune*. It was partly a modification of *o* and *u*, partly derived from older diphthongs *eu*, *iu*. For this sound *y* has been used (as in ancient English): as in *lyg* 'snake', Q. *leuca*, or *emyn* pl. of *amon* 'hill'. In Gondor this *y* was usually pronounced like *i*.

Long vowels are usually marked with the 'acute accent', as in some varieties of Fëanorian script. In Sindarin long vowels in stressed monosyllables are marked with the circumflex, since they tended in such cases to be specially prolonged;[3] so in *dûn* compared with *Dúnedan*. The use of the circumflex in other languages such as

---

[1] As in *galadhremmin ennorath* (p. 231) 'tree-woven lands of Middle-earth'. *Remmirath* (p. 80) contains *rem* 'mesh', Q. *rembe*, + *mîr* 'jewel'.

[2] A fairly widespread pronunciation of long *é* and *ó* as *ei* and *ou*, more or less as in English *say no*, both in Westron and in the renderings of Quenya names by Westron speakers, is shown by spellings such as *ei*, *ou* (or their equivalents in contemporary scripts). But such pronunciations were regarded as incorrect or rustic. They were naturally usual in the Shire. Those therefore who pronounce *yéni únótime* 'long-years innumerable', as is natural in English (*sc.* more or less as *yainy oonoatimy*) will err little more than Bilbo, Meriadoc, or Peregrin. Frodo said to have shown great 'skill with foreign sounds'.

[3] So also in *Annûn* 'sunset', *Amrûn* 'sunrise', under the influence of the related *dûn* 'west', and *rhûn* 'east'.

Adûnaic or Dwarvish has no special significance, and is used merely to mark these out as alien tongues (as with the use of *k*).

Final *e* is never mute or a mere sign of length as in English. To mark this final *e* it is often (but not consistently) written *ë*.

The groups *er*, *ir*, *ur* (finally or before a consonant) are not intended to be pronounced as in English *fern*, *fir*, *fur*, but rather as English *air*, *eer*, *oor*.

In Quenya *ui*, *oi*, *ai* and *iu*, *eu*, *au* are diphthongs (that is, pronounced in one syllable). All other pairs of vowels are dissyllabic. This is often dictated by writing *ëa* (*Eä*), *ëo*, *oë*.

In Sindarin the diphthongs are written *ae*, *ai*, *ei*, *oe*, *ui*, and *au*. Other combinations are not diphthongal. The writing of final *au* as *aw* is in accordance with English custom, but is actually not uncommon in Fëanorian spellings.

All these diphthongs[1] were 'falling' diphthongs, that is stressed on the first element, and composed of the simple vowels run together. Thus *ai*, *ei*, *oi*, *ui* are intended to be pronounced respectively as the vowels in English *rye* (not *ray*), *grey*, *boy*, *ruin*; and *au* (*aw*) as in *loud*, *how* and not as in *laud*, *haw*.

There is nothing in English closely corresponding to *ae*, *oe*, *eu*; *ae* and *oe* may be pronounced as *ai*, *oi*.

STRESS

The position of the 'accent' or stress is not marked, since in the Eldarin languages concerned its place is determined by the form of the word. In words of two syllables it falls in practically all cases on the first syllable. In longer words it falls on the last syllable but one, where that contains a long vowel, a diphthong, or a vowel followed by two (or more) consonants. Where the last syllable but one contains (as often) a short vowel followed by only one (or no) consonant, the stress falls on the syllable before it, the third from the end. Words of the last form are favoured in the Eldarin languages, especially Quenya.

In the following examples the stressed vowel is marked by a capital letter: *isIldur*, *Orome*, *erEssëa*, *fËanor*, *ancAlima*, *elentÁri*, *dEnethor*, *periAnnath*, *ecthElion*, *pelArgir*, *silIvren*. Words of the type *elentÁri* 'star-queen' seldom occur in Quenya where the vowel is *é*, *á*, *ó*, unless (as in this case) they are compounds; they are commoner with the vowels *í*, *ú*, as *andÚne* 'sunset, west'. They do not occur in Sindarin except in compounds. Note that Sindarin *dh*, *th*, *ch* are single consonants and represent single letters in the original scripts.

NOTE

In names drawn from other languages than Eldarin the same values for the letters are intended, where not specially described above, except in the case of Dwarvish.

---

[1] Originally. But *iu* in Quenya was in the Third Age usually pronounced as a rising dipthong as *yu* in English *yule*.

In Dwarvish, which did not possess the sounds represented above by *th* and *ch* (*kh*), *th* and *kh* are aspirates, that is *t* or *k* followed by an *h*, more or less as in *backhand*, *outhouse*.

Where *z* occurs the sound intended is that of English *z*. *gh* in the Black Speech and Orkish represents a 'back spirant' (related to *g* as *dh* to *d*): as in *ghâsh* and *agh*.

The 'outer' or Mannish names of the Dwarves have been given Northern forms, but the letter-values are those described. So also in the case of the personal and place-names of Rohan (where they have not been modernized), except that here *éa* and *éo* are diphthongs, which may be represented by the *ea* of English *bear*, and the *eo* of *Theobald*; *y* is the modified *u*. The modernized forms are easily recognized and are intended to be pronounced as in English. They are mostly place-names: as Dunharrow (for *Dúnharg*), except Shadowfax and Wormtongue.

II
WRITING

The scripts and letters used in the Third Age were all ultimately of Eldarin origin, and already at that time of great antiquity. They had reached the stage of full alphabetic development, but older modes in which only the consonants were denoted by full letters were still in use.

The alphabets were of two main, and in origin independent, kinds: the *Tengwar* or *Tîw*, here translated as 'letters'; and the *Certar* or *Cirth*, translated as 'runes'. The *Tengwar* were devised for writing with brush or pen, and the squared forms of inscriptions were in their case derivative from the written forms. The *Certar* were devised and mostly used only for scratched or incised inscriptions.

The *Tengwar* were the more ancient; for they had been developed by the Noldor, the kindred of the Eldar most skilled in such matters, long before their exile. The oldest Eldarin letters, the Tengwar of Rúmil, were not used in Middle-earth. The later letters, the Tengwar of Fëanor, were largely a new invention, though they owed something to the letters of Rúmil. They were brought to Middle-earth by the exiled Noldor, and so became known to the Edain and Númenoreans. In the Third Age their use had spread over much the same area as that in which the Common Speech was known.

The Cirth were devised first in Beleriand by the Sindar, and were long used only for inscribing names and brief memorials upon wood or stone. To that origin they owe their angular shapes, very similar to the runes of our times, though they differed from these in details and were wholly different in arrangement. The Cirth in their older and simpler form spread eastward in the Second Age, and became known to many peoples, to Men and Dwarves, and even to Orcs, all of whom altered them to suit their purposes and according to their skill or lack of it. One such simple form was still used by the Men of Dale, and a similar one by the Rohirrim.

But in Beleriand, before the end of the First Age, the Cirth, partly under the influence of the Tengwar of the Noldor, were rearranged and further developed. Their richest and most ordered form was known as the Alphabet of Daeron, since in Elvish tradition it was said to have been devised by Daeron, the minstrel and

THE TENGWAR

I	II	III	IV
1	2	3	4
5	6	7	8
9	10	11	12
13	14	15	16
17	18	19	20
21	22	23	24
25	26	27	28
29	30	31	32
33	34	35	36

loremaster of King Thingol of Doriath. Among the Eldar the Alphabet of Daeron did not develop true cursive forms, since for writing the Elves adopted the Fëanorian letters. The Elves of the West indeed for the most part gave up the use of runes altogether. In the country of Eregion, however, the Alphabet of Daeron was maintained in use and passed thence to Moria, where it became the alphabet most favoured by the Dwarves. It remained ever after in use among them and passed with them to the North. Hence in later times it was often called *Angerthas Moria* or the Long Rune-rows of Moria. As with their speech the Dwarves made use of such scripts as were current and many wrote the Fëanorian letters skilfully; but for their own tongue they adhered to the Cirth, and developed written pen-forms from them.

(i)
THE FËANORIAN LETTERS

The table shows, in formal book-hand shape, all the letters that were commonly used in the West-lands in the Third Age. The arrangement is the one most usual at the time, and the one in which the letters were then usually recited by name.

This script was not in origin an 'alphabet', that is, a haphazard series of letters, each with an independent value of its own, recited in a traditional order that has no reference either to their shapes or to their functions.[1] It was, rather, a system of consonantal signs, of similar shapes and style, which could be adapted at choice or convenience to represent the consonants of languages observed (or devised) by the Eldar. None of the letters had in itself a fixed value; but certain relations between them were gradually recognized.

The system contained twenty-four primary letters, 1–24, arranged in four *témar* (series), each of which had six *tyeller* (grades). There were also 'additional letters', of which 25–36 are examples. Of these 27 and 29 are the only strictly independent letters; the remainder are modifications of other letters. There was also a number of *tehtar* (signs) of varied uses. These do not appear in the table.[2]

The *primary letters* were each formed of a *telco* (stem) and a *lúva* (bow). The forms seen in 1–4 were regarded as normal. The stem could be raised, as in 9–16; or reduced, as in 17–24. The bow could be open, as in Series I and III; or closed, as in II and IV; and in either case it could be doubled, as e.g. in 5–8.

The theoretic freedom of application had in the Third Age been modified by custom to this extent that Series I was generally applied to the dental or *t*-series (*tincotéma*), and II to the labials or *p*-series (*parmatéma*). The application of Series III and IV varied according to the requirements of different languages. ·

[1] The only relation in our alphabet that would have appeared intelligible to the Eldar is that between P and B; and their separation from one another, and from F, M, V, would have seemed to them absurd.

[2] Many of them appear in the examples on the title-page, and in the inscription on p. 49, transcribed on p. 247. They were mainly used to express vowel-sounds, in Quenya usually regarded as modifications of the accompanying consonant; or to express more briefly some of the most frequent consonant combinations.

In languages like the Westron, which made much use of consonants[1] such as our *ch*, *j*, *sh*, Series III was usually applied to these; in which case Series IV was applied to the normal *k*-series (*calmatéma*). In Quenya, which possessed besides the *calmatéma* both a palatal series (*tyelpetéma*) and a labialized series (*quessetéma*), the palatals were represented by a Fëanorian diacritic denoting 'following *y*' (usually two underposed dots), while Series IV was a *kw*-series.

Within these general applications the following relations were also commonly observed. The normal letters, Grade 1, were applied to the 'voiceless stops': *t*, *p*, *k*, etc. The doubling of the bow indicated the addition of 'voice': thus if 1, 2, 3, 4=*t*, *p*, *ch*, *k* (or *t*, *p*, *k*, *kw*) then 5, 6, 7, 8 =*d*, *b*, *j*, *g* (or *d*, *b*, *g*, *gw*). The raising of the stem indicated the opening of the consonant to a 'spirant': thus assuming the above values for Grade 1, Grade 3 (9–12)=*th*, *f*, *sh*, *ch* (or *th*, *f*, *kh*, *khw/hw*), and Grade 4 (13–16)=*dh*, *v*, *zh*, *gh* (or *dh*, *v*, *gh*, *ghw/w*).

The original Fëanorian system also possessed a grade with extended stems, both above and below the line. These usually represented aspirated consonants (e.g. *t*+*h*, *p*+*h*, *k*+*h*), but might represent other consonantal variations required. They were not needed in the languages of the Third Age that used this script; but the extended forms were much used as variants (more clearly distinguished from Grade 1) of Grades 3 and 4.

Grade 5 (17–20) was usually applied to the nasal consonants: thus 17 and 18 were the most common signs for *n* and *m*. According to the principle observed above, Grade 6 should then have represented the voiceless nasals; but since such sounds (exemplified by Welsh *nh* or ancient English *hn*) were of very rare occurrence in the languages concerned, Grade 6 (21–24) was most often used for the weakest or 'semi-vocalic' consonants of each series. It consisted of the smallest and simplest shapes among the primary letters. Thus 21 was often used for a weak (untrilled) *r*, originally occurring in Quenya and regarded in the system of that language as the weakest consonant of the *tincotéma*; 22 was widely used for *w*; where Series III was used as a palatal series 23 was commonly used as consonantal *y*.[2]

Since some of the consonants of Grade 4 tended to become weaker in pronunciation, and to approach or to merge with those of Grade 6 (as described above), many of the latter ceased to have a clear function in the Eldarin languages; and it was from these letters that the letters expressing vowels were largely derived.

NOTE

The standard spelling of Quenya diverged from the applications of the letters above described. Grade 2 was used for *nd*, *mb*, *ng*, *ngw*, all of which were frequent, since

---

[1] The representation of the sounds here is the same as that employed in transcription and described above, except that here *ch* represents the *ch* in English *church*; *j* represents the sound of English *j*, and *zh* the sound heard in *azure* and *occasion*.
[2] The inscription on the West-gate of Moria gives an example of a mode, used for the spelling of Sindarin, in which Grade 6 represented the simple nasals, but Grade 5 represented the double or long nasals much used in Sindarin: 17=*nn*, but 21=*n*.

b, *g*, *gw* only appeared in these combinations, while for *rd*, *ld* the special letters 26, 28 were used. (For *lv*, not for *kv*, many speakers, especially Elves, used *lb*: this was written with 27+6, since *lmb* could not occur.) Similarly, Grade 4 was used for the extremely frequent combinations *nt*, *mp*, *nk*, *nqu*, since Quenya did not possess *dh*, *gh*, *ghw*, and for *v* used letter 22. See the Quenya letter-names pp. 1096 and 1097.

The additional letters. No. 27 was universally used for *l*. No. 25 (in origin a modification of 21) was used for 'full' trilled *r*. Nos. 26, 28 were modifications of these. They were frequently used for voiceless *r* (*rh*) and *l* (*lh*) respectively. But in Quenya they were used for *rd* and *ld*. 29 represented *s*, and 31 (with doubled curl) *z* in those languages that required it. The inverted forms, 30 and 32, though available for use as separate signs, were mostly used as mere variants of 29 and 31, according to the convenience of writing, e.g. they were much used when accompanied by superimposed *tehtar*.

No. 33 was in origin a variation representing some (weaker) variety of 11; its most frequent use in the Third Age was *h*. 34 was mostly used (if at all) for voiceless *w* (*hw*). 35 and 36 were, when used as consonants, mostly applied to *y* and *w* respectively.

The vowels were in many modes represented by *tehtar*, usually set above a consonantal letter. In languages such as Quenya, in which most words ended in a vowel, the *tehta* was placed above the preceding consonant; in those such as Sindarin, in which most words ended in a consonant, it was placed above the following consonant. When there was no consonant present in the required position, the *tehta* was placed above the 'short carrier', of which a common form was like an undotted i. The actual *tehtar* used in different languages for vowel-signs were numerous. The commonest, usually applied to (varieties of) *e*, *i*, *a*, *o*, *u*, are exhibited in the examples given. The three dots, most usual in forming writing for *a*, were variously written in quicker styles, a form like a circumflex being often employed.[1] The single dot and the 'acute accent' were frequently used for *i* and *e* (but in some modes for *e* and *i*). The curls were used for *o* and *u*. In the Ring-inscription the curl open to the right is used for *u*; but on the title-page this stands for *o*, and the curl open to the left for *u*. The curl to the right was favoured, and the application depended on the language concerned: in the Black Speech *o* was rare.

Long vowels were usually represented by placing the *tehta* on the 'long carrier', of which a common form was like an undotted *j*. But for the same purpose the *tehtar* could be doubled. This was, however, only frequently done with the curls, and sometimes with the 'accent'. Two dots was more often used as a sign for following *y*.

The West-gate inscription illustrates a mode of 'full writing' with the vowels

---

[1] In Quenya in which *a* was very frequent, its vowel sign was often omitted altogether. Thus for *calma* 'lamp' *clm* could be written. This would naturally read as *calma*, since *cl* was not in Quenya a possible initial combination, and *m* never occurred finally. A possible reading was *calama*, but no such word existed.

represented by separate letters. All the vocalic letters used in Sindarin are shown. The use of No. 30 as a sign for vocalic *y* may be noted; also the expression of diphthongs by placing the *tehta* for following *y* above the vowel-letter. The sign for following *w* (required for the expression of *au*, *aw*) was in this mode the *u*-curl or a modification of it ~. But the diphthongs were often written out in full, as in the transcription. In this mode length of vowel was usually indicated by the 'acute accent', called in that case *andaith* 'long mark'.

There were beside the *tehtar* already mentioned a number of others, chiefly used to abbreviate the writing, especially by expressing frequent consonant combinations without writing them out in full. Among these, a bar (or a sign like a Spanish *tilde*) placed above a consonant was often used to indicate that it was preceded by the nasal of the same series (as in *nt*, *mp*, or *nk*); a similar sign placed below was, however, mainly used to show that the consonant was long or doubled. A downward hook attached to the bow (as in *hobbits*, the last word on the title-page) was used to indicate a following *s*, especially in the combinations *ts*, *ps*, *ks* (*x*), that were favoured in Quenya.

There was of course no 'mode' for the representation of English. One adequate phonetically could be devised from the Fëanorian system. The brief example on the title-page does not attempt to exhibit this. It is rather an example of what a man of Gondor might have produced, hesitating between the values of the letters familiar in his 'mode' and the traditional spelling of English. It may be noted that a dot below (one of the uses of which was to represent weak obscured vowels) is here employed in the representation of unstressed *and*, but is also used in *here* for silent final *e*; *the*, *of*, and *of the* are expressed by abbreviations (extended *dh*, extended *v*, and the latter with an under-stroke).

The names of the letters. In all modes each letter and sign had a name; but these names were devised to fit or describe the phonetic uses in each particular mode. It was, however, often felt desirable, especially in describing the uses of the letters in other modes, to have a name for each letter in itself as a shape. For this purpose the Quenya 'full names' were commonly employed, even where they referred to uses peculiar to Quenya. Each 'full name' was an actual word in Quenya that contained the letter in question. Where possible it was the first sound of the word; but where the sound or the combination expressed did not occur initially it followed immediately after an initial vowel. The names of the letters in the table were (1) *tinco* metal, *parma* book, *calma* lamp, *quesse* feather; (2) *ando* gate, *umbar* fate, *anga* iron, *ungwe* spider's web; (3) *thúle* (*súle*) spirit, *formen* north, *harma* treasure (or *aha* rage), *hwesta* breeze; (4) *anto* mouth, *ampa* hook, *anca* jaws, *unque* a hollow; (5) *númen* west, *malta* gold, *noldo* (older *ngoldo*) one of the kindred of the Noldor, *nwalme* (older *ngwalme*) torment; (6) *óre* heart (inner mind), *vala* angelic power, *anna* gift, *vilya* air, sky (older *wilya*); *rómen* east, *arda* region, *lambe* tongue, *alda* tree; *silme* light, *silme nuquerna* (*s* reversed), *áre* sunlight (or *esse* name), *áre nuquerna*; *hyarmen* south, *hwesta sindarinwa*, *yanta* bridge, *úre* heat. Where there are variants this is due to the names being given before certain changes affected Quenya as spoken by the Exiles. Thus No. 11 was called *harma* when it represented the spirant *ch* in all positions, but when this sound became breath *h* initially[1] (though remaining medially) the name *aha* was devised. *áre* was originally *áze*, but when this *z* became merged with 21, the sign was in Quenya used for the very frequent *ss* of that language, and the name *esse* was given to it. *hwesta sindarinwa* or 'Grey-elven *hw*' was so called because in Quenya 12 had the sound of *hw*, and distinct signs for *chw* and *hw* were not required. The names of the letters most widely known and used were 17 *n*, 33 *hy*, 25 *r*, 9 *f*: *númen*, *hyarmen*, *rómen*, *formen*=west, south, east, north (cf. Sindarin *dûn* or *annûn*, *harad*, *rhûn* or *amrûn*, *forod*). These letters commonly indicated the points W, S, E, N even in languages that used quite different terms. They were, in the West-lands, named in this order, beginning with and facing west; *hyarmen* and *formen* indeed meant left-hand region and right-hand region (the opposite to the arrangement in many Mannish languages).

THE CIRTH

The *Certhas Daeron* was originally devised to represent the sounds of Sindarin only. The oldest *cirth* were Nos. 1, 2, 5, 6; 8, 9, 12; 18, 19, 22; 29, 31; 35, 36; 39, 42, 46, 50; and a *certh* varying between 13 and 15. The assignment of values was unsystematic. Nos. 39, 42, 46, 50 were vowels and remained so in all later developments. Nos. 13, 15 were used for *h* or *s*, according as 35 was used for *s* or *h*. This tendency to hesitate in the assignment of values for *s* and *h* continued in later arrangements. In those characters that consisted of a 'stem' and a 'branch', 1–31, the attachment of the branch was, if on one side only, usually made on the right side. The reverse was not infrequent, but had no phonetic significance.

The extension and elaboration of this *certhas* was called in its older form the *Angerthas Daeron*, since the additions to the old *cirth* and their reorganization was attributed to Daeron. The principal additions, however, the introductions of two new series, 13–17, and 23–28, were actually most probably inventions of the Noldor of Eregion, since they were used for the representation of sounds not found in Sindarin.

In the rearrangement of the *Angerthas* the following principles are observable (evidently inspired by the Fëanorian system): (1) adding a stroke to a branch added 'voice'; (2) reversing the *certh* indicated opening to a 'spirant'; (3) placing the branch on both sides of the stem added voice and nasality. These principles were regularly carried out, except in one point. For (archaic) Sindarin a sign for a spirant *m* (or nasal *v*) was required, and since this could best be provided by a reversal of the sign for *m*, the reversible No. 6 was given the value *m*, but No. 5 was given the value *hw*.

No. 36, the theoretic value of which was *z*, was used, in spelling Sindarin or Quenya, for *ss*: cf. Fëanorian 31. No. 39 was used for either *i* or *y* (consonant); 34, 35 were used indifferently for *s*; and 38 was used for the frequent sequence *nd*, though it was not clearly related in shape to the dentals.

---

[1] For breath *h* Quenya originally used a simple raised stem without bow, called *halla* 'tall'. This could be placed before a consonant to indicate that it was unvoiced and breathed; voiceless *r* and *l* were usually so expressed and are transcribed *hr*, *hl*. Later 33 was used for independent *h*, and the value of *hy* (its older value) was represented by adding the *tehta* for following *y*.

APPENDIX E

THE ANGERTHAS

THE ANGERTHAS

Values

1	p	16	zh	31	l	46	e
2	b	17	nj—z	32	lh	47	ę
3	f	18	k	33	ng—nd	48	a
4	v	19	g	34	s—h	49	ā
5	hw	20	kh	35	s—'	50	o
6	m	21	gh	36	z—ŋ	51	ŏ
7	(mh) mb	22	ŋ—n	37	ng*	52	ö
8	t	23	kw	38	nd—nj	53	n*
9	d	24	gw	39	i (y)	54	h—s
10	th	25	khw	40	y*	55	*
11	dh	26	ghw,w	41	hy*	56	*
12	n—r	27	ngw	42	u	57	ps*
13	ch	28	nw	43	ū	58	ts*
14	j	29	r—j	44	w		+h
15	sh	30	rh—zh	45	ŭ		&

In the Table of Values those on the left are, when separated by – , the values of the older *Angerthas*. Those on the right are the values of the Dwarvish *Angerthas Moria*.[1] The Dwarves of Moria, as can be seen, introduced a number of unsystematic changes in value, as well as certain new *cirth*: 37, 40, 41, 53, 55, 56. The dislocation in values was due mainly to two causes: (1) the alteration in the values of 34, 35, 54 respectively to *h*,' (the clear or glottal beginning of a word with an initial vowel that appeared in Khuzdul), and *s*; (2) the abandonment of the Nos. 14, 16 for which the Dwarves substituted 29, 30. The consequent use of 12 for *r*, the invention of 53 for *n* (and its confusion with 22); the use of 17 as *z*, to go with 54 in its value *s*, and the consequent use of 36 as *n* and the new *certh* 37 for *ng* may also be observed. The new 55, 56 were in origin a halved form of 46, and were used for vowels like those heard in English *butter*, which were frequent in Dwarvish and in the Westron. When weak or evanescent they were often reduced to a mere stroke without a stem. This *Angerthas Moria* is represented in the tomb-inscription.

The Dwarves of Erebor used a further modification of this system, known as the mode of Erebor, and exemplified in the Book of Mazarbul. Its chief characteristics were: the use of 43 as *z*; of 17 as *ks* (*x*); and the invention of two new *cirth*, 57, 58 for *ps* and *ts*. They also reintroduced 14, 16 for the values *j*, *zh*; but used 29, 30 for *g*, *gh*, or as mere variants of 19, 21. These peculiarities are not included in the table, except for the special Ereborian *cirth*, 57, 58.

---

[1] Those in ( ) are values only found in Elvish use; * marks *cirth* only used by Dwarves.

APPENDIX F

I

THE LANGUAGES AND PEOPLES OF THE THIRD AGE

The language represented in this history by English was the *Westron* or 'Common Speech' of the West-lands of Middle-earth in the Third Age. In the course of that age it had become the native language of nearly all the speaking-peoples (save the Elves) who dwelt within the bounds of the old kingdoms of Arnor and Gondor; that is along all the coasts from Umbar northward to the Bay of Forochel, and inland as far as the Misty Mountains and the Ephel Dúath. It had also spread north up the Anduin, occupying the lands west of the River and east of the mountains as far as the Gladden Fields.

At the time of the War of the Ring at the end of the age these were still its bounds as a native tongue, though large parts of Eriador were now deserted, and few Men dwelt on the shores of the Anduin between the Gladden and Rauros.

A few of the ancient Wild Men still lurked in the Drúadan Forest in Anórien; and in the hills of Dunland a remnant lingered of an old people, the former inhabitants of much of Gondor. These clung to their own languages; while in the plains of Rohan there dwelt now a Northern people, the Rohirrim, who had come into that land some five hundred years earlier. But the Westron was used as a second language of intercourse by all those who still retained a speech of their own, even by the Elves, not only in Arnor and Gondor but throughout the vales of Anduin, and eastward to the further eaves of Mirkwood. Even among the Wild Men and the Dunlendings who shunned other folk there were some that could speak it, though brokenly.

OF THE ELVES

The Elves far back in the Elder Days became divided into two main branches: the West-elves (the *Eldar*) and the East-elves. Of the latter kind were most of the elven-folk of Mirkwood and Lórien; but their languages do not appear in this history, in which all the Elvish names and words are of *Eldarin* form.[1]

Of the *Eldarin* tongues two are found in this book: the High-elven or *Quenya*, and the Grey-elven or *Sindarin*. The High-elven was an ancient tongue of Eldamar beyond the Sea, the first to be recorded in writing. It was no longer a birth-tongue, but had become, as it were, an 'Elven-latin', still used for ceremony, and for high matters of lore and song, by the High Elves, who had returned in exile to Middle-earth at the end of the First Age.

[1] In Lórien at this period Sindarin was spoken, though with an 'accent', since most of its folk were of Silvan origin. This 'accent' and his own limited acquaintance with Sindarin misled Frodo (as is pointed out in *The Thain's Book* by a commentator of Gondor). All the Elvish words cited in Book I, ii, chs 6, 7, 8 are in fact Sindarin, and so are most of the names of places and persons. But *Lórien, Caras Galadhon, Amroth, Nimrodel* are probably of Silvan origin, adapted to Sindarin.

The Grey-elven was in origin akin to *Quenya*; for it was the language of those Eldar who, coming to the shores of Middle-earth, had not passed over the Sea but had lingered on the coasts in the country of Beleriand. There Thingol Greycloak of Doriath was their king, and in the long twilight their tongue had changed with the changefulness of mortal lands and had become far estranged from the speech of the Eldar from beyond the Sea.

The Exiles, dwelling among the more numerous Grey-elves, had adopted the *Sindarin* for daily use; and hence it was the tongue of all those Elves and Elf-lords that appear in this history. For these were all of Eldarin race, even where the folk that they ruled were of the lesser kindreds. Noblest of all was the Lady Galadriel of the royal house of Finarfin and sister of Finrod Felagund, King of Nargothrond. In the hearts of the Exiles the yearning for the Sea was an unquiet never to be stilled; in the hearts of the Grey-elves it slumbered, but once awakened it could not be appeased.

OF MEN

The *Westron* was a Mannish speech, though enriched and softened under Elvish influence. It was in origin the language of those whom the Eldar called the *Atani* or *Edain*, 'Fathers of Men', being especially the people of the Three Houses of the Elf-friends who came west into Beleriand in the First Age, and aided the Eldar in the War of the Great Jewels against the Dark Power of the North.

After the overthrow of the Dark Power, in which Beleriand was for the most part drowned or broken, it was granted as a reward to the Elf-friends that they also, as the Eldar, might pass west over Sea. But since the Undying Realm was forbidden to them, a great isle was set apart for them, most westerly of all mortal lands. The name of that isle was *Númenor* (Westernesse). Most of the Elf-friends, therefore, departed and dwelt in Númenor, and there they became great and powerful, mariners of renown and lords of many ships. They were fair of face and tall, and the span of their lives was thrice that of the Men of Middle-earth. These were the Númenoreans, the Kings of Men, whom the Elves called the *Dúnedain*.

The *Dúnedain* alone of all races of Men knew and spoke an Elvish tongue; for their forefathers had learned the Sindarin tongue, and this they handed on to their children as a matter of lore, changing little with the passing of the years. And their men of wisdom learned also the High-elven Quenya and esteemed it above all other tongues, and in it they made names for many places of fame and reverence, and for many men of royalty and great renown.[1]

But the native speech of the Númenoreans remained for the most part their ancestral Mannish tongue, the Adûnaic, and to this in the latter days of their pride their kings and lords returned, abandoning the Elven-speech, save only those few that held still to their ancient friendship with the Eldar. In the years of their power

---

[1] Quenya, for example, are the names *Númenor* (or in full *Númenóre*), and *Elendi*, *Isildur*, and *Anárion*, and all the royal names of *Gondor*, including *Elessar* 'Elfstone'. Most of the names of the other men and women of the Dúnedain, such as *Aragorn*, *Denethor*, *Gilraen* are of Sindarin form, being often the names of Elves or Men remembered in the songs and histories of the First Age (as *Beren*, *Húrin*). Some few are of mixed forms, as *Boromir*.

the Númenoreans had maintained many forts and havens upon the western coasts of Middle-earth for the help of their ships; and one of the chief of these was at Pelargir near the Mouths of Anduin. There Adûnaic was spoken, and mingled with many words of the languages of lesser men it became a Common Speech that spread thence along the coasts among all that had dealings with Westernesse.

After the Downfall of Númenor, Elendil led the survivors of the Elf-friends back to the North-western shores of Middle-earth. There many already dwelt who were in whole or part of Númenorean blood; but few of them remembered the Elvish speech. All told the Dúnedain were thus from the beginning far fewer in number than the lesser men among whom they dwelt and whom they ruled, being lords of long life and great power and wisdom. They used therefore the Common Speech in their dealing with other folk and in the government of their wide realms; but they enlarged the language and enriched it with many words drawn from Elven-tongues.

In the days of the Númenorean kings this ennobled Westron speech spread far and wide, even among their enemies; and it became used more and more by the Dúnedain themselves, so that at the time of the War of the Ring the Elven-tongue was known to only a small part of the peoples of Gondor, and spoken daily by fewer. These dwelt mostly in Minas Tirith and the townlands adjacent, and in the land of the tributary princes of Dol Amroth. Yet the names of nearly all places and persons in the realm of Gondor were of Elvish form and meaning. A few were of forgotten origin, and descended doubtless from the days before the ships of the Númenoreans sailed the Sea; among these were *Umbar, Arnach* and *Erech*; and the mountain-names *Eilenach* and *Rimmon. Forlong* was also a name of the same sort.

Most of the Men of the northern regions of the West-lands were descended from the *Edain* of the First Age, or from their close kin. Their languages were, therefore, related to the Adûnaic, and some still preserved a likeness to the Common Speech. Of this kind were the peoples of the upper vales of Anduin: the Beornings, and the Woodmen of Western Mirkwood; and further north and east the Men of the Long Lake and of Dale. From the lands between the Gladden and the Carrock came the folk that were known in Gondor as the Rohirrim, Masters of Horses. They still spoke their ancestral tongue, and gave new names in it to nearly all the places in their new country; and they called themselves the Eorlings, or the Men of the Riddermark. But the lords of that people used the Common Speech freely, and spoke it nobly after the manner of their allies in Gondor; for in Gondor whence it came the Westron kept still a more gracious and antique style.

Wholly alien was the speech of the Wild Men of Drúadan Forest. Alien, too, or only remotely akin, was the language of the Dunlendings. These were a remnant of the peoples that had dwelt in the vales of the White Mountains in ages past. The Dead Men of Dunharrow were of their kin. But in the Dark Years others had removed to the southern dales of the Misty Mountains; and thence some had passed into the empty lands as far north as the Barrow-downs. From them came the Men of Bree; but long before these had become subjects of the North Kingdom of Arnor and had taken up the Westron tongue. Only in Dunland did Men of this race hold to their old speech and manners: a secret folk, unfriendly to the Dúnedain, hating the Rohirrim.

Of their language nothing appears in this book, save the name *Forgoil* which they gave to the Rohirrim (meaning Strawheads, it is said). *Dunland* and *Dunlending* are the names that the Rohirrim gave to them, because they were swarthy and dark-haired; there is thus no connexion between the word *dunn* in these names and the Grey-elven word *Dûn* 'west'.

OF HOBBITS

The Hobbits of the Shire and of Bree had at this time, for probably a thousand years, adopted the Common Speech. They used it in their own manner freely and carelessly; though the more learned among them had still at their command a more formal language when occasion required.

There is no record of any language peculiar to Hobbits. In ancient days they seem always to have used the languages of Men near whom, or among whom, they lived. Thus they quickly adopted the Common Speech after they entered Eriador, and by the time of their settlement at Bree they had already begun to forget their former tongue. This was evidently a Mannish language of the upper Anduin, akin to that of the Rohirrim; though the southern Stoors appear to have adopted a language related to Dunlendish before they came north to the Shire.[1]

Of these things in the time of Frodo there were still some traces left in local words and names, many of which closely resembled those found in Dale or in Rohan. Most notable were the names of days, months, and seasons; several other words of the same sort (such as *mathom* and *smial*) were also still in common use, while more were preserved in the place-names of Bree and the Shire. The personal names of the Hobbits were also peculiar and many had come down from ancient days.

Hobbit was the name usually applied by the Shire-folk to all their kind. Men called them *Halflings* and the Elves *Periannath*. The origin of the word *hobbit* was by most forgotten. It seems, however, to have been at first a name given to the Harfoots by the Fallohides and Stoors, and to be a worn-down form of a word preserved more fully in Rohan: *holbytla* 'hole-builder'.

OF OTHER RACES

Ents. The most ancient people surviving in the Third Age were the *Onodrim* or *Enyd. Ent* was the form of their name in the language of Rohan. They were known to the Eldar in ancient days, and to the Eldar indeed the Ents ascribed not their own language but the desire for speech. The language that they had made was unlike all others: slow, sonorous, agglomerated, repetitive, indeed long-winded; formed of a multiplicity of vowel-shades and distinctions of tone and quality which even the masters of the Eldar had not attempted to represent in writing. They used it only among themselves; but they had no need to keep it secret, for no others could learn it.

---

[1] The Stoors of the Angle, who returned to Wilderland, had already adopted the Common Speech; but *Déagol* and *Sméagol* are names in the Mannish language of the region near the Gladden.

Ents were, however, themselves skilled in tongues, learning them swiftly and never forgetting them. But they preferred the languages of the Eldar, and loved best the ancient High-elven tongue. The strange words and names that the Hobbits record as used by Treebeard and other Ents are thus Elvish, or fragments of Elf-speech strung together in Ent-fashion.[1] Some are Quenya: as *Taurelilómëa-tumbalemorna Tumbaletaurëa Lómëanor*, which may be rendered 'Forestmany-shadowed-deepvalleyblack Deepvalleyforested Gloomyland', and by which Tree-beard meant, more or less: 'there is a black shadow in the deep dales of the forest'. Some are Sindarin: as *Fangorn* 'beard-(of)-tree', or *Fimbrethil* 'slender-beech'.

Orcs and the Black Speech. Orc is the form of the name that other races had for this foul people as it was in the language of Rohan. In Sindarin it was *orch*. Related, no doubt, was the word *uruk* of the Black Speech, though this was applied as a rule only to the great soldier-orcs that at this time issued from Mordor and Isengard. The lesser kinds were called, especially by the Uruk-hai, *snaga* 'slave'.

The Orcs were first bred by the Dark Power of the North in the Elder Days. It is said that they had no language of their own, but took what they could of other tongues and perverted it to their own liking; yet they made only brutal jargons, scarcely sufficient even for their own needs, unless it were for curses and abuse. And these creatures, being filled with malice, hating even their own kind, quickly developed as many barbarous dialects as there were groups or settlements of their race, so that their Orkish speech was of little use to them in intercourse between different tribes.

So it was that in the Third Age Orcs used for communication between breed and breed the Westron tongue; and many indeed of the older tribes, such as those that still lingered in the North and in the Misty Mountains, had long used the Westron as their native language, though in such a fashion as to make it hardly less unlovely than Orkish. In this jargon *tark*, 'man of Gondor', was a debased form of *tarkil*, a Quenya word used in Westron for one of Númenorean descent; see p. 885.

It is said that the Black Speech was devised by Sauron in the Dark Years, and that he had desired to make it the language of all those that served him, but he failed in that purpose. From the Black Speech, however, were derived many of the words that were in the Third Age wide-spread among the Orcs, such as *ghâsh* 'fire', but after the first overthrow of Sauron this language in its ancient form was forgotten by all but the Nazgûl. When Sauron arose again, it became once more the language of Barad-dûr and of the captains of Mordor. The inscription on the Ring was in the ancient Black Speech, while the curse of the Mordor-orc on p. 435 was in the more debased form used by the soldiers of the Dark Tower, of whom Grishnákh was the captain. Sharku in that tongue means *old man.*

Trolls. Troll has been used to translate the Sindarin *Torog.* In their beginning far back in the twilight of the Elder Days, these were creatures of dull and lumpish

---

[1] Except where the Hobbits seem to have made some attempts to represent shorter murmurs and calls made by the Ents; *a-lalla-lalla-rumba-kamanda-lindor-burúme* also is not Elvish, and is the only extant (probably very inaccurate) attempt to represent a fragment of actual Entish.

nature and had no more language than beasts. But Sauron had made use of them, teaching them what little they could learn and increasing their wits with wickedness. Trolls therefore took such language as they could master from the Orcs; and in the Westlands the Stone-trolls spoke a debased form of the Common Speech.

But at the end of the Third Age a troll-race not before seen appeared in southern Mirkwood and in the mountain borders of Mordor. Olog-hai they were called in the Black Speech. That Sauron bred them none doubted, though from what stock was not known. Some held that they were not Trolls but giant Orcs; but the Olog-hai were in fashion of body and mind quite unlike even the largest of Orc-kind, whom they far surpassed in size and power. Trolls they were, but filled with the evil will of their master: a fell race, strong, agile, fierce and cunning, but harder than stone. Unlike the older race of the Twilight they could endure the Sun, so long as the will of Sauron held sway over them. They spoke little, and the only tongue that they knew was the Black Speech of Barad-dûr.

Dwarves. The Dwarves are a race apart. Of their strange beginning, and why they are both like and unlike Elves and Men, the Silmarillion tells; but of this tale the lesser Elves of Middle-earth had no knowledge, while the tales of later Men are confused with memories of other races.

They are a tough, thrawn race for the most part, secretive, laborious, retentive of the memory of injuries (and of benefits), lovers of stone, of gems, of things that take shape under the hands of the craftsmen rather than things that live by their own life. But they are not evil by nature, and few ever served the Enemy of free will, whatever the tales of Men may have alleged. For Men of old lusted after their wealth and the work of their hands, and there has been enmity between the races.

But in the Third Age close friendship still was found in many places between Men and Dwarves; and it was according to the nature of the Dwarves that, travelling and labouring and trading about the lands, as they did after the destruction of their ancient mansions, they should use the languages of men among whom they dwelt. Yet in secret (a secret which unlike the Elves, they did not willingly unlock, even to their friends) they used their own strange tongue, changed little by the years; for it had become a tongue of lore rather than a cradle-speech, and they tended it and guarded it as a treasure of the past. Few of other race have succeeded in learning it. In this history it appears only in such place-names as Gimli revealed to his companions; and in the battle-cry which he uttered in the siege of the Hornburg. That at least was not secret, and had been heard on many a field since the world was young. *Baruk Khazâd! Khazâd ai-mênu!* 'Axes of the Dwarves! The Dwarves are upon you!'

Gimli's own name, however, and the names of all his kin, are of Northern (Mannish) origin. Their own secret and 'inner' names, their true names, the Dwarves have never revealed to any one of alien race. Not even on their tombs do they inscribe them.

II
ON TRANSLATION

In presenting the matter of the Red Book, as a history for people of today to read, the whole of the linguistic setting has been translated as far as possible into terms of our own times. Only the languages alien to the Common Speech have been left in their original form; but these appear mainly in the names of persons and places.

The Common Speech, as the language of the Hobbits and their narratives, has inevitably been turned into modern English. In the process the difference between the varieties observable in the use of the Westron has been lessened. Some attempt has been made to represent varieties by variations in the kind of English used; but the divergence between the pronunciation and idiom of the Shire and the Westron tongue in the mouths of the Elves or of the high men of Gondor was greater than has been shown in this book. Hobbits indeed spoke for the most part a rustic dialect, whereas in Gondor and Rohan a more antique language was used, more formal and more terse.

One point in the divergence may here be noted, since, though important, it has proved impossible to represent. The Westron tongue made in the pronouns of the second person (and often also in those of the third) a distinction, independent of number, between 'familiar' and 'deferential' forms. It was, however, one of the peculiarities of Shire-usage that the deferential forms had gone out of colloquial use. They lingered only among the villagers, especially of the Westfarthing, who used them as endearments. This was one of the things referred to when people of Gondor spoke of the strangeness of Hobbit-speech. Peregrin Took, for instance, in his first few days in Minas Tirith used the familiar for people of all ranks, including the Lord Denethor himself. This may have amused the aged Steward, but it must have astonished his servants. No doubt this free use of the familiar forms helped to spread the popular rumour that Peregrin was a person of very high rank in his own country.[1]

It will be noticed that Hobbits such as Frodo, and other persons such as Gandalf and Aragorn, do not always use the same style. This is intentional. The more learned and able among the Hobbits had some knowledge of 'book-language', as it was termed in the Shire; and they were quick to note and adopt the style of those whom they met. It was in any case natural for much-travelled folk to speak more or less after the manner of those among whom they found themselves, especially in the case of men who, like Aragorn, were often at pains to conceal their origin and their business. Yet in those days all the enemies of the Enemy revered what was ancient, in language no less than in other matters, and they took pleasure in it according to their knowledge. The Eldar, being above all skilled in words, had the command of many styles, though they spoke most naturally in a manner nearest to their own speech, one even more antique than that of Gondor. The Dwarves, too, spoke with

---

[1] In one or two places an attempt has been made to hint at these distinctions by an inconsistent use of *thou*. Since this pronoun is now unusual and archaic it is employed mainly to represent the use of ceremonious language; but a change from *you* to *thou*, *thee* is sometimes meant to show, there being no other means of doing this, a significant change from the deferential, or between men and women normal, forms to the familiar.

skill, readily adapting themselves to their company, though their utterance seemed to some rather harsh and guttural. But Orcs and Trolls spoke as they would, without love of words or things; and their language was actually more degraded and filthy than I have shown it. I do not suppose that any will wish for a closer rendering, though models are easy to find. Much the same sort of talk can still be heard among the orc-minded; dreary and repetitive with hatred and contempt, too long removed from good to retain even verbal vigour, save in the ears of those to whom only the squalid sounds strong.

Translation of this kind is, of course, usual because inevitable in any narrative dealing with the past. It seldom proceeds any further. But I have gone beyond it. I have also translated all Westron names according to their senses. When English names or titles appear in this book it is an indication that names in the Common Speech were current at the time, beside, or instead of, those in alien (usually Elvish) languages.

The Westron names were as a rule translations of older names: as Rivendell, Hoarwell, Silverlode, Langstrand, The Enemy, the Dark Tower. Some differed in meaning: as Mount Doom for *Orodruin* 'burning mountain', or Mirkwood for *Taur e-Ndaedelos* 'forest of the great fear'. A few were alterations of Elvish names: as Lune and Brandywine derived from *Lhûn* and *Baranduin*.

This procedure perhaps needs some defence. It seemed to me that to present all the names in their original forms would obscure an essential feature of the times as perceived by the Hobbits (whose point of view I was mainly concerned to preserve): the contrast between a wide-spread language, to them as ordinary and habitual as English is to us, and the living remains of far older and more reverend tongues. All names if merely transcribed would seem to modern readers equally remote: for instance, if the Elvish name *Imladris* and the Westron translation *Karningul* had both been left unchanged. But to refer to Rivendell as Imladris was as if one now was to speak of Winchester as Camelot, except that the identity was certain, while in Rivendell there still dwelt a lord of renown far older than Arthur would be, were he still king at Winchester today.

The name of the Shire (*Sûza*) and all other places of the Hobbits have thus been Englished. This was seldom difficult, since such names were commonly made up of elements similar to those used in our simpler English place-names; either words still current like *hill* or *field*; or a little worn down like *ton* beside *town*. But some were derived, as already noted, from old hobbit-words no longer in use, and these have been represent by similar English things, such as *wich*, or *bottle* 'dwelling', or *michel* 'great'.

In the case of persons, however, Hobbit-names in the Shire and in Bree were for those days peculiar, notably in the habit that had grown up, some centuries before this time, of having inherited names for families. Most of these surnames had obvious meanings (in the current language being derived from jesting nicknames, or from place-names, or – especially in Bree – from the names of plants and trees). Translation of these presented little difficulty; but there remained one or two older names of forgotten meaning, and these I have been content to anglicize in spelling: as Took for *Tûk*, or Boffin for *Bophin*.

I have treated Hobbit first-names, as far as possible, in the same way. To their maid-children Hobbits commonly gave the names of flowers or jewels. To their man-children they usually gave names that had no meaning at all in their daily language; and some of their women's names were similar. Of this kind are Bilbo, Bungo, Polo, Lotho, Tanta, Nina, and so on. There are many inevitable but accidental resemblances to names we now have or know: for instance Otho, Odo, Drogo, Dora, Cora, and the like. These names I have retained, though I have usually anglicized them by altering their endings, since in Hobbit-names *a* was a masculine ending, and *o* and *e* were feminine.

In some old families, especially those of Fallohide origin such as the Tooks and the Bolgers, it was, however, the custom to give high-sounding first-names. Since most of these seem to have been drawn from legends of the past, of Men as well as of Hobbits, and many while now meaningless to Hobbits closely resembled the names of Men in the Vale of Anduin, or in Dale, or in the Mark, I have turned them into those old names, largely of Frankish and Gothic origin, that are still used by us or are met in our histories. I have thus at any rate preserved the often comic contrast between the first-names and surnames, of which the Hobbits themselves were well aware. Names of classical origin have rarely been used; for the nearest equivalents to Latin and Greek in Shire-lore were the Elvish tongues, and these the Hobbits seldom used in nomenclature. Few of them at any time knew the 'languages of the kings', as they called them.

The names of the Bucklanders were different from those of the rest of the Shire. The folk of the Marish and their offshoot across the Brandywine were in many ways peculiar, as has been told. It was from the former language of the southern Stoors, no doubt, that they inherited many of their very odd names. These I have usually left unaltered, for if queer now, they were queer in their own day. They had a style that we should perhaps feel vaguely to be 'Celtic'.

Since the survival of traces of the older language of the Stoors and the Bree-men resembled the survival of Celtic elements in England, I have sometimes imitated the latter in my translation. Thus Bree, Combe (Coomb), Archet, and Chetwood are modelled on relics of British nomenclature, chosen according to sense: *bree* 'hill' *chet* 'wood'. But only one personal name has been altered in this way. Meriadoc was chosen to fit the fact that this character's shortened name, Kali, meant in the Westron 'jolly, gay', though it was actually an abbreviation of the now unmeaning Buckland name Kalimac.

I have not used names of Hebraic or similar origin in my transpositions. Nothing in Hobbit-names corresponds to this element in our names. Short names such as Sam, Tom, Tim, Mat were common as abbreviations of actual Hobbit-names, such as Tomba, Tolma, Matta, and the like. But Sam and his father Ham were really called Ban and Ran. These were shortenings of *Banazîr* and *Ranugad*, originally nicknames, meaning 'halfwise, simple' and 'stay-at-home'; but being words that had fallen out of colloquial use they remained as traditional names in certain families. I have therefore tried to preserve these features by using Samwise and Hamfast, modernizations of ancient English *samwís* and *hámfoest* which corresponded closely in meaning.

Having gone so far in my attempt to modernize and make familiar the language and names of Hobbits, I found myself involved in a further process. The Mannish

languages that were related to the Westron should, it seemed to me, be turned into
forms related to English. The language of Rohan I have accordingly made to
resemble ancient English, since it was related both (more distantly) to the Common
Speech, and (very closely) to the former tongue of the northern Hobbits, and was
in comparison with the Westron archaic. In the Red Book it is noted in several
places that when Hobbits heard the speech of Rohan they recognized many words
and felt the language to be akin to their own, so that it seemed absurd to leave the
recorded names and words of the Rohirrim in a wholly alien style.

In several cases I have modernized the forms and spellings of place-names in
Rohan: as in *Dunharrow* or *Snowbourn*; but I have not been consistent, for I have
followed the Hobbits. They altered the names that they heard in the same way, if
they were made of elements that they recognized, or if they resembled place-names
in the Shire; but many they left alone, as I have done, for instance, in *Edoras* 'the
courts'. For the same reasons a few personal names have also been modernized, as
Shadowfax and Wormtongue.[1]

This assimilation also provided a convenient way of representing the peculiar
local hobbit-words that were of northern origin. They have been given the forms
that lost English words might well have had, if they had come down to our day.
Thus *mathom* is meant to recall ancient English *máthm*, and so to represent the
relationship of the actual Hobbit *kast* to R. *kastu*. Similarly *smial* (or *smile*) 'burrow'
is a likely form for a descendant of *smygel*, and represents well the relationship of
Hobbit *trân* to R. *trahan*. *Sméagol* and *Déagol* are equivalents made up in the same
way for the names *Trahald* 'burrowing, worming in', and *Nahald* 'secret' in the
Northern tongues.

The still more northerly language of Dale is in this book seen only in the names
of the Dwarves that came from that region and so used the language of the Men
there, taking their 'outer' names in that tongue. It may be observed that in this
book as in *The Hobbit* the form *dwarves* is used, although the dictionaries tell us
that the plural of *dwarf* is *dwarfs*. It should be *dwarrows* (or *dwerrows*), if singular
and plural had each gone its own way down the years, as have *man* and *men*, or
goose and *geese*. But we no longer speak of a dwarf as often as we do of a man, or
even of a goose, and memories have not been fresh enough among Men to keep
hold of a special plural for a race now abandoned to folk-tales, where at least a
shadow of truth is preserved, or at last to nonsense-stories in which they have
become mere figures of fun. But in the Third Age something of their old character
and power is still glimpsed, if already a little dimmed; these are the descendants of
the Naugrim of the Elder Days, in whose hearts still burns ancient fire of Aulë the
Smith, and the embers smoulder of their long grudge against the Elves; and in
whose hands still lives the skill in work of stone that none have surpassed.

It is to mark this that I have ventured to use the form *dwarves*, and remove them
a little, perhaps, from the sillier tales of these latter days. *Dwarrows* would have

---

[1] This linguistic procedure does not imply that the Rohirrim closely resembled the ancient
English otherwise, in culture or art, in weapons or modes of warfare, except in a general way
due to their circumstances: a simpler and more primitive people living in contact with a higher
and more venerable culture, and occupying lands that had once been part of its domain.

been better; but I have used that form only in the name *Dwarrowdelf*, to represent the name of Moria in the Common Speech: *Phurunargian*. For that meant 'Dwarf-delving' and yet was already a word of antique form. But Moria is an Elvish name, and given without love; for the Eldar, though they might at need, in their bitter wars with the Dark Power and his servants, contrive fortresses underground, were not dwellers in such places of choice. They were lovers of the green earth and the lights of heaven; and Moria in their tongue means the Black Chasm. But the Dwarves themselves, and this name at least was never kept secret, called it *Khazad-dûm*, the Mansion of the Khazâd; for such is their own name for their own race, and has been so, since Aulë gave it to them at their making in the deeps of time.

Elves has been used to translate both *Quendi*, 'the speakers', the High-elven name of all their kind, and *Eldar*, the name of the Three Kindreds that sought for the Undying Realm and came there at the beginning of Days (save the *Sindar* only). This old word was indeed the only one available, and was once fitted to apply to such memories of this people as Men preserved, or to the making of Men's minds not wholly dissimilar. But it has been diminished, and to many it may now suggest fancies either pretty or silly, as unlike to the Quendi of old as are butterflies to the falcon – not that any of the Quendi ever possessed wings of the body, as unnatural to them as to Men. They were a race high and beautiful, the older Children of the world, and among them the Eldar were as kings, who now are gone: the People of the Great Journey, the People of the Stars. They were tall, fair of skin and grey-eyed, though their locks were dark, save in the golden house of Finarfin; and their voices had more melodies than any mortal voice that now is heard. They were valiant, but the history of those that returned to Middle-earth in exile was grievous; and though it was in far-off days crossed by the fate of the Fathers, their fate is not that of Men. Their dominion passed long ago, and they dwell now beyond the circles of the world, and do not return.

Note on three names: *Hobbit*, *Gamgee*, and *Brandywine*.

Hobbit is an invention. In the Westron the word used, when this people was referred to at all, was *banakil* 'halfling'. But at this date the folk of the Shire and of Bree used the word *kuduk*, which was not found elsewhere. Meriadoc, however, actually records that the King of Rohan used the word *kûd-dûkan* 'hole-dweller'. Since, as has been noted, the Hobbits had once spoken a language closely related to that of the Rohirrim, it seems likely that *kuduk* was a worn-down form of *kûd-dûkan*. The latter I have translated, for reasons explained, by *holbytla*; and *hobbit* provides a word that might well be a worn-down form of *holbytla*, if that name had occurred in our own ancient language.

Gamgee. According to family tradition, set out in the Red Book, the surname *Galbasi*, or in reduced form *Galpsi*, came from the village of *Galabas*, popularly supposed to be derived from *galab-* 'game' and an old element *bas-*, more or less equivalent to our *wick*, *wich*. *Gamwich* (pronounced *Gammidge*) seemed therefore a very fair rendering. However, in reducing *Gammidgy* to *Gamgee*, to represent *Galpsi*, no reference was intended to the connexion of Samwise with the family of Cotton, though a jest of that kind would have been hobbit-like enough, had there been any warrant in their language.

Cotton, in fact, represents *Hlothran*, a fairly common village-name in the Shire, derived from *hloth*, 'a two-roomed dwelling or hole', and *ran(u)* a small group of such dwellings on a hill-side. As a surname it may be an alteration of *hlothram(a)* 'cottager'. *Hlothram*, which I have rendered Cotman, was the name of Farmer Cotton's grandfather.

Brandywine. The hobbit-names of this river were alterations of the Elvish *Baranduin* (accented on *and*), derived from *baran* 'golden brown' and *duin* '(large) river'. Of *Baranduin* Brandywine seemed a natural corruption in modern times. Actually the older hobbit-name was *Branda-nîn* 'border-water', which would have been more closely rendered by Marchbourn; but by a jest that had become habitual, referring again to its colour, at this time the river was usually called *Bralda-hîm* 'heady ale'.

It must be observed, however, that when the Oldbucks (*Zaragamba*) changed their name to Brandybuck (*Brandagamba*), the first element meant 'borderland', and Marchbuck would have been nearer. Only a very bold hobbit would have ventured to call the Master of Buckland *Braldagamba* in his hearing.

INDEX

I SONGS AND VERSES

Through Rohan over fen and field
where the long grass grows,
407–8
To the Sea, to the Sea! The white
gulls are crying, 935
Troll sat alone on his seat of stone,
201–3

Upon the hearth the fire is red,
76

We come, we come with roll of
drum: ta-runda runda runda
rom! 473

We heard of the horns in the hills
ringing, 831
When evening in the Shire was grey,
350
When spring unfolds the beechen
leaf, and sap is in the bough, 466
When the black breath blows, 847
When winter first begins to bite,
266
Where now are the Dúnedain,
Elessar, Elessar? 491
Where now the horse and the rider?
Where is the horn that was
blowing? 497

II PERSONS BEASTS AND MONSTERS

references are selective

Aldor, 955
Amroth, 330–1, 341
Anárion, 236f., 384, 655, 663. House
of Anárion (dynasty), 835. *See
also palantír*
Anborn, 660, 670–6
Ancalagon the Black, 59
Angbor, 857, 859, 863. *See also* Lord
of Lamedon
Appledore, 152
  Rowlie, 970
Aragorn, 57, 166–7, 205, 215, 218,
231, 240–8, 255–6, 258, 265,
269–92, 297, 302–4, 315–34,
343, 346–7, 358–96, 403–33,
477–532, 539, 546–53, 557, etc.,
580–2, 629–30, 643, 648–9, 655,
662, 664, 692, 737f., 744,
756–73, 779–80, 784, 792, 797,
830, 843–72, 877, 927–8, 933,
945–60, 964–5; Aragorn son of
Arathorn, 168, 215, 240, 269,
270, 334, 346, 384, 423, 426,
489, 498, 499, 511, 530, 648,
757, 829, 945; the Lord Aragorn,
760, 779f., 943, 945. For titles
see 499, 528, 648, 945; *see also*
Appendix A, 1012, 1019, 1032–7

Nicknames: Strider (used in Bree
and by his hobbit-companions),
153–209, 214–15, 218, 221, 226,
242, 257, 266, 268, 277, 335,
374, 384, 392, 396, 397, 421,
426, 435, 439, 443, 471, 558,
561, 575, 664, 737, 779, 851,
856, 932–3, 968, 972; adopted by
A., 845; Stick-at-naught S., 177;
Longshanks, 176; Wingfoot, 426.
See also Elendil, Elessar, Isildur,
Thorongil, 1012, 1032
Arathorn *See also* Aragorn
Araw, 738, 1015 (note)
Argeleb II, 4 (note)
Arod, 429, 769, 954
Arvedui, 4 (note)
Arwen (Lady), 221, 223, 226, 232,
829, 951–4, 1031—3; Arwen
Evenstar, 366, 953, 956; (of her
people), 221, 951, 953, 951,
1034; Undómiel, 951, 1033–7 (c.
undóme 1084); Lady of Rivendell,
759, 1034
Asfaloth, 207

Baggins, 9, 28ff.
  Angelica, 37

III PLACES

references are given to the first occurrence: for some names references are added to other occurrences of interest

IV THINGS

MAPS

NOTE ON THE MAPS

Maps accompanying *The Lord of the Rings* were drawn by Christopher Tolkien for the original edition published in 1954–5. They consisted of a general map of the western regions of Middle-earth and a more detailed map of Rohan, Gondor, and Mordor; printed in red and black on large folded sheets pasted in at the end of each of the three books, *The Fellowship of the Ring* and *The Two Towers* carried the general map, while *The Return of the King* carried the other. In addition, there was a map of the Shire in red and black preceding Book I of *The Fellowship of the Ring*. Christopher Tolkien redrew the general map expressly for inclusion in *Unfinished Tales* (1980), but subsequently this·replaced the original form in editions of *The Lord of the Rings*.

With paperback editions the arrangement was introduced whereby the general map was divided into four sections, in black only, fitting the size of the pages, while the whole map in greatly reduced form was also printed as a guide to the sections. The map of Rohan, Gondor, and Mordor was reduced to fit two facing pages. This arrangement is found in all current paperback and one-volume hardback editions.

The original maps, however, were not drawn and lettered in such a way as to make such reduction satisfactory. Mr Stephen Raw has therefore redrawn them all, very closely following the originals, and greatly increasing their clarity. As a guide to the four sections of the general map he has drawn a new outline map that provides all necessary indications in a simplified form.

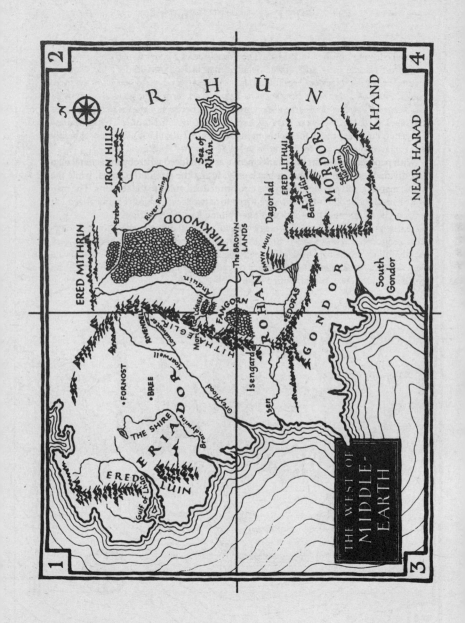

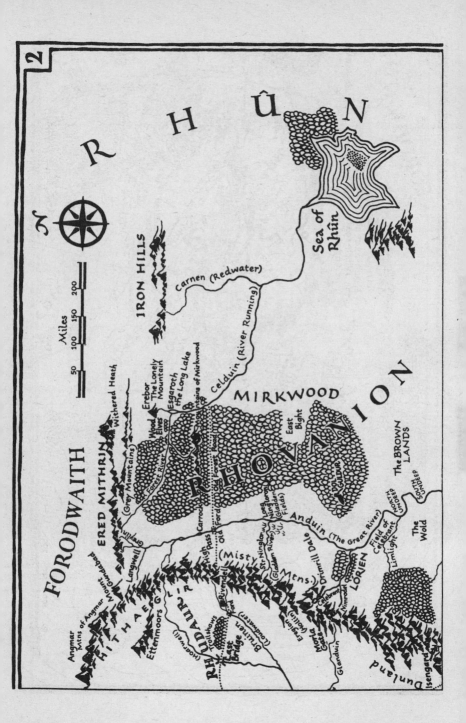

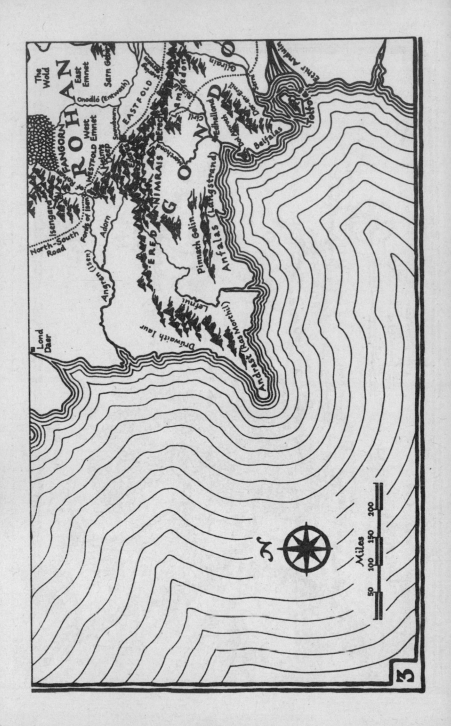

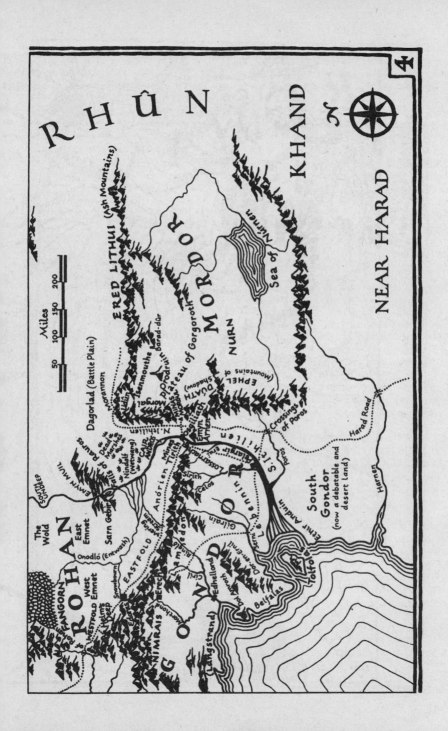

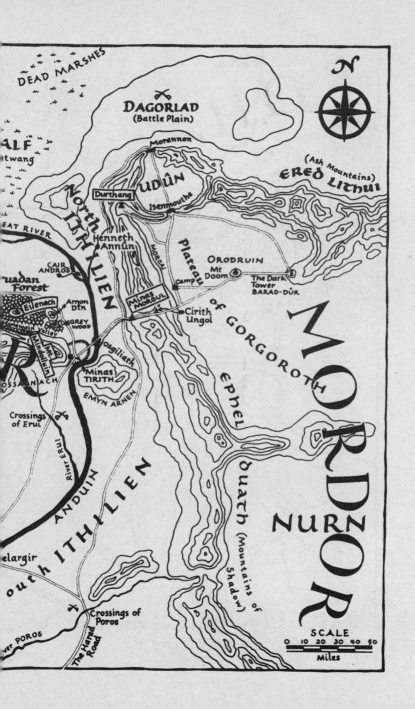

THE SILMARILLION
J. R. R. Tolkien

The Silmarillion is the central stock of J. R. R. Tolkien's imaginative writing. Although published posthumously it is the story of the First Age in Tolkien's world, the ancient drama to which the characters in *The Lord of the Rings* look back, and in whose events, some of them, such as Elrond and Galadriel, took part.

'How, given little over half a century of work, did one man become the creative equivalent of a people?' – *The Guardian*

'Demanding to be compared with English mythologies...at times rises to the greatness of true myth.' – *Financial Times*

'A creation myth of singular beauty . . . magnificent in its best moments.'
                                        – *Washingon Post*

'A grim, tragic, brooding and beautiful book, shot through with heroism and hope . . . its power is almost that of mysticism.'
                                        – *Toronto Globe & Mail*

'Stern, sweeping myth . . . an imaginative work of staggering comprehensiveness.'
                                        – *Sydney Morning Herald*

UNFINISHED TALES
J. R. R. Tolkien

Unfinished Tales of Númenor and Middle-earth is a collection of narratives ranging in time from the Elder Days of Middle-earth to the end of the War of the Ring, and comprising such various elements as Gandalf's lively account of how it was that he came to send the Dwarves to the celebrated party at Bag-End, the emergence of the sea-god Ulmo before the eyes of Tuor on the coast of Beleriand, and an exact description of the military organisation of the Riders of Rohan. The book contains the only story that survived from the long ages of Númenor before its downfall, and all that is known of such matters as the Five Wizards, the Palantíri, or the legend of Amroth.

Writing of the Appendices to *The Lord of the Rings* J. R. R. Tolkien said in 1955: 'Those who enjoy the book as a "heroic romance" only, and find "unexplained vistas" part of the literary effect, will neglect the Appendices very properly.' *Unfinished Tales* is avowedly for those who, on the contrary, have not yet sufficiently explored Middle-earth, its language, its legends, its politics, and its kings.

Christopher Tolkien has edited and introduces this collection. He has also redrawn the map for *The Lord of the Rings* to a larger scale and reproduced the only map of Númenor that J. R. R. Tolkien ever made.

'Moments of mythic grandeur.'   *– The Sunday Times*

'A series of essays, snatches of stories . . . another monument to the incredible imagination of Tolkien.'
                                        – The Sunday Telegraph